THE MODERN LIBRARY
of the World's Best Books

▶▶

THE COMPLETE NOVELS OF
JANE AUSTEN

>>>

*The publishers will be pleased to send, upon
request, an illustrated folder setting forth
the purpose and scope of* THE MODERN
LIBRARY, *and listing each volume in the
series. Every reader of books will find
titles he has been looking for, handsomely
printed, in unabridged editions, and
at an unusually low price.*

>>>

The
COMPLETE NOVELS
OF JANE AUSTEN

>>>>>>>>>>>:·>>>>>>>>>>> >>

>>

BENNETT A. CERF · DONALD S. KLOPFER

THE MODERN LIBRARY

NEW YORK

THE MODERN LIBRARY
is published by RANDOM HOUSE, INC.
BENNETT CERF · DONALD S. KLOPFER

Manufactured in the United States of America by H. Wolff

CONTENTS

SENSE AND SENSIBILITY

(First Published 1811*)*

SENSE AND SENSIBILITY

Chapter i

THE family of Dashwood had been long settled in Sussex. Their estate was large, and their residence was at Norland Park, in the centre of their property, where for many generations they had lived in so respectable a manner as to engage the general good opinion of their surrounding acquaintances. The late owner of this estate was a single man, who lived to a very advanced age, and who for many years of his life had a constant companion and housekeeper in his sister. But her death, which happened ten years before his own, produced a great alteration in his home; for to supply her loss, he invited and received into his house the family of his nephew, Mr. Henry Dashwood, the legal inheritor of the Norland estate, and the person to whom he intended to bequeath it. In the society of his nephew and niece, and their children, the old gentleman's days were comfortably spent. His attachment to them all increased. The constant attention of Mr. and Mrs. Henry Dashwood to his wishes, which proceeded not merely from interest, but from goodness of heart, gave him every degree of solid comfort which his age could receive; and the cheerfulness of the children added a relish to his existence.

By a former marriage, Mr. Henry Dashwood had one son; by his present lady, three daughters. The son, a steady, respectable young man, was amply provided for by the fortune of his mother, which had been large, and half of which devolved on him on his coming of age. By his own marriage, likewise, which happened soon afterwards, he added to his wealth. To him, therefore, the succession to the Norland estate was not so really important as to his sisters; for their fortune, independent on what might arise to them from their father's inheriting that property, could be but small. Their mother had nothing, and their father only seven thousand pounds in his own disposal; for the remaining moiety of his first wife's fortune was also secured to her child, and he had only a life interest in it.

The old gentleman died; his will was read, and like almost every other will, gave as much disappointment as pleasure. He was neither so unjust, nor so ungrateful, as to leave his estate from his nephew; but he left it to him on such terms as destroyed half the value of the bequest. Mr. Dashwood had wished for it more for the sake of his wife and daughters than for himself or his son; but to his son, and his son's son, a child of four years old, it was secured, in such a way, as to leave to himself no power of providing for those who were most dear to him, and who most needed a provision, by any charge on the estate, or by any sale of its valuable woods. The whole was tied up for the benefit of this child, who, in occasional visits with his father and mother at Norland had so far gained on the affections of his uncle, by such attractions as are by no means unusual in children of two or three years old: an imperfect articulation, an earnest desire of having his own way, many cunning tricks, and a great deal of noise, as to outweigh all the value of all the attention which, for years, he had received from his niece and her daughters. He meant not to be unkind, however, and as a mark of his affection for the three girls, he left them a thousand pounds apiece.

Mr. Dashwood's disappointment was at first severe; but his temper was cheerful and sanguine, and he might reasonably hope to live many years, and by living economically, lay by a considerable sum from the produce of an estate already large, and capable of almost immediate improvement. But the fortune, which had been so tardy in coming, was his only one twelvemonth. He survived his uncle no longer; and ten thousand pounds, including the late legacies, was all that remained for his widow and daughters.

His son was sent for, as soon as his danger was known, and to him Mr. Dashwood recommended, with all the strength and urgency which illness could command, the interest of his mother-in-law and sisters.

Mr. John Dashwood had not the strong feelings of the rest of the family; but he was affected by a recommendation of such a nature at such a time, and he promised to do everything in his power to make them comfortable. His father was rendered easy by such an assurance, and Mr. John Dashwood had then leisure to consider how much there might prudently be in his power to do for them.

He was not an ill-disposed young man, unless to be rather cold-hearted, and rather selfish, is to be ill-disposed: but he was, in general, well respected; for he conducted himself with propriety in the discharge of his ordinary duties. Had he married a more amiable woman, he might have been made still more respectable than he was; he might even have been made amiable himself; for he was very young when he married, and very fond of his wife. But Mrs. John Dashwood was a strong caricature of himself; more narrow-minded and selfish.

When he gave his promise to his father, he meditated within himself to increase the fortunes of his sisters by the present of a thousand pounds apiece. He then really thought himself equal to it. The prospect of four thousand a year, in addition to his present income, besides the remaining half of his own mother's fortune, warmed his heart and made him feel capable of generosity. "Yes, he would give them three thousand pounds: it would be liberal and handsome! It would be enough to make them completely easy. Three thousand pounds! He could spare so considerable a sum with little inconvenience." He thought of it all day long, and for many days successively, and he did not repent.

No sooner was his father's funeral over, than Mrs. John Dashwood, without sending any notice of her intention to her mother-in-law, arrived with her child and their attendants. No one could dispute her right to come; the house was her husband's from the moment of his father's decease; but the indelicacy of her conduct was so much the greater, and to a woman in Mrs. Dashwood's situation, with only common feelings, must have been highly unpleasing; but in *her* mind there was a sense of honour so keen, a generosity so romantic, that any offence of the kind, by whomsoever given or received, was to her a source of immovable disgust. Mrs. John Dashwood had never been a favourite with any of her husband's family: but she had had no opportunity till the present, of showing them with how little attention to the comfort of other people she could act when occasion required it.

So acutely did Mrs. Dashwood feel this ungracious behaviour, and so earnestly did she despise her daughter-in-law for it, that, on the arrival of the latter, she would have quitted the house for ever, had not the entreaty of her eldest girl induced her first to reflect on the propriety of going, and her own tender love for all her three children determined her afterwards to stay, and for their sakes avoid a breach with their brother.

Elinor, this eldest daughter whose advice was so effectual, possessed a strength of understanding, and coolness of judgment, which qualified her, though only nineteen, to be the counsellor of her mother, and enabled her frequently to counteract, to the advantage of them all, that eagerness of mind in Mrs. Dashwood which must generally have led to imprudence. She had an excellent heart; her disposition was affectionate, and her feelings were strong: but she knew how to govern them: it was a knowledge which her mother had yet to learn, and which one of her sisters had resolved never to be taught.

Marianne's abilities were, in many respects, quite equal to Elinor's. She was sensible and clever, but eager in everything; her sorrows, her joys, could have no moderation. She was generous, amiable, interesting: she was everything but prudent. The resemblance between her and her mother was strikingly great.

Elinor saw, with concern, the excess of her sister's sensibility; but by Mrs. Dashwood it was valued and cherished. They encouraged each other now in the violence of their affliction. The agony of grief which overpowered them at first, was voluntarily renewed, was sought for, was created again and again. They gave themselves up wholly to their sorrow, seeking increase of wretchedness in every reflection that could afford it, and resolved against ever admitting consolation in future. Elinor, too, was deeply afflicted; but still she could struggle, she could exert herself. She could consult with her brother, could receive her sister-in-law on her arrival, and treat her with proper attention: and could strive to rouse her mother to similar exertion, and encourage her to similar forbearance.

Margaret, the other sister, was a good-humoured, well-disposed girl;

but as she had already imbibed a good deal of Marianne's romance, without having much of her sense, she did not, at thirteen, bid fair to equal her sisters at a more advanced period of life.

Chapter 2

MRS. JOHN DASHWOOD now installed herself mistress of Norland; and her mother and sister-in-law were degraded to the condition of visitors. As such, however, they were treated by her with quiet civility; and by her husband with as much kindness as he could feel towards anybody beyond himself, his wife, and their child. He really pressed them, with some earnestness, to consider Norland as their home; and, as no plan appeared so eligible to Mrs. Dashwood as remaining there till she could accommodate herself with a house in the neighbourhood, his invitation was accepted.

A continuance in a place where everything reminded her of former delight, was exactly what suited her mind. In seasons of cheerfulness, no temper could be more cheerful than hers, or possess, in a greater degree, that sanguine expectation of happiness which is happiness itself. But in sorrow she must be equally carried away by her fancy, and as far beyond consolation as in pleasure she was beyond alloy.

Mrs. John Dashwood did not at all approve of what her husband intended to do for his sisters. To take three thousand pounds from the fortune of their dear little boy, would be impoverishing him to the most dreadful degree. She begged him to think again on the subject. How could he answer it to himself to rob his child, and his only child too, of so large a sum? And what possible claim could the Miss Dashwoods, who were related to him only by half blood, which she considered as no relationship at all, have on his generosity to so large an amount? It was very well known that no affection was ever supposed to exist between the children of any man by different marriages; and why was he to ruin himself, and their poor little Harry, by giving away all his money to his half-sisters?

"It was my father's last request to me," replied her husband, "that I should assist his widow and daughters."

"He did not know what he was talking of, I dare say; ten to one but he was lightheaded at the time. Had he been in his right senses, he could not have thought of such a thing as begging you to give away half your fortune from your own child."

"He did not stipulate for any particular sum, my dear Fanny; he only requested me, in general terms, to assist them, and make their situation more comfortable than it was in his power to do. Perhaps it would have been as well if he had left it wholly to myself. He could hardly suppose I should neglect them. But as he required the promise, I could not do less than give it: at least I thought so at the time. The promise, therefore, was

given, and must be performed. Something must be done for them whenever they leave Norland and settle in a new home."

"Well, then, *let* something be done for them; but *that* something need
not be three thousand pounds. Consider," she added, "that when the
money is once parted with, it never can return. Your sisters will marry,
and it will be gone for ever. If, indeed, it could ever be restored to our
poor little boy . . ."

"Why, to be sure," said her husband, very gravely, "that would make
a great difference. The time may come when Harry will regret that so
large a sum was parted with. If he should have a numerous family, for
instance, it would be a very convenient addition."

"To be sure it would."

"Perhaps, then, it would be better for all parties if the sum were
diminished one half. Five hundred pounds would be a prodigious increase
to their fortunes."

"Oh, beyond anything great! What brother on earth would do half as
much for his sisters, even if *really* his sisters! And as it is—only half
blood! But you have such a generous spirit!"

"I would not wish to do anything mean," he replied. "One had rather,
on such occasions, do too much than too little. No one, at least, can think
I have not done enough for them: even themselves, they can hardly expect
more."

"There is no knowing what *they* may expect," said the lady, "but we
are not to think of their expectations: the question is, what you can
afford to do."

"Certainly, and I think I may afford to give them five hundred pounds
apiece. As it is, without any addition of mine, they will each have above
three thousand pounds on their mother's death: a very comfortable
fortune for any young woman."

"To be sure it is: and, indeed, it strikes me that they can want no
addition at all. They will have ten thousand pounds divided amongst
them. If they marry, they will be sure of doing well; and if they do not,
they may all live very comfortably together on the interest of ten thousand pounds."

"That is very true, and, therefore, I do not know whether, upon the
whole, it would not be more advisable to do something for their mother
while she lives rather than for them; something of the annuity kind, I
mean. My sisters would feel the good effects of it as well as herself. A
hundred a year would make them all perfectly comfortable."

His wife hesitated a little, however, in giving her consent to this plan.

"To be sure," said she, "it is better than parting with fifteen hundred
pounds at once. But then, if Mrs. Dashwood should live fifteen years, we
shall be completely taken in."

"Fifteen years! My dear Fanny; her life cannot be worth half that
purchase."

"Certainly not; but if you observe, people always live for ever when there is any annuity to be paid them; and she is very stout and healthy, and hardly forty. An annuity is a very serious business; it comes over and over every year, and there is no getting rid of it. You are not aware of what you are doing. I have known a great deal of the trouble of annuities; for my mother was clogged with the payment of three to old super-annuated servants by my father's will, and it is amazing how disagreeable she found it. Twice every year, these annuities were to be paid; and then there was the trouble of getting it to them; and then one of them was said to have died, and afterwards it turned out to be no such thing. My mother was quite sick of it. Her income was not her own, she said, with such perpetual claims on it; and it was the more unkind in my father, because, otherwise, the money would have been entirely at my mother's disposal, without any restriction whatever. It has given me such an abhorrence of annuities, that I am sure I would not pin myself down to the payment of one for all the world."

"It is certainly an unpleasant thing," replied Mr. Dashwood, "to have those kind of yearly drains on one's income. One's fortune, as your mother justly says, is *not* one's own. To be tied down to the regular payment of such a sum, on every rent day, is by no means desirable: it takes away one's independence."

"Undoubtedly; and, after all, you have no thanks for it. They think themselves secure, you do no more than what is expected, and it raises no gratitude at all. If I were you, whatever I did should be done at my own discretion entirely. I would not bind myself to allow them anything yearly. It may be very inconvenient some years to spare a hundred, or even fifty pounds, from our own expenses."

"I believe you are right, my love; it will be better that there should be no annuity in the case; whatever I may give them occasionally will be of far greater assistance than a yearly allowance, because they would only enlarge their style of living if they felt sure of a larger income, and would not be sixpence the richer for it at the end of the year. It will certainly be much the best way. A present of fifty pounds, now and then, will prevent their ever being distressed for money, and will, I think, be amply discharging my promise to my father."

"To be sure it will. Indeed, to say the truth, I am convinced within myself, that your father had no idea of your giving them any money at all. The assistance he thought of, I dare say, was only such as might be reasonably expected of you; for instance, such as looking out for a comfortable small house for them, helping them to move their things, and sending them presents of fish and game, and so forth, whenever they are in season. I'll lay my life that he meant nothing further; indeed, it would be very strange and unreasonable if he did. Do but consider, my dear Mr. Dashwood, how excessively comfortable your mother-in-law and her daughters may live on the interest of seven thousand pounds, besides the thousand pounds belonging to each of the girls, which brings them in fifty pounds a year apiece, and, of course, they will pay their mother for their board out of it. Altogether, they will have five hundred a year amongst them, and what on earth can four women want for more than that? They will live so cheap! Their housekeeping will be nothing at all. They will have no carriage, no horses, and hardly any servants; they will keep no company, and can have no expenses of any kind! Only conceive how comfortable they will be! Five hundred a year! I am sure I cannot imagine how they will spend half of it; and as to your giving them more, it is quite absurd to think of it. They will be much more able to give *you* something."

"Upon my word," said Mr. Dashwood, "I believe you are perfectly right. My father certainly could mean nothing more by his request to me than what you say. I clearly understand it now, and I will strictly fulfil my engagement by such acts of assistance and kindness to them as you have described. When my mother removes into another house, my services shall be readily given to accommodate her as far as I can. Some little present of furniture, too, may be acceptable then."

"Certainly," returned Mrs. John Dashwood. "But, however, *one* thing must be considered. When your father and mother moved to Norland, though the furniture of Stanhill was sold, all the china, plate, and linen was saved, and is now left to your mother. Her house will therefore be almost completely fitted up as soon as she takes it."

"That is a material consideration, undoubtedly. A valuable legacy indeed! And yet some of the plate would have been a very pleasant addition to our own stock here."

"Yes; and the set of breakfast china is twice as handsome as what belongs to this house. A great deal too handsome, in my opinion, for any place *they* can ever afford to live in. But, however, so it is. Your father thought only of *them*. And I must say this: that you owe no particular gratitude to him, nor attention to his wishes, for we very well know that if he could, he would have left almost everything in the world to *them*."

This argument was irresistible. It gave to his intentions whatever of decision was wanting before; and he finally resolved, that it would be absolutely unnecessary, if not highly indecorous, to do more for the widow and children of his father, than such kind of neighbourly acts as his own wife pointed out.

Chapter 3

Mrs. Dashwood remained at Norland several months; not from any disinclination to move when the sight of every well-known spot ceased to raise the violent emotion which it produced for a while; for when her spirits began to revive, and her mind became capable of some other exertion than that of heightening its affliction by melancholy remembrances, she was impatient to be gone, and indefatigable in her inquiries for a suitable dwelling in the neighbourhood of Norland; for to remove far from that beloved spot was impossible. But she could hear of no situation that at once answered her notions of comfort and ease, and suited the prudence of her eldest daughter, whose steadier judgment rejected several houses as too large for their income, which her mother would have approved.

Mrs. Dashwood had been informed by her husband of the solemn promise on the part of his son in their favour, which gave comfort to his last earthly reflections. She doubted the sincerity of this assurance no more than he had doubted it himself, and she thought of it for her daughters' sake with satisfaction, though, as for herself, she was persuaded that a much smaller provision than seven thousand pounds would support her in affluence. For their brother's sake too, for the sake of his own heart, she rejoiced; and she reproached herself for being unjust to his merit before, in believing him incapable of generosity. His attentive behaviour to herself and his sisters, convinced her that their welfare was dear to him, and, for a long time, she firmly relied on the liberality of his intentions.

The contempt which she had, very early in their acquaintance, felt for her daughter-in-law was very much increased by the further knowledge of her character, which half-a-year's residence in her family afforded; and, perhaps, in spite of every consideration of politeness or maternal affection on the side of the former, the two ladies might have found it impossible to have lived together so long, had not a particular circumstance occurred to give still greater eligibility, according to the opinions of Mrs. Dashwood, to her daughters' continuance at Norland.

This circumstance was a growing attachment between her eldest girl and the brother of Mrs. John Dashwood, a gentlemanlike and pleasing young man, who was introduced to their acquaintance soon after his sister's establishment at Norland, and who had since spent the greatest part of his time there.

Some mothers might have encouraged the intimacy from motives of interest, for Edward Ferrars was the eldest son of a man who had died very rich; and some might have repressed it from motives of prudence, for, except a trifling sum, the whole of his fortune depended on the will of his mother. But Mrs. Dashwood was alike uninfluenced by either consideration. It was enough for her that he appeared to be amiable, that he loved her daughter, and that Elinor returned the partiality. It was contrary to every doctrine of hers, that difference of fortune should keep any couple asunder who were attracted by resemblance of disposition; and that Elinor's merit should not be acknowledged by everyone who knew her, was to her comprehension impossible.

Edward Ferrars was not recommended to their good opinion by any peculiar graces of person or address. He was not handsome, and his manners required intimacy to make them pleasing. He was too diffident to do justice to himself; but when his natural shyness was overcome, his behaviour gave every indication of an open, affectionate heart. His understanding was good, and his education had given it solid improvement. But he was neither fitted by abilities nor disposition to answer the wishes of his mother and sister, who longed to see him distinguished—as—they hardly knew what. They wanted him to make a fine figure in the world in some manner or other. His mother wished to interest him in political concerns, to get him into parliament, or to see him connected with some of the great men of the day. Mrs. John Dashwood wished it likewise; but in the meanwhile, till one of these superior blessings could be attained, it would have quieted her ambition to see him driving a barouche. But Edward had no turn for great men or barouches. All his wishes centred in domestic comfort and the quiet of private life. Fortunately he had a younger brother who was more promising.

Edward had been staying several weeks in the house before he engaged much of Mrs. Dashwood's attention; for she was, at that time, in such affliction as rendered her careless of surrounding objects. She saw only that he was quiet and unobtrusive, and she liked him for it. He did not disturb the wretchedness of her mind by ill-timed conversation. She was first called to observe and approve him farther, by a reflection which Elinor chanced one day to make on the difference between him and his sister. It was a contrast which recommended him most forcibly to her mother.

"It is enough," said she; "to say that he is unlike Fanny is enough. It implies everything amiable. I love him already."

"I think you will like him," said Elinor, "when you know more of him."

"Like him!" replied her mother, with a smile. "I can feel no sentiment of approbation inferior to love."

"You may esteem him."

"I have never yet known what it was to separate esteem and love."

Mrs. Dashwood now took pains to get acquainted with him. Her manners were attaching, and soon banished his reserve. She speedily comprehended all his merits; the persuasion of his regard for Elinor perhaps assisted her penetration; but she really felt assured of his worth: and even that quietness of manner which militated against all her established ideas of what a young man's address ought to be, was no longer uninteresting when she knew his heart to be warm and his temper affectionate.

No sooner did she perceive any symptom of love in his behaviour to Elinor, than she considered their serious attachment as certain, and looked forward to their marriage as rapidly approaching.

"In a few months, my dear Marianne," said she, "Elinor will in all probability be settled for life. We shall miss her; but *she* will be happy."

"O mamma! How shall we do without her?"

"My love, it will be scarcely a separation. We shall live within a few miles of each other, and shall meet every day of our lives. You will gain a brother—a real, affectionate brother. I have the highest opinion in th world of Edward's heart. But you look grave, Marianne; do you disapprove your sister's choice?"

"Perhaps," said Marianne, "I may consider it with some surprise. Edward is very amiable, and I love him tenderly. But yet, he is not the kind of young man—there is a something wanting, his figure is not striking—it has none of that grace which I should expect in the man who could seriously attach my sister. His eyes want all that spirit, that fire, which at once announce virtue and intelligence. And besides all this, I am afraid, mamma, he has no real taste. Music seems scarcely to attract him, and though he admires Elinor's drawings very much, it is not the admiration of a person who can understand their worth. It is evident, in spite of his frequent attention to her while she draws, that in fact he knows nothing of the matter. He admires as a lover, not as a connoisseur. To satisfy me, those characters must be united. I could not be happy with a man whose taste did not in every point coincide with my own. He must enter into all my feelings; the same books, the same music must charm us both. O mamma! how spiritless, how tame was Edward's manner in reading to us last night! I felt for my sister most severely. Yet she bore it with so much composure, she seemed scarcely to notice it. I could hardly keep my seat. To hear those beautiful lines which have frequently almost driven me wild, pronounced with such impenetrable calmness, such dreadful indifference!"

"He would certainly have done more justice to simple and elegant prose. I thought so at the time; but you *would* give him Cowper."

"Nay, mamma, if he is not to be animated by Cowper!—but we must allow for difference of taste. Elinor has not my feelings, and therefore she may overlook it, and be happy with him. But it would have broke *my* heart had I loved him, to hear him read with so little sensibility. Mamma, the more I know of the world, the more I am convinced that I shall never see a man whom I can really love. I require so much! He must have all Edward's virtues, and his person and manners must ornament his goodness with every possible charm."

"Remember, my love, that you are not seventeen. It is yet too early in life to despair of such an happiness. Why should you be less fortunate than your mother? In one circumstance only, my Marianne, may your destiny be different from hers!"

Chapter 4

"WHAT a pity it is, Elinor," said Marianne, "that Edward should have no taste for drawing."

"No taste for drawing," replied Elinor; "why should you think so? He does not draw himself, indeed, but he has great pleasure in seeing the performances of other people, and I assure you, he is by no means deficient in natural taste, though he has not had opportunities of improving it. Had he ever been in the way of learning, I think he would have drawn very well. He distrusts his own judgment in such matters so much, that he is always unwilling to give his opinion on any picture; but he has an innate propriety and simplicity of taste, which in general direct him perfectly right."

Marianne was afraid of offending, and said no more on the subject; but the kind of approbation which Elinor described as excited in him by the drawings of other people, was very far from that rapturous delight, which, in her opinion, could alone be called taste. Yet, though smiling within herself at the mistake, she honoured her sister for that blind partiality to Edward which produced it.

"I hope, Marianne," continued Elinor, "you do not consider him as deficient in general taste. Indeed, I think I may say that you cannot, for your behaviour to him is perfectly cordial, and if *that* were your opinion, I am sure you could never be civil to him."

Marianne hardly knew what to say. She would not wound the feelings of her sister on any account, and yet to say what she did not believe was impossible. At length she replied:

"Do not be offended, Elinor, if my praise of him is not in everything equal to your sense of his merits. I have not had so many opportunities of estimating the minuter propensities of his mind, his inclinations, and tastes, as you have; but I have the highest opinion in the world of his goodness and sense. I think him everything that is worthy and amiable."

"I am sure," replied Elinor, with a smile, "that his dearest friends could not be dissatisfied with such commendation as that. I do not perceive how you could express yourself more warmly."

Marianne was rejoiced to find her sister so easily pleased.

"Of his sense and goodness," continued Elinor, "no one can, I think, be in doubt, who has seen him often enough to engage him in unreserved conversation. The excellence of his understanding, and his principles can be concealed only by that shyness which too often keeps him silent. You know enough of him to do justice to his solid worth. But of his minuter propensities, as you call them, you have from peculiar circumstances been kept more ignorant than myself. He and I have been at times thrown a good deal together, while you have been wholly engrossed on the most affectionate principle by my mother. I have seen a great deal of him, have studied his sentiments, and heard his opinions on subjects of literature and taste; and, upon the whole, I venture to pronounce that his mind is well informed, his enjoyment of books exceeding great, his imagination lively, his observation just and correct, and his taste delicate and pure. His abilities in every respect improve as much upon acquaintance as his manners and person. At first sight, his address is certainly not striking; and his person can hardly be called handsome, till the expression of his eyes, which are uncommonly good, and the general sweetness of his countenance is perceived. At present, I know him so well, that I think him really handsome; or, at least, almost so. What say you, Marianne?"

"I shall very soon think him handsome, Elinor, if I do not now. When you tell me to love him as a brother, I shall no more see imperfection in his face, than I now do in his heart."

Elinor started at this declaration, and was sorry for the warmth she had been betrayed into, in speaking of him. She felt that Edward stood very high in her opinion. She believed the regard to be mutual; but she required greater certainty to it to make Marianne's conviction of their attachment agreeable to her. She knew that what Marianne and her mother conjectured one moment, they believed the next—that with them, to wish was to hope, and to hope was to expect. She tried to explain the real state of the case to her sister.

"I do not attempt to deny," said she, "that I think very highly of him —that I greatly esteem, that I like him."

Marianne here burst forth with indignation:

"Esteem him! Like him! Cold-hearted Elinor. Oh! worse than cold-hearted! Ashamed of being otherwise. Use those words again, and I will leave the room this moment."

Elinor could not help laughing. "Excuse me," said she, "and be assured that I meant no offence to you, by speaking, in so quiet a way, of my own feelings. Believe them to be stronger than I have declared; believe them, in short, to be such as his merit, and the suspicion—the hope of his affection for me may warrant, without imprudence or folly. But further than this you must *not* believe. I am by no means assured of his regard for me. There are moments when the extent of it seems doubtful; and till his sentiments are fully known, you cannot wonder at my wishing to avoid any encouragement of my own partiality, by believing or calling it more than it is. In my heart I feel little—scarcely any doubt of his preference. But there are other points to be considered besides his inclination. He is very far from being independent. What his mother really is we cannot know; but, from Fanny's occasional mention of her conduct and opinions, we have never been disposed to think her amiable; and I am very much mistaken, if Edward is not himself aware that there would be many difficulties in his way, if he were to wish to marry a woman who had not either a great fortune or high rank."

Marianne was astonished to find how much the imagination of her mother and herself had outstripped the truth.

"And you really are not engaged to him!" said she. "Yet it certainly soon will happen. But two advantages will proceed from this delay. *I* shall not lose you so soon, and Edward will have greater opportunity of improving that natural taste for your favourite pursuit, which must be so indispensably necessary to your future felicity. Oh! if he should be so far stimulated by your genius as to learn to draw himself, how delightful it would be!"

Elinor had given her real opinion to her sister. She could not consider her partiality for Edward in so prosperous a state as Marianne had believed it. There was, at times, a want of spirits about him, which, if it did not denote indifference, spoke a something almost as unpromising. A doubt of her regard, supposing him to feel it, need not give him more than inquietude. It would not be likely to produce that dejection of mind which frequently attended him. A more reasonable cause might be found in the dependent situation which forbade the indulgence of his affection. She knew that his mother neither behaved to him so as to make his home comfortable at present, nor to give him any assurance that he might form a home for himself, without strictly attending to her views for his aggrandisement. With such a knowledge as this, it was impossible for Elinor to feel easy on the subject. She was far from depending on that result of his preference of her, which her mother and sister still considered as certain. Nay, the longer they were together, the more doubtful seemed the nature of his regard; and sometimes, for a few painful minutes, she believed it to be no more than friendship.

But, whatever might really be its limits, it was enough, when perceived by his sister, to make her uneasy; and at the same time (which was still more common), to make her uncivil. She took the first opportunity of affronting her mother-in-law on the occasion, talking to her so expressively of her brother's great expectations, of Mrs. Ferrars's resolution that both her sons should marry well, and of the danger attending any young woman who attempted to *draw him in,* that Mrs. Dashwood could neither pretend to be unconscious, nor endeavour to be calm. She gave her an answer which marked her contempt, and instantly left the room, resolving that, whatever might be the inconvenience or expense of so sudden a removal, her beloved Elinor should not be exposed another week to such insinuations.

In this state of her spirits, a letter was delivered to her from the post, which contained a proposal particularly well-timed. It was the offer of a small house, on very easy terms, belonging to a relation of her own, a gentleman of consequence and property in Devonshire. The letter was from this gentleman himself, and written in the true spirit of friendly accommodation. He understood that she was in need of a dwelling, and though the house he now offered her was merely a cottage, he assured her that everything should be done to it which she might think necessary, if the situation pleased her. He earnestly pressed her, after giving the particulars of the house and garden, to come with her daughters to Barton Park, the place of his own residence, from whence she might judge herself whether Barton Cottage, for the houses were in the same parish, could by any alteration be made comfortable to her. He seemed really anxious to accommodate them, and the whole of his letter was written in so friendly a style as could not fail of giving pleasure to his cousin; more especially at a moment when she was suffering under the cold and unfeeling behaviour of her nearer connections. She needed no time for deliberation or inquiry. Her resolution was formed as she read. The situation of Barton, in a county so far distant from Sussex as Devonshire, which but a few hours before would have been a sufficient objection to outweigh every

possible advantage belonging to the place, was now its first recommendation. To quit the neighbourhood of Norland was no longer an evil;
it was an object of desire; it was a blessing in comparison of the misery
of continuing her daughter-in-law's guest; and to remove for ever from
that beloved place would be less painful than to inhabit or visit it while
such a woman was its mistress. She instantly wrote Sir John Middleton
her acknowledgment of his kindness, and her acceptance of his proposal;
and then hastened to show both letters to her daughters, that she might
be secure of their approbation before her answer were sent.

Elinor had always thought it would be more prudent for them to settle
at some distance from Norland than immediately amongst their present
acquaintances. On *that* head, therefore, it was not for her to oppose her
mother's intention of removing into Devonshire. The house, too, as described by Sir John, was on so simple a scale, and the rent so uncommonly moderate, as to leave her no right of objection on either point;
and, therefore, though it was not a plan which brought any charm to her
fancy, though it was a removal from the vicinity of Norland beyond
her wishes, she made no attempt to dissuade her mother from sending her
letter of acquiescence.

Chapter 5

No sooner was her answer dispatched, than Mrs. Dashwood indulged
herself in the pleasure of announcing to her son-in-law and his wife that
she was provided with a house, and should incommode them no longer
than till everything was ready for her inhabiting it. They heard her with
surprise. Mrs. John Dashwood said nothing; but her husband civilly
hoped that she would not be settled far from Norland. She had great
satisfaction in replying that she was going into Devonshire. Edward
turned hastily towards her on hearing this, and in a voice of surprise and
concern, which required no explanation to her, repeated, "Devonshire!
Are you indeed going there? So far from hence! And to what part of it?"
She explained the situation. It was within four miles northward of Exeter.

"It is but a cottage," she continued, "but I hope to see many of my
friends in it. A room or two can easily be added; and if my friends find
no difficulty in travelling so far to see me, I am sure I will find none in
accommodating them."

She concluded with a very kind invitation to Mr. and Mrs. John Dashwood to visit her at Barton; and to Edward she gave one with still
greater affection. Though her late conversation with her daughter-in-law
had made her resolve on remaining at Norland no longer than was unavoidable, it had not produced the smallest effect on her in that point to
which it principally tended. To separate Edward and Elinor was as far
from being her object as ever; and she wished to show Mrs. John Dash-

wood by this pointed invitation to her brother, how totally she disregarded her disapprobation of the match.

Mr. John Dashwood told his mother again and again how exceedingly
sorry he was that she had taken a house at such a distance from Norland
as to prevent his being of any service to her in removing her furniture.
He really felt conscientiously vexed on the occasion; for the very exertion
to which he had limited the performance of his promise to his father was
by this arrangement rendered impracticable. The furniture was all sent
round by water. It chiefly consisted of household linen, plate, china, and
books, with an handsome pianoforte of Marianne's. Mrs. John Dashwood
saw the packages depart with a sigh; she could not help feeling it hard
that as Mrs. Dashwood's income would be so trifling in comparison with
their own, she should have any handsome article of furniture.

Mrs. Dashwood took the house for a twelvemonth; it was ready furnished, and she might have immediate possession. No difficulty arose on
either side in the agreement; and she waited only for the disposal of her
effects at Norland, and to determine her future household, before she set
off for the west; and this, as she was exceedingly rapid in the performance
of everything that interested her, was soon done. The horses which were
left her by her husband had been sold soon after his death, and an opportunity now offering of disposing of her carriage, she agreed to sell that
likewise at the earnest advice of her eldest daughter. For the comfort of
her children, had she consulted only her own wishes, she would have kept
it; but the discretion of Elinor prevailed. *Her* wisdom, too, limited the
number of their servants to three—two maids and a man, with whom they
were speedily provided from amongst those who had formed their establishment at Norland.

The man and one of the maids were sent off immediately into Devonshire, to prepare the house for their mistress's arrival; for, as Lady
Middleton was entirely unknown to Mrs. Dashwood, she preferred going
directly to the cottage to being a visitor at Barton Park; and she relied so
undoubtingly on Sir John's description of the house, as to feel no curiosity
to examine it herself till she entered it as her own. Her eagerness to be
gone from Norland was preserved from diminution by the evident satisfaction of her daughter-in-law in the prospect of her removal; a satisfaction which was but feebly attempted to be concealed under a cold invitation to her to defer her departure. Now was the time when her
son-in-law's promise to his father might with particular propriety be
fulfilled. Since he had neglected to do it on first coming to the estate,
their quitting his house might be looked on as the most suitable period
for its accomplishment. But Mrs. Dashwood began shortly to give over
every hope of the kind, and to be convinced, from the general drift of his
discourse, that his assistance extended no further than their maintenance
for six months at Norland. He so frequently talked of the increasing
expense of housekeeping, and of the perpetual demands upon his purse
which a man of any consequence in the world was beyond calculation

exposed to, that he seemed rather to stand in need of more money himself than to have any design of giving money away.

In a very few weeks from the day which brought Sir John Middleton's first letter to Norland, everything was so far settled in their future abode, as to enable Mrs. Dashwood and her daughters to begin their journey.

Many were the tears shed by them in their last adieux to a place so much beloved. "Dear, dear Norland!" said Marianne, as she wandered alone before the house, on the last evening of their being there; "when shall I cease to regret you? when learn to feel at home elsewhere? O happy house! could you know what I suffer in now viewing you from this spot, from whence perhaps I may view you no more! and you, ye well-known trees! but you will continue the same. No leaf will decay because we are removed, nor any branch become motionless although we can observe you no longer! No; you will continue the same; unconscious of the pleasure or the regret you occasion, and insensible of any change in those who walk under your shade! But who will remain to enjoy you?"

Chapter 6

THE first part of their journey was performed in too melancholy a disposition to be otherwise than tedious and unpleasant. But as they drew towards the end of it, their interest in the appearance of a country which they were to inhabit overcame their dejection, and a view of Barton Valley as they entered it gave them cheerfulness. It was a pleasant, fertile spot, well wooded, and rich in pasture. After winding along it for more than a mile, they reached their own house. A small green court was the whole of its demesne in front; and a neat wicket gate admitted them into it.

As a house, Barton Cottage, though small, was comfortable and compact; but as a cottage it was defective, for the building was regular, the roof was tiled, the window-shutters were not painted green, nor were the walls covered with honeysuckles. A narrow passage led directly through the house into the garden behind. On each side of the entrance was a sitting-room, about sixteen feet square; and beyond them were the offices and the stairs. Four bedrooms and two garrets formed the rest of the house. It had not been built many years, and was in good repair. In comparison of Norland, it was poor and small indeed! but the tears which recollection called forth as they entered the house were soon dried away. They were cheered by the joy of the servants on their arrival, and each for the sake of the others resolved to appear happy. It was very early in September; the season was fine, and from first seeing the place under the advantage of good weather, they received an impression in its favour which was of material service in recommending it to their lasting approbation.

The situation of the house was good. High hills rose immediately behind, and at no great distance on each side; some of which were open downs, the others cultivated and woody. The village of Barton was chiefly on one of these hills, and formed a pleasant view from the cottage windows. The prospect in front was more extensive; it commanded the whole of the valley, and reached into the country beyond. The hills which surrounded the cottage terminated the valley in that direction; under another name, and in another course, it branched out again between two of the steepest of them.

With the size and furniture of the house Mrs. Dashwood was upon the whole well satisfied; for though her former style of life rendered many additions to the latter indispensable, yet to add and improve was a delight to her; and she had at this time ready money enough to supply all that was wanted of greater elegance to the apartments. "As for the house itself, to be sure," said she, "it is too small for our family; but we will make ourselves tolerably comfortable for the present, as it is too late in the year for improvements. Perhaps in the spring if I have plenty of money, as I dare say I shall, we may think about building. These parlours are both too small for such parties of our friends as I hope to see often collected here; and I have some thoughts of throwing the passage into one of them, with perhaps a part of the other, and so leave the remainder of that other for an entrance; this, with a new drawing-room, which may be easily added, and a bed-chamber and garret above, will make it a very snug little cottage. I could wish the stairs were handsome. But one must not expect everything; though I suppose it would be no difficult matter to widen them. I shall see how much I am beforehand with the world in the spring, and we will plan our improvements accordingly."

In the meanwhile, till all these alterations could be made from the savings of an income of five hundred a year by a woman who never saved in her life, they were wise enough to be contented with the house as it was; and each of them was busy in arranging their particular concerns, and endeavouring, by placing around them their books and other possessions, to form themselves a home. Marianne's pianoforte was unpacked and properly disposed of; and Elinor's drawings were affixed to the walls of their sitting-room.

In such employments as these they were interrupted soon after breakfast the next day by the entrance of their landlord, who called to welcome them to Barton, and to offer them every accommodation from his own house and garden in which theirs might at present be deficient. Sir John Middleton was a good-looking man about forty. He had formerly visited at Stanhill, but it was too long ago for his young cousins to remember him. His countenance was thoroughly good-humoured; and his manners were as friendly as the style of his letter. Their arrival seemed to afford him real satisfaction, and their comfort to be an object of real solicitude to him. He said much of his earnest desire of their living on the most sociable terms with his family, and pressed them so cordially to dine at

Barton Park every day till they were better settled at home, that, though his entreaties were carried to a point of perseverance beyond civility, they could not give offence. His kindness was not confined to words; for within an hour after he left them, a large basket full of garden stuff and fruit arrived from the Park, which was followed before the end of the day by a present of game. He insisted, moreover, on conveying all their letters to and from the post for them, and would not be denied the satisfaction of sending them his newspaper every day.

Lady Middleton had sent a very civil message by him, denoting her intention of waiting on Mrs. Dashwood as soon as she could be assured that her visit would be no inconvenience; and as this message was answered by an invitation equally polite, her ladyship was introduced to them the next day.

They were of course very anxious to see a person on whom so much of their comfort at Barton must depend; and the elegance of her appearance was favourable to their wishes. Lady Middleton was not more than six or seven and twenty; her face was handsome, her figure tall and striking, and her address graceful. Her manners had all the elegance which her husband's wanted. But they would have been improved by some share of his frankness and warmth; and her visit was long enough to detract something from their first admiration, by showing that, though perfectly well-bred, she was reserved, cold, and had nothing to say for herself beyond the most common-place inquiry or remark.

Conversation, however, was not wanted, for Sir John was very chatty, and Lady Middleton had taken the wise precaution of bringing with her their eldest child, a fine little boy about six years old, by which means there was one subject always to be recurred to by the ladies in case of extremity; for they had to inquire his name and age, admire his beauty, and ask him questions, which his mother answered for him, while he hung about her and held down his head, to the great surprise of her ladyship, who wondered at his being so shy before company, as he could make noise enough at home. On every formal visit a child ought to be of the party, by way of provision for discourse. In the present case it took up ten minutes to determine whether the boy were most like his father or mother, and in what particular he resembled either; for of course everybody differed, and everybody was astonished at the opinion of the others.

An opportunity was soon to be given to the Dashwoods of debating on the rest of the children, as Sir John would not leave the house without securing their promise of dining at the Park the next day.

Chapter 7

BARTON PARK was about half a mile from the cottage. The ladies had passed near it on their way along the valley, but it was screened from their view at home by the projection of an hill. The house was large and handsome; and the Middletons lived in a style of equal hospitality and elegance. The former was for Sir John's gratification, the latter for that of his lady. They were scarcely ever without some friends staying with them in the house, and they kept more company of every kind than any other family in the neighbourhood. It was necessary to the happiness of both; for, however dissimilar in temper and outward behaviour, they strongly resembled each other in that total want of talent and taste which confined their employments, unconnected with such as society produced, within a very narrow compass. Sir John was a sportsman, Lady Middleton a mother. He hunted and shot, and she humoured her children; and these were their only resources. Lady Middleton had the advantage of being able to spoil her children all the year round, while Sir John's independent employments were in existence only half the time. Continual engagements at home and abroad, however, supplied all the deficiencies of nature and education; supported the good spirits of Sir John, and gave exercise to the good breeding of his wife.

Lady Middleton piqued herself upon the elegance of her table, and of all her domestic arrangements; and from this kind of vanity was her greatest enjoyment in any of their parties. But Sir John's satisfaction in society was much more real; he delighted in collecting about him more young people than his house would hold, and the noisier they were the better was he pleased. He was a blessing to all the juvenile part of the neighbourhood, for in summer he was for ever forming parties to eat cold ham and chicken out of doors, and in winter his private balls were numerous enough for any young lady who was not suffering under the insatiable appetite of fifteen.

The arrival of a new family in the country was always a matter of joy to him, and in every point of view he was charmed with the inhabitants he had now procured for his cottage at Barton. The Miss Dashwoods were young, pretty, and unaffected. It was enough to secure his good opinion, for to be unaffected was all that a pretty girl could want to make her mind as captivating as her person. The friendliness of his disposition made him happy in accommodating those whose situation might be considered, in comparison with the past, as unfortunate. In showing kindness to his cousins, therefore, he had the real satisfaction of a good heart; and in settling a family of females only in his cottage, he had all the satisfaction of a sportsman; for a sportsman, though he esteems only those of his sex who are sportsman likewise, is not often desirous of encouraging their taste by admitting them to a residence within his own manor.

Mrs. Dashwood and her daughters were met at the door of the house by Sir John, who welcomed them to Barton Park with unaffected sincerity; and as he attended them to the drawing-room, repeated to the young ladies the concern which the same subject had drawn from him the day before, at being unable to get any smart young men to meet them. They would see, he said, only one gentleman there besides himself; a particular friend who was staying at the Park, but who was neither very young nor very gay. He hoped they would all excuse the smallness of the party, and could assure them it should never happen so again. He had been to several families that morning, in hopes of procuring some addition to their number; but it was moonlight, and everybody was full of engagements. Luckily, Lady Middleton's mother had arrived at Barton within the last hour, and as she was a very cheerful, agreeable woman, he hoped the young ladies would not find it so very dull as they might imagine. The young ladies, as well as their mother, were perfectly satisfied with having two entire strangers of the party, and wished no more.

Mrs. Jennings, Lady Middleton's mother, was a good-humoured, merry, fat, elderly woman, who talked a great deal, seemed very happy, and rather vulgar. She was full of jokes and laughter, and before dinner was over had said many witty things on the subject of lovers and husbands; hoped they had not left their hearts behind them in Sussex, and pretended to see them blush whether they did or not. Marianne was vexed at it for her sister's sake, and turned her eyes towards Elinor, to see how she bore these attacks, with an earnestness which gave Elinor far more pain than could arise from such commonplace raillery as Mrs. Jennings's.

Colonel Brandon, the friend of Sir John, seemed no more adapted by resemblance of manner to be his friend than Lady Middleton was to be his wife, or Mrs. Jennings to be Lady Middleton's mother. He was silent and grave. His appearance, however, was not unpleasing, in spite of his being, in the opinion of Marianne and Margaret, an absolute old bachelor, for he was on the wrong side of five-and-thirty; but though his face was not handsome, his countenance was sensible, and his address was particularly gentlemanlike.

There was nothing in any of the party which could recommend them as companions to the Dashwoods; but the cold insipidity of Lady Middleton was so particularly repulsive that in comparison of it the gravity of Colonel Brandon, and even the boisterous mirth of Sir John and his mother-in-law, was interesting. Lady Middleton seemed to be roused to enjoyment only by the entrance of her four noisy children after dinner, who pulled her about, tore her clothes, and put an end to every kind of discourse except what related to themselves.

In the evening, as Marianne was discovered to be musical, she was invited to play. The instrument was unlocked, everybody prepared to be charmed, and Marianne, who sang very well, at their request went through the chief of the songs which Lady Middleton had brought into the family on her marriage, and which perhaps had lain ever since in the same position on the pianoforte; for her ladyship had celebrated that event by giving up music, although by her mother's account she had played extremely well, and by her own was very fond of it.

Marianne's performance was highly applauded. Sir John was loud in his admiration at the end of every song, and as loud in his conversation with the others while every song lasted. Lady Middleton frequently called him to order, wondered how any one's attention could be diverted from music for a moment, and asked Marianne to sing a particular song which Marianne had just finished. Colonel Brandon alone, of all the party, heard her without being in raptures. He paid her only the compliment of attention; and she felt a respect for him on the occasion which the others had reasonably forfeited by their shameless want of taste. His pleasure in music, though it amounted not to that ecstatic delight which alone could sympathise with her own, was estimable when contrasted against the horrible insensibility of the others; and she was reasonable enough to allow that a man of five-and-thirty might well have outlived all acuteness of feeling and every exquisite power of enjoyment. She was perfectly disposed to make every allowance for the colonel's advanced state of life which humanity required.

Chapter 8

MRS. JENNINGS was a widow, with an ample jointure. She had only two daughters, both of whom she had lived to see respectably married, and she had now therefore nothing to do but to marry all the rest of the world. In the promotion of this object, she was zealously active, as far as her ability reached, and missed no opportunity of projecting weddings among all the young people of her acquaintance. She was remarkably quick in the discovery of attachments, and had enjoyed the advantage of raising the blushes and the vanity of many a young lady by insinuations of her power over such a young man; and this kind of discernment enabled her soon after her arrival at Barton, decisively to pronounce that Colonel Brandon was very much in love with Marianne Dashwood. She rather suspected it to be so, on the very first evening of their being together, from his listening so attentively while she sang to them; and when the visit was returned by the Middletons dining at the cottage, the fact was ascertained by his listening to her again. It must be so. She was perfectly convinced of it. It would be an excellent match, for *he* was rich and *she* was handsome. Mrs. Jennings had been anxious to see Colonel Brandon well married ever since her connection with Sir John first brought him to her knowledge; and she was always anxious to get a good husband for every pretty girl.

The immediate advantage to herself was by no means inconsiderable, for it supplied her with endless jokes against them both. At the Park she laughed at the colonel, and in the cottage at Marianne. To the former her raillery was probably, as far as it regarded only himself, perfectly indifferent; but to the latter it was at first incomprehensible; and when its object was understood, she hardly knew whether most to laugh at its absurdity, or censure its impertinence, for she considered it as an unfeeling reflection on the colonel's advanced years, and on his forlorn condition as an old bachelor.

Mrs. Dashwood, who could not think a man five years younger than herself so exceedingly ancient as he appeared to the youthful fancy of her daughter, ventured to clear Mrs. Jennings from the probability of wishing to throw ridicule on his age.

"But at least, mamma, you cannot deny the absurdity of the accusation, though you may not think it intentionally ill-natured. Colonel Brandon is certainly younger than Mrs. Jennings, but he is old enough to be *my* father; and if he were ever animated enough to be in love, must have long outlived every sensation of the kind. It is too ridiculous! When is a man to be safe from such wit, if age and infirmity will not protect him?"

"Infirmity!" said Elinor; "do you call Colonel Brandon infirm? I can easily suppose that his age may appear much greater to you than to my mother; but you can hardly deceive yourself as to his having the use of his limbs?"

"Did not you hear him complain of the rheumatism? and is not that the commonest infirmity of declining life?"

"My dearest child," said her mother, laughing, "at this rate, you must be in continual terror of *my* decay; and it must seem to you a miracle that my life has been extended to the advanced age of forty."

"Mamma, you are not doing me justice. I know very well that Colonel Brandon is not old enough to make his friends yet apprehensive of losing him in the course of Nature. He may live twenty years longer. But thirty-five has nothing to do with matrimony."

"Perhaps," said Elinor, "thirty-five and seventeen had better not have anything to do with matrimony together. But if there should by any chance happen to be a woman who is single at seven-and-twenty, I should not think Colonel Brandon's being thirty-five any objection to his marrying *her*."

"A woman of seven-and-twenty," said Marianne, after pausing a moment, "can never hope to feel or inspire affection again; and if her home be uncomfortable, or her fortune small, I can suppose that she might bring herself to submit to the offices of a nurse, for the sake of the provision and security of a wife. In his marrying such a woman, therefore, there would be nothing unsuitable. It would be a compact of convenience, and the world would be satisfied. In my eyes it would be no marriage at all, but that would be nothing. To me it would seem only a commercial exchange, in which each wished to be benefited at the expense of the other."

"It would be impossible, I know," replied Elinor, "to convince you that a woman of seven-and-twenty could feel for a man of thirty-five anything near enough to love to make him a desirable companion to her. But I must object to your dooming Colonel Brandon and his wife to the constant confinement of a sick chamber, merely because he chanced to complain yesterday (a very cold, damp day) of a slight rheumatic feel in one of his shoulders."

"But he talked of flannel waistcoats," said Marianne; "and with me a flannel waistcoat is invariably connected with aches, cramps, rheumatisms, and every species of ailment that can afflict the old and the feeble."

"Had he been only in a violent fever, you would not have despised him half so much. Confess, Marianne, is not there something interesting to you in the flushed cheek, hollow eye, and quick pulse of a fever?"

Soon after this, upon Elinor's leaving the room,

"Mamma," said Marianne, "I have an alarm on the subject of illness, which I cannot conceal from you. I am sure Edward Ferrars is not well. We have now been here almost a fortnight, and yet he does not come. Nothing but real indisposition could occasion this extraordinary delay. What else can detain him at Norland?"

"Had you any idea of his coming so soon?" said Mrs. Dashwood. "*I* had none. On the contrary, if I have felt any anxiety at all on the subject, it has been in recollecting that he sometimes showed a want of pleasure and readiness in accepting my invitation, when I talked of his coming to Barton. Does Elinor expect him already?"

"I have never mentioned it to her; but of course she must."

"I rather think you are mistaken, for, when I was talking to her yesterday of getting a new grate for the spare bed-chamber, she observed that there was no immediate hurry for it, as it was not likely that the room would be wanted for some time."

"How strange this is! What can be the meaning of it? But the whole of their behaviour to each other has been unaccountable! How cold, how composed were their last adieux! How languid their conversation the last evening of their being together! In Edward's farewell there was no distinction between Elinor and me: it was the good wishes of an affectionate brother to both. Twice did I leave them purposely together in the course of the last morning, and each time did he most unaccountably follow me out of the room. And Elinor, in quitting Norland and Edward, cried not as I did. Even now her self-command is invariable. When is she dejected or melancholy? When does she try to avoid society, or appear restless and dissatisfied in it?"

Chapter 9

THE Dashwoods were now settled at Barton with tolerable comfort to themselves. The house and the garden, with all the objects surrounding them, were now become familiar; and the ordinary pursuits which had given to Norland half its charms, were engaged in again with far greater enjoyment than Norland had been able to afford since the loss of their father. Sir John Middleton, who called on them every day for the first fortnight, and who was not in the habit of seeing much occupation at home, could not conceal his amazement on finding them always employed.

Their visitors, except those from Barton Park, were not many; for, in spite of Sir John's urgent entreaties that they would mix more in the neighbourhood, and repeated assurances of his carriage being always at their service, the independence of Mrs. Dashwood's spirit overcame the wish of society for her children; and she was resolute in declining to visit any family beyond the distance of a walk. There were but few who could be so classed; and it was not all of them that were attainable. About a mile and a half from the cottage, along the narrow winding valley of Allenham, which issued from that of Barton, as formerly described, the girls had, in one of their earliest walks, discovered an ancient respectable-looking mansion, which, by reminding them a little of Norland, interested their imagination, and made them wish to be better acquainted with it. But they learnt, on inquiry, that its possessor, an elderly lady of very good character, was unfortunately too infirm to mix with the world, and never stirred from home.

The whole country about them abounded in beautiful walks. The high downs, which invited them from almost every window of the cottage to seek the exquisite enjoyment of air on their summits, were a happy alternative when the dirt of the valleys beneath shut up their superior beauties; and towards one of these hills did Marianne and Margaret one memorable morning direct their steps, attracted by the partial sunshine of a showery sky, and unable longer to bear the confinement which the settled rain of the two preceding days had occasioned. The weather was not tempting enough to draw the two others from their pencil and their book, in spite of Marianne's declaration that the day would be lastingly fair, and that every threatening cloud would be drawn off from their hills; and the two girls set off together.

They gaily ascended the downs, rejoicing in their own penetration at every glimpse of blue sky: and when they caught in their faces the ani-mating gales of an high south-westerly wind, they pitied the fears which had prevented their mother and Elinor from sharing such delightful sensations.

"Is there a felicity in the world," said Marianne, "superior to this? Margaret, we will walk here at least two hours."

Margaret agreed, and they pursued their way against the wind, resist-ing it with laughing delight for about twenty minutes longer, when suddenly the clouds united over their heads, and a driving rain set full in their faces. Chagrined and surprised, they were obliged, though un-willingly, to turn back, for no shelter was nearer than their own house. One consolation, however, remained for them, to which the exigence of the moment gave more than usual propriety; it was that of running with all possible speed down the steep side of the hill which led immediately to their garden gate.

They set off. Marianne had at first the advantage, but a false step brought her suddenly to the ground, and Margaret, unable to stop her-self to assist her, was involuntarily hurried along, and reached the bottom in safety.

A gentleman carrying a gun, with two pointers playing round him, was passing up the hill and within a few yards of Marianne, when her accident happened. He put down his gun and ran to her assistance. She had raised herself from the ground, but her foot had been twisted in the fall, and she was scarcely able to stand. The gentleman offered his services, and perceiving that her modesty declined what her situation rendered necessary, took her up in his arms without further delay, and carried her down the hill. Then passing through the garden, the gate of which had been left open by Margaret, he bore her directly into the house, whither Margaret was just arrived, and quitted not his hold till he had seated her in a chair in the parlour.

Elinor and her mother rose up in amazement at their entrance, and while the eyes of both were fixed on him with an evident wonder and a secret admiration which equally sprung from his appearance, he apologised for his intrusion by relating its cause, in a manner so frank and so graceful, that his person, which was uncommonly handsome, received additional charms from his voice and expression. Had he been even old, ugly, and vulgar, the gratitude and kindness of Mrs. Dashwood would have been secured by any act of attention to her child; but the influence of youth, beauty, and elegance, gave an interest to the action which came home to her feelings.

She thanked him again and again, and with a sweetness of address which always attended her, invited him to be seated. But this he declined, as he was dirty and wet. Mrs. Dashwood then begged to know to whom she was obliged. His name, he replied, was Willoughby, and his present home was at Allenham, from whence he hoped she would allow him the honour of calling to-morrow to inquire after Miss Dashwood. The honour was readily granted, and he then departed, to make himself still more interesting, in the midst of an heavy rain.

His manly beauty and more than common gracefulness were instantly the theme of general admiration and the laugh which his gallantry raised against Marianne received particular spirit from his exterior attractions. Marianne herself had seen less of his person than the rest, for the confusion which crimsoned over her face, on his lifting her up, had robbed her of the power of regarding him after their entering the house. But she had seen enough of him to join in all the admiration of the others, and with an energy which always adorned her praise. His person and air were equal to what her fancy had ever drawn for the hero of a favourite story; and in his carrying her into the house with so little previous formality, there was a rapidity of thought which particularly recommended the action to her. Every circumstance belonging to him was interesting. His name was good, his residence was in their favourite village, and she soon found out that of all manly dresses a shooting-jacket was the most becoming. Her imagination was busy, her reflections were pleasant, and the pain of a sprained ankle was disregarded.

Sir John called on them as soon as the next interval of fair weather that morning allowed him to get out of doors; and Marianne's accident being related to him, he was eagerly asked whether he knew any gentleman of the name of Willoughby at Allenham.

"Willoughby!" cried Sir John; "what, is *he* in the country? That is good news, however; I will ride over to-morrow, and ask him to dinner on Thursday."

"You know him then?" said Mrs. Dashwood.

"Know him! to be sure I do. Why, he is down here every year."

"And what sort of a young man is he?"

"As good a kind of fellow as ever lived, I assure you. A very decent shot, and there is not a bolder rider in England."

"And is *that* all you can say for him!" cried Marianne indignantly. "But what are his manners on more intimate acquaintance? what his pursuits, his talents, and genius?"

Sir John was rather puzzled.

"Upon my soul," said he, "I do not know much about him as to all *that*. But he is a pleasant, good-humoured fellow, and has got the nicest little black bitch of a pointer I ever saw. Was she out with him to-day?"

But Marianne could no more satisfy him as to the colour of Mr. Willoughby's pointer than he could describe to her the shades of his mind.

"But who is he?" said Elinor. "Where does he come from? Has he a house at Allenham?"

On this point Sir John could give more certain intelligence; and he told them that Mr. Willoughby had no property of his own in the country; that he resided there only while he was visiting the old lady at Allenham Court, to whom he was related, and whose possessions he was to inherit; adding, "Yes, yes, he is very well worth catching, I can tell you, Miss Dashwood; he has a pretty little estate of his own in Somersetshire besides; and, if I were you, I would not give him up to my younger sister in spite of all this tumbling down hills. Miss Marianne must not expect to have all the men to herself. Brandon will be jealous, if she does not take care."

"I do not believe," said Mrs. Dashwood, with a good-humoured smile, "that Mr. Willoughby will be incommoded by the attempts of either of *my* daughters towards what you call *catching him*. It is not an employment to which they have been brought up. Men are very safe with us, let them be ever so rich. I am glad to find, however, from what you say, that he is a respectable young man, and one whose acquaintance will not be ineligible."

"He is as good a sort of fellow, I believe, as ever lived," repeated Sir John. "I remember last Christmas, at a little hop at the Park, he danced from eight o'clock till four, without once sitting down."

"Did he, indeed?" cried Marianne, with sparkling eyes, "and with elegance, with spirit?"

"Yes; and he was up again at eight to ride to covert."

"That is what I like; that is what a young man ought to be. Whatever be his pursuits, his eagerness in them should know no moderation, and leave him no sense of fatigue."

"Aye, aye, I see how it will be," said Sir John, "I see how it will be. You will be setting your cap at him now, and never think of poor Brandon."

"That is an expression, Sir John," said Marianne warmly, "which I particularly dislike. I abhor every commonplace phrase by which wit is intended; and 'setting one's cap at a man,' or 'making a conquest,' are the most odious of all. Their tendency is gross and illiberal; and if their construction could ever be deemed clever, time has long ago destroyed all its ingenuity."

Sir John did not much understand this reproof; but he laughed as heartily as if he did, and then replied,—

"Aye, you will make conquests enough, I dare say, one way or other. Poor Brandon! he is quite smitten already, and he is very well worth setting your cap at, I can tell you, in spite of all this tumbling about and spraining of ankles."

Chapter 10

MARIANNE's preserver, as Margaret, with more elegance than precision, styled Willoughby, called at the cottage early the next morning to make his personal inquiries. He was received by Mrs. Dashwood with more than politeness—with a kindness which Sir John's account of him and her own gratitude prompted; and everything that passed during the visit tended to assure him of the sense, elegance, mutual affection, and domestic comfort of the family to whom accident had now introduced him. Of their personal charms he had not required a second interview to be convinced.

Miss Dashwood had a delicate complexion, regular features, and a remarkably pretty figure. Marianne was still handsomer. Her form, though not so correct as her sister's, in having the advantage of height, was more striking; and her face was so lovely, that when, in the common cant of praise, she was called a beautiful girl, truth was less violently outraged than usually happens. Her skin was very brown, but, from its transparency, her complexion was uncommonly brilliant; her features were all good; her smile was sweet and attractive; and in her eyes, which were very dark, there was a life, a spirit, an eagerness, which could hardly be seen without delight. From Willoughby their expression was at first held back, by the embarrassment which the remembrance of his assistance created. But when this passed away, when her spirits became collected—when she saw that to the perfect good-breeding of the gentleman, he united frankness and vivacity, and, above all, when she heard him declare that of music and dancing he was passionately fond, she gave him such a look of approbation as secured the largest share of his discourse to herself for the rest of his stay.

It was only necessary to mention any favourite amusement to engage her to talk. She could not be silent when such points were introduced, and she had neither shyness nor reserve in their discussion. They speedily discovered that their enjoyment of dancing and music was mutual, and that it arose from a general conformity of judgment in all that related to either. Encouraged by this to a further examination of his opinions, she proceeded to question him on the subject of books; her favourite authors were brought forward and dwelt upon with so rapturous a delight, that any young man of five-and-twenty must have been insensible indeed, not to become an immediate convert to the excellence of such works, however disregarded before. Their taste was strikingly alike. The same books, the same passages were idolised by each—or, if any difference appeared, any objection arose, it lasted no longer than till the force of her arguments and the brightness of her eyes could be displayed. He acquiesced in all her decisions, caught all her enthusiasm, and long before his visit concluded, they conversed with the familiarity of a long-established acquaintance.

"Well, Marianne," said Elinor, as soon as he had left them, "for *one* morning I think you have done pretty well. You have already ascertained Mr. Willoughby's opinion in almost every matter of importance. You know what he thinks of Cowper and Scott; you are certain of his estimating their beauties as he ought, and you have received every assurance of his admiring Pope no more than is proper. But how is your acquaintance to be long supported, under such extraordinary dispatch of every subject for discourse! You will soon have exhausted each favourite topic. Another meeting will suffice to explain his sentiments on picturesque beauty and second marriages, and then you can have nothing farther to ask——"

"Elinor," cried Marianne, "is this fair? is this just? are my ideas so scanty? But I see what you mean. I have been too much at my ease, too happy, too frank. I have erred against every commonplace notion of decorum! I have been open and sincere when I ought to have been reserved, spiritless, dull, and deceitful. Had I talked only of the weather and the roads, and had I spoken only once in ten minutes this reproach would have been spared."

"My love," said her mother, "you must not be offended with Elinor—she was only in jest. I should scold her myself, if she were capable of wishing to check the delight of your conversation with our new friend." Marianne was softened in a moment.

Willoughby, on his side, gave every proof of his pleasure in their acquaintance which an evident wish of improving it could offer. He came to them every day. To inquire after Marianne was at first his excuse; but the encouragement of his reception, to which every day gave greater kindness, made such an excuse unnecessary before it had ceased to be possible by Marianne's perfect recovery. She was confined for some days to the house: but never had any confinement been less irksome. Willoughby was a young man of good abilities, quick imagination, lively spirits, and open, affectionate manners. He was exactly formed to engage Marianne's heart; for, with all this, he joined not only a captivating person, but a natural ardour of mind, which was now roused and increased by the example of her own, and which recommended him to her affection beyond everything else.

His society became gradually her most exquisite enjoyment. They read, they talked, they sang together; his musical talents were considerable; and he read with all the sensibility and spirit which Edward had unfortunately wanted.

In Mrs. Dashwood's estimation, he was as faultless as in Marianne's; and Elinor saw nothing to censure in him but a propensity in which he strongly resembled and peculiarly delighted her sister, of saying too much what he thought on every occasion, without attention to persons or circumstances. In hastily forming and giving his opinion of other people, in sacrificing general politeness to the enjoyment of undivided attention where his heart was engaged, and in slighting too easily the forms of worldly propriety, he displayed a want of caution which Elinor could not approve, in spite of all that he and Marianne could say in its support.

Marianne began now to perceive that the desperation which had seized her at sixteen and a half, of ever seeing a man who could satisfy her ideas of perfection, had been rash and unjustifiable. Willoughby was all that her fancy had delineated in that unhappy hour, and in every brighter period, as capable of attaching her; and his behaviour declared his wishes to be in that respect as earnest as his abilities were strong.

Her mother, too, in whose mind not one speculative thought of their marriage had been raised by his prospect of riches, was led before the end of a week to hope and expect it, and secretly to congratulate herself on having gained two such sons-in-law as Edward and Willoughby.

Colonel Brandon's partiality for Marianne, which had so early been discovered by his friends, now first became perceptible to Elinor, when it ceased to be noticed by them. Their attention and wit were drawn off to his more fortunate rival; and the raillery which the other had incurred before any partiality arose, was removed when his feelings began really to call for the ridicule so justly annexed to sensibility. Elinor was obliged, though unwillingly, to believe that the sentiments which Mrs. Jennings had assigned him for her own satisfaction, were now actually excited by her sister; and that however a general resemblance of disposition between the parties might forward the affection of Mr. Willoughby, an equally striking opposition of character was no hindrance to the regard of Colonel Brandon. She saw it with concern; for what could a silent man of five-and-thirty hope, when opposed by a very lively one of five-and-twenty? and as she could not even wish him successful, she heartily wished him indifferent. She liked him—in spite of his gravity and reserve, she beheld in him an object of interest. His manners, though serious, were mild; and his reserve appeared rather the result of some oppression of spirits, than of any natural gloominess of temper. Sir John had dropped hints of past injuries and disappointments, which justified her belief of his being an unfortunate man, and she regarded him with respect and compassion.

Perhaps she pitied and esteemed him the more because he was slighted by Willoughby and Marianne, who, prejudiced against him for being neither lively nor young, seemed resolved to undervalue his merits.

"Brandon is just the kind of man," said Willoughby one day, when they were talking of him together, "whom everybody speaks well of, and nobody cares about; whom all are delighted to see, and nobody remembers to talk to."

"That is exactly what I think of him," cried Marianne.

"Do not boast of it, however," said Elinor, "for it is injustice in both of you. He is highly esteemed by all the family at the Park, and I never see him myself without taking pains to converse with him."

"That he is patronised by *you*," replied Willoughby, "is certainly in his favour; but as for the esteem of the others, it is a reproach in itself. Who would submit to the indignity of being approved by such women as Lady Middleton and Mrs. Jennings, that could command the indifference of anybody else?"

"But perhaps the abuse of such people as yourself and Marianne will make amends for the regard of Lady Middleton and her mother. If their praise is censure, your censure may be praise; for they are not more undiscerning than you are prejudiced and unjust."

"In defence of your protégé, you can even be saucy."

"My protégé, as you call him, is a sensible man; and sense will always have attractions for me. Yes, Marianne, even in a man between thirty and forty. He has seen a great deal of the world; has been abroad; has read, and has a thinking mind, I have found him capable of giving me much information on various subjects, and he has always answered my inquiries with the readiness of good-breeding and good-nature."

"That is to say," cried Marianne contemptuously, "he has told you that in the East Indies the climate is hot, and the mosquitoes are troublesome."

"He *would* have told me so, I doubt not, had I made any such inquiries; but they happened to be points on which I had been previously informed."

"Perhaps," said Willoughby, "his observations may have extended to the existence of nabobs, gold mohrs, and palanquins."

"I may venture to say that *his* observations have stretched much farther than *your* candour. But why should you dislike him?"

"I do not dislike him. I consider him, on the contrary, as a very respectable man, who has everybody's good word and nobody's notice; who has more money than he can spend, more time than he knows how to employ, and two new coats every year."

"Add to which," cried Marianne, "that he has neither genius, taste, nor spirit. That his understanding has no brilliancy, his feelings no ardour, and his voice no expression."

"You decide on his imperfections so much in the mass," replied Elinor, "and so much on the strength of your own imagination, that the commendation *I* am able to give of him is comparatively cold and insipid. I can only pronounce him to be a sensible man, well-bred, well-informed, of gentle address, and, I believe, possessing an amiable heart."

"Miss Dashwood," cried Willoughby, "you are now using me unkindly. You are endeavouring to disarm me by reason, and to convince me against my will. But it will not do. You shall find me as stubborn as you can be artful. I have three unanswerable reasons for disliking Colonel Brandon: he has threatened me with rain when I wanted it to be fine; he has found fault with the hanging of my curricle, and I cannot persuade him to buy my brown mare. If it will be any satisfaction to you, however, to be told that I believe his character to be in other respects irreproachable, I am ready to confess it. And in return for an acknowledgment which must give me some pain, you cannot deny me the privilege of disliking him as much as ever."

Chapter 11

LITTLE had Mrs. Dashwood or her daughters imagined, when they came first into Devonshire, that so many engagements would arise to occupy their time as shortly presented themselves, or that they should have such frequent invitations and such constant visitors as to leave them little leisure for serious employment. Yet such was the case. When Marianne was recovered, the schemes of amusements at home and abroad which Sir John had been previously forming were put in execution. The private balls at the Park then began; and parties on the water were made and accomplished as often as a showery October would allow. In every meeting of the kind, Willoughby was included; and the ease and familiarity which naturally attended these parties were exactly calculated to give increasing intimacy to his acquaintance with the Dashwoods, to afford him opportunity of witnessing the excellences of Marianne, of marking his animated admiration of her, and of receiving, in her behaviour to himself, the most pointed assurance of her affection.

Elinor could not be surprised at their attachment. She only wished that it were less openly shown, and once or twice did venture to suggest the propriety of some self-command to Marianne. But Marianne abhorred all concealment where no real disgrace could attend unreserve; and to aim at the restraint of sentiments which were not in themselves illaudable, appeared to her not merely an unnecessary effort, but a disgraceful subjection of reason to commonplace and mistaken notions. Willoughby thought the same; and their behaviour, at all times, was an illustration of their opinions.

When he was present, she had no eyes for any one else. Everything he did was right. Everything he said was clever. If their evenings at the Park were concluded with cards, he cheated himself and all the rest of the party to get her a good hand. If dancing formed the amusement of the night, they were partners for half the time; and when obliged to separate for a couple of dances, were careful to stand together, and scarcely spoke a word to anybody else. Such conduct made them of course most exceedingly laughed at; but ridicule could not shame, and seemed hardly to provoke them.

Mrs. Dashwood entered into all their feelings with a warmth which left her no inclination for checking this excessive display of them. To her it was but the natural consequence of a strong affection in a young and ardent mind.

This was the season of happiness to Marianne. Her heart was devoted to Willoughby, and the fond attachment to Norland which she brought with her from Sussex, was more likely to be softened than she had thought it possible before, by the charms which his society bestowed on her present home.

Elinor's happiness was not so great. Her heart was not so much at ease, nor her satisfaction in their amusements so pure. They afforded her no companion that could make amends for what she had left behind, nor that could teach her to think of Norland with less regret than ever. Neither Lady Middleton nor Mrs. Jennings could supply to her the conversation she missed; although the latter was an everlasting talker, and from the first had regarded her with a kindness which ensured her a large share of her discourse. She had already repeated her own history to Elinor three or four times; and had Elinor's memory been equal to her means of improvement, she might have known very early in her acquaintance all the particulars of Mr. Jennings's last illness, and what he said to his wife a few minutes before he died. Lady Middleton was more agreeable than her mother only in being more silent. Elinor needed little observation to perceive that her reserve was a mere calmness of manner with which sense had nothing to do. Towards her husband and mother she was the same as to them; an intimacy was therefore neither to be looked for nor desired. She had nothing to say one day that she had not said the day before. Her insipidity was invariable, for even her spirits were always the same; and though she did not oppose the parties arranged by her husband, provided everything were conducted in style and her two eldest children attended her, she never appeared to receive more enjoyment from them, than she might have experienced in sitting at home; and so little did her presence add to the pleasure of the others, by any share in their conversation, that they were sometimes only reminded of her being amongst them by her solicitude about her troublesome boys.

In Colonel Brandon alone, of all her new acquaintance, did Elinor find

a person who could in any degree claim the respect of abilities, excite the
interest of friendship, or give pleasure as a companion. Willoughby was
out of the question. Her admiration and regard, even her sisterly regard,
was all his own: but he was a lover; his attentions were wholly Marianne's,
and a far less agreeable man might have been more generally pleasing.
Colonel Brandon, unfortunately for himself, had no such encouragement
to think only of Marianne, and in conversing with Elinor, he found the
greatest consolation for the total indifference of her sister.

Elinor's compassion for him increased, as she had reason to suspect
that the misery of disappointed love had already been known by him. This
suspicion was given by some words which accidentally dropped from him
one evening at the Park, when they were sitting down together by mutual
consent, while the others were dancing. His eyes were fixed on Marianne,
and, after a silence of some minutes, he said with a faint smile, "Your
sister, I understand, does not approve of second attachments."

"No," replied Elinor; "her opinions are all romantic."

"Or rather, as I believe, she considers them impossible to exist."

"I believe she does. But how she contrives it without reflecting on the
character of her own father, who had himself two wives, I know not. A
few years, however, will settle her opinions on the reasonable basis of
common sense and observation; and then they may be more easy to
define and to justify than they now are, by anybody but herself."

"This will probably be the case," he replied; "and yet there is something so amiable in the prejudices of a young mind, that one is sorry to
see them give way to the reception of more general opinions."

"I cannot agree with you there," said Elinor. "There are inconveniences
attending such feelings as Marianne's, which all the charms of enthusiasm
and ignorance of the world cannot atone for. Her systems have all the
unfortunate tendency of setting propriety at nought; and a better
acquaintance with the world is what I look forward to as her greatest
possible advantage."

After a short pause, he resumed the conversation, by saying—

"Does your sister make no distinction in her objections against a
second attachment? or is it equally criminal in everybody? Are those who
have been disappointed in their first choice, whether from the inconstancy
of its object, or the perverseness of circumstances, to be equally indifferent during the rest of their lives?"

"Upon my word, I am not acquainted with the minutiæ of her principles. I only know that I never yet heard her admit any instance of a
second attachment's being pardonable."

"This," said he, "cannot hold; but a change, a total change of sentiments—No, no, do not desire it, for when the romantic refinements of a
young mind are obliged to give way, how frequently are they succeeded
by such opinions as are but too common, and too dangerous! I speak from
experience. I once knew a lady who in temper and mind greatly resembled
your sister, who thought and judged like her, but who from an enforced

change—from a series of unfortunate circumstances——" Here he stopped suddenly; appeared to think that he had said too much, and by his countenance gave rise to conjectures which might not otherwise have entered Elinor's head. The lady would probably have passed without suspicion, had he not convinced Miss Dashwood that what concerned her ought not to escape his lips. As it was, it required but a slight effort of fancy to connect his emotion with the tender recollection of past regard. Elinor attempted no more. But Marianne, in her place, would not have done so little. The whole story would have been speedily formed under her active imagination, and everything established in the most melancholy order of disastrous love.

Chapter 12

As Elinor and Marianne were walking together the next morning, the latter communicated a piece of news to her sister, which, in spite of all that she knew before of Marianne's imprudence and want of thought, surprised her by its extravagant testimony of both. Marianne told her, with the greatest delight, that Willoughby had given her a horse, one that he had bred himself on his estate in Somersetshire, and which was exactly calculated to carry a woman. Without considering that it was not in her mother's plan to keep any horse—that if she were to alter her resolution in favour of this gift, she must buy another for the servant, and keep a servant to ride it, and after all, build a stable to receive them—she had accepted the present without hesitation, and told her sister of it in raptures.

"He intends to send his groom into Somersetshire immediately for it," she added, "and when it arrives, we will ride every day. You shall share its use with me. Imagine to yourself, my dear Elinor, the delight of a gallop on some of these downs."

Most unwilling was she to awaken from such a dream of felicity, to comprehend all the unhappy truths which attended the affair, and for some time she refused to submit to them. As to an additional servant, the expense would be a trifle; mamma, she was sure, would never object to it; and any horse would do for *him;* he might always get one at the Park; as to a stable, the merest shed would be sufficient. Elinor then ventured to doubt the propriety of her receiving such a present from a man so little, or at least so lately known to her. This was too much.

"You are mistaken, Elinor," said she warmly, "in supposing I know very little of Willoughby. I have not known him long indeed, but I am much better acquainted with him than I am with any other creature in the world, except yourself and mamma. It is not time or opportunity that is to determine intimacy: it is disposition alone. Seven years would be insufficient to make some people acquainted with each other, and seven days are more than enough for others. I should hold myself guilty of greater impropriety in accepting a horse from my brother than from Willoughby. Of John I know very little, though we have lived together for years; but of Willoughby, my judgment has long been formed."

Elinor thought it wisest to touch that point no more. She knew her sister's temper. Opposition on so tender a subject would only attach her the more to her own opinion. But by an appeal to her affection for her mother, by representing the inconveniences which that indulgent mother must draw on herself, if (as would probably be the case) she consented to this increase of establishment, Marianne was shortly subdued; and she promised not to tempt her mother to such imprudent kindness by men- tioning the offer, and to tell Willoughby when she saw him next, that it must be declined.

She was faithful to her word; and when Willoughby called at the cottage, the same day, Elinor heard her express her disappointment to him in a low voice, on being obliged to forego the acceptance of his present. The reasons for this alteration were at the same time related, and they were such as to make further entreaty on his side impossible. His concern, however, was very apparent; and after expressing it with earnestness, he added in the same low voice—"But, Marianne, the horse is still yours though you cannot use it now. I shall keep it only till you can claim it. When you leave Barton to form your own establishment in a more lasting home, Queen Mab shall receive you."

This was all overheard by Miss Dashwood; and in the whole of the sentence, in his manner of pronouncing it, and in his addressing her sister by her Christian name alone, she instantly saw an intimacy so decided, a meaning so direct, as marked a perfect agreement between them. From that moment she doubted not of their being engaged to each other; and the belief of it created no other surprise, than that she, or any of their friends, should be left by tempers so frank to discover it by accident.

Margaret related something to her the next day, which placed this matter in a still clearer light. Willoughby had spent the preceding evening with them, and Margaret, by being left some time in the parlour with only him and Marianne, had had opportunity for observations, which, with a most important face, she communicated to her eldest sister, when they were next by themselves.

"Oh! Elinor," she cried, "I have such a secret to tell you about Marianne. I am sure she will be married to Mr. Willoughby very soon."

"You have said so," replied Elinor, "almost every day since they first met on High-church Down; and they had not known each other a week, I believe, before you were certain that Marianne wore his picture round her neck; but it turned out to be only the miniature of our great-uncle."

"But indeed this is quite another thing. I am sure they will be married very soon, for he has got a lock of her hair."

"Take care, Margaret. It may be only the hair of some great-uncle of *his*."

"But indeed, Elinor, it is Marianne's. I am almost sure it is, for I saw him cut it off. Last night after tea, when you and mamma went out of the room, they were whispering and talking together as fast as could be, and he seemed to be begging something of her, and presently he took up her scissors and cut off a long lock of her hair, for it was all tumbled down her back; and he kissed it, and folded it up in a piece of white paper, and put it into his pocket-book."

From such particulars, stated on such authority, Elinor could not withhold her credit: nor was she disposed to it, for the circumstance was in perfect unison with what she had heard and seen herself.

Margaret's sagacity was not always displayed in a way so satisfactory to her sister. When Mrs. Jennings attacked her one evening at the Park, to give the name of the young man who was Elinor's particular favourite, which had been long a matter of great curiosity to her, Margaret answered by looking at her sister, and saying, "I must not tell, may I, Elinor?"

This, of course, made everybody laugh; and Elinor tried to laugh too. But the effort was painful. She was convinced that Margaret had fixed on a person whose name she could not bear with composure to become a standing joke with Mrs. Jennings.

Marianne felt for her most sincerely; but she did more harm than good to the cause, by turning very red, and saying in an angry manner to Margaret,

"Remember, that whatever your conjectures may be, you have no right to repeat them."

"I never had any conjectures about it," replied Margaret; "it was you who told me of it yourself."

This increased the mirth of the company, and Margaret was eagerly pressed to say something more.

"Oh! pray, Miss Margaret, let us know all about it," said Mrs. Jennings. "What is the gentleman's name?"

"I must not tell, ma'am. But I know very well what it is; and I know where he is too."

"Yes, yes, we can guess where he is; at his own house at Norland, to be sure. He is the curate of the parish, I dare say."

"No, *that* he is not. He is of no profession at all."

"Margaret," said Marianne, with great warmth, "you know that all this is an invention of your own, and that there is no such person in existence."

"Well, then, he is lately dead, Marianne, for I am sure there was such a man once, and his name begins with an F."

Most grateful did Elinor feel to Lady Middleton for observing at this moment, "that it rained very hard," though she believed the interruption to proceed less from any attention to her, than from her ladyship's great dislike of all such inelegant subjects of raillery as delighted her husband and mother. The idea, however, started by her, was immediately pursued by Colonel Brandon, who was on every occasion mindful of the feelings of others; and much was said on the subject of rain by both of them.

Willoughby opened the pianoforte, and asked Marianne to sit down to it; and thus, amidst the various endeavours of different people to quit the topic, it fell to the ground. But not so easily did Elinor recover from the alarm into which it had thrown her.

A party was formed this evening for going on the following day to see a very fine place about twelve miles from Barton, belonging to a brother-in-law of Colonel Brandon, without whose interest it could not be seen, as the proprietor, who was then abroad, had left strict orders on that head. The grounds were declared to be highly beautiful, and Sir John, who was particularly warm in their praise, might be allowed to be a tolerable judge, for he had formed parties to visit them, at least, twice every summer for the last ten years. They contained a noble piece of water; a sail on which was to form a great part of the morning's amusement; cold provisions were to be taken, open carriages only to be employed, and everything conducted in the usual style of a complete party of pleasure.

To some few of the company it appeared rather a bold undertaking, considering the time of year, and that it had rained every day for the last fortnight; and Mrs. Dashwood, who had already a cold, was persuaded by Elinor to stay at home.

Chapter 13

THEIR intended excursion to Whitwell turned out very differently from what Elinor had expected. She was prepared to be wet through, fatigued, and frightened; but the event was still more unfortunate, for they did not go at all.

By ten o'clock the whole party were assembled at the Park, where they were to breakfast. The morning was rather favourable, though it had rained all night, as the clouds were then dispersing across the sky, and the sun frequently appeared. They were all in high spirits and good humour, eager to be happy, and determined to submit to the greatest inconveniences and hardships rather than be otherwise.

While they were at breakfast, the letters were brought in. Among the rest there was one for Colonel Brandon; he took it, looked at the direction, changed colour, and immediately left the room.

"What is the matter with Brandon?" said Sir John.

Nobody could tell.

"I hope he has had no bad news," said Lady Middleton. "It must be something extraordinary that could make Colonel Brandon leave my breakfast-table so suddenly."

In about five minutes he returned.

"No bad news, Colonel, I hope?" said Mrs. Jennings, as soon as he entered the room.

"None at all, ma'am, I thank you."

"Was it from Avignon? I hope it is not to say that your sister is worse?"

"No, ma'am. It came from town, and is merely a letter of business."

"But how came the hand to discompose you so much, if it was only a letter of business? Come, come, this won't do, Colonel; so let us hear the truth of it."

"My dear madam," said Lady Middleton, "recollect what you are saying."

"Perhaps it is to tell you that your cousin Fanny is married?" said Mrs. Jennings, without attending to her daughter's reproof.

"No, indeed, it is not."

"Well, then, I know who it is from, Colonel. And I hope she is well."

"Whom do you mean, ma'am?" said he, colouring a little.

"Oh! you know who I mean."

"I am particularly sorry, ma'am," said he, addressing Lady Middleton, "that I should receive this letter to-day, for it is on business which requires my immediate attendance in town."

"In town!" cried Mrs. Jennings. "What can you have to do in town at this time of year?"

"My own loss is great," he continued, "in being obliged to leave so agreeable a party; but I am the more concerned, as I fear my presence is necessary to gain your admittance at Whitwell."

What a blow upon them all was this!

"But if you write a note to the housekeeper, Mr. Brandon," said Marianne, eagerly, "will it not be sufficient?"

He shook his head.

"We must go," said Sir John. "It shall not be put off when we are so near it. You cannot go to town till to-morrow, Brandon, that is all."

"I wish it could be so easily settled. But it is not in my power to delay my journey for one day!"

"If you would but let us know what your business is," said Mrs. Jennings, "we might see whether it could be put off or not."

"You would not be six hours later," said Willoughby, "if you were to defer your journey till our return."

"I cannot afford to lose *one* hour."

Elinor then heard Willoughby say in a low voice to Marianne, "There are some people who cannot bear a party of pleasure. Brandon is one of them. He was afraid of catching cold, I dare say, and invented this trick for getting out of it. I would lay fifty guineas the letter was of his own writing."

"I have no doubt of it," replied Marianne.

"There is no persuading you to change your mind, Brandon, I know of old," said Sir John, "when once you are determined on anything. But, however, I hope you will think better of it. Consider, here are the two Miss Careys come over from Newton, the three Miss Dashwoods walked up from the cottage, and Mr. Willoughby got up two hours before his usual time, on purpose to go to Whitwell."

Colonel Brandon again repeated his sorrow at being the cause of disappointing the party, but at the same time declared it to be unavoidable.

"Well then, when will you come back again?"

"I hope we shall see you at Barton," added her ladyship, "as soon as you can conveniently leave town; and we must put off the party to Whitwell till you return."

"You are very obliging. But it is so uncertain when I may have it in my power to return, that I dare not engage for it at all."

"Oh! he must and shall come back," cried Sir John. "If he is not here by the end of the week, I shall go after him."

"Aye, so do, Sir John," cried Mrs. Jennings, "and then perhaps you may find out what his business is."

"I do not want to pry into other men's concerns; I suppose it is something he is ashamed of."

Colonel Brandon's horses were announced.

"You do not go to town on horseback, do you?" added Sir John.

"No—only to Honiton. I shall then go post."

"Well, as you are resolved to go, I wish you a good journey. But you had better change your mind."

"I assure you it is not in my power."

He then took leave of the whole party.

"Is there no chance of my seeing you and your sisters in town this winter, Miss Dashwood?"

"I am afraid none at all."

"Then I must bid you farewell for a longer time than I should wish to do."

To Marianne he merely bowed and said nothing.

"Come, Colonel," said Mrs. Jennings, "before you go, do let us know what you are going about."

He wished her a good morning, and, attended by Sir John, left the room.

The complaints and lamentations which politeness had hitherto restrained, now burst forth universally; and they all agreed again and again how provoking it was to be so disappointed.

"I can guess what his business is, however," said Mrs. Jennings exultingly.

"Can you, ma'am?" said almost everybody.

"Yes; it is about Miss Williams, I am sure."

"And who is Miss Williams?" asked Marianne.

"What! do not you know who Miss Williams is? I am sure you must have heard of her before. She is a relation of the Colonel's, my dear—a very near relation. We will not say how near, for fear of shocking the young ladies." Then lowering her voice a little, she said to Elinor, "She is his natural daughter."

"Indeed!"

"Oh! yes; and as like him as she can stare. I dare say the Colonel will leave her all his fortune."

When Sir John returned, he joined most heartily in the general regret on so unfortunate an event; concluding, however, by observing, that as they were all got together, they must do something by way of being happy; and after some consultation it was agreed, that although happiness could only be enjoyed at Whitwell, they might procure a tolerable composure of mind by driving about the country. The carriages were then ordered; Willoughby's was first, and Marianne never looked happier than when she got into it. He drove through the Park very fast, and they were soon out of sight; and nothing more of them was seen till their return, which did not happen till after the return of all the rest. They both seemed delighted with their drive, but said only in general terms that they had kept in the lanes, while the others went on the downs.

It was settled that there should be a dance in the evening, and that everybody should be extremely merry all day long. Some more of the Careys came to dinner, and they had the pleasure of sitting down nearly twenty to table, which Sir John observed with great contentment. Willoughby took his usual place between the two elder Miss Dashwoods. Mrs. Jennings sat on Elinor's right hand; and they had not been long seated, before she leant behind her and Willoughby, and said to Marianne, loud enough for them both to hear: "I have found you out, in spite of all your tricks. I know where you spent the morning."

Marianne coloured, and replied very hastily, "Where, pray?"

"Did not you know," said Willoughby, "that we had been out in my curricle?"

"Yes, yes, Mr. Impudence, I know that very well, and I was determined to find out *where* you had been to. I hope you like your house, Miss Marianne. It is a very large one, I know, and when I come to see you, I hope you will have new-furnished it, for it wanted it very much when I was there six years ago."

Marianne turned away in great confusion. Mrs. Jennings laughed heartily; and Elinor found that in her resolution to know where they had been, she had actually made her own woman inquire of Mr. Willoughby's groom, and that she had by that method been informed that they had gone to Allenham, and spent a considerable time there in walking about the garden, and going all over the house.

Elinor could hardly believe this to be true, as it seemed very unlikely that Willoughby should propose, or Marianne consent, to enter the house while Mrs. Smith was in it, with whom Marianne had not the smallest acquaintance.

As soon as they left the dining-room, Elinor inquired of her about it; and great was her surprise when she found that every circumstance related by Mrs. Jennings was perfectly true. Marianne was quite angry with her for doubting it.

"Why should you imagine, Elinor, that we did not go there, or that we did not see the house? Is not it what you have often wished to do yourself?"

"Yes, Marianne, but I would not go while Mrs. Smith was there, and with no other companion than Mr. Willoughby."

"Mr. Willoughby, however, is the only person who can have a right to show that house; and as he went in an open carriage, it was impossible to have any other companion. I never spent a pleasanter morning in my life."

"I am afraid," replied Elinor, "that the pleasantness of an employment does not always evince its propriety."

"On the contrary, nothing can be a stronger proof of it, Elinor; for if there had been any real impropriety in what I did, I should have been sensible of it at the time, for we always know when we are acting wrong, and with such a conviction I could have had no pleasure."

"But, my dear Marianne, as it has already exposed you to some very impertinent remarks, do you not now begin to doubt the discretion of your own conduct?"

"If the impertinent remarks of Mrs. Jennings are to be the proof of impropriety in conduct, we are all offending every moment of all our lives. I value not her censure any more than I should do her commendation. I am not sensible of having done anything wrong in walking over Mrs. Smith's grounds, or in seeing her house. They will one day be Mr. Willoughby's, and——"

"If they were one day to be your own, Marianne, you would not be justified in what you have done."

She blushed at this hint; but it was even visibly gratifying to her; and after a ten minutes' interval of earnest thought, she came to her sister again, and said with great good humour, "Perhaps, Elinor, it *was* rather ill-judged in me to go to Allenham; but Mr. Willoughby wanted particularly to show me the place; and it is a charming house, I assure you. There is one remarkably pretty sitting-room upstairs, of a nice comfortable size for constant use, and with modern furniture it would be delightful. It is a corner room, and has windows on two sides. On one side you look across the bowling-green, behind the house, to a beautiful hanging wood; and on the other you have a view of the church and village, and, beyond them, of those fine bold hills that we have so often admired. I did not see it to advantage, for nothing could be more forlorn than the furniture—but if it were newly fitted up—a couple of hundred pounds, Willoughby says, would make it one of the pleasantest summer-rooms in England."

Could Elinor have listened to her without interruption from the others, she would have described every room in the house with equal delight.

Chapter 14

THE sudden termination of Colonel Brandon's visit at the Park, with his steadiness in concealing its cause, filled the mind and raised the

wonder of Mrs. Jennings for two or three days: she was a great won-
derer, as everyone must be who takes a very lively interest in all the
comings and goings of all their acquaintance. She wondered with little
intermission what could be the reason of it; was sure there must be some
bad news, and thought over every kind of distress that could have
befallen him, with a fixed determination that he should not escape
them all.

"Something very melancholy must be the matter, I am sure," said she.
"I could see it in his face. Poor man! I am afraid his circumstances may
be bad. The estate at Delaford was never reckoned more than two thousand a year, and his brother left everything sadly involved. I do think he
must have been sent for about money matters, for what else can it be?
I wonder whether it is so. I would give anything to know the truth of it.
Perhaps it is about Miss Williams—and, by the bye, I dare say it is,
because he looked so conscious when I mentioned her. Maybe she is ill in
town; nothing in the world more likely, for I have a notion she is always
rather sickly. I would lay any wager it is about Miss Williams. It is not
so very likely he should be distressed in his circumstances *now*, for he is
a very prudent man, and to be sure must have cleared the estate by this
time. I wonder what it can be! Maybe his sister is worse at Avignon, and
has sent for him over. His setting off in such a hurry seems very like it.
Well, I wish him out of all his trouble with all my heart, and a good wife
into the bargain."

So wondered, so talked Mrs. Jennings; her opinion varying with every
fresh conjecture, and all seeming equally probable as they arose. Elinor,
though she felt really interested in the welfare of Colonel Brandon, could
not bestow all the wonder on his going so suddenly away which Mrs.
Jennings was desirous of her feeling; for besides that the circumstances
did not in her opinion justify such lasting amazement or variety of specu-
ulation, her wonder was otherwise disposed of. It was engrossed by the
extraordinary silence of her sister and Willoughby on the subject, which
they must know to be peculiarly interesting to them all. As this silence
continued, every day made it appear more strange and more incompatible
with the disposition of both. Why they should not openly acknowledge
to her mother and herself, what their constant behaviour to each other
declared to have taken place, Elinor could not imagine.

She could easily conceive that marriage might not be immediately in
their power; for though Willoughby was independent, there was no reason
to believe him rich. His estate had been rated by Sir John at about six
or seven hundred a year; but he lived at an expense to which that income
could hardly be equal, and he had himself often complained of his poverty.
But for this strange kind of secrecy maintained by them relative to their
engagement, which in fact concealed nothing at all, she could not account;
and it was so wholly contradictory to their general opinions and practice,
that a doubt sometimes entered her mind of their being really engaged,

and this doubt was enough to prevent her making any inquiry of Marianne.

Nothing could be more expressive of attachment to them all than Willoughby's behaviour. To Marianne it had all the distinguishing tenderness which a lover's heart could give, and to the rest of the family it was the affectionate attention of a son and a brother. The cottage seemed to be considered and loved by him as his home; many more of his hours were spent there than at Allenham; and if no general engagement collected them at the Park, the exercise which called him out in the morning was almost certain of ending there, where the rest of the day was spent by himself at the side of Marianne, and by his favourite pointer at her feet.

One evening in particular, about a week after Colonel Brandon had left the country, his heart seemed more than usually open to every feeling of attachment to the objects around him; and on Mrs. Dashwood's happening to mention her design of improving the cottage in the spring, he warmly opposed every alteration of a place which affection had established as perfect with him.

"What!" he exclaimed; "improve this dear cottage. No—*that* I will never consent to. Not a stone must be added to its walls, not an inch to its size, if my feelings are regarded."

"Do not be alarmed," said Miss Dashwood; "nothing of the kind will be done; for my mother will never have money enough to attempt it."

"I am heartily glad of it," he cried. "May she always be poor if she can employ her riches no better."

"Thank you, Willoughby. But you may be assured that I would not sacrifice one sentiment of local attachment of yours, or of anyone whom I loved, for all the improvements in the world. Depend upon it, that whatever unemployed sum may remain when I make up my accounts in the spring, I would even rather lay it uselessly by than dispose of it in a manner so painful to you. But are you really so attached to this place as to see no defect in it?"

"I am," said he. "To me it is faultless. Nay, more, I consider it as the only form of building in which happiness is attainable; and were I rich enough, I would instantly pull Combe down, and build it up again in the exact plan of this cottage."

"With dark narrow stairs, and a kitchen that smokes, I suppose," said Elinor.

"Yes," cried he in the same eager tone, "with all and everything belonging to it; in no one convenience or *in*convenience about it, should the least variation be perceptbile. Then, and then only, under such a roof, I might perhaps be as happy at Combe as I have been at Barton."

"I flatter myself," replied Elinor, "that even under the disadvantage of better rooms and a broader staircase, you will hereafter find your own house as faultless as you now do this."

"There certainly are circumstances," said Willoughby, "which might greatly endear it to me; but this place will always have one claim on my affection which no other can possibly share."

Mrs. Dashwood looked with pleasure at Marianne, whose fine eyes were fixed so expressively on Willoughby, as plainly denoted how well she understood him.

"How often did I wish," added he, "when I was at Allenham this time twelvemonth, that Barton Cottage were inhabited! I never passed within view of it without admiring its situation, and grieving that no one should live in it. How little did I then think that the very first news I should hear from Mrs. Smith, when I next came into the country, would be that Barton Cottage was taken! And I felt an immediate satisfaction and interest in the event, which nothing but a kind of prescience of what happiness I should experience from it can account for. Must it not have been so, Marianne?" speaking to her in a lowered voice. Then continuing his former tone, he said: "And yet this house you would spoil, Mrs. Dashwood! You would rob it of its simplicity by imaginary improvement! And this dear parlour, in which our acquaintance first began, and in which so many happy hours have been since spent by us together, you would degrade to a condition of common entrance, and everybody would be eager to pass through the room which has hitherto contained within itself more real accommodation and comfort than any other apartment of the handsomest dimensions in the world could possibly afford."

Mrs. Dashwood again assured him that no alteration of the kind should be attempted.

"You are a good woman," he warmly replied. "Your promise makes me easy. Extend it a little farther, and it will make me happy. Tell me that not only your house will remain the same, but that I shall ever find you and yours as unchanged as your dwelling; and that you will always consider me with the kindness which has made everything belonging to you so dear to me."

The promise was readily given, and Willoughby's behaviour during the whole of the evening declared at once his affection and happiness.

"Shall we see you to-morrow to dinner?" said Mrs. Dashwood, when he was leaving them. "I do not ask you to come in the morning, for we must walk to the Park, to call on Lady Middleton."

He engaged to be with them by four o'clock.

Chapter 15

MRS. DASHWOOD's visit to Lady Middleton took place the next day, and two of her daughters went with her; but Marianne excused herself from being of the party, under some trifling pretext of employment; and her mother, who concluded that a promise had been made by Willoughby the night before, of calling on her while they were absent, was perfectly satisfied with her remaining at home.

On their return from the Park they found Willoughby's curricle and servant in waiting at the cottage, and Mrs. Dashwood was convinced that her conjecture had been just. So far it was all as she had foreseen; but on entering the house, she beheld what no foresight had taught her to expect. They were no sooner in the passage than Marianne came hastily out of the parlour, apparently in violent affliction, with her handkerchief at her eyes, and without noticing them ran upstairs. Surprised and alarmed, they proceeded directly into the room she had just quitted, where they found only Willoughby, who was leaning against the mantelpiece with his back towards them. He turned round on their coming in, and his countenance showed that he strongly partook of the emotion which overpowered Marianne.

"Is anything the matter with her?" cried Mrs. Dashwood as she entered. "Is she ill?"

"I hope not," he replied, trying to look cheerful; and with a forced smile, presently added: "It is I who may rather expect to be ill—for I am now suffering under a very heavy disappointment!"

"Disappointment?"

"Yes, for I am unable to keep my engagement with you. Mrs. Smith has this morning exercised the privilege of riches upon a poor dependent cousin, by sending me on business to London. I have just received my dispatches, and taken my farewell of Allenham; and by way of exhilaration, I am now come to take my farewell of you."

"To London—and are you going this morning?"

"Almost this moment."

"This is very unfortunate. But Mrs. Smith must be obliged; and her business will not detain you from us long, I hope."

He coloured as he replied: "You are very kind, but I have no idea of returning into Devonshire immediately. My visits to Mrs. Smith are never repeated within the twelvemonth."

"And is Mrs. Smith your only friend? Is Allenham the only house in the neighbourhood to which you will be welcomed? For shame, Willoughby. Can you wait for an invitation here?"

His colour increased; and with his eyes fixed on the ground, he only replied, "You are too good."

Mrs. Dashwood looked at Elinor with surprise. Elinor felt equal amazement. For a few moments everyone was silent. Mrs. Dashwood first spoke.

"I have only to add, my dear Willoughby, that at Barton Cottage you will always be welcome; for I will not press you to return here immediately, because you only can judge how far *that* might be pleasing to Mrs. Smith and on this head I shall be no more disposed to question your judgment than to doubt your inclination."

"My engagements at present," replied Willoughby, confusedly, "are of such a nature—that—I dare not flatter myself——"

He stopped. Mrs. Dashwood was too much astonished to speak, and another pause succeeded. This was broken by Willoughby, who said with a faint smile, "It is folly to linger in this manner. I will not torment myself any longer by remaining among friends whose society it is impossible for me now to enjoy."

He then hastily took leave of them all and left the room. They saw him step into his carriage, and in a minute it was out of sight.

Mrs. Dashwood felt too much for speech, and instantly quitted the parlour, to give way in solitude to the concern and alarm which this sudden departure occasioned.

Elinor's uneasiness was at least equal to her mother's. She thought of what had just passed with anxiety and distrust. Willoughby's behaviour in taking leave of them, his embarrassment, and affectation of cheerfulness, and, above all, his unwillingness to accept her mother's invitation, a backwardness so unlike a lover—so unlike himself, greatly disturbed her. One moment she feared that no serious design had ever been formed on his side; and the next, that some unfortunate quarrel had taken place between him and her sister; the distress in which Marianne had quitted the room was such as a serious quarrel could most reasonably account for; though when she considered what Marianne's love for him was, a quarrel seemed almost impossible.

But whatever might be the particulars of their separation, her sister's affliction was indubitable; and she thought with the tenderest compassion of that violent sorrow which Marianne was in all probability not merely giving way to as a relief, but feeding and encouraging as a duty.

In about half an hour her mother returned, and though her eyes were red, her countenance was not uncheerful.

"Our dear Willoughby is now some miles from Barton, Elinor," said she, as she sat down to work, "and with how heavy a heart does he travel!"

"It is all very strange. So suddenly to be gone! It seems but the work of a moment. And last night he was with us so happy, so cheerful, so affectionate! And now after only ten minutes' notice—gone too without intending to return? Something more than what he owned to us must have happened. He did not speak, he did not behave like himself. *You* must have seen the difference as well as I. What can it be? Can they have quarrelled? Why else should he have shown such unwillingness to accept your invitation here?"

"It was not inclination that he wanted, Elinor! I could plainly see *that*. He had not the power of accepting it. I have thought it all over, I assure you, and I can perfectly account for everything that at first seemed strange to me as well as to you."

"Can you indeed?"

"Yes. I have explained it to myself in the most satisfactory way; but you, Elinor, who love to doubt where you can—it will not satisfy *you*, I know; but you shall not talk *me* out of my trust in it. I am persuaded that Mrs. Smith suspects his regard for Marianne, disapproves of it (perhaps because she has other views for him), and on that account is eager to get him away; and that the business which she sends him off to transact is invented as an excuse to dismiss him. This is what I believe to have happened. He is, moreover, aware that she *does* disapprove the connection, he dares not therefore at present confess to her his engagement with Marianne, and he feels himself obliged, from his dependent situation, to give in to her schemes, and absent himself from Devonshire for a while. You will tell me, I know, that this may or may *not* have happened; but I will listen to no cavil unless you can point out any other method of understanding the affair as satisfactory as this. And now, Elinor, what have you to say?"

"Nothing."

"Then you would have told me, that it might or might not have happened. Oh! Elinor, how incomprehensible are your feelings! You had rather take evil upon credit than good. You had rather look out for misery for Marianne and guilt for poor Willoughby, than an apology for the latter. You are resolved to think him blameable, because he took leave of us with less affection than his usual behaviour has shown. And is no allowance to be made for inadvertence, or for spirits depressed by recent disappointment? Are no probabilities to be accepted, merely because they are not certainties? Is nothing due to the man whom we have all so much reason to love, and no reason in the world to think ill of?—to the possibility of motives unanswerable in themselves, though unavoidably secret for a while? And, after all, what is it you suspect him of?"

"I can hardly tell you myself. But suspicion of something unpleasant is the inevitable consequence of such an alteration as we have just witnessed in him. There is great truth, however, in what you have now urged of the allowances which ought to be made for him, and it is my wish to be candid in my judgment of everybody. Willoughby may undoubtedly have very sufficient reasons for his conduct, and I will hope that he has. But it would have been more like Willoughby to acknowledge them at once. Secrecy may be advisable; but still I cannot help wondering at its being practised by him."

"Do not blame him, however, for departing from his character, where the deviation is necessary. But you really do admit the justice of what I have said in his defence? I am happy—and he is acquitted."

"Not entirely. It may be proper to conceal their engagement (if they *are* engaged) from Mrs. Smith—and if that is the case, it must be highly expedient for Willoughby to be but little in Devonshire at present. But this is no excuse for their concealing it from us."

"Concealing it from us! My dear child, do you accuse Willoughby and Marianne of concealment? This is strange indeed, when your eyes have been reproaching them every day for incautiousness."

"I want no proof of their affection," said Elinor; "but of their engagement I do."

"I am perfectly satisfied of both."

"Yet not a syllable has been said to you on the subject, by either of them."

"I have not wanted syllables where actions have spoken so plainly. Has not his behaviour to Marianne and to all of us, for at least the last fortnight, declared that he loved and considered her as his future wife, and that he felt for us the attachment of the nearest relation? Have we not perfectly understood each other? Has not my consent been daily asked by his looks, his manner, his attentive and affectionate respect? My Elinor, is it possible to doubt their engagement? How could such a thought occur to you? How is it to be supposed that Willoughby, persuaded as he must be of your sister's love, should leave her, and leave her perhaps for months, without telling her of his affection—that they should part without a mutual exchange of confidence."

"I confess," replied Elinor, "that every circumstance except *one* is in favour of their engagement, but that *one* is the total silence of both on the subject, and with me it almost outweighs every other."

"How strange this is! You must think wretchedly indeed of Willoughby, if, after all that has openly passed between them, you can doubt the nature of the terms on which they are together. Has he been acting a part in his behaviour to your sister all this time? Do you suppose him really indifferent to her?"

"No, I cannot think that. He must and does love her, I am sure."

"But with a strange kind of tenderness, if he can leave her with such indifference, such carelessness of the future, as you attribute to him."

"You must remember, my dear mother, that I have never considered this matter as certain. I have had my doubts, I confess; but they are fainter than they were, and they may soon be entirely done away. If we find they correspond, every fear of mine will be removed."

"A mighty concession indeed! If you were to see them at the altar, you would suppose they were going to be married. Ungracious girl! But *I* require no such proof. Nothing, in my opinion, has ever passed to justify doubt; no secrecy has been attempted; all has been uniformly open and unreserved. You cannot doubt your sister's wishes. It must be Willoughby, therefore, whom you suspect. But why? Is he not a man of honour and feeling? Has there been an inconsistency on his side to create alarm? Can he be deceitful?"

"I hope not, I believe not," cried Elinor. "I love Willoughby, sincerely love him; and suspicion of his integrity cannot be more painful to yourself than to me. It has been involuntary, and I will not encourage it. I was startled, I confess, by the alteration in his manners this morning; he did not speak like himself, and did not return your kindness with any cordiality. But all this may be explained by such a situation of his affairs as you have supposed. He had just parted from my sister, had seen her leave him in the greatest affliction; and if he felt obliged, from a fear of offending Mrs. Smith, to resist the temptation of returning here soon, and yet aware that by declining your invitation, by saying that he was

going away for some time, he should seem to act an ungenerous, a suspicious, part by our family, he might well be embarrassed and disturbed.
In such a case, a plain and open avowal of his difficulties would have
been more to his honour, I think, as well as more consistent with his
general character—but I will not raise objections against anyone's conduct on so illiberal a foundation, as a difference in judgment from myself, or a deviation from what I may think right and consistent."

"You speak very properly. Willoughby certainly does not deserve to be
suspected. Though *we* have not known him long, he is no stranger in this
part of the world; and who has ever spoken to his disadvantage? Had he
been in a situation to act independently and marry immediately, it might
have been odd that he should leave us without acknowledging everything
to me at once: but this is not the case. It is an engagement in some
respects not prosperously begun, for their marriage must be at a very
uncertain distance; and even secrecy, as far as it can be observed, may
now be very advisable."

They were interrupted by the entrance of Margaret; and Elinor was
then at liberty to think over the representations of her mother, to
acknowledge the probability of many, and hope for the justice of all.

They saw nothing of Marianne till dinner time, when she entered the
room and took her place at the table without saying a word. Her eyes
were red and swollen; and it seemed as if her tears were even then restrained with difficulty. She avoided the looks of them all, could neither
eat nor speak, and after some time, on her mother's silently pressing her
hand with tender compassion, her small degree of fortitude was quite
overcome—she burst into tears and left the room.

This violent oppression of spirits continued the whole evening. She
was without any power, because she was without any desire of command
over herself. The slightest mention of anything relative to Willoughby
overpowered her in an instant; and though her family were most
anxiously attentive to her comfort, it was impossible for them, if they
spoke at all, to keep clear of every subject which her feelings connected
with him.

Chapter 16

MARIANNE would have thought herself very inexcusable had she been
able to sleep at all the first night after parting from Willoughby. She
would have been ashamed to look her family in the face the next morning, had she not risen from her bed in more need of repose than when
she lay down in it. But the feelings which made such composure a disgrace, left her in no danger of incurring it. She was awake the whole
night, and she wept the greatest part of it. She got up with an headache,
was unable to talk, and unwilling to take any nourishment; giving pain
every moment to her mother and sisters, and forbidding all attempt at
consolation from either. Her sensibility was potent enough!

When breakfast was over, she walked out by herself, and wandered about the village of Allenham, indulging the recollection of past enjoyment and crying over the present reverse for the chief of the morning.

The evening passed off in the equal indulgence of feeling. She played over every favourite song that she had been used to play to Willoughby, every air in which their voices had been oftenest joined, and sat at the instrument gazing on every line of music that he had written out for her, till her heart was so heavy that no further sadness could be gained; and this nourishment of grief was every day applied. She spent whole hours at the pianoforte alternately singing and crying, her voice often totally suspended by her tears. In books, too, as well as in music, she courted the misery which a contrast between the past and present was certain of giving. She read nothing but what they had been used to read together.

Such violence of affliction indeed could not be supported for ever; it sunk within a few days into a calmer melancholy; but these employments, to which she daily recurred, her solitary walks and silent meditations, still produced occasional effusions of sorrow as lively as ever.

No letter from Willoughby came, and none seemed expected by Marianne. Her mother was surprised, and Elinor again became uneasy. But Mrs. Dashwood could find explanations whenever she wanted them, which at least satisfied herself.

"Remember, Elinor," said she, "how very often Sir John fetches our letters himself from the post, and carries them to it. We have already agreed that secrecy may be necessary, and we must acknowledge that it could not be maintained if their correspondence were to pass through Sir John's hand."

Elinor could not deny the truth of this, and she tried to find in it a motive sufficient for their silence. But there was one method so direct, so simple, and in her opinion so eligible of knowing the real state of the affair, and of instantly removing all mystery, that she could not help suggesting it to her mother.

"Why do you not ask Marianne at once," said she, "whether she is or not engaged to Willoughby? From you, her mother, and so kind, so indulgent a mother, the question could not give offence. It would be the natural result of your affection for her. She used to be all unreserve, and to you more especially."

"I would not ask such a question for the world. Supposing it possible that they are not engaged, what distress would not such an inquiry inflict! At any rate, it would be most ungenerous. I should never deserve her confidence again, after forcing from her a confession of what is meant at present to be unacknowledged to anyone. I know Marianne's heart: I know that she dearly loves me, and that I shall not be the last to whom the affair is made known, when circumstances make the revealment of it eligible. I would not attempt to force the confidence of anyone, of a child much less, because a sense of duty would prevent the denial which her wishes might direct."

Elinor thought this generosity overstrained, considering her sister's youth, and urged the matter farther, but in vain; common sense, common care, common prudence, were all sunk in Mrs. Dashwood's romantic delicacy.

It was several days before Willoughby's name was mentioned before Marianne by any of her family; Sir John and Mrs. Jennings, indeed, were not so nice; their witticisms added pain to many a painful hour; but one evening, Mrs. Dashwood, accidentally taking up a volume of Shakespeare, exclaimed:

"We have never finished Hamlet, Marianne; our dear Willoughby went away before we could get through it. We will put it by, that when he comes again . . . But it may be months, perhaps, before *that* happens."

"Months!" cried Marianne, with strong surprise. "No—nor many weeks."

Mrs. Dashwood was very sorry for what she had said, but it gave Elinor pleasure, as it produced a reply from Marianne so expressive of confidence in Willoughby and knowledge of his intentions.

One morning, about a week after his leaving the country, Marianne was prevailed on to join her sisters in their usual walk. instead of wandering away by herself. Hitherto she had carefully avoided every companion in her rambles. If her sisters intended to walk on the downs, she directly stole away towards the lanes; if they talked of the valley, she was as speedy in climbing the hills, and could never be found when the others set off. But at length she was secured by the exertions of Elinor, who greatly disapproved such continual seclusion. They walked along the road through the valley, and chiefly in silence, for Marianne's *mind* could not be controlled, and Elinor, satisfied with gaining one point, would not then attempt more. Beyond the entrance of the valley, where the country, though still rich, was less wild and more open, a long stretch of the road which they had travelled on first coming to Barton lay before them; and on reaching that point, they stopped to look around them, and examine a prospect which formed the distance of their view from the cottage, from a spot which they had never happened to reach in any of their walks before.

Amongst the objects in the scene, they soon discovered an animated one; it was a man on horseback, riding towards them. In a few minutes they could distinguish him to be a gentleman; and in a moment afterwards Marianne rapturously exclaimed:

"It is he; indeed it is; I know it is!"—and was hastening to meet him, when Elinor cried out:

"Indeed, Marianne, I think you are mistaken. It is not Willoughby The person is not tall enough for him, and has not his air."

"He has, he has," cried Marianne, "I am sure he has! His air, his coat, his horse. I knew how soon he would come."

She walked eagerly on as she spoke; and Elinor, to screen Marianne from particularity, as she felt almost certain of its not being Willoughby, quickened her pace and kept up with her. They were soon within thirty yards of the gentleman. Marianne looked again; her heart sunk within her: and abruptly turning round, she was hurrying back, when as the voices of both her sisters were raised to detain her, a third, almost as well known as Willoughby's, joined them in begging her to stop, and she turned round with surprise to see and welcome Edward Ferrars.

He was the only person in the world who could at that moment be forgiven for not being Willoughby; the only one who could have gained a smile from her; but she dispersed her tears to smile on *him*, and in her sister's happiness forgot for a time her own disappointment.

He dismounted, and giving his horse to his servant walked back with them to Barton, whither he was purposely coming to visit them.

He was welcomed by them all with great cordiality, but especially by Marianne, who showed more warmth of regard in her reception of him than even Elinor herself. To Marianne, indeed, the meeting between Edward and her sister was but a continuation of that unaccountable coldness which she had often observed at Norland in their mutual behaviour. On Edward's side, more particularly, there was a deficiency of all that a lover ought to look and say on such an occasion. He was confused, seemed scarcely sensible of pleasure in seeing them, looked neither rapturous nor gay, said little but what was forced from him by questions, and distinguished Elinor by no mark of affection. Marianne saw and listened with increasing surprise. She began almost to feel a dislike of Edward; and it ended, as every feeling must end with her, by carrying back her thoughts to Willoughby, whose manners formed a contrast sufficiently striking to those of his brother elect.

After a short silence which succeeded the first surprise and inquiries of meeting, Marianne asked Edward if he came directly from London. No, he had been in Devonshire a fortnight.

"A fortnight!" she repeated, surprised at his being so long in the same county with Elinor without seeing her before.

He looked rather distressed as he added, that he had been staying with some friends near Plymouth.

"Have you been lately in Sussex?" said Elinor.

"I was at Norland about a month ago."

"And how does dear, dear Norland look?" cried Marianne.

"Dear, dear Norland," said Elinor, "probably looks much as it always does at this time of year—the woods and walks thickly covered with dead leaves."

"Oh!" cried Marianne, "with what transporting sensations have I formerly seen them fall! How have I delighted, as I walked, to see them driven in showers about me by the wind! What feelings have they, the season, the air altogether inspired! Now there is no one to regard them.

They are seen only as a nuisance, swept hastily off, and driven as much as possible from the sight."

"It is not everyone," said Elinor, "who has your passion for dead leaves."

"No; my feelings are not often shared, not often understood. But *sometimes* they are." As she said this, she sank into a reverie for a few moments; but rousing herself again, "Now, Edward," said she, calling his attention to the prospect, "here is Barton valley. Look up it, and be tranquil if you can. Look at those hills! Did you ever see their equals? To the left is Barton Park, amongst those woods and plantations. You may see one end of the house. And there, beneath that farthest hill which rises with such grandeur, is our cottage."

"It is a beautiful country," he replied; "but these bottoms must be dirty in winter."

"How can you think of dirt, with such objects before you?"

"Because," replied he, smiling, "amongst the rest of the objects before me, I see a very dirty lane."

"How strange!" said Marianne to herself as she walked on.

"Have you an agreeable neighbourhood here? Are the Middletons pleasant people?"

"No, not at all," answered Marianne; "we could not be more unfortunately situated."

"Marianne," cried her sister, "how can you say so? How can you be so unjust? They are a very respectable family, Mr. Ferrars, and towards us have behaved in the friendliest manner. Have you forgot, Marianne, how many pleasant days we have owed to them?"

"No," said Marianne, in a low voice, "nor how many painful moments."

Elinor took no notice of this, and directing her attention to their visitor, endeavoured to support something like discourse with him by talking of their present residence, its conveniences, etc., extorting from him occasional questions and remarks. His coldness and reserve mortified her severely: she was vexed and half angry; but resolving to regulate her behaviour to him by the past rather than the present, she avoided every appearance of resentment or displeasure, and treated him as she thought he ought to be treated from the family connection.

Chapter 17

MRS. DASHWOOD was surprised only for a moment at seeing him; for his coming to Barton was, in her opinion, of all things the most natural. Her joy and expressions of regard long outlived her wonder. He received the kindest welcome from her; and shyness, coldness, reserve, could not stand against such a reception. They had begun to fail him before he entered the house, and they were quite overcome by the captivating manners of Mrs. Dashwood. Indeed, a man could not very well be in love with either of her daughters, without extending the passion to her; and Elinor had the satisfaction of seeing him soon become more like himself. His affections seemed to reanimate towards them all, and his interest in their welfare again became perceptible. He was not in spirits, however; he praised their house, admired its prospect, was attentive and kind; but still he was not in spirits. The whole family perceived it, and Mrs. Dashwood, attributing it to some want of liberality in his mother, sat down to table indignant against all selfish parents.

"What are Mrs. Ferrars's views for you at present, Edward?" said she, when dinner was over, and they had drawn round the fire; "are you still to be a great orator in spite of yourself?"

"No. I hope my mother is now convinced that I have no more talents than inclination for a public life."

"But how is your fame to be established? For famous you must be to satisfy all your family; and with no inclination for expense, no affection for strangers, no profession, and no assurance, you may find it a difficult matter."

"I shall not attempt it. I have no wish to be distinguished; and I have every reason to hope I never shall. Thank Heaven! I cannot be forced into genius and eloquence."

"You have no ambition, I well know. Your wishes are all moderate."

"As moderate as those of the rest of the world, I believe. I wish, as well as everybody else, to be perfectly happy; but, like everybody else, it must be in my own way. Greatness will not make me so."

"Strange if it would!" cried Marianne. "What have wealth or grandeur to do with happiness?"

"Grandeur has but little," said Elinor, "but wealth has much to do with it."

"Elinor, for shame!" said Marianne; "money can only give happiness where there is nothing else to give it. Beyond a competence, it can afford no real satisfaction, as far as mere self is concerned."

"Perhaps," said Elinor, smiling, "we may come to the same point. *Your* competence and *my* wealth are very much alike, I dare say; and without them, as the world goes now, we shall both agree that every kind of external comfort must be wanting. Your ideas are only more noble than mine. Come, what is your competence?"

"About eighteen hundred or two thousand a year; not more than *that*."

Elinor laughed. "*Two* thousand a year! *One* is my wealth! I guessed how it would end."

"And yet two thousand a year is a very moderate income," said Marianne. "A family cannot well be maintained on a smaller. I am sure I am not extravagant in my demands. A proper establishment of servants, a carriage, perhaps two, and hunters, cannot be supported on less."

Elinor smiled again, to hear her sister describing so accurately their future expenses at Combe Magna.

"Hunters!" repeated Edward. "But why must you have hunters? Everybody does not hunt."

Marianne coloured as she replied, "But most people do."

"I wish," said Margaret, striking out a novel thought, "that somebody would give us all a large fortune apiece!"

"O that they would!" cried Marianne, her eyes sparkling with animation, and her cheeks glowing with the delight of such imaginary happiness.

"We are all unanimous in that wish, I suppose," said Elinor, "in spite of the insufficiency of wealth."

"Oh dear," cried Margaret, "how happy I should be. I wonder what I should do with it!"

Marianne looked as if she had no doubt on that point.

"I should be puzzled to spend a large fortune myself," said Mrs. Dashwood, "if my children were all to be rich without my help."

"You must begin your improvements on this house," observed Elinor, "and your difficulties will soon vanish."

"What magnificent orders would travel from this family to London," said Edward, "in such an event! What a happy day for booksellers, music-sellers, and print-shops! You, Miss Dashwood, would give a general commission for every new print of merit to be sent you; and as for Marianne, I know her greatness of soul—there would not be music enough in London to content her. And books! Thomson, Cowper, Scott— she would buy them all over and over again; she would buy up every copy, I believe, to prevent their falling into unworthy hands; and she would have every book that tells her how to admire an old twisted tree. Should not you, Marianne? Forgive me, if I am very saucy. But I was willing to show you that I had not forgot our old disputes."

"I love to be reminded of the past, Edward—whether it be melancholy or gay, I love to recall it—and you will never offend me by talking of former times. You are very right in supposing how my money would be spent—some of it, at least my loose cash, would certainly be employed in improving my collection of music and books."

"And the bulk of your fortune would be laid out in annuities on the authors or their heirs."

"No, Edward, I should have something else to do with it."

"Perhaps, then, you would bestow it as a reward on that person who wrote the ablest defence of your favourite maxim, that no one can ever be in love more than once in their life—for your opinion on that point is unchanged, I presume?"

"Undoubtedly. At my time of life, opinions are tolerably fixed. It is not likely that I should now see or hear anything to change them."

"Marianne is as steadfast as ever, you see," said Elinor, "she is not at all altered."

"She has only grown a little more grave than she was."

"Nay, Edward," said Marianne, "*you* need not reproach me. You are not very gay yourself."

"Why should you think so?" replied he, with a sigh. "But gaiety never was a part of *my* character."

"Nor do I think it a part of Marianne's," said Elinor. "I should hardly call her a lively girl; she is very earnest, very eager in all she does— sometimes talks a great deal, and always with animation—but she is not often really merry."

"I believe you are right," he replied, "and yet I have always set her down as a lively girl."

"I have frequently detected myself in such kind of mistakes," said Elinor, "in a total misapprehension of character in some points or other: fancying people so much more gay or grave, or ingenious or stupid than they really are, and I can hardly tell why, or in what the deception originated. Sometimes one is guided by what they say of themselves, and very frequently by what other people say of them, without giving oneself time to deliberate and judge."

"But I thought it was right, Elinor," said Marianne, "to be guided wholly by the opinion of other people. I thought our judgments were given us merely to be subservient to those of our neighbours. This has always been your doctrine, I am sure."

"No, Marianne, never. My doctrine has never aimed at the subjection of the understanding. All I have ever attempted to influence has been the behaviour. You must not confound my meaning. I am guilty, I confess, of having often wished you to treat our acquaintance in general with greater attention; but when have I advised you to adopt their sentiments or conform to their judgment in serious matters?"

"You have not been able then to bring your sister over to your plan of general civility," said Edward to Elinor. "Do you gain no ground?"

"Quite the contrary," replied Elinor, looking expressively at Marianne.

"My judgment," he returned, "is all on your side of the question; but I am afraid my practice is much more on your sister's. I never wish to offend, but I am so foolishly shy, that I often seem negligent, when I am only kept back by my natural awkwardness. I have frequently thought that I must have been intended by nature to be fond of low company, I am so little at my ease among strangers of gentility!"

"Marianne has not shyness to excuse any inattention of hers," said Elinor.

"She knows her own worth too well for false shame," replied Edward. "Shyness is only the effect of a sense of inferiority in some way or other. If I could persuade myself that my manners were perfectly easy and graceful, I should not be shy."

"But you would still be reserved," said Marianne, "and that is worse."

Edward stared. "Reserved? Am I reserved, Marianne?"

"Yes, very."

"I do not understand you," replied he, colouring. "Reserved! How, in what manner? What am I to tell you? What can you suppose?"

Elinor looked surprised at his emotion, but trying to laugh off the subject, she said to him, "Do not you know my sister well enough to understand what she means? Do not you know she calls everyone re-served, who does not talk as fast, and admire what she admires as rapturously as herself?"

Edward made no answer. His gravity and thoughtfulness returned on him in their fullest extent, and he sat for some time silent and dull.

Chapter 18

ELINOR saw with great uneasiness the low spirits of her friend. His visit afforded her but a very partial satisfaction, while his own enjoyment in it appeared so imperfect. It was evident that he was unhappy; she wished it were equally evident that he still distinguished her by the same affection which once she had felt no doubt of inspiring; but hitherto the continuance of his preference seemed very uncertain, and the reserved-ness of his manner towards her contradicted one moment what a more animated look had intimated the preceding one.

He joined her and Marianne in the breakfast-room the next morning before the others were down; and Marianne, who was always eager to promote their happiness as far as she could, soon left them to themselves. But, before she was halfway upstairs, she heard the parlour door open, and, turning round, was astonished to see Edward himself come out.

"I am going into the village to see my horses," said he, "as you are not yet ready for breakfast; I shall be back again presently."

Edward returned to them with fresh admiration of the surrounding country; in his walk to the village, he had seen many parts of the valley to advantage; and the village itself, in a much higher situation than the cottage, afforded a general view of the whole, which had exceedingly pleased him. This was a subject which ensured Marianne's attention, and she was beginning to describe her own admiration of these scenes, and to question him more minutely on the objects that had particularly struck him, when Edward interrupted her by saying, "You must not inquire too far, Marianne—remember, I have no knowledge in the picturesque, and I shall offend you by my ignorance and want of taste, if we come to par-ticulars. I shall call hills steep, which ought to be bold; surfaces strange and uncouth, which ought to be irregular and rugged; and distant objects out of sight, which ought only to be indistinct through the soft medium of a hazy atmosphere. You must be satisfied with such admiration as I can honestly give. I call it a very fine country—the hills are steep, the woods seem full of fine timber, and the valley looks comfortable and snug —with rich meadows and several neat farm-houses scattered here and there. It exactly answers my idea of a fine country, because it unites beauty with utility—and I dare say it is a picturesque one too, because you admire it; I can easily believe it to be full of rocks and promontories, grey moss and brushwood, but these are all lost on me. I know nothing of the picturesque."

"I am afraid it is but too true," said Marianne; "but why should you boast of it?"

"I suspect," said Elinor, "that to avoid one kind of affectation, Edward here falls into another. Because he believes many people pretend to more admiration of the beauties of nature than they really feel, and is disgusted with such pretensions, he affects greater indifference and less discrimination in viewing them himself than he possesses. He is fastidious and will have an affectation of his own."

"It is very true," said Marianne, "that admiration of landscape scenery is become a mere jargon. Everybody pretends to feel and tries to describe with the taste and elegance of him who first defined what picturesque beauty was. I detest jargon of every kind, and sometimes I have kept my feelings to myself, because I could find no language to describe them in but what was worn and hackneyed out of all sense and meaning."

"I am convinced," said Edward, "that you really feel all the delight in a fine prospect which you profess to feel. But, in return, your sister must allow me to feel no more than I profess. I like a fine prospect, but not on picturesque principles. I do not like crooked, twisted, blasted trees. I admire them much more if they are tall, straight, and flourishing. I do not like ruined, tattered cottages. I am not fond of nettles, or thistles, or heath blossoms. I have more pleasure in a snug farmhouse than a watch-tower—and a troop of tidy, happy villagers please me better than the finest banditti in the world."

Marianne looked with amazement at Edward, with compassion at her sister. Elinor only laughed.

The subject was continued no further; and Marianne remained thoughtfully silent, till a new object suddenly engaged her attention. She was sitting by Edward, and in taking his tea from Mrs. Dashwood, his hand passed so directly before her as to make a ring, with a plait of hair in the centre, very conspicuous on one of his fingers.

"I never saw you wear a ring before, Edward," she cried. "Is that Fanny's hair? I remember her promising to give you some. But I should have thought her hair had been darker."

Marianne spoke inconsiderately what she really felt—but when she saw how much she had pained Edward, her own vexation at her want of thought could not be surpassed by his. He coloured very deeply, and giving a momentary glance at Elinor, replied: "Yes, it is my sister's hair. The setting always casts a different shade on it, you know."

Elinor had met his eye, and looked conscious likewise. That the hair was her own, she instantaneously felt as well satisfied as Marianne; the only difference in their conclusions was, that what Marianne considered as a free gift from her sister, Elinor was conscious must have been procured by some theft or contrivance unknown to herself. She was not in a humour, however, to regard it as an affront, and affecting to take no notice of what had passed, by instantly talking of something else, she internally resolved henceforward to catch every opportunity of eyeing the hair, and satisfying herself, beyond all doubt, that it was exactly the shade of her own.

Edward's embarrassment lasted some time, and it ended in an absence of mind still more settled. He was particularly grave the whole morning. Marianne severely censured herself for what she had said; but her own forgiveness might have been more speedy, had she known how little offence it had given her sister.

Before the middle of the day, they were visited by Sir John and Mrs. Jennings, who, having heard of the arrival of a gentleman at the cottage, came to take a survey of the guest. With the assistance of his mother-in-law, Sir John was not long in discovering that the name of Ferrars began with an F, and this prepared a future mine of raillery against the devoted Elinor, which nothing but the newness of their acquaintance with Edward could have prevented from being immediately sprung. But, as it was, she only learned from some very significant looks, how far their penetration, founded on Margaret's instructions, extended.

Sir John never came to the Dashwoods without either inviting them to dine at the Park the next day, or to drink tea with them that evening. On the present occasion, for the better entertainment of their visitor, towards whose amusement he felt himself bound to contribute, he wished to engage them for both.

"You *must* drink tea with us to-night," said he, "for we shall be quite alone—and to-morrow you must absolutely dine with us, for we shall be a large party."

Mrs. Jennings enforced the necessity. "And who knows but you may raise a dance?" said she. "And that will tempt *you*, Miss Marianne."

"A dance!" cried Marianne. "Impossible! Who is to dance?"

"Who? Why, yourselves, and the Careys, and Whitakers, to be sure. What! You thought nobody could dance because a certain person that shall be nameless is gone!"

"I wish with all my soul," cried Sir John, "that Willoughby were among us again."

This, and Marianne's blushing, gave new suspicions to Edward. "And who is Willoughby?" said he, in a low voice to Miss Dashwood, by whom he was sitting.

She gave him a brief reply. Marianne's countenance was more communicative. Edward saw enough to comprehend not only the meaning of others, but such of Marianne's expressions as had puzzled him before; and when their visitors left them, he went immediately round to her, and said, in a whisper, "I have been guessing. Shall I tell you my guess?"

"What do you mean?"

"Shall I tell you?"

"Certainly."

"Well, then, I guess that Mr. Willoughby hunts."

Marianne was surprised and confused, yet she could not help smiling at the quiet archness of his manner, and, after a moment's silence, said:

"Oh! Edward! How can you? But the time will come, I hope. . . . I am sure you will like him."

"I do not doubt it," replied he, rather astonished at her earnestness and warmth; for had he not imagined it to be a joke for the good of her acquaintance in general, founded only on a something or a nothing between Mr. Willoughby and herself, he would not have ventured to mention it.

Chapter 19

EDWARD remained a week at the cottage; he was earnestly pressed by Mrs. Dashwood to stay longer; but as if he were bent only on self-mortification, he seemed resolved to be gone when his enjoyment among his friends was at the height. His spirits, during the last two or three days, though still very unequal, were greatly improved—he grew more and more partial to the house and environs—never spoke of going away without a sigh—declared his time to be wholly disengaged—even doubted to what place he should go when he left them—but still go he must. Never had any week passed so quickly—he could hardly believe it to be gone. He said so repeatedly; other things he said too, which marked the turn of his feelings and gave the lie to his actions. He had no pleasure at Norland; he detested being in town; but either to Norland or London he must go. He valued their kindness beyond anything, and his greatest happiness was in being with them. Yet he must leave them at the end of a week, in spite of their wishes and his own, and without any restraint on his time.

Elinor placed all that was astonishing in this way of acting to his mother's account; and it was happy for her that he had a mother whose character was so imperfectly known to her, as to be the general excuse for everything strange on the part of her son. Disappointed, however, and vexed as she was, and sometimes displeased with his uncertain behaviour to herself, she was very well disposed on the whole to regard his actions with all the candid allowances and generous qualifications, which had been rather more painfully extorted from her, for Willoughby's service, by her mother. His want of spirits, of openness, and of consistency, were most usually attributed to his want of independence, and his better knowledge of Mrs. Ferrars's dispositions and designs. The shortness of his visit, the steadiness of his purpose in leaving them, originated in the same fettered inclination, the same inevitable necessity of temporising with his mother. The old well-established grievance of duty against will, parent against child, was the cause of all. She would have been glad to know when these difficulties were to cease, this opposition was to yield—when Mrs. Ferrars would be reformed, and her son be at liberty to be happy. But from such vain wishes she was forced to turn for comfort to the renewal of her confidence in Edward's affection, to the remembrance of every mark of regard in look or word which fell from him while at Barton, and above all to that flattering proof of it which he constantly wore round his finger.

"I think, Edward," said Mrs. Dashwood, as they were at breakfast the last morning, "you would be a happier man if you had any profession to engage your time and give an interest to your plans and actions. Some inconvenience to your friends, indeed, might result from it—you would not be able to give them so much of your time. But" (with a smile) "you would be materially benefited in one particular at least—you would know where to go when you left them."

"I do assure you," he replied, "that I have long thought on this point as you think now. It has been, and is, and probably will always be a heavy misfortune to me, that I have had no necessary business to engage me, no profession to give me employment or afford me anything like independence. But unfortunately my own nicety and the nicety of my friends, have made me what I am, an idle, helpless being. We never could agree in our choice of a profession. I always preferred the church, as I still do. But that was not smart enough for my family. They recommended the army. That was a great deal too smart for me. The law was allowed to be genteel enough; many young men, who had chambers in the Temple, made a very good appearance in the first circles, and drove about town in very knowing gigs. But I had no inclination for the law, even in this less abstruse study of it, which my family approved. As for the navy, it had fashion on its side, but I was too old when the subject was first started to enter it, and, at length, as there was no necessity for my having any profession at all, as I might be as dashing and expensive without a red coat on my back as with one, idleness was pronounced on the whole to be the most advantageous and honourable, and a young man of eighteen is not in general so earnestly bent on being busy as to resist the solicitations of his friends to do nothing. I was therefore entered at Oxford, and have been properly idle ever since."

"The consequence of which, I suppose, will be," said Mrs. Dashwood, "since leisure has not promoted your own happiness, that your sons will be brought up to as many pursuits, employments, professions, and trades as Columella's."

"They will be brought up," said he, in a serious accent, "to be as unlike myself as is possible—in feeling, in action, in condition, in everything."

"Come, come; this is all an effusion of immediate want of spirits, Edward. You are in a melancholy humour, and fancy that anyone unlike yourself must be happy. But remember that the pain of parting from friends will be felt by everybody at times, whatever be their education or state. Know your own happiness. You want nothing but patience—or give it a more fascinating name, call it hope. Your mother will secure to you, in time, that independence you are so anxious for; it is her duty, and it will, it must ere long become her happiness to prevent your whole youth from being wasted in discontent. How much may not a few months do!"

"I think," replied Edward, "that I may defy many months to produce any good to me."

This desponding turn of mind, though it could not be communicated to Mrs. Dashwood, gave additional pain to them all in the parting, which shortly took place, and left an uncomfortable impression on Elinor's feelings especially, which required some trouble and time to subdue. But as it was her determination to subdue it, and to prevent herself from appearing to suffer more than what all her family suffered on his going away, she did not adopt the method so judiciously employed by Marianne, on a similar occasion, to augment and fix her sorrow, by seeking silence, solitude, and idleness. Their means were as different as their objects, and equally suited to the advancement of each.

Elinor sat down to her drawing-table as soon as he was out of the house, busily employed herself the whole day, neither sought nor avoided the mention of his name, appeared to interest herself almost as much as ever in the general concerns of the family, and if, by this conduct, she did not lessen her own grief, it was at least prevented from unnecessary increase, and her mother and sisters were spared much solicitude on her account.

Such behaviour as this, so exactly the reverse of her own, appeared no more meritorious to Marianne than her own had seemed faulty to her. The business of self-command she settled very easily; with strong affections it was impossible, with calm ones it could have no merit. That her sister's affections *were* calm, she dared not deny, though she blushed to acknowledge it; and of the strength of her own, she gave a very striking proof, by still loving and respecting that sister in spite of this mortifying conviction.

Without shutting herself up from her family, or leaving the house in determined solitude to avoid them, or lying awake the whole night to indulge meditation, Elinor found every day afforded her leisure enough to think of Edward, and of Edward's behaviour, in every possible variety which the different state of her spirits at different times could produce; with tenderness, pity, approbation, censure, and doubt. There were moments in abundance, when, if not by the absence of her mother and sisters, at least by the nature of their employments, conversation was forbidden among them, and every effect of solitude was produced. Her mind was inevitably at liberty; her thoughts could not be chained elsewhere; and the past and the future, on a subject so interesting, must be before her, must force her attention, and engross her memory, her reflection, and her fancy.

From a reverie of this kind, as she sat at her drawing-table, she was roused one morning, soon after Edward's leaving them, by the arrival of company. She happened to be quite alone. The closing of the little gate, at the entrance of the green court in front of the house, drew her eyes to the window, and she saw a large party walking up to the door. Amongst them were Sir John and Lady Middleton, and Mrs. Jennings; but there were two others, a gentleman and lady, who were quite unknown to her. She was sitting near the window, and as soon as Sir John perceived her, he left the rest of the party to the ceremony of knocking at the door, and stepping across the turf, obliged her to open the casement to speak to him, though the space was so short between the door and the window as to make it hardly possible to speak at one without being heard at the other.

"Well," said he, "we have brought you some strangers. How do you like them?"

"Hush! They will hear you."

"Never mind if they do. It is only the Palmers. Charlotte is very pretty, I can tell you. You may see her if you look this way."

As Elinor was certain of seeing her in a couple of minutes, without taking that liberty, she begged to be excused.

"Where is Marianne? Has she run away because we are come? I see her instrument is open."

"She is walking, I believe."

They were now joined by Mrs. Jennings, who had not patience enough to wait till the door was open before she told *her* story. She came hallooing to the window, "How do you do, my dear? How does Mrs. Dashwood do? And where are your sisters? What! All alone! You will be glad of a little company to sit with you. I have brought my other son and daughter to see you. Only think of their coming so suddenly! I thought I heard a carriage last night, while we were drinking our tea, but it never entered my head that it could be them. I thought of nothing but whether it might not be Colonel Brandon come back again; so I said to Sir John, 'I do think I hear a carriage; perhaps it is Colonel Brandon come back again——' "

Elinor was obliged to turn from her, in the middle of her story, to receive the rest of the party; Lady Middleton introduced the two strangers; Mrs. Dashwood and Margaret came downstairs at the same time, and they all sat down to look at one another, while Mrs. Jennings continued her story as she walked through the passage into the parlour, attended by Sir John.

Mrs. Palmer was several years younger than Lady Middleton, and totally unlike her in every respect. She was short and plump, had a very pretty face, and the finest expression of good-humour in it that could possibly be. Her manners were by no means so elegant as her sister's, but they were much more prepossessing. She came in with a smile—smiled all the time of her visit, except when she laughed, and smiled when she went away. Her husband was a grave-looking young man of five or six and twenty, with an air of more fashion and sense than his wife, but of less willingness to please or be pleased. He entered the room with a look of self-consequence, slightly bowed to the ladies without speaking a word, and, after briefly surveying them and their apartments, took up a newspaper from the table and continued to read it as long as he stayed.

Mrs. Palmer, on the contrary, who was strongly endowed by nature with a turn for being uniformly civil and happy, was hardly seated before her admiration of the parlour and everything in it burst forth.

"Well! what a delightful room this is! I never saw anything so charming! Only think, mamma, how it is improved since I was here last! I always thought it such a sweet place, ma'am" (turning to Mrs. Dashwood), "but you have made it so charming! Only look, sister, how delightful everything is! How I should like such a house for myself. Should not you, Mr. Palmer?"

Mr. Palmer made her no answer, did not even raise his eyes from the newspaper.

"Mr. Palmer does not hear me," said she, laughing. "He never does, sometimes. It is so ridiculous!"

This was quite a new idea to Mrs. Dashwood; she had never been used to find wit in the inattention of any one, and could not help looking with surprise at them both.

Mrs. Jennings, in the meantime, talked on as loud as she could, and continued her account of their surprise the evening before, on seeing their friends, without ceasing till everything was told. Mrs. Palmer laughed heartily at the recollection of their astonishment, and everybody agreed two or three times over, that it had been quite an agreeable surprise.

"You may believe how glad we all were to see them," added Mrs. Jennings, leaning forward towards Elinor, and speaking in a low voice as if she meant to be heard by no one else, though they were seated on different sides of the room; "but, however, I can't help wishing they had not travelled quite so fast, nor made such a long journey of it, for they came all round by London upon account of some business, for you know" (nodding significantly and pointing to her daughter) "it was wrong in her situation. I wanted her to stay at home and rest this morning, but she would come with us; she longed so much to see you all!"

Mrs. Palmer laughed, and said it would not do her any harm.

"She expects to be confined in February," continued Mrs. Jennings.

Lady Middleton could no longer endure such a conversation, and therefore exerted herself to ask Mr. Palmer if there was any news in the paper.

"No, none at all," he replied, and read on.

"Here comes Marianne," cried Sir John. "Now, Palmer, you shall see a monstrous pretty girl."

He immediately went into the passage, opened the front door, and ushered her in himself. Mrs. Jennings asked her, as soon as she appeared, if she had not been to Allenham; and Mrs. Palmer laughed so heartily at the question as to show she understood it. Mr. Palmer looked up on her entering the room, stared at her some minutes, and then returned to his newspaper. Mrs. Palmer's eye was now caught by the drawings which hung round the room. She got up to examine them.

"Oh! dear, how beautiful these are! Well, how delightful! Do but look, mamma, how sweet! I declare they are quite charming; I could look at them for ever." And then sitting down again, she very soon forgot that there were any such things in the room.

When Lady Middleton rose to go away, Mr. Palmer rose also, laid down the newspaper, stretched himself, and looked at them all round.

"My love, have you been asleep?" said his wife, laughing.

He made her no answer, and only observed, after again examining the room, that it was very low-pitched, and that the ceiling was crooked. He then made his bow and departed with the rest.

Sir John had been very urgent with them all to spend the next day at the Park. Mrs. Dashwood, who did not choose to dine with them oftener than they dined at the cottage, absolutely refused on her own account; her daughters might do as they pleased. But they had no curiosity to see how Mr. and Mrs. Palmer ate their dinner, and no expectation of pleasure from them in any other way. They attempted, therefore, likewise to excuse themselves; the weather was uncertain and not likely to be good. But Sir John would not be satisfied—the carriage should be sent for them, and they must come. Lady Middleton too, though she did not press their mother, pressed them. Mrs. Jennings and Mrs. Palmer joined their entreaties, all seemed equally anxious to avoid a family party, and the young ladies were obliged to yield.

"Why should they ask us?" said Marianne, as soon as they were gone. "The rent of this cottage is said to be low; but we have it on very hard terms, if we are to dine at the Park whenever any one is staying either with them or with us."

"They mean no less to be civil and kind to us now," said Elinor, "by these frequent invitations than by those which we received from them a few weeks ago. The alteration is not in them, if their parties are grown tedious and dull. We must look for the change elsewhere."

Chapter 20

As the Miss Dashwods entered the drawing-room of the Park the next day, at one door, Mrs. Palmer came running in at the other, looking as good-humoured and merry as before. She took them all most affectionately by the hand, and expressed great delight at seeing them again.

"I am so glad to see you!" said she, seating herself between Elinor and Marianne, "for it is so bad a day I was afraid you might not come.

which would be a shocking thing, as we go away again to-morrow. We must go, for the Westons come to us next week, you know. It was quite a sudden thing our coming at all, and I knew nothing of it till the carriage was coming to the door, and then Mr. Palmer asked me if I would go with him to Barton. He is so droll! He never tells me anything! I am so sorry we cannot stay longer; however, we shall meet again in town very soon, I hope."

They were obliged to put an end to such an expectation.

"Not go to town!" cried Mrs. Palmer, with a laugh; "I shall be quite disappointed if you do not. I could get the nicest house in the world for you next door to ours, in Hanover Square. You must come, indeed. I am sure I shall be very happy to chaperon you at any time till I am confined, if Mrs. Dashwood should not like to go into public."

They thanked her, but were obliged to resist all her entreaties.

"Oh! my love," cried Mrs. Palmer to her husband, who just then entered the room; "you must help me to persuade the Miss Dashwoods to go to town this winter."

Her love made no answer; and after slightly bowing to the ladies, began complaining of the weather.

"How horrid all this is!" said he. "Such weather makes everything and everybody disgusting. Dullness is as much produced within doors as without by rain. It makes one detest all one's acquaintance. What the devil does Sir John mean by not having a billiard-room in his house? How few people know what comfort is! Sir John is as stupid as the weather."

The rest of the company soon dropped in.

"I am afraid, Miss Marianne," said Sir John, "you have not been able to take your usual walk to Allenham to-day."

Marianne looked very grave, and said nothing.

"Oh! don't be so sly before us," said Mrs. Palmer: "for we know all about it, I assure you; and I admire your taste very much, for I think he is extremely handsome. We do not live a great way from him in the country, you know, not above ten miles, I dare say."

"Much nearer thirty," said her husband.

"Ah! well! there is not much difference. I never was at his house; but they say it is a sweet, pretty place."

"As vile a spot as ever I saw in my life," said Mr. Palmer.

Marianne remained perfectly silent, though her countenance betrayed her interest in what was said.

"Is it very ugly?" continued Mrs. Palmer—"then it must be some other place that is so pretty, I suppose."

When they were seated in the dining-room, Sir John observed with regret that they were only eight all together.

"My dear," said he to his lady, "it is very provoking that we should be so few. Why did not you ask the Gilberts to come to us to-day?"

"Did not I tell you, Sir John, when you spoke to me about it before, that it could not be done? They dined with us last."

"You and I, Sir John," said Mrs. Jennings, "should not stand upon such ceremony."

"Then you would be very ill-bred," cried Mr. Palmer.

"My love, you contradict everybody," said his wife, with her usual laugh. "Do you know that you are quite rude?"

"I did not know I contradicted anybody in calling your mother ill-bred."

"Aye, you may abuse me as you please," said the good-natured old lady. "You have taken Charlotte off my hands, and cannot give her back again. So there I have the whip hand of you."

Charlotte laughed heartily to think that her husband could not get rid of her, and exultingly said, she did not care how cross he was to her, as they must live together. It was impossible for any one to be more thoroughly good-natured or more determined to be happy than Mrs. Palmer. The studied indifference, insolence, and discontent of her husband gave her no pain; and when he scolded or abused her, she was highly diverted.

"Mr. Palmer is so droll!" said she, in a whisper, to Elinor. "He is always out of humour."

Elinor was not inclined, after a little observation, to give him credit for being so genuinely and unaffectedly ill-natured or ill-bred as he wished to appear. His temper might perhaps be a little soured by finding, like many others of his sex, that through some unaccountable bias in favour of beauty, he was the husband of a very silly woman—but she knew that this kind of blunder was too common for any sensible man to be lastingly hurt by it. It was rather a wish of distinction, she believed, which produced his contemptuous treatment of everybody, and his general abuse of everything before him. It was the desire of appearing superior to other people. The motive was too common to be wondered at; but the means, however they might succeed by establishing his superiority in ill-breeding, were not likely to attach any one to him, except his wife.

"Oh! my dear Miss Dashwood," said Mrs. Palmer soon afterwards, "I have got such a favour to ask of you and your sister. Will you come and spend some time at Cleveland this Christmas? Now, pray do—and come while the Westons are with us. You cannot think how happy I shall be! It will be quite delightful!——My love," applying to her husband, "don't you long to have the Miss Dashwoods come to Cleveland?"

"Certainly," he replied with a sneer—"I came into Devonshire with no other view."

"There now," said his lady, "you see Mr. Palmer expects you; so you cannot refuse to come."

They both eagerly and resolutely declined her invitation.

"But indeed, you must and shall come. I am sure you will like it of all things. The Westons will be with us, and it will be quite delightful. You

cannot think what a sweet place Cleveland is; and we are so gay now, for
Mr. Palmer is always going about the country canvassing against the
election; and so many people come to dine with us that I never saw before, it is quite charming! But, poor fellow! it is very fatiguing to him!
for he is forced to make everybody like him."

Elinor could hardly keep her countenance as she assented to the hardship of such an obligation.

"How charming it will be," said Charlotte, "when he is in Parliament!
—won't it? How I shall laugh! It will be so ridiculous to see all his letters
directed to him with an M.P. But do you know, he says he will never
frank for me. He declares he won't. Don't you, Mr. Palmer?"

Mr. Palmer took no notice of her.

"He cannot bear writing, you know," she continued—"he says it is
quite shocking."

"No," said he, "I never said anything so irrational. Don't palm all your
abuses of language upon me."

"There now; you see how droll he is. This is always the way with him!
Sometimes he won't speak to me for half a day together, and then he
comes out with something so droll—all about anything in the world."

She surprised Elinor very much, as they returned into the drawing-
room, by asking her whether she did not like Mr. Palmer excessively.

"Certainly," said Elinor, "he seems very agreeable."

"Well—I am so glad you do. I thought you would, he is so pleasant;
and Mr. Palmer is excessively pleased with you and your sisters, I can tell
you, and you can't think how disappointed he will be if you don't come to
Cleveland. I can't imagine why you should object to it."

Elinor was again obliged to decline her invitation; and by changing the
subject, put a stop to her entreaties. She thought it probable that, as they
lived in the same country, Mrs. Palmer might be able to give some more
particular account of Willoughby's general character than could be
gathered from the Middletons' partial acquaintance with him, and she
was eager to gain from any one such a confirmation of his merits as might
remove the possibility of fear for Marianne. She began by inquiring if
they saw much of Mr. Willoughby at Cleveland, and whether they were
intimately acquainted with him.

"Oh! dear, yes; I know him extremely well," replied Mrs. Palmer.
"Not that I ever spoke to him, indeed; but I have seen him for ever in
town. Somehow or other, I never happened to be staying at Barton while
he was at Allenham. Mamma saw him here once before; but I was with
my uncle at Weymouth. However, I dare say we should have seen a great
deal of him in Somersetshire, if it had not happened very unluckily that
we should never have been in the country together. He is very little at
Combe, I believe; but if he were ever so much there, I do not think Mr.
Palmer would visit him, for he is in the Opposition, you know, and besides it is such a way off. I know why you inquire about him, very well:

your sister is to marry him. I am monstrous glad of it, for then I shall have her for a neighbour, you know."

"Upon my word," replied Elinor, "you know much more of the matter than I do, if you have any reason to expect such a match."

"Don't pretend to deny it, because you know it is what everybody talks of. I assure you I heard of it in my way through town."

"My dear Mrs. Palmer!"

"Upon my honour I did. I met Colonel Brandon, Monday morning in Bond Street, just before we left town, and he told me of it directly."

"You surprise me very much. Colonel Brandon tell you of it! Surely you must be mistaken. To give such intelligence to a person who could not be interested in it, even if it were true, is not what I should expect Colonel Brandon to do."

"But I do assure you it was so, for all that, and I will tell you how it happened. When we met him, he turned back and walked with us; and so we began talking of my brother and sister, and one thing and another, and I said to him, 'So, Colonel, there is a new family come to Barton Cottage I hear, and mamma sends me word they are very pretty, and that one of them is going to be married to Mr. Willoughby, of Combe Magna. Is it true, pray? for of course you must know, as you have been in Devonshire so lately.' "

"And what did the Colonel say?"

"Oh! he did not say much; but he looked as if he knew it to be true, so from that moment I set it down as certain. It will be quite delightful, I declare! When is it to take place?"

"Mr. Brandon was very well, I hope?"

"Oh! yes, quite well; and so full of your praises, he did nothing but say fine things of you."

"I am flattered by his commendation. He seems an excellent man; and I think him uncommonly pleasing."

"So do I. He is such a charming man, that is it quite a pity he should be so grave and so dull. Mamma says *he* was in love with your sister too. I assure you it was a great compliment if he was, for he hardly ever falls in love with anybody."

"Is Mr. Willoughby much known in your part of Somersetshire?" said Elinor.

"Oh! yes, extremely well; that is, I do not believe many people are acquainted with him, because Combe Magna is so far off; but they all think him extremely agreeable, I assure you. Nobody is more liked than Mr. Willoughby wherever he goes, and so you may tell your sister. She is a monstrous lucky girl to get him, upon my honour; not but that he is much more lucky in getting her, because she is so very handsome and agreeable that nothing can be good enough for her. However, I don't think her hardly at all handsomer than you, I assure you; for I think you both excessively pretty, and so does Mr. Palmer too, I am sure, though we could not get him to own it last night."

Mrs. Palmer's information respecting Willoughby was not very material; but any testimony in his favour, however small, was pleasing to her.

"I am so glad we are got acquainted at last," continued Charlotte. "And now I hope we shall always be great friends. You can't think how much I longed to see you! It is so delightful that you should live at the cottage! Nothing can be like it, to be sure! And I am so glad your sister is going to be well married! I hope you will be a great deal at Combe Magna. It is a sweet place, by all accounts."

"You have been long acquainted with Colonel Brandon, have you not?"

"Yes, a great while; ever since my sister married. He was a particular friend of Sir John's. I believe," she added in a low voice, "he would have been very glad to have had me, if he could. Sir John and Lady Middleton wished it very much. But mamma did not think the match good enough for me, otherwise Sir John would have mentioned it to the colonel, and we should have been married immediately."

"Did not Colonel Brandon know of Sir John's proposal to your mother before it was made? Had he never owned his affection to yourself?"

"Oh! no; but if mamma had not objected to it, I dare say he would have liked it of all things. He had not seen me then above twice, for it was before I left school. However, I am much happier as I am. Mr. Palmer is just the kind of man I like."

Chapter 21

THE Palmers returned to Cleveland the next day, and the two families at Barton were again left to entertain each other. But this did not last long; Elinor had hardly got their last visitors out of her head—had hardly done wondering at Charlotte's being so happy without a cause, at Mr. Palmer's acting so simply with good abilities, and at the strange unsuitableness which often existed between husband and wife, before Sir John's and Mrs. Jennings's active zeal in the cause of society procured her some other new acquaintance to see and observe.

In a morning's excursion to Exeter, they had met with two young ladies whom Mrs. Jennings had the satisfaction of discovering to be her relations, and this was enough for Sir John to invite them directly to the Park, as soon as their present engagements at Exeter were over. Their engagements at Exeter instantly gave way before such an invitation, and Lady Middleton was thrown into no little alarm on the return of Sir John, by hearing that she was very soon to receive a visit from two girls whom she had never seen in her life, and of whose elegance—whose tolerable gentility even, she could have no proof; for the assurances of her husband and mother on that subject went for nothing at all. Their being her relations too, made it so much the worse; and Mrs. Jennings's attempts at consolation were therefore unfortunately founded, when she advised her daughter not to care about their being so fashionable, because they were all cousins and must put up with one another.

As it was impossible however now to prevent their coming, Lady Middleton resigned herself to the idea of it with all the philosophy of a well-bred woman, contenting herself with merely giving her husband a gentle reprimand on the subject five or six times every day.

The young ladies arrived, their appearance was by no means ungenteel or unfashionable. Their dress was very smart, their manners very civil, they were delighted with the house and in raptures with the furniture, and they happened to be so dotingly fond of children that Lady Middleton's good opinion was engaged in their favour before they had been an hour at the Park. She declared them to be very agreeable girls indeed, which for her ladyship was enthusiastic admiration. Sir John's confidence in his own judgment rose with this animated praise, and he set off directly for the cottage to tell the Miss Dashwoods of the Miss Steeles's arrival, and to assure them of their being the sweetest girls in the world. From such commendation as this, however, there was not much to be learned; Elinor well knew that the sweetest girls in the world were to be met with in every part of England, under every possible variation of form, face, temper, and understanding. Sir John wanted the whole family to walk to the Park directly and look at his guests. Benevolent, philanthropic man! It was painful to him even to keep a third cousin to himself.

"Do come now," said he—"pray come—you must come—I declare you shall come. You can't think how you will like them. Lucy is monstrous pretty, and so good-humoured and agreeable! The children are all hanging about her already, as if she was an old acquaintance. And they both long to see you of all things, for they have heard at Exeter that you are the most beautiful creatures in the world; and I have told them it is all very true, and a great deal more. You will be delighted with them, I am sure. They have brought the whole coach full of playthings for the children. How can you be so cross as not to come! Why, they are your cousins, you know, after a fashion. *You* are my cousins, and they are my wife's, so you must be related."

But Sir John could not prevail. He could only obtain a promise of their calling at the Park within a day or two, and then left them in amazement at their indifference, to walk home and boast anew of their attractions to the Miss Steeles, as he had been already boasting of the Miss Steeles to them.

When their promised visit to the Park and consequent introduction to these young ladies took place, they found in the appearance of the eldest, who was nearly thirty, with a very plain and not a sensible face, nothing to admire, but in the other, who was not more than two or three and twenty, they acknowledged considerable beauty; her features were pretty, and she had a sharp, quick eye, and a smartness of air, which, though it did not give actual elegance or grace, gave distinction to her person. Their manners were particularly civil, and Elinor soon allowed them credit for some kind of sense, when she saw with what constant and judicious attentions they were making themselves agreeable to Lady Middleton. With her children they were in continual raptures, extolling their beauty, courting their notice, and humouring all their whims; and such of their time as could be spared from the importunate demands which this politeness made on it, was spent in admiration of whatever her ladyship was doing, if she happened to be doing anything, or in taking patterns of some elegant new dress, in which her appearance the day before had thrown them into unceasing delight. Fortunately for those who pay their court through such foibles, a fond mother, though in pursuit of praise for her children, the most rapacious of human beings, is likewise the most credulous; her demands are exorbitant; but she will swallow anything; and the excessive affection and endurance of the Miss Steeles towards her offspring, were viewed therefore by Lady Middleton without the smallest surprise or distrust. She saw with maternal complacency all the impertinent incroachments and mischievous tricks to which her cousins submitted. She saw their sashes untied, their hair pulled about their ears, their work-bags searched, and their knives and scissors stolen away, and felt no doubt of its being a reciprocal enjoyment. It suggested no other surprise than that Elinor and Marianne should sit so composedly by without claiming a share in what was passing.

"John is in such spirits to-day!" said she, on his taking Miss Steele's pocket handkerchief, and throwing it out of window. "He is full of monkey tricks."

And soon afterwards, on the second boy's violently pinching one of the same lady's fingers, she fondly observed, "How playful William is!"

"And here is my sweet little Annamaria," she added, tenderly caressing a little girl of three years old, who had not made a noise for the last two minutes. "And she is always so gentle and quiet—never was there such a quiet little thing!"

But unfortunately, in bestowing these embraces, a pin in her ladyship's head-dress slightly scratching the child's neck, produced from this pattern of gentleness such violent screams as could hardly be outdone by any creature professedly noisy. The mother's consternation was excessive; but it could not surpass the alarm of the Miss Steeles, and everything was done by all three, in so critical an emergency, which affection could suggest as likely to assuage the agonies of the little sufferer. She was seated in her mother's lap, covered with kisses, her wound bathed with lavender-water by one of the Miss Steeles, who was on her knees to attend her, and her mouth stuffed with sugar-plums by the other. With such a reward for her tears, the child was too wise to cease crying. She still screamed and sobbed lustily, kicked her two brothers for offering to touch her, and all their united soothings were ineffectual till Lady Middleton luckily remembering that in a scene of similar distress last week, some apricot marmalade had been successfully applied for a bruised temple, the same remedy was eagerly proposed for this unfortunate scratch, and a slight intermission of screams in the young lady on hearing it, gave them reason to hope that it would not be rejected. She was carried out of the room therefore in her mother's arms, in quest of this medicine, and as the two boys chose to follow, though earnestly entreated by their mother to stay behind, the four young ladies were left in a quietness which the room had not known for many hours.

"Poor little creature!" said Miss Steele, as soon as they were gone. "It might have been a very sad accident."

"Yet I hardly know how," cried Marianne, "unless it had been under totally different circumstances. But this is the usual way of heightening alarm, where there is nothing to be alarmed at in reality."

"What a sweet woman Lady Middleton is," said Lucy Steele.

Marianne was silent; it was impossible for her to say what she did not feel, however trivial the occasion; and upon Elinor, therefore, the whole task of telling lies when politeness required it always fell. She did her best, when thus called on, by speaking of Lady Middleton with more warmth than she felt, though with far less than Miss Lucy.

"And Sir John, too," cried the elder sister, "what a charming man he is!"

Here, too, Miss Dashwood's commendation being only simple and just, came in without any *éclat*. She merely observed that he was perfectly good-humoured and friendly.

"And what a charming little family they have! I never saw such fine children in my life. I declare I quite dote upon them already, and indeed I am always distractedly fond of children."

"I should guess so," said Elinor with a smile, "from what I have witnessed this morning."

"I have a notion," said Lucy, "you think the little Middletons rather too much indulged; perhaps they may be the outside of enough; but it is so natural in Lady Middleton; and for my part, I love to see children full of life and spirits; I cannot bear them if they are tame and quiet."

"I confess," replied Elinor, "that while I am at Barton Park, I never think of tame and quiet children with any abhorrence."

A short pause succeeded this speech, which was first broken by Miss Steele, who seemed very much disposed for conversation, and who now said rather abruptly, "And how do you like Devonshire, Miss Dashwood? I suppose you were very sorry to leave Sussex."

In some surprise at the familiarity of this question, or at least of the manner in which it was spoken, Elinor replied that she was.

"Norland is a prodigious beautiful place, is not it?" added Miss Steele.

"We have heard Sir John admire it excessively," said Lucy, who seemed to think some apology necessary for the freedom of her sister.

"I think every one *must* admire it," replied Elinor, "who ever saw the place; though it is not to be supposed that any one can estimate its beauties as we do."

"And had you a great many smart beaux there? I suppose you have not so many in this part of the world; for my part, I think they are a vast addition always."

"But why should you think," said Lucy, looking ashamed of her sister, "that there are not as many genteel young men in Devonshire as Sussex?"

"Nay, my dear, I'm sure I don't pretend to say that there an't. I'm sure there's a vast many smart beaux in Exeter; but you know, how could I tell what smart beaux there might be about Norland? and I was only afraid the Miss Dashwoods might find it dull at Barton, if they had not so many as they used to have. But perhaps you young ladies may not care about the beaux, and had as lief be without them as with them. For my part, I think they are vastly agreeable, provided they dress smart and behave civil. But I can't bear to see them dirty and nasty. Now, there's Mr. Rose at Exeter, a prodigious smart young man, quite a beau, clerk to Mr. Simpson, you know, and yet if you do but meet him of a morning, he is not fit to be seen. I suppose your brother was quite a beau, Miss Dashwood, before he married, as he was so rich?"

"Upon my word," replied Elinor, "I cannot tell you, for I do not perfectly comprehend the meaning of the word. But this I can say, that if he ever was a beau before he married, he is one still, for there is not the smallest alteration in him."

"Oh! dear! one never thinks of married men's being beaux—they have something else to do."

"Lord! Anne," cried her sister, "you can talk of nothing but beaux; you will make Miss Dashwood believe you think of nothing else." And then, to turn the discourse, she began admiring the house and furniture.

This specimen of the Miss Steeles was enough. The vulgar freedom and folly of the eldest left her no recommendation, and as Elinor was not blinded by the beauty or the shrewd look of the youngest, to her want of real elegance and artlessness, she left the house without any wish of knowing them better.

Not so the Miss Steeles. They came from Exeter, well provided with admiration for the use of Sir John Middleton, his family, and all his relations, and no niggardly proportion was now dealt out to his fair cousins, whom they declared to be the most beautiful, elegant, accomplished and agreeable girls they had ever beheld, and with whom they were particularly anxious to be better acquainted. And to be better acquainted therefore, Elinor soon found was their inevitable lot; for as Sir John was entirely on the side of the Miss Steeles, their party would be too strong for opposition, and that kind of intimacy must be submitted to, which consists of sitting an hour or two together in the same room almost every day. Sir John could do no more; but he did not know that any more was required; to be together was, in his opinion, to be intimate, and while his continual schemes for their meeting were effectual, he had not a doubt of their being established friends.

To do him justice, he did everything in his power, to promote their unreserve, by making the Miss Steeles acquainted with whatever he knew or supposed of his cousins' situations in the most delicate particulars, and Elinor had not seen them more than twice, before the eldest of them wished her joy on her sister's having been so lucky as to make a conquest of a very smart beau since she came to Barton.

" 'Twill be a fine thing to have her married so young, to be sure," said she, "and I hear he is quite a beau, and prodigious handsome. And I hope you may have as good luck yourself soon, but perhaps you may have a friend in the corner already."

Elinor could not suppose that Sir John would be more nice in proclaiming his suspicions of her regard for Edward, than he had been with respect to Marianne; indeed it was rather his favourite joke of the two, as being somewhat newer and more conjectural: and since Edward's visit, they had never dined together without his drinking to her best affections with so much significancy, and so many nods and winks, as to excite general attention. The letter F—had been likewise invariably brought forward, and found productive of such countless jokes, that its character as the wittiest letter in the alphabet had been long established with Elinor.

The Miss Steeles, as she expected, had now all the benefit of these jokes, and in the eldest of them they raised a curiosity to know the name of the gentleman alluded to, which, though often impertinently expressed, was perfectly of a piece with her general inquisitiveness into the concerns of their family. But Sir John did not sport long with the curiosity which he delighted to raise, for he had at least as much pleasure in telling the name, as Miss Steele had in hearing it.

"His name is Ferrars," said he, in a very audible whisper; "but pray do not tell it, for it's a great secret."

"Ferrars!" repeated Miss Steele; "Mr. Ferrars is the happy man, is he? What! your sister-in-law's brother, Miss Dashwood? a very agreeable young man, to be sure; I know him very well."

"How can you say so, Anne?" cried Lucy, who generally made an amendment to all her sister's assertions. "Though we have seen him once or twice at my uncle's, it is rather too much to pretend to know him very well."

Elinor heard all this with attention and surprise. "And who was this uncle? where did he live? how came they acquainted!" She wished very much to have the subject continued, though she did not choose to join in it herself; but nothing more of it was said, and, for the first time in her life, she thought Mrs. Jennings deficient either in curiosity after petty information, or in a disposition to communicate it. The manner in which Miss Steele had spoken of Edward increased her curiosity; for it struck her as being rather ill-natured, and suggested the suspicion of that lady's knowing, or fancying herself to know, something to his disadvantage. But her curiosity was unavailing, for no farther notice was taken of Mr. Ferrars's name by Miss Steele when alluded to or even openly mentioned by Sir John.

Chapter 22

MARIANNE, who had never much toleration for anything like impertinence, vulgarity, inferiority of parts, or even difference of taste from
herself, was at this time particularly ill-disposed, from the state of her
spirits, to be pleased with the Miss Steeles, or to encourage their advances; and to the invariable coldness of her behaviour towards them,
which checked every endeavour at intimacy on their side, Elinor principally attributed that preference of herself which soon became evident
in the manners of both, but especially of Lucy, who missed no opportunity of engaging her in conversation, or of striving to improve their
acquaintance by an easy and frank communication of her sentiments.

Lucy was naturally clever; her remarks were often just and amusing;
and as a companion for half an hour Elinor frequently found her agreeable; but her powers had received no aid from education, she was ignorant and illiterate, and her deficiency of all mental improvement, her
want of information in the most common particulars could not be concealed from Miss Dashwood, in spite of her constant endeavour to appear
to advantage. Elinor saw, and pitied her for the neglect of abilities which
education might have rendered so respectable; but she saw, with less
tenderness of feeling, the thorough want of delicacy, of rectitude, and
integrity of mind, which her attentions, her assiduities, her flatteries at
the Park betrayed; and she could have no lasting satisfaction in the
company of a person who joined insincerity with ignorance, whose want
of instruction prevented their meeting in conversation on terms of equality, and whose conduct towards others made every show of attention
and deference towards herself prefectly valueless.

"You will think my question an odd one, I dare say," said Lucy to her
one day as they were walking together from the Park to the cottage—
"but, pray, are you personally acquainted with your sister-in-law's
mother, Mrs. Ferrars?"

Elinor *did* think the question a very odd one, and her countenance
expressed it, as she answered that she had never seen Mrs. Ferrars.

"Indeed!" replied Lucy; "I wonder at that, for I thought you must
have seen her at Norland sometimes. Then perhaps you cannot tell me
what sort of a woman she is?"

"No," returned Elinor, cautious of giving her real opinion of Edward's
mother, and not very desirous of satisfying what seemed impertinent
curiosity—"I know nothing of her."

"I am sure you think me very strange, for inquiring about her in such
a way," said Lucy, eyeing Elinor attentively as she spoke; "but perhaps
there may be reasons—I wish I might venture; but however I hope you
will do me the justice of believing that I do not mean to be impertinent."

Elinor made her a civil reply, and they walked on a few minutes in silence. It was broken by Lucy, who renewed the subject again by saying with some hesitation:

"I cannot bear to have you think me impertinently curious; I am sure I would rather do anything in the world than be thought so by a person whose good opinion is so well worth having as yours. And I am sure I should not have the smallest fear of trusting *you;* indeed I should be very glad of your advice how to manage in such an uncomfortable situation as I am; but however there is no occasion to trouble *you.* I am sorry you do not happen to know Mrs. Ferrars."

"I am sorry I do *not*," said Elinor in great astonishment, "if it could be of any use to *you* to know my opinion of her. But really, I never understood that you were at all connected with that family, and therefore I am a little surprised, I confess, at so serious an inquiry into her char-acter."

"I dare say you are, and I am sure I do not at all wonder at it. But if I dared tell you all, you would not be so much surprised. Mrs. Ferrars is certainly nothing to me at present—but the time *may* come—how soon it will come must depend upon herself—when we may be very intimately connected."

She looked down as she said this, amiably bashful, with only one side-glance at her companion to observe its effect on her.

"Good heavens!" cried Elinor, "what do you mean? Are you acquainted with Mr. Robert Ferrars? Can you be?" And she did not feel much de-lighted with the idea of such a sister-in-law.

"No," replied Lucy, "not with Mr. *Robert* Ferrars—I never saw him in my life; but," fixing her eyes upon Elinor, "with his elder brother."

What felt Elinor at that moment? Astonishment, that would have been as painful as it was strong had not an immediate disbelief of the assertion attended it. She turned towards Lucy in silent amazement, unable to divine the reason or object of such a declaration; and though her com-plexion varied, she stood firm in incredulity, and felt in no danger of an hysterical fit or a swoon.

"You may well be surprised," continued Lucy; "for, to be sure, you could have had no idea of it before; for I dare say he never dropped the smallest hint of it to you or any of your family; because it was always meant to be a great secret, and I am sure has been faithfully kept so by me to this hour. Not a soul of all my relations know of it but Anne, and I never should have mentioned it to you, if I had not felt the greatest dependence in the world upon your secrecy; and I really thought my behaviour in asking so many questions about Mrs. Ferrars must seem so odd that it ought to be explained. And I do not think Mr. Ferrars can be displeased when he knows I have trusted you, because I know he has the highest opinion in the world of all your family, and looks upon yourself and the other Miss Dashwoods quite as his own sisters." She paused.

Elinor for a few moments remained silent. Her astonishment at what she heard was at first too great for words; but at length forcing herself to speak, and to speak cautiously, she said with a calmness of manner which tolerably well concealed her surprise and solicitude—"May I ask if your engagement is of long standing?"

"We have been engaged these four years."

"Four years?"

"Yes."

Elinor, though greatly shocked, still felt unable to believe it.

"I did not know," said she, "that you were even acquainted till the other day."

"Our acquaintance, however, is of many years' date. He was under my uncle's care, you know, a considerable while."

"Your uncle!"

"Yes; Mr. Pratt. Did you never hear him talk of Mr. Pratt?"

"I think I have," replied Elinor, with an exertion of spirits which increased with her increase of emotion.

"He was four years with my uncle, who lives at Longstaple, near Plymouth. It was there our acquaintance begun, for my sister and me was often staying with my uncle, and it was there our engagement was formed, though not till a year after he had quitted as a pupil; but he was almost always with us afterwards. I was very unwilling to enter into it, as you may imagine, without the knowledge and approbation of his mother; but I was too young and loved him too well to be so prudent as I ought to have been. Though you do not know him so well as me, Miss Dashwood, you must have seen enough of him to be sensible he is very capable of making a woman sincerely attached to him."

"Certainly," answered Elinor, without knowing what she said; but after a moment's reflection, she added with revived security of Edward's honour and love, and her companion's falsehood—"Engaged to Mr. Edward Ferrars! I confess myself so totally surprised at what you tell me, that really—I beg your pardon; but surely there must be some mistake of person or name. We cannot mean the same Mr. Ferrars."

"We can mean no other," cried Lucy, smiling. "Mr Edward Ferrars, the eldest son of Mrs. Ferrars of Park Street, and brother of your sister-in-law, Mrs. John Dashwood, is the person I mean; you must allow that *I* am not likely to be deceived as to the name of the man on who all my happiness depends."

"It is strange," replied Elinor, in a most painful perplexity, "that I should never have heard him even mention your name."

"No; considering our situation, it was not strange. Our first care has been to keep the matter secret. You knew nothing of me or my family, and therefore there could be no *occasion* for ever mentioning my name to you; and as he was always particularly afraid of his sister's suspecting anything, *that* was reason enough for his not mentioning it."

She was silent. Elinor's security sunk; but her self-command did not sink with it.

"Four years you have been engaged," said she with a firm voice.

"Yes; and heaven knows how much longer we may have to wait. Poor Edward! it puts him quite out of heart." Then taking a small miniature from her pocket she added, "To prevent the possibility of mistake, be so good as to look at this face. It does not do him justice, to be sure, but yet I think you cannot be deceived as to the person it was drew for. I have had it above these three years."

She put it into her hands as she spoke, and when Elinor saw the painting whatever other doubts her fear of a too hasty decision or her wish of detecting falsehood might suffer to linger in her mind, she could have none of its being Edward's face. She returned it almost instantly, acknowledging the likeness.

"I have never been able," continued Lucy, "to give him my picture in return, which I am very much vexed at, for he has been always so anxious to get it! But I am determined to sit for it the very first opportunity."

"You are quite in the right," replied Elinor calmly. They then proceeded a few paces in silence. Lucy spoke first.

"I am sure," said she, "I have no doubt in the world of your faithfully keeping this secret, because you must know of what importance it is to us not to have it reach his mother; for she would never approve of it, I dare say. I shall have no fortune, and I fancy she is an exceeding proud woman."

"I certainly did not seek your confidence," said Elinor; "but you do me no more than justice in imagining that I may be depended on. Your secret is safe with me; but pardon me if I express some surprise at so unnecessary a communication. You must at least have felt that my being acquainted with it could not add to its safety."

As she said this, she looked earnestly at Lucy, hoping to discover something in her countenance—perhaps the falsehood of the greatest part of what she had been saying; but Lucy's countenance suffered no change.

"I was afraid you would think I was taking a great liberty with you," said she, "in telling you all this. I have not known you long to be sure, personally at least, but I have known you all and your family by description a great while; and as soon as I saw you, I felt almost as if you was an old acquaintance. Besides, in the present case, I really thought some explanation was due to you after my making such particular inquiries about Edward's mother; and I am so unfortunate that I have not a creature whose advice I can ask. Anne is the only person that knows of it, and she has no judgment at all; indeed, she does me a great deal more harm than good, for I am in constant fear of her betraying me. She does not know how to hold her tongue, as you must perceive; and I am sure I was in the greatest fright in the world t'other day, when Edward's name was mentioned by Sir John, lest she should out with it all. You can't think how much I go through in my mind from it altogether. I only wonder that I am alive after what I have suffered for Edward's sake these last four years. Everything in such suspense and uncertainty, and seeing him so seldom—we can hardly meet above twice a year. I am sure I wonder my heart is not quite broke."

Here she took out her handkerchief; but Elinor did not feel very compassionate.

"Sometimes," continued Lucy, after wiping her eyes, "I think whether it would not be better for us both, to break off the matter entirely." As she said this, she looked directly at her companion. "But then, at other times, I have not resolution enough for it. I cannot bear the thoughts of making him so miserable, as I know the very mention of such a thing would do. And on my own account too—so dear as he is to me—I don't think I could be equal to it. What would you advise me to do in such a case, Miss Dashwood? What would you do yourself?"

"Pardon me," replied Elinor, startled by the question; "but I can give you no advice under such circumstances. Your own judgment must direct you."

"To be sure," continued Lucy, after a few minutes' silence on both sides, "his mother must provide for him some time or other; but poor Edward is so cast down about it! Did not you think him dreadful low-spirited when he was at Barton? he was so miserable when he left us at Longstaple, to go to you, that I was afraid you would think him quite ill."

"Did he come from your uncle's then when he visited us?"

"Oh, yes; he had been staying a fortnight with us. Did you think he came directly from town?"

"No," replied Elinor, most feelingly sensible of every fresh circumstance in favour of Lucy's veracity. "I remember he told us that he had been staying a fortnight with some friends near Plymouth." She remembered, too, her own surprise at the time, at his mentioning nothing further of those friends, at his total silence with respect even to their names.

"Did not you think him sadly out of spirits?" repeated Lucy.

"We did indeed, particularly so when he first arrived."

"I begged him to exert himself for fear you should suspect what was the matter; but it made him so melancholy, not being able to stay more than a fortnight with us, and seeing me so much affected. Poor fellow! I am afraid it is just the same with him now; for he writes in wretched spirits. I heard from him just before I left Exeter"; taking a letter from her pocket and carelessly showing the direction to Elinor. "You know his hand, I dare say, a charming one it is; but that is not written so well as usual. He was tired, I dare say, for he had just filled the sheet to me as full as possible."

Elinor saw that it *was* his hand, and she could doubt no longer. The picture, she had allowed herself to believe, might have been accidentally obtained; it might not have been Edward's gift; but a correspondence between them by letter could subsist only under a positive engagement, could be authorised by nothing else; for a few moments she was almost overcome—her heart sunk within her, and she could hardly stand; but exertion was indispensably necessary, and she struggled so resolutely against the oppression of her feelings that her success was speedy, and for the time complete.

"Writing to each other," said Lucy, returning the letter into her pocket, "is the only comfort we have in such long separations. Yes. *I* have one other comfort in his picture; but poor Edward has not even *that*. If he had but my picture, he says he should be easy. I gave him a lock of my hair set in a ring when he was at Longstaple last, and that was some comfort to him, he said, but not equal to a picture. Perhaps you might notice the ring when you saw him?"

"I did," said Elinor, with a composure of voice under which was concealed an emotion and distress beyond anything she had ever felt before. She was mortified, shocked, confounded.

Fortunately for her they had now reached the cottage, and the conversation could be continued no farther. After sitting with them a few minutes, the Miss Steeles returned to the Park, and Elinor was then at liberty to think and be wretched.

Chapter 23

HOWEVER small Elinor's general dependence on Lucy's veracity might be, it was impossible for her on serious reflection to suspect it in the present case, where no temptation could be answerable to the folly of inventing a falsehood of such a description. What Lucy had asserted to be true, therefore, Elinor could not, dared not longer doubt; supported as it was too on every side by such probabilities and proofs, and contradicted by nothing but her own wishes. Their opportunity of acquaintance in the house of Mr. Pratt was a foundation for the rest, at once indisputable and alarming; and Edward's visit near Plymouth, his melancholy state of mind, his dissatisfaction at his own prospects, his uncertain behaviour towards herself, the intimate knowledge of the Miss Steeles as to Norland and their family connections, which had often surprised her, the picture, the letter, the ring, formed altogether such a body of evidence as overcame every fear of condemning him unfairly, and established as a fact which no partiality could set aside, his ill-treatment of herself. Her resentment of such behaviour, her indignation at having been its dupe, for a short time made her feel only for herself; but other ideas, other considerations, soon arose. Had Edward been intentionally deceiving her? Had he feigned a regard for her which he did not feel? Was his engagement to Lucy an engagement of the heart? No; whatever it might once have been, she could not believe it such at present. His affection was all her own. She could not be deceived in that. Her mother, sisters, Fanny, all had been conscious of his regard for her at Norland; it was not an illusion of her own vanity. He certainly loved her. What a softener of the heart was this persuasion! How much could it not tempt her to forgive! He had been blameable, highly blameable in remaining at Norland after he first felt her influence over him to be more than it ought to be. In that, he could not be defended; but if he had injured her, how much more had he injured himself! If her case were pitiable, his was hopeless. His imprudence had made her miserable for a while; but it seemed to have deprived himself of all chance of ever being otherwise. She might in time regain tranquillity; but *he,* what had he to look forward to? Could he ever be tolerably happy with Lucy Steele? Could he, were his affection for herself out of the question, with his integrity, his delicacy, and well-informed mind, be satisfied with a wife like her—illiterate, artful, and selfish?

The youthful infatuation of nineteen would naturally blind him to everything but her beauty and good-nature; but the four succeeding years—years which, if rationally spent, give such improvement to the understanding, must have opened his eyes to her defects of education: while the same period of time, spent on her side in inferior society and more frivolous pursuits, had perhaps robbed her of that simplicity which might once have given an interesting character to her beauty.

If, in the supposition of his seeking to marry herself, his difficulties from his mother had seemed great, how much greater were they now likely to be, when the object of his engagement was undoubtedly inferior in connections, and probably inferior in fortune to herself! These diffi⸱ culties, indeed, with a heart so alienated from Lucy, might not press very hard upon his patience; but melancholy was the state of the person by whom the expectation of family opposition and unkindness could be felt as a relief!

As these considerations occurred to her in painful succession, she wept for him more than for herself. Supported by the conviction of having done nothing to merit her present unhappiness, and consoled by the belief that Edward had done nothing to forfeit her esteem, she thought she could even now, under the first smart of the heavy blow, command herself enough to guard every suspicion of the truth from her mother and sisters. And so well was she able to answer her own expectations, that when she joined them at dinner only two hours after she had first suffered the extinction of all her dearest hopes, no one would have supposed from the appearance of the sisters, that Elinor was mourning in secret over obstacles which must divide her for ever from the object of her love, and that Marianne was internally dwelling on the perfections of a man of whose whole heart she felt thoroughly possessed, and whom she expected to see in every carriage which drove near their house.

The necessity of concealing from her mother and Marianne what had been entrusted in confidence to herself, though it obliged her to unceasing exertion, was no aggravation of Elinor's distress. On the contrary, it was a relief to her to be spared the communication of what would give such affliction to them, and to be saved likewise from hearing that condemnation of Edward which would probably flow from the excess of their partial affection for herself, and which was more than she felt equal to support.

From their counsel or their conversation she knew she could receive no assistance; their tenderness and sorrow must add to her distress, while her self-command would neither receive encouragement from their example nor from their praise. She was stronger alone, and her own good sense so well supported her, that her firmness was as unshaken, her appearance of cheerfulness as invariable, as, with regrets so poignant and so fresh, it was possible for them to be.

Much as she had suffered from her first conversation with Lucy on the subject, she soon felt an earnest wish of renewing it, and this for more reasons than one. She wanted to hear many particulars of their engagement repeated again, she wanted more clearly to understand what Lucy really felt for Edward, whether there were any sincerity in her declaration of tender regard for him, and she particularly wanted to convince Lucy, by her readiness to enter on the matter again, and her calmness in conversing on it, that she was no otherwise interested in it than as a friend, which she very much feared her involuntary agitation, in their morning discourse must have left at least doubtful. That Lucy was disposed to be jealous of her, appeared very probable; it was plain that Edward had always spoken highly in her praise, not merely from Lucy's assertion, but from her venturing to trust her on so short a personal acquaintance, with a secret so confessedly and evidently important. And even Sir John's joking intelligence must have had some weight. But indeed, while Elinor remained so well assured within herself, of being really beloved by Edward, it required no other consideration of probabilities to make it natural that Lucy should be jealous; and that she was so, her very confidence was a proof. What other reason for the disclosure of the affair could there be, but that Elinor might be informed by it of Lucy's superior claims on Edward, and be taught to avoid him in future? She had little difficulty in understanding thus much of her rival's intentions, and while she was firmly resolved to act by her as every principle of honour and honesty directed, to combat her own affection for Edward and to see him as little as possible; she could not deny herself the comfort of endeavouring to convince Lucy that her heart was unwounded. And as she could now have nothing more painful to hear on the subject than had already been told, she did not mistrust her own ability of going through a repetition of particulars with composure.

But it was not immediately that an opportunity of doing so could be commanded, though Lucy was as well disposed as herself to take advantage of any that occurred; for the weather was not often fine enough to allow of their joining in a walk, where they might most easily separate themselves from the others; and though they met at least every other evening either at the Park or cottage, and chiefly at the former, they could not be supposed to meet for the sake of conversation. Such a thought would never enter either Sir John or Lady Middleton's head, and therefore very little leisure was ever given for general chat, and none at all for particular discourse. They met for the sake of eating, drinking, and laughing together, playing at cards or consequences, or any other game that was sufficiently noisy.

One or two meetings of this kind had taken place without affording Elinor any chance of engaging Lucy in private, when Sir John called at the cottage one morning, to beg in the name of charity, that they would all dine with Lady Middleton that day, as he was obliged to attend the club at Exeter, and she would otherwise be quite alone, except her mother and the two Miss Steeles. Elinor, who foresaw a fairer opening for the point she had in view, in such a party as this was likely to be, more at liberty among themselves under the tranquil and well-bred direction of Lady Middleton than when her husband united them together in one noisy purpose, immediately accepted the invitation; Margaret, with her mother's permission, was equally compliant, and Marianne, though always unwilling to join any of their parties, was persuaded by her mother, who could not bear to have her seclude herself from any chance of amusement, to go likewise.

The young ladies went, and Lady Middleton was happily preserved from the frightful solitude which had threatened her. The insipidity of the meeting was exactly such as Elinor had expected; it produced not one novelty of thought or expression, and nothing could be less interesting than the whole of their discourse both in the dining-parlour and drawing-room: to the latter, the children accompanied them, and while they remained there, she was too well convinced of the impossibility of engaging Lucy's attention to attempt it. They quitted it only with the removal of the tea-things. The card-table was then placed, and Elinor began to wonder at herself for having ever entertained a hope of finding time for conversation at the Park. They all rose up in preparation for a round game.

"I am glad," said Lady Middleton to Lucy, "you are not going to finish poor little Annamaria's basket this evening; for I am sure it must hurt your eyes to work fillagree by candlelight. And we will make the dear little love some amends for her disappointment to-morrow, and then I hope she will not much mind it."

This hint was enough; Lucy recollected herself instantly and replied, "Indeed, you are very much mistaken, Lady Middleton; I am only waiting to know whether you can make your party without me, or I should have been at my fillagree already. I would not disappoint the little angel for all the world; and if you want me at the card-table now, I am resolved to finish the basket after supper."

"You are very good; I hope it won't hurt your eyes—will you ring the bell for some working candles? My poor little girl would be sadly disappointed, I know, if the basket was not finished to-morrow, for though I told her it certainly would not, I am sure she depends upon having it done."

Lucy directly drew her work-table near her, and reseated herself with an alacrity and cheerfulness which seemed to infer that she could taste no greater delight than in making a fillagree basket for a spoilt child.

Lady Middleton proposed a rubber of casino to the others. No one made any objection but Marianne, who, with her usual inattention to the forms of general civility, exclaimed, "Your ladyship will have the goodness to excuse *me*—you know I detest cards. I shall go to the pianoforte; I have not touched it since it was tuned." And without further ceremony, she turned away and walked to the instrument.

Lady Middleton looked as if she thanked heaven that *she* had never made so rude a speech.

"Marianne can never keep long from that instrument, you know, ma'am," said Elinor, endeavouring to smooth away the offence; "and I do not much wonder at it, for it is the very best-toned pianoforte I ever heard."

The remaining five were now to draw their cards.

"Perhaps," continued Elinor, "if I should happen to cut out, I may be of some use to Miss Lucy Steele, in rolling her papers for her; and there is so much still to be done to the basket, that it must be impossible, I think, for her labour singly, to finish it this evening. I should like the work exceedingly, if she would allow me a share in it."

"Indeed I shall be very much obliged to you for your help," cried Lucy, "for I find there is more to be done to it than I thought there was; and it would be a shocking thing to disappoint dear Annamaria after all."

"Oh! that would be terrible indeed," said Miss Steele. "Dear little soul, how I do love her!"

"You are very kind," said Lady Middleton to Elinor; "and as you really like the work, perhaps you will be as well pleased not to cut in till another rubber, or will you take your chance now?"

Elinor joyfully profited by the first of these proposals, and thus, by a little of that address which Marianne could never condescend to practise, gained her own end and pleased Lady Middleton at the same time. Lucy made room for her with ready attention, and the two fair rivals were thus seated side by side at the same table, and with the utmost harmony engaged in forwarding the same work. The pianoforte, at which Marianne, wrapped up in her own music and her own thoughts, had by this time forgotten that anybody was in the room besides herself, was luckily so near them that Miss Dashwood now judged she might safely, under the shelter of its noise, introduce the interesting subject, without any risk of being heard at the card-table.

Chapter 24

In a firm, though cautious, tone Elinor thus began:

"I should be undeserving of the confidence you have honoured me with, if I felt no desire for its continuance, or no further curiosity on its subject. I will not apologise therefore for bringing it forward again."

"Thank you," cried Lucy warmly, "for breaking the ice; you have set my heart at ease by it; for I was somehow or other afraid I had offended you by what I told you that Monday."

"Offended me! How could you suppose so? Believe me," and Elinor spoke it with the truest sincerity, "nothing could be farther from my intention than to give you such an idea. Could you have a motive for the trust that was not honourable and flattering to me?"

"And yet I do assure you," replied Lucy, her little sharp eyes full of meaning, "there seemed to me to be a coldness and displeasure in your manner that made me quite uncomfortable. I felt sure that you was angry with me; and have been quarrelling with myself ever since, for having took such a liberty as to trouble you with my affairs. But I am very glad to find it was only my own fancy, and that you do not really blame me. If you knew what a consolation it was to me to relieve my heart by speaking to you of what I am always thinking of every moment of my life, your compassion would make you overlook everything else, I am sure."

"Indeed I can easily believe that it was a very great relief to you to acknowledge your situation to me, and be assured that you shall never have reason to repent it. Your case is a very unfortunate one; you seem to me to be surrounded with difficulties, and you will have need of all your mutual affection to support you under them. Mr. Ferrars, I believe, is entirely dependent on his mother."

"He has only two thousand pounds of his own; it would be madness to marry upon that, though for my own part I could give up every prospect of more without a sigh. I have been always used to a very small income, and could struggle with any poverty for him; but I love him too well to be the selfish means of robbing him, perhaps, of all that his mother might give him if he married to please her. We must wait, it may be for many years. With almost every other man in the world, it would be an alarming prospect; but Edward's affection and constancy nothing can deprive me of, I know."

"That conviction must be everything to you; and he is undoubtedly supported by the same trust in yours. If the strength of your reciprocal attachment had failed, as between many people and under many circumstances it naturally would during a four years' engagement, your situation would have been pitiable indeed."

Lucy here looked up; but Elinor was careful in guarding her countenance from every expression that could give her words a suspicious tendency.

"Edward's love for me," said Lucy, "has been pretty well put to the test, by our long, very long absence since we were first engaged, and it has stood the trial so well that I should be unpardonable to doubt it now. I can safely say that he has never gave me one moment's alarm on that account from the first."

Elinor hardly knew whether to smile or sigh at this assertion.

Lucy went on. "I am rather of a jealous temper, too, by nature, and from our different situations in life, from his being so much more in the world than me, and our continual separation, I was enough inclined for suspicion to have found out the truth in an instant, if there had been the slightest alteration in his behaviour to me when we met, or any lowness of spirits that I could not account for, or if he had talked more of one lady than another, or seemed in any respect less happy at Longstaple than he used to be. I do not mean to say that I am particularly observant or quick-sighted in general, but in such a case I am sure I could not be deceived."

"All this," thought Elinor, "is very pretty; but it can impose upon neither of us."

"But what," said she, after a short silence, "are your views? or have you none but that of waiting for Mrs. Ferrars's death, which is a melancholy and shocking extremity? Is her son determined to submit to this, and to all the tediousness of the many years of suspense in which it may involve you, rather than run the risk of her displeasure for a while by owning the truth?"

"If we could be certain that it would be only for a while! But Mrs. Ferrars is a very headstrong, proud woman, and in her first fit of anger upon hearing it, would very likely secure everything to Robert; and the idea of that, for Edward's sake, frightens away all my inclination for hasty measures."

"And for your own sake too, or you are carrying your disinterestedness beyond reason."

Lucy looked at Elinor again, and was silent.

"Do you know Mr. Robert Ferrars?" asked Elinor.

"Not at all—I never saw him; but I fancy he is very unlike his brother—silly and a great coxcomb."

"A great coxcomb!" repeated Miss Steele, whose ear had caught those words by a sudden pause in Marianne's music. "Oh! they are talking of their favourite beaux, I dare say."

"No, sister," cried Lucy, "you are mistaken there, our favourite beaux are *not* great coxcombs."

"I can answer for it that Miss Dashwood's is not," said Mrs. Jennings, laughing heartily; "for he is one of the modestest, prettiest-behaved young men I ever saw. But as for Lucy, she is such a sly little creature, there is no finding out who *she* likes."

"Oh!" cried Miss Steele, loking significantly round at them, "I dare say Lucy's beau is quite as modest and pretty-behaved as Miss Dashwood's."

Elinor blushed in spite of herself. Lucy bit her lip, and looked angrily at her sister. A mutual silence took place for some time. Lucy first put

an end to it by saying in a lower tone, though Marianne was then giving
them the powerful protection of a very magnificent concerto:

"I will honestly tell you of one scheme which has lately come into my
head for bringing matters to bear; indeed, I am bound to let you into
the secret, for you are a party concerned. I dare say you have seen
enough of Edward to know that he would prefer the church to every
other profession. Now, my plan is that he should take orders as soon as
he can, and then through your interest, which I am sure you would be
kind enough to use out of friendship for him, and, I hope, out of some
regard to me, your brother might be persuaded to give him Norland
living; which I understand is a very good one, and the present incumbent not likely to live a great while. That would be enough for us to
marry upon, and we might trust to time and chance for the rest."

"I should be always happy," replied Elinor, "to show any mark of my
esteem and friendship for Mr. Ferrars; but do not you perceive that my
interest on such an occasion would be perfectly unnecessary? He is brother
to Mrs. John Dashwood—*that* must be recommendation enough to her
husband."

"But Mrs. John Dashwood would not much approve of Edward's going
into orders."

"Then I rather suspect that my interest would do very little."

They were again silent for many minutes. At length Lucy exclaimed
with a deep sigh:

"I believe it would be the wisest way to put an end to the business at
once by dissolving the engagement. We seem so beset with difficulties on
every side, that though it would make us miserable for a time, we should
be happier perhaps in the end. But will you not give me your advice,
Miss Dashwood?"

"No," answered Elinor, with a smile which concealed very agitated
feelings, "on such a subject I certainly will not. You know very well that
my opinion would have no weight with you, unless it were on the side of
your wishes."

"Indeed, you wrong me," replied Lucy with great solemnity; "I know
nobody of whose judgment I think so highly as I do of yours; and I do
really believe, that if you was to say to me, 'I advise you by all means to
put an end to your engagement with Edward Ferrars, it will be more
for the happiness of both of you,' I should resolve upon doing it immediately."

Elinor blushed for the insincerity of Edward's future wife, and replied,
"This compliment would effectually frighten me from giving any opinion
on the subject, had I formed one. It raises my influence much too high;
the power of dividing two people so tenderly attached is too much for an
indifferent person."

" 'Tis because you are an indifferent person," said Lucy, with some
pique, and laying a particular stress on those words, "that your judgment
might justly have such weight with me. If you could be supposed to be

biased in any respect by your own feelings, your opinion would not be worth having."

Elinor thought it wisest to make no answer to this, lest they might provoke each other to an unsuitable increase of ease and unreserve, and was even partly determined never to mention the subject again. Another pause, therefore, of many minutes' duration succeeded this speech, and Lucy was still the first to end it.

"Shall you be in town this winter, Miss Dashwood?" said she, with all her accustomary complacency.

"Certainly not."

"I am sorry for that," returned the other, while her eyes brightened at the information; "it would have gave me such pleasure to meet you there! But I dare say you will go for all that. To be sure, your brother and sister will ask you to come to them."

"It will not be in my power to accept their invitation if they do."

"How unlucky that is! I had quite depended upon meeting you there Anne and me are to go the latter end of January to some relations who have been wanting us to visit them these several years! But I only go for the sake of seeing Edward. He will be there in February; otherwise London would have no charms for me, I have not spirits for it."

Elinor was soon called to the card-table by the conclusion of the first rubber, and the confidential discourse of the two ladies was therefore at an end, to which both of them submitted without any reluctance, for nothing had been said on either side to make them dislike each other less than they had done before; and Elinor sat down to the card-table with the melancholy persuasion that Edward was not only without affection for the person who was to be his wife, but that he had not even the chance of being tolerably happy in marriage, which sincere affection on *her* side would have given, for self-interest alone could induce a woman to keep a man to an engagement of which she seemed so thoroughly aware that he was weary.

From this time the subject was never revived by Elinor; and when entered on by Lucy, who seldom missed an opportunity of introducing it, and was particularly careful to inform her confidante of her happiness whenever she received a letter from Edward, it was treated by the former with calmness and caution, and dismissed as soon as civility would allow; for she felt such conversations to be an indulgence which Lucy did not deserve, and which were dangerous to herself.

The visit of the Miss Steeles at Barton Park was lengthened far beyond what the first invitation implied. Their favour increased, they could not be spared; Sir John would not hear of their going; and in spite of their numerous and long-arranged engagements in Exeter, in spite of the absolute necessity of their returning to fulfil them immediately, which was in full force at the end of every week, they were prevailed on to stay nearly two months at the Park, and to assist in the due celebration of that festival

which requires a more than ordinary share of private balls and large
dinners to proclaim its importance.

Chapter 25

Though Mrs. Jennings was in the habit of spending a large portion
of the year at the houses of her children and friends, she was not without
a settled habitation of her own. Since the death of her husband, who had
traded with success in a less elegant part of the town, she had resided
every winter in a house in one of the streets near Portman Square.
Towards this home, she began on the approach of January to turn her
thoughts, and thither she one day abruptly, and very unexpectedly by
them, asked the elder Miss Dashwoods to accompany her. Elinor, without observing the varying complexion of her sister, and the animated
look which spoke no indifference to the plan, immediately gave a grateful
but absolute denial for both, in which she believed herself to be speaking
their united inclinations. The reason alleged, was their determined resolution of not leaving their mother at that time of year. Mrs. Jennings
received the refusal with some surprise and repeated her invitation immediately.

"O Lord! I am sure your mother can spare you very well, and I *do* beg
you will favour me with your company, for I've quite set my heart upon
it. Don't fancy that you will be any inconvenience to me, for I shan't put
myself at all out of my way for you. It will only be sending Betty by the
coach, and I hope I can afford *that*. We three shall be able to go very well
in my chaise; and when we are in town, if you do not like to go wherever
I do, well and good, you may always go with one of my daughters. I am
sure your mother will not object to it; for I have had such good luck in
getting my own children off my hands, that she will think me a very fit
person to have the charge of you: and if I don't get one of you at least
well married before I have done with you, it shall not be my fault. I shall
speak a good word for you to all the young men, you may depend upon it."

"I have a notion," said Sir John, "that Miss Marianne would not object
to such a scheme, if her elder sister would come into it. It is very hard
indeed that she should not have a little pleasure, because Miss Dashwood
does not wish it. So I would advise you two to set off for town when you
are tired of Barton, without saying a word to Miss Dashwood about it."

"Nay," cried Mrs. Jennings, "I am sure I shall be monstrous glad of
Miss Marianne's company, whether Miss Dashwood will go or not, only
the more the merrier say I, and I thought it would be more comfortable
for them to be together; because if they got tired of me, they might talk
to one another, and laugh at my odd ways behind my back. But one or the
other, if not both of them, I must have. Lord bless me! How do you think
I can live poking by myself, I who have been always used till this winter
to have Charlotte with me. Come, Miss Marianne, let us strike hands

upon the bargain, and if Miss Dashwood will change her mind by and by, why, so much the better."

"I thank you, ma'am, sincerely thank you," said Marianne, with warmth; "your invitation has insured my gratitude for ever, and it would give me such happiness—yes, almost the greatest happiness I am capable of, to be able to accept it. But my mother, my dearest, kindest mother—I feel the justice of what Elinor has urged, and if she were to be made less happy, less comfortable by our absence—Oh! no, nothing should tempt me to leave her. It should not, must not be a struggle."

Mrs. Jennings repeated her assurance that Mrs. Dashwood could spare them perfectly well; and Elinor, who now understood her sister, and saw to what indifference to almost everything else she was carried by her eagerness to be with Willoughby again, made no further direct opposition to the plan, and merely referred it to her mother's decision, from whom however she scarcely expected to receive any support in her endeavour to prevent a visit which she could not approve of for Marianne, and which on her own account she had particular reasons to avoid. Whatever Marianne was desirous of her mother would be eager to promote—she could not expect to influence the latter to cautiousness of conduct in an affair respecting which she had never been able to inspire her with distrust: and she dared not explain the motive of her own disinclination for going to London. That Marianne, fastidious as she was, thoroughly acquainted with Mrs. Jennings's manners, and invariably disgusted by them, should overlook every inconvenience of that kind, should disregard whatever must be most wounding to her irritable feelings, in her pursuit of one object, was such a proof, so strong, so full, of the importance of that object to her, as Elinor, in spite of all that had passed, was not prepared to witness.

On being informed of the invitation, Mrs. Dashwood persuaded that such an excursion would be productive of much amusement to both her daughters, and perceiving through all her affectionate attention to herself, how much the heart of Marianne was in it, would not hear of their declining the offer upon *her* account; insisted on their both accepting it directly, and then began to foresee, with her usual cheerfulness, a variety of advantages that would accrue to them all from this separation.

"I am delighted with the plan," she cried, "it is exactly what I could wish. Margaret and I shall be as much benefited by it as yourselves. When you and the Middletons are gone, we shall go on so quietly and happily together with our books and our music! You will find Margaret so improved when you come back again! And I have a little plan of alteration for your bedrooms too, which may now be performed without inconvenience to anyone. It is very right that you *should* go to town; I would have every young woman of your condition in life acquainted with the manners and amusements of London. You will be under the care of a motherly, good sort of woman, of whose kindness to you I can have no doubt. And in all probability you will see your brother, and whatever may be his faults, or the faults of his wife, when I consider whose son he is, I cannot bear to have you so wholly estranged from each other."

"Though, with your usual anxiety for our happiness," said Elinor, "you have been obviating every impediment to the present scheme which occurred to you, there is still one objection which, in my opinion, cannot be so easily removed."

Marianne's countenance sank.

"And what," said Mrs. Dashwood, "is my dear prudent Elinor going to suggest? What formidable obstacle is she now to bring forward? Do not let me hear a word about the expense of it."

"My objection is this: though I think very well of Mrs. Jennings's heart, she is not a woman whose society can afford us pleasure, or whose protection will give us consequence."

"That is very true," replied her mother; "but of her society, separately from that of other people, you will scarcely have anything at all, and you will almost always appear in public with Lady Middleton."

"If Elinor is frightened away by her dislike of Mrs. Jennings," said Marianne, "at least it need not prevent *my* accepting her invitation. I have no such scruples, and I am sure I could put up with every unpleasantness of that kind with very little effort."

Elinor could not help smiling at this display of indifference towards the manners of a person to whom she had often had difficulty in persuading Marianne to behave with tolerable politeness, and resolved within herself, that if her sister persisted in going, she would go likewise, as she did not think it proper that Marianne should be left to the sole guidance of her own judgment, or that Mrs. Jennings should be abandoned to the mercy of Marianne for all the comfort of her domestic hours. To this determination she was the more easily reconciled, by recollecting that Edward Ferrars, by Lucy's account, was not to be in town before February, and that their visit, without any unreasonable abridgment, might be previously finished.

"I will have you *both* go," said Mrs. Dashwood; "these objections are nonsensical. You will have much pleasure in being in London, and especially in being together; and if Elinor would ever condescend to anticipate enjoyment, she would foresee it there from a variety of sources; she would perhaps expect some from improving her acquaintance with her sister-in-law's family."

Elinor had often wished for an opportunity of attempting to weaken her mother's dependence on the attachment of Edward and herself, that the shock might be the less when the whole truth were revealed, and now on this attack, though almost hopeless of success, she forced herself to begin her design by saying, as calmly as she could, "I like Edward Ferrars very much, and shall always be glad to see him; but as to the rest of the family, it is a matter of perfect indifference to me whether I am ever known to them or not."

Mrs. Dashwood smiled and said nothing. Marianne lifted up her eyes in astonishment, and Elinor conjectured that she might as well have held her tongue.

After very little farther discourse, it was finally settled that the invitation should be fully accepted. Mrs. Jennings received the information with a great deal of joy, and many assurances of kindness and care; nor was it a matter of pleasure merely to her. Sir John was delighted; for to a man whose prevailing anxiety was the dread of being alone, the acquisition of two to the number of inhabitants in London was something. Even Lady Middleton took the trouble of being delighted, which was putting herself rather out of her way; and as for the Miss Steeles, especially Lucy, they had never been so happy in their lives as this intelligence made them.

Elinor submitted to the arrangement which counteracted her wishes with less reluctance than she had expected to feel. With regard to herself, it was now a matter of unconcern whether she went to town or not; and when she saw her mother so thoroughly pleased with the plan, and her sister exhilarated by it in look, voice, and manner, restored to all her usual animation, and elevated to more than her usual gaiety, she could not be dissatisfied with the cause, and would hardly allow herself to distrust the consequence.

Marianne's joy was almost a degree beyond happiness, so great was the perturbation of her spirits and her impatience to be gone. Her unwillingness to quit her mother was her only restorative to calmness; and at the moment of parting her grief on that score was excessive. Her mother's affliction was hardly less, and Elinor was the only one of the three who seemed to consider the separation as anything short of eternal.

Their departure took place in the first week in January. The Middletons were to follow in about a week. The Miss Steeles kept their station at the Park, and were to quit it only with the rest of the family.

Chapter 26

ELINOR could not find herself in the carriage with Mrs. Jennings, and beginning a journey to London under her protection, and as her guest, without wondering at her own situation, so short had their acquaintance with that lady been, so wholly unsuited were they in age and disposition, and so many had been her objections against such a measure only a few days before! But these objections had all, with that happy ardour of youth which Marianne and her mother equally shared, been overcome or overlooked; and Elinor, in spite of every occasional doubt of Willoughby's constancy, could not witness the rapture of delightful expectation which filled the whole soul and beamed in the eyes of Marianne, without feeling how blank was her own prospect, how cheerless her own state of mind in the comparison, and how gladly she would engage in the solicitude of Marianne's situation to have the same animating object in view, the same possibility of hope. A short, a very short time, however, must now decide what Willoughby's intentions were: in all probability he was already in town. Marianne's eagerness to be gone declared her dependence on finding him there; and Elinor was resolved not only upon gaining every new light as to his character which her own observation or the intelligence of others could give her, but likewise upon watching his behaviour to her sister with such zealous attention, as to ascertain what he was, and what he meant, before many meetings had taken place. Should the result of her observations be unfavourable, she was determined at all events to open the eyes of her sister; should it be otherwise, her exertions would be of a different nature—she must then learn to avoid every selfish comparison, and banish every regret which might lessen her satisfaction in the happiness of Marianne.

They were three days on their journey, and Marianne's behaviour as they travelled was a happy specimen of what her future complaisance and companionableness to Mrs. Jennings might be expected to be. She sat in silence almost all the way, wrapt in her own meditations, and scarcely ever voluntarily speaking, except when any object of picturesque beauty within their view drew from her an exclamation of delight exclusively addressed to her sister. To atone for this conduct, therefore, Elinor took immediate possession of the post of civility which she had assigned herself, behaved with the greatest attention to Mrs. Jennings, talked with her, laughed with her, and listened to her whenever she could; and Mrs. Jennings on her side treated them both with all possible kindness, was solicitous on every occasion for their ease and enjoyment, and only disturbed that she could not make them choose their own dinners at the inn, nor extort a confession of their preferring salmon to cod, or boiled fowls to veal cutlets. They reached town by three o'clock the third day, glad to be released, after such a journey, from the confinement of a carriage, and ready to enjoy all the luxury of a good fire.

The house was handsome and handsomely fitted up, and the young ladies were immediately put in possession of a very comfortable apartment. It had formerly been Charlotte's, and over the mantelpiece still hung a landscape in coloured silks of her performance, in proof of her having spent seven years at a great school in town to some effect.

As dinner was not to be ready in less than two hours from their arrival, Elinor determined to employ the interval in writing to her mother, and sat down for that purpose. In a few moments Marianne did the same. "I am writing home, Marianne," said Elinor; "had not you better defer your letter for a day or two?"

"I am *not* going to write to my mother," replied Marianne hastily, and as if wishing to avoid any further inquiry. Elinor said no more; it immediately struck her that she must then be writing to Willoughby, and the conclusion which as instantly followed was, that however mysteriously they might wish to conduct the affair, they must be engaged. This conviction, though not entirely satisfactory, gave her pleasure, and she continued her letter with greater alacrity. Marianne's was finished in a very few minutes; in length it could be no more than a note: it was then folded up, sealed and directed with eager rapidity. Elinor thought she could distinguish a large W in the direction, and no sooner was it complete than Marianne, ringing the bell, requested the footman who answered it, to get that letter conveyed for her to the twopenny post. This decided the matter at once.

Her spirits still continued very high, but there was a flutter in them which prevented their giving much pleasure to her sister, and this agitation increased as the evening drew on. She could scarcely eat any dinner, and when they afterwards returned to the drawing-room, seemed anxiously listening to the sound of every carriage.

It was a great satisfaction to Elinor that Mrs. Jennings, by being much engaged in her own room, could see little of what was passing. The teathings were brought in, and already had Marianne been disappointed more than once by a rap at a neighbouring door, when a loud one was suddenly heard which could not be mistaken for one at any other house. Elinor felt secure of its announcing Willoughby's approach, and Marianne, starting up, moved towards the door. Everything was silent; this could not be borne many seconds, she opened the door, advanced a few steps towards the stairs, and after listening half a minute, returned into the room in all the agitation which a conviction of having heard him would naturally produce; in the ecstasy of her feelings at that instant she could not help exclaiming, "O Elinor, it is Willoughby, indeed it is!" and seemed almost ready to throw herself into his arms, when Colonel Brandon appeared.

It was too great a shock to be borne with calmness, and she immediately left the room. Elinor was disappointed too; but at the same time her regard for Colonel Brandon ensured his welcome with her, and she felt particularly hurt that a man so partial to her sister should perceive that she experienced nothing but grief and disappointment in seeing him. She instantly saw that it was not unnoticed by him, that he even observed Marianne as she quitted the room, with such astonishment and concern, as hardly left him the recollection of what civility demanded towards herself.

"Is your sister ill?" said he.

Elinor answered in some distress that she was, and then talked of headaches, low spirits, and over-fatigues, and of everything to which she could decently attribute her sister's behaviour.

He heard her with the most earnest attention, but seeming to recollect himself, said no more on the subject, and began directly to speak of his pleasure at seeing them in London, making the usual inquiries about their journey and the friends they had left behind.

In this calm kind of way, with very little interest on either side, they continued to talk, both of them out of spirits, and the thoughts of both engaged elsewhere. Elinor wished very much to ask whether Willoughby were then in town, but she was afraid of giving him pain by any inquiry after his rival; and at length by way of saying something, she asked if he had been in London ever since she had seen him last. "Yes," he replied with some embarrassment, "almost ever since; I have been once or twice at Delaford for a few days, but it has never been in my power to return to Barton."

This, and the manner in which it was said, immediately brought back to her remembrance all the circumstances of his quitting that place, with the uneasiness and suspicions they had caused to Mrs. Jennings, and she was fearful that her question had implied much more curiosity on the subject than she had ever felt.

Mrs. Jennings soon came in. "O Colonel!" said she, with her usual noisy cheerfulness, "I am monstrous glad to see you—sorry I could not come before—beg your pardon, but I have been forced to look about me a little, and settle my matters; for it is a long while since I have been at home, and you know one has always a world of little odd things to do after one has been away for any time; and then I have had Cartwright to settle with. Lord, I have been as busy as a bee ever since dinner! But pray, Colonel, how came you to conjure out that I should be in town to-day?"

"I had the pleasure of hearing it at Mr. Palmer's, where I have been dining."

"Oh! you did; well, and how do they all do at their house? How does Charlotte do? I warrant you she is a fine size by this time."

"Mrs. Palmer appeared quite well, and I am commissioned to tell you that you will certainly see her to-morrow."

"Aye, to be sure, I thought as much. Well, Colonel, I have brought two young ladies with me, you see—that is, you see but one of them now, but there is another somewhere. Your friend Miss Marianne, too— which you will not be sorry to hear. I do not know what you and Mr. Willoughby will do between you about her. Aye, it is a fine thing to be young and handsome. Well! I was young once, but I never was very handsome—worse luck for me. However, I got a very good husband, and I don't know what the greatest beauty can do more. Ah! poor man! He has been dead these eight years and better. But, Colonel, where have you been to since we parted? And how does your business go on? Come, come, let's have no secrets among friends."

He replied with his accustomary mildness to all her inquiries, but without satisfying her in any. Elinor now began to make the tea, and Marianne was obliged to appear again.

After her entrance, Colonel Brandon became more thoughtful and silent than he had been before, and Mrs. Jennings could not prevail on him to stay long. No other visitor appeared that evening, and the ladies were unanimous in agreeing to go early to bed.

Marianne rose the next morning with recovered spirits and happy looks. The disappointment of the evening before seemed forgotten in the expectation of what was to happen that day. They had not long finished their breakfast before Mrs. Palmer's barouche stopped at the door, and in a few minutes she came laughing into the room; so delighted to see them all, that it was hard to say whether she received most pleasure from meeting her mother or the Miss Dashwoods again. So surprised at their coming to town, though it was what she had rather expected all along; so angry at their accepting her mother's invitation after having declined her own, though at the same time she would never have forgiven them if they had not come!

"Mr. Palmer will be so happy to see you," said she; "what do you think he said when he heard of your coming with mamma? I forget what it was now, but it was something so droll!"

After an hour or two spent in what her mother called comfortable chat, or in other words, in every variety of inquiry concerning all their acquaintances on Mrs. Jennings's side, and in laughter without cause on Mrs. Palmer's, it was proposed by the latter that they should all accompany her to some shops where she had business that morning, to which Mrs. Jennings and Elinor readily consented, as having likewise some purchases to make themselves; and Marianne, though declining it at first, was induced to go likewise.

Wherever they went, she was evidently always on the watch. In Bond Street especially, where much of their business lay, her eyes were in constant inquiry; and in whatever shop the party engaged, her mind was equally abstracted from everything actually before them, from all that interested and occupied the others. Restless and dissatisfied everywhere her sister could never obtain her opinion of any article of purchase, however it might equally concern them both; she received no pleasure from anything; was only impatient to be at home again, and could with difficulty govern her vexation at the tediousness of Mrs. Palmer, whose eye was caught by everything pretty, expensive, or new; who was wild to buy all, could determine on none, and dawdled away her time in rapture and indecision.

It was late in the morning before they returned home; and no sooner had they entered the house than Marianne flew eagerly upstairs, and when Elinor followed, she found her turning from the table with a sorrowful countenance, which declared that no Willoughby had been there.

"Has no letter been left here for me since we went out?" said she to the footman who then entered with the parcels. She was answered in the negative. "Are you quite sure of it?" she replied. "Are you certain that no servant, no porter has left any letter or note?"

The man replied that none had.

"How very odd," said she in a low and disappointed voice, as she turned away to the window.

"How odd indeed!" repeated Elinor within herself, regarding her sister with uneasiness. "If she had not known him to be in town, she would not have written to him, as she did; she would have written to Combe Magna;

and if he is in town, how odd that he should neither come nor write! Oh, my dear mother, you must be wrong in permitting an engagement between a daughter so young, a man so little known, to be carried on in so doubtful, so mysterious a manner! *I* long to inquire; but how will *my* interference be borne!"

She determined, after some consideration, that if appearances continued many days longer as unpleasant as they now were she would represent in the strongest manner to her mother the necessity of some serious inquiry into the affair.

Mrs. Palmer and two elderly ladies of Mrs. Jennings's intimate acquaintance, whom she had met and invited in the morning, dined with them. The former left them soon after tea to fulfil her evening engagements; and Elinor was obliged to assist in making a whist-table for the others. Marianne was of no use on these occasions, as she would never learn the game; but though her time was therefore at her own disposal, the evening was by no means more productive of pleasure to her than to Elinor, for it was spent in all the anxiety of expectation and the pain of disappointment. She sometimes endeavoured for a few minutes to read; but the book was soon thrown aside, and she returned to the more interesting employment of walking backwards and forwards across the room, pausing for a moment whenever she came to the window, in hopes of distinguishing the long-expected rap.

Chapter 27

"IF this open weather holds much longer," said Mrs. Jennings, when they met at breakfast the following morning, "Sir John will not like leaving Barton next week; 'tis a sad thing for sportsmen to lose a day's pleasure. Poor souls! I always pity them when they do—they seem to take it so much to heart."

"That is true," cried Marianne in a cheerful voice, and walking to the window as she spoke, to examine the day. "I had not thought of *that*. This weather will keep many sportsmen in the country."

It was a lucky recollection, all her good spirits were restored by it. "It is charming weather for *them* indeed," she continued, as she sat down to the breakfast table with a happy countenance. "How much they must enjoy it! But (with a little return of anxiety) it cannot be expected to last long. At this time of year, and after such a series of rain, we shall certainly have very little more of it. Frosts will soon set in, and in all probability with severity. In another day or two, perhaps; this extreme mildness can hardly last longer—nay, perhaps it may freeze to-night!"

"At any rate," said Elinor, wishing to prevent Mrs. Jennings from seeing her sister's thoughts as clearly as she did, "I dare say we shall have Sir John and Lady Middleton in town by the end of next week."

"Aye, my dear, I'll warrant you we do. Mary always has her own way."

"And now," silently conjectured Elinor, "she will write to Combe by this day's post."

But if she *did*, the letter was written and sent away with a privacy that eluded all her watchfulness to ascertain the fact. Whatever the truth of it might be, and far as Elinor was from feeling thorough contentment about it, yet while she saw Marianne in spirits, she could not be very uncomfortable herself. And Marianne was in spirits, happy in the mildness of the weather, and still happier in her expectation of a frost.

The morning was chiefly spent in leaving cards at the houses of Mrs. Jennings's acquaintances to inform them of her being in town; and Marianne was all the time busy in observing the direction of the wind, watching the variations of the sky, and imagining an alteration in the air.

"Don't you find it colder than it was in the morning, Elinor? There seems to me a very decided difference. I can hardly keep my hands warm even in my muff. It was not so yesterday, I think. The clouds seem parting too, the sun will be out in a moment, and we shall have a clear afternoon."

Elinor was alternately diverted and pained; but Marianne persevered, and saw every night in the brightness of the fire, and every morning in the appearance of the atmosphere, the certain symptoms of approaching frost.

The Miss Dashwoods had no greater reason to be dissatisfied with Mrs. Jennings's style of living and set of acquaintances than with her behaviour to themselves, which was invariably kind. Everything in her household arrangements was conducted on the most liberal plan, and excepting a few old city friends, whom, to Lady Middleton's regret, she had never dropped, she visited no one to whom an introduction could at all discompose the feelings of her young companions. Pleased to find herself more comfortably situated in that particular than she had expected, Elinor was very willing to compound for the want of much real enjoyment from any of their evening parties, which, whether at home or abroad, formed only for cards, could have little to amuse her.

Colonel Brandon, who had a general invitation to the house, was with them almost every day; he came to look at Marianne and talk to Elinor, who often derived more satisfaction from conversing with him than from any other daily occurrence, but who saw at the same time with much concern his continued regard for her sister. She feared it was a strengthening regard. It grieved her to see the earnestness with which he often watched Marianne, and his spirits were certainly worse than when at Barton.

About a week after their arrival, it became certain that Willoughby was also arrived. His card was on the table when they came in from the morning's drive.

"Good God!" cried Marianne, "he has been here while we were out."

Elinor, rejoiced to be assured of his being in London, now ventured to say, "Depend upon it, he will call again to-morrow." But Marianne seemed hardly to hear her, and on Mrs. Jennings's entrance, escaped with the precious card.

This event, while it raised the spirits of Elinor, restored to those of her sister all, and more than all, their former agitation. From this moment her mind was never quiet; the expectation of seeing him every hour of the day made her unfit for anything. She insisted on being left behind the next morning, when the others went out.

Elinor's thoughts were full of what might be passing in Berkeley Street during their absence; but a moment's glance at her sister when they returned was enough to inform her that Willoughby had paid no second visit there A note was just then brought in, and laid on the table.

"For me!" cried Marianne, stepping hastily forward.

"No, ma'am, for my mistress."

But Marianne, not convinced, took it instantly up.

"It is indeed for Mrs. Jennings; how provoking!"

"You are expecting a letter then?" said Elinor, unable to be longer silent.

"Yes! a little—not much."

After a short pause, "You have no confidence in me, Marianne."

"Nay, Elinor, this reproach from *you!* you who have confidence in no one!"

"Me!" returned Elinor in some confusion; "indeed, Marianne, I have nothing to tell."

"Nor I," answered Marianne with energy; "our situations then are alike. We have neither of us anything to tell; you, because you communicate, and I, because I conceal nothing."

Elinor, distressed by this charge of reserve in herself, which she was not at liberty to do away, knew not how, under such circumstances, to press for greater openness in Marianne.

Mrs. Jennings soon appeared, and the note being given her, she read it aloud. It was from Lady Middleton, announcing their arrival in Conduit Street the night before, and requesting the company of her mother and cousins the following evening. Business on Sir John's part, and a violent cold on her own, prevented their calling in Berkeley Street. The invitation was accepted: but when the hour of appointment drew near, necessary as it was in common civility to Mrs. Jennings that they should both attend her on such a visit, Elinor had some difficulty in persuading her sister to go, for still she had seen nothing of Willoughby, and therefore was not more indisposed for amusement abroad, than unwilling to run the risk of his calling again in her absence.

Elinor found, when the evening was over, that disposition is not materially altered by change of abode; for although scarcely settled in town, Sir John had contrived to collect around him nearly twenty young people, and to amuse them with a ball. This was an affair, however, of which

Lady Middleton did not approve. In the country, an unpremeditated dance was very allowable; but in London, where the reputation of elegance was more important and less easily obtained, it was risking too much, for the gratification of a few girls, to have it known that Lady Middleton had given a small dance of eight or nine couples, with two violins, and a mere sideboard collation.

Mr. and Mrs. Palmer were of the party; from the former, whom they had not seen before since their arrival in town, as he was careful to avoid the appearance of any attention to his mother-in-law, and therefore never came near her, they received no mark of recognition on their entrance. He looked at them slightly, without seeming to know who they were, and merely nodded to Mrs. Jennings from the other side of the room. Marianne gave one glance round the apartment as she entered; it was enough, *he* was not there—and she sat down, equally ill-disposed to receive or communicate pleasure. After they had been assembled about an hour, Mr. Palmer sauntered towards the Miss Dashwoods, to express his surprise on seeing them in town, though Colonel Brandon had been first informed of their arrival at his house, and he had himself said something very droll on hearing that they were to come.

"I thought you were both in Devonshire," said he.

"Did you?" replied Elinor.

"When do you go back again?"

"I do not know." And thus ended their discourse.

Never had Marianne been so unwilling to dance in her life as she was that evening, and never so much fatigued by the exercise. She complained of it as they returned to Berkeley Street.

"Aye, aye," said Mrs. Jennings, "we know the reason of all that very well; if a certain person who shall be nameless had been there, you would not have been a bit tired; and to say the truth, it was not very pretty of him not to give you the meeting when he was invited."

"Invited!" cried Marianne.

"So my daughter Middleton told me, for it seems Sir John met him somewhere in the street this morning."

Marianne said no more, but looked exceedingly hurt. Impatient in this situation to be doing something that might lead to her sister's relief, Elinor resolved to write the next morning to her mother, and hoped by awakening her fears for the health of Marianne, to procure those inquiries which had been so long delayed; and she was still more eagerly bent on this measure, by perceiving after breakfast on the morrow, that Marianne was again writing to Willoughby, for she could not suppose it to be to any other person.

About the middle of the day, Mrs. Jennings went out by herself on business, and Elinor began her letter directly; while Marianne, too restless for employment, too anxious for conversation, walked from one window to the other, or sat down by the fire in melancholy meditation. Elinor was very earnest in her application to her mother, relating all that had passed,

her suspicions of Willoughby's inconstancy, urging her by every plea of
duty and affection to demand from Marianne an account of her real situation with respect to him.

Her letter was scarcely finished when a rap foretold a visitor, and
Colonel Brandon was announced. Marianne, who had seen him from the
window, and who hated company of any kind, left the room before he
entered it. He looked more than usually grave, and though expressing
satisfaction at finding Miss Dashwood alone, as if he had somewhat in
particular to tell her, sat for some time without saying a word. Elinor,
persuaded that he had some communication to make in which her sister
was concerned, impatiently expected its opening. It was not the first time
of her feeling the same kind of conviction; for more than once before,
beginning with the observation of "Your sister looks unwell to-day," or
"Your sister seems out of spirits," he had appeared on the point, either
of disclosing, or of inquiring, something particular about her. After a
pause of several minutes their silence was broken by his asking her, in a
voice of some agitation, when he was to congratulate her on the acquisition
of a brother? Elinor was not prepared for such a question, and having no
answer ready, was obliged to adopt the simple and common expedient of
asking what he meant? He tried to smile as he replied, "Your sister's
engagement to Mr. Willoughby is very generally known."

"It cannot be generally known," returned Elinor, "for her own family
do not know it."

He looked surprised, and said, "I beg your pardon, I am afraid my
inquiry has been impertinent; but I had not supposed any secrecy intended
as they openly correspond, and their marriage is universally talked of."

"How can that be? By whom can you have heard it mentioned?"

"By many—by some of whom you know nothing, by others with whom
you are most intimate—Mrs. Jennings, Mrs. Palmer, and the Middletons.
But still I might not have believed it—for where the mind is perhaps
rather unwilling to be convinced, it will always find something to support
its doubts—if I had not, when the servant let me in to-day, accidentally
seen a letter in his hand, directed to Mr. Willoughby in your sister's
writing. I came to inquire, but I was convinced before I could ask the
question. Is everything finally settled? Is it impossible to——? But I have
no right and I could have no chance of succeeding. Excuse me, Miss
Dashwood. I believe I have been wrong in saying so much, but I hardly
know what to do, and on your prudence I have the strongest dependence.
Tell me that it is all absolutely resolved on, that any attempt—that in
short concealment, if concealment be possible, is all that remains."

These words, which conveyed to Elinor a direct avowal of his love for
her sister, affected her very much. She was not immediately able to say
anything, and even when her spirits were recovered, she debated for a
short time on the answer it would be most proper to give. The real state of
things between Willoughby and her sister was so little known to herself,
that in endeavouring to explain it, she might be as liable to say too much

as too little. Yet as she was convinced that Marianne's affection for Willoughby could leave no hope of Colonel Brandon's success, whatever the event of that affection might be, and at the same time wished to shield her conduct from censure, she thought it most prudent and kind, after some consideration, to say more than she really knew or believed. She acknowledged, therefore, that though she had never been informed by themselves of the terms on which they stood with each other, of their mutual affection she had no doubt, and of their correspondence she was not astonished to hear.

He listened to her with silent attention, and on her ceasing to speak, rose directly from his seat, and after saying in a voice of emotion, "To your sister I wish all imaginable happiness; to Willoughby, that he may endeavour to deserve her," took leave, and went away.

Elinor derived no comfortable feelings from this conversation to lessen the uneasiness of her mind on other points; she was left, on the contrary, with a melancholy impression of Colonel Brandon's unhappiness, and was prevented from even wishing it removed, by her anxiety for the very event that must confirm it.

Chapter 28

NOTHING occurred during the next three or four days to make Elinor regret what she had done in applying to her mother; for Willoughby neither came nor wrote. They were engaged about the end of that time to attend Lady Middleton to a party, from which Mrs. Jennings was kept away by the indisposition of her youngest daughter; and for this party, Marianne, wholly dispirited, careless of her appearance, and seeming equally indifferent whether she went or stayed, prepared, without one look of hope, or one expression of pleasure. She sat by the drawing-room fire after tea, till the moment of Lady Middleton's arrival, without once stirring from her seat, or altering her attitude, lost in her own thoughts and insensible of her sister's presence: and when at last they were told that Lady Middleton waited for them at the door, she started as if she had forgotten that any one was expected.

They arrived in due time at the place of destination, and as soon as the string of carriages before them would allow, alighted, ascended the stairs, heard their names announced from one landing-place to another in an audible voice, and entered a room splendidly lit up, quite full of company, and insufferably hot. When they had paid their tribute of politeness by curtseying to the lady of the house, they were permitted to mingle in the crowd, and take their share of the heat and inconvenience, to which their arrival must necessarily add. After some time spent in saying little and doing less, Lady Middleton sat down to casino, and as Marianne was not in spirits for moving about, she and Elinor, luckily succeeding to chairs, placed themselves at no great distance from the table.

They had not remained in this manner long, before Elinor perceived Willoughby, standing within a few yards of them, in earnest conversation with a very fashionable-looking young woman. She soon caught his eye, and he immediately bowed, but without attempting to speak to her, or to approach Marianne, though he could not but see her; and then continued his discourse with the same lady. Elinor turned involuntarily to Marianne, to see whether it could be unobserved by her. At that moment she first perceived him, and her whole countenance glowing with sudden delight, she would have moved towards him instantly, had not her sister caught hold of her.

"Good heavens!" she exclaimed, "he is there—he is there. Oh! why does he not look at me? why cannot I speak to him?"

"Pray, pray be composed," cried Elinor, "and do not betray what you feel to everybody present. Perhaps he has not observed you yet."

This, however, was more than she could believe herself, and to be composed at such a moment was not only beyond the reach of Marianne, it was beyond her wish. She sat in agony of impatience which affected every feature.

At last he turned round again, and regarded them both; she started up, and pronouncing his name in a tone of affection, held out her hand to him. He approached, and addressing himself rather to Elinor than Marianne, as if wishing to avoid her eye, and determined not to observe her attitude, inquired in a hurried manner after Mrs. Dashwood, and asked how long they had been in town. Elinor was robbed of all presence of mind by such an address, and was unable to say a word. But the feelings of her sister were instantly expressed. Her face crimsoned over, and she exclaimed in a voice of the greatest emotion, "Good God! Willoughby, what is the meaning of this? Have you not received my letters? Will you not shake hands with me?"

He could not then avoid it, but her touch seemed painful to him, and he held her hand only for a moment. During all this time he was evidently struggling for composure. Elinor watched his countenance, and saw its expression becoming more tranquil. After a moment's pause, he spoke with calmness.

"I did myself the honour of calling in Berkeley Street last Tuesday, and very much regretted that I was not fortunate enough to find yourselves and Mrs. Jennings at home. My card was not lost, I hope."

"But have you not received my notes?" cried Marianne in the wildest anxiety. "Here is some mistake, I am sure—some dreadful mistake. What can be the meaning of it? Tell me, Willoughby—for heaven's sake, tell me, what is the matter?"

He made no reply; his complexion changed and all his embarrassment returned; but as if, on catching the eye of the young lady with whom he had been previously talking, he felt the necessity of instant exertion, he recovered himself again, and after saying, "Yes, I had the pleasure of receiving the information of your arrival in town, which you were so good as to send me," turned hastily away with a slight bow and joined his friend.

Marianne, now looking dreadfully white, and unable to stand, sank into her chair, and Elinor, expecting every moment to see her faint, tried to screen her from the observation of others, while reviving her with lavender water.

"Go to him, Elinor," she said, as soon as she could speak, "and force him to come to me. Tell him I must see him again—must speak to him instantly. I cannot rest—I shall not have a moment's peace till this is explained—some dreadful misapprehension or other. Oh, go to him this moment."

"How can that be done? No, my dearest Marianne, you must wait. This is not a place for explanations. Wait only till to-morrow."

With difficulty, however, could she prevent her from following him herself; and to persuade her to check her agitation—to wait, at least, with the appearance of composure—till she might speak to him with more privacy and more effect, was impossible; for Marianne continued incessantly to give way in a low voice to the misery of her feelings, by exclamations of wretchedness. In a short time Elinor saw Willoughby quit the room by the door towards the staircase, and telling Marianne that he was gone, urged the impossibility of speaking to him again that evening, as a fresh argument for her to be calm. She instantly begged her sister would entreat Lady Middleton to take them home, as she was too miserable to stay a minute longer.

Lady Middleton, though in the middle of a rubber, on being informed that Marianne was unwell, was too polite to object for a moment to her wish of going away, and making over her cards to a friend, they departed as soon as the carriage could be found. Scarcely a word was spoken during their return to Berkeley Street. Marianne was in a silent agony, too much oppressed even for tears; but as Mrs. Jennings was luckily not come home, they could go directly to their own room, where hartshorn restored her a little to herself. She was soon undressed and in bed, and as she seemed desirous of being alone, her sister then left her, and while she waited the return of Mrs. Jennings, had leisure enough for thinking over the past.

That some kind of engagement had subsisted between Willoughby and Marianne, she could not doubt; and that Willoughby was weary of it, seemed equally clear; for however Marianne might still feed her own wishes, *she* could not attribute such behaviour to mistake or misapprehension of any kind. Nothing but a thorough change of sentiment could account for it. Her indignation would have been still stronger than it was, had she not witnessed that embarrassment which seemed to speak a consciousness of his own misconduct, and prevented her from believing him so unprincipled as to have been sporting with the affections of her sister from the first, without any design that would bear investigation. Absence might have weakened his regard, and convenience might have determined him to overcome it, but that such a regard had formerly existed she could not bring herself to doubt.

As for Marianne, on the pangs which so unhappy a meeting must already have given her, and on those still more severe which might await her in its probable consequence, she could not reflect without the deepest concern. Her own situation gained in the comparison; for while she could *esteem* Edward as much as ever, however they might be divided in future, her mind might be always supported. But every circumstance that could embitter such an evil seemed uniting to heighten the misery of Marianne in a final separation from Willoughby—in an immediate and irreconcilable rupture with him.

Chapter 29

BEFORE the house-maid had lit their fire the next day, or the sun gained any power over a cold, gloomy morning in January, Marianne, only half dressed, was kneeling against one of the window-seats for the sake of all the little light she could command from it, and writing as fast as a continual flow of tears would permit her. In this situation, Elinor, roused from sleep by her agitation and sobs, first perceived her; and after observing her for a few moments with silent anxiety, said, in a tone of the most considerate gentleness:

"Marianne, may I ask——?"

"No, Elinor," she replied, "ask nothing; you will soon know all."

The sort of desperate calmness with which this was said lasted no longer than while she spoke, and was immediately followed by a return of the same excessive affliction. It was some minutes before she could go on with her letter, and the frequent bursts of grief which still obliged her, at intervals, to withhold her pen, were proofs enough of her feeling how more than probable it was that she was writing for the last time to Willoughby.

Elinor paid her every quiet and unobtrusive attention in her power; and she would have tried to soothe and tranquillise her still more, had not Marianne entreated her, with all the eagerness of the most nervous irritability, not to speak to her for the world. In such circumstances, it was better for both that they should not be long together; and the restless state of Marianne's mind not only prevented her from remaining in the room a moment after she was dressed, but requiring at once solitude and continual change of place, made her wander about the house till breakfast time, avoiding the sight of everybody.

At breakfast she neither ate nor attempted to eat anything; and Elinor's attention was then all employed, not in urging her, not in pitying her, nor in appearing to regard her, but in endeavouring to engage Mrs. Jennings's notice entirely to herself.

As this was a favourite meal with Mrs. Jennings, it lasted a considerable time, and they were just setting themselves, after it, round the common work table, when a letter was delivered to Marianne, which she eagerly caught from the servant, and, turning of a death-like paleness, instantly ran out of the room. Elinor, who saw as plainly by this, as if she had seen the direction, that it must come from Willoughby, felt immediately such a sickness at heart as made her hardly able to hold up her head, and sat in such a general tremor as made her fear it impossible to escape Mrs. Jennings's notice. That good lady, however, saw only that Marianne had received a letter from Willoughby, which appeared to her a very good joke, and which she treated accordingly, by hoping, with a laugh, that she would find it to her liking. Of Elinor's distress, she was too busily employed in measuring lengths of worsted for her rug, to see anything at all; and calmly continuing her talk, as soon as Marianne dis-apeared, she said:

"Upon my word, I never saw a young woman so desperately in love in my life! *My* girls were nothing to her, and yet they used to be foolish enough; but as for Miss Marianne, she is quite an altered creature. I hope, from the bottom of my heart, he won't keep her waiting much longer, for it is quite grievous to see her look so ill and forlorn. Pray, when are they to be married?"

Elinor, though never less disposed to speak than at that moment, obliged herself to answer such an attack as this, and, therefore, trying to smile, replied, "And have you really, ma'am, talked yourself into a persuasion of my sister's being engaged to Mr. Willoughby? I thought it had been only a joke, but so serious a question seems to imply more: and I must beg, therefore, that you will not deceive yourself any longer. I do assure you that nothing would surprise me more than to hear of their being going to be married."

"For shame, for shame, Miss Dashwood! How can you talk so! Don't we all know that it must be a match—that they were over head and ears in love with each other from the first moment they met? Did not I see them together in Devonshire every day, and all day long? And did not I know that your sister came to town with me on purpose to buy wedding clothes? Come, come, this won't do. Because you are so sly about it your-self, you think nobody else has any senses; but it is no such thing, I can tell you, for it has been known all over the town this ever so long. I tell everybody of it, and so does Charlotte."

"Indeed, ma'am," said Elinor very seriously, "you are mistaken. Indeed, you are doing a very unkind thing in spreading the report, and you will find that you have though you will not believe me now."

Mrs. Jennings laughed again, but Elinor had not spirits to say more, and eager at all events to know what Willoughby had written, hurried away to their room, where, on opening the door, she saw Marianne stretched on the bed, almost choked by grief, one letter in her hand, and two or three others lying by her. Elinor drew near, but without saying a word; and seating herself on the bed, took her hand, kissed her affectionately several times, and then gave way to a burst of tears, which at first was scarcely less violent than Marianne's. The latter, though unable to speak, seemed to feel all the tenderness of this behaviour, and after some time thus spent in joint affliction, she put all the letters into Elinor's hands; and then covering her face with her handkerchief, almost screamed with agony. Elinor, who knew that such grief, shocking as it was to witness it, must have its course, watched by her till this excess of suffering had somewhat spent itself, and then turning eagerly to Willoughby's letter, read as follows:

"BOND STREET, *January.*

"MY DEAR MADAM,—I have just had the honour of receiving your letter, for which I beg to return my sincere acknowledgments. I am much concerned to find there was anything in my behaviour last night that did not meet your approbation; and though I am quite at a loss to discover in what point I could be so unfortunate as to offend you, I entreat your forgiveness of what I can assure you to have been perfectly unintentional. I shall never reflect on my former acquaintance with your family in Devonshire without the most grateful pleasure, and flatter myself it will not be broken by any mistake or misapprehension of my actions. My esteem for your whole family is very sincere; but if I have been so unfortunate as to give rise to a belief of more than I felt, or meant to express, I shall reproach myself for not having been more guarded in my professions of that esteem. That I should ever have meant more, you will allow to be impossible, when you understand that my affections have been long engaged elsewhere, and it will not be many weeks, I believe, before this engagement is fulfilled. It is with great regret that I obey your commands of returning the letters with which I have been honoured from you, and the lock of hair which you so obligingly bestowed on me.

"I am, dear Madam,
"Your most obedient
"humble Servant,
"JOHN WILLOUGHBY."

With what indignation such a letter as this must be read by Miss Dashwood, may be imagined. Though aware, before she began it, that it must bring a confession of his inconstancy, and confirm their separation for ever, she was not aware that such language could be suffered to announce it! nor could she have supposed Willoughby capable of departing so far from the appearance of every honourable and delicate feeling—so far from the common decorum of a gentleman, as to send a letter so impudently cruel: a letter which, instead of bringing with his desire of a release any professions of regret, acknowledged no breach of faith, denied all peculiar affection whatever—a letter of which every line was an insult, and which proclaimed its writer to be deep in hardened villainy.

She paused over it for some time with indignant astonishment; then read it again and again; but every perusal only served to increase her abhorrence of the man, and so bitter were her feelings against him, that she dared not trust herself to speak, lest she might wound Marianne still deeper by treating their disengagement, not as a loss to her of any possible good, but as an escape from the worst and most irremediable of evils, a connection, for life, with an unprincipled man, as a deliverance the most real, a blessing the most important.

In her earnest meditations on the contents of the letter, on the depravity of that mind which could dictate it, and, probably, on the very different mind of a very different person, who had no other connection whatever with the affair than what her heart gave him with everything that passed, Elinor forgot the immediate distress of her sister, forgot that she had three letters on her lap yet unread, and so entirely forgot how long she had been in the room, that when, on hearing a carriage drive up to the door, she went to the window to see who could be coming so unreasonably early, she was all astonishment to perceive Mrs. Jennings's chariot, which she knew had not been ordered till one. Determined not to quit Marianne, though hopeless of contributing, at present, to her ease, she hurried away to excuse herself from attending Mrs. Jennings, on account of her sister being indisposed. Mrs. Jennings, with a thoroughly good-humoured concern for its cause, admitted the excuse most readily, and Elinor, after seeing her safe off, returned to Marianne, whom she found attempting to rise from the bed, and whom she reached just in time to prevent her from falling on the floor, faint and giddy from a long want of proper rest and food; for it was many days since she had any appetite, and many nights since she had really slept; and now, when her mind was no longer supported by the fever of suspense, the consequence of all this was felt in an aching head, a weakened stomach, and general nervous faintness. A glass of wine, which Elinor procured for her directly, made her more comfortable, and she was at last able to express some sense of her kindness by saying:

"Poor Elinor! How unhappy I make you!"

"I only wish," replied her sister, "there were anything I *could* do which might be of comfort to you."

This, as everything else would have been, was too much for Marianne, who could only exclaim, in the anguish of her heart, "O Elinor, I am miserable indeed," before her voice was entirely lost in sobs.

Elinor could no longer witness this torrent of unresisted grief in silence.

"Exert yourself, dear Marianne," she cried, "if you would not kill yourself and all who love you. Think of your mother; think of her misery while *you* suffer; for her sake you must exert yourself."

"I cannot, I cannot," cried Marianne; "leave me, leave me, if I distress you; leave me, hate me, forget me; but do not torture me so. Oh! how easy for those who have no sorrow of their own to talk of exertion! Happy, happy Elinor, *you* cannot have an idea of what I suffer."

"Do you call *me* happy, Marianne! Ah; if you knew! And can you believe me to be so while I see you so wretched!"

"Forgive me, forgive me," throwing her arms round her sister's neck; "I know you feel for me; I know what a heart you have; but yet you are—you must be happy; Edward loves you—what, oh! what can do away such happiness as that!"

"Many, many circumstances," said Elinor solemnly.

"No, no, no," cried Marianne wildly; "he loves you, and only you. You *can* have no grief."

"I can have no pleasure while I see you in this state."

"And you will never see me otherwise. Mine is a misery which nothing can do away."

"You must not talk so, Marianne. Have you no comforts? no friends? Is your loss such as leaves no opening for consolation? Much as you suffer now, think of what you would have suffered if the discovery of his character had been delayed to a later period—if your engagement had been carried on for months and months, as it might have been, before he chose to put an end to it. Every additional day of unhappy confidence, on your side, would have made the blow more dreadful."

"Engagement!" cried Marianne, "there has been no engagement."

"No engagement!"

"No, he is not so unworthy as you believe him. He has broken no faith with me."

"But he told you that he loved you?"

"Yes—no—never—absolutely. It was every day implied, but never professedly declared. Sometimes I thought it had been—but it never was."

"Yet you wrote to him?"

"Yes—could that be wrong after all that had passed? But I cannot talk."

Elinor said no more, and turning again to the three letters which now raised a much stronger curiosity than before, directly ran over the contents of all. The first, which was what her sister had sent him on their arrival in town, was to this effect:

"Berkeley Street, *January*.
"How surprised you will be, Willoughby, on receiving this! and I think you will feel something more than surprise when you know I am in town. An opportunity of coming hither, though with Mrs. Jennings, was a temptation we could not resist. I wish you may receive this in time to come here to-night, but I will not depend on it. At any rate I shall expect you to-morrow. For the present, adieu.   M. D."

Her second note, which had been written on the morning after the dance at the Middletons', was in these words.

"I cannot express my disappointment in having missed you the day before yesterday, nor my astonishment at not having received any answer to a note which I sent you above a week ago. I have been expecting to hear from you, and still more to see you, every hour of the day. Pray call again as soon as possible, and explain the reason of my having expected this in vain. You had better come earlier another time, because we are generally out by one. We were last night at Lady Middleton's where there was a dance. I have been told that you were asked to be of the party. But could it be so? You must be very much altered indeed since we parted, if that could be the case, and you not there. But I will not suppose this possible, and I hope very soon to receive your personal assurance of its being otherwise.   M. D."

The contents of her last note to him were these:

"What am I to imagine, Willoughby, by your behaviour last night? Again I demand an explanation of it. I was prepared to meet you with the pleasure which our separation naturally produced, with the familiarity which our intimacy at Barton appeared to me to justify. I was repulsed indeed! I have passed a wretched night in endeavouring to excuse a conduct which can scarcely be called less than insulting; but though I have not yet been able to form any reasonable apology for your behaviour, I am perfectly ready to hear your justification of it. You have perhaps been misinformed, or purposely deceived, in something concerning me, which may have lowered me in your opinion. Tell me what it is, explain the grounds on which you acted, and I shall be satisfied in being able to satisfy you. It would grieve me indeed to be obliged to think ill of you; but if I am to do it, if I am to learn that you are not what we have hitherto believed you, that your regard for us all was insincere, that your behaviour to me was intended only to deceive, let it be told as soon as possible. My feelings are at present in a state of dreadful indecision; I wish to acquit you, but certainty on either side will be ease to what I now suffer. If your sentiments are no longer what they were, you will return my notes, and the lock of my hair which is in your possession.   M. D."

That such letters, so full of affection and confidence, could have been so answered, Elinor, for Willoughby's sake, would have been unwilling to believe. But her condemnation of him did not blind her to the impropriety of their having been written at all; and she was silently grieving over the imprudence which had hazarded such unsolicited proofs of tenderness, not warranted by anything preceding, and most severely condemned by the event, when Marianne, perceiving that she had finished the letters, observed to her that they contained nothing but what any one would have written in the same situation.

"I felt myself," she added, "to be as solemnly engaged to him as if the strictest legal covenant had bound us to each other."

"I can believe it," said Elinor; "but unfortunately, he did not feel the same."

"He *did* feel the same, Elinor—for weeks and weeks he felt it. I know he did. Whatever may have changed him now (and nothing but the blackest art employed against me can have done it), I was once as dear to him as my own soul could wish. This lock of hair, which now he can so readily give up, was begged of me with the most earnest supplication. Had you seen his look, his manner, had you heard his voice at that moment! Have you forgot the last evening of our being together at Barton? The morning that we parted too! When he told me that it might be many weeks before we met again—his distress—can I ever forget his distress!"

For a moment or two she could say no more; but when this emotion had passed away, she added, in a firmer tone:

"Elinor, I have been cruelly used, but not by Willoughby."

"Dearest Marianne, who but himself? By whom can he have been instigated?"

"By all the world, rather than by his own heart. I could rather believe every creature of my acquaintance leagued together to ruin me in his opinion, than believe his nature capable of such cruelty. This woman of whom he writes—whoever she be—or any one, in short, but your own dear self, mamma, and Edward, may have been so barbarous to belie me. Beyond you three, is there a creature in the world whom I would not rather suspect of evil than Willoughby, whose heart I know so well?"

Elinor would not contend, and only replied, "Whoever may have been so detestably your enemy, let them be cheated of their malignant triumph, my dear sister, by seeing how nobly the consciousness of your own innocence and good intentions supports your spirits. It is a reasonable and laudable pride which resists such malevolence."

"No, no," cried Marianne, "misery such as mine has no pride. I care not who knows that I am wretched. The triumph of seeing me so may be open to all the world. Elinor, Elinor, they who suffer little may be proud and independent as they like—may resist insult, or return mortification—but I cannot. I must feel—I must be wretched—and they are welcome to enjoy the consciousness of it that can."

"But for my mother's sake and mine——"

"I would do more than for my own. But to appear happy when I am so miserable—Oh! who can require it?"

Again they were both silent. Elinor was employed in walking thoughtfully from the fire to the window, from the window to the fire, without knowing that she received warmth from one, or discerning objects through the other; and Marianne, seated at the foot of the bed, with her head leaning against one of its posts, again took up Willoughby's letter, and after shuddering over every sentence, exclaimed:

"It is too much! O Willoughby, Willoughby, could this be yours! Cruel, cruel—nothing can acquit you. Elinor, nothing can. Whatever he might have heard against me—ought he not to have suspended his belief? ought he not to have told me of it, to have given me the power of clear-

ing myself? 'The lock of hair (repeating it from the letter) which you
so obligingly bestowed on me'—that is unpardonable. Willoughby, where
was your heart when you wrote those words? Oh! barbarously insolent!
Elinor, can he be justified?"

"No, Marianne, in no possible way."

"And yet this woman—who knows what her art may have been—how
long it may have been premeditated, and how deeply contrived by her!
Who is she? Who can she be? Whom did I ever hear him talk of as young
and attractive among his female acquaintances? Oh! no one, no one—he
talked to me only of myself."

Another pause ensued; Marianne was greatly agitated, and it ended
thus:

"Elinor, I must go home. I must go and comfort mamma. Cannot we
be gone to-morrow?"

"To-morrow, Marianne!"

"Yes; why should I stay here? I came only for Willoughby's sake—
and now who cares for me? Who regards me?"

"It would be impossible to go to-morrow. We owe Mrs. Jennings much
more than civility; and civility of the commonest kind must prevent such
a hasty removal as that."

"Well, then, another day or two perhaps; but I cannot stay here long,
I cannot stay to endure the questions and remarks of all these people.
The Middletons and Palmers—how am I to bear their pity? The pity of
such a woman as Lady Middleton! oh! what would *he* say to that!"

Elinor advised her to lie down again, and for a moment she did so; but
no attitude could give her ease, and in restless pain of mind and body she
moved from one posture to another, till growing more and more hysterical, her sister could with difficulty keep her on the bed at all, and for
some time was fearful of being constrained to call for assistance. Some
lavender drops, however, which she was at length persuaded to take,
were of use; and from that time till Mrs. Jennings returned, she continued on the bed quiet and motionless.

Chapter 30

MRS. JENNINGS came immediately to their room on her return, and
without waiting to have her request of admittance answered, opened the
door and walked in with a look of real concern.

"How do you do, my dear?" said she, in a voice of great compassion,
to Marianne, who turned away her face without attempting to answer.

"How is she, Miss Dashwood? Poor thing! she looks very bad. No
wonder. Aye, it is but too true. He is to be married very soon—a good-for-
nothing fellow! I have no patience with him. Mrs. Taylor told me of it
half an hour ago, and she was told it by a particular friend of Miss Grey
herself, else I am sure I should not have believed it; and I was almost

ready to sink as it was. Well, said I, all I can say is, that if it is true, he had used a young lady of my acquaintance abominably ill, and I wish with all my soul his wife may plague his heart out. And so I shall always say, my dear, you may depend on it. I have no notion of men's going on in this way; and if ever I meet him again, I will give him such a dressing as he has not had this many a day. But there is one comfort, my dear Miss Marianne; he is not the only young man in the world worth having; and with your pretty face you will never want admirers. Well, poor thing! I won't disturb her any longer, for she had better have her cry out at once and have done with it. The Parrys and Sandersons luckily are coming to-night, you know, and that will amuse her."

She then went away, walking on tiptoe out of the room, as if she supposed her young friend's affliction could be increased by noise.

Marianne, to the surprise of her sister, determined on dining with them. Elinor even advised her against it. But "no, she would go down; she could bear it very well, and the bustle about her would be less." Elinor, pleased to have her governed for a moment by such a motive, though believing it hardly possible that she could sit out the dinner, said no more; and adjusting her dress for her as well as she could while Marianne still remained on the bed, was ready to assist her into the dining-room as soon as they were summoned to it.

When there, though looking most wretchedly, she ate more and was calmer than her sister had expected. Had she tried to speak, or had she been conscious of half Mrs. Jennings's well-meant but ill-judged attentions to her, this calmness could not have been maintained; but not a syllable escaped her lips, and the abstraction of her thoughts preserved her in ignorance of everything that was passing before her.

Elinor, who did justice to Mrs. Jennings's kindness though its effusions were often distressing, and sometimes almost ridiculous, made her those acknowledgments, and returned her those civilities, which her sister could not make or return for herself. Their good friend saw that Marianne was unhappy, and felt that everything was due to her which might make her at all less so. She treated her, therefore, with all the indulgent fondness of a parent towards a favourite child on the last day of its holidays. Marianne was to have the best place by the fire, was to be tempted to eat by every delicacy in the house, and to be amused by the relation of all the news of the day. Had not Elinor, in the sad countenance of her sister, seen a check to all mirth, she could have been entertained by Mrs. Jennings's endeavours to cure a disappointment in love, by a variety of sweetmeat and olives, and a good fire. As soon, however, as the consciousness of all this was forced by continual repetition on Marianne she could stay no longer. With an hasty exclamation of misery, and a sign to her sister not to follow her, she directly got up and hurried out of the room.

"Poor soul!" cried Mrs. Jennings, as soon as she was gone, "how it grieves me to see her! And I declare if she is not gone away without

SENSE AND SENSIBILITY 115

finishing her wine! And the dried cherries too! Lord! nothing seems to do her any good. I am sure if I knew of anything she would like, I would send all over the town for it. Well, it is the oddest thing for me, that a man should use such a pretty girl so ill! But when there is plenty of money on one side, and next to none on the other, Lord, bless you! they care no more about such things!"

"The lady then—Miss Grey I think you called her—is very rich?"

"Fifty thousand pounds, my dear. Did you ever see her? A smart, stylish girl, they say, but not handsome. I remember her aunt very well, Biddy Henshawe; she married a very wealthy man. But the family are all rich together. Fifty thousand pounds! and by all accounts it won't come before it's wanted; for they say he is all to pieces. No wonder! dashing about with his curricle and hunters! Well, it don't signify talking, but when a young man, be he who he will, comes and makes love to a pretty girl, and promises marriage, he has no business to fly off from his word only because he grows poor, and a richer girl is ready to have him. Why don't he, in such a case, sell his horses, let his house, turn off his servants, and make a thorough reform at once? I warrant you, Miss Marianne would have been ready to wait till matters came round. But that won't do now-a-days; nothing in the way of pleasure can ever be given up by the young men of this age."

"Do you know what kind of a girl Miss Grey is? Is she said to be amiable?"

"I never heard any harm of her; indeed, I hardly ever heard her mentioned; except that Mrs. Taylor did say this morning, that one day Miss Walker hinted to her that she believed Mr. and Mrs. Ellison would not be sorry to have Miss Grey married, for she and Mrs. Ellison could never agree."

"And who are the Ellisons?"

"Her guardians, my dear. But now she is of age and may choose for herself; and a pretty choice she has made! What now," after pausing a moment—"your poor sister has gone to her own room, I suppose, to moan by herself. Is there nothing one can get to comfort her? Poor dear, it seems quite cruel to let her be alone. Well, by and by we shall have a few friends, and that will amuse her a little. What shall we play at? She hates whist, I know; but is there no round game she cares for?"

"Dear ma'am, this kindness is quite unnecessary. Marianne, I dare say, will not leave her room again this evening. I shall persuade her, if I can, to go early to bed, for I am sure she wants rest."

"Aye, I believe that will be best for her. Let her name her own supper, and go to bed. Lord! no wonder she has been looking so bad and so cast-down this last week or two, for this matter I suppose has been hanging over her head as long as that. And so the letter that came to-day finished it! Poor soul! I am sure if I had had a notion of it, I would not have joked her about it for all my money. But then, you know, how should I guess such a thing? I made sure of its being nothing but a common love-letter, and you know young people like to be laughed at about them. Lord! how concerned Sir John and my daughters will be when they hear it! If I had had my senses about me, I might have called in Conduit Street in my way home, and told them of it. But I shall see them to-morrow."

"It would be unnecessary, I am sure, for you to caution Mrs. Palmer and Sir John against ever naming Mr. Willoughby, or making the slightest allusion to what has passed, before my sister. Their own good-nature must point out to them the real cruelty of appearing to know anything about it when she is present; and the less that may ever be said to myself on the subject, the more my feelings will be spared, as you, my dear madam, will easily believe."

"O Lord! yes, that I do indeed. It must be terrible for you to hear it talked of; and as for your sister, I am sure I would not mention a word about it to her for the world. You saw I did not all dinner-time. No more would Sir John nor my daughters, for they are all very thoughtful and considerate—especially if I give them a hint, as I certainly will. For my part, I think the less that is said about such things, the better, the sooner 'tis blown over and forgot. And what good does talking ever do, you know?"

"In this affair it can only do harm—more so perhaps than in many cases of a similar kind, for it has been attended by circumstances which, for the sake of every one concerned in it, make it unfit to become the public conversation. I must do *this* justice to Mr. Willoughby—he has broken no positive engagement with my sister."

"Law, my dear! Don't pretend to defend him. No positive engagement indeed! after taking her all over Allenham House, and fixing on the very rooms they were to live in hereafter!"

Elinor, for her sister's sake, could not press the subject farther, and she hoped it was not required of her for Willoughby's; since, though Marianne might lose much, he could gain very little by the enforcement of the real truth. After a short silence on both sides, Mrs. Jennings, with all her natural hilarity, burst forth again:

"Well, my dear, 'tis a true saying about an ill wind, for it will be all the better for Colonel Brandon. He will have her at last; aye, that he will. Mind me, now, if they an't married by Midsummer. Lord! how he'll chuckle over this news! I hope he will come to-night. It will be all to one a better match for your sister. Two thousand a-year without debt or drawback—except the little love-child, indeed; aye, I had forgot her; but she may be 'prenticed out at small cost, and then what does it signify? Delaford is a nice place, I can tell you; exactly what I call a nice old-fashioned place, full of comforts and conveniences; quite shut in with great garden walls that are covered with the best fruit-trees in the country; and such a mulberry tree in one corner! Lord! how Charlotte and I did stuff the only time we were there! Then, there is a dovecote, some delightful stewponds, and a very pretty canal; and everything, in short, that one could wish for: and, moreover, it is close to the church, and only a quarter of a mile from the turnpike-road, so 'tis never dull, for if you only go and sit up in an old yew harbour behind the house, you may see all the carriages that pass along. Oh! 'tis a nice place! A butcher hard by in the village, and the parsonage-house within a stone's throw. To my fancy, a thousand times prettier than Barton Park, where they are forced to send three miles for their meat, and have not a neighbour nearer than your mother. Well, I shall spirit up the Colonel as soon as I can. One shoulder of mutton you know, drives another down. If we *can* but put Willoughby out of her head!"

"Aye, if we can but do *that*, ma'am," said Elinor, "we shall do very well with or without Colonel Brandon." And then rising, she went away to join Marianne, whom she found, as she expected, in her own room, leaning, in silent misery, over the small remains of a fire which, till Elinor's entrance, had been her only light.

"You had better leave me," was all the notice that her sister received from her.

"I will leave you," said Elinor, "if you will go to bed." But this, from the momentary perverseness of impatient suffering, she at first refused to do. Her sister's earnest, though gentle persuasion, however, soon softened her to compliance, and Elinor saw her lay her aching head on the pillow, and saw her, as she hoped, in a way to get some quiet rest before she left her.

In the drawing-room, whither she then repaired, she was soon joined by Mrs. Jennings, with a wine-glass, full of something, in her hand.

"My dear," said she, entering, "I have just recollected that I have some of the finest old Constantia wine in the house that ever was tasted —so I have brought a glass of it for your sister. My poor husband! how fond he was of it! Whenever he had a touch of his old cholicky gout, he said it did him more good than anything else in the world. Do take it to your sister."

"Dear ma'am," replied Elinor, smiling at the difference of the complaints for which it was recommended, "how good you are! But I have just left Marianne in bed, and, I hope, almost asleep; and as I think nothing will be of so much service to her as rest, if you will give me leave, I will drink the wine myself."

Mrs. Jennings, though regretting that she had not been five minutes earlier, was satisfied with the compromise; and Elinor, as she swallowed the chief of it, reflected that, though its good effects on a cholicky gout were at present of little importance to her, its healing powers on a disappointed heart might be as reasonably tried on herself as on her sister.

Colonel Brandon came in while the party were at tea, and by his manner of looking round the room for Marianne, Elinor immediately fancied that he neither expected nor wished to see her there, and, in short, that he was already aware of what occasioned her absence. Mrs. Jennings was not struck by the same thought; for, soon after his entrance, she walked across the room to the tea-table where Elinor presided, and whispered: "The Colonel looks as grave as ever, you see. He knows nothing of it; do tell him, my dear."

He shortly afterwards drew a chair close to hers, and with a look which perfectly assured her of his good information, inquired after her sister.

"Marianne is not well," said she. "She has been indisposed all day; and we have persuaded her to go to bed."

"Perhaps, then," he hesitatingly replied, "what I heard this morning may be true—there may be more truth in it than I could believe possible at first."

"What did you hear?"

"That a gentleman, whom I had reason to think—in short, that a man, whom I *knew* to be engaged—but how shall I tell you? If you know it already, as surely you must, I may be spared."

"You mean," answered Elinor, with forced calmness, "Mr. Willoughby's marriage with Miss Grey. Yes, we *do* know it all. This seems to have been a day of general elucidation, for this very morning first unfolded it to us. Mr. Willoughby is unfathomable! Where did you hear it?"

"In a stationer's shop in Pall Mall, where I had business. Two ladies were waiting for their carriage, and one of them was giving the other an account of the intended match, in a voice so little attempting concealment, that it was impossible for me not to hear all. The name of Willoughby, John Willoughby, frequently repeated, first caught my attention, and what followed was a positive assertion that everything was now finally settled respecting his marriage with Miss Grey—it was no longer to be a secret—it would take place even within a few weeks, with many particulars of preparation and other matters. One thing, especially, I remember, because it served to identify the man still more; as soon as the ceremony was over, they were to go to Combe Magna, his seat in Somersetshire. My astonishment! But it would be impossible to describe what I felt. The communicative lady, I learnt on inquiry, for I stayed in the shop till they were gone, was a Mrs. Ellison, and that, as I have been since informed, is the name of Miss Grey's guardian."

"It is. But have you likewise heard that Miss Grey has fifty thousand pounds? In that, if in anything, we may find an explanation."

"It may be so; but Willoughby is capable—at least I think"—he stopped a moment; then added in a voice which seemed to distrust itself, "And your sister—how did she——"

"Her sufferings have been very severe. I have only to hope that they may be proportionably short. It has been, it is a most cruel affliction. Till yesterday, I believe, she never doubted his regard; and even now, perhaps—but *I* am almost convinced that he never was really attached to her. He has been very deceitful! and, in some points, there seems a hardness of heart about him."

"Ah!" said Colonel Brandon, "there is, indeed! But your sister does not—I think you said so—she does not consider it quite as you do?"

"You know her disposition, and may believe how eagerly she would still justify him if she could."

He made no answer; and soon afterwards, by the removal of the tea-things, and the arrangement of the card parties, the subject was necessarily dropped. Mrs. Jennings, who had watched them with pleasure while they were talking, and who expected to see the effect of Miss Dashwood's communication, in such an instantaneous gaiety on Colonel Brandon's side as might have become a man in the bloom of youth, of hope and happiness, saw him, with amazement, remain the whole evening more serious and thoughtful than usual.

Chapter 31

From a night of more sleep than she had expected, Marianne awoke the next morning to the same consciousness of misery in which she had closed her eyes. Elinor encouraged her as much as possible to talk of what she felt; and before breakfast was ready, they had gone through the subject again and again; with the same steady conviction and affectionate counsel on Elinor's side, the same impetuous feelings and varying opinions on Marianne's, as before. Sometimes she could believe Willoughby to be as unfortunate and as innocent as herself, and at others, lost every consolation in the impossibility of acquitting him. At one moment she was absolutely indifferent to the observation of all the world, at another she would seclude herself from it for ever, and at a third could resist it with energy. In one thing, however, she was uniform, when it came to the point, in avoiding, where it was possible, the presence of Mrs. Jennings, and in a determined silence when obliged to endure it. Her heart was hardened against the belief of Mrs. Jennings's entering into her sorrows with any compassion.

"No, no, no, it cannot be," she cried; "she cannot feel. Her kindness is not sympathy; her good-nature is not tenderness. All that she wants is gossip, and she only likes me now because I supply it."

Elinor had not needed this to be assured of the injustice to which her sister was often led in her opinion of others, by the irritable refinement of her own mind, and the too great importance placed by her on the delicacies of a strong sensibility, and the graces of a polished manner. Like half the rest of the world, if more than half there be that is clever and good, Marianne with excellent abilities and an excellent disposition, was neither reasonable nor candid. She expected from other people the same opinions and feelings as her own, and she judged of their motives by the immediate effect of their actions on herself. Thus a circumstance occurred, while the sisters were together in their own room after breakfast, which sunk the heart of Mrs. Jennings still lower in her estimation; because, through her own weakness, it chanced to prove a source of fresh pain to herself, though Mrs. Jennings was governed in it by an impulse of the utmost good-will.

With a letter in her outstretched hand, and countenance gaily smiling, from the persuasion of bringing comfort, she entered their room, saying: "Now, my dear, I bring you something that I am sure will do you good."

Marianne heard enough. In one moment her imagination placed before her a letter from Willoughby, full of tenderness and contrition, explanatory of all that had passed, satisfactory, convincing; and instantly followed by Willoughby himself, rushing eagerly into the room to inforce, at her feet, by the eloquence of his eyes, the assurances of his letter. The work of one moment was destroyed by the next. The handwriting of her mother, never till then unwelcome, was before her; and, in the acuteness of the disappointment which followed such an ecstasy of more than hope, she felt as if, till that instant, she had never suffered.

The cruelty of Mrs. Jennings no language, within her reach in her moments of happiest eloquence, could have expressed; and now she could reproach her only by the tears which streamed from her eyes with passionate violence—a reproach, however, so entirely lost on its object, that after many expressions of pity, she withdrew, still referring her to the letter for comfort. But the letter, when she was calm enough to read it, brought little comfort. Willoughby filled every page. Her mother, still confident of her engagement, and relying as warmly as ever on his constancy, had only been roused by Elinor's application, to entreat from Marianne greater openness towards them both, and this, with such tenderness towards her, such affection for Willoughby, and such a conviction of their future happiness in each other, that she wept with agony through the whole of it.

All her impatience to be at home again now returned; her mother was dearer to her than ever—dearer through the very excess of her mistaken confidence in Willoughby, and she was wildly urgent to be gone. Elinor, unable herself to determine whether it were better for Marianne to be in London or at Barton, offered no counsel of her own except of patience till their mother's wishes could be known; and at length she obtained her sister's consent to wait for that knowledge.

Mrs. Jennings left them earlier than usual; for she could not be easy till the Middletons and Palmers were able to grieve as much as herself; and positively refusing Elinor's offered attendance, went out alone for the rest of the morning. Elinor, with a very heavy heart, aware of the pain she was going to communicate, and perceiving by Marianne's letter how ill she had succeeded in laying any foundation for it, then sat down to write her mother an account of what had passed, and entreat her directions for the future; while Marianne, who came into the drawing-room on Mrs. Jennings's going away, remained fixed at the table where Elinor wrote, watching the advancement of her pen, grieving over her for the hardship of such a task, and grieving still more fondly over its effect on her mother.

In this manner they had continued about a quarter of an hour, when Marianne, whose nerves could not then bear any sudden noise, was startled by a rap at the door.

"Who can this be?" cried Elinor. "So early too! I thought we *had* been safe."

Marianne moved to the window.

"It is Colonel Brandon!" said she, with vexation. "We are never safe from *him*."

"He will not come in, as Mrs. Jennings is from home."

"I will not trust to *that*," retreating to her own room. "A man who has nothing to do with his own time has no conscience in his intrusion on that of others."

The event proved her conjecture right, though it was founded on injustice and error, for Colonel Brandon *did* come in; and Elinor, who was convinced that solicitude for Marianne brought him thither, and who saw *that* solicitude in his disturbed and melancholy look, and in his anxious though brief inquiry after her, could not forgive her sister for esteeming him so lightly.

"I met Mrs. Jennings in Bond Street," said he, after the first salutation, "and she encouraged me to come on; and I was the more easily encouraged, because I thought it probable that I might find you alone, which I was very desirous of doing. My object—my wish—my sole wish in desiring it—I hope, I believe it is—is to be a means of giving comfort—no, I must not say comfort—not present comfort—but conviction, lasting conviction to your sister's mind. My regard for her, for yourself, for your mother—will you allow me to prove it by relating some circumstances, which nothing but a *very* sincere regard—nothing but an earnest desire of being useful—I think I am justified—though where so many hours have been spent in convincing myself that I am right, is there not some reason to fear I may be wrong?" He stopped.

"I understand you," said Elinor. "You have something to tell me of Mr. Willoughby, that will open his character farther. Your telling it will be the greatest act of friendship that can be shown Marianne. *My* gratitude will be insured immediately by any information tending to that end and *hers* must be gained by it in time. Pray, pray let me hear it."

"You shall; and, to be brief, when I quitted Barton last October—but this will give you no idea. I must go farther back. You will find me a very awkward narrator, Miss Dashwood; I hardly know where to begin. A short account of myself, I believe, will be necessary, and it *shall* be a short one. On such a subject," sighing heavily, "I can have little temptation to be diffuse."

He stopped a moment for recollection, and then, with another sigh, went on.

"You have probably entirely forgotten a conversation—(it is not to be supposed that it could make any impression on you)—a conversation between us one evening at Barton Park—it was the evening of a dance—in which I alluded to a lady I had once known, as resembling in some measure, your sister Marianne."

"Indeed," answered Elinor, "I have *not* forgotten it." He looked pleased by this remembrance, and added:

"If I am not deceived by the uncertainty, the partiality of tender recollection, there is a very strong resemblance between them as well in mind as person—the same warmth of heart, the same eagerness of fancy and spirits. This lady was one of my nearest relations, an orphan from her infancy, and under the guardianship of my father. Our ages were nearly the same, and from our earliest years we were playfellows and friends. I cannot remember the time when I did not love Eliza; and my affection for her, as we grew up, was such, as perhaps, judging from my present forlorn and cheerless gravity, you might think me incapable of having ever felt. Hers, for me, was, I believe, fervent as the attachment of your sister to Mr. Willoughby, and it was, though from a different cause, no less unfortunate. At seventeen she was lost to me for ever. She was married—married against her inclination to my brother. Her fortune was large, and our family estate much encumbered. And this, I fear, is all that can be said for the conduct of one who was at once her uncle and guardian. My brother did not deserve her; he did not even love her. I had hoped that her regard for me would support her under any difficulty, and for some time it did; but at last the misery of her situation, for she experienced great unkindness, overcame all her reso-lution, and though she had promised me that nothing—but how blindly I relate! I have never told you how this was brought on. We were within a few hours of eloping together for Scotland. The treachery, or the folly, of my cousin's maid betrayed us. I was banished to the house of a rela-tion far distant, and she was allowed no liberty, no society, no amuse-ment, till my father's point was gained. I had depended on her fortitude too far, and the blow was a severe one—but had her marriage been happy, so young as I then was, a few months must have reconciled me to it, or at least I should not have now to lament it. This, however, was not the case. My brother had no regard for her; his pleasures were not what they ought to have been, and from the first he treated her unkindly. The consequence of this, upon a mind so young, so lively, so inexperienced as Mrs. Brandon's, was but too natural. She resigned herself at first to all the misery of her situation; and happy had it been if she had not lived to overcome those regrets which the remembrance of me occasioned. But can we wonder that with such a husband to provoke inconstancy, and without a friend to advise or restrain her (for my father lived only a few months after their marriage, and I was with my regiment in the East Indies), she should fall? Had I remained in England, perhaps—but I meant to promote the happiness of both by removing from her for

years, and for that purpose had procured my exchange. The shock which
her marriage had given me," he continued in a voice of great agitation,
"was of trifling weight—was nothing—to what I felt when I heard, about
two years afterwards, of her divorce. It was *that* which threw this gloom,
even now the recollection of what I suffered——"

He could say no more, and rising hastily walked for a few minutes
about the room. Elinor, affected by his relation, and still more by his
distress, could not speak. He saw her concern, and coming to her, took
her hand, pressed it, and kissed it with grateful respect. A few minutes
more of silent exertion enabled him to proceed with composure.

"It was nearly three years after this unhappy period before I returned
to England. My first care, when I *did* arrive, was of course to seek for
her; but the search was as fruitless as it was melancholy. I could not
trace her beyond her first seducer, and there was every reason to fear
that she had removed from him only to sink deeper in a life of sin. Her
legal allowance was not adequate to her fortune, nor sufficient for her
comfortable maintenance, and I learnt from my brother that the power
of receiving it had been made over some months before to another person.
He imagined, and calmly could he imagine it, that her extravagance and
consequent distress had obliged her to dispose of it for some immediate
relief. At last, however, and after I had been six months in England, I
did find her. Regard for a former servant of my own, who had since
fallen into misfortune, carried me to visit him in a spunging-house,
where he was confined for debt, and there, in the same house, under a
similar confinement, was my unfortunate sister. So altered—so faded—
worn down by acute suffering of every kind! hardly could I believe the
melancholy and sickly figure before me, to be the remains of the lovely,
blooming, healthful girl, on whom I had once doted. What I endured in
so beholding her—but I have no right to wound your feelings by attempting to describe it—I have pained you too much already. That she was,
to all appearance, in the last stage of consumption, was—yes, in such
a situation it was my greatest comfort. Life could do nothing for her,
beyond giving time for a better preparation for death; and that was
given. I saw her placed in comfortable lodgings, and under proper
attendants; I visited her every day during the rest of her short life: I
was with her in her last moments."

Again he stopped to recover himself; and Elinor spoke her feelings in
an exclamation of tender concern at the fate of his unfortunate friend.

"Your sister, I hope, cannot be offended," said he, "by the resemblance
I have fancied between her and my poor disgraced relation. Their fates,
their fortunes cannot be the same; and had the natural sweet disposition
of the one been guarded by a firmer mind, or a happier marriage, she
might have been all that you will live to see the other be. But to what
does all this lead? I seem to have been distressing you for nothing. Ah!
Miss Dashwood—a subject such as this—untouched for fourteen years
—it is dangerous to handle it at all! I *will* be more collected—more

concise. She left to my care her only little child, a little girl, the offspring
of her first guilty connection, who was then about three years old. She
loved the child, and had always kept it with her. It was a valued, a
precious trust to me; and gladly would I have discharged it in the
strictest sense, by watching over her education myself, had the nature
of our situations allowed it; but I had no family, no home; and my
little Eliza was therefore placed at school. I saw her there whenever
I could, and after the death of my brother (which happened about five
years ago, and which left me the possession of the family property), she
frequently visited me at Delaford. I called her a distant relation; but I
am well aware that I have in general been suspected of a much nearer
connection with her. It is now three years ago (she had just reached her
fourteenth year), that I removed her from school, to place her under the
care of a very respectable woman, residing in Dorsetshire, who had the
charge of four or five other girls of about the same time of life; and
for two years I had every reason to be pleased with her situation. But
last February, almost a twelvemonth back, she suddenly disappeared.
I had allowed her (imprudently, as it has since turned out), at her earnest
desire to go to Bath with one of her young friends, who was attending
her father there for his health. I knew him to be a very good sort of
man, and I thought well of his daughter—better than she deserved, for,
with a most obstinate and ill-judged secrecy, she would tell nothing,
would give no clue, though she certainly knew all. He, her father, a well-
meaning, but not a quick-sighted man, could really, I believe, give no
information; for he had been generally confined to the house, while the
girls were ranging over the town and making what acquaintances they
chose; and he tried to convince me, as thoroughly as he was convinced
himself, of his daughter's being entirely unconcerned in the business. In
short, I could learn nothing but that she was gone; all the rest, for eight
long months, was left to conjecture. What I thought, what I feared, may
be imagined; and what I suffered too."

"Good heavens!" cried Elinor, "could it be! Could Willoughby——"

"The first news that reached me of her," he continued, "came in a
letter from herself last October. It was forwarded to me from Delaford;
and I received it on the very morning of our intended party to Whitwell;
and this was the reason of my leaving Barton so suddenly, which I am
sure must at the time have appeared strange to everybody, and which
I believe gave offence to some. Little did Mr. Willoughby imagine, I
suppose, when his looks censured me for incivility in breaking up the
party, that I was called away to the relief of one whom he had made
poor and miserable; but *had* he known it, what would it have availed?
Would he have been less gay or less happy in the smiles of your sister?
No, he had already done that which no man who *can* feel for another
would do. He had left the girl whose youth and innocence he had seduced,
in a situation of the utmost distress, with no creditable home, no help,

no friends, ignorant of his address! He had left her, promising to return; he neither returned, nor wrote, nor relieved her."

"This is beyond everything!" exclaimed Elinor.

"His character is now before you—expensive, dissipated, and worse than both. Knowing all this, as I have now known it many weeks, guess what I must have felt on seeing your sister as fond of him as ever, and on being assured that she was to marry him; guess what I must have felt for all your sakes. When I came to you last week and found you alone, I came determined to know the truth, though irresolute what to do when it *was* known. My behaviour must have seemed strange to you then; but now you will comprehend it. To suffer you all to be so deceived; to see your sister—but what could I do? I had no hope of interfering with success; and sometimes I thought your sister's influence might yet reclaim him. But now, after such dishonourable usage, who can tell what were his designs on her? Whatever they may have been, however, she may now, and hereafter doubtless *will*, turn with gratitude towards her own condition, when she compares it with that of my poor Eliza, when she considers the wretched and hopeless situation of this poor girl, and pictures her to herself, with an affection for him as strong, still as strong as her own, and with a mind tormented by self-reproach, which must attend her through life. Surely this comparison must have its use with her. She will feel her own sufferings to be nothing. They proceed from no misconduct, and can bring no disgrace. On the contrary, every friend must be made still more her friend by them. Concern for her unhappiness, and respect for her fortitude under it, must strengthen every attachment. Use your own discretion, however, in communicating to her what I have told you. You must know best what will be its effect; but had I not seriously and from my heart believed it might be of service, might lessen her regrets, I would not have suffered myself to trouble you with this account of my family afflictions, with a recital which may seem to have been intended to raise myself at the expense of others."

Elinor's thanks followed this speech with grateful earnestness; attended too with the assurance of her expecting material advantage to Marianne, from the communication of what had passed.

"I have been more pained," said she, "by her endeavours to acquit him than by all the rest; for it irritates her mind more than the most perfect conviction of his unworthiness can do. Now, though at first she will suffer much, I am sure she will soon become easier. Have you," she continued, after a short silence, "ever seen Mr. Willoughby since you left him at Barton?"

"Yes," he replied gravely, "once I have. One meeting was unavoidable."

Elinor, startled by his manner, looked at him anxiously, saying:

"What! have you met him to——"

"I could meet him in no other way. Eliza had confessed to me, though most reluctantly, the name of her lover; and when he returned to town, which was within a fortnight after myself, we met by appointment, he to defend, I to punish his conduct. We returned unwounded, and the meeting, therefore, never got abroad."

Elinor sighed over the fancied necessity of this; but to a man and a soldier, she presumed not to censure it.

"Such," said Colonel Brandon, after a pause, "has been the unhappy resemblance between the fate of mother and daughter! And so imperfectly have I discharged my trust!"

"Is she still in town?"

"No; as soon as she recovered from her lying-in, for I found her near her delivery, I removed her and her child into the country, and there she remains."

Recollecting, soon afterwards, that he was probably dividing Elinor from her sister, he put an end to his visit, receiving from her again the same grateful acknowledgments, and leaving her full of compassion and esteem for him.

Chapter 32

WHEN the particulars of this conversation were repeated by Miss Dashwood to her sister, as they very soon were, their effect on her was not entirely such as the former had hoped to see. Not that Marianne appeared to distrust the truth of any part of it, for she listened to it all with the most steady and submissive attention, made neither objection nor remark, attempted no vindication of Willoughby, and seemed to show by her tears that she felt it to be impossible. But though this behaviour assured Elinor that the conviction of his guilt *was* carried home to her mind; though she saw with satisfaction the effect of it, in her no longer avoiding Colonel Brandon when he called, in her speaking to him, even voluntarily speaking, with a kind of compassionate respect, and though she saw her spirits less violently irritated than before; she did not see her less wretched. Her mind did become settled, but it was settled in a gloomy dejection. She felt the loss of Willoughby's character yet more heavily than she had felt the loss of his heart; his seduction and desertion of Miss Williams, the misery of that poor girl, and the doubt of what his designs might *once* have been on herself, preyed together so much on her spirits, that she could not bring herself to speak of what she felt even to Elinor; and brooding over her sorrows in silence, gave more pain to her sister than could have been communicated by the most open and most frequent confession of them.

To give the feelings or the language of Mrs. Dashwood on receiving and answering Elinor's letter, would be only to give a repetition of what her daughters had already felt and said; of a disappointment hardly less painful than Marianne's, and an indignation even greater than Elinor's. Long letters from her, quickly succeeding each other, arrived to tell all that she suffered and thought: to express her anxious solicitude for

Marianne, and entreat she would bear up with fortitude under this mis, fortune. Bad indeed must the nature of Marianne's affliction be, when her mother could talk of fortitude! Mortifying and humilating must be the origin of those regrets, which *she* could wish her not to indulge!

Against the interest of her own individual comfort, Mrs. Dashwood had determined that it would be better for Marianne to be anywhere at that time than at Barton, where everything within her view would be bringing back the past in the strongest and most afflicting manner, by constantly placing Willoughby before her, such as she had always seen him there. She recommended it to her daughters, therefore, by all means not to shorten their visit to Mrs. Jennings; the length of which, though never exactly fixed, had been expected by all to comprise at least five or six weeks. A variety of occupations, of objects, and of company, which could not be procured at Barton, would be inevitable there, and might yet, she hoped, cheat Marianne, at times, into some interest beyond herself, and even into some amusement, much as the idea of both might now be spurned by her.

From all danger of seeing Willoughby again, her mother considered her to be at least equally safe in town as in the country, since his acquaintance must now be dropped by all who called themselves her friends. Design could never bring them in each other's way; negligence could never leave them exposed to a surprise; and chance had less in its favour in the crowd of London than even in the retirement of Barton, where it might force him before her while paying that visit at Allenham on his marriage, which Mrs. Dashwood, from foreseeing at first as a probable event, had brought herself to expect as a certain one.

She had yet another reason for wishing her children to remain where they were; a letter from her son-in-law had told her that he and his wife were to be in town before the middle of February, and she judged it right that they should sometimes see their brother.

Marianne had promised to be guided by her mother's opinion, and she submitted to it therefore without opposition, though it proved perfectly different from what she wished and expected, though she felt it to be entirely wrong, formed on mistaken grounds, and that by requiring her longer continuance in London it deprived her of the only possible alleviation of her wretchedness, the personal sympathy of her mother, and doomed her to such society and such scenes as must prevent her ever knowing a moment's rest.

But it was a matter of great consolation to her, that what brought evil to herself would bring good to her sister; and Elinor, on the other hand, suspecting that it would not be in her power to avoid Edward entirely, comforted herself by thinking, that though their longer stay would therefore militate against her own happiness, it would be better for Marianne than an immediate return into Devonshire.

Her carefulness in guarding her sister from ever hearing Willoughby's name mentioned, was not thrown away. Marianne, though without knowing it herself, reaped all its advantage; for neither Mrs. Jennings, nor Sir John, nor even Mrs. Palmer herself, ever spoke of him before her. Elinor wished that the same forbearance could have extended towards herself, but that was impossible, and she was obliged to listen day after day to the indignation of them all.

Sir John could not have thought it possible. "A man of whom he had always had such reason to think well! Such a good-natured fellow! He did not believe there was a bolder rider in England! It was an unaccountable business. He wished him at the devil with all his heart. He would not speak another word to him, meet him where he might, for all the world! No, not if it were to be by the side of Barton covert, and they were kept waiting for two hours together. Such a scoundrel of a fellow! Such a deceitful dog! It was only the last time they met that he had offered him one of Folly's puppies! And this was the end of it!"

Mrs. Palmer, in her way, was equally angry. "She was determined to drop his acquaintance immediately, and she was very thankful that she had never been acquainted with him at all. She wished with all her heart Combe Magna was not so near Cleveland; but it did not signify, for it was a great deal too far off to visit; she hated him so much that she was resolved never to mention his name again, and she should tell everybody she saw how good-for-nothing he was."

The rest of Mrs. Palmer's sympathy was shown in procuring all the particulars in her power of the approaching marriage, and communicating them to Elinor. She could soon tell at what coachmaker's the new carriage was building, by what painter Mr. Willoughby's portrait was drawn, and at what warehouse Miss Grey's clothes might be seen.

The calm and polite unconcern of Lady Middleton on the occasion was a happy relief to Elinor's spirits, oppressed as they often were by the clamorous kindness of the others. It was a great comfort to her to be sure of exciting no interest in *one* person at least among their circle of friends; a great comfort to know that there was *one* who would meet her without feeling any curiosity after particulars, or any anxiety for her sister's health.

Every qualification is raised at times, by the circumstances of the moment, to more than its real value; and she was sometimes worried down by officious condolence to rate good breeding as more indispensable to comfort than good nature.

Lady Middleton expressed her sense of the affair about once every day, or twice, if the subject occurred very often, by saying, "It is very shocking indeed!" and by the means of this continual though gentle vent, was able not only to see the Miss Dashwoods from the first without the smallest emotion, but very soon to see them without recollecting a word of the matter; and having thus supported the dignity of her own sex, and spoken her decided censure of what was wrong in the other, she thought herself at liberty to attend to the interest of her own assemblies, and therefore determined (though rather against the opinion of Sir John), as Mrs.

Willoughby would at once be a woman of elegance and fortune, to leave her card with her as soon as she married.

Colonel Brandon's delicate unobtrusive inquiries were never unwelcome to Miss Dashwood. He had abundantly earned the privilege of intimate discussion of her sister's disappointment, by the friendly zeal with which he had endeavoured to soften it, and they always conversed with confidence. His chief reward for the painful exertion of disclosing past sorrows and present humiliations, was given in the pitying eye with which Marianne sometimes observed him, and the gentleness of her voice whenever (though it did not often happen) she was obliged, or could oblige herself to speak to him. *These* assured him that his exertion had produced an increase of good-will towards himself, and *these* gave Elinor hopes of its being further augmented hereafter; but Mrs. Jennings, who knew nothing of all this—who knew only that the Colonel continued as grave as ever, and that she could never prevail on him to make the offer himself, nor commission her to make it for him—began at the end of two days to think that, instead of Midsummer, they would not be married till Michaelmas, and by the end of a week that it would not be a match at all. The good understanding between the Colonel and Miss Dashwood seemed rather to declare that the honours of the mulberry-tree, the canal, and the yew arbour, would all be made over to *her;* and Mrs. Jennings had for some time ceased to think at all of Mr. Ferrars.

Early in February, within a fortnight from the receipt of Willoughby's letter, Elinor had the painful office of informing her sister that he was married. She had taken care to have the intelligence conveyed to herself, as soon as it was known that the ceremony was over, as she was desirous that Marianne should not receive the first notice of it from the public papers, which she saw her eagerly examining every morning.

She received the news with resolute composure; made no observation on it, and at first shed no tears; but after a short time they would burst out, and for the rest of the day she was in a state hardly less pitiable than when she first learnt to expect the event.

The Willoughbys left town as soon as they were married; and Elinor now hoped, as there could be no danger of her seeing either of them, to prevail on her sister, who had never yet left the house since the blow first fell, to go out again by degrees as she had done before.

About this time, the two Miss Steeles, lately arrived at their cousin's house in Bartlett's Buildings, Holborn, presented themselves again before their more grand relations in Conduit and Berkeley Street, and were welcomed by them with all great cordiality.

Elinor only was sorry to see them. Their presence always gave her pain, and she hardly knew how to make a very gracious return to the overpowering delight of Lucy in finding her *still* in town.

"I should have been quite disappointed if I had not found you here *still,*" said she repeatedly, with a strong emphasis on the word. "But I always thought I *should*. I was almost sure you would not leave London yet awhile; though you *told* me, you know, at Barton, that you should not stay above a *month*. But I thought, at the time, that you would most likely change your mind when it came to the point. It would have been such a great pity to have went away before your brother and sister came. And now, to be sure, you will be in no *hurry* to be gone. I am amazingly glad you did not keep to *your word*."

Elinor perfectly understood her, and was forced to use all her self-command to make it appear that she did *not*.

"Well, my dear," said Mrs. Jennings, "and how did you travel?"

"Not in the stage, I assure you," replied Miss Steele, with quick exultation; "we came post all the way, and had a very smart beau to attend us. Dr. Davies was coming to town, and so we thought we'd join him in a post-chaise; and he behaved very genteelly, and paid ten or twelve shillings more than we did."

"Oh, oh!" cried Mrs. Jennings, "very pretty, indeed! And the Doctor is a single man, I warrant you."

"There now," said Miss Steele, affectedly simpering; "everybody laughs at me so about the Doctor, and I cannot think why. My cousins say they are sure I have made a conquest; but for my part I declare I never think about him from one hour's end to another. 'Lord! here comes your beau, Nancy,' my cousin said t'other day, when she saw him crossing the street to the house. 'My beau, indeed!' said I, 'I cannot think who you mean. The Doctor is no beau of mine.'"

"Aye, aye, that is very pretty talking—but it won't do—the Doctor is the man, I see."

"No, indeed!" replied her cousin, with affected earnestness, "and I beg you will contradict it, if you ever hear it talked of."

Mrs. Jennings directly gave her the gratifying assurance that she certainly would *not*, and Miss Steele was made completely happy.

"I suppose you will go and stay with your brother and sister, Miss Dashwood, when they come to town," said Lucy, returning, after a cessation of hostile hints, to the charge.

"No, I do not think we shall."

"Oh, yes, I dare say you will."

Elinor would not humour her by further opposition.

"What a charming thing it is that Mrs. Dashwood can spare you both for so long a time together!"

"Long a time, indeed!" interposed Mrs. Jennings. "Why, their visit is but just begun!"

Lucy was silenced.

"I am sorry we cannot see your sister, Miss Dashwood," said Miss Steele. "I am sorry she is not well"; for Marianne had left the room on their arrival.

"You are very good. My sister will be equally sorry to miss the pleasure of seeing you; but she has been very much plagued lately with nervous headaches, which make her unfit for company or conversation."

"Oh, dear, that is a great pity! But such old friends as Lucy and me! I think she might see *us;* and I am sure we would not speak a word."

Elinor, with great civility, declined the proposal. "Her sister was perhaps laid down upon the bed, or in her dressing-gown, and therefore not able to come to them."

"Oh, if that's all." cried Miss Steele, "we can just as well go and see *her.*"

Elinor began to find this impertinence too much for her temper; but she was saved the trouble of checking it, by Lucy's sharp reprimand, which now, as on many occasions, though it did not give much sweetness to the manners of one sister, was of advantage in governing those of the other.

Chapter 33

AFTER some opposition, Marianne yielded to her sister's entreaties, and consented to go out with her and Mrs. Jennings one morning for half an hour. She expressly conditioned, however, for paying no visits, and would do no more than accompany them to Gray's in Sackville Street, where Elinor was carrying on a negotiation for the exchange of a few old-fashioned jewels of her mother.

When they stopped at the door, Mrs. Jennings recollected that there was a lady at the other end of the street on whom she ought to call; and as she had no business at Gray's, it was resolved, that while her young friends transacted theirs, she should pay her visit, and return to them.

On ascending the stairs, the Miss Dashwoods found so many people before them in the room, that there was not a person at liberty to attend to their orders; and they were obliged to wait. All that could be done was, to sit down at that end of the counter which seemed to promise the quickest succession; one gentleman only was standing there, and it is probable that Elinor was not without hope of exciting his politeness to a quicker dispatch. But the correctness of his eye, and the delicacy of his taste, proved to be beyond his politeness. He was giving orders for a toothpick-case for himself, and till its size, shape, and ornaments were determined— all of which, after examining and debating for a quarter of an hour over every toothpick-case in the shop, were finally arranged by his own inventive fancy—he had no leisure to bestow any other attention on the two ladies, than what was comprised in three or four very broad stares; a kind of notice which served to imprint on Elinor the remembrance of a person and face of strong, natural, sterling insignificance, though adorned in the first style of fashion.

Marianne was spared from the troublesome feelings of contempt and resentment, on this impertinent examination of their features, and on the puppyism of his manner in deciding on all the different horrors of the different toothpick-cases presented to his inspection, by remaining unconscious of it all; for she was as well able to collect her thoughts within herself, and be as ignorant of what was passing around her, in Mr. Gray's shop, as in her own bedroom.

At last the affair was decided. The ivory, the gold, and the pearls, all received their appointment, and the gentleman having named the last day on which his existence could be continued without the possession of the toothpick-case, drew on his gloves with leisurely care, and bestowing another glance on the Miss Dashwoods, but such a one as seemed rather to demand than express admiration, walked off with a happy air of real conceit and affected indifference.

Elinor lost no time in bringing her business forward, and was on the point of concluding it, when another gentleman presented himself at her side. She turned her eyes towards his face, and found him with some surprise to be her brother.

Their affection and pleasure in meeting was just enough to make a very creditable appearance in Mr. Gray's shop. John Dashwood was really far from being sorry to see his sisters again; it rather gave them satisfaction; and his inquiries after their mother were respectful and attentive.

Elinor found that he and Fanny had been in town two days.

"I wished very much to call upon you yesterday," said he, "but it was impossible, for we were obliged to take Harry to see the wild beasts at Exeter Exchange; and we spent the rest of the day with Mrs. Ferrars. Harry was vastly pleased. *This* morning I had fully intended to call on you, if I could possibly find a spare half-hour, but one has always so much to do on first coming to town! I am come here to bespeak Fanny a seal. But to-morrow I think I shall certainly be able to call in Berkeley Street, and be introduced to your friend Mrs. Jennings. I understand she is a woman of very good fortune. And the Middletons too, you must introduce me to *them*. As my mother-in-law's relations, I shall be happy to show them every respect. They are excellent neighbours to you in the country, I understand."

"Excellent indeed. Their attention to our comfort, their friendliness in every particular, is more than I can express."

"I am extremely glad to hear it, upon my word; extremely glad indeed. But so it ought to be; they are people of large fortune, they are related to you, and every civility and accommodation that can serve to make your situation pleasant, might be reasonably expected. And so you are most comfortably settled in your little cottage, and want for nothing. Edward brought us a most charming account of the place; the most complete thing of its kind, he said, that ever was, and you all seemed to enjoy it beyond anything. It was a great satisfaction to us to hear it, I assure you."

Elinor did feel a little ashamed of her brother; and was not sorry to be spared the necessity of answering him, by the arrival of Mrs. Jennings's servant, who came to tell her that his mistress waited for them at the door.

Mr. Dashwood attended them downstairs, was introduced to Mrs. Jennings at the door of her carriage, and repeating his hope of being able to call on them the next day, took leave.

His visit was duly paid. He came with a pretence of an apology from their sister-in-law, for not coming too; "but she was so much engaged with her mother, that really she had no leisure for going anywhere." Mrs. Jennings, however, assured him directly, that she should not stand upon ceremony, for they were all cousins, or something like it, and she should certainly wait on Mrs. John Dashwood very soon, and bring her sisters to see her. His manners to *them,* though calm, were perfectly kind; to Mrs. Jennings, most attentively civil; and on Colonel Brandon's coming in soon after himself, he eyed him with a curiosity which seemed to say, that he only wanted to know him to be rich to be equally civil to *him*.

After staying with them half an hour, he asked Elinor to walk with him to Conduit Street, and introduce him to Sir John and Lady Middleton. The weather was remarkably fine, and she readily consented. As soon as they were out of the house, his inquiries began.

"Who is Colonel Brandon? Is he a man of fortune?"

"Yes; he has a very good property in Dorsetshire."

"I am glad of it. He seems a most gentlemanlike man, and I think, Elinor, I may congratulate you on the prospect of a very respectable establishment in life."

"Me, brother—what do you mean?"

"He likes you. I observed him narrowly, and am convinced of it. What is the amount of his fortune?"

"I believe about two thousand a year."

"Two thousand a year"; and then working himself up to a pitch of enthusiastic generosity, he added:

"Elinor, I wish with all my heart it were *twice* as much for your sake."

"Indeed I believe you," replied Elinor, "but I am very sure that Colonel Brandon has not the smallest wish of marrying *me*."

"You are mistaken, Elinor; you are very much mistaken. A very little trouble on your side secures him. Perhaps just at present he may be undecided; the smallness of your fortune may make him hang back; his friends may all advise him against it. But some of those little attentions and encouragements which ladies can so easily give, will fix him, in spite of himself. And there can be no reason why you should not try for him. It is not to be supposed that any prior attachment on your side—in short, you know as to an attachment of that kind, it is quite out of the question, the objections are insurmountable—you have too much sense not to see all that. Colonel Brandon must be the man; and no civility shall be wanting on my part, to make him pleased with you and your family. It is a match that must give universal satisfaction. In short, it is a kind of thing that"—lowering his voice to an important whisper—"will be exceedingly welcome to *all parties*." Recollecting himself, however, he added, "That is, I mean to say—your friends are all truly anxious to see you well settled,

Fanny particularly, for she has your interest very much at heart, I assure you. And her mother too, Mrs. Ferrars, a very good-natured woman, I am sure it would give her great pleasure; she said as much the other day."

Elinor would not vouchsafe any answer.

"It would be something remarkable now," he continued, "something droll, if Fanny should have a brother and I a sister settling at the same time. And yet it is not very unlikely."

"Is Mr. Edward Ferrars," said Elinor with resolution, "going to be married?"

"It is not actually settled, but there is such a thing in agitation. He has a most excellent mother. Mrs. Ferrars, with the utmost liberality, will come forward, and settle on him a thousand a year, if the match takes place. The lady is the Honourable Miss Morton, only daughter of the late Lord Morton, with thirty thousand pounds—a very desirable connection on both sides, and I have not a doubt of its taking place in time. A thousand a year is a great deal for a mother to give away, to make over for ever; but Mrs. Ferrars has a noble spirit. To give you another instance of her liberality: The other day, as soon as we came to town, aware that money could not be very plenty with us just now, she put bank-notes into Fanny's hands to the amount of two hundred pounds. And extremely acceptable it is, for we must live at a great expense while we are here."

He paused for her assent and compassion; and she forced herself to say:

"Your expenses both in town and country must certainly be considerable, but your income is a large one."

"Not so large, I dare say, as many people suppose. I do not mean to complain, however; it is undoubtedly a comfortable one, and, I hope, will in time be better. The inclosure of Norland Common, now carrying on, is a most serious drain. And then I have made a little purchase within this half-year—East Kingham Farm, you must remember the place, where old Gibson used to live. The land was so very desirable for me in every respect, so immediately adjoining my own property, that I felt it my duty to buy it. I could not have answered it to my conscience to let it fall into any other hands. A man must pay for his convenience, and it *has* cost me a vast deal of money."

"More than you think it really and intrinsically worth?"

"Why, I hope not that. I might have sold it again, the next day, for more than I gave: but with regard to the purchase-money, I might have been very unfortunate indeed; for the stocks were at that time so low, that if I had not happened to have the necessary sum in my banker's hands, I must have sold out to very great loss."

Elinor could only smile.

"Other great and inevitable expenses too we have had on first coming to Norland. Our respected father, as you well know, bequeathed all the Stanhill effects that remained at Norland (and very valuable they were) to your mother. Far be it for me to repine at his doing so; he had an undoubted right to dispose of his own property as he chose. But, in conse-quence of it, we have been obliged to make large purchases of linen, china, etc., to supply the place of what was taken away. You may guess, after all these expenses, how very far we must be from being rich, and how acceptable Mrs. Ferrars's kindness is."

"Certainly," said Elinor; "and assisted by her liberality I hope you may yet live to be in easy circumstances."

"Another year or two may do much towards it," he gravely replied; "but however there is still a great deal to be done. There is not a stone laid of Fanny's greenhouse, and nothing but the plan of the flower garden marked out."

"Where is the greenhouse to be?"

"Upon the knoll behind the house. The old walnut trees are all come down to make room for it. It will be a very fine object from many parts of the park, and the flower garden will slope down just before it, and be exceedingly pretty. We have cleared away all the old thorns that grew in patches over the brow."

Elinor kept her concern and her censure to herself, and was very thankful that Marianne was not present to share the provocation.

Having now said enough to make his poverty clear, and to do away the necessity of buying a pair of ear-rings for each of his sisters, in his next visit at Gray's, his thoughts took a more cheerful turn, and he began to congratulate Elinor on having such a friend as Mrs. Jennings.

"She seems a most valuable woman indeed. Her house, her style of living, all bespeak an exceeding good income, and it is an acquaintance that has not only been of great use to you hitherto, but in the end may prove materially advantageous. Her inviting you to town is certainly a vast thing in your favour; and, indeed, it speaks altogether so great a regard for you, that in all probability when she dies you will not be for-gotten. She must have a great deal to leave."

"Nothing at all, I should rather suppose; for she has only her jointure, which will descend to her children."

"But it is not to be imagined that she lives up to her income. Few people of common prudence will do *that;* and whatever she saves, she will be able to dispose of."

"And do you not think it more likely that she should leave it to her daughters, than to us?"

"Her daughters are both exceedingly well married, and therefore I cannot perceive the necessity of her remembering them further. Whereas, in my opinion, by her taking so much notice of you, and treating you in this kind of way, she has given you a sort of claim on her future consideration, which a conscientious woman would not disregard. Nothing can be kinder than her behaviour; and she can hardly do all this, without being aware of the expectations she raises."

"But she raises none in those most concerned. Indeed, brother, your anxiety for our welfare and prosperity carries you too far."

"Why, to be sure," said he, seeming to recollect himself, "people have little, have very little in their power. But, my dear Elinor, what is the matter with Marianne? She looks very unwell, has lost her colour, and is grown quite thin. Is she ill?"

"She is not well, she has had a nervous complaint on her for several weeks."

"I am sorry for that. At her time of life, anything of an illness destroys the bloom for ever! Hers has been a very short one! She was as handsome a girl last September as any I ever saw, and as likely to attract the men. There was something in her style of beauty to please them particularly. I remember Fanny used to say that she would marry sooner and better than you did; not but what she is exceeding fond of *you*—but so it happened to strike her. She will be mistaken, however. I question whether Marianne *now* will marry a man worth more than five or six hundred a year at the utmost, and I am very much deceived if *you* do not do better. Dorsetshire! I know very little of Dorsetshire, but, my dear Elinor, I shall be exceedingly glad to know more of it; and I think I can answer for your having Fanny and myself among the earliest and best pleased of your visitors."

Elinor tried very seriously to convince him that there was no likelihood of her marrying Colonel Brandon; but it was an expectation of too much pleasure to himself to be relinquished, and he was really resolved on seeking an intimacy with that gentleman, and promoting the marriage by every possible attention. He had just compunction enough for having done nothing for his sisters himself, to be exceedingly anxious that everybody else should do a great deal; and an offer from Colonel Brandon, or a legacy from Mrs. Jennings, was the easiest means of atoning for his own neglect.

They were lucky enough to find Lady Middleton at home, and Sir John came in before their visit ended. Abundance of civilities passed on all sides. Sir John was ready to like anybody, and though Mr. Dashwood did not seem to know much about horses, he soon set him down as a very good-natured fellow; while Lady Middleton saw enough of fashion in his appearance to think his acquaintance worth having; and Mr. Dashwood went away delighted with both.

"I shall have a charming account to carry to Fanny," said he, as he walked back with his sister. "Lady Middleton is really a most elegant woman! such a woman as I am sure Fanny will be glad to know. And Mrs. Jennings too, an exceedingly well-behaved woman, though not so elegant as her daughter. Your sister need not have any scruple even of visiting *her*, which, to say the truth, has been a little the case, and very naturally; for we only knew that Mrs. Jennings was the widow of a man who had got all his money in a low way; and Fanny and Mrs. Ferrars were both strongly prepossessed that neither she nor her daughters were such kind of women as Fanny would like to associate with. But now I can carry her a most satisfactory account of both."

Chapter 34

MRS. JOHN DASHWOOD had so much confidence in her husband's judgment, that she waited the very next day both on Mrs. Jennings and her
daughter; and her confidence was rewarded by finding even the former,
even the woman with whom her sisters were staying, by no means unworthy her notice; and as for Lady Middleton, she found her one of the
most charming women in the world!

Lady Middleton was equally pleased with Mrs. Dashwood. There was
a kind of coldhearted selfishness on both sides, which mutually attracted
them; and they sympathised with each other in an insipid propriety of
demeanour, and a general want of understanding.

The same manners, however, which recommended Mrs. John Dashwood
to the good opinion of Lady Middleton, did not suit the fancy of Mrs.
Jennings, and to *her* she appeared nothing more than a little proud-
looking woman of uncordial address, who met her husband's sisters without any affection, and almost without having anything to say to them;
for of the quarter of an hour bestowed on Berkeley Street, she sat a least
seven minutes and a half in silence.

Elinor wanted very much to know, though she did not choose to ask,
whether Edward was then in town; but nothing would have induced
Fanny voluntarily to mention his name before her, till able to tell her
that his marriage with Miss Morton was resolved on, or till her husband's
expectations on Colonel Brandon were answered; because she believed
them still so very much attached to each other, that they could not be
too sedulously divided in word and deed on every occasion. The intelligence, however, which *she* would not give, soon flowed from another
quarter. Lucy came very shortly to claim Elinor's compassion on being
unable to see Edward, though he had arrived in town with Mr. and Mrs.
Dashwood. He dared not come to Bartlett's Buildings for fear of detection, and though their mutual impatience to meet was not to be told, they
could do nothing at present but write.

Edward assured them himself of his being in town, within a very short
time, by twice calling in Berkeley Street. Twice was his card found on
the table, when they returned from their morning's engagements. Elinor
was pleased that he had called, and still more pleased that she had missed
him.

The Dashwoods were so prodigiously delighted with the Middletons,
that though not much in the habit of giving anything, they determined
to give them a dinner, and soon after their acquaintance began, invited
them to dine in Harley Street, where they had taken a very good house
for three months. Their sisters and Mrs. Jennings were invited likewise,
and John Dashwood was careful to secure Colonel Brandon, who, always
glad to be where the Miss Dashwoods were, received his eager civilities
with some surprise, but much more pleasure. They were to meet Mrs.

Ferrars; but Elinor could not learn whether her sons were to be of the party. The expectation of seeing *her,* however, was enough to make her interested in the engagement; for though she could now meet Edward's mother without that strong anxiety which had once promised to attend such an introduction, though she could now see her with perfect indifference, as to her opinion of herself, her desire of being in company with Mrs. Ferrars, her curiosity to know what she was like, was as lively as ever.

The interest with which she thus anticipated the party, was soon afterwards increased, more powerfully than pleasantly, by her hearing that the Miss Steeles were also to be at it.

So well had they recommended themselves to Lady Middleton, so agreeable had their assiduities made them to her, that though Lucy was certainly not elegant, and her sister not even genteel, she was as ready as Sir John to ask them to spend a week or two in Conduit Street; and it happened to be particularly convenient to the Miss Steeles, as soon as the Dashwoods' invitation was known, that their visit should begin a few days before the party took place.

Their claims to the notice of Mrs. John Dashwood as the nieces of the gentleman who for many years had had the care of her brother, might not have done much, however, towards procuring them seats at her table; but as Lady Middleton's guests they must be welcome; and Lucy, who had long wanted to be personally known to the family, to have a nearer view of their characters and her own difficulties, and to have an opportunity of endeavouring to please them, had seldom been happier in her life than she was on receiving Mrs. John Dashwood's card.

On Elinor its effect was very different. She began immediately to determine that Edward, who lived with his mother, must be asked, as his mother was, to a party given by his sister; and to see him for the first time, after all that had passed, in the company of Lucy!—she hardly knew how she could bear it!

These apprehensions perhaps were not founded entirely on reason, and certainly not at all on truth. They were relieved, however, not by her own recollection, but by the goodwill of Lucy, who believed herself to be inflicting a severe disappointment when she told her that Edward certainly would not be in Harley Street on Tuesday, and even hoped to be carrying the pain still further by persuading her, that he was kept away by that extreme affection for herself, which he could not conceal when they were together.

The important Tuesday came that was to introduce the two young ladies to this formidable mother-in-law.

"Pity me, dear Miss Dashwood!" said Lucy, as they walked up the stairs together—for the Middletons arrived so directly after Mrs. Jennings, that they all followed the servant at the same time. "There is nobody here but you, that can feel for me. I declare I can hardly stand. Good gracious! In a moment I shall see the person that all my happiness depends on—that is to be my mother!"

Elinor could have given her immediate relief by suggesting the possibility of its being Miss Morton's mother, rather than her own, whom they
were about to behold; but instead of doing that, she assured her, and with
great sincerity, that she did pity her, to the utter amazement of Lucy,
who, though really uncomfortable herself, hoped at least to be an object
of irrepressible envy to Elinor.

Mrs. Ferrars was a little, thin woman, upright, even to formality, in her
figure, and serious, even to sourness, in her aspect. Her complexion was
sallow; and her features small, without beauty, and naturally without
expression; but a lucky contraction of the brow had rescued her countenance from the disgrace of insipidity, by giving it the strong characters
of pride and ill-nature. She was not a woman of many words; for, unlike
people in general, she proportioned them to the number of her ideas; and
of the few syllables that did escape her, not one fell to the share of Miss
Dashwood, whom she eyed with the spirited determination of disliking
her at all events.

Elinor could not *now* be made unhappy by this behaviour. A few months
ago it would have hurt her exceedingly; but it was not in Mrs. Ferrars's
power to distress her by it now; and the difference of her manners to the
Miss Steeles—a difference which seemed purposely made to humble her
more—only amused her. She could not but smile to see the graciousness
of both mother and daughter towards the very person—for Lucy was
particularly distinguished—whom of all others, had they known as much
as she did, they would have been most anxious to mortify; while she
herself, who had comparatively no power to wound them, sat pointedly
slighted by both. But while she smiled at a graciousness so misapplied,
she could not reflect on the mean-spirited folly from which it sprung, nor
observe the studied attentions with which the Miss Steeles courted its
continuance, without thoroughly despising them all four.

Lucy was all exultation on being so honourably distinguished; and Miss
Steele wanted only to be teased about Dr. Davies to be perfectly happy.

The dinner was a grand one, the servants were numerous, and everything bespoke the Mistress's inclination for show, and the Master's ability
to support it. In spite of the improvements and additions which were
making to the Norland estate, and in spite of its owner having once been
within some thousand pounds of being obliged to sell out at a loss, nothing
gave any symptom of that indigence which he had tried to infer from it;
no poverty of any kind, except of conversation, appeared—but there the
deficiency was considerable. John Dashwood had not much to say for
himself that was worth hearing, and his wife had still less. But there was
no peculiar disgrace in this, for it was very much the case with the chief
of their visitors, who almost all laboured under one or other of these dis-
qualifications for being agreeable—want of sense, either natural or improved, want of elegance, want of spirits, or want of temper.

When the ladies withdrew to the drawing-room after dinner, this
poverty was particularly evident, for the gentlemen *had supplied* the

discourse with some variety—the variety of politics, inclosing land, and breaking horses—but then it was all over, and one subject only engaged the ladies till coffee came in, which was the comparative heights of Harry Dashwood, and Lady Middleton's second son William, who were nearly of the same age.

Had both the children been there, the affair might have been determined too easily by measuring them at once; but as Harry only was present, it was all conjectural assertion on both sides, and everybody had a right to be equally positive in their opinion, and to repeat it over and over again as often as they liked.

The parties stood thus:

The two mothers, though each really convinced that her own son was the tallest, politely decided in favour of the other.

The two grandmothers, with not less partiality, but more sincerity, were equally earnest in support of their own descendant.

Lucy, who was hardly less anxious to please one parent than the other, thought the boys were both remarkably tall for their age, and could not conceive that there could be the smallest difference in the world between them; and Miss Steele, with yet greater address, gave it, as fast as she could, in favour of each.

Elinor, having once delivered her opinion on William's side, by which she offended Mrs. Ferrars, and Fanny still more, did not see the necessity of enforcing it by any further assertion; and Marianne, when called on for hers, offended them all by declaring that she had no opinion to give, as she had never thought about it.

Before her removing from Norland, Elinor had painted a very pretty pair of screens for her sister-in-law, which being now just mounted and brought home, ornamented her present drawing-room; and these screens catching the eye of John Dashwood on his following the other gentlemen into the room, were officiously handed by him to Colonel Brandon for his admiration.

"These are done by my eldest sister," said he; "and you, as a man of taste, will, I dare say, be pleased with them. I do not know whether you ever happened to see any of her performances before, but she is in general reckoned to draw extremely well."

The Colonel, though disclaiming all pretensions to connoisseurship, warmly admired the screens, as he would have done anything painted by Miss Dashwood; and the curiosity of the others being of course excited, they were handed round for general inspection. Mrs. Ferrars, not aware of their being Elinor's work, particularly requested to look at them; and after they had received the gratifying testimony of Lady Middleton's approbation, Fanny presented them to her mother, considerately informing her at the same time that they were done by Miss Dashwood.

"Hum"—said Mrs. Ferrars—"very pretty"—and without regarding them at all, returned them to her daughter.

Perhaps Fanny thought for a moment that her mother had been quite rude enough—for, colouring a little, she immediately said:

"They are very pretty, ma'am—an't they?" But then again, the dread of having been too civil, too encouraging herself, probably came over her, for she presently added:

"Do you not think they are something in Miss Morton's style of paint ing, ma'am? *She does* paint most delightfully. How beautifully her last landscape is done!"

"Beautifully indeed. But *she* does everything well."

Marianne could not bear this. She was already greatly displeased with Mrs. Ferrars; and such ill-timed praise of another, at Elinor's expense, though she had not any notion of what was principally meant by it, provoked her immediately to say with warmth:

"This is admiration of a very particular kind! What is Miss Morton to us? Who knows or who cares for her? It is Elinor of whom *we* think and speak."

And so saying, she took the screens out of her sister-in-law's hand to admire them herself as they ought to be admired.

Mrs. Ferrars looked exceedingly angry, and drawing herself up more stiffly than ever, pronounced in retort this bitter philippic: "Miss Morton is Lord Morton's daughter."

Fanny looked very angry too, and her husband was all in a fright at his sister's audacity. Elinor was much more hurt by Marianne's warmth, than she had been by what produced it; but Colonel Brandon's eyes, as they were fixed on Marianne, declared that he noticed only what was amiable in it; the affectionate heart which could not bear to see a sister slighted in the smallest point.

Marianne's feeling did not stop here. The cold insolence of Mrs. Ferrars's general behaviour to her sister, seemed to her to foretell such difficulties and distresses to Elinor, as her own wounded heart taught her to think of with horror; and urged by a strong impulse of affectionate sensibility, she moved, after a moment, to her sister's chair, and putting one arm round her neck, and one cheek close to hers, said in a low, but eager voice:

"Dear, dear Elinor, don't mind them. Don't let them make *you* un-happy."

She could say no more; her spirits were quite overcome, and hiding her face on Elinor's shoulder, she burst into tears. Everybody's attention was called, and almost everybody was concerned. Colonel Brandon rose up and went to them without knowing what he did. Mrs. Jennings, with a very intelligent "Ah! poor dear," immediately gave her her salts; and Sir John felt so desperately enraged against the author of this nervous distress, that he instantly changed his seat to one close by Lucy Steele, and gave her, in a whisper, a brief account of the whole shocking affair.

In a few minutes, however, Marianne was recovered enough to put an end to the bustle, and sit down among the rest; though her spirits retained the impression of what had passed the whole evening.

"Poor Marianne!" said her brother to Colonel Brandon in a low voice, as soon as he could secure his attention. "She has not such good health as her sister—she is very nervous—she has not Elinor's constitution; and one must allow that there is something very trying to a young woman who *has been* a beauty, in the loss of her personal attractions. You would not think it perhaps, but Marianne *was* remarkably handsome a few months ago—quite as handsome as Elinor. Now you see it is all gone."

Chapter 35

ELINOR's curiosity to see Mrs. Ferrars was satisfied. She had found in her everything that could tend to make a further connection between the families undesirable. She had seen enough of her pride, her meanness, and her determined prejudice against herself, to comprehend all the difficulties that must have perplexed the engagement, and retarded the marriage of Edward and herself, had he been otherwise free; and she had seen almost enough to be thankful for her *own* sake, that one greater obstacle preserved her from suffering under any other of Mrs. Ferrars's creation, preserved her from all dependence upon her caprice, or any solicitude for her good opinion. Or at least, if she did not bring herself quite to rejoice in Edward's being fettered to Lucy, she determined, that had Lucy been more amiable, she *ought* to have rejoiced.

She wondered that Lucy's spirits could be so very much elevated by the civility of Mrs. Ferrars; that her interest and her vanity should so very much blind her, as to make the attention which seemed only paid her because she was *not Elinor*, appear a compliment to herself—or to allow her to derive encouragement from a preference only given her, because her real situation was unknown. But that it was so, had not only been declared by Lucy's eyes at the time, but was declared over again the next morning more openly; for, at her particular desire, Lady Middleton set her down in Berkeley Street on the chance of seeing Elinor alone, to tell her how happy she was.

The chance proved a lucky one, for a message from Mrs. Palmer, soon after she arrived, carried Mrs. Jennings away.

"My dear friend," cried Lucy as soon as they were by themselves, "I come to talk to you of my happiness. Could anything be so flattering as Mrs. Ferrars's way of treating me yesterday? So exceedingly affable as she was! You know how I dreaded the thoughts of seeing her; but the very moment I was introduced, there was such an affability in her behaviour as really should seem to say, she had quite took a fancy to me. Now was not it so? You saw it all; and was not you quite struck with it?"

"She was certainly very civil to you."

"Civil! Did you see nothing but only civility? I saw a vast deal more—

such kindness as fell to the share of nobody but me! No pride, no hauteur, and your sister just the same—all sweetness and affability!"

Elinor wished to talk of something else, but Lucy still pressed her to own that she had reason for her happiness, and Elinor was obliged to go on.

"Undoubtedly, if they had known your engagement," said she, "nothing could be more flattering than their treatment of you; but as that was not the case——"

"I guessed you would say so," replied Lucy quickly; "but there was no reason in the world why Mrs. Ferrars should seem to like me, if she did not—and her liking me is everything. You shan't talk me out of my satisfaction. I am sure it will all end well, and there will be no difficulties at all, to what I used to think. Mrs. Ferrars is a charming woman, and so is your sister. They are both delightful women indeed! I wonder I should never hear you say how agreeable Mrs. Dashwood was!"

To this Elinor had no answer to make, and did not attempt any.

"Are you ill, Miss Dashwood? You seem low—you don't speak; sure, you an't well."

"I never was in better health."

"I am glad of it with all my heart, but really you did not look it. I should be so sorry to have *you* ill—you, that have been the greatest comfort to me in the world! Heaven knows what I should have done without your friendship."

Elinor tried to make a civil answer, though doubting her own success. But it seemed to satisfy Lucy, for she directly replied:

"Indeed I am perfectly convinced of your regard for me, and next to Edward's love, it is the greatest comfort I have. Poor Edward! But now, there is one good thing—we shall be able to meet, and meet pretty often, for Lady Middleton's delighted with Mrs. Dashwood, so we shall be a good deal in Harley Street, I dare say, and Edward spends half his time with his sister; besides, Lady Middleton and Mrs. Ferrars will visit now; and Mrs. Ferrars and your sister were both so good to say more than once, they should always be glad to see me. They are such charming women! I am sure if ever you tell your sister what I think of her, you cannot speak too high."

But Elinor would not give her any encouragement to hope that she *should* tell her sister. Lucy continued:

"I am sure I should have seen it in a moment, if Mrs. Ferrars had took a dislike to me. If she had only made me a formal curtsey, for instance, without saying a word, and never after had took any notice of me, and never looked at me in a pleasant way—you know what I mean——if I had been treated in that forbidding sort of way, I should have gave it all up in despair. I could not have stood it. For where she *does* dislike, I know it is most violent."

Elinor was prevented from making any reply to this civil triumph, by the door being thrown open, the servant's announcing Mr. Ferrars, and Edward immediately walking in.

It was a very awkward moment; and the countenance of each showed that it was so. They all looked exceedingly foolish; and Edward seemed to have as great an inclination to walk out of the room again, as to advance further into it. The very circumstance, in its unpleasant form, which they would each have been most anxious to avoid, had fallen on them—they were not only all three together, but were together without the relief of any other person. The ladies recovered themselves first. It was not Lucy's business to put herself forward, and the appearance of secrecy must still be kept up. She could therefore only *look* her tenderness, and after slightly addressing him, said no more.

But Elinor had more to do; and so anxious was she, for his sake and her own, to do it well, that she forced herself after a moment's recollection, to welcome him, with a look and manner, that were almost easy and almost open; and another struggle, another effort still improved them. She would not allow the presence of Lucy, nor the consciousness of some injustice towards herself, to deter her from saying that she was happy to see him, and that she had very much regretted being from home, when he called before in Berkeley Street. She would not be frightened from paying him those attentions which, as a friend and almost a relation, were his due, by the observant eyes of Lucy, though she soon perceived them to be narrowly watching her.

Her manners gave some reassurance to Edward, and he had courage enough to sit down; but his embarrassment still exceeded that of the ladies in a proportion which the case rendered reasonable, though his sex might make it rare; for his heart had not the indifference of Lucy's, nor could his conscience have quite the ease of Elinor's.

Lucy, with a demure and settled air, seemed determined to make no contribution to the comfort of the others, and would not say a word; and almost everything that *was* said, proceeded from Elinor, who was obliged to volunteer all the information about her mother's health, their coming to town, etc., which Edward ought to have inquired about, but never did.

Her exertions did not stop here; for she soon afterwards felt herself so heroically disposed as to determine, under pretence of fetching Marianne, to leave the others by themselves; and she really did it, and *that* in the handsomest manner, for she loitered away several minutes on the landing place, with the most high-minded fortitude, before she went to her sister. When that was once done, however, it was time for the raptures of Edward to cease; for Marianne's joy hurried her into the drawing-room immediately. Her pleasure in seeing him was like every other of her feelings, strong in itself and strongly spoken. She met him with a hand that would be taken, and a voice that expressed the affection of a sister.

"Dear Edward!" she cried, "this is a moment of great happiness! This would almost make amends for everything!"

Edward tried to return her kindness as it deserved, but before such

witnesses he dared not say half what he really felt. Again they all sat down, and for a moment or two all were silent; while Marianne was looking with the most speaking tenderness, sometimes at Edward and sometimes at Elinor, regretting only that their delight in each other should be checked by Lucy's unwelcome presence. Edward was the first to speak, and it was to notice Marianne's altered looks, and express his fear of her not finding London agree with her.

"Oh! don't think of me!" she replied, with spirited earnestness, though her eyes were filled with tears as she spoke, "don't think of *my* health. Elinor is well, you see. That must be enough for us both."

This remark was not calculated to make Edward or Elinor more easy, nor to conciliate the good-will of Lucy, who looked up at Marianne with no very benignant expression.

"Do you like London?" said Edward, willing to say anything that might introduce another subject.

"Not at all. I expected much pleasure in it, but I have found none. The sight of you, Edward, is the only comfort it has afforded; and, thank heaven! you are what you always were!"

She paused—no one spoke.

"I think, Elinor," she presently added, "we must employ Edward to take care of us in our return to Barton. In a week or two, I suppose, we shall be going; and, I trust, Edward will not be very unwilling to accept the charge."

Poor Edward muttered something; but what it was, nobody knew, not even himself. But Marianne, who saw his agitation, and could easily trace it to whatever cause best pleased herself, was perfectly satisfied, and soon talked of something else.

"We spent such a day, Edward, in Harley Street, yesterday! So dull, so wretchedly dull! But I have much to say to you on that head, which cannot be said now."

And with this admirable discretion did she defer the assurance of her finding their mutual relatives more disagreeable than ever, and of her being particularly disgusted with his mother, till they were more in private.

"But why were you not there, Edward? Why did you not come?"

"I was engaged elsewhere."

"Engaged! But what was that, when such friends were to be met?"

"Perhaps, Miss Marianne," cried Lucy, eager to take some revenge on her, "you think young men never stand upon engagements, if they have no mind to keep them, little as well as great."

Elinor was very angry, but Marianne seemed entirely insensible of the sting; for she calmly replied,

"Not so, indeed; for, seriously speaking, I am very sure that conscience only kept Edward from Harley Street. And I really believe he *has* the most delicate conscience in the world; the most scrupulous in performing every engagement, however minute, and however it may make against his interest or pleasure. He is the most fearful of giving pain, of wounding expectation, and the most incapable of being selfish of anybody I ever saw. Edward, it is so, and I will say it. What! are you never to hear yourself praised? Then you must be no friend of mine; for those who will accept of my love and esteem, must submit to my open commendation."

The nature of her commendation in the present case, however, happened to be particularly ill-suited to the feelings of two-thirds of her auditors, and was so very unexhilarating to Edward, that he very soon got up to go away.

"Going so soon!" said Marianne; "my dear Edward, this must not be."

And drawing him a little aside, she whispered her persuasion that Lucy could not stay much longer. But even this encouragement failed, for he would go; and Lucy, who would have outstayed him had his visit lasted two hours, soon afterwards went away.

"What can bring her here so often!" said Marianne, on her leaving them. "Could she not see that we wanted her gone! How teasing to Edward!"

"Why so? we were all his friends, and Lucy has been the longest known to him of any. It is but natural that he should like to see her as well as ourselves."

Marianne looked at her steadily, and said, "You know, Elinor, that this is a kind of talking which I cannot bear. If you only hope to have your assertion contradicted, as I must suppose to be the case, you ought to recollect that I am the last person in the world to do it. I cannot descend to be tricked out of assurances that are not really wanted."

She then left the room; and Elinor dared not follow her to say more, for bound as she was by her promise of secrecy to Lucy, she could give no information that would convince Marianne; and painful as the consequences of her still continuing in an error might be, she was obliged to submit to it. All that she could hope was that Edward would not often expose her or himself to the distress of hearing Marianne's mistaken warmth, nor to the repetition of any other part of the pain that had attended their recent meeting—and this she had every reason to expect.

Chapter 36

WITHIN a few days after this meeting, the newspapers announced to the world, that the lady of Thomas Palmer, Esq., was safely delivered of a son and heir; a very interesting and satisfactory paragraph, at least to all those intimate connections who knew it before.

This event, highly important to Mrs. Jennings's happiness, produced a temporary alteration in the disposal of her time, and influenced in a like degree the engagements of her young friends; for as she wished to be as much as possible with Charlotte, she went thither every morning as soon as she was dressed, and did not return till late in the evening; and the

Miss Dashwoods, at the particular request of the Middletons, spent the whole of every day in Conduit Street. For their own comfort they would much rather have remained, at least all the morning, in Mrs. Jennings's house; but it was not a thing to be urged against the wishes of everybody. Their hours were therefore made over to Lady Middleton and the two Miss Steeles, by whom their company was in fact as little valued, as it was professedly sought.

They had too much sense to be desirable companions to the former; and by the latter they were considered with a jealous eye, as intruding on *their* ground, and sharing the kindness which they wanted to monopolise. Though nothing could be more polite than Lady Middleton's behaviour to Elinor and Marianne, she did not really like them at all. Because they neither flattered herself nor her children, she could not believe them good-natured; and because they were fond of reading, she fancied them satiri-cal: perhaps without knowing what it was to be satirical; but *that* did not signify. It was censure in common use, and easily given.

Their presence was a restraint both on her and on Lucy. It checked the idleness of one, and the business of the other. Lady Middleton was ashamed of doing nothing before them, and the flattery which Lucy was proud to think of and administer at other times, she feared they would despise her for offering. Miss Steele was the least discomposed of the three by their presence; and it was in their power to reconcile her to it entirely. Would either of them only have given her a full and minute account of the whole affair between Marianne and Mr. Willoughby, she would have thought herself amply rewarded for the sacrifice of the best place by the fire after dinner, which their arrival occasioned. But this conciliation was not granted; for though she often threw out expressions of pity for her sister to Elinor, and more than once dropped a reflection on the incon-stancy of beaux before Marianne, no effect was produced, but a look of indifference from the former or of disgust in the latter. An effort even yet lighter might have made her their friend. Would they only have laughed at her about the Doctor! But so little were they, any more than the others, inclined to oblige her, that if Sir John dined from home, she might spend a whole day without hearing any other raillery on the subject than what she was kind enough to bestow on herself.

All these jealousies and discontents, however, were so totally unsus-pected by Mrs. Jennings, that she thought it a delightful thing for the girls to be together; and generally congratulated her young friends every night on having escaped the company of a stupid old woman so long. She joined them sometimes at Sir John's, and sometimes at her own house; but wherever it was, she always came in excellent spirits, full of delight and importance, attributing Charlotte's well-doing to her own care, and ready to give so exact, so minute a detail of her situation, as only Miss Steele had curiosity enough to desire. One thing *did* disturb her; and of that she made her daily complaint. Mr. Palmer maintained the common, but unfatherly opinion among his sex, of all infants being alike; and though she could plainly perceive at different times the most striking resemblance between this baby and every one of his relations on both sides, there was no convincing his father of it; no persuading him to believe that it was not exactly like every other baby of the same age; nor could he even be brought to acknowledge the simple proposition of its being the finest child in the world.

I come now to the relation of a misfortune which about this time befell Mrs. John Dashwood. It so happened that while her two sisters with Mrs. Jennings were first calling on her in Harley Street, another of her acquaintances had dropped in—a circumstance in itself not apparently likely to produce evil to her. But while the imaginations of other people will carry them away to form wrong judgments of our conduct, and to decide on it by slight appearances, one's happiness must in some measure be always at the mercy of chance. In the present instance, this last-arrived lady allowed her fancy so far to outrun truth and probability, that on merely hearing the name of the Miss Dashwoods, and understanding them to be Mr. Dashwood's sisters, she immediately concluded them to be staying in Harley Street; and this misconstruction produced within a day or two afterwards cards of invitation for them, as well as for their brother and sister, to a small musical party at her house. The consequence of which was, that Mrs. John Dashwood was obliged to submit not only to the exceedingly great inconvenience of sending her carriage for the Miss Dashwoods, but, what was still worse, must be subject to all the unpleasantness of appearing to treat them with attention: and who could tell that they might not expect to go out with her a second time? The power of disappointing them, it was true, must always be hers. But that was not enough; for when people are determined on a mode of conduct which they know to be wrong, they feel injured by the expectation of anything better from them.

Marianne had now been brought by degrees so much into the habit of going out every day, that it was become a matter of indifference to her whether she went or not: and she prepared quietly and mechanically for every evening's engagement, though without expecting the smallest amusement from any, and very often without knowing till the last moment where it was to take her.

To her dress and appearance she was grown so perfectly indifferent, as not to bestow half the consideration on it during the whole of her toilette, which it received from Miss Steele in the first five minutes of their being together when it was finished. Nothing escaped *her* minute observation and general curiosity; she saw everything, and asked everything; was never easy till she knew the price of every part of Marianne's dress; could have guessed the number of her gowns altogether with better judgment than Marianne herself, and was not without hopes of finding out before they parted, how much her washing cost per week, and how much she had every year to spend upon herself. The impertinence of these kind of scrutinies, moreover, was generally concluded with a compliment, which though meant as its douceur, was considered by Marianne as the greatest impertinence of all; for after undergoing an examination into the value and make of her gown, the colour of her shoes and the arrangement of her hair, she was almost sure of being told that upon "her word she looked vastly smart, and she dared to say would make a great many conquests."

With such encouragement as this, was she dismissed on the present occasion to her brother's carriage; which they were ready to enter five minutes after it stopped at the door, a punctuality not very agreeable to their sister-in-law, who had preceded them to the house of her acquaintance, and was there hoping for some delay on their part that might inconvenience either herself or her coachman.

The events of the evening were not very remarkable. The party, like other musical parties, comprehended a great many people who had real taste for the performance, and a great many more who had none at all; and the performers themselves were, as usual, in their own estimation, and that of their immediate friends, the first private performers in England.

As Elinor was neither musical nor affecting to be so, she made no scruple of turning away her eyes from the grand pianoforte, whenever it suited her, and unrestrained even by the presence of a harp, and a violoncello, would fix them at pleasure on any other object in the room. In one of these excursive glances she perceived among the group of young men, the very he who had given them a lecture on toothpick-cases at Gray's. She perceived him soon afterwards looking at herself, and speaking familiarly to her brother; and had just determined to find out his name from the latter, when they both came towards her, and Mr. Dashwood introduced him to her as Mr. Robert Ferrars.

He addressed her with easy civility, and twisted his head into a bow which assured her as plainly as words could have done, that he was exactly the coxcomb she had heard him described to be by Lucy. Happy had it been for her if her regard for Edward had depended less on his own merit, than on the merit of his nearest relations. For then his brother's bow must have given the finishing stroke of what the ill-humour of his mother and sister would have begun. But while she wondered at the difference of the two young men, she did not find that the emptiness and conceit of the one put her at all out of charity with the modesty and worth of the other. Why they *were* different, Robert explained to her himself in the course of a quarter of an hour's conversation; for, talking of his brother, and lamenting the extreme *gaucherie* which he really believed kept him from mixing in proper society, he candidly and generously attributed it much less to any natural deficiency, than to the misfortune of a private education: while he himself, though probably without any particular, any material superiority by nature, merely from the advantage of a public school, was as well fitted to mix in the world as any other man.

"Upon my soul," he added, "I believe it is nothing more: and so I often tell my mother, when she is grieving about it. 'My dear madam,' I always say to her, 'you must make yourself easy. The evil is now irremediable, and it has been entirely your own doing. Why would you be persuaded by my uncle, Sir Robert, against your own judgment, to place Edward under private tuition, at the most critical time of his life? If you had only sent him to Westminster as well as myself, instead of sending him to Mr. Pratt's, all this would have been prevented.' This is the way in which I always consider the matter, and my mother is perfectly convinced of her error."

Elinor would not oppose his opinion, because whatever might be her general estimation of the advantage of a public school, she could not think of Edward's abode in Mr. Pratt's family with any satisfaction.

"You reside in Devonshire, I think," was his next observation, "in a cottage near Dawlish."

Elinor set him right as to its situation, and it seemed rather surprising to him that anybody could live in Devonshire without living near Dawlish. He bestowed his hearty approbation, however, on their species of house.

"For my own part," said he, "I am excessively fond of a cottage; there is always so much comfort, so much elegance about them. And I protest, if I had any money to spare, I should buy a little land and build one myself, within a short distance of London, where I might drive myself down at any time, and collect a few friends about me and be happy. I advise everybody who is going to build, to build a cottage. My friend Lord Courtland came to me the other day on purpose to ask my advice, and laid before me three different plans of Bonomi's. I was to decide on the best of them. 'My dear Courtland,' said I, immediately throwing them all into the fire, 'do not adopt either of them, but by all means build a cottage.' And that, I fancy, will be the end of it. Some people imagine that there can be no accommodations, no space in a cottage; but this is all a mistake. I was last month at my friend Elliott's near Dartford. Lady Elliott wished to give a dance. 'But how can it be done?' said she; 'my dear Ferrars, do tell me how it is to be managed. There is not a room in this cottage that will hold ten couple, and where can the supper be?' *I* immediately saw that there could be no difficulty in it, so I said, 'My dear Lady Elliott, do not be uneasy. The dining parlour will admit eighteen couple with ease; card-tables may be placed in the drawing-room; the library may be open for tea and other refreshments; and let the supper be set out in the saloon.' Lady Elliott was delighted with the thought. We measured the dining-room, and found it would hold exactly eighteen couples, and the affair was arranged precisely after my plan. So that in fact, you see, if people do but know how to set about it, every comfort may be as well enjoyed in a cottage as in the most spacious dwelling."

Elinor agreed to it all, for she did not think he deserved the compliment of rational opposition.

As John Dashwood had no more pleasure in music than his eldest sister, his mind was equally at liberty to fix on anything else; and a thought struck him during the evening, which he communicated to his wife, for her approbation when they got home. The consideration of Mrs. Dennison's mistake, in supposing his sisters their guests, had suggested the propriety of their being really invited to become such, while Mrs. Jennings's engagements kept her from home. The expense would be nothing, the inconvenience not more; and it was altogether an attention which the delicacy of his conscience pointed out to be requisite to its complete enfranchisement from his promise to his father. Fanny was startled at the proposal.

"I do not see how it can be done," said she, "without affronting Lady Middleton, for they spend every day with her; otherwise I should be exceedingly glad to do it. You know I am always ready to pay them any attention in my power, as my taking them out this evening shows. But they are Lady Middleton's visitors. How can I ask them away from her?"

Her husband, but with great humility, did not see the force of her objection. "They had already spent a week in this manner in Conduit Street, and Lady Middleton could not be displeased at their giving the same number of days to such near relations."

Fanny paused a moment, and then, with fresh vigour, said:

"My love, *I* would ask them with all my heart, if it was in my power. But I had just settled within myself to ask the Miss Steeles to spend a few days with us. They are very well-behaved, good kind of girls; and I think the attention is due to them, as their uncle did so very well by Edward. We can ask your sisters some other year, you know; but the Miss Steeles may not be in town any more. I am sure you will like them; indeed, you *do* like them, you know, very much already, and so does my mother; and they are such favourites with Harry!"

Mr. Dashwood was convinced. He saw the necessity of inviting the Miss Steeles immediately, and his conscience was pacified by the resolution of inviting his sisters another year; at the same time, however, slyly suspecting that another year would make the invitation needless by bringing Elinor to town as Colonel Brandon's wife, and Marianne as *their* visitor.

Fanny, rejoicing in her escape, and proud of the ready wit that had secured it, wrote the next morning to Lucy, to request her company and her sister's for some days in Harley Street, as soon as Lady Middleton could spare them. This was enough to make Lucy really and reasonably happy. Mrs. Dashwood seemed actually working for her herself, cherishing all her hopes, and promoting all her views! Such an opportunity of being with Edward and his family was, above all things, the most material to her interest, and such an invitation the most gratifying to her feelings! It was an advantage that could not be too gratefully acknowledged, nor too speedily made use of; and the visit to Lady Middleton, which had not before had any precise limits, was instantly discovered to have been always meant to end in two days' time.

When the note was shown to Elinor, as it was within ten minutes after its arrival, it gave her, for the first time, some share in the expectations of Lucy; for such a mark of uncommon kindness, vouchsafed on so short an acquaintance, seemed to declare that the good-will towards her arose from something more than merely malice against herself, and might be brought by time and address, to do everything that Lucy wished. Her flattery had already subdued the pride of Lady Middleton, and made an entry into the close heart of Mrs. John Dashwood; and these were effects that laid open the probability of greater.

The Miss Steeles removed to Harley Street, and all that reached Elinor of their influence there, strengthened her expectation of the event. Sir John, who called on them more than once, brought home such accounts of the favour they were in as must be universally striking. Mrs. Dashwood had never been so much pleased with any young women in her life as she was with them; had given each of them a needle-book, made by some emigrant; called Lucy by her Christian name; and did not know whether she should ever be able to part with them.

Chapter 37

MRS. PALMER was so well at the end of a fortnight, that her mother felt it no longer necessary to give up the whole of her time to her; and contenting herself with visiting her once or twice a day, returned from that period to her own home, and her own habits, in which she found the Miss Dashwoods very ready to reassume their former share.

About the third or fourth morning after their being thus re-settled in Berkeley Street, Mrs. Jennings, on returning from her ordinary visit to Mrs. Palmer, entered the drawing-room, where Elinor was sitting by herself, with an air of such hurrying importance as prepared her to hear something wonderful; and giving her time only to form that idea, began directly to justify it by saying,

"Lord! my dear Miss Dashwood! have you heard the news?"

"No, ma'am. What is it?"

"Something so strange! But you shall hear it all. When I got to Mr. Palmer's, I found Charlotte quite in a fuss about the child. She was sure it was very ill—it cried, and fretted, and was all over pimples. So I looked at it directly, and 'Lord! my dear,' says I, 'it is nothing in the world but the red-gum'; and nurse said just the same. But Charlotte, she would not be satisfied, so Mr. Donavan was sent for; and luckily he happened to be just come in from Harley Street, so he stepped over directly, and as soon as ever he saw the child, he said just as we did, that it was nothing in the world but the red-gum, and then Charlotte was easy. And so, just as he was going away again, it came into my head, I am sure I do not know how I happened to think of it, but it came into my head to ask him if there was any news. So upon that, he smirked, and simpered, and looked grave, and seemed to know something or other, and at last he said in a whisper, 'For fear any unpleasant report should reach the young ladies under your care as to their sister's indisposition, I think it advisable to say, that I believe there is no great reason for alarm; I hope Mrs. Dashwood will do very well.'"

"What! is Fanny ill?"

"That is exactly what I said, my dear. 'Lord!' says I, 'is Mrs. Dashwood ill?' So then it all came out; and the long and the short of the matter, by all I can learn, seems to be this:—Mr. Edward Ferrars, the very young man I used to joke with you about (but, however, as it turns out, I am monstrous glad there never was anything in it), Mr. Edward Ferrars, it seems, has been engaged above this twelvemonth to my cousin Lucy! There's for you, my dear! And not a creature knowing a syllable of the matter except Nancy! Could you have believed such a thing possible? There is no great wonder in their liking one another; but that matters should be brought so forward between them, and nobody suspect it! *That* is strange! I never happened to see them together, or I am sure I should have found it out directly. Well, and so this was kept a great secret, for fear of Mrs. Ferrars; and neither she nor your brother or sister suspected a word of the matter, till this very morning, poor Nancy, who, you know, is a well-meaning creature, but no conjurer, popped it all out. 'Lord!' thinks she to herself, 'they are all so fond of Lucy, to be sure they will make no difficulty about it'; and so, away she went to your sister, who was sitting all alone at her carpet-work, little suspecting what was to come—for she had just been saying to your brother, only five minutes be-fore, that she thought to make a match between Edward and some lord's daughter or other, I forget who. So you may think what a blow it was to all her vanity and pride. She fell into violent hysterics immediately, with such screams as reached your brother's ears, as he was sitting in his own dressing-room downstairs, thinking about writing a letter to his steward in the country. So up he flew directly, and a terrible scene took place, for Lucy was come to them by that time, little dreaming what was going on. Poor soul! I pity *her*. And I must say, I think she was used very hardly; for your sister scolded like any fury, and soon drove her into a fainting fit. Nancy, she fell upon her knees, and cried bitterly; and your brother, he walked about the room, and said he did not know what to do. Mrs. Dashwood declared they should not stay a minute longer in the house, and your brother was forced to go down upon *his* knees too, to persuade her to let them stay till they had packed up their clothes. *Then* she fell into hysterics again, and he was so frightened that he would send for Mr. Donavan, and Mr. Donavan found the house in all this uproar. The car-riage was at the door ready to take my poor cousins away, and they were just stepping in as he came off; poor Lucy in such a condition, he says, she could hardly walk; and Nancy, she was almost as bad. I declare, I have no patience with your sister; and I hope, with all my heart, it will be a match in spite of her. Lord! what a taking poor Mr. Edward will be in when he hears of it! To have his love used so scornfully! for they say he is monstrous fond of her, as well he may. I should not wonder if he was to be in the greatest of a passion! and Mr. Donavan thinks just the same. He and I had a great deal of talk about it; and the best of all is, that he is gone back again to Harley Street, that he may be within call when Mrs.

Ferrars is told of it, for she was sent for as soon as ever my cousins left the house, for your sister was sure *she* would be in hysterics too; and so she may, for what I care. I have no pity for either of them. I have no notion of people's making such a to-do about money and greatness. There is no reason on earth why Mr. Edward and Lucy should not marry; for I am sure Mrs. Ferrars may afford to do very well by her son; and though Lucy has next to nothing herself, she knows better than anybody how to make the most of everything; and I dare say, if Mrs. Ferrars would only allow him five hundred a year, she would make as good an appearance with it as anybody else would with eight. Lord! how snug they might live in such another cottage as yours—or a little bigger—with two maids and two men; and I believe I could help them to a housemaid, for my Betty has a sister out of place, that would fit them exactly."

Here Mrs. Jennings ceased, and as Elinor had had time enough to collect her thoughts, she was able to give such an answer and make such observations, as the subject might naturally be supposed to produce. Happy to find that she was not suspected of an extraordinary interest in it; that Mrs. Jennings (as she had of late often hoped might be the case) had ceased to imagine her at all attached to Edward; and happy above all the rest, in the absence of Marianne, she felt very well able to speak of the affair without embarrassment, and to give her judgment, as she believed, with impartiality on the conduct of every one concerned in it.

She could hardly determine what her own expectation of its event really was; though she earnestly tried to drive away the notion of its being possible to end otherwise at last, than in the marriage of Edward and Lucy. What Mrs. Ferrars would say and do, though there could not be a doubt of its nature, she was anxious to hear; and still more anxious to know how Edward would conduct himself. For *him* she felt much compassion; for Lucy very little—and it cost her some pains to procure that little; for the rest of the party none at all.

As Mrs. Jennings could talk on no other subject, Elinor soon saw the necessity of preparing Marianne for its discussion. No time was to be lost in undeceiving her, in making her acquainted with the real truth, and in endeavouring to bring her to hear it talked of by others, without betraying that she felt any uneasiness for her sister, or any resentment against Edward.

Elinor's office was a painful one. She was going to remove what she really believed to be her sister's chief consolation, to give such particulars of Edward, as she feared would ruin him for ever in her good opinion, and to make Marianne, by a resemblance in their situations, which to *her* fancy would seem strong, feel all her own disappointment over again. But unwelcome as such a task must be, it was necessary to be done, and Elinor therefore hastened to perform it.

She was very far from wishing to dwell on her own feelings, or to represent herself as suffering much, any otherwise than as the self-command she had practised since her first knowledge of Edward's engage-

ment, might suggest a hint of what was practicable to Marianne. Her
narration was clear and simple; and though it could not be given without
emotion, it was not accompanied by violent agitation nor impetuous grief.
That belonged rather to the hearer, for Marianne listened with horror, and
cried excessively. Elinor was to be the comforter of others in her own
distresses, no less than in theirs; and all the comfort that could be given
by assurances of her own composure of mind, and a very earnest vindication of Edward from every charge but of imprudence, was readily offered.

But Marianne for some time would give credit to neither. Edward
seemed a second Willoughby; and acknowledging as Elinor did, that she
had loved him most sincerely, could she feel less than herself! As for Lucy
Steele, she considered her so totally unamiable, so absolutely incapable of
attaching a sensible man, that she could not be persuaded at first to believe, and afterwards to pardon, any former affection of Edward for her.
She would not even admit it to have been natural; and Elinor left her to
be convinced that it was so, by that which only could convince her, a
better knowledge of mankind.

Her first communication had reached no farther than to state the fact
of the engagement, and the length of time it had existed. Marianne's
feelings had then broken in, and put an end to all regularity of detail; and
for some time all that could be done was to soothe her distress, lessen her
alarms, and combat her resentment. The first question on her side, which
led to farther particulars, was:

"How long has this been known to you, Elinor? Has he written to you?"

"I have known it these four months. When Lucy first came to Barton
Park last November, she told me in confidence of her engagement."

At these words, Marianne's eyes expressed the astonishment which her
lips could not utter. After a pause of wonder, she exclaimed:

"Four months! Have you known of this four months?"

Elinor confirmed it.

"What! while attending me in all my misery, has this been on your
heart? and I have reproached you for being happy!"

"It was not fit that you should then know how much I was the reverse."

"Four months!" cried Marianne again. "So calm! so cheerful! How
have you been supported?"

"By feeling that I was doing my duty. My promise to Lucy obliged me
to be secret. I owed it to her, therefore, to avoid giving any hint of the
truth; and I owed it to my family and friends not to create in them a
solicitude about me, which it could not be in my power to satisfy."

Marianne seemed much struck.

"I have very often wished to undeceive yourself and my mother,"
added Elinor; "and once or twice I have attempted it; but without betraying my trust, I never could have convinced you."

"Four months! and yet you loved him!"

"Yes. But I did not love only him; and while the comfort of others was
dear to me, I was glad to spare them from knowing how much I felt.

Now, I can think and speak of it with little emotion. I would not have you suffer on my account; for I assure you I no longer suffer materially myself. I have many things to support me. I am not conscious of having provoked the disappointment by any imprudence of my own, and I have borne it as much as possible without spreading it farther. I acquit Edward of all essential misconduct. I wish him very happy; and I am so sure of his always doing his duty, that though now he may harbour some regret, in the end he must become so. Lucy does not want sense, and that is the foundation on which everything good may be built. And after all, Marianne, after all that is bewitching in the idea of a single and constant attachment, and all that can be said of one's happiness depending entirely on any particular person, it is not meant—it is not fit—it is not possible that it should be so. Edward will marry Lucy; he will marry a woman superior in person and understanding to half her sex; and time and habit will teach him to forget that he ever thought another superior to *her*."

"If such is your way of thinking," said Marianne, "if the loss of what is most valued is so easily to be made up by something else, your resolution, your self-command, are perhaps a little less to be wondered at. They are brought more within my comprehension."

"I understand you. You do not suppose that I have ever felt much. For four months, Marianne, I have had all this hanging on my mind, without being at liberty to speak of it to a single creature; knowing that it would make you and my mother most unhappy whenever it were explained to you, yet unable to prepare you for it in the least. It was told me—it was in a manner forced on me by the very person herself whose prior engagement ruined all my prospects; and told me, as I thought, with triumph. This person's suspicions, therefore, I have had to oppose, by endeavouring to appear indifferent where I have been most deeply interested. And it has not been only once; I have had her hopes and exultation to listen to again and again. I have known myself to be divided from Edward for ever, without hearing one circumstance that could make me less desire the connection. Nothing has proved him unworthy; nor has anything declared him indifferent to me. I have had to contend against the unkindness of his sister, and the insolence of his mother, and have suffered the punishment of an attachment without enjoying its advantages. And all this has been going on at a time when, as you too well know, it has not been my only unhappiness. If you can think me capable of ever feeling—surely you may suppose that I have suffered *now*. The composure of mind with which I have brought myself at present to consider the matter, the consolation that I have been willing to admit, have been the effect of constant and painful exertion; they did not spring up of themselves; they did not occur to relieve my spirits at first; no, Marianne. *Then*, if I had not been bound to silence, perhaps nothing could have kept me entirely—not even what I owed to my dearest friends—from openly showing that I was *very* unhappy."

Marianne was quite subdued.

"Oh! Elinor," she cried, "you have made me hate myself for ever. How barbarous have I been to you! you, who have been my only comfort, who have borne with me in all my misery, who have seemed to be only suffering for me! Is this my gratitude? Is this the only return I can make you? Because your merit cries out upon myself, I have been trying to do it away."

The tenderest caresses followed this confession. In such a frame of mind as she was now in, Elinor had no difficulty in obtaining from her whatever promise she required; and, at her request, Marianne engaged never to speak of the affair to any one with the least appearance of bitterness; to meet Lucy without betraying the smallest increase of dislike to her; and even to see Edward himself, if chance should bring them together, without any diminution of her usual cordiality. These were great concessions, but where Marianne felt that she had injured, no reparation could be too much for her to make.

She performed her promise of being discreet to admiration. She attended to all that Mrs. Jennings had to say upon the subject with an unchanging complexion, dissented from her in nothing, and was heard three times to say, "Yes, ma'am." She listened to her praise of Lucy with only moving from one chair to another, and when Mrs. Jennings talked of Edward's affection, it cost her only a spasm in her throat. Such advances towards heroism in her sister, made Elinor feel equal to anything herself.

The next morning brought a further trial of it, in a visit from their brother, who came with a most serious aspect to talk over the dreadful affair, and bring them news of his wife.

"You have heard, I suppose," said he with great solemnity, as soon as he was seated, "of the very shocking discovery that took place under our roof yesterday."

They all looked their assent; it seemed too awful a moment for speech.

"Your sister," he continued, "has suffered dreadfully. Mrs. Ferrars too —in short, it has been a scene of such complicated distress; but I will hope that the storm may be weathered without our being, any of us, quite overcome. Poor Fanny! she was in hysterics all yesterday. But I would not alarm you too much. Donavan says there is nothing materially to be apprehended; her constitution is a good one, and her resolution equal to anything. She has borne it all with the fortitude of an angel! She says she never shall think well of anybody again; and one cannot wonder at it, after being so deceived! meeting with such ingratitude, where so much kindness had been shown, so much confidence had been placed. It was quite out of the benevolence of her heart that she had asked these young women to her house; merely because she thought they deserved some attention, were harmless, well-behaved girls, and would be pleasant companions; for otherwise we both wished very much to have invited you and Marianne to be with us, while your kind friend there was attending her daughter. And now to be so rewarded! 'I wish with all my heart,' says

poor Fanny in her affectionate way, 'that we had asked your sisters instead of them.' "

Here he stopped to be thanked; which being done, he went on.

"What poor Mrs. Ferrars suffered when first Fanny broke it to her, is
not to be described. While she with the truest affection had been planning
a most eligible connection for him, was it to be supposed that he could be
all the time secretly engaged to another person! such a suspicion could
never have entered her head! If she suspected *any* prepossession elsewhere, it could not be in *that* quarter. '*There,* to be sure,' said she, 'I
might have thought myself safe.' She was quite in an agony. We consulted together, however, as to what should be done, and at last she determined to send for Edward. He came. But I am sorry to relate what
ensued. All that Mrs. Ferrars could say to make him put an end to the
engagement, assisted too, as you may well suppose by my arguments, and
Fanny's entreaties, was of no avail. Duty, affection, everything was disregarded. I never thought Edward so stubborn, so unfeeling, before. His
mother explained to him her liberal designs, in case of his marrying Miss
Morton; told him she would settle on him the Norfolk estate, which, clear
of land-tax, brings in a good thousand a year; offered even, when matters
grew desperate, to make it twelve hundred; and in opposition to this, if he
still persisted in this low connection, represented to him the certain penury
that must attend the match. His own two thousand pounds she protested
should be his all; she would never see him again; and so far would she be
from affording him the smallest assistance, that if he were to enter into
any profession with a view of better support, she would do all in her power
to prevent his advancing in it."

Here Marianne, in an ecstasy of indignation, clapped her hands together and cried, "Gracious God! can this be possible!"

"Well may you wonder, Marianne," replied her brother, "at the obstinacy which could resist such arguments as these. Your exclamation is
very natural."

Marianne was going to retort, but she remembered her promises and
forbore.

"All this, however," he continued, "was urged in vain. Edward said
very little; but what he did say was in the most determined manner.
Nothing should prevail on him to give up his engagement. He would
stand to it, cost him what it might."

"Then," cried Mrs. Jennings, with blunt sincerity, no longer able to be
silent, "he has acted like an honest man. I beg your pardon, Mr. Dashwood, but if he had done otherwise, I should have thought him a rascal.
I have some little concern in the business, as well as yourself, for Lucy
Steele is my cousin, and I believe there is not a better kind of girl in the
world, nor one who more deserves a good husband."

John Dashwood was greatly astonished; but his nature was calm, not
open to provocation, and he never wished to offend anybody, especially
anybody of good fortune. He therefore replied, without any resentment—

"I would by no means speak disrespectfully of any relation of yours, madam. Miss Lucy Steele is, I dare say, a very deserving young woman, but in the present case, you know, the connection must be impossible. And to have entered into a secret engagement with a young man under her uncle's care, the son of a woman especially of such very large fortune as Mrs. Ferrars, is perhaps altogether a little extraordinary. In short, I do not mean to reflect upon the behaviour of any person whom you have a regard for, Mrs. Jennings. We all wish her extremely happy, and Mrs. Ferrars's conduct throughout the whole has been such as every conscientious, good mother, in like circumstances, would adopt. It has been dignified and liberal. Edward has drawn his own lot, and I fear it will be a bad one."

Marianne sighed out her similar apprehension; and Elinor's heart wrung for the feelings of Edward, while braving his mother's threats, for a woman who could not reward him.

"Well, sir," said Mrs. Jennings, "and how did it end?"

"I am sorry to say, ma'am, in a most unhappy rupture—Edward is dismissed for ever from his mother's notice. He left her house yesterday, but where he is gone, or whether he is still in town, I do not know; for we of course can make no inquiry."

"Poor young man! and what is to become of him?"

"What indeed, ma'am! It is a melancholy consideration. Born to the prospect of such affluence! I cannot conceive a situation more deplorable. The interest of two thousand pounds—how can a man live on it! and when to that is added the recollection that he might, but for his own folly, within three months have been in the receipt of two thousand five hundred a year (for Miss Morton has thirty thousand pounds), I cannot picture to myself a more wretched condition. We must all feel for him; and the more so, because it is totally out of our power to assist him."

"Poor young man!" cried Mrs. Jennings, "I am sure he should be very welcome to bed and board at my house; and so I would tell him, if I could see him. It is not fit that he should be living about at his own charge now, at lodgings and taverns."

Elinor's heart thanked her for such kindness towards Edward, though she could not forbear smiling at the form of it.

"If he would only have done as well by himself," said John Dashwood, "as all his friends were disposed to do by him, he might now have been in his proper situation, and would have wanted for nothing. But as it is, it must be out of anybody's power to assist him. And there is one thing more preparing against him, which must be worse than all—his mother has determined, with a very natural kind of spirit, to settle *that* estate upon Robert immediately, which might have been Edward's on proper conditions. I left her this morning with her lawyer, talking over the business."

"Well!" said Mrs. Jennings, "that is *her* revenge. Everybody has a way of their own. But I don't think mine would be to make one son independent, because another had plagued me."

Marianne got up, and walked about the room.

"Can anything be more galling to the spirit of a man," continued John, "than to see his younger brother in possession of an estate which might have been his own? Poor Edward! I feel for him sincerely."

A few minutes more spent in the same kind of effusion, concluded his visit; and with repeated assurances to his sisters that he really believed there was no material danger in Fanny's indisposition, and that they need not therefore be very uneasy about it, he went away; leaving the three ladies unanimous in their sentiments on the present occasion, as far at least as it regarded Mrs. Ferrars's conduct, the Dashwoods', and Edward's.

Marianne's indignation burst forth as soon as he quitted the room; and as her vehemence made reserve impossible in Elinor, and unnecessary in Mrs. Jennings, they all joined in a very spirited critique upon the party.

Chapter 38

MRS. JENNINGS was very warm in her praise of Edward's conduct, but only Elinor and Marianne understood its true merit. *They* only knew how little he had had to tempt him to be disobedient, and how small was the consolation, beyond the consciousness of doing right, that could remain to him in the loss of friends and fortune. Elinor gloried in his integrity; and Marianne forgave all his offences in compassion for his punishment. But though confidence between them was, by this public discovery, restored to its proper state, it was not a subject on which either of them were fond of dwelling when alone. Elinor avoided it upon principle, as tending to fix still more upon her thoughts, by the too warm, too positive assurances of Marianne, that belief of Edward's continued affection for herself, which she rather wished to do away; and Marianne's courage soon failed her, in trying to converse upon a topic which always left her more dissatisfied with herself than ever, by the comparison it necessarily produced between Elinor's conduct and her own.

She felt all the force of that comparison; but not as her sister had hoped, to urge her to exertion now; she felt it with all the pain of continual self-reproach, regretted most bitterly that she had never exerted herself before; but it brought only the torture of penitence, without the hope of amendment. Her mind was so much weakened that she still fancied present exertion impossible, and therefore it only dispirited her more.

Nothing new was heard by them for a day or two afterwards, of affairs in Harley Street, or Bartlett's Buildings. But though so much of the matter was known to them already, that Mrs. Jennings might have had enough to do in spreading that knowledge further, without seeking after more, she had resolved from the first to pay a visit of comfort and inquiry to her cousins as soon as she could; and nothing but the hindrance of more visitors than usual, had prevented her going to them within that time.

The third day succeeding their knowledge of the particulars, was so

fine, so beautiful a Sunday as to draw many to Kensington Gardens,
though it was only the second week in March. Mrs. Jennings and Elinor
were of the number; but Marianne, who knew that the Willoughbys were
again in town, and had a constant dread of meeting them, chose rather
to stay home, than venture into so public a place.

An intimate acquaintance of Mrs. Jennings joined them soon after they
entered the Gardens, and Elinor was not sorry that by her continuing
with them, and engaging all Mrs. Jennings's conversation, she was herself
left to quiet reflection. She saw nothing of the Willoughbys, nothing of
Edward, and for some time nothing of anybody who could by any chance,
whether grave or gay, be interesting to her. But at last, she found herself,
with some surprise, accosted by Miss Steele, who, though looking rather
shy, expressed great satisfaction in meeting them, and on receiving encouragement from the particular kindness of Mrs. Jennings, left her own
party for a short time, to join theirs. Mrs. Jennings immediately whispered
to Elinor:

"Get it all out of her, my dear. She will tell you anything if you ask.
You see I cannot leave Mrs. Clarke."

It was lucky, however, for Mrs. Jennings's curiosity, and Elinor's too,
that she would tell anything *without* being asked, for nothing would
otherwise have been learnt.

"I am so glad to meet you," said Miss Steele, taking her familiarly by
the arm, "for I wanted to see you of all things in the world"; and then
lowering her voice, "I suppose Mrs. Jennings has heard all about it. Is she
angry?"

"Not at all, I believe, with you."

"That is a good thing. And Lady Middleton, is *she* angry?"

"I cannot suppose it possible that she should be."

"I am monstrous glad of it. Good gracious! I have had such a time of it!
I never saw Lucy in such a rage in my life. She vowed at first she would
never trim me up a new bonnet, nor do anything else for me again, so long
as she lived; but now she is quite come to, and we are as good friends as
ever. Look, she made me this bow to my hat, and put in the feather last
night. There now, *you* are going to laugh at me too. But why should not I
wear pink ribbons? I do not care if it *is* the Doctor's favourite colour. I am
sure for my part, I should never have known he *did* like it better than any
other colour, if he had not happened to say so. My cousins have been so
plaguing me! I declare sometimes, I do not know which way to look before
them."

She had wandered away to a subject on which Elinor had nothing to
say, and therefore soon judged it expedient to find her way back again to
the first.

"Well, but, Miss Dashwood," speaking triumphantly, "people may say
what they choose about Mr. Ferrars's declaring he would not have Lucy,
for it's no such a thing, I can tell you; and it's quite a shame for such ill-
natured reports to be spread abroad. Whatever Lucy might think about

it herself, you know it was no business of other people to set it down for certain."

"I never heard anything of the kind hinted at before, I assure you," said Elinor.

"Oh! did not you? But it *was* said, I know very well, and by more than one; for Miss Godby told Miss Sparks, that nobody in their senses could expect Mr. Ferrars to give up a woman like Miss Morton, with thirty thousand pounds to her fortune, for Lucy Steele, that had nothing at all; and I had it from Miss Sparks myself. And besides that, my cousin Richard said himself, that when it came to the point, he was afraid Mr. Ferrars would be off; and when Edward did not come near us for three days, I could not tell what to think myself; and I believe in my heart Lucy gave it all up for lost; for we came away from your brother's Wednesday, and we saw nothing of him not all Thursday, Friday, and Saturday, and did not know what was become with him. Once Lucy thought to write to him, but then her spirit rose against that. However, this morning he came just as we came home from church; and then it all came out, how he had been sent for Wednesday to Harley Street, and been talked to by his mother and all of them, and how he had declared before them all that he loved nobody but Lucy, and nobody but Lucy would he have. And how he had been so worried by what passed, that as soon as he had went away from his mother's house, he had got upon his horse, and ridden into the country somewhere or other; and how he had stayed about at an inn all Thursday and Friday, on purpose to get the better of it. And after thinking it all over and over again, he said it seemed to him as if, now he had no fortune, and no nothing at all, it would be quite unkind to keep her on to the engagement, because it must be for her loss, for he had nothing but two thousand pounds, and no hope of anything else; and if he was to go into orders, as he had some thoughts, he could get nothing but a curacy, and how was they to live upon that? He could not bear to think of her doing no better, and so he begged, if she had the least mind for it, to put an end to the matter directly, and leave him to shift for himself. I heard him say all this as plain as could possibly be. And it was entirely for *her* sake, and upon *her* account, that he said a word about being off, and not upon his own. I will take my oath he never dropped a syllable of being tired of her, or of wishing to marry Miss Morton, or anything like it. But, to be sure, Lucy would not give ear to such kind of talking; so she told him directly (with a great deal about sweet and love, you know, and all that —Oh, la! one can't repeat such kind of things, you know)—she told him directly, she had not the least mind in the world to be off, for she could live with him upon a trifle, and how little soever he might have, she should be very glad to have it all, you know, or something of the kind. So then he was monstrous happy, and talked on some time about what they should do, and they agreed he should take orders directly, and they must wait to be married till he got a living. And just then I could not hear any more, for my cousin called from below to tell me Mrs. Richardson was come in her coach, and would take one of us to Kensington Gardens; so I was forced to go into the room and interrupt them, to ask Lucy if she would like to go, but she did not care to leave Edward; so I just run upstairs and put on a pair of silk stockings, and came oft with the Richardsons."

"I do not understand what you mean by interrupting them," said Elinor; "you were all in the same room together, were not you?"

"No indeed! not us. La! Miss Dashwood, do you think people make love when anybody else is by? Oh! for shame? To be sure, you must know better than that. (Laughing affectedly.) No, no; they were shut up in the drawing-room together, and all I heard was only by listening at the door."

"How!" cried Elinor; "have you been repeating to me what you only learnt yourself by listening at the door? I am sorry I did not know it be· fore; for I certainly would not have suffered you to give me particulars of a conversation which you ought not to have known yourself. How could you behave so unfairly by your sister?"

"Oh, la! there is nothing in *that*. I only stood at the door, and heard what I could. And I am sure Lucy would have done just the same by me; for a year or two back, when Martha Sharpe and I had so many secrets together, she never made any bones of hiding in a closet, or behind a chimney-board, on purpose to hear what we said."

Elinor tried to talk of something else; but Miss Steele could not be kept beyond a couple of minutes from what was uppermost in her mind.

"Edward talks of going to Oxford soon," said she, "but now he is lodging at No. —, Pall Mall. What an ill-natured woman his mother is, an't she? And your brother and sister were not very kind! However, I shan't say anything against them to *you;* and to be sure they did send us home in their own chariot, which was more than I looked for. And for my part, I was all in a fright for fear your sister should ask us for the house-wifes she had gave us a day or two before; but however, nothing was said about them, and I took care to keep mine out of sight. Edward have got some business at Oxford, he says, so he must go there for a time: and after *that,* as soon as he can light upon a bishop, he will be ordained. I wonder what curacy he will get! Good gracious! (giggling as she spoke) I'd lay my life I know what my cousins will say, when they hear of it. They will tell me I should write to the Doctor, to get Edward the curacy of his new living. I know they will; but I am sure I would not do such a thing for all the world. 'La!' I shall say directly, 'I wonder how you could think of such a thing. *I* write to the Doctor, indeed!' "

"Well," said Elinor, "it is a comfort to be prepared against the worst. You have got your answer ready."

Miss Steele was going to reply on the same subject, but the approach of her own party made another more necessary.

"Oh, la! here come the Richardsons. I had a vast deal more to say to you, but I must not stay away from them not any longer. I assure you they are very genteel people. He makes a monstrous deal of money, and they keep their own coach. I have not time to speak to Mrs. Jennings about it myself, but pray tell her I am quite happy to hear she is not in anger against us, and Lady Middleton the same; and if anything should happen to take you and your sister away, and Mrs. Jennings should want company, I am sure we should be very glad to come and stay with her for as long a time as she likes. I suppose Lady Middleton won't ask us any more this bout. Good-bye; I am sorry Miss Marianne was not here. Remember me kindly to her. La! if you have not got your spotted muslin on! I wonder you was not afraid of its being torn."

Such was her parting concern; for after this, she had time only to pay her farewell compliments to Mrs. Jennings, before her company was claimed by Mrs. Richardson: and Elinor was left in possession of knowledge which might feed her powers of reflection some time, though she had learnt very little more than what had been already foreseen and foreplanned in her own mind. Edward's marriage with Lucy was as firmly determined on, and the time of its taking place remained as absolutely uncertain, as she had concluded it would be; everything depended, exactly after her expectation, on his getting that preferment, of which, at present, there seemed not the smallest chance.

As soon as they returned to the carriage, Mrs. Jennings was eager for information; but as Elinor wished to spread as little as possible intelligence that had in the first place been so unfairly obtained, she confined herself to the brief repetition of such simple particulars, as she felt assured that Lucy, for the sake of her own consequence, would choose to have known. The continuance of their engagement, and the means that were to be taken for promoting its end, was all her communication; and this produced from Mrs. Jennings the following natural remark:

"Wait for his having a living! aye, we all know how *that* will end; they will wait a twelvemonth, and finding no good comes of it, will set down upon a curacy of fifty pounds a year, with the interest of his two thousand pounds, and what little matter Mr. Steele and Mr. Pratt can give her. Then they will have a child every year! and Lord help 'em! how poor they will be! I must see what I can give them towards furnishing their house. Two maids and two men indeed! as I talked of t'other day. No, no, they must get a stout girl of all works. Betty's sister would never do for them *now*."

The next morning brought Elinor a letter by the twopenny post, from Lucy herself. It was as follows:

"BARTLETT'S BUILDINGS, *March*.

"I hope my dear Miss Dashwood will excuse the liberty I take of writing to her; but I know your friendship for me will make you pleased to hear such a good account of myself and my dear Edward, after all the troubles we have went through lately, therefore will make no more apologies but proceed to say that, thank God! though we have suffered dreadfully, we are both quite well now, and as happy as we must always be in one another's love. We have had great trials, and great persecutions, but however, at the same time, gratefully acknowledge many friends, yourself not the least among them, whose great kindness I shall always thankfully remember, as will Edward too, who I have told of it. I am sure you will be glad to hear, as likewise dear Mrs. Jennings, I spent two happy hours with him yesterday afternoon, he would not hear of our parting, though earnestly did I, as I thought my duty required, urge him to it for prudence sake, and would have parted for ever on the spot, would he consent to it; but he said it should never be, he did not regard his mother's anger, while he could have my affections; our prospects are not very bright, to be sure, but we must wait, and hope for the best; he will be ordained shortly, and should it ever be in your power to recommend him to anybody that has a living to bestow, am very sure you will not forget us, and dear Mrs. Jennings too, trust she will speak a good word for us to Sir John, or Mr. Palmer, or any friend that may be able to assist us. Poor Anne was much to blame for what she did, but she did it for the best, so I say nothing; hope Mrs. Jennings won't think it too much trouble to give us a call, should she come this way any morning, 'twould be a great kindness, and my cousins would be proud to know her. My paper reminds me to conclude, and begging to be most gratefully and respectfully remembered to her, and to Sir John and Lady Middleton, and the dear children, when you chance to see them, and love to Miss Marianne,

"I am, etc., etc."

As soon as Elinor had finished it, she performed what she concluded to be its writer's real design, by placing it in the hands of Mrs. Jennings, who read it aloud, with many comments of satisfaction and praise.

"Very well indeed! how prettily she writes! aye, that was quite proper to let him be off if he would. That was just like Lucy. Poor soul! I wish I *could* get him a living with all my heart. She calls me dear Mrs. Jennings, you see. She is a good-hearted girl as ever lived. Very well, upon my word. That sentence is very prettily turned. Yes, yes, I will go and see her sure enough. How attentive she is, to think of everybody! Thank you, my dear, for showing it me. It is as pretty a letter as ever I saw, and does Lucy's head and heart great credit."

Chapter 39

THE Miss Dashwoods had now been rather more than two months in town, and Marianne's impatience to be gone increased every day. She sighed for the air, the liberty, the quiet of the country; and fancied that if any place could give her ease, Barton must do it. Elinor was hardly less anxious than herself for their removal, and only so much less bent on its being effected immediately, as that she was conscious of the difficulties of so long a journey, which Marianne could not be brought to acknowledge.

She began, however, seriously to turn her thoughts towards its accomplishment, and had already mentioned their wishes to their kind hostess, who resisted them with all the eloquence of her good-will, when a plan was suggested, which though detaining them from home yet a few weeks longer, appeared to Elinor altogether much more eligible than any other. The Palmers were to remove to Cleveland about the end of March, for the Easter holidays; and Mrs. Jennings, with both her friends, received a very warm invitation from Charlotte to go with them. This would not, in itself, have been sufficient for the delicacy of Miss Dashwood; but it was enforced with so much real politeness by Mr. Palmer himself, as, joined to the very great amendment of his manners towards them since her sister had been known to be unhappy, induced her to accept it with pleasure.

When she told Marianne what she had done, however, her first reply was not very auspicious.

"Cleveland!" she cried, with great agitation. "No, I cannot go to Cleveland."

"You forget," said Elinor gently, "that its situation is not . . . that it is not in the neighbourhood of . . ."

"But it is in Somersetshire. I cannot go into Somersetshire. There, where I looked forward to going . . . No, Elinor, you cannot expect me to go there."

Elinor would not argue upon the propriety of overcoming such feelings; she only endeavoured to counteract them by working on others; and represented it, therefore, as a measure which would fix the time of her returning to that dear mother, whom she so much wished to see, in a more eligible, more comfortable manner, than any other plan could do, and perhaps without any greater delay. From Cleveland, which was within a few miles of Bristol, the distance to Barton was not beyond one day, though a long day's journey; and their mother's servant might easily come there to attend them down; and as there could be no occasion for their staying above a week at Cleveland, they might now be at home in little more than three weeks' time. As Marianne's affection for her mother was sincere, it must triumph, with little difficulty, over the imaginary evils she had started.

Mrs. Jennings was so far from being weary of her guests, that she pressed them very earnestly to return with her again from Cleveland. Elinor was grateful for the attention, but it could not alter their design; and their mother's concurrence being readily gained, everything relative to their return was arranged as far as it could be; and Marianne found some relief in drawing up a statement of the hours that were yet to divide her from Barton.

"Ah! Colonel, I do not know what you and I shall do without the Miss Dashwoods," was Mrs. Jennings's address to him when he first called on her, after their leaving her was settled, "for they are quite resolved upon going home from the Palmers; and how forlorn we shall be when I come back! Lord! we shall sit and gape at one another as dull as two cats."

Perhaps Mrs. Jennings was in hopes, by this vigorous sketch of their future ennui, to provoke him to make that offer which might give himself an escape from it—and if so, she had soon afterwards good reason to think her object gained; for, on Elinor's moving to the window to take more expeditiously the dimensions of a print which she was going to copy for her friend, he followed her to it with a look of particular meaning, and conversed with her there for several minutes. The effect of this discourse on the lady too, could not escape her observation; for though she was too honourable to listen, and had even changed her seat on purpose that she might *not* hear, to one close by the pianoforte on which Marianne was playing, she could not keep herself from seeing that Elinor changed colour, attended with agitation, and was too intent on what he said, to pursue her employment. Still further in confirmation of her hopes, in the interval of Marianne's turning from one lesson to another, some words of the Colonel's inevitably reached her ear, in which he seemed to be apologising for the badness of his house. This set the matter beyond a doubt. She wondered indeed at his thinking it necessary to do so; but supposed it to be the proper etiquette. What Elinor said in reply she could not distinguish, but judged from the motion of her lips that she did not think *that* any material objection; and Mrs. Jennings commended her in her heart for being so honest. They then talked on for a few minutes longer without her catching a syllable, when another lucky stop in Marianne's performance brought her these words in the Colonel's calm voice:

"I am afraid it cannot take place very soon."

Astonished and shocked at so unlover-like a speech, she was almost ready to cry out, "Lord! what should hinder it!"—but checking her desire, confined herself to this silent ejaculation:

"This is very strange! Sure he need not wait to be older."

This delay on the Colonel's side, however, did not seem to offend or mortify his fair companion in the least; for on their breaking up the conference soon afterwards, and moving different ways, Mrs. Jennings very plainly heard Elinor say, and in a voice which showed her to feel what she said:

"I shall always think myself very much obliged to you."

Mrs. Jennings was delighted with her gratitude, and only wondered, that after hearing such a sentence, the Colonel should be able to take leave of them, as he immediately did, with the utmost sang-froid, and go without making her any reply! She had not thought her old friend could have made so indifferent a suitor.

What had really passed between them was to this effect:

"I have heard," said he, with great compassion, "of the injustice your friend Mr. Ferrars has suffered from his family; for if I understand the matter right, he has been entirely cast off by them for persevering in his engagement with a very deserving young woman. Have I been rightly informed? Is it so?"

Elinor told him that it was.

"The cruelty, the impolite cruelty," he replied, with great feeling, "of dividing, or attempting to divide, two young people long attached to each other, is terrible; Mrs. Ferrars does not know what she may be doing—what she may drive her son to. I have seen Mr. Ferrars two or three times in Harley Street, and am much pleased with him. He is not a young man with whom one can be intimately acquainted in a short time, but I have seen enough of him to wish him well for his own sake, and as a friend of yours, I wish it still more. I understand that he intends to take orders. Will you be so good as to tell him that the living of Delaford, now just vacant, as I am informed by this day's post, is his, if he thinks it worth his acceptance; but *that*, perhaps, so unfortunately circumstanced as he is now, it may be nonsense to appear to doubt; I only wish it were more valuable. It is a rectory, but a small one; the late incumbent, I believe, did not make more than two hundred pounds per annum, and though it is certainly capable of improvement, I fear, not to such an amount as to afford him a very comfortable income. Such as it is, however, my pleasure in presenting him to it will be very great. Pray assure him of it."

Elinor's astonishment at this commission could hardly have been greater, had the Colonel been really making her an offer of his hand. The preferment, which only two days before she had considered as hopeless for Edward, was already provided to enable him to marry; and *she*, of all people in the world, was fixed on to bestow it! Her emotion was such as Mrs. Jennings had attributed to a very different cause; but whatever minor feelings less pure, less pleasing, might have a share in that emotion, her esteem for the general benevolence, and her gratitude for the particular friendship, which together prompted Colonel Brandon to this act, were strongly felt, and warmly expressed. She thanked him for it with all her heart, spoke of Edward's principles and disposition with that praise which she knew them to deserve, and promised to undertake the commission with pleasure, if it were really his wish to put off so agreeable an office to another. But, at the same time, she could not help thinking that no one could so well perform it as himself. It was an office, in short, from which, unwilling to give Edward the pain of receiving an obligation from *her,* she would have been very glad to be spared herself; but Colonel Brandon, on motives of equal delicacy declining it likewise, still seemed so desirous of its being given through her means, that she would not on any account make further opposition. Edward, she believed, was still in town, and fortunately she had heard his address from Miss Steele. She could undertake, therefore, to inform him of it in the course of the day. After this had been settled, Colonel Brandon began to talk of his own advantage in securing so respectable and agreeable a neighbour; and *then* it was that he mentioned with regret, that the house was small and indifferent; an evil which Elinor, as Mrs. Jennings had supposed her to do, made very light of, at least as far as regarded its size.

"The smallness of the house," said she, "I cannot imagine any inconvenience to them, for it will be in proportion to their family and income."

By which the Colonel was surprised to find that *she* was considering their marriage as the certain consequence of the presentation; for he did not suppose it possible that Delaford living could supply such an income as anybody in his style of life would venture to settle on—and he said so.

"This little rectory *can* do no more than make Mr. Ferrars comfortable as a bachelor; it cannot enable him to marry. I am sorry to say that my patronage ends with this; and my interest is hardly more extensive. If, however, by any unforeseen chance it should be in my power to serve him further, I must think very differently of him from what I now do, if I am not as ready to be useful to him then, as I sincerely wish I could be at present. What I am now doing indeed seems nothing at all, since it can advance him so little towards what must be his principal, his only object of happiness. His marriage must still be a distant good; at least I am afraid it cannot take place very soon."

Such was the sentence which, when misunderstood, so justly offended the delicate feelings of Mrs. Jennings; but after this narration of what really passed between Colonel Brandon and Elinor, while they stood at the window, the gratitude expressed by the latter on their parting may perhaps appear, in general, not less reasonably excited, nor less properly worded, than if it had arisen from an offer of marriage.

Chapter 40

"WELL, Miss Dashwood," said Mrs. Jennings, sagaciously smiling, as soon as the gentleman had withdrawn, "I do not ask you what the Colonel has been saying to you; for though, upon my honour, I *tried* to keep out of hearing, I could not help catching enough to understand his business. And I assure you I never was better pleased in my life, and I wish you joy of it with all my heart."

"Thank you, ma'am," said Elinor. "It *is* a matter of great joy to me; and I feel the goodness of Colonel Brandon most sensibly. There are not many men who would act as he has done. Few people have so compassionate a heart! I never was more astonished in my life."

"Lord! my dear, you are very modest! I ain't the least astonished at it in the world, for I have often thought, of late, there was nothing more likely to happen."

"You judged from your knowledge of the Colonel's general benevolence; but at least you could not foresee that the opportunity would so very soon occur."

"Opportunity!" repeated Mrs. Jennings. "Oh! as to that, when a man has once made up his mind to such a thing, somehow or other he will soon find an opportunity. Well, my dear, I wish you joy of it again and again; and if ever there was a happy couple in the world, I think I shall soon know where to look for them."

"You mean to go to Delaford after them, I suppose," said Elinor, with a faint smile.

"Aye, my dear, that I do, indeed. And as to the house being a bad one, I do not know what the Colonel would be at, for it is as good a one as ever I saw."

"He spoke of its being out of repair."

"Well, and whose fault is that? Why don't he repair it? Who should do it but himself?"

They were interrupted by the servant's coming in, to announce the carriage being at the door; and Mrs. Jennings, immediately preparing to go, said:

"Well, my dear, I must be gone before I have had half my talk out. But, however, we may have it all over in the evening, for we shall be quite alone. I do not ask you to go with me, for I dare say your mind is too full of the matter to care for company; and besides, you must long to tell your sister all about it."

Marianne had left the room before the conversation began.

"Certainly, ma'am, I shall tell Marianne of it; but I shall not mention it at present to anybody else."

"Oh! very well," said Mrs. Jennings, rather disappointed. "Then you would not have me tell it Lucy, for I think of going as far as Holborn to-day."

"No, ma'am, not even Lucy, if you please. One day's delay will not be very material; and till I have written to Mr. Ferrars, I think it ought not to be mentioned to anybody else. I shall do *that* directly. It is of importance that no time should be lost with him, for he will, of course, have much to do relative to his ordination."

This speech at first puzzled Mrs. Jennings exceedingly. Why Mr. Ferrars was to be written to about it in such a hurry she could not immediately comprehend. A few moments' reflection, however, produced a very happy idea, and she exclaimed:

"Oh, ho! I understand you. Mr. Ferrars is to be the man. Well, so much the better for him. Aye, to be sure, he must be ordained in readiness; and I am very glad to find things are so forward between you. But, my dear, is not this rather out of character? Should not the Colonel write himself? Sure, he is the proper person."

Elinor did not quite understand the beginning of Mrs. Jennings's speech; neither did she think it worth inquiring into; and therefore only replied to its conclusion.

"Colonel Brandon is so delicate a man, that he rather wished anyone to announce his intentions to Mr. Ferrars than himself."

"And so *you* are forced to do it. Well, *that* is an odd kind of delicacy! However, I will not disturb you" (seeing her prepare to write). "You know your own concerns best. So good-bye, my dear. I have not heard of anything to please me so well since Charlotte was brought to bed."

And away she went, but returning again in a moment:

"I have just been thinking of Betty's sister, my dear. I should be very glad to get her so good a mistress. But whether she would do for a lady's maid, I am sure I can't tell. She is an excellent housemaid, and works very well at her needle. However, you will think of all that at your leisure."

"Certainly, ma'am," replied Elinor, not hearing much of what she said, and more anxious to be alone than to be mistress of the subject.

How she should begin—how she should express herself in her note to Edward was now all her concern. The particular circumstances between them made a difficulty of that which to any other person would have been the easiest thing in the world; but she equally feared to say too much or too little, and sat deliberating over her paper, with the pen in her hand, till broken in on by the entrance of Edward himself.

He had met Mrs. Jennings at the door in her way to the carriage, as he came to leave his farewell card; and she, after apologising for not returning herself, had obliged him to enter by saying that Miss Dashwood was above, and wanted to speak with him on very particular business.

Elinor had just been congratulating herself in the midst of her perplexity, that however difficult it might be to express herself properly by letter, it was at least preferable to giving the information by word of mouth, when her visitor entered, to force her upon this greatest exertion of all. Her astonishment and confusion were very great on his so sudden appearance. She had not seen him before since his engagement became public, and therefore not since his knowing her to be acquainted with it; which, with the consciousness of what she had been thinking of, and what she had to tell him, made her feel particularly uncomfortable for some minutes. He, too, was much distressed, and they sat down together in a most promising state of embarrassment. Whether he had asked her pardon for his intrusion on first coming into the room, he could not recollect; but determining to be on the safe side, he made his apology in form as soon as he could say anything, after taking a chair.

"Mrs. Jennings told me," said he, "that you wished to speak with me, at least I understood her so—or I certainly should not have intruded on you in such a manner; though, at the same time, I should have been extremely sorry to leave London without seeing you and your sister; especially as it will most likely be some time—it is not probable that I should soon have the pleasure of meeting you again. I go to Oxford to-morrow."

"You would not have gone, however," said Elinor, recovering herself, and determined to get over what she so much dreaded as soon as possible, "without receiving our good wishes, even if we had not been able to give them in person. Mrs. Jennings was quite right in what she said. I have something of consequence to inform you of, which I was on the point of communicating by paper. I am charged with a most agreeable office" (breathing rather faster than usual as she spoke). "Colonel Brandon, who was here only ten minutes ago, has desired me to say, that, understanding you mean to take orders, he has great pleasure in offering you the living of Delaford, now just vacant, and only wishes it were more valuable. Allow me to congratulate you on having so respectable and well-judging a friend, and to join in his wish that the living—it is about two hundred a year—were much more considerable, and such as might better enable you to—as might be more than a temporary accommodation to yourself—such, in short, as might establish all your views of happiness."

What Edward felt, as he could not say it himself, it cannot be expected that anyone else should say it for him. He *looked* all the astonishment which such unexpected, such unthought-of information could not fail of exciting; but he said only these two words:

"Colonel Brandon!"

"Yes," continued Elinor, gathering more resolution, as some of the worst was over; "Colonel Brandon means it as a testimony of his concern for what has lately passed—for the cruel situation in which the unjustifiable conduct of your family has placed you—a concern which, I am sure, Marianne, myself, and all your friends must share; and likewise as a proof of his high esteem for your general character, and his particular approbation of your behaviour on the present occasion."

"Colonel Brandon give *me* a living! Can it be possible?"

"The unkindness of your own relations has made you astonished to find friendship anywhere."

"No," replied he, with sudden consciousness, "not to find it in *you;* for I cannot be ignorant that to you, to your goodness, I owe it all. I feel it—I would express it if I could—but, as you well know, I am no orator."

"You are very much mistaken. I do assure you that you owe it entirely, at least almost entirely, to your own merit, and Colonel Brandon's discernment of it. I have had no hand in it. I did not even know, till I understood his design, that the living was vacant; nor had it ever occurred to me that he might have such a living in his gift. As a friend of mine, of my family, he may perhaps—indeed I know he *has,* still greater pleasure in bestowing it; but, upon my word, you owe nothing to my solicitation."

Truth obliged her to acknowledge some small share in the action; but she was at the same time so unwilling to appear as the benefactress of Edward, that she acknowledged it with hesitation; which probably contributed to fix that suspicion in his mind which had recently entered it. For a short time he sat deep in thought, after Elinor had ceased to speak; at last, as if it were rather an effort, he said:

"Colonel Brandon seems a man of great worth and respectability. I have always heard him spoken of as such, and your brother, I know, esteems him highly. He is undoubtedly a sensible man, and in his manners perfectly the gentleman."

"Indeed," replied Elinor, "I believe that you will find him, on further acquaintance, all that you have heard him to be; and as you will be such very near neighbours (for I understand the parsonage is almost close to the mansion house), it is particularly important that he *should* be all this."

Edward made no answer; but when she had turned away her head, gave her a look so serious, so earnest, so uncheerful, as seemed to say, that he might hereafter wish the distance between the parsonage and the mansion house much greater.

"Colonel Brandon, I think, lodges in St. James's Street?" said he, soon afterwards, rising from his chair.

Elinor told him the number of the house.

"I must hurry away then, to give him those thanks which you will not allow me to give *you;* to assure him that he has made me a very—an exceedingly happy man."

Elinor did not offer to detain him; and they parted, with a very earnest assurance on *her* side of her unceasing good wishes for his happiness in every change of situation that might befall him; on *his,* with rather an attempt to return the same goodwill, than the power of expressing it.

"When I see him again," said Elinor to herself, as the door shut him out, "I shall see him the husband of Lucy."

And with this pleasing anticipation, she sat down to reconsider the past, recall the words, and endeavoured to comprehend all the feelings of Edward; and, of course, to reflect on her own discontent.

When Mrs. Jennings came home, though she returned from seeing people whom she had never seen before, and of whom therefore she must have had a great deal to say, her mind was so much more occupied by the important secret in her possession, than by anything else, that she reverted to it again as soon as Elinor appeared.

"Well, my dear," she cried, "I sent you up the young man. Did not I do right? And I suppose you had no great difficulty. You did not find him very unwilling to accept your proposal?"

"No, ma'am; *that* was not very likely."

"Well, and how soon will he be ready? For it seems all to depend upon that."

"Really," said Elinor, "I know so little of these kind of forms, that I can hardly even conjecture as to the time, or the preparation necessary; but I suppose two or three months will complete his ordination."

"Two or three months?" cried Mrs. Jennings; "Lord! my dear, how calmly you talk of it! And can the Colonel wait two or three months! Lord bless me! I am sure it would put *me* quite out of patience. And though one would be very glad to do a kindness by poor Mr. Ferrars, I do think it is not worth while to wait two or three months for him. Sure, somebody else might be found that would do as well—somebody that is in orders already."

"My dear ma'am," said Elinor, "what can you be thinking of? Why, Colonel Brandon's only object is to be of use to Mr. Ferrars."

"Lord bless you, my dear! Sure you do not mean to persuade me that the Colonel only marries you for the sake of giving ten guineas to Mr. Ferrars!"

The deception could not continue after this; and an explanation immediately took place, by which both gained considerable amusement for the moment, without any material loss of happiness to either, for Mrs. Jennings only exchanged one form of delight for another, and still without forfeiting her expectation of the first.

"Aye, aye, the parsonage is but a small one," said she, after the first ebullition of surprise and satisfaction was over, "and very likely *may* be out of repair; but to hear a man apologising, as I thought, for a house that to my knowledge has five sitting-rooms on the ground-floor, and, I think the housekeeper told me, could make up fifteen beds! And to you too, that had been used to live in Barton Cottage! It seemed quite ridiculous. But, my dear, we must touch up the Colonel to do something to the parsonage, and make it comfortable for them, before Lucy goes to it."

"But Colonel Brandon does not seem to have any idea of the living's being enough to allow them to marry."

"The Colonel is a ninny, my dear; because he has two thousand a year himself, he thinks that nobody else can marry on less Take my word for it, that, if I am alive, I shall be paying a visit to Delaford parsonage before Michaelmas; and I am sure I shan't go if Lucy ain't there."

Elinor was quite of her opinion, as to the probability of their not waiting for anything more.

Chapter 41

EDWARD having carried his thanks to Colonel Brandon, proceeded with his happiness to Lucy; and such was the excess of it by the time he reached Bartlett's Buildings, that she was able to assure Mrs. Jennings, who called on her again the next day with her congratulations, that she had never seen him in such spirits before in her life.

Her own happiness, and her own spirits, were at least very certain; and she joined Mrs. Jennings most heartily in her expectation of their being all comfortably together in Delaford parsonage before Michaelmas. So far was she, at the same time, from any backwardness to give Elinor that credit which Edward *would* give her, that she spoke of her friendship for them both with the most grateful warmth, was ready to own all their obligation to her, and openly declared that no exertion for their good on Miss Dashwood's part, either present or future, would ever surprise her, for she believed her capable of doing anything in the world for those she really valued. As for Colonel Brandon, she was not only ready to worship him as a saint, but was moreover truly anxious that he should be treated as one in all worldly concerns; anxious that his tithes should be raised to the utmost; and secretly resolved to avail herself at Delaford as far as she possibly could, of his servants, his carriage, his cows, and his poultry.

It was now above a week since John Dashwood had called in Berkeley Street, and as since that time no notice had been taken by them of his wife's indisposition, beyond one verbal inquiry, Elinor began to feel it necessary to pay her a visit. This was an obligation, however, which not only opposed her own inclination, but which had not the assistance of any encouragement from her companions. Marianne, not contented with absolutely refusing to go herself, was very urgent to prevent her sister's going at all; and Mrs. Jennings, though her carriage was always at Elinor's service, so very much disliked Mrs. John Dashwood, that not even her curiosity to see how she looked after the late discovery, nor her strong desire to affront her by taking Edward's part, could overcome her unwillingness to be in her company again. The consequence was, that Elinor set out by herself to pay a visit, for which no one could really have less inclination, and to run the risk of a *tête-à-tête* with a woman whom neither of the others had so much reason to dislike.

Mrs. Dashwood was denied; but before the carriage could turn from the house, her husband accidentally came out. He expressed great pleasure in meeting Elinor, told her that he had been just going to call in Berkeley Street, and assuring her that Fanny would be very glad to see her, invited her to come in.

They walked upstairs into the drawing-room. Nobody was there.

"Fanny is in her own room, I suppose," said he; "I will go to her presently, for I am sure she will not have the least objection in the world to seeing *you*—very far from it indeed. *Now* especially there cannot be— but however, you and Marianne were always great favourites. Why would not Marianne come?"

Elinor made what excuse she could for her.

"I am not sorry to see you alone," he replied, "for I have a good deal to say to you. This living of Colonel Brandon's—can it be true? has he really given it to Edward? I heard it yesterday by chance, and was coming to you on purpose to inquire further about it."

"It is perfectly true. Colonel Brandon has given the living of Delaford to Edward."

"Really! Well, this is very astonishing! no relationship! no connection between them! and now that livings fetch such a price! what was the value of this?"

"About two hundred a year."

"Very well—and for the next presentation to a living of that value— supposing the late incumbent to have been old and sickly and likely to vacate it soon—he might have got, I dare say—fourteen hundred pounds. And how came he not to have settled that matter before this person's death? *Now* indeed it would be too late to sell it, but a man of Colonel Brandon's sense! I wonder he should be so improvident in a point of such common, such natural concern! Well, I am convinced that there is a vast deal of inconsistency in almost every human character. I suppose, however —on recollection—that the case may probably be *this*. Edward is only to hold the living till the person to whom the Colonel has really sold the presentation is old enough to take it. Aye, aye, that is the fact, depend upon it."

Elinor contradicted it, however, very positively; and by relating that she had herself been employed in conveying the offer from Colonel Brandon to Edward, and therefore must understand the terms on which it was given, obliged him to submit to her authority.

"It is truly astonishing!" he cried, after hearing what she said, "what could be the Colonel's motive?"

"A very simple one—to be of use to Mr. Ferrars."

"Well, well; whatever Colonel Brandon may be, Edward is a very lucky man! You will not mention the matter to Fanny, however; for though I have broke it to her, and she bears it vastly well, she will not like to hear it much talked of."

Elinor had some difficulty here to refrain from observing that, she thought Fanny might have borne with composure an acquisition of wealth to her brother, by which neither she nor her child could be possibly impoverished.

"Mrs. Ferrars," added he, lowering his voice to the tone becoming so important a subject, "knows nothing about it at present, and I believe it will be best to keep it entirely concealed from her as long as may be. When the marriage takes place, I fear she must hear of it all."

"But why should such precaution be used? Though it is not to be supposed that Mrs. Ferrars can have the smallest satisfaction in knowing that her son has money enough to live upon, for *that* must be quite out of the question; yet why, after her late behaviour, is she supposed to feel at all? She has done with her son, she has cast him off for ever, and has made all those over whom she had any influence cast him off likewise. Surely, after doing so, she cannot be imagined liable to any impression of sorrow or of joy on his account; she cannot be interested in anything that befalls him. She would not be so weak as to throw away the comfort of a child, and yet retain the anxiety of a parent!"

"Ah! Elinor," said John, "your reasoning is very good, but it is founded on ignorance of human nature. When Edward's unhappy match takes place, depend upon it his mother will feel as much as if she had never discarded him; and therefore every circumstance that may accelerate that dreadful event must be concealed from her as much as possible. Mrs. Ferrars can never forget that Edward is her son."

"You surprise me; I should think it must nearly have escaped her memory by *this* time."

"You wrong her exceedingly. Mrs. Ferrars is one of the most affectionate mothers in the world."

Elinor was silent.

"We think *now*," said Mr. Dashwood, after a short pause, "of *Robert's* marrying Miss Morton."

Elinor, smiling at the grave and decisive importance of her brother's tone, calmly replied:

"The lady, I suppose, has no choice in the affair."

"Choice! how do you mean?"

"I only mean, that I suppose from your manner of speaking, it must be the same to Miss Morton whether she marry Edward or Robert."

"Certainly, there can be no difference; for Robert will now to all intents and purposes be considered as the eldest son; and as to anything else, they are both very agreeable young men—I do not know that one is superior to the other."

Elinor said no more, and John was also for a short time silent. His reflections ended thus:

"Of *one* thing, my dear sister," kindly taking her hand and speaking in an awful whisper, "I may assure you: and I *will* do it, because I know it must gratify you. I have good reason to think—indeed I have it from the best authority, or I should not repeat it, for otherwise it would be very wrong to say anything about it—but I have it from the very best authority —not that I ever precisely heard Mrs. Ferrars say it herself, but her daughter *did*, and I have it from her. That, in short, whatever objections there might be against a certain—a certain connection—you understand me—it would have been far preferable to her, it would not have given her half the vexation that *this* does. I was exceedingly pleased to hear that Mrs. Ferrars considered it in that light—a very gratifying circumstance, you know, to us all. 'It would have been beyond comparison,' she said, 'the least evil of the two, and she would be glad to compound *now* for nothing worse.' But, however, all that is quite out of the question—not to be thought of or mentioned; as to any attachment, you know—it never could be—all that is gone by. But I thought I would just tell you of this, because I knew how much it must please you. Not that you have any reason to regret, my dear Elinor. There is no doubt of your doing exceedingly well—quite as well, or better, perhaps, all things considered. Has Colonel Brandon been with you lately?"

Elinor had heard enough, if not to gratify her vanity and raise her self-importance, to agitate her nerves and fill her mind; and she was therefore glad to be spared from the necessity of saying much in reply herself, and from the danger of hearing anything more from her brother, by the entrance of Mr. Robert Ferrars. After a few moments' chat, John Dashwood, recollecting that Fanny was yet uninformed of his sister being there, quitted the room in quest of her, and Elinor was left to improve her acquaintance with Robert, who, by the gay unconcern, the happy self-complacency of his manner while enjoying so unfair a division of his mother's love and liberality, to the prejudice of his banished brother, earned only by his own dissipated course of life, and that brother's integrity, was confirming her most unfavourable opinion of his head and heart.

They had scarcely been two minutes by themselves before he began to

speak of Edward; for he too had heard of the living, and was very in-
quisitive on the subject. Elinor repeated the particulars of it, as she had
given them to John, and their effect on Robert, though very different, was
not less striking than it had been on *him*. He laughed most immoderately.
The idea of Edward's being a clergyman, and living in a small parsonage
house, diverted him beyond measure; and when to that was added the
fanciful imagery of Edward reading prayers in a white surplice, and
publishing the banns of marriage between John Smith and Mary Brown,
he could conceive nothing more ridiculous.

Elinor, while she waited in silence, and immovable gravity, the conclusion of such folly, could not restrain her eyes from being fixed on him
with a look that spoke all the contempt it excited. It was a look, however,
very well bestowed, for it relieved her own feelings, and gave no intelligence to him. He was recalled from wit to wisdom, not by any reproof
of hers, but by his own sensibility.

"We may treat it as a joke," said he at last, recovering from the affected
laugh which had considerably lengthened out the genuine gaiety of the
moment—"but, upon my soul, i is a most serious business. Poor Edward!
he is ruined for ever. I am extremely sorry for it, for I know him to be a
very good-hearted creature; as well meaning a fellow, perhaps, as any in
the world. You must not judge of him, Miss Dashwood, from *your* slight
acquaintance. Poor Edward! His manners are certainly not the happiest
in nature. But we are not all born, you know, with the same powers—the
same address. Poor fellow! to see him in a circle of strangers! to be sure it
was pitiable enough! but, upon my soul, I believe he has as good a heart
as any in the kingdom; and I declare and protest to you I never was so
shocked in my life, as when it all burst forth. I could not believe it. My
mother was the first person who told me of it, and I, feeling myself called
on to act with resolution, immediately said to her, 'My dear madam, I do
not know what you may intend to do on the occasion, but as for myself, I
must say, that if Edward does marry this young woman, *I* never will see
him again.' That was what I said immediately. I was most uncommonly
shocked indeed! Poor Edward! he has done for himself completely! shut
himself out for ever from all decent society! but as I directly said to my
mother, I am not in the least surprised at it; from his style of education
it was always to be expected. My poor mother was half frantic."

'Have you ever seen the lady?"

"Yes, once; while she was staying in this house. I happened to drop in
for ten minutes; and I saw quite enough of her. The merest awkward
country girl, without style or elegance, and almost without beauty. I
remember her perfectly. Just the kind of girl I should suppose likely to
captivate poor Edward. I offered immediately as soon as my mother
related the affair to me, to talk to him myself, and dissuade him from the
match; but it was too late *then*, I found, to do anything, for unluckily,
I was not in the way at first, and knew nothing of it till after the breach
had taken place, when it was not for me, you know, to interfere. But had

I been informed of it a few hours earlier, I think it is most probable that something might have been hit on. I certainly should have represented it to Edward in a very strong light. 'My dear fellow,' I should have said, 'consider what you are doing. You are making a most disgraceful connection, and such a one as your family are unanimous in disapproving.' I cannot help thinking, in short, that means might have been found. But now it is all too late. He must be starved, you know; that is certain; absolutely starved."

He had just settled this point with great composure, when the entrance of Mrs. John Dashwood put an end to the subject. But though *she* never spoke of it out of her own family, Elinor could see its influence on her mind, in the something like confusion of countenance with which she entered, and an attempt at cordiality in her behaviour to herself. She even proceeded so far as to be concerned to find that Elinor and her sister were so soon to leave town, as she had hoped to see more of them; an exertion in which her husband, who attended her into the room, and hung enamoured over her accents, seemed to distinguish everything that was most affectionate and graceful.

Chapter 42

One other short call in Harley Street, in which Elinor received her brother's congratulations on their travelling so far towards Barton without any expense, and on Colonel Brandon's being to follow them to Cleveland in a day or two, completed the intercourse of the brother and sisters in town; and a faint invitation from Fanny, to come to Norland whenever it should happen to be in their way, which of all things was the most unlikely to occur, with a more warm, though less public assurance, from John to Elinor of the promptitude with which he should come to see her at Delaford, was all that foretold any meeting in the country.

It amused her to observe that all her friends seemed determined to send her to Delaford; a place in which, of all others, she would now least choose to visit or wish to reside; for not only was it considered as her future home by her brother and Mrs. Jennings, but even Lucy, when they parted, gave her a pressing invitation to visit her there.

Very early in April, and tolerably early in the day, the two parties from Hanover Square and Berkeley Street set out from their respective homes, to meet by appointment on the road. For the convenience of Charlotte and her child, they were to be more than two days on their journey, and Mr. Palmer, travelling more expeditiously with Colonel Brandon, was to join them at Cleveland soon after their arrival.

Marianne, few as had been her hours of comfort in London, and eager as she had long been to quit it, could not, when it came to the point, bid adieu to the house in which she had for the last time enjoyed those hopes and that confidence in Willoughby, which were now extinguished for ever.

without great pain. Nor could she leave the place in which Willoughby
remained busy in new engagements, and new schemes, in which *she* could
have no share, without shedding many tears.

Elinor's satisfaction at the moment of removal was more positive. She
had no such object for her lingering thoughts to fix on, she left no creature
behind from whom it would give her a moment's regret to be divided for
ever, she was pleased to be free herself from the persecution of Lucy's
friendship, she was grateful for bringing her sister away unseen by Willoughby since his marriage, and she looked forward with hope to what
a few months of tranquillity at Barton might do towards restoring Marianne's peace of mind, and confirming her own.

Their journey was safely performed. The second day brought them into
the cherished, or the prohibited, county of Somerset, for as such was it
dwelt on by turns in Marianne's imagination; and in the forenoon of the
third they drove up to Cleveland.

Cleveland was a spacious modern-built house, situated on a sloping
lawn. It had no park, but the pleasure-grounds were tolerably extensive;
and like every other place of the same degree of importance, it had its open
shrubbery, and closer wood-walk; a road of smooth gravel winding round
a plantation, led to the front; the lawn was dotted over with timber; the
house itself was under the guardianship of the fir, the mountain-ash, and
the acacia, and a thick screen of them altogether, interspersed with tall
Lombardy poplars, shut out the offices.

Marianne entered the house with a heart swelling with emotion from
the consciousness of being only eighty miles from Barton, and not thirty
from Combe Magna; and before she had been five minutes within its
walls, while the others were busily helping Charlotte show her child to the
house-keeper, she quitted it again, stealing away through the winding
shrubberies, now just beginning to be in beauty, to gain a distant eminence
where from its Grecian temple, her eye, wandering over a wide tract of
country to the south-east, could fondly rest on the farthest ridge of hills
in the horizon, and fancy that from their summits Combe Magna might
be seen.

In such moments of precious, of invaluable misery, she rejoiced in tears
of agony to be at Cleveland; and as she returned by a different circuit to
the house, feeling all the happy privilege of country liberty, of wandering
from place to place in free and luxurious solitude, she resolved to spend
almost every hour of every day while she remained with the Palmers, in
the indulgence of such solitary rambles.

She returned just in time to join the others as they quitted the house, on
an excursion through its more immediate premises; and the rest of the
morning was easily whiled away, in lounging round the kitchen garden,
examining the bloom upon its walls, and listening to the gardener's
lamentations upon blights, in dawdling through the greenhouse, where the
loss of her favourite plants, unwarily exposed, and nipped by the lingering
frost, raised the laughter of Charlotte, and in visiting her poultry-yard.

where in the disappointed hopes of her dairy-maid, by hens forsaking their nests, or being stolen by a fox, or in the rapid decease of a promising young brood, she found fresh sources of merriment.

The morning was fine and dry, and Marianne, in her plan of employment abroad, had not calculated for any change of weather during their stay at Cleveland. With great surprise, therefore, did she find herself prevented by a settled rain from going out again after dinner. She had depended on a twilight walk to the Grecian temple, and perhaps all over the grounds, and an evening merely cold or damp would not have deterred her from it; but a heavy and settled rain even *she* could not fancy dry or pleasant weather for walking.

Their party was small, and the hours passed quietly away. Mrs. Palmer had her child, and Mrs. Jennings her carpet-work; they talked of the friends they had left behind, arranged Lady Middleton's engagements, and wondered whether Mr. Palmer and Colonel Brandon would get further than Reading that night. Elinor, however little concerned in it, joined in their discourse, and Marianne, who had the knack of finding her way in every house to the library, however it might be avoided by the family in general, soon procured herself a book.

Nothing was wanting on Mrs. Palmer's side, that constant and friendly good humour could do, to make them feel themselves welcome. The openness and heartiness of her manner more than atoned for that want of recollection and elegance, which made her often deficient in the forms of politeness; her kindness, recommended by so pretty a face, was engaging; her folly, though evident, was not disgusting because it was not conceited; and Elinor could have forgiven everything but her laugh.

The two gentlemen arrived the next day to a very late dinner, affording a pleasant enlargement of the party, and a very welcome variety to their conversation, which a long morning of the same continued rain had reduced very low.

Elinor had seen so little of Mr. Palmer, and in that little had seen so much variety in his address to her sister and herself, that she knew not what to expect to find him in his own family. She found him, however, perfectly the gentleman in his behaviour to all his visitors, and only occasionally rude to his wife and her mother; she found him very capable of being a pleasant companion, and only prevented from being so always, by too great an aptitude to fancy himself as much superior to people in general, as he must feel himself to be to Mrs. Jennings and Charlotte. For the rest of his character and habits, they were marked, as far as Elinor could perceive, with no traits at all unusual in his sex and time of life. He was nice in his eating, uncertain in his hours; fond of his child, though affecting to slight it; and idled away the mornings at billiards, which ought to have been devoted to business. She liked him, however, upon the whole much better than she had expected, and in her heart was not sorry that she could like him no more; not sorry to be driven by the observation of his epicurism, his selfishness, and his conceit, to rest with complacency on the remembrance of Edward's generous temper, simple taste, and diffident feelings.

Of Edward, or at least of some of his concerns, she now received intelligence from Colonel Brandon, who had been into Dorsetshire lately; and who, treating her at once as the disinterested friend of Mr. Ferrars, and the kind confidante of himself, talked to her a great deal of the parsonage at Delaford, described its deficiencies, and told her what he meant to do himself towards removing them. His behaviour to her in this as well as in every other particular, his open pleasure in meeting her after an absence of only ten days, his readiness to converse with her, and his reference for her opinion, might very well justify Mrs. Jennings's persuasion of his attachment, and would have been enough, perhaps, had not Elinor still, as from the first, believed Marianne his real favourite, to make her suspect it herself. But as it was, such a notion had scarcely ever entered her head, except by Mrs. Jennings's suggestion; and she could not help believing herself the nicest observer of the two; she watched his eyes, while Mrs. Jennings thought only of his behaviour; and while his looks of anxious solicitude on Marianne's feeling in her head and throat the beginning of a heavy cold, because unexpressed by words, entirely escaped the latter lady's observation, *she* could discover in them the quick feelings and needless alarm of a lover.

Two delightful twilight walks on the third and fourth evenings of her being there, not merely on the dry gravel of the shrubbery, but all over the grounds, and especially in the most distant parts of them, where there was something more of wildness than in the rest, where the trees were the oldest, and the grass was the longest and wettest, had—assisted by the still greater imprudence of sitting in her wet shoes and stockings—given Marianne a cold so violent, as, though for a day or two trifled with or denied, would force itself by increasing ailments on the concern of everybody, and the notice of herself. Prescriptions poured in from all quarters, and as usual were all declined. Though heavy and feverish, with a pain in her limbs, a cough and a sore throat, a good night's rest was to cure her entirely; and it was with difficulty that Elinor pervailed on her, when she went to bed, to try one or two of the simplest of the remedies.

Chapter 43

MARIANNE got up the next morning at her usual time; to every inquiry replied that she was better, and tried to prove herself so, by engaging in her accustomary employments. But a day spent in sitting shivering over the fire with a book in her hand which she was unable to read, or in lying, weary and languid, on a sofa, did not speak much in favour of her amendment; and when, at last, she went early to bed, more and more indisposed, Colonel Brandon was only astonished at her sister's composure, who though attending and nursing her the whole day, against Marianne's inclination, and forcing proper medicines on her at night, trusted like Marianne to the certainty and efficacy of sleep, and felt no real alarm.

A very restless and feverish night, however, disappointed the expectation of both; and when Marianne, after persisting in rising, confessed herself unable to sit up, and returned voluntarily to her bed, Elinor was very ready to adopt Mrs. Jennings's advice, of sending for the Palmers apothecary.

He came, examined his patient, and though encouraging Miss Dashwood to expect that a very few days would restore her sister to health, yet by pronouncing her disorder to have a putrid tendency, and allowing the word "infection" to pass his lips, gave instant alarm to Mrs. Palmer on her baby's account. Mrs. Jennings, who had been inclined from the first to think Marianne's complaint more serious than Elinor, now looked very grave on Mr. Harris's report, and confirming Charlotte's fears and caution, urged the necessity of her immediate removal with her infant; and Mr. Palmer, though treating their apprehensions as idle, found the anxiety and importunity of his wife too great to be withstood. Her departure therefore was fixed on; and within an hour after Mr. Harris's arrival, she set off, with her little boy and his nurse, for the house of a near relation of Mr. Palmer's, who lived a few miles on the other side of Bath; whither her husband promised, at her earnest entreaty, to join her in a day or two; and whither she was almost equally urgent with her mother to accompany her. Mrs. Jennings, however, with a kindness of heart which made Elinor really love her, declared her resolution of not stirring from Cleveland as long as Marianne remained ill, and of endeavouring, by her own attentive care, to supply to her the place of the mother she had taken her from; and Elinor found her on every occasion a most willing and active helpmate, desirous to share in all her fatigues, and often, by her better experience in nursing, of material use.

Poor Marianne, languid and low from the nature of her malady, and feeling herself universally ill, could no longer hope that to-morrow would find her recovered; and the idea of what to-morrow would have produced but for this unlucky illness, made every ailment more severe; for on that day they were to have begun their journey home, and, attended the whole way by a servant of Mrs. Jennings, were to have taken their mother by surprise on the following forenoon. The little that she said, was all in lamentation of this inevitable delay; though Elinor tried to raise her spirits, and make her believe, as she *then* really believed herself, that it would be a very short one.

The next day produced little or no alteration in the state of the patient; she certainly was not better, and except that there was no amendment, did not appear worse. Their party was now further reduced; for Mr. Palmer, though very unwilling to go, as well from real humanity and good-nature, as from a dislike of appearing to be frightened away by his wife, was persuaded at last by Colonel Brandon, to perform his promise of following her: and while he was preparing to go, Colonel Brandon himself, with a much greater exertion, began to talk of going likewise. Here, however, the kindness of Mrs. Jennings interposed most acceptably; for to send the Colonel away while his love was in so much uneasiness on her sister's account, would be to deprive them both, she thought, of every comfort; and therefore telling him at once that his stay at Cleveland was necessary to herself, that she should want him to play at piquet of an evening while Miss Dashwood was above with her sister, etc., she urged him so strongly to remain, that he, who was gratifying the first wish of his own heart by a compliance, could not long even affect to demur; especially as Mrs. Jennings's entreaty was warmly seconded by Mr. Palmer, who seemed to feel a relief to himself in leaving behind him a person so well able to assist or advise Miss Dashwood in any emergence.

Marianne was of course kept in ignorance of all these arrangements. She knew not that she had been the means of sending the owners of Cleveland away, in about seven days from the time of their arrival. It gave her no surprise that she saw nothing of Mrs. Palmer; and as it gave her likewise no concern, she never mentioned her name.

Two days passed away from the time of Mr. Palmer's departure, and her situation continued, with little variation, the same. Mr. Harris, who attended her every day, still talked boldly of a speedy recovery, and Miss Dashwood was equally sanguine; but the expectation of the others was by no means so cheerful. Mrs. Jennings had determined very early in the seizure that Marianne would never get over it, and Colonel Brandon, who was chiefly of use in listening to Mrs. Jennings's forebodings, was not in a state of mind to resist their influence. He tried to reason himself out of fears which the different judgment of the apothecary seemed to render absurd; but the many hours of each day in which he was left entirely alone were but too favourable for the admission of every melancholy idea, and he could not expel from his mind the persuasion that he should see Marianne no more.

On the morning of the third day, however, the gloomy anticipations of both were almost done away; for when Mr. Harris arrived, he declared his patient materially better. Her pulse was much stronger and every symptom more favourable than on the preceding visit. Elinor, confirmed in every pleasant hope, was all cheerfulness; rejoicing that in her letters to her mother, she had pursued her own judgment rather than her friend's, in making very light of the indisposition which delayed them at Cleveland, and almost fixing on the time when Marianne would be able to travel.

But the day did not close so auspiciously as it began. Towards the evening Marianne became ill again, growing more heavy, restless, and uncomfortable than before. Her sister, however, still sanguine, was willing to attribute the change to nothing more than the fatigue of having sat up to have her bed made; and carefully administering the cordials prescribed, saw her with satisfaction sink at last into a slumber, from which she expected the most beneficial effects. Her sleep, though not so quiet as Elinor wished to see it, lasted a considerable time; and anxious to observe

the result of it herself, she resolved to sit with her during the whole of it.
Mrs. Jennings, knowing nothing of any change in the patient, went unusually early to bed; her maid, who was one of the principal nurses, was
recreating herself in the housekeeper's room, and Elinor remained alone
with Marianne.

The repose of the latter became more and more disturbed; and her
sister, who watched with unremitting attention her continual change of
posture, and heard the frequent but inarticulate sounds of complaint
which passed her lips, was almost wishing to rouse her from so painful a
slumber when Marianne, suddenly awakened by some accidental noise in
the house, started hastily up, and, with feverish wildness, cried out:

"Is mamma coming?"

"Not yet," replied the other, concealing her terror, and assisting Marianne to lie down again; "but she will be here I hope, before long. It is a
great way, you know, from hence to Barton."

"But she must not go round by London," cried Marianne, in the same
hurried manner. "I shall never see her, if she goes to London."

Elinor perceived with alarm that she was not quite herself, and while
attempting to soothe her, eagerly felt her pulse. It was lower and quicker
than ever; and Marianne, still talking wildly of mamma, her alarm increased so rapidly, as to determine her on sending instantly for Mr. Harris,
and dispatching a messenger to Barton for her mother. To consult with
Colonel Brandon on the best means of effecting the latter, was a thought
which immediately followed the resolution of its performance; and as
soon as she had rung up the maid to take her place by her sister, she
hastened down to the drawing-room, where she knew he was generally to
be found at a much later hour than at present.

It was no time for hesitation. Her fears and her difficulties were immediately before him. Her fears, he had no courage, no confidence to
attempt the removal of; he listened to them in silent despondence; but
her difficulties were instantly obviated, for with a readiness that seemed to
speak the occasion and the service pre-arranged in his mind, he offered
himself as the messenger who should fetch Mrs. Dashwood. Elinor made
no resistance that was not easily overcome. She thanked him with a brief,
though fervent gratitude, and while he went to hurry off his servant with
a message to Mr. Harris, and an order for post-horses directly, she wrote
a few lines to her mother.

The comfort of such a friend at that moment as Colonel Brandon—of
such a companion for her mother, how gratefully was it felt! a companion
whose judgment would guide, whose attendance must relieve, and whose
friendship might soothe her! as far as the shock of such a summons *could*
be lessened to her, his presence, his manners, his assistance, would lessen it.

He, meanwhile, whatever he might feel, acted with all the firmness of a
collected mind, made every necessary arrangement with the utmost dispatch, and calculated with exactness the time in which she might look
for his return. Not a moment was lost in delay of any kind. The horses

arrived, even before they were expected, and Colonel Brandon only pressing her hand with a look of solemnity, and a few words spoken too low to reach her ear, hurried into the carriage. It was then about twelve o'clock, and she returned to her sister's apartment to wait for the arrival of the apothecary, and to watch by her the rest of the night. It was a night of almost equal suffering to both. Hour after hour passed away in sleepless pain and delirium on Marianne's side, and in the most cruel anxiety on Elinor's, before Mr. Harris appeared. Her apprehensions once raised, paid by their excess for all her former security, and the servant who sat up with her, for she would not allow Mrs. Jennings to be called, only tortured her more, by hints of what her mistress had always thought.

Marianne's ideas were still, at intervals, fixed incoherently on her mother, and whenever she mentioned her name, it gave a pang to the heart of poor Elinor, who, reproaching herself for having trifled with so many days of illness, and wretched for some immediate relief, fancied that all relief might soon be in vain, that everything had been delayed too long, and pictured to herself her suffering mother, arriving too late to see this darling child, or to see her rational.

She was on the point of sending again for Mr. Harris, or if *he* could not come, for some other advice, when the former—but not till after five o'clock—arrived. His opinion, however, made some little amends for his delay, for though acknowledging a very unexpected and unpleasant alteration in his patient, he would not allow the danger to be material, and talked of the relief which a fresh mode of treatment must procure, with a confidence which, in a lesser degree, was communicated to Elinor. He promised to call again, in the course of three or four hours, and left both the patient and her anxious attendant more composed than he had found them.

With strong concern, and with many reproaches for not being called to their aid, did Mrs. Jennings hear in the morning of what had passed. Her former apprehensions, now with greater reason restored, left her no doubt of the event; and though trying to speak comfort to Elinor, her conviction of her sister's danger would not allow her to offer the comfort of hope. Her heart was really grieved. The rapid decay, the early death of a girl so young, so lovely as Marianne, must have struck a less interested person with concern. On Mrs. Jennings's compassion she had other claims. She had been for three months her companion, was still under her care, and she was known to have been greatly injured, and long unhappy. The distress of her sister too, particularly a favourite, was before her; and as for their mother, when Mrs. Jennings considered that Marianne might probably be to *her* what Charlotte was to herself, her sympathy in *her* sufferings was very sincere.

Mr. Harris was punctual in his second visit; but he came to be disappointed in his hopes of what the last would produce. His medicines had failed; the fever was unabated; and Marianne only more quiet—no more herself—remained in a heavy stupor. Elinor catching all, and more than all, his fears in a moment, proposed to call in further advice. But he judged it unnecessary; he had still something more to try, some fresh application, of whose success he was almost as confident as the last, and his visit concluded with encouraging assurances which reached the ear, but could not enter the heart of Miss Dashwood. She was calm, except when she thought of her mother, but she was almost hopeless; and in this state she continued till noon, scarcely stirring from her sister's bed, her thoughts wandering from one image of grief, one suffering friend to another, and her spirits oppressed to the utmost by the conversation of Mrs. Jennings, who scrupled not to attribute the severity and danger of this attack to the many weeks of previous indisposition which Marianne's disappointment had brought on. Elinor felt all the reasonableness of the idea, and it gave fresh misery to her reflections.

About noon, however, she began—but with a caution, a dread of some disappointment which for some time kept her silent, even to her friend—to fancy, to hope she could perceive a slight amendment in her sister's pulse; she waited, watched, examined it again and again; and at last, with an agitation more difficult to bury under exterior calmness than all her foregoing distress, ventured to communicate her hopes. Mrs. Jennings, though forced on examination to acknowledge a temporary revival, tried to keep her young friend from indulging a thought of its continuance; and Elinor, conning over every injunction of distrust, told herself likewise not to hope. But it was too late. Hope had already entered; and feeling all its anxious flutter, she bent over her sister to watch—she hardly knew for what. Half an hour passed away, and the favourable symptom yet blessed her. Others even arose to confirm it. Her breath, her skin, her lips, all flattered Elinor with signs of amendment, and Marianne fixed her eyes on her with a rational though languid gaze. Anxiety and hope now oppressed her in equal degrees, and left her no moment of tranquillity till the arrival of Mr. Harris at four o'clock; when his assurances, his felicitations on a recovery in her sister even surpassing his expectation, gave her confidence, comfort, and tears of joy.

Marianne was in every respect materially better, and he declared her entirely out of danger. Mrs. Jennings, perhaps satisfied with the partial justification of her forebodings, which had been found in their late alarm, allowed herself to trust in his judgment, and admitted with unfeigned joy, and soon with unequivocal cheerfulness, the probability of an entire recovery.

Elinor could not be cheerful. Her joy was of a different kind, and led to anything rather than to gaiety. Marianne restored to life, health, friends, and to her doting mother, was an idea to fill her heart with sensations of exquisite comfort, and expand it in fervent gratitude; but it led to no outward demonstrations of joy, no words, no smiles. All within Elinor's breast was satisfaction, silent and strong.

She continued by the side of her sister with little intermission the whole afternoon, calming every fear, satisfying every inquiry of her enfeebled spirits, supplying every succour, and watching almost every look and every breath. The possibility of a relapse would, of course, in some moments, occur to remind her of what anxiety was—but when she saw on her frequent and minute examination, that every symptom of recovery continued, and saw Marianne at six o'clock, sink into a quiet, steady, and to all appearance comfortable sleep, she silenced every doubt.

The time was now drawing on when Colonel Brandon might be expected back. At ten o'clock, she trusted, or at least not much later, her mother would be relieved from the dreadful suspense in which she must now be travelling towards them. The Colonel too! perhaps scarcely less an object of pity! Oh! how slow was the progress of time which yet kept them in ignorance!

At seven o'clock, leaving Marianne still sweetly asleep, she joined Mrs. Jennings in the drawing-room to tea. Of breakfast she had been kept by her fears, and of dinner by their sudden reverse, from eating much; and the present refreshment, therefore, with such feelings of content as she brought to it, was particularly welcome. Mrs. Jennings would have persuaded her at its conclusion to take some rest before her mother's arrival, and allow *her* to take her place by Marianne; but Elinor had no sense of fatigue, no capability of sleep at that moment about her, and she was not to be kept away from her sister an unnecessary instant. Mrs. Jennings therefore attending her upstairs into the sick chamber, to satisfy herself that all continued right, left her there again to her charge and her thoughts, and retired to her own room to write letters and sleep.

The night was cold and stormy. The wind roared round the house, and the rain beat against the windows; but Elinor, all happiness within, regarded it not. Marianne slept through every blast, and the travellers— they had a rich reward in store, for every present inconvenience.

The clock struck eight. Had it been ten, Elinor would have been convinced that at that moment she heard a carriage driving up to the house; and so strong was the persuasion that she *did*, in spite of the *almost* impossibility of their being already come, that she moved into the adjoining dressing-closet and opened a window-shutter, to be satisfied of the truth. She instantly saw that her ears had not deceived her. The flaring lamps of a carriage were immediately in view. By their uncertain light she thought she could discern it to be drawn by four horses; and this, while it told the excess of her poor mother's alarm, gave some explanation to such unexpected rapidity.

Never in her life had Elinor found it so difficult to be calm, as at that moment. The knowledge of what her mother must be feeling as the carriage stopped at the door, of her doubt—her dread—perhaps her despair! and of what *she* had to tell! with such knowledge it was impossible to be calm. All that remained to be done was to be speedy; and therefore staying only till she could leave Mrs. Jennings's maid with her sister, she hurried downstairs.

The bustle in the vestibule, as she passed along an inner lobby, assured her that they were already in the house. She rushed forwards towards the drawing-room—she entered it, and saw only Willoughby.

Chapter 44

ELINOR, starting back with a look of horror at the sight of him, obeyed the first impulse of her heart in turning instantly to quit the room, and her hand was already on the lock, when its action was suspended by his hastily advancing, and saying, in a voice rather of command than supplication:

"Miss Dashwood, for half an hour—for ten minutes—I entreat you to stay."

"No, sir," she replied with firmness, "I shall *not* stay. Your business cannot be with *me*. The servants, I suppose, forgot to tell you that Mr. Palmer was not in the house."

"Had they told me," he cried with vehemence, "that Mr. Palmer and all his relations were at the devil, it would not have turned me from the door. My business is with you, and only you."

"With me!" in the utmost amazement—"well, sir—be quick—and if you can—less violent."

"Sit down, and I will be both."

She hesitated; she knew not what to do. The possibility of Colonel Brandon's arriving and finding him there, came across her. But she had promised to hear him, and her curiosity no less than her honour was engaged. After a moment's recollection, therefore, concluding that prudence required dispatch, and that her acquiescence would best promote it, she walked silently towards the table and sat down. He took the opposite chair, and for half a minute not a word was said by either.

"Pray be quick, sir," said Elinor impatiently. "I have no time to spare."

He was sitting in an attitude of deep meditation, and seemed not to hear her.

"Your sister," said he, with abruptness, a moment afterwards—"is out of danger. I heard it from the servant. God be praised! But is it true! is it really true?"

Elinor would not speak. He repeated the inquiry with yet greater eagerness.

"For God's sake tell me, is she out of danger, or is she not?"

"We hope she is."

He rose up, and walked across the room.

"Had I known as much half an hour ago—But since I *am* here"—speaking with a forced vivacity as he returned to his seat—"what does it signify? For once, Miss Dashwood—it will be the last time, perhaps—let us be cheerful together. I am in a fine mood for gaiety. Tell me honestly"—a deeper glow overspreading his cheeks—"do you think me most a knave or a fool?"

Elinor looked at him with greater astonishment than ever. She began to think that he must be in liquor; the strangeness of such a visit, and of such manners, seemed no otherwise intelligible; and with this impression, she immediately rose, saying:

"Mr. Willoughby, I advise you at present to return to Combe. I am not at leisure to remain with you longer. Whatever your business may be with me, it will be better recollected and explained to-morrow."

"I understand you," he replied with an expressive smile, and a voice perfectly calm. "Yes, I am very drunk. A pint of porter with my cold beef at Marlborough was enough to overset me."

"At Marlborough!" cried Elinor, more and more at a loss to understand what he would be at.

"Yes—I left London this morning at eight o'clock, and the only ten minutes I have spent out of my chaise since that time procured me a nuncheon * at Marlborough."

The steadiness of his manner, and the intelligence of his eye as he spoke, convincing Elinor, that whatever other unpardonable folly might bring him to Cleveland, he was not brought there by intoxication, she said, after a moment's recollection:

"Mr. Willoughby, you *ought* to feel, and I certainly *do*—that after what has passed—your coming here in this manner, and forcing yourself upon my notice, requires a very particular excuse. What is it that you mean by it?"

"I mean," said he, with serious energy, "if I can, to make you hate me one degree less than you do *now*. I mean to offer some kind of explanation, some kind of apology, for the past—to open my whole heart to you, and by convincing you, that though I have been always a blockhead, I have not been always a rascal—to obtain something like forgiveness from Ma—from your sister."

"Is this the real reason of your coming?"

"Upon my soul it is," was his answer, with a warmth which brought all the former Willoughby to her remembrance, and in spite of herself made her think him sincere.

"If that is all, you may be satisfied already, for Marianne *does*—she has *long* forgiven you."

"Has she!" he cried, in the same eager tone. "Then she has forgiven me before she ought to have done it. But she shall forgive me again, and on more reasonable grounds. *Now*, will you listen to me?"

Elinor bowed her assent.

"I do not know," said he, after a pause of expectation on her side, and thoughtfulness on his own, "how *you* may have accounted for my behaviour to your sister, or what diabolical motive you may have imputed to me. Perhaps you will hardly think the better of me; it is worth the trial, however, and you shall hear everything. When I first became inti-

* A piece of victuals eaten between meals—*Johnson's Dictionary.*

mate in your family, I had no other intention, no other view in the acquaintance than to pass my time pleasantly while I was obliged to remain in Devonshire, more pleasantly than I had ever done before. Your sister's lovely person and interesting manners could not but please me; and her behaviour to me, almost from the first, was of a kind—— It is astonishing, when I reflect on what it was, and what *she* was, that my heart should have been so insensible! But at first, I must confess, my vanity only was elevated by it. Careless of her happiness, thinking only of my own amusement, giving way to feelings which I had always been too much in the habit of indulging, I endeavoured by every means in my power, to make myself pleasing to her, without any design of returning her affection."

Miss Dashwood at this point, turning her eyes on him with the most angry contempt, stopped him, by saying:

"It is hardly worth while, Mr. Willoughby, for you to relate, or for me to listen any longer. Such a beginning as this cannot be followed by anything. Do not let me be pained by hearing anything more on the subject."

"I insist on your hearing the whole of it," he replied. "My fortune was never large, and I had always been expensive, always in the habit of associating with people of better income than myself. Every year since my coming of age, or even before, I believe, had added to my debts; and though the death of my old cousin, Mrs. Smith, was to set me free, yet that event being uncertain, and possibly far distant, it had been for some time my intention to re-establish my circumstances by marrying a woman of fortune. To attach myself to your sister, therefore, was not a thing to be thought of; and, with a meanness, selfishness, cruelty—which no indignant, no contemptuous look, even of yours, Miss Dashwood, can ever reprobate too much—I was acting in this manner, trying to engage her regard, without a thought of returning it. But one thing may be said for me, even in that horrid state of selfish vanity, I did not know the extent of the injury I meditated, because I did not *then* know what it was to love. But have I ever known it? Well may it be doubted; for, had I really loved could I have sacrificed my feelings to vanity, to avarice? or, what is more, could I have sacrificed hers? But I have done it. To avoid a comparative poverty, which her affection and her society would have deprived of all its horrors, I have by raising myself to affluence lost everything that could make it a blessing."

"You did then," said Elinor, a little softened, "believe yourself at one time attached to her."

"To have resisted such attractions, to have withstood such tenderness! Is there a man on earth who could have done it! Yes, I found myself, by insensible degrees, sincerely fond of her; and the happiest hours of my life were what I spent with her, when I felt my intentions were strictly honourable, and my feelings blameless. Even *then*, however, when fully determined on paying my addresses to her, I allowed myself most improperly to put off, from day to day, the moment of doing it, from an unwillingness to enter into an engagement while my circumstances were so greatly embarrassed. I will not reason here—nor will I stop for *you* to expatiate on the absurdity, and the worse than absurdity, of scrupling to engage my faith where my honour was already bound. The event has proved that I was a cunning fool, providing with great circumspection for a possible opportunity of making myself contemptible and wretched for ever. At last, however, my resolution was taken, and I had determined, as soon as I could engage her alone, to justify the attentions I had so invariably paid her, and openly assure her of an affection which I had already taken such pains to display. But in the interim—in the interim of the very few hours that were to pass, before I could have an opportunity of speaking with her in private—a circumstance occurred—an unlucky circumstance, to ruin all my resolution, and with it all my comfort. A discovery took place"—here he hesitated and looked down. "Mrs. Smith had somehow or other been informed, I imagine by some distant relation, whose interest it was to deprive me of her favour, of an affair, a connection—but I need not explain myself further," he added, looking at her with a heightened colour and an inquiring eye, "your particular intimacy —you have probably heard the whole story long ago."

"I have," returned Elinor, colouring likewise, and hardening her heart anew against any compassion for him, "I have heard it all. And how you will explain away any part of your guilt in that dreadful business, I confess is beyond my comprehension."

"Remember," cried Willoughby, "from whom you received the account. Could it be an impartial one? I acknowledge that her situation and her character ought to have been respected by me. I do not mean to justify myself, but at the same time cannot leave you to suppose that I have nothing to urge, that because she was injured, she was irreproachable; and because *I* was a libertine, *she* must be a saint. If the violence of her passions, the weakness of her understanding—I do not mean, however, to defend myself. Her affection for me deserved better treatment, and I often, with great self-reproach, recall the tenderness which, for a very short time, had the power of creating any return. I wish—I heartily wish it had never been. But I have injured more than myself; and I have injured one whose affection for me (may I say it?) was scarcely less warm than hers, and whose mind—Oh! how infinitely superior!"

"Your indifference, however, towards that unfortunate girl—I must say it, unpleasant to me as the discussion of such a subject may well be—your indifference is no apology for your cruel neglect of her. Do not think yourself excused by any weakness, any natural defect of understanding on her side, in the wanton cruelty so evident on yours. You must have known, that while you were enjoying yourself in Devonshire, pursuing fresh schemes, always gay, always happy, she was reduced to the extremest indigence."

"But, upon my soul, I did *not* know it," he warmly replied; "I did not recollect that I had omitted to give her my direction; and common-sense might have told her how to find it out."

"Well, sir, and what said Mrs. Smith?"

"She taxed me with the offence, at once, and my confusion may be guessed. The purity of her life, the formality of her notions, her ignorance of the world—everything was against me. The matter itself I could not deny, and vain was every endeavour to soften it. She was previously disposed, I believe, to doubt the morality of my conduct in general, and was moreover discontented with the very little attention, the very little portion of my time that I had bestowed on her, in my present visit. In short, it ended in a total breach. By one measure I might have saved myself. In the height of her morality, good woman! she offered to forgive the past if I would marry Eliza. That could not be—and I was formally dismissed from her favour and her house. The night following this affair—I was to go the next morning—was spent by me in deliberating on what my future conduct should be. The struggle was great—but it ended too soon. My affection for Marianne, my thorough conviction of her attachment to me—it was all insufficient to outweigh that dread of poverty, or get the better of those false ideas of the necessity of riches, which I was naturally inclined to feel, and expensive society had increased. I had reason to believe myself secure of my present wife, if I choose to address her, and I persuaded myself to think that nothing else in common prudence remained for me to do. An heavy scene however awaited me, before I could leave Devonshire; I was engaged to dine with you on that very day, some apology was therefore necessary for my breaking the engagement. But whether I should write this apology, or deliver it in person, was a point of long debate. To see Marianne, I felt would be dreadful, and I even doubted whether I could see her again, and keep to my resolution. In that point, however, I undervalued my own magnanimity, as the event declared; for I went, I saw her, and saw her miserable, and left her miserable—and left her, hoping never to see her again."

"Why did you call, Mr. Willoughby?" said Elinor, reproachfully; "a note would have answered every purpose. Why was it necessary to call?"

"It was necessary to my own pride. I could not bear to leave the country in a manner that might lead you, or the rest of the neighbourhood, to suspect any part of what had really passed between Mrs. Smith and myself, and I resolved therefore on calling at the cottage, in my way to Honiton. The sight of your dear sister, however, was really dreadful; and to heighten the matter, I found her alone. You were all gone, I do not know where. I had left her only the evening before, so fully, so firmly resolved within myself on doing right! A few hours were to have engaged her to me for ever; and I remember how happy, how gay were my spirits, as I walked from the cottage to Allenham, satisfied with myself, delighted with everybody! But in this, our last interview of friendship, I approached her with a sense of guilt that almost took from me the power of dissembling. Her sorrow, her disappointment, her deep regret, when I told her that I was obliged to leave Devonshire so immediately—I never shall forget it; united, too, with such reliance, such confidence in me! O God! what an hard-hearted rascal I was!"

They were both silent for a few moments. Elinor first spoke.

"Did you tell her that you should soon return?"

"I do not know what I told her," he replied, impatiently; "less than was due to the past, beyond a doubt, and in all likelihood much more than was justified by the future. I cannot think of it—it won't do. Then came your dear mother to torture me further, with all her kindness and confidence. Thank heaven! it *did* torture me. I was miserable. Miss Dashwood, you cannot have an idea of the comfort it gives me to look back on my own misery. I owe such a grudge to myself for the stupid, rascally folly of my own heart, that all my past sufferings under it are only triumph and exultation to me now. Well, I went, left all that I loved, and went to those to whom, at best, I was only indifferent. My journey to town—travelling with my own horses, and therefore so tediously—no creature to speak to— my own reflections so cheerful—when I looked forward everything so inviting! when I looked back at Barton, the picture so soothing! oh! it was a blessed journey."

He stopped.

"Well, sir," said Elinor, who, though pitying him, grew impatient for his departure, "and this is all?"

"All! no—have you forgot what passed in town? That infamous letter! Did she show it you?"

"Yes, I saw every note that passed."

"When the first of hers reached me (as it immediately did, for I was in town the whole time), what I felt is—in the common phrase, not to be expressed; in a more simple one—perhaps too simple to raise any emotion —my feelings were very, very painful. Every line, every word was—in the hackneyed metaphor which their dear writer were she here, would forbid, a dagger to my heart. To know that Marianne was in town was, in the same language—a thunderbolt. Thunderbolts and daggers! what a re-proof would she have given me! her taste, her opinions—I believe they are better known to me than my own, and I am sure they are dreaded."

Elinor's heart, which had undergone many changes in the course of this extraordinary conversation, was now softened again; yet she felt it her duty to check such ideas in her companion as the last.

"This is not right, Mr. Willoughby. Remember that you are married. Relate only what in your conscience you think necessary for me to hear."

"Marianne's note, by assuring me that I was still as dear to her as in former days—that in spite of the many, many weeks we had been sep-arated, she was as constant in her own feelings and as full of faith in the constancy of mine as ever, awakened all my remorse. I say awakened, because time and London, business and dissipation had in some manner quieted it, and I had been growing a fine hardened villain, fancying myself indifferent to her, and choosing to fancy that she too must have become indifferent to me; talking to myself of our past attachments as a mere idle, trifling business, shrugging up my shoulders in proof of its being so, and silencing every reproach, overcoming every scruple, by secretly saying now and then, 'I shall be heartily glad to hear she is well married.' But this note made me know myself better. I felt that she was infinitely dearer to me than any other woman in the world, and that I was using her infamously. But everything was then just settled between Miss Grey and me. To retreat was impossible. All that I had to do, was to avoid you both. I sent no answer to Marianne, intending by that means to preserve myself from her further notice; and for some time I was even determined not to call in Berkeley Street: but at last, judging it wiser to affect the air of a cool, common acquaintance than anything else, I watched you all safely out of the house one morning and left my name."

"Watched us out of the house!"

"Even so. You would be surprised to hear how often I watched you, how often I was on the point of falling in with you. I have entered many a shop to avoid your sight, as the carriage drove by. Lodging as I did in Bond Street there was hardly a day in which I did not catch a glimpse of one or other of you; and nothing but the most constant watchfulness on my side, a most invariably prevailing desire to keep out of your sight, could have separated us so long. I avoided the Middletons as much as possible, as well as everybody else who was likely to prove an acquaintance in common. Not aware of their being in town, however, I blundered on Sir John, I believe, the first day of his coming, and the day after I called at Mrs. Jennings's. He asked me to a party, a dance at his house in the evening. Had he *not* told me as an inducement that you and your sister were to be there, I should have felt it too certain a thing to trust myself near him. The next morning brought another short note from Marianne—still affectionate, open, artless, confiding—everything that could make *my* conduct most hateful. I could not answer it. I tried, but could not frame a sentence. But I thought of her, I believe, every moment of the day. If *you* can pity me, Miss Dashwood, pity my situation as it was *then*. With my head and heart full of your sister, I was forced to play the happy lover to another woman! Those three or four weeks were worse than all. Well, at last, as I need not tell you, you were forced on me: and what a sweet figure I cut! What an evening of agony it was! Marianne, beautiful as an angel, on one side, calling me Willoughby in such a tone! O God! Holding out her hand to me, asking me for an explanation with those bewitching eyes fixed in such speaking solicitude on my face! And Sophia, jealous as the devil, on the other hand, looking all that was—well, it does not signify; it is over now. Such an evening! I ran away from you all as soon as I could, but not before I had seen Marianne's sweet face as white as death. *That* was the last, last look I ever had of her—the last manner in which she appeared to me. It was a horrid sight! Yet when I thought of her to-day as really dying, it was a kind of comfort to me to imagine that I knew exactly how she would appear to those who saw her last in this world. She was before me, constantly before me, as I travelled, in the same look and hue."

A short pause of mutual thoughtfulness succeeded. Willoughby, first rousing himself, broke it thus:

"Well, let me make haste and be gone. Your sister is certainly better, certainly out of danger?"

"We are assured of it."

"Your poor mother too!—doting on Marianne."

"But the letter, Mr. Willoughby, your own letter; have you anything to say about that?"

"Yes, yes, *that* in particular. Your sister wrote to me again, you know, the very next morning. You saw what she said. I was breakfasting at the Ellisons'; and her letter, with some others, was brought to me there from my lodgings. It happened to catch Sophia's eye before it caught mine; and its size, the elegance of the paper, the handwriting, altogether immediately gave her a suspicion. Some vague report had reached her before of my attachment to some young lady in Devonshire, and what had passed within her observation the preceding evening had marked who the young lady was, and made her more jealous than ever. Affecting that air of playfulness, therefore, which is delightful in a woman one loves, she opened the letter directly, and read its contents. She was well paid for her impudence. She read what made her wretched. Her wretchedness I could have borne, but her passion—her malice—at all events it must be appeased. And in short, what do you think of my wife's style of letter-writing? Delicate, tender, truly feminine—was it not?"

"Your wife! The letter was in your own handwriting."

"Yes, but I had only the credit of servilely copying such sentences as I was ashamed to put my name to. The original was all her own, her own happy thoughts and gentle diction. But what could I do? We were engaged, everything in preparation, the day almost fixed—but I am talking like a fool. Preparation! Day! In honest words, her money was necessary to me, and in a situation like mine anything was to be done to prevent a rupture. And after all, what did it signify to my character in the opinion of Marianne and her friends, in what language my answer was couched? It must have been only to one end. My business was to declare myself a scoundrel, and whether I did it with a bow or a bluster was of little importance. 'I am ruined for ever in their opinion,' said I to myself; 'I am shut out for ever from their society; they already think me an unprincipled fellow, this letter will only make them think me a blackguard one.' Such were my reasonings as, in a sort of desperate carelessness, I copied my wife's words, and parted with the last relics of Marianne. Her three notes—unluckily they were all in my pocket-book, or I should have denied their existence, and hoarded them for ever; I was forced to put them up, and could not even kiss them. And the lock of hair —that, too, I had always carried about me in the same pocket-book, which was now searched by Madam with the most ingratiating virulence—the dear lock—all, every memento was torn from me."

"You are very wrong, Mr. Willoughby, very blameable," said Elinor, while her voice, in spite of herself, betrayed her compassionate emotion; "you ought not to speak in this way, either of Mrs. Willoughby or my sister. You have made your own choice. It was not forced on you. Your wife has a claim to your politeness, to your respect, at least. She must be attached to you, or she would not have married you. To treat her with unkindness, to speak of her slightingly, is no atonement to Marianne, nor can I suppose it a relief to your own conscience."

"Do not talk to me of my wife," said he, with a heavy sigh. "She does not deserve your compassion. She knew I had no regard for her when we married. Well, married we were, and came down to Combe Magna to be happy, and afterwards returned to town to be gay. And, now do you pity me, Miss Dashwood? Or have I said all this to no purpose? Am I—be it only one degree—am I less guilty in your opinion than I was before? My intentions were not always wrong. Have I explained away any part of my guilt?"

"Yes, you have certainly removed something—a little. You have proved yourself, on the whole, less faulty than I had believed you. You have proved your heart less wicked, much less wicked. But I hardly know—the misery that you have inflicted—I hardly know what could have made it worse."

"Will you repeat to your sister, when she is recovered, what I have been telling you? Let me be a little lightened, too, in her opinion as well as in yours. You tell me that she has forgiven me already. Let me be able to fancy that a better knowledge of my heart, and of my present feelings, will draw from her a more spontaneous, more natural, more gentle, less dignified forgiveness. Tell her of my misery and my penitence, tell her that my heart was never inconstant to her, and if you will, that at this moment she is dearer to me than ever."

"I will tell her all that is necessary to what may comparatively be called your justification. But you have not explained to me the particular reason of your coming now, nor how you heard of her illness."

"Last night, in Drury Lane lobby, I ran against Sir John Middleton, and when he saw who I was (for the first time these two months) he spoke to me. That he had cut me ever since my marriage, I had seen without surprise or resentment. Now, however, his good-natured, honest, stupid soul, full of indignation against me, and concern for your sister, could not resist the temptation of telling me what he knew ought to, though probably he did not think it *would*, vex me horribly. As bluntly as he could speak it, therefore, he told me that Marianne Dashwood was dying of a putrid fever at Cleveland—a letter that morning received from Mrs. Jennings declared her danger most imminent—the Palmers all gone off in a fright, etc. I was too much shocked to be able to pass myself off as insensible, even to the undiscerning Sir John. His heart was softened in seeing mine suffer; and so much of his ill-will was done away, that when we parted, he almost shook me by the hand, while he reminded me of an old promise about a pointer puppy. What I felt on hearing that your sister was dying—and dying, too, believing me the greatest villain upon earth, scorning, hating me in her latest moments—for how could I tell what horrid projects might not have been imputed? *One* person I was sure would represent me as capable of anything. What I felt was dreadful! My resolution was soon made, and at eight o'clock this morning I was in my carriage. Now you know all."

Elinor made no answer. Her thoughts were silently fixed on the **irreparable** injury which too early an independence and its consequent habits of idleness, dissipation, and luxury, had made in the mind, the character, the happiness, of a man who, to every advantage of person and talents, united a disposition naturally open and honest, and a feeling, affectionate temper. The world had made him extravagant and vain; extravagance and vanity had made him cold-hearted and selfish. Vanity, while seeking its own guilty triumph at the expense of another, had involved him in a real attachment, which extravagance, or at least its offspring necessity, had required to be sacrificed. Each faulty propensity, in leading him to evil, had led him likewise to punishment. The attachment from which against honour, against feeling, against every better interest he had outwardly torn himself, now, when no longer allowable, governed every thought; and the connection, for the sake of which he had, with little scruple, left her sister to misery, was likely to prove a source of unhappiness to himself of a far more incurable nature. From a reverie of this kind she was recalled at the end of some minutes by Willoughby, who, rousing himself from a reverie at least equally painful, started up in preparation for going, and said:

"There is no use in staying here; I must be off."

"Are you going back to town?"

"No, to Combe Magna. I have business there; from thence to town in a day of two. Good-bye."

He held out his hand. She could not refuse to give him hers; he pressed it with affection.

"And you *do* think something better of me than you did?" said he, letting it fall, and leaning against the mantelpiece, as if forgetting he was to go.

Elinor assured him that she did; that she forgave, pitied him, wished him well—was even interested in his happiness—and added some gentle counsel as to the behaviour most likely to promote it. His answer was not very encouraging.

"As to that," said he, "I must rub through the world as well as I can. Domestic happiness is out of the question. If, however, I am allowed to think that you and yours feel an interest in my fate and actions, it may be the means—it may put me on my guard—at least, it may be something to live for. Marianne, to be sure, is lost to me for ever. Were I even, by any blessed chance, at liberty again——"

Elinor stopped him with a reproof.

"Well," he replied, "once more good-bye. I shall now go away and live in dread of one event."

"What do you mean?"

"Your sister's marriage."

"You are very wrong. She can never be more lost to you than she is now."

"But she will be gained by some one else. And if that some one should be the very he whom, of all others, I could least bear—— But I will not stay to rob myself of all your compassionate goodwill, by showing that where I have most injured I can least forgive. Good-bye; God bless you!"

And with these words, he almost ran out of the room.

Chapter 45

ELINOR, for some time after he left her, for some time even after the sound of his carriage had died away, remained too much oppressed by a crowd of ideas, widely differing in themselves, but of which sadness was the general result, to think even of her sister.

Willoughby—he whom only half-an-hour ago she had abhorred as the most worthless of men—Willoughby, in spite of all his faults, excited a degree of commiseration for the sufferings produced by them, which made her think of him as now separated for ever from her family with a tenderness, a regret, rather in proportion, as she soon acknowledged within herself, to his wishes than to his merits. She felt that his influence over her mind was heightened by circumstances which ought not in reason to have weight; by that person of uncommon attraction—that open, affectionate, and lively manner which it was no merit to possess; and by that still ardent love for Marianne, which it was not even innocent to indulge. But she felt that it was so, long, long before she could feel his influence less.

When at last she returned to the unconscious Marianne, she found her just awaking, refreshed by so long and sweet a sleep to the extent of her hopes. Elinor's heart was full. The past, the present, the future—Willoughby's visit, Marianne's safety, and her mother's expected arrival, threw her altogether into an agitation of spirits which kept off every indication of fatigue, and made her only fearful of betraying herself to her sister. Short was the time, however, in which that fear could affect her, for within half-an-hour after Willoughby's leaving the house, she was again called downstairs by the sound of another carriage. Eager to save her mother from every unnecessary moment's horrible suspense, she ran immediately into the hall, and reached the outward door just in time to receive and support her as she entered it.

Mrs. Dashwood, whose terror as they drew near the house had produced almost the conviction of Marianne's being no more, had no voice to inquire after her, no voice even for Elinor; but *she,* waiting neither for salutation nor inquiry, instantly gave the joyful relief; and her mother, catching it with all her usual warmth, was in a moment as much overcome by her happiness as she had been before by her fears. She was supported into the drawing-room between her daughter and her friend; and there, shedding tears of joy, though still unable to speak, embraced Elinor again and again, turning from her at intervals to press Colonel Brandon's hand, with a look which spoke at once her gratitude, and her conviction of his sharing with herself in the bliss of the moment. He shared it, however, in a silence even greater than her own.

As soon as Mrs. Dashwood had recovered herself, to see Marianne was her first desire; and in two minutes she was with her beloved child, rendered dearer to her than ever by absence, unhappiness and danger. Elinor's delight, as she saw what each felt in the meeting, was only checked by an apprehension of its robbing Marianne of further sleep; but Mrs. Dashwood could be calm, could be even prudent, when the life of a child was at stake, and Marianne, satisfied in knowing her mother was near her, and conscious of being too weak for conversation, submitted readily to the silence and quiet prescribed by every nurse around her. Mrs. Dashwood *would* sit up with her all night, and Elinor, in compliance with her mother's entreaty, went to bed. But the rest, which one night entirely sleepless and many hours of the most wearying anxiety seemed to make requisite, was kept off by irritation of spirits. Willoughby, "poor Willoughby," as she now allowed herself to call him, was constantly in her thoughts; she would not but have heard his vindication for the world, and now blamed, now acquitted herself, for having judged him so harshly before. But her promise of relating it to her sister was invariably painful. She dreaded the performance of it, dreaded what its effect on Marianne might be; doubted whether, after such an explanation, she could ever be happy with another, and for a moment, wished Willoughby a widower; then remembering Colonel Brandon, reproved herself, felt that to *his* sufferings and *his* constancy, far more than to his rival's, the reward of her sister was due, and wished anything rather than Mrs. Willoughby's death.

The shock of Colonel Brandon's errand at Barton had been much softened to Mrs. Dashwood by her own previous alarm; for so great was her uneasiness about Marianne, that she had already determined to set out for Cleveland on that very day, without waiting for any further intelligence, and had so far settled her journey before his arrival, that the Careys were then expected every moment to fetch Margaret away, as her mother was unwilling to take her where there might be infection.

Marianne continued to mend every day, and the brilliant cheerfulness of Mrs. Dashwood's looks and spirits proved her to be, as she repeatedly declared herself, one of the happiest women in the world. Elinor could not hear the declaration, nor witness its proofs, without sometimes wondering whether her mother ever recollected Edward. But Mrs. Dashwood, trusting to the temperate account of her own disappointment which Elinor had sent her, was led away by the exuberance of her joy to think only of what would increase it. Marianne was restored to her from a danger in which, as she now began to feel, her own mistaken judgment in encouraging the unfortunate attachment to Willoughby had contributed to place her; and in her recovery she had yet another source of joy unthought of by Elinor. It was thus imparted to her, as soon as any opportunity of private conference between them occurred.

"At last we are alone. My Elinor, you do not yet know all my happiness. Colonel Brandon loves Marianne; he has told me so himself."

Her daughter, feeling by turns both pleased and pained, surprised and not surprised, was all silent attention.

"You are never like me, dear Elinor, or I should wonder at your composure now. Had I sat down to wish for any possible good to my family, I should have fixed on Colonel Brandon's marrying one of you as the object most desirable. And I believe Marianne will be the most happy with him of the two."

Elinor was half inclined to ask her reason for thinking so, because satisfied that none founded on an impartial consideration of their age, characters or feelings, could be given; but her mother must always be carried away by her imagination on any interesting subject, and therefore, instead of an inquiry, she passed it off with a smile.

"He opened his whole heart to me yesterday as we travelled. It came out quite unawares, quite undesignedly. I, you may well believe, could talk of nothing but my child; he could not conceal his distress; I saw that it equalled my own, and he, perhaps, thinking that mere friendship, as the world now goes, would not justify so warm a sympathy—or rather not thinking at all, I suppose—giving way to irresistible feelings, made me acquainted with his earnest, tender, constant affection for Marianne. He has loved her, my Elinor, ever since the first moment of seeing her."

Here, however, Elinor perceived, not the language, not the professions of Colonel Brandon, but the natural embellishments of her mother's active fancy, which fashioned everything delightful to her, as it chose.

"His regard for her, infinitely surpassing anything that Willoughby ever felt or feigned, as much more warm, as more sincere or constant— whichever we are to call it—has subsisted through all the knowledge of dear Marianne's unhappy prepossession for that worthless young man!— and without selfishness—without encouraging a hope!—could he have seen her happy with another? Such a noble mind! Such openness, such sincerity! No one can be deceived in *him*."

"Colonel Brandon's character," said Elinor, "as an excellent man, is well established."

" I know it is," replied her mother seriously, "or after such a warning, *I* should be the last to encourage such affection, or even to be pleased by it. But his coming for me as he did, with such active, such ready friendship, is enough to prove him one of the worthiest of men."

"His character, however," answered Elinor, "does not rest on *one* act of kindness, to which his affection for Marianne, were humanity out of the case, would have prompted him. To Mrs. Jennings, to the Middletons, he has been long and intimately known; they equally love and respect him; and even my knowledge of him, though lately acquired, is very considerable; and so highly do *I* value and esteem him, that if Marianne can be happy with him, I shall be as ready as yourself to think our connection the greatest blessing to us in the world. What answer did you give him? Did you allow him to hope?"

"Oh! my love, I could not then talk of hope to him or to myself. Marianne might at that moment be dying. But he did not ask for hope or encouragement. His was an involuntary confidence, an irrepressible effusion to a soothing friend—not an application to a parent. Yet after a time I *did* say, for at first I was quite overcome, that if she lived, as I trusted she might, my greatest happiness would lie in promoting their marriage; and since our arrival, since our delightful security, I have repeated it to him more fully, have given him every encouragement in my power. Time, a very little time, I tell him, will do everything; Marianne's heart is not to be wasted for ever on such a man as Willoughby. His own merits must soon secure it."

"To judge from the Colonel's spirits, however, you have not yet made him equally sanguine."

"No. He thinks Marianne's affection too deeply rooted for any change in it under a great length of time; and even supposing her heart again free, is too diffident of himself to believe, that with such a difference of age and disposition, he could ever attach her. There, however, he is quite mistaken. His age is only so much beyond hers as to be an advantage, as to make his character and principles fixed; and his disposition, I am well convinced, is exactly the very one to make your sister happy. And his person, his manners too, are all in his favour. My partiality does not blind me; he certainly is not so handsome as Willoughby; but, at the same time, there is something much more pleasing in his countenance. There was always a something, if you remember, in Willoughby's eyes at times, which I did not like."

Elinor could *not* remember it; but her mother, without waiting for her assent, continued:

"And his manners, the Colonel's manners, are not only more pleasing to me than Willoughby's ever were, but they are of a kind I well know to be more solidly attaching to Marianne. Their gentleness, their genuine attention to other people, and their manly unstudied simplicity, is much more accordant with her real disposition, than the liveliness, often artificial, and often ill-timed, of the other. I am very sure myself, that had Willoughby turned out as really amiable as he has proved himself the contrary, Marianne would yet never have been so happy with *him*, as she will be with Colonel Brandon."

She paused. Her daughter could not quite agree with her, but her dissent was not heard, and therefore gave no offence.

"At Delaford, she will be within an easy distance of me," added Mrs. Dashwood, "even if I remain at Barton; and in all probability, for I hear it is a large village—indeed, there certainly *must* be some small house or cottage close by, that would suit us quite as well as our present situation."

Poor Elinor! Here was a new scheme for getting her to Delaford! But her spirit was stubborn.

"His fortune too! for at my time of life, you know, everybody cares about *that;* and though I neither know, nor desire to know, what it really is, I am sure it must be a good one."

Here they were interrupted by the entrance of a third person, and Elinor withdrew to think it all over in private, to wish success to her friend, and yet, in wishing it, to feel a pang for Willoughby.

Chapter 46

MARIANNE's illness, though weakening in its kind, had not been long enough to make her recovery slow; and with youth, natural strength, and her mother's presence in aid, it proceeded so smoothly as to enable her to remove, within four days after the arrival of the latter, into Mrs. Palmer's dressing-room. When there, at her own particular request, for she was impatient to pour forth her thanks to him for fetching her mother, Colonel Brandon was invited to visit her.

His emotion in entering the room, in seeing her altered looks, and in receiving the pale hand which she immediately held out to him, was such as in Elinor's conjecture must arise from something more than his affection for Marianne, or the consciousness of its being known to others; and she soon discovered in his melancholy eye and varying complexion as he looked at her sister, the probable recurrence of many past scenes of misery to his mind, brought back by that resemblance between Marianne and Eliza already acknowledged, and now strengthened by the hollow eye, the sickly skin, the posture of reclining weakness, and the warm acknowledgment of peculiar obligation.

Mrs. Dashwood, not less watchful of what passed than her daughter, but with a mind very differently influenced, and therefore watching to very different effect, saw nothing in the Colonel's behaviour but what arose from the most simple and self-evident sensations, while in the actions and words of Marianne she persuaded herself to think that something more than gratitude already dawned.

At the end of another day or two, Marianne growing visibly stronger every twelve hours, Mrs. Dashwood, urged equally by her own and her daughter's wishes, began to talk of removing to Barton. On *her* measures depended those of her two friends; Mrs. Jennings could not quit Cleveland during the Dashwoods' stay, and Colonel Brandon was soon brought by their united request to consider his own abode there as equally determinate, if not equally indispensable. At his and Mrs. Jennings's united request in return, Mrs. Dashwood was prevailed on to accept the use of his carriage on her journey back, for the better accommodation of her sick child; and the Colonel, at the joint invitation of Mrs. Dashwood and Mrs. Jennings, whose active good nature made her friendly and hospitable for other people as well as herself, engaged with pleasure to redeem it by a visit at the cottage, in the course of a few weeks.

The day of separation and departure arrived; and Marianne, after taking so particular and lengthened a leave of Mrs. Jennings—one so earnestly grateful, so full of respect and kind wishes as seemed due to her own heart from a secret acknowledgment of past inattention—and bidding Colonel Brandon farewell with the cordiality of a friend, was carefully assisted by him into the carriage, of which he seemed anxious that she should engross at least half. Mrs. Dashwood and Elinor then followed, and the others were left by themselves, to talk of the travellers, and feel their own dullness, till Mrs. Jennings was summoned to her chaise to take comfort in the gossip of her maid for the loss of her two young companions; and Colonel Brandon immediately afterwards took his solitary way to Delaford.

The Dashwoods were two days on the road, and Marianne bore her journey on both without essential fatigue. Everything that the most zealous affection, the most solicitous care, could do to render her comfortable, was the office of each watchful companion, and each found their reward in her bodily ease and her calmness of spirits. To Elinor, the observation of the latter was particularly grateful. She, who had seen her week after week so constantly suffering, oppressed by anguish of heart which she had neither courage to speak of, nor fortitude to conceal, now saw, with a joy which no other could equally share, an apparent composure of mind, which in being the result as she trusted of serious reflection, must eventually lead her to contentment and cheerfulness.

As they approached Barton, indeed, and entered on scenes of which every field and every tree brought some peculiar, some painful recollection, she grew silent and thoughtful, and turning away her face from their notice, sat earnestly gazing through the window. But here, Elinor could neither wonder nor blame; and when she saw, as she assisted Marianne from the carriage, that she had been crying, she saw only an emotion too natural in itself to raise anything less tender than pity, and in its unobtrusiveness entitled to praise. In the whole of her subsequent manner, she traced the direction of a mind awakened to reasonable exertion; for no sooner had they entered their common sitting-room than Marianne turned her eyes around it with a look of resolute firmness, as if determined at once to accustom herself to the sight of every object with which the remembrance of Willoughby could be connected. She said little, but every sentence aimed at cheerfulness, and though a sigh sometimes escaped her, it never passed away without the atonement of a smile. After dinner, she would try her pianoforte. She went to it; but the music on which her eye first rested was an opera, procured for her by Willoughby, containing some of their favourite duets, and bearing on its outward leaf her own name in his handwriting. That would not do. She shook her head, put the music aside, and, after running over the keys for a minute, complained of feebleness in her fingers, and closed the instrument again; declaring, however, with firmness as she did so, that she should in future practise much.

The next morning produced no abatement in these happy symptoms. On the contrary with a mind and body alike strengthened by rest, she looked and spoke with more genuine spirit, anticipating the pleasure of Margaret's return, and talking of the dear family party which would then be restored, of their mutual pursuits and cheerful society as the only happiness worth a wish.

"When the weather is settled, and I have recovered my strength," said she, "we will take long walks together every day. We will walk to the farm at the edge of the down, and see how the children go on; we will walk to Sir John's new plantation at Barton Cross, and the Abbeyland; and we will often go to the old ruins of the Priory, and try to trace its founda-tions as far as we are told they once reached. I know we shall be happy. I know the summer will pass happily away. I mean never to be later in rising than six, and from that time till dinner I shall divide every moment between music and reading. I have formed my plan, and am determined to enter on a course of serious study. Our own library is too well known to me to be resorted to for anything beyond mere amusement. But there are many works well worth reading at the Park; and there are others of more modern production which I know I can borrow of Colonel Brandon. By reading only six hours a day, I shall gain in the course of a twelvemonth a great deal of instruction which I now feel myself to want."

Elinor honoured her for a plan which originated so nobly as this; though smiling to see the same eager fancy which had been leading her to the extreme of languid indolence and selfish repining, now at work in in-troducing excess into a scheme of such rational employment and virtuous self-control. Her smile, however, changed to a sigh when she remembered that her promise to Willoughby was yet unfulfilled, and feared she had that to communicate which might again unsettle the mind of Marianne, and ruin at least for a time this fair prospect of busy tranquillity. Willing therefore to delay the evil hour, she resolved to wait till her sister's health were more secure, before she appointed it. But the resolution was made only to be broken.

Marianne had been two or three days at home, before the weather was fine enough for an invalid like herself to venture out. But at last a soft, genial morning appeared—such as might tempt the daughter's wishes and the mother's confidence; and Marianne, leaning on Elinor's arm, was authorised to walk as long as she could without fatigue, in the lane before the house.

The sisters set out at a pace slow as the feebleness of Marianne in an exercise hitherto untried since her illness required; and they had advanced only so far beyond the house as to admit a full view of the hill, the important hill behind, when, pausing with her eyes turned towards it, Marianne calmly said:

"There, exactly there"—pointing with one hand—"on that projecting mound—there I fell; and there I first saw Willoughby."

Her voice sunk with the word, but presently reviving, she added:

"I am thankful to find that I can look with so little pain on the spot! Shall we ever talk on that subject, Elinor?" Hesitatingly it was said. "Or will it be wrong? I *can* talk of it now, I hope, as I ought to do."

Elinor tenderly invited her to be open.

"As for regret," said Marianne, "I have done with that, as far as *he* is concerned. I do not mean to talk to you of what my feelings have been for him, but what they are *now*. At present, if I could be satisfied on one point —if I could be allowed to think that he was not *always* acting a part, not *always* deceiving me; but above all, if I could be assured that he never was so *very* wicked as my fears have sometimes fancied him, since the story of that unfortunate girl——"

She stopped. Elinor joyfully treasured her words as she answered:

"If you could be assured of that, you think you should be easy?"

"Yes. My peace of mind is doubly involved in it; for not only is it horrible to suspect a person, who has been what *he* has been to *me*, of such designs, but what must it make me to appear myself? What in a situation like mine, but a most shamefully unguarded affection could expose me to——"

"How then," asked her sister, "would you account for his behaviour?"

"I would suppose him—oh! how gladly would I suppose him, only fickle —very, very fickle."

Elinor said no more. She was debating within herself on the eligibility of beginning her story directly, or postponing it till Marianne were in stronger health; and they crept on for a few minutes in silence.

"I am not wishing him too much good," said Marianne at last with a sigh, "when I wish his secret reflections may be no more unpleasant than my own. He will suffer enough in them."

"Do you compare your conduct with his?"

"No. I compare it with what it ought to have been; I compare it with yours."

"Our situations have borne little resemblance."

"They have borne more than our conduct. Do not, my dearest Elinor, let your kindness defend what I know your judgment must censure. My illness has made me think—it has given me leisure and calmness for serious recollection. Long before I was enough recovered to talk, I was perfectly able to reflect. I considered the past; I saw in my own behaviour, since the beginning of our acquaintance with him last autumn, nothing but a series of imprudence towards myself, and want of kindness to others. I saw that my own feelings had prepared my sufferings, and that my want of fortitude under them had almost led me to the grave. My illness, I well knew, had been entirely brought on by myself, by such negligence of my own health as I felt even at the time to be wrong. Had I died, it would have been self-destruction. I did not know my danger till the danger was removed; but with such feelings as these reflections gave me, I wonder at my recovery—wonder that the very eagerness of my desire to live, to have time for atonement to my God, and to you all, did not kill me at once. Had I died, in what peculiar misery should I have left you, my nurse, my friend, my sister! You, who had seen all the fretful selfishness of my latter days; who had known all the murmurings of my heart! How should I have lived in *your* remembrance! My mother too! How could you have consoled her! I cannot express my own abhorrence of myself. Whenever I looked towards the past I saw some duty neglected, or some failing indulged. Everybody seemed injured by me. The kindness, the unceasing kindness of Mrs. Jennings, I had repaid with ungrateful contempt. To the Middletons, the Palmers, the Steeles, to every common acquaintance even, I had been insolent and unjust; with an heart hardened against their merits, and a temper irritated by their very attention. To John, to Fanny, yes, even to them, little as they deserve, I had given less than their due. But you, you above all, above my mother, had been wronged by me. I, and only I, knew your heart and its sorrows; yet, to what did it influence me? not to any compassion that could benefit you or myself. Your example was before me; but to what avail? Was I more considerate of you and your comfort? Did I imitate your forbearance, or lessen your restraints, by taking any part in those offices of general complaisance or particular gratitude which you had hitherto been left to discharge alone? No; not less when I knew you to be unhappy, than when I had believed you at ease, did I turn away from every exertion of duty or friendship; scarcely allowed sorrow to exist but with me, regretting only *that* heart which deserted and wronged me, and leaving you, for whom I professed an unbounded affection, to be miserable for my sake."

Here ceased the rapid flow of her self-reproving spirit; and Elinor, impatient to soothe, though too honest to flatter, gave her instantly that praise and support which her frankness and her contrition so well deserved. Marianne pressed her hand and replied:

"You are very good. The future must be my proof. I have laid down my plan, and if I am capable of adhering to it, my feelings shall be governed and my temper improved. They shall no longer worry others, nor torture myself. I shall now live solely for my family. You, my mother, and Margaret, must henceforth be all the world to me; you will share my affections entirely between you. From you, from my home, I shall never again have the smallest incitement to move; and if I do mix in other society, it will be only to show that my spirit is humbled, my heart amended, and that I can practise the civilities, the lesser duties of life, with gentleness and forbearance. As for Willoughby, to say that I shall soon or that I shall ever forget him, would be idle. His remembrance can be overcome by no change of circumstances or opinions. But it shall be regulated, it shall be checked by religion, by reason, by constant employment."

She paused, and added in a lower voice, "If I could but know *his* heart, everything would become easy."

Elinor who had now been some time reflecting on the propriety or impropriety of speedily hazarding her narration, without feeling at all nearer decision than at first, heard this; and perceiving that as reflection did nothing, resolution must do all, soon found herself leading to the fact.

She managed the recital, as she hoped, with address; prepared her anxious listener with caution; related simply and honestly the chief points on which Willoughby grounded his apology; did justice to his repentance, and softened only his protestations of present regard. Marianne said not a word; she trembled, her eyes were fixed on the ground, and her lips became whiter than even sickness had left them. A thousand inquiries sprung up from her heart, but she dared not urge one. She caught every syllable with panting eagerness; her hand, unknowingly to herself, closely pressed her sister's, and tears covered her cheeks.

Elinor, dreading her being tired, led her towards home; and till they reached the door of the cottage, easily conjecturing what her curiosity must be, though no question was suffered to speak it, talked of nothing but Willoughby, and their conversation together; and was carefully minute in every particular of speech and look, where minuteness could be safely indulged. As soon as they entered the house, Marianne, with a kiss of gratitude, and these two words just articulate through her tears, "Tell mamma," withdrew from her sister and walked slowly upstairs. Elinor would not attempt to disturb a solitude so reasonable as what she now sought; and with a mind anxiously pre-arranging its result, and a resolution of reviving the subject again should Marianne fail to do it, she turned into the parlour to fulfil her parting injunction.

Chapter 47

MRS. DASHWOOD did not hear unmoved the vindication of her former favourite. She rejoiced in his being cleared from some part of his imputed guilt; she was sorry for him; she wished him happy. But the feelings of the past could not be recalled. Nothing could restore him with a faith unbroken—a character unblemished to Marianne. Nothing could do away the knowledge of what the latter had suffered through his means, nor remove the guilt of his conduct towards Eliza. Nothing could replace him, therefore, in her former esteem, nor injure the interest of Colonel Brandon.

Had Mrs. Dashwood, like her daughter, heard Willoughby's story from himself—had she witnessed his distress, and been under the influence of his countenance and his manner, it is probable that her compassion would have been greater. But it was neither in Elinor's power, nor in her wish, to rouse such feelings in another, by her retailed explanation, as had at first been called forth in herself. Reflection had given calmness to her judgment, and sobered her own opinion of Willoughby's deserts; she wished, therefore, to declare only the simple truth, and lay open such facts as were really due to his character, without any embellishment of tenderness to lead the fancy astray.

In the evening, when they were all together, Marianne began voluntarily to speak of him again; but that it was not without an effort, the restless, unquiet thoughtfulness in which she had been for some time previously sitting, her rising colour as she spoke, and her unsteady voice, plainly showed.

"I wish to assure you both," said she, "that I see everything—as you can desire me to do."

Mrs. Dashwood would have interrupted her instantly with soothing tenderness, had not Elinor, who really wished to hear her sister's unbiased opinion, by an eager sign, engaged her silence. Marianne slowly continued:

"It is a great relief to me—what Elinor told me this morning. I have now heard exactly what I wished to hear." For some moments her voice was lost; but, recovering herself, she added, and with greater calmness than before: "I am now perfectly satisfied. I wish for no change. I never could have been happy with him, after knowing as sooner or later I must have known, all this. I should have had no confidence, no esteem. Nothing could have done it away to my feelings."

"I know it; I know it," cried her mother. "Happy with a man of libertine practices! With one who had so injured the peace of the dearest of our friends, and the best of men? No—my Marianne has not a heart to be made happy by such a man! Her conscience, her sensitive conscience, would have felt all that the conscience of her husband ought to have felt."

Marianne sighed, and repeated, "I wish for no change."

"You consider the matter," said Elinor, "exactly as a good mind and a sound understanding must consider it; and I dare say you perceive, as well as myself, not only in this, but in many other circumstances, reason enough to be convinced that your marriage must have involved you in many certain troubles and disappointments in which you would have been poorly supported by an affection, on his side, much less certain. Had you married, you must have been always poor. His expensiveness is acknowledged even by himself, and his whole conduct declares that self-denial is a word hardly understood by him. His demands and your inexperience together on a small, very small income, must have brought on distresses which would not be the *less* grievous to you from having been entirely unknown and unthought of before. *Your* sense of honour and honesty would have led you, *I* know, when aware of your situation, to attempt all the economy that would appear to you possible; and perhaps, as long as your frugality retrenched only on your own comfort, you might have been suffered to practise it, but beyond that—and how little could the utmost of your single management do to stop the ruin which had begun before your marriage? beyond *that,* had you endeavoured, however reasonably, to abridge *his* enjoyments is it not to be feared, that instead of prevailing on feelings so selfish to consent to it, you would have lessened your own influence on his heart, and made him regret the connection which had involved him in such difficulties?"

Marianne's lips quivered, and she repeated the word "Selfish?" in a tone that implied "Do you really think him selfish?"

"The whole of his behaviour," replied Elinor, "from the beginning to the end of the affair, has been grounded on selfishness. It was selfishness which first made him sport with your affections—which afterwards, when his own were engaged, made him delay the confession of it, and which finally carried him from Barton. His own enjoyment, or his own ease, was in every particular his ruling principle."

"It is very true. *My* happiness never was his object."

"At present," continued Elinor, "he regrets what he has done. And why does he regret it? Because he finds it has not answered towards himself. It has not made him happy. His circumstances are now un-embarrassed—he suffers from no evil of that kind, and he thinks only that he has married a woman of a less amiable temper than yourself. But does it thence follow that, had he married you, he would have been happy? The inconveniences would have been different. He would then have suffered under the pecuniary distresses which, because they are removed, he now reckons as nothing. He would have had a wife of whose temper he could make no complaint, but he would have been always necessitous—always poor; and probably would soon have learnt to rank the innumerable comforts of a clear estate and good income as of far more importance, even to domestic happiness, than the mere temper of a wife."

"I have not a doubt of it," said Marianne; "and I have nothing to regret—nothing but my own folly."

"Rather say your mother's imprudence, my child," said Mrs. Dash-wood; "*she* must be answerable."

Marianne would not let her proceed; and Elinor, satisfied that each felt their own error, wished to avoid any survey of the past that might weaken her sister's spirits; she therefore, pursuing the first subject, immediately continued:

"*One* observation may, I think, be fairly drawn from the whole of the story—that all Willoughby's difficulties have arisen from the first offence against virtue, in his behaviour to Eliza Williams. That crime has been the origin of every lesser one, and of all his present discontents."

Marianne assented most feelingly to the remark; and her mother was led by it to an enumeration of Colonel Brandon's injuries and merits, warm as friendship and design could unitedly dictate. Her daughter did not look, however, as if much of it were heard by her.

Elinor, according to her expectation, saw on the two or three following days that Marianne did not continue to gain strength as she had done; but while her resolution was unsubdued, and she still tried to appear cheerful and easy, her sister could safely trust to the effect of time upon her health.

Margaret returned, and the family were again all restored to each other, again quietly settled at the cottage, and if not pursuing their usual studies with quite so much vigour as when they first came to Barton, at least planning a vigorous prosecution of them in future.

Elinor grew impatient for some tidings of Edward. She had heard nothing of him since her leaving London, nothing new of his plans, nothing certain even of his present abode. Some letters had passed between her and her brother, in consequence of Marianne's illness; and in the first of John's, there had been this sentence:—"We know nothing of our unfortunate Edward, and can make no inquiries on so prohibited a subject, but conclude him to be still at Oxford"; which was all the intelligence of Edward afforded her by the correspondence, for his name was not even mentioned in any of the succeeding letters. She was not doomed, however, to be long in ignorance of his measures.

Their man-servant had been sent one morning to Exeter on business; and when, as he waited at table, he had satisfied the inquiries of his mistress as to the event of his errand, this was his voluntary communication:

"I suppose you know, ma'am, that Mr. Ferrars is married."

Marianne gave a violent start, fixed her eyes upon Elinor, saw her turning pale, and fell back in her chair in hysterics. Mrs. Dashwood, whose eyes, as she answered the servant's inquiry, had intuitively taken the same direction, was shocked to perceive by Elinor's countenance how much she really suffered, and in a moment afterwards, alike distressed by Marianne's situation, knew not on which child to bestow her principal attention.

The servant, who saw only that Miss Marianne was taken ill, had sense enough to call one of the maids, who, with Mrs. Dashwood's assistance, supported her into the other room. By that time, Marianne was rather better, and her mother leaving her to the care of Margaret and the maid, returned to Elinor, who though still much disordered, had so far recovered the use of her reason and voice as to be just beginning an inquiry of Thomas as to the source of his intelligence. Mrs. Dashwood immediately took all that trouble on herself: and Elinor had the benefit of the information without the exertion of seeking it.

"Who told you that Mr. Ferrars was married, Thomas?"

"I see Mr. Ferrars myself, ma'am, this morning in Exeter, and his lady too, Miss Steele as was. They was stopping in a chaise at the door of the New London Inn, as I went there with a message from Sally at the Park to her brother, who is one of the postboys. I happened to look up as I went by the chaise, and so I see directly it was the youngest Miss Steele; so I took off my hat, and she knew me and called to me, and inquired after you, ma'am, and the young ladies, especially Miss Marianne, and bid me I should give her compliments and Mr. Ferrars's, their best compliments and service, and how sorry they was they had not time to come on and see you—but they was in a great hurry to go forwards, for they was going further down for a little while—but howsever, when they come back, they'd make sure to come and see you."

"But did she tell you she was married, Thomas?"

"Yes, ma'am. She smiled, and said how she had changed her name since she was in these parts. She was always a very affable and free-spoken young lady, and very civil-behaved. So, I made free to wish her joy."

"Was Mr. Ferrars in the carriage with her?"

"Yes, ma'am, I just see him leaning back in it, but he did not look up; he never was a gentleman much for talking."

Elinor's heart could easily account for his not putting himself forward; and Mrs. Dashwood probably found the same explanation.

"Was there no one else in the carriage?"

"No, ma'am, only they two."

"Do you know where they came from?"

"They come straight from town, as Miss Lucy—Mrs. Ferrars told me."

"And are going further westward?"

"Yes, ma'am—but not to bide long. They will soon be back again, and then they'd be sure and call here."

Mrs. Dashwood now looked at her daughter; but Elinor knew better than to expect them. She recognised the whole of Lucy in the message, and was very confident that Edward would never come near them. She observed, in a low voice, to her mother, that they were probably going down to Mr. Pratt's, near Plymouth.

Thomas's intelligence seemed over. Elinor looked as if she wished to hear more.

"Did you see them off before you came away?"

"No, ma'am—the horses was just coming out, but I could not bide any longer; I was afraid of being late."

"Did Mrs. Ferrars look well?"

"Yes, ma'am, she said how she was very well; and to my mind she was always a very handsome young lady—and she seemed vastly contented."

Mrs. Dashwood could think of no other question and Thomas and the table-cloth, now alike needless, were soon after dismissed. Marianne had already sent to say that she should eat nothing more; Mrs. Dashwood's and Elinor's appetites were equally lost, and Margaret might think herself very well off, that with so much uneasiness as both her sisters had lately experienced, so much reason as they had often had to be careless of the meals, she had never been obliged to go without her dinner before.

When the dessert and the wine were arranged, and Mrs. Dashwood and Elinor were left to themselves, they remained long together in a similarity

of thoughtfulness and silence. Mrs. Dashwood feared to hazard any remark, and ventured not to offer consolation. She now found that she had
erred in relying on Elinor's representation of herself; and justly concluded
that everything had been expressly softened at the time, to spare her from
an increase of unhappiness, suffering as she then had suffered for Marianne. She found that she had been misled by the careful, the considerate
attention of her daughter, to think the attachment which once she had so
well understood, much slighter in reality than she had been wont to believe, or than it was now proved to be. She feared that under this persuasion she had been unjust, inattentive—nay, almost unkind to her
Elinor:—that Marianne's affliction, because more acknowledged, more
immediately before her, had too much engrossed her tenderness, and led
her away to forget that in Elinor she might have a daughter suffering almost as much, certainly with less self-provocation, and greater fortitude.

Chapter 48

ELINOR now found the difference between the expectation of an unpleasant event, however certain the mind may be told to consider it, and
certainty itself. She now found, that in spite of herself, she had always
admitted a hope, while Edward remained single, that something would
occur to prevent his marrying Lucy; that some resolution of his own,
some mediation of friends, or some eligible opportunity of establishment
for the lady, would arise to assist the happiness of all. But he was now
married, and she condemned her heart for the lurking flattery which so
much heightened the pain of the intelligence.

That he should be married so soon, before (as she imagined) he could
be in orders, and consequently before he could be in possession of the
living, surprised her a little at first. But she soon saw how likely it was
that Lucy, in her self-provident care, in her haste to secure him, should
everlook everything but the risk of delay. They were married, married
in town, and now hastening down to her uncle's. What had Edward felt
on being within four miles of Barton, on seeing her mother's servant, or
hearing Lucy's message!

They would soon, she supposed, be settled at Delaford—Delaford, that
place in which so much conspired to give her an interest—which she
wished to be acquainted with, and yet desired to avoid. She saw them in
an instant in their parsonage house; saw in Lucy the active, contriving
manager, uniting at once a desire of smart appearance with the utmost
frugality, and ashamed to be suspected of half her economical practices;
pursuing her own interest in every thought, courting the favour of Colonel
Brandon, of Mrs. Jennings, and every wealthy friend. In Edward, she
knew not what she saw, nor what she wished to see; happy or unhappy—
nothing pleased her; she turned away her head from every sketch of him

Elinor flattered herself that some one of their connections in London would write to them to announce the event, and give further particulars; but day after day passed off, and brought no letter, no tidings. Though uncertain that any one were to blame, she found fault with every absent friend. They were all thoughtless or indolent.

"When do you write to Colonel Brandon, ma'am?" was an inquiry which sprung from the impatience of her mind to have something going on.

"I wrote to him, my love, last week, and rather expect to see, than to hear from him again. I earnestly pressed his coming to us, and should not be surprised to see him walk in to-day or to-morrow, or any day."

This was gaining something, something to look forward to. Colonel Brandon *must* have some information to give.

Scarcely had she so determined it when the figure of a man on horse-back drew her eyes to the window. He stopped at their gate. It was a gentleman, it was Colonel Brandon himself. Now she should hear more; and she trembled in expectation of it. But—it was *not* Colonel Brandon—neither his air, not his height. Were it possible, she should say it must be Edward. She looked again. He had just dismounted; she could not be mistaken—it *was* Edward. She moved away and sat down. "He comes from Mr. Pratt's purposely to see us. I *will* be calm; I *will* be mistress of myself."

In a moment she perceived that the others were likewise aware of the mistake. She saw her mother and Marianne change colour; saw them look at herself, and whisper a few sentences to each other. She would have given the world to be able to speak—and to make them understand that she hoped no coolness, no slight, would appear in their behaviour to him; but she had no utterance, and was obliged to leave all to their own discretion.

Not a syllable passed aloud. They all waited in silence for the appearance of their visitor. His footsteps were heard along the gravel path; in a moment he was in the passage, and in another he was before them.

His countenance, as he entered the room, was not too happy, even for Elinor. His complexion was white with agitation, and he looked as if fearful of his reception, and conscious that he merited no kind one. Mrs. Dashwood, however, conforming, as she trusted, to the wishes of that daughter by whom she then meant, in the warmth of her heart, to be guided in everything, met him with a look of forced complacency, gave him her hand, and wished him joy.

He coloured, and stammered out an unintelligible reply. Elinor's lips had moved with her mother's and when the moment of action was over, she wished that she had shaken hands with him too. But it was then too late, and with a countenance meaning to be open, she sat down again and talked of the weather.

Marianne had retreated as much as possible out of sight to conceal her distress; and Margaret, understanding some part, but not the whole, of the case, thought it incumbent on her to be dignified, and therefore took a seat as far from him as she could, and maintained a strict silence.

When Elinor had ceased to rejoice in the dryness of the season, a very awful pause took place. It was put an end to by Mrs. Dashwood, who felt obliged to hope that he had left Mrs. Ferrars very well. In a hurried manner he replied in the affirmative.

Another pause.

Elinor, resolving to exert herself, though fearing the sound of her own voice, now said:

"Is Mrs. Ferrars at Longstaple?"

"At Longstaple!" he replied, with an air of surprise. "No, my mother is in town."

"I meant," said Elinor, taking up some work from the table, "to inquire after Mrs. *Edward* Ferrars."

She dared not look up; but her mother and Marianne both turned their eyes on him. He coloured, seemed perplexed, looked doubtingly, and, after some hesitation said:

"Perhaps you mean—my brother—you mean Mrs.—Mrs. *Robert* Ferrars."

"Mrs. Robert Ferrars!" was repeated by Marianne and her mother in an accent of the utmost amazement; and though Elinor could not speak, even *her* eyes were fixed on him with the same impatient wonder. He rose from his seat and walked to the window, apparently from not knowing what to do; took up a pair of scissors that lay there, and while spoiling both them and their sheath by cutting the latter to pieces as he spoke, said, in an hurried voice:

"Perhaps you do not know—you may not have heard that my brother is lately married to—to the youngest—to Miss Lucy Steele."

His words were echoed with unspeakable astonishment by all but Elinor, who sat with her head leaning over her work, in a state of such agitation as made her hardly know where she was.

"Yes," said he, "they were married last week and are now at Dawlish."

Elinor could sit it no longer. She almost ran out of the room, and as soon as the door was closed, burst into tears of joy, which at first she thought would never cease. Edward, who had till then looked anywhere rather than at her, saw her hurry away, and perhaps saw—or even heard—her emotion; for immediately afterwards he fell into a reverie, which no remarks, no inquiries, no affectionate address of Mrs. Dashwood could penetrate, and at last, without saying a word, quitted the room, and walked out towards the village, leaving the others in the greatest astonishment and perplexity on a change in his situation so wonderful and so sudden—a perplexity which they had no means of lessening but by their own conjectures

Chapter 49

UNACCOUNTABLE, however, as the circumstances of his release might appear to the whole family, it was certain that Edward was free; and to what purpose that freedom would be employed was easily predetermined by all; for after experiencing the blessings of *one* imprudent engagement, contracted without his mother's consent, as he had already done for more than four years, nothing less could be expected of him in the failure of *that*, than the immediate contraction of another.

His errand at Barton, in fact, was a simple one. It was only to ask Elinor to marry him; and considering that he was not altogether inexperienced in such a question, it might be strange that he should feel so uncomfortable in the present case as he really did, so much in need of encouragement and fresh air.

How soon he had walked himself into the proper resolution, however, how soon an opportunity of exercising it occurred, in what manner he expressed himself, and how he was received, need not be particularly told. This only need be said:—that when they all sat down to table at four o'clock, about three hours after his arrival, he had secured his lady, engaged her mother's consent, and was not only in the rapturous profession of the lover, but in the reality of reason and truth, one of the happiest of men. His situation indeed was more than commonly joyful. He had more than the ordinary triumph of accepted love to swell his heart, and raise his spirits. He was released, without any reproach to himself, from an entanglement which had long formed his misery, from a woman whom he had long ceased to love—and elevated at once to that security with another, which he must have thought of almost with despair, as soon as he had learnt to consider it with desire. He was brought, not from doubt or suspense, but from misery to happiness; and the change was openly spoken in such a genuine, flowing, grateful cheerfulness, as his friends had never witnessed in him before.

His heart was now open to Elinor—all its weaknesses, all its errors confessed—and his first boyish attachment to Lucy treated with all the philosophic dignity of twenty-four.

"It was foolish, idle inclination on my side," said he, "the consequence of ignorance of the world—and want of employment. Had my mother given me some active profession when I was removed at eighteen from the care of Mr. Pratt, I think, nay, I am sure, it would never have happened; for, though I left Longstaple with what I thought, at the time, a most unconquerable preference for his niece, yet had I then had any pursuit, any object to engage my time and keep me at a distance from her for a few months, I should very soon have outgrown the fancied attachment, especially by mixing more with the world, as in such a case I must have done. But instead of having anything to do—instead of having any profession chosen for me, or being allowed to choose any myself, I returned home to be completely idle; and for the first twelvemonth afterwards I had not even the nominal employment which belonging to the university would have given me, for I was not entered at Oxford till I was nineteen. I had therefore nothing in the world to do, but to fancy myself in love; and as my mother did not make my home in every respect comfortable—

as I had no friend, no companion in my brother, and disliked new acquaintances, it was not unnatural for me to be very often at Longstaple,
where I always felt myself at home, and was always sure of a welcome;
and accordingly I spent the greatest part of my time there from eighteen
to nineteen. Lucy appeared everything that was amiable and obliging.
She was pretty too—at least I thought so *then;* and I had seen so little of
other women that I could make no comparisons, and see no defects. Considering everything, therefore, I hope, foolish as our engagement was,
foolish as it has since in every way been proved, it was not at the time an
unnatural or an inexcusable piece of folly."

The change which a few hours had wrought in the minds and the happiness of the Dashwoods was such—so great—as promised them all the
satisfaction of a sleepless night. Mrs. Dashwood, too happy to be comfortable, knew not how to love Edward nor praise Elinor enough—how to
be enough thankful for his release without wounding his delicacy, nor
how at once to give them leisure for unrestrained conversation together,
and yet enjoy, as she wished, the sight and society of both.

Marianne could speak *her* happiness only by tears. Comparisons would
occur, regrets would arise; and her joy, though sincere as her love for her
sister, was of a kind to give her neither spirits nor language.

But Elinor, how are *her* feelings to be described? From the moment of
learning that Lucy was married to another, that Edward was free, to the
moment of his justifying the hopes which had so instantly followed, she
was everything by turns but tranquil. But when the second moment had
passed—when she found every doubt, every solicitude removed—compared her situation with what so lately it had been—saw him honourably
released from his former engagement—saw him instantly profiting by the
release, to address herself and declare an affection as tender, as constant
as she had ever supposed it to be—she was oppressed, she was overcome
by her own felicity; and happily disposed as is the human mind to be
easily familiarised with any change for the better, it required several
hours to give sedateness to her spirits, or any degree of tranquillity to her
heart.

Edward was now fixed at the cottage at least for a week; for whatever
other claims might be made on him, it was impossible that less than a
week should be given up to the enjoyment of Elinor's company, or suffice
to say half that was to be said of the past, the present, and the future; for
though a very few hours spent in the hard labour of incessant talking will
dispatch more subjects than can really be in common between any two
rational creatures, yet with lovers it is different. Between *them* no subject
is finished, no communication is even made, till it has been made at least
twenty times over.

Lucy's marriage, the unceasing and reasonable wonder among them all,
formed of course one of the earliest discussions of the lovers; and Elinor's
particular knowledge of each party made it appear to her, in every view,
as one of the most extraordinary and unaccountable circumstances she

had ever heard. How they could be thrown together, and by what attraction Robert could be drawn on to marry a girl of whose beauty she had herself heard him speak without any admiration—a girl, too, already engaged to his brother, and on whose account that brother had been thrown off by his family—it was beyond her comprehension to make out. To her own heart it was a delightful affair, to her imagination it was even a ridiculous one; but to her reason, her judgment, it was completely a puzzle.

Edward could only attempt an explanation by supposing that perhaps at first accidentally meeting, the vanity of the one had been so worked on by the flattery of the other, as to lead by degrees to all the rest. Elinor remembered what Robert had told her in Harley Street, of his opinion of what his own mediation in his brother's affairs might have done, if applied to in time. She repeated it to Edward.

"*That* was exactly like Robert," was his immediate observation. "And *that*," he presently added, "might perhaps be in *his* head when the acquaintance between them first began. And Lucy perhaps at first might think only of procuring his good offices in my favour. Other designs might afterwards arise."

How long it had been carrying on between them, however, he was equally at a loss with herself to make out; for at Oxford, where he had remained by choice ever since his quitting London, he had had no means of hearing of her but from herself, and her letters to the very last were neither less frequent nor less affectionate than usual. Not the smallest suspicion, therefore, had ever occurred to prepare him for what followed; and when at last it burst on him in a letter from Lucy herself, he had been for some time, he believed, half stupefied between the wonder, the horror, and the joy, of such a deliverance. He put the letter into Elinor's hands:

"DEAR SIR,—Being very sure I have long lost your affections, I have thought myself at liberty to bestow my own on another, and have no doubt of being as happy with him as I once used to think I might be with you; but I scorn to accept a hand while the heart was another's. Sincerely wish you happy in your choice, and it shall not be my fault if we are not always good friends, as our near relationship now makes proper. I can safely say I owe you no ill-will, and am sure you will be too generous to do us any ill offices. Your brother has gained my affections entirely, and as we could not live without one another, we are just returned from the altar, and are now on our way to Dawlish for a few weeks, which place your dear brother has great curiosity to see, but thought I would first trouble you with these few lines, and shall always remain,—Your sincere well-wisher, friend, and sister,

"LUCY FERRARS.

"I have burnt all your letters, and will return your picture the first opportunity. Please to destroy my scrawls; but the ring, with my hair, you are very welcome to keep."

Elinor read and returned it without any comment.

"I will not ask your opinion of it as a composition," said Edward. "For worlds would not I have had a letter of hers seen by *you* in former days. In a sister it is bad enough, but in a wife! How I have blushed over the pages of her writing! and I believe I may say that since the first half-year of our foolish business—this is the only letter I ever received from her, of which the substance made me any amends for the defect of the style."

"However it may have come about," said Elinor, after a pause, "they are certainly married. And your mother has brought on herself a most appropriate punishment. The independence she settled on Robert, through resentment against you, has put it in his power to make his own choice; and she has actually been bribing one son with a thousand a year to do the very deed which she disinherited the other for intending to do. She will hardly be less hurt, I suppose, by Robert's marrying Lucy than she would have been by your marrying her."

"She will be more hurt by it, for Robert always was her favourite. She will be more hurt by it, and on the same principle will forgive him much sooner."

In what state the affair stood at present between them Edward knew not, for no communication with any of his family had yet been attempted by him. He had quitted Oxford within four-and-twenty hours after Lucy's letter arrived, and with only one object before him, the nearest road to Barton, had had no leisure to form any scheme of conduct with which that road did not hold the most intimate connection. He could do nothing till he were assured of his fate with Miss Dashwood; and by his rapidity in seeking *that* fate, it is to be supposed, in spite of the jealousy with which he had once thought of Colonel Brandon—in spite of the modesty with which he rated his own deserts, and the politeness with which he talked of his doubts, he did not, upon the whole, expect a very cruel reception. It was his business, however, to say that he *did*, and he said it very prettily. What he might say on the subject a twelvemonth after, must be referred to the imagination of husbands and wives.

That Lucy had certainly meant to deceive, to go off with a flourish of malice against him in her message by Thomas was perfectly clear to Elinor; and Edward himself, now thoroughly enlightened on her character, had no scruple in believing her capable of the utmost meanness of wanton ill-nature. Though his eyes had been long opened, even before his acquaintance with Elinor began, to her ignorance and a want of liberality in some of her opinions, they had been equally imputed by him to her want of education; and till her last letter reached him he had always believed her to be a well-disposed, good-hearted girl, and thoroughly attached to himself. Nothing but such a persuasion could have prevented his putting an end to an engagement which, long before the discoverey of it laid him open to his mother's anger, had been a continual source of disquiet and regret to him.

"I thought it my duty," said he, "independent of my feelings, to give her the option of continuing the engagement or not, when I was renounced by my mother, and stood to all appearance without a friend in the world to assist me. In such a situation as that, where there seemed nothing to tempt the avarice or the vanity of any living creature, how could I suppose, when she so earnestly, so warmly insisted on sharing my fate, whatever it might be, that anything but the most disinterested affection was her inducement? And even now, I cannot comprehend on what motive she acted, or what fancied advantage it could be to her, to be fettered to a man for whom she had not the smallest regard, and who had only two thousand pounds in the world. She could not foresee that Colonel Brandon would give me a living."

"No, but she might suppose that something would occur in your favour; that your own family might in time relent. And at any rate, she lost nothing by continuing the engagement, for she has proved that it fettered neither her inclination nor her actions. The connection was certainly a respectable one, and probably gained her consideration among her friends; and if nothing more advantageous occurred, it would be better for her to marry *you* than be single."

Edward was of course immediately convinced that nothing could have been more natural than Lucy's conduct, nor more self-evident than the motive of it.

Elinor scolded him, harshly as ladies always scold the imprudence which compliments themselves, for having spent so much time with them at Norland, when he must have felt his own inconstancy.

"Your behaviour was certainly very wrong," said she, "because—to say nothing of my own conviction—our relations were all led away by it to fancy and expect *what*, as you were *then* situated, could never be."

He could only plead an ignorance of his own heart, and a mistaken confidence in the force of his engagement.

"I was simple enough to think that, because my *faith* was plighted to another, there could be no danger in my being with you; and that the consciousness of my engagement was to keep my heart as safe and sacred as my honour. I felt that I admired you, but I told myself it was only friendship; and till I began to make comparisons between yourself and Lucy, I did not know how far I was got. After that, I suppose, I *was* wrong in remaining so much in Sussex, and the arguments with which I reconciled myself to the expediency of it were no better than these:—The danger is my own; I am doing no injury to anybody but myself."

Elinor smiled and shook her head.

Edward heard with pleasure of Colonel Brandon's being expected at the cottage, as he really wished not only to be better acquainted with him, but to have an opportunity of convincing him that he no longer resented his giving him the living of Delaford—"Which at present," said he, "after thanks so ungraciously delivered as mine were on the occasion he must think I have never forgiven him for offering."

Now he felt astonished himself that he had never yet been to the place.

But so little interest had he taken in the matter, that he owed all his knowledge of the house, garden, and glebe, extent of the parish, condition of the land, and rate of the tithes, to Elinor herself, who had heard so much of it from Colonel Brandon, and heard it with so much attention as to be entirely mistress of the subject.

One question after this only remained undecided between them, one difficulty only was to be overcome. They were brought together by mutual affection, with the warmest approbation of their real friends; their intimate knowledge of each other seemed to make their happiness certain —and they only wanted something to live upon. Edward had two thousand pounds, and Elinor one, which, with Delaford living, was all that they could call their own; for it was impossible that Mrs. Dashwood should advance anything, and they were neither of them quite enough in love to think that three hundred and fifty pounds a year would supply them with the comforts of life.

Edward was not entirely without hopes of some favourable change in his mother towards him; and on *that* he rested for the residue of their income. But Elinor had no such dependence; for, since Edward would still be unable to marry Miss Morton, and his choosing herself had been spoken of in Mrs. Ferrars's flattering language as only a lesser evil than his choosing Lucy Steele, she feared that Robert's offence would serve no other purpose than to enrich Fanny.

About four days after Edward's arrival, Colonel Brandon appeared, to complete Mrs. Dashwood's satisfaction, and to give her the dignity of having, for the first time since her living at Barton, more company with her than her house would hold. Edward was allowed to retain the privilege of first-comer, and Colonel Brandon therefore walked every night to his old quarters at the Park; from whence he usually returned in the morning, early enough to interrupt the lovers' first *tête-à-tête* before breakfast.

A three weeks' residence at Delaford, where, in his evening hours at least, he had little to do but to calculate the disproportion between thirty-six and seventeen, brought him to Barton in a temper of mind which needed all the improvement in Marianne's looks, all the kindness of her welcome, and all the encouragement of her mother's language, to make it cheerful. Among such friends, however, and such flattery, he did revive. No rumour of Lucy's marriage had yet reached him; he knew nothing of what had passed, and the first hours of his visit were consequently spent in hearing and in wondering. Everything was explained to him by Mrs. Dashwood, and he found fresh reason to rejoice in what he had done for Mr. Ferrars, since eventually it promoted the interest of Elinor.

It would be needless to say that the gentlemen advanced in the good opinion of each other as they advanced in each other's acquaintance, for it could not be otherwise. Their resemblance in good principles and good sense, in disposition and manner of thinking, would probably have been sufficient to unite them in friendship, without any other attraction; but their being in love with two sisters, and two sisters fond of each other, made that mutual regard inevitable and immediate, which might otherwise have waited the effect of time and judgment.

The letters from town, which a few days before would have made every nerve in Elinor's body thrill with transport, now arrived to be read with less emotion than mirth. Mrs. Jennings wrote to tell the wonderful tale, to vent her honest indignation against the jilting girl, and pour forth her compassion towards poor Mr. Edward, who, she was sure, had quite doted upon the worthless hussy, and was now, by all accounts, almost brokenhearted, at Oxford. "I do think," she continued, "nothing was ever carried on so sly; for it was but two days before Lucy called and sat a couple of hours with me. Not a soul suspected anything of the matter, not even Nancy, who, poor soul! came crying to me the day after, in a great fright for fear of Mrs. Ferrars, as well as not knowing how to get to Plymouth; for Lucy, it seems, borrowed all her money before she went off to be married, on purpose, we suppose, to make a show with, and poor Nancy had not seven shillings in the world; so I was very glad to give her five guineas, to take her down to Exeter, where she thinks of staying three or four weeks with Mrs. Burgess, in hopes, as I tell her, to fall in with the Doctor again. And I must say that Lucy's crossness not to take her along with them in the chaise, is worse than all. Poor Mr. Edward! I cannot get him out of my head, but you must send for him to Barton, and Miss Marianne must try to comfort him."

Mr. Dashwood's strains were more solemn. Mrs. Ferrars was the most unfortunate of women—poor Fanny had suffered agonies of sensibility—and he considered the existence of each, under such a blow, with grateful wonder. Robert's offence was unpardonable, but Lucy's was infinitely worse. Neither of them was ever again to be mentioned to Mrs. Ferrars; and, even if she might hereafter be induced to forgive her son, his wife should never be acknowledged as her daughter, nor be permitted to appear in her presence. The secrecy with which everything had been carried on between them was rationally treated as enormously heightening the crime, because had any suspicion of it occurred to the others, proper measures would have been taken to prevent the marriage; and he called on Elinor to join with him in regretting that Lucy's engagement with Edward had not rather been fulfilled, than that she should thus be the means of spreading misery further in the family. He thus continued:

"Mrs. Ferrars has never yet mentioned Edward's name, which does not surprise us: but, to our great astonishment, not a line has been received from him on the occasion. Perhaps, however, he is kept silent by his fear of offending, and I shall therefore give him a hint, by a line to Oxford, that his sister and I both think a letter of proper submission from him, addressed perhaps to Fanny, and by her shown to her mother, might not be taken amiss; for we all know the tenderness of Mrs. Ferrars's heart, and that she wishes for nothing so much as to be on good terms with her children."

This paragraph was of some importance to the prospects and conduct of Edward. It determined him to attempt a reconciliation, though not exactly in the manner pointed out by their brother and sister.

"A letter of proper submission!" repeated he; "would they have me beg my mother's pardon for Robert's ingratitude to *her*, and breach of honour to *me?* I can make no submission—I am grown neither humble nor penitent by what has passed. I am grown very happy, but that would not interest. I know of no submission that *is* proper for me to make."

"You may certainly ask to be forgiven," said Elinor, "because you have offended; and I should think you might *now* venture so far as to profess some concern for having ever formed the engagement which drew on you your mother's anger."

He agreed that he might.

"And when she has forgiven you, perhaps a little humility may be convenient while acknowledging a second engagement, almost as imprudent in *her* eyes as the first."

He had nothing to urge against it, but still resisted the idea of a letter of proper submission; and therefore to make it easier to him, as he declared a much greater willingness to make mean concessions by word of mouth than on paper, it was resolved that, instead of writing Fanny, he should go to London, and personally intreat her good offices in his favour. "And if they really *do* interest themselves," said Marianne, in her new character of candour, "in bringing about a reconciliation, I shall think that even John and Fanny are not entirely without merit."

After a visit on Colonel Brandon's side of only three or four days, the two gentlemen quitted Barton together. They were to go immediately to Delaford, that Edward might have some personal knowledge of his future home, and assist his patron and friend in deciding on what improvements were needed to it; and from thence, after staying a couple of nights he was to proceed on his journey to town.

Chapter 50

AFTER a proper resistance on the part of Mrs. Ferrars, just so violent and so steady as to preserve her from that reproach which she always seemed fearful of incurring, the reproach of being too amiable, Edward was admitted to her presence, and pronounced to be again her son.

Her family had of late been exceedingly fluctuating. For many years of her life she had had two sons; but the crime and annihilation of Edward, a few weeks ago, had robbed her of one; the similar annihilation of Robert had left her for a fortnight without any; and now, by the resuscitation of Edward, she had one again.

In spite of his being allowed once more to live, however, he did not feel the continuance of his existence secure, till he had revealed his present engagement; for the publication of that circumstance, he feared might give a sudden turn to his constitution, and carry him off as rapidly as before. With apprehensive caution therefore it was revealed, and he was listened to with unexpected calmness. Mrs. Ferrars at first reasonably endeavoured to dissuade him from marrying Miss Dashwood, by every argument in her power; told him, that in Miss Morton he would have a woman of higher rank and larger fortune; and enforced the assertion by observing that Miss Morton was the daughter of a nobleman with thirty thousand pounds, while Miss Dashwood was only the daughter cf a private gentleman, with no more than *three;* but when she found that, though perfectly admitting the truth of her representation, he was by no means inclined to be guided by it, she judged it wisest, from the experience of the past, to submit—and therefore, after such an ungracious delay as she owed to her own dignity, and as served to prevent every suspicion of good-will, she issued her decree of consent to the marriage of Edward and Elinor.

What she would engage to do towards augmenting their income was next to be considered: and here it plainly appeared, that though Edward was now her only son, he was by no means her eldest; for while Robert was inevitably endowed with a thousand pounds a year, not the smallest objection was made against Edward's taking orders for the sake of two hundred and fifty at the utmost; nor was anything promised either for the present or in future, beyond the ten thousand pounds, which had been given with Fanny.

It was as much, however, as was desired, and more than was expected, by Edward and Elinor; and Mrs. Ferrars herself, by her shuffling excuses, seemed the only person surprised at her not giving more.

With an income quite sufficient to their wants thus secured to them, they had nothing to wait for after Edward was in possession of the living, but the readiness of the house, to which Colonel Brandon, with an eager desire for the accommodation of Elinor, was making considerable improvements; and after waiting some time for their completion—after experiencing, as usual, a thousand disappointments and delays, from the unaccountable dilatoriness of the workmen, Elinor, as usual, broke through the first positive resolution of not marrying till everything was ready, and the ceremony took place in Barton church early in the autumn.

The first month after their marriage was spent with their friend at the mansion-house, from whence they could superintend the progress of the parsonage, and direct everything as they liked on the spot; could choose papers, project shrubberies, and invent a sweep. Mrs. Jennings's prophecies, though rather jumbled together, were chiefly fulfilled; for she was able to visit Edward and his wife in their parsonage by Michaelmas, and she found in Elinor and her husband, as she really believed, one of the happiest couples in the world. They had in fact nothing to wish for, but the marriage of Colonel Brandon and Marianne, and rather better pasturage for their cows.

They were visited on their first settling by almost all their relations.and friends. Mrs. Ferrars came to inspect the happiness which she was almost ashamed of having authorised, and even the Dashwoods were at the expense of a journey from Sussex to do them honour.

"I will not say that I am disappointed, my dear sister," said John, as they were walking together one morning before the gates of Delaford House—"*that* would be saying too much, for certainly you have been one of the most fortunate young women in the world, as it is. But, I confess, it would give me great pleasure to call Colonel Brandon brother. His property here, his place, his house, everything in such respectable and excellent condition! and his woods! I have not seen such timber anywhere in Dorsetshire as there is now standing in Delaford hangar! And though, perhaps, Marianne may not seem exactly the person to attract him, yet I think it would altogether be advisable for you to have them now frequently staying with you, for as Colonel Brandon seems a great deal at home, nobody can tell what may happen—for, when people are much thrown together, and see little of anybody else—and it will always be in your power to set her off to advantage, and so forth; in short, you may as well give her a chance. You understand me."

But though Mrs. Ferrars *did* come to see them, and always treated them with the make-believe of decent affection, they were never insulted by her real favour and preference. *That* was due to the folly of Robert, and the cunning of his wife; and it was earned by them before many months had passed away. The selfish sagacity of the latter, which had at first drawn Robert into the scrape, was the principal instrument of his deliverance from it, for her respectful humility, assiduous attentions, and endless flatteries, as soon as the smallest opening was given for their exercise, reconciled Mrs. Ferrars to his choice, and re-established him completely in her favour.

The whole of Lucy's behaviour in the affair, and the prosperity which crowned it, therefore, may be held forth as a most encouraging instance of what an earnest, an unceasing attention to self-interest, however its progress may be apparently obstructed, will do in securing every advantage of fortune, with no other sacrifice than that of time and conscience. When Robert first sought her acquaintance, and privately visited her in Bartlett's Buildings, it was only with the view imputed to him by his brother. He merely meant to persuade her to give up the engagement; and as there could be nothing to overcome but the affection of both, he naturally expected that one or two interviews would settle the matter. In that point, however, and that only, he erred; for though Lucy soon gave him hopes that his eloquence would convince her in *time*, another visit, another conversation, was always wanted to produce this conviction. Some doubts always lingered in her mind when they parted, which could only be removed by another half-hour's discourse with himself. His attendance was by this means secured, and the rest followed in course. Instead of talking of Edward, they came gradually to talk only of Robert, a subject on which he had always more to say than on any other, and in which she soon betrayed an interest even equal to his own; and in short, it became speedily evident to both, that he had entirely supplanted his brother. He was proud of his conquest, proud of tricking Edward, and very proud of marrying privately without his mother's consent. What immediately followed is known. They passed some months in great happiness at Dawlish; for she had many relations and old acquaintances to cut—and he drew several plans for magnificent cottages; and from thence returning to town, procured the forgiveness of Mrs. Ferrars, by the simple expedient of asking it, which, at Lucy's instigation, was adopted. The forgiveness at first, indeed, as was reasonable, comprehended only Robert; and Lucy, who had owed his mother no duty, and therefore could have transgressed none, still remained some weeks longer unpardoned. But perseverance in humility of conduct, and messages, in self-condemnation for Robert's offence, and gratitude for the unkindness she was treated with, procured her in time the haughty notice which overcame her by its graciousness, and led soon afterwards, by rapid degrees, to the highest state of affection and influence. Lucy became as necessary to Mrs. Ferrars, as either Robert or Fanny; and while Edward was never cordially forgiven for having once intended to marry her, and Elinor, though superior to her in fortune and birth, was spoken of as an intruder, *she* was in everything considered, and always openly acknowledged, to be a favourite child. They settled in town, received very liberal assistance from Mrs. Ferrars, were on the best of terms imaginable with the Dashwoods, and setting aside the jealousies and ill-will continually subsisting between Fanny and Lucy, in which their husbands of course took a part, as well as the frequent domestic disagreements between Robert and Lucy themselves, nothing could exceed the harmony in which they all lived together.

What Edward had done to forfeit the right of eldest son, might have puzzled many people to find out; and what Robert had done to succeed to it, might have puzzled them still more. It was an arrangement, however, justified in its effects, if not in its cause; for nothing ever appeared in Robert's style of living, or of talking, to give a suspicion of his regretting the extent of his income, as either leaving his brother too little, or bringing himself too much; and if Edward might be judged from the ready discharge of his duties in every particular, from an increasing attachment to his wife and his home, and from the regular cheerfulness of his spirits, he might be supposed no less contented with his lot, no less free from every wish of an exchange.

Elinor's marriage divided her as little from her family as could well be contrived, without rendering the cottage at Barton entirely useless, for her mother and sisters spent much more than half their time with her. Mrs. Dashwood was acting on motives of policy as well as pleasure in the frequency of her visits at Delaford: for her wish of bringing Marianne and Colonel Brandon together was hardly less earnest, though rather more liberal, than what John had expressed. It was now her darling object. Precious as was the company of her daughter to her, she desired nothing so much as to give up its constant enjoyment to her valued friend; and to see Marianne settled at the mansion-house was equally the wish of Edward and Elinor. They each felt his sorrows and their own obligations, and Marianne, by general consent, was to be the reward of all.

With such a confederacy against her—with a knowledge so intimate of his goodness—with a conviction of his fond attachment to herself, which at last, though long after it was observable to everybody else, burst on her—what could she do?

Marianne Dashwood was born to an extraordinary fate. She was born to discover the falsehood of her own opinions, and to counteract, by her conduct, her most favourite maxims. She was born to overcome an affection formed so late in life as at seventeen, and with no sentiment superior to strong esteem and lively friendship, voluntarily to give her hand to another! and *that* other, a man who had suffered no less than herself under the event of a former attachment, whom, two years before, she had considered too old to be married, and who still sought the constitutional safeguard of a flannel waistcoat.

But so it was. Instead of falling a sacrifice to an irresistible passion, as once she had fondly flattered herself with expecting, instead of remaining even for ever with her mother, and finding her only pleasures in retirement and study, as afterwards in her more calm and sober judgment she had determined on, she found herself, at nineteen, submitting to new attachments, entering on new duties, placed in a new home, a wife, the mistress of a family, and the patroness of a village.

Colonel Brandon was now as happy as all those who best loved him believed he deserved to be; in Marianne he was consoled for every past affliction; her regard and her society restored his mined to animation, and his spirits to cheerfulness: and that Marianne found her own happiness in forming his, was equally the persuasion and delight of each observing friend. Marianne could never love by halves; and her whole heart became in time, as much devoted to her husband, as it had once been to Willoughby.

Willoughby could not hear of her marriage without a pang; and his punishment was soon afterwards complete in the voluntary forgiveness of Mrs. Smith, who, by stating his marriage with a woman of character, as the source of her clemency, gave him reason for believing, that had he behaved with honour towards Marianne, he might at once have been happy and rich. That his repentance of misconduct, which thus brought its own punishment, was sincere, need not be doubted; nor that he long thought of Colonel Brandon with envy, and of Marianne with regret. But that he was for ever inconsolable—that he fled from society, or contracted an habitual gloom of temper, or died of a broken heart, must not be depended on—for he did neither. He lived to exert, and frequently to enjoy himself. His wife was not always out of humour, nor his home always uncomfortable! and in his breed of horses and dogs, and in sporting of every kind, he found no inconsiderable degree of domestic felicity.

For Marianne, however—in spite of his incivility in surviving her loss—he always retained that decided regard which interested him in everything that befell her, and made her his secret standard of perfection in woman; and many a rising beauty would be slighted by him in after days as bearing no comparison with Mrs. Brandon.

Mrs. Dashwood was prudent enough to remain at the cottage, without attempting a removal to Delaford; and fortunately for Sir John and Mrs. Jennings, when Marianne was taken from them, Margaret had reached an age highly suitable for dancing, and not very ineligible for being supposed to have a lover.

Between Barton and Delaford, there was that constant communication which strong family affection would naturally dictate; and among the merits and the happiness of Elinor and Marianne, let it not be ranked as the least considerable, that though sisters, and living almost within sight of each other, they could live without disagreement between themselves, or producing coolness between their husbands.

FINIS

PRIDE AND PREJUDICE

(First Published 1813)

PRIDE AND PREJUDICE

Chapter 1

It is a truth universally acknowledged, that a single man in possession of a good fortune must be in want of a wife.

However little known the feelings or views of such a man may be on his first entering a neighbourhood, this truth is so well fixed in the minds of the surrounding families, that he is considered as the rightful property of someone or other of their daughters.

"My dear Mr. Bennet," said his lady to him one day, "have you heard that Netherfield Park is let at last?"

Mr. Bennet replied that he had not.

"But it is," returned she; "for Mrs. Long has just been here, and she told me all about it."

Mr. Bennet made no answer.

"Do not you want to know who has taken it?" cried his wife impatiently.

"*You* want to tell me, and I have no objection to hearing it."

This was invitation enough.

"Why, my dear, you must know, Mrs. Long says that Netherfield is taken by a young man of large fortune from the north of England; that he came down on Monday in a chaise and four to see the place, and was so much delighted with it, that he agreed with Mr. Morris immediately; that he is to take possession before Michaelmas, and some of his servants are to be in the house by the end of next week."

"What is his name?"

"Bingley."

"Is he married or single?"

"Oh! single, my dear, to be sure! A single man of large fortune; four or five thousand a year. What a fine thing for our girls!"

"How so? How can it affect them?"

"My dear Mr. Bennet," replied his wife, "how can you be so tiresome! You must know that I am thinking of his marrying one of them."

"Is that his design in settling here?"

"Design! Nonsense, how can you talk so! But it is very likely that he *may* fall in love with one of them, and therefore you must visit him as soon as he comes."

"I see no occasion for that. You and the girls may go, or you may send them by themselves, which perhaps will be still better, for as you are as handsome as any of them, Mr. Bingley might like you the best of the party."

"My dear, you flatter me. I certainly *have* had my share of beauty, but I do not pretend to be anything extraordinary now. When a woman has five grown-up daughters, she ought to give over thinking of her own beauty."

"In such cases, a woman has not often much beauty to think of."

"But, my dear, you must indeed go and see Mr. Bingley when he comes into the neighbourhood."

"It is more than I engage for, I assure you."

"But consider your daughters. Only think what an establishment it would be for one of them. Sir William and Lady Lucas are determined to go, merely on that account, for in general, you know, they visit no new-comers. Indeed you must go, for it will be impossible for *us* to visit him if you do not."

"You are over-scrupulous, surely. I dare say Mr. Bingley will be very glad to see you; and I will send a few lines by you to assure him of my hearty consent to his marrying whichever he chooses of the girls: though I must throw in a good word for my little Lizzy."

"I desire you will do no such thing. Lizzy is not a bit better than the others; and I am sure she is not half so handsome as Jane, nor half so good-humoured as Lydia. But you are always giving *her* the preference."

"They have none of them much to recommend them," replied he; "they are all silly and ignorant, like other girls; but Lizzy has something more of quickness than her sisters."

"Mr. Bennet, how can you abuse your own children in such a way? You take delight in vexing me. You have no compassion of my poor nerves."

"You mistake me, my dear. I have a high respect for your nerves. They are my old friends. I have heard you mention them with consideration these twenty years at least."

"Ah! You do not know what I suffer."

"But I hope you will get over it, and live to see many young men of four thousand a year come into the neighbourhood."

"It will be no use to us, if twenty such should come, since you will not visit them."

"Depend upon it, my dear, that when there are twenty, I will visit them all."

Mr. Bennet was so odd a mixture of quick parts, sarcastic humour, reserve, and caprice, that the experience of three-and-twenty years had been insufficient to make his wife understand his character. *Her* mind was less difficult to develop. She was a woman of mean understanding, little information, and uncertain temper. When she was discontented, she fancied herself nervous. The business of her life was to get her daughters married; its solace was visiting and news.

Chapter 2

Mr. Bennet was among the earliest of those who waited on Mr. Bingley. He had always intended to visit him, though to the last always assuring his wife that he should not go; and till the evening after the visit was paid she had no knowledge of it. It was then disclosed in the following manner:—Observing his second daughter employed in trimming a hat, he suddenly addressed her with:

"I hope Mr. Bingley will like it, Lizzy."

"We are not in a way to know *what* Mr. Bingley likes," said her mother resentfully, "since we are not to visit."

"But you forget, mamma," said Elizabeth, "that we shall meet him at the assemblies, and that Mrs. Long has promised to introduce him."

"I do not believe Mrs. Long will do any such thing. She has two nieces of her own. She is a selfish, hypocritical woman, and I have no opinion of her."

"No more have I," said Mr. Bennet; "and I am glad to find that you do not depend on her serving you."

Mrs. Bennet deigned not to make any reply, but, unable to contain herself, began scolding one of her daughters.

"Don't keep coughing so, Kitty, for Heaven's sake! Have a little compassion on my nerves. You tear them to pieces."

"Kitty has no discretion in her coughs," said her father; "she times them ill."

"I do not cough for my own amusement," replied Kitty fretfully. "When is your next ball to be, Lizzy?"

"To-morrow fortnight."

"Aye, so it is," cried her mother, "and Mrs. Long does not come back till the day before; so it will be impossible for her to introduce him, for she will not know him herself."

"Then, my dear, you may have the advantage of your friend, and introduce Mr. Bingley to *her*."

"Impossible, Mr. Bennet, impossible, when I am not acquainted with him myself; how can you be so teasing?"

"I honour your circumspection. A fortnight's acquaintance is certainly very little. One cannot know what a man really is by the end of a fortnight. But if we do not venture somebody else will; and after all, Mrs. Long and her nieces must stand their chance; and, therefore, as she will think it an act of kindness, if you decline the office, I will take it on myself."

The girls stared at their father. Mrs. Bennet said only, "Nonsense, nonsense!"

"What can be the meaning of that emphatic exclamation?" cried he. "Do you consider the forms of introduction, and the stress that is laid on them, as nonsense? I cannot quite agree with you *there*. What say you,

Mary? For you are a young lady of deep reflection, I know, and read great books and make extracts."

Mary wished to say something very sensible, but knew not how.

"While Mary is adjusting her ideas," he continued, "let us return to Mr. Bingley."

"I am sick of Mr. Bingley," cried his wife.

"I am sorry to hear *that;* but why did not you tell me so before? If I had known as much this morning I certainly would not have called on him. It is very unlucky; but as I have actually paid the visit, we cannot escape the acquaintance now."

The astonishment of the ladies was just what he wished; that of Mrs. Bennet perhaps surpassing the rest; though, when the first tumult of joy was over, she began to declare that it was what she had expected all the while.

"How good it was in you, my dear Mr. Bennet! But I knew I should persuade you at last. I was sure you loved your girls too well to neglect such an acquaintance. Well, how pleased I am! and it is such a good joke, too, that you should have gone this morning and never said a word about it till now."

"Now, Kitty, you may cough as much as you choose," said Mr. Bennet; and, as he spoke, he left the room, fatigued with the raptures of his wife.

"What an excellent father you have, girls!" said she, when the door was shut. "I do not know how you will ever make him amends for his kindness; or me either, for that matter. At our time of life it is not so pleasant, I can tell you, to be making new acquaintances every day; but for your sakes, we would do anything. Lydia, my love, though you *are* the youngest, I dare say Mr. Bingley will dance with you at the next ball."

"Oh!" said Lydia stoutly, "I am not afraid; for though I *am* the youngest, I'm the tallest."

The rest of the evening was spent in conjecturing how soon he would return Mr. Bennet's visit, and determining when they should ask him to dinner.

Chapter 3

Not all that Mrs. Bennet, however, with the assistance of her five daughters, could ask on the subject, was sufficient to draw from her husband any satisfactory description of Mr. Bingley. They attacked him in various ways—with barefaced questions, ingenious suppositions, and distant surmises; but he eluded the skill of them all, and they were at last obliged to accept the second-hand intelligence of their neighbour, Lady Lucas. Her report was highly favourable. Sir William had been delighted with him. He was quite young, wonderfully handsome, extremely agreeable, and, to crown the whole, he meant to be at the next assembly with a large party. Nothing could be more delightful! To be fond of dancing was a certain step towards falling in love; and very lively hopes of Mr. Bingley's heart were entertained.

"If I can but see one of my daughters happily settled at Netherfield," said Mrs. Bennet to her husband, "and all the others equally well married, I shall have nothing to wish for."

In a few days Mr. Bingley returned Mr. Bennet's visit, and sat about ten minutes with him in his library. He had entertained hopes of being admitted to a sight of the young ladies, of whose beauty he had heard much; but he saw only the father. The ladies were somewhat more fortunate, for they had the advantage of ascertaining from an upper window that he wore a blue coat, and rode a black horse.

An invitation to dinner was soon afterwards dispatched; and already had Mrs. Bennet planned the courses that were to do credit to her housekeeping, when an answer arrived which deferred it all. Mr. Bingley was obliged to be in town the following day, and, consequently, unable to accept the honour of their invitation, etc. Mrs. Bennet was quite disconcerted. She could not imagine what business he could have in town so soon after his arrival in Hertfordshire; and she began to fear that he might be always flying about from one place to another, and never settled at Netherfield as he ought to be. Lady Lucas quieted her fears a little by starting the idea of his being gone to London only to get a large party for the ball; and a report soon followed, that Mr. Bingley was to bring twelve ladies and seven gentlemen with him to the assembly. The girls grieved over such a number of ladies, but were comforted the day before the ball by hearing, that instead of twelve he had brought only six with him from London—his five sisters and a cousin. And when the party entered the assembly room it consisted only of five altogether—Mr. Bingley, his two sisters, the husband of the eldest, and another young man.

Mr. Bingley was good-looking and gentlemanlike; he had a pleasant countenance, and easy, unaffected manners. His sisters were fine women, with an air of decided fashion. His brother-in-law, Mr. Hurst, merely looked the gentleman; but his friend Mr. Darcy soon drew the attention of the room by his fine, tall person, handsome features, noble mien, and the report which was in general circulation within five minutes after his entrance, of his having ten thousand a year. The gentlemen pronounced him to be a fine figure of a man, the ladies declared he was much handsomer than Mr. Bingley, and he was looked at with great admiration for about half the evening, till his manners gave a disgust which turned the tide of his popularity; for he was discovered to be proud; to be above his company, and above being pleased; and not all his large estate in Derbyshire could then save him from having a most forbidding, disagreeable countenance, and being unworthy to be compared with his friend.

Mr. Bingley had soon made himself acquainted with all the principal people in the room; he was lively and unreserved, danced every dance, was angry that the ball closed so early, and talked of giving one himself at Netherfield. Such amiable qualities must speak for themselves. What a contrast between him and his friend! Mr. Darcy danced only once with Mrs. Hurst and once with Miss Bingley, declined being introduced to any other lady, and spent the rest of the evening in walking about the room, speaking occasionally to one of his own party. His character was decided. He was the proudest, most disagreeable man in the world, and everybody hoped that he would never come there again. Amongst the most violent against him was Mrs. Bennet, whose dislike of his general behaviour was sharpened into particular resentment by his having slighted one of her daughters.

Elizabeth Bennet had been obliged, by the scarcity of gentlemen, to sit down for two dances; and during part of that time, Mr. Darcy had been standing near enough for her to overhear a conversation between him and Mr. Bingley, who came from the dance for a few minutes, to press his friend to join it.

"Come, Darcy," said he, "I must have you dance. I hate to see you standing about by yourself in this stupid manner. You had much better dance."

"I certainly shall not. You know how I detest it, unless I am particularly acquainted with my partner. At such an assembly as this it would be insupportable. Your sisters are engaged, and there is not another woman in the room whom it would not be a punishment to me to stand up with."

"I would not be so fastidious as you are," cried Bingley, "for a kingdom! Upon my honour, I never met with so many pleasant girls in my life as I have this evening; and there are several of them you see uncommonly pretty."

"*You* are dancing with the only handsome girl in the room," said Mr. Darcy, looking at the eldest Miss Bennet.

"Oh! she is the most beautiful creature I ever beheld! But there is one of her sisters sitting down just behind you, who is very pretty, and I dare say very agreeable. Do let me ask my partner to introduce you."

"Which do you mean?" and turning round he looked for a moment at Elizabeth, till catching her eye, he withdrew his own and coldly said: "She is tolerable, but not handsome enough to tempt *me;* I am in no humour at present to give consequence to young ladies who are slighted by other men. You had better return to your partner and enjoy her smiles, for you are wasting your time with me."

Mr. Bingley followed his advice. Mr. Darcy walked off; and Elizabeth remained with no very cordial feelings towards him. She told the story, however, with great spirit among her friends; for she had a lively, playful disposition, which delighted in anything ridiculous.

The evening altogether passed off pleasantly to the whole family. Mrs. Bennet had seen her eldest daughter much admired by the Netherfield party. Mr. Bingley had danced with her twice, and she had been distinguished by his sisters. Jane was as much gratified by this as her mother could be, though in a quieter way. Elizabeth felt Jane's pleasure. Mary had heard herself mentioned to Miss Bingley as the most accomplished girl in the neighbourhood; and Catherine and Lydia had been fortunate enough to be never without partners, which was all that they had yet learnt to care for at a ball. They returned, therefore, in good spirits to Longbourn, the village where they lived, and of which they were the principal inhabitants. They found Mr. Bennet still up. With a book he was regardless of time; and on the present occasion he had a good deal of curiosity as to the event of an evening which had raised such splendid expectations. He had rather hoped that all his wife's views on the stranger would be disappointed; but he soon found that he had a very different story to hear.

"Oh! my dear Mr. Bennet," as she entered the room, "we have had a most delightful evening, a most excellent ball. I wish you had been there. Jane was so admired, nothing could be like it. Everybody said how well she looked; and Mr. Bingley thought her quite beautiful, and danced with her twice! Only think of *that*, my dear; he actually danced with her twice! and she was the only creature in the room that he asked a second time. First of all, he asked Miss Lucas. I was so vexed to see him stand up with her! But, however, he did not admire her at all; indeed, nobody can, you know; and he seemed quite struck with Jane as she was going down the dance. So he inquired who she was, and got introduced, and asked her for the two next. Then the two third he danced with Miss King, and the two fourth with Maria Lucas, and the two fifth with Jane again, and the two sixth with Lizzy, and the *Boulanger*——"

"If he had had any compassion for *me*," cried her husband impatiently, "he would not have danced half so much! For God's sake, say no more of his partners. O that he had sprained his ankle in the first place!"

"Oh! my dear," continued Mrs. Bennet, "I am quite delighted with him. He is so excessively handsome! And his sisters are charming women. I never in my life saw anything more elegant than their dresses. I dare say the lace upon Mrs. Hurst's gown——"

Here she was interrupted again. Mr. Bennet protested against any description of finery. She was therefore obliged to seek another branch of the subject, and related, with much bitterness of spirit and some exaggeration, the shocking rudeness of Mr. Darcy.

"But I can assure you," she added, "that Lizzy does not lose much by not suiting *his* fancy; for he is a most disagreeable, horrid man, not at all worth pleasing. So high and so conceited that there was no enduring him! He walked here, and he walked there, fancying himself so very great! Not handsome enough to dance with! I wish you had been there, my dear, to have given him one of your set-downs. I quite detest the man."

Chapter 4

WHEN Jane and Elizabeth were alone, the former, who had been cautious in her praise of Mr. Bingley before, expressed to her sister how very much she admired him.

"He is just what a young man ought to be," said she, "sensible, good-humoured, lively; and I never saw such happy manners!—so much ease, with such perfect good breeding!"

"He is also handsome," replied Elizabeth; "which a young man ought likewise to be, if he possibly can. His character is thereby complete."

"I was very much flattered by his asking me to dance a second time. I did not expect such a compliment."

"Did not you? *I* did for you. But that is one great difference between us. Compliments always take *you* by surprise, and *me* never. What could be more natural than his asking you again? He could not help seeing that you were about five times as pretty as every other woman in the room. No thanks to his gallantry for that. Well, he certainly is very agreeable, and I give you leave to like him. You have liked many a stupider person."

"Dear Lizzy!"

"Oh! you are a great deal too apt, you know, to like people in general. You never see a fault in anybody. All the world are good and agreeable in your eyes. I never heard you speak ill of a human being in my life."

"I would wish not to be hasty in censuring anyone; but I always speak what I think."

"I know you do; and it is *that* which makes the wonder. With *your* good sense, to be so honestly blind to the follies and nonsense of others! Affectation of candour is common enough—one meets it everywhere. But to be candid without ostentation or design—to take the good of everybody's character and make it still better, and say nothing of the bad—belongs to you alone. And so you like this man's sisters, too, do you? Their manners are not equal to his."

"Certainly not—at first. But they are very pleasing women when you converse with them. Miss Bingley is to live with her brother, and keep his house; and I am much mistaken if we shall not find a very charming neighbour in her."

Elizabeth listened in silence, but was not convinced; their behaviour at the assembly had not been calculated to please in general; and with more quickness of observation and less pliancy of temper than her sister, and with a judgment too unassailed by any attention to herself, she was very little disposed to approve them. They were in fact very fine ladies; not deficient in good humour when they were pleased, nor in the power of being agreeable when they chose it, but proud and conceited. They were rather handsome, had been educated in one of the first private seminaries in town, had a fortune of twenty thousand pounds, were in the habit of spending more than they ought, and of associating with people of rank, and were therefore in every respect entitled to think well of themselves, and meanly of others. They were of a respectable family in the north of England; a circumstance more deeply impressed on their memories than that their brother's fortune and their own had been acquired by trade.

Mr. Bingley inherited property to the amount of nearly a hundred thousand pounds from his father, who had intended to purchase an estate, but did not live to do it. Mr. Bingley intended it likewise, and sometimes made choice of his county; but as he was now provided with a good house and the liberty of a manor, it was doubtful to many of those who best knew the easiness of his temper, whether he might not spend the remainder of his days at Netherfield, and leave the next generation to purchase.

His sisters were very anxious for his having an estate of his own; but, though he was now established only as a tenant, Miss Bingley was by no means unwilling to preside at his table—nor was Mrs. Hurst, who had married a man of more fashion than fortune, less disposed to consider his house as her home when it suited her. Mr. Bingley had not been of age two years, when he was tempted by an accidental recommendation to look at Netherfield House. He did look at it, and into it for half-an-hour—was pleased with the situation and the principal rooms, satisfied with what the owner said in its praise, and took it immediately.

Between him and Darcy there was a very steady friendship, in spite of great opposition of character. Bingley was endeared to Darcy by the easiness, openness, and ductility of his temper, though no disposition could offer a greater contrast to his own, and though with his own he never appeared dissatisfied. On the strength of Darcy's regard, Bingley had the firmest reliance, and of his judgment the highest opinion. In understanding, Darcy was the superior. Bingley was by no means deficient, but Darcy was clever. He was at the same time haughty, reserved, and fastidious, and his manners, though well-bred, were not inviting. In that respect his friend had greatly the advantage. Bingley was sure of being liked wherever he appeared, Darcy was continually giving offence.

The manner in which they spoke of the Meryton assembly was sufficiently characteristic. Bingley had never met with more pleasant people or prettier girls in his life; everybody had been most kind and attentive to him; there had been no formality, no stiffness; he had soon felt acquainted with all the room; and as to Miss Bennet, he could not conceive an angel more beautiful. Darcy, on the contrary, had seen a collection of people in whom there was little beauty and no fashion, for none of whom he had felt the smallest interest, and from none received either attention or pleasure. Miss Bennet he acknowledged to be pretty, but she smiled too much.

Mrs. Hurst and her sister allowed it to be so—but still they admired her and liked her, and pronounced her to be a sweet girl, and one whom they should not object to know more of. Miss Bennet was therefore estab-

lished as a sweet girl, and their brother felt authorised by such commendation to think of her as he chose.

Chapter 5

WITHIN a short walk of Longbourn lived a family with whom the
Bennets were particularly intimate. Sir William Lucas had been formerly
in trade in Meryton, where he had made a tolerable fortune, and risen
to the honour of knighthood by an address to the king, during his mayor-
alty. The distinction had perhaps been felt too strongly. It had given
him a disgust to his business, and to his residence in a small market
town; and, quitting them both, he had removed with his family to a house
about a mile from Meryton, denominated from that period Lucas Lodge,
where he could think with pleasure of his own importance, and, unshackled by business, occupy himself solely in being civil to all the world.
For, though elated by his rank, it did not render him supercilious; on the
contrary, he was all attention to everybody. By nature inoffensive,
friendly, and obliging, his presentation at St. James's had made him
courteous.

Lady Lucas was a very good kind of woman, not too clever to be a
valuable neighbour to Mrs. Bennet. They had several children. The eldest
of them, a sensible, intelligent young woman, about twenty-seven, was
Elizabeth's intimate friend.

That the Miss Lucases and the Miss Bennets should meet to talk over
a ball was absolutely necessary; and the morning after the assembly
brought the former to Longbourn to hear and to communicate.

"*You* began the evening well, Charlotte," said Mrs. Bennet with civil
self-command to Miss Lucas. "*You* were Mr. Bingley's first choice."

"Yes; but he seemed to like his second better."

"Oh! you mean Jane, I suppose, because he danced with her twice. To
be sure that *did* seem as if he admired her—indeed I rather believe he
did—I heard something about it—but I hardly know what—something
about Mr. Robinson."

"Perhaps you mean what I overheard between him and Mr. Robinson;
did not I mention it to you? Mr. Robinson's asking him how he liked our
Meryton assemblies, and whether he did not think there were a great
many pretty women in the room, and *which* he thought the prettiest?
and his answering immediately to the last question: 'Oh! the eldest Miss
Bennet, beyond a doubt; there cannot be two opinions on that point.' "

"Upon my word! Well, that was very decided indeed—that does seem
as if—but, however, it may all come to nothing, you know."

"*My* overhearings were more to the purpose than *yours,* Eliza," said
Charlotte. "Mr. Darcy is not so well worth listening to as his friend, is he?
—poor Eliza!—to be only just *tolerable.*"

"I beg you would not put it into Lizzy's head to be vexed by his ill-treatment, for he is such a disagreeable man, that it would be quite a misfortune to be liked by him. Mrs. Long told me last night that he sat close to her for half-an-hour without once opening his lips."

"Are you quite sure, ma'am?—is not there a little mistake?" said Jane. "I certainly saw Mr. Darcy speaking to her."

"Aye—because she asked him at last how he liked Netherfield, and he could not help answering her; but she said he seemed very angry at being spoke to."

"Miss Bingley told me," said Jane, "that he never speaks much, unless among his intimate acquaintances. With *them* he is remarkably agreeable."

"I do not beileve a word of it, my dear. If he had been so very agreeable, he would have talked to Mrs. Long. But I can guess how it was; everybody says that he is eat up with pride, and I dare say he had heard somehow that Mrs. Long does not keep a carriage, and had come to the ball in a hack chaise."

"I do not mind his not talking to Mrs. Long," said Miss Lucas, "but I wish he had danced with Eliza."

"Another time, Lizzy," said her mother, "I would not dance with *him*, if I were you."

"I believe, ma'am, I may safely promise you *never* to dance with him."

"His pride," said Miss Lucas, "does not offend *me* so much as pride often does, because there is an excuse for it. One cannot wonder that so very fine a young man, with family, fortune, everything in his favour, should think highly of himself. If I may so express it, he has a *right* to be proud."

"That is very true," replied Elizabeth, "and I could easily forgive *his* pride, if he had not mortified *mine*."

"Pride," observed Mary, who piqued herself upon the solidity of her reflections, "is a very common failing, I believe. By all that I have ever read, I am convinced that it is very common indeed; that human nature is particularly prone to it, and that there are very few of us who do not cherish a feeling of self-complacency on the score of some quality or the other, real or imaginary. Vanity and pride are different things, though the words are often used synonymously. A person may be proud without being vain. Pride relates more to our opinion of ourselves, vanity to what we would have others think of us."

"If I were as rich as Mr. Darcy," cried a young Lucas, who came with his sisters, "I should not care how proud I was. I would keep a pack of foxhounds, and drink a bottle of wine every day."

"Then you would drink a great deal more than you ought," said Mrs. Bennet; "and if I were to see you at it, I should take away your bottle directly."

The boy protested that she should not; she continued to declare that she would, and the argument ended only with the visit.

Chapter 6

THE ladies of Longbourn soon waited on those of Netherfield. The visit was soon returned in due form. Miss Bennet's pleasing manners grew on the goodwill of Mrs. Hurst and Miss Bingley; and though the mother was found to be intolerable, and the younger sisters not worth speaking to, a wish of being better acquainted with *them* was expressed towards the two eldest. By Jane, this attention was received with the greatest pleasure; but Elizabeth still saw superciliousness in their treatment of everybody, hardly excepting even her sister, and could not like them; though their kindness to Jane, such as it was, had a value as arising in all probability from the influence of their brother's admiration. It was generally evident whenever they met, that he *did* admire her; and to *her* it was equally evident that Jane was yielding to the preference which she had begun to entertain for him from the first, and was in a way to be very much in love; but she considered with pleasure that it was not likely to be discovered by the world in general, since Jane united, with great strength of feeling, a composure of temper and a uniform cheerfulness of manner which would guard her from the suspicions of the impertinent. She mentioned this to her friend Miss Lucas.

"It may perhaps be pleasant," replied Charlotte, "to be able to impose on the public in such a case; but it is sometimes a disadvantage to be so very guarded. If a woman conceals her affection with the same skill from the object of it, she may lose the opportunity of fixing him; and it will then be but poor consolation to believe the world equally in the dark. There is so much of gratitude or vanity in almost every attachment, that it is not safe to leave any to itself. We can all *begin* freely—a slight preference is natural enough: but there are very few of us who have heart enough to be really in love without encouragement. In nine cases out of ten a woman had better show *more* affection than she feels. Bingley likes your sister, undoubtedly; but he may never do more than like her, if she does not help him on."

"But she does help him on, as much as her nature will allow. If *I* can perceive her regard for him, he must be a simpleton, indeed, not to discover it too."

"Remember, Eliza, that he does not know Jane's disposition as you do."

"But if a woman is partial to a man, and does not endeavour to conceal it, he must find it out."

"Perhaps he must, if he sees enough of her. But, though Bingley and Jane meet tolerably often, it is never for many hours together; and as they always see each other in large mixed parties, it is impossible that every moment should be employed in conversing together. Jane should therefore make the most of every half-hour in which she can command his attention. When she is secure of him, there will be leisure for falling in love as much as she chooses."

"Your plan is a good one," replied Elizabeth, "where nothing is in question but the desire of being well married, and if I were determined to get a rich husband, or any husband, I dare say I should adopt it. But these are not Jane's feelings; she is not acting by design. As yet, she cannot even be certain of the degree of her own regard nor of its reasonableness. She has known him only a fortnight. She danced four dances with him at Meryton; she saw him one morning at his own house, and has since dined in company with him four times. This is not quite enough to make her understand his character."

"Not as you represent it. Had she merely *dined* with him, she might only have discovered whether he had a good appetite; but you must remember that four evenings have been also spent together—and four evenings may do a great deal."

"Yes; these four evenings have enabled them to ascertain that they both like Vingt-un better than Commerce; but with respect to any other leading characteristic, I do not imagine that much has been unfolded."

"Well," said Charlotte, "I wish Jane success with all my heart; and if she were married to him to-morrow, I should think she had as good a chance of happiness as if she were to be studying his character for a twelvemonth. Happiness in marriage is entirely a matter of chance. If the dispositions of the parties are ever so well known to each other or ever so similar beforehand, it does not advance their felicity in the least. They always continue to grow sufficiently unlike afterwards to have their share of vexation; and it is better to know as little as possible of the defects of the person with whom you are to pass your life."

"You make me laugh, Charlotte; but it is not sound. You know it is not sound, and that you would never act in this way yourself."

Occupied in observing Mr. Bingley's attentions to her sister, Elizabeth was far from suspecting that she was herself becoming an object of some interest in the eyes of his friend. Mr. Darcy had at first scarcely allowed her to be pretty; he had looked at her without admiration at the ball; and when they next met, he looked at her only to criticise. But no sooner had he made it clear to himself and his friends that she had hardly a good feature in her face, than he began to find it was rendered uncommonly intelligent by the beautiful expression of her dark eyes. To this discovery succeeded some others equally mortifying. Though he had detected with a critical eye more than one failure of perfect symmetry in her form, he was forced to acknowledge her figure to be light and pleasing; and in spite of his asserting that her manners were not those of the fashionable world, he was caught by their easy playfulness. Of this was she perfectly unaware; to her he was only the man who made himself agreeable nowhere, and who had not thought her handsome enough to dance with.

He began to wish to know more of her, and as a step towards conversing with her himself, attended to her conversation with others. His doing so drew her notice. It was at Sir William Lucas's, where a large party were assembled.

"What does Mr. Darcy mean," said she to Charlotte, "by listening to my conversation with Colonel Forster?"

"That is a question which Mr. Darcy only can answer."

"But if he does it any more I shall certainly let him know that I see what he is about. He has a very satirical eye, and if I do not begin by being impertinent myself, I shall soon grow afraid of him."

On his approaching them soon afterwards, though without seeming to have any intention of speaking, Miss Lucas defied her friend to mention such a subject to him; which immediately provoking Elizabeth to do it, she turned to him and said:

"Did not you think, Mr. Darcy, that I expressed myself uncommonly well just now, when I was teasing Colonel Forster to give us a ball at Meryton?"

"With great energy; but it is a subject which always makes a lady energetic."

"You are severe on us."

"It will be *her* turn soon to be teased," said Miss Lucas. "I am going to open the instrument, Eliza, and you know what follows."

"You are a very strange creature by way of a friend!—always wanting me to play and sing before anybody and everybody! If my vanity had taken a musical turn, you would have been invaluable; but as it is, I would really rather not sit down before those who must be in the habit of hearing the very best performers." On Miss Lucas's persevering, however, she added, "Very well; if it must be so, it must." And gravely glancing at Mr. Darcy, "There is a fine old saying, which everybody here is of course familiar with: 'Keep your breath to cool your porridge'; and I shall keep mine to swell my song."

Her performance was pleasing, though by no means capital. After a song or two, and before she could reply to the entreaties of several that she would sing again, she was eagerly succeeded at the instrument by her sister Mary, who having, in consequence of being the only plain one in the family, worked hard for knowledge and accomplishments, was always impatient for display.

Mary had neither genius nor taste; and though vanity had given her application, it had given her likewise a pedantic air and conceited manner, which would have injured a higher degree of excellence than she had reached. Elizabeth, easy and unaffected, had been listened to with much more pleasure, though not playing half so well; and Mary, at the end of a long concerto, was glad to purchase praise and gratitude by Scotch and Irish airs, at the request of her younger sisters, who, with some of the Lucases, and two or three officers, joined eagerly in dancing at one end of the room.

Mr. Darcy stood near them in silent indignation at such a mode of passing the evening, to the exclusion of all conversation, and was too much engrossed by his thoughts to perceive that Sir William Lucas was his neighbour, till Sir William thus began:

"What a charming amusement for young people this is, Mr. Darcy! There is nothing like dancing after all. I consider it as one of the first refinements of polished societies."

"Certainly, sir; and it has the advantage also of being in vogue amongst the less polished societies of the world. Every savage can dance."

Sir William only smiled. "Your friend performs delightfully," he continued after a pause, on seeing Bingley join the group; "and I doubt not that you are an adept in the science yourself, Mr. Darcy."

"You saw me dance at Meryton, I believe, sir."

"Yes, indeed, and received no inconsiderable pleasure from the sight. Do you often dance at St. James's?"

"Never, sir."

"Do you not think it would be a proper compliment to the place?"

"It is a compliment which I never pay to any place if I can avoid it."

"You have a house in town, I conclude?"

Mr. Darcy bowed.

"I had once some thoughts of fixing in town myself—for I am fond of superior society; but I did not feel quite certain that the air of London would agree with Lady Lucas."

He paused in hopes of an answer; but his companion was not disposed to make any; and Elizabeth at that instant moving towards them, he was struck with the action of doing a very gallant thing, and called out to her:

"My dear Miss Eliza, why are not you dancing? Mr. Darcy, you must allow me to present this young lady to you as a very desirable partner. You cannot refuse to dance, I am sure, when so much beauty is before you." And, taking her hand, he would have given it to Mr. Darcy who, though extremely surprised, was not unwilling to receive it, when she instantly drew back, and said with some discomposure to Sir William:

"Indeed, sir, I have not the least intention of dancing. I entreat you not to suppose that I moved this way in order to beg for a partner."

Mr. Darcy, with grave propriety, requested to be allowed the honour of her hand, but in vain. Elizabeth was determined; nor did Sir William at all shake her purpose by his attempt at persuasion.

"You excel so much in the dance, Miss Eliza, that it is cruel to deny me the happiness of seeing you; and though this gentleman dislikes the amusement in general, he can have no objection, I am sure, to oblige us for one half-hour."

"Mr. Darcy is all politeness," said Elizabeth, smiling.

"He is indeed; but considering the inducement, my dear Miss Eliza, we cannot wonder at his complaisance—for who would object to such a partner?"

Elizabeth looked archly, and turned away. Her resistance had not injured her with the gentleman, and he was thinking of her with some complacency, when thus accosted by Miss Bingley:

"I can guess the subject of your reverie."

"I should imagine not."

"You are considering how insupportable it would be to pass many evenings in this manner—in such society; and indeed I am quite of your opinion. I was never more annoyed! The insipidity, and yet the noise— the nothingness, and yet the self-importance of all those people! What would I give to hear your strictures on them!"

"Your conjecture is totally wrong, I assure you. My mind was more agreeably engaged. I have been meditating on the very great pleasure which a pair of fine eyes in the face of a pretty woman can bestow."

Miss Bingley immediately fixed her eyes on his face, and desired he would tell her what lady had the credit of inspiring such reflections. Mr. Darcy replied with great intrepidity:

"Miss Elizabeth Bennet."

"Miss Elizabeth Bennet!" repeated Miss Bingley. "I am all astonishment. How long has she been such a favourite?—and pray, when am I to wish you joy?"

"That is exactly the question which I expected you to ask. A lady's imagination is very rapid; it jumps from admiration to love, from love to matrimony, in a moment. I knew you would be wishing me joy."

"Nay, if you are serious about it, I shall consider the matter is absolutely settled. You will have a charming mother-in-law, indeed; and, of course, she will be always at Pemberley with you."

He listened to her with perfect indifference while she chose to entertain herself in this manner; and as his composure convinced her that all was safe, her wit flowed long.

Chapter 7

Mr. Bennet's property consisted almost entirely in an estate of two thousand a year, which, unfortunately for his daughters, was entailed, in default of heirs male, on a distant relation; and their mother's fortune, though ample for her situation in life, could but ill supply the deficiency of his. Her father had been an attorney in Meryton, and had left her four thousand pounds.

She had a sister married to a Mr. Philips, who had been a clerk to their father and succeeded him in the business, and a brother settled in London in a respectable line of trade.

The village of Longbourn was only one mile from Meryton; a most convenient distance for the young ladies, who were usually tempted thither three or four times a week, to pay their duty to their aunt and to a milliner's shop just over the way. The two youngest of the family, Catherine and Lydia, were particularly frequent in these attentions; their minds were more vacant than their sisters', and when nothing better offered, a walk to Meryton was necessary to amuse their morning hours and furnish conversation for the evening; and however bare of news the country in general might be, they always contrived to learn some from their aunt. At present, indeed, they were well supplied both with news and happiness by the recent arrival of a militia regiment in the neighbour-hood; it was to remain the whole winter, and Meryton was the head-quarters.

Their visits to Mrs. Philips were now productive of the most interesting intelligence. Every day added something to their knowledge of the officers' names and connections. Their lodgings were not long a secret, and at length they began to know the officers themselves. Mr. Philips visited them all, and this opened to his nieces a source of felicity unknown before. They could talk of nothing but officers; and Mr. Bingley's large fortune, the mention of which gave animation to their mother, was worthless in their eyes when opposed to the regimentals of an ensign.

After listening one morning to their effusions on this subject, Mr. Bennet coolly observed:

"From all that I can collect by your manner of talking, you must be two of the silliest girls in the country. I have suspected it some time, but I am now convinced."

Catherine was disconcerted, and made no answer; but Lydia, with perfect indifference, continued to express her admiration of Captain Carter, and her hope of seeing him in the course of the day, as he was going the next morning to London.

"I am astonished, my dear," said Mrs. Bennet, "that you should be so ready to think your own children silly. If I wished to think slightingly of anybody's children, it should not be of my own, however."

"If my children are silly, I must hope to be always sensible of it."

"Yes—but as it happens, they are all of them very clever."

"This is the only point, I flatter myself, on which we do not agree. I had hoped that our sentiments coincided in every particular, but I must so far differ from you as to think our two youngest daughters uncom-monly foolish."

"My dear Mr. Bennet, you must not expect such girls to have the sense of their father and mother. When they get to our age, I dare say they will not think about officers any more than we do. I remember the time when I liked a red coat myself very well—and, indeed, so I do still at my heart; and if a smart young colonel, with five or six thousand a year, should want one of my girls I shall not say nay to him; and I thought Colonel Forster looked very becoming the other night at Sir William's in his regimentals."

"Mamma," cried Lydia, "my aunt says that Colonel Forster and Captain Carter do not go so often to Miss Watson's as they did when they first came; she sees them now very often standing in Clarke's library."

Mrs. Bennet was prevented replying by the entrance of the footman with a note for Miss Bennet; it came from Netherfield, and the servant waited for an answer. Mrs. Bennet's eyes sparkled with pleasure, and she was eagerly calling out, while her daughter read:

"Well, Jane, who is it from? What is it about? What does he say? Well, Jane, make haste and tell us; make haste, my love."

"It is from Miss Bingley," said Jane, and then read it aloud.

"MY DEAR FRIEND,—

"If you are not so compassionate as to dine to-day with Louisa and me, we shall be in danger of hating each other for the rest of our lives, for a whole day's *tête-à-tête* between two women can never end without a quarrel. Come as soon as you can on receipt of this. My brother and the gentlemen are to dine with the officers.—Yours ever,

"CAROLINE BINGLEY."

"With the officers!" cried Lydia. "I wonder my aunt did not tell us of *that*."

"Dining out," said Mrs. Bennet, "that is very unlucky."

"Can I have the carriage?" said Jane.

"No, my dear, you had better go on horseback, because it seems likely to rain; and then you must stay all night."

"That would be a good scheme," said Elizabeth, "if you were sure that they would not offer to send her home."

"Oh! but the gentlemen will have Mr. Bingley's chaise to go to Meryton; and the Hursts have no horses to theirs."

"I had much rather go in the coach."

"But, my dear, your father cannot spare the horses, I am sure. They are wanted in the farm, Mr. Bennet, are not they?"

"They are wanted in the farm much oftener than I can get them."

"But if you have got them to-day," said Elizabeth, "my mother's purpose will be answered."

She did at last extort from her father an acknowledgment that the horses were engaged; Jane was therefore obliged to go on horseback, and her mother attended her to the door with many cheerful prognostics of a bad day. Her hopes were answered; Jane had not been gone long before it rained hard. Her sisters were uneasy for her, but her mother was delighted. The rain continued the whole evening without intermission; Jane certainly could not come back.

"This was a lucky idea of mine, indeed!" said Mrs. Bennet more than once, as if the credit of making it rain were all her own. Till the next morning, however, she was not aware of all the felicity of her contrivance. Breakfast was scarcely over when a servant from Netherfield brought the following note for Elizabeth:

"MY DEAREST LIZZY,—

"I find myself very unwell this morning, which, I suppose, is to be imputed to my getting wet through yesterday. My kind friends will not hear of my returning home till I am better. They insist also on my seeing Mr. Jones—therefore do not be alarmed if you should hear of his having been to me—and, excepting a sore throat and headache, there is not much the matter with me.—Yours, etc."

"Well, my dear," said Mr. Bennet, when Elizabeth had read the note aloud, "if your daughter should have a dangerous fit of illness—if she should die, it would be a comfort to know that it was all in pursuit of Mr. Bingley, and under your orders."

"Oh! I am not at all afraid of her dying. People do not die of little trifling colds. She will be taken good care of. As long as she stays there, it is all very well. I would go and see her if I could have the carriage."

Elizabeth, feeling really anxious, was determined to go to her, though the carriage was not to be had; and as she was no horsewoman, walking was her only alternative. She declared her resolution.

"How can you be so silly," cried her mother, "as to think of such a thing, in all this dirt! You will not be fit to be seen when you get there."

"I shall be very fit to see Jane—which is all I want."

"Is this a hint to me, Lizzy," said her father, "to send for the horses?"

"No, indeed. I do not wish to avoid the walk. The distance is nothing when one has a motive; only three miles. I shall be back by dinner."

"I admire the activity of your benevolence," observed Mary, "but every impulse of feeling should be guided by reason; and, in my opinion, exertion should always be in proportion to what is required."

"We will go as far as Meryton with you," said Catherine and Lydia. Elizabeth accepted their company, and the three young ladies set off together.

"If we make haste," said Lydia, as they walked along, "perhaps we may see something of Captain Carter before he goes."

In Meryton they parted; the two youngest repaired to the lodgings of one of the officers' wives, and Elizabeth continued her walk alone, crossing field after field at a quick pace, jumping over stiles and springing over puddles with impatient activity, and finding herself at last within view of the house, with weary ankles, dirty stockings, and a face glowing with the warmth of exercise.

She was shown into the breakfast-parlour, where all but Jane were assembled, and where her appearance created a great deal of surprise. That she should have walked three miles so early in the day, in such dirty weather, and by herself, was almost incredible to Mrs. Hurst and Miss Bingley; and Elizabeth was convinced that they held her in contempt for it. She was received, however, very politely by them; and in their brother's manners there was something better than politeness; there was good humour and kindness. Mr. Darcy said very little, and Mr. Hurst nothing at all. The former was divided between admiration of the brilliancy which exercise had given to her complexion, and doubt as to the occasion's justifying her coming so far alone. The latter was thinking only of his breakfast.

Her inquiries after her sister were not very favourably answered. Miss

Bennet had slept ill, and though up, was very feverish, and not well enough to leave her room. Elizabeth was glad to be taken to her immediately; and Jane, who had only been withheld by the fear of giving alarm or incon-venience from expressing in her note how much she longed for such a visit, was delighted at her entrance. She was not equal, however, to much conversation, and when Miss Bingley left them together, could attempt little besides expressions of gratitude for the extraordinary kindness she was treated with. Elizabeth silently attended her.

When breakfast was over they were joined by the sisters; and Elizabeth began to like them herself, when she saw how much affection and solicitude they showed for Jane. The apothecary came, and having examined his patient, said, as might be supposed, that she had caught a violent cold, and that they must endeavour to get the better of it; advised her to return to bed, and promised her some draughts. The advice was followed readily, for the feverish symptoms increased, and her head ached acutely. Eliza-beth did not quit her room for a moment; nor were the other ladies often absent; the gentlemen being out, they had, in fact, nothing to do else-where.

When the clock struck three, Elizabeth felt that she must go, and very unwillingly said so. Miss Bingley offered her the carriage, and she only wanted a little pressing to accept it, when Jane testified such concern in parting with her, that Miss Bingley was obliged to convert the offer of the chaise into an invitation to remain at Netherfield for the present. Elizabeth most thankfully consented, and a servant was dispatched to Longbourn to acquaint the family with her stay and bring back a supply of clothes.

Chapter 8

At five o'clock the two ladies retired to dress, and at half-past six Elizabeth was summoned to dinner. To the civil inquiries which then poured in, and amongst which she had the pleasure of distinguishing the much superior solicitude of Mr. Bingley's, she could not make a very favourable answer. Jane was by no means better. The sisters, on hearing this, repeated three or four times how much they were grieved, how shocking it was to have a bad cold, and how excessively they disliked being ill themselves; and then thought no more of the matter: and their indifference towards Jane when not immediately before them restored Elizabeth to the enjoyment of all her original dislike.

Their brother, indeed, was the only one of the party whom she could regard with any complacency. His anxiety for Jane was evident, and his attentions to herself most pleasing, and they prevented her feeling herself so much an intruder as she believed she was considered by the others. She had very little notice from any but him. Miss Bingley was engrossed by Mr. Darcy, her sister scarcely less so; and as for Mr. Hurst, by whom Elizabeth sat, he was an indolent man, who lived only to eat, drink, and play at cards; who, when he found her prefer a plain dish to a ragout, had nothing to say to her.

When dinner was over, she returned directly to Jane, and Miss Bingley began abusing her as soon as she was out of the room. Her manners were pronounced to be very bad indeed, a mixture of pride and impertinence; she had no conversation, no style, no taste, no beauty. Mrs. Hurst thought the same, and added:

"She has nothing, in short, to recommend her, but being an excellent walker. I shall never forget her appearance this morning. She really looked almost wild."

"She did, indeed, Louisa. I could hardly keep my countenance. Very nonsensical to come at all! Why must *she* be scampering about the country, because her sister had a cold? Her hair, so untidy, so blowsy!"

"Yes, and her petticoat; I hope you saw her petticoat, six inches deep in mud, I am absolutely certain; and the gown which had been let down to hide it not doing its office."

"Your picture may be very exact, Louisa," said Bingley; "but this was all lost upon me. I thought Miss Elizabeth Bennet looked remarkably well when she came into the room this morning. Her dirty petticoat quite escaped my notice."

"*You* observed it, Mr. Darcy, I am sure," said Miss Bingley; "and I am inclined to think that you would not wish to see *your sister* make such an exhibition."

"Certainly not."

"To walk three miles, or four miles, or five miles, or whatever it is, above her ankles in dirt, and alone, quite alone! What could she mean by it? It seems to me to show an abominable sort of conceited independence, a most country-town indifference to decorum."

"It shows an affection for her sister that is very pleasing," said Bingley.

"I am afraid, Mr. Darcy," observed Miss Bingley, in a half whisper, "that this adventure has rather affected your admiration of her fine eyes."

"Not at all," he replied; "they were brightened by the exercise." A short pause followed this speech, and Mrs. Hurst began again:

"I have an excessive regard for Jane Bennet, she is really a very sweet girl, and I wish with all my heart she were well settled. But with such a father and mother, and such low connections, I am afraid there is no chance of it."

"I think I have heard you say that their uncle is an attorney in Meryton."

"Yes; and they have another, who lives somewhere near Cheapside."

"That is capital," added her sister, and they both laughed heartily.

"If they had uncles enough to fill *all* Cheapside," cried Bingley, "it would not make them one jot less agreeable."

"But it must very materially lessen their chance of marrying men of any consideration in the world," replied Darcy.

To this speech Bingley made no answer; but his sisters gave it their hearty assent, and indulged their mirth for some time at the expense of their dear friend's vulgar relations.

With a renewal of tenderness, however, they repaired to her room on leaving the dining-parlour, and sat with her till summoned to coffee. She was still very poorly, and Elizabeth would not quit her at all, till late in the evening, when she had the comfort of seeing her sleep, and when it appeared to her rather right than pleasant that she should go downstairs herself. On entering the drawing-room she found the whole party at loo, and was immediately invited to join them; but suspecting them to be playing high, she declined it, and making her sister the excuse, said she would amuse herself, for the short time she could stay below, with a book. Mr. Hurst looked at her with astonishment.

"Do you prefer reading to cards?" said he; "that is rather singular."

"Miss Eliza Bennet," said Miss Bingley, "despises cards. She is a great reader, and has no pleasure in anything else."

"I deserve neither such praise nor such censure," cried Elizabeth; "I am *not* a great reader, and I have pleasure in many things."

"In nursing your sister I am sure you have pleasure," said Bingley; "and I hope it will soon be increased by seeing her quite well."

Elizabeth thanked him from her heart, and then walked towards a table where a few books were lying. He immediately offered to fetch her others —all that his library afforded.

"And I wish my collection were larger for your benefit and my own credit; but I am an idle fellow, and though I have not many, I have more than I ever look into."

Elizabeth assured him that she could suit herself perfectly with those in the room.

"I am astonished," said Miss Bingley, "that my father should have left so small a collection of books. What a delightful library you have at Pemberley, Mr. Darcy!"

"It ought to be good," he replied, "it has been the work of many generations."

"And then you have added so much to it yourself, you are always buying books."

"I cannot comprehend the neglect of a family library in such days as these."

"Neglect! I am sure you neglect nothing that can add to the beauties of that noble place. Charles, when you build *your* house, I wish it may be half as delightful as Pemberley."

"I wish it may."

"But I would really advise you to make your purchase in that neighbourhood, and take Pemberley for a kind of model. There is not a finer county in England than Derbyshire."

"With all my heart; I will buy Pemberley itself if Darcy will sell it."

"I am talking of possibilities, Charles."

"Upon my word, Caroline, I should think it more possible to get Pemberley by purchase than by imitation."

Elizabeth was so much caught by what passed, as to leave her very little attention for her book; and soon laying it wholly aside, she drew near the card-table, and stationed herself between Mr. Bingley and his eldest sister, to observe the game.

"Is Miss Darcy much grown since the spring?" said Miss Bingley; "will she be as tall as I am?"

"I think she will. She is now about Miss Elizabeth Bennet's height, or rather taller."

"How I long to see her again! I never met with anybody who delighted me so much. Such a countenance, such manners! And so extremely accomplished for her age! Her performance on the pianoforte is exquisite."

"It is amazing to me," said Bingley, "how young ladies can have patience to be so very accomplished as they all are."

"All young ladies accomplished! My dear Charles, what do you mean?"

"Yes, all of them, I think. They all paint tables, cover screens, and net purses. I scarcely know anyone who cannot do all this, and I am sure I never heard a young lady spoken of for the first time, without being informed that she was very accomplished."

"Your list of the common extent of accomplishments," said Darcy, "has too much truth. The word is applied to many a woman who deserves it no otherwise than by netting a purse or covering a screen. But I am very far from agreeing with you in your estimation of ladies in general. I cannot boast of knowing more than half-a-dozen, in the whole range of my acquaintance, that are really accomplished."

"Nor I, I am sure," said Miss Bingley.

"Then," observed Elizabeth, "you must comprehend a great deal in your idea of an accomplished woman."

"Yes, I do comprehend a great deal in it."

"Oh! certainly," cried his faithful assistant, "no one can be really esteemed accomplished who does not greatly surpass what is usually met with. A woman must have a thorough knowledge of music, singing, drawing, dancing, and the modern languages, to deserve the word; and besides all this, she must possess a certain something in her air and manner of walking, the tone of her voice, her address and expressions, or the word will be but half-deserved."

"All this she must possess," added Darcy, "and to all this she must yet add something more substantial, in the improvement of her mind by extensive reading."

"I am no longer surprised at your knowing *only* six accomplished women. I rather wonder now at your knowing *any*."

"Are you so severe upon your own sex as to doubt the possibility of all this?"

"*I* never saw such a woman. *I* never saw such capacity, and taste, and application, and elegance, as you describe united."

Mrs. Hurst and Miss Bingley both cried out against the injustice of her implied doubt, and were both protesting that they knew many women who answered this description, when Mr. Hurst called them to order, with bitter complaints of their inattention to what was going forward. As all conversation was thereby at an end, Elizabeth soon afterwards left the room.

"Eliza Bennet," said Miss Bingley, when the door was closed on her, "is one of those young ladies who seek to recommend themselves to the other sex by undervaluing their own; and with many men, I dare say, it succeeds. But, in my opinion, it is a paltry device, a very mean art."

"Undoubtedly," replied Darcy, to whom this remark was chiefly addressed, "there is meanness in *all* the arts which ladies sometimes condescend to employ for captivation. Whatever bears affinity to cunning is despicable."

Miss Bingley was not so entirely satisfied with this reply as to continue the subject.

Elizabeth joined them again only to say that her sister was worse, and that she could not leave her. Bingley urged Mr. Jones being sent for immediately; while his sisters, convinced that no country advice could be of any service, recommended an express to town for one of the most eminent physicians. This she would not hear of; but she was not so unwilling to comply with their brother's proposal; and it was settled that Mr. Jones should be sent for early in the morning, if Miss Bennet were not decidedly better. Bingley was quite uncomfortable; his sisters declared that they were miserable: They solaced their wretchedness, however, by duets after supper, while he could find no better relief to his feelings than by giving his housekeeper directions that every possible attention might be paid to the sick lady and her sister.

Chapter 9

ELIZABETH passed the chief of the night in her sister's room, and in the morning had the pleasure of being able to send a tolerable answer to the inquiries which she very early received from Mr. Bingley by a housemaid, and some time afterwards from the two elegant ladies who waited on his sisters. In spite of this amendment, however, she requested to have a note sent to Longbourn, desiring her mother to visit Jane, and form her own judgment of her situation. The note was immediately dispatched, and its contents as quickly complied with. Mrs. Bennet, accompanied by her two youngest girls, reached Netherfield soon after the family breakfast.

Had she found Jane in any apparent danger, Mrs. Bennet would have been very miserable; but being satisfied on seeing her that her illness was not alarming, she had no wish of her recovering immediately, as her restoration to health would probably remove her from Netherfield. She would not listen, therefore, to her daughter's proposal of being carried home; neither did the apothecary, who arrived about the same time, think it at all advisable. After sitting a little while with Jane, on Miss Bingley's appearance and invitation, the mother and three daughters all attended her into the breakfast parlour. Bingley met them with hopes that Mrs. Bennet had not found Miss Bennet worse than she expected.

"Indeed I have, sir," was her answer. "She is a great deal too ill to be moved. Mr. Jones says we must not think of moving her. We must trespass a little longer on your kindness."

"Removed!" cried Bingley. "It must not be thought of. My sister, I am sure, will not hear of her removal."

"You may depend upon it, madam," said Miss Bingley, with cold civility, "that Miss Bennet shall receive every possible attention while she remains with us."

Mrs. Bennet was profuse in her acknowledgments.

"I am sure," she added, "if it was not for such good friends I do not know what would become of her, for she is very ill indeed, and suffers a vast deal, though with the greatest patience in the world, which is always the way with her, for she has, without exception, the sweetest temper I ever met with. I often tell my other girls they are nothing to *her*. You have a sweet room here, Mr. Bingley, and a charming prospect over the gravel walk. I do not know a place in the country that is equal to Netherfield. You will not think of quitting it in a hurry, I hope, though you have but a short lease."

"Whatever I do is done in a hurry," replied he; "and therefore if I should resolve to quit Netherfield, I should probably be off in five minutes. At present, however, I consider myself as quite fixed here."

"That is exactly what I should have supposed of you," said Elizabeth.

"You begin to comprehend me, do you?" cried he, turning towards her.

"Oh! yes—I understand you perfectly."

"I wish I might take this for a compliment; but to be so easily seen through I am afraid is pitiful."

"That is as it happens. It does not necessarily follow that a deep, intricate character is more or less estimable than such a one as yours."

"Lizzy," cried her mother, "remember where you are, and do not run on in the wild manner that you are suffered to do at home."

"I did not know before," continued Bingley immediately, "that you were a studier of character. It must be an amusing study."

"Yes, but intricate characters are the *most* amusing. They have at least that advantage."

"The country," said Darcy, "can in general supply but a few subjects for such a study. In a country neighbourhood you move in a very confined and unvarying society."

"But people themselves alter so much, that there is something new to be observed in them for ever."

"Yes, indeed," cried Mrs. Bennet, offended by his manner of mentioning a country neighbourhood. "I assure you there is quite as much of *that* going on in the country as in town."

Everybody was surprised, and Darcy, after looking at her for a moment, turned silently away. Mrs. Bennet, who fancied she had gained a complete victory over him, continued her triumph.

"I cannot see that London has any great advantage over the country, for my part, except the shops and public places. The country is a vast deal pleasanter, is not it, Mr. Bingley?"

"When I am in the country," he replied, "I never wish to leave it; and when I am in town it is pretty much the same. They have each their advantages, and I can be equally happy in either."

"Aye—that is because you have the right disposition. But that gentleman," looking at Darcy, "seemed to think the country was nothing at all."

"Indeed, mamma, you are mistaken," said Elizabeth, blushing for her mother. "You quite mistook Mr. Darcy. He only meant that there was not such a variety of people to be met with in the country as in town, which you must acknowledge to be true."

"Certainly, my dear, nobody said there were; but as to not meeting with many people in this neighbourhood, I believe there are few neighbourhoods larger. I know we dine with four-and-twenty families."

Nothing but concern for Elizabeth could enable Bingley to keep his countenance. His sister was less delicate, and directed her eyes towards Mr. Darcy with a very expressive smile. Elizabeth, for the sake of saying something that might turn her mother's thoughts, now asked her if Charlotte Lucas had been at Longbourn since *her* coming away.

"Yes, she called yesterday with her father. What an agreeable man Sir William is, Mr. Bingley—is not he? So much the man of fashion! So genteel and so easy! He had always something to say to everybody. *That* is my idea of good breeding; and those persons who fancy themselves very important, and never open their mouths, quite mistake the matter."

"Did Charlotte dine with you?"

"No, she would go home. I fancy she was wanted about the mince-pies. For my part, Mr. Bingley, *I* always keep servants that can do their own work; *my* daughters are brought up differently. But everybody is to judge for themselves, and the Lucases are a very good sort of girls, I assure you. It is a pity they are not handsome! Not that *I* think Charlotte so *very* plain—but then she is our particular friend."

"She seems a very pleasant young woman," said Bingley.

"Oh! dear, yes; but you must own she is very plain. Lady Lucas herself has often said so, and envied me Jane's beauty. I do not like to boast of my own child, but to be sure, Jane—one does not often see anybody better looking. It is what everybody says. I do not trust my own partiality. When she was only fifteen, there was a gentleman at my brother Gardiner's in town so much in love with her that my sister-in-law was sure he would make her an offer before we came away. But, however, he did not. Perhaps he thought her too young. However, he wrote some verses on her, and very pretty they were."

"And so ended his affection," said Elizabeth impatiently. "There has been many a one, I fancy, overcome in the same way. I wonder who first discovered the efficacy of poetry in driving away love!"

"I have been used to consider poetry as the *food* of love," said Darcy.

"Of a fine, stout, healthy love it may. Everything nourishes what is strong already. But if it be only a slight, thin sort of inclination, I am convinced that one good sonnet will starve it entirely away."

Darcy only smiled; and the general pause which ensued made Elizabeth tremble lest her mother should be exposing herself again. She longed to speak, but could think of nothing to say; and after a short silence Mrs. Bennet began repeating her thanks to Mr. Bingley for his kindness to Jane, with an apology for troubling him also with Lizzy. Mr. Bingley was unaffectedly civil in his answer, and forced his younger sister to be civil also, and say what the occasion required. She performed her part indeed without much graciousness, but Mrs. Bennet was satisfied, and soon afterwards ordered her carriage. Upon this signal, the youngest of her daughters put herself forward. The two girls had been whispering to each other during the whole visit, and the result of it was, that the youngest should tax Mr. Bingley with having promised on his first coming into the country to give a ball at Netherfield.

Lydia was a stout, well-grown girl of fifteen, with a fine complexion and good-humoured countenance; a favourite with her mother, whose affection had brought her into public at an early age. She had high animal spirits, and a sort of natural self-consequence, which the attention of the officers, to whom her uncle's good dinners and her own easy manners recommended her, had increased into assurance. She was very equal, therefore, to address Mr. Bingley on the subject of the ball, and abruptly reminded him of his promise; adding, that it would be the most shameful thing in the world if he did not keep it. His answer to this sudden attack was delightful to her mother's ear:

"I am perfectly ready, I assure you, to keep my engagement; and when your sister is recovered, you shall, if you please, name the very day of the ball. But you would not wish to be dancing while she is ill."

Lydia declared herself satisfied. "Oh! yes—it would be much better to wait till Jane was well, and by that time most likely Captain Carter would be at Meryton again. And when you have given *your* ball," she added, "I shall insist on their giving one also. I shall tell Colonel Forster it will be quite a shame if he does not."

Mrs. Bennet and her daughters then departed, and Elizabeth returned instantly to Jane, leaving her own and her relations' behaviour to the remarks of the two ladies and Mr. Darcy; the latter of whom, however, could not be prevailed on to join in their censure of *her,* in spite of all Miss Bingley's witticisms on *fine eyes.*

Chapter 10

THE day passed much as the day before had done. Mrs. Hurst and Miss Bingley had spent some hours of the morning with the invalid, who continued, though slowly, to mend; and in the evening Elizabeth joined their party in the drawing-room. The loo-table, however, did not appear. Mr. Darcy was writing, and Miss Bingley, seated near him, was watching the progress of his letter and repeatedly calling off his attention by messages to his sister. Mr. Hurst and Mr. Bingley were at piquet, and Mrs. Hurst was observing their game.

Elizabeth took up some needlework, and was sufficiently amused in attending to what passed between Darcy and his companion. The perpetual commendations of the lady, either on his handwriting, or on the evenness of his lines, or on the length of his letter, with the perfect unconcern with which her praises were received, formed a curious dialogue, and was exactly in unison with her opinion of each.

"How delighted Miss Darcy will be to receive such a letter!"

He made no answer.

"You write uncommonly fast."

"You are mistaken. I write rather slowly."

"How many letters you must have occasion to write in the course of a year! Letters of business, too! How odious I should think them!"

"It is fortunate, then, that they fall to my lot instead of to yours."

"Pray tell your sister that I long to see her."

"I have already told her so once, by your desire."

"I am afraid you do not like your pen. Let me mend it for you. I mend pens remarkably well."

"Thank you—but I always mend my own."

"How can you contrive to write so even?"

He was silent.

"Tell your sister I am delighted to hear of her improvement on the harp; and pray let her know that I am quite in raptures with her beautiful little design for a table, and I think it infinitely superior to Miss Grantley's."

"Will you give me leave to defer your raptures till I write again? At present I have not room to do them justice."

"Oh! It is of no consequence. I shall see her in January. But do you always write such charming long letters to her, Mr. Darcy?"

"They are generally long; but whether always charming it is not for me to determine."

"It is a rule with me, that a person who can write a long letter with ease, cannot write ill."

"That will not do for a compliment to Darcy, Caroline," cried her brother, "because he does not write with ease. He studies too much for words of four syllables. Do not you, Darcy?"

"My style of writing is very different from yours."

"Oh!" cried Miss Bingley, "Charles writes in the most careless way imaginable. He leaves out half his words, and blots the rest."

"My ideas flow so rapidly that I have not time to express them—by which means my letters sometimes convey no ideas at all to my correspondents."

"Your humility, Mr. Bingley," said Elizabeth, "must disarm reproof."

"Nothing is more deceitful," said Darcy, "than the appearance of humility. It is often only carelessness of opinion, and sometimes an indirect boast."

"And which of the two do you call *my* little recent piece of modesty?"

"The indirect boast; for you are really proud of your defects in writing, because you consider them as proceeding from a rapidity of thought and carelessness of execution, which, if not estimable, you think at least highly interesting. The power of doing anything with quickness is always much prized by the possessor, and often without any attention to the imperfection of the performance. When you told Mrs. Bennet this morning, that if you ever resolved on quitting Netherfield you should be gone in five minutes, you meant it to be a sort of panegyric, of compliment to yourself—and yet what is there so very laudable in a precipitance which must leave very necessary business undone, and can be of no real advantage to yourself or anyone else?"

"Nay," cried Bingley, "this is too much, to remember at night all the foolish things that were said in the morning. And yet, upon my honour, I believed what I said of myself to be true, and I believe it at this moment. At least, therefore, I did not assume the character of needless precipitance merely to show off before the ladies."

"I dare say you believed it; but I am by no means convinced that you would be gone with such celerity. Your conduct would be quite as dependent on chance as that of any man I know; and if, as you were mounting your horse, a friend were to say, 'Bingley, you had better stay till next week,' you would probably do it, you would probably not go—and at another word, might stay a month."

"You have only proved by this," cried Elizabeth, "that Mr. Bingley did not do justice to his own disposition. You have shown him off now much more than he did himself."

"I am exceedingly gratified," said Bingley, "by your converting what my friend says into a compliment on the sweetness of my temper. But I am afraid you are giving it a turn which that gentleman did by no means intend; for he would certainly think the better of me, if under such a circumstance I were to give a flat denial, and ride off as fast as I could."

"Would Mr. Darcy then consider the rashness of your original intention as atoned for by your obstinacy in adhering to it?"

"Upon my word, I cannot exactly explain the matter; Darcy must speak for himself."

"You expect me to account for opinions which you choose to call mine, but which I have never acknowledged. Allowing the case, however, to stand according to your representation, you must remember, Miss Bennet, that the friend who is supposed to desire his return to the house, and the delay of his plan, has merely desired it, asked it without offering one argument in favour of its propriety."

"To yield readily—easily—to the *persuasion* of a friend is no merit with you."

"To yield without conviction is no compliment to the understanding of either."

"You appear to me, Mr. Darcy, to allow nothing for the influence of friendship and affection. A regard for the requester would often make one readily yield to a request, without waiting for arguments to reason one into it. I am not particularly speaking of such a case as you have supposed about Mr. Bingley. We may as well wait, perhaps, till the circumstance occurs before we discuss the discretion of his behaviour thereupon. But in general and ordinary cases between friend and friend, where one of them is desired by the other to change a resolution of no very great moment, should you think ill of that person for complying with the desire, without waiting to be argued into it?"

"Will it not be advisable, before we proceed on this subject, to arrange with rather more precision the degree of importance which is to appertain to this request, as well as the degree of intimacy subsisting between the parties?"

"By all means," cried Bingley; "let us hear all the particulars, not forgetting their comparative height and size; for that will have more weight in the argument, Miss Bennet, than you may be aware of. I assure you, that if Darcy were not such a great tall fellow, in comparison with myself, I should not pay him half so much deference. I declare I do not know a more awful object than Darcy, on particular occasions, and in particular places; at his own house especially, and of a Sunday evening, when he has nothing to do."

Mr. Darcy smiled; but Elizabeth thought she could perceive that he was rather offended, and therefore checked her laugh. Miss Bingley warmly resented the indignity he had received, in an expostulation with her brother for talking such nonsense.

"I see your design, Bingley," said his friend. "You dislike an argument, and want to silence this."

"Perhaps I do. Arguments are too much like disputes. If you and Miss Bennet will defer yours till I am out of the room, I shall be very thankful; and then you may say whatever you like of me."

"What you ask," said Elizabeth, "is no sacrifice on my side; and Mr. Darcy had much better finish his letter."

Mr. Darcy took her advice, and did finish his letter.

When that business was over, he applied to Miss Bingley and Elizabeth for the indulgence of some music. Miss Bingley moved with alacrity to the pianoforte: and, after a polite request that Elizabeth would lead the way, which the other as politely and more earnestly negatived, she seated herself.

Mrs. Hurst sang with her sister, and while they were thus employed, Elizabeth could not help observing, as she turned over some music-books that lay on the instrument, how frequently Mr. Darcy's eyes were fixed on her. She hardly knew how to suppose that she could be an object of admiration to so great a man; and yet that he should look at her because he disliked her, was still more strange. She could only imagine, however, at last that she drew his notice because there was a something about her more wrong and reprehensible, according to his ideas of right, than in any other person present. The supposition did not pain her. She liked him too little to care for his approbation.

After playing some Italian songs, Miss Bingley varied the charm by a lively Scotch air; and soon afterwards Mr. Darcy, drawing near Elizabeth, said to her:

"Do not you feel a great inclination, Miss Bennet, to seize such an opportunity of dancing a reel?"

She smiled, but made no answer. He repeated the question, with some surprise at her silence.

"Oh!" said she, "I heard you before, but I could not immediately determine what to say in reply. You wanted me, I know, to say 'Yes,' that you might have the pleasure of despising my taste; but I always delight in overthrowing those kind of schemes, and cheating a person of their premeditated contempt. I have, therefore, made up my mind to tell you, that I do not want to dance a reel at all—and now despise me if you dare."

"Indeed I do not dare."

Elizabeth, having rather expected to affront him, was amazed at his gallantry; but there was a mixture of sweetness and archness in her manner which made it difficult for her to affront anybody; and Darcy had never been so bewitched by any woman as he was by her. He really believed, that were it not for the inferiority of her connections, he should be in some danger.

Miss Bingley saw, or suspected enough to be jealous; and her great anxiety for the recovery of her dear friend Jane received some assistance from her desire of getting rid of Elizabeth.

She often tried to provoke Darcy into disliking her guest, by talking of their supposed marriage, and planning his happiness in such an alliance.

"I hope," said she, as they were walking together in the shrubbery the next day, "you will give your mother-in-law a few hints, when this desirable event takes place, as to the advantage of holding her tongue; and if you can compass it, do cure the younger girls of running after the officers. And, if I may mention so delicate a subject, endeavour to check that little something, bordering on conceit and impertinence, which your lady possesses."

"Have you anything else to propose for my domestic felicity?"

"Oh! yes. Do let the portraits of your uncle and aunt Philips get placed in the gallery at Pemberley. Put them next to your great-uncle the judge. They are in the same profession, you know; only in different lines. As for your Elizabeth's picture, you must not attempt to have it taken, for what painter could do justice to those beautiful eyes?"

"It would not be easy, indeed, to catch their expression, but their colour and shape, and the eyelashes, so remarkably fine, might be copied."

At that moment they were met from another walk by Mrs. Hurst and Elizabeth herself.

"I did not know that you intended to walk," said Miss Bingley, in some confusion, lest they had been overheard.

"You used us abominably ill," answered Mrs. Hurst, "running away without telling us that you were coming out."

Then taking the disengaged arm of Mr. Darcy, she left Elizabeth to walk by herself. The path just admitted three. Mr. Darcy felt their rudeness, and immediately said:

"This walk is not wide enough for our party. We had better go into the avenue."

But Elizabeth, who had not the least inclination to remain with them, laughingly answered:

"No, no; stay where you are. You are charmingly grouped, and appear to uncommon advantage. The picturesque would be spoilt by admitting a fourth. Good-bye."

She then ran gaily off, rejoicing, as she rambled about, in the hope of being at home again in a day or two. Jane was already so much recovered as to intend leaving her room for a couple of hours that evening.

Chapter 11

WHEN the ladies removed after dinner, Elizabeth ran up to her sister, and seeing her well guarded from cold, attended her into the drawing-room, where she was welcomed by her two friends with many professions of pleasure; and Elizabeth had never seen them so agreeable as they were during the hour which passed before the gentlemen appeared. Their powers of conversation were considerable. They could describe an entertainment with accuracy, relate an anecdote with humour, and laugh at their acquaintance with spirit.

But when the gentlemen entered, Jane was no longer the first object; Miss Bingley's eyes were instantly turned toward Darcy, and she had something to say to him before he had advanced many steps. He addressed himself to Miss Bennet, with a polite congratulation; Mr. Hurst also made her a slight bow, and said he was "very glad"; but diffuseness and warmth remained for Bingley's salutation. He was full of joy and attention. The first half-hour was spent in piling up the fire, lest she should suffer from the change of room; and she removed at his desire to the other side of the fireplace, that she might be farther from the door. He then sat down by her, and talked scarcely to anyone else. Elizabeth, at work in the opposite corner, saw it all with great delight.

When tea was over, Mr. Hurst reminded his sister-in-law of the card-table—but in vain. She had obtained private intelligence that Mr. Darcy did not wish for cards; and Mr. Hurst soon found even his open petition rejected. She assured him that no one intended to play, and the silence of the whole party on the subject seemed to justify her. Mr. Hurst had therefore nothing to do, but to stretch himself on one of the sofas and go to sleep. Darcy took up a book; Miss Bingley did the same; and Mrs. Hurst, principally occupied in playing with her bracelets and rings, joined now and then in her brother's conversation with Miss Bennet.

Miss Bingley's attention was quite as much engaged in watching Mr. Darcy's progress through *his* book, as in reading her own; and she was perpetually either making some inquiry, or looking at his page. She could not win him, however, to any conversation; he merely answered her question, and read on. At length, quite exhausted by the attempt to be amused with her own book, which she had only chosen because it was the second volume of his, she gave a great yawn and said, "How pleasant it is to spend an evening in this way! I declare after all there is no enjoyment like reading! How much sooner one tires of anything than of a book! When I have a house of my own, I shall be miserable if I have not an excellent library."

No one made any reply. She then yawned again, threw aside her book, and cast her eyes round the room in quest of some amusement; when hearing her brother mentioning a ball to Miss Bennet, she turned suddenly towards him and said:

"By the bye, Charles, are you really serious in meditating a dance at Netherfield? I would advise you, before you determine on it, to consult the wishes of the present party; I am much mistaken if there are not some among us to whom a ball would be rather a punishment than a pleasure."

"If you mean Darcy," cried her brother, "he may go to bed, if he chooses, before it begins—but as for the ball, it is quite a settled thing; and as soon as Nicholls has made white soup enough, I shall send round my cards."

"I should like balls infinitely better," she replied, "if they were carried on in a different manner; but there is something insufferably tedious in the usual process of such a meeting. It would surely be much more rational if conversation instead of dancing were made the order of the day."

"Much more rational, my dear Caroline, I dare say, but it would not be near so much like a ball."

Miss Bingley made no answer, and soon afterwards got up and walked about the room. Her figure was elegant, and she walked well; but Darcy, at whom it was all aimed, **was** still inflexibly studious. In the desperation of her feelings, she resolved on one effort more, and, turning to Elizabeth, said:

"Miss Eliza Bennet, let me persuade you to follow my example, and take a turn about the room. I assure you it is very refreshing after sitting so long in one attitude."

Elizabeth was surprised, but agreed to it immediately. Miss Bingley succeeded no less in the real object of her civility; Mr. Darcy looked up. He was as much awake to the novelty of attention in that quarter as Elizabeth herself could be, and unconsciously closed his book. He was directly invited to join their party, but he declined it, observing that he could imagine but two motives for their choosing to walk up and down the room together, with either of which motives his joining them would interfere. "What could he mean? She was dying to know what could be his meaning"—and asked Elizabeth whether she could at all understand him?

"Not at all," was her answer; "but depend upon it, he means to be severe on us, and our surest way of disappointing him will be to ask nothing about it."

Miss Bingley, however, was incapable of disappointing Mr. Darcy in anything, and persevered therefore in requiring an explanation of his two motives.

"I have not the smallest objection to explaining them," said he, as soon as she allowed him to speak. "You either choose this method of passing the evening because you are in each other's confidence, and have secret affairs to discuss, or because you are conscious that your figures appear to the greatest advantage in walking; if the first, I should be completely in your way, and if the second, I can admire you much better as I sit by the fire."

"Oh! shocking!" cried Miss Bingley. "I never heard anything so abominable. How shall we punish him for such a speech?"

"Nothing so easy, if you have but the inclination," said Elizabeth. "We can all plague and punish one another. Tease him—laugh at him. Intimate as you are, you must know how it is to be done."

"But upon my honour I do *not*. I do assure you that my intimacy has not yet taught me *that*. Tease calmness of temper and presence of mind! No, no—I feel he may defy us there. And as to laughter, we will not expose ourselves, if you please, by attempting to laugh without a subject. Mr. Darcy may hug himself."

"Mr. Darcy is not to be laughed at!" cried Elizabeth. "That is an uncommon advantage, and uncommon I hope it will continue, for it would be a great loss to *me* to have many such acquaintances. I dearly love a laugh."

"Miss Bingley," said he, "has given me credit for more than can be. The wisest and the best of men—nay, the wisest and best of their actions —may be rendered ridiculous by a person whose first object in life is a joke."

"Certainly," replied Elizabeth—"there are such people, but I hope I am not one of *them*. I hope I never ridicule what is wise or good. Follies and nonsense, whims and inconsistencies, *do* divert me, I own, and I laugh at them whenever I can. But these, I suppose, are precisely what you are without."

"Perhaps that is not possible for anyone. But it has been the study of my life to avoid those weaknesses which often expose a strong understanding to ridicule."

"Such as vanity and pride."

"Yes, vanity is a weakness indeed. But pride—where there is a real superiority of mind, pride will be always under good regulation."

Elizabeth turned away to hide a smile.

"Your examination of Mr. Darcy is over, I presume," said Miss Bingley; "and pray what is the result?"

"I am perfectly convinced by it that Mr. Darcy has no defect. He owns it himself without disguise."

"No," said Darcy, "I have made no such pretension. I have faults enough, but they are not, I hope, of understanding. My temper I dare not vouch for. It is, I believe, too little yielding—certainly too little for the convenience of the world. I cannot forget the follies and vices of others so soon as I ought, nor their offences against myself. My feelings are not puffed about with every attempt to move them. My temper would perhaps be called resentful. My good opinion once lost, is lost for ever."

"*That* is a failing indeed!" cried Elizabeth. "Implacable resentment *is* a shade in a character. But you have chosen your fault well. I really cannot *laugh* at it. You are safe from me."

"There is, I believe, in every disposition a tendency to some particular evil—a natural defect, which not even the best education can overcome."

"And *your* defect is a propensity to hate everybody."

"And yours," he replied, with a smile, "is wilfully to misunderstand them."

"Do let us have a little music," cried Miss Bingley, tired of a conversation in which she had no share. "Louisa, you will not mind my waking Mr. Hurst?"

Her sister made not the smallest objection, and the pianoforte was opened; and Darcy, after a few moments' recollection, was not sorry for it. He began to feel the danger of paying Elizabeth too much attention.

Chapter 12

IN consequence of an agreement between the sisters, Elizabeth wrote the next morning to her mother, to beg that the carriage might be sent for them in the course of the day. But Mrs. Bennet, who had calculated on her daughters remaining at Netherfield till the following Tuesday, which would exactly finish Jane's week, could not bring herself to receive them with pleasure before. Her answer, therefore, was not propitious, at least not to Elizabeth's wishes, for she was impatient to get home. Mrs. Bennet sent them word that they could not possibly have the carriage before Tuesday; and in her postscript it was added, that if Mr. Bingley and his sister pressed them to stay longer, she could spare them very well. Against staying longer, however, Elizabeth was positively resolved—nor did she much expect it would be asked; and fearful, on the contrary, as being considered as intruding themselves needlessly long, she urged Jane to borrow Mr. Bingley's carriage immediately, and at length it was settled that their original design of leaving Netherfield that morning should be mentioned, and the request made.

The communication excited many professions of concern; and enough was said of wishing them to stay at least till the following day to work on Jane; and till the morrow their going was deferred. Miss Bingley was then sorry that she had proposed the delay, for her jealousy and dislike of one sister much exceeded her affection for the other.

The master of the house heard with real sorrow that they were to go so soon, and repeatedly tried to persuade Miss Bennet that it would not be safe for her—that she was not enough recovered; but Jane was firm where she felt herself to be right.

To Mr. Darcy it was welcome intelligence—Elizabeth had been at Netherfield long enough. She attracted him more than he liked—and Miss Bingley was uncivil to *her,* and more teasing than usual to himself. He wisely resolved to be particularly careful that no sign of admiration should *now* escape him, nothing that could elevate her with the hope of influencing his felicity; sensible that if such an idea had been suggested, his behaviour during the last day must have material weight in confirming or crushing it. Steady to his purpose, he scarcely spoke ten words to her through the whole of Saturday, and though they were at one time left by themselves for half-an-hour, he adhered most conscientiously to his book, and would not even look at her.

On Sunday, after morning service, the separation, so agreeable to almost all, took place. Miss Bingley's civility to Elizabeth increased at last very rapidly, as well as her affection for Jane; and when they parted, after assuring the latter of the pleasure it would always give her to see her either at Longbourn or Netherfield, and embracing her most tenderly, she even shook hands with the former. Elizabeth took leave of the whole party in the liveliest spirits.

They were not welcomed home very cordially by their mother. Mrs. Bennet wondered at their coming, and thought them very wrong to give so much trouble, and was sure Jane would have caught cold again. But their father, though very laconic in his expressions of pleasure, was really glad to see them; he had felt their importance in the family circle. The evening conversation, when they were all assembled, had lost much of its animation, and almost all its sense by the absence of Jane and Elizabeth.

They found Mary, as usual, deep in the study of thorough-bass and human nature; and had some new extracts to admire, and some new observations of threadbare morality to listen to. Catherine and Lydia had information for them of a different sort. Much had been done and much had been said in the regiment since the preceding Wednesday; several of the officers had dined lately with their uncle, a private had been flogged, and it had actually been hinted that Colonel Forster was going to be married.

Chapter 13

"I HOPE, my dear," said Mr. Bennet to his wife, as they were at break-fast the next morning, "that you have ordered a good dinner to-day, because I have reason to expect an addition to our family party."

"Who do you mean, my dear? I know of nobody that is coming, I am sure, unless Charlotte Lucas should happen to call in—and I hope *my* dinners are good enough for her. I do not believe she often sees such at home."

"The person of whom I speak is a gentleman, and a stranger."

Mrs. Bennet's eyes sparkled. "A gentleman and a stranger! It is Mr. Bingley, I am sure. Why, Jane—you never dropped a word of this; you sly thing! Well, I am sure I shall be extremely glad to see Mr. Bingley. But—good Lord! how unlucky! There is not a bit of fish to be got to-day. Lydia, my love, ring the bell—I must speak to Hill this moment."

"It is *not* Mr. Bingley," said her husband; "it is a person whom I never saw in the whole course of my life."

This roused a general astonishment; and he had the pleasure of being eagerly questioned by his wife and five daughters at once.

After amusing himself some time with their curiosity, he thus explained:

"About a month ago I received this letter; and about a fortnight ago I answered it, for I thought it a case of some delicacy, and requiring early attention. It is from my cousin, Mr. Collins, who, when I am dead, may turn you all out of this house as soon as he pleases."

"Oh! my dear," cried his wife, "I cannot bear to hear that mentioned. Pray do not talk of that odious man. I do think it is the hardest thing in the world, that your estate should be entailed away from your own children; and I am sure, if I had been you, I should have tried long ago to do something or other about it."

Jane and Elizabeth attempted to explain to her the nature of an entail. They had often attempted it before, but it was a subject on which Mrs. Bennet was beyond the reach of reason, and she continued to rail bitterly against the cruelty of settling an estate away from a family of five daughters, in favour of a man whom nobody cared anything about.

"It certainly is a most iniquitous affair," said Mr. Bennet, "and nothing can clear Mr. Collins from the guilt of inheriting Longbourn. But if you will listen to his letter, you may perhaps be a little softened by his manner of expressing himself."

"No, that I am sure I shall not; and I think it was very impertinent of him to write to you at all, and very hypocritical. I hate such false friends. Why could not he keep on quarrelling with you, as his father did before him?"

"Why, indeed; he does seem to have had some filial scruples on that head, as you will hear."

"Hunsford, near Westerham, Kent,
"15th October.

"DEAR SIR,—

"The disagreement subsisting between yourself and my late honoured father always gave me much uneasiness, and since I have had the misfortune to lose him, I have frequently wished to heal the breach; but for some time I was kept back by my own doubts, fearing lest it might seem disrespectful to his memory for me to be on good terms with anyone with whom it had always pleased him to be at variance.—'There, Mrs. Bennet.' —My mind, however, is now made up on the subject, for having received ordination at Easter, I have been so fortunate as to be distinguished by the patronage of the Right Honourable Lady Catherine de Bourgh, widow of Sir Lewis de Bourgh, whose bounty and beneficence has preferred me to the valuable rectory of this parish, where it shall be my earnest endeavour to demean myself with grateful respect towards her Ladyship, and be ever ready to perform those rites and ceremonies which are instituted by the Church of England. As a clergyman, moreover, I feel it my duty to promote and establish the blessing of peace in all families within the reach of my influence; and on these grounds I flatter myself that my present overtures of goodwill are highly commendable, and that the circumstance of my being next in the entail of Longbourn estate will be kindly overlooked on your side, and not lead you to reject the offered olive-branch. I cannot be otherwise than concerned at being the means of injuring your amiable daughters, and beg leave to apologise for it, as well as to assure you of my readiness to make them every possible amends— but of this hereafter. If you should have no objection to receive me into your house, I propose myself the satisfaction of waiting on you and your family, Monday, November 18th, by four o'clock, and shall probably trespass on your hospitality till the Saturday se'nnight following, which I can do without any inconvenience, as Lady Catherine is far from objecting to my occasional absence on a Sunday, provided that some other clergyman is engaged to do the duty of the day.—I remain, dear sir, with respectful compliments to your lady and daughters, your well-wisher and friend,

"WILLIAM COLLINS."

"At four o'clock, therefore, we may expect this peace-making gentleman." said Mr. Bennet, as he folded up the letter. "He seems to be a most conscientious and polite young man, upon my word, and I doubt not will prove a valuable acquaintance, especially if Lady Catherine should be so indulgent as to let him come to us again."

"There is some sense in what he says about the girls, however, and if he is disposed to make them any amends, I shall not be the person to discourage him."

"Though it is difficult," said Jane, "to guess in what way he can mean to make us the atonement he thinks our due, the wish is certainly to his credit."

Elizabeth was chiefly struck with his extraordinary deference for Lady Catherine, and his kind intention of christening, marrying, and burying his parishioners whenever it were required.

"He must be an oddity, I think," said she. "I cannot make him out. There is something very pompous in his style. And what can he mean by apologising for being next in the entail? We cannot suppose he would help it if he could. Can he be a sensible man, sir?"

"No, my dear, I think not. I have great hopes of finding him quite the reverse. There is a mixture of servility and self-importance in his letter, which promises well. I am impatient to see him."

"In point of composition," said Mary, "his letter does not seem defective. The idea of the olive-branch perhaps is not wholly new, yet I think it is well expressed."

To Catherine and Lydia, neither the letter nor its writer were in any degree interesting. It was next to impossible that their cousin should come in a scarlet coat, and it was now some weeks since they had received pleasure from the society of a man in any other colour. As for their mother, Mr. Collins's letter had done away much of her ill-will, and she was preparing to see him with a degree of composure which astonished her husband and daughters.

Mr. Collins was punctual to his time, and was received with great politeness by the whole family. Mr. Bennet indeed said little; but the ladies were ready enough to talk, and Mr. Collins seemed neither in need of encouragement, nor inclined to be silent himself. He was a tall, heavy-looking young man of five-and-twenty. His air was grave and stately, and his manners were very formal. He had not been long seated before he complimented Mrs. Bennet on having so fine a family of daughters; said he had heard much of their beauty, but that in this instance fame had fallen short of the truth; and added, that he did not doubt her seeing them all in due time well disposed of in marriage. This gallantry was not much to the taste of some of his hearers; but Mrs. Bennet, who quarrelled with no compliments, answered most readily.

"You are very kind, I am sure; and I wish with all my heart it may prove so, for else they will be destitute enough. Things are settled so oddly."

"You allude, perhaps, to the entail of this estate."

"Ah! sir, I do indeed. It is a grievous affair to my poor girls, you must confess. Not that I mean to find fault with *you*, for such things I know are all chance in this world. There is no knowing how estates will go when once they come to be entailed."

"I am very sensible, madam, of the hardship to my fair cousins, and could say much on the subject, but that I am cautious of appearing forward and precipitate. But I can assure the young ladies that I come prepared to admire them. At present I will not say more; but, perhaps, when we are better acquainted——"

He was interrupted by a summons to dinner; and the girls smiled on each other. They were not the only objects of Mr. Collins's admiration. The hall, the dining-room, and all its furniture, were examined and praised; and his commendation of everything would have touched Mrs. Bennet's heart, but for the mortifying supposition of his viewing it all as his own future property. The dinner too in its turn was highly admired; and he begged to know to which of his fair cousins the excellency of its cooking was owing. But here he was set right by Mrs. Bennet, who assured him with some asperity that they were very well able to keep a good cook, and that her daughters had nothing to do in the kitchen. He begged pardon for having displeased her. In a softened tone she declared herself not at all offended; but he continued to apologise for about a quarter of an hour.

Chapter 14

DURING dinner, Mr. Bennet scarcely spoke at all; but when the servants were withdrawn, he thought it time to have some conversation with his guest, and therefore started a subject in which he expected him to shine, by observing that he seemed very fortunate in his patroness. Lady Catherine de Bourgh's attention to his wishes, and consideration for his comfort, appeared very remarkable. Mr. Bennet could not have chosen better. Mr. Collins was eloquent in her praise. The subject elevated him to more than usual solemnity of manner, and with a most important aspect he protested that "he had never in his life witnessed such behaviour in a person of rank—such affability and condescension, as he had himself experienced from Lady Catherine. She had been graciously pleased to approve of both the discourses which he had already had the honour of preaching before her. She had also asked him twice to dine at Rosings, and had sent for him only the Saturday before, to make up her pool of quadrille in the evening. Lady Catherine was reckoned proud by many people he knew, but *he* had never seen anything but affability in her. She had always spoken to him as she would to any other gentleman; she made not the smallest objection to his joining in the society of the neighbourhood nor to his leaving his parish occasionally for a week or two, to visit his relations. She had even condescended to advise him to marry as soon as he could, provided he chose with discretion; and had once paid him a visit in his humble parsonage. where she had perfectly approved all the alterations he had been making, and had even vouchsafed to suggest some herself—some shelves in the closets upstairs."

"That is all very proper and civil, I am sure," said Mrs. Bennet, "and I dare say she is a very agreeable woman. It is a pity that great ladies in general are not more like her. Does she live near you, sir?"

"The garden in which stands my humble abode is separated only by a lane from Rosings Park, her ladyship's residence."

"I think you said she was a widow, sir? Has she any family?"

"She has only one daughter, the heiress of Rosings, and of very exten-sive property."

"Ah!" cried Mrs. Bennet, shaking her head, "then she is better off than many girls. And what sort of young lady is she? Is she handsome?"

"She is a most charming young lady indeed. Lady Catherine herself says that, in point of true beauty, Miss de Bourgh is far superior to the handsomest of her sex, because there is that in her features which marks the young woman of distinguished birth. She is unfortunately of a sickly constitution, which has prevented her making that progress in many accomplishments which she could not otherwise have failed of, as I am informed by the lady who superintended her education, and who still resides with them. But she is perfectly amiable, and often condescends to drive by my humble abode in her little phaeton and ponies."

"Has she been presented? I do not remember her name among the ladies at court."

"Her indifferent state of health unhappily prevents her being in town; and by that means, as I told Lady Catherine myself one day, has deprived the British court of its brightest ornament. Her ladyship seemed pleased with the idea; and you may imagine that I am happy on every occasion to offer those little delicate compliments which are always acceptable to ladies. I have more than once observed to Lady Catherine, that her charming daughter seemed born to be a duchess, and that the most elevated rank, instead of giving her consequence, would be adorned by her. These are the kind of little things which please her ladyship, and it is a sort of attention which I conceive myself peculiarly bound to pay."

"You judge very properly," said Mr. Bennet, "and it is happy for you that you possess the talent of flattering with delicacy. May I ask whether these pleasing attentions proceed from the impulse of the moment, or are the result of previous study?"

"They arise chiefly from what is passing at the time, and though I sometimes amuse myself with suggesting and arranging such little elegant compliments as may be adapted to ordinary occasions, I always wish to give them as unstudied an air as possible."

Mr. Bennet's expectations were fully answered. His cousin was as absurd as he had hoped, and he listened to him with the keenest enjoy-ment, maintaining at the same time the most resolute composure of countenance, and, except in an occasional glance at Elizabeth, requiring no partner in his pleasure.

By tea-time, however, the dose had been enough, and Mr. Bennet was glad to take his guest into the drawing-room again, and, when tea was over, glad to invite him to read aloud to the ladies. Mr. Collins readily assented, and a book was produced; but on beholding it (for everything announced it to be from a circulating library), he started back, and begging pardon, protested that he never read novels. Kitty stared at him, and Lydia exclaimed. Other books were produced, and after some deliberation, he chose Fordyce's Sermons. Lydia gaped as he opened the volume, and before he had, with very monotonous solemnity, read three pages, she interrupted him with:

"Do you know, mamma, that my uncle Philips talks of turning away Richard; and if he does, Colonel Forster will hire him. My aunt told me so herself on Saturday. I shall walk to Meryton to-morrow to hear more about it, and to ask when Mr. Denny comes back from town."

Lydia was bid by her two eldest sisters to hold her tongue; but Mr. Collins, much offended, laid aside his book, and said:

"I have often observed how little young ladies are interested by books of a serious stamp, though written solely for their benefit. It amazes me, I confess; for, certainly, there can be nothing so advantageous to them as instruction. But I will no longer importune my young cousin."

Then turning to Mr. Bennet, he offered himself as his antagonist at backgammon. Mr. Bennet accepted the challenge, observing that he acted very wisely in leaving the girls to their own trifling amusements. Mrs. Bennet and her daughters apologised most civilly for Lydia's interruption, and promised that it should not occur again, if he would resume his book; but Mr. Collins, after assuring them that he bore his young cousin no ill-will, and should never resent her behaviour as any affront, seated himself at another table with Mr. Bennet, and prepared for backgammon.

Chapter 15

MR. COLLINS was not a sensible man, and the deficiency of nature had been but little assisted by education or society; the greatest part of his life having been spent under the guidance of an illiterate and miserly father; and though he belonged to one of the universities, he had merely kept the necessary terms, without forming at it any useful acquaintance. The subjection in which his father had brought him up had given him originally great humility of manner; but it was now a good deal counteracted by the self-conceit of a weak head, living in retirement, and the consequential feelings of early and unexpected prosperity. A fortunate chance had recommended him to Lady Catherine de Bourgh when the living of Hunsford was vacant; and the respect which he felt for her high rank, and his veneration for her as his patroness, mingling with a very good opinion of himself, of his authority as a clergyman, and his right as a rector, made him altogether a mixture of pride and obsequiousness, self-importance and humility.

Having now a good house and very sufficient income, he intended to marry; and in seeking a reconciliation with the Longbourn family he had a wife in view, as he meant to choose one of the daughters, if he found them as handsome and amiable as they were represented by common report. This was his plan of amends—of atonement—for inheriting their father's estate; and he thought it an excellent one, full of eligibility and suitableness, and excessively generous and disinterested on his own part.

His plan did not vary on seeing them. Miss Bennet's lovely face confirmed his views, and established all his strictest notions of what was due to seniority; and for the first evening *she* was his settled choice. The next morning, however, made an alteration; for in a quarter of an hour's *tête-à-tête* with Mrs. Bennet before breakfast, a conversation beginning with his parsonage-house, and leading naturally to the avowal of his hopes, that a mistress for it might be found at Longbourn, produced from her, amid very complaisant smiles and general encouragement, a caution against the very Jane he had fixed on. "As to her *younger* daughters, she could not take upon her to say—she could not positively answer—but she did not *know* of any prepossession; her *eldest* daughter, she must just mention—she felt it incumbent on her to hint, was likely to be very soon engaged."

Mr. Collins had only to change from Jane to Elizabeth—and it was soon done—done while Mrs. Bennet was stirring the fire. Elizabeth, equally next to Jane in birth and beauty, succeeded her of course.

Mrs. Bennet treasured up the hint, and trusted that she might soon have two daughters married; and the man whom she could not bear to speak of the day before was now high in her good graces.

Lydia's intention of walking to Meryton was not forgotten; every sister except Mary agreed to go with her; and Mr. Collins was to attend them, at the request of Mr. Bennet, who was most anxious to get rid of him, and have his library to himself; for thither Mr. Collins had followed him after breakfast, and there he would continue, nominally engaged with one of the largest folios in the collection, but really talking to Mr. Bennet, with little cessation, of his house and garden at Hunsford. Such doings discomposed Mr. Bennet exceedingly. In his library he had been always sure of leisure and tranquillity; and though prepared, as he told Elizabeth, to meet with folly and conceit in every other room in the house, he was used to be free from them there; his civility, therefore, was most prompt in inviting Mr. Collins to join his daughters in their walk; and Mr. Collins, being in fact much better fitted for a walker than a reader, was extremely well pleased to close his large book, and go.

In pompous nothings on his side, and civil assents on that of his cousins, their time passed till they entered Meryton. The attention of the younger ones was then no longer to be gained by him. Their eyes were immediately wandering up in the street in quest of the officers, and nothing less than a very smart bonnet indeed, or a really new muslin in a shop window, could recall them.

But the attention of every lady was soon caught by a young man, whom they had never seen before, of most gentlemanlike appearance, walking with an officer on the other side of the way. The officer was the very Mr. Denny concerning whose return from London Lydia came to inquire, and he bowed as they passed. All were struck with the stranger's air, all wondered who he could be; and Kitty and Lydia, determined if possible to find out, led the way across the street, under pretence of wanting something in an opposite shop, and fortunately had just gained the pavement when the two gentlemen, turning back, had reached the same spot. Mr. Denny addressed them directly, and entreated permission to introduce his friend, Mr. Wickham, who had returned with him the day before from town, and he was happy to say had accepted a commission in their corps. This was exactly as it should be; for the young man wanted only regimentals to make him completely charming. His appearance was greatly in his favour; he had all the best part of beauty, a fine countenance, a good figure, and very pleasing address. The introduction was followed up on his side by a happy readiness of conversation—a readiness at the same time perfectly correct and unassuming; and the whole party were still standing and talking together very agreeably, when the sound of horses drew their notice, and Darcy and Bingley were seen riding down the street. On distinguishing the ladies of the group, the two gentlemen came directly towards them, and began the usual civilities. Bingley was the principal spokesman, and Miss Bennet the principal object. He was then, he said, on his way to Longbourn on purpose to inquire after her. Mr. Darcy corroborated it with a bow, and was beginning to determine not to fix his eyes on Elizabeth, when they were suddenly arrested by the sight of the stranger, and Elizabeth happening to see the countenance of both as they looked at each other, was all astonishment at the effect of the meeting. Both changed colour, one looked white, the other red. Mr. Wickham, after a few moments, touched his hat—a salutation which Mr. Darcy just deigned to return. What could be the meaning of it? It was impossible to imagine; it was impossible not to long to know.

In another minute, Mr. Bingley, but without seeming to have noticed what passed, took leave and rode on with his friend.

Mr. Denny and Mr. Wickham walked with the young ladies to the door of Mr. Philips's house, and then made their bows, in spite of Miss Lydia's pressing entreaties that they would come in, and even in spite of Mrs. Philips's throwing up the parlour window and loudly seconding the invitation.

Mrs. Philips was always glad to see her nieces; and the two eldest, from their recent absence, were particularly welcome, and she was eagerly expressing her surprise at their sudden return home, which, as their own carriage had not fetched them, she should have known nothing about, if she had not happened to see Mr. Jones's shop-boy in the street, who had told her that they were not to send any more draughts to Netherfield because the Miss Bennets were come away, when her civility was claimed towards Mr. Collins by Jane's introduction of him. She received him with her very best politeness, which he returned with as much more. apologising for his intrusion, without any previous acquaintance with her, which he could not help flattering himself, however, might be justified by his relationship to the young ladies who introduced him to her notice. Mrs. Philips was quite awed by such an excess of good breeding; but her contemplation of one stranger was soon put an end to by exclamations and inquiries about the other; of whom, however, she could only tell her nieces what they already knew, that Mr. Denny had brought him from London, and that he was to have a lieutenant's commission in the ——shire. She had been watching him the last hour, she said, as he walked up and down the street, and had Mr. Wickham appeared, Kitty and Lydia would certainly have continued the occupation, but unluckily no one passed the windows now except a few of the officers, who, in comparison with the stranger, were become "stupid, disagreeable fellows." Some of them were to dine with the Philipses the next day, and their aunt promised to make her husband call on Mr. Wickham, and give him an invitation also, if the family from Longbourn would come in the evening. This was agreed to, and Mrs. Philips protested that they would have a nice comfortable noisy game of lottery tickets, and a little bit of hot supper afterwards. The prospect of such delights was very cheering, and they parted in mutual good spirits. Mr. Collins repeated his apologies in quitting the room, and was assured with unwearying civility that they were perfectly needless.

As they walked home, Elizabeth related to Jane what she had seen pass between the two gentlemen; but though Jane would have defended either or both, had they appeared to be wrong, she could no more explain such behaviour than her sister.

Mr. Collins on his return highly gratified Mrs. Bennet by admiring Mrs. Philips's manners and politeness. He protested that, except Lady Catherine and her daughter, he had never seen a more elegant woman; for she had not only received him with the utmost civility, but had even pointedly included him in her invitation for the next evening, although utterly unknown to her before. Something, he supposed, might be attributed to his connection with them, but yet he had never met with so much attention in the whole course of his life.

Chapter 16

As no objection was made to the young people's engagement with their aunt, and all Mr. Collins's scruples of leaving Mr. and Mrs. Bennet for a single evening during his visit were most steadily resisted, the coach conveyed him and his five cousins at a suitable hour to Meryton: and the girls had the pleasure of hearing, as they entered the drawing-room, that Mr. Wickham had accepted their uncle's invitation, and was then in the house.

When this information was given, and they had all taken their seats, Mr. Collins was at leisure to look around him and admire, and he was so much struck with the size and furniture of the apartment, that he declared he might almost have supposed himself in the small summer breakfast parlour at Rosings; a comparison that did not at first convey much gratification; but when Mrs. Philips understood from him what Rosings was, and who was its proprietor—when she had listened to the description of only one of Lady Catherine's drawing-rooms, and found that the chimney-piece alone had cost eight hundred pounds, she felt all the force of the compliment, and would hardly have resented a comparison with the housekeeper's room.

In describing to her all the grandeur of Lady Catherine and her mansion, with occasional digressions in praise of his own humble abode, and the improvements it was receiving, he was happily employed until the gentlemen joined them; and he found in Mrs. Philips a very attentive listener, whose opinion of his consequence increased with what she heard, and who was resolving to retail it all among her neighbours as soon as she could. To the girls, who could not listen to their cousin, and who had nothing to do but to wish for an instrument, and examine their own indifferent imitations of china on the mantelpiece, the interval of waiting appeared very long. It was over at last, however. The gentlemen did approach, and when Mr. Wickham walked into the room, Elizabeth felt that she had neither been seeing him before, nor thinking of him since, with the smallest degree of unreasonable admiration. The officers of the ——shire were in general a very creditable, gentlemanlike set, and the best of them were of the present party; but Mr. Wickham was as far beyond them all in person, countenance, air, and walk, as *they* were superior to the broad-faced, stuffy uncle Philips, breathing port wine, who followed them into the room.

Mr. Wickham was the happy man towards whom almost every female eye was turned, and Elizabeth was the happy woman by whom he finally seated himself; and the agreeable manner in which he immediately fell into conversation, though it was only on its being a wet night, and on the probability of a rainy season, made her feel that the commonest, dullest, most threadbare topic might be rendered interesting by the skill of the speaker.

With such rivals for the notice of the fair as Mr. Wickham and the officers, Mr. Collins seemed to sink into insignificance; to the young ladies he certainly was nothing; but he had still at intervals a kind listener in Mrs. Philips, and was by her watchfulness, most abundantly supplied with coffee and muffin.

When the card-tables were placed, he had an opportunity of obliging her in return, by sitting down to whist.

"I know little of the game at present," said he, "but I shall be glad to improve myself, for in my situation in life——" Mrs. Philips was very thankful for his compliance, but could not wait for his reason.

Mr. Wickham did not play at whist, and with ready delight was he received at the other table between Elizabeth and Lydia. At first there seemed danger of Lydia's engrossing him entirely, for she was a most determined talker; but being likewise extremely fond of lottery tickets, she soon grew too much interested in the game, too eager in making bets and exclaiming after prizes to have attention for any one in particular. Allowing for the common demands of the game, Mr. Wickham was therefore at leisure to talk to Elizabeth, and she was very willing to hear him, though what she chiefly wished to hear she could not hope to be told—the history of his acquaintance with Mr. Darcy. She dared not even mention that gentleman. Her curiosity, however, was unexpectedly relieved. Mr. Wickham began the subject himself. He inquired how far Netherfield was from Meryton; and, after receiving her answer, asked in a hesitating manner how long Mr. Darcy had been staying there.

"About a month," said Elizabeth; and then, unwilling to let the subject drop, added, "he is a man of very large property in Derbyshire, I understand."

"Yes," replied Wickham; "his estate there is a noble one. A clear ten thousand per annum. You could not have met with a person more capable of giving you certain information on that head than myself, for I have been connected with his family in a particular manner from my infancy."

Elizabeth could not but look surprised.

"You may well be surprised, Miss Bennet, at such an assertion, after seeing, as you probably might, the very cold manner of our meeting yesterday. Are you much acquainted with Mr. Darcy?"

"As much as I ever wish to be," cried Elizabeth warmly. "I have spent four days in the same house with him, and I think him very disagreeable."

"I have no right to give *my* opinion," said Wickham, "as to his being agreeable or otherwise. I am not qualified to form one. I have known him too long and too well to be a fair judge. It is impossible for *me* to be impartial. But I believe your opinion of him would in general astonish —and perhaps you would not express it quite so strongly anywhere else. Here you are in your own family."

"Upon my word, I say no more *here* than I might say in any house in the neighbourhood, except Netherfield. He is not at all liked in Hertfordshire. Everybody is disgusted with his pride. You will not find him more favourably spoken of by any one."

"I cannot pretend to be sorry," said Wickham, after a short interruption, "that he or that any man should not be estimated beyond their deserts; but with *him* I believe it does not often happen. The world is blinded by his fortune and consequence, or frightened by his high and imposing manners, and sees him only as he chooses to be seen."

"I should take him, even on *my* slight acquaintance, to be an ill-tempered man." Wickham only shook his head.

"I wonder," said he, at the next opportunity of speaking, "whether he is likely to be in this country much longer."

"I do not at all know; but I *heard* nothing of his going away when I was at Netherfield. I hope your plans in favour of the ——shire will not be affected by his being in the neighbourhood."

"Oh! no—it is not for *me* to be driven away by Mr. Darcy. If *he* wishes to avoid seeing *me*, he must go. We are not on friendly terms, and it always gives me pain to meet him, but I have no reason for avoiding *him* but what I might proclaim before all the world, a sense of very great ill-usage, and most painful regrets at his being what he is. His father, Miss Bennet, the late Mr. Darcy, was one of the best men that ever breathed, and the truest friend I ever had; and I can never be in company with this Mr. Darcy without being grieved to the soul by a thousand tender recollections. His behaviour to myself has been scandalous; but I verily believe I could forgive him anything and everything, rather than his disappointing the hopes and disgracing the memory of his father."

Elizabeth found the interest of the subject increase, and listened with all her heart; but the delicacy of it prevented further inquiry.

Mr. Wickham began to speak on more general topics, Meryton, the neighbourhood, the society, appearing highly pleased with all that he had yet seen, and speaking of the latter especially with gentle but very intelligible gallantry.

"It was the prospect of constant society, and good society," he added, "which was my chief inducement to enter the ——shire. I knew it to be a most respectable, agreeable corps, and my friend Denny tempted me further by his account of their present quarters, and the very great attentions and excellent acquaintances Meryton had procured them. Society, I own, is necessary to me. I have been a disappointed man, and my spirits will not bear solitude. I *must* have employment and society. A military life is not what I was intended for, but circumstances have now made it eligible. The church *ought* to have been my profession—I was brought up for the church, and I should at this time have been in possession of a most valuable living, had it pleased the gentleman we were speaking of just now."

"Indeed!"

"Yes—the late Mr. Darcy bequeathed me the next presentation of the best living in his gift. He was my godfather, and excessively attached to me. I cannot do justice to his kindness. He meant to provide for me amply, and thought he had done it; but when the living fell, it was given elsewhere."

"Good heavens!" cried Elizabeth; "but how could *that* be? How could his will be disregarded? Why did not you seek legal redress?"

"There was just such an informality in the terms of the bequest as to give me no hope from law. A man of honour could not have doubted the intention, but Mr. Darcy chose to doubt it—or to treat it as a merely conditional recommendation, and to assert that I had forfeited all claim to it by extravagance, imprudence—in short anything or nothing. Certain it is, that the living became vacant two years ago, exactly as I was of an age to hold it, and that it was given to another man; and no less certain is it, that I cannot accuse myself of having really done anything to deserve to lose it. I have a warm, unguarded temper, and I may perhaps have sometimes spoken my opinion *of* him, and *to* him, too freely. I can recall nothing worse. But the fact is, that we are very different sort of men, and that he hates me."

"This is quite shocking! He deserves to be publicly disgraced."

"Some time or other he *will* be—but it shall not be by *me*. Till I can forget his father, I can never defy or expose *him*."

Elizabeth honoured him for such feelings, and thought him handsomer than ever as he expressed them.

"But what," said she, after a pause, "can have been his motive? What can have induced him to behave so cruelly?"

"A thorough, determined dislike of me—a dislike which I cannot but attribute in some measure to jealousy. Had the late Mr. Darcy liked me less, his son might have borne with me better: but his father's uncommon attachment to me irritated him, I believe, very early in life. He had not a temper to bear the sort of competition in which we stood—the sort of preference which was often given me."

"I had not thought Mr. Darcy so bad as this—though I have never liked him, I had not thought so very ill of him. I had supposed him to be despising his fellow-creatures in general, but did not suspect him of descending to such malicious revenge, such injustice, such inhumanity as this."

After a few minutes' reflection, however, she continued, "I *do* remember his boasting one day, at Netherfield, of the implacability of his resentments, of his having an unforgiving temper. His disposition must be dreadful."

"I will not trust myself on the subject," replied Wickham; "*I* can hardly be just to him."

Elizabeth was again deep in thought, and after a time exclaimed, "to treat in such a manner the godson, the friend, the favourite of his father!" She could have added, "a young man, too, like *you*, whose very countenance may vouch for your being amiable"—but she contented herself with, "and one, too, who had probably been his own companion from childhood, connected together, as I think you said, in the closest manner!"

"We were born in the same parish, within the same park; the greatest part of our youth was passed together; inmates of the same house, sharing the same amusements, objects of the same parental care. *My* father began life in the profession which your uncle, Mr. Philips, appears to do so much credit to—but he gave up everything to be of use to the late Mr. Darcy, and devoted all his time to the care of the Pemberley property. He was most highly esteemed by Mr. Darcy, a most intimate, confidential friend. Mr. Darcy often acknowledged himself to be under the greatest obligations to my father's active superintendence, and when, immediately before my father's death, Mr. Darcy gave him a voluntary promise of providing for me, I am convinced that he felt it to be as much a debt of gratitude to *him,* as of affection to myself."

"How strange!" cried Elizabeth. "How abominable! I wonder that the very pride of this Mr. Darcy has not made him just to you! If from no better motive, that he should not have been too proud to be dishonest—for dishonesty I must call it."

"It *is* wonderful," replied Wickham, "for almost all his actions may be traced to pride; and pride has often been his best friend. It has connected him nearer with virtue than with any other feeling. But we are none of us consistent, and in his behavior to me there were stronger impulses even than pride."

"Can such abominable pride as his have ever done him good?"

"Yes. It has often led him to be liberal and generous, to give his money freely, to display hospitality, to assist his tenants, and relieve the poor. Family pride, and *filial* pride—for he is very proud of what his father was—have done this. Not to appear to disgrace his family, to degenerate from the popular qualities, or lose the influence of the Pemberley House, is a powerful motive. He has also *brotherly* pride, which, with some brotherly affection, makes him a very kind and careful guardian of his sister, and you will hear him generally cried up as the most attentive and best of brothers."

"What sort of a girl is Miss Darcy?"

He shook his head. "I wish I could call her amiable. It gives me pain to speak ill of a Darcy. But she is too much like her brother—very, very proud. As a child, she was affectionate and pleasing, and extremely fond of me; and I have devoted hours and hours to her amusement. But she is nothing to me now. She is a handsome girl, about fifteen or sixteen, and, I understand, highly accomplished. Since her father's death, her home has been London, where a lady lives with her, and superintends her education."

After many pauses and many trials of other subjects, Elizabeth could not help reverting once more to the first, and saying:

"I am astonished at his intimacy with Mr. Bingley! How can Mr. Bingley, who seems good-humour itself, and is, I really believe, truly amiable, be in friendship with such a man? How can they suit each other? Do you know Mr. Bingley?"

"Not at all."

"He is a sweet-tempered, amiable, charming man. He cannot know what Mr. Darcy is."

"Probably not; but Mr. Darcy can please where he chooses. He does not want abilities. He can be a conversible companion if he thinks it worth his while. Among those who are at all his equals in consequence.

he is a very different man from what he is to the less prosperous. His pride never deserts him: but with the rich he is liberal-minded, just, sincere, rational, honourable, and perhaps agreeable—allowing something for fortune and figure."

The whist party soon afterwards breaking up, the players gathered round the other table, and Mr. Collins took his station between his cousin Elizabeth and Mrs. Philips. The usual inquiries as to his success was made by the latter. It had not been very great; he had lost every point; but when Mrs. Philips began to express her concern thereupon, he assured her with much earnest gravity that it was not of the least importance, that he considered the money as a mere trifle, and begged she would not make herself uneasy.

"I know very well, madam," said he, "that when persons sit down to a card table, they must take their chance of these things, and happily I am not in such circumstances as to make five shillings any object. There are undoubtedly many who could not say the same, but thanks to Lady Catherine de Bourgh, I am removed far beyond the necessity of regarding little matters."

Mr. Wickham's attention was caught; and after observing Mr. Collins for a few moments, he asked Elizabeth in a low voice whether her relation was very intimately acquainted with the family of de Bourgh.

"Lady Catherine de Bourgh," she replied, "has very lately given him a living. I hardly know how Mr. Collins was first introduced to her notice, but he certainly has not known her long."

"You know of course that Lady Catherine de Bourgh and Lady Anne Darcy were sisters; consequently that she is aunt to the present Mr. Darcy."

"No, indeed, I did not. I knew nothing at all of Lady Catherine's connections. I never heard of her existence till the day before yesterday."

"Her daughter, Miss de Bourgh, will have a very large fortune, and it is believed that she and her cousin will unite the two estates."

This information made Elizabeth smile, as she thought of poor Miss Bingley. Vain indeed must be all her attentions, vain and useless her affection for his sister and her praise of himself, if he were already self-destined to another.

"Mr. Collins," said she, "speaks highly both of Lady Catherine and her daughter; but from some particulars that he has related of her ladyship, I suspect his gratitude misleads him, and that in spite of her being his patroness, she is an arrogant, conceited woman."

"I believe her to be both in a great degree," replied Wickham; "I have not seen her for many years, but I very well remember that I never liked her, and that her manners were dictatorial and insolent. She has the reputation of being remarkably sensible and clever; but I rather believe she derives part of her abilities from her rank and fortune, part from her authoritative manner, and the rest from the pride of her nephew, who chooses that every one connected with him should have an understanding of the first class."

Elizabeth allowed that he had given a very rational account of it, and they continued talking together, with mutual satisfaction till supper put an end to cards, and gave the rest of the ladies their share of Mr. Wickham's attentions. There could be no conversation in the noise of Mrs. Philips's supper party, but his manners recommended him to everybody. Whatever he said, was said well; and whatever he did, done gracefully. Elizabeth went away with her head full of him. She could think of nothing but of Mr. Wickham, and of what he had told her, all the way home; but there was not time for her even to mention his name as they went, for neither Lydia nor Mr. Collins were once silent. Lydia talked incessantly of lottery tickets, of the fish she had lost and the fish she had won; and Mr. Collins in describing the civility of Mr. and Mrs. Philips, protesting that he did not in the least regard his losses at whist, enumerating all the dishes at supper, and repeatedly fearing that he crowded his cousins, had more to say than he could well manage before the carriage stopped at Longbourn House.

Chapter 17

ELIZABETH related to Jane the next day what had passed between Mr. Wickham and herself. Jane listened with astonishment and concern; she knew not how to believe that Mr. Darcy could be so unworthy of Mr. Bingley's regard; and yet, it was not in her nature to question the veracity of a young man of such amiable appearance as Wickham. The possibility of his having really endured such unkindness, was enough to interest all her tender feelings; and nothing therefore remained to be done, but to think well of them both, to defend the conduct of each, and throw into the account of accident or mistake whatever could not be otherwise explained.

"They have both," said she, "been deceived, I dare say, in some way or other, of which we can form no idea. Interested people have perhaps misrepresented each to the other. It is, in short, impossible for us to conjecture the causes or circumstances which may have alienated them, without actual blame on either side."

"Very true, indeed; and now, my dear Jane, what have you got to say in behalf of the interested people who have probably been concerned in the business? Do clear *them* too, or we shall be obliged to think ill of somebody?"

"Laugh as much as you choose, but you will not laugh me out of my opinion. My dearest Lizzy, do but consider in what a disgraceful light it places Mr. Darcy, to be treating his father's favourite in such a manner, one whom his father had promised to provide for. It is impossible. No man of common humanity, no man who had any value for his character, could be capable of it. Can his most intimate friends be so excessively deceived in him? Oh! no."

"I can much more easily believe Mr. Bingley's being imposed on, than that Mr. Wickham should invent such a history of himself as he gave me last night; names, facts, everything mentioned without ceremony. If it be not so, let Mr. Darcy contradict it. Besides, there was truth in his looks '

"It is difficult indeed—it is distressing. One does not know what to think."

"I beg your pardon; one knows exactly what to think."

But Jane could think with certainty on only one point—that Mr. Bingley, if he *had been* imposed on, would have much to suffer when the affair became public.

The two young ladies were summoned from the shrubbery, where this conversation passed, by the arrival of some of the very persons of whom they had been speaking: Mr. Bingley and his sisters came to give their personal invitation for the long-expected ball at Netherfield, which was fixed for the following Tuesday. The two ladies were delighted to see their dear friend again, called it an age since they had met, and repeatedly asked what she had been doing with herself since their separation. To the rest of the family they paid little attention; avoiding Mrs. Bennet as much as possible, saying not much to Elizabeth, and nothing at all to the others. They were soon gone again, rising from their seats with an activity which took their brother by surprise, and hurrying off as if eager to escape from Mrs. Bennet's civilities.

The prospect of the Netherfield ball was extremely agreeable to every female of the family. Mrs. Bennet chose to consider it as given in compliment to her eldest daughter, and was particularly flattered by receiving the invitation from Mr. Bingley himself, instead of a ceremonious card. Jane pictured to herself a happy evening in the society of her two friends, and the attentions of their brother; and Elizabeth thought with pleasure of dancing a great deal with Mr. Wickham, and of seeing a confirmation of everything in Mr. Darcy's look and behaviour. The happiness anticipated by Catherine and Lydia depended less on any single event, or any particular person, for though they each, like Elizabeth, meant to dance half the evening with Mr. Wickham, he was by no means the only partner who could satisfy them, and a ball was, at any rate, a ball. And even Mary could assure her family that she had no disinclination for it.

"While I can have my mornings to myself," said she, "it is enough—I think it is no sacrifice to join occasionally in evening engagements. Society has claims on us all; and I profess myself one of those who consider intervals of recreation and amusement as desirable for everybody."

Elizabeth's spirits were so high on the occasion, that though she did not often speak unnecessarily to Mr. Collins, she could not help asking him whether he intended to accept Mr. Bingley's invitation, and if he did, whether he would think it proper to join in the evening's amusement; and she was rather surprised to find that he entertained no scruple whatever on that head, and was very far from dreading a rebuke either from the Archbishop, or Lady Catherine de Bourgh, by venturing to dance.

"I am by no means of opinion, I assure you," said he, "that a ball of this kind, given by a young man of character, to respectable people, can have any evil tendency; and I am so far from objecting to dancing myself, that I shall hope to be honoured with the hands of all my fair cousins in the course of the evening; and I take this opportunity of soliciting yours, Miss Elizabeth, for the two first dances especially, a preference which I trust my cousin Jane will attribute to the right cause, and not to any disrespect for her."

Elizabeth felt herself completely taken in. She had fully proposed being engaged by Mr. Wickham for those very dances; and to have Mr. Collins instead! her liveliness had been never worse timed. There was no help for it, however. Mr. Wickham's happiness and her own was perforce delayed a little longer, and Mr. Collins's proposal accepted with as good a grace as she could. She was not the better pleased with his gallantry from the idea it suggested of something more. It now first struck her, that *she* was selected from among her sisters as worthy of being the mistress of Hunsford Parsonage, and of assisting to form a quadrille table at Rosings, in the absence of more eligible visitors. The idea soon reached to conviction, as she observed his increasing civilities toward herself, and heard his frequent attempt at a compliment on her wit and vivacity; and though more astonished than gratified herself by this effect of her charms, it was not long before her mother gave her to understand that the probability of their marriage was exceedingly agreeable to *her*. Elizabeth, however, did not choose to take the hint, being well aware that a serious dispute must be the consequence of any reply. Mr. Collins might never make the offer, and, till he did, it was useless to quarrel about him.

If there had not been a Netherfield ball to prepare for and talk of, the younger Miss Bennets would have been in a pitiable state at this time, for from the day of the invitation, to the day of the ball, there was such a succession of rain as prevented their walking to Meryton once. No aunt, no officers, no news could be sought after—the very shoe-roses for Netherfield were got by proxy. Even Elizabeth might have found some trial of her patience in weather which totally suspended the improvement of her acquaintance with Mr. Wickham; and nothing less than a dance on Tuesday, could have made such a Friday, Saturday, Sunday, and Monday endurable to Kitty and Lydia.

Chapter 18

TILL Elizabeth entered the drawing-room at Netherfield, and looked in vain for Mr. Wickham among the cluster of red coats there assembled, a doubt of his being present had never occurred to her. The certainty of meeting him had not been checked by any of those recollections that might not unreasonably have alarmed her. She had dressed with more than usual care, and prepared in the highest spirits for the conquest of all that remained unsubdued of his heart, trusting that it was not more than might be won in the course of the evening. But in an instant arose the dreadful suspicion of his being purposely omitted for Mr. Darcy's pleasure in the Bingleys' invitation to the officers; and though this was not exactly the case, the absolute fact of his absence was pronounced by his friend Mr. Denny, to whom Lydia eagerly applied, and who told them that Wickham had been obliged to go to town on business the day before, and was not yet returned; adding, with a significant smile, "I do not imagine his business would have called him away just now, if he had not wished to avoid a certain gentleman here."

This part of his intelligence, though unheard by Lydia, was caught by Elizabeth, and, as it assured her that Darcy was not less answerable for Wickham's absence than if her first surmise had been just, every feeling of displeasure against the former was so sharpened by immediate disappointment, that she could hardly reply with tolerable civility to the polite inquiries which he directly afterwards approached to make. Attention, forbearance, patience with Darcy, was injury to Wickham. She was resolved against any sort of conversation with him, and turned away with a degree of ill-humour which she could not wholly surmount even in speaking to Mr. Bingley, whose blind partiality provoked her.

But Elizabeth was not formed for ill-humour; and though every prospect of her own was destroyed for the evening, it could not dwell long on her spirits; and having told all her griefs to Charlotte Lucas, whom she had not seen for a week, she was soon able to make a voluntary transition to the oddities of her cousin, and to point him out to her particular notice. The two first dances, however, brought a return of distress; they were dances of mortification. Mr. Collins, awkward and solemn, apologising instead of attending, and often moving wrong without being aware of it, gave her all the shame and misery which a disagreeable partner for a couple of dances can give. The moment of her release from him was ecstasy.

She danced next with an officer, and had the refreshment of talking of Wickham, and of hearing that he was universally liked. When those dances were over, she returned to Charlotte Lucas, and was in conversation with her, when she found herself suddenly addressed by Mr. Darcy, who took her so much by surprise in his application for her hand, that, without knowing what she did, she accepted him. He walked away again immediately, and she was left to fret over her own want of presence of mind; Charlotte tried to console her.

"I dare say you will find him very agreeable."

"Heaven forbid! *That* would be the greatest misfortune of all! To find a man agreeable whom one is determined to hate! Do not wish me such an evil."

When the dancing recommenced, however, and Darcy approached to claim her hand, Charlotte could not help cautioning her in a whisper, not to be a simpleton, and allow her fancy for Wickham to make her appear unpleasant in the eyes of a man of ten times his consequence. Elizabeth made no answer, and took her place in the set, amazed at the dignity to which she was arrived in being allowed to stand opposite to Mr. Darcy, and reading in her neighbours' looks, their equal amazement in beholding it. They stood for some time without speaking a word; and she began to imagine that their silence was to last through the two dances, and at first was resolved not to break it; till suddenly fancying that it would be the greater punishment to her partner to oblige him to talk, she made some slight observation on the dance. He replied, and was again silent. After a pause of some minutes, she addressed him a second time with:—"It is *your* turn to say something now, Mr. Darcy. I talked about the dance, and *you* ought to make some kind of remark on the size of the room, or the number of couples."

He smiled, and assured her that whatever she wished him to say should be said.

"Very well. That reply will do for the present. Perhaps by and by I may observe that private balls are much pleasanter than public ones. But *now* we may be silent."

"Do you talk by rule, then, while you are dancing?"

"Sometimes. One must speak a little, you know. It would look odd to be entirely silent for half an hour together; and yet for the advantage of *some,* conversation ought to be so arranged, as that they may have the trouble of saying as little as possible."

"Are you consulting your own feelings in the present case, or do you imagine that you are gratifying mine?"

"Both," replied Elizabeth, archly; "for I have always seen a great similarity in the turn of our minds. We are each of an unsocial, taciturn disposition, unwilling to speak, unless we expect to say something that will amaze the whole room, and be handed down to posterity with all the éclat of a proverb."

"This is no very striking resemblance of your own character, I am sure," said he. "How near it may be to *mine,* I cannot pretend to say. *You* think it a faithful portrait undoubtedly."

"I must not decide on my own performance."

He made no answer, and they were again silent till they had gone down the dance, when he asked her if she and her sisters did not very often walk to Meryton? She answered in the affirmative, and, unable to resist the temptation, added, "When you met us there the other day, we had just been forming a new acquaintance."

The effect was immediate. A deeper shade of hauteur overspread his features, but he said not a word, and Elizabeth, though blaming herself for her own weakness, could not go on. At length Darcy spoke, and in a constrained manner said, "Mr. Wickham is blessed with such happy manners as may ensure his *making* friends—whether he may be equally capable of *retaining* them, is less certain."

"He has been so unlucky as to lose *your* friendship," replied Elizabeth with emphasis, "and in a manner which he is likely to suffer from all his life."

Darcy made no answer, and seemed desirous of changing the subject. At that moment Sir William Lucas appeared close to them, meaning to pass through the set to the other side of the room; but on perceiving Mr. Darcy, he stopped with a bow of superior courtesy to compliment him on his dancing and his partner.

"I have been most highly gratified indeed, my dear sir. Such very superior dancing is not often seen. It is evident that you belong to the first circles. Allow me to say, however, that your fair partner does not disgrace you, and that I must hope to have this pleasure often repeated, especially when a certain desirable event, my dear Miss Eliza (glancing at her sister and Bingley) shall take place. What congratulations will then flow in! I appeal to Mr. Darcy:—but let me not interrupt you, sir. You will not thank me for detaining you from the bewitching converse of that young lady, whose bright eyes are also upbraiding me."

The latter part of this address was scarcely heard by Darcy; but Sir William's allusion to his friend seemed to strike him forcibly, and his eyes were directed with a very serious expression towards Bingley and Jane, who were dancing together. Recovering himself, however, shortly, he turned to his partner, and said, "Sir William's interruption has made me forget what we were talking of."

"I do not think we were speaking at all. Sir William could not have interrupted any two people in the room who had less to say for themselves. We have tried two or three subjects already without success, and what we are to talk of next I cannot imagine."

"What think you of books?" said he, smiling.

"Books—oh! no. I am sure we never read the same, or not with the same feelings."

"I am sorry you think so; but if that be the case, there can at least be no want of subject. We may compare our different opinions."

"No—I cannot talk of books in a ball-room; my head is always full of something else."

"The *present* always occupies you in such scenes—does it?" said he, with a look of doubt.

"Yes, always," she replied, without knowing what she said, for her thoughts had wandered far from the subject, as soon afterwards appeared by her suddenly exclaiming, "I remember hearing you once say, Mr. Darcy, that you hardly ever forgave, that your resentment once created was unappeasable. You are very cautious, I suppose, as to its *being created*."

"I am," said he, with a firm voice.

"And never allow yourself to be blinded by prejudice?"

"I hope not."

"It is particularly incumbent on those who never change their opinion, to be secure of judging properly at first."

"May I ask to what these questions tend?"

"Merely to the illustration of *your* character," said she, endeavouring to shake off her gravity. "I am trying to make it out."

"And what is your success?"

She shook her head, "I do not get on at all. I hear such different accounts of you as puzzle me exceedingly."

"I can readily believe," answered he gravely, "that reports may vary greatly with respect to me; and I could wish, Miss Bennet, that you were not to sketch my character at the present moment, as there is reason to fear that the performance would reflect no credit on either."

"But if I do not take your likeness now, I may never have another opportunity."

"I would by no means suspend any pleasure of yours," he coldly replied. She said no more, and they went down the other dance and parted in silence; on each side dissatisfied, though not to an equal degree, for in Darcy's breast there was a tolerable powerful feeling towards her, which soon procured her pardon, and directed all his anger against another.

They had not long separated, when Miss Bingley came towards her, and with an expression of civil disdain thus accosted her:—"So, Miss Eliza, I hear you are quite delighted with George Wickham! Your sister has been talking to me about him, and asking me a thousand questions; and I find that the young man forgot to tell you, among his other communications, that he was the son of old Wickham, the late Mr. Darcy's steward. Let me recommend you, however, as a friend, not to give implicit confidence to all his assertions; for as to Mr. Darcy's using him ill, it is perfectly false; for, on the contrary, he has been always remarkably kind to him, though George Wickham has treated Mr. Darcy in a most infamous manner. I do not know the particulars, but I know very well that Mr. Darcy is not in the least to blame, that he cannot bear to hear George Wickham mentioned, and that though my brother thought he could not well avoid including him in his invitation to the officers, he was excessively glad to find that he had taken himself out of the way. His coming into the country at all is a most insolent thing, indeed, and I wonder how he could presume to do it. I pity you, Miss Eliza, for this discovery of your favourite's guilt; but really, considering his descent, one could not expect much better."

"His guilt and his descent appear by your account to be the same," said Elizabeth angrily; "for I have heard you accuse him of nothing worse than of being the son of Mr. Darcy's steward, and of *that*, I can assure you, he informed me himself."

"I beg your pardon," replied Miss Bingley, turning away with a sneer. "Excuse my interference: it was kindly meant."

"Insolent girl!" said Elizabeth to herself. "You are much mistaken if you expect to influence me by such a paltry attack as this. I see nothing in it but your own wilful ignorance and the malice of Mr. Darcy." She then sought her eldest sister, who had undertaken to make inquiries on the same subject of Bingley. Jane met her with a smile of such sweet complacency, a glow of such happy expression, as sufficiently marked how well she was satisfied with the occurrences of the evening. Elizabeth instantly read her feelings, and at that moment solicitude for Wickham, resentment against his enemies, and everything else, gave way before the hope of Jane's being in the fairest way for happiness.

"I want to know," said she, with a countenance no less smiling than her sister's, "what you have learnt about Mr. Wickham. But perhaps you have been too pleasantly engaged to think of any third person; in which case you may be sure of my pardon."

"No," replied Jane, "I have not forgotten him; but I have nothing satisfactory to tell you. Mr. Bingley does not know the whole of his history, and is quite ignorant of the circumstances which have principally offended Mr. Darcy; but he will vouch for the good conduct, the probity, and honour of his friend, and is perfectly convinced that Mr. Wickham has deserved much less attention from Mr. Darcy than he has received; and I am sorry to say that by his account as well as his sister's, Mr. Wickham is by no means a respectable young man. I am afraid he has been very imprudent, and has deserved to lose Mr. Darcy's regard."

"Mr. Bingley does not know Mr. Wickham himself?"

"No; he never saw him till the other morning at Meryton."

"This account then is what he has received from Mr. Darcy. I am satisfied. But what does he say of the living?"

"He does not exactly recollect the circumstances, though he has heard them from Mr. Darcy more than once, but he believes that it was left to him _conditionally_ only."

"I have not a doubt of Mr. Bingley's sincerity," said Elizabeth warmly; "but you must excuse my not being convinced by assurances only. Mr. Bingley's defence of his friend was a very able one, I dare say; but since he is unacquainted with several parts of the story, and has learnt the rest from that friend himself, I shall venture still to think of both gentlemen as I did before."

She then changed the discourse to one more gratifying to each, and on which there could be no difference of sentiment. Elizabeth listened with delight to the happy, though modest hopes which Jane entertained of Bingley's regard, and said all in her power to heighten her confidence in it. On their being joined by Mr. Bingley himself, Elizabeth withdrew to Miss Lucas; to whose inquiry after the pleasantness of her last partner she had scarcely replied, before Mr. Collins came up to them, and told her with great exultation that he had just been so fortunate as to make a most important discovery.

"I have found out," said he, "by a singular accident, that there is now in the room a near relation of my patroness. I happened to overhear the gentleman himself mentioning to the young lady who does the honours of this house the names of his cousin Miss de Bourgh, and of her mother Lady Catherine. How wonderfully these sort of things occur! Who would have thought of my meeting with, perhaps, a nephew of Lady Catherine de

Bourgh in this assembly! I am most thankful that the discovery is made in time for me to pay my respects to him, which I am now going to do, and trust he will excuse my not having done it before. My total ignorance of the connection must plead my apology."

"You are not going to introduce yourself to Mr. Darcy!"

"Indeed I am. I shall entreat his pardon for not having done it earlier. I believe him to be Lady Catherine's *nephew*. It will be in my power to assure him that her ladyship was quite well yesterday se'nnight."

Elizabeth tried hard to dissuade him from such a scheme, assuring him that Mr. Darcy would consider his addressing him without introduction as an impertinent freedom, rather than a compliment to his aunt; that it was not in the least necessary there should be any notice on either side; and that if it were, it must belong to Mr. Darcy, the superior in consequence, to begin the acquaintance. Mr. Collins listened to her with the determined air of following his own inclination, and, when she ceased speaking, replied thus:—"My dear Miss Elizabeth, I have the highest opinion in the world of your excellent judgment in all matters within the scope of your understanding; but permit me to say, that there must be a wide difference between the established forms of ceremony amongst the laity, and those which regulate the clergy; for, give me leave to observe that I consider the clerical office as equal in point of dignity with the highest rank in the kingdom—provided that a proper humility of behaviour is at the same time maintained. You must therefore allow me to follow the dictates of my conscience on this occasion, which leads me to perform what I look on as a point of duty. Pardon me for neglecting to profit by your advice, which on every other subject shall be my constant guide, though in the case before us I consider myself more fitted by education and habitual study to decide on what is right than a young lady like yourself." And with a low bow he left her to attack Mr. Darcy, whose reception of his advances she eagerly watched, and whose astonishment at being so addressed was very evident. Her cousin prefaced his speech with a solemn bow: and though she could not hear a word of it, she felt as if hearing it all, and saw in the motion of his lips the words "apology," "Hunsford," and "Lady Catherine de Bourgh." It vexed her to see him expose himself to such a man. Mr. Darcy was eyeing him with unrestrained wonder, and when at last Mr. Collins allowed him time to speak, replied with an air of distant civility. Mr. Collins, however, was not discouraged from speaking again, and Mr. Darcy's contempt seemed abundantly increasing with the length of his second speech, and at the end of it he only made him a slight bow, and moved another way. Mr. Collins then returned to Elizabeth.

"I have no reason, I assure you," said he, "to be dissatisfied with my reception. Mr. Darcy seemed much pleased with the attention. He answered me with the utmost civility, and even paid me the compliment of saying that he was so well convinced of Lady Catherine's discernment as to be certain she could never bestow a favour unworthily. It was really a very handsome thought. Upon the whole, I am much pleased with him."

As Elizabeth had no longer any interest of her own to pursue, she turned her attention almost entirely on her sister and Mr. Bingley; and the train of agreeable reflections which her observations gave birth to, made her perhaps almost as happy as Jane. She saw her in idea settled in that very house, in all the felicity which a marriage of true affection could bestow; and she felt capable, under such circumstances, of endeavouring even to like Bingley's two sisters. Her mother's thoughts she plainly saw were bent the same way, and she determined not to venture near her, lest she might hear too much. When they sat down to supper, therefore, she considered it a most unlucky perverseness which placed them within one of each other; and deeply was she vexed to find that her mother was talking to that one person (Lady Lucas) freely, openly, and of nothing else but of her expectation that Jane would be soon married to Mr. Bingley. It was an animating subject, and Mrs. Bennet seemed incapable of fatigue while enumerating the advantages of the match. His being such a charming young man, and so rich, and living but three miles from them, were the first points of self-gratulation; and then it was such a comfort to think how fond the two sisters were of Jane, and to be certain that they must desire the connection as much as she could do. It was, moreover, such a promising thing for her younger daughters, as Jane's marrying so greatly must throw them in the way of other rich men; and lastly, it was so pleasant at her time of life to be able to consign her single daughters to the care of their sister, that she might not be obliged to go into company more than she liked. It was necessary to make this circumstance a matter of pleasure, because on such occasions it is the etiquette; but no one was less likely than Mrs. Bennet to find comfort in staying at home at any period of her life. She concluded with many good wishes that Lady Lucas might soon be equally fortunate, though evidently and triumphantly believing there was no chance of it.

In vain did Elizabeth endeavour to check the rapidity of her mother's words, or persuade her to describe her felicity in a less audible whisper; for, to her inexpressible vexation, she could perceive that the chief of it was overheard by Mr. Darcy, who sat opposite to them. Her mother only scolded her for being nonsensical.

"What is Mr. Darcy to me, pray, that I should be afraid of him? I am sure we owe him no such particular civility as to be obliged to say nothing *he* may not like to hear."

"For heaven's sake, madam, speak lower. What advantage can it be to you to offend Mr. Darcy? You will never recommend yourself to his friend by so doing!"

Nothing that she could say, however, had any influence. Her mother would talk of her views in the same intelligible tone. Elizabeth blushed and blushed again with shame and vexation. She could not help frequently glancing her eye at Mr. Darcy, though every glance convinced her of what she dreaded: for though he was not always looking at her mother, she was convinced that his attention was invariably fixed by her. The expression of his face changed gradually from indignant contempt to a composed and steady gravity.

At length, however, Mrs. Bennet had no more to say; and Lady Lucas, who had been long yawning at the repetition of delights which she saw no likelihood of sharing, was left to the comforts of cold ham and chicken. Elizabeth now began to revive. But not long was the interval of tranquillity; for, when supper was over, singing was talked of, and she had the mortification of seeing Mary, after very little entreaty, preparing to oblige the company. By many significant looks and silent entreaties, did she endeavour to prevent such a proof of complaisance, but in vain; Mary would not understand them; such an opportunity of exhibiting was delightful to her, and she began her song. Elizabeth's eyes were fixed on her with most painful sensations, and she watched her progress through the several stanzas with an impatience which was very ill rewarded at their close; for Mary, on receiving, amongst the thanks of the table, the hint of a hope that she might be prevailed on to favour them again, after the pause of half a minute began another. Mary's powers were by no means fitted for such a display; her voice was weak, and her manner affected. Elizabeth was in agonies. She looked at Jane, to see how she bore it; but Jane was very composedly talking to Bingley. She looked at his two sisters, and saw them making signs of derision at each other, and at Darcy, who continued, however, impenetrably grave. She looked at her father to entreat his interference, lest Mary should be singing all night. He took the hint, and when Mary had finished her second song, said aloud, "That will do extremely well, child. You have delighted us long enough. Let the other young ladies have time to exhibit."

Mary, though pretending not to hear, was somewhat disconcerted; and Elizabeth, sorry for her, and sorry for her father's speech, was afraid her anxiety had done no good. Others of the party were now applied to.

"If I," said Mr. Collins, "were so fortunate as to be able to sing, I should have great pleasure, I am sure, in obliging the company with an air; for I consider music as a very innocent diversion, and perfectly compatible with the profession of a clergyman. I do not mean, however, to assert that we can be justified in devoting too much of our time to music, for there are certainly other things to be attended to. The rector of a parish has much to do. In the first place, he must make such an agreement for tithes as may be beneficial to himself and not offensive to his patron. He must write his own sermons; and the time that remains will not be too much for his parish duties, and the care and improvement of his dwelling, which he cannot be excused from making as comfortable as possible. And I do not think it of light importance that he should have attentive and conciliatory manners towards everybody, especially towards those to whom he owes his preferment. I cannot acquit him of that duty; nor could I think well of the man who should omit an occasion of testifying his respect towards anybody connected with the family." And with a bow to

Mr. Darcy, he concluded his speech, which had been spoken so loud as to be heard by half the room. Many stared—many smiled; but no one looked more amused than Mr. Bennet himself, while his wife seriously commended Mr. Collins for having spoken so sensibly, and observed in a half-whisper to Lady Lucas, that he was a remarkably clever, good kind of young man.

To Elizabeth it appeared that, had her family made an agreement to expose themselves as much as they could during the evening, it would have been impossible for them to play their parts with more spirit or finer success; and happy did she think it for Bingley and her sister that some of the exhibition had escaped his notice, and that his feelings were not of a sort to be much distressed by the folly which he must have witnessed. That his two sisters and Mr. Darcy, however, should have such an opportunity of ridiculing her relations, was bad enough, and she could not determine whether the silent contempt of the gentleman, or the insolent smiles of the ladies, were more intolerable.

The rest of the evening brought her little amusement. She was teased by Mr. Collins, who continued most perseveringly by her side, and though he could not prevail with her to dance with him again, put it out of her power to dance with others. In vain did she entreat him to stand up with somebody else, and offer to introduce him to any young lady in the room. He assured her, that as to dancing, he was perfectly indifferent to it; that his chief object was by delicate attentions to recommend himself to her, and that he should therefore make a point of remaining close to her the whole evening. There was no arguing upon such a project. She owed her greatest relief to her friend Miss Lucas, who often joined them, and good-naturedly engaged Mr. Collins's conversation to herself.

She was at least free from the offence of Mr. Darcy's further notice; though often standing within a very short distance of her, quite disengaged, he never came near enough to speak. She felt it to be the probable consequence of her allusions to Mr. Wickham, and rejoiced in it.

The Longbourn party were the last of all the company to depart, and, by a manœuvre of Mrs. Bennet, had to wait for their carriage a quarter of an hour after everybody else was gone, which gave them time to see how heartily they were wished away by some of the family. Mrs. Hurst and her sister scarcely opened their mouths, except to complain of fatigue, and were evidently impatient to have the house to themselves. They repulsed every attempt of Mrs. Bennet at conversation, and by so doing threw a languor over the whole party, which was very little relieved by the long speeches of Mr. Collins, who was complimenting Mr. Bingley and his sisters on the elegance of their entertainment, and the hospitality and politeness which had marked their behaviour to their guests. Darcy said nothing at all. Mr. Bennet, in equal silence, was enjoying the scene. Mr. Bingley and Jane were standing together, a little detached from the rest, and talked only to each other. Elizabeth preserved as steady a silence as either Mrs. Hurst or Miss Bingley; and even Lydia was too much fatigued to utter more than the occasional exclamation of "Lord, how tired I am!" accompanied by a violent yawn.

When at length they arose to take leave, Mrs. Bennet was most pressingly civil in her hope of seeing the whole family soon at Longbourn, and addressed herself particularly to Mr. Bingley, to assure him how happy he would make them by eating a family dinner with them at any time, without the ceremony of a formal invitation. Bingley was all grateful pleasure, and he readily engaged for taking the earliest opportunity of waiting on her, after his return from London, whither he was obliged to go the next day for a short time.

Mrs. Bennet was perfectly satisfied, and quitted the house under the delightful persuasion that, allowing for the necessary preparations of settlements, new carriages, and wedding clothes, she should undoubtedly see her daughter settled at Netherfield in the course of three or four months. Of having another daughter married to Mr. Collins, she thought with equal certainty, and with considerable, though not equal, pleasure. Elizabeth was the least dear to her of all her children; and though the man and the match were quite good enough for *her,* the worth of each was eclipsed by Mr. Bingley and Netherfield.

Chapter 19

THE next day opened a new scene at Longbourn. Mr. Collins made his declaration in form. Having resolved to do it without loss of time, as his leave of absence extended only to the following Saturday, and having no feelings of diffidence to make it distressing to himself even at the moment, he set about it in a very orderly manner, with all the observances, which he supposed a regular part of the business. On finding Mrs. Bennet, Elizabeth, and one of the younger girls together, soon after breakfast, he addressed the mother in these words: "May I hope, madam, for your interest with your fair daughter Elizabeth, when I solicit for the honour of a private audience with her in the course of this morning?"

Before Elizabeth had time for anything but a blush of surprise, Mrs. Bennet instantly answered, "Oh dear!—yes—certainly. I am sure Lizzy will be very happy—I am sure she can have no objection. Come, Kitty, I want you upstairs." And, gathering her work together, she was hastening away, when Elizabeth called out:

"Dear madam, do not go. I beg you will not go. Mr. Collins must excuse me. He can have nothing to say to me that anybody need not hear. I am going away myself."

"No, no, nonsense, Lizzy. I desire you will stay where you are." And upon Elizabeth's seeming really, with vexed and embarrassed looks, about to escape, she added: "Lizzy, I *insist* upon your staying and hearing Mr. Collins."

Elizabeth would not oppose such an injunction—and a moment's consideration making her also sensible that it would be wisest to get it over as soon and as quietly as possible, she sat down again, and tried to conceal, by incessant employment, the feelings which were divided between distress and diversion. Mrs. Bennet and Kitty walked off, and as soon as they were gone Mr. Collins began.

"Believe me, my dear Miss Elizabeth, that your modesty, so far from doing you any disservice, rather adds to your other perfections. You would have been less amiable in my eyes had there *not* been this little unwillingness; but allow me to assure you, that I have your respecte' mother's permission for this address. You can hardly doubt the purpor. of my discourse, however your natural delicacy may lead you to dissemble; my attentions have been too marked to be mistaken. Almost as soon as I entered the house, I singled you out as the companion of my future life. But before I am run away with by my feelings on this subject, perhaps it would be advisable for me to state my reasons for marrying— and, moreover, for coming into Hertfordshire with the design of selecting a wife, as I certainly did."

The idea of Mr. Collins, with all his solemn composure, being run away with by his feelings, made Elizabeth so near laughing, that she could not use the short pause he allowed in any attempt to stop him farther, and he continued:

"My reasons for marrying are, first, that I think it a right thing for every clergyman in easy circumstances (like myself) to set the example of matrimony in his parish; secondly, that I am convinced it will add very greatly to my happiness; and thirdly—which perhaps I ought to have mentioned earlier, that it is the particular advice and recommendation of the very noble lady whom I have the honour of calling patroness. Twice has she condescended to give me her opinion (unasked too!) on this subject; and it was but the very Saturday night before I left Hunsford— between our pools at quadrille, while Mrs. Jenkinson was arranging Miss de Bourgh's footstool, that she said, 'Mr. Collins, you must marry. A clergyman like you must marry. Choose properly, choose a gentlewoman for *my* sake; and for your *own*, let her be an active, useful sort of person, not brought up high, but able to make a small income go a good way. This is my advice. Find such a woman as soon as you can, bring her to Hunsford, and I will visit her.' Allow me, by the way, to observe, my fair cousin, that I do not reckon the notice and kindness of Lady Catherine de Bourgh as among the least of the advantages in my power to offer. You will find her manners beyond anything I can describe; and your wit and vivacity, I think, must be acceptable to her, especially when tempered with the silence and respect which her rank will inevitably excite. Thus much for my general intention in favour of matrimony; it remains to be told why my views were directed to Longbourn instead of my own neighbourhood, where I assure you there are many amiable young women. But the fact is, that being, as I am, to inherit this estate after the death of your honoured father (who, however, may live many years longer), I.

could not satisfy myself without resolving to choose a wife from among his daughters, that the loss to them might be as little as possible, when the melancholy event takes place—which, however, as I have already said, may not be for several years. This has been my motive, my fair cousin, and I flatter myself it will not sink me in your esteem. And now nothing remains for me but to assure you in the most animated language of the violence of my affection. To fortune I am perfectly indifferent, and shall make no demand of that nature on your father, since I am well aware that it could not be complied with; and that one thousand pounds in the four per cents, which will not be yours till after your mother's decease, is all that you may ever be entitled to. On that head, therefore, I shall be uniformly silent; and you may assure yourself that no ungenerous reproach shall ever pass my lips when we are married."

It was absolutely necessary to interrupt him now.

"You are too hasty, sir," she cried. "You forget that I have made no answer. Let me do it without further loss of time. Accept my thanks for the compliment you are paying me. I am very sensible of the honour of your proposals, but it is impossible for me to do otherwise than decline them."

"I am not now to learn," replied Mr. Collins, with a formal wave of the hand, "that it is usual with young ladies to reject the addresses of the man whom they secretly mean to accept, when he first applies for their favour; and that sometimes the refusal is repeated a second or even a third time. I am therefore by no means discouraged by what you have just said, and shall hope to lead you to the altar ere long."

"Upon my word, sir," cried Elizabeth, "your hope is rather an extraordinary one after my declaration. I do assure you that I am not one of those young ladies (if such young ladies there are) who are so daring as to risk their happiness on the chance of being asked a second time. I am perfectly serious in my refusal. You could not make *me* happy, and I am convinced that I am the last woman in the world who would make you so. Nay, were your friend Lady Catherine to know me, I am persuaded she would find me in every respect ill qualified for the situation."

"Were it certain that Lady Catherine would think so," said Mr. Collins very gravely—"but I cannot imagine that her ladyship would at all disapprove of you. And you may be certain that when I have the honour of seeing her again, I shall speak in the highest terms of your modesty, economy, and other amiable qualifications."

"Indeed, Mr. Collins, all praise of me will be unnecessary. You must give me leave to judge for myself, and pay me the compliment of believing what I say. I wish you very happy and very rich, and by refusing your hand, do all in my power to prevent your being otherwise. In making me the offer, you must have satisfied the delicacy of your feelings with regard to my family, and may take possession of Longbourn estate whenever it falls, without any self-reproach. This matter may be considered, therefore, as finally settled." And rising as she thus spoke, she would have quitted the room, had not Mr. Collins thus addressed her:

"When I do myself the honour of speaking to you next on the subject, I shall hope to receive a more favourable answer than you have now given me; though I am far from accusing you of cruelty at present, because I know it to be the established custom of your sex to reject a man on the first application, and perhaps you have even now said as much to encourage my suit as would be consistent with the true delicacy of the female character."

"Really, Mr. Collins," cried Elizabeth with some warmth, "you puzzle me exceedingly. If what I have hitherto said can appear to you in the form of encouragement, I know not how to express my refusal in such a way as may convince you of its being one."

"You must give me leave to flatter myself, my dear cousin, that your refusal of my addresses is merely words of course. My reasons for believing it are briefly these: It does not appear to me that my hand is unworthy your acceptance, or that the establishment I can offer would be any other than highly desirable. My situation in life, my connections with the family of de Bourgh, and my relationship to your own, are circumstances highly in my favour; and you should take it into further consideration, that in spite of your manifold attractions, it is by no means certain that another offer of marriage may ever be made you. Your portion is unhappily so small that it will in all likelihood undo the effects of your loveliness and amiable qualifications. As I must therefore conclude that you are not serious in your rejection of me, I shall choose to attribute it to your wish of increasing my love by suspense, according to the usual practice of elegant females."

"I do assure you, sir, that I have no pretensions whatever to that kind of elegance which consists in tormenting a respectable man. I would rather be paid the compliment of being believed sincere. I thank you again and again for the honour you have done me in your proposals, but to accept them is absolutely impossible. My feelings in every respect forbid it. Can I speak plainer? Do not consider me now as an elegant female, intending to plague you, but as a rational creature, speaking the truth from her heart."

"You are uniformly charming!" cried he, with an air of awkward gallantry; "and I am persuaded that when sanctioned by the express authority of both your excellent parents, my proposals will not fail of being acceptable."

To such perseverance in wilful self-deception Elizabeth would make no reply, and immediately and in silence withdrew; determined, that if he persisted in considering her repeated refusals as flattering encouragement, to apply to her father, whose negative might be uttered in such a manner as must be decisive, and whose behaviour at least could not be mistaken for the affectation and coquetry of an elegant female.

Chapter 20

MR. COLLINS was not left long to the silent contemplation of his successful love; for Mrs. Bennet, having dawdled about in the vestibule to watch for the end of the conference, no sooner saw Elizabeth open the door and with quick step pass her towards the staircase, than she entered the breakfast-room, and congratulated both him and herself in warm terms on the happy prospect of their nearer connection. Mr. Collins received and returned these felicitations with equal pleasure, and then proceeded to relate the particulars of their interview, with the result of which he trusted he had every reason to be satisfied, since the refusal which his cousin had steadfastly given him would naturally flow from her bashful modesty and the genuine delicacy of her character.

This information, however, startled Mrs. Bennet; she would have been glad to be equally satisfied that her daughter had meant to encourage him by protesting against his proposals, but she dared not believe it, and could not help saying so.

"But, depend upon it, Mr. Collins," she added, "that Lizzy shall be brought to reason. I will speak to her about it myself directly. She is a very headstrong, foolish girl, and does not know her own interest; but I will *make* her know it."

"Pardon me for interrupting you, madam," cried Mr. Collins; "but if she is really headstrong and foolish, I know not whether she would altogether be a very desirable wife to a man in my situation, who naturally looks for happiness in the marriage state. If therefore she actually persists in rejecting my suit, perhaps it were better not to force her into accepting me, because if liable to such defects of temper, she could not contribute much to my felicity."

"Sir, you quite misunderstand me," said Mrs. Bennet, alarmed. "Lizzy is only headstrong in such matters as these. In everything else she is as good-natured a girl as ever lived. I will go directly to Mr. Bennet, and we shall very soon settle it with her, I am sure."

She would not give him time to reply, but hurrying instantly to her husband, called out as she entered the library, "Oh! Mr. Bennet, you are wanted immediately; we are all in an uproar. You must come and make Lizzy marry Mr. Collins, for she vows she will not have him, and if you do not make haste he will change his mind and not have *her*."

Mr. Bennet raised his eyes from his book as she entered, and fixed them on her face with a calm unconcern which was not in the least altered by her communication.

"I have not the pleasure of understanding you," said he, when she had finished her speech. "Of what are you talking?"

"Of Mr. Collins and Lizzy. Lizzy declares she will not have Mr. Collins, and Mr. Collins begins to say that he will not have Lizzy."

"And what am I to do on the occasion? It seems an hopeless business."

"Speak to Lizzy about it yourself. Tell her that you insist upon her marrying him."

"Let her be called down. She shall hear my opinion."

Mrs. Bennet rang the bell, and Miss Elizabeth was summoned to the library.

"Come here, child," cried her father as she appeared. "I have sent for you on an affair of importance. I understand that Mr. Collins has made you an offer of marriage. Is it true?" Elizabeth replied that it was. "Very well—and this offer of marriage you have refused?"

"I have, sir."

"Very well. We now come to the point. Your mother insists upon your accepting it. Is it not so, Mrs. Bennet?"

"Yes, or I will never see her again."

"An unhappy alternative is before you, Elizabeth. From this day you must be a stranger to one of your parents. Your mother will never see you again if you do *not* marry Mr. Collins, and I will never see you again if you *do*."

Elizabeth could not but smile at such a conclusion of such a beginning; but Mrs. Bennet, who had persuaded herself that her husband regarded the affair as she wished, was excessively disappointed.

"What do you mean, Mr. Bennet, by talking in this way? You promised me to *insist* upon her marrying him."

"My dear," replied her husband, "I have two small favours to request. First, that you will allow me the free use of my understanding on the present occasion; and secondly, of my room. I shall be glad to have the library to myself as soon as may be."

Not yet, however, in spite of her disappointment in her husband, did Mrs. Bennet give up the point. She talked to Elizabeth again and again; coaxed and threatened her by turns. She endeavoured to secure Jane in her interest; but Jane, with all possible mildness, declined interfering; and Elizabeth, sometimes with real earnestness, and sometimes with playful gaiety, replied to her attacks. Though her manner varied, however, her determination never did.

Mr. Collins, meanwhile, was meditating in solitude on what had passed. He thought too well of himself to comprehend on what motive his cousin could refuse him; and though his pride was hurt, he suffered in no other way. His regard for her was quite imaginary; and the possibility of her deserving her mother's reproach prevented his feeling any regret.

While the family were in this confusion, Charlotte Lucas came to spend the day with them. She was met in the vestibule by Lydia, who, flying to her, cried in a half whisper, "I am glad you are come, for there is such fun here! What do you think has happened this morning? Mr. Collins has made an offer to Lizzy, and she will not have him."

Charlotte had hardly time to answer, before they were joined by Kitty, who came to tell the same news; and no sooner had they entered the breakfast-room, where Mrs. Bennet was alone, than she likewise began

on the subject, calling on Miss Lucas for her compassion, and entreating
her to persuade her friend Lizzy to comply with the wishes of all her
family. "Pray do, my dear Miss Lucas," she added in a melancholy tone,
"for nobody is on my side, nobody takes part with me. I am cruelly used,
nobody feels for my poor nerves."

Charlotte's reply was spared by the entrance of Jane and Elizabeth.

"Aye, there she comes," continued Mrs. Bennet, "looking as unconcerned as may be, and caring no more for us than if we were at York,
provided she can have her own way. But I tell you what, Miss Lizzy—
if you take it into your head to go on refusing every offer of marriage in
this way, you will never get a husband at all—and I am sure I do not
know who is to maintain you when your father is dead. *I* shall not be
able to keep you—and so I warn you. I have done with you from this very
day. I told you in the library, you know, that I should never speak to you
again, and you will find me as good as my word. I have no pleasure in
talking to undutiful children. Not that I have much pleasure, indeed, in
talking to anybody. People who suffer as I do from nervous complaints
can have no great inclination for talking. Nobody can tell what I suffer!
But it is always so. Those who do not complain are never pitied."

Her daughters listened in silence to this effusion, sensible that any attempt to reason with or soothe her would only increase the irritation. She
talked on, therefore, without interruption from any of them, till they were
joined by Mr. Collins, who entered with an air more stately than usual,
and on perceiving whom, she said to the girls, "Now, I do insist upon it,
that you, all of you hold your tongues, and let Mr. Collins and me have
a little conversation together."

Elizabeth passed quietly out of the room, Jane and Kitty followed, but
Lydia stood her ground, determined to hear all she could; and Charlotte,
detained first by the civility of Mr. Collins, whose inquiries after herself
and all her family were very minute, and then by a little curiosity, satisfied herself with walking to the window and pretending not to hear. In a
doleful voice Mrs. Bennet thus began the projected conversation: "Oh!
Mr. Collins!"

"My dear madam," replied he, "let us be for ever silent on this point.
Far be it from me," he presently continued, in a voice that marked his
displeasure, "to resent the behaviour of your daughter. Resignation to
inevitable evils is the duty of us all; the peculiar duty of a young man
who has been so fortunate as I have been in early preferment; and I trust
I am resigned. Perhaps not the less so from feeling a doubt of my positive
happiness had my fair cousin honoured me with her hand; for I have often
observed that resignation is never so perfect as when the blessing denied
begins to lose somewhat of its value in our estimation. You will not, I
hope, consider me as showing any disrespect to your family, my dear
madam, by thus withdrawing my pretensions to your daughter's favour,
without having paid yourself and Mr. Bennet the compliment of requesting you to interpose your authority in my behalf. My conduct may, I fear,

be objectionable in having accepted my dismission from your daughter's lips instead of your own. But we are all liable to error. I have certainly meant well through the whole affair. My object has been to secure an amiable companion for myself, with due consideration for the advantage of all your family, and if my *manner* has been at all reprehensible, I here beg leave to apologise."

Chapter 21

THE discussion of Mr. Collins's offer was now nearly at an end, and Elizabeth had only to suffer from the uncomfortable feelings necessarily attending it, and occasionally from some peevish allusion of her mother. As for the gentleman himself, *his* feelings were chiefly expressed, not by embarrassment or dejection, or by trying to avoid her, but by stiffness of manner and resentful silence. He scarcely ever spoke to her, and the assiduous attentions which he had been so sensible of himself were transferred for the rest of the day to Miss Lucas, whose civility in listening to him was a seasonable relief to them all, and especially to her friend.

The morrow produced no abatement of Mrs. Bennet's ill humour or ill health. Mr. Collins was also in the same state of angry pride. Elizabeth had hoped that his resentment might shorten his visit, but his plan did not appear in the least affected by it. He was always to have gone on Saturday, and to Saturday he still meant to stay.

After breakfast, the girls walked to Meryton to inquire if Mr. Wickham were returned, and to lament over his absence from the Netherfield ball. He joined them on their entering the town, and attended them to their aunt's, where his regret and vexation, and the concern of everybody, was well talked over. To Elizabeth, however, he voluntarily acknowledged that the necessity of his absence *had* been self-imposed.

"I found," said he, "as the time drew near that I had better not meet Mr. Darcy; that to be in the same room, the same party with him for so many hours together, might be more than I could bear, and that scenes might arise unpleasant to more than myself."

She highly approved his forbearance, and they had leisure for a full discussion of it, and for all the commendation which they civilly bestowed on each other, as Wickham and another officer walked back with them to Longbourn, and during the walk he particularly attended to her. His accompanying them was a double advantage; she felt all the compliment it offered to herself, and it was most acceptable as an occasion of introducing him to her father and mother.

Soon after their return, a letter was delivered to Miss Bennet; it came from Netherfield, and was opened immediately. The envelope contained a sheet of elegant, little, hot-pressed paper, well covered with a lady's fair, flowing hand; and Elizabeth saw her sister's countenance change as she read it, and saw her dwelling intently on some particular passages. Jane recollected herself soon, and putting the letter away, tried to join with her usual cheerfulness in the general conversation; but Elizabeth felt an anxiety on the subject which drew off her attention even from Wickham; and no sooner had he and his companion taken leave, than a glance from Jane invited her to follow her upstairs. When they had gained their own room, Jane, taking out her letter, said, "This is from Caroline Bingley; what it contains has surprised me a good deal. The whole party have left Netherfield by this time, and are on their way to town—and without any intention of coming back again. You shall hear what she says."

She then read the first sentence aloud, which comprised the information of their having just resolved to follow their brother to town directly, and of their meaning to dine that day in Grosvenor Street, where Mr. Hurst had a house. The next was in these words: "I do not pretend to regret anything I shall leave in Hertfordshire, except your society, my dearest friend; but we will hope, at some future period, to enjoy many returns of that delightful intercourse we have known, and in the meanwhile may lessen the pain of separation by a very frequent and most unreserved correspondence. I depend on you for that." To these highflown expressions Elizabeth listened with all the insensibility of distrust; and though the suddenness of their removal surprised her, she saw nothing in it really to lament: it was not to be supposed that their absence from Netherfield would prevent Mr. Bingley's being there; and as to the loss of their society, she was persuaded that Jane must cease to regard it, in the enjoyment of his.

"It is unlucky," said she, after a short pause, "that you should not be able to see your friends before they leave the country. But may we not hope that the period of future happiness to which Miss Bingley looks forward may arrive earlier than she is aware, and that the delightful intercourse you have known as friends will be renewed with yet greater satisfaction as sisters? Mr. Bingley will not be detained in London by them."

"Caroline decidedly says that none of the party will return into Hertfordshire this winter. I will read it to you:

" 'When my brother left us yesterday, he imagined that the business which took him to London might be concluded in three or four days; but as we are certain it cannot be so, and at the same time convinced that when Charles gets to town he will be in no hurry to leave it again, we have determined on following him thither, that he may not be obliged to spend his vacant hours in a comfortless hotel. Many of my acquaintances are already there for the winter; I wish I could hear that you, my dearest friend, had any intention of making one in the crowd—but of that I despair. I sincerely hope your Christmas in Hertfordshire may abound in the gaieties which that season generally brings, and that your beaux will be so numerous as to prevent your feeling the loss of the three of whom we shall deprive you.' "

"It is evident by this," added Jane, "that he comes back no more this winter."

"It is only evident that Miss Bingley does not mean he *should*."

"Why will you think so? It must be his own doing. He is his own master. But you do not know *all*. I *will* read you the passage which particularly hurts me. I will have no reserves from *you*."

" 'Mr. Darcy is impatient to see his sister; and, to confess the truth, *we* are scarcely less eager to meet her again. I really do not think Georgiana Darcy has her equal for beauty, elegance, and accomplishments; and the affection she inspires in Louisa and myself is heightened into something still more interesting, from the hope we dare to entertain of her being hereafter our sister. I do not know whether I ever before mentioned to you my feelings on this subject; but I will not leave the country without confiding them, and I trust you will not esteem them unreasonable. My brother admires her greatly already; he will have frequent opportunity now of seeing her on the most intimate footing; her relations all wish the connection as much as his own; and a sister's partiality is not misleading me, I think, when I call Charles most capable of engaging any woman's heart. With all these circumstances to favour an attachment, and nothing to prevent it, am I wrong, my dearest Jane, in indulging the hope of an event which will secure the happiness of so many?' "

"What think you of *this* sentence, my dear Lizzy?" said Jane as she finished it. "Is it not clear enough? Does it not expressly declare that Caroline neither expects nor wishes me to be her sister; that she is perfectly convinced of her brother's indifference; and that if she suspects the nature of my feelings for him, she means (most kindly!) to put me on my guard? Can there be any other opinion on the subject?"

"Yes, there can; for mine is totally different. Will you hear it?"

"Most willingly."

"You shall have it in a few words. Miss Bingley sees that her brother is in love with you, and wants him to marry Miss Darcy. She follows him to town in the hope of keeping him there, and tries to persuade you that he does not care about you."

Jane shook her head.

"Indeed, Jane, you ought to believe me. No one who has ever seen you together can doubt his affection. Miss Bingley, I am sure, cannot. She is not such a simpleton. Could she have seen half as much love in Mr. Darcy for herself, she would have ordered her wedding clothes. But the case is this: We are not rich enough or grand enough for them; and she is the more anxious to get Miss Darcy for her brother, from the notion that when there has been *one* intermarriage, she may have less trouble in achieving a second: in which there is certainly some ingenuity, and I dare say it would succeed, if Miss de Bourgh were out of the way. But, my dearest Jane, you cannot seriously imagine that because Miss Bingley tells you her brother greatly admires Miss Darcy, he is in the smallest degree less sensible of *your* merit than when he took leave of you on Tuesday, or that it will be in her power to persuade him that, instead of being in love with you, he is very much in love with her friend."

"If we thought alike of Miss Bingley," replied Jane, "your representation of all this might make me quite easy. But I know the foundation is unjust. Caroline is incapable of wilfully deceiving anyone; and all that I can hope in this case is that she is deceived herself."

"That is right. You could not have started a more happy idea, since you will not take comfort in mine. Believe her to be deceived, by all means. You have now done your duty by her, and must fret no longer."

"But, my dear sister, can I be happy, even supposing the best, in accepting a man whose sisters and friends are all wishing him to marry elsewhere?"

"You must decide for yourself," said Elizabeth; "and if, upon mature deliberation, you find that the misery of disobliging his two sisters is more than equivalent to the happiness of being his wife, I advise you by all means to refuse him."

"How can you talk so?" said Jane, faintly smiling. "You must know that though I should be exceedingly grieved at their disapprobation, I could not hesitate."

"I did not think you would; and that being the case, I cannot consider your situation with much compassion."

"But if he returns no more this winter, my choice will never be required. A thousand things may arise in six months!"

The idea of his returning no more Elizabeth treated with the utmost contempt. It appeared to her merely the suggestion of Caroline's interested wishes, and she could not for a moment suppose that those wishes, however openly or artfully spoken, could influence a young man so totally independent of everyone.

She represented to her sister as forcibly as possible what she felt on the subject, and had soon the pleasure of seeing its happy effect. Jane's temper was not desponding, and she was gradually led to hope, though the diffidence of affection sometimes overcame the hope, that Bingley would return to Netherfield and answer every wish of her heart.

They agreed that Mrs. Bennet should only hear of the departure of the family, without being alarmed on the score of the gentleman's conduct; but even this partial communication gave her a great deal of concern, and she bewailed it as exceedingly unlucky that the ladies should happen to go away just as they were all getting so intimate together. After lamenting it, however, at some length, she had the consolation of thinking that Mr. Bingley would be soon down again and soon dining at Longbourn, and the conclusion of all was the comfortable declaration, that though he had been invited only to a family dinner, she would take care to have two full courses.

Chapter 22

THE Bennets were engaged to dine with the Lucases and again during the chief of the day was Miss Lucas so kind as to listen to Mr. Collins.

Elizabeth took an opportunity of thanking her. "It keeps him in good humour," said she, "and I am more obliged to you than I can express." Charlotte assured her friend of her satisfaction in being useful, and that it amply repaid her for the little sacrifice of her time. This was very amiable, but Charlotte's kindness extended farther than Elizabeth had any conception of; its object was nothing else than to secure her from any return of Mr. Collins's addresses, by engaging them towards herself. Such was Miss Lucas's scheme; and appearances were so favourable, that when they parted at night, she would have felt almost sure of success if he had not been to leave Hertfordshire so very soon. But here she did injustice to the fire and independence of his character, for it led him to escape out of Longbourn House the next morning with admirable slyness, and hasten to Lucas Lodge to throw himself at her feet. He was anxious to avoid the notice of his cousins, from a conviction that if they saw him depart, they could not fail to conjecture his design, and he was not willing to have the attempt known till its success could be known likewise; for though feeling almost secure, and with reason, for Charlotte had been tolerably encouraging, he was comparatively diffident since the adventure of Wednesday. His reception, however, was of the most flattering kind. Miss Lucas perceived him from an upper window as he walked towards the house, and instantly set out to meet him accidentally in the lane. But little had she dared to hope that so much love and eloquence awaited her there.

In as short a time as Mr. Collins's long speeches would allow, everything was settled between them to the satisfaction of both; and as they entered the house he earnestly entreated her to name the day that was to make him the happiest of men; and though such a solicitation must be waived for the present, the lady felt no inclination to trifle with his happiness. The stupidity with which he was favoured by nature must guard his courtship from any charm that could make a woman wish for its continuance; and Miss Lucas, who accepted him solely from the pure and disinterested desire of an establishment, cared not how soon that establishment were gained.

Sir William and Lady Lucas were speedily applied to for their consent; and it was bestowed with a most joyful alacrity. Mr. Collins's present circumstances made it a most eligible match for their daughter, to whom they could give little fortune; and his prospects of future wealth were exceedingly fair. Lady Lucas began directly to calculate, with more interest than the matter had ever excited before, how many years longer Mr. Bennet was likely to live; and Sir William gave it as his decided opinion, that whenever Mr. Collins should be in possession of the Longbourn estate, it would be highly expedient that both he and his wife should make their appearance at St. James's. The whole family, in short, were properly overjoyed on the occasion. The younger girls formed hopes of *coming out* a year or two sooner than they might otherwise have done; and the boys were relieved from their apprehension of Charlotte's dying an old maid. Charlotte herself was tolerably composed. She had gained her point, and had time to consider of it. Her reflections were in general satisfactory. Mr. Collins, to be sure, was neither sensible nor agreeable; his society was irksome, and his attachment to her must be imaginary. But still he would be her husband. Without thinking highly either of men or of matrimony, marriage had always been her object; it was the only honourable provision for well-educated young women of small fortune, and however uncertain of giving happiness, must be their pleasantest preservative from want. This preservative she had now obtained; and at the age of twenty-seven, without having ever been handsome, she felt all the good luck of it. The least agreeable circumstance in the business was the surprise it must occasion to Elizabeth Bennet, whose friendship she valued beyond that of any other person. Elizabeth would wonder, and probably would blame her; and though her resolution was not to be shaken, her feelings must be hurt by such a disapprobation. She resolved to give her the information herself, and therefore charged Mr. Collins, when he returned to Longbourn to dinner, to drop no hint of what had passed before any of the family. A promise of secrecy was of course very dutifully given, but it could not be kept without difficulty; for the curiosity excited by his long absence burst forth in such very direct questions on his return as required some ingenuity to evade, and he was at the same time exercising great self-denial, for he was longing to publish his prosperous love.

As he was to begin his journey too early on the morrow to see any of the family, the ceremony of leave-taking was performed when the ladies moved for the night; and Mrs. Bennet, with great politeness and cordiality, said how happy they should be to see him at Longbourn again, whenever his other engagements might allow him to visit them.

"My dear madam," he replied, "this invitation is particularly gratifying, because it is what I have been hoping to receive; and you may be very certain that I shall avail myself of it as soon as possible."

They were all astonished; and Mr. Bennet, who could by no means wish for so speedy a return, immediately said:

"But is there not danger of Lady Catherine's disapprobation here, my good sir? You had better neglect your relations than run the risk of offending your patroness."

"My dear sir," replied Mr. Collins, "I am particularly obliged to you for this friendly caution, and you may depend upon my not taking so material a step without her ladyship's concurrence."

"You cannot be too much on your guard. Risk anything rather than her displeasure; and if you find it likely to be raised by your coming to us again, which I should think exceedingly probable, stay quietly at home, and be satisfied that *we* shall take no offence."

"Believe me, my dear sir, my gratitude is warmly excited, by such affectionate attention; and depend upon it, you will speedily receive from me a letter of thanks for this, as for every other mark of your regard during my stay in Hertfordshire. As for my fair cousins, though my absence may not be long enough to render it necessary, I shall now take the liberty of wishing them health and happiness, not excepting my cousin Elizabeth."

With proper civilities the ladies then withdrew; all of them equally surprised to find that he meditated a quick return. Mrs. Bennet wished to understand by it that he thought of paying his addresses to one of her younger girls, and Mary might have been prevailed on to accept him. She rated his abilities much higher than any of the others; there was a solidity in his reflections which often struck her, and though by no means so clever as herself, she thought that if encouraged to read and improve himself by such an example as hers, he might become a very agreeable companion. But on the following morning, every hope of this kind was done away. Miss Lucas called soon after breakfast, and in a private conference with Elizabeth related the event of the day before.

The possibility of Mr. Collins's fancying himself in love with her friend had once occurred to Elizabeth within the last day or two; but that Charlotte could encourage him seemed almost as far from possibility as she could encourage him herself, and her astonishment was consequently so great as to overcome at first the bounds of decorum, and she could not help crying out:

"Engaged to Mr. Collins! My dear Charlotte—impossible!"

The steady countenance which Miss Lucas had commanded in telling her story, gave way to a momentary confusion here on receiving so direct a reproach; though, as it was no more than she expected, she soon regained her composure, and calmly replied:

"Why should you be surprised, my dear Eliza? Do you think it incredible that Mr. Collins should be able to procure any woman's good opinion, because he was not so happy as to succeed with you?"

But Elizabeth had now recollected herself, and making a strong effort for it, was able to assure her with tolerable firmness that the prospect of their relationship was highly grateful to her, and that she wished her all imaginable happiness.

"I see what you are feeling," replied Charlotte. "You must be surprised, very much surprised—so lately as Mr. Collins was wishing to marry you. But when you have had time to think it all over, I hope you will be satisfied with what I have done. I am not romantic, you know; I never was. I ask only a comfortable home; and considering Mr. Collins's character, connections, and situation in life, I am convinced that my chance of happiness with him is as fair as most people can boast on entering the marriage state."

Elizabeth quietly answered "Undoubtedly"; and after an awkward pause, they returned to the rest of the family. Charlotte did not stay much longer, and Elizabeth was then left to reflect on what she had heard. It was a long time before she became at all reconciled to the idea of so unsuitable a match. The strangeness of Mr. Collins's making two offers of marriage within three days was nothing in comparison of his being now accepted. She had always felt that Charlotte's opinion of matrimony was not exactly like her own, but she could not have supposed it possible that, when called into action, she would have sacrificed every better feeling to worldly advantage. Charlotte the wife of Mr. Collins was a most humiliating picture! And to the pang of a friend disgracing herself and sunk in her esteem, was added the distressing conviction that it was impossible for that friend to be tolerably happy in the lot she had chosen.

Chapter 23

ELIZABETH was sitting with her mother and sisters, reflecting on what she had heard, and doubting whether she was authorised to mention it, when Sir William Lucas himself appeared, sent by his daughter, to announce her engagement to the family. With many compliments to them, and much self-gratulation on the prospect of a connection between the houses, he unfolded the matter—to an audience not merely wondering, but incredulous; for Mrs. Bennet, with more perseverance than politeness, protested he must be entirely mistaken; and Lydia, always unguarded and often uncivil, boisterously exclaimed:

"Good Lord! Sir William, how can you tell such a story? Do not you know that Mr. Collins wants to marry Lizzy?"

Nothing less than the complaisance of a courtier could have borne without anger such treatment; but Sir William's good breeding carried him through it all; and though he begged leave to be positive as to the truth of his information, he listened to all their impertinence with the most forbearing courtesy.

Elizabeth, feeling it incumbent on her to relieve him from so unpleasant a situation, now put herself forward to confirm his account, by mentioning her prior knowledge of it from Charlotte herself; and endeavoured to put a stop to the exclamations of her mother and sisters by the earnestness of her congratulations to Sir William, in which she was readily joined by Jane, and by making a variety of remarks on the happiness that might be expected from the match, the excellent character of Mr. Collins, and the convenient distance of Hunsford from London.

Mrs. Bennet was in fact too much overpowered to say a great deal while Sir William remained; but no sooner had he left them than her feelings found a rapid vent. In the first place, she persisted in disbelieving the whole of the matter; secondly, she was very sure that Mr. Collins had been taken in; thirdly, she trusted that they would never be happy together; and fourthly, that the match might be broken off. Two inferences, however, were plainly deduced from the whole: one, that Elizabeth was the real cause of all the mischief; and the other that she herself nad been barbarously used by them all: and on these two points she principally dwelt during the rest of the day. Nothing could console and nothing appease her. Nor did that day wear out her resentment. A week elapsed before she could see Elizabeth without scolding her, a month passed away before she could speak to Sir William or Lady Lucas without being rude, and many months were gone before she could at all forgive their daughter.

Mr. Bennet's emotions were much more tranquil on the occasion, and such as he did experience he pronounced to be of a most agreeable sort; for it gratified him, he said, to discover that Charlotte Lucas, whom he had been used to think tolerably sensible, was as foolish as his wife, and more foolish than his daughter!

Jane confessed herself a little surprised at the match; but she said less of her astonishment than of her earnest desire for their happiness; nor could Elizabeth persuade her to consider it as improbable. Kitty and Lydia were far from envying Miss Lucas, for Mr. Collins was only a clergyman; and it affected them in no other way than as a piece of news to spread at Meryton.

Lady Lucas could not be insensible of triumph on being able to retort on Mrs. Bennet the comfort of having a daughter well married; and she called at Longbourn rather oftener than usual to say how happy she was, though Mrs. Bennet's sour looks and ill-natured remarks might have been enough to drive happiness away.

Between Elizabeth and Charlotte there was a restraint which kept them mutually silent on the subject; and Elizabeth felt persuaded that no real confidence could ever subsist between them again. Her disappointment in Charlotte made her turn with fonder regard to her sister, of whose rectitude and delicacy she was sure her opinion could never be shaken, and for whose happiness she grew daily more anxious, as Bingley had now been gone a week and nothing was heard of his return.

Jane had sent Caroline an early answer to her letter, and was counting the days till she might reasonably hope to hear again. The promised letter of thanks from Mr. Collins arrived on Tuesday, addressed to their father, and written with all the solemnity of gratitude which a twelvemonth's abode in the family might have prompted. After discharging his conscience on that head, he proceeded to inform them, with many rapturous expressions, of his happiness in having obtained the affection of their amiable neighbour, Miss Lucas, and then explained that it was merely with the view of enjoying her society that he had been so ready to close with their kind wish of seeing him again at Longbourn, whither he hoped to be able to return on Monday fortnight; for Lady Catherine, he added, so heartily approved his marriage, that she wished it to take place as soon as possible, which he trusted would be an unanswerable argument with his amiable Charlotte to name an early day for making him the happiest of men.

Mr. Collins's return into Hertfordshire was no longer a matter of pleasure to Mrs. Bennet. On the contrary, she was as much disposed to complain of it as her husband. It was very strange that he should come to Longbourn instead of to Lucas Lodge; it was also very inconvenient and exceedingly troublesome. She hated having visitors in the house while her health was so indifferent, and lovers were of all people the most disagreeable. Such were the gentle murmurs of Mrs. Bennet, and they gave way only to the greater distress of Mr. Bingley's continued absence.

Neither Jane nor Elizabeth were comfortable on this subject. Day after day passed away without bringing any other tidings of him than the report which shortly prevailed in Meryton of his coming no more to Netherfield the whole winter; a report which highly incensed Mrs. Bennet, and which she never failed to contradict as a most scandalous falsehood.

Even Elizabeth began to fear—not that Bingley was indifferent—but that his sisters would be successful in keeping him away. Unwilling as she was to admit an idea so destructive of Jane's happiness, and so dishonourable to the stability of her lover, she could not prevent its frequently occurring. The united efforts of his two unfeeling sisters and of his overpowering friend, assisted by the attractions of Miss Darcy and the amusements of London might be too much, she feared, for the strength of his attachment.

As for Jane, *her* anxiety under this suspense was, of course, more painful than Elizabeth's; but whatever she felt she was desirous of concealing, and between herself and Elizabeth, therefore, the subject was never alluded to. But as no such delicacy restrained her mother, an hour seldom passed in which she did not talk of Bingley, express her impatience for his arrival, or even require Jane to confess that if he did not come back she should think herself very ill used. It needed all Jane's steady mildness to bear these attacks with tolerable tranquillity.

Mr. Collins returned most punctually on the Monday fortnight, but his reception at Longbourn was not quite so gracious as it had been on his first introduction. He was too happy, however, to need much attention; and, luckily for the others, the business of love-making relieved them from a great deal of his company. The chief of every day was spent by him at Lucas Lodge, and he sometimes returned to Longbourn only in time to make an apology for his absence before the family went to bed.

Mrs. Bennet was really in a most pitiable state. The very mention of anything concerning the match threw her into an agony of ill-humour, and wherever she went she was sure of hearing it talked of. The sight of Miss Lucas was odious to her. As her successor in that house, she regarded her with jealous abhorrence. Whenever Charlotte came to see them, she concluded her to be anticipating the hour of possession; and whenever she spoke in a low voice to Mr. Collins, was convinced that they were talking of the Longbourn estate, and resolving to turn herself and her daughters out of the house, as soon as Mr. Bennet were dead. She complained bitterly of all this to her husband.

"Indeed, Mr. Bennet," said she, "it is very hard to think that Charlotte Lucas should ever be mistress of this house, that *I* should be forced to make way for *her,* and live to see her take my place in it!"

"My dear, do not give way to such gloomy thoughts. Let us hope for better things. Let us flatter ourselves that *I* may be the survivor."

This was not very consoling to Mrs. Bennet, and, therefore, instead of making any answer, she went on as before.

"I cannot bear to think that they should have all this estate. If it was not for the entail, I should not mind it."

"What should not you mind?"

"I should not mind anything at all."

"Let us be thankful that you are preserved from a state of such insensibility."

"I never can be thankful, Mr. Bennet, for anything about the entail. How anyone could have the conscience to entail away an estate from one's own daughters, I cannot understand; and all for the sake of Mr. Collins too! Why should *he* have it more than anybody else?"

"I leave it to yourself to determine," said Mr. Bennet.

Chapter 24

Miss BINGLEY's letter arrived, and put an end to doubt. The very first sentence conveyed the assurance of their being all settled in London for the winter, and concluded with her brother's regret at not having had time to pay his respects to his friends in Hertfordshire before he left the country.

Hope was over, entirely over; and when Jane could attend to the rest of the letter, she found little, except the professed affection of the writer, that could give her any comfort. Miss Darcy's praise occupied the chief of it. Her many attractions were again dwelt on, and Caroline boasted joyfully of their increasing intimacy, and ventured to predict the accomplishment of the wishes which had been unfolded in her former letter. She wrote also with great pleasure of her brother's being an inmate of Mr. Darcy's house, and mentioned with raptures some plans of the latter with regard to new furniture.

Elizabeth, to whom Jane very soon communicated the chief of all this, heard it in silent indignation. Her heart was divided between concern for her sister, and resentment against all others. To Caroline's assertion of her brother's being partial to Miss Darcy she paid no credit. That he was really fond of Jane, she doubted no more than she had ever done; and much as she had always been disposed to like him, she could not think without anger, hardly without contempt, on that easiness of temper, that want of proper resolution, which now made him the slave of his designing friends, and led him to sacrifice his own happiness to the caprice of their inclinations. Had his own happiness, however, been the only sacrifice, he might have been allowed to sport with it in whatever manner he thought best, but her sister's was involved in it, as she thought he must be sensible himself. It was a subject, in short, on which reflection would be long indulged, and must be unavailing. She could think of nothing else; and yet whether Bingley's regard had really died away, or were suppressed by his friends' interference; whether he had been aware of Jane's attachment, or whether it had escaped his observation; whatever were the case, though her opinion of him must be materially affected by the difference, her sister's situation remained the same, her peace equally wounded.

A day or two passed before Jane had courage to speak of her feelings to Elizabeth; but at last, on Mrs. Bennet's leaving them together, after a longer irritation than usual about Netherfield and its master, she could not help saying:

"Oh, that my dear mother had more command over herself! She can have no idea of the pain she gives me by her continual reflections on him. But I will not repine. It cannot last long. He will be forgot, and we shall all be as we were before."

Elizabeth looked at her sister with incredulous solicitude, but said nothing.

"You doubt me," cried Jane, slightly colouring; "indeed you have no reason. He may live in my memory as the most amiable man of my acquaintance, but that is all. I have nothing either to hope or fear, and nothing to reproach him with. Thank God! I have not *that* pain. A little time therefore—I shall certainly try to get the better."

With a stronger voice she soon added, "I have this comfort immediately, that it has not been more than an error of fancy on my side, and that it has done no harm to anyone but myself."

"My dear Jane!" exclaimed Elizabeth, "you are too good. Your sweetness and disinterestedness are really angelic; I do not know what to say to you. I feel as if I had never done you justice, or loved you as you deserve."

Miss Bennet eagerly disclaimed all extraordinary merit, and threw back the praise on her sister's warm affection.

"Nay," said Elizabeth, "this is not fair. *You* wish to think all the world respectable, and are hurt if I speak ill of anybody. *I* only want to think *you* perfect, and you set yourself against it. Do not be afraid of my running into any excess, of my encroaching on your privilege of universal good-will. You need not. There are few people whom I really love, and still fewer of whom I think well. The more I see of the world, the more am I dissatisfied with it; and every day confirms my belief of the inconsistency of all human characters, and of the little dependence that can be placed on the appearance of either merit or sense. I have met with two instances lately, one I will not mention; the other is Charlotte's marriage. It is unaccountable! In every view it is unaccountable!"

"My dear Lizzy, do not give way to such feelings as these. They will ruin your happiness. You do not make allowance enough for difference of situation and temper. Consider Mr. Collins's respectability, and Charlotte's prudent, steady character. Remember that she is one of a large family; that as to fortune, it is a most eligible match; and be ready to believe, for everybody's sake, that she may feel something like regard and esteem for our cousin."

"To oblige you, I would try to believe almost anything, but no one else could be benefited by such a belief as this; for were I persuaded that Charlotte had any regard for him, I should only think worse of her understanding than I now do of her heart. My dear Jane, Mr. Collins is a conceited, pompous, narrow-minded, silly man; you know he is, as well as I do; and you must feel, as well as I do, that the woman who marries him cannot have a proper way of thinking. You shall not defend her, though it is Charlotte Lucas. You shall not, for the sake of one individual, change the meaning of principle and integrity, nor endeavour to persuade yourself or me, that selfishness is prudence, and insensibility of danger security for happiness."

"I must think your language too strong in speaking of both," replied Jane; "and I hope you will be convinced of it, by seeing them happy together. But enough of this. You alluded to something else. You mentioned *two* instances. I cannot misunderstand you, but I entreat you, dear Lizzy, not to pain me by thinking *that person* to blame, and saying your opinion of him is sunk. We must not be so ready to fancy ourselves intentionally injured. We must not expect a lively young man to be always so guarded and circumspect. It is very often nothing but our own vanity that deceives us. Women fancy admiration means more than it does."

"And men take care that they should."

"If it is designedly done, they cannot be justified; but I have no idea of there being so much design in the world as some persons imagine."

"I am far from attributing any part of Mr. Bingley's conduct to design," said Elizabeth; "but without scheming to do wrong, or to make others unhappy, there may be error, and there may be misery. Thoughtlessness, want of attention to other people's feelings, and want of resolution, will do the business."

"And do you impute it to either of those?"

"Yes; to the last. But if I go on, I shall displease you by saying what I think of persons you esteem. Stop me whilst you can."

"You persist, then, in supposing his sisters influence him?"

"Yes, in conjunction with his friend."

"I cannot believe it. Why should they try to influence him? They can only wish his happiness; and if he is attached to me, no other woman can secure it."

"Your first position is false. They may wish many things besides his happiness; they may wish his increase of wealth and consequence; they may wish him to marry a girl who has all the importance of money, great connections, and pride."

"Beyond a doubt, they do wish him to choose Miss Darcy," replied Jane; "but this may be from better feelings than you are supposing. They have known her much longer than they have known me; no wonder if they love her better. But, whatever may be their own wishes, it is very unlikely they should have opposed their brother's. What sister would think herself at liberty to do it, unless there were something very objectionable? If they believed him attached to me, they would not try to part us; if he were so, they could not succeed. By supposing such an affection, you make everybody acting unnaturally and wrong, and me most unhappy. Do not distress me by the idea. I am not ashamed of having been mistaken—or, at least, it is light, it is nothing in comparison of what I should feel in thinking ill of him or his sisters. Let me take it in the best light, in the light in which it may be understood."

Elizabeth could not oppose such a wish; and from this time Mr. Bingley's name was scarcely ever mentioned between them.

Mrs. Bennet still continued to wonder and repine at his returning no more, and though a day seldom passed in which Elizabeth did not account for it clearly, there seemed little chance of her ever considering it with less perplexity. Her daughter endeavoured to convince her of what she did not believe herself, that his attentions to Jane had been merely the effect of a common and transient liking, which ceased when he saw her no more; but though the probability of the statement was admitted at the time, she had the same story to repeat every day. Mrs. Bennet's best comfort was that Mr. Bingley must be down again in the summer.

Mr. Bennet treated the matter differently. "So, Lizzy," said he one day, "your sister is crossed in love, I find. I congratulate her. Next to being married, a girl likes to be crossed in love a little now and then. It is something to think of, and gives her a sort of distinction among her companions. When is your turn to come? You will hardly bear to be long outdone by Jane. Now is your time. Here are officers enough at Meryton to disappoint all the young ladies in the country. Let Wickham be your man. He is a pleasant fellow, and would jilt you creditably."

"Thank you, sir, but a less agreeable man would satisfy me. We must not all expect Jane's good fortune."

"True," said Mr. Bennet, "but it is a comfort to think that whatever of that kind may befall you, you have an affectionate mother who will always make the most of it."

Mr. Wickham's society was of material service in dispelling the gloom which the late perverse occurrences had thrown on many of the Longbourn family. They saw him often, and to his other recommendations was now added that of general unreserve. The whole of what Elizabeth had already heard, his claims on Mr. Darcy, and all that he had suffered from him, was now openly acknowledged and publicly canvassed; and everybody was pleased to think how much they had always disliked Mr. Darcy before they had known anything of the matter.

Miss Bennet was the only creature who could suppose there might be any extenuating circumstances in the case, unknown to the society of Hertfordshire; her mild and steady candour always pleaded for allowances, and urged the possibility of mistakes—but by everybody else Mr. Darcy was condemned as the worst of men.

Chapter 25

AFTER a week spent in professions of love and schemes of felicity, Mr. Collins was called from his amiable Charlotte by the arrival of Saturday. The pain of separation, however, might be alleviated on his side, by preparations for the reception of his bride; as he had reason to hope, that shortly after his next return into Hertfordshire, the day would be fixed that was to make him the happiest of men. He took leave of his relations at Longbourn with as much solemnity as before; wished his fair cousins health and happiness again, and promised their father another letter of thanks.

On the following Monday, Mrs. Bennet had the pleasure of receiving her brother and his wife, who came as usual to spend the Christmas at Longbourn. Mr. Gardiner was a sensible, gentlemanlike man, greatly superior to his sister, as well by nature as education. The Netherfield ladies would have had difficulty in believing that a man who lived by trade, and within view of his own warehouses, could have been so well-bred and agreeable. Mrs. Gardiner, who was several years younger than Mrs. Bennet and Mrs. Philips, was an amiable, intelligent, elegant woman, and a great favourite with all her Longbourn nieces. Between the two eldest and herself especially, there subsisted a very particular regard. They had frequently been staying with her in town.

The first part of Mrs. Gardiner's business on her arrival was to distribute her presents and describe the newest fashions. When this was done she had a less active part to play. It became her turn to listen. Mrs. Bennet had many grievances to relate, and much to complain of. They had all been very ill-used since she last saw her sister. Two of her girls had been on the point of marriage, and after all there was nothing in it.

"I do not blame Jane," she continued, "for Jane would have got Mr. Bingley if she could. But Lizzy! Oh, sister! It is very hard to think that she might have been Mr. Collins's wife by this time, had not it been for her own perverseness. He made her an offer in this very room, and she refused him. The consequence of it is, that Lady Lucas will have a daughter married before I have, and that Longbourn estate is just as much entailed as ever. The Lucases are very artful people indeed, sister. They are all for what they can get. I am sorry to say it of them, but so it is. It makes me very nervous and poorly, to be thwarted so in my own family, and to have neighbours who think of themselves before anybody else. However, your coming just at this time is the greatest of comforts, and I am very glad to hear what you tell us, of long sleeves."

Mrs. Gardiner, to whom the chief of this news had been given before, in the course of Jane and Elizabeth's correspondence with her, made her sister a slight answer, and, in compassion to her nieces, turned the conversation.

When alone with Elizabeth afterwards, she spoke more on the subject.

"It seems likely to have been a desirable match for Jane," said she. "I am sorry it went off. But these things happen so often! A young man, such as you describe Mr. Bingley, so easily falls in love with a pretty girl for a few weeks, and when accident separates them, so easily forgets her, that these sort of inconsistencies are very frequent."

"An excellent consolation in its way," said Elizabeth, "but it will not do for *us*. We do not suffer by accident. It does not often happen that the interference of friends will persuade a young man of independent fortune to think no more of a girl whom he was violently in love with only a few days before."

"But that expression of 'violently in love' is so hackneyed, so doubtful, so indefinite, that it gives me very little idea. It is as often applied to feelings which arise from an half-hour's acquaintance, as to a real, strong attachment. Pray, how *violent was* Mr. Bingley's love?"

"I never saw a more promising inclination; he was growing quite inattentive to other people, and wholly engrossed by her. Every time they met, it was more decided and remarkable. At his own ball he offended two or three young ladies, by not asking them to dance; and I spoke to him twice myself, without receiving an answer. Could there be finer symptoms? Is not general incivility the very essence of love?"

"Oh, yes! of that kind of love which I suppose him to have felt. Poor Jane! I am sorry for her, because, with her disposition, she may not get over it immediately. It had better have happened to *you*, Lizzy; you would have laughed yourself out of it sooner. But do you think she would be prevailed on to go back with us? Change of scene might be of service—and perhaps a little relief from home may be as useful as anything."

Elizabeth was exceedingly pleased with this proposal, and felt persuaded of her sister's ready acquiescence.

"I hope," added Mrs. Gardiner, "that no consideration with regard to this young man will influence her. We live in so different a part of town, all our connections are so different, and, as you well know, we go out so little, that it is very improbable that they should meet at all, unless he really comes to see her."

"And *that* is quite impossible; for he is now in the custody of his friend, and Mr. Darcy would no more suffer him to call on Jane in such a part of London! My dear aunt, how could you think of it? Mr. Darcy may perhaps have *heard* of such a place as Gracechurch Street, but he would hardly think a month's ablution enough to cleanse him from its impurities, were he once to enter it; and depend upon it, Mr. Bingley never stirs without him."

"So much the better. I hope they will not meet at all. But does not Jane correspond with his sister? *She* will not be able to help calling."

"She will drop the acquaintance entirely."

But in spite of the certainty in which Elizabeth affected to place this point, as well as the still more interesting one of Bingley's being withheld from seeing Jane, she felt a solicitude on the subject which convinced her, on examination, that she did not consider it entirely hopeless. It was possible, and sometimes she thought it probable, that his affection might be reanimated, and the influence of his friends successfully combated by the more natural influence of Jane's attractions.

Miss Bennet accepted her aunt's invitation with pleasure; and the Bingleys were no otherwise in her thoughts at the same time, than as she hoped by Caroline's not living in the same house with her brother, she might occasionally spend a morning with her, without any danger of seeing him.

The Gardiners stayed a week at Longbourn; and what with the Philipses, the Lucases, and the officers, there was not a day without its engagement. Mrs. Bennet had so carefully provided for the entertainment of her brother and sister, that they did not once sit down to a family dinner. When the engagement was for home, some of the officers always made part of it—of which officers Mr. Wickham was sure to be one; and on these occasions, Mrs. Gardiner, rendered suspicious by Elizabeth's warm commendation of him, narrowly observed them both. Without sup-posing them, from what she saw, to be very seriously in love, their prefer-ence of each other was plain enough to make her a little uneasy; and she resolved to speak to Elizabeth on the subject before she left Hertford-shire, and represent to her the imprudence of encouraging such an attach-ment.

To Mrs. Gardiner, Wickham had one means of affording pleasure, unconnected with his general powers. About ten or a dozen years ago, before her marriage, she had spent a considerable time in that very part of Derbyshire to which he belonged. They had, therefore, many acquaint-ance in common; and though Wickham had been little there since the death of Darcy's father, five years before, it was yet in his power to give her fresher intelligence of her former friends than she had been in the way of procuring.

Mrs. Gardiner had seen Pemberley, and known the late Mr. Darcy by character perfectly well. Here consequently was an inexhaustible subject of discourse. In comparing her recollection of Pemberley with the minute description which Wickham could give, and in bestowing her tribute of praise on the character of its late possessor, she was delighting both him and herself. On being made acquainted with the present Mr. Darcy's treatment of him, she tried to remember something of that gentleman's reputed disposition when quite a lad which might agree with it, and was confident at last that she recollected having heard Mr. Fitzwilliam Darcy formerly spoken of as a very proud, ill-natured boy.

Chapter 26

MRS. GARDINER's caution to Elizabeth was punctually and kindly given on the first favourable opportunity of speaking to her alone; after honestly telling her what she thought, she thus went on:

"You are too sensible a girl, Lizzy, to fall in love merely because you are warned against it; and, therefore, I am not afraid of speaking openly. Seriously, I would have you be on your guard. Do not involve yourself or endeavour to involve him in an affection which the want of fortune would make so very imprudent. I have nothing to say against *him;* he is a most interesting young man; and if he had the fortune he ought to have, I should think you could not do better. But as it is, you must not let your fancy run away with you. You have sense, and we all expect you to use it. Your father would depend on *your* resolution and good conduct, I am sure. You must not disappoint your father."

"My dear aunt, this is being serious indeed."

"Yes, and I hope to engage you to be serious likewise."

"Well, then, you need not be under any alarm. I will take care of myself, and of Mr. Wickham too. He shall not be in love with me, if I can prevent it."

"Elizabeth, you are not serious now."

"I beg your pardon, I will try again. At present I am not in love with Mr. Wickham; no, I certainly am not. But he is, beyond all comparison, the most agreeable man I ever saw—and if he becomes really attached to me—I believe it will be better that he should not. I see the imprudence of it. Oh! *that* abominable Mr. Darcy! My father's opinion of me does me the greatest honour, and I should be miserable to forfeit it. My father, however, is partial to Mr. Wickham. In short, my dear aunt, I should be very sorry to be the means of making any of you unhappy; but since we see every day that where there is affection, young people are seldom withheld by immediate want of fortune from entering into engagements with each other, how can I promise to be wiser than so many of my fellow-creatures if I am tempted, or how am I even to know that it would be wisdom to resist? All that I can promise you, therefore, is not to be in a hurry. I will not be in a hurry to believe myself his first object. When I am in company with him, I will not be wishing. In short, I will do my best."

"Perhaps it will be as well if you discourage his coming here so very often. At least, you should not *remind* your mother of inviting him."

"As I did the other day," said Elizabeth with a conscious smile: "very true, it will be wise in me to refrain from *that*. But do not imagine that he is always here so often. It is on your account that he has been so frequently invited this week. You know my mother's ideas as to the necessity of constant company for her friends. But really, and upon my honour, I will try to do what I think to be the wisest; and now I hope you are satisfied."

Her aunt assured her that she was, and Elizabeth having thanked her for the kindness of her hints, they parted; a wonderful instance of advice being given on such a point, without being resented.

Mr. Collins returned into Hertfordshire soon after it had been quitted by the Gardiners and Jane; but as he took up his abode with the Lucases, his arrival was no great inconvenience to Mrs. Bennet. His marriage was now fast approaching, and she was at length so far resigned as to think it inevitable, and even repeatedly to say, in an ill-natured tone, that she *"wished* they might be happy." Thursday was to be the wedding day, and on Wednesday Miss Lucas paid her farewell visit; and when she rose to take leave, Elizabeth, ashamed of her mother's ungracious and reluctant good wishes, and sincerely affected herself, accompanied her out of the room. As they went downstairs together, Charlotte said:

"I shall depend on hearing from you very often, Eliza."

"*That* you certainly shall."

"And I have another favour to ask. Will you come and see me?"

"We shall often meet, I hope, in Hertfordshire."

"I am not likely to leave Kent for some time. Promise me, therefore, to come to Hunsford."

Elizabeth could not refuse, though she foresaw little pleasure in the visit.

"My father and Maria are to come to me in March," added Charlotte, "and I hope you will consent to be of the party. Indeed, Eliza, you will be as welcome to me as either of them."

The wedding took place: the bride and bridegroom set off for Kent from the church door, and everybody had as much to say, or to hear, on the subject as usual. Elizabeth soon heard from her friend; and their correspondence was as regular and frequent as it had ever been; that it should be equally unreserved was impossible. Elizabeth could never address her without feeling that all the comfort of intimacy was over, and though determined not to slacken as a correspondent, it was for the sake of what had been, rather than what was. Charlotte's first letters were received with a good deal of eagerness; there could not but be curiosity to know how she would speak of her new home, how she would like Lady Catherine, and how happy she would dare pronounce herself to be; though, when the letters were read, Elizabeth felt that Charlotte expressed herself on every point exactly as she might have foreseen. She wrote cheerfully, seemed surrounded with comforts, and mentioned nothing which she could not praise. The house, furniture, neighbourhood, and roads, were all to her taste, and Lady Catherine's behaviour was most friendly and obliging. It was Mr. Collins's picture of Hunsford and Rosings rationally softened; and Elizabeth perceived that she must wait for her own visit there to know the rest.

Jane had already written a few lines to her sister to announce their safe arrival in London; and when she wrote again, Elizabeth hoped it would be in her power to say something of the Bingleys.

Her impatience for this second letter was as well rewarded as impatience generally is. Jane had been a week in town without either seeing or hearing from Caroline. She accounted for it, however, by supposing that her last letter to her friend from Longbourn had by some accident been lost.

"My aunt," she continued, "is going to-morrow into that part of the town, and I shall take the opportunity of calling in Grosvenor Street."

She wrote again when the visit was paid, and she had seen Miss Bingley. "I did not think Caroline in spirits," were her words, "but she was very glad to see me, and reproached me for giving her no notice of my coming to London. I was right, therefore, my last letter had never reached her. I inquired after their brother, of course. He was well, but so much engaged with Mr. Darcy that they scarcely ever saw him. I found that Miss Darcy was expected to dinner. I wish I could see her. My visit was not long, as Caroline and Mrs. Hurst were going out. I dare say I shall soon see them here."

Elizabeth shook her head over this letter. It convinced her that accident only could discover to Mr. Bingley her sister's being in town.

Four weeks passed away, and Jane saw nothing of him. She endeavoured to persuade herself that she did not regret it; but she could no longer be blind to Miss Bingley's inattention. After waiting at home every morning for a fortnight, and inventing every evening a fresh excuse for her, the visitor did at last appear; but the shortness of her stay, and yet more, the alteration of her manner would allow Jane to deceive herself no longer. The letter which she wrote on this occasion to her sister will prove what she felt.

"My dearest Lizzy will, I am sure, be incapable of triumphing in her better judgment, at my expense, when I confess myself to have been entirely deceived in Miss Bingley's regard for me. But, my dear sister, though the event has proved you right, do not think me obstinate if I still assert, that, considering what her behaviour was, my confidence was as natural as your suspicion. I do not at all comprehend her reason for wishing to be intimate with me; but if the same circumstances were to happen again, I am sure I should be deceived again. Caroline did not return my visit till yesterday; and not a note, not a line, did I receive in the meantime. When she did come, it was very evident that she had no pleasure in it; she made a slight, formal apology, for not calling before, said not a word of wishing to see me again, and was in every respect so altered a creature, that when she went away I was perfectly resolved to continue the acquaintance no longer. I pity, though I cannot help blaming her. She was very wrong in singling me out as she did; I can safely say that every advance to intimacy began on her side. But I pity her, because she must feel that she has been acting wrong, and because I am very sure that anxiety for her brother is the cause of it. I need not explain myself farther; and though *we* know this anxiety to be quite needless, yet if she feels it, it will easily account for her behaviour to me; and so deservedly dear as he is to his sister, whatever anxiety she may feel on his behalf is natural and amiable. I cannot but wonder, however, at her having any such fears now, because, if he had at all cared about me, we must have met long, long ago. He knows of my being in town, I am certain, from something she said herself; and yet it would seem, by her manner of talking, as if she wanted to persuade herself that he is really partial to Miss Darcy. I cannot understand it. If I were not afraid of judging harshly, I should be almost tempted to say that there is a strong appearance of duplicity in all this. But I will endeavour to banish every painful thought, and think only of what will make me happy—your affection, and the invariable kindness of my dear uncle and aunt. Let me hear from you very soon. Miss Bingley said something of his never returning to Netherfield again, of giving up the house, but not with any certainty. We had better not mention it. I am extremely glad that you have such pleasant accounts from our friends at Hunsford. Pray go to see them, with Sir William and Maria. I am sure you will be very comfortable there.—Yours, etc."

This letter gave Elizabeth some pain; but her spirits returned as she considered that Jane would no longer be duped, by the sister at least. All expectation from the brother was now absolutely over. She would not even wish for any renewal of his attentions. His character sunk on every review of it; and as a punishment for him, as well as a possible advantage to Jane, she seriously hoped he might really soon marry Mr. Darcy's sister, as by Wickham's account, she would make him abundantly regret what he had thrown away.

Mrs. Gardiner about this time reminded Elizabeth of her promise concerning that gentleman, and required information; and Elizabeth had such to send as might rather give contentment to her aunt than to herself. His apparent partiality had subsided, his attentions were over, he was the admirer of some one else. Elizabeth was watchful enough to see it all, but she could see it and write of it without material pain. Her heart had been but slightly touched, and her vanity was satisfied with believing that *she* would have been his only choice, had fortune permitted it. The sudden acquisition of ten thousand pounds was the most remarkable charm of the young lady to whom he was now rendering himself agreeable; but Elizabeth, less clear-sighted perhaps in this case than in Charlotte's, did not quarrel with him for his wish of independence. Nothing, on the contrary, could be more natural; and while able to suppose that it cost him a few struggles to relinquish her, she was ready to allow it a wise and desirable measure for both, and could very sincerely wish him happy.

All this was acknowledged to Mrs. Gardiner; and after relating the circumstances, she thus went on:—"I am now convinced, my dear aunt, that I have never been much in love; for had I really experienced that pure and elevating passion, I should at present detest his very name, and wish him all manner of evil. But my feelings are not only cordial towards *him;* they are even impartial towards Miss King. I cannot find out that I hate her at all, or that I am in the least unwilling to think her a very good sort of girl. There can be no love in all this. My watchfulness has been effectual; and though I should certainly be a more interesting object to all my acquaintances were I distractedly in love with him, I cannot say that I regret my comparative insignificance. Importance may sometimes be purchased too dearly. Kitty and Lydia take his defection much more to heart than I do. They are young in the ways of the world, and not yet open to the mortifying conviction that handsome young men must have something to live on as well as the plain."

Chapter 27

WITH no greater events than these in the Longbourn family, and otherwise diversified by little beyond the walks to Meryton, sometimes dirty and sometimes cold, did January and February pass away. March was to take Elizabeth to Hunsford. She had not at first thought very seriously of going thither; but Charlotte, she soon found, was depending on the plan, and she gradually learned to consider it herself with greater pleasure as well as greater certainty. Absence had increased her desire of seeing Charlotte again, and weakened her disgust of Mr. Collins. There was novelty in the scheme, and as, with such a mother and such un-companionable sisters, home could not be faultless, a little change was not unwelcome for its own sake. The journey would moreover give her a peep at Jane; and, in short, as the time drew near, she would have been very sorry for any delay. Everything, however, went on smoothly, and was finally settled according to Charlotte's first sketch. She was to accompany Sir William and his second daughter. The improvement of spending a night in London was added in time, and the plan became perfect as plan could be.

The only pain was in leaving her father, who would certainly miss her, and who, when it came to the point, so little liked her going, that he told her to write to him, and almost promised to answer her letter.

The farewell between herself and Mr. Wickham was perfectly friendly; on his side even more. His present pursuit could not make him forget that Elizabeth had been the first to excite and to deserve his attention, the first to listen and to pity, the first to be admired; and in his manner of bidding her adieu, wishing her every enjoyment, reminding her of what she was to expect in Lady Catherine de Bourgh, and trusting their opinion of her—their opinion of everybody—would always coincide, there was a solicitude, an interest which she felt must ever attach her to him with a most sincere regard; and she parted from him convinced that, whether married or single, he must always be her model of the amiable and pleasing.

Her fellow-travellers the next day were not of a kind to make her think him less agreeable. Sir William Lucas, and his daughter Maria, a good-humoured girl, but as empty-headed as himself, had nothing to say that could be worth hearing, and were listened to with about as much delight as the rattle of the chaise. Elizabeth loved absurdities, but she had known Sir William's too long. He could tell her nothing new of the wonders of his presentation and knighthood; and his civilities were worn out, like his information.

It was a journey of only twenty-four miles, and they began it so early as to be in Gracechurch Street by noon. As they drove to Mr. Gardiner's door, Jane was at a drawing-room window watching their arrival; when they entered the passage she was there to welcome them, and Elizabeth, looking earnestly in her face, was pleased to see it healthful and lovely as ever. On the stairs were a troop of little boys and girls, whose eagerness for their cousin's appearance would not allow them to wait in the drawing-room, and whose shyness, as they had not seen her for a twelvemonth, prevented their coming lower. All was joy and kindness. The day passed most pleasantly away; the morning in bustle and shopping, and the evening at one of the theatres.

Elizabeth then contrived to sit by her aunt. Their first subject was her sister; and she was more grieved than astonished to hear, in reply to her minute inquiries, that though Jane always struggled to support her spirits, there were periods of dejection. It was reasonable, however, to hope that they would not continue long. Mrs. Gardiner gave her the particulars also of Miss Bingley's visit in Gracechurch Street, and repeated conversations occurring at different times between Jane and herself, which proved that the former had, from her heart, given up the acquaintance.

Mrs. Gardiner then rallied her niece on Wickham's desertion, and complimented her on bearing it so well.

"But my dear Elizabeth," she added, "what sort of girl is Miss King? I should be sorry to think our friend mercenary."

"Pray, my dear aunt, what is the difference in matrimonial affairs, between the mercenary and the prudent motive? Where does discretion end, and avarice begin? Last Christmas you were afraid of his marrying me, because it would be imprudent; and now, because he is trying to get a girl with only ten thousand pounds, you want to find out that he is mercenary."

"If you will only tell me what sort of girl Miss King is, I shall know what to think."

"She is a very good kind of girl, I believe. I know no harm of her."

"But he paid her not the smallest attention till her grandfather's death made her mistress of this fortune."

"No—why should he? If it were not allowable for him to gain *my* affections because I had no money, what occasion could there be for making love to a girl whom he did not care about, and who was equally poor?"

"But there seems indelicacy in directing his attention towards her so soon after this event."

"A man in distressed circumstances has not time for all those elegant decorums which other people may observe. If *she* does not object to it, why should *we?*"

"*Her* not objecting does not justify *him*. It only shows her being deficient in something herself—sense or feeling."

"Well," cried Elizabeth, "have it as you choose. *He* shall be mercenary, and *she* shall be foolish."

"No, Lizzy, that is what I do *not* choose. I should be sorry, you know, to think ill of a young man who has lived so long in Derbyshire."

"Oh! if that is all, I have a very poor opinion of young men who live in Derbyshire; and their intimate friends who live in Hertfordshire are not much better. I am sick of them all. Thank Heaven! I am going to-morrow where I shall find a man who has not one agreeable quality, who has neither manner nor sense to recommend him. Stupid men are the only ones worth knowing, after all."

"Take care, Lizzy; that speech savours strongly of disappointment."

Before they were separated by the conclusion of the play, she had the unexpected happiness of an invitation to accompany her uncle and aunt in a tour of pleasure which they proposed taking in the summer.

"We have not quite determined how far it shall carry us," said Mrs. Gardiner, "but, perhaps, to the Lakes."

No scheme could have been more agreeable to Elizabeth, and her acceptance of the invitation was most ready and grateful. "My dear, dear aunt," she rapturously cried, "what delight! what felicity! You give me fresh life and vigour. Adieu to disappointment and spleen. What are men to rocks and mountains? Oh! what hours of transport we shall spend! And when we *do* return, it shall not be like other travellers, without being able to give one accurate idea of anything. We *will* know where we have gone—we *will* recollect what we have seen. Lakes, mountains, and rivers shall not be jumbled together in our imaginations; nor when we attempt to describe any particular scene, will we begin quarrelling about its relative situation. Let *our* first effusions be less insupportable than those of the generality of travellers."

Chapter 28

EVERY object in the next day's journey was new and interesting to Elizabeth; and her spirits were in a state of enjoyment; for she had seen her sister looking so well as to banish all fear for her health, and the prospect of her northern tour was a constant source of delight.

When they left the high road for the lane to Hunsford, every eye was in search of the Parsonage, and every turning expected to bring it in view. The paling of Rosings Park was their boundary on one side. Elizabeth smiled at the recollection of all that she had heard of its inhabitants.

At length the Parsonage was discernible. The garden sloping to the road, the house standing in it, the green pales, and the laurel hedge, everything declared they were arriving. Mr. Collins and Charlotte appeared at the door, and the carriage stopped at the small gate which led by a short gravel walk to the house, amidst the nods and smiles of the whole party. In a moment they were all out of the chaise, rejoicing at the sight of each other. Mrs. Collins welcomed her friend with the liveliest pleasure, and Elizabeth was more and more satisfied with coming when she found herself so affectionately received. She saw instantly that her cousin's manners were not altered by his marriage; his formal civility was just what it had been, and he detained her some minutes at the gate to hear and satisfy his inquiries after all her family. They were then, with no other delay than his pointing out the neatness of the entrance taken into the house; and as soon as they were in the parlour he welcomed them a second time, with ostentatious formality to his humble abode, and punctually repeated all his wife's offers of refreshment.

Elizabeth was prepared to see him in his glory; and she could not help fancying that in displaying the good proportion of the room, its aspect and its furniture, he addressed himself particularly to her, as if wishing to make her feel what she had lost in refusing him. But though everything seemed neat and comfortable, she was not able to gratify him by any sigh of repentance, and rather looked with wonder at her friend that she could have so cheerful an air with such a companion. When Mr. Collins said anything of which his wife might reasonably be ashamed, which certainly was not unseldom, she involuntarily turned her eye on Charlotte. Once or twice she could discern a faint blush; but in general Charlotte wisely did not hear. After sitting long enough to admire every article of furniture in the room, from the sideboard to the fender, to give an account of their journey, and of all that had happened in London, Mr. Collins invited them to take a stroll in the garden, which was large and well laid out, and to the cultivation of which he attended himself. To work in his garden was one of his most respectable pleasures; and Elizabeth admired the command of countenance with which Charlotte talked of the healthfulness of the exercise, and owned she encouraged it as much as possible. Here, leading the way through every walk and cross walk, and scarcely allowing them an interval to utter the praises he asked for, every view was pointed out with a minuteness which left beauty entirely behind. He could number the fields in every direction, and could tell how many trees there were in the most distant clump. But of all the views which his garden, or which the country or the kingdom could boast, none were to be compared with the prospect of Rosings, afforded by an opening in the trees that bordered the park nearly opposite the front of his house. It was a handsome modern building, well situated on rising ground.

From his garden, Mr. Collins would have led them round his two meadows; but the ladies, not having shoes to encounter the remains of a white frost, turned back; and while Sir William accompanied him, Charlotte took her sister and friend over the house, extremely well pleased, probably, to have the opportunity of showing it without her husband's help. It was rather small, but well built and convenient; and everything was fitted up and arranged with a neatness and consistency of which Elizabeth gave Charlotte all the credit. When Mr. Collins could be forgotten, there was really a great air of comfort throughout, and by Charlotte's evident enjoyment of it, Elizabeth supposed he must be often forgotten.

She had already learnt that Lady Catherine was still in the country. It was spoken of again while they were at dinner, when Mr. Collins joining in, observed:

"Yes, Miss Elizabeth, you will have the honour of seeing Lady Catherine de Bourgh on the ensuing Sunday at church, and I need not say you will be delighted with her. She is all affability and condescension, and I doubt not but you will be honoured with some portion of her notice when service is over. I have scarcely any hesitation in saying that she will include you and my sister Maria in every invitation with which she honours us during your stay here. Her behaviour to my dear Charlotte is charming. We dine at Rosings twice every week, and are never allowed to walk home. Her ladyship's carriage is regularly ordered for us. I *should* say, one of her ladyship's carriages, for she has several."

"Lady Catherine is a very respectable, sensible woman indeed," added Charlotte, "and a most attentive neighbour."

"Very true, my dear, that is exactly what I say. She is the sort of woman whom one cannot regard with too much deference."

The evening was spent chiefly in talking over Hertfordshire news, and telling again what had been already written; and when it closed, Elizabeth, in the solitude of her chamber, had to meditate upon Charlotte's degree of contentment, to understand her address in guiding, and composure in bearing with, her husband, and to acknowledge that it was all done very well. She had also to anticipate how her visit would pass, the quiet tenor of their usual employments, the vexatious interruptions of Mr. Collins, and the gaieties of their intercourse with Rosings. A lively imagination soon settled it all.

About the middle of the next day, as she was in her room getting ready for a walk, a sudden noise below seemed to speak the whole house in confusion; and, after listening a moment, she heard somebody running upstairs in a violent hurry, and calling loudly after her. She opened the door and met Maria in the landing place, who, breathless with agitation, cried out—

"Oh, my dear Eliza! pray make haste and come into the dining-room, for there is such a sight to be seen! I will not tell you what it is. Make haste, and come down this moment."

Elizabeth asked questions in vain; Maria would tell her nothing more, and down they ran into the dining-room, which fronted the lane, in quest of this wonder! It was two ladies stopping in a low phaeton at the garden gate.

' And is this all?" cried Elizabeth. "I expected at least that the pigs were got into the garden, and here is nothing but Lady Catherine and her daughter!"

"La! my dear," said Maria, quite shocked at the mistake, "it is not Lady Catherine. The old lady is Mrs. Jenkinson, who lives with them; the other is Miss de Bourgh. Only look at her. She is quite a little creature. Who would have thought she could be so thin and small!"

"She is abominably rude to keep Charlotte out of doors in all this wind. Why does she not come in?"

"Oh, Charlotte says she hardly ever does. It is the greatest of favours when Miss de Bourgh comes in."

"I like her appearance," said Elizabeth, struck with other ideas. "She looks sickly and cross. Yes, she will do for him very well. She will make him a very proper wife."

Mr. Collins and Charlotte were both standing at the gate in conversation with the ladies; and Sir William, to Elizabeth's high diversion, was stationed in the doorway, in earnest contemplation of the greatness before him, and constantly bowing whenever Miss de Bourgh looked that way.

At length there was nothing more to be said; the ladies drove on, and the others returned into the house. Mr. Collins no sooner saw the two girls than he began to congratulate them on their good fortune, which Charlotte explained by letting them know that the whole party was asked to dine at Rosings the next day.

Chapter 29

Mr. Collins's triumph, in consequence of this invitation, was complete. The power of displaying the grandeur of his patroness to his wondering visitors, and of letting them see her civility towards himself and his wife, was exactly what he had wished for; and that an opportunity of doing it should be given so soon, was such an instance of Lady Catherine's condescension, as he knew not how to admire enough.

"I confess," said he, "that I should not have been at all surprised by her ladyship's asking us on Sunday to drink tea and spend the evening at Rosings. I rather expected, from my knowledge of her affability, that it would happen. But who could have foreseen such an attention as this? Who could have imagined that we should receive an invitation to dine there (an invitation, moreover, including the whole party) so immediately after your arrival!"

"I am the less surprised at what has happened," replied Sir William, "from that knowledge of what the manners of the great really are, which my situation in life has allowed me to acquire. About the court, such instances of elegant breeding are not uncommon."

Scarcely anything was talked of the whole day or next morning but their visit to Rosings. Mr. Collins was carefully instructing them in what they were to expect, that the sight of such rooms, so many servants, and so splendid a dinner, might not wholly overpower them.

When the ladies were separating for the toilette, he said to Elizabeth—

"Do not make yourself uneasy, my dear cousin, about your apparel. Lady Catherine is far from requiring that elegance of dress in us which becomes herself and daughter. I would advise you merely to put on whatever of your clothes is superior to the rest—there is no occasion for anything more. Lady Catherine will not think the worse of you for being simply dressed. She likes to have the distinction of rank preserved."

While they were dressing, he came two or three times to their different doors, to recommend their being quick, as Lady Catherine very much objected to be kept waiting for her dinner. Such formidable accounts of her ladyship, and her manner of living, quite frightened Maria Lucas, who had been little used to company, and she looked forward to her introduction at Rosings with as much apprehension as her father had done to his presentation at St. James's.

As the weather was fine, they had a pleasant walk of about half a mile across the park. Every park has its beauty and its prospects; and Elizabeth saw much to be pleased with, though she could not be in such raptures as Mr. Collins expected the scene to inspire, and was but slightly affected by his enumeration of the windows in front of the house, and his relation of what the glazing altogether had originally cost Sir Lewis de Bourgh.

When they ascended the steps to the hall, Maria's alarm was every moment increasing, and even Sir William did not look perfectly calm. Elizabeth's courage did not fail her. She had heard nothing of Lady Catherine that spoke her awful from any extraordinary talents or miraculous virtue, and the mere stateliness of money and rank she thought she could witness without trepidation.

From the entrance-hall, of which Mr. Collins pointed out, with a rapturous air, the fine proportion and finished ornaments, they followed the servants through an ante-chamber, to the room where Lady Catherine, her daughter, and Mrs. Jenkinson were sitting. Her ladyship, with great condescension, arose to receive them; and as Mrs. Collins had settled it with her husband that the office of introduction should be hers, it was performed in a proper manner, without any of those apologies and thanks which he would have thought necessary.

In spite of having been at St. James's Sir William was so completely awed by the grandeur surrounding him, that he had but just courage enough to make a very low bow, and take his seat without saying a word; and his daughter, frightened almost out of her senses, sat on the edge of her chair, not knowing which way to look. Elizabeth found herself quite equal to the scene, and could observe the three ladies before her composedly. Lady Catherine was a tall, large woman, with strongly-marked features, which might once have been handsome. Her air was not conciliating, nor was her manner of receiving them such as to make her visitors forget their inferior rank. She was not rendered formidable by silence; but whatever she said was spoken in so authoritative a tone, as marked her self-importance, and brought Mr. Wickham immediately to Elizabeth's mind; and from the observation of the day altogether, she believed Lady Catherine to be exactly what he had represented.

When, after examining the mother, in whose countenance and deportment she soon found some resemblance of Mr. Darcy, she turned her eyes on the daughter, she could almost have joined in Maria's astonishment at her being so thin and so small. There was neither in figure nor face any likeness between the ladies. Miss de Bourgh was pale and sickly; her features, though not plain, were insignificant; and she spoke very little, except in a low voice, to Mrs. Jenkinson, in whose appearance there was nothing remarkable, and who was entirely engaged in listening to what she said, and placing a screen in the proper direction before her eyes.

After sitting a few minutes, they were all sent to one of the windows to admire the view, Mr. Collins attending them to point out its beauties, and Lady Catherine kindly informing them that it was much better worth looking at in the summer.

The dinner was exceedingly handsome, and there were all the servants and all the articles of plate which Mr. Collins had promised; and, as he had likewise foretold, he took his seat at the bottom of the table, by her ladyship's desire, and looked as if he felt that life could furnish nothing greater. He carved, and ate, and praised with delighted alacrity; and every dish was commended, first by him and then by Sir William, who was now enough recovered to echo whatever his son-in-law said, in a manner which Elizabeth wondered Lady Catherine could bear. But Lady Catherine seemed gratified by their excessive admiration, and gave most gracious smiles, especially when any dish on the table proved a novelty to them. The party did not supply much conversation. Elizabeth was ready to speak whenever there was an opening, but she was seated between Charlotte and Miss de Bourgh—the former of whom was engaged in listening to Lady Catherine, and the latter said not a word to her all dinner-time. Mrs. Jenkinson was chiefly employed in watching how little Miss de Bourgh ate, pressing her to try some other dish, and fearing she was indisposed. Maria thought speaking out of the question, and the gentlemen did nothing but eat and admire.

When the ladies returned to the drawing-room, there was little to be done but to hear Lady Catherine talk, which she did without any intermission till coffee came in, delivering her opinion on every subject in so decisive a manner, as proved that she was not used to have her judgment controverted. She inquired into Charlotte's domestic concerns familiarly and minutely, and gave her a great deal of advice as to the management of them all; told her how everything ought to be regulated in so small a family as hers, and instructed her as to the care of her cows and her poultry. Elizabeth found that nothing was beneath this great lady's attention, which could furnish her with an occasion of dictating to others. In

the intervals of her discourse with Mrs. Collins, she addressed a variety
of questions to Maria and Elizabeth, but especially to the latter, of
whose connections she knew the least, and who she observed to Mrs.
Collins was a very genteel, pretty kind of girl. She asked her, at different
times, how many sisters she had, whether they were older or younger
than herself, whether any of them were likely to be married, whether
they were handsome, where they had been educated, what carriage her
father kept, and what had been her mother's maiden name? Elizabeth
felt all the impertinence of her questions but answered them very composedly. Lady Catherine then observed,

"Your father's estate is entailed on Mr. Collins, I think. For your
sake," turning to Charlotte, "I am glad of it; but otherwise I see no occasion for entailing estates from the female line. It was not thought necessary in Sir Lewis de Bourgh's family. Do you play and sing, Miss
Bennet?"

"A little."

"Oh! then—some time or other we shall be happy to hear you. Our
instrument is a capital one, probably superior to—— You shall try it
some day. Do your sisters play and sing?"

"One of them does."

"Why did not you all learn? You ought all to have learned. The Miss
Webbs all play, and their father has not so good an income as yours. Do
you draw?"

"No, not at all."

"What, none of you?"

"Not one."

"That is very strange. But I suppose you had no opportunity. Your
mother should have taken you to town every spring for the benefit of
masters."

"My mother would have had no objection, but my father hates
London."

"Has your governess left you?"

"We never had any governess."

"No governess! How was that possible? Five daughters brought up at
home without a governess! I never heard of such a thing. Your mother
must have been quite a slave to your education."

Elizabeth could hardly help smiling as she assured her that had not
been the case.

"Then, who taught you? who attended to you? Without a governess,
you must have been neglected."

"Compared with some families, I believe we were; but such of us as
wished to learn never wanted the means. We were always encouraged to
read, and had all the masters that were necessary. Those who chose to be
idle, certainly might."

"Aye, no doubt; but that is what a governess will prevent, and if I had
known your mother, I should have advised her most strenuously to engage

one. I always say that nothing is to be done in education without steady and regular instruction, and nobody but a governess can give it. It is wonderful how many families I have been the means of supplying in that way. I am always glad to get a young person well placed out. Four nieces of Mrs. Jenkinson are most delightfully situated through my means; and it was but the other day that I recommended another young person, who was merely accidentally mentioned to me, and the family are quite delighted with her. Mrs. Collins, did I tell you of Lady Metcalf's calling yesterday to thank me? She finds Miss Pope a treasure. 'Lady Catherine,' said she, 'you have given me a treasure.' Are any of your younger sisters out, Miss Bennet?"

"Yes, ma'am, all."

"All! What, all five out at once? Very odd! And you only the second. The younger ones out before the elder are married! Your younger sisters must be very young?"

"Yes, my youngest is not sixteen. Perhaps *she* is full young to be much in company. But really, ma'am, I think it would be very hard upon younger sisters, that they should not have their share of society and amusement, because the elder may not have the means or inclination to marry early. The last-born has as good a right to the pleasures of youth at the first. And to be kept back on *such* a motive! I think it would not be very likely to promote sisterly affection or delicacy of mind."

"Upon my word," said her ladyship, "you give your opinion very decidedly for so young a person. Pray, what is your age?"

"With three younger sisters grown up," replied Elizabeth, smiling, "your ladyship can hardly expect me to own it."

Lady Catherine seemed quite astonished at not receiving a direct answer; and Elizabeth suspected herself to be the first creature who had ever dared to trifle with so much dignified impertinence.

"You cannot be more than twenty, I am sure, therefore you need not conceal your age."

"I am not one-and-twenty."

When the gentlemen had joined them, and tea was over, the card-tables were placed. Lady Catherine, Sir William, and Mr. and Mrs. Collins sat down to quadrille; and as Miss de Bourgh chose to play at cassino, the two girls had the honour of assisting Mrs. Jenkinson to make up her party. Their table was superlatively stupid. Scarcely a syllable was uttered that did not relate to the game, except when Mrs. Jenkinson expressed her fears of Miss de Bourgh's being too hot or too cold, or having too much or too little light. A great deal more passed at the other table. Lady Catherine was generally speaking—stating the mistakes of the three others, or relating some anecdote of herself. Mr. Collins was employed in agreeing to everything her ladyship said, thanking her for every fish he won, and apologising if he thought he won too many. Sir William did not say much. He was storing his memory with anecdotes and noble names.

When Lady Catherine and her daughter had played as long as they chose, the tables were broken up, the carriage was offered to Mrs. Collins, gratefully accepted and immediately ordered. The party then gathered round the fire to hear Lady Catherine determine what weather they were to have on the morrow. From these instructions they were summoned by the arrival of the coach; and with many speeches of thankfulness on Mr. Collins's side and as many bows on Sir William's, they departed. As soon as they had driven from the door, Elizabeth was called on by her cousin to give her opinion of all that she had seen at Rosings, which, for Charlotte's sake, she made more favourable than it really was. But her commendation, though costing her some trouble, could by no means satisfy Mr. Collins, and he was very soon obliged to take her ladyship's praise into his own hands.

Chapter 30

SIR WILLIAM stayed only a week at Hunsford, but his visit was long enough to convince him of his daughter's being most comfortably settled, and of her possessing such a husband and such a neighbour as were not often met with. While Sir William was with them, Mr. Collins devoted his morning to driving him out in his gig, and showing him the country; but when he went away, the whole family returned to their usual employments, and Elizabeth was thankful to find that they did not see more of her cousin by the alteration, for the chief of the time between breakfast and dinner was now passed by him either at work in the garden or in reading and writing, and looking out of the window in his own book-room, which fronted the road. The room in which the ladies sat was backwards. Elizabeth at first had rather wondered that Charlotte should not prefer the dining-parlour for common use; it was a better sized room, and had a more pleasant aspect; but she soon saw that her friend had an excellent reason for what she did, for Mr. Collins would undoubtedly have been much less in his own apartment had they sat in one equally lively; and she gave Charlotte credit for the arrangement.

From the drawing-room they could distinguish nothing in the lane, and were indebted to Mr. Collins for the knowledge of what carriages went along, and how often especially Miss de Bourgh drove by in her phaeton, which he never failed coming to inform them of, though it happened almost every day. She not unfrequently stopped at the Parsonage, and had a few minutes' conversation with Charlotte, but was scarcely ever prevailed on to get out.

Very few days passed in which Mr. Collins did not walk to Rosings, and not many in which his wife did not think it necessary to go likewise; and till Elizabeth recollected that there might be other family livings to be disposed of, she could not understand the sacrifice of so many hours. Now and then they were honoured with a call from her ladyship, and nothing escaped her observation that was passing in the room during these visits. She examined into their employments, looked at their work, and advised them to do it differently; found fault with the arrangement of the furniture; or detected the housemaid in negligence; and if she accepted any refreshment, seemed to do it only for the sake of finding out that Mrs. Collins's joints of meat were too large for her family.

Elizabeth soon perceived, that though this great lady was not in the commission of the peace of the county, she was a most active magistrate in her own parish, the minutest concerns of which were carried to her by Mr. Collins; and whenever any of the cottagers were disposed to be quarrelsome, discontented, or too poor, she sallied forth into the village to settle their differences, silence their complaints, and scold them into harmony and plenty.

The entertainment of dining at Rosings was repeated about twice a week; and, allowing for the loss of Sir William, and there being only one card-table in the evening, every such entertainment was the counterpart of the first. Their other engagements were few, as the style of living of the neighbourhood in general was beyond the Collins's reach. This, however, was no evil to Elizabeth, and upon the whole she spent her time comfortably enough; there were half-hours of pleasant conversation with Charlotte, and the weather was so fine for the time of year that she had often great enjoyment out of doors. Her favourite walk, and where she frequently went while the others were calling on Lady Catherine, was along the open grove which edged that side of the park, where there was a nice sheltered path, which no one seemed to value but herself, and where she felt beyond the reach of Lady Catherine's curiosity.

In this quiet way, the first fortnight of her visit soon passed away. Easter was approaching, and the week preceding it was to bring an addition to the family at Rosings, which in so small a circle must be important. Elizabeth had heard soon after her arrival that Mr. Darcy was expected there in the course of a few weeks, and though there were not many of her acquaintances whom she did not prefer, his coming would furnish one comparatively new to look at in their Rosings parties, and she might be amused in seeing how hopeless Miss Bingley's designs on him were, by his behaviour to his cousin, for whom he was evidently destined by Lady Catherine, who talked of his coming with the greatest satisfaction, spoke of him in terms of the highest admiration, and seemed almost angry to find that he had already been frequently seen by Miss Lucas and herself.

His arrival was soon known at the Parsonage; for Mr. Collins was walking the whole morning within view of the lodges opening into Hunsford Lane, in order to have the earliest assurance of it, and after making his bow as the carriage turned into the Park, hurried home with the great intelligence. On the following morning he hastened to Rosings to pay his respects. There were two nephews of Lady Catherine to require them, for Mr. Darcy had brought with him a Colonel Fitzwilliam, the younger son of his uncle Lord ——, and, to the great surprise of all the party, when

Mr. Collins returned, the gentlemen accompanied him. Charlotte had seen them from her husband's room, crossing the road, and immediately running into the other, told the girls what an honour they might expect, adding:

"I may thank you, Eliza, for this piece of civility. Mr. Darcy would never have come so soon to wait upon me."

Elizabeth had scarcely time to disclaim all right to the compliment, before their approach was announced by the door-bell, and shortly afterwards the three gentlemen entered the room. Colonel Fitzwilliam, who led the way, was about thirty, not handsome, but in person and address most truly the gentleman. Mr. Darcy looked just as he had been used to look in Hertfordshire—paid his compliments, with his usual reserve, to Mrs. Collins, and whatever might be his feelings towards her friend, met her with every appearance of composure. Elizabeth merely curtseyed to him without saying a word.

Colonel Fitzwilliam entered into conversation directly with the readiness and ease of a well-bred man, and talked very pleasantly; but his cousin, after having addressed a slight observation on the house and garden to Mrs. Collins, sat for some time without speaking to anybody. At length, however, his civility was so far awakened as to inquire of Elizabeth after the health of her family. She answered him in the usual way, and after a moment's pause, added:

"My eldest sister has been in town these three months. Have you never happened to see her there?"

She was perfectly sensible that he never had; but she wished to see whether he would betray any consciousness of what had passed between the Bingleys and Jane, and she thought he looked a little confused as he answered that he had never been so fortunate as to meet Miss Bennet. The subject was pursued no farther, and the gentlemen soon afterwards went away.

Chapter 31

COLONEL FITZWILLIAM'S manners were very much admired at the Parsonage, and the ladies all felt that he must add considerably to the pleasure of their engagements at Rosings. It was some days, however, before they received any invitation thither—for while there were visitors in the house, they could not be necessary; and it was not till Easter-day, almost a week after the gentlemen's arrival, that they were honoured by such an attention, and then they were merely asked on leaving church to come there in the evening. For the last week they had seen very little of either Lady Catherine or her daughter. Colonel Fitzwilliam had called at the Parsonage more than once during the time, but Mr. Darcy they had only seen at church.

The invitation was accepted of course, and at a proper hour they joined the party in Lady Catherine's drawing-room. Her ladyship received them civilly, but it was plain that their company was by no means so acceptable as when she could get nobody else; and she was, in fact, almost engrossed by her nephews, speaking to them, especially to Darcy, much more than to any other person in the room.

Colonel Fitzwilliam seemed really glad to see them; anything was a welcome relief to him at Rosings; and Mrs. Collins's pretty friend had moreover caught his fancy very much. He now seated himself by her, and talked so agreeably of Kent and Hertfordshire, of travelling and staying at home, of new books and music, that Elizabeth had never been half so well entertained in that room before; and they conversed with so much spirit and flow, as to draw the attention of Lady Catherine herself, as well as of Mr. Darcy. *His* eyes had been soon and repeatedly turned towards them with a look of curiosity; and that her ladyship, after a while, shared the feeling, was more openly acknowledged, for she did not scruple to call out:

"What is that you are saying, Fitzwilliam? What is it you are talking of? What are you telling Miss Bennet? Let me hear what it is."

"We are speaking of music, madam," said he, when no longer able to avoid a reply.

"Of music! Then pray speak aloud. It is of all subjects my delight. I must have my share in the conversation if you are speaking of music. There are few people in England, I suppose, who have more true enjoyment of music than myself, or a better natural taste. If I had ever learnt, I should have been a great proficient. And so would Anne, if her health had allowed her to apply. I am confident that she would have performed delightfully. How does Georgiana get on, Darcy?"

Mr. Darcy spoke with affectionate praise of his sister's proficiency.

"I am very glad to hear such a good account of her," said Lady Catherine; "and pray tell her from me, that she cannot expect to excel if she does not practise a great deal."

"I assure you, madam," he replied, "that she does not need such advice. She practises very constantly."

"So much the better. It cannot be done too much; and when I next write to her, I shall charge her not to neglect it on any account. I often tell young ladies that no excellence in music is to be acquired without constant practice. I have told Miss Bennet several times, that she will never play really well unless she practises more; and though Mrs. Collins has no instrument, she is very welcome, as I have often told her, to come to Rosings every day, and play on the pianoforte in Mrs. Jenkinson's room. She would be in nobody's way, you know, in that part of the house."

Mr. Darcy looked a little ashamed of his aunt's ill-breeding, and made no answer.

When coffee was over, Colonel Fitzwilliam reminded Elizabeth of having promised to play to him; and she sat down directly to the instrument. He drew a chair near her. Lady Catherine listened to half a song, and then talked, as before, to her other nephew; till the latter walked away from her, and making with his usual deliberation towards the pianoforte, stationed himself sc as to command a full view of the fair performer's countenance. Elizabeth saw what he was doing, and at the first convenient pause, turned to him with an arch smile, and said:

"You mean to frighten me, Mr. Darcy, by coming in all this state to hear me? But I will not be alarmed though your sister *does* play so well. There is a stubbornness about me that never can bear to be frightened at the will of others. My courage always rises with every attempt to intimidate me."

"I shall not say that you are mistaken," he replied, "because you could not really believe me to entertain any design of alarming you; and I have had the pleasure of your acquaintance long enough to know that you find great enjoyment in occasionally professing opinions which in fact are not your own."

Elizabeth laughed heartily at this picture of herself, and said to Colonel Fitzwilliam, "Your cousin will give you a very pretty notion of me, and teach you not to believe a word I say. I am particularly unlucky in meeting with a person so well able to expose my real character, in a part of the world where I had hoped to pass myself off with some degree of credit. Indeed, Mr. Darcy, it is very ungenerous in you to mention all that you knew to my disadvantage in Hertfordshire—and, give me leave to say, very impolitic too—for it is provoking me to retaliate, and such things may come out as will shock your relations to hear."

"I am not afraid of you," said he, smilingly.

"Pray let me hear what you have to accuse him of," cried Colonel Fitzwilliam. "I should like to know how he behaves among strangers."

"You shall hear then—but prepare yourself for something very dreadful. The first time of my ever seeing him in Hertfordshire, you must know, was at a ball—and at this ball, what do you think he did? He danced only four dances! I am sorry to pain you—but so it was. He danced only four dances, though gentlemen were scarce; and, to my certain knowledge, more than one young lady was sitting down in want of a partner. Mr. Darcy, you cannot deny the fact."

"I had not at that time the honour of knowing any lady in the assembly beyond my own party."

"True; and nobody can ever be introduced in a ball-room. Well, Colonel Fitzwilliam, what do I play next? My fingers wait your orders."

"Perhaps," said Darcy, "I should have judged better, had I sought an introduction; but I am ill qualified to recommend myself to strangers."

"Shall we ask your cousin the reason of this?" said Elizabeth, still addressing Colonel Fitzwilliam. "Shall we ask him why a man of sense and education, and who has lived in the world, is ill qualified to recommend himself to strangers?"

"I can answer your question," said Fitzwilliam, "without applying to him. It is because he will not give himself the trouble."

"I certainly have not the talent which some people possess," said

Darcy, "of conversing easily with those I have never seen before. I cannot catch their tone of conversation, or appear interested in their concerns, as I often see done."

"My fingers," said Elizabeth, "do not move over this instrument in the masterly manner which I see so many women's do. They have not the same force or rapidity, and do not produce the same expression. But then I have always supposed it to be my own fault—because I would not take the trouble of practising. It is not that I do not believe *my* fingers as capable as any other woman's of superior execution."

Darcy smiled and said, "You are perfectly right. You have employed your time much better. No one admitted to the privilege of hearing you can think anything wanting. We neither of us perform to strangers."

Here they were interrupted by Lady Catherine, who called out to know what they were talking of. Elizabeth immediately began playing again. Lady Catherine approached, and, after listening for a few minutes, said to Darcy:

"Miss Bennet would not play at all amiss if she practised more, and could have the advantage of a London Master. She has a very good notion of fingering, though her taste is not equal to Anne's. Anne would have been a delightful performer, had her health allowed her to learn."

Elizabeth looked at Darcy to see how cordially he assented to his cousin's praise; but neither at that moment nor at any other could she discern any symptom of love; and from the whole of his behaviour to Miss de Bourgh she derived this comfort for Miss Bingley, that he might have been just as likely to marry *her*, had she been his relation.

Lady Catherine continued her remarks on Elizabeth's performance, mixing with them many instructions on execution and taste. Elizabeth received them with all the forbearance of civility, and, at the request of the gentlemen, remained at the instrument till her ladyship's carriage was ready to take them all home.

Chapter 32

Elizabeth was sitting by herself the next morning, and writing to Jane, while Mrs. Collins and Maria were gone on business into the village, when she was startled by a ring at the door, the certain signal of a visitor. As she had heard no carriage, she thought it not unlikely to be Lady Catherine, and under that apprehension was putting away her half-finished letter that she might escape all impertinent questions, when the door opened, and, to her very great surprise, Mr. Darcy, and Mr. Darcy only, entered the room.

He seemed astonished too on finding her alone, and apologised for his intrusion by letting her know that he had understood all the ladies to be within.

They then sat down, and when her inquiries after Rosings were made, seemed in danger of sinking into total silence. It was absolutely necessary, therefore, to think of something, and in this emergence recollecting *when* she had seen him last in Hertfordshire, and feeling curious to know what he would say on the subject of their hasty departure, she observed:

"How very suddenly you all quitted Netherfield last November, Mr. Darcy! It must have been a most agreeable surprise to Mr. Bingley to see you all after him so soon; for, if I recollect right, he went but the day before. He and his sisters were well, I hope, when you left London?"

"Perfectly so, I thank you."

She found that she was to receive no other answer, and, after a short pause, added:

"I think I have understood that Mr. Bingley has not much idea of ever returning to Netherfield again?"

"I have never heard him say so; but it is probable that he may spend very little of his time there in future. He has many friends, and he is at a time of life when friends and engagements are continually increasing."

"If he means to be but little at Netherfield, it would be better for the neighbourhood that he should give up the place entirely, for then we might possibly get a settled family there. But, perhaps, Mr. Bingley did not take the house so much for the convenience of the neighbourhood as for his own, and we must expect him to keep or quit it on the same principle."

"I should not be surprised," said Darcy, "if he were to give it up as soon as any eligible purchase offers."

Elizabeth made no answer. She was afraid of talking longer of his friend; and, having nothing else to say, was now determined to leave the trouble of finding a subject to him.

He took the hint, and soon began with, "This seems a very comfortable house. Lady Catherine, I believe, did a great deal to it when Mr. Collins first came to Hunsford."

"I believe she did—and I am sure she could not have bestowed her kindness on a more grateful object."

"Mr. Collins appears very fortunate in his choice of a wife."

"Yes, indeed, his friends may well rejoice in his having met with one of the very few sensible women who would have accepted him, or have made him happy if they had. My friend has an excellent understanding—though I am not certain that I consider her marrying Mr. Collins as the wisest thing she ever did. She seems perfectly happy, however, and in a prudential light it is certainly a very good match for her."

"It must be very agreeable to her to be settled within so easy a distance of her own family and friends."

"An easy distance, do you call it? It is nearly fifty miles."

"And what is fifty miles of good road? Little more than half a day's journey. Yes, I call it a very easy distance."

"I should never have considered the distance as one of the *advantages* of the match," cried Elizabeth. "I should never have said Mrs. Collins was settled *near* her family."

"It is a proof of your own attachment to Hertfordshire. Anything beyond the very neighbourhood of Longbourn, I suppose, would appear far."

As he spoke there was a sort of smile which Elizabeth fancied she understood; he must be supposing her to be thinking of Jane and Netherfield, and she blushed as she answered:

"I do not mean to say that a woman may not be settled too near her family. The far and the near must be relative, and depend on many varying circumstances. Where there is fortune to make the expenses of travelling unimportant, distance becomes no evil. But that is not the case *here*. Mr. and Mrs. Collins have a comfortable income, but not such a one as will allow of frequent journeys—and I am persuaded my friend would not call herself *near* her family under less than *half* the present distance."

Mr. Darcy drew his chair a little towards her, and said, "*You* cannot have a right to such very strong local attachment. *You* cannot have been always at Longbourn."

Elizabeth looked surprised. The gentleman experienced some change of feeling; he drew back his chair, took a newspaper from the table, and, glancing over it, said, in a colder voice:

"Are you pleased with Kent?"

A short dialogue on the subject of the county ensued, on either side calm and concise—and soon put an end to by the entrance of Charlotte and her sister, just returned from their walk. The *tête-à-tête* surprised them. Mr. Darcy related the mistake which had occasioned his intruding on Miss Bennet, and after sitting a few minutes longer without saying much to anybody, went away.

"What can be the meaning of this?" said Charlotte, as soon as he was gone. "My dear Eliza, he must be in love with you, or he would never have called on us in this familiar way."

But when Elizabeth told of his silence, it did not seem very likely, even to Charlotte's wishes, to be the case; and after various conjectures, they could at last only suppose his visit to proceed from the difficulty of finding anything to do, which was the more probable from the time of year. All field sports were over. Within doors there was Lady Catherine, books, and a billiard-table, but gentlemen cannot be always within doors; and in the nearness of the Parsonage, or the pleasantness of the walk to it, or of the people who lived in it, the two cousins found a temptation from this period of walking thither almost every day. They called at various times of the morning, sometimes separately, sometimes together, and now and then accompanied by their aunt. It was plain to them all that Colonel Fitzwilliam came because he had pleasure in their society, a persuasion which of course recommended him still more; and Elizabeth was reminded by her own satisfaction in being with him, as well as by his evident admiration of her, of her former favourite George Wickham; and though, in comparing them, she saw there was less captivating softness in Colonel

Fitzwilliam's manners, she believed he might have the best informed mind.

But why Mr. Darcy came so often to the Parsonage, it was more diffi-cult to understand. It could not be for society, as he frequently sat there ten minutes together without opening his lips; and when he did speak, it seemed the effect of necessity rather than of choice—a sacrifice to propriety, not a pleasure to himself. He seldom appeared really animated. Mrs. Collins knew not what to make of him. Colonel Fitzwilliam's occa-sionally laughing at his stupidity, proved that he was generally different, which her own knowledge of him could not have told her; and as she would have liked to believe this change the effect of love, and the object of that love her friend Eliza, she set herself seriously to work to find it out. She watched him whenever they were at Rosings, and whenever he came to Hunsford; but without much success. He certainly looked at her friend a great deal, but the expression of that look was disputable. It was an earnest, steadfast gaze, but she often doubted whether there were much admiration in it, and sometimes it seemed nothing but absence of mind.

She had once or twice suggested to Elizabeth the possibility of his being partial to her, but Elizabeth always laughed at the idea; and Mrs. Collins did not think it right to press the subject, from the danger of raising ex-pectations which might only end in disappointment; for in her opinion it admitted not of a doubt, that all her friend's dislike would vanish, if she could suppose him to be in her power.

In her kind schemes for Elizabeth, she sometimes planned her marrying Colonel Fitzwilliam. He was beyond comparison the most pleasant man; he certainly admired her, and his situation in life was most eligible; but, to counterbalance these advantages, Mr. Darcy had considerable patron-age in the church, and his cousin could have none at all.

Chapter 33

MORE than once did Elizabeth, in her ramble within the park, unex-pectedly meet Mr. Darcy. She felt all the perverseness of the mischance that should bring him where no one else was brought, and, to prevent its ever happening again, took care to inform him at first that it was a favourite haunt of hers. How it could occur a second time, therefore, was very odd! Yet it did, and even the third. It seemed like wilful ill-nature, or a voluntary penance, for on these occasions it was not merely a few formal inquiries and an awkward pause and then away, but he actually thought it necessary to turn back and walk with her. He never said a great deal, nor did she give herself the trouble of talking or of listening much; but it struck her in the course of their third rencontre that he was asking some old unconnected questions—about her pleasure in being at Hunsford, her love of solitary walks, and her opinion of Mr. and Mrs. Collins's happiness; and that in speaking of Rosings and her not perfectly understanding the house, he seemed to expect that whenever she came into Kent again she would be staying *there* too. His words seemed to imply it. Could he have Colonel Fitzwilliam in his thoughts? She supposed, if he meant anything, he must mean an allusion to what might arise in that quarter. It distressed her a little, and she was quite glad to find herself at the gate in the pales opposite the Parsonage.

She was engaged one day as she walked in reperusing Jane's last letter, and dwelling on some passage which proved that Jane had not written in spirits, when, instead of being again surprised by Mr. Darcy, she saw on looking up that Colonel Fitzwilliam was meeting her. Putting away the letter immediately and forcing a smile, she said:

"I did not know before that you ever walked this way."

"I have been making the tour of the park," he replied, "as I generally do every year, and intend to close it with a call at the Parsonage. Are you going much farther?"

"No, I should have turned in a moment."

And accordingly she did turn, and they walked towards the Parsonage together.

"Do you certainly leave Kent on Saturday?" said she.

"Yes—if Darcy does not put it off again. But I am at his disposal. He arranges the business just as he pleases."

"And if not able to please himself in the arrangement, he has at least great pleasure in the power of choice. I do not know anybody who seems more to enjoy the power of doing what he likes than Mr. Darcy."

"He likes to have his own way very well," replied Colonel Fitzwilliam. "But so we all do. It is only that he has better means of having it than many others, because he is rich, and many others are poor. I speak feelingly. A younger son, you know, must be inured to self-denial and dependence."

"In my opinion, the younger son of an earl can know very little of either. Now, seriously, what have you ever known of self-denial and dependence? When have you been prevented by want of money from going wherever you chose, or procuring anything you had a fancy for?"

"These are home questions—and perhaps I cannot say that I have experienced many hardships of that nature. But in matters of greater weight, I may suffer from the want of money. Younger sons cannot marry where they like."

"Unless where they like women of fortune, which I think they very often do."

"Our habits of expense make us too dependent, and there are not many in my rank of life who can afford to marry without some attention to money."

"Is this," thought Elizabeth, "meant for me?" and she coloured at the idea; but, recovering herself, said in a lively tone, "And pray, what is the usual price of an earl's younger son? Unless the elder brother is very sickly, I suppose you would not ask above fifty thousand pounds."

He answered her in the same style, and the subject dropped. To interrupt a silence which might make him fancy her affected with what had passed, she soon afterwards said:

"I imagine your cousin brought you down with him chiefly for the sake of having somebody at his disposal. I wonder he does not marry, to secure a lasting convenience of that kind. But, perhaps, his sister does as well for the present, and, as she is under his sole care, he may do what he likes with her."

"No," said Colonel Fitzwilliam, "that is an advantage which he must divide with me. I am joined with him in the guardianship of Miss Darcy."

"Are you indeed? And pray what sort of guardians do you make? Does your charge give you much trouble? Young ladies of her age are sometimes a little difficult to manage, and if she has the true Darcy spirit, she may like to have her own way."

As she spoke she observed him looking at her earnestly; and the manner in which he immediately asked her why she supposed Miss Darcy likely to give them any uneasiness, convinced her that she had somehow or other got pretty near the truth. She directly replied:

"You need not be frightened. I never heard any harm of her; and I dare say she is one of the most tractable creatures in the world. She is a very great favourite with some ladies of my acquaintance, Mrs. Hurst and Miss Bingley. I think I have heard you say that you know them."

"I know them a little. Their brother is a pleasant gentlemanlike man— he is a great friend of Darcy's."

"Oh! yes," said Elizabeth drily; "Mr. Darcy is uncommonly kind to Mr. Bingley, and takes a prodigious deal of care of him."

"Care of him! Yes, I really believe Darcy *does* take care of him in those points where he most wants care. From something that he told me in our journey hither, I have reason to think Bingley very much indebted to him. But I ought to beg his pardon, for I have no right to suppose that Bingley was the person meant. It was all conjecture."

"What is it you mean?"

"It is a circumstance which Darcy of course could not wish to be generally known, because if it were to get round to the lady's family, it would be an unpleasant thing."

"You may depend upon my not mentioning it."

"And remember that I have not much reason for supposing it to be Bingley. What he told me was merely this: that he congratulated himself on having lately saved a friend from the inconveniences of a most imprudent marriage, but without mentioning names or any other particulars, and I only suspected it to be Bingley from believing him the kind of young man to get into a scrape of that sort, and from knowing them to have been together the whole of last summer."

"Did Mr. Darcy give you his reasons for this interference?"

"I understood that there were some very strong objections against the lady."

"And what arts did he use to separate them?"

"He did not talk to me of his own arts," said Fitzwilliam, smiling. "He only told me what I have now told you."

Elizabeth made no answer, and walked on, her heart swelling with indignation. After watching her a little, Fitzwilliam asked her why she was so thoughtful.

"I am thinking of what you have been telling me," said she. "Your cousin's conduct does not suit my feelings. Why was he to be the judge?"

"You are rather disposed to call his interference officious?"

"I do not see what right Mr. Darcy had to decide on the propriety of his friend's inclination, or why, upon his own judgment alone, he was to determine and direct in what manner that friend was to be happy. But," she continued, recollecting herself, "as we know none of the particulars, it is not fair to condemn him. It is not to be supposed that there was much affection in the case."

"That is not an unnatural surmise," said Fitzwilliam, "but it is lessening the honour of my cousin's triumph very sadly."

This was spoken jestingly; but it appeared to her so just a picture of Mr. Darcy, that she would not trust herself with an answer, and therefore, abruptly changing the conversation, talked on indifferent matters till they reached the Parsonage. There, shut into her own room, as soon as their visitor left them, she could think without interruption of all that she had heard. It was not to be supposed that any other people could be meant than those with whom she was connected. There could not exist in the world *two* men over whom Mr. Darcy could have such boundless influence. That he had been concerned in the measures taken to separate Mr. Bingley and Jane she had never doubted; but she had always attributed to Miss Bingley the principal design and arrangement of them. If his own vanity, however, did not mislead him, *he* was the cause, his pride and caprice were the cause, of all that Jane had suffered, and still continued to suffer. He had ruined for a while every hope of happiness for the most affectionate, generous heart in the world; and no one could say how lasting an evil he might have inflicted.

"There were some very strong objections against the lady," were Colonel Fitzwilliam's words; and these strong objections probably were, her having one uncle who was a country attorney, and another who was in business in London.

"To Jane herself," she exclaimed, "there could be no possibility of objection; all loveliness and goodness as she is!—her understanding excellent, her mind improved, and her manners captivating. Neither could anything be urged against my father, who, though with some peculiarities, has abilities which Mr. Darcy himself need not disdain, and respectability which he will probably never reach." When she thought of her mother, indeed, her confidence gave way a little; but she would not allow that any objections *there* had material weight with Mr. Darcy, whose pride, she was convinced, would receive a deeper wound from the want of importance in his friend's connections, than from their want of sense; and she was quite decided, at last, that he had been partly governed by this worst kind of pride, and partly by the wish of retaining Mr. Bingley for his sister.

The agitation and tears which the subject occasioned, brought on a headache; and it grew so much worse towards the evening, that, added to her unwillingness to see Mr. Darcy, it determined her not to attend her cousins to Rosings, where they were engaged to drink tea. Mrs. Collins, seeing that she was really unwell, did not press her to go, and as much as possible prevented her husband from pressing her; but Mr. Collins could not conceal his apprehension of Lady Catherine's being rather displeased by her staying at home.

Chapter 34

When they were gone, Elizabeth, as if intending to exasperate herself as much as possible against Mr. Darcy, chose for her employment the examination of all the letters which Jane had written to her since her being in Kent. They contained no actual complaint, nor was there any revival of past occurrences, or any communication of present suffering. But in all, and in almost every line of each, there was a want of that cheerfulness which had been used to characterise her style, and which, proceeding from the serenity of a mind at ease with itself and kindly disposed towards everyone, had been scarcely ever clouded. Elizabeth noticed every sentence conveying the idea of uneasiness, with an attention which it had hardly received on the first perusal. Mr. Darcy's shameful boast of what misery he had been able to inflict gave her a keener sense of her sister's sufferings. It was some consolation to think that his visit to Rosings was to end on the day after the next—and, a still greater, that in less than a fortnight she should herself be with Jane again, and enabled to contribute to the recovery of her spirits, by all that affection could do.

She could not think of Darcy's leaving Kent without remembering that his cousin was to go with him; but Colonel Fitzwilliam had made it clear that he had no intentions at all, and agreeable as he was, she did not mean to be unhappy about him.

While settling this point, she was suddenly roused by the sound of the door-bell, and her spirits were a little fluttered by the idea of its being Colonel Fitzwilliam himself, who had once before called late in the evening, and might now come to inquire particularly after her. But this idea was soon banished, and her spirits were very differently affected, when, to her utter amazement, she saw Mr. Darcy walk into the room. In an hurried manner he immediately began an inquiry after her health, imputing his visit to a wish of hearing that she were better. She answered him with cold civility. He sat down for a few moments, and then getting up, walked about the room. Elizabeth was surprised, but said not a word.

After a silence of several minutes, he came towards her in an agitated manner, and thus began:

"In vain have I struggled. It will not do. My feelings will not be repressed. You must allow me to tell you how ardently I admire and love you."

Elizabeth's astonishment was beyond expression. She stared, coloured, doubted, and was silent. This he considered sufficient encouragement; and the avowal of all that he felt, and had long felt for her, immediately followed. He spoke well; but there were feelings besides those of the heart to be detailed, and he was not more eloquent on the subject of tenderness than of pride. His sense of her inferiority—of its being a degradation—of the family obstacles which judgment had always opposed to inclination, were dwelt on with a warmth which seemed due to the consequence he was wounding, but was very unlikely to recommend his suit.

In spite of her deeply-rooted dislike, she could not be insensible to the compliment of such a man's affection, and though her intentions did not vary for an instant, she was at first sorry for the pain he was to receive; till, roused to resentment by his subsequent language, she lost all compassion in anger. She tried, however, to compose herself to answer him with patience, when he should have done. He concluded with representing to her the strength of that attachment which, in spite of all his endeavours, he had found impossible to conquer; and with expressing his hope that it would now be rewarded by her acceptance of his hand. As he said this, she could easily see that he had no doubt of a favourable answer. He *spoke* of apprehension and anxiety, but his countenance expressed real security. Such a circumstance could only exasperate farther, and, when he ceased, the colour rose into her cheeks, and she said:

"In such cases as this, it is, I believe, the established mode to express a sense of obligation for the sentiments avowed, however unequally they may be returned. It is natural that obligation should be felt, and if I could *feel* gratitude, I would now thank you. But I cannot—I have never desired your good opinion, and you have certainly bestowed it most unwillingly. I am sorry to have occasioned pain to anyone. It has been most unconsciously done, however, and I hope will be of short duration. The feelings which, you tell me, have long prevented the acknowledgment of your regard, can have little difficulty in overcoming it after this explanation."

Mr. Darcy, who was leaning against the mantelpiece with his eyes fixed on her face, seemed to catch her words with no less resentment than surprise. His complexion became pale with anger, and the disturbance of his mind was visible in every feature. He was struggling for the appearance of composure, and would not open his lips till he believed himself to have attained it. The pause was to Elizabeth's feelings dreadful. At length, in a voice of forced calmness, he said:

"And this is all the reply which I am to have the honour of expecting!

I might, perhaps, wish to be informed why, with so little *endeavour* at civility, I am thus rejected. But it is of small importance."

"I might as well inquire," replied she, "why with so evident a design of offending and insulting me, you chose to tell me that you liked me against your will, against your reason, and even against your character? Was not this some excuse for incivility, if I *was* uncivil? But I have other provocations. You know I have. Had not my own feelings decided against you—had they been indifferent, or had they even been favourable, do you think that any consideration would tempt me to accept the man who has been the means of ruining, perhaps for ever, the happiness of a most beloved sister?"

As she pronounced these words, Mr. Darcy changed colour; but the emotion was short, and he listened without attempting to interrupt her while she continued:

"I have every reason in the world to think ill of you. No motive can excuse the unjust and ungenerous part you acted *there*. You dare not, you cannot deny that you have been the principal, if not the only means of dividing them from each other—of exposing one to the censure of the world for caprice and instability, the other to its derision for disappointed hopes, and involving them both in misery of the acutest kind."

She paused, and saw with no slight indignation that he was listening with an air which proved him wholly unmoved by any feeling of remorse. He even looked at her with a smile of affected incredulity.

"Can you deny that you have done it?" she repeated.

With assumed tranquillity he then replied: "I have no wish of denying that I did everything in my power to separate my friend from your sister, or that I rejoice in my success. Towards *him* I have been kinder than towards myself."

Elizabeth disdained the appearance of noticing this civil reflection, but its meaning did not escape, nor was it likely to conciliate her.

"But it is not merely this affair," she continued, "on which my dislike is founded. Long before it had taken place my opinion of you was decided. Your character was unfolded in the recital which I received many months ago from Mr. Wickham. On this subject, what can you have to say? In what imaginary act of friendship can you here defend yourself? or under what misrepresentation can you here impose upon others?"

"You take an eager interest in that gentleman's concerns," said Darcy, in a less tranquil tone, and with a heightened colour.

"Who that knows what his misfortunes have been, can help feeling an interest in him?"

"His misfortunes!" repeated Darcy contemptuously; "yes, his misfortunes have been great indeed."

"And of your infliction," cried Elizabeth with energy. "You have reduced him to his present state of poverty—comparative poverty. You have withheld the advantages which you must know to have been designed for him. You have deprived the best years of his life of that independence which was no less his due than his desert. You have done all this! and yet you can treat the mention of his misfortune with contempt and ridicule."

"And this," cried Darcy, as he walked with quick steps across the room, "is your opinion of me! This is the estimation in which you hold me! I thank you for explaining it so fully. My faults, according to this calculation, are heavy indeed! But perhaps," added he, stopping in his walk, and turning towards her, "these offences might have been overlooked, had not your pride been hurt by my honest confession of the scruples that had long prevented my forming any serious design. These bitter accusations might have been suppressed, had I, with greater policy, concealed my struggles, and flattered you into the belief of my being impelled by unqualified, unalloyed inclination; by reason, by reflection, by everything. But disguise of every sort is my abhorrence. Nor am I ashamed of the feelings I related. They were natural and just. Could you expect me to rejoice in the inferiority of your connections?—to congratulate myself on the hope of relations, whose condition in life is so decidedly beneath my own?"

Elizabeth felt herself growing more angry every moment; yet she tried to the utmost to speak with composure when she said:

"You are mistaken, Mr. Darcy, if you suppose that the mode of your declaration affected me in any other way, than as it spared the concern which I might have felt in refusing you, had you behaved in a more gentlemanlike manner."

She saw him start at this, but he said nothing, and she continued:

"You could not have made me the offer of your hand in any possible way that would have tempted me to accept it."

Again his astonishment was obvious; and he looked at her with an expression of mingled incredulity and mortification. She went on:

"From the very beginning—from the first moment, I may almost say—of my acquaintance with you, your manners, impressing me with the fullest belief of your arrogance, your conceit, and your selfish disdain of the feelings of others, were such as to form that groundwork of disapprobation on which succeeding events have built so immovable a dislike, and I had not known you a month before I felt that you were the last man in the world whom I could ever be prevailed on to marry."

"You have said quite enough, madam. I perfectly comprehend your feelings, and have now only to be ashamed of what my own have been. Forgive me for having taken up so much of your time, and accept my best wishes for your health and happiness."

And with these words he hastily left the room, and Elizabeth heard him the next moment open the front door and quit the house.

The tumult of her mind, was now painfully great. She knew not how to support herself, and from actual weakness sat down and cried for half-ar-hour. Her astonishment, as she reflected on what had passed, was increased by every review of it. That she should receive an offer of marriage from Mr. Darcy! That he should have been in love with her for so many

months! So much in love as to wish to marry her in spite of all the objections which had made him prevent his friend's marrying her sister, and
which must appear at least with equal force in his own case—was almost
incredible! It was gratifying to have inspired unconsciously so strong an
affection. But his pride, his abominable pride—his shameless avowal of
what he had done with respect to Jane—his unpardonable assurance in
acknowledging, though he could not justify it, and the unfeeling manner
in which he had mentioned Mr. Wickham, his cruelty towards whom he
had not attempted to deny, soon overcame the pity which the consideration of his attachment had for a moment excited. She continued in very
agitating reflections till the sound of Lady Catherine's carriage made her
feel how unequal she was to encounter Charlotte's observation, and hurried her away to her room.

Chapter 35

ELIZABETH awoke the next morning to the same thoughts and meditations which had at length closed her eyes. She could not yet recover from
the surprise of what had happened; it was impossible to think of anything else; and, totally indisposed for employment, she resolved, soon
after breakfast, to indulge herself in air and exercise. She was proceeding
directly to her favourite walk, when the recollection of Mr. Darcy's sometimes coming there stopped her, and instead of entering the park, she
turned up the lane, which led farther from the turnpike-road. The park
paling was still the boundary on one side, and she soon passed one of the
gates into the ground.

After walking two or three times along that part of the lane, she was
tempted, by the pleasantness of the morning, to stop at the gates and look
into the park. The five weeks which she had now passed in Kent had made
a great difference in the country, and every day was adding to the verdure
of the early trees. She was on the point of continuing her walk, when she
caught a glimpse of a gentleman within the sort of grove which edged the
park; he was moving that way; and, fearful of its being Mr. Darcy, she
was directly retreating. But the person who advanced was now near
enough to see her, and stepping forward with eagerness, pronounced her
name. She had turned away; but on hearing herself called, though in a
voice which proved it to be Mr. Darcy, she moved again towards the gate.
He had by that time reached it also, and, holding out a letter, which she
instinctively took, said, with a look of haughty composure, "I have been
walking in the grove some time in the hope of meeting you. Will you do
me the honour of reading that letter?" And then, with a slight bow,
turned again into the plantation, and was soon out of sight.

With no expectation of pleasure, but with the strongest curiosity,
Elizabeth opened the letter, and, to her still increasing wonder, perceived
an envelope containing two sheets of letter-paper, written quite through,

in a very close hand. The envelope itself was likewise full. Pursuing her
way along the lane, she then began it. It was dated from Rosings, at eight
o'clock in the morning, and was as follows:—

"Be not alarmed, madam, on receiving this letter, by the apprehension
of its containing any repetition of those sentiments or renewal of those
offers which were last night so disgusting to you. I write without any
intention of paining you, or humbling myself, by dwelling on wishes
which, for the happiness of both, cannot be too soon forgotten; and the
effort which the formation and the perusal of this letter must occasion,
should have been spared had not my character required it to be wri.' .n
and read. You must, therefore, pardon the freedom with which I demand
your attention; your feelings, I know, will bestow it unwillingly, but I
demand it of your justice.

"Two offences of a very different nature, and by no means of equal
magnitude, you last night laid to my charge. The first mentioned was,
that, regardless of the sentiments of either, I had detached Mr. Bingley
from your sister, and the other, that I had, in defiance of various claims,
in defiance of honour and humanity, ruined the immediate prosperity and
blasted the prospects of Mr. Wickham. Wilfully and wantonly to have
thrown off the companion of my youth, the acknowledged favourite of my
father, a young man who had scarcely any other dependence than on our
patronage, and who had been brought up to expect its exertion, would be
a depravity, to which the separation of two young persons, whose affection
could be the growth of only a few weeks, could bear no comparison. But
from the severity of that blame which was last night so liberally bestowed,
respecting each circumstance, I shall hope to be in future secured, when
the following account of my actions and their motives has been read. If,
in the explanation of them, which is due to myself, I am under the necessity of relating feelings which may be offensive to yours, I can only say
that I am sorry. The necessity must be obeyed, and further apology would
be absurd.

"I had not been long in Hertfordshire, before I saw, in common with
others, that Bingley preferred your elder sister to any other young woman
in the country. But it was not till the evening of the dance at Netherfield
that I had any apprehension of his feeling a serious attachment. I had
often seen him in love before. At that ball, while I had the honour of
dancing with you, I was first made acquainted, by Sir William Lucas's
accidental information, that Bingley's attentions to your sister had given
rise to a general expectation of their marriage. He spoke of it as a certain
event, of which the time alone could be undecided. From that moment I
observed my friend's behaviour attentively; and I could then perceive that
his partiality for Miss Bennet was beyond what I had ever witnessed in
him. Your sister I also watched. Her look and manners were open, cheerful, and engaging as ever, but without any symptom of peculiar regard,
and I remained convinced from the evening's scrutiny, that though she

received his attentions with pleasure, she did not invite them by any participation of sentiment. If *you* have not been mistaken here, *I* must have been in an error. Your superior knowledge of your sister must make the latter probable. If it be so, if I have been misled by such error to inflict pain on her, your resentment has not been unreasonable. But I shall not scruple to assert, that the serenity of your sister's countenance and air was such as might have given the most acute observer a conviction that, however amiable her temper, her heart was not likely to be easily touched. That I was desirous of believing her indifferent is certain—but I will venture to say that my investigations and decisions are not usually influenced by my hopes or fears. I did not believe her to be indifferent because I wished it; I believed it on impartial conviction, as truly as I wished it in reason. My objections to the marriage were not merely those which I last night acknowledged to have required the utmost force of passion to put aside, in my own case; the want of connection could not be so great an evil to my friend as to me. But there were other causes of repugnance; causes which, though still existing, and existing to an equal degree in both instances, I had myself endeavoured to forget, because they were not immediately before me. These causes must be stated, though briefly. The situation of your mother's family, though objectionable, was nothing in comparison of that total want of propriety so frequently, so almost uniformly betrayed by herself, by your three younger sisters, and occasionally even by your father. Pardon me. It pains me to offend you. But amidst your concern for the defects of your nearest relations, and your displeasure at this representation of them, let it give you consolation to consider that, to have conducted yourselves so as to avoid any share of the like censure, is praise no less generally bestowed on you and your eldest sister, than it is honourable to the sense and disposition of both. I will only say farther that from what passed that evening my opinion of all parties was confirmed, and every inducement heightened which could have led me before to preserve my friend from what I esteemed a most unhappy connection. He left Netherfield for London, on the day following, as you, I am certain, remember, with the design of soon returning.

"The part which I acted is now to be explained. His sisters' uneasiness had been equally excited with my own; our coincidence of feeling was soon discovered, and, alike sensible that no time was to be lost in detaching their brother, we shortly resolved on joining him directly in London. We accordingly went—and there I readily engaged in the office of pointing out to my friend the certain evils of such a choice. I described, and enforced them earnestly. But, however this remonstrance might have staggered or delayed his determination, I do not suppose that it would ultimately have prevented the marriage, had it not been seconded by the assurance which I hesitated not in giving, of your sister's indifference. He had before believed her to return his affection with sincere, if not with equal regard. But Bingley has great natural modesty, with a stronger dependence on my judgment than on his own. To convince him, therefore, that he had deceived himself, was no very difficult point. To persuade him against returning into Hertfordshire, when that conviction had been given, was scarcely the work of a moment. I cannot blame myself for having done thus much. There is but one part of my conduct in the whole affair on which I do not reflect with satisfaction; it is, that I condescended to adopt the measures of art so far as to conceal from him your sister's being in town. I knew it myself, as it was known to Miss Bingley; but her brother is even yet ignorant of it. That they might have met without ill consequence is perhaps probable; but his regard did not appear to me enough extinguished for him to see her without some danger. Perhaps this concealment, this disguise was beneath me; it is done, however, and it was done for the best. On this subject I have nothing more to say, no other apology to offer. If I have wounded your sister's feelings, it was unknowingly done; and though the motives which governed me may to you very naturally appear insufficient, I have not yet learnt to condemn them.

"With respect to that other, more weighty accusation, of having injured Mr. Wickham, I can only refute it by laying before you the whole of his connection with my family. Of what he has *particularly* accused me I am ignorant; but of the truth of what I shall relate, I can summon more than one witness of undoubted veracity.

"Mr. Wickham is the son of a very respectable man, who had for many years the management of all the Pemberley estates, and whose good conduct in the discharge of his trust naturally inclined my father to be of service to him; and on George Wickham, who was his godson, his kindness was therefore liberally bestowed. My father supported him at school, and afterwards at Cambridge—most important assistance, as his own father, always poor from the extravagance of his wife, would have been unable to give him a gentleman's education. My father was not only fond of this young man's society, whose manners were always engaging; he had also the highest opinion of him, and hoping the church would be his profession, intended to provide for him in it. As for myself, it is many, many years since I first began to think of him in a very different manner. The vicious propensities—the want of principle, which he was careful to guard from the knowledge of his best friend, could not escape the observation of a young man of nearly the same age with himself, and who had opportunities of seeing him in unguarded moments, which Mr. Darcy could not have. Here again I shall give you pain—to what degree you only can tell. But whatever may be the sentiments which Mr. Wickham has created, a suspicion of their nature shall not prevent me from unfolding his real character—it adds even another motive.

"My excellent father died about five years ago; and his attachment to Mr. Wickham was to the last so steady, that in his will he particularly recommended it to me, to promote his advancement in the best manner that his profession might allow—and if he took orders, desired that a valuable family living might be his as soon as it became vacant. There was also a legacy of one thousand pounds. His own father did not long survive mine, and within half a year from these events Mr. Wickham wrote to inform me that, having finally resolved against taking orders, he hoped I should not think it unreasonable for him to expect some more immediate pecuniary advantage, in lieu of the preferment, by which he could not be benefited. He had some intention, he added, of studying law, and I must be aware that the interest of one thousand pounds would be a very insufficient support therein. I rather wished, than believed him to be sincere—but, at any rate, was perfectly ready to accede to his proposal. I knew that Mr. Wickham ought not to be a clergyman; the business was therefore soon settled—he resigned all claim to assistance in the church, were it possible that he could ever be in a situation to receive it, and accepted in return three thousand pounds. All connection between us seemed now dissolved. I thought too ill of him to invite him to Pemberley, or admit his society in town. In town I believe he chiefly lived, but his studying the law was a mere pretence, and being now free from all restraint, his life was a life of idleness and dissipation. For about three years I heard little of him; but on the decease of the incumbent of the living which had been designed for him, he applied to me again by letter for the presentation. His circumstances, he assured me, and I had no difficulty in believing it, were exceedingly bad. He had found the law a most unprofitable study, and was now absolutely resolved on being ordained, if I would present him to the living in question—of which he trusted there could be little doubt, as he was well assured that I had no other person to provide for, and I could not have forgotten my revered father's intentions. You will hardly blame me for refusing to comply with this entreaty, or for resisting every repetition to it. His resentment was in proportion to the distress of his circumstances—and he was doubtless as violent in his abuse of me to others as in his reproaches to myself. After this period every appearance of acquaintance was dropped. How he lived I know not. But last summer he was again most painfully obtruded on my notice.

"I must now mention a circumstance which I would wish to forget myself, and which no obligation less than the present should induce me to unfold to any human being. Having said thus much, I feel no doubt of your secrecy. My sister, who is more than ten years my junior, was left to the guardianship of my mother's nephew, Colonel Fitzwilliam, and myself. About a year ago, she was taken from school, and an establishment formed for her in London; and last summer she went with the lady who presided over it, to Ramsgate; and thither also went Mr. Wickham, undoubtedly by design; for there proved to have been a prior acquaintance between him and Mrs. Younge, in whose character we were most unhappily deceived; and by her connivance and aid, he so far recommended himself to Georgiana, whose affectionate heart retained a strong impression of his kindness to her as a child, that she was persuaded to believe herself in love, and to consent to an elopement. She was then but fifteen, which must be her excuse; and after stating her imprudence, I am happy to add, that I owed the knowledge of it to herself. I joined them unexpectedly a day or two before the intended elopement, and then Georgiana, unable to support the idea of grieving and offending a brother whom she almost looked up to as a father, acknowledged the whole to me. You may imagine what I felt and how I acted. Regard for my sister's credit and feelings prevented any public exposure; but I wrote to Mr. Wickham, who left the place immediately, and Mrs. Younge was of course removed from her charge. Mr. Wickham's chief object was unquestionably my sister's fortune, which is thirty thousand pounds; but I cannot help supposing that the hope of revenging himself on me was a strong inducement. His revenge would have been complete indeed.

"This, madam, is a faithful narrative of every event in which we have been concerned together; and if you do not absolutely reject it as false, you will, I hope, acquit me henceforth of cruelty towards Mr. Wickham. I know not in what manner, under what form of falsehood he had imposed on you; but his success is not perhaps to be wondered at, ignorant as you previously were of everything concerning either. Detection could not be in your power, and suspicion certainly not in your inclination.

"You may possibly wonder why all this was not told you last night; but I was not then master enough of myself to know what could or ought to be revealed. For the truth of everything here related, I can appeal more particularly to the testimony of Colonel Fitzwilliam, who, from our near relationship and constant intimacy, and, still more, as one of the executors of my father's will, has been unavoidably acquainted with every particular of these transactions. If your abhorrence of *me* should make *my* assertions valueless, you cannot be prevented by the same cause from confiding in my cousin; and that there may be the possibility of consulting him, I shall endeavour to find some opportunity of putting this letter in your hands in the course of the morning. I will only add, God bless you.

"FITZWILLIAM DARCY."

Chapter 36

IF Elizabeth, when Mr. Darcy gave her the letter, did not expect it to contain a renewal of his offers, she had formed no expectation at all of its contents. But such as they were, it may be well supposed how eagerly she went through them, and what a contrariety of emotion they excited. Her feelings as she read were scarcely to be defined. With amazement did she first understand that he believed any apology to be in his power; and steadfastly was she persuaded, that he could have no explanation to give, which a just sense of shame would not conceal. With a strong prejudice against everything he might say, she began his account of what had happened at Netherfield. She read with an eagerness which hardly left her power of comprehension, and from impatience of knowing what the next sentence might bring, was incapable of attending to the sense of the one before her eyes. His belief of her sister's insensibility she instantly resolved to be false; and his account of the real, the worst objections to the match, made her too angry to have any wish of doing him justice. He expressed no regret for what he had done which satisfied her; his style was not pentitent, but haughty. It was all pride and insolence.

But when this subject was succeeded by his account of Mr. Wickham—when she read with somewhat clearer attention a relation of events which, if true, must overthrow every cherished opinion of his worth, and which bore so alarming an affinity to his own history of himself—her feelings were yet more acutely painful and more difficult of definition. Astonishment, apprehension, and even horror, oppressed her. She wished to discredit it entirely, repeatedly exclaiming, "This must be false! This cannot be! This must be the grossest falsehood!"—and when she had gone through the whole letter, though scarcely knowing anything of the last page or two, put it hastily away, protesting that she would not regard it, that she would never look in it again.

In this perturbed state of mind, with thoughts that could rest on nothing, she walked on; but it would not do; in half a minute the letter was unfolded again, and collecting herself as well as she could, she again began the mortifying perusal of all that related to Wickham, and commanded herself so far as to examine the meaning of every sentence. The account of his connection with the Pemberley family was exactly what he had related himself; and the kindness of the late Mr. Darcy, though she had not before known its extent, agreed equally well with his own words. So far each recital confirmed the other; but when she came to the will, the difference was great. What Wickham had said of the living was fresh in her memory, and as she recalled his very words, it was impossible not to feel that there was gross duplicity on one side or the other; and, for a few moments, she flattered herself that her wishes did not err. But when she read and re-read with the closest attention, the particulars immediately following of Wickham's resigning all pretensions to the living, of his receiving in lieu so considerable a sum as three thousand pounds, again was she forced to hesitate. She put down the letter, weighed every circumstance with what she meant to be impartiality—deliberated on the probability of each statement—but with little success. On both sides it was only assertion. Again she read on; but every line proved more clearly that the affair, which she had believed it impossible that any contrivance could so represent as to render Mr. Darcy's conduct in it less than infamous, was capable of a turn whichtmust make him entirely blameless throughout the whole.

The extravagance and general profligacy which he scrupled not to lay to Mr. Wickham's charge, exceedingly shocked her; the more so, as she could bring no proof of its injustice. She had never heard of him before his entrance into the ——shire Militia, in which he had engaged at the persuasion of the young man who, on meeting him accidentally in town, had there renewed a slight acquaintance. Of his former way of life nothing had been known in Hertfordshire but what he told himself. As to his real character, had information been in her power, she had never felt a wish of inquiring. His countenance, voice, and manner had established him at once in the possession of every virtue. She tried to recollect some instance of goodness, some distinguished trait of integrity or benevolence, that might rescue him from the attacks of Mr. Darcy; or at least, by the predominance of virtue, atone for those casual errors under which she would endeavour to class what Mr. Darcy had described as the idleness and vice of many years' continuance. But no such recollection befriended her. She could see him instantly before her, in every charm of air and address; but she could remember no more substantial good than the general approbation of the neighbourhood, and the regard which his social powers had gained him in the mess. After pausing on this point a considerable while, she once more continued to read. But, alas! the story which followed, of his designs on Miss Darcy, received some confirmation from what had passed between Colonel Fitzwilliam and herself only the morning before; and at last she was referred for the truth of every particular to Colonel Fitzwilliam himself—from whom she had previously received the information of his near concern in all his cousin's affairs, and whose character she had no reason to question. At one time she had almost resolved on applying to him, but the idea was checked by the awkwardness of the application, and at length wholly banished by the conviction that Mr. Darcy would never have hazarded such a proposal, if he had not been well assured of his cousin's corroboration.

She perfectly remembered everything that had passed in conversation between Wickham and herself, in their first evening at Mr. Philips's. Many of his expressions were still fresh in her memory. She was *now* struck with the impropriety of such communications to a stranger, and wondered it had escaped her before. She saw the indelicacy of putting himself forward as he had done, and the inconsistency of his professions with his conduct. She remembered that he had boasted of having no fear of seeing Mr. Darcy—that Mr. Darcy might leave the country, but that *he* should stand his ground: yet he had avoided the Netherfield ball the very next week. She remembered also that, till the Netherfield family had quitted the country, he had told his story to no one but herself; but that after their removal it had been everywhere discussed; that he had then no reserves, no scruples in sinking Mr. Darcy's character, though he had assured her that respect for the father would always prevent his exposing the son.

How differently did everything now appear in which he was concerned! His attentions to Miss King were now the consequence of views solely and hatefully mercenary; and the mediocrity of her fortune proved no longer the moderation of his wishes, but his eagerness to grasp at anything. His behaviour to herself could now have had no tolerable motive; he had either been deceived with regard to her fortune, or had been gratifying his vanity

by encouraging the preference which she believed she had most incau-
tiously shown. Every lingering struggle in his favour grew fainter and
fainter; and in farther justification of Mr. Darcy, she could not but allow
that Mr. Bingley, when questioned by Jane, had long ago asserted his
blamelessness in the affair; that proud and repulsive as were his manners,
she had never, in the whole course of their acquaintance—an acquaintance
which had latterly brought them much together, and given her a sort of
intimacy with his ways—seen anything that betrayed him to be unprincipled or unjust—anything that spoke him of irreligious or immoral
habits; that among his own connections he was esteemed and valued—
that even Wickham had allowed him merit as a brother, and that she had
often heard him speak so affectionately of his sister as to prove him
capable of some amiable feeling; that had his actions been what Wickham
represented them, so gross a violation of everything right could hardly
have been concealed from the world; and that friendship between a person
capable of it, and such an amiable man as Mr. Bingley, was incomprehensible.

She grew absolutely ashamed of herself. Of neither Darcy nor Wickham
could she think without feeling that she had been blind, partial, prejudiced, absurd.

"How despicably have I acted!" she cried; "I, who have prided myself
on my discernment! I, who have valued myself on my abilities! who have
often disdained the generous candour of my sister, and gratified my
vanity in useless or blameable distrust. How humiliating is this discovery!
yet, how just a humiliation! Had I been in love, I could not have been
more wretchedly blind. But vanity, not love, has been my folly. Pleased
with the preference of one, and offended by the neglect of the other, on
the very beginning of our acquaintance, I have courted prepossession and
ignorance, and driven reason away, where either were concerned. Till this
moment I never knew myself."

From herself to Jane—from Jane to Bingley, her thoughts were in a line
which soon brought to her recollection that Mr. Darcy's explanation *there*
had appeared very insufficient, and she read it again. Widely different
was the effect of a second perusal. How could she deny that credit to his
assertions, in one instance, which she had been obliged to give in the
other? He declared himself to have been totally unsuspicious of her sister's
attachment; and she could not help remembering what Charlotte's opinion
had always been. Neither could she deny the justice of his description of
Jane. She felt that Jane's feelings, though fervent, were little displayed,
and that there was a constant complacency in her air and manner not
often united with great sensibility.

When she came to that part of the letter in which her family were
mentioned in terms of such mortifying, yet merited reproach, her sense of
shame was severe. The justice of the charge struck her too forcibly for
denial, and the circumstances to which he particularly alluded as having
passed at the Netherfield ball, and as confirming all his first disapproba-

tion, could not have made a stronger impression on his mind than on hers

The compliment to herself and her sister was not unfelt. It soothed, but it could not console her for the contempt which had thus been self-attracted by the rest of her family; and as she considered that Jane's disappointment had in fact been the work of her nearest relations, and reflected how materially the credit of both must be hurt by such impropriety of conduct, she felt depressed beyond anything she had ever known before.

After wandering along the lane for two hours, giving way to every variety of thought—re-considering events, determining probabilities, and reconciling herself, as well as she could, to a change so sudden and so important, fatigue, and a recollection of her long absence, made her at length return home; and she entered the house with the wish of appearing cheerful as usual, and the resolution of repressing such reflections as must make her unfit for conversation.

She was immediately told that the two gentlemen from Rosings had each called during her absence; Mr. Darcy, only for a few minutes to take leave—but that Colonel Fitzwilliam had been sitting with them at least an hour, hoping for her return, and almost resolving to walk after her till she could be found. Elizabeth could but just *affect* concern in missing him; she really rejoiced at it. Colonel Fitzwilliam was no longer an object; she could think only of her letter.

Chapter 37

THE two gentlemen left Rosings the next morning, and Mr. Collins having been in waiting near the lodges, to make them his parting obeisance, was able to bring home the pleasing intelligence, of their appearing in very good health, and in as tolerable spirits as could be expected, after the melancholy scene so lately gone through at Rosings. To Rosings he then hastened, to console Lady Catherine and her daughter; and on his return brought back, with great satisfaction, a message from her ladyship, importing that she felt herself so dull as to make her very desirous of having them all to dine with her.

Elizabeth could not see Lady Catherine without recollecting that, had she chosen it, she might by this time have been presented to her as her future niece; nor could she think, without a smile, of what her ladyship's indignation would have been. "What would she have said? how would she have behaved?" were questions with which she amused herself.

Their first subject was the diminution of the Rosings party. "I assure you, I feel it exceedingly," said Lady Catherine; "I believe nobody feels the loss of friends so much as I do. But I am particularly attached to these young men, and know them to be so much attached to me! They were excessively sorry to go! But so they always are. The dear Colonel rallied his spirits tolerably till just at last; but Darcy seemed to feel it most acutely, more, I think, than last year. His attachment to Rosings certainly increases."

Mr. Collins had a compliment, and an allusion to throw in here, which were kindly smiled on by the mother and daughter.

Lady Catherine observed, after dinner, that Miss Bennet seemed out of spirits, and immediately accounting for it herself, by supposing that she did not like to go home again so soon, she added:

"But if that is the case, you must write to your mother to beg that you may stay a little longer. Mrs. Collins will be very glad of your company, I am sure."

"I am much obliged to your ladyship for your kind invitation," replied Elizabeth, "but it is not in my power to accept it. I must be in town next Saturday."

"Why, at that rate, you will have been here only six weeks. I expected you to stay two months. I told Mrs. Collins so before you came. There can be no occasion for your going so soon. Mrs. Bennet could certainly spare you for another fortnight."

"But my father cannot. He wrote last week to hurry my return."

"Oh! your father of course may spare you, if your mother can. Daughters are never of so much consequence to a father. And if you will stay another *month* complete, it will be in my power to take one of you as far as London, for I am going there early in June, for a week; and as Dawson does not object to the barouche-box, there will be very good room for one of you—and indeed, if the weather should happen to be cool, I should not object to taking you both, as you are neither of you large."

"You are all kindness, madam; but I believe we must abide by our original plan."

Lady Catherine seemed resigned. "Mrs. Collins, you must send a servant with them. You know I always speak my mind, and I cannot bear the idea of two young women travelling post by themselves. It is highly improper. You must contrive to send somebody. I have the greatest dislike in the world to that sort of thing. Young women should always be properly guarded and attended, according to their situation in life. When my niece Georgiana went to Ramsgate last summer, I made a point of her having two men-servants go with her. Miss Darcy, the daughter of Mr. Darcy, of Pemberley, and Lady Anne, could not have appeared with propriety in a different manner. I am excessively attentive to all those thing You must send John with the young ladies, Mrs. Collins. I am glad it occurred to me to mention it; for it would really be discreditable to *you* to let them go alone."

"My uncle is to send a servant for us."

"Oh! Your uncle! He keeps a man-servant, does he? I am very glad you have somebody who thinks of those things. Where shall you change horses? Oh! Bromley, of course. If you mention my name at the Bell, you will be attended to."

Lady Catherine had many other questions to ask respecting their journey, and as she did not answer them all herself, attention was necessary, which Elizabeth believed to be lucky for her; or, with a mind so occupied, she might have forgotten where she was. Reflection must be reserved for solitary hours; whenever she was alone, she gave way to it as the greatest relief; and not a day went by without a solitary walk, in which she might indulge in all the delight of unpleasant recollections.

Mr. Darcy's letter she was in a fair way of soon knowing by heart. She studied every sentence; and her feelings towards its writer were at times widely different. When she remembered the style of his address, she was still full of indignation; but when she considered how unjustly she had condemned and upbraided him, her anger was turned against herself; and his disappointed feelings became the object of compassion. His attachment excited gratitude, his general character respect; but she could not approve him; nor could she for a moment repent her refusal, or feel the slightest inclination ever to see him again. In her own past behaviour, there was a constant source of vexation and regret; and in the unhappy defects of her family, a subject of yet heavier chagrin. They were hopeless of remedy. Her father, contented with laughing at them, would never exert himself to restrain the wild giddiness of his youngest daughters; and her mother, with manners so far from right herself, was entirely insensible of the evil. Elizabeth had frequently united with Jane in an endeavour to check the imprudence of Catherine and Lydia; but while they were supported by their mother's indulgence, what chance could there be of improvement? Catherine, weak-spirited, irritable, and completely under Lydia's guidance, had been always affronted by their advice; and Lydia, self-willed and careless, would scarcely give them a hearing. They were ignorant, idle, and vain. While there was an officer in Meryton, they would flirt with him; and while Meryton was within a walk of Longbourn, they would be going there for ever.

Anxiety on Jane's behalf was another prevailing concern; and Mr. Darcy's explanation, by restoring Bingley to all her former good opinion, heightened the sense of what Jane had lost. His affection was proved to have been sincere, and his conduct cleared of all blame, unless any could attach to the implicitness of his confidence in his friend. How grievous then was the thought that, of a situation so desirable in every respect, so replete with advantage, so promising for happiness, Jane had been deprived, by the folly and indecorum of her own family!

When to these recollections was added the development of Wickham's character, it may be easily believed that the happy spirits which had seldom been depressed before, were now so much affected as to make it almost impossible for her to appear tolerably cheerful.

Their engagements at Rosings were as frequent during the last week of her stay as they had been at first. The very last evening was spent there; and her ladyship again inquired minutely into the particulars of their journey, gave them directions as to the best method of packing, and was so urgent on the necessity of placing gowns in the only right way, that

Maria thought herself obliged, on her return, to undo all the work of the morning, and pack her trunk afresh.

When they parted, Lady Catherine, with great condescension, wished them a good journey, and invited them to come to Hunsford again next year; and Miss de Bourgh exerted herself so far as to curtsey and hold out her hand to both.

Chapter 38

On Saturday morning Elizabeth and Mr. Collins met for breakfast a few minutes before the others appeared; and he took the opportunity of paying the parting civilities which he deemed indispensably necessary.

"I know not, Miss Elizabeth," said he, "whether Mrs. Collins has yet expressed her sense of your kindness in coming to us; but I am very certain you will not leave the house without receiving her thanks for it. The favour of your company has been much felt, I assure you. We know how little there is to tempt any one to our humble abode. Our plain manner of living, our small rooms and few domestics, and the little we see of the world, must make Hunsford extremely dull to a young lady like yourself; but I hope you will believe us grateful for the condescension, and that we have done everything in our power to prevent your spending your time unpleasantly."

Elizabeth was eager with her thanks and assurances of happiness. She had spent six weeks with great enjoyment; and the pleasure of being with Charlotte, and the kind attentions she had received, must make *her* feel the obliged. Mr. Collins was gratified, and with a more smiling solemnity replied:

"It gives me the greatest pleasure to hear that you have passed your time not disagreeably. We have certainly done our best; and most fortunately having it in our power to introduce you to very superior society, and, from our connection with Rosings, the frequent means of varying the humble home scene, I think we may flatter ourselves that your Hunsford visit cannot have been entirely irksome. Our situation with regard to Lady Catherine's family is indeed the sort of extraordinary advantage and blessing which few can boast. You see on what a footing we are. You see how continually we are engaged there. In truth I must acknowledge that, with all the disadvantages of this humble parsonage, I should not think any one abiding in it an object of compassion, while they are sharers of our intimacy at Rosings."

Words were insufficient for the elevation of his feelings; and he was obliged to walk about the room, while Elizabeth tried to unite civility and truth in a few short sentences.

"You may, in fact, carry a very favourable report of us into Hertfordshire, my dear cousin. I flatter myself at least that you will be able to do so. Lady Catherine's great attentions to Mrs. Collins you have been a daily witness of; and altogether I trust it does not appear that your friend has drawn an unfortunate—— But on this point it will be as well to be silent. Only let me assure you, my dear Miss Elizabeth, that I can from my heart most cordially wish you equal felicity in marriage. My dear Charlotte and I have but one mind and one way of thinking. There is in everything a most remarkable resemblance of character and ideas between us. We seem to have been designed for each other."

Elizabeth could safely say that it was a great happiness where that was the case, and with equal sincerity could add, that she firmly believed and rejoiced in his domestic comforts. She was not sorry, however, to have the recital of them interrupted by the entrance of the lady from whom they sprang. Poor Charlotte! it was melancholy to leave her to such society! But she had chosen it with her eyes open; and though evidently regretting that her visitors were to go, she did not seem to ask for compassion. Her home and her housekeeping, her parish and her poultry, and all their dependent concerns, had not yet lost their charms.

At length the chaise arrived, the trunks were fastened on, the parcels placed within, and it was pronounced to be ready. After an affectionate parting between the friends, Elizabeth was attended to the carriage by Mr. Collins, and as they walked down the garden, he was commissioning her with his best respects to all her family, not forgetting his thanks for the kindness he had received at Longbourn in the winter, and his compliments to Mr. and Mrs. Gardiner, though unknown. He then handed her in, Maria followed, and the door was on the point of being closed, when he suddenly reminded them, with some consternation, that they had hitherto forgotten to leave any message for the ladies at Rosings.

"But," he added, "you will of course wish to have your humble respects delivered to them, with your grateful thanks for their kindness to you while you have been here."

Elizabeth made no objection; the door was then allowed to be shut, and the carriage drove off.

"Good gracious!" cried Maria, after a few minutes' silence, "it seems but a day or two since we first came! and yet how many things have happened!"

"A great many indeed," said her companion with a sigh.

"We have dined nine times at Rosings, besides drinking tea there twice! How much I shall have to tell!"

Elizabeth privately added, "And how much I shall have to conceal!"

Their journey was performed without much conversation, or any alarm; and within four hours of their leaving Hunsford they reached Mr. Gardiner's house, where they were to remain a few days.

Jane looked well, and Elizabeth had little opportunity of studying her spirits, amidst the various engagements which the kindness of her aunt had reserved for them. But Jane was to go home with her, and at Longbourn there would be leisure enough for observation.

It was not without an effort, meanwhile, that she could wait even for

Longbourn, before she told her sister of Mr. Darcy's proposals. To know that she had the power of revealing what would so exceedingly astonish Jane, and must, at the same time, so highly gratify whatever of her own vanity she had not yet been able to reason away, was such a temptation to openness as nothing could have conquered but the state of indecision in which she remained as to the extent of what she should communicate; and her fear, if she once entered on the subject, of being hurried into repeating something of Bingley which might only grieve her sister further.

Chapter 39

I⊤ was the second week in May, in which the three young ladies set out together from Gracechurch Street for the town of ——, in Hertfordshire; and, as they drew near the appointed inn where Mr. Bennet's carriage was to meet them, they quickly perceived, in token of the coachman's punctuality, both Kitty and Lydia looking out of a dining-room upstairs. These two girls had been above an hour in the place, happily employed in visiting an opposite milliner, watching the sentinel on guard, and dressing a salad and cucumber.

After welcoming their sisters, they triumphantly displayed a table set out with such cold meat as an inn larder usually affords, exclaiming, "Is not this nice? is not this an agreeable surprise?"

"And we mean to treat you all," added Lydia; "but you must lend us the money, for we have just spent ours at the shop out there." Then, showing her purchases—"Look here, I have bought this bonnet. I do not think it is very pretty; but I thought I might as well buy it as not. I shall pull it to pieces as soon as I get home, and see if I can make it up any better."

And when her sisters abused it as ugly, she added, with perfect unconcern, "Oh! but there were two or three much uglier in the shop; and when I have bought some prettier-coloured satin to trim it with fresh, I think it will be very tolerable. Besides, it will not much signify what one wears this summer, after the ——shire have left Meryton, and they are going in a fortnight."

"Are they indeed!" cried Elizabeth, with the greatest satisfaction.

"They are going to be encamped near Brighton; and I do so want papa to take us all there for the summer! It would be such a delicious scheme, and I dare say would hardly cost anything at all. Mamma would like to go too of all things! Only think what a miserable summer else we shall have!"

"Yes," thought Elizabeth, "*that* would be a delightful scheme indeed, and completely do for us at once. Good Heaven! Brighton, and a whole campful of soldiers, to us, who have been overset already by one poor regiment of militia, and the monthly balls of Meryton!"

"Now I have got some news for you," said Lydia, as they sat down at table. "What do you think? It is excellent news—capital news—and about a certain person that we all like!"

Jane and Elizabeth looked at each other, and the waiter was told he need not stay. Lydia laughed, and said:

"Aye, that is just like your formality and discretion. You thought the waiter must not hear, as if he cared! I dare say he often hears worse things said than I am going to say. But he is an ugly fellow! I am glad he is gone. I never saw such a long chin in my life. Well, but now for my news; it is about dear Wickham; too good for the waiter, is not it? There is no danger of Wickham's marrying Mary King. There's for you! She is gone down to her uncle at Liverpool: gone to stay. Wickham is safe."

"And Mary King is safe!" added Elizabeth; "safe from a connection imprudent as to fortune."

"She is a great fool for going away, if she liked him."

"But I hope there is no strong attachment on either side," said Jane.

"I am sure there is not on *his*. I will answer for it, he never cared three straws about her—who *could* about such a nasty little freckled thing?"

Elizabeth was shocked to think that, however incapable of such coarseness of *expression* herself, the coarseness of the *sentiment* was little other than her own breast had formerly harboured and fancied liberal!

As soon as all had ate, and the elder ones paid, the carriage was ordered; and after some contrivance, the whole party, with all their boxes, work-bags, and parcels, and the unwelcome addition of Kitty's and Lydia's purchases, were seated in it.

"How nicely we are crammed in," cried Lydia. "I am glad I bought my bonnet, if it is only for the fun of having another bandbox! Well, now let us be quite comfortable and snug, and talk and laugh all the way home. And in the first place, let us hear what has happened to you all since you went away. Have you seen any pleasant men? Have you had any flirting? I was in great hopes that one of you would have got a husband before you came back. Jane will be quite an old maid soon, I declare. She is almost three-and-twenty! Lord, how ashamed I should be of not being married before three-and-twenty! My aunt Philips wants you so to get husbands, you can't think. She says Lizzy had better have taken Mr. Collins; but *I* do not think there would have been any fun in it. Lord! how I should like to be married before any of you! and then I would chaperon you about to all the balls. Dear me! we had such a good piece of fun the other day at Colonel Forster's. Kitty and me were to spend the day there, and Mrs. Forster promised to have a little dance in the evening; (by the bye, Mrs. Forster and me are *such* friends!) and so she asked the two Harringtons to come, but Harriet was ill, and so Pen was forced to come by herself; and then, what do you think we did? We dressed up Chamberlayne in woman's clothes on purpose to pass for a lady, only think what fun! Not a soul knew of it, but Colonel and Mrs. Forster, and Kitty and me, except my aunt, for we were forced to borrow one of her gowns; and you cannot imagine how well he looked! When Denny, and Wickham, and Pratt, and two or three more of the men came in, they did not know him in the least. Lord! how I laughed! and so did Mrs. Forster. I thought I should have died. And *that* made the men suspect something, and then they soon found out what was the matter."

With such kind of histories of their parties and good jokes, did Lydia, assisted by Kitty's hints and additions, endeavour to amuse her companions all the way to Longbourn. Elizabeth listened as little as she could, but there was no escaping the frequent mention of Wickham's name.

Their reception at home was most kind. Mrs. Bennet rejoiced to see Jane in undiminished beauty; and more than once during dinner did Mr. Bennet say voluntarily to Elizabeth:

"I am glad you are come back, Lizzy."

Their party in the dining-room was large, for almost all the Lucases came to meet Maria and hear the news; and various were the subjects which occupied them: Lady Lucas was inquiring of Maria, across the table, after the welfare and poultry of her eldest daughter; Mrs. Bennet was doubly engaged, on one hand collecting an account of the present fashions from Jane, who sat some way below her, and, on the other, retailing them all to the younger Miss Lucases; and Lydia, in a voice rather louder than any other person's, was enumerating the various pleasures of the morning to anybody who would hear her.

"Oh! Mary," said she, "I wish you had gone with us, for we had such fun! As we went along, Kitty and me drew up all the blinds, and pretended there was nobody in the coach; and I should have gone so all the way, if Kitty had not been sick; and when we got to the George, I do think we behaved very handsomely, for we treated the other three with the nicest cold luncheon in the world, and if you would have gone, we would have treated you too. And then when we came away it was such fun! I thought we never should have got into the coach. I was ready to die of laughter. And then we were so merry all the way home! we talked and laughed so loud, that anybody might have heard us ten miles off!"

To this Mary very gravely replied, "Far be it from me, my dear sister, to depreciate such pleasures! They would doubtless be congenial with the generality of female minds. But I confess they would have no charms for *me*—I should infinitely prefer a book."

But of this answer Lydia heard not a word. She seldom listened to anybody for more than half a minute, and never attended to Mary at all.

In the afternoon Lydia was urgent with the rest of the girls to walk to Meryton, and see how everybody went on; but Elizabeth steadily opposed the scheme. It should not be said that the Miss Bennets could not be at home half a day before they were in pursuit of the officers. There was another reason too for her opposition. She dreaded seeing Wickham again, and was resolved to avoid it as long as possible. The comfort to *her* of the regiment's approaching removal was indeed beyond expression. In a fortnight they were to go—and once gone, she hoped there could be nothing more to plague her on his account.

She had not been many hours at home before she found that the Brighton scheme, of which Lydia had given them a hint at the inn, was under frequent discussion between her parents. Elizabeth saw directly that her father had not the smallest intention of yielding; but his answers were at the same time so vague and equivocal, that her mother, though often disheartened, had never yet despaired of succeeding at last.

Chapter 40

ELIZABETH'S impatience to acquaint Jane with what had happened could no longer be overcome; and at length, resolving to suppress every particular in which her sister was concerned, and preparing her to be surprised, she related to her the next morning the chief of the scene between Mr. Darcy and herself.

Miss Bennet's astonishment was soon lessened by the strong sisterly partiality which made any admiration of Elizabeth appear perfectly natural; and all surprise was shortly lost in other feelings. She was sorry that Mr. Darcy should have delivered his sentiments in a manner so little suited to recommend them; but still more was she grieved for the unhappiness which her sister's refusal must have given him.

"His being so sure of succeeding was wrong," said she, "and certainly ought not to have appeared; but consider how much it must increase his disappointment!"

"Indeed," replied Elizabeth, "I am heartily sorry for him; but he has other feelings, which will probably soon drive away his regard for me. You do not blame me, however, for refusing him?"

"Blame you! Oh, no."

"But you blame me for having spoken so warmly of Wickham?"

"No—I do not know that you were wrong in saying what you did."

"But you *will* know it, when I have told you what happened the very next day."

She then spoke of the letter, repeating the whole of its contents as far as they concerned George Wickham. What a stroke was this for poor Jane! who would willingly have gone through the world without believing that so much wickedness existed in the whole race of mankind, as was here collected in one individual. Nor was Darcy's vindication, though grateful to her feelings, capable of consoling her for such discovery. Most earnestly did she labour to prove the probability of error, and seek to clear one without involving the other.

"This will not do," said Elizabeth; "you never will be able to make both of them good for anything. Take your choice, but you must be satisfied with only one. There is but such a quantity of merit between them; just enough to make one good sort of man; and of late it has been shifting about pretty much. For my part, I am inclined to believe it all Mr. Darcy's; but you shall do as you choose."

It was some time, however, before a smile could be extorted from Jane.

"I do not know when I have been more shocked," said she. "Wickham so very bad! It is almost past belief. And poor Mr. Darcy! Dear Lizzy, only consider what he must have suffered. Such a disappointment! and with the knowledge of your ill opinion too! and having to relate such a thing of his sister! It is really too distressing. I am sure you must feel it so."

"Oh! no, my regret and compassion are all done away by seeing you so full of both. I know you will do him such ample justice, that I am growing every moment more unconcerned and indifferent. Your profusion makes me saving; and if you lament over him much longer, my heart will be as light as a feather."

"Poor Wickham! there is such an expression of goodness in his countenance! such an openness and gentleness in his manner!"

"There certainly was some great mismanagement in the education of those two young men. One has got all the goodness, and the other all the appearance of it."

"I never thought Mr. Darcy so deficient in the *appearance* of it as you used to do."

"And yet I meant to be uncommonly clever in taking so decided a dislike to him, without any reason. It is such a spur to one's genius, such an opening for wit, to have a dislike of that kind. One may be continually abusive without saying anything just; but one cannot be always laughing at a man without now and then stumbling on something witty."

"Lizzy, when you first read that letter, I am sure you could not treat the matter as you do now."

"Indeed, I could not. I was uncomfortable enough. I was very uncomfortable, I may say unhappy. And with no one to speak to of what I felt, no Jane to comfort me and say that I had not been so very weak and vain and nonsensical as I knew I had! Oh! how I wanted you!"

"How unfortunate that you should have used such very strong expressions in speaking of Wickham to Mr. Darcy, for now they *do* appear wholly undeserved."

"Certainly. But the misfortune of speaking with bitterness is a most natural consequence of the prejudices I had been encouraging. There is one point on which I want your advice. I want to be told whether I ought, or ought not, to make our acquaintances in general understand Wickham's character."

Miss Bennet paused a little, and then replied, "Surely there can be no occasion for exposing him so dreadfully. What is your own opinion?"

"That it ought not to be attempted. Mr. Darcy has not authorised me to make his communication public. On the contrary, every particular relative to his sister was meant to be kept as much as possible to myself; and if I endeavour to undeceive people as to the rest of his conduct, who will believe me? The general prejudice against Mr. Darcy is so violent, that it would be the death of half the good people in Meryton to attempt to place him in an amiable light. I am not equal to it. Wickham will soon be gone; and therefore it will not signify to anybody here what he really is. Some time hence it will be all found out, and then we may laugh at their stupidity in not knowing it before. At present I will say nothing about it."

"You are quite right. To have his errors made public might ruin him for ever. He is now, perhaps, sorry for what he has done, and anxious to re-establish a character. We must not make him desperate."

The tumult of Elizabeth's mind was allayed by this conversation. She had got rid of two of the secrets which had weighed on her for a fortnight, and was certain of a willing listener in Jane, whenever she might wish to talk again of either. But there was still something lurking behind, of which prudence forbade the disclosure. She dared not relate the other half of Mr. Darcy's letter, nor explain to her sister how sincerely she had been valued by his friend. Here was knowledge in which no one could partake; and she was sensible that nothing less than a perfect understanding between the parties could justify her in throwing off this last encumbrance of mystery. "And then," said she, "if that very improbable event should ever take place, I shall merely be able to tell what Bingley may tell in a much more agreeable manner himself. The liberty of communication cannot be mine till it has lost all its value!"

She was now, on being settled at home, at leisure to observe the real state of her sister's spirits. Jane was not happy. She still cherished a very tender affection for Bingley. Having never even fancied herself in love before, her regard had all the warmth of first attachment, and, from her age and disposition, greater steadiness than first attachments often boast; and so fervently did she value his remembrance, and prefer him to every other man, that all her good sense, and all her attention to the feelings of her friends, were requisite to check the indulgence of those regrets which must have been injurious to her own health and their tranquillity.

"Well, Lizzy," said Mrs. Bennet one day, "what is your opinion *now* of this sad business of Jane's? For my part, I am determined never to speak of it again to anybody. I told my sister Philips so the other day. But I cannot find out that Jane saw anything of him in London. Well, he is a very undeserving young man—and I do not suppose there's the least chance in the world of her ever getting him now. There is no talk of his coming to Netherfield again in the summer; and I have inquired of everybody, too, who is likely to know."

"I do not believe that he will ever live at Netherfield any more."

"Oh, well! it is just as he chooses. Nobody wants him to come. Though I shall always say that he used my daughter extremely ill; and if I was her, I would not have put up with it. Well, my comfort is, I am sure Jane will die of a broken heart; and then he will be sorry for what he has done."

But as Elizabeth could not receive comfort from any such expectation, she made no answer.

"Well, Lizzy," continued her mother, soon afterwards, "and so the Collinses live very comfortable, do they? Well, well, I only hope it will last. And what sort of table do they keep? Charlotte is an excellent manager, I dare say. If she is half as sharp as her mother, she is saving enough. There is nothing extravagant in *their* housekeeping, I dare say."

"No, nothing at all."

"A great deal of good management, depend upon it. Yes, yes. *They* will take care not to outrun their income. *They* will never be distressed for money. Well, much good may it do them! And so, I suppose, they often talk of having Longbourn when your father is dead. They look upon it quite as their own, I dare say, whenever that happens."

"It was a subject which they could not mention before me."

"No; it would have been strange if they had: but I make no doubt they often talk of it between themselves. Well, if they can be easy with an estate that is not lawfully their own, so much the better. *I* should be ashamed of having one that was only entailed on me."

Chapter 41

THE first week of their return was soon gone. The second began. It was the last of the regiment's stay in Meryton, and all the young ladies in the neighbourhood were drooping apace. The dejection was almost universal. The elder Miss Bennets alone were still able to eat, drink, and sleep, and pursue the usual course of their employments. Very frequently were they reproached for this insensibility by Kitty and Lydia, whose own misery was extreme, and who could not comprehend such hard-heartedness in any of the family.

"Good Heaven! what is to become of us? What are we to do?" would they often exclaim in the bitterness of woe. "How can you be smiling so, Lizzy?"

Their affectionate mother shared all their grief; she remembered what she had herself endured on a similar occasion, five-and-twenty years ago.

"I am sure," said she, "I cried for two days together when Colonel Miller's regiment went away. I thought I should have broken my heart."

"I am sure I shall break *mine*," said Lydia.

"If one could but go to Brighton!" observed Mrs. Bennet.

"Oh, yes!—if one could but go to Brighton! But papa is so disagreeable."

"A little sea-bathing would set me up for ever."

"And my aunt Philips is sure it would do *me* a great deal of good," added Kitty.

Such were the kind of lamentations resounding perpetually through Longbourn House. Elizabeth tried to be diverted by them; but all sense of pleasure was lost in shame. She felt anew the justice of Mr. Darcy's objections; and never had she before been so much disposed to pardon his interference in the views of his friend.

But the gloom of Lydia's prospect was shortly cleared away; for she received an invitation from Mrs. Forster, the wife of the colonel of the regiment, to accompany her to Brighton. This invaluable friend was a very young woman, and very lately married. A resemblance in good humour and good spirits had recommended her and Lydia to each other, and out of their *three* months' acquaintance they had been intimate *two*.

The rapture of Lydia on this occasion, her adoration of Mrs. Forster, the delight of Mrs. Bennet, and the mortification of Kitty, are scarcely to be described. Wholly inattentive to her sister's feelings, Lydia flew about the house in restless ecstasy, calling for every one's congratulations, and laughing and talking with more violence than ever; whilst the luckless Kitty continued in the parlour repining at her fate in terms as unreasonable as her accent was peevish.

"I cannot see why Mrs. Forster should not ask *me* as well as Lydia," said she, "though I am *not* her particular friend. I have just as much right to be asked as she has, and more too, for I am two years older."

In vain did Elizabeth attempt to make her reasonable, and Jane to make her resigned. As for Elizabeth herself, this invitation was so far from exciting in her the same feelings as in her mother and Lydia, that she considered it as the death warrant of all possibility of common sense for the latter; and detestable as such a step must make her were it known, she could not help secretly advising her father not to let her go. She represented to him all the improprieties of Lydia's general behaviour, the little advantage she could derive from the friendship of such a woman as Mrs. Forster, and the probability of her being yet more imprudent with such a companion at Brighton, where the temptations must be greater than at home. He heard her attentively, and then said:

"Lydia will never be easy till she has exposed herself in some public place or other, and we can never expect her to do it with so little expense or inconvenience to her family as under the present circumstances."

"If you were aware," said Elizabeth, "of the very great disadvantage to us all which must arise from the public notice of Lydia's unguarded and imprudent manner—nay, which has already arisen from it, I am sure you would judge differently in the affair."

"Already arisen?" repeated Mr. Bennet. "What, has she frightened away some of your lovers? Poor little Lizzy! But do not be cast down. Such squeamish youths as cannot bear to be connected with a little absurdity are not worth a regret. Come, let me see the list of pitiful fellows who have been kept aloof by Lydia's folly."

"Indeed you are mistaken. I have no such injuries to resent. It is not of peculiar, but of general evils, which I am now complaining. Our importance, our respectability in the world must be affected by the wild volatility, the assurance and disdain of all restraint which mark Lydia's character. Excuse me, for I must speak plainly. If you, my dear father, will not take the trouble of checking her exuberant spirits, and of teaching her that her present pursuits are not to be the business of her life, she will soon be beyond the reach of amendment. Her character will be fixed, and she will, at sixteen, be the most determined flirt that ever made herself and her family ridiculous; a flirt too, in the worst and meanest degree of flirtation; without any attraction beyond youth and a tolerable person; and, from the ignorance and emptiness of her mind, wholly unable to ward off any portion of that universal contempt which her rage for admiration will excite. In this danger Kitty is also comprehended. She will follow wherever Lydia leads. Vain, ignorant, idle, and absolutely uncontrolled! Oh! my dear father, can you suppose it possible that they will not be censured and despised wherever they are known, and that their sisters will not be often involved in the disgrace?"

Mr. Bennet saw that her whole heart was in the subject, and affectionately taking her hand said in reply:

"Do not make yourself uneasy, my love. Wherever you and Jane are known you must be respected and valued; and you will not appear to less advantage for having a couple of—or I may say, three—very silly sisters. We shall have no peace at Longbourn if Lydia does not go to Brighton. Let her go, then. Colonel Forster is a sensible man, and will keep her out of any real mischief; and she is luckily too poor to be an object of prey to anybody. At Brighton she will be of less importance even as a common flirt than she has been here. The officers will find women better worth their notice. Let us hope, therefore, that her being there may teach her her own insignificance. At any rate, she cannot grow many degrees worse, without authorising us to lock her up for the rest of her life."

With this answer Elizabeth was forced to be content; but her own opinion continued the same, and she left him disappointed and sorry. It was not in her nature, however, to increase her vexations by dwelling on them. She was confident of having performed her duty, and to fret over unavoidable evils, or augment them by anxiety, was no part of her disposition.

Had Lydia and her mother known the substance of her conference with her father, their indignation would hardly have found expression in their united volubility. In Lydia's imagination, a visit to Brighton comprised every possibility of earthly happiness. She saw, with the creative eye of fancy, the streets of that gay bathing-place covered with officers. She saw herself the object of attention to tens and to scores of them at present unknown. She saw all the glories of the camp—its tents stretched forth in beauteous uniformity of lines, crowded with the young and the gay, and dazzling with scarlet; and, to complete the view, she saw herself seated beneath a tent, tenderly flirting with at least six officers at once.

Had she known that her sister sought to tear her from such prospects and such realities as these, what would have been her sensations? They could have been understood only by her mother, who might have felt nearly the same. Lydia's going to Brighton was all that consoled her for her melancholy conviction of her husband's never intending to go there himself.

But they were entirely ignorant of what had passed; and their raptures continued, with little intermission, to the very day of Lydia's leaving home.

Elizabeth was now to see Mr. Wickham for the last time. Having been frequently in company with him since her return, agitation was pretty well over; the agitations of former partiality entirely so. She had even learnt to detect, in the very gentleness which had first delighted her, an affectation and a sameness to disgust and weary. In his present behaviour to herself, moreover, she had a fresh source of displeasure, for the inclination he soon testified of renewing those attentions which had marked the early part of their acquaintance could only serve, after what had since passed, to provoke her. She lost all concern for him in finding herself thus selected as the object of such idle and frivolous gallantry; and while she steadily repressed it, could not but feel the reproof contained in his believing, that however long, and for whatever cause, his attentions had been withdrawn, her vanity would be gratified, and her preference secured at any time by their renewal.

On the very last day of the regiment's remaining at Meryton, he dined, with other of the officers, at Longbourn; and so little was Elizabeth disposed to part from him in good humour, that on his making some inquiry as to the manner in which her time had passed at Hunsford, she mentioned Colonel Fitzwilliam's and Mr. Darcy's having both spent three weeks at Rosings, and asked him if he was acquainted with the former.

He looked surprised, displeased, alarmed; but with a moment's recollection and a returning smile, replied that he had formerly seen him often; and, after observing that he was a very gentlemanlike man, asked her how she had liked him. Her answer was warmly in his favour. With an air of indifference he soon afterwards added:

"How long did you say that he was at Rosings?"

"Nearly three weeks."

"And you saw him frequently?"

"Yes, almost every day."

"His manners are very different from his cousin's."

"Yes, very different. But I think Mr. Darcy improves on acquaintance."

"Indeed!" cried Wickham, with a look which did not escape her. "And pray, may I ask?——" But checking himself, he added, in a gayer tone, "Is it in address that he improves? Has he designed to add aught of civility to his ordinary style?—for I dare not hope," he continued in a lower and more serious tone, "that he is improved in essentials."

"Oh, no!" said Elizabeth. "In essentials, I believe, he is very much what he ever was."

While she spoke, Wickham looked as if scarcely knowing whether to rejoice over her words, or to distrust their meaning. There was a something in her countenance which made him listen with an apprehensive and anxious attention, while she added:

"When I said that he improved on acquaintance, I did not mean that either his mind or manners were in a state of improvement, but that, from knowing him better, his disposition was better understood."

Wickham's alarm now appeared in a heightened complexion and agitated look; for a few minutes he was silent, till, shaking off his embarrassment, he turned to her again, and said in the gentlest of accents:

"You, who so well know my feelings towards Mr. Darcy, will readily comprehend how sincerely I must rejoice that he is wise enough to assume even the *appearance* of what is right. His pride, in that direction, may be of service, if not to himself, to many others, for it must deter him from such foul misconduct as I have suffered by. I only fear that the sort of cautiousness to which you, I imagine, have been alluding, is merely adopted on his visits to his aunt, of whose good opinion and judgment he stands much in awe. His fear of her has always operated, I know, when they were together; and a good deal is to be imputed to his wish of forwarding the match with Miss de Bourgh, which I am certain he has very much at heart."

Elizabeth could not repress a smile at this, but she answered only by a slight inclination of the head. She saw that he wanted to engage her on the old subject of his grievances, and she was in no humour to indulge him. The rest of the evening passed with the *appearance,* on his side, of usual cheerfulness, but with no further attempt to distinguish Elizabeth; and they parted at last with mutual civility, and possibly a mutual desire of never meeting again.

When the party broke up, Lydia returned with Mrs. Forster to Meryton, from whence they were to set out early the next morning. The separation between her and her family was rather noisy than pathetic. Kitty was the only one who shed tears; but she did weep from vexation and envy. Mrs. Bennet was diffuse in her good wishes for the felicity of her daughter, and impressive in her injunctions that she would not miss the opportunity of enjoying herself as much as possible—advice which there was every reason to believe would be attended to; and in the clamorous happiness of Lydia herself in bidding farewell, the more gentle adieux of her sisters were uttered without being heard.

Chapter 42

HAD Elizabeth's opinion been all drawn from her own family, she could not have formed a very pleasing picture of conjugal felicity or domestic comfort. Her father, captivated by youth and beauty, and that appearance of good humour which youth and beauty generally give, had married a woman whose weak understanding and illiberal mind had very early in their marriage put an end to all real affection for her. Respect, esteem,

and confidence had vanished for ever; and all his views of domestic happiness were overthrown. But Mr. Bennet was not of a disposition to seek
comfort for the disappointment which his own imprudence had brought
on, in any of those pleasures which too often console the unfortunate for
their folly or their vice. He was fond of the country and of brooks; and
from these tastes had arisen his principal enjoyments. To his wife he was
very little otherwise indebted, than as her ignorance and folly had contributed to his amusement. This is not the sort of happiness which a man
would in general wish to owe to his wife; but where other powers of entertainment are wanting, the true philosopher will derive benefit from such
as are given.

Elizabeth, however, had never been blind to the impropriety of her
father's behaviour as a husband. She had always seen it with pain; but
respecting his abilities, and grateful for his affectionate treatment of herself, she endeavoured to forget what she could not overlook, and to banish
from her thoughts that continual breach of conjugal obligation and decorum which, in exposing his wife to the contempt of her own children,
was so highly reprehensible. But she had never felt so strongly as now the
disadvantages which must attend the children of so unsuitable a marriage,
nor ever been so fully aware of the evils arising from so ill-judged a direction of talents; talents which, rightly used, might at least have preserved
the respectability of his daughters, even if incapable of enlarging the mind
of his wife.

When Elizabeth had rejoiced over Wickham's departure she found little
other cause for satisfaction in the loss of the regiment. Their parties
abroad were less varied than before, and at home she had a mother and
sister whose constant repinings at the dullness of everything around them
threw a real gloom over their domestic circle; and, though Kitty might in
time regain her natural degree of sense, since the disturbers of her brain
were removed, her other sister, from whose disposition greater evil might
be apprehended, was likely to be hardened in all her folly and assurance
by a situation of such double danger as a watering-place and a camp.
Upon the whole, therefore, she found, what has been sometimes found
before, that an event to which she had looked forward with impatient
desire did not, in taking place, bring all the satisfaction she had promised
herself. It was consequently necessary to name some other period for the
commencement of actual felicity—to have some other point on which her
wishes and hopes might be fixed, and by again enjoying the pleasure of
anticipation, console herself for the present, and prepare for another disappointment. Her tour to the Lakes was now the object of her happiest
thoughts; it was her best consolation for all the uncomfortable hours
which the discontentedness of her mother and Kitty made inevitable;
and could she have included Jane in the scheme, every part of it would
have been perfect.

"But it is fortunate," thought she, "that I have something to wish for.
Were the whole arrangement complete, my disappointment would be

certain. But here, by carrying with me one ceaseless source of regret in my sister's absence, I may reasonably hope to have all my expectations of pleasure realised. A scheme of which every part promises delight can never be successful; and general disappointment is only warded off by the defence of some little peculiar vexation."

When Lydia went away she promised to write very often and very minutely to her mother and Kitty; but her letters were always long expected, and always very short. Those to her mother contained little else than that they were just returned from the library, where such and such officers had attended them, and where she had seen such beautiful ornaments as made her quite wild; that she had a new gown, or a new parasol, which she would have described more fully, but was obliged to leave off in a violent hurry, as Mrs. Forster called her, and they were going to the camp; and from her correspondence with her sister there was still less to be learnt—for her letters to Kitty, though rather longer, were much too full of lines under the words to be made public.

After the first fortnight or three weeks of her absence, health, good humour, and cheerfulness began to reappear at Longbourn. Everything wore a happier aspect. The families who had been in town for the winter came back again, and summer finery and summer engagements arose. Mrs. Bennet was restored to her usual querulous serenity; and, by the middle of June, Kitty was so much recovered as to be able to enter Meryton without tears; an event of such happy promise as to make Elizabeth hope that by the following Christmas she might be so tolerably reasonable as not to mention an officer above once a day, unless, by some cruel and malicious arrangement at the War Office, another regiment should be quartered in Meryton.

The time fixed for the beginning of their northern tour was now fast approaching, and a fortnight only was wanting of it, when a letter arrived from Mrs. Gardiner, which at once delayed its commencement and curtailed its extent. Mr. Gardiner would be prevented by business from setting out till a fortnight later in July, and must be in London again within a month; and as that left too short a period for them to go so far, and see so much as they had proposed, or at least to see it with the leisure and comfort they had built on, they were obliged to give up the Lakes, and substitute a more contracted tour, and, according to the present plan, were to go no farther northwards than Derbyshire. In that county there was enough to be seen to occupy the chief of their three weeks; and to Mrs. Gardiner it had a peculiarly strong attraction. The town where she had formerly passed some years of her life, and where they were now to spend a few days, was probably as great an object of her curiosity as all the celebrated beauties of Matlock, Chatsworth, Dovedale, or the Peak.

Elizabeth was excessively disappointed; she had set her heart on seeing the Lakes, and still thought there might have been time enough. But it was her business to be satisfied—and certainly her temper to be happy; and all was soon right again.

With the mention of Derbyshire there were many ideas connected. It was impossible for her to see the word without thinking of Pemberley and its owner. "But surely," said she, "I may enter his county with impunity, and rob it of a few petrified spars without his perceiving me."

The period of expectation was now doubled. Four weeks were to pass away before her uncle and aunt's arrival. But they did pass away, and Mr. and Mrs. Gardiner, with their four children, did at length appear at Longbourn. The children, two girls of six and eight years old, and two younger boys, were to be left under the particular care of their cousin Jane, who was the general favourite, and whose steady sense and sweetness of temper exactly adapted her for attending to them in every way—teaching them, playing with them, and loving them.

The Gardiners stayed only one night at Longbourn, and set off the next morning with Elizabeth in pursuit of novelty and amusement. One enjoyment was certain—that of suitableness as companions; a suitableness which comprehended health and temper to bear inconveniences—cheerfulness to enhance every pleasure—and affection and intelligence, which might supply it among themselves if there were disappointments abroad.

It is not the object of this work to give a description of Derbyshire, nor of any of the remarkable places through which their route thither lay; Oxford, Blenheim, Warwick, Kenilworth, Birmingham, etc., are sufficiently known. A small part of Derbyshire is all the present concern. To the little town of Lambton, the scene of Mrs. Gardiner's former residence, and where she had lately learned that some acquaintances still remained, they bent their steps, after having seen all the principal wonders of the country; and within five miles of Lambton, Elizabeth found from her aunt that Pemberley was situated. It was not in their direct road, nor more than a mile or two out of it. In talking over their route the evening before, Mrs. Gardiner expressed an inclination to see the place again. Mr. Gardiner declared his willingness, and Elizabeth was applied to for her approbation.

"My love, should not you like to see a place of which you have heard so much?" said her aunt; "a place, too, with which so many of your acquaintances are connected. Wickham passed all his youth there, you know."

Elizabeth was distressed. She felt that she had no business at Pemberley, and was obliged to assume a disinclination for seeing it. She must own that she was tired of great houses; after going over so many, she really had no pleasure in fine carpets or satin curtains.

Mrs. Gardiner abused her stupidity. "If it were merely a fine house richly furnished," said she, "I should not care about it myself; but the grounds are delightful. They have some of the finest woods in the country."

Elizabeth said no more—but her mind could not acquiesce. The possibility of meeting Mr. Darcy, while viewing the place, instantly occurred. It would be dreadful! She blushed at the very idea, and thought it would be better to speak openly to her aunt than to run such a risk. But against this there were objections; and she finally resolved that it could be the last resource, if her private inquiries as to the absence of the family were unfavourably answered.

Accordingly, when she retired at night, she asked the chambermaid whether Pemberley were not a very fine place? what was the name of its proprietor? and, with no little alarm, whether the family were down for the summer? A most welcome negative followed the last question—and her alarms being now removed, she was at leisure to feel a great deal of curiosity to see the house herself; and when the subject was revived the next morning, and she was again applied to, could readily answer, and with a proper air of indifference, that she had not really any dislike to the scheme. To Pemberley, therefore, they were to go.

Chapter 43

ELIZABETH, as they drove along, watched for the first appearance of Pemberley Woods with some perturbation; and when at length they turned in at the lodge, her spirits were in a high flutter.

The park was very large, and contained great variety of ground. They entered it in one of its lowest points, and drove for some time through a beautiful wood stretching over a wide extent.

Elizabeth's mind was too full for conversation, but she saw and admired very remarkable spot and point of view. They gradually ascended for half-a-mile, and then found themselves at the top of a considerable emi-nence, where the wood ceased, and the eye was instantly caught by Pemberley House, situated on the opposite side of a valley, into which the road with some abruptness wound. It was a large, handsome stone building, standing well on rising ground, and backed by a ridge of high woody hills; and in front, a stream of some natural importance was swelled into greater, but without any artificial appearance. Its banks were neither formal nor falsely adorned. Elizabeth was delighted. She had never seen a place for which nature had done more, or where natural beauty had been so little counteracted by an awkward taste. They were all of them warm in their admiration; and at that moment she felt that to be mistress of Pemberley might be something!

They descended the hill, crossed the bridge, and drove to the door; and, while examining the nearer aspect of the house, all her apprehension of meeting its owner returned. She dreaded lest the chambermaid had been mistaken. On applying to see the place, they were admitted into the hall; and Elizabeth, as they waited for the housekeeper, had leisure to wonder at her being where she was.

The housekeeper came; a respectable-looking elderly woman, much less fine, and more civil, than she had any notion of finding her. They followed her into the dining-parlour. It was a large, well proportioned room, handsomely fitted up. Elizabeth, after slightly surveying it, went to a window to enjoy its prospect. The hill, crowned with wood, which which they had descended, receiving increased abruptness from the distance, was a beautiful object. Every disposition of the ground was good; and she looked on the whole scene, the river, the trees scattered on its banks and the winding of the valley, as far as she could trace it, with delight. As they passed into other rooms these objects were taking different positions; but from every window there were beauties to be seen. The rooms were lofty and handsome, and their furniture suitable to the fortune of their proprietor; but Elizabeth saw, with admiration of his taste, that it was neither gaudy nor uselessly fine; with less of splendour, and more real elegance, than the furniture of Rosings.

"And of this place," thought she, "I might have been mistress! With these rooms I might now have been familiarly acquainted! Instead of viewing them as a stranger, I might have rejoiced in them as my own, and welcomed to them as visitors my uncle and aunt. But no"—recollecting herself—"that could never be; my uncle and aunt would have been lost to me; I should not have been allowed to invite them."

This was a lucky recollection—it saved her from something like regret.

She longed to inquire of the housekeeper whether her master was really absent, but had not courage for it. At length, however, the question was asked by her uncle; and she turned away with alarm, while Mrs. Reynolds replied that he was, adding, "But we expect him to-morrow, with a large party of friends." How rejoiced was Elizabeth that their own journey had not by any circumstance been delayed a day!

Her aunt now called her to look at a picture. She approached and saw the likeness of Mr. Wickham suspended, amongst several other miniatures, over the mantelpiece. Her aunt asked her, smilingly, how she liked it. The housekeeper came forward, and told them it was the picture of a young gentleman, the son of her late master's steward, who had been brought up by him at his own expense. "He is now gone into the army," she added; "but I am afraid he has turned out very wild."

Mrs. Gardiner looked at her niece with a smile, but Elizabeth could not return it.

"And that," said Mrs. Reynolds, pointing to another of the miniatures, "is my master—and very like him. It was drawn at the same time as the other—about eight years ago."

"I have heard much of your master's fine person," said Mrs. Gardiner, looking at the picture; "it is a handsome face. But, Lizzy, you can tell us whether it is like or not."

Mrs. Reynolds's respect for Elizabeth seemed to increase on this intimation of her knowing her master.

"Does that young lady know Mr. Darcy?"

Elizabeth coloured, and said: "A little."

"And do not you think him a very handsome gentleman, ma'am?"

"Yes, very handsome."

"I am sure *I* know none so handsome; but in the gallery upstairs you will see a finer, larger picture of him than this. This room was my late master's favourite room, and these miniatures are just as they used to be then. He was very fond of them."

This accounted to Elizabeth for Mr. Wickham's being among them.

Mrs. Reynolds then directed their attention to one of Miss Darcy, drawn when she was only eight years old.

"And is Miss Darcy as handsome as her brother?" said Mr. Gardiner.

"Oh! yes—the handsomest young lady that ever was seen; and so accomplished! She plays and sings all day long. In the next room is a new instrument just come down for her—a present from my master; she comes here to-morrow with him."

Mr. Gardiner, whose manners were easy and pleasant, encouraged her communicativeness by his questions and remarks: Mrs. Reynolds, either from pride or attachment, had evidently great pleasure in talking of her master and his sister.

"Is your master much at Pemberley in the course of the year?"

"Not so much as I could wish, sir; but I dare say he may spend half his time here; and Miss Darcy is always down for the summer months."

"Except," thought Elizabeth, "when she goes to Ramsgate."

"If your master would marry, you might see more of him."

"Yes, sir; but I do not know when *that* will be. I do not know who is good enough for him."

Mr. and Mrs. Gardiner smiled. Elizabeth could not help saying, "It is very much to his credit, I am sure, that you should think so."

"I say no more than the truth, and what everybody will say that knows him," replied the other. Elizabeth thought this was going pretty far; and she listened with increasing astonishment as the housekeeper added, "I have never had a cross word from him in my life, and I have known him ever since he was four years old."

This was praise, of all others most extraordinary, most opposite to her ideas. That he was not a good-tempered man had been her firmest opinion. Her keenest attention was awakened; she longed to hear more, and was grateful to her uncle for saying:

"There are very few people of whom so much can be said. You are lucky in having such a master."

"Yes, sir, I know I am. If I were to go through the world, I could not meet with a better. But I have always observed, that they who are good-natured when children, are good-natured when they grow up; and he was always the sweetest-tempered, most generous-hearted boy in the world."

Elizabeth almost stared at her. "Can this be Mr. Darcy?" thought she.

"His father was an excellent man," said Mrs. Gardiner.

"Yes, ma'am, that he was indeed; and his son will be just like him—just as affable to the poor."

Elizabeth listened, wondered, doubted, and was impatient for more. Mrs. Reynolds could interest her on no other point. She related the subjects of the pictures, the dimensions of the rooms, and the price of the furniture, in vain. Mr. Gardiner, highly amused by the kind of family prejudice to which he attributed her excessive commendation of her master, soon led again to the subject; and she dwelt with energy on his many merits as they proceeded together up the great staircase.

"He is the best landlord, and the best master," said she, "that ever lived; not like the wild young men nowadays, who think of nothing but themselves. There is not one of his tenants or servants but what will give him a good name. Some people call him proud; but I am sure I never saw anything of it. To my fancy, it is only because he does not rattle away like other young men."

"In what an amiable light does this place him!" thought Elizabeth.

"This fine account of him," whispered her aunt as they walked, "is not quite consistent with his behaviour to our poor friend."

"Perhaps we might be deceived."

"That is not very likely; our authority was too good."

On reaching the spacious lobby above they were shown into a very pretty sitting-room, lately fitted up with greater elegance and lightness than the apartments below; and were informed that it was but just done to give pleasure to Miss Darcy, who had taken a liking to the room when last at Pemberley.

"He is certainly a good brother," said Elizabeth, as she walked toward one of the windows.

Mrs. Reynolds anticipated Miss Darcy's delight, when she should enter the room. "And this is always the way with him," she added. "Whatever can give his sister any pleasure is sure to be done in a moment. There is nothing he would not do for her."

The picture-gallery, and two or three of the principal bedrooms, were all that remained to be shown. In the former were many good paintings; but Elizabeth knew nothing of the art; and from such as had been already visible below, she had willingly turned to look at some drawings of Miss Darcy's, in crayons, whose subjects were usually more interesting, and also more intelligible.

In the gallery there were many family portraits, but they could have little to fix the attention of a stranger. Elizabeth walked on in quest of the only face whose features would be known to her. At last it arrested her—and she beheld a striking resemblance to Mr. Darcy, with such a smile over the face as she remembered to have sometimes seen when he looked at her. She stood several minutes before the picture, in earnest contemplation, and returned to it again before they quitted the gallery. Mrs. Reynolds informed them that it had been taken in his father's lifetime.

There was certainly at this moment, in Elizabeth's mind, a more gentle sensation towards the original than she had ever felt in the height of their acquaintance. The commendation bestowed on him by Mrs. Reynolds was of no trifling nature. What praise is more valuable than the praise of an intelligent servant? As a brother, a landlord, a master, she considered how many people's happiness were in his guardianship!—how much of pleasure or pain it was in his power to bestow!—how much of good or evil must be done by him! Every idea that had been brought forward by the housekeeper was favourable to his character, and as she stood before the canvas on which he was represented, and fixed his eyes upon herself, she thought of his regard with a deeper sentiment of gratitude than it had ever raised before; she remembered its warmth, and softened its impropriety of expression.

When all of the house that was open to general inspection had been seen, they returned downstairs, and, taking leave of the housekeeper, were consigned over to the gardener, who met them at the hall-door.

As they walked across the lawn towards the river, Elizabeth turned back to look again; her uncle and aunt stopped also, and while the former was conjecturing as to the date of the building, the owner of it himself suddenly came forward from the road, which led behind it to the stables.

They were within twenty yards of each other, and so abrupt was his appearance that it was impossible to avoid his sight. Their eyes instantly met, and the cheeks of each were overspread with the deepest blush. He absolutely started, and for a moment seemed immovable from surprise; but shortly recovering himself, advanced towards the party, and spoke to Elizabeth, if not in terms of perfect composure, at least of perfect civility.

She had instinctively turned away; but stopping on his approach, received his compliments with an embarrassment impossible to be overcome. Had his first appearance, or his resemblance to the picture they had just been examining, been insufficient to assure the other two that they now saw Mr. Darcy, the gardener's expression of surprise, on beholding his master, must immediately have told it. They stood a little aloof while he was talking to their niece, who, astonished and confused, scarcely dared lift her eyes to his face, and knew not what answer she returned to his civil inquiries after her family. Amazed at the alteration of his manner since they last parted, every sentence that he uttered was increasing her embarrassment; and every idea of the impropriety of her being found there recurring to her mind, the few minutes in which they continued together were some of the most uncomfortable of her life. Nor did he seem much more at ease: when he spoke, his accent had none of its usual sedateness; and he repeated his inquiries as to the time of her having left Longbourn, and of her stay in Derbyshire, so often, and in so hurried a way, as plainly spoke the distraction of his thoughts.

At length every idea seemed to fail him; and, after standing a few moments without saying a word, he suddenly recollected himself, and took leave.

The others then joined her, and expressed their admiration of his figure; but Elizabeth heard not a word, and, wholly engrossed by her own feelings, followed them in silence. She was overpowered by shame and vexation. Her coming there was the most unfortunate, the most ill-judged thing in the world! How strange must it appear to him! In what a disgraceful light might it not strike so vain a man! It might seem as if she had purposely thrown herself in his way again! Oh! why did she come? Or, why did he thus come a day before he was expected? Had they been only ten minutes sooner, they should have been beyond the reach of his discrimination; for it was plain that he was that moment arrived—that moment alighted from his horse or his carriage. She blushed again and again over the perverseness of the meeting. And his behaviour, so strikingly altered—what could it mean? That he should even speak to her was amazing!—but to speak with such civility, to inquire after her family! Never in her life had she seen his manners so little dignified, never had he spoken with such gentleness as on this unexpected meeting. What a contrast did it offer to his last address in Rosings Park, when he put his letter into her hand! She knew not what to think, or how to account for it.

They had now entered a beautiful walk by the side of the water, and every step was bringing forward a nobler fall of ground, or a finer reach of the woods to which they were approaching; but it was some time before Elizabeth was sensible of any of it; and, though she answered mechanically to the repeated appeals of her uncle and aunt, and seemed to direct her eyes to such objects as they pointed out, she distinguished no part of the scene. Her thoughts were all fixed on that one spot of Pemberley House, whichever it might be, where Mr. Darcy then was. She longed to know what at that moment was passing in his mind—in what manner he thought of her, and whether, in defiance of everything, she was still dear to him. Perhaps he had been civil only because he felt himself at ease; yet there had been *that* in his voice which was not like ease. Whether he had felt more of pain or of pleasure in seeing her she could not tell, but he certainly had not seen her with composure.

At length, however, the remarks of her companions on her absence of mind aroused her, and she felt the necessity of appearing more like herself.

They entered the woods, and bidding adieu to the river for a while ascended some of the higher grounds; when, in spots where the opening of the trees gave the eye power to wander, were many charming views of the valley, the opposite hills, with the long range of woods overspreading many, and occasionally part of the stream. Mr. Gardiner expressed a wish of going round the whole park, but feared it might be beyond a walk. With a triumphant smile, they were told that it was ten miles round. It settled the matter; and they pursued the accustomed circuit; which brought them again, after some time, in a descent among hanging woods, to the edge of the water, and one of its narrowest parts. They crossed it by a simple bridge, in character with the general air of the scene; it was a spot less adorned than any they had yet visited; and the valley, here contracted into a glen, allowed room only for the stream, and a narrow walk amidst the rough coppice-wood which bordered it. Elizabeth longed to explore its windings; but when they had crossed the bridge, and perceived their distance from the house, Mrs. Gardiner, who was not a great walker, could go no farther, and thought only of returning to the carriage as quickly as possible. Her niece was, therefore, obliged to submit, and they took their way towards the house on the opposite side of the river, in the nearest direction; but their progress was slow, for Mr. Gardiner, though seldom able to indulge the taste, was very fond of fishing, and was so much engaged in watching the occasional appearance of some trout in the water, and talking to the man about them, that he advanced but little. Whilst wandering on in this slow manner, they were again surprised, and Elizabeth's astonishment was quite equal to what it had been at first, by the sight of Mr. Darcy approaching them, and at no great distance. The walk being here less sheltered than on the other side, allowed them to see him before they met. Elizabeth, however astonished, was at least more prepared for an interview than before, and resolved to appear and to speak with calmness, if he really intended to meet them. For a few moments, indeed, she felt that he would probably strike into some other path. The idea lasted while a turning in the walk concealed him from their view; the turning past, he was immediately before them. With a glance, she saw that he had lost none of his recent civility; and, to imitate his politeness, she began as they met to admire the beauty of the place; but she had not got beyond the words "delightful," and "charming," when some unlucky recollections obtruded, and she fancied that praise of Pemberley from her might be mischievously construed. Her colour changed, and she said no more.

Mrs. Gardiner was standing a little behind; and on her pausing, he asked her if she would do him the honour of introducing him to her friends. This was a stroke of civility for which she was quite unprepared; and she could hardly suppress a smile at his being now seeking the acquaintance of some of those very people against whom his pride had revolted in his offer to herself. "What will be his surprise," thought she, "when he knows who they are? He takes them now for people of fashion."

The introduction, however, was immediately made; and as she named their relationship to herself, she stole a sly look at him, to see how he bore it, and was not without the expectation of his decamping as fast as he could from such disgraceful companions. That he was *surprised* by the connection was evident; he sustained it, however, with fortitude, and, so far from going away, turned back with them, and entered into conversation with Mr. Gardiner. Elizabeth could not but be pleased, could not but triumph. It was consoling that he should know she had some relations for whom there was no need to blush. She listened most attentively to all that passed between them, and gloried in every expression, every sentence of her uncle, which marked his intelligence, his taste, or his good manners.

The conversation soon turned upon fishing; and she heard Mr. Darcy invite him, with the greatest civility, to fish there as often as he chose while he continued in the neighbourhood, offering at the same time to supply him with fishing tackle, and pointing out those parts of the stream where there was usually most sport. Mrs. Gardiner, who was walking arm-

and-arm with Elizabeth, gave her a look expressive of her wonder. Elizabeth said nothing, but it gratified her exceedingly; the compliment must be all for herself. Her astonishment, however, was extreme, and continually was she repeating, "Why is he so altered? From what can it proceed? It cannot be for *me*—it cannot be for *my* sake that his manners are thus softened. My reproofs at Hunsford could not work such a change as this. It is impossible that he should still love me."

After walking some time in this way, the two ladies in front, the two gentlemen behind, on resuming their places, after descending to the brink of the river for the better inspection of some curious water-plant, there chanced to be a little alteration. It originated in Mrs. Gardiner, who, fatigued by the exercise of the morning, found Elizabeth's arm inadequate to her support, and consequently preferred her husband's. Mr. Darcy took her place by her niece, and they walked on together. After a short silence, the lady first spoke. She wished him to know that she had been assured of his absence before she came to the place, and accordingly began by observing, that his arrival had been very unexpected—"for your housekeeper," she added, "informed us that you would certainly not be here till to-morrow; and indeed, before we left Bakewell, we understood that you were not immediately expected in the country." He acknowledged the truth of it all, and said that business with his steward had occasioned his coming forward a few hours before the rest of the party with whom he had been travelling. "They will join me early to-morrow," he continued, "and among them are some who will claim an acquaintance with you—Mr. Bingley and his sisters."

Elizabeth answered only by a slight bow. Her thoughts were instantly driven back to the time when Mr. Bingley's name had been last mentioned between them; and, if she might judge from his complexion, *his* mind was not very differently engaged.

"There is also one other person in the party," he continued after a pause, "who more particularly wishes to be known to you. Will you allow me, or do I ask too much, to introduce my sister to your acquaintance during your stay at Lambton?"

The surprise of such an application was great indeed; it was too great for her to know in what manner she acceded to it. She immediately felt that whatever desire Miss Darcy might have of being acquainted with her must be the work of her brother, and, without looking farther, it was satisfactory; it was gratifying to know that his resentment had not made him think really ill of her.

They now walked on in silence, each of them deep in thought. Elizabeth was not comfortable; that was impossible; but she was flattered and pleased. His wish of introducing his sister to her was a compliment of the highest kind. They soon outstripped the others, and when they had reached the carriage, Mr. and Mrs. Gardiner were half a quarter of a mile behind.

He then asked her to walk into the house—but she declared herself not t'red, and they stood together on the lawn. At such a time much might have been said, and silence was very awkward. She wanted to talk, but there seemed an embargo on every subject. At last she recollected that she had been travelling, and they talked of Matlock and Dovedale with great perseverance. Yet time and her aunt moved slowly—and her patience and her ideas were nearly worn out before the *tête-à-tête* was over On Mr. and Mrs. Gardiner's coming up they were all pressed to go into the house and take some refreshment; but this was declined, and they parted on each side with the utmost politeness. Mr. Darcy handed the ladies into the carriage; and when it drove off, Elizabeth saw him walking slowly towards the house.

The observations of her uncle and aunt now began; and each of them pronounced him to be infinitely superior to anything they had expected. "He is perfectly well behaved, polite, and unassuming," said her uncle.

"There *is* something a little stately in him, to be sure," replied her aunt; "but it is confined to his air, and is not unbecoming. I can now say with the housekeeper, that though some people may call him proud, *I* have seen nothing of it."

"I was never more surprised than by his behaviour to us. It was more than civil; it was really attentive; and there was no necessity for such attention. His acquaintance with Elizabeth was very trifling."

"To be sure, Lizzy," said her aunt, "he is not so handsome as Wickham; or, rather, he has not Wickham's countenance, for his features are perfectly good. But how came you to tell me that he was so disagreeable?"

Elizabeth excused herself as well as she could; said that she had liked him better when they met in Kent than before, and that she had never seen him so pleasant as this morning.

"But perhaps he may be a little whimsical in his civilities," replied her uncle. "Your great men often are; and therefore I shall not take him at his word about fishing, as he might change his mind another day, and warn me off his grounds."

Elizabeth felt that they had entirely mistaken his character, but said nothing.

"From what we have seen of him," continued Mrs. Gardiner, "I really should not have thought that he could have behaved in so cruel a way by anybody as he has done by poor Wickham. He has not an ill-natured look. On the contrary, there is something pleasing about his mouth when he speaks. And there is something of dignity in his countenance, that would not give one an unfavourable idea of his heart. But, to be sure, the good lady who showed us the house did give him a most flaming character! I could hardly help laughing aloud sometimes. But he is a liberal master, I suppose, and *that* in the eye of a servant comprehends every virtue."

Elizabeth here felt herself called on to say something in vindication of his behaviour to Wickham; and therefore gave them to understand, in as guarded a manner as she could, that by what she had heard from his relations in Kent, his actions were capable of a very different construction; and that his character was by no means so faulty, nor Wickham's so amiable, as they had been considered in Hertfordshire. In confirmation of this, she related the particulars of all the pecuniary transactions in which they had been connected, without actually naming her authority, but stating it to be such as might be relied on.

Mrs. Gardiner was surprised and concerned; but as they were now approaching the scene of her former pleasures, every idea gave way to the charm of recollection; and she was too much engaged in pointing out to her husband all the interesting spots in its environs to think of anything else. Fatigued as she had been by the morning's walk, they had no sooner dined than she set off again in quest of her former acquaintance, and the evening was spent in the satisfactions of an intercourse renewed after many years' discontinuance.

The occurrences of the day were too full of interest to leave Elizabeth much attention for any of these new friends; and she could do nothing but think, and think with wonder, of Mr. Darcy's civility, and, above all, of his wishing her to be acquainted with his sister.

Chapter 44

ELIZABETH had settled it that Mr. Darcy would bring his sister to visit her the very day after her reaching Pemberley; and was consequently resolved not to be out of sight of the inn the whole of that morning. But her conclusion was false; for on the very morning after their own arrival at Lambton, these visitors came. They had been walking about the place with some of their new friends, and were just returning to the inn to dress themselves for dining with the same family, when the sound of a carriage drew them to a window, and they saw a gentleman and lady in a curricle driving up the street. Elizabeth immediately recognising the livery, guessed what it meant, and imparted no small degree of surprise to her relations by acquainting them with the honour which she expected. Her uncle and aunt were all amazement; and the embarrassment of her manner as she spoke, joined to the circumstance itself, and many of the circumstances of the preceding day, opened to them a new idea on the business. Nothing had ever suggested it before, but they now felt that there was no other way of accounting for such attentions from such a quarter than by supposing a partiality for their niece. While these newly-born notions were passing in their heads, the perturbation of Elizabeth's feelings was every moment increasing. She was quite amazed at her own discomposure; but amongst other causes of disquiet, she dreaded lest the partiality of the brother should have said too much in her favour; and, more than commonly anxious to please, she naturally suspected that every power of pleasing would fail her.

She retreated from the window, fearful of being seen; and as she walked up and down the room, endeavouring to compose herself, saw such looks of inquiring surprise in her uncle and aunt as made everything worse.

Miss Darcy and her brother appeared, and this formidable introduction took place. With astonishment did Elizabeth see that her new acquaintance was at least as much embarrassed as herself. Since her being at Lambton, she had heard that Miss Darcy was exceedingly proud; but the observation of a very few minutes convinced her that she was only exceedingly shy. She found it difficult to obtain even a word from her beyond a monosyllable.

Miss Darcy was tall, and on a larger scale than Elizabeth; and, though little more than sixteen, her figure was formed, and her appearance womanly and graceful. She was less handsome than her brother; but there was sense and good humour in her face, and her manners were perfectly unassuming and gentle. Elizabeth, who had expected to find in her as acute and unembarrassed an observer as ever Mr. Darcy had been, was much relieved by discerning such different feelings.

They had not been long together before Darcy told her that Bingley was also coming to wait on her; and she had barely time to express her satisfaction, and prepare for such a visitor, when Bingley's quick step was heard on the stairs, and in a moment he entered the room. All Elizabeth's anger against him had been long done away; but had she still felt any, it could hardly have stood its ground against the unaffected cordiality with which he expressed himself on seeing her again. He inquired in a friendly, though general way, after her family, and looked and spoke with the same good-humoured ease that he had ever done.

To Mr. and Mrs. Gardiner he was scarcely a less interesting personage than to herself. They had long wished to see him. The whole party before them, indeed, excited a lively attention. The suspicions which had just arisen of Mr. Darcy and their niece directed their observation towards each with an earnest though guarded inquiry; and they soon drew from those inquiries the full conviction that one of them at least knew what it was to love. Of the lady's sensations they remained a little in doubt; but that the gentleman was overflowing with admiration was evident enough.

Elizabeth, on her side, had much to do. She wanted to ascertain the feelings of each of her visitors; she wanted to compose her own, and to make herself agreeable to all; and in the latter object, where she feared most to fail, she was most sure of success, for those to whom she endeavoured to give pleasure were prepossessed in her favour. Bingley was ready, Georgiana was eager, and Darcy determined, to be pleased.

In seeing Bingley, her thoughts naturally flew to her sister; and oh! how ardently did she long to know whether any of his were directed in a like manner. Sometimes she could fancy that he talked less than on former occasions, and once or twice pleased herself with the notion that, as he looked at her, he was trying to trace a resemblance. But, though this might be imaginary, she could not be deceived as to his behaviour to Miss Darcy, who had been set up as a rival to Jane. No look appeared on either side that spoke particular regard. Nothing occurred between them that could justify the hopes of his sister. On this point she was soon satisfied; and two or three little circumstances occurred ere they parted, which, in her anxious interpretation, denoted a recollection of Jane not untinctured by tenderness, and a wish of saying more that might lead to the mention of her, had he dared. He observed to her, at a moment when the others were talking together, and in a tone which had something of real regret, that it "was a very long time since he had had the pleasure of seeing her"; and, before she could reply, he added, "It is above eight months. We have not met since the 26th of November, when we were all dancing together at Netherfield."

Elizabeth was pleased to find his memory so exact; and he afterwards took occasion to ask her, when unattended to by any of the rest, whether *all* her sisters were at Longbourn. There was not much in the question, nor in the preceding remark; but there was a look and a manner which gave them meaning.

It was not often that she could turn her eyes on Mr. Darcy himself; but, whenever she did catch a glimpse, she saw an expression of general complaisance, and in all that he said she heard an accent so far removed from hauteur or disdain of his companions, as convinced her that the improvement of manners which she had yesterday witnessed however temporary its existence might prove, had at least outlived one day. When she saw him thus seeking the acquaintance and courting the good opinion of people with whom any intercourse a few months ago would have been a disgrace—when she saw him thus civil, not only to herself, but to the very relations whom he had openly disdained, and recollected their last lively scene in Hunsford Parsonage—the difference, the change was so great, and struck so forcibly on her mind, that she could hardly restrain her astonishment from being visible. Never, even in the company of his dear friends at Netherfield, or his dignified relations at Rosings, had she seen him so desirous to please, so free from self-consequence or unbending reserve, as now, when no importance could result from the success of his endeavours, and when even the acquaintance of those to whom his attentions were addressed would draw down the ridicule and censure of the ladies both of Netherfield and Rosings.

Their visitors stayed with them above half-an-hour; and when they arose to depart, Mr. Darcy called on his sister to join him in expressing their wish of seeing Mr. and Mrs. Gardiner, and Miss Bennet, to dinner at Pemberley, before they left the country. Miss Darcy, though with a diffidence which marked her little in the habit of giving invitations, readily obeyed. Mrs. Gardiner looked at her niece, desirous of knowing how *she*, whom the invitation most concerned, felt disposed as to its acceptance, but Elizabeth had turned away her head. Presuming however, that this studied avoidance spoke rather a momentary embarrassment than any dislike of the proposal, and seeing in her husband, who was fond of society, a perfect willingness to accept it, she ventured to engage for her attendance, and the day after the next was fixed on.

Bingley expressed great pleasure in the certainty of seeing Elizabeth again, having still a great deal to say to her, and many inquiries to make after all their Hertfordshire friends. Elizabeth, construing all this into a wish of hearing her speak of her sister, was pleased, and on this account, as well as some others, found herself, when their visitors left them, capable of considering the last half-hour with some satisfaction, though while it was passing, the enjoyment of it had been little. Eager to be alone, and fearful of inquiries or hints from her uncle and aunt, she stayed with them only long enough to hear their favourable opinion of Bingley, and then hurried away to dress.

But she had no reason to fear Mr. and Mrs. Gardiner's curiosity; it was not their wish to force her communication. It was evident that she was much better acquainted with Mr. Darcy than they had before any idea of; it was evident that he was very much in love with her. They saw much to interest, but nothing to justify inquiry.

Of Mr. Darcy it was now a matter of anxiety to think well; and, as far as their acquaintance reached, there was no fault to find. They could not be untouched by his politeness; and had they drawn his character from their own feelings and his servant's report, without any reference to any other account, the circle in Hertfordshire to which he was known would not have recognised it for Mr. Darcy. There was now an interest, however, in believing the housekeeper; and they soon became sensible that the authority of a servant who had known him since he was four years old, and whose own manners indicated respectability, was not to be hastily rejected. Neither had anything occurred in the intelligence of their Lambton friends that could materially lessen its weight. They had nothing to accuse him of but pride; pride he probably had, and if not, it would certainly be imputed by the inhabitants of a small market-town where the family did not visit. It was acknowledged, however, that he was a liberal man, and did much good among the poor.

With respect to Wickham, the travellers soon found that he was not held there in much estimation; for though the chief of his concerns with the son of his patron were imperfectly understood, it was yet a well-known fact that, on his quitting Derbyshire, he had left many debts behind him, which Mr. Darcy afterwards discharged.

As for Elizabeth, her thoughts were at Pemberley this evening more than the last; and the evening, though as it passed it seemed long, was not long enough to determine her feelings towards *one* in that mansion; and she lay awake two whole hours endeavouring to make them out. She certainly did not hate him. No; hatred had vanished long ago, and she had almost as long been ashamed of ever feeling a dislike against him, that could be so called. The respect created by the conviction of his valuable qualities, though at first unwillingly admitted, had for some time ceased to be repugnant to her feeling; and it was now heightened into somewhat of a friendlier nature, by the testimony so highly in his favour, and bringing forward his disposition in so amiable a light, which yesterday had produced. But above all, above respect and esteem, there was a motive within her of goodwill which could not be overlooked. It was gratitude; gratitude, not merely for having once loved her, but for loving her still well enough to forgive all the petulance and acrimony of her manner in rejecting him, and all the unjust accusations accompanying her rejection. He who, she had been persuaded, would avoid her as his greatest enemy, seemed, on this accidental meeting, most eager to preserve the acquaintance, and without any indelicate display of regard, or any peculiarity of manner, where their two selves only were concerned, was soliciting the good opinion of her friends, and bent on making her known to his sister. Such a change in a man of so much pride excited not only astonishment but gratitude—for to love, ardent love, it must be attributed; and as such its impression on her was of a sort to be encouraged, as by no means unpleasing, though it could not be exactly defined. She respected, she esteemed, she was grateful to him, she felt a real interest in his welfare; and she only wanted to know how far she wished that welfare to depend upon herself, and how far it would be for the happiness of both that she should employ the power, which her fancy told her she still possessed, of bringing on the renewal of his addresses.

It had been settled in the evening between the aunt and niece, that such a striking civility as Miss Darcy's in coming to them on the very day of her arrival at Pemberley, for she had reached it only to a late breakfast, ought to be imitated, though it could not be equalled, by some exertion of politeness on their side; and, consequently, that it would be highly expedient to wait on her at Pemberley the following morning. They were, therefore, to go. Elizabeth was pleased; though when she asked herself the reason, she had very little to say in reply.

Mr. Gardiner left them soon after breakfast. The fishing scheme had been renewed the day before, and a positive engagement made of his meeting some of the gentlemen at Pemberley by noon.

Chapter 45

CONVINCED as Elizabeth now was that Miss Bingley's dislike of her had originated in jealousy, she could not help feeling how very unwelcome her appearance at Pemberley must be to her, and was curious to know with how much civility on that lady's side the acquaintance would now be renewed.

On reaching the house, they were shown through the hall into the saloon, whose northern aspect rendered it delightful for summer. Its windows opening to the ground, admitted a most refreshing view of the high woody hills behind the house, and of the beautiful oaks and Spanish chestnuts which were scattered over the intermediate lawn.

In this room they were received by Miss Darcy, who was sitting there with Mrs. Hurst and Miss Bingley, and the lady with whom she lived in London. Georgiana's reception of them was very civil, but attended with all that embarrassment which, though proceeding from shyness and the fear of doing wrong, would easily give to those who felt themselves inferior the belief of her being proud and reserved. Mrs. Gardiner and her niece, however, did her justice, and pitied her.

By Mrs. Hurst and Miss Bingley they were noticed only by a curtsey; and, on their being seated, a pause, awkward as such pauses must always be, succeeded for a few moments. It was first broken by Mrs. Annesley, a genteel, agreeable-looking woman, whose endeavour to introduce some kind of discourse proved her to be more truly well-bred than either of the others; and between her and Mrs. Gardiner, with occasional help from Elizabeth, the conversation was carried on. Miss Darcy looked as if she wished for courage enough to join in it; and sometimes did venture a short sentence when there was least danger of its being heard.

Elizabeth soon saw that she was herself closely watched by Miss Bingley, and that she could not speak a word, especially to Miss Darcy, without calling her attention. This observation would not have prevented her from trying to talk to the latter, had they not been seated at an inconvenient distance; but she was not sorry to be spared the necessity of saying much. Her own thoughts were employing her. She expected every moment that some of the gentlemen would enter the room. She wished, she feared that the master of the house might be amongst them; and whether she wished or feared it most, she could scarcely determine. After sitting in this manner a quarter of an hour without hearing Miss Bingley's voice, Elizabeth was roused by receiving from her a cold inquiry after the health of her family. She answered with equal indifference and brevity, and the others said no more.

The next variation which their visit afforded was produced by the entrance of servants with cold meat, cake, and a variety of all the finest fruits in season; but this did not take place till after many a significant look and smile from Mrs. Annesley to Miss Darcy had been given, to remind her of her post. There was now employment for the whole party —for though they could not all talk, they could all eat; and the beautiful pyramids of grapes, nectarines, and peaches soon collected them round the table.

While thus engaged, Elizabeth had a fair opportunity of deciding whether she most feared or wished for the appearance of Mr. Darcy, by the feelings which prevailed on his entering the room; and then, though but a moment before she had believed her wishes to predominate, she began to regret that he came.

He had been some time with Mr. Gardiner, who, with two or three other gentlemen from the house, was engaged by the river, and had left him only on learning that the ladies of the family intended a visit to Georgiana that morning. No sooner did he appear than Elizabeth wisely resolved to be perfectly easy and unembarrassed; a resolution the more necessary to be made, but perhaps not the more easily kept, because she saw that the suspicions of the whole party were awakened against them, and that there was scarcely an eye which did not watch his behaviour when he first came into the room. In no countenance was attentive curiosity so strongly marked as in Miss Bingley's, in spite of the smiles which overspread her face whenever she spoke to one of its objects; for jealousy had not yet made her desperate, and her attentions to Mr. Darcy were by no means over. Miss Darcy, on her brother's entrance, exerted herself much more to talk, and Elizabeth saw that he was anxious for his sister and herself to get acquainted, and forwarded as much as possible, every attempt at conversation on either side. Miss Bingley saw all this likewise; and, in the imprudence of anger, took the first opportunity of saying, with sneering civility:

"Pray, Miss Eliza, are not the ——shire Militia removed from Meryton? They must be a great loss to *your* family."

In Darcy's presence she dared not mention Wickham's name; but Elizabeth instantly comprehended that he was uppermost in her thoughts; and the various recollections connected with him gave her a moment's distress; but exerting herself vigorously to repel the ill-natured attack, she presently answered the question in a tolerably disengaged tone. While she spoke, an involuntary glance showed her Darcy, with a heightened complexion, earnestly looking at her, and his sister overcome with confusion, and unable to lift up her eyes. Had Miss Bingley known what pain she was then giving her beloved friend, she undoubtedly would have refrained from the hint; but she had merely intended to discompose Elizabeth by bringing forward the idea of a man to whom she believed her partial, to make her betray a sensibility which might injure her in Darcy's opinion, and, perhaps, to remind the latter of all the follies and absurdities by which some part of her family were connected with that corps. Not a syllable had ever reached her of Miss Darcy's meditated elopement. To no creature had it been revealed, where secrecy was possible, except to Elizabeth; and from all Bingley's connections her brother was particularly anxious to conceal it, from that very wish which Elizabeth had long ago attributed to him, of their becoming hereafter her own. He had certainly formed such a plan, and without meaning that it should effect his endeavour to separate him from Miss Bennet, it is probable that it might add something to his lively concern for the welfare of his friend.

Elizabeth's collected behaviour, however, soon quieted his emotion; and as Miss Bingley, vexed and disappointed, dared not approach nearer to Wickham, Georgiana also recovered in time, though not enough to be able to speak any more. Her brother, whose eye she feared to meet, scarcely recollected her interest in the affair, and the very circumstance which had been designed to turn his thoughts from Elizabeth seemed to have fixed them on her more and more cheerfully.

Their visit did not continue long after the question and answer above mentioned; and while Mr. Darcy was attending them to their carriage Miss Bingley was venting her feelings in criticisms on Elizabeth's person, behaviour, and dress. But Georgiana would not join her. Her brother's recommendation was enough to ensure her favour; his judgment could not err, and he had spoken in such terms of Elizabeth as to leave Georgiana without the power of finding her otherwise than lovely and amiable. When Darcy returned to the saloon, Miss Bingley could not help repeating to him some part of what she had been saying to his sister.

"How very ill Eliza Bennet looks this morning, Mr. Darcy," she cried; "I never in my life saw any one so much altered as she is since the winter. She is grown so brown and coarse! Louisa and I were agreeing that we should not have known her again."

However little Mr. Darcy might have liked such an address, he contented himself with coolly replying that he perceived no other alteration than her being rather tanned, no miraculous consequence of travelling in the summer.

"For my own part," she rejoined, "I must confess that I never could see any beauty in her. Her face is too thin; her complexion has no brilliancy; and her features are not at all handsome. Her nose wants character—there is nothing marked in its lines. Her teeth are tolerable, but not out of the common way; and as for her eyes, which have sometimes been called so fine, I never could perceive anything extraordinary in them. They have a sharp, shrewish look, which I do not like at all; and in her air altogether there is a self-sufficiency without fashion, which is intolerable."

Persuaded as Miss Bingley was that Darcy admired Elizabeth, this was not the best method of recommending herself; but angry people are not always wise; and in seeing him at last look somewhat nettled, she had all the success she expected. He was resolutely silent, however, and, from a determination of making him speak, she continued:

"I remember, when we first knew her in Hertfordshire, how amazed we all were to find that she was a reputed beauty; and I particularly recollect your saying one night, after they had been dining at Netherfield, 'She a beauty! I should as soon call her mother a wit.' But afterwards she seemed to improve on you, and I believe you thought her rather pretty at one time."

"Yes," replied Darcy, who could contain himself no longer, "but *that* was only when I first knew her, for it is many months since I have considered her as one of the handsomest women of my acquaintances."

He then went away, and Miss Bingley was left to all the satisfaction of having forced him to say what gave no one any pain but herself.

Mrs. Gardiner and Elizabeth talked of all that had occurred during their visit, as they returned, except what had particularly interested them both. The look and behaviour of everybody they had seen were discussed, except of the person who had mostly engaged their attention. They talked of his sister, his friends, his house, his fruit—of everything but himself;

yet Elizabeth was longing to know what Mrs. Gardiner thought of him, and Mrs. Gardiner would have been highly gratified by her niece's beginning the subject.

Chapter 46

ELIZABETH had been a good deal disappointed in not finding a letter from Jane on their first arrival at Lambton; and this disappointment had been renewed on each of the mornings that had now been spent there; but on the third her repining was over, and her sister justified, by the receipt of two letters from her at once, on one of which was marked that it had been missent elsewhere. Elizabeth was not surprised at it, as Jane had written the direction remarkably ill.

They had just been preparing to walk as the letters came in; and her uncle and aunt, leaving her to enjoy them in quiet, set off by themselves. The one missent must be first attended to; it had been written five days ago. The beginning contained an account of all their little parties and engagements, with such news as the country afforded; but the latter half, which was dated a day later, and written in evident agitation, gave more important intelligence. It was to this effect:

"Since writing the above, dearest Lizzy, something has occurred of a most unexpected and serious nature; but I am afraid of alarming you— be assured that we are all well. What I have to say relates to poor Lydia. An express came at twelve last night, just as we were all gone to bed, from Colonel Forster, to inform us that she was gone off to Scotland with one of his officers; to own the truth, with Wickham! Imagine our surprise. To Kitty, however, it does not seem so wholly unexpected. I am very, very sorry. So imprudent a match on both sides! But I am willing to hope the best, and that his character has been misunderstood. Thoughtless and indiscreet I can easily believe him, but this step (and let us rejoice over it) marks nothing bad at heart. His choice is disinterested at least, for he must know my father can give her nothing. Our poor mother is sadly grieved. My father bears it better. How thankful am I that we never let them know what has been said against him! we must forget it ourselves. They were off Saturday night about twelve, as is conjectured, but were not missed till yesterday morning at eight. The express was sent off directly. My dear Lizzy, they must have passed within ten miles of us. Colonel Forster gives us reason to expect him here soon. Lydia left a few lines for his wife, informing her of their intention. I must conclude, for I cannot be long from my poor mother. I am afraid you will not be able to make it out, but I hardly know what I have written."

Without allowing herself time for consideration, and scarcely knowing what she felt, Elizabeth on finishing this letter instantly seized the other; and opening it with the utmost impatience, read as follows: it had been written a day later than the conclusion of the first.

"By this time, by dearest sister, you have received my hurried letter;

I wish this may be more intelligible, but though not confined for time, my head is so bewildered that I cannot answer for being coherent. Dearest Lizzy, I hardly know what I would write, but I have bad news for you, and it cannot be delayed. Imprudent as a marriage between Mr. Wickham and our poor Lydia would be, we are now anxious to be assured it has taken place, for there is but too much reason to fear they are not gone to Scotland. Colonel Forster came yesterday, having left Brighton the day before, not many hours after the express. Though Lydia's short letter to Mrs. F. gave them to understand that they were going to Gretna Green, something was dropped by Denny expressing his belief that W. never intended to go there, or to marry Lydia at all, which was repeated to Colonel F., who, instantly, taking the alarm, set off from B., intending to trace their route. He did trace them easily to Clapham, but no further; for on entering that place, they removed into a hackney coach, and dismissed the chaise that brought them from Epsom. All that is known after this is, that they were seen to continue the London road. I know not what to think. After making every possible inquiry on that side London, Colonel F. came on into Hertfordshire, anxiously renewing them at all the turnpikes, and at the inns in Barnet and Hatfield, but without any success— no such people had been seen to pass through. With the kindest concern he came on to Longbourn, and broke his apprehensions to us in a manner most creditable to his heart. I am sincerely grieved for him and Mrs. F., but no one can throw any blame on them. Our distress, my dear Lizzy, is very great. My father and mother believe the worst, but I cannot think so ill of him. Many circumstances might make it more eligible for them to be married privately in town than to pursue their first plan; and even if *he* could form such a design against a young woman of Lydia's connections, which is not likely, can I suppose her so lost to everything? Impossible! I grieve to find, however, that Colonel F. is not disposed to depend upon their marriage; he shook his head when I expressed my hopes, and said he feared W. was not a man to be trusted. My poor mother is really ill, and keeps her room. Could she exert herself, it would be better; but this is not to be expected. And as to my father, I never in my life saw him so affected. Poor Kitty has anger for having concealed their attachment; but as it was a matter of confidence, one cannot wonder. I am truly glad, dearest Lizzy, that you have been spared something of these distressing scenes; but now, as the first shock is over, shall I own that I long for your return? I am not so selfish, however, as to press for it, if inconvenient. Adieu! I take up my pen again to do what I have just told you I would not; but circumstances are such that I cannot help earnestly begging you all to come here as soon as possible. I know my dear uncle and aunt so well, that I am not afraid of requesting it, though I have still something more to ask of the former. My father is going to London with Colonel Forster instantly, to try to discover her. What he means to do I am sure I know not; but his excessive distress will not allow him to pursue any measure in the best and safest way, and Colonel Forster is obliged to be at Brighton again to-morrow evening. In such an exigence, my uncle's advice and assistance would be everything in the world; he will immediately comprehend what I must feel, and I rely upon his goodness."

"Oh! where, where is my uncle?" cried Elizabeth, darting from her seat as she finished the letter, in eagerness to follow him, without losing a moment of the time so precious; but as she reached the door it was opened by a servant, and Mr. Darcy appeared. Her pale face and impetuous manner made him start, and before he could recover himself to speak, she, in whose mind every idea was superseded by Lydia's situation, hastily exclaimed, "I beg your pardon, but I must leave you. I must find Mr. Gardiner this moment, on business that cannot be delayed; I have not an instant to lose."

"Good God! what is the matter?" cried he, with more feeling than politeness; then recollecting himself, "I will not detain you a minute; but let me, or let the servant go after Mr. and Mrs. Gardiner. You are not well enough; you cannot go yourself."

Elizabeth hesitated, but her knees trembled under her and she felt how little would be gained by her attempting to pursue them. Calling back the servant, therefore, she commissioned him, though in so breathless an accent as made her almost unintelligible, to fetch his master and mistress home instantly.

On his quitting the room she sat down, unable to support herself, and looking so miserably ill, that it was impossible for Darcy to leave her, or to refrain from saying, in a tone of gentleness and commiseration, "Let me call your maid. Is there nothing you could take to give you present relief? A glass of wine; shall I get you one? You are very ill."

"No, I thank you," she replied, endeavouring to recover herself. "There is nothing the matter with me. I am quite well; I am only distressed by some dreadful news which I have just received from Longbourn."

She burst into tears as she alluded to it, and for a few minutes could not speak another word. Darcy, in wretched suspense, could only say something indistinctly of his concern, and observe her in compassionate silence. At length she spoke again. "I have just had a letter from Jane, with such dreadful news. It cannot be concealed from any one. My younger sister has left all her friends—has eloped; has thrown herself into the power of—of Mr. Wickham. They are gone off together from Brighton. *You* know him too well to doubt the rest. She has no money, no connections, nothing that can tempt him to—she is lost for ever."

Darcy was fixed in astonishment. "When I consider," she added in a yet more agitated voice, "that *I* might have prevented it! *I*, who knew what he was. Had I but explained some part of it only—some part of what I learnt, to my own family! Had his character been known, this could not have happened. But it is all—all too late now."

"I am grieved indeed," cried Darcy; "grieved—shocked. But is it certain—absolutely certain?"

"Oh yes! They left Brighton together on Sunday night, and were traced almost to London, but not beyond: they are certainly not gone to Scotland."

"And what has been done, what has been attempted, to recover her?"

"My father is gone to London, and Jane has written to beg my uncle's immediate assistance; and we shall be off, I hope, in half-an-hour. But nothing can be done—I know very well that nothing can be done. How is such a man to be worked on? How are they even to be discovered? I have not the smallest hope. It is every way horrible!"

Darcy shook his head in silent acquiescence.

"When *my* eyes were opened to his real character—Oh! had I known what I ought, what I dared to do! But I knew not—I was afraid of doing too much. Wretched, wretched mistake!"

Darcy made no answer. He seemed scarcely to hear her, and was walking up and down the room in earnest meditation, his brow contracted, his air gloomy. Elizabeth soon observed, and instantly understood it. Her power was sinking; everything *must* sink under such a proof of family weakness, such an assurance of the deepest disgrace. She could neither wonder nor condemn, but the belief of his self-conquest brought nothing consolatory to her bosom, afforded no palliation of her distress. It was, on the contrary, exactly calculated to make her understand her own wishes; and never had she so honestly felt that she could have loved him, as now, when all love must be vain.

But self, though it would intrude, could not engross her. Lydia—the humiliation, the misery she was bringing on them all, soon swallowed up every private care; and covering her face with her handkerchief, Elizabeth was soon lost to everything else; and, after a pause of several minutes, was only recalled to a sense of her situation by the voice of her companion, who, in a manner which, though it spoke compassion, spoke likewise restraint, said, "I am afraid you have been long desiring my absence, nor have I anything to plead in excuse of my stay, but real, though unavailing, concern. Would to Heaven that anything could be either said or done on my part that might offer consolation to such distress! But I will not torment you with vain wishes, which may seem purposely to ask for your thanks. This unfortunate affair will, I fear, prevent my sister's having the pleasure of seeing you at Pemberley to-day."

"Oh yes. Be so kind as to apologise for us to Miss Darcy. Say that urgent business calls us home immediately. Conceal the unhappy truth as long as it is possible, I know it cannot be long."

He readily assured her of his secrecy; again expressed his sorrow for her distress, wished it a happier conclusion than there was at present reason to hope, and leaving his compliments for her relations, with only one serious, parting look, went away.

As he quitted the room, Elizabeth felt how improbable it was that they should ever see each other again on such terms of cordiality as had marked their several meetings in Derbyshire; and as she threw a retrospective glance over the whole of their acquaintance, so full of contradictions and varieties, sighed at the perverseness of those feelings which would now have promoted its continuance, and would formerly have rejoiced in its termination.

If gratitude and esteem are good foundations of affection, Elizabeth's change of sentiment will be neither improbable nor faulty. But if otherwise—if the regard springing from such sources is unreasonable or unnatural, in comparison of what is so often described as arising on a first interview with its object, and even before two words have been exchanged, nothing can be said in her defence, except that she had given somewhat of a trial to the latter method in her partiality for Wickham, and that its ill success might, perhaps, authorise her to seek the other less interesting mode of attachment. Be that as it may, she saw him go with regret; and in this early example of what Lydia's infamy must produce, found additional anguish as she reflected on that wretched business. Never, since reading Jane's second letter, had she entertained a hope of Wickham's meaning to marry her. No one but Jane, she thought, could flatter herself with such an expectation. Surprise was the least of her feelings on this development. While the contents of the first letter remained on her mind, she was all surprise—all astonishment that Wickham should marry a girl whom it was impossible he could marry for money; and how Lydia could ever have attached him had appeared incomprehensible. But now it was all too natural. For such an attachment as this she might have sufficient charm; and though she did not suppose Lydia to be deliberately engaging in an elopement without the intention of marriage, she had no difficulty in believing that neither her virtue nor her understanding would preserve her from falling an easy prey.

She had never perceived, while the regiment was in Hertfordshire, that Lydia had any partiality for him; but she was convinced that Lydia had wanted only encouragement to attach herself to anybody. Sometimes one officer, sometimes another, had been her favourite, as their attentions raised them in her opinion. Her affections had been continually fluctuating but never without an object. The mischief of neglect and mistaken indulgence towards such a girl—oh! how acutely did she now feel it!

She was wild to be at home—to hear, to see, to be upon the spot to share with Jane in the cares that must now fall wholly upon her, in a family so deranged, a father absent, a mother incapable of exertion, and requiring constant attendance; and though almost persuaded that nothing could be done for Lydia, her uncle's interference seemed of the utmost importance, and till he entered the room the misery of her impatience was severe. Mr. and Mrs. Gardiner had hurried back in alarm, supposing by the servant's account that their niece was taken suddenly ill; but satisfying them instantly on that head, she eagerly communicated the cause of their summons, reading the two letters aloud, and dwelling on the postscript of the last with trembling energy, though Lydia had never been a favourite with them. Mr. and Mrs. Gardiner could not but be deeply afflicted. Not Lydia only, but all were concerned in it; and after the first exclamations of surprise and horror, Mr. Gardiner readily promised every assistance in his power. Elizabeth, though expecting no less, thanked him with tears of gratitude; and all three being actuated by one spirit, everything relating to their journey was speedily settled. They were to be off as soon as possible. "But what is to be done about Pemberley?" cried Mrs. Gardiner. "John told us Mr. Darcy was here when you sent for us; was it so?"

"Yes; and I told him we should not be able to keep our engagement. *That* is all settled."

"What is all settled?" repeated the other, as she ran into her room to prepare. "And are they upon such terms as for her to disclose the real truth? Oh, that I knew how it was!"

But wishes were vain, or at least could serve only to amuse her in the hurry and confusion of the following hour. Had Elizabeth been at leisure to be idle, she would have remained certain that all employment was impossible to one so wretched as herself; but she had her share of business as well as her aunt, and amongst the rest there were notes to be written to all their friends at Lambton, with false excuses for their sudden departure. An hour, however, saw the whole completed; and Mr. Gardiner meanwhile having settled his account at the inn, nothing remained to be done but to go; and Elizabeth, after all the misery of the morning, found herself, in a shorter space of time than she could have supposed, seated in the carriage, and on the road to Longbourn.

Chapter 47

"I HAVE been thinking it over again, Elizabeth," said her uncle, as they drove from the town; "and really, upon serious consideration, I am much more inclined than I was to judge as your eldest sister does on the matter. It appears to me so very unlikely that any young man should form such a design against a girl who is by no means unprotected or friendless, and who was actually staying in his colonel's family, that I am strongly inclined to hope the best. Could he expect that her friends would not step forward? Could be expect to be noticed again by the regiment, after such an affront to Colonel Forster? His temptation is not adequate to the risk!"

"Do you really think so?" cried Elizabeth, brightening up for a moment.

"Upon my word," said Mrs. Gardiner, "I begin to be of your uncle's opinion. It is really too great a violation of decency, honour, and interest, for him to be guilty of it. I cannot think so very ill of Wickham. Can you yourself, Lizzy, so wholly give him up, as to believe him capable of it?"

"Not, perhaps, of neglecting his own interest; but of every other neglect I can believe him capable. If, indeed, it should be so! But I dare not hope it. Why should they not go on to Scotland if that had been the case?"

"In the first place," replied Mr. Gardiner, "there is no absolute proof that they are not gone to Scotland."

"Oh! but their removing from the chaise into a hackney coach is such a presumption! And, besides, no traces of them were to be found on the Barnet road."

"Well, then—supposing them to be in London. They may be there, though for the purpose of concealment, for no more exceptional purpose. It is not likely that money should be very abundant on either side; and it might strike them that they could be more economically, though less expeditiously, married in London than in Scotland."

"But why all this secrecy? Why any fear of detection? Why must their marriage be private? Oh, no, no—this is not likely. His most particular friend, you see by Jane's account, was persuaded of his never intending to marry her. Wickham will never marry a woman without some money. He cannot afford it. And what claims has Lydia—what attraction has she beyond youth, health, and good humour that could make him, for her sake, forego every chance of benefiting himself by marrying well? As to what restraint the apprehensions of disgrace in the corps might throw on a dishonourable elopement with her, I am not able to judge; for I know nothing of the effects that such a step might produce. But as to your other objection, I am afraid it will hardly hold good. Lydia has no brothers to step forward; and he might imagine, from my father's behaviour, from his indolence and the little attention he has ever seemed to give to what was going forward in his family, that *he* would do as little, and think as little about it, as any father could do, in such a matter."

"But can you think that Lydia is so lost to everything but love of him as to consent to live with him on any other terms than marriage?"

"It does seem, and it is most shocking indeed," replied Elizabeth, with tears in her eyes, "that a sister's sense of decency and virtue in such a point should admit of doubt. But, really, I know not what to say. Perhaps I am not doing her justice. But she is very young; she has never been taught to think on serious subjects; and for the last half-year, nay, for a twelvemonth—she has been given up to nothing but amusement and vanity. She has been allowed to dispose of her time in the most idle and frivolous manner, and to adopt any opinions that came in her way. Since the ——shire were first quartered in Meryton, nothing but love, flirtation, and officers have been in her head. She has been doing everything in her power by thinking and talking on the subject, to give greater—what shall I call it? susceptibility to her feelings; which are naturally lively enough. And we all know that Wickham has every charm of person and address that can captivate a woman."

"But you see that Jane," said her aunt, "does not think so ill of Wickham as to believe him capable of the attempt."

"Of whom does Jane ever think ill? And who is there, whatever might be their former conduct, that she would believe capable of such an attempt, till it were proved against them? But Jane knows, as well as I do, what

Wickham really is. We both know that he has been profligate in every sense of the word; that he has neither integrity nor honour; that he is as false and deceitful as he is insinuating."

"And do you really know all this?" cried Mrs. Gardiner, whose curiosity as to the mode of her intelligence was all alive.

"I do indeed," replied Elizabeth, colouring. "I told you, the other day, of his infamous behaviour to Mr. Darcy; and you yourself, when last at Longbourn, heard in what manner he spoke of the man who had behaved with such forbearance and liberality towards him. And there are other circumstances which I am not at liberty—which it is not worth while to relate; but his lies about the whole Pemberley family are endless. From what he said of Miss Darcy I was thoroughly prepared to see a proud, reserved, disagreeable girl. Yet he knew to the contrary himself. He must know that she was as amiable and unpretending as we have found her."

"But does Lydia know nothing of this? can she be ignorant of what you and Jane seem so well to understand?"

"Oh yes! that, that is the worst of all. Till I was in Kent, and saw so much both of Mr. Darcy and his relation Colonel Fitzwilliam, I was ignorant of the truth myself. And when I returned home, the ——shire was to leave Meryton in a week or fortnight's time. As that was the case, neither Jane, to whom I related the whole, nor I, thought it necessary to make our knowledge public; for of what use could it apparently be to any one, that the good opinion which all the neighbourhood had of him should then be overthrown? And even when it was settled that Lydia should go with Mrs. Forster, the necessity of opening her eyes to his character never occurred to me. That *she* could be in any danger from the deception never entered my head. That such a consequence as *this* should ensue, you may easily believe, was far enough from my thoughts."

"When they all removed to Brighton, therefore, you had no reason, I suppose, to believe them fond of each other?"

"Not the slightest. I can remember no symptom of affection on either side; and had anything of the kind been perceptible, you must be aware that ours is not a family on which it could be thrown away. When first he entered the corps, she was ready enough to admire him; but so we all were. Every girl in or near Meryton was out of her senses about him for the first two months; but he never distinguished *her* by any particular attention; and, consequently, after a moderate period of extravagant and wild admiration, her fancy for him gave way, and others of the regiment, who treated her with more distinction, again became her favourites."

It may be easily believed, that however little of novelty could be added to their fears, hopes, and conjectures, on this interesting subject, by its repeated discussion, no other could detain them from it long, during the whole of the journey. From Elizabeth's thoughts it was never absent. Fixed there by the keenest of all anguish, self-reproach, she could find no interval of ease or forgetfulness.

They travelled as expeditiously as possible, and, sleeping one night on the road, reached Longbourn by dinner time the next day. It was a comfort to Elizabeth to consider that Jane could not have been wearied by long expectations.

The little Gardiners, attracted by the sight of a chaise, were standing on the steps of the house as they entered the paddock; and, when the carriage drove up to the door, the joyful surprise that lighted up their faces, and displayed itself over their whole bodies, in a variety of capers and frisks, was the first pleasing earnest of their welcome.

Elizabeth jumped out; and, after giving each of them a hasty kiss, hurried into the vestibule, where Jane, who came running downstairs from her mother's apartment, immediately met her.

Elizabeth, as she affectionately embraced her, whilst tears filled the eyes of both, lost not a moment in asking whether anything had been heard of the fugitives.

"Not yet," replied Jane. "But now that my dear uncle is come, I hope everything will be well."

"Is my father in town?"

"Yes, he went on Tuesday, as I wrote you word."

"And have you heard from him often?"

"We have heard only once. He wrote me a few lines on Wednesday, to say that he had arrived in safety, and to give me his directions, which I particularly begged him to do. He merely added that he should not write again till he had something of importance to mention."

"And my mother—how is she? How are you all?"

"My mother is tolerably well, I trust; though her spirits are greatly shaken. She is upstairs, and will have great satisfaction in seeing you all. She does not yet leave her dressing-room. Mary and Kitty, thank Heaven, are quite well."

"But you—how are you?" cried Elizabeth. "You look pale. How much you must have gone through!"

Her sister, however, assured her of her being perfectly well; and their conversation, which had been passing while Mr. and Mrs. Gardiner were engaged with their children, was now put an end to by the approach of the whole party. Jane ran to her uncle and aunt, and welcomed and thanked them both, with alternate smiles and tears.

When they were all in the drawing-room, the questions which Elizabeth had already asked were of course repeated by the others, and they soon found that Jane had no intelligence to give. The sanguine hope of good, however, which the benevolence of her heart suggested had not yet deserted her; she still expected that it would all end well, and that every morning would bring some letter, either from Lydia or her father, to explain their proceedings, and, perhaps, announce the marriage.

Mrs. Bennet, to whose apartment they all repaired, after a few minutes' conversation together, received them exactly as might be expected; with tears and lamentations of regret, invectives against the villainous conduct of Wickham, and complaints of her own sufferings and ill-usage; blaming everybody but the person to whose ill-judging indulgence the errors of her daughter must be principally owing.

"If I had been able," said she, "to carry my point in going to Brighton, with all my family, *this* would not have happened: but poor dear Lydia had nobody to take care of her. Why did the Forsters ever let her go out of their sight? I am sure there was some great neglect or other on their side, for she is not the kind of girl to do such a thing if she had been well looked after. I always thought they were very unfit to have the charge of her; but I was overruled, as I always am. Poor dear child! And now here's Mr. Bennet gone away, and I know he will fight Wickham, wherever he meets him and then he will be killed, and what is to become of us all? The Collinses will turn us out before he is cold in his grave, and if you are not kind to us, brother, I do not know what we shall do."

They all exclaimed against such terrific ideas; and Mr. Gardiner, after general assurances of his affection for her and all her family, told her that ne meant to be in London the very next day, and would assist Mr. Bennet in every endeavour for recovering Lydia.

"Do not give way to useless alarm," added he; "though it is right to be prepared for the worst, there is no occasion to look on it as certain. It is not quite a week since they left Brighton. In a few days more we may gain some news of them; and till we know that they are not married, and have no design of marrying, do not let us give the matter over as lost. As soon as I get to town I shall go to my brother, and make him come home with me to Gracechurch Street; and then we may consult together as to what is to be done."

"Oh! my dear brother," replied Mrs. Bennet, "that is exactly what I could most wish for. And now do, when you get to town, find them out, wherever they may be; and if they are not married already, *make* them marry. And as for wedding clothes, do not let them wait for that, but tell Lydia she shall have as much money as she chooses to buy them, after they are married. And, above all things, keep Mr. Bennet from fighting. Tell him what a dreadful state I am in, that I am frighted out of my wits—and have such tremblings, such flutterings, all over me—such spasms in my side and pains in my head, and such beatings at heart, that I can get no rest by night nor by day. And tell my dear Lydia not to give any directions about her clothes till she has seen me, for she does not know which are the best warehouses. Oh, brother, how kind you are! I know you will contrive it all."

But Mr. Gardiner, though he assured her again of his earnest endeavours in the cause, could not avoid recommending moderation to her, as well in her hopes as her fears; and after talking with her in this manner till dinner was on table, they left her to vent all her feelings on the housekeeper, who attended in the absence of her daughters.

Though her brother and sister were persuaded that there was no real occasion for such a seclusion from the family, they did not attempt to oppose it, for they knew that she had not prudence enough to hold her tongue before the servants, while they waited at table, and judged it better that *one* only of the household, and the one whom they could most trust should comprehend all her fears and solicitude on the subject.

In the dining-room they were soon joined by Mary and Kitty, who had been too busily engaged in their separate apartments to make their appearance before. One came from her books, and the other from her toilette. The faces of both, however, were tolerably calm; and no change was visible in either, except that the loss of her favourite sister, or the anger which she had herself incurred in the business, had given something more of fretfulness than usual to the accents of Kitty. As for Mary, she was mistress enough of herself to whisper to Elizabeth, with a countenance of grave reflection, soon after they were seated at table:

"This is a most unfortunate affair, and will probably be much talked of. But we must stem the tide of malice, and pour into the wounded bosoms of each other the balm of sisterly consolation."

Then, perceiving in Elizabeth no inclination of replying, she added, "Unhappy as the event must be for Lydia, we may draw from it this useful lesson: that loss of virtue in a female is irretrievable; that one false step involves her in endless ruin; that her reputation is no less brittle than it is beautiful; and that she cannot be too much guarded in her behaviour towards the undeserving of the other sex."

Elizabeth lifted up her eyes in amazement, but was too much oppressed to make any reply. Mary, however, continued to console herself with such kind of moral extractions from the evil before them.

In the afternoon, the two elder Miss Bennets were able to be for half-an-hour by themselves; and Elizabeth instantly availed herself of the opportunity of making any inquiries, which Jane was equally eager to satisfy. After joining in general lamentations over the dreadful sequel of this event, which Elizabeth considered as all but certain, and Miss Bennet could not assert to be wholly impossible, the former continued the subject, by saying, "But tell me all and everything about it which I have not already heard. Give me further particulars. What did Colonel Forster say? Had they no apprehension of anything before the elopement took place? They must have seen them together for ever."

"Colonel Forster did own that he had often suspected some partiality, especially on Lydia's side, but nothing to give him any alarm. I am so grieved for him! His behaviour was attentive and kind to the utmost. He *was* coming to us, in order to assure us of his concern, before he had any idea of their not being gone to Scotland: when that apprehension first got abroad, it hastened his journey."

"And was Denny convinced that Wickham would not marry? Did he know of their intending to go off? Had Colonel Forster seen Denny himself?"

"Yes: but, when questioned by *him*, Denny denied knowing anything of their plan, and would not give his real opinion about it. He did not repeat his persuasion of their not marrying—and from *that*, I am inclined to hope, he might have been misunderstood before."

"And till Colonel Forster came himself, not one of you entertained a doubt, I suppose, of their being really married?"

"How was it possible that such an idea should enter our brains? I felt a little uneasy—a little fearful of my sister's happiness with him in marriage, because I knew that his conduct had not been always quite right. My father and mother knew nothing of that; they only felt how imprudent a match it must be. Kitty then owned, with a very natural triumph on knowing more than the rest of us, that in Lydia's last letter she had prepared her for such a step. She had known, it seems, of their being in love with each other, many weeks."

"But not before they went to Brighton?"

"No, I believe not."

"And did Colonel Forster appear to think ill of Wickham himself? Does he know his real character?"

"I must confess that he did not speak so well of Wickham as he formerly did. He believed him to be imprudent and extravagant. And since this sad affair has taken place, it is said that he left Meryton greatly in debt; but I hope this may be false."

"Oh, Jane, had we been less secret, had we told what we knew of him, this could not have happened!"

"Perhaps it would have been better," replied her sister. "But to expose the former faults of any person without knowing what their present feelings were, seemed unjustifiable. We acted with the best intentions."

"Could Colonel Forster repeat the particulars of Lydia's note to his wife?"

"He brought it with him for us to see."

Jane then took it from her pocket-book, and gave it to Elizabeth. These were the contents:

"MY DEAR HARRIET,—

"You will laugh when you know where I am gone, and I cannot help laughing myself at your surprise to-morrow morning, as soon as I am missed. I am going to Gretna Green, and if you cannot guess with who, I shall think you a simpleton, for there is but one man in the world I love, and he is an angel. I should never be happy without him, so think it no harm to be off. You need not send them word at Longbourn of my going, if you do not like it, for it will make the surprise the greater, when I write to them and sign my name 'Lydia Wickham.' What a good joke it will be! I can hardly write for laughing. Pray make my excuses to Pratt for not keeping my engagement, and dancing with him to-night. Tell him I hope he will excuse me when he knows all; and tell him I will dance with him at the next ball we meet, with great pleasure. I shall send for my clothes when I get to Longbourn; but I wish you would tell Sally to mend a great slit in my worked muslin gown before they are packed up. Good-bye. Give my love to Colonel Forster. I hope you will drink to our good journey. Your affectionate friend,

"LYDIA BENNET."

"Oh! thoughtless, thoughtless Lydia!" cried Elizabeth when she had finished it. "What a letter is this, to be written at such a moment! But at least it shows that *she* was serious in the object of her journey. Whatever he might afterwards persuade her to, it was not on her side a *scheme* of infamy. My poor father! how he must have felt it!"

"I never saw any one so shocked. He could not speak a word for full ten minutes. My mother was taken ill immediately, and the whole house in such confusion!"

"Oh! Jane," cried Elizabeth, "was there a servant belonging to it who did not know the whole story before the end of the day?"

"I do not know. I hope there was. But to be guarded at such a time is very difficult. My mother was in hysterics, and though I endeavoured to give her every assistance in my power, I am afraid I did not do so much as I might have done! But the horror of what might possibly happen almost took from me my faculties."

"Your attendance upon her has been too much for you. You do not look well. Oh that I had been with you! you have had every care and anxiety upon yourself alone."

"Mary and Kitty have been very kind, and would have shared in every fatigue, I am sure, but I did not think it right for either of them. Kitty is slight and delicate; and Mary studies so much, that her hours of repose should not be broken in on. My aunt Philips came to Longbourn on Tuesday, after my father went away; and was so good as to stay till Thursday with me. She was of great use and comfort to us all. And Lady Lucas has been very kind; she walked here on Wednesday morning to condole with us, and offered her services, or any of her daughters', if they could be of use to us."

"She had better have stayed at home," cried Elizabeth; "perhaps she *meant* well, but, under such a misfortune as this, one cannot see too little of one's neighbours. Assistance is impossible; condolence insufferable. Let them triumph over us at a distance, and be satisfied."

She then proceeded to inquire into the measures which her father had intended to pursue, while in town, for the recovery of his daughter.

"He meant I believe," replied Jane, "to go to Epsom, the place where they last changed horses, see the postilions and try if anything could be made out from them. His principal object must be to discover the number of the hackney coach which took them from Clapham. It had come with a fare from London; and as he thought the circumstance of a gentleman and lady's removing from one carriage into another might be remarked he meant to make inquiries at Clapham. If he could anyhow discover at what house the coachman had before set down his fare, he determined to make inquiries there, and hoped it might not be impossible to find out the stand and number of the coach. I do not know of any other designs that he had formed; but he was in such a hurry to be gone, and his spirits so greatly discomposed, that I had difficulty in finding out even so much as this."

Chapter 48

THE whole party were in hopes of a letter from Mr. Bennet the next morning, but the post came in without bringing a single line from him. His family knew him to be, on all common occasions, a most negligent and dilatory correspondent; but at such a time they had hoped for exertion. They were forced to conclude that he had no pleasing intelligence to send; but even of *that* they would have been glad to be certain. Mr. Gardiner had waited only for the letters before he set off.

When he was gone, they were certain at least of receiving constant information of what was going on, and their uncle promised, at parting, to prevail on Mr. Bennet to return to Longbourn, as soon as he could, to the great consolation of his sister, who considered it as the only security for her husband's not being killed in a duel.

Mrs. Gardiner and the children were to remain in Hertfordshire a few days longer, as the former thought her presence might be serviceable to her nieces. She shared in their attendance on Mrs. Bennet, and was a great comfort to them in their hours of freedom. Their other aunt also visited them frequently, and always, as she said, with the design of cheering and heartening them up—though, as she never came without reporting some fresh instance of Wickham's extravagance or irregularity, she seldom went away without leaving them more dispirited than she found them.

All Meryton seemed striving to blacken the man who, but three months before, had been almost an angel of light. He was declared to be in debt to every tradesman in the place, and his intrigues all honoured with the title of seduction, had been extended into every tradesman's family. Everybody declared that he was the wickedest young man in the world; and everybody began to find out that they had always distrusted the appearance of his goodness. Elizabeth, though she did not credit above half of what was said, believed enough to make her former assurance of her sister's ruin still more certain; and even Jane, who believed still less of it, became almost hopeless, more especially as the time was now come when, if they had gone to Scotland, which she had never before entirely despaired of, they must in all probability have gained some news of them.

Mr. Gardiner left Longbourn on Sunday; on Tuesday, his wife received a letter from him; it told them that, on his arrival, he had immediately found out his brother, and persuaded him to come to Gracechurch Street; that Mr. Bennet had been to Epsom and Clapham, before his arrival, but without gaining any satisfactory information; and that he was now determined to inquire at all the principal hotels in town, as Mr. Bennet thought it possible they might have gone to one of them, on their first coming to London, before they procured lodgings. Mr. Gardiner himself did not expect any success from this measure, but as his brother was eager in it, he meant to assist him in pursuing it. He added that Mr. Bennet seemed wholly disinclined at present to leave London and promised to write again very soon. There was also a postscript to this effect:

"I have written to Colonel Forster to desire him to find out, if possible, from some of the young man's intimates in the regiment, whether Wick-ham has any relations or connections who would be likely to know in what part of the town he has now concealed himself. If there were any one that one could apply to with a probability of gaining such a clue as that, it might be of essential consequence. At present we have nothing to guide us. Colonel Forster will, I dare say, do everything in his power to satisfy us on this head. But, on second thoughts, perhaps, Lizzy could tell us what relations he has now living, better than any other person."

Elizabeth was at no loss to understand from whence this deference for her authority proceeded; but it was not in her power to give any information of so satisfactory a nature as the compliment deserved. She had never heard of his having had any relations, except a father and mother, both of whom had been dead many years. It was possible, however, that some of his companions in the ——shire might be able to give more information; and though she was not very sanguine in expecting it, the application was a something to look forward to.

Every day at Longbourn was now a day of anxiety; but the most anxious part of each was when the post was expected. The arrival of letters was the first grand object of every morning's impatience. Through letters, whatever of good or bad was to be told would be communicated, and every succeeding day was expected to bring some news of importance.

But before they heard again from Mr. Gardiner, a letter arrived for their father, from a different quarter, from Mr. Collins; which, as Jane had received directions to open all that came for him in his absence, she accordingly read; and Elizabeth, who knew what curiosities his letters always were, looked over her, and read it likewise. It was as follows:

"MY DEAR SIR,—

"I feel myself called upon, by our relationship, and my situation in life, to condole with you on the grievous affliction you are now suffering under, of which we were yesterday informed by a letter from Hertford-shire. Be assured, my dear sir, that Mrs. Collins and myself sincerely sympathise with you and all your respectable family, in your present distress, which must be of the bitterest kind, because proceeding from a cause which no time can remove. No arguments shall be wanting on my part that can alleviate so severe a misfortune—or that may comfort you, under a circumstance that must be of all others most afflicting to a parent's mind. The death of your daughter would have been a blessing in comparison of this. And it is the more to be lamented, because there is reason to suppose as my dear Charlotte informs me, that this licentiousness of behaviour in your daughter has proceeded from a faulty degree of indulgence; though, at the same time, for the consolation of yourself and Mrs. Bennet, I am inclined to think that her own disposition must be naturally bad, or she could not be guilty of such an enormity, at so early an age. Howsoever that may be, you are grievously to be pitied; in which opinion I am not only joined by Mrs. Collins, but likewise by Lady Catherine and her daughter, to whom I have related the affair. They agree with me in apprehending that this false step in one daughter will be injurious to the fortunes of all the others; for who, as Lady Catherine herself condescendingly says, will connect themselves with such a family? And this consideration leads me moreover to reflect, with augmented satisfaction, on a certain event of last November; for had it been otherwise, I must have been involved in all your sorrow and disgrace. Let me advise you then, my dear sir, to console yourself as much as possible, to throw off your unworthy child from your affection for ever, and leave her to reap the fruits of her own heinous offence.—I am. dear sir, etc., etc."

Mr. Gardiner did not write again till he had received an answer from Colonel Forster; and then he had nothing of a pleasant nature to send. It was not known that Wickham had a single relation with whom he kept up any connection, and it was certain that he had no near one living. His former acquaintances had been numerous; but since he had been in the militia, it did not appear that he was on terms of particular friendship with any of them. There was no one, therefore, who could be pointed out as likely to give any news of him. And in the wretched state of his own finances, there was a very powerful motive for secrecy, in addition to his fear of discovery by Lydia's relations, for it had just transpired that he had left gaming debts behind him to a very considerable amount. Colonel Forster believed that more than a thousand pounds would be necessary to clear his expenses at Brighton. He owed a good deal in the town, but his debts of honour were still more formidable. Mr. Gardiner did not attempt to conceal these particulars from the Longbourn family. Jane heard them with horror. "A gamester!" she cried. "This is wholly unexpected. I had not an idea of it."

Mr. Gardiner added in his letter, that they might expect to see their father at home on the following day, which was Saturday. Rendered spiritless by the ill-success of all their endeavours, he had yielded to his brother-in-law's entreaty that he would return to his family, and leave it to him to do whatever occasion might suggest to be advisable for continuing their pursuit. When Mrs. Bennet was told of this, she did not express so much satisfaction as her children expected, considering what her anxiety for his life had been before.

"What, is he coming home, and without poor Lydia?" she cried. "Sure he will not leave London before he has found them. Who is to fight Wickham, and make him marry her, if he comes away?"

As Mrs. Gardiner began to wish to be at home, it was settled that she and her children should go to London, at the same time that Mr. Bennet came from it. The coach, therefore, took them the first stage of their journey, and brought its master back to Longbourn.

Mrs. Gardiner went away in all the perplexity about Elizabeth and her Derbyshire friend that had attended her from that part of the world. His name had never been voluntarily mentioned before them by her niece; and the kind of half-expectation which Mrs. Gardiner had formed, of their being followed by a letter from him, had ended in nothing. Elizabeth had received none since her return that could come from Pemberley.

The present unhappy state of the family rendered any other excuse for the lowness of her spirits unnecessary; nothing, therefore, could be fairly conjectured from *that,* though Elizabeth, who was by this time tolerably well acquainted with her own feelings, was perfectly aware that, had she known nothing of Darcy, she could have borne the dread of Lydia's infamy somewhat better. It would have spared her, she thought, one sleepless night out of two.

When Mr. Bennet arrived, he had all the appearance of his usual philosophic composure. He said as little as he had ever been in the habit of saying; made no mention of the business that had taken him away, and it was some time before his daughters had courage to speak of it.

It was not till the afternoon, when he joined them at tea, that Elizabeth ventured to introduce the subject; and then, on her briefly expressing her sorrow for what he must have endured, he replied, "Say nothing of that. Who should suffer but myself? It has been my own doing, and I ought to feel it."

"You must not be too severe upon yourself," replied Elizabeth.

"You may well warn me against such an evil. Human nature is so prone to fall into it! No, Lizzy, let me once in my life feel how much I have been to blame. I am not afraid of being overpowered by the impression. It will pass away soon enough."

"Do you suppose them to be in London?"

"Yes; where else can they be so well concealed?"

"And Lydia used to want to go to London," added Kitty.

"She is happy then," said her father drily; "and her residence there will probably be of some duration."

Then, after a short silence, he continued:

"Lizzy, I bear you no ill-will for being justified in your advice to me last May, which, considering the event, shows some greatness of mind."

They were interrupted by Miss Bennet, who came to fetch her mother's tea.

"This is a parade," cried he, "which does one good; it gives such an elegance to misfortune! Another day I will do the same; I will sit in my library, in my nightcap and powdering gown, and give as much trouble as I can; or, perhaps, I may defer it till Kitty runs away."

"I am not going to run away, papa," said Kitty fretfully. "If *I* should ever go to Brighton, I would behave better than Lydia."

"*You* go to Brighton. I would not trust you so near it as Eastbourne for fifty pounds! No, Kitty, I have at last learnt to be cautious, and you will feel the effects of it. No officer is ever to enter my house again, nor even to pass through the village. Balls will be absolutely prohibited, unless you stand up with one of your sisters. And you are never to stir out of doors till you can prove that you have spent ten minutes of every day in a rational manner."

Kitty, who took all these threats in a serious light, began to cry.

"Well, well," said he, "do not make yourself unhappy. If you are a good girl for the next ten years, I will take you to a review at the end of them."

Chapter 49

Two days after Mr. Bennet's return, as Jane and Elizabeth were walking together in the shrubbery behind the house, they saw the housekeeper coming towards them, and, concluding that she came to call them to their mother, went forward to meet her; but, instead of the expected summons, when they approached her, she said to Miss Bennet, "I beg your pardon, madam, for interrupting you, but I was in hopes you might have got some good news from town, so I took the liberty of coming to ask."

"What do you mean, Hill? We have heard nothing from town."

"Dear madam," cried Mrs. Hill, in great astonishment, "don't you know there is an express come for master from Mr. Gardiner? He has been here this half-hour, and master has had a letter."

Away ran the girls, too eager to get in to have time for speech. They ran through the vestibule into the breakfast-room; from thence to the library; their father was in neither; and they were on the point of seeking him upstairs with their mother, when they were met by the butler, who said:

"If you are looking for my master, ma'am, he is walking towards the little copse."

Upon this information, they instantly passed through the hall once more, and ran across the lawn after their father, who was deliberately pursuing his way towards a small wood on one side of the paddock.

Jane, who was not so light nor so much in the habit of running as Elizabeth, soon lagged behind, while her sister, panting for breath, came up with him, and eagerly cried out:

"Oh, papa, what news—what news? Have you heard from my uncle?"

"Yes I have had a letter from him by express."

"Well, and what news does it bring—good or bad?"

"What is there of good to be expected?" said he, taking the letter from his pocket. "But perhaps you would like to read it."

Elizabeth impatiently caught it from his hand. Jane now came up.

"Read it aloud," said their father, "for I hardly know myself what it is about."

> "Gracechurch Street, Monday,
> "August 2.

"MY DEAR BROTHER,—

"At last I am able to send you some tidings of my niece, and such as, upon the whole, I hope will give you satisfaction. Soon after you left me on Saturday, I was fortunate enough to find out in what part of London they were. The particulars I reserve till we meet: it is enough to know they are discovered. I have seen them both——"

"Then it is as I always hoped," cried Jane; "they are married!"

Elizabeth read on:

"I have seen them both. They are not married, nor can I find there was any intention of being so; but if you are willing to perform the engagements which I have ventured to make on your side, I hope it will not be long before they are. All that is required of you is, to assure to your daughter, by settlement, her equal share of the five thousand pounds secured among your children after the decease of yourself and my sister; and, moreover, to enter into an engagement of allowing her, during your life, one hundred pounds per annum. These are conditions which, considering everything, I had no hesitation in complying with, as far as I thought myself privileged, for you. I shall send this by express, that no time may be lost in bringing me your answer. You will easily comprehend, from these particulars, that Mr. Wickham's circumstances are not so hopeless as they are generally believed to be. The world has been deceived in that respect; and I am happy to say there will be some little money, even when all his debts are discharged, to settle on my niece, in addition to her own fortune. If, as I conclude will be the case, you send me full powers to act in your name throughout the whole of this business, I will immediately give directions to Haggerston for preparing a proper settlement. There will not be the smallest occasion for your coming to town again; therefore stay quietly at Longbourn, and depend on my diligence and care. Send back your answer as soon as you can, and be careful to write explicitly. We have judged it best that my niece should be married from this house, of which I hope you will approve. She comes to us to-day. I shall write again as soon as anything more is determined on. Yours, etc.,

> "EDW. GARDINER."

"Is it possible?" cried Elizabeth, when she had finished. "Can it be possible that he will marry her?"

"Wickham is not so undeserving, then, as we have thought him," said her sister. "My dear father, I congratulate you."

"And have you answered the letter?" said Elizabeth.

"No; but it must be done soon."

Most earnestly did she then entreat him to lose no more time before he wrote.

"Oh! my dear father," she cried, "come back and write immediately. Consider how important every moment is in such a case."

"Let me write for you," said Jane, "if you dislike the trouble yourself."

"I dislike it very much," he replied; "but it must be done."

And so saying, he turned back with them, and walked towards the house.

"And may I ask——" said Elizabeth; "but the terms, I suppose, must be complied with."

"Complied with! I am only ashamed of his asking so little."

"And they *must* marry! Yet he is *such* a man!"

"Yes, yes, they must marry. There is nothing else to be done. But there are two things that I want very much to know: one is, how much money your uncle has laid down to bring it about; and the other, how I am ever to pay him."

"Money! My uncle!" cried Jane, "what do you mean, sir?"

"I mean, that no man in his senses would marry Lydia on so slight a temptation as one hundred a year during my life, and fifty after I am gone."

"That is very true," said Elizabeth; "though it had not occurred to me before. His debts to be discharged, and something still to remain! Oh! it must be my uncle's doings! Generous, good man, I am afraid he has distressed himself. A small sum could not do all this."

"No," said her father; "Wickham's a fool if he takes her with a farthing less than ten thousand pounds. I should be sorry to think so ill of him, in the very beginning of our relationship."

"Ten thousand pounds! Heaven forbid! How is half such a sum to be repaid?"

Mr. Bennet made no answer, and each of them, deep in thought, continued silent till they reached the house. Their father then went to the library to write, and the girls walked into the breakfast-room.

"And they are really to be married!" cried Elizabeth, as soon as they were by themselves. "How strange this is! And for *this* we are to be thankful. That they should marry, small as is their chance of happiness, and wretched as is his character, we are forced to rejoice. Oh, Lydia!"

"I comfort myself with thinking," replied Jane, "that he certainly would not marry Lydia if he had not a real regard for her. Though our kind uncle has done something towards clearing him, I cannot believe that ten thousand pounds, or anything like it, has been advanced. He has children of his own, and may have more. How could he spare half ten thousand pounds?"

"If we were ever able to learn what Wickham's debts have been," said Elizabeth, "and how much is settled on his side on our sister, we shall exactly know what Mr. Gardiner has done for them, because Wickham has not sixpence of his own. The kindness of my uncle and aunt can never be requited. Their taking her home, and affording her their personal protection and countenance, is such a sacrifice to her advantage as years of gratitude cannot enough acknowledge. By this time she is actually with them! If such goodness does not make her miserable now, she will never deserve to be happy! What a meeting for her, when she first sees my aunt!"

"We must endeavour to forget all that has passed on either side," said Jane: "I hope and trust they will yet be happy. His consenting to marry her is a proof, I will believe, that he is come to a right way of thinking. Their mutual affection will steady them; and I flatter myself they will settle so quietly, and live in so rational a manner, as may in time make their past imprudence forgotten."

"Their conduct has been such," replied Elizabeth, "as neither you, nor I, nor anybody can ever forget. It is useless to talk of it."

It now occurred to the girls that their mother was in all likelihood perfectly ignorant of what had happened. They went to the library, therefore, and asked their father whether he would not wish them to make it known to her. He was writing and, without raising his head, coolly replied:

"Just as you please."

"May we take my uncle's letter to read to her?"

"Take whatever you like, and get away."

Elizabeth took the letter from his writing-table, and they went upstairs together. Mary and Kitty were both with Mrs. Bennet: one communication would, therefore, do for all. After a slight preparation for good news, the letter was read aloud. Mrs. Bennet could hardly contain herself. As soon as Jane had read Mr. Gardiner's hope of Lydia's being soon married, her joy burst forth, and every following sentence added to its exuberance. She was now in an irritation as violent from delight, as she had ever been fidgety from alarm and vexation. To know that her daughter would be married was enough. She was disturbed by no fear for her felicity, nor humbled by any remembrance of her misconduct.

"My dear, dear Lydia!" she cried. "This is delightful indeed! She will be married! I shall see her again! She will be married at sixteen! My good, kind brother! I knew how it would be. I knew he would manage everything! How I long to see her! and to see dear Wickham too! But the clothes, the wedding clothes! I will write to my sister Gardiner about them directly. Lizzy, my dear, run down to your father, and ask him how much he will give her. Stay, stay, I will go myself. Ring the bell, Kitty, for Hill. I will put on my things in a moment. My dear, dear Lydia! How merry we shall be together when we meet!"

Her eldest daughter endeavoured to give some relief to the violence of these transports, by leading her thoughts to the obligations which Mr. Gardiner's behaviour laid them all under.

"For we must attribute this happy conclusion," she added, "in a great measure to his kindness. We are persuaded that he has pledged himself to assist Mr. Wickham with money."

"Well," cried her mother, "it is all very right; who should do it but her own uncle? If he had not had a family of his own, I and my children must have had all his money, you know; and it is the first time we have ever had anything from him, except a few presents. Well! I am so happy! In a short time I shall have a daughter married. Mrs. Wickham! How well it sounds! And she was only sixteen last June. My dear Jane, I am in such a flutter, that I am sure I can't write; so I will dictate, and you write for me. We will settle with your father about the money afterwards; but the things should be ordered immediately."

She was then proceeding to all the particulars of calico, muslin, and cambric, and would shortly have dictated some very plentiful orders, had not Jane, though with some difficulty, persuaded her to wait till her father was at leisure to be consulted. One day's delay, she observed, would be of small importance; and her mother was too happy to be quite so obstinate as usual. Other schemes, too, came into her head.

"I will go to Meryton," said she, "as soon as I am dressed, and tell the good, good news to my sister Philips. And as I come back, I can call on Lady Lucas and Mrs. Long. Kitty, run down and order the carriage. An airing would do me a great deal of good, I am sure. Girls, can I do anything for you in Meryton? Oh! here comes Hill! My dear Hill, have you heard the good news? Miss Lydia is going to be married; and you shall all have a bowl of punch to make merry at her wedding."

Mrs. Hill began instantly to express her joy. Elizabeth received her congratulations amongst the rest, and then, sick of this folly, took refuge in her own room, that she might think with freedom.

Poor Lydia's situation must, at best, be bad enough; but that it was no worse, she had need to be thankful. She felt it so; and though, in looking forward, neither rational happiness nor worldly prosperity could be justly expected for her sister, in looking back to what they had feared, only two hours ago, she felt all the advantages of what they had gained.

Chapter 50

MR. BENNET had very often wished before this period of his life that, instead of spending his whole income, he had laid by an annual sum for the better provision of his children, and of his wife, if she survived him. He now wished it more than ever. Had he done his duty in that respect, Lydia need not have been indebted to her uncle for whatever of honour or credit could now be purchased for her. The satisfaction of prevailing

on one of the most worthless young men in Great Brtiain to be her husband might then have rested in its proper place.

He was seriously concerned that a cause of so little advantage to anyone
should be forwarded at the sole expense of his brother-in-law, and he was
determined, if possible, to find out the extent of his assistance, and to
discharge the obligation as soon as he could.

When first Mr. Bennet had married, economy was held to be perfectly
useless; for, of course, they were to have a son. This son was to join in
cutting off the entail, as soon as he should be of age, and the widow and
younger children would by that means be provided for. Five daughters
successively entered the world, but yet the son was to come; and Mrs.
Bennet, for many years after Lydia's birth, had been certain that he
would. This event had at last been despaired of, but it was then too late
to be saving. Mrs. Bennet had no turn for economy, and her husband's
love of independence had alone prevented their exceeding their income.

Five thousand pounds was settled by marriage articles on Mrs. Bennet
and the children. But in what proportions it should be divided amongst
the latter depended on the will of the parents. This was one point, with
regard to Lydia, at least, which was now to be settled, and Mr. Bennet
could have no hesitation in acceding to the proposal before him. In terms
of grateful acknowledgment for the kindness of his brother, though expressed most concisely, he then delivered on paper his perfect approbation
of all that was done, and his willingness to fulfil the engagements that had
been made for him. He had never before supposed that, could Wickham
be prevailed on to marry his daughter, it would be done with so little
inconvenience to himself as by the present arrangement. He would
scarcely be ten pounds a year the loser by the hundred that was to be
paid them; for, what with her board and pocket allowance, and the continual presents in money which passed to her through her mother's hands,
Lydia's expenses had been very little within that sum.

That it would be done with such trifling exertion on his side, too, was
another very welcome surprise; for his wish at present was to have as
little trouble in the business as possible. When the first transports of rage
which had produced his activity in seeking her were over, he naturally
returned to all his former indolence. His letter was soon dispatched; for,
though dilatory in undertaking business, he was quick in its execution.
He begged to know further particulars of what he was indebted to his
brother, but was too angry with Lydia to send any message to her.

The good news quickly spread through the house, and with proportionate speed through the neighbourhood. It was borne in the latter with
decent philosophy. To be sure, it would have been more for the advantage
of conversation had Miss Lydia Bennet come upon the town; or, as the
happiest alternative, been secluded from the world, in some distant farmhouse. But there was much to be talked of in marrying her; and the good-
natured wishes for her well-doing which had proceeded before from all
the spiteful old ladies in Meryton lost but a little of their spirit in this

change of circumstances, because with such an husband her misery was
considered certain.

It was a fortnight since Mrs. Bennet had been downstairs; but on this
happy day she again took her seat at the head of her table, and in spirits
oppressively high. No sentiment of shame gave a damp to her triumph.
The marriage of a daughter, which had been the first object of her wishes
since Jane was sixteen, was now on the point of accomplishment, and her
thoughts and her words ran wholly on those attendants of elegant nuptials, fine muslins, new carriages, and servants. She was busily searching
through the neighbourhood for a proper situation for her daughter, and,
without knowing or considering what their income might be, rejected
many as deficient in size and importance.

"Haye Park might do," said she, "if the Gouldings could quit it—or
the great house at Stoke, if the drawing-room were larger; but Ashworth
is too far off! I could not bear to have her ten miles from me; and as for
Pulvis Lodge, the attics are dreadful."

Her husband allowed her to talk on without interruption while the
servants remained. But when they had withdrawn, he said to her: "Mrs.
Bennet, before you take any or all of these houses for your son and
daughter, let us come to a right understanding. Into *one* house in this
neighbourhood they shall never have admittance. I will not encourage the
imprudence of either, by receiving them at Longbourn."

A long dispute followed this declaration; but Mr. Bennet was firm. It
soon led to another; and Mrs. Bennet found, with amazement and horror,
that her husband would not advance a guinea to buy clothes for his
daughter. He protested that she should receive from him no mark of
affection whatever on the occasion. Mrs. Bennet could hardly comprehend
it. That his anger could be carried to such a point of inconceivable resentment as to refuse his daughter a privilege without which her marriage
would scarcely seem valid, exceeded all that she could believe possible.
She was more alive to the disgrace which her want of new clothes must
reflect on her daughter's nuptials, than to any sense of shame at her
eloping and living with Wickham a fortnight before they took place.

Elizabeth was now most heartily sorry that she had, from the distress
of the moment, been led to make Mr. Darcy acquainted with their fears
for her sister; for since her marriage would so shortly give the proper
termination to the elopement, they might hope to conceal its unfavourable
beginning from all those who were not immediately on the spot.

She had no fear of its spreading farther through his means. There were
few people on whose secrecy she would have more confidently depended;
but, at the same time, there was no one whose knowledge of a sister's
frailty would have mortified her so much—not, however, from any fear
of disadvantage from it individually to herself, for, at any rate, there
seemed a gulf impassable between them. Had Lydia's marriage been
concluded on the most honourable terms, it was not to be supposed that

Mr. Darcy would connect himself with a family where, to every other objection, would now be added an alliance and relationship of the nearest kind with the man whom he so justly scorned.

From such a connection she could not wonder that he should shrink. The wish of procuring her regard, which she had assured herself of his feeling in Derbyshire, could not in rational expectation survive such a blow as this. She was humbled, she was grieved; she repented, though she hardly knew of what. She became jealous of his esteem, when she could no longer hope to be benefited by it. She wanted to hear of him, when there seemed the least chance of gaining intelligence. She was convinced that she could have been happy with him, when it was no longer likely they should meet.

What a triumph for him, as she often thought, could he know that the proposals which she had proudly spurned only four months ago, would now have been gladly and gratefully received! He was as generous, she doubted not, as the most generous of his sex; but while he was mortal, there must be a triumph.

She began now to comprehend that he was exactly the man who, in disposition and talents, would most suit her. His understanding and temper, though unlike her own, would have answered all her wishes. It was an union that must have been to the advantage of both: by her ease and liveliness, his mind might have been softened, his manners improved; and from his judgment, information, and knowledge of the world, she must have received benefit of greater importance.

But no such happy marriage could now teach the admiring multitude what connubial felicity really was. An union of a different tendency, and precluding the possibility of the other, was soon to be formed in their family.

How Wickham and Lydia were to be supported in tolerable independence, she could not imagine. But how little of permanent happiness could belong to a couple who were only brought together because their passions were stronger than their virtue, she could easily conjecture.

Mr. Gardiner soon wrote again to his brother. To Mr. Bennet's acknowledgments he briefly replied, with assurances of his eagerness to promote the welfare of any of his family; and concluded with entreaties that the subject might never be mentioned to him again. The principal purport of his letter was to inform them that Mr. Wickham had resolved on quitting the militia.

"It was greatly my wish that he should do so," he added, "as soon as his marriage was fixed on. And I think you will agree with me, in considering the removal from that corps as highly advisable, both on his account and my niece's. It is Mr. Wickham's intention to go into the regulars; and among his former friends, there are still some who are able and willing to assist him in the army. He has the promise of an ensigncy in

General ——'s regiment, now quartered in the North. It is an advantage to have it so far from this part of the kingdom. He promises fairly; and I hope among different people, where they may each have a character to preserve, they will both be more prudent. I have written to Colonel Forster, to inform him of our present arrangements, and to request that he will satisfy the various creditors of Mr. Wickham in and near Brighton, with assurances of speedy payment, for which I have pledged myself. And will you give yourself the trouble of carrying similar assurances to his creditors in Meryton, of whom I shall subjoin a list according to his information? He has given in all his debts; I hope at least he has not deceived us. Haggerston has our directions, and all will be completed in a week. They will then join his regiment, unless they are first invited to Longbourn; and I understand from Mrs. Gardiner, that my niece is very desirous of seeing you all before she leaves the South. She is well, and begs to be dutifully remembered to you and her mother.—Yours, etc.,

"E. GARDINER."

Mr. Bennet and his daughters saw all the advantages of Wickham's removal from the ——shire as clearly as Mr. Gardiner could do. But Mrs. Bennet was not so well pleased with it. Lydia's being settled in the North, just when she had expected most pleasure and pride in her company, for she had by no means given up her plan of their residing in Hertfordshire, was a severe disappointment; and, besides, it was such a pity that Lydia should be taken from a regiment where she was acquainted with everybody, and had so many favourites.

"She is so fond of Mrs. Forster," said she, "it will be quite shocking to send her away! And there are several of the young men, too, that she likes very much. The officers may not be so pleasant in General ——'s regiment."

His daughter's request, for such it might be considered, of being admitted into her family again before she set off for the North, received at first an absolute negative. But Jane and Elizabeth, who agreed in wishing, for the sake of their sister's feelings and consequence, that she should be noticed on her marriage by her parents, urged him so earnestly yet so rationally and so mildly, to receive her and her husband at Longbourn, as soon as they were married, that he was prevailed on to think as they thought, and act as they wished. And their mother had the satisfaction of knowing that she should be able to show her married daughter in the neighbourhood before she was banished to the North. When Mr. Bennet wrote again to his brother, therefore, he sent his permission for them to come; and it was settled, that as soon as the ceremony was over, they should proceed to Longbourn. Elizabeth was surprised, however, that Wickham should consent to such a scheme, and had she consulted only her own inclination, any meeting with him would have been the last object of her wishes.

Chapter 51

THEIR sister's wedding-day arrived; and Jane and Elizabeth felt for her, probably more than she felt for herself. The carriage was sent to meet them at ——, and they were to return in it by dinner-time. Their arrival was dreaded by the elder Miss Bennets, and Jane more especially, who gave Lydia the feelings which would have attended herself, had *she* been the culprit, and was wretched in the thought of what her sister must endure.

They came. The family were assembled in the breakfast-room to receive them. Smiles decked the face of Mrs. Bennet as the carriage drove up to the door; her husband looked impenetrably grave; her daughters, alarmed, anxious, uneasy.

Lydia's voice was heard in the vestibule; the door was thrown open, and she ran into the room. Her mother stepped forward, embraced her, and welcomed her with rapture; gave her hand with an affectionate smile to Wickham, who followed his lady, and wished them both joy, with an alacrity which showed no doubt of their happiness.

Their reception from Mr. Bennet, to whom they then turned, was not quite so cordial. His countenance rather gained an austerity, and he scarcely opened his lips. The easy assurance of the young couple, indeed, was enough to provoke him. Elizabeth was disgusted, and even Miss Bennet was shocked. Lydia was Lydia still—untamed, unabashed, wild, noisy, and fearless. She turned from sister to sister, demanding their congratulations; and when at length they all sat down, looked eagerly round the room, took notice of some little alteration in it, and observed, with a laugh, that it was a great while since she had been there.

Wickham was not at all more distressed than herself; but his manners were always so pleasing, that had his character and his marriage been exactly what they ought, his smiles and his easy address, while he claimed their relationship, would have delighted them all. Elizabeth had not before believed him quite equal to such assurance; but she sat down, resolving within herself to draw no limits in future to the impudence of an impudent man. *She* blushed, and Jane blushed; but the cheeks of the two who caused their confusion suffered no variation of colour.

There was no want of discourse. The bride and her mother could neither of them talk fast enough; and Wickham, who happened to sit near Elizabeth, began inquiring after his acquaintances in that neighbourhood with a good-humoured ease which she felt very unable to equal in her replies. They seemed each of them to have the happiest memories in the world. Nothing of the past was recollected with pain; and Lydia led voluntarily to subjects which her sisters would not have alluded to for the world.

"Only think of its being three months," she cried, "since I went away! It seems but a fortnight, I declare; and yet there have been things enough happened in the time. Good gracious! When I went away, I am sure I had no more idea of being married till I came back again—though I thought it would be very good fun if I was."

Her father lifted up his eyes, Jane was distressed, Elizabeth looked expressively at Lydia; but she, who never heard nor saw anything of which she chose to be insensible, gaily continued: "Oh! mamma, do the people hereabouts know I am married to-day! I was afraid they might not; and we overtook William Goulding in his curricle, so I was determined he should know it, and so I let down the side glass next to him, and took off my glove and let my hand just rest upon the window-frame, so that he might see the ring; and then I bowed and smiled like anything."

Elizabeth could bear it no longer. She got up and ran out of the room, and returned no more till she heard them passing through the hall to the dining-parlour. She then joined them soon enough to see Lydia, with anxious parade, walk up to her mother's right hand, and hear her say to her eldest sister: "Ah, Jane, I take your place now, and you must go lower, because I am a married woman!"

It was not to be supposed that time would give Lydia that embarrassment from which she had been so wholly free at first. Her ease and good spirits increased. She longed to see Mrs. Philips, the Lucases, and all their other neighbours, and to hear herself called "Mrs. Wickham" by each of them; and, in the meantime, she went after dinner to show her ring, and boast of being married, to Mrs. Hill and the two housemaids.

"Well, mamma," said she, when they were all returned to the breakfast room, "and what do you think of my husband? Is not he a charming man? I am sure my sisters must all envy me. I only hope they may have half my good luck. They must all go to Brighton. That is the place to get husbands. What a pity it is, mamma, we did not all go!"

"Very true; and if I had my will, we should. But, my dear Lydia, I don't at all like your going such a way off. Must it be so?"

"Oh, Lord! yes, there is nothing in that. I shall like it of all things. You and papa, and my sisters, must come down and see us. We shall be at Newcastle all the winter, and I dare say there will be some balls, and I will take care to get good partners for them all."

"I should like it beyond anything!" said her mother.

"And then, when you go away, you may leave one or two of my sisters behind you; and I dare say I shall get husbands for them before the winter is over."

"I thank you for my share of the favour," said Elizabeth; "but I do not particularly like your way of getting husbands."

Their visitors were not to remain above ten days with them. Mr. Wickham had received his commission before he left London, and he was to join his regiment at the end of a fortnight.

No one but Mrs. Bennet regretted that their stay would be so short; and she made the most of the time, by visiting about with her daughter, and having very frequent parties at home. These parties were acceptable

.o all: to avoid a family circle was even more desirable to such as did think, than such as did not.

Wickham's affection for Lydia was just what Elizabeth had expected to find it—not equal to Lydia's for him. She had scarcely needed her present observation to be satisfied, from the reason of things, that their elopement had been brought on by the strength of her love rather than by his; and she would have wondered why, without violently caring for her, he chose to elope with her at all, had she not felt certain that his flight was rendered necessary by distress of circumstances; and if that were the case, he was not the young man to resist an opportunity of having a companion.

Lydia was exceedingly fond of him. He was her dear Wickham on every occasion; no one was to be put in competition with him. He did everything best in the world; and she was sure he would kill more birds on the first of September than anybody else in the country.

One morning, soon after their arrival, as she was sitting with her two elder sisters, she said to Elizabeth:

"Lizzy, I never gave *you* an account of my wedding, I believe. You were not by when I told mamma and the others all about it. Are not you curious to hear how it was managed?"

"No, really," replied Elizabeth; "I think there cannot be too little said on the subject."

"La! You are so strange! But I must tell you how it went off. We were married, you know, at St. Clement's, because Wickham's lodgings were in that parish. And it was settled that we should all be there by eleven o'clock. My uncle and aunt, and I, were to go together; and the others were to meet us at the church. Well, Monday morning came, and I was in such a fuss! I was so afraid, you know, that something would happen to put it off, and then I should have gone quite distracted. And there was my aunt, all the time I was dressing, preaching and talking away just as if she was reading a sermon. However, I did not hear above one word in ten, for I was thinking, you may suppose, of my dear Wickham. I longed to know whether he would be married in his blue coat.

"Well, and so we breakfasted at ten, as usual. I thought it would never be over; for, by the bye, you are to understand that my uncle and aunt were horrid unpleasant all the time I was with them. If you'll believe me, I did not once put my foot out of doors, though I was there a fortnight. Not one party, or scheme, or anything! To be sure, London was rather thin; but, however, the Little Theatre was open. Well, and so, just as the carriage came to the door, my uncle was called away upon business to that horrid man, Mr. Stone. And then, you know, when once they get together, there is no end of it. Well, I was so frightened, I did not know what to do; for my uncle was to give me away; and if we were beyond the hour we could not be married all day. But, luckily, he came back again in ten minutes' time, and then we all set out. However, I recollected afterwards, that if he *had* been prevented going the wedding need not be put off, for Mr. Darcy might have done as well."

"Mr. Darcy!" repeated Elizabeth, in utter amazement.

"Oh, yes!—he was to come there with Wickham, you know. But, gracious me! I quite forgot! I ought not to have said a word about it. I promised them so faithfully! What will Wickham say? It was to be such a secret!"

"If it was to be a secret," said Jane, "say not another word on the subject. You may depend upon my seeking no further."

"Oh! certainly," said Elizabeth, though burning with curiosity; "we will ask you no questions."

"Thank you," said Lydia; "for, if you did, I should certainly tell you all, and then Wickham would be angry."

On such encouragement to ask, Elizabeth was forced to put it out of her power, by running away.

But to live in ignorance on such a point was impossible; or, at least, it was impossible not to try for information. Mr. Darcy had been at her sister's wedding. It was exactly a scene, and exactly among people, where he had apparently least to do, and least temptation to go. Conjectures as to the meaning of it, rapid and wild, hurried into her brain; but she was satisfied with none. Those that best pleased her, as placing his conduct in the noblest light, seemed most improbable. She could not bear such suspense; and hastily seizing a sheet of paper, wrote a short letter to her aunt, to request an explanation of what Lydia had dropped, if it were compatible with the secrecy which had been intended.

"You may readily comprehend," she added, "what my curiosity must be to know how a person unconnected with any of us, and (comparatively speaking) a stranger to our family, should have been amongst you at such a time. Pray write instantly, and let me understand it—unless it is, for very cogent reasons, to remain in the secrecy which Lydia seems to think necessary; and then I must endeavour to be satisfied with ignorance."

"Not that I *shall*, though," she added to herself, and she finished the letter: "and, my dear aunt, if you do not tell me in an honourable manner, I shall certainly be reduced to tricks and stratagems to find it out."

Jane's delicate sense of honour would not allow her to speak to Elizabeth privately of what Lydia had let fall: Elizabeth was glad of it; till it appeared whether her inquiries would receive any satisfaction, she had rather be without a confidante.

Chapter 52

ELIZABETH had the satisfaction of receiving an answer to her letter as soon as she possibly could. She was no sooner in possession of it than, hurrying into the little copse, where she was least likely to be interrupted, she sat down on one of the benches, and prepared to be happy; for the length of the letter convinced her that it did not contain a denial.

"Gracechurch Street, Sept. 6.

"My Dear Niece,—

"I have just received your letter, and shall devote this whole morning to answering it, as I foresee that a *little* writing will not comprise what I have to tell you. I must confess myself surprised by your application; I did not expect it from *you*. Don't think me angry, however, for I only mean to let you know that I had not imagined such inquiries to be necessary on *your* side. If you do not choose to understand me, forgive my impertinence. Your uncle is as much surprised as I am, and nothing but the belief of your being a party concerned would have allowed him to act as he has done. But if you are really innocent and ignorant, I must be more explicit.

"On the very day of my coming home from Longbourn, your uncle had a most unexpected visitor. Mr. Darcy called, and was shut up with him several hours. It was all over before I arrived; so my curiosity was not so dreadfully racked as *yours* seems to have been. He came to tell Mr. Gardiner that he had found out where your sister and Mr. Wickham were, and that he had seen and talked with them both—Wickham repeatedly, Lydia once. From what I can collect, he left Derbyshire only one day after ourselves, and came to town with the resolution of hunting for them. The motive professed was his conviction of its being owing to himself that Wickham's worthlessness had not been so well known as to make it impossible for any young woman of character to love or confide in him. He generously imputed the whole to his mistaken pride, and confessed that he had before thought it beneath him to lay his private actions open to the world. His character was to speak for itself. He called it, therefore, his duty to step forward, and endeavour to remedy an evil which had been brought on by himself. If he *had another* motive, I am sure it would never disgrace him. He had been some days in town before he was able to discover them; but he had something to direct his search, which was more than *we* had; and the consciousness of this was another reason for his resolving to follow us.

"There is a lady, it seems, a Mrs. Younge, who was some time ago governess to Miss Darcy, and was dismissed from her charge on some cause of disapprobation, though he did not say what. She then took a large house in Edward Street, and has since maintained herself by letting lodgings. This Mrs. Younge was, he knew, intimately acquainted with Wickham; and he went to her for intelligence of him, as soon as he got to town. But it was two or three days before he could get from her what he wanted. She would not betray her trust, I suppose, without bribery and corruption, for she really did know where her friend was to be found. Wickham, indeed, had gone to her on their first arrival in London, and had she been able to receive them into her house, they would have taken up their abode with her. At length, however, our kind friend procured the wished-for direction. They were in —— Street. He saw Wickham, and afterwards insisted on seeing Lydia. His first object with her, he acknowledged, had been to persuade her to quit her present disgraceful situation, and return to her friends as soon as they could be prevailed on to receive her, offering his assistance as far it would go. But he found Lydia absolutely resolved on remaining where she was. She cared for none of her friends; she wanted no help of his; she would not hear of leaving Wickham; she was sure they should be married some time or other, and it did not much signify when. Since such were her feelings, it only remained, he thought, to secure and expedite a marriage, which, in his very first conversation with Wickham, he easily learnt had never been *his* design. He confessed himself obliged to leave the regiment on account of some debts of honour which were very pressing, and scrupled not to lay all the ill consequences of Lydia's flight on her own folly alone. He meant to resign his commission immediately; and as to his future situation, he could conjecture very little about it. He must go somewhere, but he did not know where, and he knew he should have nothing to live on.

"Mr. Darcy asked him why he had not married your sister at once? Though Mr. Bennet was not imagined to be very rich, he would have been able to do something for him, and his situation must have been benefited by marriage. But he found, in reply to this question, that Wickham still cherished the hope of more effectually making his fortune by marriage in some other country. Under such circumstances, however, he was not likely to be proof against the temptation of immediate relief.

"They met several times, for there was much to be discussed. Wickham, of course, wanted more than he could get, but at length was reduced to be reasonable.

"Everything being settled between *them*, Mr. Darcy's next step was to make your uncle acquainted with it, and he first called in Gracechurch Street the evening before I came home. But Mr. Gardiner could not be seen, and Mr. Darcy found, on further inquiry, that your father was still with him, but would quit town the next morning. He did not judge your father to be a person whom he could so properly consult as your uncle, and therefore readily postponed seeing him till after the departure of the former. He did not leave his name, and till the next day it was only known that a gentleman had called on business.

"On Saturday he came again. Your father was gone, your uncle at home, and, as I said before, they had a great deal of talk together.

"They met again on Sunday, and then *I* saw him too. It was not all settled before Monday; as soon as it was, the express was sent off to Longbourn. But our visitor was very obstinate. I fancy, Lizzy, that obstinacy is the real defect of his character after all. He has been accused of many faults at different times, but *this* is the true one. Nothing was to be done that he did not do himself; though I am sure (and I do not speak it to be

thanked, therefore say nothing about it) your uncle would most readily
have settled the whole.

"They battled it together for a long time, which was more than either
the gentleman or lady concerned in it deserved. But at last your uncle
was forced to yield, and instead of being allowed to be of use to his niece,
was forced to put up with only having the probable credit of it, which
went sorely against the grain; and I really believe your letter this morning
gave him great pleasure, because it required an explanation that would
rob him of his borrowed feathers, and give the praise where it was due.
But, Lizzy, this must go no farther than yourself, or Jane at most.

"You know pretty well, I suppopse, what has been done for the young
people. His debts are to be paid, amounting, I believe, to considerably
more than a thousand pounds, another thousand in addition to her own
settled upon her and his commission purchased. The reason why all this
was to be done by him alone was such as I have given above. It was owing
to him, to his reserve and want of proper consideration, that Wickham's
character had been so misunderstood, and, consequently, that he had been
received and noticed, as he was. Perhaps there was some truth in *this;*
though I doubt whether *his* reserve, or *anybody's* reserve, can be answerable for the event. But in spite of all this fine talking, my dear Lizzy, you
may rest perfectly assured that your uncle would never have yielded, if
we had not given him credit for *another interest* in the affair.

"When all this was resolved on, he returned again to his friends, who
were still staying at Pemberley; but it was agreed that he should be in
London once more when the wedding took place, and all money matters
were then to receive the last finish.

"I believe I have now told you everything. It is a relation which you
tell me is to give you great surprise; I hope at least it will not afford you
any displeasure. Lydia came to us; and Wickham had constant admission
to the house. *He* was exactly what he had been when I knew him in
Hertfordshire; but I would not tell you how little I was satisfied with *her*
behaviour while she stayed with us, if I had not perceived, by Jane's
letter last Wednesday, that her conduct on coming home was exactly of
a piece with it, and therefore what I now tell you can give you no fresh
pain. I talked to her repeatedly in the most serious manner, representing
to her the wickedness of what she had done and all the unhappiness she
had brought on her family. If she heard me, it was by good luck, for I
am sure she did not listen. I was sometimes quite provoked, but then I
recollected my dear Elizabeth and Jane, and for their sakes had patience
with her.

"Mr. Darcy was punctual in his return, and, as Lydia informed you,
attended the wedding. He dined with us the next day, and was to leave
town again on Wednesday or Thursday. Will you be very angry with me,
my dear Lizzy, if I take this opportunity of saying (what I was never bold
enough to say before) how much I like him? His behaviour to us has
in every respect, been as pleasing as when we were in Derbyshire. His

understanding and opinions all please me; he wants nothing but a little more liveliness, and *that*, if he marry *prudently*, his wife may teach him. I thought him very sly; he hardly ever mentioned your name. But slyness seems the fashion.

"Pray forgive me if I have been very presuming; or at least do not punish me so far as to exclude me from P. I shall never be quite happy till I have been all round the park. A low phaeton, with a nice little pair of ponies, would be the very thing.

"But I must write no more. The children have been wanting me this half-hour.

"Yours, very sincerely,

"M. GARDINER."

The contents of this letter threw Elizabeth into a flutter of spirits, in which it was difficult to determine whether pleasure or pain bore the greatest share. The vague and unsettled suspicions which uncertainty had produced of what Mr. Darcy might have been doing to forward her sister's match, which she had feared to encourage as an exertion of goodness too great to be probable, and at the same time dreaded to be just, from the pain of obligation, were proved beyond their greatest extent to be true! He had followed them purposely to town, he had taken on himself all the trouble and mortification attendant on such a research; in which supplication had been necessary to a woman whom he must abominate and despise, and where he was reduced to meet—frequently meet, reason with, persuade, and finally bribe—the man whom he always most wished to avoid, and whose very name it was punishment to him to pronounce. He had done all this for a girl whom he could neither regard nor esteem. Her heart did whisper that he had done it for her. But it was a hope shortly checked by other considerations, and she soon felt that even her vanity was insufficient, when required to depend on his affection for her, for a woman who had already refused him, as able to overcome a sentiment so natural as abhorrence against relationship with Wickham. Brother-in-law of Wickham! Every kind of pride must revolt from the connection. He had, to be sure, done much—she was ashamed to think how much. But he had given a reason for this interference, which asked no extraordinary stretch of belief. It was reasonable that he should feel he had been wrong; he had liberality, and he had the means of exercising it; and though she would not place herself as his principal inducement, she could, perhaps, believe that remaining partiality for her might assist his endeavours in a cause where her peace of mind must be materially concerned. It was painful, exceedingly painful, to know that they were under obligations to a person who could never receive a return. They owed the restoration of Lydia, her character, everything to him. Oh! how heartily did she grieve over every ungracious sensation she had ever encouraged, every saucy speech she had ever directed towards him. For herself, she was humbled; but she was proud of him. Proud that in a cause of compassion and honour he had been able to get the better of himself. She read over her aunt's commendation of him again and again. It was hardly enough; but it pleased her. She was even sensible of some pleasure, though mixed with regret, on finding how steadfastly both she and her uncle had been persuaded that affection and confidence subsisted between Mr. Darcy and herself.

She was roused from her seat and her reflections by someone's approach; and before she could strike into another path she was overtaken by Wickham.

"I am afraid I interrupt your solitary ramble, my dear sister," said he, as he joined her.

"You certainly do," she replied with a smile; "but it does not follow that the interruption must be unwelcome."

"I should be sorry indeed if it were. *We* were always good friends; and now we are better."

"True. Are the others coming out?"

"I do not know. Mrs. Bennet and Lydia are going in the carriage to Meryton. And so, my dear sister, I find from our uncle and aunt that you have actually seen Pemberley."

She replied in the affirmative.

"I almost envy you the pleasure, and yet I believe it would be too much for me, or else I could take it in my way to Newcastle. And you saw the old housekeeper, I suppose? Poor Reynolds, she was always very fond of me. But of course she did not mention my name to you."

"Yes, she did."

"And what did she say?"

"That you were gone into the army, and, she was afraid, had—not turned out well. At such a distance as *that*, you know, things are strangely misrepresented."

"Certainly," he replied, biting his lips.

Elizabeth hoped she had silenced him; but he soon afterwards said:

"I was surprised to see Darcy in town last month. We passed each other several times. I wonder what he can be doing there?"

"Perhaps preparing for his marriage with Miss de Bourgh," said Elizabeth. "It must be something particular to take him there at this time of year."

"Undoubtedly. Did you see him while you were at Lambton? I thought I understood from the Gardiners that you had."

"Yes; he introduced us to his sister."

"And do you like her?"

"Very much."

"I have heard, indeed, that she is uncommonly improved within this year or two. When I last saw her she was not very promising. I am very glad you liked her. I hope she will turn out well."

"I dare say she will; she has got over the most trying age."

"Did you go by the village of Kympton?"

"I do not recollect that we did."

"I mention it because it is the living which I ought to have had. A most delightful place! Excellent parsonage house! It would have suited me in every respect."

"How should you have liked making sermons?"

"Exceedingly well. I should have considered it as part of my duty, and the exertion would soon have been nothing. One ought not to repine; but, to be sure, it would have been such a thing for me! The quiet, the retirement of such a life, would have answered all my ideas of happiness! But it was not to be. Did you ever hear Darcy mention the circumstance when you were in Kent?"

"I *have* heard, from authority which I thought *as good,* that it was left you conditionally only, and at the will of the present patron."

"You have! Yes, there was something in *that;* I told you so from the first, you may remember."

"I *did* hear, too, that there was a time when sermon-making was not so palatable to you as it seems to be at present—that you actually declared your resolution of never taking orders, and that the business had been compromised accordingly."

"You did! And it was not wholly without foundation. You may remember what I told you on that point, when first we talked of it."

They were now almost at the door of the house, for she had walked fast to get rid of him, and, unwilling for her sister's sake, to provoke him, she only said in reply, with a good-humoured smile:

"Come, Mr. Wickham, we are brother and sister, you know. Do not let us quarrel about the past. In future, I hope we shall be always of one mind."

She held out her hand; he kissed it with affectionate gallantry, though he hardly knew how to look, and they entered the house.

Chapter 53

MR. WICKHAM was so perfectly satisfied with this conversation, that he never again distressed himself or provoked his dear sister Elizabeth by introducing the subject of it; and she was pleased to find that she had said enough to keep him quiet.

The day of his and Lydia's departure soon came, and Mrs. Bennet was forced to submit to a separation which, as her husband by no means entered into her scheme of their all going to Newcastle, was likely to continue at least a twelvemonth.

"Oh! my dear Lydia," she cried, "when shall we meet again?"

"Oh, Lord! I don't know. Not these two or three years, perhaps."

"Write to me very often, my dear."

"As often as I can. But you know married women have never much time for writing. My sisters may write to *me*. They will have nothing else to do."

Mr. Wickham's adieux were much more affectionate than his wife's. He smiled, looked handsome, and said many pretty things.

"He is as fine a fellow," said Mr. Bennet, as soon as they were out of the house, "as ever I saw. He simpers, and smirks, and makes love to us all. I am prodigiously proud of him. I defy even Sir William Lucas himself to produce a more valuable son-in-law."

The loss of her daughter made Mrs. Bennet very dull for several days.

"I often think," said she, "that there is nothing so bad as parting with one's friends. One seems so forlorn without them."

"This is the consequence, you see, madam, of marrying a daughter," said Elizabeth. "It must make you better satisfied that your other four are single."

"It is no such thing. Lydia does not leave me because she is married, but only because her husband's regiment happen to be so far off. If that had been nearer, she would not have gone so soon."

But the spiritless condition which this event threw her into was shortly relieved, and her mind opened again to the agitation of hope, by an article of news which then began to be in circulation. The housekeeper at Netherfield had received orders to prepare for the arrival of her master, who was coming down in a day or two, to shoot there for several weeks. Mrs. Bennet was quite in the fidgets. She looked at Jane, and smiled, and shook her head by turns.

"Well, well and so Mr. Bingley is coming down, sister" (for Mrs. Philips first brought the news). "Well, so much the better. Not that I care about it, though. He is nothing to us, you know, and I am sure I never want to see him again. But, however, he is very welcome to come to Netherfield, if he likes it. And who knows what *may* happen? But that is nothing to us. You know, sister, we agreed long ago never to mention a word about it. And so, is it quite certain he is coming?"

"You may depend on it," replied the other, "for Mrs. Nicholls was in Meryton last night: I saw her passing by, and went out myself on purpose to know the truth of it; and she told me that it was certainly true. He comes down on Thursday at the latest, very likely on Wednesday. She was going to the butcher's, she told me, on purpose to order in some meat on Wednesday, and she has got three couple of ducks just fit to be killed."

Miss Bennet had not been able to hear of his coming without changing colour. It was many months since she had mentioned his name to Elizabeth, but now, as soon as they were alone together, she said:

"I saw you look at me to-day, Lizzy, when my aunt told us of the present report; and I know I appeared distressed; but don't imagine it was from any silly cause. I was only confused for the moment, because I felt that I *should* be looked at. I do assure you that the news does not affect me either with pleasure or pain. I am glad of one thing—that he comes alone; because we shall see the less of him. Not that I am afraid of *myself*, but I dread other people's remarks."

Elizabeth did not know what to make of it. Had she not seen him in Derbyshire, she might have supposed him capable of coming there with no other view than what was acknowledged; but she still thought him partial to Jane, and she wavered as to the greater probability of his coming there *with* his friend's permission, or being bold enough to come without it.

"Yet it is hard," she sometimes thought, "that this poor man cannot come to a house which he has legally hired without raising all this speculation! I *will* leave him to himself."

In spite of what her sister declared, and really believed to be her feelings, in the expectation of his arrival, Elizabeth could easily perceive that her spirits were affected by it. They were more disturbed, more unequal, than she had often seen them.

The subject which had been so warmly canvassed between their parents about a twelvemonth ago was now brought forward again.

"As soon as ever Mr. Bingley comes, my dear," said Mrs. Bennet, "you will wait on him, of course."

"No, no. You forced me into visiting him last year, and promised, if I went to see him, he should marry one of my daughters. But it ended in nothing, and I will not be sent on a fool's errand again."

His wife represented to him how absolutely necessary such an attention would be from all the neighbouring gentlemen, on his returning to Netherfield.

" 'Tis an *etiquette* I despise," said he. "If he wants our society, let him seek it. He knows where we live. I will not spend *my* hours in running after my neighbours every time they go away and come back again."

"Well, all I know is, that it will be abominably rude if you do not wait on him. But, however, that shan't prevent my asking him to dine here, I am determined. We must have Mrs. Long and the Gouldings soon. That will make thirteen with ourselves, so there will be just room at table for him."

Consoled by this resolution, she was the better able to bear her husband's incivility; though it was very mortifying to know that her neighbours might all see Mr. Bingley, in consequence of it, before *they* did. As the day of his arrival drew near:

"I begin to be sorry that he comes at all," said Jane to her sister. "It would be nothing; I could see him with perfect indifference; but I can hardly bear to hear it thus perpetually talked of. My mother means well; but she does not know—no one can know—how much I suffer from what she says. Happy shall I be when his stay at Netherfield is over!"

"I wish I could say anything to comfort you," replied Elizabeth; "but it is wholly out of my power. You must feel it; and the usual satisfaction of preaching patience to a sufferer is denied me, because you have always so much."

Mr. Bingley arrived. Mrs. Bennet, through the assistance of servants, contrived to have the earliest tidings of it, that the period of anxiety and fretfulness on her side might be as long as it could. She counted the days that must intervene before their invitation could be sent—hopeless of seeing him before. But, on the third morning after his arrival in Hertfordshire, she saw him from her dressing-room window enter the paddock and ride towards the house.

Her daughters were eagerly called to partake of her joy. Jane resolutely kept her place at the table; but Elizabeth, to satisfy her mother, went to the window—she looked—she saw Mr. Darcy with him, and sat down again by her sister.

"There is a gentleman with him, mamma," said Kitty; "who can it be?"

"Some acquaintance or other, my dear, I suppose; I am sure I do not know."

"La!" replied Kitty, "it looks just like that man that used to be with him before—Mr. what's his name. That tall, proud man."

"Good gracious! Mr. Darcy! And so it does, I vow. Well, any friend of Mr. Bingley's will always be welcome here, to be sure; but else I must say that I hate the very sight of him."

Jane looked at Elizabeth with surprise and concern. She knew but little of their meeting in Derbyshire, and therefore felt for the awkwardness which must attend her sister, in seeing him almost for the first time after receiving his explanatory letter. Both sisters were uncomfortable enough. Each felt for the other, and of course for themselves; and their mother talked on, of her dislike of Mr. Darcy, and her resolution to be civil to him only as Mr. Bingley's friend, without being heard by either of them. But Elizabeth had sources of uneasiness which could not be suspected by Jane, to whom she had never yet had courage to show Mrs. Gardiner's letter, or to relate her own change of sentiment towards him. To Jane, he could be only a man whose proposals she had refused, and whose merit she had undervalued; but to her own more extensive information, he was the person to whom the whole family were indebted for the first of benefits, and whom she regarded herself with an interest, if not quite so tender, at least as reasonable and just as what Jane felt for Bingley. Her astonishment at his coming—at his coming to Netherfield, to Longbourn, and voluntarily seeking her again, was almost equal to what she had known on first witnessing his altered behaviour in Derbyshire.

The colour which had been driven from her face, returned for half a minute with an additional glow, and a smile of delight added lustre to her eyes, as she thought for that space of time, that his affection and wishes must still be unshaken. But she would not be secure.

"Let me first see how he behaves," said she; "it will then be early enough for expectations."

She sat intently at work striving to be composed, and without daring to lift up her eyes, till anxious curiosity carried them to the face of her sister, as the servant was approaching the door. Jane looked a little paler

than usual, but more sedate than Elizabeth had expected. On the gentlemen's appearing, her colour increased; yet she received them with tolerable ease, and with a propriety of behaviour equally free from any symptom of resentment, or any unnecessary complaisance.

Elizabeth said as little to either as civility would allow, and sat down
again to her work, with an eagerness which it did not often command.
She had ventured only one glance at Darcy. He looked serious as usual,
and, she thought, more as he had been used to look in Hertfordshire than
as she had seen him at Pemberley. But, perhaps, he could not in her
mother's presence be what he was before her uncle and aunt. It was a
painful, but not an improbable, conjecture.

Bingley she had likewise seen for an instant, and in that short period
saw him looking both pleased and embarrassed. He was received by Mrs.
Bennet with a degree of civility which made her two daughters ashamed,
especially when contrasted with the cold and ceremonious politeness of
her curtsey and address of his friend.

Elizabeth particularly, who knew that her mother owed to the latter
the preservation of her favourite daughter from irremediable infamy, was
hurt and distressed to a most painful degree by a distinction so ill-applied.

Darcy, after inquiring of her how Mr. and Mrs. Gardiner did—a question which she could not answer without confusion—said scarcely anything. He was not seated by her; perhaps that was the reason of his
silence; but it had not been so in Derbyshire. There he had talked to her
friends, when he could not to herself. But now several minutes elapsed,
without bringing the sound of his voice; and when occasionally, unable
to resist the impulse of curiosity, she raised her eyes to his face, she as
often found him looking at Jane as at herself, and frequently on no object
but the ground. More thoughtfulness, and less anxiety to please than
when they last met, were plainly expressed. She was disappointed, and
angry with herself for being so.

"Could I expect it to be otherwise!" said she. "Yet why did he come?"

She was in no humour for conversation with anyone but himself; and
to him she had hardly courage to speak.

She inquired after his sister, but could do no more.

"It is a long time, Mr. Bingley, since you went away," said Mrs. Bennet.

He readily agreed to it. "I began to be afraid you would never come
back again. People *did* say, you meant to quit the place entirely at
Michaelmas; but, however, I hope it is not true. A great many changes
have happened in the neighbourhood since you went away. Miss Lucas
is married and settled. And one of my own daughters. I suppose you have
heard of it; indeed, you must have seen it in the papers. It was in *The
Times* and the *Courier*, I know; though it was not put in as it ought to be.
It was only said, 'Lately, George Wickham, Esq., to Miss Lydia Bennet,'
without there being a syllable said of her father, or the place where she
lived, or anything. It was my brother Gardiner's drawing up too, and I

wonder how he came to make such an awkward business of it. Did you see it?"

Bingley replied that he did, and made his congratulations. Elizabeth dared not lift up her eyes. How Mr. Darcy looked, therefore, she could not tell.

"It is a delightful thing, to be sure, to have a daughter well married," continued her mother; "but, at the same time, Mr. Bingley, it is very hard to have her taken away from me. They are gone down to Newcastle, a place quite northward, it seems, and there they are to stay I do not know how long. His regiment is there; for I suppose you have heard of his leaving the ——shire, and of his being gone into the regulars. Thank Heaven; he has *some* friends, though, perhaps, not so many as he deserves."

Elizabeth, who knew this to be levelled at Mr. Darcy, was in such misery of shame that she could hardly keep her seat. It drew from her, however, the exertion of speaking, which nothing else had so effectually done before; and she asked Bingley whether he meant to make any stay in the country at present. A few weeks, he believed.

"When you have killed all your own birds, Mr. Bingley," said her mother, "I beg you will come here, and shoot as many as you please, on Mr. Bennet's manor. I am sure he will be vastly happy to oblige you, and will save all the best of the covies for you."

Elizabeth's misery increased at such unnecessary, such officious attention! Were the same fair prospect to arise at present as had flattered them a year ago, everything, she was persuaded, would be hastening to the same vexatious conclusions. At that instant she felt that years of happiness could not make Jane or herself amends for moments of such painful confusion.

"The first wish of my heart," said she to herself, "is never more to be in company with either of them. Their society can afford no pleasure that will atone for such wretchedness as this! Let me never see either one or the other again!"

Yet the misery, for which years of happiness were to offer no compensation, received soon afterwards material relief from observing how much the beauty of her sister rekindled the admiration of her former lover. When first he came in, he had spoken to her but little, but every five minutes seemed to be giving her more of his attention. He found her as handsome as she had been last year—as good-natured and as unaffected, though not quite so chatty. Jane was anxious that no difference should be perceived in her at all, and was really persuaded that she talked as much as ever. But her mind was so busily engaged that she did not always know when she was silent.

When the gentlemen rose to go away, Mrs. Bennet was mindful of her intended civility, and they were invited and engaged to dine at Longbourn in a few days' time.

"You are quite a visit in my debt, Mr. Bingley," she added; "for when you went to town last winter you promised to take a family dinner with us as soon as you returned. I have not forgot, you see; and I assure you I was very much disappointed that you did not come back and keep your engagement."

Bingley looked a little silly at this reflection, and said something of his concern at having been prevented by business. They then went away.

Mrs. Bennet had been strongly inclined to ask them to stay and dine there that day; but, though she always kept a very good table, she did not think anything less than two courses could be good enough for a man on whom she had such anxious designs, or satisfy the appetite and pride of one who had ten thousand a-year.

Chapter 54

As soon as they were gone Elizabeth walked out to recover her spirits, or, in other words, to dwell without interruption on those subjects that must deaden them more. Mr. Darcy's behaviour astonished and vexed her.

"Why, if he came only to be silent, grave, and indifferent," said she, "did he come at all?"

She could settle it in no way that gave her pleasure.

"He could be still amiable, still pleasing to my uncle and aunt, when he was in town; and why not to me? If he fears me, why come hither? If he no longer cares for me, why silent? Teasing, teasing man! I will think no more about him."

Her resolution was for a short time involuntarily kept by the approach of her sister, who joined her with a cheerful look, which showed her better satisfied with their visitors than Elizabeth.

"Now," said she, "that this first meeting is over, I feel perfectly easy. I know my own strength, and I shall never be embarrassed again by his coming. I am glad he dines here on Tuesday: it will then be publicly seen that on both sides we met only as common and indifferent acquaintances."

"Yes, very indifferent indeed," said Elizabeth, laughingly. "Oh, Jane! take care."

"My dear Lizzy, you cannot think me so weak as to be in danger now."

"I think you are in very great danger of making him as much in love with you as ever."

They did not see the gentlemen again till Tuesday; and Mrs. Bennet, in the meanwhile, was giving way to all the happy schemes which the good humour and common politeness of Bingley, in half-an-hour's visit, had revived.

On Tuesday there was a large party assembled at Longbourn; and the two, who were most anxiously expected, to the credit of their punctuality as sportsmen, were in very good time. When they repaired to the dining-room, Elizabeth eagerly watched to see whether Bingley would take the place which, in all their former parties, had belonged to him, by her sister. Her prudent mother, occupied by the same ideas, forbore to invite him to sit by herself. On entering the room, he seemed to hesitate; but Jane happened to look round, and happened to smile; it was decided—he placed himself by her.

Elizabeth, with a triumphant sensation, looked towards his friend. He bore it with noble indifference, and she would have imagined that Bingley had received his sanction to be happy, had she not seen his eyes likewise turned towards Mr. Darcy, with an expression of half-laughing alarm.

His behaviour to her sister was such, during dinnertime, as showed an admiration of her which, though more guarded than formerly, persuaded Elizabeth, that if left wholly to himself, Jane's happiness, and his own, would be speedily secured. Though she dared not depend upon the consequence, she yet received pleasure from observing his behaviour. It gave her all the animation that her spirits could boast; for she was in no cheerful humour. Mr. Darcy was almost as far from her as the table could divide them. He was on one side of her mother. She knew how little such a situation would give pleasure to either, or make either appear to advantage. She was not near enough to hear any of their discourse; but she could see how seldom they spoke to each other, and how formal and cold was their manner whenever they did. Her mother's ungraciousness made the sense of what they owed him more painful to Elizabeth's mind; and she would, at times, have given anything to be privileged to tell him that his kindness was neither unknown nor unfelt by the whole of the family.

She was in hopes that the evening would afford some opportunity of bringing them together; that the whole of the visit would not pass away without enabling them to enter into something more of conversation, than the mere ceremonious salutation attending his entrance. Anxious and uneasy, the period which passed in the drawing-room, before the gentlemen came, was wearisome and dull to a degree that almost made her uncivil. She looked forward to their entrance as the point on which all her chance of pleasure for the evening must depend.

"If he does not come to me *then*," said she, "I shall give him up for ever."

The gentlemen came; and she thought he looked as if he would have answered her hopes; but, alas! the ladies had crowded round the table, where Miss Bennet was making tea, and Elizabeth pouring out the coffee, in so close a confederacy, that there was not a single vacancy near her which would admit of a chair. And on the gentlemen's approaching, one of the girls moved closer to her than ever, and said, in a whisper:

"The men shan't come and part us, I am determined. We want none of them; do we?"

Darcy had walked away to another part of the room. She followed him with her eyes, envied every one to whom he spoke, had scarcely patience enough to help anybody to coffee, and then was enraged against herself for being so silly!

"A man who has once been refused! How could I ever be foolish enough to expect a renewal of his love? Is there one among the sex who would not protest against such a weakness as a second proposal to the same woman? There is no indignity so abhorrent to their feelings!"

She was a little revived, however, by his bringing back his coffee-cup himself; and she seized the opportunity of saying, "Is your sister at Pemberley still?"

"Yes, she will remain there till Christmas."

"And quite alone? Have all her friends left her?"

"Mrs. Annesley is with her. The others have been gone on to Scarborough these three weeks."

She could think of nothing more to say; but if he wished to converse with her, he might have better success. He stood by her, however, for some minutes, in silence; and, at last, on the young ladies whispering to Elizabeth again, he walked away.

When the tea-things were removed, and the card-tables placed, the ladies all rose, and Elizabeth was then hoping to be soon joined by him, when all her views were overthrown by seeing him fall a victim to her mother's rapacity for whist-players, and in a few moments after seated with the rest of the party. She now lost every expectation of pleasure. They were confined for the evening at different tables, and she had nothing to hope, but that his eyes were so often turned towards her side of the room, as to make him play as unsuccessfully as herself.

Mrs. Bennet had designed to keep the two Netherfield gentlemen to supper; but their carriage was unluckily ordered before any of the others, and she had no opportunity of detaining them.

"Well, girls," said she, as soon as they were left to themselves, "what say you to the day? I think everything has passed off uncommonly well, I assure you. The dinner was as well dressed as any I ever saw. The venison was roasted to a turn—and everybody said, they never saw so fat a haunch. The soup was fifty times better than what we had at the Lucases' last week; and even Mr. Darcy acknowledged that the partridges were remarkably well done; and I suppose he has two or three French cooks at least. And, my dear Jane, I never saw you look in greater beauty. Mrs. Long said so too, for I asked her whether you did not. And what do you think she said besides? 'Ah! Mrs. Bennet, we shall have her at Netherfield at last.' She did indeed. I do think Mrs. Long is as good a creature as ever lived—and her nieces are very pretty behaved girls, and not at all handsome: I like them prodigiously."

Mrs. Bennet, in short, was in very great spirits. She had seen enough of Bingley's behaviour to Jane, to be convinced that she would get him at last; and her expectations of advantage to her family, when in a happy humour, were so far beyond reason, that she was quite disappointed at not seeing him there again the next day to make his proposals.

"It has been a very agreeable day," said Miss Bennet to Elizabeth.

"The party seemed so well selected, so suitable one with the other. I hope we may often meet again."

Elizabeth smiled.

"Lizzy, you must not do so. You must not suspect me. It mortifies me. I assure you that I have now learnt to enjoy his conversation as an agreeable and sensible young man, without having a wish beyond it. I am perfectly satisfied from what his manners now are, that he never had any design of engaging my affection. It is only that he is blessed with greater sweetness of address, and a stronger desire of generally pleasing, than any other man."

"You are very cruel," said her sister; "you will not let me smile, and are provoking me to it every moment."

"How hard it is in some cases to be believed!"

"And how impossible in others!"

"But why should you wish to persuade me that I feel more than I acknowledge?"

"That is a question which I hardly know how to answer. We all love to instruct, though we can teach only what is not worth knowing. Forgive me; and if you persist in indifference, do not make *me* your confidante."

Chapter 55

A FEW days after this visit, Mr. Bingley called again, and alone. His friend had left him that morning for London, but was to return home in ten days' time. He sat with them above an hour, and was in remarkably good spirits. Mrs. Bennet invited him to dine with them; but, with many expressions of concern, he confessed himself engaged elsewhere.

"Next time you call," said she, "I hope we shall be more lucky."

He should be particularly happy at any time, etc., etc., and if she would give him leave, would take an early opportunity of waiting on them.

"Can you come to-morrow?"

Yes, he had no engagement at all for to-morrow; and her invitation was accepted with alacrity.

He came, and in such very good time, that the ladies were none of them dressed. In ran Mrs. Bennet to her daughters' room, in her dressing gown, and with her hair half finished, crying out, "My dear Jane, make haste and hurry down. He is come—Mr. Bingley is come. He is indeed. Make haste, make haste. Here, Sarah, come to Miss Bennet this moment, and help her on with her gown. Never mind Miss Lizzy's hair."

"We will be down as soon as we can," said Jane; "but I dare say Kitty is forwarder than either of us, for she went upstairs half an hour ago."

"Oh! hang Kitty! what has she to do with it! Come, be quick, be quick! where is your sash, my dear?"

But when her mother was gone, Jane would not be prevailed on to go down without one of her sisters.

The same anxiety to get them by themselves, was visible again in the evening. After tea, Mr. Bennet retired to the library, as was his custom, and Mary went upstairs to her instrument. Two obstacles of the five being thus removed, Mrs. Bennet sat looking and winking at Elizabeth and Catherine for a considerable time, without making any impression on them. Elizabeth would not observe her; and when at last Kitty did, she very innocently said, "What is the matter, mamma? What do you keep winking at me for? What am I to do?"

"Nothing, child, nothing. I did not wink at you."

She then sat still five minutes longer; but, unable to waste such a precious occasion, she suddenly got up, and saying to Kitty, "Come here, my love, I want to speak to you," took her out of the room. Jane instantly gave a look at Elizabeth, which spoke her distress at such premeditation, and her entreaty that *she* would not give in to it.

In a few minutes, Mrs. Bennet half opened the door, and called out, "Lizzy, my dear, I want to speak with you."

Elizabeth was forced to go. "We may as well leave them by themselves, you know," said her mother as soon as she was in the hall. "Kitty and I are going upstairs to sit in my dressing-room."

Elizabeth made no attempt to reason with her mother, but remained quietly in the hall till she and Kitty were out of sight, then returned into the drawing-room.

Mrs. Bennet's schemes for this day were ineffectual. Bingley was everything that was charming, except the professed lover of her daughter. His ease and cheerfulness rendered him a most agreeable addition to their evening party; and he bore with the ill-judged officiousness of the mother, and heard all her silly remarks with a forbearance and command of countenance particularly grateful to the daughter.

He scarcely needed an invitation to stay to supper; and before he went away, an engagement was formed, chiefly through his own and Mrs. Bennet's means, for his coming next morning to shoot with her husband.

After this day, Jane said no more of her indifference. Not a word passed between the sisters concerning Bingley; but Elizabeth went to bed in the happy belief that all must speedily be concluded, unless Mr. Darcy returned within the stated time. Seriously, however, she felt tolerably persuaded that all this must have taken place with that gentleman's concurrence.

Bingley was punctual to his appointment; and he and Mr. Bennet spent the morning together, as had been agreed on. The latter was much more agreeable than his companion expected. There was nothing of presumption or folly in Bingley, that could provoke his ridicule, or disgust him into silence; and he was more communicative and less eccentric than the other had ever seen him. Bingley, of course, returned with him to dinner; and in the evening Mrs. Bennet's invention was again at work to get everybody away from him and her daughter. Elizabeth, who had a letter to write, went into the breakfast room for that purpose soon after tea; for as the others were all going to sit down to cards, she could not be wanted to counteract her mother's schemes.

But on returning to the drawing-room when her letter was finished, she saw, to her infinite surprise, there was reason to fear that her mother had been too ingenious for her. On opening the door, she perceived her sister and Bingley standing together over the hearth as if engaged in earnest conversation; and had this led to no suspicion, the faces of both, as they hastily turned round and moved away from each other, would have told it all. *Their* situation was awkward enough; but *hers*, she thought, was still worse. Not a syllable was uttered by either; and Elizabeth was on the point of going away again, when Bingley, who as well as the other had sat down, suddenly rose, and whispering a few words to her sister, ran out of the room.

Jane could have no reserves from Elizabeth, where confidence would give pleasure; and instantly embracing her, acknowledged with the liveliest emotion, that she was the happiest creature in the world.

" 'Tis too much," she added, "by far too much. I do not deserve it. Oh! why is not everybody as happy!"

Elizabeth's congratulations were given with a sincerity, a warmth, a delight, which words could but poorly express. Every sentence of kindness was a fresh source of happiness to Jane. But she would not allow nerself to stay with her sister, or say half that remained to be said, for the present.

"I must go instantly to my mother," she cried; "I would not on any account trifle with her affectionate solicitude, or allow her to hear it from any one but myself. He is gone to my father already. Oh! Lizzy, to know that what I have to relate will give such pleasure to all my dear family! how shall I bear so much happiness!"

She then hastened away to her mother, who had purposely broken up the card party, and was sitting upstairs with Kitty.

Elizabeth, who was left by herself, now smiled at the rapidity and case with which an affair was finally settled that had given them so many previous months of suspense and vexation.

"And this," said she, "is the end of all his friend's anxious circumspection! of all his sister's falsehood and contrivance! the happiest, wisest, and most reasonable end!"

In a few minutes she was joined by Bingley, whose conference with her father had been short and to the purpose.

"Where is your sister?" said he hastily, as he opened the door.

"With my mother upstairs. She will be down in a moment, I dare say."

He then shut the door, and coming up to her, claimed the good wishes and affection of a sister. Elizabeth honestly and heartily expressed her delight in the prospect of their relationship. They shook hands with great cordiality; and then till her sister came down, she had to listen to all he had to say of his own happiness, and of Jane's perfections; and in spite of his being a lover, Elizabeth really believed all his expectations of felicity to be rationally founded, because they had for basis the excellent understanding and super-excellent disposition of Jane, and a general similarity of feeling and taste between her and himself.

It was an evening of no common delight to them all. The satisfaction of Miss Bennet's mind gave such a glow of sweet animation to her face, as made her look handsomer than ever. Kitty simpered and smiled, and hoped her turn was coming soon. Mrs. Bennet could not give her consent or speak her approbation in terms warm enough to satisfy her feelings, though she talked to Bingley of nothing else for half-an-hour, and when Mr. Bennet joined them at supper, his voice and manner plainly showed how really happy he was.

Not a word, however, passed his lips in allusion to it, till their visitor took his leave for the night; but as soon as he was gone, he turned to his daughter and said:

"Jane, I congratulate you. You will be a very happy woman."

Jane went to him instantly, kissed him, and thanked him for his goodness.

"You are a good girl," he replied, "and I have great pleasure in thinking you will be so happily settled. I have not a doubt of your doing very well together. Your tempers are by no means unlike. You are each of you so complying, that nothing will ever be resolved on; so easy, that every servant will cheat you; and so generous, that you will always exceed your income."

"I hope not so. Imprudence or thoughtlessness in money matters would be unpardonable in *me*."

"Exceed their income! My dear Mr. Bennet," cried his wife, "what are you talking of? Why, he has four or five thousand a-year, and very likely more." Then addressing her daughter, "Oh! my dear, dear Jane, I am so happy, I am sure I shan't get a wink of sleep all night. I knew how it would be. I always said it must be so, at last. I was sure you could not be so beautiful for nothing! I remember, as soon as ever I saw him, when he first came into Hertfordshire last year, I thought how likely it was that you should come together. Oh! he is the handsomest young man that ever was seen!"

Wickham, Lydia, were all forgotten. Jane was beyond competition her favourite child. At that moment she cared for no other. Her younger sisters soon began to make interest with her for objects of happiness which she might in future be able to dispense.

Mary petitioned for the use of the library at Netherfield; and Kitty begged very hard for a few balls there every winter.

Bingley, from this time, was of course a daily visitor at Longbourn, coming frequently before breakfast, and always remaining till after supper, unless when some barbarous neighbour, who could not be enough detested, had given him an invitation to dinner, which he thought himself obliged to accept.

Elizabeth had now but little time for conversation with her sister; for while he was present, Jane had no attention to bestow on any one else; but she found herself considerably useful to both of them, in those hours of separation that must sometimes occur. In the absence of Jane, he always attached himself to Elizabeth for the pleasure of talking to her; and when Bingley was gone, Jane constantly sought the same means of relief.

"He has made me so happy," said she, one evening, "by telling me, that he was totally ignorant of my being in town last spring! I had not believed it possible."

"I suspected as much," replied Elizabeth. "But how did he account for it?"

"It must have been his sisters' doing. They were certainly no friends to his acquaintance with me, which I cannot wonder at, since he might have chosen so much more advantageously in many respects. But when they see, as I trust they will, that their brother is happy with me, they will learn to be contented, and we shall be on good terms again; though we can never be what we once were to each other."

"That is the most unforgiving speech," said Elizabeth, "that I ever heard you utter. Good girl! It would vex me, indeed, to see you again the dupe of Miss Bingley's pretended regard!"

"Would you believe it, Lizzy, that when he went to town last November, he really loved me, and nothing but a persuasion of *my* being indifferent would have prevented his coming down again!"

"He made a little mistake, to be sure; but it is to the credit of his modesty."

This naturally introduced a panegyric from Jane on his diffidence, and the little value he put on his own good qualities.

Elizabeth was pleased to find that he had not betrayed the interference of his friend; for, though Jane had the most generous and forgiving heart in the world, she knew it was a circumstance which must prejudice her against him.

"I am certainly the most fortunate creature that ever existed!" cried Jane. "Oh! Lizzy, why am I thus singled from my family, and blessed above them all! If I could but see *you* as happy! If there *were* but such another man for you!"

"If you were to give me forty such men, I never could be so happy as you. Till I have your disposition, your goodness, I never can have your happiness. No, no, let me shift for myself; and perhaps, if I have very good luck, I may meet with another Mr. Collins in time."

The situation of affairs in the Longbourn family could not be long a secret. Mrs. Bennet was privileged to whisper it to Mrs. Philips, and *she* ventured, without any permission, to do the same by all her neighbours in Meryton.

The Bennets were speedily pronounced to be the luckiest family in the world, though only a few weeks before, when Lydia had first run away, they had been generally proved to be marked out for misfortune.

Chapter 56

ONE morning, about a week after Bingley's engagement with Jane had been formed, as he and the females of the family were sitting together in the breakfast-room, their attention was suddenly drawn to the window, by the sound of a carriage; and they perceived a chaise-and-four driving up the lawn. It was too early in the morning for visitors, and besides, the equipage did not answer to that of any of their neighbours. The horses were post; and neither the carriage nor the livery of the servant who preceded it, were familiar to them. As it was certain, however, that somebody was coming, Bingley instantly prevailed on Miss Bennet to avoid the confinement of such an intrusion, and walk away with him into the shrubbery. They both set off, and the conjecture of the remaining three continued, though with little satisfaction, till the door was thrown open, and their visitor entered. It was Lady Catherine de Bourgh.

They were of course all intending to be surprised; but their astonishment was beyond their expectation; and on the part of Mrs. Bennet and Kitty, though she was perfectly unknown to them, even inferior to what Elizabeth felt.

She entered the room with an air more than usually ungracious, made no other reply to Elizabeth's salutation than a slight inclination of the head, and sat down without saying a word. Elizabeth had mentioned her name to her mother on her ladyship's entrance, though no request of introduction had been made.

Mrs. Bennet, all amazement, though flattered by having a guest of such high importance, received her with the utmost politeness. After sitting for a moment in silence, she said very stiffly to Elizabeth:

"I hope you are well, Miss Bennet. That lady, I suppose, is your mother?"

Elizabeth replied very concisely that she was.

"And *that*, I suppose, is one of your sisters?"

"Yes, madam," said Mrs. Bennet, delighted to speak to a Lady Catherine. "She is my youngest girl but one, my youngest of all is lately married, and my eldest is somewhere about the ground, walking with a young man, who, I believe, will soon become a part of the family."

"You have a very small park here," returned Lady Catherine, after a short silence.

"It is nothing in comparison of Rosings, my lady, I dare say; but, I assure you, it is much larger than Sir William Lucas's."

"This must be a most inconvenient sitting-room for the evening in summer: the windows are full west."

Mrs. Bennet assured her that they never sat there after dinner, and then added:

"May I take the liberty of asking your ladyship whether you left Mr. and Mrs. Collins well?"

"Yes, very well. I saw them the night before last."

Elizabeth now expected that she would produce a letter for her from Charlotte, as it seemed the only probable motive for her calling. But no letter appeared, and she was completely puzzled.

Mrs. Bennet, with great civility, begged her ladyship to take some refreshment; but Lady Catherine very resolutely and not very politely, declined eating anything; and then rising up, said to Elizabeth:

"Miss Bennet, there seemed to be a prettyish kind of a little wilderness on one side of your lawn. I should be glad to take a turn in it, if you will favour me with your company."

"Go, my dear," cried her mother, "and show her ladyship about the different walks. I think she will be pleased with the hermitage."

Elizabeth obeyed, and, running into her own room for her parasol, attended her noble guest downstairs. As they passed through the hall, Lady Catherine opened the doors into the dining-parlour and drawing-room, and pronouncing them, after a short survey, to be decent-looking rooms, walked on.

Her carriage remained at the door, and Elizabeth saw that her waiting-woman was in it. They proceeded in silence along the gravel-walk that led to the copse; Elizabeth was determined to make no effort for conversation with a woman who was now more than usually insolent and disagreeable.

"How could I ever think her like her nephew?" said she, as she looked in her face.

As soon as they entered the copse, Lady Catherine began in the following manner:—

"You can be at no loss, Miss Bennet, to understand the reason of my journey hither. Your own heart, your own conscience, must tell you why I come."

Elizabeth looked with unaffected astonishment.

"Indeed, you are mistaken, madam. I have not been at all able to account for the honour of seeing you here."

"Miss Bennet," replied her ladyship, in an angry tone, "you ought to know that I am not to be trifled with. But, however insincere *you* may choose to be, you shall not find *me* so. My character has ever been celebrated for its sincerity and frankness, and in a cause of such moment as this I shall certainly not depart from it. A report of a most alarming nature reached me two days ago. I was told that not only your sister was on the point of being most advantageously married, but that *you,* that Miss Elizabeth Bennet, would, in all likelihood, be soon afterwards united to my nephew—my own nephew—Mr. Darcy. Though I *know* it must be a scandalous falsehood—though I would not injure him so much as to suppose the truth of it possible, I instantly resolved on setting off for this place, that I might make my sentiments known to you."

"If you believed it impossible to be true," said Elizabeth, colouring with astonishment and disdain, "I wonder you took the trouble of coming so far. What could your ladyship propose by it?"

"At once to insist upon having such a report universally contradicted."

"Your coming to Longbourn, to see me and my family," said Elizabeth coolly, "will be rather a confirmation of it; if, indeed, such a report is in existence."

"If! do you, then, pretend to be ignorant of it? Has it not been industriously circulated by yourselves? Do you not know that such a report is spread abroad?"

"I never heard that it was."

"And can you likewise declare, that there is no *foundation* for it?"

"I do not pretend to possess equal frankness with your ladyship. *You* may ask questions, which *I* shall not choose to answer."

"This is not to be borne! Miss Bennet, I insist on being satisfied. Has he, has my nephew, made you an offer of marriage?"

"Your ladyship has declared it to be impossible."

"It ought to be so; it must be so, while he retains the use of his reason. But *your* arts and allurements may, in a moment of infatuation, have made him forget what he owes to himself and to all his family. You may have drawn him in."

"If I have, I shall be the last person to confess it."

"Miss Bennet, do you know who I am? I have not been accustomed to such language as this. I am almost the nearest relation he has in the world, and am entitled to know all his dearest concerns."

"But you are not entitled to know *mine;* nor will such behaviour as this ever induce me to be explicit."

"Let me be rightly understood. This match, to which you have the presumption to aspire, can never take place. No, never. Mr. Darcy is engaged to *my daughter*. Now, what have you to say?"

"Only this: that if he is so, you can have no reason to suppose he will make an offer to me."

Lady Catherine hesitated for a moment, and then replied:

"The engagement between them is of a peculiar kind. From their infancy, they have been intended for each other. It was the favourite wish of *his* mother, as well as of hers. While in their cradles, we planned the union: and now, at the moment when the wishes of both sisters would be accomplished in their marriage, to be prevented by a young woman of inferior birth, of no importance in the world, and wholly unallied to the family! Do you pay no regard to the wishes of his friends—to his tacit engagement with Miss de Bourgh? Are you lost to every feeling of propriety and delicacy? Have you not heard me say that from his earliest hours he was destined for his cousin?"

"Yes, and I had heard it before. But what is that to me? If there is no other objection to my marrying your nephew, I shall certainly not be kept from it by knowing that his mother and aunt wished him to marry Miss de Bourgh. You both did as much as you could, in planning the marriage; its completion depended on others. If Mr. Darcy is neither by honour nor inclination confined to his cousin, why is not he to make another choice? and if I am that choice, why may I not accept him?"

"Because honour, decorum, prudence—nay, interest, forbid it. Yes, Miss Bennet, interest; for do not expect to be noticed by his family or friends if you wilfully act against the inclinations of all. You will be censured, slighted, and despised by every one connected with him. Your alliance will be a disgrace; your name will never even be mentioned by any of us."

"These are heavy misfortunes," replied Elizabeth. "But the wife of Mr. Darcy must have such extraordinary sources of happiness necessarily attached to her situation, that she could, upon the whole, have no cause to repine."

"Obstinate, headstrong girl! I am ashamed of you! Is this your gratitude for my attentions to you last spring? Is nothing due to me on that score? Let us sit down. You are to understand, Miss Bennet, that I came here with the determined resolution of carrying my purpose; nor will I be dissuaded from it. I have not been used to submit to any person's whims. I have not been in the habit of brooking disappointment."

"*That* will make your ladyship's situation at present more pitiable: but it will have no effect on *me*."

"I will not be interrupted! Hear me in silence. My daughter and my nephew are formed for each other. They are descended, on the maternal side, from the same noble line; and, on the fathers', from respectable, honourable, and ancient, though untitled families. Their fortune on both sides is splended. They are destined for each other by the voice of every member of their respective houses; and what is to divide them? The upstart pretensions of a young woman without family, connections, or fortune. Is this to be endured? But it must not, shall not be! If you were sensible of your own good, you would not wish to quit the sphere in which you have been brought up."

"In marrying your nephew I should not consider myself as quitting that sphere. He is a gentleman; I am a gentleman's daughter: so far we are equal."

"True. You *are* a gentleman's daughter. But who was your mother? Who are your uncles and aunts? Do not imagine me ignorant of their condition."

"Whatever my connections may be," said Elizabeth, "if your nephew does not object to them, they can be nothing to *you*."

"Tell me, once for all, are you engaged to him?"

Though Elizabeth would not, for the mere purpose of obliging Lady Catherine, have answered this question, she could not but say, after a moment's delberation, "I am not."

Lady Catherine seemed pleased.

"And will you promise me never to enter into such an engagement?"

"I will make no promise of the kind."

"Miss Bennet, I am shocked and astonished. I expected to find a more reasonable young woman. But do not deceive yourself into a belief that I will ever recede. I shall not go away till you have given me the assurance I require."

"And I certainly *never* shall give it. I am not to be intimidated into anything so wholly unreasonable. Your ladyship wants Mr. Darcy to marry your daughter; but would my giving you the wished-for promise make *their* marriage at all more probable? Supposing him to be attached to me, would *my* refusing to accept his hand make him wish to bestow it on his cousin? Allow me to say, Lady Catherine, that the arguments with which you have supported this extraordinary application have been as frivolous as the application was ill-judged. You have widely mistaken my character, if you think I can be worked on by such persuasions as these. How far your nephew might approve of your interference in *his* affairs I cannot tell; but you have certainly no right to concern yourself in mine. I must beg, therefore, to be importuned no farther on the subject."

"Not so hasty, if you please. I have by no means done. To all the objections I have already urged, I have still another to add. I am no stranger to the particulars of your youngest sister's infamous elopement. I know it all; that the young man's marrying her was a patched-up business, at the expense of your father and uncle. And is *such* a girl to be my nephew's sister? Is *her* husband, who is the son of his late father's steward, to be his brother? Heaven and earth—of what are you thinking? Are the shades of Pemberley to be thus polluted?"

"You can *now* have nothing further to say," Elizabeth resentfully answered. "You have insulted me in every possible method. I must beg to return to the house."

And she rose as she spoke. Lady Catherine rose also, and they turned back. Her ladyship was highly incensed.

"You have no regard, then, for the honour and credit of my nephew! Unfeeling, selfish girl! Do you not consider that a connection with you must disgrace him in the eye of everybody?"

"Lady Catherine, I have nothing further to say. You know my sentiments."

"You are, then, resolved to have him?"

"I have said no such thing. I am only resolved to act in that manner which will, in my own opinion, constitute my happiness, without reference to *you*, or to any person so wholly unconnected with me."

"It is well. You refuse, then, to oblige me. You refuse to obey the claims of duty, honour, and gratitude. You are determined to ruin him in the opinion of all his friends, and make him the contempt of the world."

"Neither duty, nor honour, nor gratitude," replied Elizabeth, "has any possible claim on me in the present instance. No principle of either would be violated by my marriage with Mr. Darcy. And with regard to the resentment of his family or the indignation of the world, if the former *were* excited by his marrying me, it would not give me one moment's concern and the world in general would have too much sense to join in the scorn."

"And this is your real opinion! This is your final resolve! Very well. I shall now know how to act. Do not imagine, Miss Bennet, that your ambition will ever be gratified. I came to try you. I hoped to find you reasonable; but, depend upon it, I will carry my point."

In this manner Lady Catherine talked on, till they were at the door of the carriage, when, turning hastily round, she added:

"I take no leave of you, Miss Bennet. I send no compliments to your mother. You deserve no such attention. I am seriously displeased."

Elizabeth made no answer, and, without attempting to persuade her ladyship to return into the house, walked quietly into it herself. She heard the carriage drive away as she proceeded upstairs. Her mother impatiently met her at the door of the dressing-room, to ask why Lady Catherine would not come in again and rest herself.

"She did not choose it," said her daughter; "she would go."

"She is a very fine-looking woman! and her calling here was prodigiously civil! for she only came, I suppose, to tell us the Collinses were well. She is on her road somewhere, I dare say, and so, passing through Meryton, thought she might as well call on you. I suppose she had nothing particular to say to you, Lizzy?"

Elizabeth was forced to give in to a little falsehood here; for to acknowledge the substance of their conversation was impossible.

Chapter 57

The discomposure of spirts which this extraordinary visit threw Elizabeth into could not be easily overcome, nor could she for many hours learn to think of it less than incessantly. Lady Catherine, it appeared, had actually taken the trouble of this journey from Rosings for the sole purpose of breaking off her supposed engagement with Mr. Darcy. It was a rational scheme, to be sure; but from what the report of their engagement could originate, Elizabeth was at a loss to imagine; till she recollected that *his* being the intimate friend of Bingley, and *her* being the sister of Jane, was enough, at a time when the expectation of one wedding made everybody eager for another, to supply the idea. She had not herself forgotten to feel that the marriage of her sister must bring them more frequently together. And her neighbours at Lucas Lodge, therefore (for through their communication with the Collinses the report, she concluded, had reached Lady Catherine), had only set *that* down as almost certain and immediate, which *she* had looked forward to as possible, at some future time.

In revolving Lady Catherine's expressions, however, she could not help feeling some uneasiness as to the possible consequence of her persisting in this interference. From what she had said of her resolution to prevent their marriage, it occurred to Elizabeth that she must meditate an application to her nephew; and how *he* might take a similar representation of the evils attached to a connection with her, she dared not pronounce. She knew not the exact degree of his affection for his aunt, or his dependence on her judgment, but it was natural to suppose that he thought much higher of her ladyship than *she* could do; and it was certain that, in enumerating the miseries of a marriage with *one* whose immediate connections were so unequal to his own, his aunt would address him on his weakest side. With his notions of dignity, he would probably feel that the arguments which to Elizabeth had appeared weak and ridiculous, contained much good sense and solid reasoning.

If he had been wavering before as to what he should do, which had often seemed likely, the advice and entreaty of so near a relation might settle every doubt, and determine him at once to be as happy as dignity unblemished could make him. In that case, he would return no more. Lady Catherine might see him in her way through town, and his engagement to Bingley of coming again to Netherfield must give way.

"If, therefore, an excuse for not keeping his promise should come to his friend within a few days," she added, "I shall know how to understand it. I shall then give over every expectation, every wish of his constancy. If he is satisfied with only regretting me, when he might have obtained my affections and hand, I shall soon cease to regret him at all."

The surprise of the rest of the family, on hearing who their visitor had been, was very great; but they obligingly satisfied it with the same kind of supposition which had appeased Mrs. Bennet's curiosity; and Elizabeth was spared from much teasing on the subject.

The next morning, as she was going downstairs, she was met by her father, who came out of his library with a letter in his hand.

"Lizzy," said he, "I was going to look for you; come into my room."

She followed him thither; and her curiosity to know what he had to tell her was heightened by the supposition of its being in some manner connected with the letter he held. It suddenly struck her that it might be from Lady Catherine; and she anticipated with dismay all the consequent explanations.

She followed her father to the fireplace, and they both sat down. He then said:

"I have received a letter this morning that has astonished me exceedingly. As it principally concerns yourself, you ought to know its contents. I did not know before that I had *two* daughters on the brink of matrimony. Let me congratulate you on a very important conquest."

The colour now rushed into Elizabeth's cheeks in the instantaneous conviction of its being a letter from the nephew, instead of the aunt; and she was undetermined whether most to be pleased that he explained himself at all or offended that his letter was not rather addressed to herself; when her father continued:

"You look conscious. Young ladies have great penetration in such matters as these! but I think I may defy even *your* sagacity to discover the name of your admirer. This letter is from Mr. Collins."

"From Mr. Collins! and what can *he* have to say?"

"Something very much to the purpose, of course. He begins with congratulations on the approaching nuptials of my eldest daughter, of which it seems he has been told, by some of the good-natured, gossiping Lucases. I shall not sport with your impatience by reading what he says on that point. What relates to yourself is as follows: 'Having thus offered you the sincere congratulations of Mrs. Collins and myself on this happy event, let me now add a short hint on the subject of another; for which we have been advertised by the same authority. Your daughter Elizabeth, it is presumed, will not long bear the name of Bennet, after her elder sister has resigned it, and the chosen partner of her fate may be reasonably looked up to as one of the most illustrious personages in this land.'

"Can you possibly guess, Lizzy, who is meant by this? '—This young gentleman is blessed, in a peculiar way, with everything the heart of mortal can most desire, splendid property, noble kindred, and extensive patronage. Yet, in spite of all these temptations, let me warn my cousin Elizabeth, and yourself, of what evils you may incur by a precipitate closure with this gentleman's proposals, which, of course, you will be inclined to take immediate advantage of.'

"Have you any idea, Lizzy, who this gentleman is? But now it comes out:

" 'My motive for cautioning you is as follows: we have reason to imagine that his aunt, Lady Catherine de Bourgh, does not look on the match with a friendly eye.'

"*Mr. Darcy,* you see, is the man! Now, Lizzy, I think I *have* surprised you. Could he or the Lucases have pitched on any man, within the circle of our acquaintances, whose name would have given the lie more effectually to what they related? Mr. Darcy, who never looks at any woman but to see a blemish, and who probably never looked at *you* in his life? It is admirable!"

Elizabeth tried to join in her father's pleasantry, but could only force one most reluctant smile. Never had his wit been directed in a manner so little agreeable to her.

"Are you not diverted?"

"Oh! yes. Pray read on."

" 'After mentioning the likelihood of this marriage to her ladyship last night, she immediately, with her usual condescension, expressed what she felt on the occasion; when it became apparent, that on the score of some family objections on the part of my cousin, she would never give her consent to what she termed so disgraceful a match. I thought it my duty to give the speediest intelligence of this to my cousin, that she and her noble admirer may be aware of what they are about, and not run hastily into a marriage which has not been properly sanctioned.' Mr. Collins, moreover adds, 'I am truly rejoiced that my cousin Lydia's sad business has been so well hushed up, and am only concerned that their living together before the marriage took place should be so generally known. I must not, however, neglect the duties of my station, or refrain from declaring my amazement, at hearing that you received the young couple into your house as soon as they were married. It was an encouragement of vice; and had I been the rector of Longbourn, I should very strenuously have opposed it. You ought certainly to forgive them, as a Christian, but never to admit them in your sight, or allow their names to be mentioned in your hearing.' *That* is his notion of Christian forgiveness! The rest of his letter is only about his dear Charlotte's situation, and his expectation of a young olive-branch. But, Lizzy, you look as if you did not enjoy it. You are not going to be *missish,* I hope, and pretend to be affronted at an idle report. For what do we live, but to make sport for our neighbours, and laugh at them in our turn?"

"Oh!" cried Elizabeth, "I am excessively diverted. But it is so strange!"

"Yes—*that* is what makes it amusing. Had they fixed on any other man, it would have been nothing; but *his* perfect indifference, and *your* pointed dislike, make it so delightfully absurd! Much as I abominate writing, I would not give up Mr. Collins's correspondence for any consideration. Nay, when I read a letter of his, I cannot help giving him the preference even over Wickham, much as I value the impudence and hypocrisy of my son-in-law. And pray, Lizzy, what said Lady Catherine about this report? Did she call to refuse her consent?"

To this question his daughter replied only with a laugh; and as it had been asked without the least suspicion, she was not distressed by his repeating it. Elizabeth had never been more at a loss to make her feelings appear what they were not. It was necessary to laugh, when she would rather have cried. Her father had most cruelly mortified her by what he said of Mr. Darcy's indifference, and she could do nothing but wonder at such a want of penetration, or fear that, perhaps, instead, of his seeing too *little,* she might have fancied too *much.*

Chapter 58

INSTEAD of receiving any such letter of excuse from his friend, as Elizabeth half expected Mr. Bingley to do, he was able to bring Darcy with him to Longbourn before many days had passed after Lady Catherine's visit. The gentlemen arrived early; and before Mrs. Bennet had time to tell him of their having seen his aunt, of which her daughter sat in momentary dread, Bingley, who wanted to be alone with Jane, proposed their all walking out. It was agreed to. Mrs. Bennet was not in the habit of walking. Mary could never spare time, but the remaining five set off together. Bingley and Jane, however, soon allowed the others to outstrip them. They lagged behind, while Elizabeth, Kitty, and Darcy were to entertain each other. Very little was said by either: Kitty was too much afraid of him to talk; Elizabeth was secretly forming a desperate resolution; and, perhaps he might be doing the same.

They walked towards the Lucases, because Kitty wished to call upon Maria; and as Elizabeth saw no occasion for making it a general concern, when Kitty left them she went boldly on with him alone. Now was the moment for her resolution to be executed; and, while her courage was high, she immediately said:

"Mr. Darcy, I am a very selfish creature; and for the sake of giving relief to my own feelings, care not how much I may be wounding yours. I can no longer help thanking you for your unexampled kindness to my poor sister. Ever since I have known it, I have been most anxious to acknowledge to you how gratefully I feel it. Were it known to the rest of my family, I should not have merely my own gratitude to express."

"I am sorry, exceedingly sorry," replied Darcy, in a tone of surprise and emotion, "that you have ever been informed of what may, in a mistaken light, have given you uneasiness, I did not think Mrs. Gardiner was so little to be trusted."

"You must not blame my aunt. Lydia's thoughtlessness first betrayed to me that you had been concerned in the matter; and, of course, I could not rest till I knew the particulars. Let me thank you again and again, in the name of all my family, for that generous compassion which induced you to take so much trouble and bear so many mortifications, for the sake of discovering them."

"If you *will* thank me," he replied, "let it be for yourself alone. That the wish of giving happiness to you might add force to the other inducements which led me on, I shall not attempt to deny. But your *family* owe me nothing. Much as I respect them, I believe I thought only of *you*."

Elizabeth was too much embarrassed to say a word. After a short pause, her companion added, "You are too generous to trifle with me. If your feelings are still what they were last April, tell me so at once. *My* affections and wishes are unchanged; but one word from you will silence me on this subject for ever."

Elizabeth, feeling all the more than common awkwardness and anxiety of his situation, now forced herself to speak; and immediately, though not very fluently, gave him to understand that her sentiments had undergone so material a change since the period to which he alluded, as to make her receive with gratitude and pleasure his present assurances. The happiness which this reply produced was such as he had probably never felt before, and he expressed himself on the occasion as sensibly and as warmly as a man violently in love can be supposed to do. Had Elizabeth been able to encounter his eyes, she might have seen how well the expression of heartfelt delight diffused over his face became him; but, though she could not look, she could listen, and he told her of feelings which, in proving of what importance she was to him, made his affection every moment more valuable.

They walked on, without knowing in what direction. There was too much to be thought, and felt, and said, for attention to any other objects. She soon learnt that they were indebted for their present good understanding to the efforts of his aunt, who *did* call on him in her return through London, and there relate her journey to Longbourn, its motive, and the substance of her conversation with Elizabeth; dwelling emphatically on every expression of the latter which, in her ladyship's apprehension, peculiarly denoted her perverseness and assurance, in the belief that such a relation must assist her endeavours to obtain that promise from her nephew which *she* had refused to give. But unluckily for her ladyship, its effect had been exactly contrarywise.

"It taught me to hope," said he, "as I had scarcely ever allowed myself to hope before. I knew enough of your disposition to be certain, that had you been absolutely, irrevocably decided against me, you would have acknowledged it to Lady Catherine, frankly and openly."

Elizabeth coloured and laughed as she replied, "Yes, you know enough of my *frankness* to believe me capable of *that*. After abusing you so abominably to your face, I could have no scruple in abusing you to all your relations."

"What did you say of me that I did not deserve? For, though your accusations were ill-founded, formed on mistaken premises, my behaviour to you at the time had merited the severest reproof. It was unpardonable. I cannot think of it without abhorrence."

"We will not quarrel for the greater share of blame annexed to that evening," said Elizabeth; "the conduct of neither, if strictly examined, will be irreproachable. But since then we have both, I hope, improved in civility."

"I cannot be so easily reconciled to myself. The recollection of what I then said—of my conduct, my manners, my expressions during the whole of it—is now, and has been many months, inexpressibly painful to me. Your reproof, so well applied, I shall never forget: 'Had you behaved in a more gentlemanlike manner.' Those were your words. You know not, you can scarcely conceive, how they have tortured me; though it was some time, I confess, before I was reasonable enough to allow their justice."

"I was certainly very far from expecting them to make so strong an impression. I had not the smallest idea of their being ever felt in such a way."

"I can easily believe it. You thought me then devoid of every proper feeling; I am sure you did. The turn of your countenance I shall never forget, as you said that I could not have addressed you in any possible way that would induce you to accept me."

"Oh! do not repeat what I then said. These recollections will not do at all. I assure you, that I have long been most heartily ashamed of it."

Darcy mentioned his letter. "Did it," said he, "did it *soon* make you think better of me? Did you, on reading it, give any credit to its contents?"

She explained what its effect on her had been, and how gradually all her former prejudices had been removed.

"I knew," said he, "that what I wrote must give you pain; but it was necessary. I hope you have destroyed the letter. There was one part, especially the opening of it, which I should dread your having the power of reading again. I can remember some expressions which might justly make you hate me."

"The letter shall certainly be burnt, if you believe it essential to the preservation of my regard; but, though we have both reason to think my opinions not entirely unalterable, they are not, I hope, quite so easily changed as that implies."

"When I wrote that letter," replied Darcy, "I believed myself perfectly calm and cool; but I am since convinced that it was written in a dreadful bitterness of spirit."

"The letter, perhaps, began in bitterness; but it did not end so. The adieu is charity itself. But think no more of the letter. The feelings of the person who wrote and the person who received it are now so widely different from what they were then, that every unpleasant circumstance attending it ought to be forgotten. You must learn some of my philosophy. Think only of the past as its remembrance gives you pleasure."

"I cannot give you credit for any philosophy of the kind. *Your* retrospections must be so totally void of reproach, that the contentment arising from them is not of philosophy, but, what is much better, of ignorance. But with *me* it is not so. Painful recollections will intrude, which cannot, which ought not, to be repelled. I have been a selfish being all my life, in practice, though not in principle. As a child, I was taught what was *right;* but I was not taught to correct my temper. I was given good principles, but left to follow them in pride and conceit. Unfortunately, an only son (for many years an only *child*), I was spoiled by my parents, who, though good themselves (my father particularly, all that was benevolent and amiable), allowed, encouraged, almost taught me to be selfish and overbearing—to care for none beyond my own family circle, to think meanly of all the rest of the world, to *wish* at least to think meanly of their sense and worth compared with my own. Such I was, from eight to eight-and-twenty; and such I might still have been but for you, dearest, loveliest Elizabeth! What do I not owe you? You taught me a lesson, hard indeed at first, but most advantageous. By you I was properly humbled. I came to you without a doubt of my reception. You showed me how insufficient were all my pretensions to please a woman worthy of being pleased."

"Had you then persuaded yourself that I should?"

"Indeed I had. What will you think of my vanity? I believed you to be wishing, expecting my addresses."

"My manners must have been in fault, but not intentionally, I assure you. I never meant to deceive you, but my spirits might often lead me wrong. How you must have hated me after *that* evening!"

"Hate you! I was angry, perhaps, at first, but my anger soon began to take a proper direction."

"I am almost afraid of asking what you thought of me when we met at Pemberley. You blamed me for coming?"

"No, indeed, I felt nothing but surprise."

"Your surprise could not be greater than *mine* in being noticed by you. My conscience told me that I deserved no extraordinary politeness, and I confess that I did not expect to receive *more* than my due."

"My object *then*," replied Darcy, "was to show you, by every civility in my power, that I hoped to obtain your forgiveness, to lessen your ill-opinion by letting you see that your reproofs had been attended to. How soon any other wishes introduced themselves I can hardly tell, but I believe in about half-an-hour after I had seen you."

He then told her of Georgiana's delight in her acquaintance, and of her disappointment at its sudden interruption; which naturally leading to the cause of that interruption, she soon learnt that his resolution of following her from Derbyshire in quest of her sister had been formed before he quitted the inn, and that his gravity and thoughtfulness there had arisen from no other struggles than what such a purpose must comprehend.

She expressed her gratitude again; but it was too painful a subject to each to be dwelt on farther.

After walking several miles in a leisurely manner, and too busy to know anything about it, they found at last, on examining their watches, that it was time to be at home.

"What could have become of Mr. Bingley and Jane!" was a wonder which introduced the discussion of *their* affairs. Darcy was delighted with their engagement; his friend had given him the earliest information of it.

"I must ask whether you were surprised?" said Elizabeth.

"Not at all. When I went away, I felt that it would soon happen."

"That is to say, you had given your permission. I guessed as much."

And though he exclaimed at the term, she found that it had been pretty much the case.

"On the evening before my going to London," said he, "I made a confession to him which I believe I ought to have made long ago. I told him of all that had occurred to make my former interference in his affairs absurd and impertinent. His surprise was great. He had never had the slightest suspicion. I told him, moreover, that I believed myself mistaken in supposing as I had done, that your sister was indifferent to him; and as I could easily perceive that his attachment to her was unabated, I felt no doubt of their happiness together."

Elizabeth could not help smiling at his easy manner of directing his friend.

"Did you speak from your own observation," said she, "when you told him that my sister loved him or merely from my information last spring?"

"From the former. I had narrowly observed her during the two visits which I had lately made her here, and I was convinced of her affection."

"And your assurance of it, I suppose, carried immediate conviction to him."

"It did. Bingley is most unaffectedly modest. His diffidence had prevented his depending on his own judgment in so anxious a case, but his reliance on mine made everything easy. I was obliged to confess one thing which for a time, and not unjustly, offended him. I could not allow myself to conceal that your sister had been in town three months last winter—that I had known it, and purposely kept it from him. He was angry. But his anger, I am persuaded, lasted no longer than he remained in any doubt of your sister's sentiments. He has heartily forgiven me now."

Elizabeth longed to observe that Mr. Bingley had been a most delightful friend—so easily guided, that his worth was invaluable; but she checked herself. She remembered that he had yet to learn to be laughed at, and it was rather too early to begin. In anticipating the happiness of Bingley, which of course was to be inferior only to his own, he continued the conversation till they reached the house. In the hall they parted.

Chapter 59

"My dear Lizzy, where can you have been walking to?" was a question which Elizabeth received from Jane as soon as she entered the room, and from all the others when they sat down to table. She had only to say in reply, that they had wandered about till she was beyond her own knowledge. She coloured as she spoke; but neither that, nor anything else, awakened a suspicion of the truth.

The evening passed quietly, unmarked by anything extraordinary. The acknowledged lovers talked and laughed; the unacknowledged were silent. Darcy was not of a disposition in which happiness overflows in mirth; and Elizabeth, agitated and confused, rather *knew* that she was happy, than *felt* herself to be so; for, besides the immediate embarrassment, there were other evils before her. She anticipated what would be felt in the family when her situation became known; she was aware that no one liked him but Jane; and even feared that with the others it was a *dislike* which not all his fortune and consequence might do away.

At night she opened her heart to Jane. Though suspicion was very far from Miss Bennet's general habits, she was absolutely incredulous here.

"You are joking, Lizzy. This cannot be! engaged to Mr. Darcy! No, no, you shall not deceive me. I know it to be impossible."

"This is a wretched beginning indeed! My sole dependence was on you; and I am sure nobody else will believe me, if you do not. Yet, indeed, I am in earnest. I speak nothing but the truth. He still loves me, and we are engaged."

Jane looked at her doubtingly. "Oh, Lizzy! it cannot be. I know how much you dislike him."

"You know nothing of the matter. *That* is all to be forgot. Perhaps I did not always love him so well as I do now. But in such cases as these a good memory is unpardonable. This is the last time I shall ever remember it myself."

Miss Bennet still looked all amazement. Elizabeth again, and more seriously, assured her of its truth.

"Good Heaven! can it be really so? Yet now I must believe you," cried Jane. "My dear, dear Lizzy, I would—I do congratulate you—but are you certain—forgive the question—are you quite certain that you can be happy with him?"

"There can be no doubt of that. It is settled between us already that we are to be the happiest couple in the world. But are you pleased, Jane? Shall you like to have such a brother?"

"Very, very much. Nothing could give either Bingley or myself more delight. But we considered it, we talked of it as impossible. And do you really love him quite well enough? Oh, Lizzy! do anything rather than marry without affection. Are you quite sure that you feel what you ought to do?"

"Oh, yes! You will only think I feel *more* than I ought to do, when I tell you all."

"What do you mean?"

"Why, I must confess that I love him better than I do Bingley. I am afraid you will be angry."

"My dearest sister, now *be*, be serious. I want to talk very seriously. Let me know everything that I am to know, without delay. Will you tell me how long you have loved him?"

"It has been coming on so gradually, that I hardly know when it began. But I believe I must date it from my first seeing his beautiful grounds at Pemberley."

Another entreaty that she would be serious, however, produced the desired effect, and she soon satisfied Jane by her solemn assurances of attachment. When convinced on that article, Miss Bennet had nothing further to wish.

"Now I am quite happy," said she, "for you will be as happy as myself. I always had a value for him. Were it for nothing but his love of you, must always have esteemed him; but now, as Bingley's friend and your husband, there can be only Bingley and yourself more dear to me. But, Lizzy, you have been very sly, very reserved with me. How little did you tell me of what passed at Pemberley and Lambton! I owe all that I know of it to another, not to you."

Elizabeth told her the motives of her secrecy. She had been unwilling to mention Bingley; and the unsettled state of her own feelings had made her equally avoid the name of his friend. But now she would no longer conceal from her his share in Lydia's marriage. All was acknowledged, and half the night spent in conversation.

"Good gracious!" cried Mrs. Bennet, as she stood at a window the next morning, "if that disagreeable Mr. Darcy is not coming here again with our dear Bingley! What can he mean by being so tiresome as to be always coming here? I had no notion but he would go a-shooting, or something or other, and not disturb us with his company. What shall we do with him? Lizzy, you must walk out with him again, that he may not be in Bingley's way."

Elizabeth could hardly help laughing at so convenient a proposal, yet was really vexed that her mother should be always giving him such an epithet.

As soon as they entered, Bingley looked at her so expressively, and shook hands with such warmth, as left no doubt of his good information; and he soon afterwards said aloud, "Mrs. Bennet, have you no more lanes hereabouts in which Lizzy may lose her away again to-day?"

"I advise Mr. Darcy, and Lizzy, and Kitty," said Mrs. Bennet, "to walk to Oakham Mount this morning. It is a nice long walk, and Mr. Darcy has never seen the view."

"It may do very well for the others," replied Mr. Bingley; "but I am sure it will be too much for Kitty. Won't it, Kitty?"

Kitty owned that she had rather stay at home. Darcy professed a great curiosity to see the view from the Mount, and Elizabeth silently consented. As she went upstairs to get ready, Mrs. Bennet followed her, saying:

"I am quite sorry, Lizzy, that you should be forced to have that disagreeable man all to yourself. But I hope you will not mind: it is all for Jane's sake, you know; and there is no occasion for talking to him, except just now and then. So do not put yourself to inconvenience."

During their walk, it was resolved that Mr. Bennet's consent should be asked in the course of the evening. Elizabeth reserved to herself the application for her mother's. She could not determine how her mother would take it; sometimes doubting whether all his wealth and grandeur would be enough to overcome her abhorrence of the man. But whether she were violently set against the match, or violently delighted with it, it was certain that her manner would be equally ill adapted to do credit to her sense; and she could no more bear that Mr. Darcy should hear the first raptures of her joy than the first vehemence of her disapprobation.

In the evening, soon after Mr. Bennet withdrew to the library, she saw Mr. Darcy rise also and follow him, and her agitation on seeing it was extreme. She did not fear her father's opposition, but he was going to be made unhappy, and that it should be through her means that *she*, his favourite child, should be distressing him by her choice, should be filling him with fears and regrets in disposing of her, was a wretched reflection, and she sat in misery till Mr. Darcy appeared again, when, looking at him, she was a little relieved by his smile. In a few minutes he approached the table where she was sitting with Kitty, and, while pretending to admire her work, said in a whisper, "Go to your father; he wants you in the library." She was gone directly.

Her father was walking about the room, looking grave and anxious. "Lizzy," said he, "what are you doing? Are you out of your senses, to be accepting this man? Have not you always hated him?"

How earnestly did she then wish that her former opinions had been more reasonable, her expressions more moderate! It would have spared her from explanations and professions which it was exceedingly awkward to give; but they were now necessary, and she assured him, with some confusion, of her attachment to Mr. Darcy.

"Or, in other words, you are determined to have him. He is rich, to be sure, and you may have more fine clothes and fine carriages than Jane. But will they make you happy?"

"Have you any other objection," said Elizabeth, "than your belief of my indifference?"

"None at all. We all know him to be a proud, unpleasant sort of man; but this would be nothing, if you really liked him."

"I do, I do like him," she replied, with tears in her eyes; "I love him. Indeed, he has no improper pride. He is perfectly amiable. You do not know what he really is; then pray do not pain me by speaking of him in such terms."

"Lizzy," said her father, "I have given him my consent. He is the kind of man, indeed, to whom I should never dare refuse anything which he condescended to ask. I now give it to *you*, if you are resolved on having him. But let me advise you to think better of it. I know your disposition, Lizzy. I know that you could be neither happy nor respectable unless you truly esteemed your husband—unless you looked up to him as a superior. Your lively talents would place you in the greatest danger in an unequal marriage. You could scarcely escape discredit and misery. My child, let me not have the grief of seeing *you* unable to respect your partner in life. You know not what you are about."

Elizabeth, still more affected, was earnest and solemn in her reply; and at length, by repeated assurances that Mr. Darcy was really the object of her choice, by explaining the gradual change which her estimation of him had undergone, relating her absolute certainty that his affection was not the work of a day, but had stood the test of many months' suspense, and enumerating with energy all his good qualities, she did conquer her father's incredulity, and reconcile him to the match.

"Well, my dear," said he, when she ceased speaking, "I have no more to say. If this be the case, he deserves you. I could not have parted with you, my Lizzy, to any one less worthy." To complete the favourable impression, she then told him what Mr. Darcy had voluntarily done for Lydia. He heard her with astonishment.

"This is an evening of wonders, indeed! And so, Darcy did everything —made up the match, gave the money, paid the fellow's debts, and got him his commission! So much the better. It will save me a world of trouble and economy. Had it been your uncle's doing, I must and *would* have paid him; but these violent young lovers carry everything their own way. I shall offer to pay him to-morrow: he will rant and storm about his love for you, and there will be an end of the matter." He then recollected her embarrassment a few days before, on his reading Mr. Collins's letter; and after laughing at her some time, allowed her at last to go, saying, as she quitted the room, "If any young men come for Mary or Kitty, send them in, for I am quite at leisure."

Elizabeth's mind was now relieved from a very heavy weight, and, after half-an-hour's quiet reflection in her own room, she was able to join the others with tolerable composure. Everything was too recent for gaiety, but the evening passed tranquilly away; there was no longer anything material to be dreaded, and the comfort of ease and familiarity would come in time.

When her mother went up to her dressing-room at night she followed her, and made the important communication. Its effect was most extraordinary; for, on first hearing it, Mrs. Bennet sat quite still, and unable to utter a syllable. Nor was it under many, many minutes, that she could comprehend what she heard, though not in general backward to credit what was for the advantage of her family, or that came in the shape of a lover to any of them. She began at length to recover, to fidget about in her chair, get up, sit down again, wonder, and bless herself.

"Good gracious! Lord bless me! Only think! Dear me! Mr. Darcy! Who would have thought it? And is it really true? Oh, my sweetest Lizzy! How rich and how great you will be! What pin-money, what jewels, what carriages you will have! Janes's is nothing to it—nothing at all. I am so pleased—so happy! Such a charming man! So handsome! So tall! Oh, my dear Lizzy! Pray apologise for my having disliked him so much before. I hope he will overlook it. Dear, dear Lizzy! A house in town! Everything that is charming! Three daughters married! Ten thousand a year! Oh, Lord! what will become of me? I shall go distracted."

This was enough to prove that her approbation need not be doubted; and Elizabeth, rejoicing that such an effusion was heard only by herself, soon went away. But before she had been three minutes in her own room, her mother followed her.

"My dearest child," she cried, "I can think of nothing else! Ten thousand a year, and very likely more! 'Tis as good as a lord! And a special license! You must and shall be married by a special license! But, my dearest love, tell me what dish Mr. Darcy is particularly fond of, that I may have it to-morrow."

This was a sad omen of what her mother's behaviour to the gentleman himself might be; and Elizabeth found, that though in the certain possession of his warmest affection, and secure of her relations' consent, there was still something to be wished for. But the morrow passed off much better than she expected; for Mrs. Bennet luckily stood in such awe of her intended son-in-law that she ventured not to speak to him, unless it was in her power to offer him any attention, to mark her deference for his opinion.

Elizabeth had the satisfaction of seeing her father taking pains to get acquainted with him; and Mr. Bennet soon assured her that he was rising every hour in his esteem.

"I admire all my sons-in-law highly," said he. "Wickham, perhaps, is my favourite; but I think I shall like *your* husband quite as well as Jane's."

Chapter 60

ELIZABETH's spirits soon rising to playfulness again, she wanted Mr. Darcy to account for his having ever fallen in love with her. "How could you begin?" said she. "I can comprehend your going on charmingly, when you had once made a beginning; but what could set you off in the first place?"

"I cannot fix on the hour, or the spot, or the look, or the words, which laid the foundation. It is too long ago. I was in the middle before I knew that I *had* begun."

"My beauty you had early withstood, and as for my manners—my behaviour to *you* was at least always bordering on the uncivil, and I never spoke to you without rather wishing to give you pain than not. Now, be sincere; did you admire me for my impertinence?"

"For the liveliness of your mind, I did."

"You may as well call it impertinence at once. It was very little less. The fact is, that you were sick of civility, of deference, of officious attention. You were disgusted with the women who were always speaking and looking and thinking for *your* approbation alone. I roused and interested you, because I was so unlike *them*. Had you not been really amiable, you would have hated me for it; but, in spite of the pains you took to disguise yourself, your feelings were always noble and just; and, in your heart, you thoroughly despised the persons who so assiduously courted you. There—I have saved you the trouble of accounting for it; and really, all things considered, I begin to think it perfectly reasonable. To be sure, you know no actual good of me—but nobody thinks of *that* when they fall in love."

"Was there no good in your affectionate behaviour to Jane, while she was ill at Netherfield?"

"Dearest Jane! Who could have done less for her? But make a virtue of it by all means. My good qualities are under your protection, and you are to exaggerate them as much as possible; and, in return, it belongs to me to find occasions for teasing and quarrelling with you as often as may be; and I shall begin directly, by asking you what made you so unwilling to come to the point at last? What made you so shy of me when you first called, and afterwards dined here? Why, especially, when you called, did you look as if you did not care about me?"

"Because you were grave and silent, and gave me no encouragement."

"But I was embarrassed."

"And so was I."

"You might have talked to me more when you came to dinner."

"A man who had felt less, might."

"How unlucky that you should have a reasonable answer to give, and that I should be so reasonable as to admit. But I wonder how long you *would* have gone on if you had been left to yourself! I wonder when you *would* have spoken, if I had not asked you! My resolution of thanking you for your kindness to Lydia had certainly great effect—*too much,* I am afraid; for what becomes of the moral, if our comfort springs from a breach of promise? For I ought not to have mentioned the subject. This will never do."

"You need not distress yourself. The moral will be perfectly fair. Lady Catherine's unjustifiable endeavours to separate us were the means of removing all my doubts. I am not indebted for my present happiness to your eager desire of expressing your gratitude. I was not in a humour to wait for an opening of yours. My aunt's intelligence had given me hope, and I was determined at once to know everything."

"Lady Catherine has been of infinite use which ought to make her happy, for she loves to be of use. But tell me, what did you come down to Netherfield for? Was it merely to ride to Longbourn, and be embarrassed—or had you intended any more serious consequences?"

"My real purpose was to see *you,* and to judge, if I could, whether I might ever hope to make you love me. My avowed one, or what I avowed to myself, was to see whether your sister was still partial to Bingley, and, if she were, to make the confession to him which I have since made."

"Shall you ever have courage to announce to Lady Catherine what is to befall her?"

"I am more likely to want time than courage, Elizabeth. But it ought to be done; and if you will give me a sheet of paper, it shall be done directly. "

"And if I had not a letter to write myself, I might sit by you, and admire the evenness of your writing, as another young lady once did. But I have an aunt, too, who must not be longer neglected."

From an unwillingness to confess how much her intimacy with Mr. Darcy had been overrated, Elizabeth had never yet answered Mrs. Gardiner's long letter, but now, having *that* to communicate which she knew would be most welcome, she was almost ashamed to find that her uncle and aunt had already lost three days of happiness, and immediately wrote as follows:—

"I would have thanked you before, my dear aunt, as I ought to have done, for your long, kind, satisfactory detail of particulars; but, to say the truth, I was too cross to write. You supposed more than really existed. But *now* suppose as much as you choose; give a loose rein to your fancy, indulge your imagination in every possible flight which the subject will afford, and unless you believe me actually married, you cannot greatly err. You must write again very soon, and praise him a great deal more than you did in your last. I thank you, again and again, for not going to the Lakes. How could I be so silly as to wish it! Your idea of the ponies is delightful. We will go round the Park every day. I am the happiest creature in the world. Perhaps other people have said so before, but no one with such justice. I am happier even than Jane; she only smiles. I laugh. Mr. Darcy sends you all the love in the world that can be spared from me. You are all to come to Pemberley at Christmas.—Yours, etc."

Mr. Darcy's letter to Lady Catherine was in a different style, and still different from either was what Mr. Bennet sent to Mr. Collins, in reply to his last.

'DEAR SIR,—
"I must trouble you once more for congratulations. Elizabeth will soon be the wife of Mr. Darcy. Console Lady Catherine as well as you can. But, if I were you, I would stand by the nephew; he has more to give. —Yours sincerely, etc."

Miss Bingley's congratulations to her brother on his approaching marriage were all that was affectionate and insincere. She wrote even to Jane on the occasion, to express her delight, and repeat all her former professions of regard. Jane was not deceived, but she was affected, and, though feeling no reliance on her, could not help writing her a much kinder answer than she knew was deserved.

The joy which Miss Darcy expressed on receiving similar information was as sincere as her brother's in sending it. Four sides of paper were insufficient to contain all her delight, and all her earnest desire of being loved by her sister.

Before any answer could arrive from Mr. Collins, or any congratulations to Elizabeth, from his wife, the Longbourn family heard that the Collinses were come themselves to Lucas Lodge. The reason of this sudden removal was soon evident. Lady Catherine had been rendered so exceedingly angry by the contents of her nephew's letter, that Charlotte, really rejoicing in the match, was anxious to get away till the storm was blown over. At such a moment the arrival of her friend was a sincere pleasure to Elizabeth, though in the course of their meetings she must sometimes think the pleasure dearly bought, when she saw Mr. Darcy exposed to all the parading and obsequious civility of her husband. He bore it, however, with admirable calmness. He could even listen to Sir William Lucas, when he complimented him on carrying away the brightest jewel of the country, and expressed his hopes of their all meeting frequently at St. James's with very decent composure. If he did shrug his shoulders, it was not till Sir William was out of sight.

Mrs. Philips's vulgarity was another, and, perhaps, a greater tax on his forbearance; and though Mrs. Philips, as well as her sister, stood in too much awe of him to speak with the familiarity which Bingley's good humour encouraged, yet, whenever she *did* speak, she must be vulgar. Nor was her respect for him, though it made her more quiet, at all likely to make her more elegant. Elizabeth did all she could to shield him from the frequent notice of either, and was ever anxious to keep him to herself, and to those of her family with whom he might converse without mortification; and though the uncomfortable feelings arising from all this took from the season of courtship much of its pleasure, it added to the hope of the future; and she looked forward with delight to the time when they should be removed from society so little pleasing to either, to all the comfort and elegance of their family party at Pemberley.

Chapter 61

HAPPY for all her maternal feelings was the day on which Mrs. Bennet got rid of her two most deserving daughters. With what delighted pride she afterwards visited Mrs. Bingley, and talked of Mrs. Darcy, may be guessed. I wish I could say, for the sake of her family, that the accomplishment of her earnest desire in the establishment of so many of her children produced so happy an effect as to make her a sensible, amiable, well-informed woman for the rest of her life; though, perhaps, it was lucky for her husband, who might not have relished domestic felicity in so unusual a form, that she still was occasionally nervous, and invariably silly.

Mr. Bennet missed his second daughter exceedingly; his affection for her drew him oftener from home than anything else could do. He delighted in going to Pemberley, especially when he was least expected.

Mr. Bingley and Jane remained at Netherfield only a twelvemonth. So near a vicinity to her mother and Meryton relations was not desirable even to *his* easy temper, or *her* affectionate heart. The darling wish of his sisters was then gratified; he bought an estate in a neighbouring county to Derbyshire; and Jane and Elizabeth, in addition to every other source of happiness, were within thirty miles of each other.

Kitty, to her very material advantage, spent the chief of her time with her two elder sisters. In society so superior to what she had generally known, her improvement was great. She was not of so ungovernable a temper as Lydia; and, removed from the influence of Lydia's example, she became, by proper attention and management, less irritable, less ignorant, and less insipid. From the further disadvantage of Lydia's society she was of course carefully kept; and though Mrs. Wickham frequently invited her to come and stay with her, with the promise of balls and young men, her father would never consent to her going.

Mary was the only daughter who remained at home; and she was necessarily drawn from the pursuit of accomplishments by Mrs. Bennet's being quite unable to sit alone. Mary was obliged to mix more with the world, but she could still moralise over every morning visit; and as she was no longer mortified by comparisons between her sisters' beauty and her own, it was suspected by her father that she submitted to the change without much reluctance.

As for Wickham and Lydia, their characters suffered no revolution from the marriage of her sisters. He bore with philosophy the conviction that Elizabeth must now become acquainted with whatever of his ingratitude and falsehood had before been unknown to her, and, in spite of everything, was not wholly without hope that Darcy might yet be prevailed on to make his fortune. The congratulatory letter which Elizabeth received from Lydia on her marriage explained to her that, by his wife at least, if not by himself, such a hope was cherished. The letter was to this effect:

"MY DEAR LIZZY,—

"I wish you joy. If you love Mr. Darcy half so well as I do my dear Wickham, you must be very happy. It is a great comfort to have you so rich, and when you have nothing else to do, I hope you will think of us. I am sure Wickham would like a place at court very much, and I do not think we shall have quite enough money to live upon without some help. Any place would do, of about three or four hundred a year; but, however, do not speak to Mr. Darcy about it, if you had rather not.—Yours, etc."

As it happened that Elizabeth had *much* rather not, she endeavoured in her answer to put an end to every entreaty and expectation of the kind. Such relief, however, as it was in her power to afford, by the practice of what might be called economy in her own private expenses, she frequently sent them. It had always been evident to her that such an income as theirs, under the direction of two persons so extravagant in their wants, and heedless of the future, must be very insufficient to their support; and whenever they changed their quarters, either Jane or herself were sure of being applied to, for some little assistance towards discharging their bills. Their manner of living, even when the restoration of peace dismissed them to a home, was unsettled in the extreme. They were always moving from place to place in quest of a cheap situation, and always spending more than they ought. His affection for her soon sunk into indifference; hers lasted a little longer; and in spite of her youth and her manners, she retained all the claims to reputation which her marriage had given her.

Though Darcy could never receive *him* at Pemberley, yet, for Elizabeth's sake, he assisted him further in his profession. Lydia was occasionally a visitor there, when her husband was gone to enjoy himself in London or Bath; and with the Bingleys they both of them frequently stayed so long, that even Bingley's good humour was overcome, and he proceeded so far as to *talk* of giving them a hint to be gone.

Miss Bingley was very deeply mortified by Darcy's marriage; but as she thought it advisable to retain the right of visiting at Pemberley, she dropped all her resentment; was fonder than ever of Georgiana, almost as attentive to Darcy as heretofore, and paid off every arrear of civility to Elizabeth.

Pemberley was now Georgiana's home; and the attachment of the sisters was exactly what Darcy had hoped to see. They were able to love each other, even as well as they intended. Georgiana had the highest opinion in the world of Elizabeth; though at first she often listened with an astonishment bordering on alarm at her lively, sportive manner of talking to her brother. He, who had always inspired in herself a respect which almost overcame her affection, she now saw the object of open pleasantry. Her mind received knowledge which had never before fallen in her way. By Elizabeth's instructions she began to comprehend that a woman may take liberties with her husband, which a brother will not allow in a sister more than ten years younger than himself.

Lady Catherine was extremely indignant on the marriage of her nephew; and as she gave way to all the genuine frankness of her character, in her reply to the letter which announced its arrangement, she sent him language so very abusive, especially of Elizabeth, that for some time all intercourse was at an end. But at length, by Elizabeth's persuasion, he was prevailed on to overlook the offence, and seek a reconciliation; and, after a little further resistance on the part of his aunt, her resentment gave way, either to her affection for him, or her curiosity to see how his wife conducted herself: and she condescended to wait on them at Pemberley, in spite of that pollution which its woods had received, not merely from the presence of such a mistress, but the visits of her uncle and aunt from the city.

With the Gardiners they were always on the most intimate terms. Darcy, as well as Elizabeth, really loved them; and they were both ever sensible of the warmest gratitude towards the persons who, by bringing her into Derbyshire, had been the means of uniting them.

FINIS

MANSFIELD PARK

(First Published 1814*)*

MANSFIELD PARK

Chapter 1

ABOUT thirty years ago, Miss Maria Ward, of Huntingdon, with only seven thousand pounds. had the good luck to captivate Sir Thomas Bertram, of Mansfield Park, in the county of Northampton, and to be thereby raised to the rank of a baronet's lady, with all the comforts and consequences of an handsome house and large income. All Huntingdon exclaimed on the greatness of the match, and her uncle, the lawyer, himself allowed her to be at least three thousand pounds short of any equitable claim to it. She had two sisters to be benefited by her elevation; and such of their acquaintances as thought Miss Ward and Miss Frances quite as handsome as Miss Maria, did not scruple to predict their marrying with almost equal advantage. But there certainly are not so many men of large fortune in the world as there are pretty women to deserve them. Miss Ward, at the end of half-a-dozen years, found herself obliged to be attached to the Rev. Mr. Norris, a friend of her brother-in-law, with scarcely any private fortune, and Miss Frances fared yet worse. Miss Ward's match, indeed, when it came to the point, was not contemptible; Sir Thomas being happily able to give his friend an income in the living of Mansfield; and Mr. and Mrs. Norris began their career of conjugal felicity with very little less than a thousand a year. But Miss Frances married, in the common phrase, to disoblige her family, and by fixing on a lieutenant of marines, without education, fortune, or connections, did it very thoroughly. She could hardly have made a more untoward choice. Sir Thomas Bertram had interest which, from principle as well as pride—from a general wish of doing right, and a desire of seeing all that were connected with him in situations of respectability, he would have been glad to exert for the advantage of Lady Bertram's sister; but her husband's profession was such as no interest could reach; and before he had time to devise any other method of assisting them, an absolute breach between the sisters had taken place. It was the natural result of the conduct of each party, and such as a very imprudent marriage almost always produces. To save herself from useless remonstrance, Mrs. Price never wrote to her family on the subject till actually married. Lady Bertram, who was a woman of very tranquil feelings, and a temper remarkably easy and indolent, would have contented herself with merely giving up her sister, and thinking no more of the matter; but Mrs. Norris had a spirit of activity, which could not be satisfied till she had written a long and angry letter to Fanny, to point out the folly of her conduct, and threaten her with all its possible ill consequences. Mrs. Price, in her turn, was injured and angry;

and an answer, which comprehended each sister in its bitterness, and
bestowed such very disrespectful reflections on the pride of Sir Thomas,
as Mrs. Norris could not possibly keep to herself, put an end to all intercourse between them for a considerable period.

Their homes were so distant, and the circles in which they moved so
distinct, as almost to preclude the means of ever hearing of each other's
existence during the eleven following years, or, at least, to make it very
wonderful to Sir Thomas, that Mrs. Norris should ever have it in her
power to tell them, as she now and then did, in an angry voice, that Fanny
had got another child. By the end of eleven years, however, Mrs. Price
could no longer afford to cherish pride or resentment, or to lose one connection that might possibly assist her. A large and still increasing family,
an husband disabled for active service, but not the less equal to company
and good liquor, and a very small income to supply their wants, made her
eager to regain the friends she had so carelessly sacrificed; and she addressed Lady Bertram in a letter which spoke so much contrition and
despondence, such a superfluity of children, and such a want of almost
everything else, as could not but dispose them all to a reconciliation. She
was preparing for her ninth lying-in; and after bewailing the circumstance,
and imploring their countenance as sponsors to the expected child, she
could not conceal how important she felt they might be to the future
maintenance of the eight already in being. Her eldest was a boy of ten
years old, a fine spirited fellow, who longed to be out in the world; but
what could she do? Was there any chance of his being hereafter useful to
Sir Thomas in the concerns of his West Indian property? No situation
would be beneath him; or what did Sir Thomas think of Woolwich? or
how could a boy be sent out to the East?

The letter was not unproductive. It re-established peace and kindness.
Sir Thomas sent friendly advice and professions, Lady Bertram dispatched money and baby-linen, and Mrs. Norris wrote the letters.

Such were its immediate effects, and within a twelvemonth a more
important advantage to Mrs. Price resulted from it. Mrs. Norris was often
observing to the others that she could not get her poor sister and her
family out of her head, and that, much as they had all done for her, she
seemed to be wanting to do more; and at length she could not but own it
to be her wish that poor Mrs. Price should be relieved from the charge
and expense of one child entirely out of her great number.

"What if they were among them to undertake the care of her eldest
daughter, a girl now nine years old, of an age to require more attention
than her poor mother could possibly give? The trouble and expense of it
to them would be nothing, compared with the benevolence of the action."
Lady Bertram agreed with her instantly. "I think we cannot do better,"
said she; "let us send for the child."

Sir Thomas could not give so instantaneous and unqualified a consent.
He debated and hesitated: it was a serious charge; a girl so brought up
must be adequately provided for, or there would be cruelty instead of

kindness in taking her from her family. He thought of his own four children, of his two sons, of cousins in love, etc.; but no sooner had he deliberately begun to state his objections, than Mrs. Norris interrupted him with a reply to them all, whether stated or not.

"My dear Sir Thomas, I perfectly comprehend you, and do justice to the generosity and delicacy of your notions, which, indeed, are quite of a piece with your general conduct; and I entirely agree with you in the main as to the propriety of doing everything one could by way of providing for a child one had in a manner taken into one's own hands; and I am sure I should be the last person in the world to withhold my mite upon such an occasion. Having no children of my own, who should I look to in any little matter I may ever have to bestow, but the children of my sisters? And I am sure Mr. Norris is too just—but you know I am a woman of few words and professions. Do not let us be frightened from a good deed by a trifle. Give a girl an education, and introduce her properly into the world, and ten to one but she has the means of settling well, without further expense to anybody. A niece of ours, Sir Thomas, I may say, or, at least, of *yours*, would not grow up in this neighbourhood without many advantages. I don't say she would be so handsome as her cousins. I dare say she would not; but she would be introduced into the society of this country under such very favourable circumstances as, in all human probability, would get her a creditable establishment. You are thinking of your sons; but do not you know that of all things upon earth *that* is the least likely to happen, brought up as they would be, always together like brothers and sisters? It is morally impossible. I never knew an instance of it. It is, in fact, the only sure way of providing against the connection. Suppose her a pretty girl, and seen by Tom or Edmund for the first time seven years hence, and I dare say there would be mischief. The very idea of her having been suffered to grow up at a distance from us all in poverty and neglect, would be enough to make either of the dear, sweet-tempered boys in love with her. But breed her up with them from this time, and suppose her even to have the beauty of an angel, and she will never be more to either than a sister."

"There is a great deal of truth in what you say," replied Sir Thomas, "and far be it from me to throw any fanciful impediment in the way of a plan which would be so consistent with the relative situations of each. I only meant to observe, that it ought not to be lightly engaged in, and that to make it really serviceable to Mrs. Price, and creditable to ourselves, we must secure to the child, or consider ourselves engaged to secure to her hereafter, as circumstances may arise, the provision of a gentlewoman, if no such establishment should offer as you are so sanguine in expecting."

"I thoroughly understand you," cried Mrs. Norris; "You are everything that is generous and considerate, and I am sure we shall never disagree on this point. Whatever I can do, as you well know, I am always ready enough to do for the good of those I love; and, though I could never feel for this little girl the hundredth part of the regard I bear your own dear children, nor consider her, in any respect, so much my own, I should hate myself if I were capable of neglecting her. Is not she a sister's child? And could I bear to see her want while I had a bit of bread to give her? My dear Sir Thomas, with all my faults I have a warm heart; and, poor as I am, would rather deny myself the necessaries of life than do an ungenerous thing. So, if you are not against it, I will write to my poor sister to-morrow, and make the proposal; and, as soon as matters are settled, *I* will engage to get the child to Mansfield; *you* shall have no trouble about it. My own trouble, you know, I never regard. I will send Nanny to London on purpose, and she may have a bed at her cousin the saddler's, and the child be appointed to meet her there. They may easily get her from Portsmouth to town by the coach, under the care of any creditable person that may chance to be going. I dare say there is always some reputable tradesman's wife or other going up."

Except to the attack on Nanny's cousin, Sir Thomas no longer made any objection, and a more respectable, though less economical rendezvous being accordingly substituted, everything was considered as settled, and the pleasures of so benevolent a scheme were already enjoyed. The division of gratifying sensations ought not, in strict justice, to have been equal; for Sir Thomas was fully resolved to be the real and consistent patron of the selected child, and Mrs. Norris had not the least intention of being at any expense whatever in her maintenance. As far as walking, talking, and contriving reached, she was thoroughly benevolent, and nobody knew better how to dictate liberality to others; but her love of money was equal to her love of directing, and she knew quite as well how to save her own as to spend that of her friends. Having married on a narrower income than she had been used to look forward to, she had, from the first, fancied a very strict line of economy necessary; and what was begun as a matter of prudence, soon grew into a matter of choice, as an object of that needful solicitude which there were no children to supply. Had there been a family to provide for, Mrs. Norris might never have saved her money; but having no care of that kind, there was nothing to impede her frugality, or lessen the comfort of making a yearly addition to an income which they had never lived up to. Under this infatuating principle, counteracted by no real affection for her sister, it was impossible for her to aim at more than the credit of projecting and arranging so expensive a charity; though perhaps she might so little know herself, as to walk home to the Parsonage, after this conversation, in the happy belief of being the most liberal-minded sister and aunt in the world.

When the subject was brought forward again, her views were more fully explained; and, in reply to Lady Bertram's calm inquiry of "Where shall the child come to first, sister, to you or to us?" Sir Thomas heard with some surprise that it would be totally out of Mrs. Norris's power to take any share in the personal charge of her. He had been considering her as a particularly welcome addition at the Parsonage, as a desirable com-

panion to an aunt who had no children of her own; but he found himself
wholly mistaken. Mrs. Norris was sorry to say, that the little girl's staying
with them, at least as things were then, was quite out of the question. Poor
Mr. Norris's indifferent state of health made it an impossibility; he could
no more bear the noise of a child than he could fly; if, indeed, he should
ever get well of his gouty complaints, it would be a different matter; she
should then be glad to take her turn, and think nothing of the inconvenience; but just now poor Mr. Norris took up every moment of her
time, and the very mention of such a thing she was sure would distract him.

"Then she had better come to us," said Lady Bertram, with the utmost
composure. After a short pause, Sir Thomas added with dignity: "Yes;
let her home be in this house. We will endeavour to do our duty by her,
and she will, at least, have the advantage of companions of her own age,
and of a regular instructress."

"Very true," cried Mrs. Norris, "which are both very important considerations; and it will be just the same to Miss Lee, whether she has three
girls to teach or only two—there can be no difference. I only wish I could
be more useful; but you see I do all in my power. I am not one of those
that spare their own trouble; and Nanny shall fetch her, however it may
put me to inconvenience to have my chief counsellor away for three days.
I suppose, sister, you will put the child in the little white attic, near the
old nurseries. It will be much the best place for her, so near Miss Lee, and
not far from the girls, and close by the housemaids, who could either of
them help to dress her, you know, and take care of her clothes, for I
suppose you would not think it fair to expect Ellis to wait on her as well
as the others. Indeed, I do not see that you could possibly place her anywhere else."

Lady Bertram made no opposition.

"I hope she will prove a well-disposed girl," continued Mrs. Norris,
"and be sensible of her uncommon good fortune in having such friends."

"Should her disposition be really bad," said Sir Thomas, "we must not,
for our own children's sake, continue her in the family; but there is no
reason to expect so great an evil. We shall probably see much to wish
altered in her, and must prepare ourselves for gross ignorance, some
meanness of opinions, and very distressing vulgarity of manner; but these
are not incurable faults; nor, I trust, can they be dangerous for her associates. Had my daughters been *younger* than herself, I should have considered the introduction of such a companion as a matter of very serious
moment; but, as it is, I hope there can be nothing to fear for *them*, and
everything to hope for *her*, from the association."

"That is exactly what I think," cried Mrs. Norris, "and what I was
saying to my husband this morning. It will be an education for the child,
said I, only being with her cousins; if Miss Lee taught her nothing, she
would learn to be good and clever from *them*."

"I hope she will not tease my poor pug," said Lady Bertram; "I have
but just got Julia to leave it alone."

"There will be some difficulty in our way, Mrs. Norris," observed Sir Thomas, "as to the distinction proper to be made between the girls as they grow up: how to preserve in the minds of my *daughters* the consciousness of what they are, without making them think too lowly of their cousin; and how, without depressing her spirits too far, to make her remember that she is not a *Miss Bertram.* I should wish to see them very good friends, and would, on no account, authorise in my girls the smallest degree of arrogance towards their relation; but still they cannot be equals. Their rank, fortune, rights, and expectations will always be different. It is a point of great delicacy, and you must assist us in our endeavours to choose exactly the right line of conduct."

Mrs. Norris was quite at his service; and though she perfectly agreed with him as to its being a most difficult thing, encouraged him to hope that between them it would be easily managed.

It will be readily believed that Mrs. Norris did not write to her sister in vain. Mrs. Price seemed rather surprised that a girl should be fixed on, when she had so many fine boys, but accepted the offer most thankfully, assuring them of her daughter's being a very well-disposed, good-humoured girl, and trusting they would never have cause to throw her off. She spoke of her further as somewhat delicate and puny, but was sanguine in the hope of her being materially better for change of air. Poor woman! She probably thought change of air might agree with many of her children.

Chapter 2

THE little girl performed her long journey in safety; and at Northampton was met by Mrs. Norris, who thus regaled in the credit of being foremost to welcome her, and in the importance of leading her into the others, and recommending her to their kindness.

Fanny Price was at this time just ten years old, and though there might not be much in her first appearance to captivate, there was at least nothing to disgust her relations. She was small for her age, with no glow of complexion, nor any other striking beauty; exceedingly timid and shy, and shrinking from notice; but her air, though awkward, was not vulgar, her voice was sweet, and when she spoke her countenance was pretty. Sir Thomas and Lady Bertram received her very kindly; and Sir Thomas, seeing how much she needed encouragement, tried to be all that was conciliating; but he had to work against a most untoward gravity of deportment; and Lady Bertram, without taking half so much trouble, or speaking one word where he spoke ten, by the mere aid of a good-humoured smile, became immediately the less awful character of the two.

The young people were all at home, and sustained their share in the introduction very well, with much good humour, and no embarrassment, at least on the part of the sons, who, at seventeen and sixteen, and tall for their age, had all the grandeur of men in the eyes of their little cousin. The two girls were more at a loss from being younger and in greater awe of their father, who addressed them on the occasion with rather an injudicious particularity. But they were too much used to company and praise to have anything like natural shyness; and their confidence increasing from their cousin's total want of it, they were soon able to take a full survey of her face and her frock in easy indifference.

They were a remarkably fine family, the sons very well-looking, the daughters decidedly handsome, and all of them well grown and forward for their age, which produced as striking a difference between the cousins in person, as education had given to their address; and no one would have supposed the girls so nearly of an age as they really were. There was in fact but two years between the youngest and Fanny. Julia Bertram was only twelve, and Maria but a year older. The little visitor meanwhile was as unhappy as possible. Afraid of everybody, ashamed of herself, and longing for the home she had left, she knew not how to look up, and could scarcely speak to be heard, or without crying. Mrs. Norris had been talking to her the whole way from Northampton of her wonderful good fortune, and the extraordinary degree of gratitude and good behaviour which it ought to produce, and her consciousness of misery was therefore increased by the idea of its being a wicked thing for her not to be happy. The fatigue, too, of so long a journey, became soon no trifling evil. In vain were the well-meant condescensions of Sir Thomas, and all the officious prognostications of Mrs. Norris that she would be a good girl; in vain did Lady Bertram smile and make her sit on the sofa with herself and pug, and vain was even the sight of a gooseberry tart towards giving her comfort; she could scarcely swallow two mouthfuls before tears interrupted her, and sleep seeming to be her likeliest friend, she was taken to finish her sorrows in bed.

"This is not a very promising beginning," said Mrs. Norris, when Fanny had left the room. "After all that I said to her as we came along, I thought she would have behaved better; I told her how much might depend upon her acquitting herself well at first. I wish there may not be a little sulkiness of temper—her poor mother had a good deal; but we must make allowances for such a child—and I do not know that her being sorry to leave her home is really against her, for, with all its faults, it *was* her home, and she cannot as yet understand how much she has changed for the better; but then there is moderation in all things."

It required a longer time, however, than Mrs. Norris was inclined to allow, to reconcile Fanny to the novelty of Mansfield Park, and the separation from everybody she had been used to. Her feelings were very acute, and too little understood to be properly attended to. Nobody meant to be unkind, but nobody put themselves out of their way to secure her comfort.

The holiday allowed to the Miss Bertrams the next day, on purpose to afford leisure for getting acquainted with, and entertaining their young cousin, produced little union. They could not but hold her cheap on finding that she had but two sashes, and had never learned French; and when they perceived her to be little struck with the duet they were so good as to play, they could do no more than make her a generous present of some of their least valued toys, and leave her to herself, while they adjourned to whatever might be the favourite holiday sport of the moment, making artificial flowers or wasting gold paper.

Fanny, whether near or from her cousins, whether in the schoolroom, the drawing-room, or the shrubbery, was equally forlorn, finding something to fear in every person and place. She was disheartened by Lady Bertram's silence, awed by Sir Thomas's grave looks, and quite overcome by Mrs. Norris's admonitions. Her elder cousins mortified her by reflections on her size, and abashed her by noticing her shyness; Miss Lee wondered at her ignorance, and the maidservants sneered at her clothes; and when to these sorrows was added the idea of the brothers and sisters among whom she had always been important as playfellow, instructress, and nurse, the despondence that sunk her little heart was severe.

The grandeur of the house astonished, but could not console her. The rooms were too large for her to move in with ease; whatever she touched she expected to injure, and she crept about in constant terror of something or other; often retreating towards her own chamber to cry; and the little girl who was spoken of in the drawing-room when she left it at night, as seeming so desirably sensible of her peculiar good fortune, ended every day's sorrows by sobbing herself to sleep. A week had passed in this way, and no suspicion of it conveyed by her quiet passive manner, when she was found one morning by her cousin Edmund, the youngest of the sons, sitting crying on the attic stairs.

"My dear little cousin," said he, with all the gentleness of an excellent nature, "what can be the matter?" And sitting down by her, was at great pains to overcome her shame in being so surprised, and persuade her to speak openly. "Was she ill? Or was anybody angry with her? Or had she quarrelled with Maria and Julia? Or was she puzzled about anything in her lesson that he could explain? Did she, in short, want anything he could possibly get her, or do for her?" For a long while no answer could be obtained beyond a "No, no—not at all—no, thank you"; but he still persevered; and no sooner had he begun to revert to her own home, than her increased sobs explained to him where the grievance lay. He tried to console her.

"You are sorry to leave mamma, my dear little Fanny," said he, "which shows you to be a very good girl; but you must remember that you are with relations and friends, who all love you, and wish to make you happy. Let us walk out in the park, and you shall tell me all about your brothers and sisters."

On pursuing the subject, he found that, dear as all these brothers and sisters generally were, there was one among them who ran more in her thoughts than the rest. It was William whom she talked of most, and wanted most to see. William, the eldest, a year older than herself, her constant companion and friend; her advocate with her mother (of whom he was the darling) in every distress. "William did not like she should come away; he had told her he should miss her very much indeed." "But William will write to you, I dare say." "Yes, he had promised he would, but he had told *her* to write first." "And when shall you do it?" She hung her head and answered, hesitatingly, "She did not know; she had not any paper."

"If that will be all your difficulty, I will furnish you with paper and every other material, and you may write your letter whenever you choose. Would it make you happy to write to William?"

"Yes, very."

"Then let it be done now. Come with me into the breakfast-room, we shall find everything there, and be sure of having the room to ourselves."

"But, cousin, will it go to the post?"

"Yes, depend upon me it shall; it shall go with the other letters; and, as your uncle will frank it, it will cost William nothing."

"My uncle!" repeated Fanny, with a frightened look.

"Yes, when you have written the letter, I will take it to my father to frank."

Fanny thought it a bold measure, but offered no further resistance; and they went together into the breakfast-room, where Edmund prepared her paper and ruled her lines with all the good-will that her brother could himself have felt, and probably with somewhat more exactness. He continued with her the whole time of her writing, to assist her with his pen-knife or his orthography, as either were wanted; and added to these attentions, which she felt very much, a kindness to her brother which delighted her beyond all the rest. He wrote with his own hand his love to his cousin William, and sent him half a guinea under the seal. Fanny's feelings on the occasion were such as she believed herself incapable of expressing; but her countenance and a few artless words fully conveyed all their gratitude and delight, and her cousin began to find her an interesting object. He talked to her more, and, from all that she said, was convinced of her having an affectionate heart, and a strong desire of doing right; and he could perceive her to be further entitled to attention, by great sensibility of her situation, and great timidity. He had never knowingly given her pain, but he now felt that she required more positive kindness and with that view endeavoured, in the first place, to lessen her fears of them all, and gave her especially a great deal of good advice as to playing with Maria and Julia, and being as merry as possible.

From this day Fanny grew more comfortable. She felt that she had a friend, and the kindness of her cousin Edmund gave her better spirits with everybody else. The place became less strange, and the people less formidable; and if there were some amongst them whom she could not cease to fear, she began at least to know their ways, and to catch the best manner of conforming to them. The little rusticities and awkwardnesses which had at first made grievous inroads on the tranquillity of all, and not least of herself, necessarily wore away, and she was no longer materially afrait to appear before her uncle, nor did her Aunt Norris's voice make her start very much. To her cousins she became occasionally an acceptable companion. Though unworthy, from inferiority of age and strength, to be their constant associate, their pleasures and schemes were sometimes of a nature to make a third very useful, especially when that third was of an obliging, yielding temper; and they could not but own, when their aunt inquired into her faults, or their brother Edmund urged her claims to their kindness, that "Fanny was good natured enough."

Edmund was uniformly kind himself; and she had nothing worse to endure on the part of Tom than that sort of merriment which a young man of seventeen will always think fair with a child of ten. He was just entering into life, full of spirits, and with all the liberal dispositions of an eldest son, who feels born only for expense and enjoyment. His kindness to his little cousin was consistent with his situation and rights: he made her some very pretty presents, and laughed at her.

As her appearance and spirits improved, Sir Thomas and Mrs. Norris thought with greater satisfaction of their benevolent plan; and it was pretty soon decided between them that, though far from clever, she showed a tractable disposition, and seemed likely to give them little trouble. A mean opinion of her abilities was not confined to *them*. Fanny could read, work, or write, but she had been taught nothing more; and as her cousins found her ignorant of many things with which they had been long familiar, they thought her prodigiously stupid, and for the first two or three weeks were continually bringing some fresh report of it into the drawing-room. "Dear mamma, only think, my cousin cannot put the map of Europe together—or my cousin cannot tell the principal rivers in Russia—or she never heard of Asia Minor—or she does not know the difference between water-colours and crayons! How strange! Did you ever hear anything so stupid?"

"My dear," their considerate aunt would reply, "it is very bad, but you must not expect everybody to be as forward and quick at learning as yourself."

"But, aunt, she is really so very ignorant! Do you know, we asked her last night which way she would go to get to Ireland; and she said she should cross to the Isle of Wight. She thinks of nothing but the Isle of Wight, and she calls it *the Island,* as if there were no other island in the world. I am sure I should have been ashamed of myself, if I had not known better long before I was so old as she is. I cannot remember the time when I did not know a great deal that she has not the least notion of yet. How long ago it is, aunt, since we used to repeat the chronological order of the kings of England, with the dates of their accession, and most of the principal events of their reigns!"

"Yes," added the other; "and of the Roman emperors as low as Severus; besides a great deal of the heathen mythology, and all the metals, semi-metals, planets, and distinguished philosophers."

"Very true, indeed, my dears, but you are blessed with wonderful memories, and your poor cousin has probably none at all. There is a vast deal of difference in memories, as well as in everything else, and therefore you must make allowance for your cousin, and pity her deficiency. And remember that, if you are ever so forward and clever yourselves, you should always be modest; for, much as you know already, there is a great deal more for you to learn."

"Yes, I know there is, till I am seventeen. But I must tell you another thing of Fanny, so odd and so stupid. Do you know, she says she does not want to learn either music or drawing."

"To be sure, my dear, that is very stupid indeed, and shows a great want of genius and emulation. But, all things considered, I do not know whether it is not as well that it should be so, for, though you know (owing to me) your papa and mamma are so good as to bring her up with you, it is not at all necessary that she should be as accomplished as you are; on the contrary, it is much more desirable that there should be a difference."

Such were the counsels by which Mrs. Norris assisted to form her nieces' minds; and it is not very wonderful that, with all their promising talents and early information, they should be entirely deficient in the less common acquirements of self-knowledge, generosity and humility. In everything but disposition, they were admirably taught. Sir Thomas did not know what was wanting, because, though a truly anxious father, he was not outwardly affectionate, and the reserve of his manner repressed all the flow of their spirits before him.

To the education of her daughters Lady Bertram paid not the smallest attention. She had not time for such cares. She was a woman who spent her days in sitting, nicely dressed, on a sofa, doing some long piece of needlework, of little use and no beauty, thinking more of her pug than her children, but very indulgent to the latter, when it did not put herself to inconvenience, guided in everything important by Sir Thomas and in smaller concerns by her sister. Had she possessed greater leisure for the service of her girls, she would probably have supposed it unnecessary, for they were under the care of a governess, with proper masters, and could want nothing more. As for Fanny's being stupid at learning, "she could only say it was very unlucky, but some people *were* stupid, and Fanny must take more pains: she did not know what else was to be done; and, except her being so dull, she must add she saw no harm in the poor little thing, and always found her very handy, and quick in carrying messages, and fetching what she wanted."

Fanny, with all her faults of ignorance and timidity, was fixed at Mansfield Park, and learning to transfer in its favour much of her attachment to her former home, grew up there not unhappily among her cousins. There was no positive ill-nature in Maria or Julia; and though Fanny was often mortified by their treatment of her, she thought too lowly of her own claims to feel injured by it.

From about the time of her entering the family, Lady Bertram, in consequence of a little ill-health, and a greater deal of indolence, gave up the house in town, which she had been used to occupy every spring, and remained wholly in the country, leaving Sir Thomas to attend his duty in Parliament with whatever increase or diminution of comfort might arise from her absence. In the country, therefore, the Miss Bertrams continued to exercise their memories, practise their duets, and grow tall and womanly; and their father saw them becoming in person, manner and accomplishments everything that could satisfy his anxiety. His eldest son was careless and extravagant, and had already given him much uneasiness; but his other children promised him nothing but good. His daughters, he felt, while they retained the name of Bertram, must be giving it new grace, and in quitting it, he trusted, would extend its respectable alliances; and the character of Edmund, his strong good sense and uprightness of mind, bid most fairly for utility, honour and happiness to himself and all his connections. He was to be a clergyman.

Amid the cares and the complacency which his own children suggested, Sir Thomas did not forget to do what he could for the children of Mrs. Price: he assisted her liberally in the education and disposal of her sons as they became old enough for a determinate pursuit; and Fanny, though almost totally separated from her family, was sensible of the truest satisfaction in hearing of any kindness towards them, or of anything at all promising in their situation or conduct. Once, and once only in the course of many years, had she the happiness of being with William. Of the rest she saw nothing; nobody seemed to think of her ever going amongst them again, even for a visit, nobody at home seemed to want her; but William determining, soon after her removal, to be a sailor, was invited to spend a week with his sister in Northamptonshire, before he went to sea. Their eager affection and meeting, their exquisite delight in being together, their hours of happy mirth, and moments of serious conference, may be imagined; as well as the sanguine views and spirits of the boy even to the last, and the misery of the girl when he left her. Luckily the visit happened in the Christmas holidays, when she could directly look for comfort to her cousin Edmund; and he told her such charming things of what William was to do and be hereafter, in consequence of his profession, as made her gradually admit that the separation might have some use. Edmund's friendship never failed her: his leaving Eton for Oxford made no change in his kind disposition, and only afforded more frequent opportunities of proving them. Without any display of doing more than the rest, or any fear of doing too much, he was always true to her interests, and considerate of her feelings, trying to make her good qualities understood, and to conquer the diffidence which prevented their being more apparent; giving her advice, consolation and encouragement.

Kept back as she was by everybody else, his single support could not bring her forward; but his attentions were otherwise of the highest importance in assisting the improvement of her mind, and extending its pleasures. He knew her to be clever, to have a quick apprehension as well as good sense, and a fondness for reading, which, properly directed, must be an education in itself. Miss Lee taught her French, and heard her read the daily portion of history; but he recommended the books which charmed her leisure hours, he encouraged her taste, and corrected her judgment; he made reading useful by talking to her of what she read and heightened its attraction by judicious praise. In return for such services, she loved him better than anybody in the world except William; her heart was divided between the two.

Chapter 3

THE first event of any importance in the family was the death of Mr. Norris, which happened when Fanny was about fifteen, and necessarily introduced alterations and novelties. Mrs. Norris, on quitting the Parsonage, removed first to the Park, and afterwards to a small house of Sir Thomas's in the village, and consoled herself for the loss of her husband by considering that she could do very well without him; and for her reduction of income by the evident necessity of stricter economy.

The living was hereafter for Edmund; and, had his uncle died a few years sooner, it would have been duly given to some friend to hold till he were old enough for orders. But Tom's extravagance had, previous to that event, been so great as to render a different disposal of the next presenta-tion necessary, and the younger brother must help to pay for the pleasures of the elder. There was another family living actually held for Edmund; but though this circumstance had made the arrangement somewhat easier to Sir Thomas's conscience, he could not but feel it to be an act of injustice and he earnestly tried to impress his eldest son with the same conviction, in the hope of its producing a better effect than anything he had yet been able to say or do.

"I blush for you, Tom," said he, in his most dignified manner; "I blush for the expedient which I am driven on, and I trust I may pity your feelings as a brother on the occasion. You have robbed Edmund for ten, twenty, thirty years, perhaps for life, of more than half the income which ought to be his. It may hereafter be in my power, or in yours (I hope it will) to procure him better preferment; but it must not be forgotten, that no benefit of that sort would have been beyond his natural claims on us, and that nothing can, in fact, be an equivalent for the certain advantage which he is now obliged to forego through the urgency of your debts."

Tom listened with some shame and some sorrow; but escaping as quickly as possible, could soon with cheerful selfishness reflect, firstly, that he had not been half so much in debt as some of his friends; secondly, that his father had made a most tiresome piece of work of it; and thirdly, that the future incumbent, whoever he might be, would, in all probability, die very soon.

On Mr. Norris's death, the presentation became the right of a Dr. Grant, who came consequently to reside at Mansfield; and on proving to be a hearty man of forty-five, seemed likely to disappoint Mr. Bertram's calculations. But "no, he was a short-necked, apoplectic sort of fellow, and, plied well with good things, would seen pop off."

He had a wife about fifteen years his junior, but no children; and they entered the neighbourhood with the usual fair report of being very respectable, agreeable people.

The time was now come when Sir Thomas expected his sister-in-law to claim her share in their niece, the change in Mrs. Norris's situation, and the improvement in Fanny's age, seeming not merely to do away any former objection to their living together, but even to give it the most decided eligibility; and as his own circumstances were rendered less fair than heretofore, by some recent losses on his West India estate, in addition to his eldest son's extravagance, it became not undesirable to himself to be relieved from the expense of her support, and the obligation of her future provision. In the fullness of his belief that such a thing must be, he mentioned its probability to his wife; and the first time of the subject's occurring to her again happening to be when Fanny was present, she calmly observed to her: "So, Fanny, you are going to leave us, and live with my sister. How shall you like it?"

Fanny was too much surprised to do more than repeat her aunt's words, "Going to leave you?"

"Yes, my dear; why should you be astonished? You have been five years with us, and my sister always meant to take you when Mr. Norris died. But you must come up and tack on my patterns all the same."

The news was as disagreeable to Fanny as it had been unexpected. She had never received kindness from her Aunt Norris, and could not love her.

"I shall be very sorry to go away," said she, with a faltering voice.

"Yes, I dare say you will; *that's* natural enough. I suppose you have had as little to vex you since you came into this house as any creature in the world."

"I hope I am not ungrateful, aunt," said Fanny, modestly.

"No, my dear; I hope not. I have always found you a very good girl."

"And I am never to live here again?"

"Never, my dear; but you are sure of a comfortable home. It can make very little difference to you, whether you are in one house or the other."

Fanny left the room with a very sorrowful heart: she could not feel the difference to be so small, she could not think of living with her aunt with anything like satisfaction. As soon as she met with Edmund, she told him her distress.

"Cousin," said she, "something is going to happen which I do not like at all; and though you have often persuaded me into being reconciled to things that I disliked at first, you will not be able to do it now. I am going to live entirely with my Aunt Norris."

"Indeed!"

"Yes: my Aunt Bertram has just told me so. It is quite settled. I am to leave Mansfield Park, and go to the White House, I suppose, as soon as she is removed there."

"Well, Fanny, and if the plan were not unpleasant to you, I should call it an excellent one."

"Oh, cousin!"

"It has everything else in its favour. My aunt is acting like a sensible woman in wishing for you. She is choosing a friend and companion exactly where she ought, and I am glad her love of money does not interfere. You will be what you ought to be to her. I hope it does not distress you very much, Fanny."

"Indeed it does; I cannot like it. I love this house and everything in it: I shall love nothing there. You know how uncomfortable I feel with her."

"I can say nothing for her manner to you as a child; but it was the same with us all, or nearly so. She never knew how to be pleasant to children. But you are now of an age to be treated better; I think she *is* behaving better already; and when you are her only companion, you *must* be impor tant to her."

"I can never be important to anyone."

"What is to prevent you?"

"Everything. My situation, my foolishness, and awkwardness."

"As to your foolishness and awkwardness, my dear Fanny, believe me, you never have a shadow of either, but in using the words so improperly. There is no reason in the world why you should not be important where you are known. You have good sense, and a sweet temper, and I am sure you have a grateful heart, that could never receive kindness without wish ing to return it. I do not know any better qualification for a friend and companion."

"You are too kind," said Fanny, colouring at such praise; "how shall I ever thank you as I ought, for thinking so well of me? Oh! cousin, if I am to go away, I shall remember your goodness to the last moment of my life."

"Why, indeed, Fanny, I should hope to be remembered at such a distance as the White House. You speak as if you were going two hundred miles off instead of only across the park; but you will belong to us almost as much as ever. The two families will be meeting every day in the year. The only difference will be that living with your aunt, you will necessarily be brought forward as you ought to be. *Here*, there are too many whom you can hide behind; but with *her* you will be forced to speak for yourself."

"Oh! do not say so."

"I must say it, and say it with pleasure. Mrs. Norris is much better fitted than my mother for having the charge of you now. She is of a temper to do a great deal for anybody she really interests herself about, and she will force you to do justice to your natural powers."

Fanny sighed, and said, "I cannot see things as you do; but I ought to believe you to be right rather than myself, and I am very much obliged to you for trying to reconcile me to what must be. If I could suppose my aunt really to care for me, it would be delightful to feel myself of consequence to anybody. *Here,* I know, I am of none, and yet I love the place so well."

"The place, Fanny, is what you will not quit, though you quit the house. You will have as free a command of the park and gardens as ever. Even *your* constant little heart need not take fright at such a nominal change. You will have the same walks to frequent, the same library to choose from, the same people to look at, the same horse to ride."

"Very true. Yes, dear old grey pony! Ah! cousin, when I remember how much I used to dread riding, what terrors it gave me to hear it talked of as likely to do me good (oh! how I have trembled at my uncle's opening his lips if horses were talked of), and then think of the kind pains you took to reason and persuade me out of my fears, and convince me that I should like it after a little while, and feel how right you proved to be, I am inclined to hope you may always prophesy as well."

"And I am quite convinced that your being with Mrs. Norris will be as good for your mind as riding has been for your health, and as much for your ultimate happiness, too."

So ended their discourse, which, for any very appropriate service it could render Fanny, might as well have been spared, for Mrs. Norris had not the smallest intention of taking her. It had never occurred to her, on the present occasion, but as a thing to be carefully avoided. To prevent its being expected, she had fixed on the smallest habitation which could rank as genteel among the buildings of Mansfield parish, the White House being only just large enough to receive herself and her servants, and allow a spare room for a friend, of which she made a very particular point. The spare rooms at the Parsonage had never been wanted, but the absolute necessity of a spare room for a friend was now never forgotten. Not all her precautions, however, could save her from being suspected of something better; or, perhaps, her very display of the importance of a spare room might have misled Sir Thomas to suppose it really intended for Fanny. Lady Bertram soon brought the matter to a certainty, by carelessly observing to Mrs. Norris:

"I think, sister, we need not keep Miss Lee any longer, when Fanny goes to live with you."

Mrs. Norris almost started. "Live with me, dear Lady Bertram? What do you mean?"

"Is she not to live with you? I thought you had settled it with Sir Thomas."

"Me! never. I never spoke a syllable about it to Sir Thomas, nor he to me. Fanny live with me! The last thing in the world for me to think of, or for anybody to wish that really knows us both. Good heaven! What could I do with Fanny? Me? A poor, helpless, forlorn widow, unfit for anything, my spirits quite broken down; what could I do with a girl at her time of life? A girl of fifteen! The very age of all others to need most attention and care, and put the cheerfullest spirits to the test! Sure Sir Thomas could not seriously expect such a thing! Sir Thomas is too much my friend. Nobody that wishes me well, I am sure, would propose it. How came Sir Thomas to speak to you about it?"

"Indeed, I do not know. I suppose he thought it best."

"But what did he say? He could not say he *wished* me to take Fanny. I am sure in his heart he could not wish me to do it."

"No; he only said he thought it very likely; and I thought so too. We both thought it would be a comfort to you. But if you do not like it, there is no more to be said. She is no incumbrance here."

"Dear sister, if you consider my unhappy state, how can she be any comfort to me? Here am I, a poor desolate widow, deprived of the best of husbands, my health gone in attending and nursing him, my spirits still worse, all my peace in this world destroyed, with hardly enough to support me in the rank of a gentlewoman, and enable me to live so as not to disgrace the memory of the dear departed—what possible comfort could I have in taking such a charge upon me as Fanny? If I could wish it for my own sake, I would not do so unjust a thing by the poor girl. She is in good hands, and sure of doing well. I must struggle through my sorrows and difficulties as I can."

"Then you will not mind living by yourself quite alone?"

"Dear Lady Bertram, what am I fit for but solitude? Now and then I shall hope to have a friend in my little cottage (I shall always have a bed for a friend); but the most part of my future days will be spent in utter seclusion. If I can but make both ends meet, that's all I ask for."

"I hope, sister, things are not so very bad with you neither, considering Sir Thomas says you will have six hundred a year."

"Lady Bertram, I do not complain. I know I cannot live as I have done, but I must retrench where I can, and learn to be a better manager. I *have been* a liberal housekeeper enough, but I shall not be ashamed to practise economy now. My situation is as much altered as my income. A great many things were due from poor Mr. Norris, as clergyman of the parish, that cannot be expected from me. It is unknown how much was consumed in our kitchen by odd comers and goers. At the White House, matters must be better looked after. I *must* live within my income, or I shall be miserable; and I own it would give me great satisfaction to be able to do rather more, to lay by a little at the end of the year."

"I dare say you will. You always do, don't you?"

"My object, Lady Bertram, is to be of use to those that come after me. It is for your children's good that I wish to be richer. I have nobody else to care for; but I should be very glad to think I could leave a little trifle among them worth their having."

"You are very good, but do not trouble yourself about them. They are sure of being well provided for. Sir Thomas will take care of that."

"Why, you know, Sir Thomas's means will be rather straitened if the Antigua estate is to make such poor returns."

"Oh! *that* will soon be settled. Sir Thomas has been writing about it, I know."

"Well, Lady Bertram," said Mrs. Norris, moving to go, "I can only say that my sole desire is to be of use to your family; and so, if Sir Thomas should ever speak again about my taking Fanny, you will be able to say that my health and spirits put it quite out of the question; besides that, I really should not have a bed to give her, for I must keep a spare room for a friend."

Lady Bertram repeated enough of this conversation to her husband to convince him how much he had mistaken his sister-in-law's views; and she was from that moment perfectly safe from all expectation, or the slightest allusion to it from him. He could not but wonder at her refusing to do anything for a niece whom she had been so forward to adopt; but, as she took early care to make him, as well as Lady Bertram, understand, that whatever she possessed was designed for their family, he soon grew reconciled to a distinction which, at the same time that it was advantageous and complimentary to them, would enable him better to provide for Fanny himself.

Fanny soon learnt how unnecessary had been her fears of a removal: and her spontaneous, untaught felicity on the discovery, conveyed some consolation to Edmund for his disappointment in what he had expected to be so essentially serviceable to her. Mrs. Norris took possession of the White House, the Grants arrived at the Parsonage, and these events over, everything at Mansfield went on for some time as usual.

The Grants, showing a disposition to be friendly and sociable, gave great satisfaction in the main among their new acquaintances. They had their faults, and Mrs. Norris soon found them out. The Doctor was very fond of eating, and would have a good dinner every day; and Mrs. Grant, instead of contriving to gratify him at little expense, gave her cook as high wages as they did at Mansfield Park, and was scarcely ever seen in her offices. Mrs. Norris could not speak with any temper of such grievances, nor of the quantity of butter and eggs that were regularly consumed in the house. "Nobody loved plenty and hospitality more than herself; nobody more hated pitiful doings; the Parsonage, she believed, had never been wanting in comforts of any sort, had never borne a bad character in *her time,* but this was a way of going on that she could not understand. A fine lady in a country parsonage was quite out of place. *Her* store-room, she thought, might have been good enough for Mrs. Grant to go into. Enquire where she would, she could not find out that Mrs. Grant had ever had more than five thousand pounds."

Lady Bertram listened without much interest to this sort of invective. She could not enter into the wrongs of an economist, but she felt all the injuries of beauty in Mrs. Grant's being so well settled in life without being handsome, and expressed her astonishment on that point almost as often, though not so diffusely, as Mrs. Norris discussed the other.

These opinions had been hardly canvassed a year before another event arose of such importance in the family, as might fairly claim some place in the thoughts and conversation of the ladies. Sir Thomas found it expedient to go to Antigua himself, for the better arrangement of his affairs, and he took his eldest son with him, in the hope of detaching him from some bad connections at home. They left England with the probability of being nearly a twelvemonth absent.

The necessity of the measure in a pecuniary light, and the hope of its utility to his son, reconciled Sir Thomas to the effort of quitting the rest of his family, and of leaving his daughters to the direction of others at their present most interesting time of life. He could not think Lady Bertram quite equal to supply his place with them, or rather, to perform what should have been her own; but, in Mrs. Norris's watchful attention, and in Edmund's judgment, he had sufficient confidence to make him go without fears for their conduct.

Lady Bertram did not at all like to have her husband leave her; but she was not disturbed by any alarm for his safety, or solicitude for his comfort, being one of those persons who think nothing can be dangerous or difficult, or fatiguing, to anybody but themselves.

The Miss Bertrams were much to be pitied on the occasion; not for their sorrow, but for their want of it. Their father was no object of love to them; he had never seemed the friend of their pleasures, and his absence was unhappily most welcome. They were relieved by it from all restraint; and without aiming at one gratification that would probably have been forbidden by Sir Thomas, they felt themselves immediately at their own disposal, and to have every indulgence within their reach. Fanny's relief, and her consciousness of it, was quite equal to her cousins'; but a more tender nature suggested that her feelings were ungrateful, and she really grieved because she could not grieve. "Sir Thomas, who had done so much for her and her brothers, and who was gone perhaps never to return! That she should see him go without a tear! It was a shameful insensibility." He had said to her, moreover, on the very last morning, that he hoped she might see William again in the course of the ensuing winter, and had charged her to write and invite him to Mansfield, as soon as the squadron to which he belonged should be known to be in England. "This was so thoughtful and kind!" and would he only have smiled upon her, and called her "my dear Fanny" while he said it, every former frown or cold address might have been forgotten. But he had ended his speech in a way to sink her in sad mortification, by adding, "If William does come to Mansfield, I hope you may be able to convince him that the many years which have passed since you parted have not been spent on your side entirely without improvement; though, I fear, he must find his sister at sixteen in some respects too much like his sister at ten." She cried bitterly over this reflection when her uncle was gone; and her cousins, on seeing her with red eyes, set her down as a hypocrite.

Chapter 4

Tom Bertram had of late spent so little of his time at home, that he could be only nominally missed; and Lady Bertram was soon astonished to find how very well they did even without his father, how well Edmund could supply his place in carving, talking to the steward, writing to the attorney, settling with the servants, and equally saving her from all possible fatigue or exertion in every particular, but that of directing her letters.

The earliest intelligence of the travellers' safe arrival at Antigua, after a favourable voyage, was received; though not before Mrs. Norris had been indulging in very dreadful fears, and trying to make Edmund participate them whenever she could get him alone; and as she depended on being the first person made acquainted with any fatal catastrophe, she had already arranged the manner of breaking it to all the others, when Sir Thomas's assurances of their both being alive and well, made it necessary to lay by her agitation and affectionate preparatory speeches for a while.

The winter came and passed without their being called for; the accounts continued perfectly good; and Mrs. Norris, in promoting gaieties for her nieces, assisting their toilets, displaying their accomplishments, and looking about for their future husbands, had so much to do as, in addition to all her own household cares, some interference in those of her sister, and Mrs. Grant's wasteful doings to overlook, left her very little occasion to be occupied in fears for the absent.

The Miss Bertrams were now fully established among the belles of the neighbourhood; and as they joined to beauty and brilliant acquirements a manner naturally easy, and carefully formed to general civility and obligingness, they possessed its favour as well as its admiration. Their vanity was in such good order, that they seemed to be quite free from it, and gave themselves no airs; while the praise attending such behaviour, secured and brought round by their aunt, served to strengthen them in believing they had no faults.

Lady Bertram did not go into public with her daughters. She was too indolent even to accept a mother's gratification in witnessing their success and enjoyment at the expense of any personal trouble, and the charge was made over to her sister, who desired nothing better than a post of such honourable representation, and very thoroughly relished the means it afforded her of mixing in society without having horses to hire.

Fanny had no share in the festivities of the season; but she enjoyed being avowedly useful as her aunt's companion, when they called away the rest of the family; and, as Miss Lee had left Mansfield, she naturally became everything to Lady Bertram during the night of a ball or a party. She talked to her, listened to her, read to her; and the tranquillity of such evenings, her perfect security in such a *tête-à-tête* from any sound of unkindness, was unspeakably welcome to a mind which had seldom known a pause in its alarms or embarrassments. As to her cousins' gaieties, she loved to hear an account of them, especially of the balls, and whom Edmund had danced with; but thought too lowly of her own situation to imagine she should ever be admitted to the same, and listened, therefore, without an idea of any nearer concern in them. Upon the whole, it was a comfortable winter to her; for though it brought no William to England, the never-failing hope of his arrival was worth much.

The ensuing spring deprived her of her valued friend the old grey pony; and for some time she was in danger of feeling the loss in her health as well as in her affections; for in spite of the acknowledged importance of her riding on horseback, no measures were taken for mounting her again, "because," as it was observed by her aunts, "she might ride one of her cousins' horses at any time when they did not want them," and as the Miss Bertrams regularly wanted their horses every fine day, and had no idea of carrying their obliging manners to the sacrifice of any real pleasure, that time, of course, never came. They took their cheerful rides in the fine mornings of April and May; and Fanny either sat at home the whole day with one aunt, or walked beyond her strength at the instigation of the other; Lady Bertram holding exercise to be as unnecessary for everybody as it was unpleasant to herself; and Mrs. Norris, who was walking all day, thinking everybody ought to walk as much. Edmund was absent at this time, or the evil would have been earlier remedied. When he returned, to understand how Fanny was situated, and perceived its ill effects, there seemed with him but one thing to be done; and that "Fanny must have a horse," was the resolute declaration with which he opposed whatever could be urged by the supineness of his mother, or the economy of his aunt, to make it appear unimportant. Mrs. Norris could not help thinking that some steady old thing might be found among the numbers belonging to the Park, that would do vastly well; or, that one might be borrowed of the steward; or that perhaps Dr. Grant might now and then lend them the pony he sent to the post. She could not but consider it as absolutely unnecessary, and even improper, that Fanny should have a regular lady's horse of her own, in the style of her cousins. She was sure Sir Thomas never intended it: and she must say, that to be making such a purchase in his absence, and adding to the great expenses of his stable, at a time when a large part of his income was unsettled, seemed to her very unjustifiable. "Fanny must have a horse," was Edmund's only reply. Mrs. Norris could not see it in the same light. Lady Bertram did: she entirely agreed with her son as to the necessity of it, and as to its being considered necessary by his father; she only pleaded against there being any hurry; she only wanted him to wait till Sir Thomas's return, and then Sir Thomas might settle it all himself. He would be at home in September, and where would be the harm of only waiting till September?

Though Edmund was much more displeased with his aunt than with his mother, as evincing least regard for her niece, he could not help paying more attention to what she said, and at length determined on a method of proceeding which would obviate the risk of his father's thinking he had done too much, and at the same time procure for Fanny the immediate means of exercise, which he could not bear she should be without. He had three horses of his own, but not one that would carry a woman. Two of them were hunters; the third, a useful road-horse. This third he resolved to exchange for one that his cousin might ride; he knew where such a one was to be met with; and having once made up his mind, the whole business was soon completed. The new mare proved a treasure; with a very little trouble she became exactly calculated for the purpose, and Fanny was then put in almost full possession of her. She had not supposed before, that anything could ever suit her like the old grey pony; but her delight in Edmund's mare was far beyond any former pleasure of the sort; and the addition it was ever receiving in the consideration of that kindness from which her pleasure sprung, was beyond all her words to express. She regarded her cousin as an example of everything good and great, as possessing worth, which no one but herself could ever appreciate, and as entitled to such gratitude from her, as no feelings could be strong enough to pay. Her sentiments towards him were compounded of all that was respectful, grateful, confiding and tender.

As the horse continued in name, as well as fact, the property of Edmund, Mrs. Norris could tolerate its being for Fanny's use; and had Lady Bertram ever thought about her own objection again, he might have been excused in her eyes for not waiting till Sir Thomas' return in September, for when September came, Sir Thomas was still abroad, and without any near prospect of finishing his business. Unfavourable circumstances had suddenly arisen at a moment when he was beginning to turn all his thoughts towards England; and the very great uncertainty in which everything was then involved determined him on sending home his son, and waiting the final arrangement by himself. Tom arrived safely, bringing an excellent account of his father's health; but to very little purpose, as far as Mrs. Norris was concerned. Sir Thomas's sending away his son seemed to her so like a parent's care, under the influence of a foreboding of evil to himself, that she could not help feeling dreadful presentiments; and as the long evenings of autumn came on, was so terribly haunted by these ideas, in the sad solitariness of her cottage, as to be obliged to take daily refuge in the dining-room of the Park. The return of winter engagements, however, was not without its effects; and in the course of their progress, her mind became so pleasantly occupied in superintending the fortunes of her eldest niece, as tolerably to quiet her nerves. "If poor Sir Thomas were fated never to return, it would be peculiarly consoling to see their dear Maria well married," she very often thought; always when they were in the company of men of fortune, and particularly on the introduction of a young man who had recently succeeded to one of the largest estates and finest places in the country.

Mr. Rushworth was from the first struck with the beauty of Miss Bertram, and, being inclined to marry, soon fancied himself in love. He was a heavy young man, with not more than common sense; but as there was nothing disagreeable in his figure or address, the young lady was well pleased with her conquest. Being now in her twenty-first year, Maria Bertram was beginning to think matrimony a duty, and as a marriage with Mr. Rushworth would give her the enjoyment of a larger income than her father's, as well as ensure her the house in town, which was now a prime object, it became, by the same rule of moral obligation, her evident duty to marry Mr. Rushworth if she could. Mrs. Norris was most zealous in promoting the match, by every suggestion and contrivance likely to enhance its desirableness to either party; and, among other means, by seeking an intimacy with the gentleman's mother, who at present lived with him, and to whom she even forced Lady Bertram to go through ten miles of indifferent road to pay a morning visit. It was not long before a good understanding took place between this lady and herself. Mrs. Rushworth acknowledged herself very desirous that her son should marry, and declared that of all the young ladies she had ever seen, Miss Bertram seemed, by her amiable qualities and accomplishments, the best adapted to make him happy. Mrs. Norris accepted the compliment, and admired the nice discernment of character which could so well distinguish merit. Maria was indeed the pride and delight of them all—perfectly faultless— an angel; and, of course, so surrounded by admirers, must be difficult in her choice: but yet, as far as Mrs. Norris could allow herself to decide on so short an acquaintance, Mr. Rushworth appeared precisely the young man to deserve and attach her.

After dancing with each other at a proper number of balls, the young people justified these opinions, and an engagement, with a due reference to the absent Sir Thomas, was entered into, much to the satisfaction of their respective families, and of the general lookers-on of the neighbourhood, who had, for many weeks past, felt the expediency of Mr. Rushworth's marrying Miss Bertram.

It was some months before Sir Thomas's consent could be received; but, in the meanwhile, as no one felt a doubt of his most cordial pleasure in the connection, the intercourse of the two families was carried on without restraint, and no other attempt made at secrecy, than Mrs. Norris's talking of it everywhere as a matter not to be talked of at present.

Edmund was the only one of the family who could see a fault in the business; but no representation of his aunt's could induce him to find Mr. Rushworth a desirable companion. He could allow his sister to be the best judge of her own happiness, but he was not pleased that her happiness should centre in a large income; nor could he refrain from often saying to himself, in Mr. Rushworth's company, "If this man had not twelve thousand a year, he would be a very stupid fellow."

Sir Thomas, however, was truly happy in the prospect of an alliance so unquestionably advantageous, and of which he heard nothing but the perfectly good and agreeable. It was a connection exactly of the right sort—in the same county, and the same interest—and his most hearty concurrence was conveyed as soon as possible. He only conditioned that the marriage should not take place before his return, which he was again looking eagerly forward to. He wrote in April, and had strong hopes of settling everything to his entire satisfaction, and leaving Antigua before the end of the summer.

Such was the state of affairs in the month of July; and Fanny had just reached her eighteenth year, when the society of the village received an addition in the brother and sister of Mrs. Grant, a Mr. and Miss Crawford, the children of her mother by a second marriage. They were young people of fortune. The son had a good estate in Norfolk, the daughter twenty thousand pounds. As children, their sister had been always very fond of them; but, as her own marriage had been soon followed by the death of their common parent, which left them to the care of a brother of their father, of whom Mrs. Grant knew nothing, she had scarcely seen them since. In their uncle's house they had found a kind home. Admiral and Mrs. Crawford, though agreeing in nothing else, were united in affection for these children, or, at least, were no further adverse in their feelings than that each had their favourite, to whom they showed the greatest fondness of the two. The Admiral delighted in the boy, Mrs. Crawford doted on the girl; and it was the lady's death which now obliged her *protégée*, after some months' further trial at her uncle's house, to find another home. Admiral Crawford was a man of vicious conduct, who chose, instead of retaining his niece, to bring his mistress under his own roof; and to this Mrs. Grant was indebted for her sister's proposal of coming to her, a measure quite as welcome on one side as it could be expedient on the other; for Mrs. Grant, having by this time run through the usual resources of ladies residing in the country without a family of children—having more than filled her favourite sitting-room with pretty furniture, and made a choice collection of plants and poultry—was very much in want of some variety at home. The arrival, therefore, of a sister whom she had always loved, and now hoped to retain with her as long as she remained single, was highly agreeable; and her chief anxiety was, lest Mansfield should not satisfy the habits of a young woman who had been mostly used to London.

Miss Crawford was not entirely free from similar apprehensions, though they arose principally from doubts of her sister's style of living and tone of society; and it was not till after she had tried in vain to persuade her brother to settle with her at his own country house, that she could resolve to hazard herself among her other relations. To anything like a permanence of abode, or limitation of society, Henry Crawford had, unluckily, a great dislike; he could not accommodate his sister in an article of such importance; but he escorted her, with the utmost kindness, into North-amptonshire and as readily engaged to fetch her away again, at half an hour's notice, whenever she were weary of the place.

The meeting was very satisfactory on each side. Miss Crawford found a sister without preciseness or rusticity—a sister's husband who looked the gentleman, and a house commodious and well fitted up; and Mrs. Grant received in those whom she hoped to love better than ever, a young man and woman of very prepossessing appearance. Mary Crawford was remarkably pretty; Henry, though not handsome, had air and counte-nance; the manners of both were lively and pleasant, and Mrs. Grant immediately gave them credit for everything else. She was delighted with each, but Mary was her dearest object; and having never been able to glory in beauty of her own, she thoroughly enjoyed the power of being proud of her sister's. She had not waited for her arrival to look out for a suitable match for her; she had fixed on Tom Bertram; the eldest son of a baronet was not too good for a girl of twenty thousand pounds, with all the elegance and accomplishments which Mrs. Grant foresaw in her; and being a warmhearted, unreserved woman, Mary had not been there three hours in the house before she told her what she had planned.

Miss Crawford was glad to find a family of such consequence so very near them, and not at all displeased either at her sister's early care, or the choice it had fallen on. Matrimony was her object, provided she could marry well: and having seen Mr. Bertram in town, she knew that objec-tion could no more be made to his person than to his situation in life. While she treated it as a joke, therefore, she did not forget to think of it seriously. The scheme was soon repeated to Henry.

"And now," added Mrs. Grant, "I have thought of something to make it complete. I should dearly love to settle you both in this country; and therefore, Henry, you shall marry the youngest Miss Bertram, a nice, handsome, good-humoured, accomplished girl, who will make you very happy."

Henry bowed and thanked her.

"My dear sister," said Mary, "if you can persuade him into anything of the sort, it will be a fresh matter of delight to me to find myself allied to anybody so clever, and I shall only regret that you have not half-a-dozen daughters to dispose of. If you can persuade Henry to marry, you must have the address of a Frenchwoman. All that English abilities can do has been tried already. I have three very particular friends who have been all dying for him in their turn; and the pains which they, their mothers (very clever women), as well as my dear aunt and myself, have taken to reason, coax, or trick him into marrying, is inconceivable! He is the most horrible flirt that can be imagined. If your Miss Bertrams do not like to have their hearts broke let them avoid Henry."

"My dear brother, I will not believe this of you."

"No, I am sure you are too good. You will be kinder than Mary. You will allow for the doubts of youth and inexperience. I am of a cautious temper, and unwilling to risk my happiness in a hurry. Nobody can think more highly of the matrimonial state than myself. I consider the blessing of a wife as most justly described in those discreet lines of the poet 'Heaven's *last* best gift.' "

"There, Mrs. Grant, you see how he dwells on one word, and only look at his smile. I assure you he is very detestable; the Admiral's lessons have quite spoiled him."

"I pay very little regard," said Mrs. Grant, "to what any young person says on the subject of marriage. If they profess a disinclination for it, I only set it down that they have not yet seen the right person."

Dr. Grant laughingly congratulated Miss Crawford on feeling no disinclination to the state herself.

"Oh yes! I am not at all ashamed of it. I would have everybody marry if they can do it properly: I do not like to have people throw themselves away: but everybody should marry as soon as they can do it to advantage."

Chapter 5

THE young people were pleased with each other from the first. On each side there was much to attract, and their acquaintance soon promised as early an intimacy as good manners would warrant. Miss Crawford's beauty did her no disservice with the Miss Bertrams. They were too handsome themselves to dislike any woman for being so too, and were almost as much charmed as their brothers with her lively dark eyes, clear-brown complexion, and general prettiness. Had she been tall, full formed, and fair, it might have been more of a trial: but as it was, there could be no comparison; and she was most allowably a sweet, pretty girl, while they were the finest young women in the country.

Her brother was not handsome; no, when they first saw him he was absolutely plain, black and plain; but still he was the gentleman, with a pleasing address. The second meeting proved him not so very plain; he was plain, to be sure, but then he had so much countenance, and his teeth were so good, and he was so well made, that one soon forgot he was plain; and after a third interview, after dining in company with him at the Parsonage, he was no longer allowed to be called so by anybody. He was, in fact, the most agreeable young man the sisters had ever known, and they were equally delighted with him. Miss Bertram's engagement made him in equity the property of Julia, of which Julia was fully aware; and before he had been at Mansfield a week, she was quite ready to be fallen in love with.

Maria's notions on the subject were more confused and indistinct. She did not want to see or understand. "There could be no harm in her liking an agreeable man—everybody knew her situation—Mr. Crawford must take care of himself." Mr. Crawford did not mean to be in any danger!

the Miss Bertrams were worth pleasing, and were ready to be pleased; and he began with no object of making them like him. He did not want them to die of love; but with sense and temper which ought to have made him judge and feel better, he allowed himself great latitude on such points.

"I like your Miss Bertrams exceedingly, sister," said he, as he returned from attending them to their carriage after the said dinner visit; "they are very elegant, agreeable girls."

"So they are, indeed, and I am delighted to hear you say it. But you like Julia best."

"Oh yes! I like Julia best."

"But do you really? for Miss Bertram is in general thought the handsomest."

"So I should suppose. She has the advantage in every feature, and 1 prefer her countenance; but I like Julia best; Miss Bertram is certainly the handsomest, and I have found her the most agreeable, but I shall always like Julia best, because you order me."

"I shall not talk to you, Henry, but I know you *will* like her best at last."

"Do not I tell you that I like her best at *first?*"

"And besides, Miss Bertram is engaged. Remember that, my dear brother. Her choice is made."

"Yes, and I like her the better for it. An engaged woman is always more agreeable than a disengaged. She is satisfied with herself. Her cares are over, and she feels that she may exert all her powers of pleasing without suspicion. All is safe with a lady engaged; no harm can be done."

"Why, as to that, Mr. Rushworth is a very good sort of young man, and it is a great match for her."

"But Miss Bertram does not care three straws for him; *that* is your opinion of your intimate friend. *I* do not subscribe to it. I am sure Miss Bertram is very much attached to Mr. Rushworth. I could see it in her eyes, when he was mentioned. I think too well of Miss Bertram to suppose she would ever give her hand without her heart."

"Mary, how shall we manage him?"

"We must leave him to himself, I believe. Talking does no good. He will be taken in at last."

"But I would not have him *taken in;* I would not have him duped; I would have it all fair and honourable."

"Oh dear! let him stand his chance and be taken in. It will do just as well. Everybody is taken in at some period or other."

"Not always in marriage, dear Mary."

"In marriage especially. With all due respect to such of the present company as chance to be married, my dear Mrs. Grant, there is not one in a hundred of either sex who is not taken in when they marry. Look where I will, I see that it *is* so; and I feel that it *must* be so, when I consider that it is, of all transactions, the one in which people expect most from others, and are least honest themselves."

"Ah! You have been in a bad school for matrimony, in Hill Street."

"My poor aunt had certainly little cause to love the state; but, however, speaking from my own observation, it is a manœuvring business. I know so many who have married in the full expectation and confidence of some one particular advantage in the connection, or accomplishment, or good quality in the person, who have found themselves entirely deceived, and been obliged to put up with exactly the reverse. What is this but a take in?"

"My dear child, there must be a little imagination here. I beg your pardon, but I cannot quite believe you. Depend upon it, you see but half. You see the evil, but you do not see the consolation. There will be little rubs and disappointments everywhere, and we are all apt to expect too much; but then, if one scheme of happiness fails, human nature turns to another; if the first calculation is wrong we make a second better; we find comfort somewhere—and those evil-minded observers, dearest Mary, who make much of a little, are more taken in and deceived than the parties themselves."

"Well done, sister! I honour your *esprit de corps*. When I am a wife, I mean to be just as staunch myself; and I wish my friends in general would be so too. It would save me many a heart-ache."

"You are as bad as your brother, Mary; but we will cure you both. Mansfield shall cure you both, and without any taking in. Stay with us, and we will cure you."

The Crawfords, without wanting to be cured, were very willing to stay. Mary was satisfied with the Parsonage as a present home and Henry equally ready to lengthen his visit. He had come, intending to spend only a few days with them; but Mansfield promised well, and there was nothing to call him elsewhere. It delighted Mrs. Grant to keep them both with her, and Dr. Grant was exceedingly well contented to have it so: a talking pretty young woman like Miss Crawford is always pleasant society to an indolent, stay-at-home man; and Mr. Crawford's being his guest was an excuse for drinking claret every day.

The Miss Bertrams' admiration of Mr. Crawford was more rapturous than anything which Miss Crawford's habits made her likely to feel. She acknowledged, however, that the Mr. Bertrams were very fine young men, that two such young men were not often seen together even in London, and that their manners, particularly those of the eldest, were very good. *He* had been much in London, and had more liveliness and gallantry than Edmund, and must, therefore, be preferred; and indeed, his being the eldest was another strong claim. She had felt an early presentiment that she *should* like the eldest best. She knew it was her way.

Tom Bertram must have been thought pleasant, indeed, at any rate; he was the sort of young man to be generally liked, his agreeableness was of the kind to be oftener found agreeable than some endowments of a higher stamp, for he had easy manners, excellent spirits, a large acquaintance, and a great deal to say: and the reversion of Mansfield Park, and a baronetcy, did no harm to all this. Miss Crawford soon felt that he and his situation might do. She looked about her with due consideration, and found almost everything in his favour, a park, a real park, five miles round, a spacious modern-built house, so well placed and well screened as to deserve to be in any collection of engravings of gentlemen's seats in the kingdom, and wanting only to be completely new furnished—pleasant sisters, a quiet mother, and an agreeable man himself—with the advantage of being tied up from much gaming at present by a promise to his father, and of being Sir Thomas hereafter. It might do very well; she believed she should accept him; and she began accordingly to interest herself a little about the horse which he had to run at the B—— races.

These races were to call him away not long after their acquaintance began; and as it appeared that the family did not, from his usual goings on, expect him back again for many weeks, it would bring his passion to an early proof. Much was said on his side to induce her to attend the races, and schemes were made for a large party to them, with all the eagerness of inclination, but it would only do to be talked of.

And Fanny, what was *she* doing and thinking all this while? and what was *her* opinion of the new-comers? Few young ladies of eighteen could be less called on to speak their opinion than Fanny. In a quiet way, very little attended to, she paid her tribute of admiration to Miss Crawford's beauty; but as she still continued to think Mr. Crawford very plain, in spite of her two cousins having repeatedly proved the contrary, she never mentioned *him*. The notice which she excited herself, was to this effect. "I begin now to understand you all, except Miss Price," said Miss Crawford, as she was walking with the Mr. Bertrams. "Pray, is she out, or is she not? I am puzzled. She dined at the Parsonage, with the rest of you, which seemed like being *out*; and yet she says so little, that I can hardly suppose she *is*."

Edmund, to whom this was chiefly addressed, replied, "I believe I know what you mean, but I will not undertake to answer the question. My cousin is grown up. She has the age and sense of a woman, but the outs and not outs are beyond me."

"And yet, in general, nothing can be more easily ascertained. The distinction is so broad. Manners as well as appearance are, generally speaking, so totally different. Till now, I could not have supposed it possible to be mistaken as to a girl's being out or not. A girl not out, has always the same sort of dress: a close bonnet, for instance; looks very demure, and never says a word. You may smile, but it is so, I assure you; and except that it is sometimes carried a little too far, it is all very proper. Girls should be quiet and modest. The most objectionable part is, that the alteration of manners on being introduced into company is frequently too sudden. They sometimes pass in such very little time from reserve to quite the opposite—to confidence! *That* is the faulty part of the present system. One does not like to see a girl of eighteen or nineteen so immediately up to everything—and perhaps when one has seen her hardly able to speak the year before. Mr. Bertram, I dare say *you* have sometimes met with such changes."

"I believe I have, but this is hardly fair; I see what you are at. You are quizzing me and Miss Anderson."

"No, indeed. Miss Anderson! I do not know who or what you mean. I am quite in the dark. But I *will* quiz you with a great deal of pleasure, if you will tell me what about."

"Ah! you carry it off very well, but I cannot be quite so far imposed on. You must have had Miss Anderson in your eye, in describing an altered young lady. You paint too accurately for mistake. It was exactly so. The Andersons of Baker Street. We were speaking of them the other day, you know. Edmund, you have heard me mention Charles Anderson. The circumstance was precisely as this lady has represented it. When Anderson first introduced me to his family, about two years ago, his sister was not *out*, and I could not get her to speak to me. I sat there an hour one morning waiting for Anderson, with only her and a little girl or two in the room, the governess being sick or run away, and the mother in and out every moment with letters of business, and I could hardly get a word or a look from the young lady—nothing like a civil answer—she screwed up her mouth, and turned from me with such an air! I did not see her again for a twelvemonth. She was then *out*. I met her at Mrs. Holford's, and did not recollect her. She came up to me, claimed me as an acquaintance, stared me out of countenance, and talked and laughed till I did not know which way to look. I felt that I must be the jest of the room at the time, and Miss Crawford, it is plain, has heard the story."

"And a very pretty story it is, and with more truth in it, I dare say, than does credit to Miss Anderson. It is too common a fault. Mothers certainly have not yet got quite the right way of managing their daughters. I do not know where the error lies. I do not pretend to set people right, but I do see that they are often wrong."

"Those who are showing the world what female manners *should* be," said Mr. Bertram gallantly, "are doing a great deal to set them right."

"The error is plain enough," said the less courteous Edmund; "such girls are ill brought up. They are given wrong notions from the beginning. They are always acting upon motives of vanity, and there is no more real modesty in their behaviour *before* they appear in public than afterwards."

"I do not know," replied Miss Crawford, hesitatingly. "Yes, I cannot agree with you there. It is certainly the modestest part of the business. It is much worse to have girls *not out*, give themselves the same airs and take the same liberties as if they were, which I *have* seen done. *That* is worse than anything—quite disgusting!"

"Yes, *that* is very inconvenient, indeed," said Mr. Bertram. "It leads one astray; one does not know what to do. The close bonnet and demure air you described so well (and nothing was ever juster), tell one what is expected; but I got into a dreadful scrape last year from the want of them. I went down to Ramsgate for a week with a friend last September, just after my return from the West Indies. My friend Sneyd—you have heard me speak of Sneyd, Edmund—his father, and mother, and sisters, were there all new to me. When we reached Albion Place, they were out: we went after them, and found them on the pier; Mrs. and the two Miss Sneyds, with others of their acquaintances. I made my bow in form; and as Mrs. Sneyd was surrounded by men, attached myself to one of her daughters, walked by her side all the way home, and made myself as agreeable as I could; the young lady, perfectly easy in her manners, and as ready to talk as to listen. I had not a suspicion that I could be doing anything wrong. They looked just the same: both well dressed, with veils and parasols like other girls; but I afterwards found that I had been giving all my attention to the youngest, who was not *out,* and had most excessively offended the eldest. Miss Augusta ought not to have been noticed for the next six months; and Miss Sneyd, I believe, has never forgiven me."

"That was bad, indeed. Poor Miss Sneyd! Though I have no younger sister, I feel for her. To be neglected before one's time must be very vexatious; but it was entirely her mother's fault. Miss Augusta should have been with her governess. Such half and half doings never prosper. But now I must be satisfied about Miss Price. Does she go to balls? Does she dine out everywhere, as well as at my sister's?"

"No," replied Edmund; "I do not think she has ever been to a ball. My mother seldom goes into company herself, and dines nowhere but with Mrs. Grant, and Fanny stays at home with *her.*"

"Oh! then the point is clear. Miss Price is *not* out."

Chapter 6

MR. BERTRAM set off for B——, and Miss Crawford was prepared to find a great chasm in their society, and to miss him decidedly in the meetings which were now becoming almost daily between the families; and on their all dining together at the Park soon after his going, she re-took her chosen place near the bottom of the table, fully expecting to feel a most melancholy difference in the change of masters. It would be a very flat business, she was sure. In comparison with his brother, Edmund would have nothing to say. The soup would be sent round in a most spiritless manner, wine drank without any smiles or agreeable trifling, and the venison cut up without supplying one pleasant anecdote of any former haunch, or a single entertaining story, about "my friend such a one." She must try to find amusement in what was passing at the upper end of the table, and in observing Mr. Rushworth, who was now making his appearance at Mansfield for the first time since the Crawfords' arrival. He had been visiting a friend in the neighbouring county, and that friend having recently had his grounds laid out by an improver, Mr. Rushworth was returned with his head full of the subject, and very eager to be improving his own place in the same way; and though not saying much to the purpose, could talk of nothing else. The subject had been already handled in the drawing-room; it was revived in the dining-parlour. Miss Bertram's attention and opinion was evidently his chief aim; and though her deportment showed rather conscious superiority than any solicitude to oblige him, the mention of Sotherton Court, and the ideas attached to it, gave her a feeling of complacency, which prevented her from being very ungracious.

"I wish you could see Compton," said he, "it is the most complete thing! I never saw a place so altered in my life. I told Smith I did not know where I was. The approach, *now*, is one of the finest things in the country; you see the house in the most surprising manner. I declare, when I got back to Sotherton yesterday, it looked like a prison—quite a dismal old prison."

"Oh, for shame!" cried Mrs. Norris. "A prison, indeed! Sotherton Court is the noblest old place in the world."

"It wants improvement, ma'am, beyond anything. I never saw a place that wanted so much improvement in my life: and it is so forlorn, that I do not know what can be done with it."

"No wonder that Mr. Rushworth should think so at present," said Mrs. Grant to Mrs. Norris, with a smile; "but depend upon it, Sotherton will have *every* improvement in time which his heart can desire."

"I must try to do something with it," said Mr. Rushworth, "but I do not know what. I hope I shall have some good friend to help me."

"Your best friend upon such an occasion," said Miss Bertram calmly, "would be Mr. Repton, I imagine."

"That is what I was thinking of. As he has done so well by Smith, I think I had better have him at once. His terms are five guineas a day."

"Well, and if they were *ten*," cried Mrs. Norris, "I am sure *you* need not regard it. The expense need not be any impediment. If I were you, I should not think of the expense. I would have everything done in the best style, and made as nice as possible. Such a place as Sotherton Court deserves everything that taste and money can do. You have space to work upon there, and grounds that will well reward you. For my own part, if I had anything within the fiftieth part of the size of Sotherton, I should be always planting and improving, for, naturally, I am excessively fond of it. It would be too ridiculous for me to attempt anything where I am now with my little half acre. It would be quite a burlesque. But if I had more room, I should take a prodigious delight in improving and planting. We did a vast deal in that way at the Parsonage: we made it quite a place from what it was when we first had it. You young ones do not remember much about it, perhaps; but if dear Sir Thomas were here, he could tell you what improvements we made: and a great deal more would have been done, but for poor Mr. Norris's sad state of health. He could hardly ever get out, poor man, to enjoy anything, and *that* disheartened me from doing several things that Sir Thomas and I used to talk of. If it had not been for *that,* we should have carried on the garden wall, and made the plantation to shut out the churchyard, just as Dr. Grant has done. We were always doing something as it was. It was only the spring twelvemonth before Mr. Norris's death, that we put in the apricot against the stable wall, which is now grown such a noble tree, and getting to such perfection, sir," addressing herself then to Dr. Grant.

"The tree thrives well, beyond a doubt, madam," replied Dr. Grant. "The soil is good; and I never pass it without regretting that the fruit should be so little worth the trouble of gathering."

"Sir, it is a Moor Park, we bought it as a Moor Park, and it cost us— that is, it was a present from Sir Thomas, but I saw the bill—and I know it cost seven shillings, and was charged as a Moor Park."

"You were imposed on, ma'am," replied Dr. Grant: "these potatoes have as much the flavour of a Moor Park apricot as the fruit from that tree. It is an insipid fruit at the best; but a good apricot is eatable, which none from my garden are."

"The truth is, ma'am," said Mrs. Grant, pretending to whisper across the table to Mrs. Norris, "that Dr. Grant hardly knows what the natural taste of our apricot is: he is scarcely ever indulged with one, for it is so valuable a fruit, with a little assistance, and ours is such a remarkably large, fair sort, that what with early tarts and preserves, my cook contrives to get them all."

Mrs. Norris, who had begun to redden, was appeased; and, for a little while, other subjects took place of the improvements of Sotherton. Dr. Grant and Mrs. Norris were seldom good friends; their acquaintance had begun in dilapidations, and their habits were totally dissimilar.

After a short interruption, Mr. Rushworth began again. "Smith's place is the admiration of all the country; and it was a mere nothing before Repton took it in hand. I think I shall have Repton."

"Mr. Rushworth," said Lady Bertram, "if I were you, I would have a very pretty shrubbery. One likes to get out into a shrubbery in fine weather."

Mr. Rushworth was eager to assure her ladyship of his acquiescence, and tried to make out something complimentary; but, between his submission to *her* taste, and his having always intended the same himself, with superadded objects of professing attention to the comfort of ladies in general, and of insinuating that there was one only whom he was anxious to please, he grew puzzled, and Edmund was glad to put an end to his speech by a proposal of wine. Mr. Rushworth, however, though not usually a great talker, had still more to say on the subject next his heart; "Smith has not much above a hundred acres altogether, in his grounds, which is little enough, and makes it more surprising that the place can have been so improved. Now, at Sotherton, we have a good seven hundred, without reckoning the water meadows; so that I think, if so much could be done at Compton, we need not despair. There have been two or three fine old trees cut down, that grew too near the house, and it opens the prospect amazingly, which makes me think that Repton, or anybody of that sort, would certainly have the avenue at Sotherton down; the avenue that leads from the west front to the top of the hill, you know," turning to Miss Bertram particularly as he spoke. But Miss Bertram thought it most becoming to reply:

"The avenue! Oh! I do not recollect it. I really know very little of Sotherton."

Fanny, who was sitting on the other side of Edmund, exactly opposite Miss Crawford, and who had been attentively listening, now looked at him, and said, in a low voice:

"Cut down an avenue! What a pity! Does it not make you think of Cowper? 'Ye fallen avenues, once more I mourn your fate unmerited.' "

He smiled as he answered, "I am afraid the avenue stands a bad chance, Fanny."

"I should like to see Sotherton before it is cut down, to see the place as it is now, in its old state; but I do not suppose I shall."

"Have you never been there? No, you never can; and, unluckily, it is out of distance for a ride. I wish we could contrive it."

"Oh! it does not signify. Whenever I do see it, you will tell me how it has been altered."

"I collect," said Miss Crawford, "that Sotherton is an old place, and a place of some grandeur. In any particular style of building?"

"The house was built in Elizabeth's time, and is a large, regular, brick building; heavy, but respectable looking, and has many good rooms. It is ill placed. It stands in one of the lowest spots of the park; in that respect, unfavourable for improvement. But the woods are fine, and there is a stream, which, I dare say, might be made a good deal of. Mr. Rushworth is quite right, I think, in meaning to give it a modern dress, and I have no doubt that it will be all done extremely well."

Miss Crawford listened with submission, and said to herself, "He is a well-bred man; he makes the best of it."

"I do not wish to influence Mr. Rushworth," he continued; "but, had I a place to new-fashion, I should not put myself into the hands of an improver. I would rather have an inferior degree of beauty, of my own choice, and acquired progressively. I would rather abide by my own blunders than by his."

"*You* would know what you were about, of course; but that would not suit *me*. I have no eye of ingenuity for such matters, but as they are before me; and had I a place of my own in the country, I should be most thankful to any Mr. Repton who would undertake it, and give me as much beauty as he could for my money; and I should never look at it till it was complete."

"It would be delightful to *me* to see the progress of it all," said Fanny.

"Ay, you have been brought up to it. It was no part of my education; and the only dose I ever had, being administered by not the first favourite in the world, has made me consider improvements *in hand* as the greatest of nuisances. Three years ago, the Admiral, my honoured uncle, bought a cottage at Twickenham for us all to spend our summers in; and my aunt and I went down to it quite in raptures; but it being excessively pretty, it was soon found necessary to be improved, and for three months we were all dirt and confusion, without a gravel walk to step on, or a bench fit for use. I would have everything as complete as possible in the country, shrubberies and flower-gardens, and rustic seats innumerable: but it must all be done without my care. Henry is different, he loves to be doing."

Edmund was sorry to hear Miss Crawford, whom he was much disposed to admire, speak so freely of her uncle. It did not suit his sense of propriety, and he was silenced, till induced by further smiles and liveliness, to put the matter by for the present.

"Mr. Bertram," said she, "I have tidings of my harp at last. I am assured that it is safe at Northampton; and there it has probably been these ten days, in spite of the solemn assurances we have so often received to the contrary." Edmund expressed his pleasure and surprise. "The truth is, that our inquiries were too direct; we sent a servant, we went ourselves: this will not do seventy miles from London; but this morning we heard of it in the right way. It was seen by some farmer, and he told the miller, and the miller told the butcher, and the butcher's son-in-law left word at the shop."

"I am very glad that you have heard of it, by whatever means, and hope there will be no further delay."

"I am to have it to-morrow; but, how do you think it is to be conveyed? Not by a wagon or cart: oh no! nothing of that kind could be hired in the village. I might as well have asked for porters and a hand-barrow."

"You would find it difficult, I dare say, just now, in the middle of a very late hay harvest, to hire a horse and cart?"

"I was astonished to find what a piece of work was made of it! To want a horse and cart in the country seemed impossible, so I told my maid to speak for one directly; and as I cannot look out of my dressing-closet without seeing one farm-yard, nor walk in the shrubbery without passing another, I thought it would be only ask and have, and was rather grieved that I could not give the advantage to all. Guess my surprise when I found that I had been asking the most unreasonable, most impossible thing in the world; had offended all the farmers, all the labourers, all the hay in the parish! As for Dr. Grant's bailiff, I believe I had better keep out of *his* way; and my brother-in-law himself, who is all kindness in general, looked rather black upon me, when he found what I had been at."

"You could not be expected to have thought on the subject before; but when you *do* think of it, you must see the importance of getting in the grass. The hire of a cart at any time might not be so easy as you suppose; our farmers are not in the habit of letting them out: but, in harvest, it must be quite out of their power to spare a horse."

"I shall understand all your ways in time; but, coming down with the true London maxim, that everything is to be got with money, I was a little embarrassed at first by the sturdy independence of your country customs. However, I am to have my harp fetched to-morrow. Henry, who is good nature itself, has offered to fetch it in his barouche. Will it not be honourably conveyed?"

Edmund spoke of the harp as his favourite instrument, and hoped to be soon allowed to hear her. Fanny had never heard the harp at all, and wished for it very much.

"I shall be most happy to play to you both," said Miss Crawford; "at least as long as you can like to listen: probably much longer, for I dearly love music myself, and where the natural taste is equal the player must always be best off, for she is gratified in more ways than one. Now, Mr. Bertram, if you write to your brother, I entreat you to tell him that my harp *is* come; he heard so much of my misery about it. And you may say, if you please, that I shall prepare my most plaintive airs against his return, in compassion to his feelings, as I know his horse will lose."

"If I write, I will say whatever you wish me; but I do not, at present, foresee any occasion for writing."

"No, I dare say, not if he were to be gone a twelvemonth would you ever write to him, nor he to you, if it could be helped. The occasion would never be foreseen. What strange creatures brothers are! You would not write to each other but upon the most urgent necessity in the world; and when obliged to take up a pen to say that such a horse is ill, or such a relation dead, it is done in the fewest possible words. You have but one style among you. I know it perfectly. Henry, who is in every other respect exactly what a brother should be, who loves me, consults me, confides in me, and will talk to me by the hour together, has never yet turned the page in a letter; and very often it is nothing more than—'Dear Mary, I am just arrived. Bath seems full and everything as usual. Yours sincerely.' That is the true manly style; that is a complete brother's letter."

"When they are at a distance from all their family," said Fanny, colouring for William's sake, "they can write long letters."

"Miss Price has a brother at sea," said Edmund, "whose excellence as a correspondent makes her think you too severe upon us."

"At sea, has she? In the king's service, of course?"

Fanny would rather have had Edmund tell the story, but his determined silence obliged her to relate her brother's situation; her voice was animated in speaking of his profession, and the foreign stations he had been on; but she could not mention the number of years that he had been absent without tears in her eyes. Miss Crawford civilly wished him an early promotion.

"Do you know anything of my cousin's captain?" said Edmund; "Captain Marshall? You have a large acquaintance in the navy, I conclude?"

"Among admirals, large enough; but," with an air of grandeur, "we know very little of the inferior ranks. Post-captains may be very good sort of men, but they do not belong to *us*. Of various admirals I could tell you a great deal; of them and their flags, and the gradation of their pay, and their bickerings and jealousies. But, in general, I can assure you that they are all passed over, and all very ill used. Certainly, my home at my uncle's brought me acquainted with a circle of admirals. Of *Rears* and *Vices*, I saw enough. Now do not be suspecting me of a pun, I entreat."

Edmund again felt grave, and only replied, "It is a noble profession."

"Yes, the profession is well enough under two circumstances; if it make the fortune, and there be discretion in spending it; but, in short, it is not a favourite profession of mine. It has never worn an amiable form to *me*."

Edmund reverted to the harp, and was again very happy in the prospect of hearing her play.

The subject of improving grounds, meanwhile, was still under consideration among the others; and Mrs. Grant could not help addressing her brother, though it was calling his attention from Miss Julia Bertram.

"My dear Henry, have *you* nothing to say? You have been an improver yourself, and from what I hear of Everingham, it may vie with any place in England. Its natural beauties, I am sure, are great. Everingham, as it *used* to be, was perfect in my estimation; such a happy fall of ground, and such timber! What would I not give to see it again."

"Nothing could be so gratifying to me as to hear your opinion of it," was his answer; "but I fear there would be some disappointment: you would not find it equal to your present ideas. In extent, it is a mere nothing; you would be surprised at its insignificance; and, as for improvement, there was very little for me to do—too little; I should like to have been busy much longer."

"You are fond of the sort of thing?" said Julia.

"Excessively; but what with the natural advantages of the ground, which pointed out, even to a very young eye, what little remained to be done, and my own consequent resolutions, I had not been of age three months before Everingham was all that it is now. My plan was laid at Westminster, a little altered, perhaps, at Cambridge, and at one-and-twenty executed. I am inclined to envy Mr. Rushworth for having so much happiness yet before him. I have been a devourer of my own."

"Those who see quickly, will resolve quickly, and act quickly," said Julia. "*You* can never want employment. Instead of envying Mr. Rushworth, you should assist him with your opinion."

Mrs. Grant, hearing the latter part of this speech, enforced it warmly; persuaded that no judgment could be equal to her brother's; and as Miss Bertram caught at the idea likewise, and gave it her full support, declaring that, in her opinion, it was infinitely better to consult with friends and disinterested advisers, than immediately to throw the business into the hands of a professional man, Mr. Rushworth was very ready to request the favour of Mr. Crawford's assistance; and Mr. Crawford, after properly depreciating his own abilities, was quite at his service in any way that could be useful. Mr. Rushworth then began to propose Mr. Crawford's doing him the honour of coming over to Sotherton, and taking a bed there; when Mrs. Norris, as if reading in her two nieces' minds their little approbation of a plan which was to take Mr. Crawford away, interposed with an amendment.

"There can be no doubt of Mr. Crawford's willingness; but why should not more of us go? Why should not we make a little party? Here are many that would be interested in your improvements, my dear Mr. Rushworth, and that would like to hear Mr. Crawford's opinion on the spot, and that might be of some small use to you with *their* opinions; and for my own part, I have been long wishing to wait upon your good mother again; nothing but having no horses of my own could have made me so remiss; but now I could go and sit a few hours with Mrs. Rushworth, while the rest of you walked about and settled things, and then we could all return to a late dinner here, or dine at Sotherton, just as might be most agreeable to your mother, and have a pleasant drive home by moonlight. I dare say Mr. Crawford would take my two nieces and me in his barouche, and Edmund can go on horseback, you know, sister, and Fanny will stay at home with you."

Lady Bertram made no objection; and every one concerned in the going was forward in expressing their ready concurrence, excepting Edmund, who heard it all and said nothing.

Chapter 7

"WELL, Fanny, and how do you like Miss Crawford *now?*" said Edmund the next day, after thinking some time on the subject himself. "How did you like her yesterday?"

"Very well—very much. I like to hear her talk. She entertains me; and she is so extremely pretty, that I have great pleasure in looking at her."

"It is her countenance that is so attractive. She has a wonderful play of feature! But was there nothing in her conversation that struck you, Fanny, as not quite right?"

"Oh, yes! she ought not to have spoken of her uncle as she did. I was quite astonished. An uncle with whom she has been living so many years, and who, whatever his faults may be, is so very fond of her brother, treating him, they say, quite like a son. I could not have believed it!"

"I thought you would be struck. It was very wrong; very indecorous."

"And very ungrateful, I think."

"Ungrateful is a strong word. I do not know that her uncle has any claim to her *gratitude;* his wife certainly had; and it is the warmth of her respect for her aunt's memory which misleads her here. She is awkwardly circumstanced. With such warm feelings and lively spirits it must be difficult to do justice to her affection for Mrs. Crawford, without throwing a shade on the Admiral. I do not pretend to know which was most to blame in their disagreements, though the Admiral's present conduct might incline one to the side of his wife; but it is natural and amiable that Miss Crawford should acquit her aunt entirely. I do not censure her *opinions:* but there certainly *is* impropriety in making them public."

"Do not you think," said Fanny, after a little consideration, "that this impropriety is a reflection itself upon Mrs. Crawford, as her niece has been entirely brought up by her? She cannot have given her right notions of what was due to the Admiral."

"That is a fair remark. Yes, we must suppose the faults of the niece to have been those of the aunt; and it makes one more sensible of the disadvantages she has been under. But I think her present home must do her good. Mrs. Grant's manners are just what they ought to be. She speaks of her brother with a very pleasing affection."

"Yes, except as to his writing her such short letters. She made me almost laugh; but I cannot rate so very highly the love or good nature of a brother, who will not give himself the trouble of writing anything worth reading to his sisters, when they are separated. I am sure William would never have used *me* so, under any circumstances. And what right had she to suppose that *you* would not write long letters when you were absent?"

"The right of a lively mind, Fanny, seizing whatever may contribute to its own amusement or that of others; perfectly allowable, when untinctured by ill humour or roughness; and there is not a shadow of either in the countenance or manner of Miss Crawford: nothing sharp, or loud, or coarse. She is perfectly feminine, except in the instances we have been speaking of. *There* she cannot be justified. I am glad you saw it all as I did."

Having formed her mind and gained her affections, he had a good chance of her thinking like him; though at this period, and on this subject, there began now to be some danger of dissimilarity, for he was in a line of admiration of Miss Crawford, which might lead him where Fanny could not follow. Miss Crawford's attractions did not lessen. The harp arrived, and rather added to her beauty, wit, and good humour; for she played with the greatest obligingness, with an expression and taste which were peculiarly becoming, and there was something clever to be said at the close of every air. Edmund was at the Parsonage every day, to be indulged with his favourite instrument: one morning secured an invitation for the next; for the lady could not be unwilling to have a listener, and everything was soon in a fair train.

A young woman, pretty, lively, with a harp as elegant as herself, and both placed near a window cut down to the ground and opening on a little lawn, surrounded by shrubs in the rich foliage of summer, was enough to catch any man's heart. The season, the scene, the air, were all favourable to tenderness and sentiment. Mrs. Grant and her tambour frame were not without their use: it was all in harmony; and as everything will turn to account when love is once set going, even the sandwich tray, and Dr. Grant doing the honours of it, were worth looking at. Without studying the business, however, or knowing what he was about, Edmund was beginning, at the end of a week of such intercourse, to be a good deal in love; and to the credit of the lady it may be added, that, without his being a man of the world or an elder brother, without any of the arts of flattery or the gaieties of small talk, he began to be agreeable to her. She felt it to be so, though she had not foreseen, and could hardly understand it; for he was not pleasant by any common rule; he talked no nonsense; he paid no compliments; his opinions were unbending, his attentions tranquil and simple. There was a charm, perhaps, in his sincerity, his steadiness, his integrity, which Miss Crawford might be equal to feel, though not equal to discuss with herself. She did not think very much about it, however: he pleased her for the present; she liked to have him near her; it was enough.

Fanny could not wonder that Edmund was at the Parsonage every morning; she would gladly have been there too, might she have gone in uninvited and unnoticed, to hear the harp; neither could she wonder that, when the evening stroll was over, and the two families parted again, he should think it right to attend Mrs. Grant and her sister to their home, while Mr. Crawford was devoted to the ladies of the Park; but she thought it a very bad exchange; and if Edmund were not there to mix the wine and water for her, would rather go without it than not. She was a little surprised that he could spend so many hours with Miss Crawford, and not see more of the sort of fault which he had already observed, and of which *she* was almost always reminded by a something of the same nature whenever she was in her company; but so it was. Edmund was fond of speaking to her of Miss Crawford, but he seemed to think it enough that the Admiral had since been spared; and she scrupled to point out her own remarks to him, lest it should appear like ill nature. The first actual pain which Miss Crawford occasioned her was the consequence of an inclination to learn to ride, which the former caught soon after her being settled at Mansfield, from the example of the young ladies at the Park, and which, when Edmund's acquaintance with her increased, led to his encouraging the wish, and the offer of his own quiet mare for the purpose of her first attempts, as the best fitted for a beginner, that either stable could furnish. No pain, no injury, however, was designed by him to his cousin in this offer: *she* was not to lose a day's exercise by it. The mare was only to be taken down to the Parsonage half an hour before her rides were to begin; and Fanny on its being first proposed, so far from feeling slighted, was almost overpowered with gratitude that he should be asking her leave for it.

Miss Crawford made her first essay with great credit to herself, and no inconvenience to Fanny. Edmund, who had taken down the mare and presided at the whole, returned with it in excellent time, before either Fanny or the steady old coachman, who always attended her when she rode without her cousins, were ready to set forward. The second days' trial was not so guiltless. Miss Crawford's enjoyment of riding was such, that she did not know how to leave off. Active and fearless, and, though rather small, strongly made, she seemed formed for a horsewoman; and to the pure genuine pleasure of the exercise, something was probably added in Edmund's attendance and instructions, and something more in the conviction of very much surpassing her sex in general by her early progress, to make her unwilling to dismount. Fanny was ready and waiting and Mrs. Norris was beginning to scold her for not being gone, and still no horse was announced, no Edmund appeared. To avoid her aunt, and look for him, she went out.

The houses, though scarcely half a mile apart, were not within sight of each other; but, by walking fifty yards from the hall door, she could look down the park, and command a view of the Parsonage and all its demesnes, gently rising beyond the village road; and in Dr. Grant's meadow she immediately saw the group: Edmund and Miss Crawford both on horseback, riding side by side, Dr. and Mrs. Grant, and Mr. Crawford, with two or three grooms, standing about and looking on. A happy party it appeared to her, all interested in one object: cheerful beyond a doubt, for the sound of merriment ascended even to her. It was a sound which did not make *her* cheerful; she wondered that Edmund should forget her, and felt a pang. She could not turn her eyes from the meadow; she could not help watching all that passed. At first Miss Crawford and her companion made the circuit of the field, which was not small, at a foot's pace; then, at *her* apparent suggestion, they rose into a canter; and to Fanny's timid nature it was most astonishing to see how well she sat. After a few minutes, they stopped entirely. Edmund was close to her; he was speaking to her; he was evidently directing her management of the bridle; he had hold of her hand; she saw it, or the imagination supplied what the eye could not reach. She must not wonder at all this; what could be more natural than that Edmund should be making himself useful, and proving his good nature by any one? She could not but think, indeed, that Mr. Crawford might as well have saved him the trouble; that it would have been particularly proper and becoming in a brother to have done it himself; but Mr. Crawford, with all his boasted good-nature, and all his coachmanship, probably knew nothing of the matter, and had no active kindness in comparison of Edmund. She began to think it rather hard upon the mare to have such double duty; if she were forgotten, the poor mare should be remembered.

Her feelings for one and the other were soon a little tranquillised, by seeing the party in the meadow disperse, and Miss Crawford still on horseback, but attended by Edmund on foot, pass through a gate into the lane, and so into the park, and make towards the spot where she stood. She began then to be afraid of appearing rude and impatient; and walked to meet them with a great anxiety to avoid the suspicion.

"My dear Miss Price," said Miss Crawford, as soon as she was at all within hearing, "I am come to make my own apologies for keeping you waiting; but I have nothing in the world to say for myself. I knew it was very late, and that I was behaving extremely ill; and therefore, if you please, you must forgive me. Selfishness must always be forgiven, you know, because there is no hope of a cure."

Fanny's answer was extremely civil, and Edmund added his conviction that she could be in no hurry. "For there is more than time enough for my cousin to ride twice as far as she ever goes," said he, "and you have been promoting her comfort by preventing her from setting off half-an-hour sooner; clouds are now coming up, and she will not suffer from the heat as she would have done then. I wish *you* may not be fatigued by so much exercise. I wish you had saved yourself this walk home."

"No part of it fatigues me but getting off this horse, I assure you," said she, as she sprang down with his help; "I am very strong. Nothing ever fatigues me, but doing what I do not like. Miss Price, I give way to you with a very bad grace; but I sincerely hope you will have a pleasant ride, and that I may have nothing but good to hear of this dear, delightful, beautiful animal."

The old coachman, who had been waiting about with his own horse, now joining them, Fanny was lifted on hers, and they set off across another part of the park; her feelings of discomfort not lightened by seeing, as she looked back, that the others were walking down the hill together to the village; nor did her attendant do her much good by his comments on Miss Crawford's great cleverness as a horsewoman, which he had been watching with an interest almost equal to her own.

"It is a pleasure to see a lady with such a good heart for riding!" said he. "I never see one sit a horse better. She did not seem to have thought of fear. Very different from you, miss, when you first began, six years ago come next Easter. Lord bless you! how you did tremble when Sir Thomas first had you put on!"

In the drawing-room Miss Crawford was also celebrated. Her merit in being gifted by Nature with strength and courage, was fully appreciated by the Miss Bertrams; her delight in riding was like their own; her early excellence in it was like their own, and they had great pleasure in praising it.

"I was sure she would ride well," said Julia; "she has the make for it. Her figure is as neat as her brother's."

"Yes," added Maria, "and her spirits are as good, and she has the same energy of character. I cannot but think that good horsemanship has a great deal to do with the mind."

When they parted at night, Edmund asked Fanny whether she meant to ride the next day.

"No, I do not know—not if you want the mare," was her answer. "I do not want her at all for myself," said he; "but whenever you are next inclined to stay at home, I think Miss Crawford would be glad to have her a longer time—for a whole morning, in short. She has a great desire to get as far as Mansfield Common; Mrs. Grant has been telling her of its fine views, and I have no doubt of her being perfectly equal to it. But any morning will do for this. She would be extremely sorry to interfere with you. It would be very wrong if she did. *She* rides only for pleasure; *you* for health."

"I shall not ride to-morrow, certainly," said Fanny; "I have been out very often lately, and would rather stay at home. You know I am strong enough now to walk very well."

Edmund looked pleased, which must be Fanny's comfort, and the ride to Mansfield Common took place the next morning: the party included all the young people but herself, and was much enjoyed at the time, and doubly enjoyed again in the evening discussion. A successful scheme of this sort generally brings on another; and the having been to Mansfield Common disposed them all for going somewhere else the day after. There were many other views to be shown; and though the weather was hot, there were shady lanes wherever they wanted to go. A young party is always provided with a shady lane. Four fine mornings successively were spent in this manner, in showing the Crawfords the country, and doing the honours of its finest spots. Everything answered; it was all gaiety and good humour, the heat only supplying inconvenience enough to be talked of with pleasure—till the fourth day, when the happiness of one of the party was exceedingly clouded. Miss Bertram was the one. Edmund and Julia were invited to dine at the Parsonage, and *she* was excluded. It was meant and done by Mrs. Grant, with perfect good humour, on Mr. Rushworth's account, who was partly expected at the Park that day; but it was felt as a very grievous injury, and her good manners were severely taxed to conceal her vexation and anger till she reached home. As Mr. Rushworth did *not* come, the injury was increased, and she had not even the relief of showing her power over him; she could only be sullen to her mother, aunt, and cousin, and throw as great a gloom as possible over their dinner and dessert.

Between ten and eleven, Edmund and Julia walked into the drawing-room, fresh with the evening air, glowing and cheerful, the very reverse of what they found in the three ladies sitting there, for Maria would scarcely raise her eyes from her book, and Lady Bertram was half asleep; and even Mrs. Norris discomposed by her niece's ill humour, and having asked one or two questions about the dinner, which were not immediately attended to, seemed almost determined to say no more. For a few minutes, the brother and sister were too eager in their praise of the night and their remarks on the stars, to think beyond themselves; but when the first pause came, Edmund, looking around, said, "But where is Fanny? Is she gone to bed?"

"No, not that I know of," replied Mrs. Norris; "she was here a moment ago."

Her own gentle voice speaking from the other end of the room, which was a very long one, told them that she was on the sofa. Mrs. Norris began scolding.

"That is a very foolish trick, Fanny, to be idling away all the evening upon a sofa. Why cannot you come and sit here, and employ yourself as *we* do? If you have no work of your own, I can supply you from the poor basket. There is all the new calico, that was bought last week, not touched yet. I am sure I almost broke my back by cutting it out. You should learn to think of other people; and take my word for it, it is a shocking trick for a young person to be always lolling upon a sofa."

Before half this was said, Fanny was returned to her seat at the table, and had taken up her work again; and Julia, who was in high good humour, from the pleasures of the day, did her the justice of exclaiming, "I must say, ma'am, that Fanny is as little upon the sofa as anybody in the house."

"Fanny," said Edmund, after looking at her attentively, "I am sure you have the headache."

She could not deny it, but said it was not very bad.

"I can hardly believe you," he replied; "I know your looks too well. How long have you had it?"

"Since a little before dinner. It is nothing but the heat."

"Did you go out in the heat?"

"Go out! to be sure she did," said Mrs. Norris: "would you have her stay within such a fine day as this? Were not we *all* out? Even your mother was out to-day for above an hour."

"Yes, indeed, Edmund," added her ladyship, who had been thoroughly awakened by Mrs. Norris's sharp reprimand to Fanny; "I was out above an hour. I sat three-quarters of an hour in the flower-garden, while Fanny cut the roses, and very pleasant it was, I assure you, but very hot. It was shady enough in the alcove, but I declare I quite dreaded the coming home again."

"Fanny has been cutting roses, has she?"

"Yes, and I am afraid they will be the last this year. Poor thing! *She* found it hot enough; but they were so full blown that one could not wait."

"There was no help for it, certainly," rejoined Mrs. Norris, in a rather softened voice; "but I question whether her headache might not be caught *then,* sister. There is nothing so likely to give it as standing and stooping in a hot sun; but I dare say it will be well to-morrow. Suppose you let her have your aromatic vinegar; I always forget to have mine filled."

"She has got it," said Lady Bertram; "she has had it ever since she came back from your house the second time."

"What!" cried Edmund; "has she been walking as well as cutting roses, walking across the hot park to your house, and doing it twice, ma'am! No wonder her head aches."

Mrs. Norris was talking to Julia, and did not hear.

"I was afraid it would be too much for her," said Lady Bertram; "but when the roses were gathered, your aunt wished to have them, and then you know they must be taken home."

"But were there roses enough to oblige her to go twice?"

"No, but they were to be put into the spare room to dry; and, unluckily,

Fanny forgot to lock the door of the room and bring away the key, so she was obliged to go again."

Edmund got up and walked about the room, saying, "And could nobody be employed on such an errand but Fanny? Upon my word, ma'am, it has been a very ill-managed business."

"I am sure I do not know how it was to have been done better," cried Mrs. Norris, unable to be longer deaf; "unless I had gone myself, indeed, but I cannot be in two places at once; and I was talking to Mr. Green at that very time about your mother's dairymaid, by *her* desire, and had promised John Groom to write to Mrs. Jefferies about his son, and the poor fellow was waiting for me half an hour. I think nobody can justly accuse me of sparing myself upon any occasion, but really I cannot do everything at once. And as for Fanny's just stepping down to my house for me—it is not much above a quarter of a mile—I cannot think I was unreasonable to ask it. How often do I pace it three times a day, early and late, ay, and in all weathers too, and say nothing about it?"

"I wish Fanny had half your strength, ma'am."

"If Fanny would be more regular in her exercise, she would not be knocked up so soon. She has not been out on horseback now this long while, and I am persuaded, that when she does not ride, she ought to walk. If she had been riding before, I should not have asked it of her. But I thought it would rather do her good after being stooping among the roses; for there is nothing so refreshing as a walk after a fatigue of that kind; and though the sun was strong, it was not so very hot. Between ourselves, Edmund," nodding significantly at his mother, "it was cutting the roses, and dawdling about in the flower-garden, that did the mischief."

"I am afraid it was, indeed," said the more candid Lady Bertram, who had overheard her; "I am very much afraid she caught the headache there, for the heat was enough to kill anybody. It was as much as I could bear myself. Sitting and calling to pug, and trying to keep him from the flower-beds, was almost too much for me."

Edmund said no more to either lady; but going quietly to another table, on which the supper tray yet remained, brought a glass of Madeira to Fanny, and obliged her to drink the greater part. She wished to be able to decline it; but the tears, which a variety of feelings created, made it easier to swallow than to speak.

Vexed as Edmund was with his mother and aunt, he was still more angry with himself. His own forgetfulness of her was worse than anything which they had done. Nothing of this would have happened had she been properly considered; but she had been left four days together without any choice of companions or exercise, and without any excuse for avoiding whatever her unreasonable aunts might require. He was ashamed to think that for four days together she had not had the power of riding, and very seriously resolved, however unwilling he must be to check a pleasure of Miss Crawford's, that it should never happen again.

Fanny went to bed with her heart as full as on the first evening of her arrival at the Park. The state of her spirits had probably had its share in her indisposition; for she had been feeling neglected and been struggling against discontent and envy for some days past. As she leant on the sofa, to which she had retreated that she might not be seen, the pain of her mind had been much beyond that in her head; and the sudden change which Edmund's kindness had then occasioned, made her hardly know how to support herself.

Chapter 8

FANNY's rides recommenced the very next day; and as it was a pleasant fresh-feeling morning, less hot than the weather had lately been, Edmund trusted that her losses both of health and pleasure would be soon made good. While she was gone, Mr. Rushworth arrived, escorting his mother, who came to be civil and to show her civility especially, in urging the execution of the plan for visiting Sotherton, which had been started a fortnight before, and which, in consequence of her subsequent absence from home, had since lain dormant. Mrs. Norris and her nieces were all well pleased with its revival, and an early day was named, and agreed to, provided Mr. Crawford should be disengaged; the young ladies did not forget that stipulation, and though Mrs. Norris would willingly have answered for his being so, they would neither authorise the liberty, nor run the risk; and at last, on a hint from Miss Bertram, Mr. Rushworth discovered that the most proper thing to be done was for him to walk down to the Parsonage directly, and call on Mr. Crawford, and inquire whether Wednesday would suit him or not.

Before his return, Mrs. Grant and Miss Crawford came in. Having been out some time, and taken a different route to the house, they had not met him. Comfortable hopes, however, were given that he would find Mr. Crawford at home. The Sotherton scheme was mentioned of course. It was hardly possible, indeed, that anything else should be talked of, for Mrs. Norris was in high spirits about it; and Mrs. Rushworth, a well-meaning, civil, prosing, pompous woman, who thought nothing of consequence but as it related to her own and her son's concerns, had not yet given over pressing Lady Bertram to be of the party. Lady Bertram constantly declined it; but her placid manner of refusal made Mrs. Rushworth still think she wished to come, till Mrs. Norris's more numerous words and louder tone convinced her of the truth.

"The fatigue would be too much for my sister, a great deal too much, I assure you, my dear Mrs. Rushworth. Ten miles there, and ten back, you know. You must excuse my sister on this occasion, and accept of our two dear girls and myself without her. Sotherton is the only place that could give her a *wish* to go so far, but it cannot be, indeed. She will have a companion in Fanny Price, you know, so it will all do very well; and as for

Edmund, as he is not here to speak for himself, I will answer for his being most happy to join the party. He can go on horseback, you know."

Mrs. Rushworth being obliged to yield to Lady Bertram's staying at home, could only be sorry. "The loss of her ladyship's company would be a great drawback, and she should have been extremely happy to have seen the young lady too, Miss Price, who had never been at Sotherton yet, and it was a pity she should not see the place."

"You are very kind, you are all kindness, my dear madam," cried Mrs. Norris; "but as to Fanny, she will have opportunities in plenty of seeing Sotherton. She has time enough before her; and her going now is quite out of the question. Lady Bertram could not possibly spare her."

"Oh no! I cannot do without Fanny."

Mrs. Rushworth proceeded next, under the conviction that everybody must be wanting to see Sotherton, to include Miss Crawford in the invitation; and though Mrs. Grant, who had not been at the trouble of visiting Mrs. Rushworth on her coming into the neighbourhood, civilly declined it on her own account, she was glad to secure any pleasure for her sister; and Mary, properly pressed and persuaded, was not long in accepting her share of the civility. Mr. Rushworth came back from the Parsonage successful; and Edmund made his appearance just in time to learn what had been settled for Wednesday, to attend Mrs. Rushworth to her carriage, and walk half-way down the park with the two other ladies.

On his return to the breakfast-room, he found Mrs. Norris trying to make up her mind as to whether Miss Crawford's being of the party were desirable or not, or whether her brother's barouche would not be full without her. The Miss Bertrams laughed at the idea, assuring her that the barouche would hold four perfectly well, independent of the box, on which *one* might go with him."

"But why is it necessary," said Edmund, "that Crawford's carriage, or his *only*, should be employed? Why is no use to be made of my mother's chaise? I could not, when the scheme was first mentioned the other day, understand why a visit from the family were not to be made in the carriage of the family."

"What!" cried Julia; "go, boxed up three in a postchaise in this weather, when we may have seats in a barouche! No, my dear Edmund, that will not quite do."

"Besides," said Maria, "I know that Mr. Crawford depends upon taking us. After what passed at first, he would claim it as a promise."

"And, my dear Edmund," added Mrs. Norris, "taking out *two* carriages when *one* will do, would be trouble for nothing; and, between ourselves, coachman is not very fond of the roads between this and Sotherton; he always complains bitterly of the narrow lanes scratching his carriage, and you know one should not like to have dear Sir Thomas, when he comes home, find all the varnish scratched off."

"That would not be a very handsome reason for using Mr. Crawford's," said Maria; "but the truth is, that Wilcox is a stupid old fellow, and does not know how to drive. I will answer for it, that we shall find no inconvenience from narrow roads on Wednesday."

"There is no hardship, I suppose, nothing unpleasant," said Edmund, "in going on the barouche box."

"Unpleasant!" cried Maria; "oh dear! I believe it would be generally thought the favourite seat. There can be no comparison as to one's view of the country. Probably Miss Crawford will choose the barouche box herself."

"There can be no objection, then, to Fanny's going with you; there can be no doubt of your having room for her."

"Fanny!" repeated Mrs. Norris; "my dear Edmund, there is no idea of her going with us. She stays with her aunt. I told Mrs. Rushworth so. She is not expected."

"You can have no reason, I imagine, madam," said he, addressing his mother, "for wishing Fanny *not* to be of the party, but as it relates to yourself, to your own comfort. If you could do without her, you would not wish to keep her at home?"

"To be sure not, but I *cannot* do without her."

"You can, if I stay at home with you, as I mean to do."

There was a general cry out at this. "Yes," he continued, "there is no necessity for my going, and I mean to stay at home. Fanny has a great desire to see Sotherton. I know she wishes it very much. She has not often a gratification of the kind, and I am sure, ma'am, you would be glad to give her the pleasure now?"

"Oh yes! very glad, if your aunt sees no objection."

Mrs. Norris was very ready with the only objection which could remain —their having positively assured Mrs. Rushworth that Fanny could not go, and the very strange appearance there would consequently be in taking her, which seemed to her a difficulty quite impossible to be got over. It must have the strangest appearance! It would be something so very unceremonious, so bordering on disrespect for Mrs. Rushworth, whose own manners were such a pattern of good breeding and attention, that she really did not feel equal to it. Mrs. Norris had no affection for Fanny, and no wish of procuring her pleasure at any time; but her opposition to Edmund *now,* arose more from partiality for her own scheme, because it *was* her own, than from anything else. She felt that she had arranged everything extremely well, and that any alteration must be for the worse. When Edmund, therefore, told her in reply, as he did when she would give him the hearing, that she need not distress herself on Mrs. Rushworth's account, because he had taken the opportunity as he walked with her through the hall of mentioning Miss Price as one who would probably be of the party, and had directly received a very sufficient invitation for his cousin, Mrs. Norris was too much vexed to submit with a very good grace, and would only say, "Very well, very well, just as you choose, settle it your own way, I am sure I do not care about it."

"It seems very odd," said Maria, "that you should be staying at home instead of Fanny."

"I am sure she ought to be very much obliged to you," added Julia, hastily leaving the room as she spoke, from a consciousness that she ought to offer to stay at home herself.

"Fanny will feel quite as grateful as the occasion requires," was Edmund's reply only, and the subject dropped.

Fanny's gratitude, when she heard the plan, was in fact much greater than her pleasure. She felt Edmund's kindness with all, and more than all, the sensibility which he, unsuspicious of her fond attachment, could be aware of; but that he should forego any enjoyment on her account gave her pain, and her own satisfaction in seeing Sotherton would be nothing without him.

The next meeting of the two Mansfield families produced another alteration in the plan, and one that was admitted with general approbation. Mrs. Grant offered herself as companion for the day to Lady Bertram in lieu of her son, and Dr. Grant was to join them at dinner. Lady Bertram was very well pleased to have it so, and the young ladies were in spirits again. Even Edmund was very thankful for an arrangement which restored him to his share of the party; and Mrs. Norris thought it an excellent plan, and had it at her tongue's end, and was on the point of proposing it, when Mrs. Grant spoke.

Wednesday was fine, and soon after breakfast the barouche arrived, Mr. Crawford driving his sisters; and as everybody was ready, there was nothing to be done but for Mrs. Grant to alight, and the others to take their places. The place of all places, the envied seat, the post of honour, was unappropriated. To whose happy lot was it to fall? While each of the Miss Bertrams were meditating how best, and with the most appearance of obliging the others, to secure it, the matter was settled by Mrs. Grant's saying, as she stepped from the carriage, "As there are five of you, it will be better that one should sit with Henry; and as you were saying lately that you wished you could drive, Julia, I think this will be a good opportunity for you to take a lesson."

Happy Julia! Unhappy Maria! The former was on the barouche-box in a moment, the latter took her seat within, in gloom and mortification; and the carriage drove off amid the good wishes of the two remaining ladies, and the barking of pug in his mistress's arms.

Their road was through a pleasant country; and Fanny, whose rides had never been extensive, was soon beyond her knowledge, and was very happy in observing all that was new, and admiring all that was pretty. She was not often invited to join in the conversation of the others, nor did she desire it. Her own thoughts and reflections were habitually her best companions; and, in observing the appearance of the country, the bearings of the roads, the difference of soil, the state of the harvest, the cottages, the cattle, the children, she found entertainment that could only have been heightened by having Edmund to speak to of what she felt.

That was the only point of resemblance between her and the lady who sat by her; in everything but a value for Edmund, Miss Crawford was very unlike her. She had none of Fanny's delicacy of taste, of mind, of feeling; she saw Nature, inanimate Nature, with little observation; her attention was all for men and women, her talents for the light and lively. In looking back after Edmund, however, when there was any stretch of road behind them, or when he gained on them in ascending a considerable hill, they were united, and a "there he is" broke at the same moment from them both, more than once.

For the first seven miles Miss Bertram had very little real comfort; her prospect always ended in Mr. Crawford and her sister sitting side by side, full of conversation and merriment; and to see only his expressive profile as he turned with a smile to Julia, or to catch the laugh of the other, was a perpetual source of irritation, which her own sense of propriety could but just smooth over. When Julia looked back, it was with a countenance of delight, and whenever she spoke to them, it was in the highest spirits: "her view of the country was charming, she wished they could all see it," etc.; but her only offer of exchange was addressed to Miss Crawford, as they gained the summit of a long hill, and was not more inviting than this: "Here is a fine burst of country. I wish you had my seat, but I dare say you will not take it, let me press you ever so much"; and Miss Crawford could hardly answer, before they were moving again at a good pace.

When they came within the influence of Sotherton associations, it was better for Miss Bertram, who might be said to have two strings to her bow. She had Rushworth-feelings, and Crawford-feelings, and in the vicinity of Sotherton, the former had considerable effect. Mr. Rushworth's consequence was hers. She could not tell Miss Crawford that "those woods belonged to Sotherton"; she could not carelessly observe that "she believed that it was now all Mr. Rushworth's property on each side of the road," without elation of heart; and it was a pleasure to increase with their approach to the capital freehold mansion, and ancient manorial residence of the family, with all its rights of court-leet and court-baron.

"Now, we shall have no more rough road, Miss Crawford; our difficulties are over. The rest of the way is such as it ought to be. Mr. Rushworth has made it since he succeeded to the estate. Here begins the village. Those cottages are really a disgrace. The church spire is reckoned remarkably handsome. I am glad the church is not so close to the great house as often happens in old places. The annoyance of the bells must be terrible. There is the Parsonage; a tidy-looking house, and I understand the clergyman and his wife are very decent people. Those are almshouses, built by some of the family. To the right is the steward's house; he is a very respectable man. Now we are coming to the lodge-gates; but we have nearly a mile through the park still. It is not ugly, you see, at this end; there is some fine timber, but the situation of the house is dreadful. We go down hill to it for half a mile, and it is a pity, for it would not be an ill-looking place if it had a better approach."

Miss Crawford was not slow to admire; she pretty well guessed Miss Bertram's feelings, and made it a point of honour to promote her enjoyment to the utmost. Mrs. Norris was all delight and volubility; and even Fanny had something to say in admiration, and might be heard with complacency. Her eye was eagerly taking in everything within her reach; and after being at some pains to get a view of the house, and observing that "it was a sort of building which she could not look at but with respect," she added: "Now, where is the avenue? The house fronts the east, I perceive. The avenue, therefore, must be at the back of it. Mr. Rushworth talked of the west front."

"Yes, it is exactly behind the house; begins at a little distance, and ascends for half a mile to the extremity of the grounds. You may see something of it here—something of the more distant trees. It is oak entirely."

Miss Bertram could now speak with decided information of what she had known nothing about when Mr. Rushworth had asked her opinion; and her spirits were in as happy a flutter as vanity and pride could furnish, when they drove up to the spacious stone steps before the principal entrance.

Chapter 9

MR. RUSHWORTH was at the door to receive his fair lady; and the whole party were welcomed by him with due attention. In the drawing-room they were met with equal cordiality by the mother, and Miss Bertram had all the distinction with each that she could wish. After the business of arriving was over, it was first necessary to eat, and the doors were thrown open to admit them through one or two intermediate rooms into the appointed dining-parlour, where a collation was prepared with abundance and elegance. Much was said, and much was ate, and all went well. The particular object of the day was then considered. How would Mr. Crawford like, in what manner would he choose, to take a survey of the grounds? Mr. Rushworth mentioned his curricle, Mr. Crawford suggested the greater desirableness of some carriage which might convey more than two. "To be depriving themselves of the advantage of other eyes and other judgments, might be an evil even beyond the loss of present pleasure."

Mrs. Rushworth proposed that the chaise should be taken also; but this was scarcely received as an amendment: the young ladies neither smiled nor spoke. Her next proposition, of showing the house to such of them as had not been there before, was more acceptable, for Miss Bertram was pleased to have its size displayed, and all were glad to be doing something.

The whole party rose accordingly, and under Mrs. Rushworth's guidance were shown through a number of rooms, all lofty, and many large, and amply furnished in the taste of fifty years back, with shining floors, solid mahogany, rich damask, marble, gilding and carving, each handsome in its way. Of pictures there were abundance, and some few good, but the larger part were family portraits, no longer anything to anybody except Mrs. Rushworth, who had been at great pains to learn all that the housekeeper could teach, and was now almost equally well qualified to show the house. On the present occasion, she addressed herself chiefly to Miss Crawford and Fanny, but there was no comparison in the willingness of their attention; for Miss Crawford, who had seen scores of great houses, and cared for none of them, had only the appearance of civilly listening, while Fanny, to whom everything was almost as interesting as it was new, attended with unaffected earnestness to all that Mrs. Rushworth could relate of the family in former times, its rise and grandeur, regal visits and loyal efforts, delighted to connect anything with history already known, or warm her imagination with scenes of the past.

The situation of the house excluded the possibility of much prospect from any of the rooms; and while Fanny and some of the others were attending Mrs. Rushworth, Henry Crawford was looking grave and shaking his head at the windows. Every room on the west front looked across a lawn to the beginning of the avenue immediately beyond tall iron palisades and gates.

Having visited many more rooms than could be supposed to be of any other use than to contribute to the window tax, and find employment for housemaids, "Now," said Mrs. Rushworth, "we are coming to the chapel, which properly we ought to enter from above, and look down upon; but as we are quite among friends, I will take you in this way, if you will excuse me."

They entered. Fanny's imagination had prepared her for something grander than a mere spacious, oblong room, fitted up for the purpose of devotion; with nothing more striking or more solemn than the profusion of mahogany, and the crimson velvet cushions appearing over the ledge of the family gallery above. "I am disappointed," said she, in a low voice to Edmund. "This is not my idea of a chapel. There is nothing awful here, nothing melancholy, nothing grand. Here are no aisles, no arches, no inscriptions, no banners. No banners, cousin, to be 'blown by the night wind of heaven.' No signs that a 'Scottish monarch sleeps below.' "

"You forget, Fanny, how lately all this has been built, and for how confined a purpose, compared with the old chapels of castles and monasteries. It was only for the private use of the family. They have been buried, I suppose, in the parish church. *There* you must look for the banners and the achievements."

"It was foolish of me not to think of all that; but I am disappointed."

Mrs. Rushworth began her relation. "This chapel was fitted up as you see it, in James the Second's time. Before that period, as I understand, the pews were only wainscot; and there is some reason to think that the linings and cushions of the pulpit and family seat were only purple cloth; but this is not quite certain. It is a handsome chapel, and was formerly in constant use both morning and evening. Prayers were always read in it by the domestic chaplain, within the memory of many; but the late Mr. Rushworth left it off."

"Every generation has its improvements," said Miss Crawford, with a smile, to Edmund.

Mrs. Rushworth was gone to repeat her lesson to Mr. Crawford; and Edmund, Fanny and Miss Crawford remained in a cluster together.

"It is a pity," cried Fanny, "that the custom should have been discontinued. It was a valuable part of former times. There is something in a chapel and chaplain so much in character with a great house, with one's ideas of what such a household should be! A whole family assembling regularly for the purpose of prayer is fine!"

"Very fine, indeed," said Miss Crawford, laughing. "It must do the heads of the family a great deal of good to force all the poor housemaids and footmen to leave business and pleasure, and say their prayers here twice a day, while they are inventing excuses themselves for staying away."

"*That* is hardly Fanny's idea of a family assembling," said Edmund. "If the master and mistress do *not* attend themselves, there must be more harm than good in the custom."

"At any rate, it is safer to leave people to their own devices on such subjects. Everybody likes to go their own way—to choose their own time and manner of devotion. The obligation of attendance, the formality, the restraint, the length of time—altogether it is a formidable thing, and what nobody likes; and if the good people who used to kneel and gape in that gallery could have foreseen that the time would ever come when men and women might lie another ten minutes in bed when they woke with a headache, without danger of reprobation because chapel was missed, they would have jumped with joy and envy. Cannot you imagine with what unwilling feelings the former belles of the house of Rushworth did many a time repair to this chapel? The young Mrs. Eleanors and Mrs. Bridgets —starched up into seeming piety, but with heads full of something very different—especially if the poor chaplain were not worth looking at— and, in those days, I fancy parsons were very inferior even to what they are now."

For a few moments she was unanswered. Fanny coloured and looked at Edmund, but felt too angry for speech; and *he* needed a little recollection before he could say, "Your lively mind can hardly be serious even on serious subjects. You have given us an amusing sketch, and human nature cannot say it was not so. We must all feel *at times* the difficulty of fixing our thoughts as we could wish; but if you are supposing it a frequent thing, that is to say, a weakness grown into a habit from neglect, what could be expected from the *private* devotions of such persons? Do you think the minds which are suffered, which are indulged in wanderings in a chapel, would be more collected in a closet?"

"Yes, very likely. They would have two chances at least in their favour.

There would be less to distract the attention from without, and it would not be tried so long."

"The mind which does not struggle against itself under *one* circumstance, would find objects to distract it in the *other*, I believe; and the influence of the place and of example may often rouse better feelings than are begun with. The greater length of the service, however, I admit to be sometimes too hard a stretch upon the mind. One wishes it were not so; but I have not yet left Oxford long enough to forget what chapel prayers are."

While this was passing, the rest of the party being scattered about the chapel, Julia called Mr. Crawford's attention to her sister, by saying, "Do look at Mr. Rushworth and Maria, standing side by side, exactly as if the ceremony were going to be performed. Have not they completely the air of it?"

Mr. Crawford smiled his acquiescence, and stepping forward to Maria, said, in a voice which she only could hear, "I do not like to see Miss Bertram so near the altar."

Starting, the lady instinctively moved a step or two, but recovering herself in a moment, affected to laugh, and asked him in a tone not much louder, "If he would give her away?"

"I am afraid I should do it very awkwardly," was his reply, with a look of meaning.

Julia, joining them at the moment, carried on the joke. "Upon my word, it is really a pity that it should not take place directly, if we had but a proper licence, for here we are all together, and nothing in the world could be more snug and pleasant." And she talked and laughed about it with so little caution, as to catch the comprehension of Mr. Rushworth and his mother, and expose her sister to the whispered gallantries of her lover, while Mrs. Rushworth spoke with proper smiles and dignity of its being a most happy event to her whenever it took place.

"If Edmund were but in orders!" cried Julia, and running to where he stood with Miss Crawford and Fanny: "My dear Edmund, if you were but in orders now, you might perform the ceremony directly. How unlucky that you are not ordained; Mr. Rushworth and Maria are quite ready."

Miss Crawford's countenance, as Julia spoke, might have amused a disinterested observer. She looked almost aghast under the new idea she was receiving. Fanny pitied her. "How distressed she will be at what she said just now," passed across her mind.

"Ordained!" said Miss Crawford; "what, are you to be a clergyman?"

"Yes; I shall take orders soon after my father's return; probably at Christmas."

Miss Crawford rallying her spirits, and recovering her complexion, replied only, "If I had known this before, I would have spoken of the cloth with more respect," and turned the subject.

The chapel was soon afterwards left to the silence and stillness which reigned in it, with few interruptions, throughout the year. Miss Bertram, displeased with her sister, led the way, and all seemed to feel that they had been there long enough.

The lower part of the house had been now entirely shown, and Mrs. Rushworth, never weary in the cause, would have proceeded towards the principal staircase, and taken them through all the rooms above, if her son had not interposed with a doubt of there being time enough. "For if," said he, with a sort of self-evident proposition which many a clearer head does not always avoid, "we are *too long* going over the house, we shall not have time for what is to be done out of doors. It is past two, and we are to dine at five."

Mrs. Rushworth submitted; and the question of surveying the grounds, with the who and the how was likely to be more fully agitated, and Mrs. Norris was beginning to arrange by what junction of carriages and horses most could be done, when the young people, meeting with an outward door, temptingly open on a flight of steps which led immediately to turf and shrubs, and all the sweets of pleasure-grounds, as by one impulse, one wish for air and liberty, all walked out.

"Suppose we turn down here for the present," said Mrs. Rushworth, civilly taking the hint and following them. "Here are the greatest number of our plants, and here are the curious pheasants."

"Query," said Mr. Crawford, looking round him, "whether we may not find something to employ us here, before we go further? I see walls of great promise. Mr. Rushworth, shall we summon a council on this lawn?"

"James," said Mrs. Rushforth to her son, "I believe the wilderness will be new to all the party. The Miss Bertrams have never seen the wilderness yet."

No objection was made, but for some time there seemed no inclination to move in any plan, or to any distance. All were attracted at first by the plants or the pheasants, and all dispersed about in happy independence. Mr. Crawford was the first to move forward, to examine the capabilities of that end of the house. The lawn, bounded on each side by a high wall, contained beyond the first planted area a bowling-green, and beyond the bowling-green a long terrace walk, backed by iron palisades, and commanding a view over them into the tops of the trees of the wilderness immediately adjoining. It was a good spot for fault-finding. Mr. Crawford was soon followed by Miss Bertram and Mr. Rushworth; and when, after a little time, the others began to form into parties, these three were found in busy consultation on the terrace by Edmund, Miss Crawford, and Fanny, who seemed as naturally to unite, and who, after a short participation of their regrets and difficulties, left them and walked on. The remaining three, Mrs. Rushworth, Mrs. Norris, and Julia, were still far behind; for Julia, whose happy star no longer prevailed, was obliged to keep by the side of Mrs. Rushworth, and restrain her impatient feet to that lady's slow pace, while her aunt, having fallen in with the housekeeper, who was come out to feed the pheasants, was lingering behind in gossip with her. Poor Julia, the only one out of the nine not tolerably satisfied with their lot, was now in a state of complete penance, and as different from the Julia of the barouche-box as could well be imagined. The politeness which she had been brought up to practise as a duty made it impossible for her to escape; while the want of that higher species of self-command, that just consideration of others, that knowledge of her own heart, that principle of right, which had not formed any essential part of her education, made her miserable under it.

"This is insufferably hot," said Miss Crawford, when they had taken one turn on the terrace, and were drawing a second time to the door in the middle which opened to the wilderness. "Shall any of us object to being comfortable? Here is a nice little wood, if one can but get into it. What happiness if the door should not be locked! But of course it is; for in these great places the gardeners are the only people who can go where they like."

The door, however, proved not to be locked, and they were all agreed in turning joyfully through it, and leaving the unmitigated glare of day behind. A considerable flight of steps landed them in the wilderness, which was a planted wood of about two acres, and though chiefly of larch and laurel, and beech cut down, and though laid out with too much regularity, was darkness and shade, and natural beauty, compared with the bowling-green and the terrace. They all felt the refreshment of it, and for some time could only walk and admire. At length, after a short pause, Miss Crawford began with: "So you are to be a clergyman, Mr. Bertram. This is rather a surprise to me."

"Why should it surprise you? You must suppose me designed for some profession, and might perceive that I am neither a lawyer, nor a soldier, nor a sailor."

"Very true; but, in short, it had not occurred to me. And you know there is generally an uncle or a grandfather to leave a fortune to the second son."

"A very praiseworthy practice," said Edmund, "but not quite universal. I am one of the exceptions, and *being* one, must do something for myself."

"But why are you to be a clergyman? I thought *that* was always the lot of the youngest, where there were many to choose before him."

"Do you think the church itself never chosen, then?"

"*Never* is a black word. But yes, in the *never* of conversation, which means *not very often,* I do think it. For what is to be done in the church? Men love to distinguish themselves, and in either of the other lines distinction may be gained, but not in the church. A clergyman is nothing."

"The *nothing* of conversation has its gradations, I hope, as well as the *never.* A clergyman cannot be high in state or fashion. He must not head mobs, or set the ton in dress. But I cannot call that situation nothing which has the charge of all that is of the first importance to mankind individually or collectively considered, temporally and eternally, which has the guardianship of religion and morals, and consequently of the manners which result from their influence. No one here can call the *office* nothing. If the man who holds it is so, it is by the neglect of his duty, by foregoing its just importance, and stepping out of his place to appear what he ought not to appear."

"*You* assign greater consequence to the clergyman than one has been used to hear given, or than I can quite comprehend. One does not see much of this influence and importance in society, and how can it be acquired where they are so seldom seen themselves? How can two sermons a week, even supposing them worth hearing, supposing the preacher to have the sense to prefer Blair's to his own, do all that you speak of—govern the conduct and fashion the manners of a large congregation for the rest of the week? One scarcely sees a clergyman out of his pulpit."

"*You* are speaking of London, *I* am speaking of the nation at large."

"The metropolis, I imagine, is a pretty fair sample of the rest."

"Not, I should hope, of the proportion of virtue to vice throughout the kingdom. We do not look in great cities for our best morality. It is not there that respectable people of any denomination can do most good; and it certainly is not there that the influence of the clergy can be most felt. A fine preacher is followed and admired; but it is not in fine preaching only that a good clergyman will be useful in his parish and his neighbourhood, where the parish and neighbourhood are of a size capable of knowing his private character, and observing his general conduct, which in London can rarely be the case. The clergy are lost there in the crowds of their parishioners. They are known to the largest part only as preachers. And with regard to their influencing public matters, Miss Crawford must not misunderstand me, or suppose I mean to call them the arbiters of good breeding, the regulators of refinement and courtesy, the masters of the ceremonies of life. The *manners* I speak of might rather be called *conduct*, perhaps, the result of good principles; the effect, in short, of those doctrines which it is their duty to teach and recommend; and it will, I believe, be everywhere found, that as the clergy are, or are not what they ought to be, so are the rest of the nation."

"Certainly," said Fanny, with gentle earnestness.

"There," cried Miss Crawford, "you have quite convinced Miss Price already."

"I wish I could convince Miss Crawford too."

"I do not think you ever will," said she, with an arch smile; "I am just as much surprised now as I was at first that you should intend to take orders. You really are fit for something better. Come, do change your mind. It is not too late. Go into the law."

"Go into the law! With as much ease as I was told to go into this wilderness."

"Now you are going to say something about law being the worst wilderness of the two, but I forestall you; remember, I have forestalled you."

"You need not hurry when the object is only to prevent my saying a bon-mot, for there is not the least wit in my nature. I am a very matter-of-fact, plain-spoken being, and may blunder on the borders of a repartee for half-an-hour together without striking it out."

A general silence succeeded. Each was thoughtful. Fanny made the first interruption by saying: "I wonder that I should be tired with only walking in this sweet wood; but the next time we come to a seat, if it is not disagreeable to you, I should be glad to sit down for a little while."

"My dear Fanny," cried Edmund, immediately drawing her arm within his, "how thoughtless I have been! I hope you are not very tired. Perhaps," turning to Miss Crawford, "my other companion may do me the honour of taking an arm."

"Thank you, but I am not at all tired." She took it, however, as she spoke, and the gratification of having her do so, of feeling such a connection for the first time, made him a little forgetful of Fanny. "You scarcely touch me," said he. "You do not make me of any use. What a difference in the weight of a woman's arm from that of a man! At Oxford I have been a good deal used to have a man lean on me for the length of a street, and you are only a fly in comparison."

"I am really not tired, which I almost wonder at; for we must have walked at least a mile in this wood. Do not you think we have?"

"Not half a mile," was his sturdy answer; for he was not yet so much in love as to measure distance, or reckon time, with feminine lawlessness.

"Oh! you do not consider how much we have wound about. We have taken such a very serpentine course, and the wood itself must be half a mile long in a straight line, for we have never seen the end of it yet since we left the first great path."

"But if you remember, before we left that first great path, we saw directly to the end of it. We looked down the whole vista, and saw it closed by iron gates, and it could not have been more than a furlong in length."

"Oh! I know nothing of your furlongs, but I am sure it is a very long wood, and that we have been winding in and out ever since we came into it; and therefore, when I say that we have walked a mile in it, I must speak within compass."

"We have been exactly a quarter of an hour here," said Edmund, taking out his watch. "Do you think we are walking four miles an hour?"

"Oh! do not attack me with your watch. A watch is always too fast or too slow. I cannot be dictated to by a watch."

A few steps further brought them out at the bottom of the very walk they had been talking of; and standing back, well shaded and sheltered, and looking over a ha-ha into the park, was a comfortable-sized bench on which they all sat down.

"I am afraid you are very tired, Fanny," said Edmund, observing her; "why would you not speak sooner? This will be a bad day's amusement for you if you are to be knocked up. Every sort of exercise fatigues her so soon, Miss Crawford, except riding."

"How abominable in you, then, to let me engross her horse as I did all last week! I am ashamed of you and of myself, but it shall never happen again."

"*Your* attentiveness and consideration make me more sensible of my own neglect. Fanny's interest seems in safer hands with you than with me."

"That she should be tired now, however, gives me no surprise; for there is nothing in the course of one's duties so fatiguing as what we have been doing this morning: seeing a great house, dawdling from one room to another, straining one's eyes and one's attention, hearing what one does not understand, admiring what one does not care for. It is generally allowed to be the greatest bore in the world, and Miss Price has found it so, though she did not know it."

"I shall soon be rested," said Fanny; "to sit in the shade on a fine day, and look upon verdure, is the most perfect refreshment."

After sitting a little while, Miss Crawford was up again. "I must move," said she, "resting fatigues me. I have looked across the ha-ha till I am weary. I must go and look through that iron gate at the same view, without being able to see it so well."

Edmund left the seat likewise. "Now, Miss Crawford, if you will look up the walk, you will convince yourself that it cannot be half a mile long, or half half a mile."

"It is an immense distance," said she; "I see *that* with a glance."

He still reasoned with her, but in vain. She would not calculate, she would not compare. She would only smile and assert. The greatest degree of rational consistency could not have been more engaging, and they talked with mutual satisfaction. At last it was agreed that they should endeavour to determine the dimensions of the wood by walking a little more about it. They would go to the end of it, in the line they were then in (for there was a straight green walk along the bottom by the side of the ha-ha), and perhaps turn a little way in some other direction, if it seemed likely to assist them, and be back in a few minutes. Fanny said she was rested, and would have moved too, but this was not suffered. Edmund urged her remaining where she was with an earnestness which she could not resist, and she was left on the bench to think with pleasure of her cousin's care, but with great regret that she was not stronger. She watched them till they had turned the corner, and listened till all sound of them had ceased.

Chapter 10

A QUARTER of an hour, twenty minutes, passed away, and Fanny was still thinking of Edmund, Miss Crawford, and herself, without interruption from anyone. She began to be surprised at being left so long, and to listen with an anxious desire of hearing their steps and their voices again. She listened, and at length she heard; she heard voices and feet approach·

ing; but she had just satisfied herself that it was not those she wanted, when Miss Bertram, Mr. Rushworth, and Mr. Crawford, issued from the same path which she had trod herself, and were before her.

"Miss Price all alone!" and "My dear Fanny, how comes this?" were the first salutations. She told her story. "Poor dear Fanny," cried her cousin, "how ill you have been used by them! You had better have stayed with us."

Then seating herself with a gentleman on each side, she resumed the conversation which had engaged them before, and discussed the possibility of improvements with much animation. Nothing was fixed on; but Henry Crawford was full of ideas and projects, and, generally speaking, whatever he proposed was immediately approved, first by her, and then by Mr. Rushworth, whose principal business seemed to be to hear the others, and who scarcely risked an original thought of his own beyond a wish that they had seen his friend Smith's place.

After some minutes spent in this way, Miss Bertram, observing the iron gate, expressed a wish of passing through it into the park, that their views and their plans might be more comprehensive. It was the very thing of all others to be wished, it was the best, it was the only way of proceeding with any advantage, in Henry Crawford's opinion, and he directly saw a knoll not half a mile off, which would give them exactly the requisite command of the house. Go therefore they must to that knoll, and through that gate; but the gate was locked. Mr. Rushworth wished he had brought the key; he had been very near thinking whether he should not bring the key; he was determined he would never come without the key again; but still this did not remove the present evil. They could not get through; and as Miss Bertram's inclination for so doing did by no means lessen, it ended in Mr. Rushworth's declaring outright that he would go and fetch the key. He set off accordingly.

"It is undoubtedly the best thing we can do now, as we are so far from the house already," said Mr. Crawford, when he was gone.

"Yes, there is nothing else to be done. But now, sincerely, do not you find the place altogether worse than you expected?"

"No, indeed, far otherwise. I find it better, grander, more complete in its style, though that style may not be the best. And to tell you the truth," speaking rather lower, "I do not think that *I* shall ever see Sotherton again with so much pleasure as I do now. Another summer will hardly improve it to me."

After a moment's embarrassment the lady replied: "You are too much a man of the world not to see with the eyes of the world. If other people think Sotherton improved, I have no doubt that you will."

"I am afraid I am not quite so much the man of the world as might be good for me in some points. My feelings are not quite so evanescent, nor my memory of the past under such easy dominion as one finds to be the case with men of the world."

This was followed by a short silence. Miss Bertram began again. "You seemed to enjoy your drive here very much this morning. I was glad to see you so well entertained. You and Julia were laughing the whole way."

"Were we? Yes, I believe we were; but I have not the least recollection at what. Oh! I believe I was relating to her some ridiculous stories of an old Irish groom of my uncle's. Your sister loves to laugh."

"You think her more lighthearted than I am."

"More easily amused," he replied, "consequently, you know," smiling, "better company. I could not have hoped to entertain *you* with Irish anecdotes during a ten miles' drive."

"Naturally, I believe, I am as lively as Julia, but I have more to think of now."

"You have, undoubtedly; and there are situations in which very high spirits would denote insensibility. Your prospects, however, are too fair to justify want of spirits. You have a very smiling scene before you."

"Do you mean literally or figuratively? Literally, I conclude. Yes, certainly the sun shines, and the park looks very cheerful. But unluckily that iron gate, that ha-ha, give me a feeling of restraint and hardship. 'I cannot get out,' as the starling said." As she spoke, and it was with expression, she walked to the gate: he followed her. "Mr. Rushworth is so long fetching this key?"

"And for the world you would not get out without the key and without Mr. Rushworth's authority and protection, or I think you might with little difficulty pass round the edge of the gate, here, with my assistance; I think it might be done, if you really wished to be more at large, and could allow yourself to think it not prohibited."

"Prohibited! Nonsense! I certainly can get out that way, and I will. Mr. Rushworth will be here in a moment, you know; we shall not be out of sight."

"Or if we are, Miss Price will be so good as to tell him that he will find us near that knoll: the grove of oak on the knoll."

Fanny, feeling all this to be wrong, could not help making an effort to prevent it. "You will hurt yourself, Miss Bertram," she cried, "you will certainly hurt yourself against those spikes; you will tear your gown; you will be in danger of slipping into the ha-ha. You had better not go."

Her cousin was safe on the other side while these words were spoken, and, smiling with all the good humour of success, she said: "Thank you, my dear Fanny, but I and my gown are alive and well, and so good-bye."

Fanny was again left to her solitude, and with no increase of pleasant feelings, for she was sorry for almost all that she had seen and heard, astonished at Miss Bertram, and angry with Mr. Crawford. By taking a circuitous route, and, as it appeared to her, very unreasonable direction to the knoll, they were soon beyond her eye; and for some minutes longer she remained without sight or sound of any companion. She seemed to have the little wood all to herself. She could almost have thought that

Edmund and Miss Crawford had left it, but that it was impossible for Edmund to forget her so entirely.

She was again roused from disagreeable musings by sudden footsteps: somebody was coming at a quick pace down the principal walk. She expected Mr. Rushworth, but it was Julia, who, hot and out of breath, and with a look of disappointment, cried out on seeing her: "Heyday! Where are the others? I thought Maria and Mr. Crawford were with you."

Fanny explained.

"A pretty trick, upon my word! I cannot see them anywhere," looking eagerly into the park. "But they cannot be very far off, and I think I am equal to as much as Maria, even without help."

"But, Julia, Mr. Rushworth will be here in a moment with the key. Do wait for Mr. Rushworth."

"Not I, indeed. I have had enough of the family for one morning. Why, child, I have but this moment escaped from his horrible mother. Such a penance as I have been enduring, while you were sitting here so composed and so happy! It might have been as well, perhaps, if you had been in my place, but you always contrive to keep out of these scrapes."

This was a most unjust reflection, but Fanny could allow for it, and let it pass: Julia was vexed, and her temper was hasty; but she felt that it would not last, and therefore taking no notice, only asked her if she had not seen Mr. Rushworth.

"Yes, yes, we saw him. He was posting away as if upon life and death, and could but just spare time to tell us his errand, and where you all were."

"It is a pity he should have so much trouble for nothing."

"*That* is Miss Maria's concern. I am not obliged to punish myself for *her* sins. The mother I could not avoid, as long as my tiresome aunt was dancing about with the housekeeper, but the son I *can* get away from."

And she immediately scrambled across the fence, and walked away, not attending to Fanny's last question of whether she had seen anything of Miss Crawford and Edmund. The sort of dread in which Fanny now sat of seeing Mr. Rushworth, prevented her thinking so much of their continued absence, however, as she might have done. She felt that he had been very ill used, and was quite unhappy in having to communicate what had passed. He joined her within five minutes after Julia's exit; though she made the best of the story, he was evidently mortified and displeased in no common degree. At first he scarcely said anything; his looks only expressed his extreme surprise and vexation, and he walked to the gate and stood there, without seeming to know what to do.

"They desired me to stay; my cousin Maria charged me to say that you would find them at that knoll, or thereabouts."

"I do not believe I shall go any further," said he, sullenly; "I see nothing of them. By the time I get to the knoll, they may be gone somewhere else. I have had walking enough."

And he sat down with a most gloomy countenance by Fanny.

"I am very sorry," said she; "it is very unlucky." And she longed **to** be able to say something more to the purpose.

After an interval of silence, "I think they might as well have stayed for me," said he.

"Miss Bertram thought you would follow her."

"I should not have had to follow her if she had stayed."

This could not be denied, and Fanny was silenced. After another pause, he went on: "Pray, Miss Price, are you such a great admirer of this Mr. Crawford as some people are? For my part, I can see nothing in him."

"I do not think him at all handsome."

"Handsome! Nobody can call such an undersized man handsome. He is not five foot nine. I should not wonder if he was not more than five foot eight. I think he is an ill-looking fellow. In my opinion, these Crawfords are no addition at all. We did very well without them."

A small sigh escaped Fanny here, and she did not know how to contra-dict him.

"If I had made any difficulty about fetching the key, there might have been some excuse, but I went the very moment she said she wanted it."

"Nothing could be more obliging than your manner, I am sure, and I dare say you walked as fast as you could; but still it is some distance, you know, from this spot, to the house, quite into the house; and when people are waiting they are bad judges of time, and every half minute seems like five."

He got up and walked to the gate again, and "wished he had had the key about him at the time." Fanny thought she discerned in his standing there an indication of relenting, which encouraged her to another attempt, and she said, therefore: "It is a pity you should not join them. They expected to have a better view of the house from that part of the park, and will be thinking how it may be improved; and nothing of that sort, you know, can be settled without you."

She found herself more successful in sending away, than in retaining a companion. Mr. Rushworth was worked on. "Well," said he, "if you really think I had better go: it would be foolish to bring the key for nothing." And letting himself out, he walked off without further ceremony.

Fanny's thoughts were now all engrossed by the two who had left her so long ago, and getting quite impatient, she resolved to go in search of them. She followed their steps along the bottom walk, and had just turned up into another, when the voice and the laugh of Miss Crawford once more caught her ear; the sound approached, and a few more windings brought them before her. They were just returned into the wilderness from the park, to which a side gate, not fastened, had tempted them very soon after their leaving her, and they had been across a portion of the park into the very avenue which Fanny had been hoping the whole morn-ing to reach at last, and had been sitting down under one of the trees. This was their history. It was evident that they had been spending their time pleasantly, and were not aware of the length of their absence. Fanny's best consolation was in being assured that Edmund had wished for her very much, and that he should certainly have come back for her, had she not been tired already; but this was not quite sufficient to do away with the pain of having been left a whole hour, when he had talked of only a few minutes, nor to banish the sort of curiosity she felt, to know what they had been conversing about all that time; and the result of the whole was to her disappointment and depression, as they prepared by general agreement to return to the house.

On reaching the bottom of the steps to the terrace, Mrs. Rushworth and Mrs. Norris presented themselves at the top, just ready for the wilderness, at the end of an hour and a half from their leaving the house. Mrs. Norris had been too well employed to move faster. Whatever cross accidents had occurred to intercept the pleasures of her nieces, she had found a morning of complete enjoyment; for the housekeeper, after a great many courtesies on the subject of pheasants, had taken her to the dairy, told her all about their cows, and given her the receipt for a famous cream cheese; and since Julia's leaving them, they had been met by the gardener, with whom she had made a most satisfactory acquaintance, for she had set him right as to his grandson's illness, convinced him that it was an ague, and promised him a charm for it; and he, in return, had shown her all his choicest nursery of plants, and actually presented her with a very curious specimen of heath.

On this rencontre they all returned to the house together, there to lounge away the time as they could with sofas, and chit-chat, and *Quarterly Reviews,* till the return of the others, and the arrival of dinner. It was late before the Miss Bertrams and the two gentlemen came in, and their ramble did not appear to have been more than partially agreeable, or at all productive of anything useful with regard to the object of the day. By their own accounts they had been all walking after each other, and the junction which had taken place at last seemed, to Fanny's observation, to have been as much too late for re-establishing harmony, as it confessedly had been for determining on any alteration. She felt, as she looked at Julia and Mr. Rushworth, that hers was not the only dissatisfied bosom amongst them; there was gloom on the face of each. Mr. Crawford and Miss Bertram were much more gay, and she thought that he was taking particular pains, during dinner, to do away any little resentment of the other two, and restore general good humour.

Dinner was soon followed by tea and coffee, a ten miles' drive home allowed no waste of hours; and from the time of their sitting down to table, it was a quick succession of busy nothings till the carriage came to the door, and Mrs. Norris, having fidgeted about, and obtained a few pheasants' eggs and a cream cheese from the housekeeper, and made abundance of civil speeches to Mrs. Rushworth, was ready to lead the way. At the same moment, Mr. Crawford, approaching Julia, said: "I hope I am not to lose my companion, unless she is afraid of the evening air in so exposed a seat." The request had not been foreseen, but was very graciously received, and Julia's day was likely to end almost as well as it began. Miss Bertram had made up her mind to something different, and was a little disappointed; but her conviction of being really the one preferred comforted her under it, and enabled her to receive Mr. Rushworth's parting attentions as she ought. He was certainly better pleased to hand her into the barouche than to assist her in ascending the box, and his complacency seemed confirmed by the arrangement.

"Well, Fanny, this has been a fine day for you, upon my word," said Mrs. Norris, as they drove through the park. "Nothing but pleasure from beginning to end! I am sure you ought to be very much obliged to your Aunt Bertram and me, for contriving to let you go. A pretty good day's amusement you have had!"

Maria was just discontented enough to say directly: "I think *you* have done pretty well yourself, ma'am. Your lap seems full of good things, and here is a basket of something between us, which has been knocking my elbow unmercifully."

"My dear, it is only a beautiful little heath, which that nice old gardener would make me take; but if it is in your way, I will have it in my lap directly. There, Fanny, you shall carry that parcel for me; take great care of it; do not let it fall; it is a cream cheese, just like the excellent one we had at dinner. Nothing would satisfy that good old Mrs. Whitaker, but my taking one of the cheeses. I stood out as long as I could, till the tears almost came into her eyes, and I knew it was just the sort that my sister would be delighted with. That Mrs. Whitaker is a treasure! She was quite shocked when I asked her whether wine was allowed at the second table, and she has turned away two housemaids for wearing white gowns. Take care of the cheese, Fanny. Now I can manage the other parcel and the basket very well."

"What else have you been spunging?" said Maria, half pleased that Sotherton should be so complimented.

"Spunging, my dear! It is nothing but four of those beautiful pheasants' eggs, which Mrs. Whitaker would quite force upon me; she would not take a denial. She said it must be such an amusement to me, as she understood I lived quite alone, to have a few living creatures of that sort; and so to be sure it will. I shall get the dairymaid to set them under the first spare hen, and if they come to good I can have them moved to my own house and borrow a coop; and it will be a great delight to me in my lonely hours to attend to them. And if I have good luck your mother shall have some."

It was a beautiful evening, mild and still, and the drive was as pleasant as the serenity of Nature could make it; but when Mrs. Norris ceased speaking, it was altogether a silent drive to those within. Their spirits were in general exhausted; and to determine whether the day had afforded most pleasure or pain, might occupy the meditations of almost all.

Chapter 11

THE day at Sotherton, with all its imperfections, afforded the Miss Bertrams much more agreeable feelings than were derived from the letters from Antigua, which soon afterwards reached Mansfield. It was much pleasanter to think of Henry Crawford than of their father; and to think of their father in England again within a certain period, which these letters obliged them to do, was a most unwelcome exercise.

November was the black month fixed for his return. Sir Thomas wrote of it with as much decision as experience and anxiety could authorise. His business was so nearly concluded as to justify him in proposing to take his passage in the September packet, and he consequently looked forward with the hope of being with his beloved family again early in November.

Maria was more to be pitied than Julia; for to her the father brought a husband, and the return of the friend most solicitous for her happiness would unite her to the lover, on whom she had chosen that happiness should depend. It was a gloomy prospect, and all she could do was to throw a mist over it, and hope when the mist cleared away she should see something else. It would hardly be *early* in November, there were generally delays, a bad passage or *something;* that favouring *something* which everybody who shuts their eyes while they look, or their understandings while they reason, feels the comfort of. It would probably be the middle of November at least; the middle of November was three months off. Three months comprised thirteen weeks. Much might happen in thirteen weeks.

Sir Thomas would have been deeply mortified by a suspicion of half that his daughters felt on the subject of his return, and would hardly have found consolation in a knowledge of the interest it excited in the breast of another young lady. Miss Crawford, on walking up with her brother to spend the evening at Mansfield Park, heard the good news; and though seeming to have no concern in the affair beyond politeness, and to have vented all her feelings in a quiet congratulation, heard it with an attention not so easily satisfied. Mrs. Norris gave the particulars of the letters, and the subject was dropped; but after tea, as Miss Crawford was standing at an open window with Edmund and Fanny looking out on a twilight scene, while the Miss Bertrams, Mr. Rushworth, and Henry Crawford were all busy with candles at the pianoforte, she suddenly revived it by turning round towards the group, and saying, "How happy Mr. Rushworth looks! He is thinking of November."

Edmund looked round at Mr. Rushworth too, but had nothing to say. "Your father's return will be a very interesting event."

"It will, indeed, after such an absence; an absence not only long, but including so many dangers."

"It will be the forerunner also of other interesting events; your sister's marriage, and your taking orders."

"Yes."

"Don't be affronted," said she, laughing, "but it does put me in mind of some of the old heathen heroes, who, after performing great exploits in a foreign land, offered sacrifices to the gods on their safe return."

"There is no sacrifice in the case," replied Edmund, with a serious smile, and glancing at the pianoforte again, "it is entirely her own doing."

"Oh yes! I know it is. I was merely joking. She has done no more than what every young woman would do; and I have no doubt of her being extremely happy. My other sacrifice of course you do not understand."

"My taking orders, I assure you, is quite as voluntary as Maria's marrying."

"It is fortunate that your inclination and your father's convenience should accord so well. There is a very good living kept for you, I understand, hereabouts."

"Which you suppose has biassed me?"

"But *that* I am sure it has not," cried Fanny.

"Thank you for your good word, Fanny, but it is more than I would affirm myself. On the contrary, the knowing that there was such provision for me probably did bias me. Nor can I think it wrong that it should. There was no natural disinclination to be overcome, and I see no reason why a man should make a worse clergyman for knowing that he will have a competence early in life. I was in safe hands. I hope I should not have been influenced myself in a wrong way, and I am sure my father was too conscientious to have allowed it. I have no doubt that I was biassed, but I think it was blamelessly."

"It is the same sort of thing," said Fanny, after a short pause, "as for the son of an admiral to go into the navy or the son of a general to be in the army, and nobody sees anything wrong in that. Nobody wonders that they should prefer the line where their friends can serve them best, or suspects them to be less in earnest in it than they appear."

"No, my dear Miss Price, and for reasons good. The profession, either navy or army, is its own justification. It has everything in its favour; heroism, danger, bustle, fashion. Soldiers and sailors are always acceptable in society. Nobody can wonder that men are soldiers and sailors."

"But the motives of a man who takes orders with the certainty of preferment may be fairly suspected, you think?" said Edmund. "To be justified in your eyes, he must do it in the most complete uncertainty of any provision."

"What! take orders without a living! No; that is madness indeed; absolute madness."

"Shall I ask you how the church is to be filled, if a man is neither to take orders with a living, nor without? No; for you certainly would not know what to say. But I must beg some advantage to the clergyman from your own argument. As he cannot be influenced by those feelings which you rank highly as temptation and reward to the soldier and sailor, in their choice of a profession, as heroism, and noise, and fashion, are all against him, he ought to be less liable to the suspicion of wanting sincerity or good intentions in the choice of his."

"Oh! no doubt he is very sincere in preferring an income ready made, to the trouble of working for one: and has the best intentions of doing nothing all the rest of his days but eat, drink, and grow fat. It is indolence, Mr. Bertram, indeed. Indolence and love of ease; a want of all laudable ambition, of taste for good company, or of inclination to take the trouble of being agreeable, which makes men clergymen. A clergyman has nothing to do but be slovenly and selfish; read the newspaper, watch the weather, and quarrel with his wife. His curate does all the work, and the business of his own life is to dine."

"There are such clergymen, no doubt, but I think they are not so common as to justify Miss Crawford in esteeming it their general character. I suspect that in this comprensive and (may I say) commonplace censure, you are not judging from yourself, but from prejudiced persons, whose opinions you have been in the habit of hearing. It is impossible that your own observation can have given you much knowledge of the clergy. You can have been personally acquainted with very few of a set of men you condemn so conclusively. You are speaking what you have been told at your uncle's table."

"I speak what appears to me the general opinion; and where an opinion is general, it is usually correct. Though *I* have not seen much of the domestic lives of clergymen, it is seen by too many to leave any deficiency of information."

"Where any one body of educated men, of whatever denomination, are condemned indiscriminately, there must be a deficiency of information, or (smiling) of something else. Your uncle, and his brother admirals, perhaps knew little of clergymen beyond the chaplains whom, good or bad, they were always wishing away."

"Poor William! He has met with great kindness from the chaplain of the Antwerp," was a tender apostrophe of Fanny's, very much to the purpose of her own feelings if not of the conversation.

"I have been so little addicted to take my opinions from my uncle," said Miss Crawford, "that I can hardly suppose——and since you push me so hard, I must observe, that I am not entirely without the means of seeing what clergymen are, being at this present time the guest of my own brother, Dr. Grant. And though Dr. Grant is most kind and obliging to me, and though he is really a gentleman, and, I dare say, a good scholar and clever, and often preaches good sermons, and is very respectable, *I* see him to be an indolent, selfish bon vivant, who must have his palate consulted in everything; who will not stir a finger for the convenience of any one; and who, moreover, if the cook makes a blunder, is out of humour with his excellent wife. To own the truth, Henry and I were partly driven out this very evening by a disappointment about a green goose, which he could not get the better of. My poor sister was forced to stay and bear it."

"I do not wonder at your disapprobation, upon my word. It is a great defect of temper, made worse by a very faulty habit of self-indulgence; and to see your sister suffering from it must be exceedingly painful to such feelings as yours. Fanny, it goes against us. We cannot attempt to defend Dr. Grant."

"No," replied Fanny, "but we need not give up his profession for all that; because, whatever profession Dr. Grant had chosen, he would have taken a—not a good temper into it; and as he must, either in the navy or army, have had a great many more people under his command than he has now, I think more would have been made unhappy by him as a sailor or soldier than as a clergyman. Besides, I cannot but suppose that what-ever there may be to wish otherwise in Dr. Grant, would have been in a greater danger of becoming worse in a more active and worldly profession, where he would have had less time and obligation—where he might have escaped that knowledge of himself, the *frequency*, at least, of that knowl-edge which it is impossible he should escape as he is now. A man—a sensi-ble man like Dr. Grant, cannot be in the habit of teaching others, their duty every week, cannot go to church twice every Sunday, and preach such very good sermons in so good a manner as he does, without being the better for it himself. It must make him think; and I have no doubt that he oftener endeavours to restrain himself than he would if he had been anything but a clergyman."

"We cannot prove to the contrary, to be sure; but I wish you a better fate, Miss Price, than to be the wife of a man whose amiableness depends upon his own sermons; for, though he may preach himself into a good humour every Sunday, it will be bad enough to have him quarrelling about green geese from Monday morning till Saturday night."

"I think the man who could often quarrel with Fanny," said Edmund, affectionately, "must be beyond the reach of any sermons."

Fanny turned further into the window; and Miss Crawford had only time to say, in a pleasant manner, "I fancy Miss Price has been more used to deserve praise than to hear it;" when being earnestly invited by the Miss Bertrams to join in a glee, she tripped off to the instrument, leaving Edmund looking after her in an ecstasy of admiration of all her many virtues, from her obliging manners down to her light and graceful tread.

"There goes good humour, I am sure," said he presently. "There goes a temper which would never give pain! How well she walks! and how readily she falls in with the inclination of others! joining them the moment she is asked. What a pity," he added, after an instant's reflection, "that she should have been in such hands!"

Fanny agreed to it, and had the pleasure of seeing him continue at the window with her, in spite of the expected glee; and of having his eyes soon turned, like hers, towards the scene without, where all that was solemn, and soothing, and lovely, appeared in the brilliancy of an unclouded night, and the contrast of the deep shade of the woods. Fanny spoke her feelings. "Here's harmony!" said she; "here's repose! Here's what may leave all painting and all music behind, and what poetry can only attempt to describe! Here's what may tranquillise every care, and lift the heart to rapture! When I look out on such a night as this, I feel as if there could be neither wickedness nor sorrow in the world; and there certainly would be less of both if the sublimity of Nature were more attended to, and people were carried more out of themselves by contemplating such a scene."

"I like to hear your enthusiasm, Fanny. It is a lovely night, and they are much to be pitied who have not been taught to feel, in some degree, as you do; who have not, at least, been given a taste for Nature in early life. They lose a great deal."

"*You* taught me to think and feel on the subject, cousin."

"I had a very apt scholar. There's Arcturus looking very bright."

"Yes, and the Bear. I wish I could see Cassiopeia."

"We must go out on the lawn for that. Should you be afraid?"

"Not in the least. It is a great while since we have had any star-gazing."

"Yes, I do not know how it has happened." The glee began. "We will stay till this is finished, Fanny," said he, turning his back on the window; and as it advanced, she had the mortification of seeing him advance too, moving forward by gentle degrees towards the instrument, and when it ceased, he was close by the singers, among the most urgent in requesting to hear the glee again.

Fanny sighed alone at the window till scolded away by Mrs. Norris's threats of catching cold.

Chapter 12

Sir Thomas was to return in November, and his eldest son had duties to call him earlier home. The approach of September brought tidings of Mr. Bertram, first in a letter to the gamekeeper and then in a letter to Edmund; and by the end of August he arrived himself, to be gay, agreeable, and gallant again as occasion served, or Miss Crawford demanded; to tell of races and Weymouth, and parties and friends, to which she might have listened six weeks before with some interest, and altogether to give her the fullest conviction, by the power of actual comparison, of her preferring his younger brother.

It was very vexatious, and she was heartily sorry for it; but so it was; and so far from now meaning to marry the elder, she did not even want to attract him beyond what the simplest claims of conscious beauty required; his lengthened absence from Mansfield, without anything but pleasure in view, and his own will to consult, made it perfectly clear that he did not care about her; and his indifference was so much more than equalled by her own, that, were he now to step forth the owner of Mansfield Park, the

Sir Thomas complete, which he was to be in time, she did not believe she could accept him.

The season and duties which brought Mr. Bertram back to Mansfield took Mr. Crawford into Norfolk. Everingham could not do without him in the beginning of September. He went for a fortnight—a fortnight of such dullness to the Miss Bertrams as ought to have put them both on their guard, and made even Julia admit, in her jealousy of her sister, the absolute necessity of distrusting his attentions, and wishing him not to return; and a fortnight of sufficient leisure, in the intervals of shooting and sleeping, to have convinced the gentleman that he ought to keep longer away, had he been more in the habit of examining his own motives, and of reflecting to what the indulgence of his idle vanity was tending; but, thoughtless and selfish from prosperity and bad example, he would not look beyond the present moment. The sisters, handsome, clever, and encouraging, were an amusement to his sated mind; and finding nothing in Norfolk to equal the social pleasures of Mansfield, he gladly returned to it at the time appointed, and was welcomed thither quite as gladly by those whom he came to trifle with further.

Maria, with only Mr. Rushworth to attend to her, and doomed to the repeated details of his day's sport, good or bad, his boast of his dogs, his jealousy of his neighbours, his doubts of their qualifications, and his zeal after poachers, subjects which will not find their way to female feelings without some talent on one side or some attachment on the other, had missed Mr. Crawford grievously; and Julia, unengaged and unemployed, felt all the right of missing him much more. Each sister believed herself the favourite. Julia might be justified in so doing by the hints of Mrs. Grant, inclined to credit what she wished, and Maria by the hints of Mr. Crawford himself. Everything returned into the same channel as before his absence; his manners being to each so animated and agreeable as to lose no ground with either, and just stopping short of the consistence, the steadiness, the solicitude, and the warmth which might excite general notice.

Fanny was the only one of the party who found anything to dislike; but since the day at Sotherton, she could never see Mr. Crawford with either sister without observation, and seldom without wonder or censure; and had her confidence in her own judgment been equal to her exercise of it in every other respect, had she been sure that she was seeing clearly, and judging candidly, she would probably have made some important communications to her usual confidant. As it was, however, she only hazarded a hint, and the hint was lost. "I am rather surprised," said she, "that Mr. Crawford should come back again so soon, after being here so long before, full seven weeks; for I had understood he was so very fond of change and moving about, that I thought something would certainly occur when he was once gone, to take him elsewhere. He is used to much gayer places than Mansfield."

"It is to his credit," was Edmund's answer; "and I dare say it gives his sister pleasure. She does not like his unsettled habits."

"What a favourite he is with my cousins!"

"Yes, his manners to women are such as must please. Mrs. Grant, I believe, suspects him of a preference for Julia; I have never seen much symptom of it, but I wish it may be so. He has no faults but what a serious attachment would remove."

"If Miss Bertram were not engaged," said Fanny, cautiously, "I could sometimes almost think that he admired her more than Julia."

"Which is, perhaps, more in favour of his liking Julia best, than you, Fanny, may be aware; for I believe it often happens, that a man, before he has quite made up his own mind, will distinguish the sister or intimate friend of the woman he is really thinking of, more than the woman herself. Crawford has too much sense to stay here if he found himself in any danger from Maria; and I am not at all afraid for her, after such a proof as she has given, that her feelings are not strong."

Fanny supposed she must have been mistaken, and meant to think differently in future; but with all that submission to Edmund could do, and all the help of the coinciding looks and hints which she occasionally noticed in some of the others, and which seemed to say that Julia was Mr. Crawford's choice, she knew not always what to think. She was privy, one evening, to the hopes of her Aunt Norris on the subject, as well as to her feelings, and the feelings of Mrs. Rushworth, on a point of some similarity, and could not help wondering as she listened; and glad would she have been not to be obliged to listen, for it was while all the other young people were dancing, and she sitting, most unwillingly, among the chaperons at the fire, longing for the re-entrance of her elder cousin, on whom all her own hopes of a partner then depended. It was Fanny's first ball, though without the preparation or splendour of many a young lady's first ball, being the thought only of the afternoon, built on the late acquisition of a violin player in the servants' hall, and the possibility of raising five couples with the help of Mrs. Grant and a new intimate friend of Mr. Bertram's just arrived on a visit. It had, however, been a very happy one to Fanny through four dances, and she was quite grieved to be losing even a quarter of an hour. While waiting and wishing, looking now at the dancers and now at the door, this dialogue between the two above-mentioned ladies was forced on her:

"I think, ma'am," said Mrs. Norris—her eyes directed towards Mr. Rushworth and Maria, who were partners for the second time, "we shall see some happy faces again now."

"Yes, ma'am, indeed," replied the other, with a stately simper, "there will be some satisfaction in looking on *now*, and I think it was rather a pity they should have been obliged to part. Young folks in their situation should be excused complying with the common forms. I wonder my son did not propose it."

"I dare say he did, ma'am. Mr. Rushworth is never remiss. But dear

Maria has such a strict sense of propriety, so much of that true delicacy which one seldom meets with now-a-days, Mrs. Rushworth—that wish of avoiding particularity! Dear ma'am, only look at her face at this moment; how different from what it was the two last dances!"

Miss Bertram did indeed look happy, her eyes were sparkling with pleasure, and she was speaking with great animation, for Julia and her partner, Mr. Crawford, were close to her; they were all in a cluster together. How she had looked before, Fanny could not recollect, for she had been dancing with Edmund herself, and had not thought about her.

Mrs. Norris continued, "It is quite delightful, ma'am, to see young people so properly happy, so well suited, and so much the thing! I cannot but think of dear Sir Thomas's delight. And what do you say, ma'am, to the chance of another match? Mr. Rushworth has set a good example and such things are very catching."

Mrs. Rushworth, who saw nothing but her son, was quite at a loss. "The couple above, ma'am. Do you see no symptoms there?"

"Oh dear! Miss Julia and Mr. Crawford. Yes, indeed, a very pretty match. What is his property?"

"Four thousand a year."

"Very well. Those who have not more, must be satisfied with what they have. Four thousand a year is a pretty estate, and he seems a very genteel, steady young man, so I hope Miss Julia will be very happy."

"It is not a settled thing, ma'am, yet. We only speak of it among friends. But I have very little doubt it *will be*. He is growing extremely particular in his attentions."

Fanny could listen no further. Listening and wondering were all suspended for a time, for Mr. Bertram was in the room again; and though feeling it would be a great honour to be asked by him, she thought it must happen. He came towards their little circle; but instead of asking her to dance, drew a chair near her, and gave her an account of the present state of a sick horse, and the opinion of the groom, from whom he had just parted. Fanny found that it was not to be, and in the modesty of her nature immediately felt that she had been unreasonable in expecting it.

When he had told of his horse, he took a newspaper from the table, and looking over it, said in a languid way, "If you want to dance, Fanny, I will stand up with you." With more than equal civility the offer was declined; she did not wish to dance. "I am glad of it," said he, in a much brisker tone, and throwing down the newspaper again, "for I am tired to death. I only wonder how the good people can keep it up so long. They had need be *all* in love, to find any amusement in such folly; and so they are, I fancy. If you look at them you may see they are so many couple of lovers—all but Yates and Mrs. Grant—and, between ourselves, she, poor woman, must want a lover as much as any one of them. A desperate dull life hers must be with the doctor," making a sly face as he spoke towards the chair of the latter, who proving, however, to be close at his elbow, made so instantaneous a change of expression and subject necessary, as Fanny in spite of everything, could hardly help laughing at. "A strange business this in America, Dr. Grant! What is your opinion? I always come to you to know what I am to think of public matters."

"My dear Tom," cried his aunt soon afterwards, "as you are not dancing, I dare say you will have no objection to join us in a rubber; shall you?" Then leaving her seat, and coming to him to enforce the proposal, added in a whisper, "We want to make a table for Mrs. Rushworth, you know. Your mother is quite anxious about it, but cannot very well spare time to sit down herself, because of her fringe. Now, you, and I, and Dr. Grant, will just do; and though *we* play but half-crowns, you know, you may bet half-guineas with *him*."

"I should be most happy," replied he aloud, and jumping up with alacrity, "it would give me the greatest pleasure; but that I am this moment going to dance. Come, Fanny," taking her hand, "do not be dawdling any longer, or the dance will be over."

Fanny was led off very willingly, though it was impossible for her to feel much gratitude towards her cousin, or distinguish, as he certainly did, between the selfishness of another person and his own.

"A pretty modest request upon my word," he indignantly exclaimed as they walked away. "To want to nail me to a card table for the next two hours with herself and Dr. Grant, who are always quarrelling, and that poking old woman, who knows no more of whist than of algebra. I wish my good aunt would be a little less busy! And to ask me in such a way too! without ceremony, before them all, so as to leave me no possibility of refusing. *That* is what I dislike most particularly. It raises my spleen more than anything to have the pretence of being asked, of being given a choice, and at the same time addressed in such a way as to oblige one to do the very thing, whatever it be! If I had not luckily thought of standing up with you I could not have got out of it. It is a great deal too bad. But when my aunt has got a fancy in her head, nothing can stop her."

Chapter 13

THE Honourable John Yates, this new friend, had not much to recommend him beyond habits of fashion and expense, and being the younger son of a lord with a tolerable independence; and Sir Thomas would probably have thought his introduction at Mansfield by no means desirable. Mr. Bertram's acquaintance with him had begun at Weymouth, where they had spent ten days together in the same society, and the friendship, if friendship it might be called, had been proved and perfected by Mr. Yates's being invited to take Mansfield in his way, whenever he could, and by his promising to come; and he did come rather earlier than had been expected, in consequence of the sudden breaking-up of a large party assembled for gaiety at the house of another friend, which he had left Weymouth to join. He came on the wings of disappointment, and with his head full of acting, for it had been a theatrical party; and the play in which he had borne a part was within two days of representation, when the sudden death of one of the nearest connections of the family had destroyed the scheme and dispersed the performers. To be so near happiness, so near fame, so near the long paragraph in praise of the private theatricals at Ecclesford, the seat of the Right Hon. Lord Ravenshaw, in Cornwall, which would of course have immortalised the whole party for at least a twelvemonth! and being so near, to lose it all, was an injury to be keenly felt, and Mr. Yates could talk of nothing else. Ecclesford and its theatre, with its arrangements and dresses, rehearsals, and jokes, was his never-failing subject, and to boast of the past his only consolation.

Happily for him, a love of the theatre is so general, an itch for acting so strong among young people, that he could hardly out-talk the interest of his hearers. From the first casting of the parts, to the epilogue, it was all bewitching, and there were few who did not wish to have been a party concerned, or would have hesitated to try their skill. The play had been *Lovers' Vows*, and Mr. Yates was to have been Count Cassel. "A trifling part," said, he, "and not at all to my taste, and such a one as I certainly would not accept again; but I was determined to make no difficulties. Lord Ravenshaw and the duke had appropriated the only two characters worth playing before I reached Ecclesford; and though Lord Ravenshaw offered to resign his to me, it was impossible to take it, you know. I was sorry for *him* that he should have so mistaken his powers, for he was no more equal to the Baron—a little man with a weak voice, always hoarse after the first ten minutes. It must have injured the piece materially; but *I* was resolved to make no difficulties. Sir Henry thought the duke not equal to Frederick, but that was because Sir Henry wanted the part himself; whereas it was certainly in the best hands of the two. I was surprised to see Sir Henry such a stick. Luckily the strength of the piece did not depend upon him. Our Agatha was inimitable, and the duke was thought very great by many. And upon the whole it would certainly have gone off wonderfully."

"It was a hard case, upon my word;" and, "I do think you were very much to be pitied," were the kind responses of listening sympathy.

"It is not worth complaining about; but to be sure the poor old dowager could not have died at a worse time; and it is impossible to help wishing that the news could have been suppressed for just the three days we wanted. It was but three days; and being only a grandmother, and all happening two hundred miles off, I think there would have been no great harm, and it *was* suggested, I know; but Lord Ravenshaw, who I suppose is one of the most correct men in England, would not hear of it."

"An afterpiece instead of a comedy," said Mr. Bertram. "Lovers' vows were at an end, and Lord and Lady Ravenshaw left to act My Grandmother by themselves. Well, the jointure may comfort *him;* and, perhaps, between friends, he began to tremble for his credit and his lungs in the Baron, and was not sorry to withdraw; and to make *you* amends, Yates,

I think we must raise a little theatre at Mansfield, and ask you to be our manager."

This, though the thought of the moment, did not end with the moment; for the inclination to act was awakened, and in no one more strongly than in him who was now master of the house; and who having so much leisure as to make almost any novelty a certain good, had likewise such a degree of lively talents and comic taste, as were exactly adapted to the novelty of acting. The thought returned again and again. "Oh, for the Ecclesford theatre and scenery to try something with!" Each sister could echo the wish; and Henry Crawford, to whom, in all the riot of his gratifications it was yet an untasted pleasure, was quite alive at the idea. "I really believe," said he, "I could be fool enough at this moment to undertake any character that ever was written, from Shylock or Richard III down to the singing hero of a farce in his scarlet coat and cocked hat. I feel as if I could be anything or everything; as if I could rant and storm, or sigh, or cut capers in any tragedy or comedy in the English language. Let us be doing something. Be it only half a play, an act, a scene; what should prevent us? Not these countenances, I am sure," looking towards the Miss Bertrams, "and for a theatre, what signifies a theatre? We shall be only amusing ourselves. Any room in this house might suffice."

"We must have a curtain," said Tom Bertram; "a few yards of green baize for a curtain, and perhaps that may be enough."

"Oh, quite enough!" cried Mr. Yates, "with only just a side wing or two run up, doors in flat, and three or four scenes to be let down; nothing more would be necessary on such a plan as this. For mere amusement among ourselves, we should want nothing more."

"I believe we must be satisfied with *less*," said Maria. "There would not be time, and other difficulties would arise. We must rather adopt Mr. Crawford's views, and make the *performance*, not the *theatre*, our object. Many parts of our best plays are independent of scenery."

"Nay," said Edmund, who began to listen with alarm. "Let us do nothing by halves. If we are to act, let it be in a theatre completely fitted up with pit, boxes, and gallery, and let us have a play entire from beginning to end; so as it be a German play, no matter what, with a good tricking, shifting afterpiece, and a figure-dance, and a hornpipe, and a song between the acts. If we do not outdo Ecclesford, we do nothing."

"Now, Edmund, do not be disagreeable," said Julia. "Nobody loves a play better than you do, or can have gone much further to see one."

"True, to see real acting, good hardened real acting; but I would hardly walk from this room to the next to look at the raw efforts of those who have not been bred to the trade: a set of gentlemen and ladies, who have all the disadvantages of education and decorum to struggle through."

After a short pause, however, the subject still continued, and was discussed with unabated eagerness, every one's inclination increasing by the discussion, and a knowledge of the inclination of the rest; and though nothing was settled but that Tom Bertram would prefer a comedy, and his sisters and Henry Crawford a tragedy, and that nothing in the world could be easier than to find a piece which would please them all, the resolution to act something or other seemed so decided, as to make Edmund quite uncomfortable. He was determined to prevent it, if possible, though his mother, who equally heard the conversation, which passed at table, did not evince the least disapprobation.

The same evening afforded him an opportunity of trying his strength. Maria, Julia, Henry Crawford, and Mr. Yates were in the billiard-room. Tom returning from them into the drawing-room, where Edmund was standing thoughtfully by the fire, while Lady Bertram was on the sofa at a little distance, and Fanny close beside her, arranging her work, thus began as he entered:

"Such a horribly vile billiard-table as ours is not to be met with, I believe, above ground. I can stand it no longer, and I think, I may say, that nothing shall ever tempt me to it again; but one good thing I have just ascertained; it is the very room for a theatre, precisely the shape and length for it; and the doors at the further end, communicating with each other, as they may be made to do in five minutes, by merely moving the bookcase in my father's room, is the very thing we could have desired, if we had set down to wish for it; and my father's room will be an excellent green room. It seems to join the billiard-room on purpose."

"You are not serious, Tom, in meaning to act?" said Edmund, in a low voice, as his brother approached the fire.

"Not serious! never more so, I assure you. What is there to surprise you in it?"

"I think it would be very wrong. In a *general* light, private theatricals are open to some objections, but as *we* are circumstanced, I must think it would be highly injudicious, and more than injudicious, to attempt anything of the kind. It would show great want of feeling on my father's account, absent as he is, and in some degree of constant danger; and it would be imprudent, I think, with regard to Maria, whose situation is a very delicate one, considering everything, extremely delicate."

"You take up a thing so seriously! as if we were going to act three times a week till my father's return, and invite all the country. But it is not to be a display of that sort. We mean nothing but a little amusement among ourselves, just to vary the scene, and exercise our powers in something new. We want no audience, no publicity. We may be trusted, I think, in choosing some play most perfectly unexceptionable; and I can conceive no greater harm or danger to any of us in conversing in the elegant written language of some respectable author than in chattering in words of our own. I have no fears, and no scruples. And as to my father's being absent, it is so far from an objection, that I consider it rather as a motive; for the expectation of his return must be a very anxious period to my mother; and if we can be the means of amusing that anxiety, and keeping up her spirits for the next few weeks, I shall think our time very well spent, and so, I am sure, will he. It is a *very* anxious period for her."

As he said this, each looked towards their mother. Lady Bertram, sunk back in one corner of the sofa, the picture of health, wealth, ease, and tranquillity, was just falling into a gentle doze, while Fanny was getting through the few difficulties of her work for her.

Edmund smiled and shook his head.

"By jove! this won't do," cried Tom, throwing himself into a chair with a hearty laugh. "To be sure, my dear mother, your anxiety—I was unlucky there."

"What is the matter?" asked her ladyship, in the heavy tone of one half roused, "I was not asleep."

"Oh, dear no, ma'am, nobody suspected you! Well, Edmund," he continued, returning to the former subject, posture, and voice, as soon as Lady Bertram began to nod again, "but *this* I *will* maintain, that we shall be doing no harm."

"I cannot agree with you; I am convinced that my father would totally disapprove it."

"And I am convinced to the contrary. Nobody is fonder of the exercise of talent in young people, or promotes it more than my father, and for anything of the acting, spouting, reciting kind, I think he has always a decided taste. I am sure he encouraged it in us as boys. How many a time have we mourned over the dead body of Julius Cæsar, and *to be'd* and not *to be'd*, in this very room, for his amusement? And I am sure, *my name was Norval*, every evening of my life through one Christmas holidays."

"It was a very different thing. You must see the difference yourself. My father wished us, as schoolboys, to speak well, but he would never wish his grown-up daughters to be acting plays. His sense of decorum is strict."

"I know all that," said Tom, displeased. "I know my father as well as you do; and I'll take care that his daughters do nothing to distress him. Manage your own concerns, Edmund, and I'll take care of the rest of the family."

"If you are resolved on acting," replied the persevering Edmund, "I must hope it will be in a very small and quiet way; and I think a theatre ought not to be attempted. It would be taking liberties with my father's house in his absence which could not be justified."

"For everything of that nature, I will be answerable," said Tom, in a decided tone. "His house shall not be hurt. I have quite as great an interest in being careful of his house as you can have; and as to such alterations as I was suggesting just now, such as moving a bookcase, or unlocking a door; or even as using the billiard-room for the space of a week without playing at billiards in it, you might just as well suppose he would object to our sitting more in this room, and less in the breakfast-room, than we did before he went away, or to my sister's pianoforte being moved from one side of the room to the other. Absolute nonsense!"

"The innovation, if not wrong as an innovation, will be wrong as an expense."

"Yes, the expense of such an undertaking would be prodigious! Perhaps it might cost a whole twenty pounds. Something of a theatre we must have undoubtedly, but it will be on the simplest plan; a green curtain and a little carpenter's work, and that's all; and as the carpenter's work may be all done at home by Christopher Jackson himself, it will be too absurd to talk of expense; and as long as Jackson is employed, everything will be right with Sir Thomas. Don't imagine that nobody in this house can see or judge but yourself. Don't act yourself, if you do not like it, but don't expect to govern everybody else."

"No, as to acting myself," said Edmund, "*that* I absolutely protest against."

Tom walked out of the room as he said it, and Edmund was left to sit down and stir the fire in thoughtful vexation.

Fanny, who had heard it all, and borne Edmund company in every feeling throughout the whole, now ventured to say, in her anxiety to suggest some comfort, "Perhaps they may not be able to find any play to suit them. Your brother's taste, and your sisters', seem very different."

"I have no hope there, Fanny. If they persist in the scheme, they will find something. I shall speak to my sisters and try to dissuade *them*, and that is all I can do."

"I should think my Aunt Norris would be on your side."

"I dare say she would, but she has no influence with either Tom or my sisters that could be of any use; and if I cannot convince them myself, I shall let things take their course, without attempting it through her. Family squabbling is the greatest evil of all, and we had better do anything than be altogether by the ears."

His sisters, to whom he had an opportunity of speaking the next morning, were quite as impatient of his advice, quite as unyielding to his representation, quite as determined in the cause of pleasure, as Tom. Their mother had no objection to the plan, and they were not in the least afraid of their father's disapprobation. There could be no harm in what had been done in so many respectable families, and by so many women of the first consideration; and it must be scrupulousness run mad, that could see anything to censure in a plan like theirs, comprehending only brothers and sisters, and intimate friends, and which would never be heard of beyond themselves. Julia *did* seem inclined to admit that Maria's situation might require particular caution and delicacy—but that could not extend to *her*—*she* was at liberty; and Maria evidently considered her engagement as only raising her so much more above restraint, and leaving her less occasion than Julia, to consult either father or mother. Edmund had little to hope, but he was still urging the subject, when Henry Crawford entered the room, fresh from the Parsonage, calling out, "No want of hands in our theatre, Miss Bertram. No want of understrappers; my sister desires her love, and hopes to be admitted into the company, and will be happy to take the part of any old duenna, or tame confidante, that you may not like to do yourselves."

Maria gave Edmund a glance, which meant, "What say you now? Can we be wrong if Mary Crawford feels the same?" And Edmund, silenced, was obliged to acknowledge that the charm of acting might well carry fascination to the mind of genius; and with the ingenuity of love, to dwell more on the obliging, accommodating purport of the message than on anything else.

The scheme advanced. Opposition was vain; and as to Mrs. Norris, he was mistaken in supposing she would wish to make any. She started no difficulties that were not talked down in five minutes by her eldest nephew and niece, who were all-powerful with her; and, as the whole arrangement was to bring very little expense to anybody, and none at all to herself, as she foresaw in it all the comfort of hurry, bustle, and importance, and derived the immediate advantage of fancying herself obliged to leave her own house, where she had been living a month at her own cost, and take up her abode in theirs, that every hour might be spent in their service, she was, in fact, exceedingly delighted with the project.

Chapter 14

FANNY seemed nearer being right than Edmund had supposed. The business of finding a play that would suit everybody proved to be no trifle; and the carpenter had received his orders and taken his measurements, had suggested and removed at least two sets of difficulties and having made the necessity of an enlargement of plan and expense fully evident, was already at work, while a play was still to seek. Other preparations were also in hand. An enormous roll of green baize had arrived from Northampton, and been cut out by Mrs. Norris (with a saving by her good management, of full three quarters of a yard), and was actually forming into a curtain by the housemaids, and still the play was wanting; and as two or three days passed away in this manner, Edmund began almost to hope that none might ever be found.

There were, in fact, so many things to be attended to, so many people to be pleased, so many best characters required, and above all, such a need that the play should be at once both tragedy and comedy, that there did seem as little chance of a decision as anything pursued by youth and zeal could hold out.

On the tragic side were the Miss Bertrams, Henry Crawford and Mr. Yates; on the comic, Tom Bertram, not *quite* alone, because it was evident that Mary Crawford's wishes, though politely kept back, inclined the same way: but his determinateness and his power seemed to make allies unnecessary; and, independent of this great irreconcilable difference, they wanted a piece containing very few characters in the whole, but every character first-rate, and three principal women. All the best plays were run over in vain. Neither *Hamlet*, nor *Macbeth*, nor *Othello*, nor *Douglas*, nor *The Gamester*, presented anything that could satisfy even the tragedians; and *The Rivals, The School for Scandal, Wheel of Fortune, Heir at Law,* and a long et cetera, were successively dismissed with yet warmer objections. No piece could be proposed that did not supply somebody with a difficulty, and on one side or the other it was a continual repetition of, "Oh no, *that* will never do! Let us have no ranting tragedies. Too many characters. Not a tolerable woman's part in the play. Anything but *that,* my dear Tom. It would be impossible to fill it up. One could not expect anybody to take such a part. Nothing but buffoonery from beginning to end. *That* might do, perhaps, but for the low parts. If I *must* give my opinion, I have always thought it the most insipid play in the English language, *I* do not wish to make objections; I shall be happy to be of any use, but I think we could not choose worse."

Fanny looked on and listened, not unamused to observe the selfishness which, more or less disguised, seemed to govern them all, and wondering how it would end. For her own gratification she could have wished that something might be acted, for she had never seen even half a play, but everything of higher consequence was against it.

"This will never do," said Tom Bertram at last. "We are wasting time most abominably. Something must be fixed on. No matter what, so that something is chosen. We must not be so nice. A few characters too many must not frighten us. We must *double* them. We must descend a little. If a part is insignificant, the greater our credit in making anything of it. From this moment, *I* make no difficulties. I take any part you choose to give me, so as it be comic. Let it but be comic, I condition for nothing more."

For about the fifth time he then proposed *The Heir at Law,* doubting only whether to prefer Lord Duberley or Dr. Pangloss for himself; and very earnestly, but very unsuccessfully, trying to persuade the others that there were some fine tragic parts in the rest of the dramatis personæ.

The pause which followed this fruitless effort was ended by the same speaker, who taking up one of the many volumes of plays that lay on the table, and turning it over, suddenly exclaimed—"*Lovers' Vows!* And why should not *Lovers' Vows* do for *us* as well as for the Ravenshaws? How came it never to be thought of before? It strikes me as if it would do exactly. What say you all? Here are two capital tragic parts for Yates and Crawford, and here is the rhyming Butler for me, if nobody else wants it; a trifling part, but the sort of thing I should not dislike, and, as I said before, I am determined to take anything and do my best. And as for the rest, they may be filled up by anybody. It is only Count Cassel and Anhalt."

The suggestion was generally welcome. Everybody was growing weary of indecision, and the first idea with everybody was, that nothing had been proposed before so likely to suit them all. Mr. Yates was particularly pleased: he had been sighing and longing to do the Baron at Ecclesford, had grudged every rant of Lord Ravenshaw's and been forced to re-rant it all in his own room. To storm through Baron Wildenheim was the height of his theatrical ambition; and with the advantage of knowing half the scenes by heart already, he did now with the greatest alacrity, offer his services for the part. To do him justice, however, he did not resolve to appropriate it; for remembering that there was some very good ranting ground in Frederick, he professed an equal willingness for that. Henry Crawford was ready to take either. Whichever Mr. Yates did not choose would perfectly satisfy him, and a short parley of compliment ensued. Miss Bertram, feeling all the interest of an Agatha in the question, took on her to decide it, by observing to Mr. Yates, that this was a point in which height and figure ought to be considered, and that *his* being the tallest, seemed to fit him peculiarly for the Baron. She was acknowledged to be quite right, and the two parts being accepted accordingly, she was certain of the proper Frederick. Three of the characters were now cast, besides Mr. Rushworth, who was always answered for by Maria as willing to do anything, when Julia, meaning, like her sister, to be Agatha, began to be scrupulous on Miss Crawford's account.

"This is not behaving well by the absent," said she. "Here are not women enough. Amelia and Agatha may do for Maria and me, but here is nothing for your sister, Mr. Crawford."

Mr. Crawford desired *that* might not be thought of: he was very sure his sister had no wish of acting but as she might be useful, and that she would not allow herself to be considered in the present case. But this was immediately opposed by Tom Bertram, who asserted the part of Amelia to be in every respect the property of Miss Crawford, if she would accept it. "It falls as naturally, as necessarily, to her," said he, "as Agatha does to one or other of my sisters. It can be no sacrifice on their side, for it is highly comic."

A short silence followed. Each sister looked anxious; for each felt the best claim to Agatha, and was hoping to have it pressed on her by the rest. Henry Crawford, who meanwhile had taken up the play, and with seeming carelessness was turning over the first act, soon settled the business.

"I must entreat Miss *Julia* Bertram," said he, "not to engage in the part of Agatha, or it will be the ruin of all my solemnity. You must not, indeed you must not (turning to her). I could not stand your countenance dressed up in woe and paleness. The many laughs we have had together would infallibly come across me, and Frederick and his knapsack would be obliged to run away."

Pleasantly, courteously, it was spoken; but the manner was lost in the matter to Julia's feelings. She saw a glance at Maria, which confirmed the injury to herself: it was a scheme, a trick; she was slighted, Maria was preferred; the smile of triumph which Maria was trying to suppress showed how well it was understood; and before Julia could command herself enough to speak, her brother gave his weight against her too, by saying, "Oh yes! Maria must be Agatha. Maria will be the best Agatha. Though Julia fancies she prefers tragedy, I would not trust her in it. There is nothing of tragedy about her. She has not the look of it. Her features are not tragic features, and she walks too quick, and speaks too quick, and would not keep her countenance. She had better do the old country-woman: the Cottager's Wife; you had, indeed, Julia. Cottager's Wife is a very pretty part, I assure you. The old lady relieves the high-flown benevolence of her husband with a good deal of spirit. You shall be Cottager's Wife."

"Cottager's Wife!" cried Mr. Yates. "What are you talking of? The most trivial, paltry, insignificant part; the merest commonplace; not a tolerable speech in the whole. Your sister do that! It is an insult to pro-pose it. At Ecclesford the governess was to have done it. We all agreed that it could not be offered to anybody else. A little more justice, Mr. Manager, if you please. You do not deserve the office, if you cannot appre-ciate the talents of your company a little better."

"Why, as to *that*, my good friend, till I and my company have really acted there must be some guess work; but I mean no disparagement to Julia. We cannot have two Agatha's, and we must have one Cottager's Wife; and I am sure I set her the example of moderation myself in being satisfied with the old Butler. If the part is trifling she will have more credit in making something of it; and if she is so desperately bent against every-thing humorous, let her take Cottager's speeches instead of Cottager's Wife's and so change the parts all through; *he* is solemn and pathetic enough, I am sure. It could make no difference in the play, and as for Cottager himself, when he has got his wife's speeches, *I* would undertake him with all my heart."

"With all your partiality for Cottager's Wife," said Henry Crawford, "it will be impossible to make anything of it fit for your sister, and we must not suffer her good nature to be imposed on. We must not *allow* her to accept the part. She must not be left to her own complaisance. Her talents will be wanted in Amelia. Amelia is a character more difficult to be well represented than even Agatha. I consider Amelia is the most difficult character in the whole piece. It requires great powers, great nicety, to give her playfulness and simplicity without extravagance. I have seen good actresses fail in the part. Simplicity, indeed, is beyond the reach of almost every actress by profession. It requires a delicacy of feeling which they have not. It requires a gentlewoman—a Julia Bertram. You *will* undertake it, I hope?" turning to her with a look of anxious entreaty, which softened her a little; but while she hesitated what to say, her brother again interposed with Miss Crawford's better claim.

"No, no, Julia must not be Amelia. It is not at all the part for her. She would not like it. She would not do well. She is too tall and robust. Amelia should be a small, light, girlish, skipping figure. It is fit for Miss Crawford, and Miss Crawford only. She looks the part, and I am persuaded will do it admirably."

Without attending to this, Henry Crawford continued his supplication. "You must oblige us," said he, "indeed you must. When you have studied the character, I am sure you will feel it suit you. Tragedy may be your choice, but it will certainly appear that comedy chooses *you*. You will be to visit me in prison with a basket of provisions; you will not refuse to visit me in prison? I think I see you coming in with your basket?"

The influence of his voice was felt. Julia wavered; but was he only trying to soothe and pacify her, and make her overlook the previous affront? She distrusted him. The slight had been most determined. He was, perhaps, but at treacherous play with her. She looked suspiciously at her sister; Maria's countenance was to decide it; if she were vexed and alarmed—but Maria looked all serenity and satisfaction, and Julia well knew that on this ground Maria could not be happy but at her expense. With hasty indignation, therefore, and a tremulous voice, she said to him, "You do not seem afraid of not keeping your countenance when I come in with a basket of provisions—though one might have supposed—but it is only as Agatha that I was to be so overpowering!" She stopped, Henry Crawford looked rather foolish, and as if he did not know what to say. Tom Bertram began again:

"Miss Crawford must be Amelia. She will be an excellent Amelia."

"Do not be afraid of *my* wanting the character," cried Julia, with angry quickness: "I am *not* to be Agatha, and I am sure I will do nothing else; and as to Amelia, it is of all parts in the world most disgusting to me. I quite detest her. An odious, little, pert, unnatural, impudent girl. I have always protested against comedy, and this is comedy in its worst form." And so saying, she walked hastily out of the room, leaving awkward feelings to more than one, but exciting small compassion in any except Fanny, who had been a quiet auditor of the whole, and who could not think of her as under the agitations of *jealousy* without great pity.

A short silence succeeded her leaving them; but her brother soon returned to business and *Lovers' Vows*, and was eagerly looking over the play, with Mr. Yates' help, to ascertain what scenery would be necessary, while Maria and Henry Crawford conversed together in an under voice, and the declaration with which she began of, "I am sure I would give up the part of Julia most willingly, but that though I shall probably do it very ill, I feel persuaded *she* would do it worse," was doubtless receiving all the compliments it called for.

When this had lasted some time, the division of the party was completed by Tom Bertram and Mr. Yates walking off together to consult further in the room now beginning to be called *the Theatre*, and Miss Bertram's resolving to go down to the Parsonage herself with the offer of Amelia to Miss Crawford; and Fanny remained alone.

The first use she made of her solitude was to take up the volume which had been left on the table, and begin to acquaint herself with the play of which she had heard so much. Her curiosity was all awake, and she ran through it with an eagerness which was suspended only by intervals of astonishment, that it could be chosen in the present instance, that it could be proposed and accepted in a private theatre! Agatha and Amelia appeared to her in their different ways so totally improper for home representation; the situation of one, and the language of the other, so unfit to be expressed by any woman of modesty, that she could hardly suppose her cousins could be aware of what they were engaging in; and longed to have them roused as soon as possible by the remonstrance which Edmund would certainly make.

Chapter 15

Miss CRAWFORD accepted the part very readliy; and soon after Miss Bertram's return from the Parsonage, Mr. Rushworth arrived, and another character was consequently cast. He had the offer of Count Cassel and Anhalt, and at first did not know which to choose, and wanted Miss Bertram to direct him; but upon being made to understand the different style of the characters, and which was which, and recollecting that he had once seen the play in London, and had thought Anhalt a very stupid fellow, he soon decided for the Count. Miss Bertram approved the decision, for the less he had to learn the better; and though she could not sympathise in his wish that the Count and Agatha might be to act together, nor wait very patiently while he was slowly turning over the leaves with the hope of still discovering such a scene, she very kindly took his part in hand, and curtailed every speech that admitted being shortened; besides pointing out the necessity of his being very much dressed, and choosing his colours. Mr. Rushworth liked the idea of his finery very well, though affecting to despise it; and was too much engaged with what his own appearance would be to think of the others, or draw any of those conclusions, or feel any of that displeasure which Maria had been half prepared for.

Thus much was settled before Edmund, who had been out all the morning, knew anything of the matter; but when he entered the drawing-room before dinner, the buzz of discussion was high between Tom, Maria, and Mr. Yates; and Mr. Rushworth stepped forward with great alacrity to tell him the agreeable news.

"We have got a play," said he. "It is to be *Lovers' Vows;* and I am to be Count Cassel, and am to come in first with a blue dress, and a pink satin cloak, and afterwards am to have another fine fancy suit, by way of a shooting-dress. I do not know how I shall like it."

Fanny's eyes followed Edmund, and her heart beat for him as she heard this speech, and saw his look and felt what his sensations must be.

"*Lovers' Vows!*" in a tone of the greatest amazement, was his only reply to Mr. Rushworth, and he turned towards his brother and sisters as if hardly doubting a contradiction.

"Yes," cried Mr. Yates. "After all our debatings and difficulties, we find there is nothing that will suit us altogether so well, nothing so unexceptionable as *Lovers' Vows*. The wonder is that it should not have been thought of before. My stupidity was abominable, for here we have all th advantage of what I saw at Ecclesford; and it is so useful to have anything of a model! We have cast almost every part."

"But what do you do for women?" said Edmund gravely, and looking at Maria.

Maria blushed in spite of herself as she answered, "I take the part which Lady Ravenshaw was to have done, and (with a bolder eye) Miss Crawford is to be Amelia."

"I should not have thought it the sort of play to be so easily filled up, with *us*," replied Edmund, turning away to the fire, where sat his mother, aunt, and Fanny, and seating himself with a look of great vexation.

Mr. Rushworth followed him to say, "I come in three times, and have two-and-forty speeches. That's something, is not it? But I do not much like the idea of being so fine. I shall hardly know myself in a blue dress, and a pink satin cloak."

Edmund could not answer him. In a few minutes Mr. Bertram was called out of the room to satisfy some doubts of the carpenter; and being accompanied by Mr. Yates, and followed soon afterwards by Mr. Rushworth, Edmund almost immediately took the opportunity of saying, "I cannot before Mr. Yates speak what I feel as to this play, without reflecting on his friends at Ecclesford; but I must now, my dear Maria, tell *you*, that I think it exceedingly unfit for private representation, and that I hope you will give it up. I cannot but suppose you *will* when you have read it carefully over. Read only the first act aloud to either mother or aunt, and see how you can approve it. It will not be necessary to send you to your *father's* judgment, I am convinced."

"We see things very differently," cried Maria. "I am perfectly acquainted with the play, I assure you; and with a very few omissions, and so forth, which will be made, of course, I can see nothing objectionable in it; and *I* am not the *only* young woman you find, who thinks it very fit for private representation."

"I am sorry for it," was his answer; "but in this matter it is *you* who are to lead. *You* must set the example. If others have blundered, it is your place to put them right, and show them what true delicacy is. In all points of decorum, *your* conduct must be law to the rest of the party."

This picture of her consequence had some effect, for no one loved better to lead than Maria; and with far more good humour she answered, "I am much obliged to you, Edmund; you mean very well, I am sure; but I still think you see things too strongly; and I really cannot undertake to harangue all the rest upon a subject of this kind. *There* would be the greatest indecorum, I think."

"Do you imagine that I could have such an idea in my head? No: let your conduct be the only harangue. Say that, on examining the part, you feel yourself unequal to it; that you find it requiring more exertion and confidence than you can be supposed to have. Say this with firmness, and it will be quite enough. All who can distinguish will understand your motive. The play will be given up, and your delicacy honoured as it ought."

"Do not act anything improper, my dear," said Lady Bertram. "Sir Thomas would not like it. Fanny, ring the bell; I must have my dinner. To be sure Julia is dressed by this time."

"I am convinced, madam," said Edmund, preventing Fanny, "that Sir Thomas would not like it."

"There, my dear, do you hear what Edmund says?"

"If I were to decline the part," said Maria, with renewed zeal, "Julia would certainly take it."

"What!" cried Edmund, "if she knew your reasons!"

"Oh! she might think the difference between us—the difference in our situations—that *she* need not be so scrupulous as *I* might feel necessary. I am sure she would argue so. No: you must excuse me; I cannot retract my consent; it is too far settled, everybody would be so disappointed, Tom would be quite angry; and if we are so very nice, we shall never act anything."

"I was just going to say the very same thing," said Mrs. Norris. "If every play is to be objected to, you will act nothing, and the preparations will be all so much money thrown away, and I am sure *that* would be a discredit to us all. I do not know the play; but, as Maria says, if there is anything a little too warm (and it is so with most of them) it can be easily left out. We must not be over precise, Edmund. As Mr. Rushworth is to act too, there can be no harm. I only wish Tom had known his own mind when the carpenters began, for there was the loss of half a day's work about those side-doors. The curtain will be a good job, however. The maids do their work very well, and I think we shall be able to send back some dozens of the rings. There is no occasion to put them so very close together. I *am* of some use, I hope, in preventing waste and making the most of things. There should always be one steady head to superintend so many young ones. I forgot to tell Tom of something that happened to me this very day. I had been looking about me in the poultry yard, and was just coming out, when who should I see but Dick Jackson, making up to the servants' hall-door with two bits of deal board in his hand, bringing them to father you may be sure; mother had chanced to send him on a message to father, and then father had bid him bring up them two bits of board, for he could not know how do without them. I knew what all this meant, for the servants' dinner-bell was ringing at the very moment over our heads; and as I hate such encroaching people (the Jacksons are very encroaching, I have always said so: just the sort of people to get all they can), I said to the boy directly (a great lubberly fellow of ten years old, you know, who ought to be ashamed of himself); 'I'll take the boards to your father, Dick, so get you home again as fast as you can.' The boy looked very silly, and turned away without offering a word, for I believe I might speak pretty sharp; and I dare say it will cure him of coming marauding about the house for one while. I hate such greediness; so good as your father is to the family, employing the man all the year round!"

Nobody was at the trouble of an answer; the others soon returned; and Edmund found that to have endeavoured to set them right must be his only satisfaction.

Dinner passed heavily. Mrs. Norris related again her triumph over Dick Jackson, but neither play nor preparation were otherwise much talked of, for Edmund's disapprobation was felt even by his brother, though he would not have owned it. Maria, wanting Henry Crawford's animating support, thought the subject better avoided. Mr. Yates, who was trying to make himself agreeable to Julia, found her gloom less impenetrable on any topic than that of her regret at her secession from their company; and Mr. Rushworth, having only his own part and his own dress in his head, had soon talked away all that could be said of either.

But the concerns of the theatre were suspended only for an hour or two: there was still a great deal to be settled; and the spirits of evening giving fresh courage, Tom, Maria, and Mr. Yates, soon after their being reassembled in the drawing-room, seated themselves in committee at a separate table, with the play open before them, and were just getting deep in the subject, when a most welcome interruption was given by the entrance of Mr. and Miss Crawford, who, late and dark and dirty as it was, could not help coming, and were received with the most grateful joy.

"Well, how do you go on?" and "What have you settled?" and "Oh! we can do nothing without you," followed the first salutations; and Henry Crawford was soon seated with the other three at the table, while his sister made her way to Lady Bertram, and with pleasant attention complimenting *her*. "I must really congratulate your ladyship," said she, "on the play being chosen; for though you have borne it with exemplary patience, I am sure you must be sick of all our noise and difficulties. The actors may be glad, but the by-standers must be infinitely more thankful for a decision; and I do sincerely give you joy, madam, as well as Mrs. Norris, and everybody else who is in the same predicament," glancing half fearfully, half slyly, beyond Fanny to Edmund.

She was very civilly answered by Lady Bertram, but Edmund said nothing. His being only a by-stander was not disclaimed. After continuing in chat with the party round the fire a few minutes, Miss Crawford returned to the party round the table; and standing by them, seemed to interest herself in their arrangements till, as if struck by a sudden recollection, she exclaimed, "My good friends, you are most composedly at work upon these cottages and ale-houses, inside and out; but pray, let me know my fate in the meanwhile. Who is to be Anhalt? What gentleman among you am I to have the pleasure of making love to?"

For a moment no one spoke; and then many spoke together to tell the same melancholy truth, that they had not yet got any Anhalt. "Mr. Rushworth was to be Count Cassel, but no one had yet undertaken Anhalt."

"I had my choice of the parts," said Mr. Rushworth; "but I thought I should like the Count best, though I do not much relish the finery I am to have."

"You choose very wisely, I am sure," replied Miss Crawford, with a brightened look; "Anhalt is a heavy part."

"*The Count* has two-and-forty speeches," returned Mr. Rushworth, "which is no trifle."

"I am not at all surprised," said Miss Crawford, after a short pause, "at this want of an Anhalt. Amelia deserves no better. Such a forward young lady might well frighten the men."

"I should be but too happy in taking the part, if it were possible," cried Tom; "but, unluckily, the Butler and Anhalt are in together. I will not entirely give it up, however; I will try what can be done—I will look it over again."

"Your *brother* should take the part," said Mr. Yates, in a low voice. "Do you not think he would?"

"*I* shall not ask him," replied Tom, in a cold determined manner.

Miss Crawford talked of something else, and soon afterwards rejoined the party at the fire.

"They do not want me at all," said she, seating herself. "I only puzzle them, and oblige them to make civil speeches. Mr. Edmund Bertram, as you do not act yourself, you will be a disinterested adviser; and, therefore, I apply to *you*. What shall we do for an Anhalt? Is it practicable for any of the others to double it? What is your advice?"

"My advice," said he calmly, "is that you change the play."

"*I* should have no objection," she replied; "for though I should not particularly dislike the part of Amelia, if well supported, that is, if every-thing went well, I shall be sorry to be an inconvenience; but as they do not choose to hear your advice at *that table* (looking round), it certainly will not be taken."

Edmund said no more.

"If *any* part could tempt *you* to act, I suppose it would be Anhalt," observed the lady archly, after a short pause; "for he is a clergyman, you know."

"*That* circumstance would by no means tempt me," he replied, "for I should be sorry to make the character ridiculous by bad acting. It must be very difficult to keep Anhalt from appearing a formal solemn lecturer; and the man who chooses the profession itself, is, perhaps, one of the last who would wish to represent it on the stage."

Miss Crawford was silenced, and with some feelings of resentment and mortification, moved her chair considerably nearer the tea-table, and gave all her attention to Mrs. Norris, who was presiding there.

"Fanny," cried Tom Bertram, from the other table, where the con-ference was eagerly carrying on, and the conversation incessant, "we want your services."

Fanny was up in a moment, expecting some errand; for the habit of employing her in that way was not yet overcome, in spite of all that Edmund could do.

"Oh! we do not want to disturb you from your seat. We do not want your *present* services. We shall only want you in our play. You must be Cottager's Wife."

"Me!" cried Fanny, sitting down again with a most frightened look. "Indeed you must excuse me. I could not act anything if you were to give me the world. No, indeed, I cannot act."

"Indeed, but you must, for we cannot excuse you. It need not frighten you; it is a nothing of a part, a mere nothing, not above half-a-dozen speeches altogether, and it will not much signify if nobody hears a word you say, so you may be as creep-mouse as you like, but we must have you to look at."

"If you are afraid of half-a-dozen speeches," cried Mr. Rushworth, "what would you do with such a part as mine? I have forty-two to learn."

"It is not that I am afraid of learning by heart," said Fanny, shocked to find herself at that moment the only speaker in the room, and to feel that almost every eye was upon her; "but I really cannot act."

"Yes, yes, you can act well enough for *us*. Learn your part, and we will teach you all the rest. You have only two scenes, and as I shall be Cottager, I'll put you in and push you about, and you will do it very well, I'll answer for it."

"No, indeed, Mr. Bertram, you must excuse me. You cannot have an idea. It would be absolutely impossible for me. If I were to undertake it, I should only disappoint you."

"Phoo! Phoo! Do not be so shamefaced. You'll do it very well. Every allowance will be made for you. We do not expect perfection. You must get a brown gown, and a white apron, and a mob cap, and we must make you a few wrinkles, and a little of the crowsfoot at the corner of your eyes, and you will be a very proper, little old woman."

"You must excuse me, indeed you must excuse me," cried Fanny, growing more and more red from excessive agitation, and looking distressfully at Edmund, who was kindly observing her; but unwilling to exasperate his brother by interference, gave her only an encouraging smile. Her entreaty had no effect on Tom; he only said again what he had said before, and it was not merely Tom, for the requisition was now backed by Maria, and Mr. Crawford, and Mr. Yates, with an urgency which differed from his but in being more gentle or more ceremonious, and which altogether was quite overpowering to Fanny; and before she could breathe after it, Mrs. Norris completed the whole by thus addressing her in a whisper at once angry and audible: "What a piece of work here is about nothing; I am quite ashamed of you, Fanny, to make such a difficulty of obliging your cousins in a trifle of this sort—so kind as they are to you! Take the part with a good grace, and let us hear no more of the matter, I entreat."

"Do not urge her, madam," said Edmund. "It is not fair to urge her in this manner. You see she does not like to act. Let her choose for herself, as well as the rest of us. Her judgment may be quite as safely trusted. Do not urge her any more."

"I am not going to urge her," replied Mrs. Norris sharply; "but I shall think her a very obstinate, ungrateful girl, if she does not do what her aunt and cousins wish her; very ungrateful, indeed, considering who and what she is."

Edmund was too angry to speak; but Miss Crawford looking for a moment with astonished eyes at Mrs. Norris, and then at Fanny, whose tears were beginning to show themselves, immediately said, with some keenness, "I do not like my situation; this *place* is too hot for me," and moved away her chair to the opposite side of the table, close to Fanny, saying to her, in a kind, low whisper, as she placed herself, "Never mind, my dear Miss Price, this is a cross evening; everybody is cross and teasing, but do not let us mind them"; and with pointed attention continued to talk to her and endeavour to raise her spirits, in spite of being out of spirits herself. By a look at her brother, she prevented any further entreaty from the theatrical board, and the really good feelings by which she was almost purely governed, were rapidly restoring her to all the little she had lost in Edmund's favour.

Fanny did not love Miss Crawford; but she felt very much obliged to her for her present kindness; and when, from taking notice of her work, and wishing *she* could work as well, and begging for the pattern, and supposing Fanny was now preparing for her *appearance*, as of course she would come out when her cousin was married, Miss Crawford proceeded to inquire if she had heard lately from her brother at sea, and said that she had quite a curiosity to see him, and imagined him a very fine young man, and advised Fanny to get his picture drawn before he went to sea again, she could not help admitting it to be very agreeable flattery, or help listening, and answering with more animation than she had intended.

The consultation upon the play still went on, and Miss Crawford's attention was first called from Fanny, by Tom Bertram's telling her, with infinite regret, that he found it absolutely impossible for him to undertake the part of Anhalt in addition to the Butler: he had been most anxiously trying to make it out to be feasible, but it would not do; he must give it up. "But there will not be the smallest difficulty in filling it," he added. "We have but to speak the word; we may pick and choose. I could name, at this moment, at least six young men within six miles of us, who are wild to be admitted into our company, and there are one or two that would not disgrace us; I should not be afraid to trust either of the Olivers or Charles Maddox. Tom Oliver is a very clever fellow, and Charles Maddox is as gentlemanlike a man as you will see anywhere, so I will take my horse early to-morrow morning and ride over to Stoke, and settle with one of them."

While he spoke, Maria was looking apprehensively round at Edmund in full expectation that he must oppose such an enlargement of the plan as this: so contrary to all their first protestations; but Edmund said nothing. After a moment's thought, Miss Crawford calmly replied, "As far as I am concerned, I can have no objection to anything that you all think eligible. Have I ever seen either of the gentlemen? Yes, Mr. Charles Maddox dined at my sister's one day, did not he, Henry? A quiet looking young man. I remember him. Let *him* be applied to, if you please, for it will be less unpleasant for me than to have a perfect stranger."

Charles Maddox was to be the man. Tom repeated his resolution of going to him early on the morrow; and though Julia, who had scarcely opened her lips before, observed in a sarcastic manner, and with a glance first at Maria, and then at Edmund, that "the Mansfield theatricals would enliven the whole neighbourhood exceedingly," Edmund still held his peace, and showed his feelings only by a determined gravity.

"I am not very sanguine as to our play," said Miss Crawford, in an under voice to Fanny, after some consideration; "and I can tell Mr. Maddox that I shall shorten some of *his* speeches, and a great many of *my own* before we rehearse together. It will be very disagreeable, and by no means what I expected."

Chapter 16

It was not in Miss Crawford's power to talk Fanny into any real forgetfulness of what had passed. When the evening was over, she went to bed, full of it, her nerves still agitated by the shock of such an attack from her cousin Tom, so public and so persevered in, and her spirits sinking under her aunt's unkind reflection and reproach. To be called into notice in such a manner, to hear that it was but the prelude to something so infinitely worse, to be told that she must do what was so impossible as to act; and then to have the charge of obstinacy and ingratitude follow it, enforced with such a hint at the dependence of her situation, had been too distressing at the time to make the remembrance when she was alone much less so, especially with the superadded dread of what the morrow might produce in continuation of the subject. Miss Crawford had protected her only for the time; and if she were applied to again among themselves with all the authoritative urgency that Tom and Maria were capable of, and Edmund perhaps away, what should she do? She fell asleep before she could answer the question, and found it quite as puzzling when she awoke the next morning. The little white attic, which had continued her sleeping room ever since her first entering the family, proving incompetent to suggest any reply, she had recourse, as soon as she was dressed, to another apartment more spacious and more meet for walking about in and thinking, and of which she had now for some time been almost equally mistress. It had been their schoolroom; so called till the Miss Bertrams would not allow it to be called so any longer, and inhabited as such to a later period. There Miss Lee had lived, and there they had read and written, and talked and laughed, till within the last three years, when she had quitted them. The room had then become useless, and for some time was quite deserted, except by Fanny, when she visited her plants, or wanted one of the books, which she was still glad to keep there, from the deficiency of space and accommodation in her little chamber above; but gradually, as her value for the comforts of it increased, she had added to her possessions, and spent more of her time there; and having nothing to oppose her, had so naturally and so artlessly worked herself into it, that it was now generally admitted to be hers. The East Room, as it had been called ever since Maria Bertram was sixteen, was now considered Fanny's, almost as decidedly as the white attic: the smallness of the one making the use of the other so evidently reasonable, that the Miss Bertrams, with every superiority in their own apartments which their own sense of superiority could demand, were entirely approving it; and Mrs. Norris, having stipulated for there never being a fire in it on Fanny's account, was tolerably resigned to her having the use of what nobody else wanted, though the terms in which she sometimes spoke of the indulgence seemed to imply that it was the best room in the house.

The aspect was so favourable, that even without a fire it was habitable in many an early spring and late autumn morning, to such a willing mind as Fanny's; and while there was a gleam of sunshine, she hoped not to be driven from it entirely, even when winter came. The comfort of it in her hours of leisure was extreme. She could go there after anything unpleasant below, and find immediate consolation in some pursuit, or some train of thought at hand. Her plants, her books—of which she had been a collector from the first hour of her commanding a shilling—her writing-desk, and her works of charity and ingenuity, were all within her reach; or if indisposed for employment, if nothing but musing would do, she could scarcely see an object in that room which had not an interesting remembrance connected with it. Everything was a friend, or bore her thoughts to a friend; and though there had been sometimes much of suffering to her, though her motives had often been misunderstood, her feelings disregarded; and her comprehension undervalued; though she had known the pains of tyranny, or ridicule, and neglect; yet almost every recurrence of either had led to something consolatory; her Aunt Bertram had spoken for her, or Miss Lee had been encouraging, or, what was yet more frequent or more dear, Edmund had been her champion and her friend; he had supported her cause or explained her meaning; he had told her not to cry, or had given her some proof of affection which made her tears delightful, and the whole was now so blended together, so harmonised by distance, that every former affliction had its charm. The room was most dear to her, and she would not have changed its furniture for the handsomest in the house, though what had been originally plain, had suffered all the ill-usage of children; and its greatest elegancies and ornaments were a faded footstool of Julia's work, too ill done for the drawing-room, three transparencies, made in a rage for transparencies, for the three lower panes of one window, where Tintern Abbey held its station between a cave in

Italy and a moonlight lake in Cumberland, a collection of family profiles, thought unworthy of being anywhere else, over the mantelpiece, and by their side, and pinned against the wall, a small sketch of a ship sent four years ago from the Mediterranean by William, with H.M.S. *Antwerp* at the bottom, in letters as tall as the mainmast.

To this nest of comforts Fanny now walked down to try its influence on an agitated, doubting spirit, to see if by looking at Edmund's profile she could catch any of his counsel, or by giving air to her geraniums she might inhale a breeze of mental strength herself. But she had more than fears of her own perseverance to remove: she had begun to feel undecided as to what she *ought to do;* and as she walked round the room her doubts were increasing. Was she *right* in refusing what was so warmly asked, so strongly wished for—what might be so essential to a scheme on which some of those to whom she owed the greatest complaisance had set their hearts? Was it not ill-nature, selfishness, and a fear of exposing herself? And would Edmund's judgment, would his persuasion of Sir Thomas's disapprobation of the whole, be enough to justify her in a determined denial in spite of all the rest? It would be so horrible to her to act, that she was inclined to suspect the truth and purity of her own scruples; and as she looked around her, the claims of her cousins to being obliged were strengthened by the sight of present upon present that she had received from them. The table between the windows was covered with work-boxes and netting-boxes which had been given her at different times, principally by Tom; and she grew bewildered as to the amount of the debt which all these kind remembrances produced. A tap at the door roused her in the midst of this attempt to find her way to her duty, and her gentle "come in" was answered by the appearance of one, before whom all her doubts were wont to be laid. Her eyes brightened at the sight of Edmund.

"Can I speak with you, Fanny, for a few minutes?" said he.

"Yes, certainly."

"I want to consult. I want your opinion."

"My opinion!" she cried, shrinking from such a compliment, highly as it gratified her.

"Yes, your advice and opinion. I do not know what to do. This acting scheme gets worse and worse, you see. They have chosen almost as bad a play as they could, and now, to complete the business, are going to ask the help of a young man very slightly known to any of us. This is the end of all the privacy and propriety which was talked about at first. I know no harm of Charles Maddox; but the excessive intimacy which must spring from his being admitted among us in this manner is highly objectionable, the *more* than intimacy—the familiarity. I cannot think of it with any patience; and it does appear to me an evil of such magnitude as must, *if possible*, be prevented. Do not you see it in the same light?"

"Yes; but what can be done? Your brother is so determined."

"There is but *one* thing to be done, Fanny. I must take Anhalt myself. I am well aware that nothing else will quiet Tom."

Fanny could not answer him.

"It is not at all what I like," he continued. "No man can like being driven into the *appearance* of such inconsistency. After being known to oppose the scheme from the beginning, there is absurdity in the face of my joining them *now*, when they are exceeding their first plan in every respect; but I can think of no other alternative. Can you, Fanny?"

"No," said Fanny slowly, "not immediately, but——"

"But what? I see your judgment is not with me. Think it a little over. Perhaps you are not so much aware as I am of the mischief that *may*, of the unpleasantness that *must* arise from a young man's being received in this manner; domesticated among us; authorised to come at all hours, and placed suddenly on a footing which must do away all restraints. To think only of the licence which every rehearsal must tend to create. It is all very bad! Put yourself in Miss Crawford's place, Fanny. Consider what it would be to act Amelia with a stranger. She has a right to be felt for, because she evidently feels for herself. I heard enough of what she said to you last night to understand her unwillingness to be acting with a stranger; and as she probably engaged in the part with different expectations—perhaps without considering the subject enough to know what was likely to be—it would be ungenerous, it would be really wrong to expose her to it. Her feelings ought to be respected. Does it not strike you so, Fanny? You hesitate."

"I am sorry for Miss Crawford; but I am more sorry to see you drawn in to do what you had resolved against, and what you are known to think will be disagreeable to my uncle. It will be such a triumph to the others!"

"They will not have much cause of triumph when they see how infamously I act. But, however, triumph there certainly will be, and I must brave it. But if I can be the means of restraining the publicity of the business, of limiting the exhibition, of concentrating our folly, I shall be well repaid. As I am now, I have no influence, I can do nothing: I have offended them, and they will not hear me; but when I have put them in good humour by this concession, I am not without hopes of persuading them to confine the representation within a much smaller circle than they are now in the high road for. This will be a material gain. My object is to confine it to Mrs. Rushworth and the Grants. Will not this be worth gaining?"

"Yes, it will be a great point."

"But still it has not your approbation. Can you mention any other measure by which I have a chance of doing equal good?"

"No, I cannot think of anything else."

"Give me your approbation, then, Fanny. I am not comfortable without it."

"Oh, cousin!"

"If you are against me, I ought to distrust myself, and yet—— But it is absolutely impossible to let Tom go on in this way, riding about the country in quest of anybody who can be persuaded to act—no matter whom: the look of a gentleman is to be enough. I thought *you* would have entered more into Miss Crawford's feelings."

"No doubt she will be very glad. It must be a great relief to her," said Fanny, trying for greater warmth of manner.

"She never appeared more amiable than in her behaviour to you last night. It gave her a very strong claim on my goodwill."

"She *was* very kind, indeed, and I am glad to have her spared——"

She could not finish the generous effusion. Her conscience stopped her in the middle, but Edmund was satisfied.

"I shall walk down immediately after breakfast," said he, "and am sure of giving pleasure there. And now, dear Fanny, I will not interrupt you any longer. You want to be reading. But I could not be easy till I had spoken to you, and come to a decision. Sleeping or waking, my head has been full of this matter all night. It is an evil, but I am certainly making it less than it might be. If Tom is up, I shall go to him directly and get it over, and when we meet at breakfast we shall be all in high good humour at the prospect of acting the fool together with such unanimity. *You* in the meanwhile will be taking a trip into China, I suppose. How does Lord Macartney go on? (opening a volume on the table and then taking up some others). And here are Crabbe's *Tales*, and *The Idler*, at hand to relieve you, if you tire of your great book. I admire your little establishment exceedingly; and as soon as I am gone, you will empty your head of all this nonsense of acting, and sit comfortably down to your table. But do not stay here to be cold."

He went; but there was no reading, no China, no composure for Fanny. He had told her the most extraordinary, the most inconceivable, the most unwelcome news; and she could think of nothing else. To be acting! After all his objections—-objections so just and so public! After all that she had heard him say, and seen him look, and known him to be feeling. Could it be possible? Edmund so inconsistent! Was he not deceiving himself? Was he not wrong? Alas! it was all Miss Crawford's doing. She had seen her influence in every speech, and was miserable. The doubts and alarms as to her own conduct, which had previously distressed her, and which had all slept while she listened to him, were become of little consequence now. This deeper anxiety swallowed them up. Things should take their course; she cared not how it ended. Her cousins might attack, but could hardly teaze her. She was beyond their reach; and if at last obliged to yield—no matter—it was all misery *now*.

Chapter 17

IT was, indeed, a triumphant day to Mr. Bertram and Maria. Such a victory over Edmund's discretion had been beyond their hopes, and was most delightful. There was no longer anything to disturb them in their darling project, and they congratulated each other in private on the jealous weakness to which they attributed the change, with all the glee of feelings gratified in every way. Edmund might still look grave, and say he did not like the scheme in general, and must disapprove the play in particular; their point was gained; he was to act, and he was driven to it by the force of selfish inclinations only. Edmund had descended from that moral elevation which he had maintained before, and they were both as much the better as the happier for the descent.

They behaved very well, however, *to him* on the occasion, betraying no exultation beyond the lines about the corners of the mouth, and seemed to think it as great an escape to be quit of the intrusion of Charles Maddox, as if they had been forced into admitting him against their inclination. "To have it quite in their own family circle was what they had particularly wished. A stranger among them would have been the destruction of all their comfort"; and when Edmund, pursuing that idea, gave a hint of his hope as to the limitation of the audience, they were ready, in the complaisance of the moment, to promise anything. It was all good humour and encouragement. Mrs. Norris offered to contrive his dress, Mr. Yates assured him that Anhalt's last scene with the Baron admitted a good deal of action and emphasis, and Mr. Rushworth undertook to count his speeches.

"Perhaps," said Tom, "*Fanny* may be more disposed to oblige us now Perhaps you may persuade *her*."

"No, she is quite determined. She certainly will not act."

"Oh! very well." And not another word was said; but Fanny felt herself again in danger, and her indifference to the danger was beginning to fail her already.

There were not fewer smiles at the Parsonage than at the Park on this change in Edmund; Miss Crawford looked very lovely in hers, and entered with such an instantaneous renewal of cheerfulness into the whole affair, as could have but one effect on him. "He was certainly right in respecting such feelings; he was glad he had determined on it." And the morning wore away in satisfactions very sweet, if not very sound. One advantage resulted from it to Fanny; at the earnest request of Miss Crawford, Mrs. Grant had, with her usual good humour, agreed to undertake the part for which Fanny had been wanted; and this was all that occurred to gladden *her* heart during the day; and even this, when imparted by Edmund, brought a pang with it, for it was Miss Crawford to whom she was obliged; it was Miss Crawford whose kind exertions were to excite her gratitude and whose merit in making them was spoken of with a glow of admiration. She was safe; but peace and safety were unconnected here. Her mind had been never farther from peace. She could not feel that she had done wrong herself, but she was disquieted in every other way. Her heart and her judgment were equally against Edmund's decision: she could not acquit his unsteadiness, and his happiness under it made her wretched. She was full of jealousy and agitation. Miss Crawford came with looks of gaiety which seemed an insult, with friendly expressions towards herself which she could hardly answer calmly. Everybody around her was gay and busy, prosperous and important; each had their object of interest, their part, their dress, their favourite scene, their friends and confederates: all were finding employment in consultations and comparisons, or diversion in the playful conceits they suggested. She alone was sad and insignificant; she had no share in anything; she might go or stay; she might be in the midst of their noise, or retreat from it to the solitude of the East Room, without being seen or missed. She could almost think anything would have been preferable to this. Mrs. Grant was of consequence: *her* good nature had honourable mention: her taste and her time were considered; her presence was wanted; she was sought for, and attended, and praised; and Fanny was at first in some danger of envying her the character she had accepted. But reflection brought better feelings, and showed her that Mrs. Grant was entitled to respect, which could never have belonged to *her;* and that, had she received even the greatest, she could never have been easy in joining a scheme which, considering only her uncle, she must condemn altogether.

Fanny's heart was not absolutely the only saddened one amongst them, as she soon began to acknowledge to herself. Julia was a sufferer, too, though not quite so blamelessly.

Henry Crawford had trifled with her feelings; but she had very long allowed, and even sought his attentions with a jealousy of her sister so reasonable as ought to have been their cure; and now that the conviction of his preference for Maria had been forced on her, she submitted to it without any alarm for Maria's situation, or any endeavour at rational tranquillity for herself. She either sat in gloomy silence, wrapped in such gravity as nothing could subdue, no curiosity touch, no wit amuse; or allowing the attentions of Mr. Yates, was talking with forced gaiety to him alone, and ridiculing the acting of the others.

For a day or two after the affront was given Henry Crawford had endeavoured to do it away by the usual attack of gallantry and compliment, but he had not cared enough about it to persevere against a few repulses; and becoming soon too busy with his play to have time for more than one flirtation, he grew indifferent to the quarrel, or rather thought it a lucky occurrence, as quietly putting an end to what might ere long have raised expectations in more than Mrs. Grant. She was not pleased to see Julia excluded from the play, and sitting by disregarded; but as it was not a matter which really involved her happiness, as Henry must be the best judge of his own, and as he did assure her, with a most persuasive smile, that neither he nor Julia had ever had a serious thought of each other, she could only renew her former caution as to the elder sister, entreat him not to risk his tranquillity by too much admiration there, and then gladly take her share in anything that brought cheerfulness to the young people in general, and that did so particularly promote the pleasure of the two so dear to her.

"I rather wonder Julia is not in love with Henry," was her observation to Mary.

"I dare say she is," replied Mary coldly. "I imagine both sisters are."

"Both! No, no, that must not be. Do not give him a hint of it. Think of Mr. Rushworth!"

"You had better tell Miss Bertram to think of Mr. Rushworth. It may do *her* some good. I often think of Mr. Rushworth's property and independence and wish them in other hands; but I never think of *him*. A man might represent the county with such an estate; a man might escape a profession and represent the county."

"I dare say he *will* be in parliament soon. When Sir Thomas comes, I dare say he will be in for some borough, but there has been nobody to put him in the way of doing anything yet."

"Sir Thomas is to achieve many mighty things when he comes home," said Mary, after a pause. "Do you remember Hawkins Browne's 'Address to Tobacco,' in imitation of Pope?

> 'Blest leaf! whose aromatic gales dispense
> To Templars modesty, to Parsons sense.'

I will parody them:

> Blest Knight! whose dictatorial looks dispense
> To Children affluence, to Rushworth sense.

Will not that do, Mrs. Grant? Everything seems to depend upon Sir Thomas's return."

"You will find his consequence very just and reasonable when you see him in his family, I assure you. I do not think we do so well without him. He has a fine dignified manner, which suits the head of such a house, and keeps everybody in their place. Lady Bertram seems more of a cypher now than when he is at home; and nobody else can keep Mrs. Norris in order. But, Mary, do not fancy that Maria Bertram cares for Henry. I am sure *Julia* does not, or she would not have flirted as she did last night with Mr. Yates; and though he and Maria are very good friends, I think she likes Sotherton too well to be inconstant."

"I would not give much for Mr. Rushworth's chance, if Henry stepped in before the articles were signed."

"If you have such a suspicion, something must be done; and as soon as the play is all over, we will talk to him seriously, and make him know his own mind; and if he means nothing, we will send him off, though he is Henry, for a time."

Julia *did* suffer, however, though Mrs. Grant discerned it not, and though it escaped the notice of many of her own family likewise. She had loved, she did love still, and she had all the suffering which a warm temper and a high spirit were likely to endure under the disappointment of a dear, though irrational hope, with a strong sense of ill-usage. Her heart was sore and angry, and she was capable only of angry consolations. The sister with whom she was used to be on easy terms was now become her greatest enemy: they were alienated from each other; and Julia was not superior to the hope of some distressing end to the attentions which were still carrying on there, some punishment to Maria for conduct so shameful towards herself as well as towards Mr. Rushworth. With no material fault of temper, or difference of opinion, to prevent their being very good friends while their interests were the same, the sisters, under such a trial as this, had not affection or principle enough to make them merciful or just, to give them honour or compassion. Maria felt her triumph, and pursued her purpose, careless of Julia; and Julia could never see Maria distinguished by Henry Crawford without trusting that it would create jealousy, and bring a public disturbance at last.

Fanny saw and pitied much of this in Julia; but there was no outward fellowship between them. Julia made no communication, and Fanny took no liberties. They were two solitary sufferers, or connected only by Fanny's consciousness.

The inattention of the two brothers and the aunt to Julia's discomposure, and their blindness to its true cause, must be imputed to the fullness of their own minds. They were totally preoccupied. Tom was engrossed by the concerns of his theatre, and saw nothing that did not immediately relate to it. Edmund, between his theatrical and his real part—between Miss Crawford's claims and his own conduct—between love and consistency, was equally unobservant; and Mrs. Norris was too busy in contriving and directing the general little matters of the company, superintending their various dresses with economical expedience, for which nobody thanked her, and saving, with delighted integrity, half-a-crown here and there to the absent Sir Thomas, to have leisure for watching the behaviour, or guarding the happiness of his daughters.

Chapter 18

EVERYTHING was now in a regular train; theatre, actors, actresses and dresses were all getting forward; but though no other great impediments arose, Fanny found, before many days were past, that it was not all uninterrupted enjoyment to the party themselves, and that she had not to witness the continuance of such unanimity and delight, as had been almost too much for her at first. Everybody began to have their vexation. Edmund had many. Entirely against *his* judgment, a scene painter arrived from town, and was at work, much to the increase of the expenses, and, what was worse, of the éclat of their proceedings; and his brother, instead of being really guided by him as to the privacy of the representation, was giving an invitation to every family who came in his way. Tom himself began to fret over the scene painter's slow progress, and to feel the miseries of waiting. He had learned his part—all his parts, for he took every trifling one that could be united with the Butler, and began to be impatient to be acting; and every day thus unemployed was tending to increase his sense of the insignificance of all his parts together, and make him more ready to regret that some other play had not been chosen.

Fanny, being always a very courteous listener, and often the only listener at hand, came in for the complaints and the distresses of most of them. *She* knew that Mr. Yates was in general thought to rant dreadfully; that Mr. Yates was disappointed in Henry Crawford; that Tom Bertram spoke so quick he would be unintelligible; that Mrs. Grant spoiled everything by laughing; that Edmund was behind-hand with his part, and that it was a misery to have anything to do with Mr. Rushworth, who was wanting a prompter through every speech. She knew, also, that poor Mr. Rushworth could seldom get anybody to rehearse with him; *his* complaint came before her as well as the rest; and so decided to her eye was her cousin Maria's avoidance of him, and so needlessly often the rehearsal of the first scene between her and Mr. Crawford, that she had soon all the terror of other complaints from *him*. So far from being all satisfied and all enjoying, she found everybody requiring something they had not, and giving occasion of discontent to the others. Everybody had a part either too long or too short; nobody would attend as they ought; nobody would remember on which side they were to come in; nobody but the complainer would observe any directions.

Fanny believed herself to derive as much innocent enjoyment from the play as any of them; Henry Crawford acted well, and it was a pleasure to her to creep into the theatre, and attend the rehearsal of the first act, in spite of the feelings it excited in some speeches for Maria. Maria, she also thought, acted well, too well; and after the first rehearsal or two, Fanny began to be their only audience, and sometimes as prompter, sometimes as spectator, was often very useful. As far as she could judge, Mr. Crawford was considerably the best actor of all; he had more confidence than Edmund, more judgment than Tom, more talent and taste than Mr. Yates. She did not like him as a man, but she must admit him to be the best actor, and on this point there were not many who differed from her. Mr. Yates, indeed, exclaimed against his tameness and insipidity; and the day came at last when Mr. Rushworth turned to her with a black look and said: "Do you think there is anything so very fine in all this? For the life and soul of me, I cannot admire him; and between ourselves, to see such an undersized, little, mean-looking man, set up for a fine actor, is very ridiculous in my opinion."

From this moment there was a return of his former jealousy, which Maria, from increasing hopes of Crawford, was at little pains to remove, and the chances of Mr. Rushworth's ever attaining to the knowledge of his two-and-forty speeches became much less. As to his ever making anything *tolerable* of them, nobody had the smallest idea of that except his mother; *she*, indeed, regretted that his part was not more considerable, and deferred coming over to Mansfield till they were forward enough in their rehearsal to comprehend all his scenes; but the others aspired at nothing beyond his remembering the catch-word, and the first line of his speech, and being able to follow the prompter through the rest. Fanny, in her pity and kindheartedness, was at great pains to teach him how to learn, giving him all the helps and directions in her power, trying to make an artificial memory for him, and learning every word of his part herself, but without his being much the forwarder.

Many uncomfortable, anxious, apprehensive feelings she certainly had; but with all these, and other claims on her time and attention, she was as far from finding herself without employment or utility amongst them, as without a companion in uneasiness; quite as far from having no demand on her leisure as on her compassion. The gloom of her first anticipations was proved to have been unfounded. She was occasionally useful to all; she was perhaps as much at peace as any.

There was a great deal of needlework to be done, moreover, in which her help was wanted; and that Mrs. Norris thought her quite as well off as the rest was evident by the manner in which she claimed it: "Come, Fanny," she cried, "these are fine times for you, but you must not be always walking from one room to the other, and doing the lookings-on at your ease, in this way; I want you here. I have been slaving myself till I can hardly stand, to contrive Mr. Rushworth's cloak without sending for any more satin; and now I think you may give me your help in putting it together. There are but three seams, you may do them in a trice. It would be lucky for me if I had nothing but the executive part to do. *You* are best off, I can tell you; but if nobody did more than *you*, we should not get on very fast."

Fanny took the work very quietly, without attempting any defence; but her kinder Aunt Bertram observed on her behalf:

"One cannot wonder, sister, that Fanny *should* be delighted; it is all new to her, you know; you and I used to be very fond of a play ourselves, and so am I still; and as soon as I am a little more at leisure, *I* mean to look in at their rehearsals too. What is the play about, Fanny, you have never told me?"

"Oh! sister, pray do not ask her now; for Fanny is not one of those who can talk and work at the same time. It is about lovers' vows."

"I believe," said Fanny to her Aunt Bertram, "there will be three acts rehearsed to-morrow evening, and that will give you an opportunity of seeing all the actors at once."

"You had better stay till the curtain is hung," interposed Mrs. Norris; "the curtain will be hung in a day or two—there is very little sense in a play without a curtain—and I am much mistaken if you do not find it drawn up into very handsome festoons."

Lady Bertram seemed quite resigned to waiting. Fanny did not share her aunt's composure; she thought of the morrow a great deal, for if the three acts were rehearsed, Edmund and Miss Crawford would then be acting together for the first time; the third act would bring a scene be-tween them which interested her most particularly, and which she was longing and dreading to see how they would perform. The whole subject of it was love—a marriage of love was to be described by the gentleman, and very little short of a declaration of love be made by the lady.

She had read, and read the scene again with many painful, many wondering emotions, and looked forward to their representation of it as a circumstance almost too interesting. She did not *believe* they had yet rehearsed it, even in private.

The morrow came, the plan for the evening continued, and Fanny's consideration of it did not become less agitated. She worked very diligently under her aunt's directions, but her diligence and her silence concealed a very absent, anxious mind; and about noon she made her escape with her work to the East Room, that she might have no concern in another, and, as she deemed it, most unnecessary rehearsal of the first act, which Henry Crawford was just proposing, desirous at once of having her time to herself, and of avoiding the sight of Mr. Rushworth. A glimpse, as she passed through the hall, of the two ladies walking up from the Parsonage, made no change in her wish of retreat, and she worked and meditated in the East Room, undisturbed, for a quarter of an hour, when a gentle tap at the door was followed by the entrance of Miss Crawford.

"Am I right? Yes; this is the East Room. My dear Miss Price, I beg your pardon, but I have made my way to you on purpose to entreat your help."

Fanny, quite surprised, endeavoured to show herself mistress of the room by her civilities, and looked at the bright bars of her empty grate with concern.

"Thank you; I am quite warm, very warm. Allow me to stay here a little while, and do have the goodness to hear my third act. I have brought my book, and if you would but rehearse it with me, I should be so obliged! I came here to-day intending to rehearse it with Edmund—by ourselves—against the evening, but he is not in the way; and if he *were,* I do not think I could go through it with *him,* till I have hardened myself a little; for really there *is* a speech or two—— You will be so good, won't you?"

Fanny was most civil in her assurances, though she could not give them in a very steady voice.

"Have you ever happened to look at the part I mean?" continued Miss Crawford, opening her book. "Here it is. I did not think much of it at first—but, upon my word—— There, look at *that* speech, and *that,* and *that.* How am I ever to look him in the face and say such things? Could you do it? But then he is your cousin, which makes all the difference. You must rehearse it with me, that I may fancy *you* him, and get on by degrees. You *have* a look of *his* sometimes."

"Have I? I will do my best with the greatest readiness; but I must *read* the part, for I can *say* very little of it."

"None of it, I suppose. You are to have the book, of course. Now for it. We must have two chairs at hand for you to bring forward to the front of the stage. There——very good schoolroom chairs, not made for a theatre,

I dare say; much more fitted for little girls to sit and kick their feet against when they are learning a lesson. What would your governess and your uncle say to see them used for such a purpose? Could Sir Thomas look in upon us just now, he would bless himself, for we are rehearsing all over the house. Yates is storming away in the dining-room. I heard him as I came upstairs, and the theatre is engaged of course by those indefatigable rehearsers, Agatha and Frederick. If *they* are not perfect, I *shall* be surprised. By the bye, I looked in upon them five minutes ago, and it happened to be exactly at one of the times when they were trying *not* to embrace, and Mr. Rushworth was with me. I thought he began to look a little queer, so I turned it off as well as I could, by whispering to him, 'We shall have an excellent Agatha, there is something so *maternal* in her manner, so completely *maternal* in her voice and countenance.' Was not that well done of me? He brightened up directly. Now for my soliloquy."

She began, and Fanny joined in with all the modest feeling which the idea of representing Edmund was so strongly calculated to inspire; but with looks and voice as truly feminine, as to be no very good picture of a man. With such an Anhalt, however, Miss Crawford had courage enough; and they had got through half the scene, when a tap at the door brought a pause, and the entrance of Edmund, the next moment, suspended it all.

Surprise, consciousness, and pleasure appeared in each of the three on this unexpected meeting; and as Edmund was come on the very same business that had brought Miss Crawford, consciousness and pleasure were likely to be more than momentary in *them*. He, too, had his book, and was seeking Fanny, to ask her to rehearse with him, and help him to prepare for the evening, without knowing Miss Crawford to be in the house; and great was the joy and animation of being thus thrown together, of comparing schemes, and sympathising in praise of Fanny's kind offices.

She could not equal them in their warmth. *Her* spirits sank under the glow of theirs, and she felt herself becoming too nearly nothing to both, to have any comfort in having been sought by either. They must now rehearse together. Edmund proposed, urged, entreated it, till the lady, not very unwilling at first, could refuse no longer, and Fanny was wanted only to prompt and observe them. She was invested, indeed, with the office of judge and critic, and earnestly desired to exercise it and tell them all their faults; but from doing so every feeling within her shrank—she could not, would not, dared not, attempt it; had she been otherwise qualified for criticism, her conscience must have restrained her from venturing at disapprobation. She believed herself to feel too much of it in the aggregate for honesty or safety in particulars. To prompt them must be enough for her; and it was sometimes *more* than enough; for she could not always pay attention to the book. In watching them she forgot herself; and, agitated by the increasing spirit of Edmund's manner, had once closed the page and turned away exactly as he wanted help. It was imputed to very reasonable weariness, and she was thanked and pitied; but she deserved their pity more than she hoped they would ever surmise. At last the scene was over, and Fanny forced herself to add her praise to the compliments each was giving the other; and when again alone, and able to recall the whole, she was inclined to believe their performance would, indeed, have such nature and feeling in it as must ensure their credit, and make it a very suffering exhibition to herself. Whatever might be its effect, however, she must stand the brunt of it again that very day.

The first regular rehearsal of the three first acts was certainly to take place in the evening: Mrs. Grant and the Crawfords were engaged to return for that purpose as soon as they could after dinner; and everyone concerned was looking forward with eagerness. There seemed a general diffusion of cheerfulness on the occasion. Tom was enjoying such an advance towards the end; Edmund was in spirits from the morning's rehearsal, and little vexations seemed everywhere smoothed away. All were alert and impatient; the ladies moved soon, the gentlemen soon followed them, and with the exception of Lady Bertram, Mrs. Norris and Julia, everybody was in the theatre at an early hour; and, having lighted it up as well as its unfinished state admitted, were waiting only the arrival of Mrs. Grant and the Crawfords to begin.

They did not wait long for the Crawfords, but there was no Mrs. Grant. She could not come. Dr. Grant, professing an indisposition, for which he had little credit with his fair sister-in-law, could not spare his wife.

"Dr. Grant is ill," said she, with mock solemnity. "He has been ill ever since he did not eat any of the pheasant to-day. He fancied it tough, sent away his plate, and has been suffering ever since."

Here was disappointment! Mrs. Grant's non-attendance was sad indeed. Her pleasant manners and cheerful conformity made her always valuable amongst them; but *now* she was absolutely necessary. They could not act, they could not rehearse with any satisfaction without her. The comfort of the whole evening was destroyed. What was to be done? Tom, as Cottager, was in despair. After a pause of perplexity, some eyes began to be turned towards Fanny, and a voice or two to say, "If Miss Price would be so good as to *read* the part." She was immediately surrounded by supplications, everybody asked it, even Edmund said, "Do, Fanny, if it is not *very* disagreeable to you."

But Fanny still hung back. She could not endure the idea of it. Why was not Miss Crawford to be applied to as well? Or why had not she rather gone to her own room, as she had felt to be safest, instead of attending the rehearsal at all? She had known it would irritate and distress her; she had known it her duty to keep away. She was properly punished.

"You have only to *read* the part," said Henry Crawford, with renewed entreaty.

"And I do believe she can say every word of it," added Maria, "for she could put Mrs. Grant right the other day in twenty places. Fanny, I am sure you know the part."

Fanny could not say she did *not ;* and as they all persevered, as Edmund repeated his wish, and with a look of even fond dependence on her good nature, she must yield. She would do her best. Everybody was satisfied; and she was left to the tremors of a most palpitating heart, while the others prepared to begin.

They *did* begin; and being too much engaged in their own noise to be struck by an unusual noise in the other part of the house, had proceeded some way, when the door of the room was thrown open, and Julia, appearing at it, with a face all aghast, exclaimed, "My father is come! He is in the hall at this moment."

Chapter 19

How is the consternation of the party to be described? To the greater number it was a moment of absolute horror. Sir Thomas in the house! All felt the instantaneous conviction. Not a hope of imposition or mistake was harboured anywhere. Julia's looks were an evidence of the fact that made it indisputable; and after the first starts and exclamations, not a word was spoken for half a minute; each with an altered countenance was looking at some other, and almost each was feeling it a stroke the most unwelcome, most ill-timed, most appalling! Mr. Yates might consider it only as a vexatious interruption for the evening, and Mr. Rushworth might imagine it a blessing; but every other heart was sinking under some degree of self-condemnation or undefined alarm, every other heart was suggesting, "What will become of us? What is to be done now?" It was a terrible pause; and terrible to every ear were the corroborating sounds of opening doors and passing footsteps.

Julia was the first to move and speak again. Jealousy and bitterness had been suspended: selfishness was lost in the common cause; but at the moment of her appearance, Frederick was listening with looks of devotion to Agatha's narrative, and pressing her hand to his heart; and as soon as she could notice this, and see that, in spite of the shock of her words, he still kept his station and retained her sister's hand, her wounded heart swelled again with injury, and looking as red as she had been white before, she turned out of the room, saying, "*I* need not be afraid of appearing before him."

Her going roused the rest; and at the same moment the two brothers stepped forward, feeling the necessity of doing something. A very few words between them were sufficient. The case admitted no difference of opinion; they must go to the drawing-room directly. Maria joined them with the same intent, just then the stoutest of the three; for the very circumstance which had driven Julia away was to her the sweetest support. Henry Crawford's retaining her hand at such a moment, a moment of such peculiar proof and importance, was worth ages of doubt and anxiety. She hailed it as an earnest of the most serious determination, and was equal even to encounter her father. They walked off, utterly heedless of Mr. Rushworth's repeated question of, "Shall I go too? Had not I better go too? Will not it be right for me to go too?" But they were no sooner through the door than Henry Crawford undertook to answer the anxious enquiry, and, encouraging him by all means to pay his respects to Sir Thomas without delay, sent him after the others with delighted haste.

Fanny was left with only the Crawfords and Mr. Yates. She had been quite overlooked by her cousins; and as her own opinion of her claims on Sir Thomas's affection was much too humble to give her any idea of classing herself with his children, she was glad to remain behind and gain a little breathing time. Her agitation and alarm exceeded all that was endured by the rest, by the right of a disposition which not even innocence could keep from suffering. She was nearly fainting: all her former habitual dread of her uncle was returning, and with it compassion for him and for almost every one of the party on the development before him, with solicitude on Edmund's account indescribable. She had found a seat, where in excessive trembling she was enduring all these fearful thoughts, while the other three, no longer under any restraint, were giving vent to their feelings of vexation, lamenting over such an unlooked-for premature arrival as a most untoward event, and without mercy wishing poor Sir Thomas had been twice as long on his passage, or were still in Antigua.

The Crawfords were more warm on the subject than Mr. Yates, from better understanding the family, and judging more clearly of the mischief that must ensue. The ruin of the play was to them a certainty: they felt the total destruction of the scheme to be inevitably at hand; while Mr. Yates considered it only as a temporary interruption, a disaster for the evening, and could even suggest the possibility of the rehearsal being renewed after tea, when the bustle of receiving Sir Thomas were over, and he might be at leisure to be amused by it. The Crawfords laughed at the idea; and having soon agreed on the propriety of their walking quietly home and leaving the family to themselves, proposed Mr. Yates's accompanying them and spending the evening at the Parsonage. But Mr. Yates, having never been with those who thought much of parental claims, or family confidence, could not perceive that anything of the kind was necessary; and therefore, thanking them, said: "He preferred remaining where he was, that he might pay his respects to the old gentleman handsomely, since he *was* come; and besides, he did not think it would be fair by the others to have everybody run away."

Fanny was just beginning to collect herself, and to feel that if she stayed longer behind it might seem disrespectful, when this point was settled, and being commissioned with the brother and sister's apology, saw them preparing to go as she quitted the room herself to perform the dreadful duty of appearing before her uncle.

Too soon did she find herself at the drawing-room door; and after pausing a moment for what she knew would not come, for a courage which the outside of no door had ever supplied to her, she turned the lock in desperation, and the lights of the drawing-room, and all the collected family, were before her. As she entered, her own name caught her ear.

Sir Thomas was at that moment looking round him and saying, "But where is Fanny? Why do not I see my little Fanny?"—and on perceiving her, came forward with a kindness which astonished and penetrated her, calling her his dear Fanny, kissing her affectionately, and observing with decided pleasure how much she was grown! Fanny knew not how to feel, nor where to look. She was quite oppressed. He had never been so kind, so *very* kind to her in his life. His manner seemed changed, his voice was quick from the agitation of joy; and all that had been awful in his dignity seemed lost in tenderness. He led her nearer the light and looked at her again—enquired particularly after her health, and then correcting himself, observed that he need *not* enquire, for her appearance spoke sufficiently on that point. A fine blush having succeeded the previous paleness of her face, he was justified in his belief of her equal improvement in health and beauty. He enquired next after her family, especially William; and his kindness altogether was such as made her reproach herself for loving him so little, and thinking his return a misfortune; and when, on having courage to lift her eyes to his face, she saw that he was grown thinner, and had the burnt, fagged, worn look of fatigue and a hot climate, every tender feeling was increased, and she was miserable in considering how much unsuspected vexation was probably ready to burst on him.

Sir Thomas was indeed the life of the party, who at his suggestion now seated themselves round the fire. He had the best right to be the talker; and the delight of his sensations in being again in his own house, in the centre of his family, after such a separation, made him communicative and chatty in a very unusual degree; and he was ready to give every information as to his voyage, and answer every question of his two sons almost before it was put. His business in Antigua had latterly been prosperously rapid, and he came directly from Liverpool, having had an opportunity of making his passage thither in a private vessel, instead of waiting for the packet; and all the little particulars of his proceedings and events, his arrivals and departures, were most promptly delivered, as he sat by Lady Bertram and looked with heartfelt satisfaction on the faces around him—interrupting himself more than once, however, to remark on his good fortune in finding them all at home—coming unexpectedly as he did —all collected together exactly as he could have wished, but dared not depend on. Mr. Rushworth was not forgotten; a most friendly reception and warmth of hand-shaking had already met him, and with pointed attention he was now included in the objects most intimately connected with Mansfield. There was nothing disagreeable in Mr. Rushworth's appearance, and Sir Thomas was liking him already.

By not one of the circle was he listened to with such unbroken, unalloyed enjoyment as by his wife, who was really extremely happy to see him, and whose feelings were so warmed by his sudden arrival as to place her nearer agitation than she had been for the last twenty years. She had been *almost* fluttered for a few minutes, and still remained so sensibly animated as to put away her work, move pug from her side, and give all her attention and all the rest of her sofa to her husband. She had no anxieties for anybody to cloud *her* pleasure: her own time had been irreproachably spent during his absence: she had done a great deal of carpet work, and made many yards of fringe; and she would have answered as freely for the good conduct and useful pursuits of all the young people as for her own. It was so agreeable to her to see him again, and hear him talk, to have her ear amused and her whole comprehensions filled by his narratives, that she began particularly to feel how dreadfully she must have missed him, and how impossible it would have been for her to bear a lengthened absence.

Mrs. Norris was by no means to be compared in happiness to her sister. Not that *she* was incommoded by many fears of Sir Thomas's disapprobation when the present state of his house should be known, for her judgment had been so blinded that, except by the instinctive caution with which she had whisked away Mr. Rushworth's pink satin cloak as her brother-in-law entered, she could hardly be said to show any sign of alarm; but she was vexed by the *manner* of his return. It had left her nothing to do. Instead of being sent for out of the room, and seeing him first, and having to spread the happy news through the house, Sir Thomas, with a very reasonable dependence, perhaps, on the nerves of his wife and children, had sought no confidant but the butler, and had been following him almost instantaneously into the drawing-room. Mrs. Norris felt herself defrauded of an office on which she had always depended, whether his arrival or his death were to be the thing unfolded; and was now trying to be in a bustle without having anything to bustle about, and labouring to be important where nothing was wanted but tranquillity and silence. Would Sir Thomas have consented to eat, she might have gone to the housekeeper with troublesome directions, and insulted the footmen with injunctions of despatch; but Sir Thomas resolutely declined all dinner; he would take nothing, nothing till tea came—he would rather wait for tea. Still Mrs. Norris was at intervals urging something different; and in the most interesting moment of his passage to England, when the alarm of a French privateer was at the height, she burst through his recital with the proposal of soup. "Sure, my dear Sir Thomas, a basin of soup would be a much better thing for you than tea. Do have a basin of soup."

Sir Thomas could not be provoked. "Still the same anxiety for everybody's comfort, my dear Mrs. Norris," was his answer. "But, indeed, I would rather have nothing but tea."

"Well, then, Lady Bertram, suppose you speak for tea directly; suppose you hurry Baddeley a little; he seems behindhand to-night." She carried this point, and Sir Thomas's narrative proceeded.

At length there was a pause. His immediate communications were exhausted, and it seemed enough to be looking joyfully around him, now at one, now at another of the beloved circle; but the pause was not long: in the elation of her spirits Lady Bertram became talkative, and what were the sensations of her children upon hearing her say: "How do you

think the young people have been amusing themselves lately, Sir Thomas?
They have been acting. We have been all alive with acting."

"Indeed! And what have you been acting?"

"Oh! They'll tell you all about it."

"The *all* will soon be told," cried Tom hastily, and with affected unconcern; "but it is not worth while to bore my father with it now. You
will hear enough of it to-morrow, sir. We have just been trying, by way
of doing something, and amusing my mother, just within the last week,
to get up a few scenes, a mere trifle. We have had such incessant rains
almost since October began, that we have been nearly confined to the
house for days together. I have hardly taken out a gun since the third.
Tolerable sport the first three days, but there has been no attempting
anything since. The first day I went over Mansfield Wood, and Edmund
took the copses beyond Easton, and we brought home six brace between
us, and might each have killed six times as many; but we respect your
pheasants, sir, I assure you, as much as you could desire. I do not think
you will find your woods by any means worse stocked than they were.
I never saw Mansfield Wood so full of pheasants in my life as this year.
I hope you will take a day's sport there yourself, sir, soon."

For the present the danger was over, and Fanny's sick feelings subsided; but when tea was soon afterwards brought in, and Sir Thomas,
getting up, said that he found that he could not be any longer in the house
without just looking into his own dear room, every agitation was returning. He was gone before anything had been said to prepare him for the
change he must find there; and a pause of alarm followed his disappearance. Edmund was the first to speak:

"Something must be done," said he.

"It is time to think of our visitors," said Maria, still feeling her hand
pressed to Henry Crawford's heart, and caring little for anything else.
"Where did you leave Miss Crawford, Fanny?"

Fanny told of their departure, and delivered their message.

"Then poor Yates is all alone," cried Tom. "I will go and fetch him.
He will be no bad assistant when it all comes out."

To the theatre he went, and reached it just in time to witness the first
meeting of his father and his friend. Sir Thomas had been a good deal
surprised to find candles burning in his room; and on casting his eye
round it, to see other symptoms of recent habitation and a general air of
confusion in the furniture. The removal of the bookcase from before the
billiard-room door struck him especially, but he had scarcely more than
time to feel astonished at all this, before there were sounds from the billiard-room to astonish him still further. Someone was talking there in a
very loud accent; he did not know the voice—*more* than talking—almost
hallooing. He stepped to the door, rejoicing at that moment in having the
means of immediate communication, and, opening it, found himself on the
stage of a theatre, and opposed to a ranting young man, who appeared
likely to knock him down backwards. At the very moment of Yates per-

ceiving Sir Thomas, and giving perhaps the very best start he had ever given in the whole course of his rehearsals, Tom Bertram entered at the other end of the room; and never had he found greater difficulty in keeping his countenance. His father's looks of solemnity and amazement on this, his first appearance on any stage, and the gradual metamorphosis of the impassioned Baron Wildenheim into the well-bred and easy Mr. Yates, making his bow and apology to Sir Thomas Bertram, was such an exhibition, such a piece of true acting, as he would not have lost upon any account. It would be the last—in all probability the last scene on that stage; but he was sure there could not be a finer. The house would close with the greatest éclat.

There was little time, however, for the indulgence of any images of merriment. It was necessary for him to step forward, too, and assist the introduction, and with many awkward sensations he did his best. Sir Thomas received Mr. Yates with all the appearance of cordiality which was due to his own character, but was really as far from pleased with the necessity of the acquaintance as with the manner of its commencement. Mr. Yates's family and connections were sufficiently known to him, to render his introduction as the "particular friend," another of the hundred particular friends of his son, exceedingly unwelcome; and it needed all the felicity of being again at home, and all the forbearance it could supply, to save Sir Thomas from anger on finding himself thus bewildered in his own house, making part of a ridiculous exhibition in the midst of theatrical nonsense, and forced in so untoward a moment to admit the acquaintance of a young man whom he felt sure of disapproving, and whose easy indifference and volubility in the course of the first five minutes seemed to mark him the most at home of the two.

Tom understood his father's thoughts, and heartily wishing he might be always as well disposed to give them but partial expression, began to see more clearly than he had ever done before, that there might be some ground of offence, that there might be some reason for the glance his father gave towards the ceiling and stucco of the room; and that when he enquired with mild gravity after the fate of the billiard-table, he was not proceeding beyond a very allowable curiosity. A few minutes were enough for such unsatisfactory sensations on each side; and Sir Thomas having exerted himself so far as to speak a few words of calm approbation in reply to an eager appeal of Mr. Yates, as to the happiness of the arrangement, the three gentlemen returned to the drawing-room together, Sir Thomas with an increase of gravity which was not lost on all.

"I come from your theatre," said he, composedly, as he sat down; "I found myself in it rather unexpectedly. Its vicinity to my own room—— but in every respect, indeed, it took me by surprise, as I had not the smallest suspicion of your acting having assumed so serious a character. It appears a neat job, however, as far as I could judge by candle-light, and does my friend Christopher Jackson credit." And then he would have changed the subject, and sipped his coffee in peace over domestic matters of a calmer hue; but Mr. Yates, without discernment to catch Sir Thomas's meaning, or diffidence, or delicacy, or discretion enough to allow him to lead the discourse while he mingled among the others with the least obtrusiveness himself, would keep him on the topic of the theatre, would torment him with questions and remarks relative to it, and finally would make him hear the whole history of his disappointment at Ecclesford. Sir Thomas listened most politely, but found much to offend his ideas of decorum, and confirm his ill opinion of Mr. Yates's habits of thinking, from the beginning to the end of the story; and when it was over, could give him no other assurance of sympathy than what a slight bow conveyed.

"This was, in fact, the origin of *our* acting," said Tom, after a moment's thought. "My friend Yates brought the infection from Ecclesford, and it spread—as those things always spread, you know, sir—the faster, probably, from *your* having so often encouraged the sort of thing in us formerly. It was like treading old ground again."

Mr. Yates took the subject from his friend as soon as possible, and immediately gave Sir Thomas an account of what they had done and were doing; told him of the gradual increase of their views, the happy conclusion of their first difficulties, and present promising state of affairs; relating everything with so blind an interest as made him not only totally unconscious of the uneasy movements of many of his friends as they sat, the change of countenance, the fidget, the hem! of unquietness, but prevented him even from seeing the expression of the face on which his own eyes were fixed—from seeing Sir Thomas's dark brows contract as he looked with enquiring earnestness at his daughters and Edmund, dwelling particularly on the latter, and speaking a language, a remonstrance, a reproof, which *he* felt at his heart. Not less acutely was it felt by Fanny, who had edged back her chair behind her aunt's end of the sofa, and, screened from notice herself, saw all that was passing before her. Such a look of reproach at Edmund from his father she could never have expected to witness; and to feel that it was in any degree deserved was an aggravation indeed. Sir Thomas's look implied, "On your judgment, Edmund, I depended; what have you been about?" She knelt in spirit to her uncle, and her bosom swelled to utter, "Oh, not to *him!* Look so to all the others, but not to *him!*"

Mr. Yates was still talking. "To own the truth, Sir Thomas, we were in the middle of a rehearsal when you arrived this evening. We were going through the three first acts, and not unsuccessfully upon the whole. Our company is now so dispersed, from the Crawfords being gone home, that nothing more can be done to-night; but if you will give us the honour of your company to-morrow evening, I should not be afraid of the result. We bespeak your indulgence, you understand, as young performers; we bespeak your indulgence."

"My indulgence shall be given, sir," replied Sir Thomas gravely, "but without any other rehearsal." And with a relenting smile he added, "I come home to be happy and indulgent." Then turning away towards any or all of the rest, he tranquilly said, "Mr. and Miss Crawford were mentioned in my last letters from Mansfield. Do you find them agreeable acquaintances?"

Tom was the only one at all ready with an answer, but he being entirely without particular regard for either, without jealousy either in love or acting, could speak very handsomely of both. "Mr. Crawford was a most pleasant gentlemanlike man; his sister a sweet, pretty, elegant, lively girl."

Mr. Rushworth could be silent no longer. "I do not say he is not gentlemanlike, considering; but you should tell your father he is not above five feet eight, or he will be expecting a well-looking man."

Sir Thomas did not quite understand this, and looked with some surprise at the speaker.

"If I must say what I think," continued Mr. Rushworth, "in my opinion it is very disagreeable to be always rehearsing. It is having too much of a good thing. I am not so fond of acting as I was at first. I think we are a great deal better employed, sitting comfortably here among ourselves and doing nothing."

Sir Thomas looked again, and then replied with an approving smile, "I am happy to find our sentiments on this subject so much the same. It gives me sincere satisfaction. That I should be cautious and quick-sighted, and feel many scruples which my children do *not* feel, is perfectly natural; and equally so that *my* value for domestic tranquillity, for a home which shuts out noisy pleasures, should much exceed theirs. But at your time of life to feel all this, is a most favourable circumstance for yourself, and for everybody connected with you; and I am sensible of the importance of having an ally of such weight."

Sir Thomas meant to be giving Mr. Rushworth's opinion in better words than he could find himself. He was aware that he must not expect a genius in Mr. Rushworth; but as a well-judging, steady young man, with better notions than his elocution would do justice to, he intended to value him very highly. It was impossible for many of the others not to smile. Mr. Rushworth hardly knew what to do with so much meaning; but by looking, as he really felt, most exceedingly pleased with Sir Thomas's good opinion, and saying scarcely anything, he did his best towards preserving that good opinion a little longer.

Chapter 20

EDMUND'S first object the next morning was to see his father alone, and give him a fair statement of the whole acting scheme, defending his own share in it as far only as he could then, in a soberer moment, feel his motives to deserve, and acknowledging, with perfect ingenuousness, that his concession had been attended with such partial good as to make his judgment in it very doubtful. He was anxious, while vindicating himself, to say nothing unkind of the others; but there was only one amongst them whose conduct he could mention without some necessity of defence or palliation. "We have all been more or less to blame," said he, "every one of us, excepting Fanny. Fanny is the only one who has judged rightly throughout; who has been consistent. *Her* feelings have been steadily against it from first to last. She never ceased to think of what was due to you. You will find Fanny everything you could wish."

Sir Thomas saw all the impropriety of such a scheme among such a party, and at such a time, as strongly as his son had ever supposed he must; he felt it too much, indeed, for many words; and having shaken hands with Edmund, meant to try to lose the disagreeable impression, and forget how much he had been forgotten himself as soon as he could, after the house had been cleared of every object enforcing the remembrance, and restored to its proper state. He did not enter into any remonstrance with his other children: he was more willing to believe they felt their error, than to run the risk of investigation. The reproof of an immediate conclusion of everything, the sweep of every preparation, would be sufficient.

There was one person, however, in the house, whom he could not leave to learn his sentiments merely through his conduct. He could not help giving Mrs. Norris a hint of his having hoped that her advice might have been interposed to prevent what her judgment must certainly have disapproved. The young people had been very inconsiderate in forming the plan; they ought to have been capable of a better decision themselves; but they were young; and, excepting Edmund, he believed, of unsteady characters; and with greater surprise, therefore, he must regard her acquiescence in their wrong measures, her countenance of their unsafe amusements, than that such measures and such amusements should have been suggested. Mrs. Norris was a little confounded and as nearly being silenced as ever she had been in her life; for she was ashamed to confess having never seen any of the impropriety which was so glaring to Sir Thomas, and would not have admitted that her influence was insufficient —that she might have talked in vain. Her only resource was to get out of the subject as fast as possible, and turn the current of Sir Thomas's ideas into a happier channel. She had a great deal to insinuate in her own praise as to *general* attention to the interest and comfort of his family, much exertion and many sacrifices to glance at in the form of hurried walks and sudden removals from her own fireside, and many excellent hints of distrust and economy to Lady Bertram and Edmund to detail, whereby a most considerable saving had always arisen, and more than one bad servant been detected. But her chief strength lay in Sotherton. Her greatest support and glory was in having formed the connection with the Rushworths. *There* she was impregnable. She took to herself all the credit of bringing Mr. Rushworth's admiration of Maria to any effect. "If I had not been active," said she, "and made a point of being introduced to his mother, and then prevailed on my sister to pay the first visit, I am as certain as I sit here that nothing would have come of it; for Mr. Rushworth is the sort of amiable modest young man who wants a great deal of encouragement, and there were girls enough on the catch for him if we had been idle. But I left no stone unturned. I was ready to move heaven and earth to persuade my sister, and at last I did persuade her. You know the distance to Sotherton; it was in the middle of winter, and the roads almost impassable, but I did persuade her."

"I know how great, how justly great, your influence is with Lady Bertram and her children, and am the more concerned that it should not have been——"

"My dear Sir Thomas, if you had seen the state of the roads *that* day! I thought we should never have got through them, though we had the four horses of course; and poor old coachman would attend us, out of his great love and kindness, though he was hardly able to sit the box on account of the rheumatism which I had been doctoring him for ever since Michaelmas. I cured him at last; but he was very bad all the winter—and this was such a day, I could not help going to him up in his room before we set off to advise him not to venture: he was putting on his wig; so I said, 'Coachman, you had much better not go; your Lady and I shall be very safe; you know how steady Stephen is, and Charles has been upon the leaders so often now, that I am sure there is no fear.' But, however, I soon found it would not do; he was bent upon going, and as I hate to be worrying and officious, I said no more; but my heart quite ached for him at every jolt, and when we got into the rough lanes about Stoke, where, what with frost and snow upon beds of stones, it was worse than anything you can imagine, I was quite in an agony about him. And then the poor horses too! To see them straining away! You know how I always feel for the horses. And when we got to the bottom of Sandcroft Hill, what do you think I did? You will laugh at me; but I got out and walked up. I did indeed. It might not be saving them much, but it was something, and I could not bear to sit at my ease, and be dragged up at the expense of those noble animals. I caught a dreadful cold, but *that* I did not regard. My object was accomplished in the visit."

"I hope we shall always think the acquaintance worth any trouble that might be taken to establish it. There is nothing very striking in Mr. Rushworth's manners, but I was pleased last night with what appeared to be his opinion on *one* subject; his decided preference of a quiet family party to the bustle and confusion of acting. He seemed to feel exactly as one could wish."

"Yes, indeed, and the more you know of him the better you will like him. He is not a shining character, but he has a thousand good qualities; and is so disposed to look up to you, that I am quite laughed at about it, for everybody considers it as my doing. 'Upon my word, Mrs. Norris,' said Mrs. Grant, the other day, 'if Mr. Rushworth were a son of your own, he could not hold Sir Thomas in greater respect.'"

Sir Thomas gave up the point, foiled by her evasions, disarmed by her flattery; and was obliged to rest satisfied with the conviction that where the present pleasure of those she loved was at stake, her kindness did sometimes overpower her judgment.

It was a busy morning with him. Conversation with any of them occupied but a small part of it. He had to reinstate himself in all the wonted concerns of his Mansfield life; to see his steward and his bailiff; to examine and compute, and, in the intervals of business, to walk into his stables and his gardens, and nearest plantations; but active and method-ical, he had not only done all this before he resumed his seat as master of the house at dinner, he had also set the carpenter to work in pulling down what had been so lately put up in the billiard-room, and given the scene-painter his dismissal, long enough to justify the pleasing belief of his being then at least as far off as Northampton. The scene-painter was gone, hav-ing spoilt only the floor of one room, ruined all the coachman's sponges, and made five of the under-servants idle and dissatisfied; and Sir Thomas was in hopes that another day or two would suffice to wipe away every outward memento of what had been, even to the destruction of every unbound copy of *Lovers' Vows* in the house, for he was burning all that met his eye.

Mr. Yates was beginning now to understand Sir Thomas's intentions, though as far as ever from understanding their source. He and his friend had been out with their guns the chief of the morning, and Tom had taken the opportunity of explaining, with proper apologies for his father's par-ticularity, what was to be expected. Mr. Yates felt is as acutely as might be supposed. To be a second time disappointed in the same way was an instance of very severe ill luck; and his indignation was such, that had it not been for delicacy towards his friend, and his friend's youngest sister, he believed he should certainly attack the baronet on the absurdity of his proceedings, and argue him into a little more rationality. He believed this very stoutly while he was in Mansfield Wood, and all the way home; but there was a something in Sir Thomas, when they sat round the same table, which made Mr. Yates think it wiser to let him pursue his own way, and feel the folly of it without question. He had known many disagreeable fathers before, and often been struck with the inconveniences they oc-casioned, but never, in the whole course of his life, had he seen one of that class, so unintelligibly moral, so infamously tyrannical as Sir Thomas. He was not a man to be endured but for his children's sake, and he might be thankful to his fair daughter Julia that Mr. Yates did yet mean to stay a few days longer under his roof.

The evening passed with external smoothness, though almost every mind was ruffled; and the music which Sir Thomas called for from his daughters helped to conceal the want of real harmony. Maria was in a good deal of agitation. It was of the utmost consequence to her that Crawford should now lose no time in declaring himself, and she was dis-turbed that even a day should be gone by without seeming to advance that point. She had been expecting to see him the whole morning, and all the evening, too, was still expecting him. Mr. Rushworth had set off early with the great news for Sotherton; and she had fondly hoped for such an immediate éclaircissement as might save him the trouble of ever coming back again. But they had seen no one from the Parsonage, not a creature, and had heard no tidings beyond a friendly note of congratulation and enquiry from Mrs. Grant to Lady Bertram. It was the first day for many, many weeks, in which the families had been wholly divided. Four-and-twenty hours had never passed before, since August began, without bringing them together in some way or other. It was a sad, anxious day; and the morrow, though differing in the sort of evil, did by no means bring less. A few moments of feverish enjoyment were followed by hours of acute suffering. Henry Crawford was again in the house; he walked up with Dr. Grant, who was anxious to pay his respects to Sir Thomas, and at rather an early hour they were ushered into the breakfast-room, where were most of the family. Sir Thomas soon appeared, and Maria saw with delight and agitation the introduction of the man she loved to her father. Her sensations were indefinable, and so were they a few minutes afterwards upon hearing Henry Crawford, who had a chair between herself and Tom, ask the latter in an under voice, whether there were any plans for resuming the play after the present happy interruption (with a courteous glance at Sir Thomas), because, in that case, he should make a point of returning to Mansfield at any time required by the party: he was going away immediately, being to meet his uncle at Bath without delay: but if there were any prospect of a renewal of *Lovers' Vows*, he should hold himself positively engaged, he should break through every other claim; he should absolutely condition with his uncle for attending them whenever he might be wanted. The play should not be lost by *his* absence.

"From Bath, Norfolk, London, York; wherever I may be," said he: "I will attend you from any place in England, at an hour's notice."

It was well at that moment that Tom had to speak and not his sister. He could immediately say with easy fluency, "I am sorry you are going; but as to our play, *that* is all over—entirely at an end—(looking significantly at his father). The painter was sent off yesterday, and very little will remain of the theatre to-morrow. I knew how *that* would be from the first. It is early for Bath. You will find nobody there."

"It is about my uncle's usual time."

"When do you think of going?"

"I may, perhaps, get as far as Banbury to-day."

"Whose stables do you use at Bath?" was the next question; and while this branch of the subject was under discussion, Maria, who wanted neither pride nor resolution, was preparing to encounter her share of it with tolerable calmness.

To her he soon turned, repeating much of what he had already said with only a softened air and stronger expression of regret. But what availed his expressions or his air? He was going, and, if not voluntarily going, voluntarily intending to stay away; for, excepting what might be due to his uncle, his engagements were all self-imposed. He might talk of necessity, but she knew his independence. The hand which had so pressed hers to his heart! the hand and the heart were alike motionless and passive now! Her spirit supported her, but the agony of her mind was severe. She had not long to endure what arose from listening to language which his actions contradicted, or to bury the tumult of her feelings under the restraint of society; for general civilities soon called his notice from her. and the farewell visit, as it then became openly acknowledged, was a very short one. He was gone—he had touched her hand for the last time, he had made his parting bow, and she might seek directly all that solitude could do for her. Henry Crawford was gone, gone from the house, and within two hours afterwards from the parish; and so ended all the hopes his selfish vanity had raised in Maria and Julia Bertram.

Julia could rejoice that he was gone. His presence was beginning to be odious to her; and if Maria gained him not, she was now cool enough to dispense with any other revenge. She did not want exposure to be added to desertion. Henry Crawford gone, she could even pity her sister.

With a purer spirit did Fanny rejoice in the intelligence. She heard it at dinner, and felt it a blessing. By all the others it was mentioned with regret; and his merits honoured with due gradation of feeling, from the sincerity of Edmund's too partial regard, to the unconcern of his mother speaking entirely by rote. Mrs. Norris began to look about her, and wonder that his falling in love with Julia had come to nothing; and could almost fear that she had been remiss herself in forwarding it; but with so many to care for, how was it possible for even *her* activity to keep pace with her wishes?

Another day or two, and Mr. Yates was gone likewise. In *his* departure Sir Thomas felt the chief interest; wanting to be alone with his family, the presence of a stranger superior to Mr. Yates must have been irksome; but of him, trifling and confident, idle and expensive, it was every way vexatious. In himself he was wearisome, but as the friend of Tom and the admirer of Julia he became offensive. Sir Thomas had been quite indifferent to Mr. Crawford's going or staying; but his good wishes for Mr. Yates's having a pleasant journey, as he walked with him to the hall door, were given with genuine satisfaction. Mr. Yates had stayed to see the destruction of every theatrical preparation at Mansfield, the removal of everything appertaining to the play: he left the house in all the soberness of its general character; and Sir Thomas hoped, in seeing him out of it, to be rid of the worst object connected with the scheme, and the last that must be inevitably reminding him of its existence.

Mrs. Norris contrived to remove one article from his sight that might have distressed him. The curtain over which she had presided with such talent and such success, went off with her to her cottage, where she happened to be particularly in want of green baize.

Chapter 21

Sir Thomas's return made a striking change in the ways of the family, independent of *Lovers' Vows*. Under his government, Mansfield was an altered place. Some members of their society sent away, and the spirits of many others saddened—it was all sameness and gloom compared with the past—a sombre family party rarely enlivened. There was little intercourse with the Parsonage. Sir Thomas, drawing back from intimacies in general, was particularly disinclined, at this time, for any engagements but in one quarter. The Rushworths were the only addition to his own domestic circle which he could solicit.

Edmund did not wonder that such should be his father's feelings, nor could he regret anything but the exclusion of the Grants. "But they," he observed to Fanny, "have a claim. They seem to belong to us; they seem to be part of ourselves. I could wish my father were more sensible of their very great attention to my mother and sisters while he was away. I am afraid they may feel themselves neglected. But the truth is, that my father hardly knows them. They had not been here a twelvemonth when he left England. If he knew them better, he would value their society as it deserves; for they are in fact exactly the sort of people he would like. We are sometimes a little in want of animation among ourselves: my sisters seem out of spirits, and Tom is certainly not at his ease. Dr. and Mrs. Grant would enliven us, and make our evenings pass away with more enjoyment even to my father."

"Do you think so?" said Fanny: "in my opinion, my uncle would not like *any* addition. I think he values the very quietness you speak of, and that the repose of his own family circle is all he wants. And it does not appear to me that we are more serious than we used to be—I mean before my uncle went abroad. As well as I can recollect it was always much the same. There was never much laughing in his presence; or, if there is any difference it is not more I think than such an absence has a tendency to produce at first. There must be a sort of shyness; but I cannot recollect that our evenings formerly were ever merry, except when my uncle was in town. No young people's are, I suppose, when those they look up to are at home."

"I believe you are right, Fanny," was his reply, after a short consideration. "I believe our evenings are rather returned to what they were, than assuming a new character. The novelty was in their being lively. Yet, how strong the impression that only a few weeks will give! I have been feeling as if we had never lived so before."

"I suppose I am graver than other people," said Fanny. "The evenings do not appear long to me. I love to hear my uncle talk of the West Indies. I could listen to him for an hour together. It entertains *me* more than many other things have done; but then I am unlike other people, I dare say."

"Why should you dare say *that?*" (smiling). "Do you want to be told that you are only unlike other people in being more wise and discreet? But when did you, or anybody, ever get a compliment from me, Fanny? Go to my father if you want to be complimented. He will satisfy you. Ask your uncle what he thinks, and you will hear compliments enough: and though they may be chiefly on your person, you must put up with it, and trust to his seeing as much beauty of mind in time."

Such language was so new to Fanny that it quite embarrassed her.

"Your uncle thinks you very pretty, dear Fanny—and that is the long and the short of the matter. Anybody but myself would have made something more of it, and anybody but you would resent that you had not been thought very pretty before; but the truth is, that your uncle never did admire you till now—and now he does. Your complexion is so improved! and you have gained so much countenance! and your figure—nay, Fanny, do not turn away about it—it is but an uncle. If you cannot bear an uncle's admiration, what is to become of you? You must really begin to harden yourself to the idea of being worth looking at. You must try not to mind growing up into a pretty woman."

"Oh! don't talk so, don't talk so," cried Fanny, distressed by more feelings than he was aware of; but seeing that she was distressed, he had done with the subject, and only added more seriously—

"Your uncle is disposed to be pleased with you in every respect; and I only wish you would talk to him more. You are one of those who are too silent in the evening circle."

"But I do talk to him more than I used. I am sure I do. Did not you hear me ask him about the slave-trade last night?"

"I did—and was in hopes the question would be followed up by others. It would have pleased your uncle to be enquired of farther."

"And I longed to do it—but there was such a dead silence! And while my cousins were sitting by without speaking a word, or seeming at all interested in the subject, I did not like—I thought it would appear as if I wanted to set myself off at their expense, by showing a curiosity and pleasure in his information which he must wish his own daughters to feel."

"Miss Crawford was very right in what she said of you the other day: that you seemed almost as fearful of notice and praise as other women were of neglect. We were talking of you at the Parsonage, and those were her words. She has great discernment. I know nobody who distinguishes characters better. For so young a woman it is remarkable! She certainly understands *you* better than you are understood by the greater part of those who have known you so long; and with regard to some others, I can perceive, from occasional lively hints, the unguarded expressions of the moment, that she could define *many* as accurately did not delicacy forbid it. I wonder what she thinks of my father! She must admire him as a fine-looking man, with most gentlemanlike, dignified, consistent manners, but, perhaps, having seen him so seldom, his reserve may be a little repulsive. Could they be much together, I feel sure of their liking each other. He

would enjoy her liveliness, and she has talents to value his powers. I wish
they met more frequertly! I hope she does not suppose there is any dislike
cn his side."

"She must know herself too secure of the regard of all the rest of you,"
said Fanny, with half a sigh, "to have any such apprehension. And Sir
Thomas's wishing just at first to be only with his family is so very natural,
that she can argue nothing from that. After a little while I dare say we
shall be meeting again in the same sort of way, allowing for the difference
of the time of year."

"This is the first October that she has passed in the country since her
infancy. I do not call Tunbridge or Cheltenham the country; and November is a still more serious month, and I can see that Mrs. Grant is very
anxious for her not finding Mansfield dull as winter comes on."

Fanny could have said a great deal, but it was safer to say nothing, and
leave untouched all Miss Crawford's resources, her accomplishments, her
spirits, her importance, her friends, lest it should betray her into any observations seemingly unhandsome. Miss Crawford's kind opinion of herself deserved at least a grateful forbearance, and she began to talk of
something else.

"To-morrow, I think, my uncle dines at Sothertcn and you and Mr.
Bertram too. We shall be quite a small party at home. I hope my uncle
may continue to like Mr. Rushworth."

"That is impossible, Fanny. He must like him less after to-morrow's
visit, for we shall be five hours in his company. I should dread the stupidity
of the day, if there were not a much greater evil to follow—the impression
it must leave on Sir Thomas. He cannot much longer deceive himself. I am
sorry for them all, and would give something that Rushworth and Maria
had never met."

In this quarter, indeed, disappointment was impending over Sir
Thomas. Not all his good-will for Mr. Rushworth, not all Mr. Rushworth's
deference for him, could prevent him from soon discerning some part of
the truth—that Mr. Rushworth was an inferior young man, as ignorant
in business as in books, with opinions in general unfixed, and without
seeming much aware of it himself.

He had expected a very different son-in-law; and beginning to feel grave
on Maria's account, tried to understand *her* feelings. Little observation
there was necessary to tell him that indifference was the most favourable
state they could be in. Her behaviour to Mr. Rushworth was careless and
cold. She could not, did not like him. Sir Thomas resolved to speak seriously to her. Advantageous as would be the alliance, and long standing
and public as was the engagement, her happiness must not be sacrificed to
it. Mr. Rushworth had, perhaps, been accepted on too short an acquaintance, and, on knowing him better, she was repenting.

With solemn kindness Sir Thomas addressed her; told her his fears,
enquired into her wishes, entreated her to be open and sincere, and assured her that every inconvenience should be braved, and the connection

entirely given up, if she felt herself unhappy in the prospect of it. He would act for her and release her. Maria had a moment's struggle as she listened, and only a moment's; when her father ceased, she was able to give her answer immediately, decidedly, and with no apparent agitation. She thanked him for his great attention, his paternal kindness, but he was quite mistaken in supposing she had the smallest desire of breaking through her engagement, or was sensible of any change of opinion or inclination since her forming it. She had the highest esteem for Mr. Rushworth's character and disposition, and could not have a doubt of her happiness with him.

Sir Thomas was satisfied; too glad to be satisfied, perhaps, to urge the matter quite so far as his judgment might have dictated to others. It was an alliance which he could not have relinquished without pain; and thus he reasoned. Mr. Rushworth was young enough to improve: Mr. Rushworth must and would improve in good society; and if Maria could now speak so securely of her happiness with him, speaking certainly without the prejudice, the blindness of love, she ought to be believed. Her feelings, probably, were not acute; he had never supposed them to be so; but her comforts might not be less on that account; and if she could dispense with seeing her husband a leading, shining character, there would certainly be everything else in her favour. A well-disposed young woman, who did not marry for love, was in general but the more attached to her own family; and the nearness of Sotherton to Mansfield must naturally hold out the greatest temptation, and would, in all probability, be a continual supply of the most amiable and innocent enjoyments. Such and such-like were the reasonings of Sir Thomas, happy to escape the embarrassing evils of a rupture, the wonder, the reflections, the reproach that must attend it; happy to secure a marriage which would bring him such an addition of respectability and influence, and very happy to think anything of his daughter's disposition that was most favourable for the purpose.

To her the conference closed as satisfactorily as to him. She was in a state of mind to be glad that she had secured her fate beyond recall; that she had pledged herself anew to Sotherton; that she was safe from the possibility of giving Crawford the triumph of governing her actions, and destroying her prospects; and retired in proud resolve, determined only to behave more cautiously to Mr. Rushworth in future, that her father might not be again suspecting her.

Had Sir Thomas applied to his daughter within the first three or four days after Henry Crawford's leaving Mansfield, before her feelings were at all tranquillised, before she had given up every hope of him, or absolutely resolved on enduring his rival, her answer might have been different; but after another three or four days, when there was no return, no letter, no message, no symptom of a softened heart, no hope of advantage from separation her mind became cool enough to seek all the comfort that pride and self-revenge could give.

Henry Crawford had destroyed her happiness, but he should not know that he had done it; he should not destroy her credit, her appearance, her prosperity too. He should not have to think of her as pining in the retirement of Mansfield for *him*, rejecting Sotherton and London, independence and splendour, for *his* sake. Independence was more needful than ever; the want of it at Mansfield more sensibly felt. She was less and less able to endure the restraint which her father imposed. The liberty which his absence had given was now become absolutely necessary. She must escape from him and Mansfield as soon as possible, and find consolation in fortune and consequence, bustle and the world, for a wounded spirit. Her mind was quite determined, and varied not.

To such feelings delay, even the delay of much preparation, would have been an evil, and Mr. Rushworth could hardly be more impatient for the marriage than herself. In all the important preparations of the mind she was complete: being prepared for matrimony by an hatred of home, restraint, and tranquillity; by the misery of disappointed affection, and contempt of the man she was to marry. The rest might wait. The preparation of new carriages and furniture might wait for London and spring, when her own taste could have fairer play.

The principals being all agreed in this respect, it soon appeared that a very few weeks would be sufficient for such arrangements as must precede the wedding.

Mrs. Rushworth was quite ready to retire, and make way for the fortunate young woman whom her dear son had selected; and very early in November removed herself, her maid, her footman, and her chariot, with true dowager propriety, to Bath, there to parade over the wonders of Sotherton in her evening parties; enjoying them as thoroughly, perhaps, in the animation of a card-table as she had ever done on the spot; and before the middle of the same month the ceremony had taken place which gave Sotherton another mistress.

It was a very proper wedding. The bride was elegantly dressed; the two bridesmaids were duly inferior; her father gave her away; her mother stood with salts in her hand, expecting to be agitated; her aunt tried to cry; and the service was impressively read by Dr. Grant. Nothing could be objected to when it came under the discussion of the neighbourhood, except that the carriage which conveyed the bride and bridegroom and Julia from the church door to Sotherton was the same chaise which Mr. Rushworth had used for a twelvemonth before. In everything else the etiquette of the day might stand the strictest investigation.

It was done, and they were gone. Sir Thomas felt as an anxious father must feel, and was indeed experiencing much of the agitation which his wife had been apprehensive of for herself, but had fortunately escaped. Mrs. Norris, most happy to assist in the duties of the day, by spending it at the Park to support her sister's spirits, and drinking the health of Mr. and Mrs. Rushworth in a supernumerary glass or two, was all joyous delight; for she had made the match; she had done everything and no one would have supposed, from her confident triumph, that she had ever heard of conjugal infelicity in her life or could have the smallest insight into the disposition of the niece who had been brought up under her eye.

The plan of the young couple was to proceed, after a few days, to Brighton, and take a house there for some weeks. Every public place was new to Maria, and Brighton is almost as gay in winter as in summer. When the novelty of amusement there was over, it would be time for the wider range of London.

Julia was to go with them to Brighton. Since rivalry between the sisters had ceased, they had been gradually recovering much of their former good understanding; and were at least sufficiently friends to make each of them exceedingly glad to be with the other at such a time. Some other companion than Mr. Rushworth was of the first consequence to his lady; and Julia was quite as eager for novelty and pleasure as Maria, though she might not have struggled through so much to obtain them, and could better bear a subordinate situation.

Their departure made another material change at Mansfield, a chasm which required some time to fill up. The family circle became greatly contracted; and though the Miss Bertrams had latterly added little to its gaiety, they could not but be missed. Even their mother missed them; and how much more their tender-hearted cousin, who wandered about the house, and thought of them, and felt for them, with a degree of affectionate regret which they had never done much to deserve!

Chapter 22

FANNY's consequence increased on the departure of her cousins. Becoming, as she then did, the only young woman in the drawing-room, the only occupier of that interesting division of a family in which she had hitherto held so humble a third, it was impossible for her not to be more looked at, more thought of and attended to, than she had ever been before; and "Where is Fanny?" became no uncommon question even without her being wanted for any one's convenience.

Not only at home did her value increase, but at the Parsonage too. In that house which she had hardly entered twice a year since Mr. Norris's death, she became a welcome, an invited guest, and in the gloom and dirt of a November day, most acceptable to Mary Crawford. Her visits there, beginning by chance, were continued by solicitation. Mrs. Grant, really eager to get any change for her sister, could, by the easiest self-deceit, persuade herself that she was doing the kindest thing by Fanny, and giving her the most important opportunities of improvement in pressing her frequent calls.

Fanny having been sent into the village on some errand by her Aunt Norris, was overtaken by a heavy shower close to the Parsonage; and being descried from one of the windows endeavouring to find shelter under the branches and lingering leaves of an oak just beyond their premises, was forced, though not without some modest reluctance on her part, to come in. A civil servant she had withstood; but when Dr. Grant himself went out with an umbrella, there was nothing to be done but to be very much ashamed, and to get into the house as fast as possible; and to poor Miss Crawford, who had just been contemplating the dismal rain in a very desponding state of mind, sighing over the ruin of all her plan of exercise for that morning, and of every chance of seeing a single creature beyond themselves for the next twenty-four hours, the sound of a little bustle at the front door, and the sight of Miss Price dripping with wet in the vestibule, was delightful. The value of an event on a wet day in the country was most forcibly brought before her. She was all alive again directly, and among the most active in being useful to Fanny, in detecting her to be wetter than she would at first allow, and providing her with dry clothes; and Fanny, after being obliged to submit to all this attention, and to being assisted and waited on by mistresses and maids, being also obliged, on returning downstairs, to be fixed in their drawing-room for an hour while the rain continued, the blessing of something fresh to see and think of was thus extended to Miss Crawford, and might carry on her spirits to the period of dressing and dinner.

The two sisters were so kind to her, and so pleasant, that Fanny might have enjoyed her visit could she have believed herself not in the way, and could she have foreseen that the weather would certainly clear at the end of the hour, and save her from the shame of having Dr. Grant's carriage and horses out to take her home, with which she was threatened. As to anxiety for any alarm that her absence in such weather might occasion at home, she had nothing to suffer on that score; for as her being out was known only to her two aunts, she was perfectly aware that none would be felt, and that in whatever cottage Aunt Norris might choose to establish her during the rain, her being in such a cottage would be indubitable to Aunt Bertram.

It was beginning to look brighter, when Fanny, observing a harp in the room, asked some questions about it, which soon led to an acknowledgment of her wishing very much to hear it, and a confession, which could hardly be believed, of her having never yet heard it since its being in Mansfield. To Fanny herself it appeared a very simple and natural circumstance. She had scarcely ever been at the Parsonage since the instrument's arrival, there had been no reason that she should; but Miss Crawford, calling to mind an early expressed wish on the subject, was concerned at her own neglect; and "Shall I play to you now?" and "What will you have?" were questions immediately following with the readiest good humour.

She played accordingly; happy to have a new listener, and a listener who seemed so much obliged, so full of wonder at the performance, and who showed herself not wanting in taste. She played till Fanny's eyes, straying to the window on the weather's being evidently fair, spoke what she felt must be done.

"Another quarter of an hour," said Miss Crawford, "and we shall see how it will be. Do not run away the first moment of its holding up. Those clouds look alarming."

"But they are passed over," said Fanny. "I have been watching them. This weather is all from the south."

"South or north, I know a black cloud when I see it; and you must not set forward while it is so threatening. And besides I want to play something more to you—a very pretty piece—and your cousin Edmund's prime favourite. You must stay and hear your cousin's favourite."

Fanny felt that she must; and though she had not waited for that sentence to be thinking of Edmund, such a memento made her particularly awake to his idea, and she fancied him sitting in that room again and again, perhaps in the very spot where she sat now, listening with constant delight to the favourite air, played, as it appeared to her, with superior tone and expression; and though pleased with it herself, and glad to like whatever was liked by him, she was more sincerely impatient to go away at the conclusion of it than she had been before; and on this being evident, she was so kindly asked to call again, to take them in her walk whenever she could, to come and hear more of the harp, that she felt it necessary to be done, if no objection arose at home.

Such was the origin of the sort of intimacy which took place between them within the first fortnight after the Miss Bertrams' going away—an intimacy resulting principally from Miss Crawford's desire of something new, and which had little reality in Fanny's feelings. Fanny went to her every two or three days: it seemed a kind of fascination: she could not be easy without going, and yet it was without loving her, without ever thinking like her, without any sense of obligation for being sought after now when nobody else was to be had; and deriving no higher pleasure from her conversation than occasional amusement, and *that* often at the expense of her judgment, when it was raised by pleasantry on people or subjects which she wished to be respected. She went, however, and they sauntered about together many an half-hour in Mrs. Grant's shrubbery, the weather being unusually mild for the time of year; and venturing sometimes even to sit down on one of the benches now comparatively unsheltered, remaining there perhaps till, in the midst of some tender ejaculation of Fanny's, on the sweets of so protracted an autumn, they were forced by the sudden swell of a cold gust shaking down the last few yellow leaves about them, to jump up and walk for warmth.

"This is pretty, very pretty," said Fanny, looking around her as they were thus sitting together one day; "every time I come into this shrubbery I am more struck with its growth and beauty. Three years ago this was nothing but a rough hedgerow along the upper side of the field, never thought of as anything or capable of becoming anything; and now it is converted into a walk, and it would be difficult to say whether most valuable as a convenience or an ornament; and perhaps, in another three years we may be forgetting—almost forgetting what it was before. How wonderful, how very wonderful the operations of time and the changes of the human mind!" And following the latter train of thought, she soon afterwards added: "If any one faculty of our nature may be called *more* wonderful than the rest, I do think it is memory. There seems something more speakingly incomprehensible in the powers, the failures, the inequalities of memory, than in any other of our intelligences. The memory is sometimes so retentive, so serviceable, so obedient: at others, so bewildered and so weak; and at others again, so tyrannic, so beyond control! We are, to be sure, a miracle every way; but our powers of recollecting and of forgetting do seem peculiarly past finding out."

Miss Crawford, untouched and inattentive, had nothing to say; and Fanny, perceiving it, brought back her own mind to what she thought must interest.

"It may seem impertinent in *me* to praise, but I must admire the taste Mrs. Grant has shown in all this. There is such a quiet simplicity in the plan of the walk! Not too much attempted!"

"Yes," replied Miss Crawford, carelessly, "it does very well for a place of this sort. One does not think of extent *here;* and between ourselves, till I came to Mansfield, I had not imagined a country parson ever aspired to a shrubbery, or anything of the kind."

"I am so glad to see the evergreens thrive!" said Fanny, in reply. "My uncle's gardener always says the soil here is better than his own, and so it appears from the growth of the laurels and evergreens in general. The evergreen! How beautiful, how welcome, how wonderful the evergreen! When one thinks of it, how astonishing a variety of nature! In some countries we know the tree that sheds its leaf is the variety, but that does not make it less amazing, that the same soil and the same sun should nurture plants differing in the first rule and law of their existence. You will think me rhapsodising; but when I am out of doors, especially when I am sitting out of doors, I am very apt to get into this sort of wondering strain. One cannot fix one's eyes on the commonest natural production without finding food for a rambling fancy."

"To say the truth," replied Miss Crawford, "I am something like the famous Doge at the court of Louis XIV; and may declare that I see no wonder in this shrubbery equal to seeing myself in it. If anybody had told me a year ago that this place would be my home, that I should be spending month after month here, as I have done, I certainly should not have believed them. I have now been here nearly five months; and, moreover, the quietest five months I ever passed."

"*Too* quiet for you, I believe."

"I should have thought so *theoretically* myself, but," and her eyes brightened as she spoke, "take it all and all, I never spent so happy a summer. But then," with a more thoughtful air and lowered voice, "there is no saying what it may lead to."

Fanny's heart beat quick, and she felt quite unequal to surmising or soliciting anything more. Miss Crawford, however, with renewed animation, soon went on—

"I am conscious of being far better reconciled to a country residence than I had ever expected to be. I can even suppose it pleasant to spend *half* the year in the country, under certain circumstances, very pleasant. An elegant, moderate-sized house in the centre of family connections; continual engagements among them; commanding the first society in the neighbourhood; looked-up to, perhaps, as leading it even more than those of larger fortune, and turning from the cheerful round of such amusements to nothing worse than a *tête-à-tête* with the person one feels most agreeable in the world. There is nothing frightful in such a picture, is there, Miss Price? One need not envy the new Mrs. Rushworth with such a home as *that*." "Envy Mrs. Rushworth!" was all that Fanny attempted to say. "Come, come, it would be very unhandsome in us to be severe on Mrs. Rushworth, for I look forward to our owing her a great many gay, brilliant, happy hours. I expect we shall be all very much at Sotherton another year. Such a match as Miss Bertram has made is a public blessing; for the first pleasures of Mr. Rushworth's wife must be to fill her house, and give the best balls in the country."

Fanny was silent, and Miss Crawford relapsed into thoughtfulness, till suddenly looking up at the end of a few minutes, she exclaimed, "Ah, here he is." It was not Mr. Rushworth, however, but Edmund, who then appeared walking towards them with Mrs. Grant. "My sister and Mr. Bertram. I am so glad your eldest cousin is gone, that he *may* be Mr. Bertram again. There is something in the sound of Mr. *Edmund* Bertram so formal, so pitiful, so younger-brother-like, that I detest it."

"How differently we feel!" cried Fanny. "To me, the sound of *Mr.* Bertram is so cold and nothing-meaning, so entirely without warmth or character! It just stands for a gentleman, and that's all. But there is nobleness in the name of Edmund. It is a name of heroism and renown; of kings, princes, and knights; and seems to breathe the spirit of chivalry and warm affections."

"I grant you the name is good in itself, and *Lord* Edmund or *Sir* Edmund sound delightfully; but sink it under the chill, the annihilation of a Mr. and Mr. Edmund is not more than Mr. John or Mr. Thomas. Well, shall we join and disappoint them of half their lecture upon sitting down out of doors at this time of year, by being up before they can begin?"

Edmund met them with particular pleasure. It was the first time of his seeing them together since the beginning of that better acquaintance which he had been hearing of with great satisfaction. A friendship between two so very dear to him was exactly what he could have wished: and to the credit of the lover's understanding, be it stated, that he did not by any means consider Fanny as the only, or even as the greater gainer by such a friendship.

"Well," said Miss Crawford, "and do you not scold us for our imprudence? What do you think we have been sitting down for but to be talked to about it, and entreated and supplicated never to do so again?"

"Perhaps I might have scolded," said Edmund, "if either of you had been sitting down alone; but while you do wrong together, I can overlook a great deal."

"They cannot have been sitting long," cried Mrs. Grant, "for when I went up for my shawl I saw them from the staircase window, and then they were walking."

"And really," added Edmund, "the day is so mild, that your sitting down for a few minutes can be hardly thought imprudent. Our weather must not always be judged by the calendar. We may sometimes take greater liberties in November than in May."

"Upon my word," cried Miss Crawford, "you are two of the most disappointing and unfeeling kind friends I ever met with! There is no giving you a moment's uneasiness. You do not know how much we have been suffering, nor what chills we have felt! But I have long thought Mr. Bertram one of the worst subjects to work on, in any little manœuvre against common sense, that a woman could be plagued with. I had very little hope of *him* from the first; but you, Mrs. Grant, my sister, my own sister, I think I had a right to alarm you a little."

"Do not flatter yourself, my dearest Mary. You have not the smallest chance of moving me. I have my alarms, but they are quite in a different quarter; and if I could have altered the weather, you would have had a good sharp east wind blowing on you the whole time—for here are some of my plants which Robert *will* leave out because the nights are so mild, and I know the end of it will be, that we shall have a sudden change of weather, a hard frost setting in all at once, taking everybody (at least Robert) by surprise, and I shall lose every one; and what is worse, cook has just been telling me that the turkey, which I particularly wished not to be dressed till Sunday, because I know how much more Dr. Grant would enjoy it on Sunday after the fatigues of the day, will not keep beyond to-morrow. These are something like grievances, and make me think the weather most unseasonably close."

"The sweets of housekeeping in a country village!" said Miss Crawford, archly. "Commend me to the nurseryman and the poulterer."

"My dear child, commend Dr. Grant to the deanery of Westminster or St. Paul's, and I should be as glad of your nurseryman and poulterer as you could be. But we have no such people in Mansfield. What would you have me do?"

"Oh! you can do nothing but what you do already: be plagued very often, and never lose your temper."

"Thank you; but there is no escaping these little vexations, Mary, live where we may; and when you are settled in town and I come to see you, I dare say I shall find you with yours, in spite of the nurseryman and the poulterer—or perhaps on their very account. Their remoteness and unpunctuality, or their exorbitant charges and frauds, will be drawing forth bitter lamentations."

"I mean to be too rich to lament or to feel anything of the sort. A large income is the best recipe for happiness I ever heard of. It certainly may secure all the myrtle and turkey part of it."

"You intend to be very rich?" said Edmund, with a look which, to Fanny's eye, had a great deal of serious meaning.

"To be sure. Do not you? Do not we all?"

"I cannot intend anything which it must be so completely beyond my power to command. Miss Crawford may choose her degree of wealth. She has only to fix on her number of thousands a year, and there can be no doubt of their coming. My intentions are only not to be poor."

"By moderation and economy, and bringing down your wants to your income, and all that. I understand you—and a very proper plan it is for a person at your time of life, with such limited means and indifferent connections. What can *you* want but a decent maintenance? You have not much time before you; and your relations are in no situation to do anything for you, or to mortify you by the contrast of their own wealth and consequence. Be honest and poor, by all means—but I shall not envy you; I do not much think I shall even respect you. I have a much greater respect for those that are honest and rich."

"Your degree of respect for honesty, rich or poor, is precisely what I have no manner of concern with. I do not mean to be poor. Poverty is exactly what I have determined against. Honesty, in the something between, in the middle state of worldly circumstances, is all that I am anxious for your not looking down on."

"But I do look down upon it, if it might have been higher. I must look down upon anything contented with obscurity when it might rise to distinction."

"But how may it rise? How may my honesty at least rise to any distinction?"

This was not so very easy a question to answer, and occasioned an "Oh!" of some length from the fair lady before she could add, "You ought to be in parliament, or you should have gone into the army ten years ago."

"*That* is not much to the purpose now; and as to my being in parliament, I believe I must wait till there is an especial assembly for the representation of younger sons who have little to live on. No, Miss Crawford," he added, in a more serious tone, "there *are* distinctions which I should be miserable if I thought myself without any chance—absolutely without chance or possibility of obtaining—but they are of a different character."

A look of consciousness, as he spoke, and what seemed a consciousness of manner on Miss Crawford's side as she made some laughing answer, was sorrowful food for Fanny's observation; and finding herself quite unable to attend as she ought to Mrs. Grant, by whose side she was now following the others, she had nearly resolved on going home immediately, and only waited for courage to say so, when the sound of the great clock at Mansfield Park, striking three, made her feel that she had really been much longer absent than usual, and brought the previous self-enquiry, of whether she should take leave or not just then, and how, to a very speedy issue. With undoubting decision she directly began her adieus; and Edmund began at the same time to recollect that his mother had been enquiring for her, and that he had walked down to the Parsonage on purpose to bring her back.

Fanny's hurry increased; and without in the least expecting Edmund's attendance, she would have hastened away alone; but the general pace was quickened, and they all accompanied her into the house through which it was necessary to pass. Dr. Grant was in the vestibule, and as they stopped to speak to him she found from Edmund's manner that he *did* mean to go with her. He, too, was taking leave. She could not but be thankful. In the moment of parting, Edmund was invited by Dr. Grant to eat his mutton with him the next day; and Fanny had barely time for an unpleasant feeling on the occasion, when Mrs. Grant, with sudden recollection, turned to her and asked for the pleasure of her company too. This was so new an attention, so perfectly new a circumstance in the events of Fanny's life, that she was all surprise and embarrassment; and while stammering out her great obligation, and her—"but she did not suppose it would be in her power," was looking at Edmund for his opinon and help. But Edmund, delighted with her having such an happiness offered, and ascertaining with half a look and half a sentence, that she had no objection but on her aunt's account, could not imagine that his mother would make any difficulty of sparing her, and therefore gave his decided open advice that the invitation should be accepted; and though Fanny would not venture, even on his encouragement, to such a flight of audacious independence, it was soon settled, that if nothing were heard to the contrary, Mrs. Grant might expect her.

"And you know what your dinner will be," said Mrs. Grant, smiling— "the turkey, and I assure you a very fine one; for, my dear," turning to her husband, "cook insists upon the turkey's being dressed to-morrow."

"Very well, very well," cried Dr. Grant, "all the better; I am glad to hear you have anything so good in the house. But Miss Price and Mr. Edmund Bertram, I dare say, would take their chance. We none of us want to hear the bill of fare. A friendly meeting, and not a fine dinner, is all we have in view. A turkey, or a goose, or a leg of mutton, or whatever you and your cook choose to give us."

The two cousins walked home together; and, except in the immediate discussion of this engagement, which Edmund spoke of with the warmest satisfaction, as so particularly desirable for her in the intimacy which he saw with so much pleasure established, it was a silent walk; for having finished that subject, he grew thoughtful and indisposed for any other.

Chapter 23

"BUT why should Mrs. Grant ask Fanny?" said Lady Bertram. "How came she to think of asking Fanny? Fanny never dines there, you know, in this sort of way. I cannot spare her, and I am sure she does not want to go. Fanny, you do not want to go, do you?"

"If you put such a question to her," cried Edmund, preventing his cousin's speaking, "Fanny will immediately say No; but I am sure, my dear mother, she would like to go; and I can see no reason why she should not."

"I cannot imagine why Mrs. Grant should think of asking her? She never did before. She used to ask your sisters now and then, but she never asked Fanny."

"If you cannot do without me, ma'am——" said Fanny, in a self-denying tone.

"But my mother will have my father with her all the evening."

"To be sure, so I shall."

"Suppose you take my father's opinion, ma'am."

"That's well thought of. So I will, Edmund. I will ask Sir Thomas, as soon as he comes in, whether I can do without her."

"As you please, ma'am, on that head; but I meant my father's opinion as to the *propriety* of the invitation's being accepted or not; and I think he will consider it a right thing by Mrs. Grant, as well as by Fanny, that being the *first* invitation it should be accepted."

"I do not know. We will ask him. But he will be very much surprised that Mrs. Grant should ask Fanny at all."

There was nothing more to be said, or that could be said, to any purpose, till Sir Thomas were present; but the subject involving, as it did, her own evening's comfort for the morrow, was so much uppermost in Lady Bertram's mind, that half an hour afterwards, on his looking in for a minute in his way from his plantation to his dressing-room, she called him back again, when he had almost closed the door, with "Sir Thomas, stop a moment—I have something to say to you."

Her tone of calm languor, for she never took the trouble of raising her voice, was always heard and attended to; and Sir Thomas came back. Her story began; and Fanny immediately slipped out of the room; for to her herself the subject of any discussion with her uncle was more than her nerves could bear. She was anxious, she knew—more anxious perhaps than she ought to be—for what was it after all whether she went or stayed? but if her uncle were to be a great while considering and deciding, and with very grave looks, and those grave looks directed to her, and at last decide against her, she might not be able to appear properly submissive and indifferent. Her cause, meanwhile, went on well. It began, on Lady Bertram's part, with—"I have something to tell you that will surprise you. Mrs. Grant has asked Fanny to dinner."

"Well," said Sir Thomas, as if waiting more to accomplish the surprise.
"Edmund wants her to go. But how can I spare her?"

"She will be late," said Sir Thomas, taking out his watch, "but what is your difficulty?"

Edmund found himself obliged to speak and fill up the blanks in his mother's story. He told the whole; and she had only to add, "So strange! for Mrs. Grant never used to ask her."

"But is it not very natural," observed Edmund, "that Mrs. Grant should wish to procure so agreeable a visitor for her sister?"

"Nothing can be more natural," said Sir Thomas, after a short deliberation; "nor, were there no sister in the case, could anything, in my opinion, be more natural. Mrs. Grant's showing civility to Miss Price, to Lady Bertram's niece, could never want explanation. The only surprise I can feel is, that this should be the *first* time of its being paid. Fanny was perfectly right in giving only a conditional answer. She appears to feel as she ought. But as I conclude that she must wish to go, since all young people like to be together, I can see no reason why she should be denied the indulgence."

"But can I do without her, Sir Thomas?"

"Indeed I think you may."

"She always makes tea, you know, when my sister is not here."

"Your sister, perhaps, may be prevailed on to spend the day with us, and I shall certainly be at home."

"Very well, then, Fanny may go, Edmund."

The good news soon followed her. Edmund knocked at her door in his way to his own.

"Well, Fanny, it is all happily settled, and without the smallest hesitation on your uncle's side. He had but one opinion. You are to go."

"Thank you, I am *so* glad," was Fanny's instinctive reply; though when she had turned from him and shut the door, she could not help feeling, "And yet why should I be glad? for am I not certain of seeing or hearing something there to pain me?"

In spite of this conviction, however, she was glad. Simple as such an engagement might appear in other eyes, it had novelty and importance in hers, for excepting the day at Sotherton, she had scarcely ever dined out before; and though now going only half a mile, and only to three people, still it was dining out, and all the little interests of preparation were enjoyments in themselves. She had neither sympathy nor assistance from those who ought to have entered into her feelings and directed her taste; for Lady Bertram never thought of being useful to anybody, and Mrs. Norris, when she came on the morrow, in consequence of an early call and invitation from Sir Thomas, was in a very ill humour, and seemed intent only on lessening her niece's pleasure, both present and future, as much as possible.

"Upon my word, Fanny, you are in high luck to meet with such attention and indulgence! You ought to be very much obliged to Mrs. Grant for thinking of you, and to your aunt for letting you go, and you ought to look upon it as something extraordinary; for I hope you are aware that there is no real occasion for your going into company in this sort of way, or ever dining out at all; and it is what you must not depend upon ever being repeated. Nor must you be fancying that the invitation is meant as any particular compliment to *you;* the compliment is intended to your uncle and aunt and me. Mrs. Grant thinks it a civility due to *us* to take a little notice of you, or else it would never have come into her head, and you may be very certain, that if your cousin Julia had been at home, you would not have been asked at all."

Mrs. Norris had now so ingeniously done away all Mrs. Grant's part of the favour, that Fanny, who found herself expected to speak, could only say that she was very much obliged to her Aunt Bertram for sparing her, and that she was endeavouring to put her aunt's evening work in such a state as to prevent her being missed.

"Oh! depend upon it, your aunt can do very well without you, or you would not be allowed to go. *I* shall be here, so you may be quite easy about your aunt. And I hope you will have a very *agreeable* day, and find it all mighty *delightful.* But I must observe that five is the very awkwardest of all possible numbers to sit down to table; and I cannot but be surprised that such an *elegant* lady as Mrs. Grant should not contrive better! And round their enormous great wide table, too, which fills up the room so dreadfully! Had the Doctor been contented to take my dining table when I came away, as anybody in their senses would have done, instead of having that absurd new one of his own, which is wider, literally wider than the dinner table here, how infinitely better it would have been! and how much more he would have been respected! for people are never respected when they step out of their proper sphere. Remember *that*, Fanny. Five—only five to be sitting round that table. However, you will have dinner enough on it for ten, I dare say."

Mrs. Norris fetched breath, and went on again.

"The nonsense and folly of people's stepping out of their rank and trying to appear above themselves, makes me think it right to give *you* a hint, Fanny, now that you are going into company without any of us; and I do beseech and entreat you not to be putting yourself forward, and talking and giving your opinion as if you were one of your cousins, as if you were dear Mrs. Rushworth or Julia. *That* will never do, believe me. Remember, wherever you are, you must be the lowest and last; and though Miss Crawford is in a manner at home at the Parsonage, you are not to be taking place of her. And as to coming away at night, you are to stay just as long as Edmund chooses. Leave him to settle *that*."

"Yes, ma'am, I should not think of anything else."

"And if it should rain, which I think exceedingly likely, for I never saw it more threatening for a wet evening in my life, you must manage as well as you can, and not be expecting the carriage to be sent for you. I certainly do not go home to-night, and, therefore, the carriage will not be out on my account; so you must make up your mind to what may happen, and take your things accordingly."

Her niece thought it perfectly reasonable. She rated her own claims to comfort as low even as Mrs. Norris could; and when Sir Thomas, soon afterwards, just opening the door, said, "Fanny, at what time would you have the carriage come round?" she felt a degree of astonishment which made it impossible for her to speak.

"My dear Sir Thomas!" cried Mrs. Norris, red with anger, "Fanny can walk."

"Walk!" repeated Sir Thomas, in a tone of most unanswerable dignity, and coming farther into the room. "My niece walk to a dinner engagement at this time of the year! Will twenty minutes after four suit you?"

"Yes, sir," was Fanny's humble answer, given with the feelings almost of a criminal towards Mrs. Norris; and not bearing to remain with her in what might seem a state of triumph, she followed her uncle out of the room, having stayed behind him only long enough to hear these words spoken in angry agitation:—

"Quite unnecessary! a great deal too kind! But Edmund goes; true, it is upon Edmund's account. I observed he was hoarse on Thursday night."

But this could not impose on Fanny. She felt that the carriage was for herself alone; and her uncle's consideration of her, coming immediately after such representations from her aunt, cost her some tears of gratitude when she was alone.

The coachman drove round to a minute; another minute brought down the gentleman; and as the lady had, with a most scrupulous fear of being late, been many minutes seated in the drawing-room, Sir Thomas saw them off in as good time as his own correctly punctual habits required.

"Now I must look at you, Fanny," said Edmund, with the kind smile of an affectionate brother, "and tell you how I like you; and as well as I can judge by this light, you look very nicely indeed. What have you got on?"

"The new dress that my uncle was so good as to give me on my cousin's marriage. I hope it is not too fine; but I thought I ought to wear it as soon as I could, and that I might not have such another opportunity all the winter. I hope you do not think me too fine."

"A woman can never be too fine while she is all in white. No, I see no finery about you; nothing but what is perfectly proper. Your gown seems very pretty. I like these glossy spots. Has not Miss Crawford a gown something the same?"

In approaching the Parsonage they passed close by the stable-yard and coach-house.

"Hey-day!" said Edmund, "here's company, here's a carriage! who have they got to meet us?" And letting down the side-glass to distinguish, "'Tis Crawford's, Crawford's barouche, I protest! There are his own two men pushing it back into its old quarters. He is here, of course. This is quite a surprise, Fanny. I shall be very glad to see him."

There was no occasion, there was no time for Fanny to say how very differently she felt; but the idea of having such another to observe her, was a great increase of the trepidation with which she performed the very awful ceremony of walking into the drawing-room.

In the drawing-room Mr. Crawford certainly was; having been just long enough arrived to be ready for dinner; and the smiles and pleased looks of the three others standing round him, showed how welcome was his sudden resolution of coming to them for a few days on leaving Bath. A very cordial meeting passed between him and Edmund; and with the exception of Fanny, the pleasure was general; and even to *her*, there might be some advantage in his presence, since every addition to the party must rather forward her favourite indulgence of being suffered to sit silent and un-attended to. She was soon aware of this herself; for though she must submit, as her own propriety of mind directed, in spite of her Aunt Norris's opinion, to being the principal lady in company, and to all the little distinctions consequent thereon, she found, while they were at table, such a happy flow of conversation prevailing in which she was not required to take any part—there was so much to be said between the brother and sister about Bath, so much between the two young men about hunting, so much of politics between Mr. Crawford and Dr. Grant, and of every-thing and all together between Mr. Crawford and Mrs. Grant, as to leave her the fairest prospect of having only to listen in quiet, and of passing a very agreeable day. She could not compliment the newly-arrived gentle-man, however, with any appearance of interest in a scheme for extending his stay at Mansfield, and sending for his hunters from Norfolk, which, suggested by Dr. Grant, advised by Edmund, and warmly urged by the two sisters, was soon in possession of his mind, and which he seemed to want to be encouraged even by her to resolve on. Her opinion was sought as to the probable continuance of the open weather, but her answers were as short and indifferent as civility allowed. She could not wish him to stay, and would much rather not have him speak to her.

Her two absent cousins, especially Maria, were much in her thoughts on seeing him; but no embarrassing remembrance affected *his* spirits. Here he was again on the same ground where all had passed before, and appar-ently as willing to stay and be happy without the Miss Bertrams, as if he had never known Mansfield in any other state. She heard them spoken of by him only in a general way, till they were all re-assembled in the draw-ing-room, when Edmund, being engaged apart in some matter of business with Dr. Grant, which seemed entirely to engross them, and Mrs. Grant occupied at the tea-table, he began talking of them with more particu-larity to his other sister. With a significant smile, which made Fanny quite hate him, he said, "So Rushworth and his fair bride are at Brighton, I understand; happy man!"

"Yes, they have been there about a fortnight, Miss Price, have they not? And Julia is with them."

"And Mr. Yates, I presume, is not far off."

"Mr. Yates! Oh! we hear nothing of Mr. Yates. I do not imagine he figures much in the letters to Mansfield Park; do you, Miss Price? I think my friend Julia knows better than to entertain her father with Mr. Yates."

"Poor Rushworth and his two-and-forty speeches!" continued Crawford. "Nobody can ever forget them. Poor fellow! I see him now—his toil and his despair. Well, I am much mistaken if his lovely Maria will ever want him to make two-and-forty speeches to her;" adding, with a momentary seriousness, "She is too good for him—much too good." And then changing his tone again to one of gentle gallantry, and addressing Fanny, he said, "You were Mr. Rushworth's best friend. Your kindness and patience can never be forgotten, your indefatigable patience in trying to make it possible for him to learn his part—in trying to give him a brain which nature had denied—to mix up an understanding for him out of the superfluity of your own! *He* might not have sense enough himself to estimate your kindness, but I may venture to say that it had honour from all the rest of the party."

Fanny coloured, and said nothing.

"It is as a dream, a pleasant dream!" he exclaimed, breaking forth again, after a few minutes' musing. "I shall always look back on our theatricals with exquisite pleasure. There was such an interest, such an animation, such a spirit diffused. Everybody felt it. We were all alive. There was employment, hope, solicitude, bustle, for every hour of the day. Always some little objection, some little doubt, some little anxiety to be got over. I never was happier."

With silent indignation Fanny repeated to herself, "Never happier!— never happier than when doing what you must know was not justifiable! —never happier than when behaving so dishonourably and unfeelingly! Oh! what a corrupted mind!"

"We were unlucky, Miss Price," he continued, in a lower tone, to avoid the possibility of being heard by Edmund, and not at all aware of her feelings, "we certainly were very unlucky. Another week, only one other week, would have been enough for us. I think if we had had the disposal of events—if Mansfield Park had had the government of the winds just for a week or two, about the equinox, there would have been a difference. Not that we would have endangered his safety by any tremendous weather —but only by a steady contrary wind, or a calm. I think, Miss Price, we would have indulged ourselves with a week's calm in the Atlantic at that season."

He seemed determined to be answered; and Fanny, averting her face, said with a firmer tone than usual, "As far as *I* am concerned, sir, I would not have delayed his return for a day. My uncle disapproved it all so entirely when he did arrive, that in my opinion everything had gone quite far enough."

She had never spoken so much at once to him in her life before, and never so angrily to anyone; and when her speech was over, she trembled and blushed at her own daring. He was surprised; but after a few moments' silent consideration of her, replied in a calmer, graver tone, and as if the candid result of conviction, "I believe you are right. It was more pleasant than prudent. We were getting too noisy." And then turning the conversation, he would have engaged her on some other subject, but her answers were so shy and reluctant that he could not advance in any.

Miss Crawford, who had been repeatedly eyeing Dr. Grant and Edmund, now observed: "Those gentlemen must have some very interesting point to discuss."

"The most interesting in the world," replied her brother—"how to make money; how to turn a good income into a better. Dr. Grant is giving Bertram instructions about the living he is to step into so soon. I find he takes orders in a few weeks. They were at it in the dining-parlour. I am glad to heart Bertram will be so well off. He will have a very pretty income to make ducks and drakes with, and earned without much trouble. I apprehend he will not have less than seven hundred a year. Seven hundred a year is a fine thing for a younger brother; and as of course he will still live at home, it will be all his for *menus plaisirs;* and a sermon at Christmas and Easter, I suppose, will be the sum total of sacrifice."

His sister tried to laugh off her feelings by saying, "Nothing amuses me more than the easy manner with which everybody settles the abundance of those who have a great deal less than ourselves. You would look rather blank, Henry, if your *menus plaisirs* were to be limited to seven hundred a year."

"Perhaps I might; but all *that* you know is entirely comparative. Birthright and habit must settle the business. Bertram is certainly well off for a cadet of even a baronet's family. By the time he is four or five and twenty he will have seven hundred a year, and nothing to do for it."

Miss Crawford *could* have said that there would be a something to do and to suffer for it, which she could not think lightly of; but she checked herself and let it pass; and tried to look calm and unconcerned when the two gentlemen shortly afterwards joined them.

"Bertram," said Henry Crawford, "I shall make a point of coming to Mansfield to hear you preach your first sermon. I shall come on purpose to encourage a young beginner. When is it to be? Miss Price, will not you join me in encouraging your cousin? Will not you engage to attend with your eyes steadily fixed on him the whole time—as I shall do—not to lose a word; or only looking off just to note down any sentence preeminently beautiful? We will provide ourselves with tablets and a pencil. When will it be? You must preach at Mansfield, you know, that Sir Thomas and Lady Bertram may hear you."

"I shall keep clear of you, Crawford, as long as I can," said Edmund; "for you would be more likely to disconcert me, and I should be more sorry to see you trying at it than almost any other man."

"Will he not feel this?" thought Fanny. "No, he can feel nothing as he ought."

The party being now all united, and the chief talkers attracting each other, she remained in tranquillity; and as a whist table was formed after tea—formed really for the amusement of Dr. Grant, by his attentive wife, though it was not to be supposed so—and Miss Crawford took her harp, she had nothing to do but to listen; and her tranquillity remained undisturbed the rest of the evening, except when Mr. Crawford now and then addressed to her a question or observation, which she could not avoid answering. Miss Crawford was too much vexed by what had passed to be in a humour for anything but music. With that she soothed herself and amused her friend.

The assurance of Edmund's being so soon to take orders, coming upon her like a blow that had been suspended, and still hoped uncertain and at a distance, was felt with resentment and mortification. She was very angry with him. She had thought her influence more. She *had* begun to think of him; she felt that she had, with great regard, with almost decided intentions; but she would now meet him with his own cool feelings. It was plain that he could have no serious views, no true attachment, by fixing himself in a situation which he must know she would never stoop to. She would learn to match him in his indifference. She would henceforth admit his attentions without any idea beyond immediate amusement. If h~ could so command his affections, *hers* should do her no harm.

Chapter 24

HENRY CRAWFORD had quite made up his mind by the next morning to give another fortnight to Mansfield, and having sent for his hunters, and written a few lines of explanation to the Admiral, he looked round at his sister as he sealed and threw the letter from him, and seeing the coast clear of the rest of the family, said, with a smile: "And how do you think I mean to amuse myself, Mary, on the days that I do not hunt? I am grown too old to go out more than three times a week; but I have a plan for the intermediate days, and what do you think it is?"

"To walk and ride with me, to be sure."

"Not exactly, though I shall be happy to do both, but *that* would be exercise only to my body, and I must take care of my mind. Besides, *that* would be all recreation and indulgence, without the wholesome alloy of labour, and I do not like to eat the bread of idleness. No, my plan is to make Fanny Price in love with me."

"Fanny Price! Nonsense! No, no. You ought to be satisfied with her two cousins."

"But I cannot be satisfied without Fanny Price, without making a small hole in Fanny Price's heart. You do not seem properly aware of her claims to notice. When we talked of her last night, you none of you seemed sensible of the wonderful improvement that has taken place in her looks within the last six weeks. You see her every day, and therefore do not notice it; but I assure you she is quite a different creature from what she was in the autumn. She was then merely a quiet, modest, not plain-looking girl, but she is now absolutely pretty. I used to think she had neither complexion nor countenance; but in that soft skin of hers, so frequently tinged with a blush as it was yesterday, there is decided beauty; and from what I observed of her eyes and mouth I do not despair of their being capable of expression enough when she has anything to express. And then, her air, her manner, her *tout ensemble*, is so indescribably improved! She must be grown two inches, at least, since October."

"Phoo! phoo! This is only because there were no tall women to compare her with, and because she has got a new gown, and you never saw her so well dressed before. She is just what she was in October, believe me. The truth is, that she was the only girl in company for you to notice, and you must have a somebody. I have always thought her pretty—not strikingly pretty—but 'pretty enough,' as people say; a sort of beauty that grows on one. Her eyes should be darker, but she has a sweet smile; but as for this wonderful degree of improvement, I am sure it may all be resolved into a better style of dress, and your having nobody else to look at; and therefore, if you do set about a flirtation with her, you never will persuade me that it is in compliment to her beauty, or that it proceeds from anything but your own idleness and folly."

Her brother gave only a smile to this accusation, and soon afterwards said, "I do not quite know what to make of Miss Fanny. I do not understand her. I could not tell what she would be at yesterday. What is her character? Is she solemn? Is she queer? Is she prudish? Why did she draw back and look so grave at me? I could hardly get her to speak. I never was so long in company with a girl in my life, trying to entertain her, and succeed so ill! Never met with a girl who looked so grave on me! I must try to get the better of this. Her looks say, 'I will not like you, I am determined not to like you'; and I say she shall."

"Foolish fellow! And so this is her attraction after all! This it is, her not caring about you, which gives her such a soft skin, and makes her so much taller, and produces all these charms and graces! I do desire that you will not be making her really unhappy; a *little* love, perhaps, may animate and do her good, but I will not have you plunge her deep, for she is as good a little creature as ever lived, and has a great deal of feeling."

"It can be but for a fortnight," said Henry; "and if a fortnight can kill her, she must have a constitution which nothing could save. No, I will not do her any harm, dear little soul! I only want her to look kindly on me, to give me smiles as well as blushes, to keep a chair for me by herself wherever we are, and be all animation when I take it and talk to her; to think as I think, be interested in all my possessions and pleasures, try to keep me longer at Mansfield, and feel when I go away that she shall be never happy again. I want nothing more."

"Moderation itself!" said Mary. "I can have no scruples now. Well, you will have opportunities enough of endeavouring to recommend yourself, for we are a great deal together."

And without attempting any further remonstrance, she left Fanny to her fate, a fate which, had not Fanny's heart been guarded in a way unsuspected by Miss Crawford, might have been a little harder than she deserved; for although there doubtless are such unconquerable young ladies of eighteen (or one should not read about them) as are never to be persuaded into love against their judgment by all that talent, manner, attention, and flattery can do, I have no inclination to believe Fanny one of them, or to think that with so much tenderness of disposition, and so much taste as belonged to her, she could have escaped heartwhole from the courtship (though the courtship only of a fortnight) of such a man as Crawford, in spite of there being some previous ill opinion of him to be overcome, had not her affection been engaged elsewhere. With all the security which love of another and dis-esteem of him could give to the peace of mind he was attacking, his continued attentions—continued, but not obtrusive, and adapting themselves more and more to the gentleness and delicacy of her character—obliged her very soon to dislike him less than formerly. She had by no means forgotten the past, and she thought as ill of him as ever; but she felt his powers: he was entertaining; and his manners were so improved, so polite, so seriously and blamelessly polite, that it was impossible not to be civil to him in return.

A very few days were enough to effect this; and at the end of those few days, circumstances arose which had a tendency rather to forward his views of pleasing her, inasmuch as they gave her a degree of happiness which must dispose her to be pleased with everybody. William, her brother, the so long absent and dearly loved brother, was in England again. She had a letter from him herself, a few hurried happy lines, written as the ship came up Channel, and sent into Portsmouth with the first boat that left the *Antwerp* at anchor in Spithead; and when Crawford walked up with the newspaper in his hand, which he had hoped would bring the first tidings, he found her trembling with joy over this letter, and listening with a glowing, grateful countenance to the kind invitation which her uncle was most collectedly dictating in reply.

It was but the day before that Crawford had made himself thoroughly master of the subject, or had in fact become at all aware of her having such a brother, or his being in such a ship, but the interest then excited had been very properly lively, determining him on his return to town to apply for information as to the probable period of the *Antwerp's* return from the Mediterranean, etc.; and the good luck which attended his early examination of ship news the first morning, seemed the reward of his ingenuity in finding out such a method of pleasing her, as well as of his dutiful attention to the Admiral, in having for many years taken in the paper esteemed to have the earliest naval intelligence. He proved, however, to be too late. All those fine first feelings, of which he had hoped to be the exciter, were already given. But his intention, the kindness of his intention, was thankfully acknowledged: quite thankfully and warmly, for she was elevated beyond the common timidity of her mind by the flow of her love for William.

This dear William would soon be amongst them. There could be no doubt of his obtaining leave of absence immediately, for he was still only a midshipman; and as his parents, from living on the spot, must already have seen him, and be seeing him perhaps daily, his direct holidays might with justice be instantly given to the sister who had been his best correspondent through a period of seven years, and the uncle who had done most for his support and advancement; and accordingly the reply to her reply, fixing a very early day for his arrival, came as soon as possible; and scarcely ten days had passed since Fanny had been in the agitation of her first dinner visit, when she found herself in an agitation of a higher nature, watching in the hall, in the lobby, on the stairs, for the first sound of the carriage which was to bring her a brother.

It came happily while she was thus waiting; and there being neither ceremony nor fearfulness to delay the moment of meeting, she was with him as he entered the house, and the first minutes of exquisite feeling had no interruption and no witnesses, unless the servants chiefly intent upon opening the proper doors could be called such. This was exactly what Sir Thomas and Edmund had been separately conniving at, as each proved to the other by the sympathetic alacrity with which they both advised Mrs. Norris's continuing where she was, instead of rushing out into the hall as soon as the noises of the arrival reached them.

William and Fanny soon showed themselves; and Sir Thomas had the pleasure of receiving, in his protégé, certainly a very different person from the one he had equipped seven years ago, but a young man of an open, pleasant countenance, and frank, unstudied, but feeling and respectful manners, and such as confirmed him his friend.

It was long before Fanny could recover from the agitated happiness of such an hour as was formed by the last thirty minutes of expectation, and the first of fruition; it was some time even before her happiness could be said to make her happy, before the disappointment inseparable from the alteration of person had vanished, and she could see in him the same William as before, and talk to him, as her heart had been yearning to do, through many a past year. That time, however, did gradually come, forwarded by an affection on his side as warm as her own, and much less encumbered by refinement or self-distrust. She was the first object of his love, but it was a love which his stronger spirits and bolder temper made it as natural for him to express as to feel. On the morrow, they were walking about together with true enjoyment, and every succeeding morrow renewed a tête-à-tête, which Sir Thomas could not but observe with complacency, even before Edmund had pointed it out to him.

Excepting the moments of peculiar delight, which any marked or unlooked-for instance of Edmund's consideration of her in the last few months had excited, Fanny had never known so much felicity in her life, as in this unchecked, equal, fearless intercourse with the brother and

friend, who was opening all his heart to her, telling her all his hopes and
fears, plans, and solicitudes respecting that long thought of, dearly earned,
and justly valued blessing of promotion; who could give her direct and
minute information of the father and mother, brothers and sisters, of
whom she very seldom heard; who was interested in all the comforts and
all the little hardships of her home, at Mansfield; ready to think of every
member of that home as she directed, or differing only by a less scrupulous
opinion, and more noisy abuse of their Aunt Norris, and with whom (perhaps the dearest indulgence of the whole) all the evil and good of their
earliest years could be gone over again, and every former united pain and
pleasure retraced with the fondest recollection. An advantage this, a
strengthener of love, in which even the conjugal tie is beneath the fraternal. Children of the same family, the same blood, with the same first
associations and habits, have some means of enjoyment in their power,
which no subsequent connections can supply; and it must be by a long
and unnatural estrangement, by a divorce which no subsequent connection
can justify, if such precious remains of the earliest attachments are ever
entirely outlived. Too often, alas! it is so. Fraternal love, sometimes
almost everything, is at others worse than nothing. But with William and
Fanny Price it was still a sentiment in all its prime and freshness, wounded
by no opposition of interest, cooled by no separate attachment, and feeling
the influence of time and absence only in its increase.

An affection so amiable was advancing each in the opinion of all who
had hearts to value anything good. Henry Crawford was as much struck
with it as any. He honoured the warm-hearted, blunt fondness of the
young sailor, which led him to say, with his hands stretched towards
Fanny's head: "Do you know, I begin to like that queer fashion already,
though when I first heard of such things being done in England, I could
not believe it, and when Mrs. Brown, and the other women at the Commissioner's at Gibraltar, appeared in the same trim, I thought they were
mad; but Fanny can reconcile me to anything"; and saw, with lively
admiration, the glow of Fanny's cheek, the brightness of her eye, the deep
interest, the absorbed attention, while her brother was describing any of
the imminent hazards, or terrific scenes, which such a period at sea must
supply.

It was a picture which Henry Crawford had moral taste enough to
value. Fanny's attractions increased—increased twofold; for the sensibility which beautified her complexion and illumined her countenance was
an attraction in itself. He was no longer in doubt of the capabilities of her
heart. She had feeling, genuine feeling. It would be something to be loved
by such a girl, to excite the first ardours of her young, unsophisticated
mind! She interested him more than he had foreseen. A fortnight was not
enough. His stay became indefinite.

William was often called on by his uncle to be the talker. His recitals
were amusing in themselves to Sir Thomas, but the chief object in seeking

them was to understand the reciter, to know the young man by his histories; and he listened to his clear, simple, spirited details with full satisfaction, seeing in them the proof of good principles, professional
knowledge, energy, courage and cheerfulness, everything that could
deserve or promise well. Young as he was, William had already seen a great
deal. He had been in the Mediterranean; in the West Indies; in the Mediterranean again; had been often taken on shore by the favour of his captain, and in the course of seven years had known every variety of danger
which sea and war together could offer. With such means in his power he
had a right to be listened to; and though Mrs. Norris could fidget about the
room, and disturb everybody in quest of two needlefuls of thread or a
second-hand shirt button, in the midst of her nephew's account of a
shipwreck or an engagement, everybody else was attentive; and even Lady
Bertram could not hear of such horrors unmoved, or without sometimes
lifting her eyes from her work to say, "Dear me! how disagreeable! I
wonder anybody can ever go to sea."

To Henry Crawford they gave a different feeling. He longed to have
been at sea, and seen and done and suffered as much. His heart was
warmed, his fancy fired, and he felt the highest respect for a lad who,
before he was twenty, had gone through such bodily hardships, and given
such proofs of mind. The glory of heroism, of usefulness, of exertion, of
endurance, made his own habits of selfish indulgence appear in shameful
contrast and he wished he had been a William Price, distinguishing himself and working his way to fortune and consequence with so much self-
respect and happy ardour, instead of what he was!

The wish was rather eager than lasting. He was roused from the reverie
of retrospection and regret produced by it, by some enquiry from Edmund
as to his plans for the next day's hunting; and he found it was as well to
be a man of fortune at once with horses and grooms at his command. In
one respect it was better, as it gave him the means of conferring a kindness
where he wished to oblige. With spirits, courage and curiosity up to anything, William expressed an inclination to hunt and Crawford could
mount him without the slightest inconvenience to himself, and with only
some scruples to obviate in Sir Thomas, who knew better than his nephew
the value of such a loan, and some alarms to reason away in Fanny. She
feared for William; by no means convinced by all that he could relate of
his own horsemanship in various countries, of the scrambling parties in
which he had been engaged, the rough horses and mules he had ridden,
or his many narrow escapes from dreadful falls, that he was at all equal
to the management of a high-fed hunter in an English fox-chase; nor
till he returned safe and well, without accident or discredit, could she be
reconciled to the risk, or feel any of that obligation to Mr. Crawford for
lending the horse, which he had fully intended it should produce. When it
was proved, however, to have done William no harm, she could allow
it to be a kindness, and even reward the owner with a smile when the

animal was one minute tendered to his use again; and the next, with the greatest cordiality, and in a manner not to be resisted, made over to his use entirely so long as he remained in Northamptonshire.

Chapter 25

THE intercourse of the two families was at this period more nearly restored to what it had been in the autumn, than any member of the old intimacy had thought ever likely to be again. The return of Henry Crawford, and the arrival of William Price, had much to do with it, but much was still owing to Sir Thomas's more than toleration of the neighbourly attempts at the Parsonage. His mind, now disengaged from the cares which had pressed on him at first, was at leisure to find the Grants and their young inmates really worth visiting; and though infinitely above scheming or contriving for any the most advantageous matrimonial establishment that could be among the apparent possibilities of anyone most dear to him, and disdaining even as a littleness the being quick-sighted on such points, he could not avoid perceiving, in a grand and careless way, that Mr. Crawford was somewhat distinguishing his niece—nor perhaps refrain (though unconsciously) from giving a more willing assent to invitations on that account.

His readiness, however, in agreeing to dine at the Parsonage, when the general invitation was at last hazarded, after many debates and many doubts as to whether it were worth while, "because Sir Thomas seemed so ill inclined, and Lady Bertram was so indolent!" proceeded from good breeding and good will alone, and had nothing to do with Mr. Crawford, but as being one in an agreeable group; for it was in the course of that very visit, that he first began to think, that anyone in the habit of such idle observations *would have thought* that Mr. Crawford was the admirer of Fanny Price.

The meeting was generally felt to be a pleasant one, being composed in a good proportion of those who would talk and those who would listen; and the dinner itself was elegant and plentiful, according to the usual style of the Grants, and too much according to the usual habits of all to raise any emotion except in Mrs. Norris, who could never behold either the wide table or the number of dishes on it with patience, and who did always contrive to experience some evil from the passing of the servants behind her chair, and to bring away some fresh conviction of its being impossible among so many dishes but that some must be cold.

In the evening it was found, according to the predetermination of Mrs. Grant and her sister, that after making up the whist table there would remain sufficient for a round game, and everybody being as perfectly complying and without a choice as on such occasions they always are, speculation was decided on almost as soon as whist; and Lady Bertram soon found herself in the critical situation of being applied to for her own choice between the games, and being required either to draw a card for whist or not. She hesitated. Luckily Sir Thomas was at hand.

"What shall I do, Sir Thomas? Whist and speculation; which will amuse me most?"

Sir Thomas, after a moment's thought, recommended speculation. He was a whist player himself, and perhaps might feel that it would not much amuse him to have her for a partner.

"Very well," was her ladyship's contented answer; "then speculation, if you please, Mrs. Grant. I know nothing about it, but Fanny must teach me."

Here Fanny interposed, however, with anxious protestations of her own equal ignorance; she had never played the game nor seen it played in her life; and Lady Bertram felt a moment's indecision again; but upon everybody's assuring her that nothing could be so easy, that it was the easiest game on the cards, and Henry Crawford's stepping forward with a most earnest request to be allowed to sit between her ladyship and Miss Price, and teach them both, it was so settled; and Sir Thomas, Mrs. Norris and Dr. and Mrs. Grant being seated at the table of prime intellectual state and dignity, the remaining six, under Miss Crawford's direction, were arranged round the other. It was a fine arrangement for Henry Crawford, who was close to Fanny, and with his hands full of business, having two persons' cards to manage as well as his own; for though it was impossible for Fanny not to feel herself mistress of the rules of the game in three minutes, he had yet to inspirit her play, sharpen her avarice, and harden her heart, which, especially in any competition with William, was a work of some difficulty; and as for Lady Bertram, he must continue in charge of all her fame and fortune through the whole evening; and if quick enough to keep her from looking at her cards when the deal began, must direct her in whatever was to be done with them to the end of it.

He was in high spirits, doing everything with happy ease, and preeminent in all the lively turns, quick resources, and playful impudence that could do honour to the game; and the round table was altogether a very comfortable contrast to the steady sobriety and orderly silence of the other.

Twice had Sir Thomas enquired into the enjoyment and success of his lady, but in vain; no pause was long enough for the time his measured manner needed; and very little of her state could be known till Mrs. Grant was able, at the end of the first rubber, to go to her and pay her compliments.

"I hope your ladyship is pleased with the game."

"Oh dear, yes! Very entertaining, indeed. A very odd game. I do not know what it is all about. I am never to see my cards; and Mr. Crawford does all the rest."

"Bertram," said Crawford, some time afterwards, taking the opportunity of a little languor in the game, "I have never told you what happened to me yesterday in my ride home." They had been hunting together,

and were in the midst of a good run, and at some distance from Mansfield
when his horse being found to have flung a shoe, Henry Crawford had been
obliged to give up, and make the best of his way back. "I told you I lost
my way after passing that old farmhouse, with the yew-trees, because I
can never bear to ask; but I have not told you that, with my usual luck—
for I never do wrong without gaining by it—I found myself in due time
in the very place which I had a curiosity to see. I was suddenly, upon
turning the corner of a steepish downy field, in the midst of a retired
little village between gently rising hills; a small stream before me to be
forded, a church standing on a sort of knoll to my right—which church
was strikingly large and handsome for the place, and not a gentleman or
half a gentleman's house to be seen excepting one—to be presumed the
Parsonage—within a stone's throw of the said knoll and church. I found
myself, in short, in Thornton Lacey."

"It sounds like it," said Edmund; "but which way did you turn after
passing Sewell's farm?"

"I answer no such irrelevant and insidious questions; though were I to
answer all that you could put in the course of an hour, you would never
be able to prove that it was *not* Thornton Lacey—for such it certainly
was."

"You enquired, then?"

"No, I never enquire. But I *told* a man mending a hedge that it was
Thornton Lacey, and he agreed to it."

"You have a good memory. I had forgotten having ever told you half
so much of the place."

Thornton Lacey was the name of his impending living, as Miss Crawford
well knew; and her interest in a negotiation for William Price's knave
increased.

"Well," continued Edmund, "and how did you like what you saw?"

"Very much, indeed. You are a lucky fellow. There will be work for
five summers at least before the place is livable."

"No, no, not so bad as that. The farmyard must be moved, I grant
you; but I am not aware of anything else. The house is by no means bad,
and when the yard is removed, there may be a very tolerable approach
to it."

"The farmyard must be cleared away entirely, and planted up to shut
out the blacksmith's shop. The house must be turned to front the east
instead of the north; the entrance and principal rooms, I mean, must be
on that side, where the view is really very pretty; I am sure it may be
done. And *there* must be your approach, through what is at present
the garden. You must make a new garden at what is now the back of the
house; which will be giving it the best aspect in the world, sloping to the
south-east. The ground seems precisely formed for it. I rode fifty yards up
the lane, between the church and the house, in order to look about me;
and saw how it might all be. Nothing can be easier. The meadows beyond
what *will be* the garden, as well as what now *is*, sweeping round from the

lane I stood in to the north-east, that is, to the principal road through the village, must be all laid together of course; very pretty meadows they are, finely sprinkled with timber. They belong to the living, I suppose; if not, you must purchase them. Then the stream—something must be done with the stream; but I could not quite determine what. I had two or three ideas."

"And I have two or three ideas also," said Edmund, "and one of them is, that very little of your plan for Thornton Lacey will ever be put in practice. I must be satisfied with rather less ornament and beauty. I think the house and premises may be made comfortable, and given the air of a gentleman's residence without any very heavy expense, and that must suffice me; and, I hope, may suffice all who care about me."

Miss Crawford, a little suspicious and resentful of a certain tone of voice, and a certain half-look attending the last expression of his hope, made a hasty finish of her dealings with William Price; and securing his knave at an exorbitant rate, exclaimed, "There, I will stake my last like a woman of spirit. No cold prudence for me. I am not born to sit still and do nothing. If I lose the game, it shall not be from not striving for it."

The game was hers, and only did not pay her for what she had given to secure it. Another deal proceeded, and Crawford began again about Thornton Lacey.

"My plan may not be the best possible; I had not many minutes to form it in; but you must do a good deal. The place deserves it, and you will find yourself not satisfied with much less than it is capable of. (Excuse me, your ladyship must not see your cards. There, let them lie just before you.) The place deserves it, Bertram. You talk of giving it the air of a gentleman's residence. *That* will be done by the removal of the farmyard; for, independent of that terrible nuisance, I never saw a house of the kind which had in itself so much the air of a gentleman's residence, so much the look of a something above a mere parsonage house; above the expenditure of a few hundreds a year. It is not a scrambling collection of low single rooms, with as many roofs as windows; it is not cramped into the vulgar compactness of a square farmhouse; it is a solid, roomy, mansion-like looking house, such as one might suppose a respectable old country family had lived in from generation to generation, through two centuries at least, and were now spending from two to three thousand a year in."

Miss Crawford listened, and Edmund agreed to this. "The air of a gentleman's residence, therefore, you cannot but give it, if you do anything. But it is capable of much more. (Let me see, Mary; Lady Bertram bids a dozen for that queen; no, no, a dozen is more than it is worth. Lady Bertram does *not* bid a dozen. She will have nothing to say to it. Go on, go on.) By some such improvements as I have suggested (I do not really require you to proceed upon my plan, though, by the by, I doubt anybody's striking out a better)—you may give it a higher character. You may raise it into a *place*. From being the mere gentleman's residence, it becomes, by judicious improvement, the residence of a man of education, taste, modern manners, good connections. All this may be stamped on it; and that house receive such an air as to make its owner be set down as the great land-holder of the parish, by every creature travelling the road; especially as there is no real squire's house to dispute the point; a circumstance, between ourselves, to enhance the value of such a situation in point of privilege and independence beyond all calculation. *You* think with me, I hope—(turning with a softened voice to Fanny). Have you ever seen the place?"

Fanny gave a quick negative, and tried to hide her interest in the subject by an eager attention to her brother, who was driving as hard a bargain, and imposing on her as much as he could; but Crawford pursued with, "No, no, you must not part with the queen. You have bought her too dearly, and your brother does not offer half her value. No, no, sir, hands off, hands off. Your sister does not part with the queen. She is quite deter-mined. The game will be yours," turning to her again—"it will certainly be yours."

"And Fanny had much rather it were William's," said Edmund, smiling at her. "Poor Fanny! Not allowed to cheat herself as she wishes!"

"Mr. Bertram," said Miss Crawford, a few minutes afterwards, "you know Henry to be such a capital improver, that you cannot possibly engage in anything of the sort at Thornton Lacey without accepting his help. Only think how useful he was at Sotherton! Only think what grand things were produced there by our all going with him one hot day in August to drive about the grounds, and see his genius take fire. There we went, and there we came home home again; and what was done there is not to be told!"

Fanny's eyes were turned on Crawford for a moment with an expression more than grave—even reproachful; but on catching his, were instantly withdrawn. With something of consciousness, he shook his head at his sister, and laughingly replied, "I cannot say there was much done at Sotherton; but it was a hot day, and we were all walking after each other, and bewildered." As soon as a general buzz gave him shelter, he added, in a low voice, directed solely at Fanny, "I should be sorry to have my powers of *planning* judged of by the day at Sotherton. I see things very differently now. Do not think of me as I appeared then."

Sotherton was a word to catch Mrs. Norris, and being just then in the happy leisure which followed securing the odd trick by Sir Thomas's capital play and her own, against Dr. and Mrs. Grant's great hands, she called out, in high good humour, "Sotherton! Yes, that is a place, indeed, and we had a charming day there. William, you are quite out of luck; but the next time you come, I hope dear Mr. and Mrs. Rushworth will be at home, and I am sure I can answer for your being kindly received by both. Your cousins are not of a sort to forget their relations, and Mr. Rushworth is a most amiable man. They are at Brighton now, you know; in one of the best houses there, as Mr. Rushworth's fine fortune gives them a right to be. I do not exactly know the distance, but when you get back to Portsmouth, if it is not very far off, you ought to go over, and pay your respects to them; and I could send a little parcel by you that I want to get conveyed to your cousins."

"I should be very happy, aunt; but Brighton is almost by Beachy Head; and if I could get so far, I could not expect to be welcome in such a smart place as that—poor scrubby midshipman as I am."

Mrs. Norris was beginning an eager assurance of the affability he might depend on, when she was stopped by Sir Thomas's saying with authority, "I do not advise your going to Brighton, William, as I trust you may soon have more convenient opportunities of meeting; but my daughters would be happy to see their cousins anywhere; and you will find Mr. Rushworth most sincerely disposed to regard all the connections of our family as his own."

"I would rather find him private secretary to the First Lord than anything else," was William's only answer, in an under voice, not meant to reach far, and the subject dropped.

As yet Sir Thomas had seen nothing to remark in Mr. Crawford's behaviour; but when the whist table broke up at the end of the second rubber, and leaving Dr. Grant and Mrs. Norris to dispute over their last play, he became a looker-on at the other, he found his niece the object of attentions, or rather of professions, of a somewhat pointed character.

Henry Crawford was in the first glow of another scheme about Thornton Lacey; and not being able to catch Edmund's ear, was detailing it to his fair neighbour with a look of considerable earnestness. His scheme was to rent the house himself the following winter, that he might have a home of his own in that neighbourhood; and it was not merely for the use of it in the hunting season (as he was then telling her), though *that* consideration had certainly some weight, feeling as he did that, in spite of all Dr. Grant's very great kindness, it was impossible for him and his horses to be accommodated where they now were without material inconvenience; but his attachment to that neighbourhood did not depend upon one amusement or one season of the year; he had set his heart upon having a something there that he could come to at any time, a little homestall at his command, where all the holidays of his year might be spent, and he might find himself continuing, improving, and *perfecting* that friendship and intimacy with the Mansfield Park family which was increasing in value to him every day. Sir Thomas heard and was not offended. There was no want of respect in the young man's address; and Fanny's reception of it was so proper and modest, so calm and uninviting, that he had nothing to censure in her. She said little, assented only here and there, and betrayed no inclination either of appropriating any part of the compliment to herself, or of strengthening his views in favour of Northamptonshire. Finding by whom he was observed, Henry Crawford addressed himself on the same subject to Sir Thomas, in a more everyday tone, but still with feeling.

"I want to be your neighbour, Sir Thomas, as you have, perhaps, heard me telling Miss Price. May I hope for your acquiescence, and for your not influencing your son against such a tenant?"

Sir Thomas, politely bowing, replied: "It is the only way, sir, in which I could *not* wish you established as a permanent neighbour; but I hope, and believe, that Edmund will occupy his own house at Thornton Lacey. Edmund, am I saying too much?"

Edmund, on this appeal, had first to hear what was going on; but, on understanding the question, was at no loss for an answer.

"Certainly, sir, I have no idea but of residence. But, Crawford, though I refuse you as a tenant, come to me as a friend. Consider the house as half your own every winter; and we will add to the stables on your own improved plan, and with all the improvements of your improved plan that may occur to you this spring."

"We shall be the losers," continued Sir Thomas. "His going, though only eight miles, will be an unwelcome contraction of our family circle; but I should have been deeply mortified if any son of mine could reconcile himself to doing less. It is perfectly natural that you should not have thought much on the subject, Mr. Crawford. But a parish has wants and claims which can be known only by a clergyman constantly resident, and which no proxy can be capable of satisfying to the same extent. Edmund might, in the common phrase, do the duty of Thornton, that is, he might read prayers and preach, without giving up Mansfield Park; he might ride over every Sunday, to a house nominally inhabited, and go through divine service; he might be the clergyman of Thornton Lacey every seventh day, for three or four hours, if that would content him. But it will not. He knows that human nature needs more lessons than a weekly sermon can convey; and that if he does not live among his parishioners, and prove himself, by constant attention, their well-wisher and friend, he does very little either for their good or his own."

Mr. Crawford bowed his acquiescence.

"I repeat again," added Sir Thomas, "that Thornton Lacey is the only house in the neighbourhood in which I should not be happy to wait on Mr. Crawford as occupier."

Mr. Crawford bowed his thanks.

"Sir Thomas," said Edmund, "undoubtedly understands the duty of a parish priest. We must hope his son may prove that *he* knows it too."

Whatever effect Sir Thomas's little harangue might really produce on Mr. Crawford, it raised some awkward sensations in two of the others, two of his most attentive listeners—Miss Crawford and Fanny. One of whom, having never before understood that Thornton was so soon and so completely to be his home, was pondering with downcast eyes on what it would be *not* to see Edmund every day; and the other, startled from the agreeable fancies she had been previously indulging on the strength of her brother's description, no longer able, in the picture she had been forming of a future Thornton, to shut out the church, sink the clergyman, and see only the respectable, elegant, modernised and occasional residence of a man of independent fortune, was considering Sir Thomas, with decided ill-will, as the destroyer of all this, and suffering the more from that involuntary forbearance which his character and manner commanded, and from not daring to relieve herself by a single attempt at throwing ridicule on his cause.

All the agreeable of *her* speculation was over for that hour. It was time to have done with cards, if sermons prevailed; and she was glad to find it necessary to come to a conclusion, and be able to refresh her spirits by a change of place and neighbour.

The chief of the party were now collected irregularly round the fire, and waiting the final break-up. William and Fanny were the most detached. They remained together at the otherwise deserted card-table, talking very comfortably, and not thinking of the rest, till some of the rest began to think of them. Henry Crawford's chair was the first to be given a direction towards them, and he sat silently observing them for a few minutes; himself, in the meanwhile, observed by Sir Thomas, who was standing in chat with Dr. Grant.

"This is the assembly night," said William. "If I were at Portsmouth I should be at it, perhaps."

"But you do not wish yourself at Portsmouth, William."

"No, Fanny, that I do not. I shall have enough of Portsmouth and of dancing, too, when I cannot have you. And I do not know that there would be any good in going to the assembly, for I might not get a partner. The Portsmouth girls turn up their noses at anybody who has not a commission. One might as well be nothing as a midshipman. One *is* nothing, indeed. You remember the Gregorys; they are grown up amazing fine girls, but they will hardly speak to *me*, because Lucy is courted by a lieutenant."

"Oh! shame, shame! But never mind it, William (her own cheeks in a glow of indignation as she spoke). It is not worth minding. It is no reflection on *you;* it is no more than what the greatest admirals have all experienced, more or less, in their time. You must think of that, you must try to make up your mind to it as one of the hardships which fall to every sailor's share, like bad weather and hard living, only with this advantage, that there will be an end to it, and there will come a time when you will have nothing of that sort to endure. When you are a lieutenant! Only think, William, when you are a lieutenant, how little you will care for any nonsense of this kind."

"I begin to think I shall never be a lieutenant, Fanny. Everybody gets made but me."

"Oh! my dear William, do not talk so; do not be so desponding. My uncle says nothing, but I am sure he will do everything in his power to get you made. He knows, as well as you do, of what consequence it is."

She was checked by the sight of her uncle much nearer to them than she had any suspicion of, and each found it necessary to talk of something else.

"Are you fond of dancing, Fanny?"

"Yes, very; only I am soon tired."

"I should like to go to a ball with you and see you dance. Have you never any balls at Northampton? I should like to see you dance, and I'd dance with you if you *would,* for nobody would know who I was here, and I should like to be your partner once more. We used to jump about together many a time, did not we? When the hand-organ was in the street? I am a pretty good dancer in my way, but I dare say you are a better." And turning to his uncle, who was now close to them, "Is not Fanny a very good dancer, sir?"

Fanny, in dismay at such an unprecedented question, did not know which way to look, or how to be prepared for the answer. Some very grave reproof, or at least the coldest expression of indifference, must be coming to distress her brother, and sink her to the ground. But, on the contrary, it was no worse than, "I am sorry to say that I am unable to answer your question. I have never seen Fanny dance since she was a little girl; but I trust we shall both think she acquits herself like a gentlewoman when we do see her, which, perhaps, we may have an opportunity of doing ere long."

"I have had the pleasure of seeing your sister dance, Mr. Price," said Henry Crawford, leaning forward, "and will engage to answer every enquiry which you can make on the subject, to your entire satisfaction. But I believe" (seeing Fanny looked distressed) "it must be at some other time. There is *one* person in company who does not like to have Miss Price spoken of."

True enough, he had once seen Fanny dance; and it was equally true that he would now have answered for her gliding about with quiet, light elegance, and in admirable time; but in fact he could not for the life of him recall what her dancing had been, and rather took it for granted that she had been present than remembered anything about her.

He passed, however, for an admirer of her dancing; and Sir Thomas, by no means displeased, prolonged the conversation on dancing in general, and was so well engaged in describing the balls of Antigua, and listening to what his nephew could relate of the different modes of dancing which had fallen within his observation, that he had not heard his carriage announced, and was first called to the knowledge of it by the bustle of Mrs. Norris.

"Come, Fanny, Fanny, what are you about? We are going. Do not you see your aunt is going? Quick, quick! I cannot bear to keep good old Wilcox waiting. You should always remember the coachman and horses. My dear Sir Thomas, we have settled it that the carriage should come back for you and Edmund and William."

Sir Thomas could not dissent, as it had been his own arrangement, previously communicated to his wife and sister; but *that* seemed forgotten by Mrs. Norris, who must fancy that she settled it all herself.

Fanny's last feeling in the visit was disappointment: for the shawl which

Edmund was quietly taking from the servant to bring and put round her shoulders was seized by Mr. Crawford's quicker hand, and she was obliged to be indebted to his more prominent attention.

Chapter 26

WILLIAM'S desire of seeing Fanny dance made more than a momentary impression on his uncle. The hope of an opportunity, which Sir Thomas had then given, was not given to be thought of no more. He remained steadily inclined to gratify so amiable a feeling; to gratify anybody else who might wish to see Fanny dance, and to give pleasure to the young people in general; and having thought the matter over, and taken his resolution in quiet independence, the result of it appeared the next morning at breakfast, when, after recalling and commending what his nephew had said, he added, "I do not like, William, that you should leave Northamptonshire without this indulgence. It would give me pleasure to see you both dance. You spoke of the balls at Northampton. Your cousins have occasionally attended them: but they would not altogether suit us now. The fatigue would be too much for your aunt. I believe we must not think of a Northampton ball. A dance at home would be more eligible; and if— –"

"Ah, my dear Sir Thomas!" interrupted Mrs. Norris, "I knew what was coming. I knew what you were going to say. If dear Julia were at home, or dearest Mrs. Rushworth at Sotherton, to afford a reason, an occasion for such a thing, you would be tempted to give the young people a dance at Mansfield. I knew you would. If *they* were at home to grace the ball, a ball you would have this very Christmas. Thank your uncle, William, thank your uncle!"

"My daughters,' replied Sir Thomas, gravely interposing, "have their pleasures at Brighton, and I hope are very happy; but the dance which I think of giving at Mansfield will be for their cousins. Could we be all assembled, our satisfaction would undoubtedly be more complete, but the absence of some is not to debar the others of amusement."

Mrs. Norris had not another word to say. She saw decision in his looks, and her surprise and vexation required some minutes' silence to be settled into composure. A ball at such a time! His daughters absent and herself not consulted! There was comfort, however, soon at hand. *She* must be the doer of everything: Lady Bertram would of course be spared all thought and exertion, and it would all fall upon *her*. She should have to do the honours of the evening; and this reflection quickly restored so much of her good humour as enabled her to join in with the others, before their happiness and thanks were all expressed.

Edmund, William and Fanny did, in their different ways, look and speak as much grateful pleasure in the promised ball as Sir Thomas could desire. Edmund's feelings were for the other two. His father had never conferred a favour or shown a kindness more to his satisfaction.

Lady Bertram was perfectly quiescent and contented, and had no objections to make. Sir Thomas engaged for its giving her very little trouble; and she assured him "that she was not at all afraid of the trouble; indeed, she could not imagine there would be any."

Mrs. Norris was ready with her suggestions as to the rooms he would think fittest to be used, but found it all prearranged; and when she would have conjectured and hinted about the day, it appeared that the day was settled too. Sir Thomas had been amusing himself with shaping a very complete outline of the business; and as soon as she would listen quietly, could read his list of the families to be invited, from whom he calculated, with all necessary allowance for the shortness of the notice, to collect young people enough to form twelve or fourteen couple: and could detail the considerations which had induced him to fix on the 22nd as the most eligible day. William was required to be at Portsmouth on the 24th; the 22nd would therefore be the last day of his visit; but where the days were so few it would be unwise to fix on any earlier. Mrs. Norris was obliged to be satisfied with thinking just the same, and with having been on the point of proposing the 22nd herself, as by far the best day for the purpose.

The ball was now a settled thing, and before the evening a proclaimed thing to all whom it concerned. Invitations were sent with despatch, and many a young lady went to bed that night with her head full of happy cares as well as Fanny. To her, the cares were sometimes almost beyond the happiness; for young and inexperienced, with small means of choice, and no confidence in her own taste, the "how she should be dressed," was a point of painful solicitude; and the almost solitary ornament in her possession, a very pretty amber cross which William had brought her from Sicily, was the greatest distress of all, for she had nothing but a bit of ribbon to fasten it to; and though she had worn it in that manner once, would it be allowable at such a time, in the midst of all the rich ornaments which she supposed all the other young ladies would appear in? And yet not to wear it! William had wanted to buy her a gold chain too, but the purchase had been beyond his means, and therefore not to wear the cross might be mortifying him. These were anxious considerations; enough to sober her spirits even under the prospect of a ball given principally for her gratification.

The preparations meanwhile went on, and Lady Bertram continued to sit on her sofa without any inconvenience from them. She had some extra visits from the housekeeper, and her maid was rather hurried in making up a new dress for her: Sir Thomas gave orders, and Mrs. Norris ran about; but all this gave *her* no trouble, and as she had foreseen, "there was, in fact, no trouble in the business."

Edmund was at this time particularly full of cares; his mind being deeply occupied in the consideration of two important events now at hand, which were to fix his fate in life—ordination and matrimony—events of such a serious character as to make the ball, which would be very quickly followed by one of them, appear of less moment in his eyes than in those of any other person in the house. On the 23rd he was going to a friend near Peterborough, in the same situation as himself, and they were to receive ordination in the course of the Christmas week. Half his destiny would then be determined, but the other half might not be so very smoothly wooed. His duties would be established, but the wife who was to share, and animate, and reward those duties, might yet be unattainable. He knew his own mind, but he was not always perfectly assured of knowing Miss Crawford's. There were points on which they did not quite agree; there were moments in which she did not seem propitious; and though trusting altogether to her affection, so far as to be resolved (almost resolved) on bringing it to a decision within a very short time as soon as the variety of business before him were arranged, and he knew what he had to offer her, he had many anxious feelings, many doubting hours as to the result. His conviction of her regard for him was sometimes very strong; he could look back on a long course of encouragement, and she was as perfect in disinterested attachment as in everything else. But at other times doubt and alarm intermingled with his hopes; and when he thought of her acknowledged disinclination for privacy and retirement, her decided preference of a London life, what could he expect but a determined rejection? Unless it were an acceptance even more to be deprecated, demanding such sacrifices of situation and employment on his side as conscience must forbid.

The issue of all depended on one question. Did she love him well enough to forgo what had used to be essential points? Did she love him well enough to make them no longer essential? And this question, which he was continually repeating to himself, though oftenest answered with a "Yes," had sometimes its "No."

Miss Crawford was soon to leave Mansfield, and on this circumstance the "no" and the "yes" had been very recently in alternation. He had seen her eyes sparkle as she spoke of the dear friend's letter, which claimed a long visit from her in London, and of the kindness of Henry, in engaging to remain where he was till January, that he might convey her thither; he had heard her speak of the pleasure of such a journey with an animation which had "no" in every tone. But this had occurred on the first day of its being settled, within the first hour of the burst of such enjoyment, when nothing but the friends she was to visit was before her. He had since heard her express herself differently, with other feelings, more checkered feelings; he had heard her tell Mrs. Grant that she should leave her with regret; that she began to believe neither the friends nor the pleasures she was going to were worth those she left behind; and that though she felt she must go, and knew she should enjoy herself when once away, she was already looking forward to being at Mansfield again. Was there not a "yes" in all this?

With such matters to ponder over, and arrange, and rearrange, Edmund could not, on his own account, think very much of the evening which the rest of the family were looking forward to with a more equal degree of strong interest. Independent of his two cousins' enjoyment in it, the evening was to him of no higher value than any other appointed meeting of the two families might be. In every meeting there was a hope of receiving further confirmation of Miss Crawford's attachment; but the whirl of a ballroom, perhaps, was not particularly favourable to the excitement or expression of serious feelings. To engage her early for the two first dances, was all the command of individual happiness which he felt in his power, and the only preparation for the ball which he could enter into, in spite of all that was passing around him on the subject, from morning till night.

Thursday was the day of the ball, and on Wednesday morning Fanny, still unable to satisfy herself as to what she ought to wear, determined to seek the counsel of the more enlightened, and apply to Mrs. Grant and her sister, whose acknowledged taste would certainly bear her blameless; and as Edmund and William were gone to Northampton, and she had reason to think Mr. Crawford likewise out, she walked down to the Parsonage without much fear of wanting an opportunity for private discussion; and the privacy of such a discussion was a most important part of it to Fanny, being more than half ashamed of her own solicitude.

She met Miss Crawford within a few yards of the Parsonage, just setting out to call on her, and as it seemed to her that her friend, though obliged to insist on turning back, was unwilling to lose her walk, she explained her business at once, and observed that if she would be so kind as to give her opinion, it might be all talked over as well without doors as within. Miss Crawford appeared gratified by the application, and after a moment's thought urged Fanny's returning with her in a much more cordial manner than before, and proposed their going up into her room, where they might have a comfortable cose, without disturbing Dr. and Mrs. Grant, who were together in the drawing-room. It was just the plan to suit Fanny; and with a great deal of gratitude on her side for such ready and kind attention, they proceeded indoors, and upstairs, and were soon deep in the interesting subject. Miss Crawford, pleased with the appeal, gave her all her best judgment and taste, made everything easy by her suggestions, and tried to make everything agreeable by her encouragement. The dress being settled in all its grander parts—"But what shall you have by way of necklace?" said Miss Crawford. "Shall not you wear your brother's cross?" And as she spoke she was undoing a small parcel, which Fanny had observed in her hand when they met. Fanny acknowledged her wishes and doubts on this point; she did not know how either to wear the cross, or to refrain from wearing it. She was answered by having a small trinket-box placed before her, and being requested to choose from among several gold chains and necklaces. Such had been the parcel with which Miss Crawford was provided, and such the object of her intended visit: and in the kindest manner she now urged Fanny's taking one for the cross and to keep for her sake, saying everything she could think of to obviate the scruples which were making Fanny start back at first with a look of horror at the proposal.

"You see what a collection I have," said she, "more by half than I ever use or think of. I do not offer them as new. I offer nothing but an old necklace. You must forgive the liberty, and oblige me."

Fanny still resisted, and from her heart. The gift was too valuable. But Miss Crawford persevered, and argued the case with so much affectionate earnestness through all the heads of William and the cross, and the ball, and herself, as to be finally successful. Fanny found herself obliged to yield, that she might not be accused of pride or indifference, or some other littleness; and having with modest reluctance given her consent, proceeded to make the selection. She looked and looked, longing to know which might be least valuable; and was determined in her choice at last, by fancying there was one necklace more frequently placed before her eyes than the rest. It was of gold, prettily worked; and though Fanny would have preferred a longer and a plainer chain as more adapted for her purpose, she hoped, in fixing on this, to be choosing what Miss Crawford least wished to keep. Miss Crawford smiled her perfect approbation; and hastened to complete the gift by putting the necklace round her, and making her see how well it looked. Fanny had not a word to say against its becomingness, and excepting what remained of her scruples, was exceedingly pleased with an acquisition so very apropos. She would rather perhaps have been obliged to some other person. But this was an unworthy feeling. Miss Crawford had anticipated her wants with a kindness which proved her a real friend. "When I wear this necklace I shall always think of you," said she, "and feel how very kind you were."

"You must think of somebody else, too, when you wear that necklace," replied Miss Crawford. "You must think of Henry, for it was his choice in the first place. He gave it to me, and with the necklace I make over to you all the duty of remembering the original giver. It is to be a family remembrancer. The sister is not to be in your mind without bringing the brother too."

Fanny, in great astonishment and confusion, would have returned the present instantly. To take what had been the gift of another person, of a brother too, impossible! It must not be! And with an eagerness and embarrassment quite diverting to her companion, she laid down the necklace again on its cotton, and seemed resolved either to take another or none at all. Miss Crawford thought she had never seen a prettier consciousness. "My dear child," said she, laughing, "what are you afraid of? Do you think Henry will claim the necklace as mine, and fancy you did not come honestly by it? Or are you imagining he would be too much flattered by seeing round your lovely throat an ornament which his money purchased three years ago, before he knew there was such a throat in the world? Or perhaps—looking archly—you suspect a confederacy between us, and that what I am now doing is with his knowledge and at his desire?"

With the deepest blushes Fanny protested against such a thought.

"Well, then," replied Miss Crawford more seriously, but without at all believing her, "to convince me that you suspect no trick, and are as unsuspicious of compliment as I have always found you, take the necklace and say no more about it. Its being a gift of my brother's need not make the smallest difference in your accepting it, as I assure you it makes none in my willingness to part with it. He is always giving me something or other. I have such innumerable presents from him that it is quite impossible for me to value, or for him to remember half. And as for this necklace, I do not suppose I have worn it six times; it is very pretty, but I never think of it; and though you would be most heartily welcome to any other in my trinket-box, you have happened to fix on the very one which, if I have a choice, I would rather part with and see in your possession than any other. Say no more against it, I entreat you. Such a trifle is not worth half so many words."

Fanny dared not make any further opposition; and with renewed but less happy thanks accepted the necklace again, for there was an expression in Miss Crawford's eyes which she could not be satisfied with.

It was impossible for her to be insensible of Mr. Crawford's change of manners. She had long seen it. He evidently tried to please her; he was gallant, he was attentive, he was something like what he had been to her cousins: he wanted, she supposed, to cheat her of her tranquillity as he had cheated them; and whether he might not have some concern in this necklace? She could not be convinced that he had not, for Miss Crawford, complaisant as a sister, was careless as a woman and a friend.

Reflecting and doubting, and feeling that the possession of what she had so much wished for did not bring much satisfaction, she now walked home again, with a change rather than a diminution of cares since her treading that path before.

Chapter 27

On reaching home, Fanny went immediately upstairs to deposit this unexpected acquisition, this doubtful good of a necklace, in some favourite box in the East Room, which held all her smaller treasures; but on opening the door, what was her surprise to find her cousin Edmund there writing at the table! Such a sight having never occurred before, was almost as wonderful as it was welcome.

"Fanny," said he directly, leaving his seat and his pen, and meeting her with something in his hand, "I beg your pardon for being here. I came to look for you, and after waiting a little while in hope of your coming in, was making use of your inkstand to explain my errand. You will find the beginning of a note to yourself; but I can now speak my business, which is merely to beg your acceptance of this little trifle: a chain for William's cross. You ought to have had it a week ago, but there has been a delay from my brother's not being in town by several days so soon as I expected; and I have only just now received it at Northampton. I hope you will like the chain itself, Fanny. I endeavoured to consult the simplicity of your taste; but at any rate I know you will be kind to my intentions, and consider it, as it really is, a token of the love of one of your oldest friends."

And so saying, he was hurrying away, before Fanny, overpowered by a thousand feelings of pain and pleasure, could attempt to speak; but quickened by one sovereign wish she then called out, "Oh! cousin, stop a moment, pray stop!"

He turned back.

"I cannot attempt to thank you," she continued, in a very agitated manner; "thanks are out of the question. I feel much more than I can possibly express. Your goodness in thinking of me in such a way is beyond——"

"If that is all you have to say, Fanny——" smiling, and turning away again.

"No, no, it is not. I want to consult you."

Almost unconsciously she had now undone the parcel he had just put into her hand, and seeing before her, in all the niceness of jewellers' packing, a plain gold chain, perfectly simple and neat, she could not help bursting forth again, "Oh, this is beautiful, indeed! This is the very thing, precisely what I wished for! This is the only ornament I have ever had a desire to possess. It will exactly suit my cross. They must and shall be worn together. It comes, too, in such an acceptable moment. Oh, cousin, you do not know how acceptable it is."

"My dear Fanny, you feel these things a great deal too much. I am most happy that you like the chain, and that it should be here in time for to-morrow; but your thanks are far beyond the occasion. Believe me, I have no pleasure in the world superior to that of contributing to yours. No, I can safely say, I have no pleasure so complete, so unalloyed. It is without a drawback."

Upon such expressions of affection, Fanny could have lived an hour without saying another word; but Edmund, after waiting a moment, obliged her to bring down her mind from its heavenly flight, by saying, "But what is it that you want to consult me about?"

It was about the necklace, which she was now most earnestly longing to return, and hoped to obtain his approbation of her doing. She gave the history of her recent visit, and now her raptures might well be over; for Edmund was so struck with the circumstance, so delighted with what Miss Crawford had done, so gratified by such a coincidence of conduct between them, that Fanny could not but admit the superior power of *one* pleasure over his own mind, though it might have its drawback. It was some time before she could get his attention to her plan, or any answer to her demand of his opinion: he was in a reverie of fond reflection, uttering only now

and then a few half sentences of praise; but when he did awake and understand, he was very decided in opposing what she wished.

"Return the necklace! No, my dear Fanny, upon no account. It would
be mortifying her severely. There can hardly be a more unpleasant sensation than the having anything returned on our hands which we have
given with a reasonable hope of its contributing to the comfort of a friend.
Why should she lose a pleasure which she has shown herself so deserving of?"

"If it had been given to me in the first instance," said Fanny, "I should
not have thought of returning it; but being her brother's present, is not it
fair to suppose that she would rather not part with it, when it is not
wanted?"

"She must not suppose it not wanted, not acceptable, at least; and its
having been originally her brother's gift makes no difference; for as she
was not prevented from offering, nor you from taking it on that account, it
ought not to prevent you from keeping it. No doubt it is handsomer than
mine, and fitter for a ball-room."

"No, it is not handsomer, not at all handsomer in its way, and, for my
purpose, not half so fit. The chain will agree with William's cross beyond
all comparison better than the necklace."

"For one night, Fanny, for only one night, if it *be* a sacrifice—I am sure
you will, upon consideration, make that sacrifice rather than give pain to
one who has been so studious of your comfort. Miss Crawford's attentions
to you have been—not more than you were justly entitled to—I am the
last person to think that *could be,* but they have been invariable; and to
be returning them with what must have something the *air* of ingratitude,
though I know it could never have the *meaning,* is not in your nature, I
am sure. Wear the necklace, as you are engaged to do, to-morrow evening,
and let the chain, which was not ordered with any reference to the ball, be
kept for commoner occasions. This is my advice. I would not have the
shadow of a coolness between the two whose intimacy I have been observing with the greatest pleasure, and in whose characters there is so much
general resemblance in true generosity and natural delicacy as to make
the few slight differences, resulting principally from situation, no reasonable hindrance to a perfect friendship. I would not have the shadow of a
coolness arise," he repeated, his voice sinking a little, "between the two
dearest objects I have on earth."

He was gone as he spoke; and Fanny remained to tranquillise herself as
she could. She was one of his two dearest—that must support her. But the
other: the first! She had never heard him speak so openly before, and
though it told her no more than what she had long perceived, it was a stab,
for it told of his own convictions and views. They were decided. He would
marry Miss Crawford. It was a stab, in spite of every long-standing
expectation; and she was obliged to repeat again and again, that she was
one of his two dearest, before the words gave her any sensation. Could she
believe Miss Crawford to deserve him, it would be—oh, how different

would it be—how far more tolerable! But he was deceived in her; he gave her merits which she had not; her faults were what they had ever been, but he saw them no longer. Till she had shed many tears over this deception, Fanny could not subdue her agitation; and the dejection which followed could only be relieved by the influence of fervent prayers for his happiness.

It was her intention, as she felt it to be her duty, to try to overcome all that was excessive, all that bordered on selfishness, in her affection for Edmund. To call or to fancy it a loss, a disappointment, would be a presumption for which she had not words strong enough to satisfy her own humility. To think of him as Miss Crawford might be justified in thinking would in her be insanity. To her he could be nothing under any circumstances; nothing dearer than a friend. Why did such an idea occur to her even enough to be reprobated and forbidden? It ought not to have touched on the confines of her imagination. She would endeavour to be rational, and to deserve the right of judging of Miss Crawford's character, and the privilege of true solicitude for him by a sound intellect and an honest heart.

She had all the heroism of principle, and was determined to do her duty; but having also many of the feelings of youth and nature, let her not be much wondered at, if, after making all these good resolutions on the side of self-government, she seized the scrap of paper on which Edmund had begun writing to her, as a treasure beyond all her hopes, and reading with the tenderest emotion these words, "My very dear Fanny, you must do me the favour to accept—" locked it up with the chain, as the dearest part of the gift. It was the only thing approaching to a letter which she had ever received from him; she might never receive another; it was impossible that she ever should receive another so perfectly gratifying in the occasion and the style. Two lines more prized had never fallen from the pen of the most distinguished author—never more completely blessed the researches of the fondest biographer. The enthusiasm of a woman's love is even beyond the biographer's. To her, the hand-writing itself, independent of anything it may convey, is a blessedness. Never were such characters cut by any other human being, as Edmund's commonest hand-writing gave! This specimen, written in haste as it was, had not a fault; and there was a felicity in the flow of the first four words, in the arrangement of "My very dear Fanny," which she could have looked at for ever.

Having regulated her thoughts and comforted her feelings by this happy mixture of reason and weakness, she was able, in due time, to go down and resume her usual employments near her Aunt Bertram, and pay her the usual observances without any apparent want of spirits.

Thursday, predestined to hope and enjoyment, came; and opened with more kindness to Fanny than such self-willed, unmanageable days often volunteer, for soon after breakfast a very friendly note was brought from Mr. Crawford to William, stating that as he found himself obliged to go to London on the morrow for a few days, he could not help trying to procure a companion; and therefore hoped that if William could make up his mind to leave Mansfield half a day earlier than had been proposed, he would accept a place in his carriage. Mr. Crawford meant to be in town by his uncle's accustomary late dinner hour, and William was invited to dine with him at the Admiral's. The proposal was a very pleasant one to William himself, who enjoyed the idea of travelling post with four horses, and such a good-humoured, agreeable friend; and, in likening it to going up with dispatches, was saying at once everything in favour of its happiness and dignity which his imagination could suggest; and Fanny, from a different motive, was exceedingly pleased; for the original plan was that William should go up by the mail from Northampton the following night, which would not have allowed him an hour's rest before he must have got into a Portsmouth coach; and though this offer of Mr. Crawford's would rob her of many hours of his company, she was too happy in having William spared from the fatigue of such a journey, to think of anything else. Sir Thomas approved of it for another reason. His nephew's introduction to Admiral Crawford might be of service. The Admiral, he believed, had interest. Upon the whole, it was a very joyous note. Fanny's spirits lived on it half the morning, deriving some accession of pleasure from its writer being himself to go away.

As for the ball, so near at hand, she had too many agitations and fears to have half the enjoyment in anticipation which she ought to have had, or must have been supposed to have, by the many young ladies looking forward to the same event in situations more at ease, but under circumstances of less novelty, less interest, less peculiar gratification, than would be attributed to her. Miss Price, known only by name to half the people invited, was now to make her first appearance, and must be regarded as the queen of the evening. Who could be happier than Miss Price? But Miss Price had not been brought up to the trade of *coming out;* and had she known in what light this ball was, in general, considered respecting her, it would very much have lessened her comfort by increasing the fears she already had of doing wrong and being looked at. To dance without much observation or any extraordinary fatigue, to have strength and partners for about half the evening, to dance a little with Edmund, and not a great deal with Mr. Crawford, to see William enjoy himself, and be able to keep away from her Aunt Norris, was the height of her ambition, and seemed to comprehend her greatest possibility of happiness. As these were the best of her hopes, they could not always prevail; and in the course of a long morning, spent principally with her two aunts, she was often under the influence of much less sanguine views. William, determined to make this last day a day of thorough enjoyment, was out snipe-shooting; Edmund, she had too much reason to suppose, was at the Parsonage; and left alone to bear the worrying of Mrs. Norris, who was cross because the housekeeper would have her own way with the supper, and whom *she* could not avoid though the housekeeper might, Fanny was worn down at last to think everything an evil belonging to the ball, and when sent off with a parting worry to dress, moved as languidly towards her own room, and felt as incapable of happiness as if she had been allowed no share in it.

As she walked slowly upstairs she thought of yesterday; it had been about the same hour that she had returned from the Parsonage, and found Edmund in the East Room. "Suppose I were to find him there again to-day!" said she to herself, in a fond indulgence of fancy.

"Fanny," said a voice at that moment near her. Starting and looking up, she saw across the lobby she had just reached, Edmund himself, standing at the head of a different staircase. He came towards her. "You look tired and fagged, Fanny. You have been walking too far."

"No, I have not been out at all."

"Then you have had fatigues within doors, which are worse. You had better have gone out."

Fanny, not liking to complain, found it easiest to make no answer; and though he looked at her with his usual kindness, she believed he had soon ceased to think of her countenance. He did not appear in spirits; something unconnected with her was probably amiss. They proceeded upstairs together, their rooms being on the same floor above.

"I come from Dr. Grant's," said Edmund, presently. "You may guess my errand there, Fanny." And he looked so conscious, that Fanny could think but of one errand, which turned her too sick for speech. "I wished to engage Miss Crawford for the first two dances," was the explanation that followed, and brought Fanny to life again, enabling her, as she found she was expected to speak, to utter something like an enquiry as to the result.

"Yes," he answered, "she is engaged to me; but (with a smile that did not sit easy) she says it is to be the last time that she ever will dance with me. She is not serious. I think, I hope, I am sure she is not serious; but I would rather not hear it. She never has danced with a clergyman, she says, and she never *will*. For my own sake, I could wish there had been no ball just at—I mean not this very week, this very day; to-morrow I leave home."

Fanny struggled for speech, and said, "I am very sorry that anything has occurred to distress you. This ought to be a day of pleasure. My uncle meant it so."

"Oh yes, yes! and it will be a day of pleasure. It will all end right. I'm only vexed for a moment. In fact, it is not that I consider the ball as ill-timed; what does it signify? But, Fanny," stopping her, by taking her hand, and speaking low and seriously, "you know what all this means. You see how it is; and could tell me, perhaps better than I could tell you, how and why I am vexed. Let me talk to you a little. You are a kind, kind listener. I have been pained by her manner this morning, and cannot get the better of it. I know her disposition to be as sweet and faultless as your own, but the influence of her former companions makes her seem—gives to her conversation, to her professed opinions, sometimes a tinge of wrong. She does not *think* evil, but she speaks it, speaks it in playfulness; and though I know it to be playfulness, it grieves me to the soul."

"The effect of education," said Fanny gently.

Edmund could not but agree to it. "Yes, that uncle and aunt! They have injured the finest mind; for sometimes, Fanny, I own to you, it does appear more than manner; it appears as if the mind itself was tainted."

Fanny imagined this to be an appeal to her judgment, and therefore, after a moment's consideration, said, "If you only want me as a listener, cousin, I will be as useful as I can; but I am not qualified for an adviser. Do not ask advice of *me*. I am not competent."

"You are right, Fanny, to protest against such an office, but you need not be afraid. It is a subject on which I should never ask advice; it is the sort of subject on which it had better never be asked; and few, I imagine, do ask it, but when they want to be influenced against their conscience. I only want to talk to you."

"One thing more. Excuse the liberty; but take care *how* you talk to me. Do not tell me aything now, which hereafter you may be sorry for. The time may come——"

The colour rushed into her cheeks as she spoke.

"Dearest Fanny!" cried Edmund, pressing her hand to his lips with almost as much warmth as if it had been Miss Crawford's, "you are all considerate thought! But it is unnecessary here. The time will never come. No such time as you allude to will ever come. I begin to think it most improbable; the chances grow less and less; and even if it should, there will be nothing to be remembered by either you or me that we need be afraid of, for I can never be ashamed of my own scruples; and if they are removed, it must be by changes that will only raise her character the more by the recollection of the faults she once had. You are the only being upon earth to whom I should say what I have said; but you have always known my opinion of her; you can bear me witness, Fanny, that I have never been blinded. How many a time have we talked over her little errors! You need not fear me; I have almost given up every serious idea of her; but I must be a blockhead indeed, if, whatever befell me, I could think of your kindness and sympathy without the sincerest gratitude."

He had said enough to shake the experience of eighteen. He had said enough to give Fanny some happier feelings than she had lately known, and with a brighter look, she answered, "Yes, cousin, I am convinced that *you* would be incapable of anything else, though perhaps some might not. I cannot be afraid of hearing anything you wish to say. Do not check yourself. Tell me whatever you like."

They were now on the second floor, and the appearance of a housemaid prevented any further conversation. For Fanny's present comfort it was concluded, perhaps, at the happiest moment: had he been able to talk another five minutes, there is no saying that he might not have talked away all Miss Crawford's faults and his own despondence. But as it was, they parted with looks on his side of grateful affection, and with some very precious sensations on hers. She had felt nothing like it for hours. Since the first joy from Mr. Crawford's note to William had worn away, she had been in a state absolutely the reverse; there had been no comfort around, no hope within her. Now everything was smiling. William's good fortune returned again upon her mind, and seemed of greater value than at first. The ball, too—such an evening of pleasure before her! It was now a real animation; and she began to dress for it with much of the happy flutter which belongs to a ball. All went well; she did not dislike her own looks; and when she came to the necklaces again, her good fortune seemed complete, for upon trial the one given her by Miss Crawford would by no means go through the ring of the cross. She had, to oblige Edmund, resolved to wear it; but it was too large for the purpose. His, therefore, must be worn; and having, with delightful feelings, joined the chain and the cross—those memorials of the two most beloved of her heart, those dearest tokens so formed for each other by everything real and imaginary —and put them round her neck, and seen and felt how full of William and Edmund they were, she was able, without an effort, to resolve on wearing Miss Crawford's necklace too. She acknowledged it to be right. Miss Crawford had a claim; and when it was no longer to encroach on, to interfere with the stronger claims, the truer kindness of another, she could do her justice even with pleasure to herself. The necklace really looked very well; and Fanny left her room at last, comfortably satisfied with herself and all about her.

Her Aunt Bertram had recollected her on this occasion with an unusual degree of wakefulness. It had really occurred to her, unprompted, that Fanny, preparing for a ball, might be glad of better help than the upper housemaid's, and when dressed herself, she actually sent her own maid to assist her; too late, of course, to be of any use. Mrs. Chapman had just reached the attic floor, when Miss Price came out of her room completely dressed, and only civilities were necessary; but Fanny felt her aunt's attention almost as much as Lady Bertram or Mrs. Chapman could do themselves.

Chapter 28

HER uncle and both her aunts were in the drawing-room when Fanny went down. To the former she was an interesting object, and he saw with pleasure the general elegance of her appearance, and her being in remarkably good looks. The neatness and propriety of her dress was all that he would allow himself to commend in her presence, but upon her leaving the room again soon afterwards, he spoke of her beauty with very decided praise.

"Yes," said Lady Bertram, "she looks very well. I sent Chapman to her."

"Look well! Oh, yes!" cried Mrs. Norris, "she has good reason to look well with all her advantages; brought up in this family as she has been, with all the benefit of her cousins' manners before her. Only think, my dear Sir Thomas, what extraordinary advantages you and I have been the means of giving her. The very gown you have been taking notice of is your own generous present to her when dear Mrs. Rushworth married. What would she have been if we had not taken her in hand?"

Sir Thomas said no more; but when they sat down to table the eyes of the two young men assured him that the subject might be gently touched again when the ladies withdrew, with more success. Fanny saw that she was approved; and the consciousness of looking well made her look still better. From a variety of causes she was happy, and she soon was made still happier; for in following her aunts out of the room, Edmund, who was holding open the door, said, as she passed him, "You must dance with me, Fanny; you must keep two dances for me; any two that you like, except the first." She had nothing more to wish for. She had hardly ever been in a state so nearly approaching high spirits in her life. Her cousins' former gaiety on the day of a ball was no longer surprising to her; she felt it to be indeed very charming, and was actually practising her steps about the drawing-room as long as she could be safe from the notice of her Aunt Norris, who was entirely taken up in fresh arranging and injuring the noble fire which the butler had prepared.

Half an hour followed, that would have been at least languid under any other circumstances, but Fanny's happiness still prevailed. It was but to think of her conversation with Edmund; and what was the restlessness of Mrs. Norris? What were the yawns of Lady Bertram?

The gentlemen joined them; and soon after began the sweet expectation of a carriage, when a general spirit of ease and enjoyment seemed diffused and they all stood about and talked and laughed, and every moment had its pleasure and its hope. Fanny felt that there must be a struggle in Edmund's cheerfulness, but it was delightful to see the effort so successfully made.

When the carriages were really heard, when the guests began really to assemble, her own gaiety of heart was much subdued: the sight of so many strangers threw her back into herself; and besides the gravity and formality of the first great circle, which the manners of neither Sir Thomas nor Lady Bertram were of a kind to do away, she found herself occasionally called on to endure something worse. She was introduced here and there by her uncle, and forced to be spoken to, and to curtsey, and speak again. This was a hard duty, and she was never summoned to it without looking at William, as he walked about at his ease in the background of the scene, and longing to be with him.

The entrance of the Grants and Crawfords was a favourable epoch. The stiffness of the meeting soon gave way before their popular manners and more diffused intimacies: little groups were formed, and everybody grew comfortable. Fanny felt the advantage; and, drawing back from the toils of civility, would have been again most happy, could she have kept her eyes from wandering between Edmund and Mary Crawford. *She* looked all loveliness—and what might not be the end of it? Her own musings were brought to an end on perceiving Mr. Crawford before her, and her thoughts were put into another channel by his engaging her almost instantly for the two first dances. Her happiness on this occasion was very much à-la-mortal, finely chequered. To be secure of a partner at first was a most essential good—for the moment of beginning was now growing seriously near; and she so little understood her own claims as to think that if Mr. Crawford had not asked her, she must have been the last to be sought after, and should have received a partner only through a series of enquiry, and bustle, and interference, which would have been terrible; but at the same time there was a pointedness in his manner of asking her which she did not like, and she saw his eye glancing for a moment at her necklace, with a smile—she thought there was a smile—which made her blush and feel wretched. And though there was no second glance to disturb her, though his object seemed then to be only quietly agreeable, she could not get the better of her embarrassment, heightened as it was by the idea of his perceiving it, and had no composure till he turned away to some one else. Then she could gradually rise up to the genuine satisfaction of having a partner, a voluntary partner, secured against the dancing began.

When the company were moving into the ball-room, she found herself for the first time near Miss Crawford, whose eyes and smiles were immediately and more unequivocally directed, as her brother's had been, and who was beginning to speak on the subject, when Fanny, anxious to get the story over, hastened to give the explanation of the second necklace: the real chain. Miss Crawford listened; and all her intended compliments and insinuations to Fanny were forgotten: she felt only one thing; and her eyes, bright as they had been before, showing they could yet be brighter, she exclaimed with eager pleasure, "Did he? Did Edmund? That was like himself. No other man would have thought of it. I honour him beyond expression." And she looked around as if longing to tell him so. He was not near, he was attending a party of ladies out of the room; and Mrs. Grant coming up to the two girls, and taking an arm of each, they followed with the rest.

Fanny's heart sunk, but there was no leisure for thinking long even of Miss Crawford's feelings. They were in the ball-room, the violins were playing, and her mind was in a flutter that forbade its fixing on anything serious. She must watch the general arrangements, and see how everything was done.

In a few minutes Sir Thomas came to her, and asked if she were engaged: and the "Yes, sir; to Mr. Crawford," was exactly what he had intended to hear. Mr. Crawford was not far off; Sir Thomas brought him to her, saying something which discovered to Fanny that *she* was to lead the way and open the ball; an idea that had never occurred to her before. Whenever she had thought of the minutiæ of the evening, it had been as a matter of course that Edmund would begin with Miss Crawford; and the impression was so strong, that though *her uncle* spoke the contrary, she could not help an exclamation of surprise, a hint of her unfitness, an entreaty even to be excused. To be urging her opinion against Sir Thomas's, was a proof of the extremity of the case; but such was her horror at the first suggestion, that she could actually look him in the face and say that she hoped it might be settled otherwise; in vain, however; Sir Thomas smiled, tried to encourage her, and then looked too serious, and said too decidedly—"It must be so, my dear," for her to hazard another word; and she found herself the next moment conducted by Mr. Crawford to the top of the room, and standing there to be joined by the rest of the dancers, couple after couple as they were formed.

She could hardly believe it. To be placed above so many elegant young women! The distinction was too great. It was treating her like her cousins! And her thoughts flew to those absent cousins with most unfeigned and truly tender regret, that they were not at home to take their own place in the room, and have their share of a pleasure which would have been so very delightful to them. So often as she had heard them wish for a ball at home as the greatest of all felicities! And to have them away when it was given—and for *her* to be opening the ball—and with Mr. Crawford too! She hoped they would not envy her that distinction *now;* but when she looked back to the state of things in the autumn, to what they had all been to each other when once dancing in that house before, the present arrangement was almost more than she could understand herself.

The ball began. It was rather honour than happiness to Fanny, for the first dance at least: her partner was in excellent spirits, and tried to impart them to her; but she was a great deal too much frightened to have any enjoyment, till she could suppose herself no longer looked at. Young, pretty, and gentle, however, she had no awkwardnesses that were not as good as graces, and there were few persons present that were not disposed to praise her. She was attractive, she was modest, she was Sir Thomas's niece, and she was soon said to be admired by Mr. Crawford. It was enough to give her general favour. Sir Thomas himself was watching her progress down the dance with much complacency; he was proud of his niece; and without attributing all her personal beauty, as Mrs. Norris seemed to do, to her transplantation to Mansfield, he was pleased with himself for having supplied everything else: education and manners she owed to him.

Miss Crawford saw much of Sir Thomas's thoughts as he stood and, having in spite of all his wrongs towards her, a general prevailing desire of recommending herself to him, took an opportunity of stepping aside to say something agreeable of Fanny. Her praise was warm, and he received it as she could wish, joining in it as far as discretion, and politeness, and slowness of speech would allow, and certainly appearing to greater advantage on the subject than his lady did soon afterwards, when Mary, perceiving her on a sofa very near, turned round before she began to dance, to compliment her on Miss Price's looks.

"Yes, she does look very well," was Lady Bertram's placid reply. "Chapman helped her to dress. I sent Chapman to her." Not but that she was really pleased to have Fanny admired; but she was so much more struck with her own kindness in sending Chapman to her, that she could not get it out of her head.

Miss Crawford knew Mrs. Norris too well to think of gratifying *her* by commendations of Fanny; to her, it was as the occasion offered—"Ah! ma'am, how much we want dear Mrs. Rushworth and Julia to-night!" and Mrs. Norris paid her with as many smiles and courteous words as she had time for, amid so much occupation as she found for herself in making up card-tables, giving hints to Sir Thomas, and trying to move all the chaperons to a better part of the room.

Miss Crawford blundered most towards Fanny herself in her intentions to please. She meant to be giving her little heart a happy flutter, and filling her with sensations of delightful self-consequence; and misinterpreting Fanny's blushes, still thought she must be doing so, when she went to her after the two first dances, and said, with a significant look, "Perhaps *you* can tell me why my brother goes to town to-morrow? He says he has business there, but will not tell me what. The first time he ever denied me his confidence! But this is what we all come to. All are supplanted sooner or later. Now, I must apply to you for information. Pray, what is Henry going for?"

Fanny protested her ignorance as steadily as her embarrassment allowed.

"Well, then," replied Miss Crawford, laughing, "I must suppose it to be purely for the pleasure of conveying your brother, and of talking of you by the way."

Fanny was confused, but it was the confusion of discontent; while Miss Crawford wondered she did not smile, and thought her over-anxious, or thought her odd, or thought her anything rather than insensible of pleasure in Henry's attentions. Fanny had a good deal of enjoyment in the course of the evening; but Henry's attentions had very little to do with it. She would much rather *not* have been asked by him again so very soon, and she wished she had not been obliged to suspect that his previous enquiries of Mrs. Norris about the supper hour, were all for the sake of securing her at that part of the evening. But it was not to be avoided: he made her feel that she was the object of all; though she could not say it was unpleasantly done, that there was indelicacy or ostentation in his manner; and sometimes, when he talked of William, he was really not unagreeable, and showed even a warmth of heart which did him credit. But still his attentions made no part of her satisfaction. She was happy whenever she looked at William, and saw how perfectly he was enjoying himself, in every five minutes that she could walk about with him, and hear his account of his partners; she was happy in knowing herself admired; and she was happy in having the two dances with Edmund still to look forward to, during the greatest part of the evening, her hand being so eagerly sought after, that her indefinite engagement with *him* was in continual perspective. She was happy even when they did take place;

but not from any flow of spirits on his side, or any such expressions of tender gallantry as had blessed the morning. His mind was fagged, and her happiness sprung from being the friend with whom he could find repose. "I am worn out with civility," said he. "I have been talking incessantly all night, and with nothing to say. But with *you*, Fanny, there may be peace. You will not want to be talked to. Let us have the luxury of silence." Fanny would hardly even speak her agreement. A weariness, arising probably, in great measure, from the same feelings which he had acknowledged in the morning, was peculiarly to be respected, and they went down their two dances together with such sober tranquillity as might satisfy any looker-on that Sir Thomas had been bringing up no wife for his younger son.

The evening had afforded Edmund little pleasure. Miss Crawford had been in gay spirits when they first danced together, but it was not her gaiety that could do him good; it rather sank than raised his comfort; and afterwards, for he found himself still impelled to seek her again, she had absolutely pained him by her manner of speaking of the profession to which he was now on the point of belonging. They had talked, and they had been silent; he had reasoned, she had ridiculed; and they had parted at last with mutual vexation. Fanny, not able to refrain entirely from observing them, had seen enough to be tolerably satisfied. It was barbarous to be happy when Edmund was suffering. Yet some happiness must and would arise from the very conviction that he did suffer.

When her two dances with him were over, her inclination and strength for more were pretty well at an end; and Sir Thomas, having seen her walk rather than dance down the shortening set, breathless, and with her hand at her side, gave his orders for her sitting down entirely. From that time Mr. Crawford sat down likewise.

"Poor Fanny!" cried William, coming for a moment to visit her, and working away his partner's fan as if for life, "how soon she is knocked up! Why, the sport is but just begun. I hope we shall keep it up these two hours. How can you be tired so soon?"

"So soon! my good friend," said Sir Thomas, producing his watch with all necessary caution; "it is three o'clock, and your sister is not used to these sort of hours."

"Well, then, Fanny, you shall not get up to-morrow before I go. Sleep as long as you can, and never mind me."

"Oh! William."

"What! Did she think of being up before you set off?"

"Oh! yes, sir," cried Fanny, rising eagerly from her seat to be nearer her uncle; "I must get up and breakfast with him. It will be the last time, you know; the last morning."

"You had better not. He is to have breakfasted and be gone by half-past nine. Mr. Crawford, I think you call for him at half-past nine?"

Fanny was too urgent, however, and had too many tears in her eyes for denial; and it ended in a gracious "Well, well!" which was permission.

"Yes, half-past nine," said Crawford to William, as the latter was leaving them, "and I shall be punctual for there will be no kind sister to get up for *me*." And in a lower tone to Fanny, "I shall have only a desolate house to hurry from. Your brother will find my ideas of time and his own very different to-morrow."

After a short consideration, Sir Thomas asked Crawford to join the early breakfast party in that house instead of eating alone; he should himself be of it; and the readiness with which his invitation was accepted convinced him that the suspicions whence, he must confess to himself, this very ball had in great measure sprung, were well founded. Mr. Crawford was in love with Fanny. He had a pleasing anticipation of what would be. His niece, meanwhile, did not thank him for what he had just done. She had hoped to have William all to herself the last morning. It would have been an unspeakable indulgence. But though her wishes were overthrown, there was no spirit of murmuring within her. On the contrary, she was so totally unused to have her pleasure consulted, or to have anything take place at all in the way she could desire, that she was more disposed to wonder and rejoice in having carried her point so far, than to repine at the counter-action which followed.

Shortly afterward, Sir Thomas was again interfering a little with her inclination, by advising her to go immediately to bed. "Advise" was his word, but it was the advice of absolute power, and she had only to rise, and with Mr. Crawford's very cordial adieus, pass quietly away; stopping at the entrance door, like the Lady of Branxholm Hall, "one moment and no more," to view the happy scene, and take a last look at the five or six determined couple, who were still hard at work; and then, creeping slowly up the principal staircase, pursued by the ceaseless country-dance, feverish with hopes and fears, soup and negus, sore-footed and fatigued, restless and agitated, yet feeling, in spite of everything, that a ball was indeed delightful.

In thus sending her away, Sir Thomas perhaps might not be thinking merely of her health. It might occur to him that Mr. Crawford had been sitting by her long enough, or he might mean to recommend her as a wife by showing her persuadableness.

Chapter 29

THE ball was over, and the breakfast was soon over too; the last kiss was given, and William was gone. Mr. Crawford had, as he foretold, been very punctual, and short and pleasant had been the meal.

After seeing William to the last moment, Fanny walked back to the breakfast-room with a very saddened heart to grieve over the melancholy change; and there her uncle kindly left her to cry in peace, conceiving, perhaps, that the deserted chair of each young man might exercise her tender enthusiasm, and that the remaining cold pork bones and mustard in William's plate, might but divide her feelings with the broken egg-shells in Mr. Crawford's. She sat and cried con amore as her uncle intended, but it was con amore fraternal and no other. William was gone, and she now felt as if she had wasted half his visit in idle cares and selfish solicitudes unconnected with him.

Fanny's disposition was such that she could never even think of her Aunt Norris in the meagreness and cheerlessness of her own small house, without reproaching herself for some little want of attention to her when they had been last together; much less could her feelings acquit her of having done and said and thought everything by William, that was due to him for a whole fortnight.

It was a heavy, melancholy day. Soon after the second breakfast, Edmund bade them good-bye for a week, and mounted his horse for Peterborough, and then all were gone. Nothing remained of last night but remembrances, which she had nobody to share in. She talked to her Aunt Bertram; she must talk to somebody of the ball; but her aunt had seen so little of what had passed, and had so little curiosity, that it was heavy work. Lady Bertram was not certain of anybody's dress or anybody's place at supper, but her own. "She could not recollect what it was that she had heard about one of the Miss Maddoxes, or what it was that Lady Prescott had noticed in Fanny; she was not sure whether Colonel Harrison had been talking of Mr. Crawford or of William, when he said he was the finest young man in the room; somebody had whispered something to her; she had forgot to ask Sir Thomas what it could be." And these were her longest speeches and clearest communications: the rest was only a languid "Yes, yes; very well; did you? Did he? I did not see *that;* I should not know one from the other." This was very bad. It was only better than Mrs. Norris's sharp answers would have been; but she being gone home with all the supernumerary jellies to nurse a sick maid, there was peace and good humour in their little party, though it could not boast much beside.

The evening was heavy like the day: "I cannot think what is the matter with me," said Lady Bertram, when the tea-things were removed. "I feel quite stupid. It must be sitting up so late last night. Fanny, you must do something to keep me awake. I cannot work. Fetch the cards; I feel so very stupid."

The cards were brought, and Fanny played at cribbage with her aunt till bedtime; and as Sir Thomas was reading to himself, no sounds were heard in the room for the next two hours beyond the reckonings of the game:—"And *that* makes thirty-one; four in hand and eight in crib. You are to deal, ma'am; shall I deal for you?" Fanny thought and thought again of the difference which twenty-four hours had made in that room and all that part of the house. Last night it had been hope and smiles, bustle and motion, noise and brilliancy, in the drawing-room, and out of the drawing-room and everywhere. Now it was languor, and all but solitude.

A good night's rest improved her spirits. She could think of William the next day more cheerfully; and as the morning afforded her an opportunity of talking over Thursday night with Mrs. Grant and Miss Crawford, in a very handsome style, with all the heightenings of imagination and all the laughs of playfulness, which are so essential to the shade of a departed ball, she could afterwards bring her mind without much effort into its everyday state, and easily conform to the tranquillity of the present quiet week.

They were indeed a smaller party than she had ever known there for a whole day together, and *he* was gone on whom the comfort and cheerfulness of every family meeting and every meal chiefly depended. But this must be learned to be endured. He would soon be always gone; and she was thankful that she could now sit in the same room with her uncle, hear his voice, receive his questions, and even answer them without such wretched feelings as she had formerly known.

"We miss our two young men," was Sir Thomas's observation on both the first and second day, as they formed the very reduced circle after dinner; and in consideration of Fanny's swimming eyes, nothing more was said on the first day than to drink their good health; but on the second it led to something further. William was kindly commended and his promotion hoped for. "And there is no reason to suppose," added Sir Thomas, "but that his visits to us may now be tolerably frequent. As to Edmund, we must learn to do without him. This will be the last winter of his belonging to us, as he has done."

"Yes," said Lady Bertram, "but I wish he was not going away. They are all going away, I think. I wish they would stay at home."

This wish was levelled principally at Julia, who had just applied for permission to go to town with Maria; and as Sir Thomas thought it best for each daughter that the permission should be granted, Lady Bertram, though in her own good nature she would not have prevented it, was lamenting the change it made in the prospect of Julia's return, which would otherwise have taken place about this time. A great deal of good sense followed on Sir Thomas's side, tending to reconcile his wife to the arrangements. Everything that a considerate parent *ought* to feel was advanced for her use, and everything that an affectionate mother *must* feel in promoting her children's enjoyment was attributed to her nature. Lady Bertram agreed to it all with a calm "Yes;" and at the end of a quarter of an hour's silent consideration spontaneously observed, "Sir Thomas, I have been thinking—and I am very glad we took Fanny as we did, for now the others are away we feel the good of it."

Sir Thomas immediately improved this compliment by adding, "Very true. We show Fanny what a good girl we think her by praising her to her face; she is now a very valuable companion. If we have been kind to *her*, she is now quite as necessary to *us*."

"Yes," said Lady Bertram, presently; "and it is a comfort to think that we shall always have *her*."

Sir Thomas paused, half smiled, glanced at his niece, and then gravely replied, "She will never leave us, I hope, till invited to some other home that may reasonably promise her greater happiness than she knows here."

"And *that* is not very likely to be, Sir Thomas. Who should invite her? Maria might be very glad to see her at Sotherton now and then, but she would not think of asking her to live there; and I am sure she is better off here; and besides, I cannot do without her."

The week which passed so quietly and peaceably at the great house in Mansfield had a very different character at the Parsonage. To the young lady, at least, in each family, it brought very different feelings. What was tranquillity and comfort to Fanny was tediousness and vexation to Mary. Something arose from difference of disposition and habit: one so easily satisfied, the other so unused to endure; but still more might be imputed to difference of circumstances. In some points of interest they were exactly opposed to each other. To Fanny's mind, Edmund's absence was really in its cause and its tendency a relief. To Mary it was every way painful. She felt the want of his society every day, almost every hour, and was too much in want of it to derive anything but irritation from considering the object for which he went. He could not have devised anything more likely to raise his consequence than this week's absence, occurring as it did at the very time of her brother's going away, of William Price's going too, and completing the sort of general break-up of a party which had been so animated. She felt it keenly. They were now a miserable trio, confined within doors by a series of rain and snow, with nothing to do and no variety to hope for. Angry as she was with Edmund for adhering to his own notions, and acting on them in defiance of her (and she had been so angry that they had hardly parted friends at the hall), she could not help thinking of him continually when absent, dwelling on his merits and affection, and longing again for the almost daily meetings they lately had. His absence was unnecessarily long. He should not have planned such an absence; he should not have left home for a week, when her own departure from Mansfield was so near. Then she began to blame herself. She wished she had not spoken so warmly in their last conversation. She was afraid she had used some strong, some contemptuous expressions in speaking of the clergy, and *that* should not have been. It was ill-bred; it was wrong. She wished such words unsaid with all her heart.

Her vexation did not end with the week. All this was bad, but she had still more to feel when Friday came round again and brought no Edmund; when Saturday came and still no Edmund; and when, through the slight communication with the other family which Sunday produced, she learned that he had actually written home to defer his return, having promised to remain some days longer with his friend.

If she had felt impatience and regret before—if she had been sorry for what she said, and feared its too strong effect on him—she now felt and feared it all tenfold more. She had, moreover, to contend with one disagreeable emotion entirely new to her—jealousy. His friend Mr. Owen had sisters; he might find them attractive. But at any rate his staying away at a time when, according to all preceding plans, she was to remove to London, meant something that she could not bear. Had Henry returned, as he talked of doing, at the end of three or four days, she should now have been leaving Mansfield. It became absolutely necessary for her to get to Fanny and try to learn something more. She could not live any longer in such solitary wretchedness; and she made her way to the Park, through difficulties of walking which she had deemed unconquerable a week before, for the chance of hearing a little in addition, for the sake of at least hearing his name.

The first half hour was lost, for Fanny and Lady Bertram were together, and unless she had Fanny to herself she could hope for nothing. But at last Lady Bertram left the room, and then almost immediately Miss Crawford thus began, with a voice as well regulated as she could:—

"And how do *you* like your cousin Edmund's staying away so long! Being the only young person at home, I consider *you* as the greatest sufferer. You must miss him. Does his staying longer surprise you?"

"I do not know," Fanny said hesitatingly. "Yes; I had not particularly expected it."

"Perhaps he will always stay longer than he talks of. It is the general way all young men do."

"He did not, the only time he went to see Mr. Owen before."

"He finds the house more agreeable *now*. He is a very—a very pleasing young man himself, and I cannot help being rather concerned at not seeing him again before I go to London, as will now undoubtedly be the case. I am looking for Henry every day, and as soon as he comes there will be nothing to detain me at Mansfield. I should like to have seen him once more, I confess. But you must give my compliments to him. Yes; I think it must be compliments. Is not there a something wanted, Miss Price, in our language—a something between compliments and—and love—to suit the sort of friendly acquaintance we have had together? So many months' acquaintance! But compliments may be sufficient here. Was his letter a long one? Does he give you much account of what he is doing? Is it Christmas gaieties that he is staying for?"

"I only heard a part of the letter; it was to my uncle; but I believe it was very short; indeed I am sure it was but a few lines. All that I heard was that his friend had pressed him to stay longer, and that he had agreed to do so. A *few* days longer, or *some* days longer; I am not quite sure which."

"Oh! if he wrote to his father—but I thought it might have been to Lady Bertram or you. But if he wrote to his father, no wonder he was concise. Who could write chat to Sir Thomas? If he had written to you, there would have been more particulars. You would have heard of balls and parties. He would have sent you a description of everything and everybody. How many Miss Owens are there?"

"Three grown up."

"Are they musical?"

·"I do not at all know. I never heard."

"That is the first question, you know," said Miss Crawford, trying to appear gay and unconcerned, "which every woman who plays herself is sure to ask about another. But it is very foolish to ask questions about any young ladies—about any three sisters just grown up; for one knows, without being told, exactly what they are: all very accomplished and pleasing, and *one* very pretty. There is a beauty in every family; it is a regular thing. Two play on the pianoforte, and one on the harp; and all sing, or would sing if they were taught, or sing all the better for not being taught; or something like it."

"I know nothing of the Miss Owens," said Fanny calmly.

"You know nothing and you care less as people say. Never did tone express indifference plainer. Indeed, how can one care for those one has never seen? Well, when your cousin comes back, he will find Mansfield very quiet; all the noisy ones gone, your brother and mine and myself. I do not like the idea of leaving Mrs. Grant now the time draws near. She does not like my going."

Fanny felt obliged to speak. "You cannot doubt your being missed by many," said she. "You will be very much missed."

Miss Crawford turned her eye on her, as if wanting to hear or see more, and then laughingly said, "Oh yes! missed as every noisy evil is missed when it is taken away; that is, there is a great difference felt. But I am not fishing: don't compliment me. If I *am* missed, it will appear. I may be discovered by those who want to see me. I shall not be in any doubtful, or distant, or unapproachable region."

Now Fanny could not bring herself to speak, and Miss Crawford was disappointed; for she had hoped to hear some pleasant assurance of her power, from one who she thought must know, and her spirits were clouded again.

"The Miss Owens," said she, soon afterwards; "suppose you were to have one of the Miss Owens settled at Thornton Lacey, how should you like it? Stranger things have happened. I dare say they are trying for it. And they are quite in the right, for it would be a very pretty establishment for them. I do not at all wonder or blame them. It is everybody's duty to do as well for themselves as they can. Sir Thomas Bertram's son is somebody; and now he is in their own line. Their father is a clergyman, and their brother is a clergyman, and they are all clergymen together. He is their lawful property; he fairly belongs to them. You don't speak, Fanny; Miss Price, you don's speak. But honestly now, do not you rather expect it than otherwise?"

"No," said Fanny stoutly, "I do not expect it at all."

"Not at all!" cried Miss Crawford, with alacrity. "I wonder at that. But I dare say you know exactly—I always imagine you are—perhaps you do not think him likely to marry at all—or not at present."

"No, I do not," said Fanny softly, hoping she did not err either in the belief or the acknowledgment of it.

Her companion looked at her keenly; and gathering greater spirit from the blush soon produced from such a look, only said, "He is best off as he is," and turned the subject.

Chapter 30

MISS CRAWFORD's uneasiness was much lightened by this conversation, and she walked home again in spirits which might have defied almost another week of the same small party in the same bad weather, had they been put to the proof; but as that very evening brought her brother down from London again in quite, or more than quite, his usual cheerfulness, she had nothing further to try her own. His still refusing to tell her what he had gone for was but the promotion of gaiety; a day before it might have irritated, but now it was a pleasant joke; suspected only of concealing something planned as a pleasant surprise to herself. And the next day *did* bring a surprise to her. Henry had said he should just go and ask the Bertrams how they did, and be back in ten minutes, but he was gone above an hour; and when his sister, who had been waiting for him to walk with her in the garden, met him at last most impatiently in the sweep, and cried out, "My dear Henry, where can you have been all this time?" he had only to say that he had been sitting with Lady Bertram and Fanny.

"Sitting with them an hour and a half!" exclaimed Mary.

But this was only the beginning of her surprise.

"Yes, Mary," said he, drawing her arm within his, and walking along the sweep as if not knowing where he was: "I could not get away sooner; Fanny looked so lovely! I am quite determined, Mary. My mind is entirely made up. Will it astonish you? No: you must be aware that I am quite determined to marry Fanny Price."

The surprise was now complete; for, in spite of whatever his consciousness might suggest, a suspicion of his having any such views had never entered his sister's imagination; and she looked so truly the astonishment he felt, that he was obliged to repeat what he had said and more fully and more solemnly. The conviction of his determination once admitted, it was not unwelcome. There was even pleasure with the surprise. Mary was in a state of mind to rejoice in a connection with the Bertram family, and to be not displeased with her brother's marrying a little beneath him.

"Yes, Mary," was Henry's concluding assurance. "I am fairly caught. You know with what idle designs I began; but this is the end of them. I have (I flatter myself) made no inconsiderable progress in her affections; but my own are entirely fixed."

"Lucky, lucky girl!" cried Mary, as soon as she could speak; "what a match for her! My dearest Henry, this must be my *first* feeling; but my *second,* which you shall have as sincerely, is, that I approve your choice from my soul, and foresee your happiness as heartily as I wish and desire it. You will have a sweet little wife; all gratitude and devotion. Exactly what you deserve. What an amazing match for her! Mrs. Norris often talks of her luck; what will she say now? The delight of all the family, indeed! And she has some *true* friends in it! How *they* will rejoice! But tell me all about it! Talk to me for ever. When did you begin to think seriously about her?"

Nothing could be more impossible than to answer such a question, though nothing could be more agreeable than to have it asked. "How the pleasing plague had stolen on him" he could not say; and before he had expressed the same sentiment with a little variation of words three times over, his sister eagerly interrupted him with "Ah, my dear Henry, and this is what took you to London! This was your business! You choose to consult the Admiral before you made up your mind."

But this he stoutly denied. He knew his uncle too well to consult him on any matrimonial scheme. The Admiral hated marriage, and thought it never pardonable in a young man of independent fortune.

"When Fanny is known to him," continued Henry, "he will dote on her. She is exactly the woman to do away every prejudice of such a man as the Admiral, for she is exactly such a woman as he thinks does not exist in the world. She is the very impossibility he would describe, if indeed he has now delicacy of language enough to embody his own ideas. But till it is absolutely settled—settled beyond all interference—he shall know nothing of the matter. No, Mary, you are quite mistaken. You have not discovered my business yet."

"Well, well, I am satisfied. I know now to whom it must relate, and am in no hurry for the rest. Fanny Price! wonderful, quite wonderful! That Mansfield should have done so much for—that *you* should have found your fate in Mansfield! But you are quite right; you could not have chosen better. There is not a better girl in the world, and you do not want for fortune; and as to her connections, they are more than good. The Bertrams are undoubtedly some of the first people in this country. She is niece to Sir Thomas Bertram; that will be enough for the world. But go on, go on. Tell me more. What are your plans? Does she know her own happiness?"

"No."

"What are you waiting for?"

"For—for very little more than opportunity. Mary, she is not like her cousins; but I think I shall not ask in vain."

"Oh no! you cannot. Were you even less pleasing—supposing her not to love you already (of which, however, I can have little doubt)—you would be safe. The gentleness and gratitude of her disposition would secure her all your own immediately. From my soul I do not think she would marry you *without* love; that is, if there is a girl in the world capable of being uninfluenced by ambition, I can suppose it her; but ask her to love you, and she will never have the heart to refuse."

As soon as her eagerness could rest in silence, he was as happy to tell as she could be to listen; and a conversation followed almost as deeply interesting to her as to himself, though he had in fact nothing to relate but his own sensations, nothing to dwell on but Fanny's charms. Fanny's beauty of face and figure, Fanny's graces of manner and goodness of heart, were the exhaustless theme. The gentleness, modesty, and sweetness of her character were warmly expatiated on; that sweetness which makes so essential a part of every woman's worth in the judgment of man, that though he sometimes loves where it is not, he can never believe it absent. Her temper he had good reason to depend on and to praise. He had often seen it tried. Was there one of the family, excepting Edmund, who had not in some way or other continually exercised her patience and forbearance? Her affections were evidently strong. To see her with her brother! What could more delightfully prove that the warmth of her heart was equal to its gentleness? What could be more encouraging to a man who had her love in view? Then, her understanding was beyond every suspicion, quick and clear: and her manners were the mirror of her own modest and elegant mind. Nor was this all. Henry Crawford had too much sense not to feel the worth of good principles in a wife, though he was too little accustomed to serious reflection to know them by their proper name; but when he talked of her having such a steadiness and regularity of conduct, such a high notion of honour, and such an observance of decorum as might warrant any man in the fullest dependence on her faith and integrity, he expressed what was inspired by the knowledge of her being well principled and religious.

"I could so wholly and absolutely confide in her," said he, "and *that* is what I want."

Well might his sister, believing as she really did that his opinion of Fanny Price was scarcely beyond her merits, rejoice in her prospects.

"The more I think of it," she cried, "the more am I convinced that you are doing quite right; and though I should never have selected Fanny Price as the girl most likely to attach you, I am now persuaded she is the very one to make you happy. Your wicked project upon her peace turns out a clever thought indeed. You will both find your good in it."

"It was bad, very bad in me against such a creature; but I did not know her then; and she shall have no reason to lament the hour that first put it into my head. I will make her very happy, Mary; happier than she has ever yet been herself, or ever seen anybody else. I will not take her from Northamptonshire. I shall let Everingham, and rent a place in this neighbourhood; perhaps Stanwix Lodge. I shall let a seven years' lease of Everingham. I am sure of an excellent tenant at half a word. I could name three people now, who would give me my own terms and thank me."

"Ha!" cried Mary; "settle in Northamptonshire! That is pleasant! Then we shall be all together."

When she had spoken it, she recollected herself, and wished it unsaid; but there was no need of confusion; for her brother saw her only as the supposed inmate of Mansfield Parsonage, and replied but to invite her in the kindest manner to his own house, and to claim the best right in her.

"You must give us more than half your time," said he. "I cannot admit Mrs. Grant to have an equal claim with Fanny and myself, for we shall both have a right in you. Fanny will be so truly your sister!"

Mary had only to be grateful and give general assurances; but she was now very fully purposed to be the guest of neither brother nor sister many months longer.

"You will divide your year between London and Northamptonshire?"

"Yes."

"That's right; and in London, of course, a house of your own; no longer with the Admiral. My dearest Henry, the advantage to you of getting away from the Admiral before your manners are hurt by the contagion of his, before you have contracted any of his foolish opinions, or learned to sit over your dinner, as if it were the best blessing of life! *You* are not sensible of the gain, for your regard for him has blinded you; but, in my estimation, your marrying early may be the saving of you. To have seen you grow like the Admiral in word or deed, look or gesture, would have broken my heart."

"Well, well, we do not think quite alike here. The Admiral has his faults, but he is a very good man, and has been more than a father to me. Few fathers would have let me have my own way half so much. You must not prejudice Fanny against him. I must have them love one another."

Mary refrained from saying what she felt, that there could not be two persons in existence whose characters and manners were less accordant: time would discover it to him; but she could not help *this* reflection on the Admiral. "Henry, I think so highly of Fanny Price that if I could suppose the next Mrs. Crawford would have half the reason which my poor ill-used aunt had to abhor the very name, I would prevent the marriage, if possible; but I know you: I know that a wife you *loved* would be the happiest of women, and that even when you ceased to love, she would yet find in you the liberality and good-breeding of a gentleman."

The impossibility of not doing everything in the world to make Fanny Price happy, or of ceasing to love Fanny Price, was of course the ground-work of his eloquent answer.

"Had you seen her this morning, Mary," he continued, "attending with such ineffable sweetness and patience to all the demands of her aunt's stupidity, working with her, and for her, her colour beautifully heightened as she leant over the work, then returning to her seat to finish a note which she was previously engaged in writing for that stupid woman's service, and all this with such unpretending gentleness, so much as if it were a matter of course that she was not to have a moment at her own command, her hair arranged as neatly as it always is, and one little curl falling forward as she wrote, which she now and then shook back, and in the midst of all this, still speaking at intervals to *me,* or listening, and as if she liked to listen, to what I said. Had you seen her so, Mary, you would not have implied the possibility of her power over my heart ever ceasing."

"My dearest Henry," cried Mary, stopping short, and smiling in his face, "how glad I am to see you so much in love! It quite delights me. But what will Mrs. Rushworth and Julia say?"

"I care neither what they say nor what they feel. They will now see what sort of woman it is that can attach me, that can attach a man of sense. I wish the discovery may do them any good. And they will now see their cousin treated as she ought to be, and I wish they may be heartily ashamed of their own abominable neglect and unkindness. They will be angry," he added, after a moment's silence, and in a cooler tone: "Mrs. Rushworth will be very angry. It will be a bitter pill to her; that is, like other bitter pills, it will have two moments' ill flavour, and then be swallowed and forgotten; for I am not such a coxcomb as to suppose her feelings more lasting than other women's, though *I* was the object of them. Yes, Mary, my Fanny will feel a difference, indeed; a daily, hourly difference, in the behaviour of every being who approaches her; and it will be the completion of my happiness to know that I am the doer of it; that I am the person to give the consequence so justly her due. Now she is dependent, helpless, friendless, neglected, forgotten."

"Nay, Henry, not by all; not forgotten by all; not friendless, or forgotten. Her cousin Edmund never forgets her."

"Edmund! True, I believe he is, generally speaking, kind to her, and so is Sir Thomas in his way; but it is the way of a rich, superior, long-worded, arbitrary uncle. What can Sir Thomas and Edmund together do, what *do* they do for her happiness, comfort, honour, and dignity in the world, to what I *shall* do?"

Chapter 31

HENRY CRAWFORD was at Mansfield Park again the next morning, and at an earlier hour than common visiting warrants. The two ladies were together in the breakfast-room, and, fortunately for him, Lady Bertram was on the very point of quitting it as he entered. She was almost at the door, and not choosing by any means to take so much trouble in vain, she still went on, after a civil reception, a short sentence about being waited for, and a "Let Sir Thomas know," to the servant.

Henry, overjoyed to have her go, bowed and watched her off, and without losing another moment, turned instantly to Fanny, and, taking out some letters, said, with a most animated look, "I must acknowledge myself infinitely obliged to any creature who gives me such an opportunity of seeing you alone: I have been wishing it more than you can have any idea. Knowing as I do what your feelings as a sister are, I could hardly have borne that any one in the house should share with you in the first knowledge of the news I now bring. He is made. Your brother is a lieutenant. I have the infinite satisfaction of congratulating you on your brother's promotion. Here are the letters which announce it, this moment come to hand. You will perhaps, like to see them."

Fanny could not speak, but he did not want her to speak. To see the expression of her eyes, the change of her complexion, the progress of her feelings, their doubt, confusion, and felicity was enough. She took the letters as he gave them. The first was from the Admiral to inform his nephew, in a few words, of his having succeeded in the object he had undertaken, the promotion of young Price, and enclosing two more, one from the Secretary of the First Lord to a friend, whom the Admiral had set to work in the business; the other from that friend to himself, by which it appeared that his lordship had the very great happiness of attending to the recommendation of Sir Charles; that Sir Charles was much delighted in having such an opportunity of proving his regard for Admiral Crawford, and that the circumstance of Mr. William Price's commission as Second Lieutenant of H.M. Sloop Thrush, being made out, was spreading general joy through a wide circle of great people.

While her hand was trembling under these letters, her eye running from one to the other, and her heart swelling with emotion, Crawford thus continued, with unfeigned eagerness, to express his interest in the event:—

"I will not talk of my own happiness," said he, "great as it is, for I think only of yours. Compared with you, who has a right to be happy? I have almost grudged myself my own prior knowledge of what you ought to have known before all the world. I have not lost a moment, however. The post was late this morning, but there has not been since a moment's delay. How impatient, how anxious, how wild I have been on the subject, I will not attempt to describe; how severely mortified, how cruelly disappointed, in not having it finished while I was in London! I was kept there from day to day in the hope of it, for nothing less dear to me than such an object would have detained me half the time from Mansfield. But though my uncle entered into my wishes with all the warmth I could desire, and exerted himself immediately, there were difficulties from the absence of one friend, and the engagements of another which at last I could no longer bear to stay the end of, and knowing in what good hands I left the cause, I came away on Monday, trusting that many posts would not pass before I should be followed by such very letters as these. My uncle, who is the very best man in the world, has exerted himself, as I knew he would, after seeing your brother. He was delighted with him. I would not allow myself yesterday to say *how* delighted, or to repeat half that the Admiral said in his praise. I deferred it all till his praise should be proved the praise of a friend, as this day *does* prove it. *Now* I may say that even *I* could not require William Price to excite a greater interest or be followed by warmer wishes and higher commendation, than were most voluntarily bestowed by my uncle after the evening they had passed together."

"Has this been all *your* doing, then?" cried Fanny. "Good heaven! how very, very kind! Have you really—was it by *your* desire? I beg your pardon, but I am bewildered. Did Admiral Crawford apply? How was it? I am stupefied."

Henry was most happy to make it more intelligible, by beginning at an earlier stage, and explaining very particularly what he had done. His last journey to London had been undertaken with no other view than that of introducing her brother in Hill Street, and prevailing on the Admiral to exert whatever interest he might have for getting him on. This had been his business. He had communicated it to no creature; he had not breathed a syllable of it even to Mary; while uncertain of the issue, he could not have borne any participation of his feelings, but this had been his business; and he spoke with such a glow of what his solicitude had been, and used such strong expressions, was so abounding in the *deepest interest,* in *twofold motives,* in *views and wishes more than could be told,* that Fanny could not have remained insensible of his drift, had she been able to attend; but her heart was so full and her senses still so astonished, that she could listen but imperfectly even to what he told her of William, and saying only when he paused, "How kind! how very kind! Oh, Mr. Crawford, we are infinitely obliged to you! Dearest, dearest William!" She jumped up and moved in haste towards the door, crying out, "I will go to my uncle. My uncle ought to know it as soon as possible." But this could not be suffered. The opportunity was too fair, and his feelings too impatient. He was after her immediately. "She must not go, she must allow him five minutes longer," and he took her hand and led her back to her seat, and was in the middle of his further explanation, before she had suspected for what she was detained. When she did understand it, however, and found herself expected to believe that *she* had created sensations which his heart had never known before, and that everything he had done for William was to be placed to the account of his excessive and unequalled attachment to her, she was exceedingly distressed, and for some moments unable to speak. She considered it all as nonsense, as mere trifling and gallantry, which meant only to deceive for the hour; she could not but feel that it was treating her improperly and unworthily, and in such a way as she had not deserved; but it was like himself, and entirely of a piece with what she had seen before; and she would not allow herself to show half the displeasure she felt, because he had been conferring an obligation, which no want of delicacy on his part could make a trifle to her. While her heart was still bounding with joy and gratitude on William's behalf, she could not be severely resentful of anything that injured only herself; and after having twice drawn back her hand, and twice attempted in vain to turn away from him, she got up, and said only, with much agitation, "Don't, Mr. Crawford, pray don't! I beg you would not. This is a sort of talking which is very unpleasant to me. I must go away. I cannot bear it." But he was still talking on, describing his affection, soliciting a return, and finally, in words so plain as to bear but one meaning even to *her,* offering himself, hand, fortune, everything to her acceptance. It was so; he had said it. Her astonishment and confusion increased; and though still not knowing how to suppose him serious, she could hardly stand. He pressed for an answer.

"No, no, no!" she cried, hiding her face. "This is all nonsense. Do not distress me. I can hear no more of this. Your kindness to William makes me more obliged to you than words can express; but I do not want, I cannot bear, I must not listen to such—no, no, don't think of me. But you are *not* thinking of me. I know it is all nothing."

She had burst away from him, and at that moment Sir Thomas was heard speaking to a servant in his way towards the room they were in. It was no time for further assurances or entreaty, though to part with her at a moment when her modesty alone seemed, to his sanguine and pre-assured mind, to stand in the way of the happiness he sought, was a cruel necessity. She rushed out at an opposite door from the one her uncle was approaching, and was walking up and down the East Room in the utmost confusion of contrary feeling, before Sir Thomas's politeness or apologies were over, or he had reached the beginning of the joyful intelligence which his visitor came to communicate.

She was feeling, thinking, trembling, about everything; agitated, happy, miserable, infinitely obliged, absolutely angry. It was all beyond belief! He was inexcusable, incomprehensible! But such were his habits, that he could do nothing without a mixture of evil. He had previously made her the happiest of human beings, and now he had insulted—she knew not what to say—how to class, or how to regard it. She would not have him be serious, and yet what could excuse the use of such words and offers, if they meant but to trifle?

But William was a lieutenant. *That* was a fact beyond a doubt, and without an alloy. She would think of it for ever and forget all the rest. Mr. Crawford would certainly never address her so again; he must have seen how unwelcome it was to her; and in that case, how gratefully she could esteem him for his friendship to William!

She would not stir further from the East Room than the head of the great staircase, till she had satisfied herself of Mr. Crawford's having left the house; but when convinced of his being gone, she was eager to go down and be with her uncle, and have all the happiness of his joy as well as her own, and all the benefit of his information or his conjectures as to what would now be William's destination. Sir Thomas was as joyful as she could desire, and very kind and communicative; and she had so comfortable a talk with him about William as to make her feel as if nothing had occurred to vex her, till she found, towards the close, that Mr. Crawford was engaged to return and dine there that very day. This was a most unwelcome hearing, for though *he* might think nothing of what had passed, it would be quite distressing to her to see him again so soon.

She tried to get the better of it; tried very hard, as the dinner hour approached, to feel and appear as usual; but it was quite impossible for her not to look most shy and uncomfortable when their visitor entered the room. She could not have supposed it in the power of any concurrence of circumstances to give her so many painful sensations on the first day of hearing of William's promotion.

Mr. Crawford was not only in the room—he was soon close to her. He

had a note to deliver from his sister. Fanny could not look at him, but
there was no consciousness of past folly in his voice. She opened her note
immediately, glad to have anything to do, and happy, as she read it, to
feel that the fidgetings of her Aunt Norris, who was also to dine there,
screened her a little from view.

"MY DEAR FANNY—for so I may now always call you, to the infinite
relief of a tongue that has been stumbling at *Miss Price* for at least the
last six weeks: I cannot let my brother go without sending you a few lines
of general congratulation, and giving my most joyful consent and ap-
proval. Go on, my dear Fanny, and without fear; there can be no difficulties worth naming. I choose to suppose that the assurance of *my* consent
will be something; so you may smile upon him with your sweetest smiles
this afternoon, and send him back to me even happier than he goes.—
Yours affectionately,

"M. C."

These were not expressions to do Fanny any good; for though she read
in too much haste and confusion to form the clearest judgment of Miss
Crawford's meaning, it was evident that she meant to compliment her on
her brother's attachment, and even to *appear* to believe it serious. She
did not know what to do, or what to think. There was wretchedness in the
idea of its being serious; there was perplexity and agitation every way.
She was distressed whenever Mr. Crawford spoke to her, and he spoke to
her much too often; and she was afraid there was a something in his voice
and manner in addressing her very different from what they were when
he talked to the others. Her comfort in that day's dinner was quite
destroyed: she could hardly eat anything; and when Sir Thomas good-
humouredly observed that joy had taken away her appetite she was ready
to sink with shame, from the dread of Mr. Crawford's interpretation; for
though nothing could have tempted her to turn her eyes to the right hand,
where he sat, she felt that *his* were immediately directed towards her.

She was more silent than ever. She would hardly join even when William was the subject, for his commission came all from the right hand
too, and there was pain in the connection.

She thought Lady Bertram sat longer than ever, and began to be in
despair of ever getting away; but at last they were in the drawing-room,
and she was able to think as she would, while her aunts finished the subject of William's appointment, in their own style.

Mrs. Norris seemed as much delighted with the saving it would be to
Sir Thomas as with any part of it. "*Now* William would be able to keep
himself, which would make a vast difference to his uncle, for it was unknown how much he had cost his uncle; and, indeed, it would make some
difference in *her* presents too. She was very glad that she had given
William what she did at parting, very glad, indeed, that it had been in
her power, without material inconvenience, just at that time to give him

something rather considerable; that is, for *her*, with *her* limited means, for now it would all be useful in helping to fit up his cabin. She knew he must be at some expense, that he would have many things to buy, though to be sure his father and mother would be able to put him in the way of getting everything very cheap; but she was very glad she had contributed her mite towards it."

"I am glad you gave him something considerable," said Lady Bertram, with most unsuspicious calmness, "for *I* gave him only £10."

"Indeed!" cried Mrs. Norris, reddening. "Upon my word, he must have gone off with his pockets well lined, and at no expense for his journey to London either!"

"Sir Thomas told me £10 would be enough."

Mrs. Norris being not at all inclined to question its sufficiency began to take the matter in another point.

"It is amazing," said she, "how much young people cost their friends, what with bringing them up and putting them out in the world! They little think how much it comes to, or what their parents, or their uncles and aunts pay for them in the course of the year. Now, here are my sister Price's children; take them all together, I dare say nobody would believe what a sum they cost Sir Thomas every year, to say nothing of what *I* do for them."

"Very true, sister, as you say. But, poor things! They cannot help it; and you know it makes very little difference to Sir Thomas. Fanny, William must not forget my shawl, if he goes to the East Indies; and I shall give him a commission for anything else that is worth having. I wish he may go to the East Indies, that I may have my shawl. I think I will have two shawls, Fanny."

Fanny, meanwhile, speaking only when she could not help it, was very earnestly trying to understand what Mr. and Miss Crawford were at. There was everything in the world *against* their being serious, but his words and manner. Everything natural, probable, reasonable, was against it; all their habits and ways of thinking, and all her own demerits. How could *she* have excited serious attachment in a man who had seen so many, and been admired by so many, and flirted with so many, infinitely her superiors; who seemed so little open to serious impressions, even where pains had been taken to please him; who thought so slightly, so carelessly, so unfeelingly on all such points; who was everything to everybody, and seemed to find no one essential to him? And further, how could it be supposed that his sister, with all her high and worldly notions of matrimony, would be forwarding anything of a serious nature in such a quarter? Nothing could be more unnatural in either. Fanny was ashamed of her own doubts. Everything might be possible rather than serious attachment, or serious approbation of it towards her. She had quite convinced herself of this before Sir Thomas and Mr. Crawford joined them. The difficulty was in maintaining the conviction quite so absolutely after Mr. Crawford was in the room; for once or twice a look seemed forced on her which she did not know how to class among the common meaning; in any other man, at least, she would have said that it meant something very earnest, very pointed. But she still tried to believe it no more than what he might often have expressed towards her cousins and fifty other women.

She thought he was wishing to speak to her unheard by the rest. She fancied he was trying for it the whole evening at intervals, whenever Sir Thomas was out of the room, or at all engaged with Mrs. Norris, and she carefully refused him every opportunity.

At last—it seemed an at last to Fanny's nervousness, though not remarkably late—he began to talk of going away; but the comfort of the sound was impaired by his turning to her the next moment, and saying, "Have you nothing to send to Mary? No answer to her note? She will be disappointed if she receives nothing from you. Pray write to her, if it be only a line."

"Oh yes! certainly," cried Fanny, rising in haste, the haste of embarrassment and of wanting to get away. "I will write directly."

She went accordingly to the table, where she was in the habit of writing for her aunt, and prepared her materials without knowing what in the world to say. She had read Miss Crawford's note only once, and how to reply to anything so imperfectly understood was most distressing. Quite unpractised in such sort of notewriting, had there been time for scruples and fears as to style she would have felt them in abundance; but something must be instantly written; and with only one decided feeling, that of wishing not to appear to think anything really intended, she wrote thus, in great trembling both of spirits and hand:—

"I am very much obliged to you, my dear Miss Crawford, for your kind congratulations as far as they relate to my dearest William. The rest of your note, I know, means nothing; but I am so unequal to anything of the sort, that I hope you will excuse my begging you to take no further notice. I have seen too much of Mr. Crawford not to understand his manners; if he understood me as well, he would, I dare say, behave differently. I do not know what I write, but it would be a great favour of you never to mention the subject again. With thanks for the honour of your note, I remain, dear Miss Crawford, etc., etc."

The conclusion was scarcely intelligible from increasing fright, for she found that Mr. Crawford, under pretence of receiving the note, was coming towards her.

"You cannot think I mean to hurry you," said he, in an under voice, perceiving the amazing trepidation with which she made up the note; "you cannot think I have any such object. Do not hurry yourself, I entreat."

"Oh! I thank you; I have quite done, just done; it will be ready in a moment; I am very much obliged to you; if you will be so good as to give *that* to Miss Crawford."

The note was held out, and must be taken; and as she instantly and with averted eyes walked towards the fireplace, where sat the others, he had nothing to do but to go in good earnest.

Fanny thought she had never known a day of greater agitation, both of pain and pleasure; but happily, the pleasure was not of a sort to die with the day; for every day would restore the knowledge of William's advancement, whereas the pain, she hoped, would return no more. She had no doubt that her note must appear excessively ill-written, that the language would disgrace a child, for her distress had allowed no arrangement; but at least it would assure them both of her being neither imposed on nor gratified by Mr. Crawford's attentions.

Chapter 32

FANNY had by no means forgotten Mr. Crawford when she awoke the next morning; but she remembered the purport of her note, and was not less sanguine as to its effect than she had been the night before. If Mr. Crawford would but go away! That was what she most earnestly desired; go and take his sister with him, as he was to do, and as he returned to Mansfield on purpose to do. And why it was not done already she could not devise, for Miss Crawford certainly wanted no delay. Fanny had hoped, in the course of his yesterday's visit, to hear the day named; but he had only spoken of their journey as what would take place ere long.

Having so satisfactorily settled the conviction her note would convey, she could not but be astonished to see Mr. Crawford, as she accidentally did, coming up to the house again, and at an hour as early as the day before. His coming might have nothing to do with her, but she must avoid seeing him if possible; and being then on her way upstairs, she resolved there to remain, during the whole of his visit, unless actually sent for; and as Mrs. Norris was still in the house, there seemed little danger of her being wanted.

She sat some time in a good deal of agitation, listening, trembling, and fearing to be sent for every moment; but as no footsteps approached the East Room, she grew gradually composed, could sit down, and be able to employ herself, and able to hope that Mr. Crawford had come and would go without her being obliged to know anything of the matter.

Nearly half an hour had passed, and she was growing very comfortable, when suddenly the sound of a step in regular approach was heard; a heavy step, an unusual step in that part of the house; it was her uncle's; she knew it as well as his voice; she had trembled at it as often, and began to tremble again, at the idea of his coming up to speak to her, whatever might be the subject. It was indeed Sir Thomas, who opened the door and asked if she were there, and if he might come in. The terror of his former occasional visits to that room seemed all renewed, and she felt as if he were going to examine her again in French and English.

She was all attention, however, in placing a chair for him, and trying to appear honoured; and in her agitation, had quite overlooked the deficiencies of her apartment, till he, stopping short as he entered, said, with much surprise, "Why have you no fire to-day?"

There was snow on the ground, and she was sitting in a shawl. She hestitated.

"I am not cold, sir: I never sit here long at this time of year."

"But you have a fire in general?"

"No, sir."

"How comes this about? Here must be some mistake. I understood that you had the use of this room by way of making you perfectly comfortable. In your bedchamber I know you *cannot* have a fire. Here is some great misapprehension which must be rectified. It is highly unfit for you to sit, be it only half an hour a day, without a fire. You are not strong. You are chilly. Your aunt cannot be aware of this."

Fanny would rather have been silent; but being obliged to speak, she could not forbear, in justice to the aunt she loved best, from saying something in which the words "my Aunt Norris" were distinguishable.

"I understand," cried her uncle, recollecting himself, and not wanting to hear more: "I understand. Your Aunt Norris has always been an advocate, and very judiciously, for young people's being brought up without unnecessary indulgences; but there should be moderation in everything. She is also very hardy herself, which of course will influence her in her opinion of the wants of others. And on another account, too, I can perfectly comprehend. I know what her sentiments have always been. The principle was good in itself, but it may have been, and I believe *has been*, carried too far in your case. I am aware that there has been sometimes in some points, a misplaced distinction; but I think too well of you, Fanny, to suppose you will ever harbour resentment on that account. You have an understanding which will prevent you from receiving things only in part, and judging partially by the event. You will take in the whole of the past, you will consider times, persons, and probabilities, and you will feel that *they* were not least your friends who were educating and preparing you for that mediocrity of condition which *seemed* to be your lot. Though their caution may prove eventually unnecessary, it was kindly meant; and of this you may be assured, that every advantage of affluence will be doubled by the little privations and restrictions that may have been imposed. I am sure you will not disappoint my opinion of you, by failing at any time to treat your Aunt Norris with the respect and attention that are due to her. But enough of this. Sit down, my dear. I must speak to you for a few minutes, but I will not detain you long."

Fanny obeyed, with eyes cast down and colour rising. After a moment's pause, Sir Thomas, trying to suppress a smile, went on.

"You are not aware, perhaps, that I have had a visitor this morning. I had not been long in my own room, after breakfast, when Mr. Crawford was shown in. His errand you may probably conjecture."

Fanny's colour grew deeper and deeper; and her uncle, perceiving that she was embarrassed to a degree that made either speaking or looking up quite impossible, turned away his own eyes, and without any further pause proceeded in his account of Mr. Crawford's visit.

Mr. Crawford's business had been to declare himself the lover of Fanny, make decided proposals for her, and entreat the sanction of the uncle, who seemed to stand in the place of her parents; and he had done it all so well, so openly, so liberally, so properly, that Sir Thomas, feeling, moreover, his own replies, and his own remarks to have been very much to the purpose, was exceedingly happy to give the particulars of their conversation, and, little aware of what was passing in his niece's mind, conceived, that by such details he must be gratifying her far more than himself. He talked, therefore, for several minutes, without Fanny's daring to interrupt him. She had hardly even attained the wish to do it. Her mind was in too much confusion. She had changed her position; and, with her eyes fixed intently on one of the windows, was listening to her uncle in the utmost perturbation and dismay. For a moment he ceased, but she had barely become conscious of it, when, rising from his chair, he said: "And now, Fanny, having performed one part of my commission, and shown you everything placed on a basis the most assured and satisfactory, I may execute the remainder by prevailing on you to accompany me downstairs, where, though I cannot but presume on having been no unacceptable companion myself, I must submit to your finding one still better worth listening to. Mr. Crawford, as you have perhaps foreseen, is yet in the house. He is in my room, and hoping to see you there."

There was a look, a start, an exclamation, on hearing this, which astonished Sir Thomas; but what was his increase of astonishment on hearing her exclaim: "Oh! no, sir, I cannot, indeed I cannot go down to him. Mr. Crawford ought to know—he must know that; I told him enough yesterday to convince him; he spoke to me on this subject yesterday, and I told him without disguise that it was very disagreeable to me, and quite out of my power to return his good opinion."

"I do not catch your meaning," said Sir Thomas, sitting down again. "Out of your power to return his good opinion? What is all this? I know he spoke to you yesterday, and (as far as I understand) received as much encouragement to proceed as a well-judging young woman could permit herself to give. I was very much pleased with what I collected to have been your behaviour on the occasion; it showed a discretion highly to be commended. But now, when he has made his overtures so properly, and honourably—what are your scruples *now?*"

"You are mistaken, sir," cried Fanny, forced by the anxiety of the moment even to tell her uncle that he was wrong; "you are quite mistaken. How could Mr. Crawford say such a thing? I gave him no encouragement yesterday. On the contrary, I told him, I cannot recollect my exact words, but I am sure I told him that I would not listen to him, that it was very unpleasant to me in every respect, and that I begged him never to talk to me in that manner again. I am sure I said as much as that and more; and I should have said still more, if I had been quite certain of his meaning anything seriously; but I did not like to be, I could not bear to be, imputing more than might be intended. I thought it might all pass for nothing with *him*."

She could say no more; her breath was almost gone.

"Am I to understand," said Sir Thomas, after a few moments' silence, "that you mean to *refuse* Mr. Crawford?"

"Yes, sir."

"Refuse him?"

"Yes, sir."

"Refuse Mr. Crawford! Upon what plea? For what reason?"

"I—I cannot like him, sir, well enough to marry him."

"This is very strange!" said Sir Thomas, in a voice of calm displeasure. "There is something in this which my comprehension does not reach. Here is a young man wishing to pay his addresses to you, with everything to recommend him; not merely situation in life, fortune, and character, but with more than common agreeableness, with address and conversation pleasing to everybody. And he is not an acquaintance of to-day; you have now known him some time. His sister, moreover, is your intimate friend and he has been doing *that* for your brother, which I should suppose would have been almost sufficient recommendation to you, had there been no other. It is very uncertain when my interest might have got William on. He has done it already."

"Yes," said Fanny, in a faint voice, and looking down with fresh shame; and she did feel almost ashamed of herself, after such a picture as her uncle had drawn, for not liking Mr. Crawford.

"You must have been aware," continued Sir Thomas presently, "you must have been some time aware of a particularity in Mr. Crawford's manners to you. This cannot have taken you by surprise. You must have observed his attentions; and though you always received them very properly (I have no accusation to make on that head), I never perceived them to be unpleasant to you. I am half inclined to think, Fanny, that you do not quite know your own feelings."

"Oh, yes, sir! indeed I do. His attentions were always—what I did not like."

Sir Thomas looked at her with deeper surprise. "This is beyond me," said he. "This requires explanation. Young as you are, and having seen scarcely anyone, it is hardly possible that your affections——"

He paused and eyed her fixedly. He saw her lips formed into a *no*, though the sound was inarticulate, but her face was like scarlet. That, however, in so modest a girl might be very compatible with innocence; and choosing at least to appear satisfied, he quickly added, "No, no, I know *that* is quite out of the question; quite impossible. Well, there is nothing more to be said."

And for a few minutes he did say nothing. He was deep in thought.

His niece was deep in thought likewise, trying to harden and prepare herself against further questioning. She would rather die than own the truth; and she hoped by a little reflection to fortify herself beyond betraying it.

"Independently of the interest which Mr. Crawford's *choice* seemed to justify," said Sir Thomas, beginning again, and very composedly, "his wishing to marry at all so early is recommendatory to me. I am an advocate for early marriages, where there are means in proportion, and would have every young man, with a sufficient income, settle as soon after four-and-twenty as he can. This is so much my opinion, that I am sorry to think how little likely my own eldest son, your cousin, Mr. Bertram, is to marry early; but at present, as far as I can judge, matrimony makes no part of his plans or thoughts. I wish he were more likely to fix." Here was a glance at Fanny. "Edmund, I consider, from his disposition and habits, as much more likely to marry early than his brother. *He,* indeed, I have lately thought has seen the woman he could love, which, I am convinced, my eldest son has not. Am I right? Do you agree with me, my dear?"

"Yes, sir."

It was gently, but it was calmly said, and Sir Thomas was easy on the score of the cousins. But the removal of his alarm did his niece no service; as her unaccountableness was confirmed his displeasure increased; and getting up and walking about the room, with a frown, which Fanny could picture to herself, though she dared not lift up her eyes, he shortly afterwards, and in a voice of authority, said, "Have you any reason, child, to think ill of Mr. Crawford's temper?"

"No, sir."

She longed to add, "But of his principles I have"; but her heart sank under the appalling prospect of discussion, explanation, and probably non-conviction. Her ill opinion of him was founded chiefly on observations, which, for her cousins' sake, she could scarcely dare mention to their father. Maria and Julia, and especially Maria, were so closely implicated in Mr. Crawford's misconduct, that she could not give his character, such as she believed it, without betraying them. She had hoped that, to a man like her uncle, so discerning, so honourable, so good, the simple acknowledgment of settled *dislike* on her side, would have been sufficient. To her infinite grief she found it was not.

Sir Thomas came towards the table where she sat in trembling wretchedness, and with a good deal of cold sternness, said: "It is of no use, I perceive, to talk to you. We had better put an end to this most mortifying conference. Mr. Crawford must not be kept longer waiting. I will, therefore, only add, as thinking it my duty to mark my opinion of your conduct, that you have disappointed every expectation I had formed, and proved yourself of a character the very reverse of what I had supposed. For I *had,* Fanny, as I think my behaviour must have shown, formed a very favourable opinion of you from the period of my return to England.

I had thought you peculiarly free from wilfulness of temper, self-conceit, and every tendency to that independence of spirit which prevails so much in modern days, even in young women, and which in young women is offensive and disgusting beyond all common offence. But you have now shown me that you can be wilful and perverse; that you can and will decide for yourself, without any consideration or deference for those who have surely some right to guide you, without even asking their advice. You have shown yourself very, very different from anything that I had imagined. The advantage or disadvantage of your family, of your parents, your brothers and sisters, never seems to have had a moment's share in your thoughts on this occasion. How *they* might be benefited, how *they* must rejoice in such an establishment for you, is nothing to *you*. You think only of yourself, and because you do not feel for Mr. Crawford exactly what a young heated fancy imagines to be necessary for happiness, you resolve to refuse him at once, without wishing even for a little time to consider of it, a little more time for cool consideration, and for really examining your own inclinations; and are, in a wild fit of folly, throwing away from you such an opportunity of being settled in life, eligibly, honourably, nobly settled, as will, probably, never occur to you again. Here is a young man of sense, of character, of temper, of manners, and of fortune, exceedingly attached to you, and seeking your hand in the most handsome and disinterested way; and let me tell you, Fanny, that you may live eighteen years longer in the world, without being addressed by a man of half Mr. Crawford's estate, or a tenth part of its merits. Gladly would I have bestowed either of my own daughters on him. Maria is nobly married; but had Mr. Crawford sought Julia's hand, I should have given it to him with superior and more heartfelt satisfaction than I gave Maria's to Mr. Rushworth." After half a moment's pause: "And I should have been very much surprised had either of my daughters, on receiving a proposal of marriage at any time, which might carry with it only *half* the eligibility of *this*, immediately and peremptorily, and without paying my opinion or my regard the compliment of any consultation, put a decided negative on it. I should have been much surprised and much hurt, by such a proceeding. I should have thought it a gross violation of duty and respect. *You* are not to be judged by the same rule. You do not owe me the duty of a child. But, Fanny, if your heart can acquit you of *ingratitude*——"

He ceased. Fanny was by this time crying so bitterly, that, angry as he was, he would not press that article further. Her heart was almost broken by such a picture of what she appeared to him; by such accusations, so heavy, so multiplied, so rising in dreadful gradation! Self-willed, obstinate, selfish, and ungrateful. He thought her all this. She had deceived his expectations; she had lost his good opinion. What was to become of her?

"I am very sorry," said she, inarticulately, through her tears, "I am very sorry, indeed."

"Sorry! Yes, I hope you are sorry; and you will probably have reason to be long sorry for this day's transactions."

"If it were possible for me to do otherwise——" said she, with another strong effort; "but I am so perfectly convinced that I could never make him happy, and that I should be miserable myself."

Another burst of tears; but in spite of that burst, and in spite of that great black word *miserable,* which served to introduce it, Sir Thomas began to think a little relenting, a little change of inclination, might have something to do with it; and to augur favourably from the personal entreaty of the young man himself. He knew her to be very timid, and exceedingly nervous; and thought it not improbable that her mind might be in such a state as a little time, a little pressing, a little patience, and a little impatience, a judicious mixture of all on the lover's side, might work their usual effect on. If the gentleman would but persevere, if he had but love enough to persevere, Sir Thomas began to have hopes; and these reflections having passed across his mind and cheered it, "Well," said he, in a tone of becoming gravity, but of less anger, "well, child, dry up your tears. There is no use in these tears; they can do no good. You must now come downstairs with me. Mr. Crawford has been kept waiting too long already. You must give him your own answer; we cannot expect him to be satisfied with less; and you only can explain to him the grounds of that misconception of your sentiments, which, unfortunately for himself, he certainly has imbibed. I am totally unequal to it."

But Fanny showed such reluctance, such misery, at the idea of going down to him, that Sir Thomas, after a little consideration, judged it better to indulge her. His hopes from both gentleman and lady suffered a small depression in consequence; but when he looked at his niece, and saw the state of feature and complexion which her crying had brought her into, he thought there might be as much lost as gained by an immediate interview. With a few words, therefore, of no particular meaning, he walked off by himself, leaving his poor niece to sit and cry over what had passed, with very wretched feelings.

Her mind was all disorder. The past, present, future, everything was terrible. But her uncle's anger gave her the severest pain of all. Selfish and ungrateful! to have appeared so to him! She was miserable for ever. She had no one to take her part, to counsel, or speak for her. Her only friend was absent. He might have softened his father; but all, perhaps all, would think her selfish and ungrateful. She might have to endure the reproach again and again; she might hear it, or see it, or know it to exist for ever in every connection about her. She could not but feel some resentment against Mr. Crawford; yet, if he really loved her, and were unhappy too——! It was all wretchedness together.

In about a quarter of an hour her uncle returned; she was almost ready to faint at the sight of him. He spoke calmly, however, without austerity, without reproach, and she revived a little. There was comfort, too, in his words, as well as his manner, for he began with, "Mr. Crawford is gone:

he has just left me. I need not repeat what has passed. I do not want to add to anything you may now be feeling, by an account of what he has felt. Suffice it, that he has behaved in the most gentlemanlike and generous manner, and has confirmed me in a most favourable opinion of his understanding, heart and temper. Upon my representation of what you were suffering, he immediately, and with the greatest delicacy, ceased to urge to see you for the present."

Here Fanny, who had looked up, looked down again.

"Of course," continued her uncle, "it cannot be supposed but that he should request to speak with you alone, be it only for five minutes; a request too natural, a claim too just to be denied. But there is no time fixed; perhaps to-morrow, or whenever your spirits are composed enough. For the present you have only to tranquillise yourself. Check these tears; they do but exhaust you. If, as I am willing to suppose, you wish to show me any observance, you will not give way to these emotions, but endeavour to reason yourself into a stronger frame of mind. I advise you to go out; the air will do you good; go out for an hour on the gravel; you will have the shrubbery to yourself, and will be the better for air and exercise. And, Fanny (turning back again for a moment), I shall make no mention below of what has passed; I shall not even tell your Aunt Bertram. There is no occasion for spreading the disappointment; say nothing about it yourself."

This was an order to be most joyfully obeyed; this was an act of kindness which Fanny felt at her heart. To be spared from her Aunt Norris's interminable reproaches; he left her in a glow of gratitude. Anything might be bearable rather than such reproaches. Even to see Mr. Crawford would be less overpowering.

She walked out directly as her uncle recommended, and followed his advice throughout, as far as she could; did check her tears; did earnestly try to compose her spirits and strengthen her mind. She wished to prove to him that she did desire his comfort, and sought to regain his favour; and he had given her another strong motive for exertion, in keeping the whole affair from the knowledge of her aunts. Not to excite suspicion by her look or manner, was now an object worth attaining; and she felt equal to almost anything that might save her from her Aunt Norris.

She was struck, quite struck, when, on returning from her walk and going into the East Room again, the first thing which caught her eye was a fire lighted and burning. A fire! It seemed too much; just at that time to be giving her such an indulgence was exciting even painful gratitude. She wondered that Sir Thomas could have leisure to think of such a trifle again; but she soon found, from the voluntary information of the housemaid, who came in to attend it, that so it was to be every day. Sir Thomas had given orders for it.

"I must be a brute, indeed, if I can be really ungrateful!" said she, in soliloquy. "Heaven defend me from being ungrateful!"

She saw nothing more of her uncle, nor of her Aunt Norris, till they met at dinner. Her uncle's behaviour to her was then as nearly as possible what ıt had been before; she was sure he did not mean there should be any change, and that it was only her own conscience that could fancy any; but her aunt was soon quarrelling with her; and when she found how much and how pleasantly her having only walked out without her aunt's knowledge could be dwelt on, she felt all the reason she had to bless the kindness which saved her from the same spirit of reproach, exerted on a more momentous subject.

"If I had known you were going out, I should have got you just to go as far as my house with some orders for Nanny," said she, "which I have since, to my very great inconvenience, been obliged to go and carry myself. I could very ill spare the time, and you might have saved me the trouble, if you would only have been so good as to let us know you were going out. It would have made no difference to you, I suppose, whether you had walked in the shrubbery or gone to my house."

"I recommended the shrubbery to Fanny as the driest place," said Sir Thomas.

"Oh!" said Mrs. Norris, with a moment's check, "that was very kind of you, Sir Thomas, but you do not know how dry the path is to my house. Fanny would have had quite as good a walk there, I assure you, with the advantage of being of some use, and obliging her aunt: it is all her fault. If she would but have let us know she was going out—but there is a something about Fanny, I have often observed it before—she likes to go her own way to work; she does not like to be dictated to; she takes her own independent walk whenever she can; she certainly has a little spirit of secrecy, and independence, and nonsense, about her, which I would advise her to get the better of."

As a general reflection on Fanny, Sir Thomas thought nothing could be more unjust, though he had been so lately expressing the same sentiments himself, and he tried to turn the conversation: tried repeatedly before he could succeed; for Mrs. Norris had not discernment enough to perceive, either now, or at any other time, to what degree he thought well of his niece, or how very far he was from wishing to have his own children's merits set off by the depreciation of hers. She was talking *at* Fanny, and resenting this private walk half through the dinner.

It was over, however, at last; and the evening set in with more composure to Fanny, and more cheerfulness of spirits than she could have hoped for after so stormy a morning; but she trusted, in the first place, that she had done right; that her judgment had not misled her. For the purity of her intentions she could answer; and she was willing to hope, secondly, that her uncle's displeasure was abating, and would abate further as he considered the matter with more impartiality, and felt, as a good man must feel, how wretched, and how unpardonable, how hopeless, and how wicked it was, to marry without affection.

When the meeting with which she was threatened for the morrow was past, she could not but flatter herself that the subject would be finally concluded, and Mr. Crawford once gone from Mansfield, that everything would soon be as if no such subject had existed. She would not, could not believe, that Mr. Crawford's affection for her could distress him long; his mind was not of that sort. London would soon bring its cure. In London he would soon learn to wonder at his infatuation, and be thankful for the right reason in her which had saved him from its evil consequences.

While Fanny's mind was engaged in these sort of hopes, her uncle was, soon after tea, called out of the room; an occurrence too common to strike her, and she thought nothing of it till the butler reappeared ten minutes afterwards, and advancing decidedly towards herself, said, "Sir Thomas wishes to speak with you, ma'am, in his own room." Then it occurred to her what might be going on; a suspicion rushed over her mind which drove the colour from her cheeks; but instantly rising, she was preparing to obey, when Mrs. Norris called out, "Stay, stay, Fanny! What are you about? Where are you going? Don't be in such a hurry. Depend upon it, it is not you who are wanted; depend upon it, it is me" (looking at the butler) "but you are so very eager to put yourself forward. What should Sir Thomas want you for? It is me, Baddeley, you mean; I am coming this moment. You mean me, Baddeley, I am sure; Sir Thomas wants me, not Miss Price."

But Baddeley was stout. "No, ma'am, it is Miss Price; I am certain of its being Miss Price." And there was a half smile with the words, which meant, "I do not think *you* would answer the purpose at all."

Mrs. Norris, much discontented, was obliged to compose herself to work again; and Fanny, walking off in agitating consciousness, found herself, as she anticipated, in another minute alone with Mr. Crawford.

Chapter 33

THE conference was neither so short nor so conclusive as the lady had designed. The gentleman was not so easily satisfied. He had all the disposition to persevere that Sir Thomas could wish him. He had vanity, which strongly inclined him in the first place to think she did love him, though she might not know it herself; and which, secondly, when constrained at last to admit that she did know her own present feelings, convinced him that he should be able in time to make those feelings what he wished.

He was in love, very much in love; and it was a love which, operating on an active, sanguine spirit, of more warmth than delicacy, made her affection appear of greater consequence because it was withheld, and determined him to have the glory, as well as the felicity, of forcing her to love him.

He would not despair: he would not desist. He had every well-grounded reason for solid attachment; he knew her to have all the worth that could justify the warmest hopes of lasting happiness with her; her conduct at this time by speaking the disinterestedness and delicacy of her character (qualities which he believed most rare indeed), was of a sort to heighten all his wishes, and confirm all his resolutions. He knew not that he had a pre-engaged heart to attack. Of *that* he had no suspicion. He considered her rather as one who had never thought on the subject enough to be in danger; who had been guarded by youth, a youth of mind as lovely as of person; whose modesty had prevented her from understanding his attentions, and who was still overpowered by the suddenness of addresses so wholly unexpected, and the novelty of a situation which her fancy had never taken into account.

Must it not follow of course, that, when he was understood, he should succeed? He believed it fully. Love such as his, in a man like himself, must with perseverance secure a return, and at no great distance; and he had so much delight in the idea of obliging her to love him in a very short time, that her not loving him now was scarcely regretted. A little difficulty to be overcome was no evil to Henry Crawford. He rather derived spirits from it. He had been apt to gain hearts too easily. His situation was new and animating.

To Fanny, however, who had known too much opposition all her life to find any charm in it, all this was unintelligible. She found that he did mean to persevere; but how he could, after such language from her as she felt herself obliged to use, was not to be understood. She told him that she did not love him, could not love him, was sure she never should love him; that such a change was quite impossible; that the subject was most painful to her; that she must intreat him never to mention it again, to allow her to leave him at once, and let it be considered as concluded for ever. And when further pressed, had added, that in her opinion their dispositions were so totally dissimilar, as to make mutual affection incompatible; and that they were unfitted for each other by nature, education, and habit. All this she had said, and with the earnestness of sincerity; yet this was not enough, for he immediately denied there being anything uncongenial in their characters, or anything unfriendly in their situations; and positively declared that he would still love, and still hope!

Fanny knew her own meaning, but was no judge of her own manner. Her manner was incurably gentle; and she was not aware how much it concealed the sternness of her purpose. Her diffidence, gratitude, and softness made every expression of indifference seem almost an effort of self-denial; seem, at least, to be giving nearly as much pain to herself as to him. Mr. Crawford was no longer the Mr. Crawford who, as the clandestine, insidious, treacherous admirer of Maria Bertram, had been her abhorrence, whom she had hated to see or to speak to, in whom she could believe no good quality to exist, and whose power, even of being agreeable, she had barely acknowledged. He was now the Mr. Crawford who was addressing herself with ardent, disinterested love; whose feelings were apparently become all that was honourable and upright, whose views of happiness were all fixed on a marriage of attachment; who was pouring out his sense of her merits, describing and describing again his affection, proving, as far as words could prove it, and in the language, tone, and spirit of a man of talent, too, that he sought her for her gentleness and her goodness; and to complete the whole, he was now the Mr. Crawford who had procured William's promotion!

Here was a change, and here were claims which could not but operate! She might have disdained him in all the dignity of angry virtue in the grounds of Sotherton, or the theatre at Mansfield Park; but he approached her now with rights that demanded different treatment. She must be courteous, and she must be compassionate. She must have a sensation of being honoured, and whether thinking of herself or her brother, she must have a strong feeling of gratitude. The effect of the whole was a manner so pitying and agitated, and words intermingled with her refusal so expressive of obligation and concern, that to a temper of vanity and hope like Crawford's, the truth, or at least the strength of her indifference, might well be questionable; and he was not so irrational as Fanny considered him, in the professions of persevering, assiduous, and not desponding attachment which closed the interview.

It was with reluctance that he suffered her to go; but there was no look of despair in parting to bely his words, or give her hopes of his being less unreasonable than he professed himself.

Now she was angry. Some resentment did arise at a perseverance so selfish and ungenerous. Here was again a want of delicacy and regard for others which had formerly so struck and disgusted her. Here was again a something of the same Mr. Crawford whom she had so reprobated before. How evidently was there a gross want of feeling and humanity where his own pleasure was concerned; and alas! how always known, no principle to supply as a duty what the heart was deficient in! Had her own affections been as free as perhaps they ought to have been, he never could have engaged them.

So thought Fanny, in good truth and sober sadness, as she sat musing over that too great indulgence and luxury of a fire upstairs; wondering at the past and present; wondering at what was yet to come, and in a nervous agitation which made nothing clear to her but the persuasion of her being never under any circumstances able to love Mr. Crawford, and the felicity of having a fire to sit over and think of it.

Sir Thomas was obliged, or obliged himself, to wait till the morrow for a knowledge of what had passed between the young people. He then saw Mr. Crawford, and received his account. The first feeling was disappointment: he had hoped better things; he had thought that an hour's entreaty from a young man like Crawford could not have worked so little change on a gentle-tempered girl like Fanny; but there was speedy comfort in the determined views and sanguine perseverance of the lover; and when seeing such confidence of success in the principal, Sir Thomas was soon able to depend on it himself.

Nothing was omitted, on his side, of civility, compliment, or kindness, that might assist the plan. Mr. Crawford's steadiness was honoured, and

Fanny was praised, and the connection was still the most desirable in the world. At Mansfield Park Mr. Crawford would always be welcome; he had only to consult his own judgment and feelings as to the frequency of his visits, at present or in future. In all his niece's family and friends, there could be but one opinion, one wish on the subject; the influence of all who loved her must incline one way.

Everything was said that could encourage, every encouragement received with grateful joy, and the gentlemen parted the best of friends.

Satisfied that the cause was now on a footing the most proper and hopeful, Sir Thomas resolved to abstain from all further importunity with his niece, and to show no open interference. Upon her disposition he believed kindness might be the best way of working. Intreaty should be from one quarter only. The forbearance of her family on a point, respecting which she could be in no doubt of their wishes, might be their surest means of forwarding it. Accordingly, on this principle, Sir Thomas took the first opportunity of saying to her, with a mild gravity, intended to be overcoming, "Well, Fanny, I have seen Mr. Crawford again, and learnt from him exactly how matters stand between you. He is a most extraordinary young man, and whatever be the event, you must feel that you have created an attachment of no common character; though, young as you are, and little acquainted with the transient, varying, unsteady nature of love, as it generally exists, you cannot be struck as I am with all that is wonderful in a perseverance of this sort against discouragement. With him, it is entirely a matter of feeling; he claims no merit in it; perhaps is entitled to none. Yet, having chosen so well, his constancy has a respectable stamp. Had his choice been less unexceptionable, I should have condemned his persevering."

"Indeed, sir," said Fanny, "I am very sorry that Mr. Crawford should continue to—— I know that it is paying me a very great compliment, and I feel most undeservedly honoured; but I am so perfectly convinced, and I have told him so, that it never will be in my power——"

"My dear," interrupted Sir Thomas, "there is no occasion for this. Your feelings are as well known to me as my wishes and regrets must be to you. There is nothing more to be said or done. From this hour, the subject is never to be revived between us. You will have nothing to fear, or to be agitated about. You cannot suppose me capable of trying to persuade you to marry against your inclinations. Your happiness and advantage are all that I have in view, and nothing is required of you but to bear with Mr. Crawford's endeavours to convince you that they may not be incompatible with his. He proceeds at his own risk. You are on safe ground. I have engaged for your seeing him whenever he calls, as you might have done had nothing of this sort occurred. You will see him with the rest of us, in the same manner, and, as much as you can, dismissing the recollection of everything unpleasant. He leaves Northamptonshire so soon, that even this slight sacrifice cannot be often demanded. The future must be very uncertain. And now, my dear Fanny, this subject is closed between us."

The promised departure was all that Fanny could think of with much satisfaction. Her uncle's kind expressions, however, and forbearing manner were sensibly felt; and when she considered how much of the truth was unknown to him, she believed she had no right to wonder at the line of conduct he pursued. He, who had married a daughter to Mr. Rushworth: romantic delicacy was certainly not to be expected from him. She must do her duty, and trust that time might make her duty easier than it now was.

She could not, though only eighteen, suppose Mr. Crawford's attachment would hold out for ever; she could not but imagine that steady, unceasing discouragement from herself would put an end to it in time. How much time she might, in her own fancy, allot for its dominion, is another concern. It would not be fair to inquire into a young lady's exact estimate of her own perfections.

In spite of his intended silence, Sir Thomas found himself once more obliged to mention the subject to his niece, to prepare her briefly for its being imparted to her aunts; a measure which he would still have avoided, if possible, but which became necessary from the totally opposite feelings of Mr. Crawford, as to any secrecy of proceeding. He had no idea of concealment. It was all known at the Parsonage, where he loved to talk over the future with both his sisters, and it would be rather gratifying to him to have enlightened witnesses of the progress of his success. When Sir Thomas understood this, he felt the necessity of making his own wife and sister-in-law acquainted with the business without delay; though, on Fanny's account, he almost dreaded the effect of the communication to Mrs. Norris as much as Fanny herself. He deprecated her mistaken but well-meaning zeal. Sir Thomas, indeed, was, by this time, not very far from classing Mrs. Norris as one of those well-meaning people who are always doing mistaken and very disagreeable things.

Mrs. Norris, however, relieved him. He pressed for the strictest forbearance and silence towards their niece; she not only promised, but did observe it. She only looked her increased ill-will. Angry she was: bitterly angry; but she was more angry with Fanny for having received such an offer, than for refusing it. It was an injury and affront to Julia, who ought to have been Mr. Crawford's choice; and independently of that, she disliked Fanny, because she had neglected her; and she would have grudged such an elevation to one whom she had been always trying to depress.

Sir Thomas gave her more credit for discretion on the occasion than she deserved; and Fanny could have blessed her for allowing her only to see her displeasure, and not to hear it.

Lady Bertram took it differently. She had been a beauty, and a prosperous beauty, all her life; and beauty and wealth were all that excited her respect. To know Fanny to be sought in marriage by a man of fortune, raised her, therefore, very much in her opinion. By convincing her that Fanny *was* very pretty, which she had been doubting about before, and that she would be advantageously married, it made her feel a sort of credit in calling her niece.

"Well, Fanny," said she, as soon as they were alone together afterwards, and she really had known something like impatience to be alone with her, and her countenance, as she spoke, had extraordinary animation: "Well, Fanny, I have had a very agreeable surprise this morning. I must just speak of it *once*, I told Sir Thomas I must *once*, and then I shall have done. I give you joy, my dear niece." And looking at her complacently, she added, "Humph, we certainly are a handsome family!"

Fanny coloured, and doubted at first what to say; when hoping to assail her on her vulnerable side, she presently answered—

"My dear aunt, *you* cannot wish me to do differently from what I have done, I am sure. *You* cannot wish me to marry; for you would miss me, should not you? Yes, I am sure you would miss me too much for that."

"No, my dear, I should not think of missing you, when such an offer as this comes in your way. I could do very well without you, if you were married to a man of such good estate as Mr. Crawford. And you must be aware, Fanny, that it is every young woman's duty to accept such a very unexceptionable offer as this."

This was almost the only rule of conduct, the only piece of advice, which Fanny had ever received from her aunt in the course of eight years and a half. It silenced her. She felt how unprofitable contention would be. If her aunt's feelings were against her, nothing could be hoped from attacking her understanding. Lady Bertram was quite talkative.

"I will tell you what, Fanny," said she, "I am sure he fell in love with you at the ball; I am sure the mischief was done that evening. You did look remarkably well. Everybody said so. Sir Thomas said so. And you know you had Chapman to help you to dress. I am very glad I sent Chapman to you. I shall tell Sir Thomas that I am sure it was done that evening." And still pursuing the same cheerful thoughts, she soon afterwards added, "And I will tell you what, Fanny, which is more than I did for Maria, the next time pug has a litter you shall have a puppy."

Chapter 34

EDMUND had great things to hear on his return. Many surprises were awaiting him. The first that occurred was not least in interest: the appearance of Henry Crawford and his sister walking together through the village as he rode into it. He had concluded—he had meant them to be far distant. His absence had been extended beyond a fortnight purposely to avoid Miss Crawford. He was returning to Mansfield with spirits ready to feed on melancholy remembrances, and tender associations, when her own fair self was before him, leaning on her brother's arm, and he found himself receiving a welcome, unquestionably friendly, from the woman whom, two moments before, he had been thinking of as seventy miles off, and as farther, much farther, from him in inclination than any distance could express.

Her reception of him was of a sort which he could not have hoped for, had he expected to see her. Coming as he did from such a purport fulfilled as had taken him away, he would have expected anything rather than a look of satisfaction, and words of simple, pleasant meaning. It was enough to set his heart in a glow, and to bring him home in the properest state for feeling the full value of the other joyful surprises at hand.

William's promotion, with all its particulars, he was soon master of; and with such a secret provision of comfort within his own breast to help the joy, he found in it a source of most gratifying sensation, and unvarying cheerfulness all dinner-time.

After dinner, when he and his father were alone, he had Fanny's history; and then all the great events of the last fortnight, and the present situation of matters at Mansfield were known to him.

Fanny suspected what was going on. They sat so much longer than usual in the dining-parlour, that she was sure they must be talking of her; and when tea at last brought them away, and she was to be seen by Edmund again, she felt dreadfully guilty. He came to her, sat down by her, took her hand, and pressed it kindly; and at that moment she thought that, but for the occupation and the screen which the tea-things afforded, she must have betrayed her emotion in some unpardonable excess.

He was not intending, however, by such action, to be conveying to her that unqualified approbation and encouragement which her hopes drew from it. It was designed only to express his participation in all that interested her, and to tell her that he had been hearing what quickened every feeling of affection. He was, in fact, entirely on his father's side of the question. His surprise was not so great as his father's at her refusing Crawford, because, so far from supposing her to consider him with anything like a preference, he had always believed it to be rather the reverse, and could imagine her to be taken perfectly unprepared, but Sir Thomas could not regard the connection as more desirable than he did. It had every recommendation to him; and while honouring her for what she had done under the influence of her present indifference, honouring her in rather stronger terms than Sir Thomas could quite echo, he was most earnest in hoping and sanguine in believing, that it would be a match at last, and that, united by mutual affection, it would appear that their dispositions were as exactly fitted to make them blessed in each other, as he was now beginning seriously to consider them. Crawford had been too precipitate. He had not given her time to attach herself. He had begun at the wrong end. With such powers as his, however, and such a disposition as hers, Edmund trusted that everything would work out a happy conclusion. Meanwhile, he saw enough of Fanny's embarrassment to make him scrupulously guard against exciting it a second time, by any word, or look, or movement.

Crawford called the next day, and on the score of Edmund's return, Sir

Thomas felt himself more than licensed to ask him to stay to dinner; it was really a necessary compliment. He stayed of course, and Edmund had then ample opportunity for observing how he sped with Fanny, and what degree of immediate encouragement for him might be extracted from her manners; and it was so little, so very very little (every chance, every possibility of it, resting upon her embarrassment only: if there was not hope in her confusion, there was hope in nothing else), that he was almost ready to wonder at his friend's perseverance. Fanny was worth it all; he held her to be worth every effort of patience, every exertion of mind, but he did not think he could have gone on himself with any woman breathing, without something more to warm his courage than his eyes could discern in hers. He was very willing to hope that Crawford saw clearer, and this was the most comfortable conclusion for his friend that he could come to from all that he observed to pass before, and at, and after dinner.

In the evening a few circumstances occurred which he thought more promising. When he and Crawford walked into the drawing-room, his mother and Fanny were sitting as intently and silently at work as if there were nothing else to care for. Edmund could not help noticing their apparently deep tranquillity.

"We have not been so silent all the time," replied his mother. "Fanny has been reading to me, and only put the book down upon hearing you coming." And sure enough there was a book on the table which had the air of being very recently closed: a volume of Shakespeare. "She often reads to me out of those books; and she was in the middle of a very fine speech of that man's—what's his name, Fanny?—when we heard your footsteps."

Crawford took the volume. "Let me have the pleasure of finishing that speech to your ladyship," said he. "I shall find it immediately." And by carefully giving way to the inclination of the leaves, he did find it, or within a page or two, quite near enough to satisfy Lady Bertram, who assured him, as soon as he mentioned the name of Cardinal Wolsey, that he had got the very speech. Not a look, or an offer of help had Fanny given; not a syllable for or against. All her attention was for her work. She seemed determined to be interested by nothing else. But taste was too strong in her. She could not abstract her mind five minutes; she was forced to listen; his reading was capital, and her pleasure in good reading extreme. To *good* reading, however, she had been long used; her uncle read well, her cousins all, Edmund very well, but in Mr. Crawford's reading there was a variety of excellence beyond what she had ever met with. The King, the Queen, Buckingham, Wolsey, Cromwell, all were given in turn; for with the happiest knack, the happiest power of jumping and guessing, he could always alight at will on the best scene, or the best speeches of each; and whether it were dignity or pride, or tenderness or remorse, or whatever were to be expressed, he could do it with equal beauty. It was truly dramatic. His acting had first taught Fanny what pleasure a play might give, and his reading brought all his acting before her again; nay, perhaps with greater enjoyment, for it came unexpectedly, and with no such drawback as she had been used to suffer in seeing him on the stage with Miss Bertram.

Edmund watched the progress of her attention, and was amused and gratified by seeing how she gradually slackened in the needlework, which at the beginning, seemed to occupy her totally; how it fell from her hand while she sat motionless over it, and at last, how the eyes which had appeared so studiously to avoid him throughout the day, were turned and fixed on Crawford; fixed on him for minutes, fixed on him, in short, till the attraction drew Crawford's upon her, and the book was closed, and the charm was broken. Then she was shrinking again into herself, and blushing and working as hard as ever; but it had been enough to give Edmund encouragement for his friend, and as he cordially thanked him, he hoped to be expressing Fanny's secret feelings too.

"That play must be a favourite with you," said he; "you read as if you knew it well."

"It will be a favourite, I believe, from this hour," replied Crawford; "but I do not think I have had a volume of Shakespeare in my hand before since I was fifteen. I once saw Henry the Eighth acted, or I have heard of it from somebody who did, I am not certain which. But Shakespeare one gets acquainted with without knowing how. It is a part of an Englishman's constitution. His thoughts and beauties are so spread abroad that one touches them everywhere; one is intimate with him by instinct. No man of any brain can open at a good part of one of his plays without falling into the flow of his meaning immediately."

"No doubt one is familiar with Shakespeare in a degree," said Edmund, "from one's earliest years. His celebrated passages are quoted by everybody; they are in half the books we open, and we all talk Shakespeare, use his similes, and describe with his descriptions; but this is totally distinct from giving his sense as you gave it. To know him in bits and scraps is common enough; to know him pretty thoroughly is, perhaps, not uncommon; but to read him well aloud is no every-day talent."

"Sir, you do me honour," was Crawford's answer, with a bow of mock gravity.

Both gentlemen had a glance at Fanny, to see if a word of accordant praise could be extorted from her; yet both feeling that it could not be. Her praise had been given in her attention; *that* must content them.

Lady Bertram's admiration was expressed, and strongly too. "It was really like being at a play," said she. "I wish Sir Thomas had been here."

Crawford was excessively pleased. If Lady Bertram, with all her incompetency and languor, could feel this, the inference of what her niece, alive and enlightened as she was, must feel, was elevating.

"You have a great turn for acting, I am sure, Mr. Crawford," said her ladyship soon afterwards; "and I will tell you what, I think you will have a theatre, some time or other, at your house in Norfolk. I mean when you are settled there. I do, indeed. I think you will fit up a theatre at your house in Norfolk."

"Do you, ma'am?" cried he, with quickness. "No, no, that will never be. Your ladyship is quite mistaken. No theatre at Everingham! Oh, no!" And he looked at Fanny with an expressive smile, which evidently meant, "that lady will never allow a theatre at Everingham."

Edmund saw it all, and saw Fanny so determined *not* to see it, as to make it clear that the voice was enough to convey the full meaning of the protestation; and such a quick consciousness of compliment, such a ready comprehension of a hint, he thought, was rather favourable than not.

The subject of reading aloud was further discussed. The two young men were the only talkers, but they, standing by the fire, talked over the too common neglect of the qualification, the total inattention to it, in the ordinary school-system for boys, the consequently natural yet in some instances almost unnatural, degree of ignorance and uncouthness of men, of sensible and well-informed men, when suddenly called to the necessity of reading aloud, which had fallen within their notice, giving instances of blunders, and failures with their secondary causes, the want of management of the voice, of proper modulation and emphasis, of foresight and judgment, all proceeding from the first cause: want of early attention and habit; and Fanny was listening again with great entertainment.

"Even in my profession," said Edmund, with a smile, "how little the art of reading has been studied! How little a clear manner, and good delivery, have been attended to! I speak rather of the past, however, than the present. There is now a spirit of improvement abroad; but among those who were ordained twenty, thirty, forty years ago, the larger number, to judge by their performance, must have thought reading was reading, and preaching was preaching. It is different now. The subject is more justly considered. It is felt that distinctness and energy may have weight in recommending the most solid truths; and besides there is more general observation and taste, a more critical knowledge diffused than formerly; in every congregation there is a larger proportion who know a little of the matter, and who can judge and criticise."

Edmund had already gone through the service once since his ordination; and upon this being understood, he had a variety of questions from Crawford as to his feelings and success; questions, which being made, though with the vivacity of friendly interest and quick taste, without any touch of that spirit of banter or air of levity which Edmund knew to be most offensive to Fanny, he had true pleasure in satisfying; and when Crawford proceeded to ask his opinion and give his own as to the proper-est manner in which particular passages in the service should be delivered, showing it to be a subject on which he had thought before, and thought with judgment, Edmund was still more and more pleased. This would be the way to Fanny's heart. She was not to be won by all that gallantry and wit and good-nature together could do; or at least, she would not be won by them nearly so soon, without the assistance of sentiment and feeling, and seriousness on serious subjects.

"Our liturgy," observed Crawford, "has beauties which not even a careless slovenly style of reading can destroy; but it has also redundancies and repetitions which require good reading not to be felt. For myself, at least, I must confess being not always so attentive as I ought to be" (here was a glance at Fanny); "that nineteen times out of twenty, I am thinking how such a prayer ought to be read, and longing to have it to read myself. Did you speak?" stepping eagerly to Fanny, and addressing her in a softened voice; and upon her saying "No," he added, "Are you sure you did not speak? I saw your lips move. I fancied you might be going to tell me I *ought* to be more attentive, and not *allow* my thoughts to wander. Are not you going to tell me so?"

"No, indeed, you know your duty too well for me to—even sup-posing——"

She stopped, felt herself getting into a puzzle, and could not be pre-vailed on to add another word, not by dint of several minutes of supplica-tion and waiting. He then returned to his former station, and went on as if there had been no such tender interruption.

"A sermon, well delivered, is more uncommon even than prayers well read. A sermon, good in itself, is no rare thing. It is more difficult to speak well than to compose well; that is, the rules and trick of composition are often an object of study. A thoroughly good sermon, thoroughly well delivered, is a capital gratification. I can never hear such a one without the greatest admiration and respect, and more than half a mind to take orders and preach myself. There is something in the eloquence of the pulpit, when it is really eloquence, which is entitled to the highest praise and honour. The preacher who can touch and affect such a heterogeneous mass of hearers, on subjects limited, and long worn threadbare in all common hands; who can say anything new or striking, anything that rouses the attention, without offending the taste, or wearing out the feelings of his hearers, is a man whom one could not in his public capacity honour enough. I should like to be such a man."

Edmund laughed.

"I should indeed. I never listened to a distinguished preacher in my life without a sort of envy. But then, I must have a London audience. I could not preach but to the educated; to those who were capable of estimating my composition. And I do not know that I should be fond of preaching often; now and then, perhaps, once or twice in the spring, after being anxiously expected for half-a-dozen Sundays together; but not for a constancy; it would not do for a constancy."

Here Fanny who could not but listen, involuntarily shook her head, and Crawford was instantly by her side again, intreating to know her meaning; and as Edmund perceived, by his drawing in a chair, and sitting down close by her, that it was to be a very thorough attack, that looks and undertones were to be well tried, he sank as quietly as possible into a corner, turned his back, and took up a newspaper, very sincerely wishing that dear little Fanny might be persuaded into explaining away that shake of the head to the satisfaction of her ardent lover; and as earnestly trying to bury every sound of the business from himself in murmurs of his own, over the various advertisements of "A most desirable Estate in South Wales;" "To Parents and Guardians;" and a "Capital season'd Hunter."

Fanny meanwhile, vexed with herself for not having been as motionless as she was speechless, and grieved to the heart to see Edmund's arrangements, was trying by everything in the power of her modest, gentle nature, to repulse Mr. Crawford, and avoid both his looks and enquiries; and he, unrepulsable, was persisting in both.

"What did that shake of the head mean?" said he. "What was it meant to express? Disapprobation, I fear. But of what? What had I been saying to displease you? Did you think me speaking improperly, lightly, irreverently on the subject? Only tell me if I was. Only tell me if I was wrong. I want to be set right. Nay, nay, I intreat you; for one moment put down your work. What did that shake of the head mean?"

In vain was her "Pray, sir, don't; pray, Mr. Crawford;" repeated twice over; and in vain did she try to move away. In the same low, eager voice, and the same close neighbourhood, he went on, re-urging the same questions as before. She grew more agitated and displeased.

"How can you, sir? You quite astonish me; I wonder how you can——"

"Do I astonish you?" said he. "Do you wonder? Is there anything in my present intreaty that you do not understand? I will explain to you instantly all that makes me urge you in this manner, all that gives me an interest in what you look and do, and excites my present curiosity. I will not leave you to wonder long."

In spite of herself, she could not help half a smile, but she said nothing.

"You shook your head at my acknowledging that I should not like to engage in the duties of a clergyman always for a constancy. Yes, that was the word. Constancy: I am not afraid of the word. I would spell it, read it, write it with anybody. I see nothing alarming in the word. Did you think I ought?"

"Perhaps, sir," said Fanny, wearied at last into speaking; "perhaps, sir, I thought it was a pity you did not always know yourself as well as you seemed to do at that moment."

Crawford, delighted to get her to speak at any rate, was determined to keep it up; and poor Fanny, who had hoped to silence him by such an extremity of reproof, found herself sadly mistaken, and that it was only a change from one object of curiosity and one set of words to another. He had always something to intreat the explanation of. The opportunity was too fair. None such had occurred since his seeing her in her uncle's room, none such might occur again before his leaving Mansfield. Lady Bertram's being just on the other side of the table was a trifle, for she might always be considered as only half awake, and Edmund's advertisements were still of the first utility.

"Well," said Crawford, after a course of rapid questions and reluctant answers; "I am happier than I was, because I now understand more clearly your opinion of me. You think me unsteady; easily swayed by the whim of the moment, easily tempted, easily put aside. With such an opinion, no wonder that—— But we shall see. It is not by protestations that I shall endeavour to convince you I am wronged; it is not by telling you that my affections are steady. My conduct shall speak for me; absence, distance, time shall speak for me. *They* shall prove that, as far as you can be deserved by anybody, I do deserve you. You are infinitely my superior in merit; all *that* I know. You have qualities which I had not before supposed to exist in such a degree in any human creature. You have some touches of the angel in you beyond what—not merely beyond what one sees, because one never sees anything like it—but beyond what one fancies might be. But still I am not frightened. It is not by equality of merit that you can be won. That is out of the question. It is he who sees and worships your merit the strongest, who loves you most devotedly, that has the best right to a return. There I build my confidence. By that right I do and will deserve you; and when once convinced that my attachment is what I declare it, I know you too well not to entertain the warmest hopes. Yes, dearest, sweetest Fanny. Nay—" (seeing her draw back displeased)—"forgive me. Perhaps I have as yet no right; but by what other name can I call you? Do you suppose you are ever present to my imagination under any other? No, it is 'Fanny' that I think of all day, and dream of all night. You have given the name such reality of sweetness, that nothing else can now be descriptive of you."

Fanny could hardly have kept her seat any longer, or have refrained from at least trying to get away in spite of all the too public opposition she foresaw to it, had it not been for the sound of approaching relief, the very sound which she had been long watching for, and long thinking strangely delayed.

The solemn procession, headed by Baddeley, of teaboard, urn, and cake-bearers, made its appearance, and delivered her from a grievous imprisonment of body and mind. Mr. Crawford was obliged to move. She was at liberty, she was busy, she was protected.

Edmund was not sorry to be admitted again among the number of those who might speak and hear. But though the conference had seemed full long to him, and though on looking at Fanny he saw rather a flush of vexation, he inclined to hope that so much could not have been said and listened to, without some profit to the speaker.

Chapter 35

EDMUND had determined that it belonged entirely to Fanny to choose whether her situation with regard to Crawford should be mentioned between them or not; and that if she did not lead the way, it should never be touched on by him; but after a day or two of mutual reserve, he was induced by his father to change his mind, and try what his influence might do for his friend.

A day, and a very early day, was actually fixed for the Crawfords' departure; and Sir Thomas thought it might be as well to make one more effort for the young man before he left Mansfield, that all his professions and vows of unshaken attachment might have as much hope to sustain them as possible.

Sir Thomas was most cordially anxious for the perfection of Mr. Crawford's character in that point. He wished him to be a model of constancy; and fancied the best means of effecting it would be by not trying him too long.

Edmund was not unwilling to be persuaded to engage in the business; he wanted to know Fanny's feelings. She had been used to consult him in every difficulty, and he loved her too well to bear to be denied her confidence now; he hoped to be of service to her, he thought he must be of service to her; whom else had she to open her heart to? If she did not need counsel, she must need the comfort of communication. Fanny estranged from him, silent, and reserved, was an unnatural state of things; a state which he must break through, and which he could easily learn to think she was wanting him to break through.

"I will speak to her, sir: I will take the first opportunity of speaking to her alone," was the result of such thoughts as these; and upon Sir Thomas's information of her being at that very time walking alone in the shrubbery, he instantly joined her.

"I am come to walk with you, Fanny," said he. "Shall I?" Drawing her arm within his. "It is a long while since we have had a comfortable walk together."

She assented to it all rather by look than word. Her spirits were low.

"But, Fanny," he presently added, "in order to have a comfortable walk, something more is necessary than merely pacing this gravel together. You must talk to me. I know you have something on your mind. I know what you are thinking of. You cannot suppose me uninformed. Am I to hear of it from everybody but Fanny herself?"

Fanny, at once agitated and dejected, replied, "If you hear of it from everybody, cousin, there can be nothing for me to tell."

"Not of facts, perhaps; but of feelings, Fanny. No one but you can tell me them. I do not mean to press you, however. If it is not what you wish yourself, I have done. I had thought it might be a relief."

"I am afraid we think too differently, for me to find any relief in talking of what I feel."

"Do you suppose that we think differently? I have no idea of it. I dare say that on a comparison of our opinions, they would be found as much alike as they have been used to be: to the point—I consider Crawford's proposals as most advantageous and desirable, if you could return his affection. I consider it as most natural that all your family should wish you could return it; but that as you cannot, you have done exactly as you ought in refusing him. Can there be any disagreement between us here?"

"Oh, no! But I thought you blamed me. I thought you were against me. This is such a comfort!"

"This comfort you might have had sooner, Fanny, had you sought it. But how could you possibly suppose me against you? How could you imagine me an advocate for marriage without love? Were I even careless in general on such matters, how could you imagine me so where *your* happiness was at stake?"

"My uncle thought me wrong, and I knew he had been talking to you."

"As far as you have gone, Fanny, I think you perfectly right. I may be sorry, I may be surprised: though hardly *that*, for you had not had time to attach yourself: but I think you perfectly right. Can it admit of a question? It is disgraceful to us if it does. You did not love him; nothing could have justified your accepting him."

Fanny had not felt so comfortable for days and days.

"So far your conduct has been faultless, and they were quite mistaken who wished you to do otherwise. But the matter does not end here. Crawford's is no common attachment; he perseveres, with the hope of creating that regard which had not been created before. This, we know, must be a work of time. But" (with an affectionate smile) "let him succeed at last, Fanny, let him succeed at last. You have proved yourself upright and disinterested, prove yourself grateful and tender-hearted; and then you will be the perfect model of a woman, which I have always believed you born for."

"Oh! never, never, never! he never will succeed with me." And as she spoke with a warmth which quite astonished Edmund, and which she blushed at the recollection of herself, when she saw his look, and heard him reply, "Never! Fanny! so very determined and positive! This is not like yourself, your rational self."

"I mean," she cried, sorrowfully correcting herself, "that I *think* I never shall, as far as the future can be answered for; I think I never shall return his regard."

"I must hope better things. I am aware, more aware than Crawford can be, that the man who means to make you love him (you having due notice of his intentions) must have very up-hill work, for there are all your early attachments and habits in battle array; and before he can get your heart for his own use he has to unfasten it from all the holds upon things animate and inanimate, which so many years' growth have confirmed, and which are considerably tightened for the moment by the very idea of separation. I know that the apprehension of being forced to quit Mansfield will for a time be arming you against him. I wish he had not been obliged to tell you what he was trying for. I wish he had known you as well as I do, Fanny. Between us, I think we should have won you.

My theoretical and his practical knowledge together, could not have failed. He should have worked upon my plans. I must hope, however, that time proving him (as I firmly believe it will), to deserve you by his steady affection, will give him his reward. I cannot suppose that you have not the *wish* to love him—the natural wish of gratitude. You must have some feeling of that sort. You must be sorry for your own indifference."

"We are so totally unlike," said Fanny, avoiding a direct answer, "we are so very, very different in all our inclinations and ways, that I consider it as quite impossible we should ever be tolerably happy together, even if I *could* like him. There never were two people more dissimilar. We have not one taste in common. We should be miserable."

"You are mistaken, Fanny. The dissimilarity is not so strong. You are quite enough alike. You *have* tastes in common. You have moral and literary tastes in common. You have both warm hearts and benevolent feelings; and, Fanny, who that heard him read, and saw you listen to Shakespeare the other night, will think you unfitted as companions? You forget yourself: there is a decided difference in your tempers, I allow. He is lively, you are serious; but so much the better; his spirits will support yours. It is your disposition to be easily dejected and to fancy difficulties greater than they are. His cheerfulness will counteract this. He sees difficulties nowhere: and his pleasantness and gaiety will be a constant support to you. Your being so far unlike, Fanny, does not in the smallest degree make against the probability of your happiness together: do not imagine it. I am myself convinced that it is rather a favourable circumstance. I am perfectly persuaded that the tempers had better be unlike: I mean unlike in the flow of the spirits, in the manners, in the inclination for much or little company, in the propensity to talk or to be silent, to be grave or to be gay. Some opposition here is, I am thoroughly convinced, friendly to matrimonial happiness. I exclude extremes, of course; and a very close resemblance in all those points would be the likeliest way to produce an extreme. A counteraction, gentle and continual, is the best safeguard of manners and conduct."

Full well could Fanny guess where his thoughts were now, Miss Crawford's power was all returning. He had been speaking of her cheerfully from the hour of his coming home. His avoiding her was quite at an end. He had dined at the Parsonage only the preceding day.

After leaving him to his happier thoughts for some minutes, Fanny, feeling it due to herself, returned to Mr. Crawford, and said, "It is not merely in *temper* that I consider him as totally unsuited to myself, though, in *that* respect, I think the difference between us too great, infinitely too great; his spirits often oppress me: but there is something in him which I object to still more. I must say, cousin, that I cannot approve his character. I have not thought well of him from the time of the play. I then saw him behaving, as it appeared to me, so very improperly and unfeelingly—I may speak of it now because it is all over—so improperly by poor Mr. Rushworth, not seeming to care how he exposed or hurt him, and paying attentions to my cousin Maria, which—in short, at the time of the play, I received an impression which will never be got over."

"My dear Fanny," replied Edmund, scarcely hearing her to the end, "let us not, any of us, be judged by what we appeared at that period of general folly. The time of the play is a time which I hate to recollect. Maria was wrong, Crawford was wrong, we were all wrong together; but none so wrong as myself. Compared with me, all the rest were blameless. I was playing the fool with my eyes open."

"As a bystander," said Fanny, "perhaps I saw more than you did; and I do think that Mr. Rushworth was sometimes very jealous."

"Very possibly. No wonder. Nothing could be more improper than the whole business. I am shocked whenever I think that Maria could be capable of it; but, if she could undertake the part, we must not be surprised at the rest."

"Before the play, I am much mistaken, if *Julia* did not think he was paying her attentions."

"Julia! I have heard before from some one of his being in love with Julia; but I could never see anything of it. And, Fanny, though I hope I do justice to my sisters' good qualities, I think it very possible that they might, one or both, be more desirous of being admired by Crawford, and might show that desire rather more unguardedly than was perfectly prudent. I can remember that they were evidently fond of his society; and with such encouragement, a man like Crawford, lively, and it may be, a little unthinking, might be led on to— There could be nothing very striking, because it is clear that he had no pretensions: his heart was reserved for you. And I must say, that its being for you has raised him inconceivably in my opinion. It does him the highest honour; it shows his proper estimation of the blessing of domestic happiness and pure attachment. It proves him unspoilt by his uncle. It proves him, in short, everything that I had been used to wish to believe him, and feared he was not."

"I am persuaded that he does not think, as he ought, on serious subjects."

"Say, rather, that he has not thought at all upon serious subjects, which I believe to be a good deal the case. How could it be otherwise, with such an education and adviser? Under the disadvantages, indeed, which both have had, is it not wonderful that they should be what they are? Crawford's *feelings*, I am ready to acknowledge, have hitherto been too much his guides. Happily, those feelings have generally been good. You will supply the rest; and a most fortunate man he is to attach himself to such a creature—to a woman, who, firm as a rock in her own principles, has a gentleness of character so well adapted to recommend them. He has chosen his partner, indeed, with rare felicity; he will make you happy, Fanny; I know he will make you happy; but you will make him everything."

"I would not engage in such a charge," cried Fanny, in a shrinking accent; "in such an office of high responsibility!"

'As usual, believing yourself unequal to anything! fancying everything too much for you! Well, though I may not be able to persuade you into different feelings, you will be persuaded into them, I trust. I confess myself sincerely anxious that you may. I have no common interest in Crawford's well-doing. Next to your happiness, Fanny, his has the first claim on me. You are aware of my having no common interest in Crawford."

Fanny was too well aware of it to have anything to say; and they walked on together some fifty yards in mutual silence and abstraction. Edmund first began again:—

"I was very much pleased by her manner of speaking of it yesterday, particularly pleased, because I had not depended upon her seeing everything in so just a light. I knew she was very fond of you; but yet I was afraid of her not estimating your worth to her brother quite as it deserved, and of her regretting that he had not rather fixed on some woman of distinction or fortune. I was afraid of the bias of those worldly maxims which she has been too much used to hear. But it was very different. She spoke of you, Fanny, just as she ought. She desires the connection as warmly as your uncle or myself. We had a long talk about it. I should not have mentioned the subject, though very anxious to know her sentiments, but I had not been in the room five minutes before she began introducing it with all that openness of heart, and sweet peculiarity of manner, that spirit of ingenuousness which are so much a part of herself. Mrs. Grant laughed at her for her rapidity."

"Was Mrs. Grant in the room, then?"

"Yes, when I reached the house I found the two sisters together by themselves; and when once we had begun, we had not done with you, Fanny, till Crawford and Dr. Grant came in."

"It is above a week since I saw Miss Crawford."

"Yes, she laments it; yet owns it may have been best. You will see her, however, before she goes. She is very angry with you, Fanny; you must be prepared for that. She calls herself very angry, but you can imagine her anger. It is the regret and disappointment of a sister, who thinks her brother has a right to everything he may wish for, at the first moment. She is hurt, as you would be for William; but she loves and esteems you with all her heart."

"I knew she would be very angry with me."

"My dearest Fanny," cried Edmund, pressing her arm closer to him, "do not let the idea of her anger distress you. It is anger to be talked of rather than felt. Her heart is made for love and kindness, not for resentment. I wish you could have overheard her tribute of praise; I wish you could have seen her countenance, when she said that you *should* be Henry's wife. And I observed that she always spoke of you as 'Fanny,' which she was never used to do; and it had a sound of most sisterly cordiality."

"And Mrs. Grant did she say—did she speak; was she there all the time?"

"Yes, she was agreeing exactly with her sister. The surprise of your refusal, Fanny, seems to have been unbounded. That you could refuse such a man as Henry Crawford, seems more than they can understand. I said what I could for you; but in good truth, as they stated the case—you must prove yourself to be in your senses as soon as you can, by a different conduct; nothing else will satisfy them. But this is teasing you. I have done. Do not turn away from me."

"I *should* have thought," said Fanny, after a pause of recollection and exertion, "that every woman must have felt the possibility of a man's not being approved, not being loved by some one of her sex, at least, let him be ever so generally agreeable. Let him have all the perfections in the world, I think it ought not to be set down as certain that a man must be acceptable to every woman he may happen to like himself. But, even supposing it is so, allowing Mr. Crawford to have all the claims which his sisters think he has, how was I to be prepared to meet him with any feeling answerable to his own? He took me wholly by surprise. I had not an idea that his behaviour to me before had any meaning; and surely I was not to be teaching myself to like him only because he was taking what seemed very idle notice of me. In my situation, it would have been the extreme of vanity to be forming expectations on Mr. Crawford. I am sure his sisters, rating him as they do, must have thought it so, supposing he had meant nothing. How, then, was I to be—to be in love with him the moment he said he was with me? How was I to have an attachment at his service, as soon as it was asked for? His sisters should consider me as well as him. The higher his deserts, the more improper for me ever to have thought of him. And, and—we think very differently of the nature of women, if they can imagine a woman so very soon capable of returning an affection, as this seems to imply."

"My dear, dear Fanny, now I have the truth. I know this to be the truth; and most worthy of you are such feelings. I had attributed them to you before. I thought I could understand you. You have now given exactly the explanation which I ventured to make for you to your friend and Mrs. Grant, and they were both better satisfied, though your warm-hearted friend was still run away with a little by the enthusiasm of her fondness for Henry. I told them, that you were of all human creatures the one over whom habit had most power and novelty least; and that the very circumstance of the novelty of Crawford's addresses was against him. Their being so new and so recent was all in their disfavour; that you could tolerate nothing that you were not used to; and a great deal more to the same purpose, to give them a knowledge of your character. Miss Crawford made us laugh by her plans of encouragement for her brother. She meant to urge him to persevere in the hope of being loved in time, and of having his addresses most kindly received at the end of about ten years' happy marriage."

Fanny could with difficulty give the smile that was here asked for. Her feelings were all in revolt. She feared she had been doing wrong: saying too much, overacting the caution which she had been fancying necessary; in guarding against one evil, laying herself open to another; and to have Miss Crawford's liveliness repeated to her at such a moment, and on such a subject, was a bitter aggravation.

Edmund saw weariness and distress in her face, and immediately resolved to forbear all further discussion; and not even to mention the name of Crawford again, except as it might be connected with what *must* be agreeable to her. On this principle, he soon afterwards observed—

"They go on Mondoy. You are sure, therefore, of seeing your friend either to-morrow or Sunday. They really go on Monday; and I was within a trifle of being persuaded to stay at Lessingby till that very day! I had almost promised it. What a difference it might have made! Those five or six days more at Lessingby might have been felt all my life."

"You were near staying there?"

"Very. I was most kindly pressed, and had nearly consented. Had I received any letter from Mansfield, to tell me how you were all going on, I believe I should certainly have stayed; but I knew nothing that had happened here for a fortnight, and felt that I had been away long enough."

"You spent your time pleasantly there?"

"Yes; that is, it was the fault of my own mind if I did not. They were all very pleasant. I doubt their finding me so. I took uneasiness with me, and there was no getting rid of it till I was in Mansfield again."

"The Miss Owens—you liked them, did not you?"

"Yes, very well. Pleasant, good-humoured, unaffected girls. But I am spoilt, Fanny, for common female society. Good-humoured, unaffected girls will not do for a man who has been used to sensible women. They are two distinct orders of being. You and Miss Crawford have made me too nice."

Still, however, Fanny was oppressed and wearied; he saw it in her looks, it could not be talked away; and in attempting it no more, he led her directly, with the kind authority of a privileged guardian, into the house.

Chapter 36

EDMUND now believed himself perfectly acquainted with all that Fanny could tell, or could leave to be conjectured of her sentiments, and he was satisfied. It had been, as he before presumed, too hasty a measure on Crawford's side, and time must be given to make the idea first familiar, and then agreeable to her. She must be used to the consideration of his being in love with her, and then a return of affection might not be very distant.

He gave this opinion as the result of the conversation to his father;

and recommended there being nothing more said to her: no further attempts to influence or persuade; but that everything should be left to Crawford's assiduities, and the natural workings of her own mind.

Sir Thomas promised that it should be so. Edmund's account of Fanny's disposition he could believe to be just; he supposed she had all those feelings, but he must consider it as very unfortunate that she *had;* for, less willing than his son to trust to the future, he could not help fearing that if such very long allowances of time and habit were necessary for her, she might not have persuaded herself into receiving his addresses properly, before the young man's inclination for paying them were over. There was nothing to be done, however, but to submit quietly and hope the best.

The promised visit from "her friend," as Edmund called Miss Crawford, was a formidable threat to Fanny, and she lived in continual terror of it. As a sister, so partial and so angry, and so little scrupulous of what she said, and in another light so triumphant and secure, she was in every way an object of painful alarm. Her displeasure, her penetration and her happiness were all fearful to encounter; and the dependence of having others present when they met, was Fanny's only support in looking forward to it. She absented herself as little as possible from Lady Bertram, kept away from the East Room, and took no solitary walk in the shrubbery, in her caution to avoid any sudden attack.

She succeeded. She was safe in the breakfast-room, with her aunt, when Miss Crawford did come; and the first misery over, and Miss Crawford looking and speaking with much less particularity of expression than she had anticipated, Fanny began to hope there would be nothing worse to be endured than an half hour of moderate agitation. But here she hoped too much; Miss Crawford was not the slave of opportunity. She was determined to see Fanny alone, and therefore said to her tolerably soon, in a low voice, "I must speak to you for a few minutes somewhere;" words that Fanny felt all over her, in all her pulses and all her nerves. Denial was impossible. Her habits of ready submission, on the contrary, made her almost instantly rise and lead the way out of the room. She did it with wretched feelings, but it was inevitable.

They were no sooner in the hall than all restraint of countenance was over on Miss Crawford's side. She immediately shook her head at Fanny with arch, yet affectionate reproach, and taking her hand, seemed hardly able to help beginning directly. She said nothing, however, but, "Sad, sad, girl! I do not know when I shall have done scolding you," and had discretion enough to reserve the rest till they might be secure of having four walls to themselves. Fanny naturally turned upstairs, and took her guest to the apartment which was now always fit for comfortable use; opening the door, however, with a most aching heart, and feeling that she had a more distressing scene before her than ever that spot had yet witnessed. But the evil ready to burst on her, was at least delayed by the sudden change in Miss Crawford's ideas; by the strong effect on her mind which the finding herself in the East Room again produced.

"Ha!" she cried, with instant animation, "am I here again? The East Room! Once only was I in this room before;" and after stopping to look about her, and seemingly to retrace all that had then passed, she added, "once only before. Do you remember it? I came to rehearse. Your cousin came too; and we had a rehearsal. You were our audience and prompter. A delightful rehearsal. I shall never forget it. Here we were, just in this part of the room; here was your cousin, here was I, here were the chairs. Oh! why will such things ever pass away?"

Happily for her companion, she wanted no answer. Her mind was entirely self-engrossed. She was in a reverie of sweet remembrances.

"The scene we were rehearsing was so very remarkable! The subject of it so very—very—what shall I say? He was to be describing and recommending matrimony to me. I think I see him now, trying to be as demure and composed as Anhalt ought, through the two long speeches. 'When two sympathetic hearts meet in the marriage state, matrimony may be called a happy life.' I suppose no time can ever wear out the impression I have of his looks and voice as he said those words. It was curious, very curious that we should have such a scene to play! If I had the power of recalling any one week of my existence, it should be that week—that acting week. Say what you would, Fanny, it should be *that;* for I never knew such exquisite happiness in any other. His sturdy spirit to bend as it did! Oh! it was sweet beyond expression. But alas, that very evening destroyed it all. That very evening brought your most unwelcome uncle. Poor Sir Thomas, who was glad to see you? Yet, Fanny, do not imagine I would now speak disrespectfully of Sir Thomas, though I certainly did hate him for many a week. No, I do him justice now. He is just what the head of such a family should be. Nay, in sober sadness, I believe I now love you all." And having said so, with a degree of tenderness and consciousness which Fanny had never seen in her before, and now thought only too becoming, she turned away for a moment to recover herself. "I have had a little fit since I came into this room, as you may perceive," said she presently, with a playful smile, "but it is over now; so let us sit down and be comfortable; for as to scolding you, Fanny, which I came fully intending to do, I have not the heart for it when it comes to the point." And embracing her very affectionately, "Good, gentle Fanny! when I think of this being the last time of seeing you for I do not know how long, I feel it quite impossible to do anything but love you."

Fanny was affected. She had not foreseen anything of this, and her feelings could seldom withstand the melancholy influence of the word "last." She cried as if she had loved Miss Crawford more than she possibly could; and Miss Crawford, yet further softened by the sight of such emotion, hung about her with fondness, and said, "I hate to leave you. I shall see no one half so amiable where I am going. Who says we shall not be sisters? I know we shall. I feel that we are born to be connected; and those tears convince me that you feel it too, dear Fanny."

Fanny roused herself, and replying only in part, said, "But you are only going from one set of friends to another. You are going to a very particular friend."

"Yes, very true. Mrs. Fraser has been my intimate friend for years. But I have not the least inclination to go near her. I can think only of the friends I am leaving; my excellent sister, yourself, and the Bertrams in general. You have all so much more *heart* among you than one finds in the world at large. You all give me a feeling of being able to trust and confide in you, which in common intercourse one knows nothing of. I wish I had settled with Mrs. Fraser not to go to her till after Easter, a much better time for the visit, but now I cannot put her off. And when I have done with her, I must go to her sister, Lady Stornaway, because *she* was rather my most particular friend of the two, but I have not cared much for *her* these three years."

After this speech the two girls sat many minutes silent, each thoughtful; Fanny meditating on the different sorts of friendship in the world, Mary on something of less philosophic tendency. *She* first spoke again.

"How perfectly I remember my resolving to look for you upstairs, and setting off to find my way to the East Room, without having an idea whereabouts it was! How well I remember what I was thinking of as I came along, and my looking in and seeing you here sitting at this table at work; and then your cousin's astonishment, when he opened the door, at seeing me here! To be sure, your uncle's returning that very evening! there never was anything quite like it."

Another short fit of abstraction followed, when, shaking it off, she thus attacked her companion.

"Why, Fanny, you are absolutely in a reverie. Thinking, I hope, of one who is always thinking of you. Oh! that I could transport you for a short time into our circle in town, that you might understand how your power over Henry is thought of there! Oh! the envyings and heart-burnings of dozens and dozens; the wonder, the incredulity that will be felt at hearing what you have done! For as to secrecy, Henry is quite the hero of an old romance, and glories in his chains. You should come to London to know how to estimate your conquest. If you were to see how he is courted, and how I am courted for his sake! Now, I am well aware that I shall not be half so welcome to Mrs. Fraser in consequence of his situation with you. When she comes to know the truth she will, very likely, wish me in Northamptonshire again; for there is a daughter of Mr. Fraser, by a first wife, whom she is wild to get married, and wants Henry to take. Oh! she has been trying for him to such a degree. Innocent and quiet as you sit here you cannot have an idea of the *sensation* that you will be occasioning, of the curiosity there will be to see you, of the endless questions I shall have to answer! Poor Margaret Fraser will be at me for ever about your eyes and your teeth, and how you do your hair, and who makes your shoes. I wish Margaret were married, for my poor friend's sake, for I look upon the Frasers to be about as unhappy as most other married people. And yet it was a most desirable match for Janet at the time. We were all delighted. She could not do otherwise than accept him, for he was rich, and she had nothing; but he turns out ill-tempered and exigeant, and wants a young woman, a beautiful young woman of five-and twenty, to be as steady as himself. And my friend does not manage him well; she does not seem to know how to make the best of it. There is a spirit of irritation which, to say nothing worse, is certainly very ill-bred. In their house I shall call to mind the conjugal manners of Mansfield Parsonage with respect. Even Dr. Grant does show a thorough confidence in my sister, and a certain consideration for her judgment, which makes one feel there *is* attachment; but of that I shall see nothing with the Frasers. I shall be at Mansfield for ever, Fanny. My own sister as a wife, Sir Thomas Bertram as a husband, are my standards of perfection. Poor Janet has been sadly taken in, and yet there was nothing improper on her side; she did not run into the match inconsiderately; there was no want of foresight. She took three days to consider of his proposals, and during those three days asked the advice of everybody connected with her whose opinion was worth having, and especially applied to my late dear aunt, whose knowledge of the world made her judgment very generally and deservedly looked up to by all the young people of her acquaintance, and she was decidedly in favour of Mr. Fraser. This seems as if nothing were a security for matrimonial comfort. I have not so much to say for my friend Flora, who jilted a very nice young man in the Blues for the sake of that horrid Lord Stornaway, who has about as much sense, Fanny, as Mr. Rushworth, but much worse looking, and with a blackguard character. I *had* my doubts at the time about her being right, for he has not even the air of a gentleman, and now I am sure she was wrong. By-the-bye, Flora Ross was dying for Henry the first winter she came out. But were I to attempt to tell you of all the women whom I have known to be in love with him, I should never have done. It is you, only you, insensible Fanny, who can think of him with anything like indifference. But are you so insensible as you profess yourself? No, no, I see you are not."

There was indeed so deep a blush over Fanny's face at that moment, as might warrant strong suspicion in a predisposed mind.

"Excellent creature! I will not tease you. Everything shall take its course. But, dear Fanny, you must allow that you were not so absolutely unprepared to have the question asked as your cousin fancies. It is not possible but that you must have had some thoughts on the subject, some surmises as to what might be. You must have seen that he was trying to please you by every attention in his power. Was not he devoted to you at the ball? And then before the ball, the necklace! Oh! you received it just as it was meant. You were as conscious as heart could desire. I remember it perfectly."

"Do you mean, then, that your brother knew of the necklace before-hand? Oh! Miss Crawford, *that* was not fair."

"Knew of it! It was his own doing entirely, his own thought. I am ashamed to say that it had never entered my head, but I was delighted to act on his proposal for both your sakes."

"I will not say," replied Fanny, "that I was not half afraid at the time of its being so, for there was something in your look that frightened me—but not at first—I was as unsuspicious of it at first—indeed, indeed I was. It is as true as that I sit here. And had I had an idea of it, nothing should have induced me to accept the necklace. As to your brother's behaviour, certainly I was sensible of a particularity; I had been sensible of it some little time, perhaps two or three weeks, but then I considered it as mean-ing nothing; I put it down as simply being his way, and was as far from supposing as from wishing him to have any serious thoughts of me. I had not, Miss Crawford, been an inattentive observer of what was passing between him and some part of this family in the summer and autumn. I was quiet, but I was not blind. I could not but see that Mr. Crawford allowed himself in gallantries which did mean nothing."

"Ah! I cannot deny it. He has now and then been a sad flirt, and cared very little for the havoc he might be making in young ladies' affections. I have often scolded him for it, but it is his only fault; and there is this to be said, that very few young ladies have any affections worth caring for. And then, Fanny, the glory of fixing one who has been shot at by so many; of having it in one's power to pay off the debts of one's sex! Oh! I am sure it is not in woman's nature to refuse such a triumph."

Fanny shook her head. "I cannot think well of a man who sports with any woman's feelings; and there may often be a great deal more suffered than a stander-by can judge of."

"I do not defend him. I leave him entirely to your mercy, and when he has got you at Everingham I do not care how much you lecture him. But this I will say, that his fault, the liking to make girls a little in love with him, is not half so dangerous to a wife's happiness, as a tendency to fall in love himself, which he has never been addicted to. And I do seriously and truly believe that he is attached to you in a way that he never was to any woman before; that he loves you with all his heart, and will love you as nearly for ever as possible. If any man ever loved a woman for ever, I think Henry will do so much for you."

Fanny could not avoid a faint smile, but had nothing to say.

"I cannot imagine Henry ever to have been happier," continued Mary, presently, "than when he had succeeded in getting your brother's com-mission."

She had made a sure push at Fanny's feelings here.

"Oh! yes. How very, very kind of him."

"I know he must have exerted himself very much, for I know the parties he had to move. The Admiral hates trouble, and scorns asking favours; and there are so many young men's claims to be attended to in the same way, that a friendship and energy, not very determined, is easily put by. What a happy creature William must be! I wish we could see him."

Poor Fanny's mind was thrown into the most distressing of all its varieties. The recollection of what had been done for William was always the most powerful disturber of every decision against Mr. Crawford; and she sat thinking deeply of it till Mary, who had been first watching her complacently, and then musing on something else, suddenly called her attention by saying: "I should like to sit talking with you here all day, but we must not forget the ladies below, and so good-bye, my dear, my amiable, my excellent Fanny, for though we shall nominally part in the breakfast parlour, I must take leave of you here. And I do take leave. longing for a happy re-union, and trusting that when we meet again it will be under circumstances which may open our hearts to each other, without any remnant or shadow of reserve."

A very, very kind embrace, and some agitation of manner, accompanied these words.

"I shall see your cousin in town soon: he talks of being there tolerably soon; and Sir Thomas, I dare say, in the course of the spring; and your eldest cousin, and the Rushworths, and Julia, I am sure of meeting again and again, and all but you. I have two favours to ask, Fanny: one is your correspondence. You must write to me. And the other, that you will often call on Mrs. Grant, and make her amends for my being gone."

The first, at least, of these favours Fanny would rather not have been asked; but it was impossible for her to refuse the correspondence; it was impossible for her even not to accede to it more readily than her own judgment authorised. There was no resisting so much apparent affection. Her disposition was peculiarly calculated to value a fond treatment, and from having hitherto known so little of it, she was the more overcome by Miss Crawford's. Besides, there was gratitude towards her, for having made their *tête-à-tête* so much less painful than her fears had predicted.

It was over, and she had escaped without reproaches and without detection. Her secret was still her own; and while that was the case, she thought she could resign herself to almost everything.

In the evening there was another parting. Henry Crawford came and sat some time with them; and her spirits not being previously in the strongest state, her heart was softened for a while towards him, because he really seemed to feel. Quite unlike his usual self, he scarcely said anything. He was evidently oppressed, and Fanny must grieve for him, though hoping she might never see him again, till he were the husband of some other woman.

When it came to the moment of parting, he would take her hand, he would not be denied it; he said nothing, however, or nothing that she heard, and when he had left the room, she was better pleased that such a token of friendship had passed.

On the morrow the Crawfords were gone.

Chapter 37

MR. CRAWFORD gone, Sir Thomas's next object was that he should be missed; and he entertained great hope that his niece would find a blank in the loss of those attentions which at the time she had felt, or fancied, an evil. She had tasted of consequence in its most flattering form; and he did hope that the loss of it, the sinking again into nothing, would awaken very wholesome regrets in her mind. He watched her with this idea; but he could hardly tell with what success. He hardly knew whether there were any difference in her spirits or not. She was always so gentle and retiring, that her emotions were beyond his discrimination. He did not understand her; he felt that he did not; and therefore applied to Edmund to tell him how she stood affected on the present occasion, and whether she were more or less happy than she had been.

Edmund did not discern any symptoms of regret, and thought his father a little unreasonable in supposing the first three or four days could produce any.

What chiefly surprised Edmund was, that Crawford's sister, the friend and companion, who had been so much to her, should not be more visibly regretted. He wondered that Fanny spoke so seldom of *her*, and had so little voluntarily to say of her concern at this separation.

Alas! it was this sister, this friend and companion, who was now the chief bane of Fanny's comfort. If she could have believed Mary's future fate as unconnected with Mansfield as she was determined the brother's should be, if she could have hoped her return thither to be as distant as she was much inclined to think his, she would have been light of heart indeed; but the more she recollected and observed, the more deeply was she convinced that everything was now in a fairer train for Miss Crawford's marrying Edmund than it had ever been before. On his side the inclination was stronger, on hers less equivocal. His objections, the scruples of his integrity, seemed all done away, nobody could tell how, and the doubts and hesitations of her ambition were equally got over; and equally without apparent reason. It could only be imputed to increasing attachment. His good and her bad feelings yielded to love, and such love must unite them. He was to go to town, as soon as some business relative to Thornton Lacey were completed, perhaps within a fortnight; he talked of going, he loved to talk of it; and when once with her again, Fanny could not doubt the rest. Her acceptance must be as certain as his offer; and yet there were bad feelings still remaining which made the prospect of it most sorrowful to her, independently, she believed, independently of self.

In their very last conversation, Miss Crawford, in spite of some amiable sensations, and much personal kindness, had still been Miss Crawford; still shown a mind led astray and bewildered, and without any suspicion of being so, darkened, yet fancying itself light. She might love, but she did not deserve Edmund by any other sentiment. Fanny believed there was scarcely a second feeling in common between them; and she may be for-given by older sages for looking on the chance of Miss Crawford's future improvement as nearly desperate, for thinking that if Edmund's influence in this season of love had already done so little in clearing her judgment, and regulating her notions, his worth would be finally wasted on her even in years of matrimony.

Experience might have hoped more for any young people so circum-stanced, and impartiality would not have denied to Miss Crawford's nature that participation of the general nature of women which would lead her to adopt the opinions of the man she loved and respected as her own. But as such were Fanny's persuasions, she suffered very much from them, and could never speak of Miss Crawford without pain.

Sir Thomas, meanwhile, went on with his own hopes, and his own observations, still feeling a right, by all his knowledge of human nature, to expect to see the effect of the loss of power and consequence on his niece's spirits, and the past attentions of the lover producing a craving for their return; and he was soon afterwards able to account for his not yet completely and indubitably seeing all this, by the prospect of another visitor, whose approach he could allow to be quite enough to support the spirits he was watching. William had obtained a ten days' leave of ab-sence, to be given to Northamptonshire, and was coming, the happiest of lieutenants, because the latest made, to show his happiness and describe his uniform.

He came; and he would have been delighted to show his uniform there too, had not cruel custom prohibited its appearance except on duty. So the uniform remained at Portsmouth, and Edmund conjectured that before Fanny had any chance of seeing it, all its own freshness and all the freshness of its wearer's feelings must be worn away. It would be sunk into a badge of disgrace; for what can be more unbecoming, or more worthless, than the uniform of a lieutenant, who has been a lieutenant a year or two, and sees others made commanders before him? So reasoned Edmund, till his father made him the confidant of a scheme which placed Fanny's chance of seeing the second lieutenant of H.M.S. "Thrush" in all his glory in another light.

This scheme was that she should accompany her brother back to Ports-mouth, and spend a little time with her own family. It had occurred to Sir Thomas, in one of his dignified musings, as a right and desirable measure; but before he absolutely made up his mind, he consulted his son. Edmund considered it every way, and saw nothing but what was right. The thing was good in itself, and could not be done at a better time; and he had no doubt of it being highly agreeable to Fanny. This was enough to determine Sir Thomas; and a decisive "then so it shall be" closed that stage of the business; Sir Thomas retiring from it with some feelings of satisfaction, and views of good over and above what he had communicated to his son; for his prime motive in sending her away had very little to do with the propriety of her seeing her parents again, and nothing at all with any idea of making her happy. He certainly wished her to go willingly, but he as certainly wished her to be heartily sick of home before her visit ended; and that a little abstinence from the elegancies and luxuries of Mansfield Park would bring her mind into a sober state, and incline her to a juster estimate of the value of that home of greater permanence, and equal comfort, of which she had the offer.

It was a medicinal project upon his niece's understanding, which he must consider as at present diseased. A residence of eight or nine years in the abode of wealth and plenty had a little disordered her powers of comparing and judging. Her father's house would, in all probability, teach her the value of a good income; and he trusted that she would be the wiser and happier woman, all her life, for the experiment he had devised.

Had Fanny been at all addicted to raptures, she must have had a strong attack of them when she first understood what was intended, when her uncle first made her the offer of visiting the parents, and brothers, and sisters, from whom she had been divided, almost half her life; of returning for a couple of months to the scenes of her infancy, with William for the protector and companion of her journey, and the certainty of continuing to see William to the last hour of his remaining on land. Had she ever given way to bursts of delight, it must have been then, for she was delighted, but her happiness was of a quiet, deep, heart-swelling sort, and though never a great talker, she was always more inclined to silence when feeling most strongly. At the moment she could only thank and accept. Afterwards, when familiarised with the visions of enjoyment so suddenly opened, she could speak more largely to William and Edmund of what she felt; but still there were emotions of tenderness that could not be clothed in words. The remembrance of all her earliest pleasures, and of what she had suffered in being torn from them, came over her with renewed strength, and it seemed as if to be at home again would heal every pain that had since grown out of the separation. To be in the centre of such a circle, loved by so many, and more loved by all than she had ever been before; to feel affection without fear or restraint; to feel herself the equal of those who surrounded her; to be at peace from all mention of the Crawfords, safe from every look which could be fancied a reproach on their account—this was a prospect to be dwelt on with a fondness that could be but half acknowledged.

Edmund, too—to be two months from *him*, and perhaps, she might be allowed to make her absence three, must do her good. At a distance, unassailed by his looks or his kindness, and safe from the perpetual irritation of knowing his heart, and striving to avoid his confidence, she should be able to reason herself into a proper state; she should be able to think of him as in London, and arranging everything there, without wretchedness. What might have been hard to bear at Mansfield was to become a slight evil at Portsmouth.

The only drawback was the doubt of her Aunt Bertram's being comfortable without her. She was of use to no one else; but *there* she might be missed to a degree that she did not like to think of; and that part of the arrangement was, indeed, the hardest for Sir Thomas to accomplish, and what only *he* could have accomplished at all.

But he was master at Mansfield Park. When he had really resolved on any measure, he could always carry it through; and now by dint of long talking on the subject, explaining and dwelling on the duty of Fanny's sometimes seeing her family, he did induce his wife to let her go; obtaining it rather from submission, however, than conviction, for Lady Bertram was convinced of very little more than that Sir Thomas thought Fanny ought to go, and therefore that she must. In the calmness of her own dressing-room, in the impartial flow of her own meditations, unbiassed by his bewildering statements, she could not acknowledge any necessity for Fanny's ever going near a father and mother who had done without her so long, while she was so useful to herself. And as to the not missing her, which under Mrs. Norris's discussion was the point attempted to be proved, she set herself very steadily against admitting any such thing.

Sir Thomas had appealed to her reason, conscience and dignity. He called it a sacrifice, and demanded it of her goodness and self-command as such. But Mrs. Norris wanted to persuade her that Fanny could be very well spared (*she* being ready to give up all her own time to her as requested) and in short, could not really be wanted or missed.

"That may be, sister," was all Lady Bertram's reply. "I dare say you are very right; but I am sure I shall miss her very much."

The next step was to communicate with Portsmouth. Fanny wrote to offer herself; and her mother's answer, though short, was so kind—a few simple lines expressed so natural and motherly a joy in the prospect of seeing her child again, as to confirm all the daughter's views of happiness in being with her—convincing her that she should now find a warm and affectionate friend in the "mamma" who had certainly shown no remarkable fondness for her formerly; but this she could easily suppose to have been her own fault or her own fancy. She had probably alienated love by the helplessness and fretfulness of a fearful temper, or been unreasonable in wanting a larger share than any one among so many could deserve. Now, when she knew better how to be useful, and how to forbear, and when her mother could be no longer occupied by the incessant demands of a house full of little children, there would be leisure and inclination for every comfort, and they should soon be what mother and daughter ought to be to each other.

William was almost as happy in the plan as his sister. It would be the greatest pleasure to him to have her there to the last moment before he sailed, and perhaps find her there still when he came in from his first cruise. And besides, he wanted her so very much to see the "Thrush" before she went out of harbour (the "Thrush" was certainly the finest sloop in the service); and there were several improvements in the dock·yard, too, which he quite longed to show her.

He did not scruple to add, that her being at home for a while would be a great advantage to everybody.

"I do not know how it is," said he; "but we seem to want some of your nice ways and orderliness at my father's. The house is always in confusion. You will set things going in a better way, I am sure. You will tell my mother how it all ought to be, and you will be so useful to Susan, and you will teach Betsey, and make the boys love and mind you. How right and comfortable it will all be!"

By the time Mrs. Price's answer arrived, there remained but a very few days more to be spent at Mansfield; and for part of one of those days, the young travellers were in a good deal of alarm on the subject of their journey, for when the mode of it came to be talked of, and Mrs. Norris found that all her anxiety to save her brother-in-law's money was vain, and that in spite of her wishes and hints for a less expensive conveyance of Fanny, they were to travel post; when she saw Sir Thomas actually give William notes for the purpose, she was struck with the idea of there being room for a third in the carriage, and suddenly seized with a strong inclination to go with them, to go and see her poor dear sister Price. She proclaimed her thoughts. She must say that she had more than half a mind to go with the young people; it would be such an indulgence to her; she had not seen her poor dear sister Price for more than twenty years; and it would be a help to the young people in their journey to have her older head to manage for them; and she could not help thinking her poor dear sister Price would feel it very unkind of her not to come by such an opportunity.

William and Fanny were horror-struck at the idea.

All the comfort of their comfortable journey would be destroyed at once. With woeful countenances they looked at each other. Their suspense lasted an hour or two. No one interfered to encourage or dissuade. Mrs. Norris was left to settle the matter by herself; and it ended, to the infinite joy of her nephew and niece, in the recollection that she could not possibly be spared from Mansfield Park at present; that she was a great deal too necessary to Sir Thomas and Lady Bertram for her to be able to answer it to herself to leave them even for a week, and therefore must certainly sacrifice every other pleasure to that of being useful to them.

It had, in fact, occurred to her, that though taken to Portsmouth for nothing, it would be hardly possible for her to avoid paying her own expenses back again. So her poor dear sister Price was left to all the disappointment of her missing such an opportunity, and another twenty years' absence, perhaps, begun.

Edmund's plans were affected by this Portsmouth journey, this absence of Fanny's. He, too, had a sacrifice to make to Mansfield Park as well as his aunt. He had intended, about this time, to be going to London; but he could not leave his father and mother just when everybody else of most importance to their comfort was leaving them; and with an effort, felt but not boasted of, he delayed for a week or two longer a journey which he was looking forward to with the hope of its fixing his happiness for ever.

He told Fanny of it. She knew so much already, that she must know everything. It made the substance of one other confidential discourse about Miss Crawford; and Fanny was the more affected from feeling it to be the last time in which Miss Crawford's name would ever be mentioned between them with any remains of liberty. Once afterwards she was alluded to by him. Lady Bertram had been telling her niece in the evening to write to her soon and often, and promising to be a good correspondent herself; and Edmund, at a convenient moment, then added in a whisper, "And *I* shall write to you, Fanny, when I have anything worth writing about, anything to say that I think you will like to hear, and that you will not hear so soon from any other quarter." Had she doubted his meaning while she listened, the glow in his face, when she looked up at him, would have been decisive.

For this letter she must try to arm herself. That a letter from Edmund should be a subject of terror! She began to feel that she had not yet gone through all the changes of opinion and sentiment which the progress of time and variation of circumstances occasion in this world of changes. The vicissitudes of the human mind had not yet been exhausted by her.

Poor Fanny! Though going as she did willingly and eagerly, the last evening at Mansfield Park must still be wretchedness. Her heart was completely sad at parting. She had tears for every room in the house, much more for every beloved inhabitant. She clung to her aunt, because she would miss her; she kissed the hand of her uncle with struggling sobs, because she had displeased him; and as for Edmund, she could neither speak, nor look, nor think, when the last moment came with *him;* and it was not till it was over that she knew he was giving her the affectionate farewell of a brother.

All this passed overnight, for the journey was to begin very early in the morning; and when the small, diminished party met at breakfast, William and Fanny were talked of as already advanced one stage.

Chapter 38

THE novelty of travelling, and the happiness of being with William, soon produced their natural effect on Fanny's spirits, when Mansfield Park was fairly left behind; and by the time their first stage was ended, and they were to quit Sir Thomas's carriage, she was able to take leave of the old coachman, and send back proper messages, with cheerful looks.

Of pleasant talk between the brother and sister there was no end. Everything supplied an amusement to the high glee of William's mind, and he was full of frolic and joke in the intervals of their higher-toned subjects, all of which ended, if they did not begin, in praise of the "Thrush," conjectures how she would be employed, schemes for an action with some superior force, which (supposing the first lieutenant out of the way, and William was not very merciful to the first lieutenant) was to give himself the next step as soon as possible, or speculations upon prize-money, which was to be generously distributed at home, with only the reservation of enough to make the little cottage comfortable, in which he and Fanny were to pass all their middle and latter life together.

Fanny's immediate concerns, as far as they involved Mr. Crawford, made no part of their conversation. William knew what had passed, and from his heart lamented that his sister's feelings should be so cold towards a man whom he must consider as the first of human characters; but he was of an age to be all for love, and therefore unable to blame; and knowing her wish on the subject, he would not distress her by the slightest allusion.

She had reason to suppose herself not yet forgotten by Mr. Crawford. She had heard repeatedly from his sister within the three weeks which had passed since their leaving Mansfield, and in each letter there had been a few lines from himself, warm and determined like his speeches. It was a correspondence which Fanny found quite as unpleasant as she had feared. Miss Crawford's style of writing, lively and affectionate, was itself an evil, independent of what she was thus forced into reading from the brother's pen, for Edmund would never rest till she had read the chief of the letter to him; and then she had to listen to his admiration of her language, and the warmth of her attachments. There had, in fact, been so much of message, of allusion, of recollection, so much of Mansfield in every letter, that Fanny could not but suppose it meant for him to hear; and to find herself forced into a purpose of that kind, compelled into a correspondence which was bringing her the addresses of the man she did not love, and obliging her to administer to the adverse passion of the man she did, was cruelly mortifying. Here, too, her present removal promised advantage. When no longer under the same roof with Edmund, she trusted that Miss Crawford would have no motive for writing strong enough to overcome the trouble, and that at Portsmouth their correspondence would dwindle into nothing.

With such thoughts as these, among ten hundred others, Fanny proceeded in her journey safely and cheerfully, and as expeditiously as could rationally be hoped in the dirty month of February. They entered Oxford, but she could take only a hasty glimpse of Edmund's college as they passed along, and made no stop anywhere, till they reached Newbury, where a comfortable meal uniting dinner and supper, wound up the enjoyments and fatigues of the day.

The next morning saw them off again at an early hour; and with no events, and no delays, they regularly advanced, and were in the environs of Portsmouth while there was yet daylight for Fanny to look around her, and wonder at the new buildings. They passed the drawbridge, and entered the town; and the light was only beginning to fail, as, guided by William's powerful voice, they were rattled into a narrow street, leading from the High Street, and drawn up before the door of a small house now inhabited by Mr. Price.

Fanny was all agitation and flutter; all hope and apprehension. The moment they stopped, a trollopy-looking maidservant, seemingly in waiting for them at the door, stepped forward, and more intent on telling the news than giving them any help, immediately began with "The 'Thrush' is gone out of harbour, please, sir, and one of the officers has been here to——" She was interrupted by a fine tall boy of eleven years old, who, rushing out of the house, pushed the maid aside, and while William was opening the chaise-door himself, called out, "You are just in time. We have been looking for you this half-hour. The 'Thrush' went out of harbour this morning. I saw her. It was a beautiful sight. And they think she will have her orders in a day or two. And Mr. Campbell was here at four o'clock to ask for you: he has got one of the 'Thrush's' boats, and is going off to her at six, and hoped you would be here in time to go with him."

A stare or two at Fanny, as William helped her out of the carriage, was all the voluntary notice which this brother bestowed: but he made no objection to her kissing him, though still entirely engaged in detailing further particulars of the "Thrush's" going out of harbour, in which he had a strong right of interest, being to commence his career of seamanship in her at this very time.

Another moment and Fanny was in the narrow entrance passage of the house, and in her mother's arms, who met her there with looks of true kindness, and with features which Fanny loved the more, because they brought her Aunt Bertram's before her; and there were her two sisters, Susan, a well-grown, fine girl of fourteen, and Betsey, the youngest of the family, about five—both glad to see her in their way, though with no advantage of manner in receiving her. But manner Fanny did not want. Would they but love her, she should be satisfied.

She was then taken into a parlour, so small that her first conviction was of its being only a passage-room to something better, and she stood for a moment expecting to be invited on; but when she saw there was no other door, and that there were signs of habitation before her, she called back her thoughts, reproved herself, and grieved lest they should have been suspected. Her mother, however, could not stay long enough to suspect anything. She was gone again to the street-door to welcome William. "Oh! my dear William, how glad I am to see you. But have you heard about the 'Thrush'? She is gone out of harbour already; three days before we had any thought of it; and I do not know what I am to do about Sam's things, they will never be ready in time; for she may have her orders to-morrow, perhaps. It takes me quite unawares. And now you must be off for Spithead too. Campbell has been here, quite in a worry about you; and now what shall we do? I thought to have had such a comfortable evening with you, and here everything comes upon me at once."

Her son answered cheerfully, telling her that everything was always for the best; and making light of his own inconvenience, in being obliged to hurry away so soon.

"To be sure, I had much rather she had stayed in harbour, that I might have sat a few hours with you in comfort; but as there is a boat ashore I had better go off at once, and there is no help for it. Whereabouts does the 'Thrush' lie at Spithead? Near the 'Canopus'? But no matter; here's Fanny in the parlour, and why should we stay in the passage? Come, mother, you have hardly looked at your own dear Fanny yet."

In they both came, and Mrs. Price having kindly kissed her daughter again, and commented a little on her growth, began with very natural solicitude to feel for their fatigues and wants as travellers.

"Poor dears! How tired you must both be! And now, what will you have? I began to think you would never come. Betsey and I have been watching for you this half hour. And when did you get anything to eat? And what would you like to have now? I could not tell whether you would be for some meat, or only a dish of tea after your journey, or else I would have got something ready. And now I am afraid Campbell will be here before there is time to dress a steak, and we have no butcher at hand. It is very inconvenient to have no butcher in the street. We were better off in our last house. Perhaps you would like some tea as soon as it can be got."

They both declared they should prefer it to anything. "Then, Betsey, my dear, run into the kitchen, and see if Rebecca has put the water on; and tell her to bring in the tea-things as soon as she can. I wish we could get the bell mended; but Betsey is a very handy little messenger."

Betsey went with alacrity, proud to show her abilities before her fine new sister.

"Dear me!" continued the anxious mother, "what a sad fire we have got, and I dare say you are both starved with cold. Draw your chair nearer, my dear. I cannot think what Rebecca has been about. I am sure I told her to bring some coals half an hour ago. Susan, *you* should have taken care of the fire."

"I was upstairs, mamma, moving my things," said Susan, in a fearless, self-defending tone, which startled Fanny. "You know you had but just settled that my sister Fanny and I should have the other room; and I could not get Rebecca to give me any help."

Further discussion was prevented by various bustles; first, the driver came to be paid; then there was a squabble between Sam and Rebecca about the manner of carrying up his sister's trunk, which he would manage all his own way; and lastly in walked Mr. Price himself, his own loud voice preceding him, as with something of the oath kind he kicked away his son's portmanteau and his daughter's band-box in the passage, and called out for a candle; no candle was brought, however, and he walked into the room.

Fanny with doubting feelings had risen to meet him, but sank down again on finding herself undistinguished in the dusk, and unthought of. With a friendly shake of his son's hand, and an eager voice, he instantly began: "Ha! welcome back, my boy. Glad to see you. Have you heard the news? The 'Thrush' went out of harbour this morning. Sharp is the word, you see! By G——, you are just in time! The doctor has been here enquiring for you: he has got one of the boats, and is to be off for Spithead by six, so you had better go with him. I have been to Turner's about your mess; it is all in a way to be done. I should not wonder if you had your orders to-morrow; but you cannot sail with this wind, if you are to cruise to the westward; and Captain Walsh thinks you will certainly have a cruise to the westward, with the 'Elephant.' By G——, I wish you may! But old Scholey was saying, just now, that he thought you would be sent first to the 'Texel.' Well, well, we are ready, whatever happens. But by G——, you lost a fine sight by not being here in the morning to see the 'Thrush' go out of harbour! I would not have been out of the way for a thousand pounds. Old Scholey ran in at breakfast-time, to say she had slipped her moorings and was coming out. I jumped up, and made but two steps to the platform. If ever there was a perfect beauty afloat, she is one; and there she lays at Spithead and anybody in England would take her for an eight-and-twenty. I was upon the platform two hours this afternoon looking at her. She lays close to the 'Endymion,' between her and the 'Cleopatra,' just to the eastward of the sheer hulk."

"Ha!" cried William, "*that's* just where I should have put her myself. It's the best berth at Spithead. But here is my sister, sir; here is Fanny," turning and leading her forward; "it is so dark you do not see her."

With an acknowledgment that he had quite forgot her, Mr. Price now received his daughter; and having given her a cordial hug, and observed that she was grown into a woman, and he supoposed would be wanting a husband soon, seemed very much inclined to forget her again.

Fanny shrunk back to her seat, with feelings sadly pained by his language and his smell of spirits; and he talked on only to his son, and only of the "Thrush," though William, warmly interested as he was in that subject, more than once tried to make his father think of Fanny, and her long absence and long journey.

After sitting some time longer, a candle was obtained; but as there was still no appearance of tea, nor, from Betsey's reports from the kitchen, much hope of any under a considerable period, William determined to go and change his dress, and made the necessary preparations for his removal on board directly, that he might have his tea in comfort afterwards.

As he left the room, two rosy-faced boys, ragged and dirty, about eight and nine years old, rushed into it just released from school, and coming eagerly to see their sister, and tell that the "Thrush" was gone out of harbour; Tom and Charles. Charles had been born since Fanny's going away, but Tom she had often helped to nurse, and now felt a particular pleasure in seeing again. Both were kissed very tenderly, but Tom she wanted to keep by her, to try to trace the features of the baby she had loved, and talked to, of his infant preference of herself. Tom, however, had no mind for such treatment: he came home not to stand and be talked to, but to run about and make a noise; and both boys had soon burst from her, and slammed the parlour door till her temples ached.

She had now seen all that were at home; there remained only two brothers between herself and Susan, one of whom was a clerk in a public office in London, and the other midshipman on board an Indiaman. But though she had *seen* all the members of the family, she had not yet *heard* all the noise they could make. Another quarter of an hour brought her a great deal more. William was soon calling out, from the landing-place of the second story, for his mother and for Rebecca. He was in distress for something that he had left there, and did not find again. A key was mislaid, Betsey accused of having got at his new hat, and some slight, but essential alteration of his uniform waistcoat, which he had been promised to have done for him, entirely neglected.

Mrs. Price, Rebecca, and Betsey, all went up to defend themselves, all talking together, but Rebecca loudest, and the job was to be done, as well as it could, in a great hurry; William trying in vain to send Betsey down again, or keep her from being troublesome where she was; the whole of which, as almost every door in the house was open, could be plainly distinguished in the parlour, except when drowned at intervals by the superior noise of Sam, Tom and Charles chasing each other up and down stairs, and tumbling about and hallooing.

Fanny was almost stunned. The smallness of the house and thinness of the walls brought everything so close to her, that, added to the fatigue of her journey, and all her recent agitation, she hardly knew how to bear it. *Within* the room all was tranquil enough, for Susan having disappeared with the others, there were soon only her father and herself remaining; and he taking out a newspaper, the accustomary loan of a neighbour, applied himself to studying it, without seeming to recollect her existence. The solitary candle was held between himself and the paper, without any reference to her possible convenience; but she had nothing to do, and was glad to have the light screened from her aching head, as she sat in bewildered, broken, sorrowful contemplation.

She was at home. But, alas! it was not such a home, she had not such a welcome, as—she checked herself; she was unreasonable. What right had she to be of importance to her family? She could have none, so long lost sight of! William's concerns must be dearest, they always had been, and he had every right. Yet to have so little said or asked about herself, to have scarcely an enquiry made after Mansfield! It did pain her to have Mansfield forgotten; the friends who had done so much; the dear, dear friends! But here, one subject swallowed up all the rest. Perhaps it must be so. The destination of the "Thrush" must be now pre-eminently interesting. A day or two might show the difference. *She* only was to blame. Yet she thought it would not have been so at Mansfield's. No, in her uncle's house there would have been a consideration of times and seasons, a regulation of subject, a propriety, an attention towards everybody which there was not here.

The only interruption which thoughts like these received for nearly half an hour was from a sudden burst of her father's, not at all calculated to compose them. At a more than ordinary pitch of thumping and hallooing in the passage, he exclaimed, "Devil take those young dogs! How they are singing out! Ay, Sam's voice louder than all the rest! That boy is fit for a boatswain. Halloa you there! Sam, stop your confounded pipe, or I shall be after you."

This threat was so palpably disregarded, that though within five minutes afterwards the three boys all burst into the room together and sat down, Fanny could not consider it as a proof of anything more than their being for the time thoroughly fagged, which their hot faces and panting breaths seemed to prove, especially as they were still kicking each other's shins, and hallooing out at sudden starts immediately under their father's eye.

The next opening of the door brought something more welcome; it was for the tea-things, which she had begun almost to despair of seeing that evening. Susan and an attendant girl, whose inferior appearance informed Fanny, to her great surprise, that she had previously seen the upper servant, brought in everything necessary for the meal: Susan looking, as she put the kettle on the fire and glanced at her sister, as if divided between the agreeable triumph of showing her activity and usefulness, and the dread of being thought to demean herself by such an office. "She had been into the kitchen," she said, "to hurry Sally and help make the toast, and spread the bread and butter, or she did not know when they should have got tea, and she was sure her sister must want something after her journey."

Fanny was very thankful. She could not but own that she should be very glad of a little tea, and Susan immediately set about making it, as if pleased to have the employment all to herself; and with only a little unnecessary bustle, and some few injudicious attempts at keeping her brothers in better order than she could, acquitted herself very well. Fanny's spirit was as much refreshed as her body; her head and heart were soon the better for such well-timed kindness. Susan had an open, sensible countenance; she was like William, and Fanny hoped to find her like him in disposition and good will towards herself .

In this more placid state of things William re-entered, followed not far behind by his mother and Betsey. He, complete in his lieutenant's uniform, looking and moving all the taller, firmer and more graceful for it, and with the happiest smile over his face, walked up directly to Fanny, who, rising from her seat, looked at him for a moment in speechless admiration, and then threw her arms round his neck to sob out her various emotions of pain and pleasure.

Anxious not to appear unhappy, she soon recovered herself; and wiping away her tears, was able to notice and admire all the striking parts of his dress; listening with reviving spirits to his cheerful hopes of being on

shore some part of every day before they sailed, and even of getting her to
Spithead to see the sloop.

The next bustle brought in Mr. Campbell, the surgeon of the "Thrush,"
a very well-behaved young man, who came to call for his friend, and for
whom there was with some contrivance found a chair, and with some hasty
washing of the young tea-maker's, a cup and saucer; and after another
quarter of an hour of earnest talk between the gentlemen, noise rising
upon noise, and bustle upon bustle, men and boys at last all in motion together, the moment came for setting off; everything was ready, William
took leave, and all of them were gone; for the three boys, in spite of their
mother's entreaty, determined to see their brother and Mr. Campbell to
the sally-port; and Mr. Price walked off at the same time to carry back
his neighbour's newspaper.

Something like tranquillity might now be hoped for; and accordingly,
when Rebecca had been prevailed on to carry away the tea-things, and
Mrs. Price had walked about the room some time looking for a shirt-
sleeve, which Betsey at last hunted out from a drawer in the kitchen,
the small party of females were pretty well composed, and the mother
having lamented again over the impossibility of getting Sam ready in
time, was at leisure to think of her eldest daughter and the friends she
had come from.

A few enquiries began; but one of the earliest—How did her sister Bertram manage about her servants? Was she as much plagued as herself to
get tolerable servants?—soon led her mind away from Northamptonshire,
and fixed it on her own domestic grievances, and the shocking character of all the Portsmouth servants, of whom she believed her own two
were the very worst, engrossed her completely. The Bertrams were all
forgotten in detailing the faults of Rebecca, against whom Susan had also
much to depose, and little Betsey a great deal more, and who did seem so
thoroughly without a single recommendation, that Fanny could not help
modestly presuming that her mother meant to part with her when her
year was up.

"Her year!" cried Mrs. Price; "I am sure I hope I shall be rid of her
before she has stayed a year, for that will not be up till November. Servants are come to such a pass, my dear, in Portsmouth, that it is quite a
miracle if one keeps them more than half a year. I have no hope of ever
being settled; and if I was to part with Rebecca, I should only get something worse. And yet I do not think I am a very difficult mistress to please;
and I am sure the place is easy enough, for there is always a girl under her,
and I often do half the work myself."

Fanny was silent; but not from being convinced that there might not
be a remedy found for some of these evils. As she now sat looking at
Betsey, she could not but think particularly of another sister, a very
pretty little girl, whom she had left there not much younger when she
went into Northamptonshire, who had died a few years afterwards. There
had been something remarkably amiable about her. Fanny in those early

days had preferred her to Susan; and when the news of her death had at last reached Mansfield, had for a short time been quite afflicted. The sight of Betsey brought the image of little Mary back again, but she would not have pained her mother by alluding to her for the world. While considering her with these ideas, Betsey, at a small distance, was holding out something to catch her eyes, meaning to screen it at the same time from Susan's.

"What have you got there, my love?" said Fanny, "come and show it to me."

It was a silver knife. Up jumped Susan, claiming it as her own, and trying to get it away; but the child ran to her mother's protection, and Susan could only reproach, which she did very warmly, and evidently hoping to interest Fanny on her side. "It was very hard that she was not to have her *own* knife; it was her own knife; little sister Mary had left it to her upon her death-bed, and she ought to have had it to keep herself long ago. But mamma kept it from her, and was always letting Betsey get hold of it; and the end of it would be that Betsey would spoil it, and get it for her own, though mamma had *promised* her that Betsey should not have it in her own hands."

Fanny was quite shocked. Every feeling of duty, honour, and tenderness, was wounded by her sister's speech and her mother's reply.

"Now, Susan," cried Mrs. Price in a complaining voice, "now, how can you be so cross? You are always quarrelling about that knife. I wish you would not be so quarrelsome. Poor little Betsey; how cross Susan is to you! But you should not have taken it out, my dear, when I sent you to the drawer. You know I told you not to touch it, because Susan is so cross about it. I must hide it another time, Betsey. Poor Mary little thought it would be such a bone of contention when she gave it me to keep, only two hours before she died. Poor little soul! She could but just speak to be heard, and she said so prettily, 'Let sister Susan have my knife, mamma, when I am dead and buried.' Poor little dear! She was so fond of it, Fanny, that she would have it lie by her in bed, all through her illness. It was the gift of her good godmother, old Mrs. Admiral Maxwell, only six weeks before she was taken for death. Poor little sweet creature! Well, she was taken away from evil to come. My own Betsey (fondling her), *you* have not the luck of such a good godmother. Aunt Norris lives too far off to think of such little people as you."

Fanny had indeed nothing to convey from Aunt Norris, but a message to say she hoped that her god-daughter was a good girl, and learnt her book. There had been at one moment a slight murmur in the drawing-room at Mansfield Park, about sending her a prayer-book; but no second sound had been heard of such a purpose. Mrs. Norris, however, had gone home and taken down two old prayer-books of her husband with that idea; but, upon examination, the ardour of generosity went off. One was found to have too small a print for a child's eyes, and the other to be too cumbersome for her to carry about.

Fanny, fatigued and fatigued again, was thankful to accept the first invitation of going to bed; and before Betsey had finished her cry at being allowed to sit up only one hour extraordinary in honour of sister, she was off, leaving all below in confusion and noise again; the boys begging for toasted cheese, her father calling out for his rum and water, and Rebecca never where she ought to be.

There was nothing to raise her spirits in the confined and scantily-furnished chamber that she was to share with Susan. The smallness of the rooms above and below, indeed, and the narrowness of the passage and staircase, struck her beyond her imagination. She soon learned to think with respect of her own little attic at Mansfield Park, in *that* house reckoned too small for anybody's comfort.

Chapter 39

COULD Sir Thomas have seen all his niece's feelings, when she wrote her first letter to her aunt, he would not have despaired; for though a good night's rest, a pleasant morning, the hope of soon seeing William again, and the comparatively quiet state of the house, from Tom and Charles being gone to school, Sam on some project of his own, and her father on his usual lounges, enabled her to express herself cheerfully on the subject of home, there were still, to her own perfect consciousness, many drawbacks suppressed. Could he have seen only half that she felt before the end of a week, he would have thought Mr. Crawford sure of her, and been delighted with his own sagacity.

Before the week ended, it was all disappointment. In the first place, William was gone. The "Thrush" had had her orders, the wind had changed and he was sailed within four days from their reaching Portsmouth; and during those days she had seen him only twice, in a short and hurried way, when he had come ashore on duty. There had been no free conversation, no walk on the ramparts, no visit to the dockyard, no acquaintance with the "Thrush," nothing of all that they had planned and depended on. Everything in that quarter failed her, except William's affection. His last thought on leaving home was for her. He stepped back again to the door to say, "Take care of Fanny, mother. She is tender, and not used to rough it like the rest of us. I charge you, take care of Fanny."

William was gone; and the home he had left her in was, Fanny could not conceal it from herself, in almost every respect the very reverse of what she could have wished. It was the abode of noise, disorder and impropriety. Nobody was in their right place, nothing was done as it ought to be. She could not respect her parents as she had hoped. On her father, her confidence had not been sanguine, but he was more negligent of his family, his habits were worse, and his manners coarser, than she had been prepared for. He did not want abilities; but he had no curiosity, and no information beyond his profession; he read only the newspaper and the navy-list; he talked only of the dockyard, the harbour, Spithead, and the Motherbank; he swore and he drank, he was dirty and gross. She had never been able to recall anything approaching to tenderness in his former treatment of herself. There had remained only a general impression of roughness and loudness; and now he scarcely ever noticed her, but to make her the object of a coarse joke.

Her disappointment in her mother was greater; *there* she had hoped much, and found almost nothing. Every flattering scheme of being of consequence to her soon fell to the ground. Mrs. Price was not unkind; but, instead of gaining on her affection and confidence, and becoming more and more dear, her daughter never met with greater kindness from her than on the first day of her arrival. The instinct of nature was soon satisfied, and Mrs. Price's attachment had no other source. Her heart and her time were already quite full; she had neither leisure nor affection to bestow on Fanny. Her daughters never had been much to her. She was fond of her sons, especially William, but Betsey was the first of her girls whom she had ever much regarded. To her she was most injudiciously indulgent. William was her pride; Betsey her darling; and John, Richard, Sam, Tom, and Charles occupied all the rest of her maternal solicitude, alternately her worries and her comforts. These shared her heart: her time was given chiefly to her house and her servants. Her days were spent in a kind of slow bustle; always busy without getting on; always behind hand and lamenting it, without altering her ways; wishing to be an economist, without contrivance or regularity; dissatisfied with her servants, without skill to make them better, and whether helping, or reprimanding, or indulging them, without any power of engaging their respect.

Of her two sisters, Mrs. Price very much more resembled Lady Bertram than Mrs. Norris. She was a manager by necessity, without any of Mrs. Norris's inclination for it, or any of her activity. Her disposition was naturally easy and indolent, like Lady Bertram's; and a situation of similar affluence and do-nothingness would have been much more suited to her capacity than the exertions and self-denials of the one which her imprudent marriage had placed her in. She might have made just as good a woman of consequence as Lady Bertram, but Mrs. Norris would have been a more respectable mother of nine children on a small income.

Much of all this Fanny could not but be sensible of. She might scruple to make use of the words, but she must and did feel that her mother was a partial, ill-judging parent, a dawdle, a slattern, who neither taught nor restrained her children, whose house was the scene of mismanagement and discomfort from beginning to end, and who had no talent, no conversation, no affection towards herself; no curiosity to know her better, no desire of her friendship, and no inclination for her company that could lessen her sense of such feelings.

Fanny was very anxious to be useful, and not to appear above her home, or in any way disqualified or disinclined, by her foreign education, from contributing her help to its comforts, and therefore set about working for

Sam immediately, and by working early and late, with perseverance and great despatch, did so much that the boy was shipped off at last, with more than half his linen ready. She had great pleasure in feeling her usefulness, but could not conceive how they would have managed without her.

Sam, loud and overbearing as he was, she rather regretted when he went, for he was clever and intelligent, and glad to be employed in any errand in the town; and though spurning the remonstrances of Susan, given as they were, though very reasonable in themselves, with ill-timed and powerless warmth, was beginning to be influenced by Fanny's services and gentle persuasions; and she found that the best of the three younger ones was gone in him; Tom and Charles being at least as many years as they were his juniors distant from that age of feeling and reason, which might suggest the expediency of making friends, and of endeavouring to be less disagreeable. Their sister soon despaired of making the smallest impression on *them;* they were quite untameable by any means of address which she had spirits or time to attempt. Every afternoon brought a return of their riotous games all over the house; and she very early learned to sigh at the approach of Saturday's constant half holiday.

Betsey, too, a spoiled child, trained up to think the alphabet her greatest enemy, left to be with the servants at her pleasure, and then encouraged to report any evil of them, she was almost as ready to despair of being able to love or assist; and of Susan's temper she had many doubts. Her continual disagreements with her mother, her rash squabbles with Tom and Charles, and petulance with Betsey, were at least so distressing to Fanny, that though admitting they were by no means without provocation, she feared the disposition that could push them to such length must be far from amiable, and from affording any repose to herself.

Such was the home which was to put Mansfield out of her head, and teach her to think of her cousin Edmund with moderated feelings. On the contrary, she could think of nothing but Mansfield, its beloved inmates, its happy ways. Everything where she now was was in full contrast to it. The elegance, propriety, regularity, harmony, and perhaps, above all, the peace and tranquillity of Mansfield, were brought to her remembrance every hour of the day, by the prevalence of everything opposite to them *here.*

The living in incessant noise was, to a frame and temper delicate and nervous like Fanny's, an evil which no super-added elegance or harmony could have entirely atoned for. It was the greatest misery of all. At Mansfield, no sounds of contention, no raised voice, no abrupt bursts, no tread of violence, was ever heard; all proceeded in a regular course of cheerful orderliness; everybody had their due importance; everybody's feelings were consulted. If tenderness could be ever supposed wanting, good sense and good breeding supplied its place; and as to the little irritations, sometimes introduced by Aunt Norris, they were short, they were trifling, they were as a drop of water to the ocean, compared with the ceaseless tumult of her present abode. Here, everybody was noisy, every voice was loud (excepting, perhaps, her mother's, which resembled the soft monotony of Lady Bertram's, only worn into fretfulness). Whatever was wanted was halloo'd for, and the servants halloo'd out their excuses from the kitchen The doors were in constant banging, the stairs were never at rest, nothing was done without a clatter, nobody sat still, and nobody could command attention when they spoke.

In a review of the two houses, as they appeared to her before the end of a week, Fanny was tempted to apply to them Dr. Johnson's celebrated judgment as to matrimony and celibacy, and say, that though Mansfield Park might have some pains, Portsmouth could have no pleasures.

Chapter 40

FANNY was right enough in not expecting to hear from Miss Crawford now, at the rapid rate in which their correspondence had begun; Mary's next letter was after a decidedly longer interval than the last, but she was not right in supposing that such an interval would be felt a great relief to herself. Here was another strange revolution of mind! She was really glad to receive the letter when it did come. In her present exile from good society, and distance from everything that had been wont to interest her, a letter from one belonging to the set where her heart lived, written with affection, and some degree of elegance, was thoroughly acceptable. The usual plea of increasing engagements was made in excuse for not having written to her earlier; "and now that I have begun," she continued, "my letter will not be worth your reading, for there will be no little offering of love at the end, no three or four lines passionnées from the most devoted H. C. in the world, for Henry is in Norfolk; business called him to Everingham ten days ago, or perhaps he only pretended the call, for the sake of being travelling at the same time that you were. But there he is, and, by the bye, his absence may sufficiently account for any remissness of his sister's in writing, for there has been no 'Well, Mary, when do you write Fanny? Is not it time for you to write to Fanny?' to spur me on. At last, after various attempts at meeting, I have seen your cousins, 'dear Julia and dearest Mrs. Rushworth;' they found me at home yesterday and we were glad to see each other again. We *seemed very* glad to see each other, and I do really think we were a little. We had a vast deal to say. Shall I tell you how Mrs. Rushworth looked when your name was mentioned? I did not use to think her wanting in self-possession, but she had not quite enough for the demands of yesterday. Upon the whole Julia was in the best looks of the two, at least after you were spoken of. There was no recovering the complexion from the moment that I spoke of 'Fanny,' and spoke of her as a sister should. But Mrs. Rushworth's day of good looks will come; we have cards for her first party on the 28th. Then she will be in beauty, for she will open one of the best houses in Wimpole Street. I was in it two years ago, when it was Lady Lascelles's, and prefer it to almost any I know in London, and certainly she will then feel, to use a vulgar phrase, that she has got her pennyworth for her penny. Henry could not have afforded her such a house. I hope she will recollect it, and be satisfied, as well as she may, with moving the queen of a palace, though the king may appear best in the background; and as I have no desire to tease her, I shall never *force* your name upon her again. She will grow sober by degrees. From all that I hear and guess, Baron Wildenheim's attentions to Julia continue, but I do not know that he has any serious encouragement. She ought to do better. A poor honourable is no catch, and I cannot imagine any liking in the case, for, take away his rants, and the poor baron has nothing. What a difference a vowel makes! If his rents were but equal to his rants! Your cousin Edmund moves slowly; detained, perchance, by parish duties. There may be some old woman at Thornton Lacey to be converted. I am unwilling to fancy myself neglected for a *young* one. Adieu! my dear sweet Fanny, this is a long letter from London: write me a pretty one in reply to gladden Henry's eyes, when he comes back, and send me an account of all the dashing young captains whom you disdain for his sake."

There was great food for meditation in this letter, and chiefly for unpleasant meditation; and yet, with all the uneasiness it supplied, it connected her with the absent, it told her of people and things about whom she had never felt so much curiosity as now, and she would have been glad to have been sure of such a letter every week. Her correspondence with her Aunt Bertram was her only concern of higher interest.

As for any society in Portsmouth, that could at all make amends for deficiencies at home, there were none within the circle of her father's and mother's acquaintance to afford her the smallest satisfaction; she saw nobody in whose favour she could wish to overcome her own shyness and reserve. The men appeared to her all coarse, the women all pert, everybody underbred; and she gave as little contentment as she received from introductions either to old or new acquaintances. The young ladies who approached her at first with some respect, in consideration of her coming from a baronet's family, were soon offended by what they termed "airs"; for, as she neither played on the pianoforte, nor wore fine pelisses, they could, on farther observation, admit no right of superiority.

The first solid consolation which Fanny received for the evils of home, the first which her judgment could entirely approve, and which gave any promise of durability, was in a better knowledge of Susan, and a hope of being of service to her. Susan had always behaved pleasantly to herself, but the determined character of her general manners had astonished and alarmed her, and it was at least a fortnight before she began to understand a disposition so totally different from her own. Susan saw that much was wrong at home, and wanted to set it right. That a girl of fourteen, acting only on her own unassisted reason, should err in the method of reform, was not wonderful; and Fanny soon became more disposed to admire the natural light of the mind which could so early distinguish justly, than to censure severely the faults of conduct to which it led. Susan was only acting on the same truths, and pursuing the same system, which her own judgment acknowledged, but which her more supine and yielding temper would have shrunk from asserting. Susan tried to be useful, where *she* could only have gone away and cried; and that Susan was useful she could perceive; that things, bad as they were, would have been worse but for such interposition, and that both her mother and Betsey were restrained from some excesses of very offensive indulgence and vulgarity.

In every argument with her mother, Susan had in point of reason the advantage, and never was there any maternal tenderness to buy her off. The blind fondness which was for ever producing evil around her *she* had never known. There was no gratitude for affection past or present to make her better bear with its excesses to the others.

All this became gradually evident, and gradually placed Susan before her sister as an object of mingled compassion and respect. That her manner was wrong, however, at times very wrong, her measures often ill-chosen and ill-timed, and her looks and language very often indefensible, Fanny could not cease to feel; but she began to hope they might be rectified. Susan, she found, looked up to her and wished for her good opinion; and new as anything like an office of authority was to Fanny, new as it was to imagine herself capable of guiding or informing any one, she did resolve to give occasional hints to Susan, and endeavour to exercise for her advantage the juster notions of what was due to everybody, and what would be wisest for herself, which her own more favoured education had fixed in her.

Her influence, or at least the consciousness and use of it, originated in an act of kindness by Susan, which, after many hesitations of delicacy, she at last worked herself up to. It had very early occurred to her that a small sum of money might, perhaps, restore peace for ever on the sore subject of the silver knife, canvassed as it now was continually, and the riches which she was in possession of herself, her uncle having given her £10 at parting, made her as able as she was willing to be generous. But she was so wholly unused to confer favours, except on the very poor, so unpractised in removing evils, or bestowing kindnesses among her equals, and so fearful of appearing to elevate herself as a great lady at home, that it took some time to determine that it would not be unbecoming in her to make such a present. It was made, however, at last; a silver knife was bought for Betsey, and accepted with great delight, its newness giving it every advantage over the other that could be desired; Susan was established in the full possession of her own, Betsey handsomely declaring that now she had got one so much prettier herself, she should never want *that* again; and no reproach seemed conveyed to the equally satisfied mother, which Fanny had almost feared to be impossible. The deed thoroughly answered; a source of domestic altercation was entirely done away, and it was the means of opening Susan's heart to her, and giving her something more to love and be interested in. Susan showed that she had delicacy; pleased as she was to be mistress of property which she had been struggling for at least two years, she yet feared that her sister's judgment had been against her, and that a reproof was designed for her having so struggled as to make the purchase necessary for the tranquillity of the house.

Her temper was open. She acknowledged her fears, blamed herself for having contended so warmly; and from that hour Fanny, understanding the worth of her disposition, and perceiving how fully she was inclined to seek her good opinion and refer to her judgment, began to feel again the blessing of affection, and to entertain the hope of being useful to a mind so much in need of help, and so much deserving it. She gave advice, advice too sound to be resisted by a good understanding, and given so mildly and considerately as not to irritate an imperfect temper, and she had the happiness of observing its good effects not unfrequently. More was not expected by one who, while seeing all the obligation and expediency of submission and forbearance, saw also with sympathetic acuteness of feeling all that must be hourly grating to a girl like Susan. Her greatest wonder on the subject soon became—not that Susan should have been provoked into disrespect and impatience against her better knowledge—but that so much better knowledge, so many good notions should have been hers at all; and that, brought up in the midst of negligence and error, she should have formed such proper opinions of what ought to be; she, who had had no cousin Edmund to direct her thoughts or fix her principles.

The intimacy thus begun between them was a material advantage to each. By sitting together upstairs, they avoided a great deal of the disturbance of the house; Fanny had peace, and Susan learned to think it no misfortune to be quietly employed. They sat without a fire; but *that* was a privation familiar even to Fanny, and she suffered the less because reminded by it of the East Room. It was the only point of resemblance. In space, light, furniture, and prospect, there was nothing alike in the two apartments; and she often heaved a sigh at the remembrance of all her books and boxes, and various comforts there. By degrees the girls came to spend the chief of the morning upstairs, at first only in working and talking, but after a few days, the remembrance of the said books grew so potent and stimulative, that Fanny found it impossible not to try for books again. There were none in her father's house; but wealth is luxurious and daring, and some of hers found its way to a circulating library. She became a subscriber; amazed at being anything in propria persona, amazed at her own doings in every way, to be a renter, a chooser of books! And to be having any one's improvement in view in her choice! But so it was. Susan had read nothing, and Fanny longed to give her a share in her own first pleasure, and inspire a taste for the biography and poetry which she delighted in herself.

In this occupation she hoped, moreover, to bury some of the recollec-

tions of Mansfield, which were too apt to seize her mind if her fingers
only were busy; and especially at this time, hoped it might be useful
in diverting her thoughts from pursuing Edmund to London, whither,
on the authority of her aunt's last letter, she knew he was gone. She
had no doubt of what would ensue. The promised notification was
hanging over her head. The postman's knock within the neighbourhood
was beginning to bring its daily terrors, and if reading could banish
the idea for even half an hour, it was something gained.

Chapter 41

A WEEK was gone since Edmund might be supposed in town, and Fanny
had heard nothing of him. There were three different conclusions to be
drawn from his silence, between which her mind was in fluctuation;
each of them at times being held the most probable. Either his going
had been again delayed or he had yet procured no opportunity of seeing
Miss Crawford alone, or he was too happy for letter-writing!

One morning, about this time, Fanny having now been nearly four
weeks from Mansfield, a point which she never failed to think over
and calculate every day, as she and Susan were preparing to remove, as
usual, upstairs, they were stopped by the knock of a visitor, whom they
felt they could not avoid, from Rebecca's alertness in going to the door,
a duty which always interested her beyond any other.

It was a gentleman's voice; it was a voice that Fanny was just turning pale about, when Mr. Crawford walked into the room.

Good sense, like hers, will always act when really called upon; and
she found that she had been able to name him to her mother, and recall
her remembrance of the name, as that of "William's friend," though
she could not previously have believed herself capable of uttering a
syllable at such a moment. The consciousness of his being known there
only as William's friend was some support. Having introduced him,
however, and being all reseated, the terrors that occurred of what this
visit might lead to were overpowering, and she fancied herself on the
point of fainting away.

While trying to keep herself alive, their visitor, who had at first approached her with as animated a countenance as ever, was wisely and
kindly keeping his eyes away, and giving her time to recover, while he
devoted himself entirely to her mother, addressing her, and attending
to her with the utmost politeness and propriety, at the same time with a
degree of friendliness, of interest, at least, which was making his
manner perfect.

Mrs. Price's manners were also at their best. Warmed by the sight
of such a friend to her son, and regulated by the wish of appearing to
advantage before him, she was overflowing with gratitude, artless, maternal gratitude, which could not be unpleasing. Mr. Price was out, which

she regretted very much. Fanny was just recovered enough to feel that *she* could not regret it; for to her many other sources of uneasiness was added the severe one of shame for the home in which he found her. She might scold herself for the weakness, but there was no scolding it away. She was ashamed, and she would have been yet more ashamed of her father than of all the rest.

They talked of William; a subject on which Mrs. Price could never tire; and Mr. Crawford was as warm in his commendation as even her heart could wish. She felt that she had never seen so agreeable a man in her life; and was only astonished to find, that so great and so agreeable as he was, he should be come down to Portsmouth neither on a visit to the port-admiral, nor the commissioner, nor yet with the intention of going over to the island, nor of seeing the dockyard. Nothing of all that she had been used to think of as the proof of importance, or the employment of wealth, had brought him to Portsmouth. He had reached it late the night before, was come for a day or two, was staying at the Crown, had accidentally met with a navy officer or two of his acquaintance since his arrival, but had no object of that kind in coming.

By the time he had given all this information, it was not unreasonable to suppose that Fanny might be looked at and spoken to; and she was tolerably able to bear his eye, and hear that he had spent half an hour with his sister the evening before his leaving London; that she had sent her best and kindest love, but had had no time for writing; that he thought himself lucky in seeing Mary for even half an hour, having spent scarcely twenty-four hours in London, after his return from Norfolk, before he set off again; that her cousin Edmund was in town, had been in town, he understood, a few days; that he had not seen him himself, but that he was well, had left them all well at Mansfield, and was to dine, as yesterday, with the Frasers.

Fanny listened collectedly, even to the last-mentioned circumstance; nay, it seemed a relief to her worn mind to be at any certainty; and the words, "then by this time it is all settled," passed internally, without more evidence of emotion than a faint blush.

After talking a little more about Mansfield, a subject in which her interest was most apparent, Crawford began to hint at the expediency of an early walk. "It was a lovely morning, and at that season of the year a fine morning so often turned off, that it was wisest for everybody not to delay their exercise;" and such hints producing nothing, he soon proceeded to a positive recommendation to Mrs. Price and her daughters, to take their walk without loss of time. Now they came to an understanding. Mrs. Price, it appeared, scarcely ever stirred out of doors, except on a Sunday; she owned she could seldom, with her large family, find time for a walk. "Would she not, then, persuade her daughters to take advantage of such weather, and allow him the pleasure of attending them?" Mrs. Price was greatly obliged and very complying.

"Her daughters were very much confined; Portsmouth was a sad place; they did not often get out; and she knew they had some errands in the town, which they would be very glad to do." And the consequence was that Fanny, strange as it was, strange, awkward, and distressing, found herself and Susan, within ten minutes, walking towards the High Street, with Mr. Crawford.

It was soon pain upon pain, confusion upon confusion; for they were hardly in the High Street, before they met her father, whose appearance was not the better from its being Saturday. He stopped, and, ungentlemanlike as he looked, Fanny was obliged to introduce him to Mr. Crawford. She could not have a doubt of the manner in which Mr. Crawford must be struck. He must be ashamed and disgusted altogether. He must soon give her up, and cease to have the smallest inclination for the match; and yet, though she had been so much wanting his affection to be cured, this was a sort of cure that would be almost as bad as the complaint; and I believe there is scarcely a young lady in the United Kingdoms who would not rather put up with the misfortune of being sought by a clever, agreeable man, than have him driven away by the vulgarity of her nearest relations.

Mr. Crawford probably could not regard his future father-in-law with any idea of taking him for a model in dress; but (as Fanny instantly, and to her great relief, discerned) her father was a very different man, a very different Mr. Price in his behaviour to this most highly respected stranger, from what he was in his own family at home. His manners now, though not polished, were more than passable; they were grateful, animated, manly; his expressions were those of an attached father, and a sensible man; his loud tones did very well in the open air, and there was not a single oath to be heard. Such was his instinctive compliment to the good manners of Mr. Crawford; and, be the consequence what it might, Fanny's immediate feelings were infinitely soothed.

The conclusion of the two gentlemen's civilities was an offer of Mr. Price's to take Mr. Crawford into the dockyard, which Mr. Crawford, desirous of accepting as a favour what was intended as such, though he had seen the dockyard again and again, and hoping to be so much the longer with Fanny, was very gratefully disposed to avail himself of, if the Miss Prices were not afraid of the fatigue; and as it was somehow or other ascertained or inferred, or at least acted upon, that they were not at all afraid, to the dockyard they were all to go; and but for Mr. Crawford, Mr. Price would have turned thither directly, without the smallest consideration for his daughters' errands in the High Street. He took care, however, that they should be allowed to go to the shops they came out expressly to visit; and it did not delay them long, for Fanny could so little bear to excite impatience, or be waited for, that before the gentlemen, as they stood at the door, could do more than begin upon the last naval regulations, or settle the number of three-deckers now in commission, their companions were ready to proceed.

They were then to set forward for the dockyard at once, and the walk would have been conducted (according to Mr. Crawford's opinion) in a singular manner, had Mr. Price been allowed the entire regulation of it, as the two girls, he found, would have been left to follow, and keep up with them or not, as they could, while they walked on together at their own hasty pace. He was able to introduce some improvement occasionally, though by no means to the extent he wished; he absolutely would not walk away from them; and at any crossing or any crowd, when Mr. Price was only calling out, "Come, girls; come, Fan; come, Sue, take care of yourselves; keep a sharp look out!" he would give them his particular attendance.

Once fairly in the dockyard, he began to reckon upon some happy intercourse with Fanny, as they were very soon joined by a brother lounger of Mr. Price's, who was come to take his daily survey of how things went on, and who must prove a far more worthy companion than himself; and after a time the two officers seemed very well satisfied going about together, and discussing matters of equal and never-failing interest, while the young people sat down upon some timbers in the yard, or found a seat on board a vessel in the stocks which they all went to look at. Fanny was most conveniently in want of rest. Crawford could not have wished her more fatigued or more ready to sit down; but he could have wished her sister away. A quick-looking girl of Susan's age was the very worst third in the world: totally different from Lady Bertram, all eyes and ears; and there was no introducing the main point before her. He must content himself with being only generally agreeable, and letting Susan have her share of entertainment, with the indulgence, now and then, of a look or hint for the better informed and conscious Fanny. Norfolk was what he had mostly to talk of: there he had been some time, and everything there was rising in importance from his present schemes. Such a man could come from no place, no society, without importing something to amuse; his journeys and his acquaintances were all of use, and Susan was entertained in a way quite new to her. For Fanny, somewhat more was related than the accidental agreeableness of the parties he had been in. For her approbation, the particular reason of his going into Norfolk at all, at this unusual time of year, was given. It had been real business, relative to the renewal of a lease in which the welfare of a large and (he believed) industrious family was at stake. He had suspected his agent of some underhand dealing; of meaning to bias him against the deserving; and he had determined to go himself, and thoroughly investigate the merits of the case. He had gone, had done even more good than he had foreseen, had been useful to more than his first plan had comprehended, and was now able to congratulate himself upon it, and to feel that, in performing a duty, he had secured agreeable recollections for his own mind. He had introduced himself to some tenants, whom he had never seen before; he had begun making acquaintances with cottages whose very existence, though on his own estate, had been hitherto unknown to him. This was aimed, and well aimed, at Fanny. It was pleasing to hear him speak so properly; here he had been acting as he ought to do. To be the friend of the poor and the oppressed! Nothing could be more grateful to her; and she was on the point of giving him an approving look when it was all frightened off, by his adding a something too pointed of his hoping soon to have an assistant, a friend, a guide in every plan of utility or charity for Everingham; a somebody that would make Everingham and all about it a dearer object than it had ever been yet.

She turned away, and wished he would not say such things. She was willing to allow he might have more good qualities than she had been wont to suppose. She began to feel the possibility of his turning out well at last; but he was and must ever be completely unsuited to her, and ought not to think of her.

He perceived that enough had been said of Everingham, and that it would be as well to talk of something else, and turned to Mansfield. He could not have chosen better; that was a topic to bring back her attention and her looks almost instantly. It was a real indulgence to her to hear or to speak of Mansfield. Now so long divided from everybody who knew the place, she felt it quite the voice of a friend when he mentioned it, and led the way to her fond exclamations in praise of its beauties and comforts, and by his honourable tribute to its inhabitants allowed her to gratify her own heart in the warmest eulogium, in speaking of her uncle as all that was clever and good, and her aunt as having the sweetest of all sweet tempers.

He had a great attachment to Mansfield himself; he said so; he looked forward with the hope of spending much, very much, of his time there; always there, or in the neighbourhood. He particularly built upon a very happy summer and autumn there this year; he felt that it would be so; he depended upon it; a summer and autumn infinitely superior to the last. As animated as diversified, as social, but with circumstances of superiority undescribable.

"Mansfield, Sotherton, Thornton Lacey," he continued, "what a society will be comprised in those houses! And at Michaelmas, perhaps, a fourth may be added: some small hunting-box in the vicinity of everything so dear; for as to any partnership in Thornton Lacey, as Edmund Bertram once good-humouredly proposed, I hope I foresee two objections: two fair, excellent, irresistible objections to that plan."

Fanny was doubly silenced here; though when the moment was passed, could regret that she had not forced herself into the acknowledged comprehension of one half of his meaning, and encouraged him to say something more of his sister and Edmund. It was a subject which she must learn to speak of, and the weakness that shrunk from it would soon be quite unpardonable.

When Mr. Price and his friend had seen all that they wished, or had time for, the others were ready to return; and in the course of their walk back, Mr. Crawford contrived a minute's privacy for telling Fanny that his only business in Portsmouth was to see her; that he was come down for a couple of days on her account and hers only, and because he could not endure a longer total separation. She was sorry, really sorry; and yet in spite of this and the two or three other things which she wished he had not said, she thought him altogether improved since she had seen him; he was much more gentle, obliging, and attentive to other people's feelings than he had ever been at Mansfield; she had never seen him so agreeable—so *near* being agreeable; his behaviour to her father could not offend, and there was something particularly kind and proper in the notice he took of Susan. He was decidedly improved. She wished the next day over, she wished he had come only for one day; but it was not so very bad as she would have expected: the pleasure of talking of Mansfield was so very great.

Before they parted, she had to thank him for another pleasure, and one of no trivial kind. Her father asked him to do them the honour of taking his mutton with them, and Fanny had time for only one thrill of horror, before he declared himself prevented by a prior engagement. He was engaged to dinner already both for that day and the next; he had met with some acquaintance at the Crown who would not be denied; he should have the honour, however, of waiting on them again on the morrow, etc., and so they parted—Fanny in a state of actual felicity from escaping so horrible an evil!

To have had him join their family dinner-party, and see all their deficiencies, would have been dreadful! Rebecca's cookery, and Rebecca's waiting, and Betsey's eating at table without restraint, and pulling everything about as she chose, were what Fanny herself was not yet enough inured to for her often to make a tolerable meal. *She* was nice only from natural delicacy, but *he* had been brought up in a school of luxury and epicurism.

Chapter 42

THE Prices were just setting off for church the next day when Mr. Crawford appeared again. He came, not to stop, but to join them; he was asked to go with them to the Garrison Chapel, which was exactly what he had intended, and they all walked thither together.

The family were now seen to advantage. Nature had given them no inconsiderable share of beauty, and every Sunday dressed them in their cleanest skins and best attire. Sunday always brought this comfort to Fanny, and on this Sunday she felt it more than ever. Her poor mother now did not look so very unworthy of being Lady Bertram's sister as she was but too apt to look. It often grieved her to the heart to think of the contrast between them; to think that where nature had made so little difference, circumstances should have made so much, and that her mother as handsome as Lady Bertram, and some years her junior, should have an appearance so much more worn and faded, so comfortless, so slatternly, so shabby. But Sunday made her a very creditable and tolerably cheerful-looking Mrs. Price, coming abroad with a fine family of children, feeling a little respite of her weekly cares, and only discomposed if she saw her boys run into danger, or Rebecca pass by with a flower in her hat.

In chapel they were obliged to divide, but Mr. Crawford took care not to be divided from the female branch; and after chapel he still continued with them, and made one in the family party on the ramparts.

Mrs. Price took her weekly walk on the ramparts every fine Sunday throughout the year, always going directly after morning service and staying till dinner-time. It was her public place: there she met her acquaintances, heard a little news, talked over the badness of the Portsmouth servants, and wound up her spirits for the six days ensuing.

Thither they now went; Mr. Crawford most happy to consider the Miss Prices as his peculiar charge; and before they had been there long, somehow or other, there was no saying how, Fanny could not have believed it, but he was walking between them with an arm of each under his, and she did not know how to prevent or put an end to it. It made her uncomfortable for a time, but yet there were enjoyments in the day and in the view which would be felt.

The day was uncommonly lovely. It was really March; but it was April in its mild air, brisk soft wind, and bright sun, occasionally clouded for a minute; and everything looked so beautiful under the influence of such a sky; the effects of the shadows pursuing each other on the ships at Spithead and the island beyond, with the ever-varying hues of the sea, now at high water, dancing in its glee and dashing against the ramparts with so fine a sound, produced altogether such a combination of charms for Fanny, as made her gradually almost careless of the circumstances under which she felt them. Nay, had she been without his arm, she would soon have known that she needed it, for she wanted strength for a two hours' saunter of this kind, coming, as it generally did, upon a week's previous inactivity. Fanny was beginning to feel the effect of being debarred from her usual regular exercise; she had lost ground as to health since her being in Portsmouth; and but for Mr. Crawford and the beauty of the weather would soon have been knocked up now.

The loveliness of the day, and of the view, he felt like herself. They often stopped with the same sentiment and taste, leaning against the wall some minutes, to look and admire, and considering he was not Edmund, Fanny could not but allow that he was sufficiently open to the charms of nature, and very well able to express his admiration. She had a few tender reveries now and then, which he could sometimes take advantage of to look in her face without detection; and the result of these looks was, that though as bewitching as ever, her face was less blooming than it ought to be. She *said* she was very well, and did not like to be supposed otherwise; but take it all in all, he was convinced that her present residence could not be comfortable, and therefore could not be salutary for her, and he was growing anxious for her being again at Mansfield, where her own happiness, and his in seeing her, must be so much greater.

"You have been here a month, I think?" said he.

"No; not quite a month. It is only four weeks to-morrow since I left Mansfield."

"You are a most accurate and honest reckoner. I should call that a month."

"I did not arrive here till Tuesday evening."

"And it is to be a two months' visit, is not it?"

"Yes. My uncle talked of two months. I suppose it will not be less."

"And how are you to be conveyed back again? Who comes for you?"

"I do not know. I have heard nothing about it yet from my aunt. Perhaps I may be able to stay longer. It may not be convenient for me to be fetched exactly at the two months' end."

After a moment's reflection Mr. Crawford replied, "I know Mansfield, I know its way, I know its faults towards *you*. I know the danger of your being so far forgotten, as to have your comforts give way to the imaginary convenience of any single being in the family. I am aware that you may be left here week after week, if Sir Thomas cannot settle everything for coming himself, or sending your aunt's maid for you, without involving the slightest alteration of the arrangements which he may have laid down for the next quarter of a year. This will not do. Two months is an ample allowance; I should think six weeks quite enough. I am considering your sister's health," said he, addressing himself to Susan, "which I think the confinement of Portsmouth unfavourable to. She requires constant air and exercise. When you know her as well as I do, I am sure you will agree that she does, and that she ought never to be long banished from the free air and liberty of the country. If, therefore" (turning again to Fanny), "you find yourself growing unwell, and any difficulties arise about your returning to Mansfield, without waiting for the two months to be ended, *that* must not be regarded as of any consequence, if you feel yourself at all less strong or comfortable than usual, and will only let my sister know it, give her only the slightest hint, she and I will immediately come down, and take you back to Mansfield. You know the ease and the pleasure with which this would be done. You know all that would be felt on the occasion."

Fanny thanked him, but tried to laugh it off.

"I am perfectly serious," he replied, "as you perfectly know. And I hope you will not be cruelly concealing any tendency to indisposition. Indeed, you shall *not;* it shall not be in your power; for so long only as you positively say, in every letter to Mary, 'I am well,' and I know you cannot speak or write a falsehood, so long only shall you be considered as well."

Fanny thanked him again, but was affected and distressed to a degree that made it impossible for her to say much, or even to be certain of what she ought to say. This was towards the close of their walk. He attended them to the last, and left them only at the door of their own house, when he knew them to be going to dinner, and therefore pretended to be waited for elsewhere.

"I wish you were not so tired," said he, still detaining Fanny after all the others were in the house—"I wish I felt you in stronger health. Is there anything I can do for you town? I have half an idea of going into Norfolk again soon. I am not satisfied about Maddison. I am sure he still means to impose on me if possible, and get a cousin of his own into a certain mill, which I design for somebody else. I must come to an understanding with him. I must make him know that I will not be tricked on the south side of Everingham, any more than on the north: that I will be master of my own property. I was not explicit enough with him before. The mischief such a man does on an estate, both as to the credit of his employer and the welfare of the poor, is inconceivable. I have a great mind to go back into Norfolk directly, and put everything at once on such a footing as cannot be afterwards swerved from. Maddison is a clever fellow; I do not wish to displace him, provided he does not try to displace *me;* but it would be simple to be duped by a man who has no right of creditor to dupe me, and worse than simple to let him give me a hard-hearted, griping fellow for a tenant, instead of an honest man, to whom I have given half a promise already. Would it not be worse than simple? Shall I go? Do you advise it?"

"I advise! You know very well what is right."

"Yes. When you give me your opinion, I always know what is right. Your judgment is my rule of right."

"Oh, no! do not say so. We have all a better guide in ourselves, if we would attend to it, than any other person can be. Good-bye; I wish you a pleasant journey to-morrow."

"Is there nothing I can do for you in town?"

"Nothing, I am much obliged to you."

"Have you no message for anybody?"

"My love to your sister, if you please; and when you see my cousin, my cousin Edmund, I wish you would be so good as to say that I suppose I shall soon hear from him."

"Certainly; and if he is lazy or negligent, I will write his excuses myself."

He could say no more, for Fanny would be no longer detained. He pressed her hand, looked at her, and was gone. *He* went to while away the next three hours as he could, with his other acquaintance, till the best dinner that a capital inn afforded was ready for their enjoyment, and *she* turned in to her more simple one immediately.

Their general fare bore a very different character; and could he have suspected how many privations, besides that of exercise, she endured in her father's house, he would have wondered that her looks were not much more affected than he found them. She was so little equal to Rebecca's puddings and Rebecca's hashes, brought to table, as they all were, with such accompaniments of half-cleaned plates, and not half-cleaned knives and forks, that she was very often constrained to defer her heartiest meal till she could send her brothers in the evening for biscuits and buns. After being nursed up at Mansfield, it was too late in the day to be hardened at Portsmouth; and though Sir Thomas, had he known all, might have thought his niece in the most promising way of being starved, both mind and body, into a much juster value of Mr. Crawford's good company and good fortune, he would probably have feared to push his experiment farther, lest she might die under the cure.

Fanny was out of spirits all the rest of the day. Though tolerably secure of not seeing Mr. Crawford again, she could not help being low. It was parting with somebody of the nature of a friend; and though, in one light, glad to have him gone, it seemed as if she was now deserted by everybody; it was a sort of renewed separation from Mansfield; and she could not think of his returning to town and being frequently with Mary and Edmund, without feelings so near akin to envy as made her hate herself for having them.

Her dejection had no abatement from anything passing around her; a friend or two of her father's, as always happened if he was not with them, spent the long, long evening there; and from six o'clock till half-past nine, there was little intermission of noise or grog. She was very low. The wonderful improvement which she still fancied in Mr. Crawford was the nearest to administering comfort of anything within the current of her thoughts. Not considering in how different a circle she had been just seeing him, nor how much might be owing to contrast, she was quite persuaded of his being astonishingly more gentle and regardful of others than formerly. And, if in little things, must it not be so in great? So anxious for her health and comfort, so very feeling as he now expressed himself, and really seemed, might not it be fairly supposed that he would not much longer persevere in a suit so distressing to her?

Chapter 43

It was presumed that Mr. Crawford was travelling back to London, on the morrow, for nothing more was seen of him at Mr. Price's; and two days afterwards, it was a fact ascertained to Fanny by the following letter from his sister, opened and read by her, on another account, with the most anxious curiosity:—

"I have to inform you, my dearest Fanny, that Henry has been down to Portsmouth to see you; that he had a delightful walk with you to the dockyard last Saturday, and one still more to be dwelt on the next day, on the ramparts; when the balmy air, the sparkling sea, and your sweet looks and conversation were altogether in the most delicious harmony, and afforded sensations which are to raise ecstasy even in retrospect. This, as well as I understand, is to be the substance of my information. He makes me write, but I do not know what else is to be communicated, except this said visit to Portsmouth, and these two said walks and his introduction to your family, especially to a fair sister of yours, a fine girl of fifteen, who was of the party on the ramparts, taking her first lesson, I presume, in love. I have not time for writing much, but it would be out of place if I had, for this is to be a mere letter of business, penned for the purpose of conveying necessary information, which could not be delayed without risk of evil. My dear, dear Fanny, if I had you here, how I would talk to you! You should listen to me till you were tired, and advise me till you were still tired more; but it is impossible to put a hundredth part of my great mind on paper, so I will abstain altogether, and leave you to guess what you like. I have no news for you. You have politics, of course; and it would be too bad to plague you with the names of people and parties that fill up my time. I ought to have sent you an account of your cousin's first party, but I was lazy, and now it is too long ago; suffice it, that everything was just as it ought to be, in a style that any of her connections must have been gratified to witness, and that her own dress and manners did her the greatest credit. My friend, Mrs. Fraser, is made for such a house, and it would not make *me* miserable. I go to Lady Stornaway after Easter; she seems in high spirits, and very happy. I fancy Lord S. is very good-humoured and pleasant in his own family, and I do not think him so very ill-looking as I did—at least, one sees many worse. He will not do by the side of your cousin Edmund. Of the last-mentioned hero, what shall I say? If I avoided his name entirely, it would look suspicious. I will say, then, that we have seen him two or three times, and that my friends here are very much struck with his gentlemanlike appearance. Mrs. Fraser (no bad judge) declares she knows but three men in town who have so good a person, height, and air; and I must confess, when he dined here the other day, there were none to compare with him, and we were a party of sixteen. Luckily there is no distinction of dress nowadays to tell tales, but—but—but— Yours affectionately—

"I had almost forgot (it was Edmund's fault: he gets into my head more than does me good) one very material thing I had to say from Henry and myself—I mean about our taking you back into Northamptonshire. My dear little creature, do not stay at Portsmouth to lose your pretty looks. Those vile sea-breezes are the ruin of beauty and health. My poor aunt always felt affected if within ten miles of the sea, which the Admiral of course never believed, but I know it was so. I am at your service and Henry's, at an hour's notice. I should like the scheme, and we would make a little circuit, and show you Everingham in our way, and perhaps you would not mind passing through London, and seeing the inside of St

George's, Hanover Square. Only keep your cousin Edmund from me at such a time: I should not like to be tempted. What a long letter! one word more. Henry, I find, has some idea of going into Norfolk again upon some business that *you* approve but this cannot possibly be permitted before the middle of next week; that is, he cannot anyhow be spared till after the 14th, for *we* have a party that evening. The value of a man like Henry, on such an occasion, is what you can have no conception of; so you must take it upon my word to be inestimable. He will see the Rushworths, which I own I am not sorry for—having a little curiosity, and so I think has he—though he will not acknowledge it."

This was a letter to be run through eagerly, to be read deliberately, to supply matter for much reflection, and to leave everything in greater suspense than ever. The only certainty to be drawn from it was, that nothing decisive had yet taken place. Edmund had not yet spoken. How Miss Crawford really felt, how she meant to act, or might act without or against her meaning; whether his importance to her were quite what it had been before the last separation; whether, if lessened, it were likely to lessen more, or to recover itself, were subjects for endless conjecture, and to be thought of on that day and many days to come, without producing any conclusion. The idea that returned the oftenest was that Miss Crawford, after proving herself cooled and staggered by a return to London habits, would yet prove herself in the end too much attached to him to give him up. She would try to be more ambitious than her heart would allow. She would hesitate, she would tease, she would condition, she would require a great deal, but she would finally accept.

This was Fanny's most frequent expectation. A house in town, *that*, she thought, must be impossible. Yet there was no saying what Miss Crawford might not ask. The prospect for her cousin grew worse and worse. The woman who could speak of him, and speak only of his appearance! What an unworthy attachment! To be deriving support from the commendations of Mrs. Fraser! *She* who had known him intimately half a year! Fanny was ashamed of her. Those parts of the letter which related only to Mr. Crawford and herself, touched her, in comparison, slightly. Whether Mr. Crawford went into Norfolk before or after the 14th was certainly no concern of hers, though, everything considered she thought he *would* go without delay. That Miss Crawford should endeavour to secure a meeting between him and Mrs. Rushworth was all in her worst line of conduct, and grossly unkind and ill-judged; but she hoped *he* would not be actuated by any such degrading curiosity. He acknowledged no such inducement, and his sister ought to have given him credit for better feelings than her own.

She was yet more impatient for another letter from town after receiving this than she had been before; and for a few days was so unsettled by it altogether, by what had come, and what might come, that her usual readings and conversations with Susan were much suspended. She could not command her attention as she wished. If Mr. Crawford remembered her message to her cousin, she thought it very likely, *most* likely, that he would write to her at all events; it would be most consistent with his usual kindness; and till she got rid of this idea, till it gradually wore off, by no letters appearing in the course of three or four days more, she was in a most restless, anxious state.

At length, a something like composure succeeded. Suspense must be submitted to, and must not be allowed to wear her out, and make her useless. Time did something, her own exertions something more, and she resumed her attentions to Susan, and again awakened the same interest in them.

Susan was growing very fond of her, and though without any of the early delight in books, which had been so strong in Fanny, with a disposition much less inclined to sedentary pursuits, or to information for information's sake, she had so strong a desire, of not *appearing* ignorant, as, with a good clear understanding, made her a most attentive, profitable, thankful pupil. Fanny was her oracle. Fanny's explanations and remarks were a most important addition to every essay, or every chapter of history. What Fanny told her of former times dwelt more on her mind than the pages of Goldsmith; and she paid her sister the compliment of preferring her style to that of any printed author. The early habit of reading was wanting.

Their conversations, however, were not always on subjects so high as history or morals. Others had their hour; and of lesser matters none returned so often, or remained so long between them, as Mansfield Park, a description of the people, the manners, the amusements, the ways of Mansfield Park. Susan, who had an innate taste for the genteel and well-appointed, was eager to hear, and Fanny could not but indulge herself in dwelling on so beloved a theme. She hoped it was not wrong; though, after a time, Susan's very great admiration of everything said or done in her uncle's house, and earnest longing to go into Northamptonshire, seemed almost to blame her for exciting feelings which could not be gratified.

Poor Susan was very little better fitted for home than her elder sister; and as Fanny grew thoroughly to understand this, she began to feel that when her own release from Portsmouth came, her happiness would have a material drawback in leaving Susan behind. That a girl so capable of being made everything good should be left in such hands, distressed her more and more. Were *she* likely to have a home to invite her to, what a blessing it would be! And had it been possible for her to return Mr. Crawford's regard, the probability of his being very far from objecting to such a measure would have been the greatest increase of all her own comforts. She thought he was really good-tempered, and could fancy his entering into a plan of that sort most pleasantly.

Chapter 44

SEVEN weeks of the two months were very nearly gone, when the one letter, the letter from Edmund, so long expected, was put into Fanny's hands. As she opened, and saw its length, she prepared herself for a minute detail of happiness and a profusion of love and praise towards the fortunate creature who was now mistress of his fate. These were the contents:—

MANSFIELD PARK.

"MY DEAR FANNY,—Excuse me that I have not written before. Crawford told me that you were wishing to hear from me, but I found it impossible to write from London, and persuaded myself that you would understand my silence. Could I have sent a few happy lines, they should not have been wanting, but nothing of that nature was ever in my power. I am returned to Mansfield in a less assured state than when I left it. My hopes are much weaker. You are probably aware of this already. So very fond of you as Miss Crawford is, it is most natural that she should tell you enough of her own feelings to furnish a tolerable guess at mine. I will not be prevented however, from making my own communication. Our confidences in you need not clash. I ask no questions. There is something soothing in the idea that we have the same friend, and that whatever unhappy differences of opinion may exist between us, we are united in our love of you. It will be a comfort to me to tell you how things now are, and what are my present plans, if plans I can be said to have. I have been returned since Saturday. I was three weeks in London, and saw her (for London) very often. I had every attention from the Frasers that could be reasonably expected. I dare say I was *not* reasonable in carrying with me hopes of an intercourse at all like that of Mansfield. It was her manner, however, rather than any unfrequency of meeting. Had she been different when I did see her, I should have made no complaint, but from the very first she was altered; my first reception was so unlike what I had hoped, that I had almost resolved on leaving London again directly. I need not particularise. You know the weak side of her character, and may imagine the sentiments and expressions which were torturing me. She was in high spirits, and surrounded by those who were giving all the support of their own bad sense to her too lively mind. I do not like Mrs. Fraser. She is a cold-hearted, vain woman, who has married entirely from convenience, and though evidently unhappy in her marriage, places her disappointment not to faults of judgment, or temper, or disproportion of age, but to her being, after all, less affluent than many of her acquaintance, especially than her sister, Lady Stornaway, and is the determined supporter of everything mercenary and ambitious, provided it be only mercenary and ambitious enough. I look upon her intimacy with those two sisters as the greatest misfortune of her life and mine. They have been leading her astray

for years. Could she be detached from them!—and sometimes I do not
despair of it, for the affection appears to me principally on their side. They
are very fond of her; but I am sure she does not love them as she loves
you. When I think of her great attachment to you, indeed, and the whole
of her judicious, upright conduct as a sister, she appears a very different
creature, capable of everything noble, and I am ready to blame myself for
a too harsh construction of a playful manner. I cannot give her up, Fanny.
She is the only woman in the world whom I could ever think of as a wife.
If I did not believe that she had some regard for me, of course I should
not say this, but I do believe it. I am convinced that she is not without a
decided preference. I have no jealousy of any individual. It is the influence
of the fashionable world altogether that I am jealous of. It is the habits
of wealth that I fear. Her ideas are not higher than her own fortune may
warrant, but they are beyond what our incomes united could authorise.
There is comfort, however, even here. I could better bear to lose her,
because not rich enough, than because of my profession. That would only
prove her affection not equal to sacrifices, which, in fact, I am scarcely
justified in asking; and, if I am refused, *that,* I think, will be the honest
motive. Her prejudices, I trust, are not so strong as they were. You have
my thoughts exactly as they arise, my dear Fanny; perhaps they are
sometimes contradictory, but it will not be a less faithful picture of my
mind. Having once begun, it is a pleasure to me to tell you all I feel. I
cannot give her up. Connected as we already are, and, I hope, are to be,
to give up Mary Crawford would be to give up the society of some of those
most dear to me; to banish myself from the very houses and friends whom,
under any other distress, I should turn to for consolation. The loss of Mary
I must consider as comprehending the loss of Crawford and of Fanny.
Were it a decided thing, an actual refusal, I hope I should know how to
bear it, and how to endeavour to weaken her hold on my heart, and in the
course of a few years—but I am writing nonsense. Were I refused, I must
bear it; and till I am, I can never cease to try for her. This is the truth. The
only question is *how?* What may be the likeliest means? I have sometimes
thought of going to London again after Easter, and sometimes resolved
on doing nothing till she returns to Mansfield. Even now, she speaks with
pleasure of being in Mansfield in June; but June is at a great distance, and
I believe I shall write to her. I have nearly determined on explaining
myself by letter. To be at an early certainty is a material object. My
present state is miserably irksome. Considering everything, I think a letter
will be decidedly the best method of explanation. I shall be able to write
much that I could not say, and shall be giving her time for reflection before
she resolves on her answer, and I am less afraid of the result of reflection
than of an immediate hasty impulse; I think I am. My greatest danger
would lie in her consulting Mrs. Fraser, and I at a distance unable to help
my own cause. A letter exposes to all the evil of consultation, and where
the mind is anything short of perfect decision, an adviser may, in an unlucky moment, lead it to do what it may afterwards regret. I must think

this matter over a little. This long letter, full of my own concerns alone, will be enough to tire even the friendship of a Fanny. The last time I saw Crawford was at Mrs. Fraser's party. I am more and more satisfied with all that I see and hear of him. There is not a shadow of wavering. He thoroughly knows his own mind, and acts up to his resolutions: an inestimable quality. I could not see him and my eldest sister in the same room, without recollecting what you once told me, and I acknowledge that they did not meet as friends. There was marked coolness on her side. They scarcely spoke. I saw him draw back surprised, and I was sorry that Mrs. Rushworth should resent any former supposed slight to Miss Bertram. You will wish to hear my opinion of Maria's degree of comfort as a wife. There is no appearance of unhappiness. I hope they get on pretty well together. I dined twice in Wimpole Street, and might have been there oftener, but it is mortifying to be with Rushworth as a brother. Julia seems to enjoy London exceedingly. I had little enjoyment there, but have less here. We are not a lively party. You are very much wanted. I miss you more than I can express. My mother desires her best love, and hopes to hear from you soon. She talks of you almost every hour, and I am sorry to find how many weeks more she is likely to be without you. My father means to fetch you himself, but it will not be till after Easter, when he has business in town. You are happy at Portsmouth, I hope, but this must not be a yearly visit. I want you at home, that I may have your opinion about Thornton Lacey. I have little heart for extensive improvements till I know that it will ever have a mistress. I think I shall certainly write. It is quite settled that the Grants go to Bath; they leave Mansfield on Monday. I am glad of it. I am not comfortable enough to be fit for anybody; but your aunt seems to feel out of luck that such an article of Mansfield news should fall to my pen instead of hers. Yours ever, my dearest Fanny—"

"I never will, no, I certainly never will wish for a letter again," was Fanny's secret declaration as she finished this. "What do they bring but disappointment and sorrow? Not till after Easter! How shall I bear it? And my poor aunt talking of me every hour!"

Fanny checked the tendency of these thoughts as well as she could, but she was within half a minute of starting the idea that Sir Thomas was quite unkind, both to her aunt and to herself. As for the main subject of the letter, there was nothing in that to soothe irritation. She was almost vexed into displeasure and anger against Edmund. "There is no good in this delay," said she. "Why is not it settled? He is blinded, and nothing will open his eyes; nothing can, after having had truths before him so long in vain. He will marry her, and be poor and miserable. God grant that her influence does not make him cease to be respectable!" She looked over the letter again. " 'So very fond of me!' 'tis nonsense all. She loves nobody but herself and her brother. 'Her friends leading her astray for years!' She is quite as likely to have led *them* astray. They have all, perhaps, been corrupting one another; but if they are so much fonder of her than she is of them, she is the less likely to have been hurt, except by their flattery. 'The only woman in the world whom he could ever think of as a wife.' I firmly believe it. It is an attachment to govern his whole life. Accepted or refused, his heart is wedded to her for ever. 'The loss of Mary I must consider as comprehending the loss of Crawford and Fanny.' Edmund, you do not know *me*. The families would never be connected if you did not connect them! Oh! write, write. Finish it at once. Let there be an end of this suspense. Fix, commit, condemn yourself."

Such sensations, however, were too near akin to resentment to be long guiding Fanny's soliloquies. She was soon more softened and sorrowful. His warm regard, his kind expressions, his confidential treatment, touched her strongly. He was only too good to everybody. It was a letter, in short, which she would not but have had for the world, and which could never be valued enough. This was the end of it.

Everybody at all addicted to letter-writing, without having much to say, which will include a large proportion of the female world, at least, must feel with Lady Bertram that she was out of luck in having such a capital piece of Mansfield news as the certainty of the Grants going to Bath, occur at a time when she could make no advantage of it, and will admit that it must have been very mortifying to her to see it fall to the share of her thankless son, and treated as concisely as possible at the end of a long letter, instead of having it to spread over the largest part of a page of her own. For though Lady Bertram rather shone in the epistolary line, having early in her marriage, from the want of other employment, and the circumstance of Sir Thomas's being in Parliament, got into the way of making and keeping correspondents and formed for herself a very creditable, commonplace, amplifying style, so that very little matter was enough for her: she could not do entirely without any; she must have something to write about, even to her niece; and being so soon to lose all the benefit of Dr. Grant's gouty symptoms and Mrs. Grant's morning calls, it was very hard upon her to be deprived of one of the last epistolary uses she could put them to.

There was a rich amends, however, preparing for her. Lady Bertram's hour of good luck came. Within a a few days from the receipt of Edmund's letter, Fanny had one from her aunt, beginning thus:—

"MY DEAR FANNY,—I take up my pen to communicate some very alarming intelligence, which I make no doubt will give you much concern."

This was a great deal better than to have to take up the pen to acquaint her with all the particulars of the Grants' intended journey, for the present intelligence was of a nature to promise occupation for the pen for many days to come, being no less than the dangerous illness of her eldest son, of which they had received notice by express a few hours before.

Tom had gone from London with a party of young men to Newmarket, where a neglected fall and a good deal of drinking had brought on a fever; and when the party broke up, being unable to move, had been left by himself at the house of one of these young men to the comforts of sickness and solitude, and the attendance only of servants. Instead of being soon well enough to follow his friends, as he had then hoped, his disorder in-increased considerably, and it was not long before he thought so ill of himself, as to be as ready as his physician to have a letter dispatched to Mansfield.

"This distressing intelligence, as you may suppose," observed her lady-ship, after giving the substance of it, "has agitated us exceedingly and we cannot prevent ourselves from being greatly alarmed and apprehensive for the poor invalid, whose state Sir Thomas fears may be very critical; and Edmund kindly proposes attending his brother immediately, but I am happy to add that Sir Thomas will not leave me on this distressing occasion, as it would be too trying for me. We shall greatly miss Edmund in our small circle, but I trust and hope he will find the poor invalid in a less alarming state than might be apprehended, and that he will be able to bring him to Mansfield shortly, which Sir Thomas proposes should be done, and thinks best on every account, and I flatter myself the poor sufferer will soon be able to bear the removal without material incon-venience or injury. As I have little doubt of your feeling for us, my dear Fanny, under these distressing circumstances, I will write again very soon."

Fanny's feelings on the occasion were indeed considerably more warm and genuine than her aunt's style of writing. She felt truly for them all. Tom dangerously ill, Edmund gone to attend him, and the sadly small party remaining at Mansfield, were cares to shut out every other care, or almost every other. She could just find selfishness enough to wonder whether Edmund *had* written to Miss Crawford before this summons came, but no sentiment dwelt long with her that was not purely affection-ate and disinterestedly anxious. Her aunt did not neglect her; she wrote again and again; they were receiving frequent accounts from Edmund, and these accounts were as regularly transmitted to Fanny, in the same diffuse style, and the same medley of trusts, hopes, and fears, all following and producing each other at haphazard. It was a sort of playing at being frightened. The sufferings which Lady Bertram did not see had little power over her fancy; and she wrote very comfortably about agitation, and anxiety, and poor invalids, till Tom was actually conveyed to Mans-field, and her own eyes had beheld his altered appearance. Then a letter which she had been previously preparing for Fanny was finished in a different style, in the language of real feeling and alarm; then she wrote as she might have spoken. "He is just come, my dear Fanny, and is taken upstairs; and I am so shocked to see him, that I do not know what to do. I am sure he has been very ill. Poor Tom! I am quite grieved for him, and very much frightened, and so is Sir Thomas; and how glad I should be if you were here to comfort me. But Sir Thomas hopes he will be better to-morrow, and says we must consider his journey."

The real solicitude now awakened in the maternal bosom was not soon over. Tom's extreme impatience to be removed to Mansfield, and experience those comforts of home and family which had been little thought of in uninterrupted health, had probably induced his being conveyed thither too early, as a return of fever came on, and for a week he was in a more alarming state than ever. They were all very seriously frightened. Lady Bertram wrote her daily terrors to her niece, who might now be said to live upon letters, and pass all her time between suffering from that of to-day and looking forward to to-morrow's. Without any particular affection for her eldest cousin, her tenderness of heart made her feel that she could not spare him, and the purity of her principles added yet a keener solicitude, when she considered how little useful, how little self-denying his life had (apparently) been.

Susan was her only companion and listener on this, as on more common occasions. Susan was always ready to hear and to sympathise. Nobody else could be interested in so remote an evil as illness in a family above a hundred miles off; not even Mrs. Price, beyond a brief question or two, if she saw her daughter with a letter in her hand, and now and then the quiet observation of—"My poor sister Bertram must be in a great deal of trouble."

So long divided and so differently situated, the ties of blood were little more than nothing. An attachment, originally as tranquil as their tempers, was now become a mere name. Mrs. Price did quite as much for Lady Bertram as Lady Bertram would have done for Mrs. Price. Three or four Prices might have been swept away, any or all except Fanny and William, and Lady Bertram would have thought little about it; or perhaps might have caught from Mrs. Norris's lips the cant of its being a very happy thing and a great blessing to their poor dear sister Price to have them so well provided for.

Chapter 45

At about the week's end from his return to Mansfield, Tom's immediate danger was over, and he was so far pronounced safe as to make his mother perfectly easy; for being now used to the sight of him in his suffering, helpless state, and hearing only the best, and never thinking beyond what she heard, with no disposition for alarm and no aptitude at a hint, Lady Bertram was the happiest subject in the world for a little medical imposition. The fever was subdued; the fever had been his complaint; of course he would soon be well again. Lady Bertram could think nothing less, and Fanny shared her aunt's security, till she received a few lines from Edmund, written purposely to give her a clearer idea of his brother's situation, and acquaint her with the apprehensions which he and his father had imbibed from the physician with respect to some strong hectic symptoms, which seemed to seize the frame on the departure of the fever. They judged it best that Lady Bertram should not be harassed by alarms which, it was to be hoped, would prove unfounded; but there was no reason why Fanny should not know the truth. They were apprehensive for his lungs.

A very few lines from Edmund showed her the patient and the sick room in a juster and stronger light than all Lady Bertram's sheets of paper could do. There was hardly any one in the house who might not have described, from personal observation, better than herself; not one who was not more useful at times to her son. She could do nothing but glide in quietly and look at him; but when able to talk or be talked to, or read to, Edmund was the companion he preferred. His aunt worried him by her cares, and Sir Thomas knew not how to bring down his conversation or his voice to the level of irritation and feebleness. Edmund was all in all. Fanny would certainly believe him so at least, and must find that her estimation of him was higher than ever when he appeared as the attendant, supporter, cheerer of a suffering brother. There was not only the debility of recent illness to assist; there was also, as she now learnt, nerves much affected, spirits much depressed to calm and raise, and her own imagination added that there must be a mind to be properly guided.

The family were not consumptive, and she was more inclined to hope than fear for her cousin, except when she thought of Miss Crawford; but Miss Crawford gave her the idea of being the child of good luck, and to her selfishness and vanity it would be good luck to have Edmund the only son.

Even in the sick chamber the fortunate Mary was not forgotten. Edmund's letter had this postscript. "On the subject of my last, I had actually begun a letter when called away by Tom's illness, but I have now changed my mind, and fear to trust the influence of friends. When Tom is better, I shall go."

Such was the state of Mansfield, and so it continued with scarcely any change till Easter. A line occasionally added by Edmund to his mother's letter was enough for Fanny's information. Tom's amendment was alarmingly slow.

Easter came particularly late this year, as Fanny had most sorrowfully considered on first learning that she had no chance of leaving Portsmouth till after it. It came, and she had yet heard nothing of her return, nothing even of the going to London, which was to precede her return. Her aunt often expressed a wish for her, but there was no notice, no message from the uncle on whom all depended. She supposed he could not yet leave his son, but it was a cruel, a terrible delay to her. The end of April was coming on; it would soon be almost three months, instead of two, that she had been absent from them all and that her days had been passing in a state of penance, which she loved them too well to hope they would thoroughly understand; and who could say when there might be leisure to think of or fetch her?

Her eagerness, her impatience, her longings to be with them, were such as to bring a line or two of Cowper's Tirocinium for ever before her. "With what intense desire she wants her home," was continually on her tongue, as the truest description of a yearning which she could not suppose any school-boy's bosom to feel more keenly.

When she had been coming to Portsmouth, she had loved to call it her home, had been fond of saying that she was going home; the word had been very dear to her, and so it still was, but it must be applied to Mansfield. *That* was now the home. Portsmouth was Portsmouth; Mansfield was home. They had been long so arranged in the indulgence of her secret meditations, and nothing was more consolatory to her than to find her aunt using the same language; "I cannot but say I much regret your being from home at this distressing time, so very trying to my spirits. I trust and hope, and sincerely wish you may never be absent from home so long again," were most delightful sentences to her. Still, however, it was her private regale. Delicacy to her parents made her careful not to betray such a preference for her uncle's house. It was always: "When I go back into Northamptonshire," or "when I return to Mansfield, I shall do so and so." For a great while it was so, but at last the longing grew stronger, it overthrew caution, and she found herself talking of what she should do when she went home, before she was aware. She reproached herself, coloured, and looked fearfully towards her father and mother. She need not have been uneasy. There was no sign of displeasure, or even of hearing her. They were perfectly free from any jealousy of Mansfield. She was as welcome to wish herself there as to be there.

It was sad to Fanny to lose all the pleasures of spring. She had not known before what pleasures she *had* to lose in passing March and April in a town. She had not known before how much the beginnings and progress of vegetation had delighted her. What animation, both of body and mind, she had derived from watching the advance of that season which cannot, in spite of its capriciousness, be unlovely, and seeing its increasing beauties from the earliest flowers in the warmest divisions of her aunt's garden, to the opening of leaves of her uncle's plantations and the glory of his woods. To be losing such pleasures was no trifle; to be losing them because she was in the midst of closeness and noise, to have confinement, bad air, bad smells, substituted for liberty, freshness, fragrance, and verdure, was infinitely worse: but even these incitements to regret were feeble, compared with what arose from the conviction of being missed by her best friends, and the longing to be useful to those who were wanting her!

Could she have been at home, she might have been of service to every creature in the house. She felt that she must have been of use to all. To all she must have saved some trouble of head or hand; and were it only in supporting the spirits of her Aunt Bertram, keeping her from the evil of solitude, or the still greater evil of a restless, officious companion, too apt to be heightening danger in order to enhance her own importance, her being there would have been a general good. She loved to fancy how she could have read to her aunt, how she could have talked to her, and tried at once to make her feel the blessing of what was, and prepare her mind for what might be; and how many walks up and down stairs she might have saved her, and how many messages she might have carried.

It astonished her that Tom's sisters could be satisfied with remaining in London at such a time, through an illness which had now, under different degrees of danger, lasted several weeks. *They* might return to Mansfield when they chose; travelling could be no difficulty to *them*, and she could not comprehend how both could still keep away. If Mrs. Rushworth could imagine any interfering obligations, Julia was certainly able to quit London whenever she chose. It appeared from one of her aunt's letters that Julia had offered to return if wanted, but this was all. It was evident that she would rather remain where she was.

Fanny was disposed to think the influence of London very much at war with all respectable attachments. She saw the proof of it in Miss Crawford, as well as in her cousins; *her* attachment to Edmund had been respectable, the most respectable part of her character; her friendship for herself had at least been blameless. Where was either sentiment now? It was so long since Fanny had had any letter from her, that she had some reason to think lightly of the friendship which had been so dwelt on. It was weeks since she had heard anything of Miss Crawford or of her other connections in town, except through Mansfield, and she was beginning to suppose that she might never know whether Mr. Crawford had gone into Norfolk again or not till they met, and might never hear from his sister any more this spring, when the following letter was received to revive old and create some new sensations:—

"Forgive me, my dear Fanny, as soon as you can, for my long silence, and behave as if you could forgive me directly. This is my modest request and expectation, for you are so good, that I depend upon being treated better than I deserve, and I write now to beg an immediate answer. I want to know the state of things at Mansfield Park, and you, no doubt, are perfectly able to give it. One should be a brute not to feel for the distress they are in; and from what I hear, poor Mr. Bertram has a bad chance of ultimate recovery. I thought little of his illness at first. I looked upon him as the sort of person to be made a fuss with, and to make a fuss himself in any trifling disorder, and was chiefly concerned for those who had to nurse him; but now it is confidently asserted that he is really in a decline, that the symptoms are most alarming, and that part of the family, at least, are aware of it. If it be so, I am sure you must be included in that part, that discerning part, and therefore entreat you to let me know how far I have been rightly informed. I need not say how rejoiced I shall be to hear there has been any mistake, but the report is so prevalent, that

I confess I cannot help trembling. To have such a fine young man cut off in the flower of his days, is most melancholy. Poor Sir Thomas will feel it dreadfully. I really am quite agitated on the subject. Fanny, Fanny, I see you smile and look cunning, but upon my honour I never bribed a physician in my life. Poor young man! If he is to die, there will be *two* poor young men less in the world; and with a fearless face and bold voice would I say to anyone, that wealth and consequence could fall into no hands more deserving of them. It was a foolish precipitation last Christmas, but the evil of a few days may be blotted out in part. Varnish and gilding hide many stains. It will be but the loss of the Esquire after his name. With real affection, Fanny, like mine, more might be overlooked. Write to me by return of post, judge of my anxiety, and do not trifle with it. Tell me the real truth, as you have it from the fountain-head. And now do not trouble yourself to be ashamed of either my feelings or your own. Believe me, they are not only natural, they are philanthropic and virtuous. I put it to your conscience, whether 'Sir Edmund' would not do more good with all the Bertram property than any other possible 'Sir.' Had the Grants been at home I would not have troubled you, but you are now the only one I can apply to for the truth, his sisters not being within my reach. Mrs. R. has been spending the Easter with the Aylmers at Twickenham (as to be sure you know), and is not yet returned; and Julia is with the cousins who live near Bedford Square, but I forget their name and street. Could I immediately apply to either, however, I should still prefer you because it strikes me that they have all along been so unwilling to have their own amusements cut up, as to shut their eyes to the truth. I suppose Mrs. R.'s Easter holidays will not last much longer; no doubt they are thorough holidays to her. The Aylmers are pleasant people; and her husband away, she can have nothing but enjoyment. I give her credit for promoting his going dutifully down to Bath, to fetch his mother; but how will she and the dowager agree in one house? Henry is not at hand, so I have nothing to say from him. Do not you think Edmund would have been in town again long ago, but for this illness?—Yours ever,

"MARY.

"I had actually began folding my letter when Henry walked in, but he brings no intelligence to prevent my sending it. Mrs. R. knows a decline is apprehended; he saw her this morning; she returns to Wimpole Street to-day; the old lady is come. Now do not make yourself uneasy with any queer fancies, because he has been spending a few days at Richmond. He does it every spring. Be assured he cares for nobody but you. At this very moment he is wild to see you, and occupied only in contriving the means for doing so, and for making his pleasure conduce to yours. In proof, he repeats, and more eagerly, what he said at Portsmouth, about our conveying you home, and I join him in it with all my soul. Dear Fanny, write directly, and tell us to come. It will do us all good. He and I can go to the Parsonage, you know, and be no trouble to our friends at Mansfield Park. It would really be gratifying to see them all again, and a little addition of society might be of infinite use to them, and as to yourself, you must feel yourself to be so wanted there, that you cannot in conscience (conscientious as you are) keep away, when you have the means of returning. I have not time or patience to give half Henry's messages; be satisfied that the spirit of each and everyone is unalterable affection."

Fanny's disgust at the greater part of this letter, with her extreme reluctance to bring the writer of it and her cousin Edmund together, would have made her (as she felt) incapable of judging impartially whether the concluding offer might be accepted or not. To herself, individually, it was most tempting. To be finding herself perhaps within three days transported to Mansfield, was an image of the greatest felicity, but it would have been a material drawback to be owing such felicity to persons in whose feelings and conduct, at the present moment, she saw so much to condemn; the sister's feelings, the brother's conduct, *her* coldhearted ambition, *his* thoughtless vanity. To have him still the acquaintance, the flirt, perhaps, of Mrs. Rushworth! She was mortified. She had thought better of him. Happily, however, she was not left to weigh and decide between opposite inclinations and doubtful notions of right; there was no occasion to determine whether she ought to keep Edmund and Mary asunder or not. She had a rule to apply to, which settled everything. Her awe of her uncle, and her dread of taking a liberty with him, made it instantly plain to her what she had to do. If he wanted, he would send for her; and even to offer an early return was a presumption which hardly anything would have seemed to justify. She thanked Miss Crawford, but gave a decided negative. "Her uncle, she understood, meant to fetch her; and as her cousin's illness had continued so many weeks without her being thought at all necessary, she must suppose her return would be unwelcome at present, and that she should be felt an encumbrance."

Her representation of her cousin's state at this time was exactly according to her own belief of it, and such as she supposed would convey to the sanguine mind of her correspondent the hope of everything she was wishing for. Edmund would be forgiven for being a clergyman, it seemed, under certain conditions of wealth; and this, she suspected, was all the conquest of prejudice which he was so ready to congratulate himself upon. She had only learnt to think nothing of consequence but money.

Chapter 46

As Fanny could not doubt that her answer was conveying a real disappointment, she was rather in expectation, from her knowledge of Miss Crawford's temper, of being urged again; and though no second letter arrived for the space of a week, she had still the same feeling when it did come.

On receiving it, she could instantly decide on its containing little writing, and was persuaded of its having the air of a letter of haste and business. Its object was unquestionable; and two moments were enough to start the probability of its being merely to give her notice that they should be in Portsmouth that very day, and to throw her into all the agitation of doubting what she ought to do in such a case. If two moments, however, can surround with difficulties, a third can disperse them; and before she had opened the letter, the possibility of Mr. and Miss Crawford's having applied to her uncle and obtained his permission, was giving her ease. This was the letter:

"A most scandalous, ill-natured rumour has just reached me, and I write, dear Fanny, to warn you against giving the least credit to it, should it spread into the country. Depend upon it, there is some mistake, and that a day or two will clear it up; at any rate, that Henry is blameless, and in spite of a moment's *étourderie*, thinks of nobody but you. Say not a word of it; hear nothing, surmise nothing, whisper nothing, till I write again. I am sure it will be all hushed up, and nothing proved but Rushworth's folly. If they are gone, I would lay my life they are only gone to Mansfield Park, and Julia with them. But why would not you let us come for you? I wish you may not repent it.—Yours, etc."

Fanny stood aghast. As no scandalous, ill-natured rumour had reached her, it was impossible for her to understand much of this strange letter. She could only perceive that it must relate to Wimpole Street and Mr. Crawford, and only conjecture that something very imprudent had just occurred in that quarter to draw the notice of the world, and to excite her jealousy, in Miss Crawford's apprehension, if she heard it. Miss Crawford need not be alarmed for her. She was only sorry for the parties concerned and for Mansfield, if the report should spread so far; but she hoped it might not. If the Rushworths were gone themselves to Mansfield, as was to be inferred from what Miss Crawford said, it was not likely that anything unpleasant should have preceded them, or at least should make any impression.

As to Mr. Crawford, she hoped it might give him a knowledge of his own disposition, convince him that he was not capable of being steadily attached to any one woman in the world, and shame him from persisting any longer in addressing herself.

It was very strange! She had begun to think he really loved her, and to fancy his affection for her something more than common; and his sister still said that he cared for nobody else. Yet there must have been some marked display of attentions to her cousin, there must have been some strong indiscretion, since her correspondent was not of a sort to regard a slight one.

Very uncomfortable she was, and must continue, till she heard from Miss Crawford again. It was impossible to banish the letter from her thoughts, and she could not relieve herself by speaking of it to any human being. Miss Crawford need not have urged secrecy with so much warmth; she might have trusted to her sense of what was due to her cousin.

The next day came and brought no second letter. Fanny was disappointed. She could still think of little else all the morning; but, when her father came back in the afternoon with the daily newspaper as usual, she was so far from expecting any elucidation through such a channel that the subject was for a moment out of her head.

She was deep in other musing. The remembrance of her first evening in that room, of her father and his newspaper, came across her. No candle was *now* wanted. The sun was yet an hour and a half above the horizon. She felt that she had, indeed, been three months there; and the sun's rays falling strongly into the parlour, instead of cheering, made her still more melancholy, for sunshine appeared to her a totally different thing in a town and in the country. Here its power was only a glare: a stifling, sickly glare, serving but to bring forward stains and dirt that might otherwise have slept. There was neither health nor gaiety in sunshine in a town. She sat in a blaze of oppressive heat, in a cloud of moving dust, and her eyes could only wander from the walls, marked by her father's head, to the table cut and notched by her brothers, where stood the tea-board never thoroughly cleaned, the cups and saucers wiped in streaks, the milk a mixture of motes floating in thin blue, and the bread and butter growing every minute more greasy than even Rebecca's hands had first produced it. Her father read his newspaper, and her mother lamented over the ragged carpet as usual, while the tea was in preparation, and wished Rebecca would mend it; and Fanny was first roused by his calling out to her, after humphing and considering over a particular paragraph: "What's the name of your great cousins in town, Fan?"

A moment's recollection enabled her to say, "Rushworth, sir."

"And don't they live in Wimpole Street?"

"Yes, sir."

"Then, there's the devil to pay among them, that's all! There" (holding out the paper to her); "much good may such fine relations do you. I don't know what Sir Thomas may think of such matters; he may be too much of the courtier and fine gentleman to like his daughter the less. But, by G——! if she belonged to *me,* I'd give her the rope's end as long as I could stand over her. A little flogging for man and woman, too, would be the best way of preventing such things."

Fanny read to herself that "it was with infinite concern the newspaper had to announce to the world a matrimonial fracas in the family of Mr. R. of Wimpole Street; the beautiful Mrs. R., whose name had not long been enrolled in the lists of Hymen, and who had promised to become so brilliant a leader in the fashionable world, having quitted her husband's roof in company with the well-known and captivating Mr. C., the intimate friend and associate of Mr. R., and it was not known, even to the editor of the newspaper, whither they were gone."

"It is a mistake, sir," said Fanny, instantly; "it must be a mistake, it cannot be true; it must mean some other people."

She spoke from the instinctive wish of delaying shame; she spoke with a resolution which sprung from despair, for she spoke what she did not, could not believe herself. It had been the shock of conviction as she read. The truth rushed on her; and how she could have spoken at all, how she could even have breathed, was afterwards matter of wonder to herself.

Mr. Price cared too little about the report to make her much answer. "It might be all a lie," he acknowledged, "but so many fine ladies were going to the devil nowadays that way, that there was no answering for anybody."

"Indeed, I hope it is not true," said Mrs. Price, plaintively; "it would be so very shocking! If I have spoken once to Rebecca about that carpet, I am sure I have spoken at least a dozen times; have not I, Betsey? And it would not be ten minutes' work."

The horror of a mind like Fanny's, as it received the conviction of such guilt, and began to take in some part of the misery that must ensue, can hardly be described. At first, it was a sort of stupefaction; but every moment was quickening her perception of the horrible evil. She could not doubt, she dared not indulge a hope, of the paragraph being false. Miss Crawford's letter, which she had read so often as to make every line her own, was in frightful conformity with it. Her eager defence of her brother, her hope of its being *hushed up*, her evident agitation, were all of a piece with something very bad; and if there was a woman of character in existence, who could treat as a trifle this sin of the first magnitude, who would try to gloss it over, and desire to have it unpunished, she could believe Miss Crawford to be the woman! Now she could see her own mistake as to *who* were gone, or *said* to be gone. It was not Mr. and Mrs. Rushworth; it was Mrs. Rushworth and Mr. Crawford.

Fanny seemed to herself never to have been shocked before. There was no possibility of rest. The evening passed without a pause of misery, the night was totally sleepless. She passed only from feelings of sickness to shudderings of horror; and from hot fits of fever to cold. The event was so shocking that there were moments even when her heart revolted from it as impossible; when she thought it could not be. A woman married only six months ago; a man professing himself devoted, even *engaged* to another; that other her near relation; the whole family, both families connected as they were by tie upon tie; all friends, all intimate together! It was too horrible a confusion of guilt, too gross a complication of evil, for human nature, not in a state of utter barbarism, to be capable of! Yet her judgment told her it was so. *His* unsettled affections, wavering with his vanity. *Maria's* decided attachment, and no sufficient principle on either side, gave it possibility: Miss Crawford's letter stamped it a fact.

What would be the consequence? Whom would it not injure?? Whose views might it not affect? Whose peace would it not cup up for ever? Miss Crawford, herself, Edmund; but it was dangerous, perhaps, to tread such ground. She confined herself, or tried to confine herself, to the simple, indubitable family misery which must envelop all, if it were indeed a matter of certified guilt and public exposure. The mother's sufferings, the father's; there she paused. Julia's, Tom's, Edmund's; there a yet longer pause. They were the two on whom it would fall most horribly. Sir Thomas's parental solicitude and high sense of honour and decorum, Edmund's upright principles, unsuspicious temper, and genuine strength of feeling, made her think it scarcely possible for them to support life and reason under such disgrace; and it appeared to her, that, as far as this world alone was concerned, the greatest blessing to every one of kindred with Mrs. Rushworth would be instant annihilation.

Nothing happened the next day, or the next, to weaken her terrors. Two posts came in, and brought no refutation, public or private. There was no second letter to explain away the first from Miss Crawford; there was no intelligence from Mansfield, though it was now full time for her to hear again from her aunt. This was an evil omen. She had, indeed, scarcely the shadow of a hope to soothe her mind, and was reduced to so low and wan and trembling a condition, as no mother, not unkind, except Mrs. Price, could have overlooked, when the third day did bring the sickening knock, and a letter was again put into her hands. It bore the London postmark, and came from Edmund.

"DEAR FANNY,—You know our present wretchedness. May God support you under *your* share! We have been here two days, but there is nothing to be done. They cannot be traced. You may not have heard of the last blow—Julia's elopement; she is gone to Scotland with Yates. She left London a few hours before we entered it. At any other time this would have been felt dreadfully. Now it seems nothing; yet it is a heavy aggravation. My father is not overpowered. More cannot be hoped. He is still able to think and act; and I write, by his desire, to propose your returning home. He is anxious to get you there for my mother's sake. I shall be at Portsmouth the morning after you receive this, and I hope to find you ready to set off for Mansfield. My father wishes you to invite Susan to go with you for a few months. Settle it as you like; say what is proper; I am sure you will feel such an instance of his kindness at such a moment! Do justice to his meaning, however I may confuse it. You may imagine something of my present state. There is no end of the evil let loose upon us. You will see me early by the mail.—Yours, etc."

Never had Fanny more wanted a cordial. Never had she felt such a one as this letter contained. To-morrow! To leave Portsmouth to-morrow! She was, she felt she was, in the greatest danger of being exquisitely happy, while so many were miserable. The evil which brought such good to her! She dreaded lest she should learn to be insensible to it. To be going so soon, sent for so kindly, sent for as a comfort, and with leave to take Susan, was altogether such a combination of blessings as set her heart in a glow, and for a time seemed to distance every pain, and make her incapable of suitably sharing the distress even of those whose distress she thought of most. Julia's elopement could affect her comparatively but little; she was amazed and shocked; but it could not occupy her, could not dwell on her mind. She was obliged to call herself to think of it, and acknowledge it to be terrible and grievous, or it was escaping her, in the midst of all the agitating pressing joyful cares attending this summons to herself.

There is nothing like employment, active indispensable employment, for relieving sorrow. Employment, even melancholy, may dispel melancholy, and her occupations were hopeful. She had so much to do, that not even the horrible story of Mrs. Rushworth (now fixed to the last point of certainty) could affect her as it had done before. She had no time to be miserable. Within twenty-four hours she was hoping to be gone; her father and mother must be spoken to, Susan prepared, everything got ready. Business followed business; the day was hardly long enough. The happiness she was imparting, too, happiness very little alloyed by the black communication which must briefly precede it—the joyful consent of her father and mother to Susan's going with her—the general satisfaction with which the going of both seemed regarded, and the ecstasy of Susan herself, was all serving to support her spirits.

The affliction of the Bertrams was little felt in the family. Mrs. Price talked of her poor sister for a few minutes, but how to find anything to hold Susan's clothes, because Rebecca took away all the boxes and spoilt them, was much more in her thoughts: and as for Susan, now unexpectedly gratified in the first wish of her heart, and knowing nothing personally of those who had sinned, or of those who were sorrowing—if she could help rejoicing from beginning to end, it was as much as ought to be expected from human virtue at fourteen.

As nothing was really left for the decision of Mrs. Price, or the good offices of Rebecca, everything was rationally and duly accomplished, and the girls were ready for the morrow. The advantage of much sleep to prepare them for their journey was impossible. The cousin who was travelling towards them could hardly have less than visited their agitated spirits, one all happiness, the other all varying and indescribable perturbation.

By eight in the morning Edmund was in the house. The girls heard his entrance from above, and Fanny went down. The idea of immediately seeing him, with the knowledge of what he must be suffering, brought back all her own first feelings. He so near her, and in misery. She was ready to sink as she entered the parlour. He was alone, and met her instantly; and found herself pressed to his heart with only these words, just articulate: "My Fanny, my only sister; my only comfort now!" She could say nothing; nor for some minutes could he say more.

He turned away to recover himself, and when he spoke again, though his voice still faltered, his manner showed the wish of self-command, and the resolution of avoiding any further allusion. "Have you breakfasted?

When shall you be ready? Does Susan go?" were questions following each other rapidly. His great object was to be off as soon as possible. When Mansfield was considered, time was precious; and the state of his own mind made him find relief only in motion. It was settled that he should order the carriage to the door in half an hour. Fanny answered for having breakfasted and being quite ready in half an hour. He had already ate, and declined staying for their meal. He would walk round the ramparts, and join them with the carriage. He was gone again; glad to get away even from Fanny.

He looked very ill; evidently suffering under violent emotions, which he was determined to suppress. She knew it must be so, but it was terrible to her.

The carriage came; and he entered the house again at the same moment, just in time to spend a few minutes with the family, and be a witness—but that he saw nothing—of the tranquil manner in which the daughters were parted with, and just in time to prevent their sitting down to the breakfast table, which by dint of much unusual activity, was quite and completely ready as the carriage drove from the door. Fanny's last meal in her father's house was in character with her first; she was dismissed from it as hospitably as she had been welcomed.

How her heart swelled with joy and gratitude as she passed the barriers of Portsmouth, and how Susan's face wore its broadest smiles, may be easily conceived. Sitting forwards, however, and screened by her bonnet, those smiles were unseen.

The journey was likely to be a silent one. Edmund's deep sighs often reached Fanny. Had he been alone with her, his heart must have opened in spite of every resolution; but Susan's presence drove him quite into himself, and his attempts to talk on indifferent subjects could never be long supported.

Fanny watched him with never-failing solicitude, and sometimes catching his eye, revived an affectionate smile, which comforted her; but the first day's journey passed without her hearing a word from him on the subjects that were weighing him down. The next morning produced a little more. Just before their setting out from Oxford, while Susan was stationed at a window, in eager observation of the departure of a large family from the inn, the other two were standing by the fire; and Edmund, particularly struck by the alteration in Fanny's looks, and from his ignorance of the daily evils of her father's house, attributing an undue share of the change, attributing *all* to the recent event, took her hand, and said in a low, but very expressive tone, "No wonder—you must feel it—you must suffer. How a man who had once loved, could desert you! But *yours*—your regard was new compared with——Fanny, think of *me!*"

The first division of their journey occupied a long day, and brought them, almost knocked up, to Oxford; but the second was over at a much earlier hour. They were in the environs of Mansfield long before the usual dinner-time, and as they approached the beloved place, the hearts of both sisters sank a little. Fanny began to dread the meeting with her aunts and Tom, under so dreadful a humiliation; and Susan to feel with some anxiety, that all her best manners, all her lately acquired knowledge of what was practised here, was on the point of being called into action. Visions of good and ill breeding, of old vulgarisms and new gentilities were before her; and she was meditating much upon silver forks, napkins, and finger glasses. Fanny had been everywhere awake to the difference of the country since February; but when they entered the Park her perceptions and her pleasures were of the keenest sort. It was three months, full three months, since her quitting it, and the change was from winter to summer. Her eye fell everywhere on lawns and plantations of the freshest green; and the trees, though not fully clothed, were in that delightful state when further beauty is known to be at hand, and when, while much is actually given to the sight, more yet remains for the imagination. Her enjoyment, however, was for herself alone. Edmund could not share it. She looked at him, but he was leaning back, sunk in a deeper gloom than ever, and with eyes closed, as if the view of cheerfulness oppressed him, and the lovely scenes of home must be shut out.

It made her melancholy again; and the knowledge of what must be enduring there, invested even the house, modern, airy, and well situated as it was, with a melancholy aspect.

By one of the suffering party within, they were expected with such impatience as she had never known before. Fanny had scarcely passed the solemn-looking servants, when Lady Bertram came from the drawing-room to meet her; came with no indolent step; and falling on her neck, said: "Dear Fanny! Now I shall be comfortable."

Chapter 47

IT had been a miserable party, each of the three believing themselves most miserable. Mrs. Norris, however, as most attached to Maria, was really the greatest sufferer. Maria was her first favourite, the dearest of all; the match had been her own contriving, as she had been wont with such pride of heart to feel and say, and this conclusion of it almost overpowered her.

She was an altered creature, quieted, stupefied, indifferent to everything that passed. The being left with her sister and nephew, and all the house under her care, had been an advantage entirely thrown away; she had been unable to direct or dictate, or even fancy herself useful. When really touched by affliction, her active powers had been all benumbed, and neither Lady Bertram nor Tom had received from her the smallest support or attempt at support. She had done no more for them than they had done for each other. They had been all solitary, helpless, and forlorn alike; and now the arrival of the others only established her superiority in wretchedness. Her companions were relieved, but there was no good for *her*. Edmund was almost as welcome to his brother as Fanny to her aunt; but Mrs. Norris, instead of having comfort from either, was but the more irritated by the sight of the person whom, in the blindness of her anger, she could have charged as the demon of the piece. Had Fanny accepted Mr. Crawford this could not have happened.

Susan, too, was a grievance. She had not spirits to notice her in more than a few repulsive looks, but she felt her as a spy, and an intruder, and an indigent niece, and everything most odious. By her other aunt, Susan was received with quiet kindness. Lady Bertram could not give her much time, or many words, but she felt her, as Fanny's sister, to have a claim at Mansfield, and was ready to kiss and like her; and Susan was more than satisfied, for she came perfectly aware that nothing but ill humour was to be expected from Aunt Norris; and was so provided with happiness, so strong in that best of blessings, an escape from many certain evils, that she could have stood against a great deal more indifference than she met with from the others.

She was now left a good deal to herself, to get acquainted with the house and grounds as she could, and spent her days very happily in so doing, while those who might otherwise have attended to her were shut up, or wholly occupied each with the person quite dependent on them, at this time, for everything like comfort; Edmund trying to bury his own feelings in exertions for the relief of his brother's, and Fanny devoted to her Aunt Bertram, returning to every former office with more than former zeal, and thinking she could never do enough for one who seemed so much to want her.

To talk over the dreadful business with Fanny, talk and lament, was all Lady Bertram's consolation. To be listened to and borne with, and hear the voice of kindness and sympathy in return, was everything that could be done for her. To be otherwise comforted was out of the question. The case admitted of no comfort. Lady Bertram did not think deeply, but, guided by Sir Thomas, she thought justly on all important points; and she saw therefore, in all its enormity, what had happened, and neither endeavoured herself, nor required Fanny to advise her, to think little of guilt and infamy.

Her affections were not acute, nor was her mind tenacious. After a time, Fanny found it not impossible to direct her thoughts to other subjects, and revive some interest in the usual occupations; but whenever Lady Bertram *was* fixed on the event, she could see it only in one light, as comprehending the loss of a daughter, and a disgrace never to be wiped off.

Fanny learned from her all the particulars which had yet transpired. Her aunt was no very methodical narrator, but with the help of some letters to and from Sir Thomas, and what she already knew herself, and could reasonably combine, she was soon able to understand quite as much as she wished of the circumstances attending the story.

Mrs. Rushworth had gone, for the Easter holidays, to Twickenham, with a famly whom she had just grown intimate with: a family of lively, agreeable manners, and probably of morals and discretion to suit, for to *their* house Mr. Crawford had constant access at all times. His having been in the same neighbourhood Fanny already knew. Mr. Rushworth had been gone at this time to Bath, to pass a few days with his mother, and bring her back to town, and Maria was with these friends without any restraint, without even Julia; for Julia had removed from Wimpole Street two or three weeks before, on a visit to some relations of Sir Thomas; a removal which her father and mother were now disposed to attribute to some view of convenience on Mr. Yates's account. Very soon after the Rushworths' return to Wimpole Street, Sir Thomas had received a letter from an old and most particular friend in London, who hearing and witnessing a good deal to alarm him in that quarter, wrote to recommend Sir Thomas's coming to London himself, and using his influence with his daughter to put an end to the intimacy which was already exposing her to unpleasant remarks, and evidently making Mr. Rushworth uneasy.

Sir Thomas was preparing to act upon this letter, without communicating its contents to any creature at Mansfield, when it was followed by another, sent express from the same friend, to break to him the almost desperate situation in which affairs then stood with the young people. Mrs. Rushworth had left her husband's house: Mr. Rushworth had been in great anger and distress to *him* (Mr. Harding) for his advice; Mr. Harding feared there had been *at least* very flagrant indiscretion. The maidservant of Mrs. Rushworth, senior, threatened alarmingly. He was doing all in his power to quiet everything, with the hope of Mrs. Rushworth's return, but was so much counteracted in Wimpole Street by the influence of Mr. Rushworth's mother, that the worst consequences might be apprehended.

This dreadful communication could not be kept from the rest of the family. Sir Thomas set off, Edmund would go with him, and the others had been left in a state of wretchedness, inferior only to what followed the receipt of the next letters from London. Everything was by that time public beyond a hope. The servant of Mrs. Rushworth, the mother, had exposure in her power, and supported by her mistress, was not to be silenced. The two ladies, even in the short time they had been together, had disagreed; and the bitterness of the elder against her daughter-in-law might perhaps arise almost as much from the personal disrespect with which she had herself been treated as from sensibility for her son.

However that might be, she was unmanageable. But had she been less obstinate, or of less weight with her son, who was always guided by the last speaker, by the person who could get hold of and shut him up, the case would still have been hopeless, for Mrs. Rushworth did not appear again, and there was every reason to conclude her to be concealed somewhere with Mr. Crawford, who had quitted his uncle's house, as for a journey, on the very day of her absenting herself.

Sir Thomas, however, remained yet a little longer in town, in the hope of discovering and snatching her from further vice, though all was lost on the side of character.

His present state Fanny could hardly bear to think of. There was but one of his children who was not at this time a source of misery to him. Tom's complaints had been greatly heightened by the shock of his sister's conduct, and his recovery so much thrown back by it, that even Lady Bertram had been struck by the difference, and all her alarms were regularly sent off to her husband; and Julia's elopement, the additional blow which had met him on his arrival in London, though its force had been deadened at the moment, must, she knew, be sorely felt. She saw that it was. His letters expressed how much he deplored it. Under any circumstances it would have been an unwelcome alliance; but to have it so clandestinely formed, and such a period chosen for its completion, placed Julia's feelings in a most unfavourable light, and severely aggravated the folly of her choice. He called it a bad thing, done in the worst manner, and at the worst time; and though Julia was yet as more pardonable than Maria as folly than vice, he could not but regard the step she had taken as opening the worst probabilities of a conclusion hereafter like her sister's. Such was his opinion of the set into which she had thrown herself.

Fanny felt for him most acutely. He could have no comfort but in Edmund. Every other child must be racking his heart. His displeasure against herself she trusted, reasoning differently from Mrs. Norris, would now be done away. *She* should be justified. Mr. Crawford would have fully acquitted her conduct in refusing him; but this, though most material to herself, would be poor consolation to Sir Thomas. Her uncle's displeasure was terrible to her; but what could her justification or her gratitude and attachment do for him? His stay must be on Edmund alone.

She was mistaken, however, in supposing that Edmund gave his father no present pain. It was of a much less poignant nature than what the others excited; but Sir Thomas was considering his happiness as very deeply involved in the offence of his sister and friend; cut off by it, as he must be, from the woman whom he had been pursuing with undoubted attachment and strong probability of success; and who, in everything but this despicable brother, would have been so eligible a connection. He was aware of what Edmund must be suffering on his own behalf, in addition to all the rest, when they were in town: he had seen or conjectured his feelings; and, having reason to think that *one* interview with Miss Crawford had taken place, from which Edmund derived only increased distress, had been as anxious on that account as on others to get him out of town, and had engaged him in taking Fanny home to her aunt, with a view to his relief and benefit, no less than theirs. Fanny was not in the secret of her uncle's feelings, Sir Thomas not in the secret of Miss Crawford's character. Had he been privy to her conversation with his son, he would not have wished her to belong to him, though her twenty thousand pounds had been forty.

That Edmund must be for ever divided from Miss Crawford did not admit of a doubt with Fanny; and yet, till she knew that he felt the same, her own conviction was insufficient. She thought he did, but she wanted to be assured of it. If he would now speak to her with the unreserve which had sometimes been too much for her before, it would be most consoling; but *that* she found was not to be. She seldom saw him: never alone. He probably avoided being alone with her. What was to be inferred? That his judgment submitted to all his own peculiar and bitter share of this family affliction, but that it was too keenly felt to be a subject of the slightest communication. This must be his state. He yielded, but it was with agonies which did not admit of speech. Long, long would it be ere Miss Crawford's name passed his lips again, or she could hope for a renewal of such confidential intercourse as had been.

It *was* long. They reached Mansfield on Thursday, and it was not till Sunday evening that Edmund began to talk to her on the subject. Sitting with her on Sunday evening—-a wet Sunday evening—the very time of all others when, if a friend is at hand, the heart must be opened, and everything told; no one else in the room, except his mother, who, after hearing an affecting sermon, had cried herself to sleep, it was impossible not to speak; and so, with the usual beginnings, hardly to be traced as to what came first, and the usual declaration that if she would listen to him for a few minutes, he should be very brief, and certainly never tax her kindness in the same way again; she need not fear a repetition; it would be a subject prohibited entirely: he entered upon the luxury of relating circumstances and sensations of the first interest to himself, to one of whose affectionate sympathy he was quite convinced.

How Fanny listened, with what curiosity and concern, what pain and what delight, how the agitation of his voice was watched, and how carefully her own eyes were fixed on any object but himself, may be imagined. The opening was alarming. He had seen Miss Crawford. He had been invited to see her. He had received a note from Lady Stornaway to beg him to call; and regarding it as what was meant to be the last, last interview of friendship, and investing her with all the feelings of shame and wretchedness which Crawford's sister ought to have known, he had gone to her in such a state of mind, so softened, so devoted, as made it for a few moments impossible to Fanny's fears that it should be the last. But as he proceeded in his story, these fears were over. She had met him, he said, with a serious—certainly a serious—even an agitated air; but before he had been able to speak one intelligible sentence, she had introduced the subject in a manner which he owned had shocked him. " 'I heard you were in town,' said she; 'I wanted to see you. Let us talk over this sad business. What can equal the folly of our two relations?' I could not answer, but I believe my looks spoke. She felt reproved. Sometimes how quick to feel! With a graver look and voice she then added, 'I do not mean to defend Henry at your sister's expense.' So she began, but how she went on, Fanny, is not fit, is hardly fit to be repeated to you. I cannot recall all her words. I would not dwell upon them if I could. Their substance was great anger at the *folly* of each. She reprobated her brother's folly in being drawn on by a woman whom he had never cared for, to do what must lose him the woman he adored; but still more the folly of poor Maria, in sacrificing such a situation, plunging into such difficulties, under the idea of being really loved by a man who had long ago made his indifference clear. Guess what I must have felt. To hear the woman whom—— No harsher name than folly given! So voluntarily, so freely, so coolly to canvass it! No reluctance, no horror, no feminine, shall I say, no modest loathings? This is what the world does. For where, Fanny, shall we find a woman whom nature had so richly endowed? Spoilt, spoilt!"

After a little reflection, he went on with a sort of desperate calmness. "I will tell you everything, and then have done for ever. She saw it only as folly, and that folly stamped only by exposure. The want of common discretion, of caution; his going down to Richmond for the whole time of her being at Twickenham; her putting herself in the power of a servant; it was the detection, in short—oh, Fanny! it was the detection, not the offence, which she reprobated. It was the imprudence which had brought things to extremity, and obliged her brother to give up every dearer plan in order to fly with her."

He stopped. "And what," said Fanny (believing herself required to speak), "what could you say?"

"Nothing, nothing to be understood. I was like a man stunned. She went on, began to talk of you; yes, then she began to talk of you, regretting, as well she might, the loss of such a—— There she spoke very rationally. But she has always done justice to you. 'He has thrown away,' said she, 'such a woman as he will never see again. She would have fixed him; she would have made him happy for ever.' My dearest Fanny, I am giving you, I hope, more pleasure than pain by this retrospect of what might have been—but what never can be now. You do not wish me to be silent? If you do, give me but a look, a word, and I have done."

No look or word was given.

"Thank God," said he. "We were all disposed to wonder, but it seems to have been the merciful appointment of Providence that the heart which knew no guile should not suffer. She spoke of you with high praise and warm affection; yet, even here, there was alloy, a dash of evil; for in the midst of it she could exclaim, 'Why would not she have him? It is all her fault. Simple girl! I shall never forgive her. Had she accepted him as she ought, they might now have been on the point of marriage, and Henry would have been too happy and too busy to want any other object. He would have taken no pains to be on terms with Mrs. Rushworth again. It would have all ended in a regular standing flirtation, in yearly meetings at Sotherton and Everingham.' Could you have believed it possible? But the charm is broken. My eyes are opened."

"Cruel!" said Fanny, "quite cruel. At such a moment to give way to gaiety, to speak with lightness, and to you! Absolute cruelty."

"Cruelty, do you call it? We differ there. No, hers is not a cruel nature. I do not consider her as meaning to wound my feelings. The evil lies yet deeper; in her total ignorance, unsuspiciousness of there being such feelings; in a perversion of mind which made it natural to her to treat the subject as she did. She was speaking only as she had been used to hear others speak, as she imagined everybody else would speak. Hers are not faults of temper. She would not voluntarily give unnecessary pain to anyone, and though I may deceive myself, I cannot but think that for me, for my feelings, she would—— Hers are faults of principle, Fanny; of blunted delicacy and a corrupted, vitiated mind. Perhaps it is best for me, since it leaves me so little to regret. Not so, however. Gladly would I submit to all the increased pain of losing her, rather than have to think of her as I do. I told her so."

"Did you?"

"Yes; when I left her I told her so."

"How long were you together?"

"Five-and-twenty minutes. Well, she went on to say that what remained now to be done was to bring about a marriage between them. She spoke of it, Fanny, with a steadier voice than I can." He was obliged to pause more than once as he continued. " 'We must persuade Henry to marry her,' said she; 'and what with honour, and the certainty of having shut himself out for ever from Fanny, I do not despair of it. Fanny he must give up. I do not think that even *he* could now hope to succeed with one of her stamp, and therefore I hope we may find no insuperable difficulty. My influence, which is not small, shall all go that way; and when once married, and properly supported by her own family, people of respectability as they are, she may recover her footing in society to a certain degree. In some circles, we know, she would never be admitted, but with good dinners, and large parties, there will always be those who will be glad of her acquaintance; and there is, undoubtedly, more liberality and candour on those points than formerly. What I advise is, that your father be quiet. Do not let him injure his own cause by interference. Persuade him to let things take their course. If by any officious exertions of his, she is induced to leave Henry's protection, there will be much less chance of his marrying her than if she remain with him. I know how he is likely to be influenced. Let Sir Thomas trust to his honour and compassion, and it may all end well; but if he gets his daughter away, it will be destroying the chief hold.' "

After repeating this, Edmund was so much affected that Fanny, watching him with silent, but most tender concern, was almost sorry that the subject had been entered on at all. It was long before he could speak again. At last, "Now, Fanny," said he, "I shall soon have done. I have told you the substance of all that she said. As soon as I could speak, I replied that I had not supposed it possible, coming in such a state of mind into that house as I have done, that anything could occur to make me suffer more, but that she had been inflicting deeper wounds in almost every sentence. That though I had, in the course of our acquaintance, been often sensible of some difference in our opinions, on points, too, of some moment, it had not entered my imagination to conceive the difference could be such as she had now proved it. That the manner in which she treated the dreadful crime committed by her brother and my sister (with whom lay the greater seduction I pretended not to say), but the manner in which she spoke of the crime itself, giving it every reproach but the right; considering its ill consequences only as they were to be braved or overborne by a defiance of decency and impudence in wrong; and last of all, and above all, recommending to us a compliance, a compromise, an acquiescence, in the continuance of the sin, on the chance of a marriage which, thinking as I now thought of her brother, should rather be prevented than sought; all this together most grievously convinced me that I had never understood her before, and that, as far as related to mind, it had been the creature of my own imagination, not Miss Crawford, that I had been too apt to dwell on for many months past. That, perhaps, it was best for me; I had less to regret in sacrificing a friendship, feelings, hopes which must, at any rate, have been torn from me now. And yet, that I must, and would confess, that, could I have restored her to what she had appeared to me before, I would infinitely prefer any increase of the pain of parting, for the sake of carrying with me the right of tenderness and esteem. This is what I said, the purport of it; but, as you may imagine, not spoken so collectedly or methodically as I have repeated it to you. She was astonished, exceedingly astonished—more than astonished. I saw her change countenance. She turned extremely red. I imagined I saw a mixture of many feelings: a great, though short struggle; half a wish of yielding to truths, half a sense of shame, but habit, habit carried it. She would have laughed if she could. It was a sort of laugh, as she answered, 'A pretty good lecture, upon my word. Was it part of your last sermon? At this rate you will soon reform everybody at Mansfield and Thornton Lacey; and when I hear of you next, it may be as a celebrated preacher in some great society of Methodists, or as a missionary into foreign parts.' She tried to speak carelessly, but she was not so careless as she wanted to appear. I only said in reply, that from my heart I wished her well, and earnestly hoped that she might soon learn to think more justly, and not owe the most valuable knowledge we could any of us acquire, the knowledge of ourselves and of our duty, to the lessons of affliction, and immediately left the room. I had gone a few steps, Fanny, when I heard the door open behind me. 'Mr. Bertram,' said she. I looked back. 'Mr. Bertram,' said she, with a smile; but it was a smile ill-suited to the conversation that had passed, a saucy playful smile, seeming to invite in order to subdue me; at least it appeared so to me. I resisted; it was the impulse of the moment to resist, and still walked on. I have since, sometimes, for a moment, regretted that I did not go back, but I know I was right, and such has been the end of our acquaintance. And what an acquaintance has it been! How have I been deceived! Equally in brother and sister deceived! I thank you for your patience, Fanny. This has been the greatest relief, and now we will have done."

And such was Fanny's dependence on his words, that for five minutes she thought they _had_ done. Then, however, it all came on again, or something very like it, and nothing less than Lady Bertram's rousing thoroughly up, could really close such a conversation. Till that happened, they continued to talk of Miss Crawford alone, and how she had attached him, and how delightful nature had made her, and how excellent she would have been, had she fallen into good hands earlier. Fanny, now at liberty to speak openly, felt more than justified in adding to his knowledge of her real character, by some hint of what share his brother's state of health might be supposed to have in her wish for a complete reconciliation. This was not an agreeable intimation. Nature resisted it for a while. It would have been a vast deal pleasanter to have had her more disinterested in her attachment; but his vanity was not of a strength to fight long against reason. He submitted to believe that Tom's illness had influenced her, only reserving for himself this consoling thought, that considering the many counteractions of opposing habits, she had certainly been _more_ attached to him than could have been expected, and for his sake been more near doing right. Fanny thought exactly the same; and they were also quite agreed in their opinion of the lasting effect, the indelible impression, which such a disappointment must make on his mind. Time would undoubtedly abate somewhat of his sufferings, but still it was a sort of thing which he never could get entirely the better of; and as to his ever meeting with any other woman who could—it was too impossible to be named but with indignation. Fanny's friendship was all that he had to cling to.

Chapter 48

LET other pens dwell on guilt and misery. I quit such odious subjects as soon as I can, impatient to restore everybody, not greatly in fault themselves, to tolerable comfort, and to have done with all the rest.

My Fanny, indeed, at this very time, I have the satisfaction of knowing, must have been happy in spite of everything. She must have been a happy creature in spite of all that she felt, or thought she felt, for the distress of those around her. She had sources of delight that must force their way. She was returned to Mansfield Park, she was useful, she was beloved; she was safe from Mr. Crawford; and when Sir Thomas came back she had every proof that could be given in his then melancholy state of spirits, of his perfect approbation and increased regard; and happy as all this must make her, she would still have been happy without any of it, for Edmund was no longer the dupe of Miss Crawford.

It is true that Edmund was very far from happy himself. He was suffering from disappointment and regret, grieving over what was, and wishing for what could never be. She knew it was so, and was sorry; but it was with a sorrow so founded on satisfaction, so tending to ease, and so much in harmony with every dearest sensation, that there are few who might not have been glad to exchange their greatest gaiety for it.

Sir Thomas, poor Sir Thomas, a parent, and conscious of errors in his own conduct as a parent, was the longest to suffer. He felt that he ought not to have allowed the marriage; that his daughter's sentiments had been sufficiently known to him to render him culpable in authorising it; that in so doing he had sacrificed the right to the expedient, and been governed by motives of selfishness and worldly wisdom. These were reflections that required some time to soften; but time will do almost everything; and though little comfort arose on Mrs. Rushworth's side for the misery she had occasioned, comfort was to be found greater than he had supposed in his other children. Julia's match became a less desperate business than he had considered it at first. She was humble, and wishing to be forgiven; and Mr. Yates, desirous of being really received into the family, was disposed to look up to him and be guided. He was not very solid; but there was a hope of his becoming less trifling, of his being at least tolerably domestic and quiet; and at any rate, there was comfort in finding his estate rather more, and his debts much less, than he had feared, and in being consulted and treated as the friend best worth attending to. There was comfort also in Tom, who gradually regained his health, without regaining the thoughtlessness and selfishness of his previous habits. He was the better for ever for his illness. He had suffered, and he had learned to think; two advantages that he had never known before; and the self-reproach arising from the deplorable event in Wimpole Street, to which he felt himself accessory by all the dangerous intimacy of his unjustifiable theatre, made an impression on his mind which, at the age of six-and-twenty, with no want of sense or good companions, was durable in its happy effects. He became what he ought to be: useful to his father, steady and quiet, and not living merely for himself.

Here was comfort indeed! And quite as soon as Sir Thomas could place dependence on such sources of good, Edmund was contributing to his father's ease by improvement in the only point in which *he* had given him pain before: improvement in his spirits. After wandering about and sitting under trees with Fanny all the summer evenings, he had so well talked his mind into submission, as to be very tolerably cheerful again.

These were the circumstances and the hopes which gradually brought their alleviation to Sir Thomas, deadening his sense of what was lost, and in part reconciling him to himself; though the anguish arising from the conviction of his own errors in the education of his daughters was never to be entirely done away.

Too late he became aware how unfavourable to the character of any young people must be the totally opposite treatment which Maria and Julia had been always experiencing at home, where the excessive indulgence and flattery of their aunt had been continually contrasted with his own severity. He saw how ill he had judged, in expecting to counteract what was wrong in Mrs. Norris, by its reverse in himself; clearly saw that he had but increased the evil, by teaching them to repress their spirits in his presence so as to make their real disposition unknown to him, and sending them for all their indulgences to a person who had been able to attach them only by the blindness of her affection, and the excess of her praise.

Here had been grievous mismanagement; but, bad as it was, he gradually grew to feel that it had not been the most direful mistake in his plan of education. Something must have been wanting *within,* or time would have worn away much of its ill effect. He feared that principle, active principle, had been wanting; that they had never been properly taught to govern their inclinations and tempers by that sense of duty which can alone suffice. They had been instructed theoretically in their religion, but never required to bring it into daily practice. To be distinguished for elegance and accomplishments, the authorised object of their youth, could have had no useful influence that way, no moral effect on the mind. He had meant them to be good, but his cares had been directed to the understanding and manners, not the disposition; and of the necessity of self-denial and humility, he feared they had never heard from any lips that could profit them.

Bitterly did he deplore a deficiency which now he could scarcely comprehend to have been possible. Wretchedly did he feel, that with all the cost and care of an anxious and expensive education, he had brought up his daughters without their understanding their first duties, or his being acquainted with their character and temper.

The high spirit and strong passions of Mrs. Rushworth, especially, were made known to him only in their sad result. She was not to be prevailed on to leave Mr. Crawford. She hoped to marry him, and they continued together till she was obliged to be convinced that such hope was vain, and till the disappointment and wretchedness arising from the conviction rendered her temper so bad, and her feelings for him so like hatred, as to make them for a while each other's punishment, and then induce a voluntary separation.

She had lived with him to be reproached as the ruin of all his happiness in Fanny, and carried away no better consolation in leaving him, than that she *had* divided them. What can exceed the misery of such a mind in such a situation?

Mr. Rushworth had no difficulty in procuring a divorce; and so ended a marriage contracted under such circumstances as to make any better end the effect of good luck not to be reckoned on. She had despised him, and loved another; and he had been very much aware that it was so. The indignities of stupidity, and the disappointments of selfish passion, can excite little pity. His punishment followed his conduct, as did a deeper punishment the deeper guilt of his wife. He was released from the engagement to be mortified and unhappy, till some other pretty girl could attract him into matrimony again, and he might set forward on a second, and it is to be hoped, more prosperous trial of the state: if duped, to be duped at least with good humour and good luck; while *she* must withdraw with infinitely stronger feelings to a retirement and reproach which could allow no second spring of hope or character.

Where she could be placed became a subject of most melancholy and momentous consultation. Mrs. Norris, whose attachment seemed to augment with the demerits of her niece, would have had her received at home, and countenanced by them all. Sir Thomas would not hear of it; and Mrs. Norris's anger against Fanny was so much the greater, from considering *her* residence there as the motive. She persisted in placing his scruples to *her* account, though Sir Thomas very solemnly assured her that, had there been no young woman in question, had there been no young person of either sex belonging to him, to be endangered by the society or hurt by the character of Mrs. Rushworth, he would never have offered so great an insult to the neighbourhood as to expect it to notice her. As a daughter, he hoped a penitent one, she should be protected by him, and secured in every comfort, and supported by every encouragement to do right, which their relative situations admitted; but further than *that* he could not go. Maria had destroyed her own character, and he would not, by a vain attempt to restore what never could be restored by affording his sanction to vice, or in seeking to lessen its disgrace, be anywise accessory to introducing such misery in another man's family, as he had known himself.

It ended in Mrs. Norris's resolving to quit Mansfield, and devote herself to her unfortunate Maria, and in an establishment being formed for them in another country, remote and private, where, shut up together with little society, on one side no affection, on the other no judgment, it may be reasonably supposed that their tempers became their mutual punishment. Mrs. Norris's removal from Mansfield was the great supplementary comfort of Sir Thomas's life. His opinion of her had been sinking from the day of his return from Antigua: in every transaction together from that period; in their daily intercourse, in business, or in chat, she had been regularly losing ground in his esteem, and convincing him that either time had done her much disservice, or that he had considerably over-rated her sense, and wonderfully borne with her manners before. He had felt her as an hourly evil, which was so much the worse, as there seemed no chance of its ceasing but with life; she seemed a part of himself that must be borne for ever. To be relieved from her, therefore, was so great a felicity that, had she not left bitter remembrances behind her, there might have been danger of his learning almost to approve the evil which produced such a good.

She was regretted by no one at Mansfield. She had never been able to attach even those she loved best, and since Mrs. Rushworth's elopement, her temper had been in a state of such irritation as to make her everywhere tormenting. Not even Fanny had tears for Aunt Norris, not even when she was gone for ever.

That Julia escaped better than Maria was owing, in some measure, to a favourable difference of disposition and circumstance, but in a greater to her having been less the darling of that very aunt, less flattered and less spoilt. Her beauty and acquirements had held but a second place. She had been always used to think herself a little inferior to Maria. Her temper was naturally the easiest of the two; her feelings, though quick, were more controllable, and education had not given her so very hurtful a degree of self-consequence.

She had submitted the best to the disappointment in Henry Crawford. After the first bitterness of the conviction of being slighted was over, she had been tolerably soon in a fair way of not thinking of him again; and when the acquaintance was renewed in town, and Mr. Rushworth's house became Crawford's object, she had had the merit of withdrawing herself from it, and of choosing that time to pay a visit to her other friends, in order to secure herself from being again too much attracted. This had been her motive in going to her cousins. Mr. Yates's convenience had had nothing to do with it. She had been allowing his attentions some time, but with very little idea of ever accepting him; and had not her sister's conduct burst forth as it did, and her increased dread of her father and of home, on that event, imagining its certain consequence to herself would be greater severity and restraint, made her hastily resolve on avoiding such immediate horrors at all risks, it is probable that Mr. Yates would never have succeeded. She had not eloped with any worse feelings than those of selfish alarm. It had appeared to her the only thing to be done. Maria's guilt had induced Julia's folly.

Henry Crawford, ruined by early independence and bad domestic example, indulged in the freaks of a cold-blooded vanity a little too long. Once it had, by an opening undesigned and unmerited, led him into the way of happiness. Could he have been satisfied with the conquest of one amiable woman's affections, could he have found sufficient exultation in overcoming the reluctance, in working himself into the esteem and tenderness of Fanny Price, there would have been every probabilty of success and felicity for him. His affection had already done something. Her influence over him had already given him some influence over her. Would he have deserved more, there can be no doubt that more would have been obtained, especially when that marriage had taken place, which would have given him the assistance of her conscience in subduing her first inclination, and brought them very often together. Would he have persevered, and uprightly, Fanny must have been his reward, and a reward very voluntarily bestowed, within a reasonable period from Edmund's marrying Mary. Had he done as he intended, and as he knew he ought, by going down to Everingham after his return from Portsmouth, he might have been deciding his own happy destiny. But he was pressed to stay for Mrs. Fraser's party; his staying was made of flattering consequence, and he was to meet Mrs. Rushworth there. Curiosity and vanity were both engaged, and the temptation of immediate pleasure was too strong for a mind unused to make any sacrifice to right: he resolved to defer his Norfolk journey, resolved that writing should answer the purpose of it, or that its purpose was unimportant, and stayed. He saw Mrs. Rushworth, was received by her with a coldness which ought to have been repulsive, and have established apparent indifference between them for ever; but he was mortified, he could not bear to be thrown off by the woman whose smiles had been so wholly at his command; he must exert himself to subdue so proud a display of resentment; it was anger on Fanny's account; he must get the better of it, and make Mrs. Rushworth Maria Bertram again in her treatment of himself.

In this spirit he began the attack, and by animated perseverance had soon re-established the sort of familiar intercourse of gallantry, of flirtation, which bounded his views; but in triumphing over the discretion which, though beginning in anger, might have saved them both, he had put himself in the power of feelings on her side more strong than he had supposed. She loved him; there was no withdrawing attentions avowedly dear to her. He was entangled by his own vanity, with as little excuse of love as possible, and without the smallest inconstancy of mind towards her cousin. To keep Fanny and the Bertrams from a knowledge of what was passing became his first object. Secrecy could not have been more desirable for Mrs. Rushworth's credit than he felt it for his own. When he returned from Richmond, he would have been glad to see Mrs. Rushworth no more. All that followed was the result of her imprudence, and he went off with her at last, because he could not help it, regretting Fanny even at the moment, but regretting her infinitely more when all the bustle of the intrigue was over, and a very few months had taught him, by the force of contrast, to place a yet higher value on the sweetness of her temper, the purity of her mind, and the excellence of her principles.

That punishment, the public punishment of disgrace, should in a just measure attend *his* share of the offence is, we know, not one of the barriers which society gives to virtue. In this world the penalty is less equal than could be wished; but without presuming to look forward to a juster appointment hereafter, we may fairly consider a man of sense, like Henry Crawford, to be providing for himself no small portion of vexation and regret; vexation that must rise sometimes to self-reproach, and regret to wretchedness, in having so requited hospitality, so injured family peace, so forfeited his best, most estimable, and endeared acquaintance, and so lost the woman whom he had rationally as well as passionately loved.

After what had passed to wound and alienate the two families, the continuance of the Bertrams and Grants in such close neighbourhood would have been most distressing; but the absence of the latter, for some months purposely lengthened, ended very fortunately in the necessity, or at least the practicability, of a permanent removal. Dr. Grant, through an interest on which he had almost ceased to form hopes, succeeded to a stall in Westminster, which, as affording an occasion for leaving Mansfield, an excuse for residence in London, and an increase of income to answer the expenses of the change, was highly acceptable to those who went and those who stayed.

Mrs. Grant, with a temper to love and be loved, must have gone with some regret from the scenes and people she had been used to; but the same happiness of disposition must in any place, and any society, secure her a great deal to enjoy, and she had again a home to offer Mary; and Mary had had enough of her own friends, enough of vanity, ambition, love, and disappointment in the course of the last half-year, to be in need of the true kindness of her sister's heart, and the rational tranquillity of her ways. They lived together; and when Dr. Grant had brought on apoplexy and death, by three great institutionary dinners in one week, they still lived together; for Mary, though perfectly resolved against ever attaching herself to a younger brother again, was long in finding among the dashing representatives, or idle heir-apparents, who were at the command of her beauty, and her £20,000, anyone who could satisfy the better taste she had acquired at Mansfield, whose character and manners could authorise a hope of the domestic happiness she had there learned to estimate, or put Edmund Bertram sufficiently out of her head.

Edmund had greatly the advantage of her in this respect. He had not to wait and wish with vacant affections for an object worthy to succeed her in them. Scarcely had he done regretting Mary Crawford, and observing to Fanny how impossible it was that he should ever meet with such another woman, before it began to strike him whether a very different kind of woman might not do just as well, or a great deal better; whether Fanny herself were not growing as dear, as important to him in all her smiles and all her ways, as Mary Crawford had ever been; and whether it might not be possible, a hopeful undertaking to persuade her that her warm and sisterly regard for him would be foundation enough for wedded love.

I purposely abstain from dates on this occasion, that everyone may be at liberty to fix their own, aware that the cure of unconquerable passions, and the transfer of unchanging attachments, must vary much as to time in different people I only entreat everybody to believe that exactly at the time when it was quite natural that it should be so, and not a week earlier, Edmund did cease to care about Miss Crawford, and became as anxious to marry Fanny as Fanny herself could desire.

With such a regard for her, indeed, as his had long been, a regard founded on the most endearing claims of innocence and helplessness, and completed by every recommendation of growing worth, what could be more natural than the change? Loving, guiding, protecting her, as he had been doing ever since her being ten years old, her mind in so great a degree

formed by his care, and her comfort depending on his kindness, an object
to him of such close and peculiar interest, dearer by all his own importance
with her than anyone else at Mansfield, what was there now to add, but
that he should learn to prefer soft light eyes to sparkling dark ones. And
being always with her, and always talking confidentially, and his feelings
exactly in that favourable state which a recent disappointment gives, those
soft light eyes could not be very long in obtaining the pre-eminence.

Having once set out, and felt that he had done so on this road to happiness, there was nothing on the side of prudence to stop him or make his
progress slow; no doubts of her deserving, no fears of opposition of taste,
no need of drawing new hopes of happiness from dissimilarity of temper.
Her mind, disposition, opinions, and habits wanted no half concealment,
no self-deception on the present, no reliance on future improvement. Even
in the midst of this late infatuation, he had acknowledged Fanny's mental
superiority. What must be his sense of it now, therefore! She was of course
only too good for him; but as nobody minds having what is too good for
them, he was very steadily earnest in the pursuit of the blessing, and it
was not possible that encouragement from her should be long wanting.
Timid, anxious, doubting as she was, it was still impossible that such
tenderness as hers should not, at times, hold out the strongest hope of
success, though it remained for a later period to tell him the whole delightful and astonishing truth. His happiness in knowing himself to have
been so long the beloved of such a heart, must have been great enough to
warrant any strength of language in which he could clothe it to her or to
himself; it must have been a delightful happiness. But there was happiness
elsewhere which no description can reach. Let no one presume to give the
feelings of a young woman on receiving the assurance of that affection of
which she has scarcely allowed herself to entertain a hope.

Their own inclinations ascertained, there were no difficulties behind,
no drawback of poverty or parent. It was a match which Sir Thomas's
wishes had even forestalled. Sick of ambitious and mercenary connections,
prizing more and more the sterling good of principle and temper, and
chiefly anxious to bind by the strongest securities all that remained to
him of domestic felicity, he had pondered with genuine satisfaction on the
more than possibility of the two young friends finding their mutual consolation in each other for all that had occurred of disappointment to
either; and the joyful consent which met Edmund's application, the high
sense of having realised a great acquisition in the promise of Fanny for a
daughter, formed just such a contrast with his early opinion on the subject
when the poor little girl's coming had been first agitated, as time is for
ever producing between the plans and decisions of mortals, for their own
instruction, and their neighbours' entertainment.

Fanny was indeed the daughter that he wanted. His charitable kindness
had been rearing a prime comfort for himself. His liberality had a rich
repayment, and the general goodness of his intentions by her deserved it.
He might have made her childhood happier; but it had been an error of

judgment only which had given him the appearance of harshness, and deprived him of her early love; and now, on really knowing each other, their mutual attachment became very strong. After settling her at Thornton Lacey with every kind attention to her comfort, the object of almost every day was to see her there, or to get her away from it.

Selfishly dear as she had long been to Lady Bertram, she could not be parted with willingly by *her*. No happiness of son or niece could make her wish the marriage. But it was possible to part with her, because Susan remained to supply her place. Susan became the stationary niece, delighted to be so; and equally well adapted for it by a readiness of mind, and an inclination for usefulness, as Fanny had been by sweetness of temper and strong feelings of gratitude. Susan could never be spared. First as a comfort to Fanny, then as an auxiliary, and last as her substitute, she was established at Mansfield, with every appearance of equal permanency. Her more fearless disposition and happier nerves made everything easy to her there. With quickness in understanding the tempers of those she had to deal with, and no natural timidity to restrain any consequent wishes, she was soon welcome and useful to all; and after Fanny's removal succeeded so naturally to her influence over the hourly comfort of her aunt as gradually to become, perhaps, the most beloved of the two. In *her* usefulness, in Fanny's excellence, in William's continued good conduct and rising fame, and in the general well-being and success of the other members of the family, all assisting to advance each other, and doing credit to his countenance and aid, Sir Thomas saw repeated, and for ever repeated reason to rejoice in what he had done for them all, and acknowledge the advantages of early hardship and discipline, and the consciousness of being born to struggle and endure.

With so much true merit and true love, and no want of fortune and friends, the happiness of the married cousins must appear as secure as earthly happiness can be. Equally formed for domestic life, and attached to country pleasures, their home was the home of affection and comfort; and to complete the picture of good, the acquisition of Mansfield living, by the death of Dr. Grant, occurred just after they had been married long enough to begin to want an increase of income, and feel their distance from the paternal abode an inconvenience.

On that event they removed to Mansfield; and the Parsonage there, which, under each of its two former owners, Fanny had never been able to approach but with some painful sensation of restraint or alarm, soon grew as dear to her heart, and as thoroughly perfect in her eyes, as everything else within the view and patronage of Mansfield Park had long been.

FINIS

EMMA

(First Published 1816)

EMMA

Chapter 1

EMMA WOODHOUSE, handsome, clever, and rich, with a comfortable home and happy disposition seemed to unite some of the best blessings of existence; and had lived nearly twenty-one years in the world with very little to distress or vex her.

She was the youngest of the two daughters of a most affectionate, indulgent father; and had, in consequence of her sister's marriage, been mistress of his house from a very early period. Her mother had died too long ago for her to have more than an indistinct remembrance of her caresses; and her place had been supplied by an excellent woman as governess, who had fallen little short of a mother in affection.

Sixteen years had Miss Taylor been in Mr. Woodhouse's family, less as a governess than a friend, very fond of both daughters, but particularly of Emma. Between *them* it was more the intimacy of sisters. Even before Miss Taylor had ceased to hold the nominal office of governess, the mildness of her temper had hardly allowed her to impose any restraint; and the shadow of authority being now long passed away, they had been living together as friend and friend very mutually attached, and Emma doing just what she liked; highly esteeming Miss Taylor's judgment, but directed chiefly by her own.

The real evils, indeed, of Emma's situation were the power of having rather too much her own way, and a disposition to think a little too well of herself: these were the disadvantages which threatened alloy to her many enjoyments. The danger, however, was at present so unperceived, that they did not by any means rank as misfortunes with her.

Sorrow came—a gentle sorrow—but not at all in the shape of any disagreeable consciousness. Miss Taylor married. It was Miss Taylor's loss which first brought grief. It was on the wedding day of this beloved friend that Emma first sat in mournful thought of any continuance. The wedding over, and the bride people gone, her father and herself were left to dine together, with no prospect of a third to cheer a long evening. Her father composed himself to sleep after dinner, as usual, and she had then only to sit and think of what she had lost.

The event had every promise of happiness for her friend. Mr. Weston was a man of unexceptionable character, easy fortune, suitable age, and pleasant manners; and there was some satisfaction in considering with what self-denying, generous friendship she had always wished and promoted the match; but it was a black morning's work for her. The want of Miss Taylor would be felt every hour of every day. She recalled her past kindness—the kindness, the affection of sixteen years—how she had taught and how she had played with her from five years old—how she had devoted all her powers to attach and amuse her in health—and how nursed her through the various illnesses of childhood. A large debt of gratitude was owing here; but the intercourse of the last seven years, the equal footing and perfect unreserve which had soon followed Isabella's marriage, on their being left to each other, was yet a dearer, tenderer recollection. She had been a·friend and companion such as few possessed: intelligent, well-informed, useful, gentle, knowing all the ways of the family, interested in all its concerns, and peculiarly interested in herself, in every pleasure, every scheme of hers; one to whom she could speak every thought as it arose, and who had such an affection for her as could never find fault.

How was she to bear the change? It was true that her friend was going only half a mile from them; but Emma was aware that great must be the difference between a Mrs. Weston, only half a mile from them, and a Miss Taylor in the house; and with all her advantages, natural and domestic, she was now in great danger of suffering from intellectual solitude. She dearly loved her father, but he was no companion for her. He could not meet her in conversation, rational or playful.

The evil of the actual disparity in their ages (and Mr. Woodhouse had not married early) was much increased by his constitution and habits; for having been a valetudinarian all his life, without activity of mind or body, he was a much older man in ways than in years; and though everywhere beloved for the friendliness of his heart and his amiable temper, his talents could not have recommended him at any time.

Her sister, though comparatively but little removed by matrimony, being settled in London, only sixteen miles off, was much beyond her daily reach; and many a long October and November evening must be struggled through at Hartfield, before Christmas brought the next visit from Isabella and her husband, and their little children, to fill the house, and give her pleasant society again.

Highbury, the large and populous village almost amounting to a town, to which Hartfield, in spite of its separate lawn, and shrubberies, and name, did really belong, afforded her no equals. The Woodhouses were first in consequence there. All looked up to them. She had many acquaintances in the place, for her father was universally civil, but not one among them who could be accepted in lieu of Miss Taylor for even half a day. It was a melancholy change; and Emma could not but sigh over it, and wish for impossible things, till her father awoke, and made it necessary to be cheerful. His spirits required support. He was a nervous man, easily depressed; fond of everybody that he was used to, and hating to part with them; hating change of every kind. Matrimony, as the origin of change, was always disagreeable; and he was by no means yet reconciled to his own daughter's marrying, nor could ever speak of her but with compassion. though it had been entirely a match of affection, when he was now obliged to part with Miss Taylor too; and from his habits of gentle selfishness, and of being never able to suppose that other people could feel differently from himself, he was very much disposed to think Miss Taylor had done as sad a thing for herself as for them, and would have been a great deal happier if she had spent all the rest of her life at Hartfield. Emma smiled and chatted as cheerfully as she could, to keep him from such thoughts; but when tea came, it was impossible for him not to say exactly as he had said at dinner:

"Poor Miss Taylor! I wish she were here again. What a pity it is that Mr. Weston ever thought of her!"

"I cannot agree with you, papa; you know I cannot. Mr. Weston is such a good-humoured, pleasant, excellent man, that he thoroughly deserves a good wife; and you would not have had Miss Taylor live with us for ever, and bear all my odd humours, when she might have a house of her own?"

"A house of her own! but where is the advantage of a house of her own? This is three times as large; and you have never any odd humours, my dear."

"How often we shall be going to see them, and they coming to see us! We shall be always meeting! *We* must begin; we must go and pay our wedding-visit very soon."

"My dear, how am I to get so far? Randalls is such a distance. I could not walk half so far."

"No, papa; nobody thought of your walking. We must go in the carriage, to be sure."

"The carriage! But James will not like to put the horses to for such a little way; and where are the poor horses to be while we are paying our visit?"

"They are to be put into Mr. Weston's stable, papa. You know we have settled all that already. We talked it all over with Mr. Weston last night. And as for James, you may be very sure he will always like going to Randalls, because of his daughter's being housemaid there. I only doubt whether he will ever take us anywhere else. That was your doing, papa. You got Hannah that good place. Nobody thought of Hannah till you mentioned her—James is so obliged to you!"

"I am very glad I did think of her. It was very lucky, for I would not have had poor James think himself slighted upon any account; and I am sure she will make a very good servant; she is a civil, pretty-spoken girl; I have a great opinion of her. Whenever I see her, she always curtseys and asks me how I do, in a very pretty manner; and when you have had her here to do needlework, I observe she always turns the lock of the door the right way and never bangs it. I am sure she will be an excellent servant; and it will be a great comfort to poor Miss Taylor to have somebody about her that she is used to see. Whenever James goes over to see his daughter, you know, she will be hearing of us. He will be able to tell her how we all are."

Emma spared no exertions to maintain this happier flow of ideas, and hoped, by the help of backgammon, to get her father tolerably through the evening, and be attacked by no regrets but her own. The backgammon-table was placed; but a visitor immediately afterwards walked in and made it unnecessary.

Mr. Knightley, a sensible man about seven or eight-and-thirty, was not only a very old and intimate friend of the family, but particularly con-nected with it, as the elder brother of Isabella's husband. He lived about a mile from Highbury, was a frequent visitor, and always welcome, and at this time more welcome than usual, as coming directly from their mutual connections in London. He had returned to a late dinner after some days' absence, and now walked up to Hartfield to say that all were well in Brunswick Square. It was a happy circumstance, and animated Mr. Woodhouse for some time. Mr. Knightley had a cheerful manner, which always did him good; and his many inquiries after "poor Isabella" and her children were answered most satisfactorily. When this was over, Mr. Woodhouse gratefully observed:

"It is very kind of you, Mr. Knightley, to come out at this late hour to call upon us. I am afraid you must have had a shocking walk."

"Not at all, sir. It is a beautiful moonlight night; and so mild that I must draw back from your great fire."

"But you must have found it very damp and dirty. I wish you may not catch cold."

"Dirty, sir! Look at my shoes. Not a speck on them."

"Well: that is quite surprising, for we have had a vast deal of rain here. It rained dreadfully hard for half an hour while we were at breakfast. I wanted them to put off the wedding."

"By the bye, I have not wished you joy. Being pretty well aware of what sort of joy you must both be feeling, I have been in no hurry with my congratulations; but I hope it all went off tolerably well. How did you all behave? Who cried most?"

"Ah! poor Miss Taylor! 'tis a sad business."

"Poor Mr. and Miss Woodhouse, if you please; but I cannot possibly say 'poor Miss Taylor.' I have a great regard for you and Emma; but when it comes to the question of dependence or independence! at any rate, it must be better to have only one to please than two."

"Especially when one of those two is such a fanciful, troublesome creature!" said Emma playfully. "That is what you have in your head, I know—and what you would certainly say if my father were not by."

"I believe it is very true, my dear, indeed," said Mr. Woodhouse, with a sigh. "I am afraid I am sometimes very fanciful and troublesome."

"My dearest papa! You do not think I could mean *you,* or suppose Mr. Knightley to mean *you.* What a horrible idea! Oh, no! I meant only my-self. Mr. Knightley loves to find fault with me, you know—in a joke—it is all a joke. We always say what we like to one another."

Mr. Knightley, in fact, was one of the few people who could see faults in Emma Woodhouse, and the only one who ever told her of them; and though this was not particularly agreeable to Emma herself, she knew it would be so much less so to her father, that she would not have him really suspect such a circumstance as her not being thought perfect by everybody.

"Emma knows I never flatter her," said Mr. Knightley, "but I meant no reflection on anybody. Miss Taylor has been used to have two persons to please; she will now have but one. The chances are that she must be a gainer."

"Well," said Emma, willing to let it pass, "you want to hear about the wedding; and I shall be happy to tell you, for we all behaved charmingly. Everybody was punctual, everybody in their best looks: not a tear, and hardly a long face to be seen. Oh, no; we all felt that we were going to be only half a mile apart, and were sure of meeting every day."

"Dear Emma bears everything so well," said her father. "But, Mr. Knightley, she is really very sorry to lose poor Miss Taylor, and I am sure she *will* miss her more than she thinks for."

Emma turned away her head, divided between tears and smiles.

"It is impossible that Emma should not miss such a companion," said Mr. Knightley. "We should not like her so well as we do, sir, if we could suppose it: but she knows how much the marriage is to Miss Taylor's advantage; she knows how very acceptable it must be, at Miss Taylor's time of life, to be settled in a home of her own, and how important to her to be secure of a comfortable provision, and therefore cannot allow herself to feel so much pain as pleasure. Every friend of Miss Taylor must be glad to have her so happily married."

"And you have forgotten one matter of joy to me," said Emma, "and a very considerable one—that I made the match myself. I made the match, you know, four years ago; and to have it take place, and be proved in the right, when so many people said Mr. Weston would never marry again, may comfort me for anything."

Mr. Knightley shook his head at her. Her father fondly replied, "Ah! my dear, I wish you would not make matches and foretell things, for whatever you say always comes to pass. Pray do not make any more matches."

"I promise you to make none for myself, papa; but I must, indeed, for other people. It is the greatest amusement in the world! And after such success, you know! Everybody said that Mr. Weston would never marry again. Oh dear, no! Mr. Weston, who had been a widower so long, and who seemed so perfectly comfortable without a wife, so constantly occupied either in his business in town or among his friends here, always acceptable wherever he went, always cheerful—Mr. Weston need not spend a single evening in the year alone if he did not like it. Oh no! Mr. Weston certainly would never marry again. Some people even talked of a promise to his wife on her deathbed, and others of the son and the uncle not letting him. All manner of solemn nonsense was talked on the subject, but I

believed none of it. Ever since the day (about four years ago) that Miss
Taylor and I met with him in Broadway Lane, when, because it began to
mizzle, he darted away with so much gallantry, and borrowed two umbrellas for us from Farmer Mitchell's, I made up my mind on the subject.
I planned the match from that hour; and when such success has blessed
me in this instance, dear papa, you cannot think that I shall leave off
matchmaking."

"I do not understand what you mean by 'success,' " said Mr. Knightley.
"Success supposes endeavour. Your time has been properly and delicately
spent, if you have been endeavouring for the last four years to bring about
this marriage. A worthy employment for a young lady's mind! but if,
which I rather imagine, your making the match as you call it, means only
your planning it, your saying to yourself one idle day, 'I think it would
be a very good thing for Miss Taylor if Mr. Weston were to marry her,'
and saying it again to yourself every now and then afterwards—why do
you talk of success? where is your merit? What are you proud of? You
made a lucky guess; and *that* is all that can be said."

"And have you never known the pleasure and triumph of a lucky guess?
I pity you. I thought you cleverer; for, depend upon it, a lucky guess is
never merely luck. There is always some talent in it. And as to my poor
word 'success,' which you quarrel with, I do not know that I am so entirely
without any claim to it. You have drawn two pretty pictures; but I think
there may be a third—a something between the do-nothing and the do-all.
If I had not promoted Mr. Weston's visits here, and given many little
encouragements, and smoothed many little matters, it might not have
come to anything after all. I think you must know Hartfield enough to
comprehend that."

"A straightforward, open-hearted man like Weston, and a rational,
unaffected woman like Miss Taylor may be safely left to manage their
own concerns. You are more likely to have done harm to yourself, than
good to them, by interference."

"Emma never thinks of herself, if she can do good to others," rejoined
Mr. Woodhouse, understanding but in part. "But, my dear, pray do not
make any more matches; they are silly things, and break up one's family
circle grievously."

"Only one more, papa; only for Mr. Elton. Poor Mr. Elton! You like
Mr. Elton, papa; I must look about for a wife for him. There is nobody in
Highbury who deserves him—and he has been here a whole year, and has
fitted up his house so comfortably, that it would be a shame to have him
single any longer; and I thought when he was joining their hands to-day,
he looked so very much as if he would like to have the same kind office
done for him! I think very well of Mr. Elton, and this is the only way I
have of doing him a service."

"Mr. Elton is a very pretty young man, to be sure, and a very good
young man, and I have a great regard for him. But if you want to show
him any attention, my dear, ask him to come and dine with us some day

That will be a much better thing. I dare say Mr. Knightley will be so kind as to meet him."

"With a great deal of pleasure, sir, at any time," said Mr. Knightley laughing: "and I agree with you entirely, that it will be a much better thing. Invite him to dinner, Emma, and help him to the best of the fish and the chicken, but leave him to choose his own wife. Depend upon it, a man of six or seven-and-twenty can take care of himself."

Chapter 2

Mr. WESTON was a native of Highbury, and born of a respectable family, which for the last two or three generations had been rising into gentility and property. He had received a good education, but, on succeeding early in life to a small independence, had become indisposed for any of the more homely pursuits in which his brothers were engaged; and had satisfied an active, cheerful mind and social temper by entering into the militia of his county, then embodied.

Captain Weston was a general favourite; and when the chances of his military life had introduced him to Miss Churchill, of a great Yorkshire family, and Miss Churchill fell in love with him, nobody was surprised, except her brother and his wife, who had never seen him, and who were full of pride and importance, which the connection would offend.

Miss Churchill, however, being of age, and with the full command of her fortune—though her fortune bore no proportions to the family estate —was not to be dissuaded from the marriage, and it took place, to the infinite mortification of Mr. and Mrs. Churchill, who threw her off with due decorum. It was an unsuitable connection, and did not produce much happiness. Mrs. Weston ought to have found more in it, for she had a husband whose warm heart and sweet temper made him think everything due to her in return for the great goodness of being in love with him; but though she had one sort of spirit, she had not the best. She had resolution enough to pursue her own will in spite of her brother, but not enough to refrain from unreasonable regrets at that brother's unreasonable anger, nor from missing the luxuries of her former home. They lived beyond their income, but still it was nothing in comparison of Enscombe: she did not cease to love her husband; but she wanted at once to be the wife of Captain Weston, and Miss Churchill of Enscombe.

Captain Weston, who had been considered, especially by the Churchills, as making such an amazing match, was proved to have much the worst of the bargain; for when his wife died, after a three years' marriage, he was rather a poorer man than at first, and with a child to maintain. From the expense of the child, however, he was soon relieved. The boy had, with the additional softening claim of a lingering illness of his mother's, been the means of a sort of reconciliation; and Mr. and Mrs. Churchill, having no children of their own, nor any other young creature of equal kindred to care for, offered to take the whole charge of the little Frank soon after her decease. Some scruples and some reluctance the widower-father may be supposed to have felt; but as they were overcome by other considerations the child was given up to the care and the wealth of the Churchills, and he had only his own comfort to seek, and his own situation to improve as he could.

A complete change of life became desirable. He quitted the militia and engaged in trade, having brothers already established in a good way in London, which afforded him a favourable opening. It was a concern which brought just employment enough. He had still a small house in Highbury, where most of his leisure days were spent; and between useful occupation and the pleasures of society, the next eighteen or twenty years of his life passed cheerfully away. He had by that time, realised an easy competence—enough to secure the purchase of a little estate adjoining Highbury, which he had always longed for—enough to marry a woman as portionless even as Miss Taylor, and to live according to the wishes of his own friendly and social disposition.

It was now some time since Miss Taylor had begun to influence his schemes; but as it was not the tyrannic influence of youth on youth, it had not shaken his determination of never settling till he could purchase Randalls, and the sale of Randalls was long looked forward to; but he had gone steadily on, with these objects in view, till they were accomplished. He had made his fortune, bought his house and obtained his wife; and was beginning a new period of existence, with every probability of greater happiness than in any yet passed through. He had never been an unhappy man; his own temper had secured him from that, even in his first marriage; but his second must show him how delightful a well-judging and truly amiable woman could be, and must give him the most pleasant proof of its being a great deal better to choose than to be chosen, to excite gratitude than to feel it.

He had only himself to please in his choice; his fortune was his own; for as to Frank, it was more than being tacitly brought up as his uncle's heir, it had become so avowed an adoption as to have him assume the name of Churchill on coming of age. It was most unlikely, therefore, that he should ever want his father's assistance. His father had no apprehension of it. The aunt was a capricious woman, and governed her husband entirely; but it was not in Mr. Weston's nature to imagine that any caprice could be strong enough to affect one so dear, and, as he believed, so deservedly dear. He saw his son every year in London, and was proud of him; and his fond report of him as a very fine young man had made Highbury feel a sort of pride in him too. He was looked on as sufficiently belonging to the place to make his merits and prospects a kind of common concern.

Mr. Frank Churchill was one of the boasts of Highbury and a lively curiosity to see him prevailed, though the compliment was so little returned that he had never been there in his life. His coming to visit his father had been often talked of but never achieved.

Now, upon his father's marriage, it was very generally proposed, as a most proper attention, that the visit should take place. There was not a dissentient voice on the subject, either when Mrs. Perry drank tea with Mrs. and Miss Bates, or when Mrs. and Miss Bates returned the visit. Now was the time for Mr. Frank Churchill to come among them; and the hope strengthened when it was understood that he had written to his new mother on the occasion. For a few days, every morning visit to Highbury included some mention of the handsome letter Mrs. Weston had received. "I suppose you have heard of the handsome letter Mr. Frank Churchill has written to Mrs. Weston? I understand it was a very handsome letter, indeed. Mr. Woodhouse told me of it. Mr. Woodhouse saw the letter, and he says he never saw such a handsome letter in his life."

It was, indeed, a highly-prized letter. Mrs. Weston had, of course, formed a very favourable idea of the young man; and such a pleasing attention was an irresistible proof of his great good sense, and a most welcome addition to every source and every expression of congratulation which her marriage had already secured. She felt herself a most fortunate woman; and she had lived long enough to know how fortunate she might well be thought, where the only regret was for a partial separation from friends whose friendship for her had never cooled, and who could ill bear to part with her.

She knew that at times she must be missed; and could not think, without pain, of Emma's losing a single pleasure, or suffering an hour's ennui from the want of her companionableness: but dear Emma was of no feeble character; she was more equal to her situation than most girls would have been, and had sense, and energy, and spirits that might be hoped would bear her well and happily through its little difficulties and privations. And then there was such comfort in the very easy distance of Randalls from Hartfield, so convenient for even solitary female walking, and in Mr. Weston's disposition and circumstances, which would make the approaching season no hindrance to their spending half the evenings in the week together.

Her situation was altogether the subject of hours of gratitude to Mrs. Weston, and of moments only of regret; and her satisfaction—her more than satisfaction—her cheerful enjoyment, was so just and so apparent, that Emma, well as she knew her father, was sometimes taken by surprise at his being still able to pity "poor Miss Taylor," when they left her at Randalls in the centre of every domestic comfort, or saw her go away in the evening attended by her pleasant husband to a carriage of her own. But never did she go without Mr. Woodhouse's giving a gentle sigh, and saying:

"Ah, poor Miss Taylor! She would be very glad to stay."

There was no recovering Miss Taylor—nor much likelihood of ceasing to pity her; but a few weeks brought some alleviation to Mr. Woodhouse. The compliments of his neighbours were over; he was no longer teased by being wished joy of so sorrowful an event; and the wedding-cake, which had been a great distress to him, was all ate up. His own stomach could bear nothing rich, and he could never believe other people to be different from himself. What was unwholesome to him he regarded as unfit for anybody; and he had, therefore, earnestly tried to dissuade them from having any wedding-cake at all, and when that proved vain, as earnestly tried to prevent anybody's eating it. He had been at the pains of consulting Mr. Perry, the apothecary, on the subject. Mr. Perry was an intelligent, gentlemanlike man, whose frequent visits were one of the comforts of Mr. Woodhouse's life; and, upon being applied to, he could not but acknowledge (though it seemed rather against the bias of inclination) that wedding-cake might certainly disagree with many —perhaps with most people, unless taken moderately. With such an opinion, in confirmation of his own, Mr. Woodhouse hoped to influence every visitor of the newly married pair; but still the cake was eaten; and there was no rest for his benevolent nerves till it was all gone.

There was a strange rumour in Highbury of all the little Perrys being seen with a slice of Mrs. Weston's wedding-cake in their hands; but Mr. Woodhouse would never believe it.

Chapter 3

MR. WOODHOUSE was fond of society in his own way. He liked very much to have his friends come and see him; and from various united causes, from his long residence at Hartfield, and his good-nature, from his fortune, his house, and his daughter, he could command the visits of his own little circle, in a great measure as he liked. He had not much intercourse with any families beyond that circle; his horror of late hours, and large dinner-parties, made him unfit for any acquaintance but such as would visit him on his own terms. Fortunately for him, Highbury, including Randalls in the same parish, and Donwell Abbey in the parish adjoining, the seat of Mr. Knightley, comprehended many such. Not unfrequently, through Emma's persuasion, he had some of the chosen and the best to dine with him; but evening parties were what he preferred; and, unless he fancied himself at any time unequal to company, there was scarcely an evening in the week in which Emma could not make up a card-table for him.

Real, long-standing regard brought the Westons and Mr. Knightley; and by Mr. Elton, a young man living alone without liking it, the privilege of exchanging any vacant evening of his own blank solitude for the elegancies and society of Mr. Woodhouse's drawing-room, and the smiles of his lovely daughter, was in no danger of being thrown away.

After these came a second set; among the most come-at-able of whom were Mrs. and Miss Bates, and Mrs. Goddard, three ladies almost always at the service of an invitation from Hartfield, and who were fetched and carried home so often, that Mr. Woodhouse thought it no hardship for either James or the horses. Had it taken place only once a year, it would have been a grievance.

Mrs. Bates, the widow of a former vicar of Highbury, was a very old lady, almost past everything but tea and quadrille. She lived with her single daughter in a very small way, and was considered with all the regard and respect which a harmless old lady, under such untoward circumstances, can excite. Her daughter enjoyed a most uncommon degree of popularity for a woman neither young, handsome, rich, nor married. Miss Bates stood in the very worst predicament in the world for having much of the public favour; and she had no intellectual superiority to make atonement to herself, or frighten those who might hate her into outward respect. She had never boasted either beauty or cleverness. Her youth had passed without distinction and her middle of life was devoted to the care of a failing mother, and the endeavour to make a small income go as far as possible. And yet she was a happy woman, and a woman whom no one named without good-will. It was her own universal good-will and contented temper which worked such wonders. She loved everybody, was interested in everybody's happiness, quick-sighted to everybody's merits; thought herself a most fortunate creature, and surrounded with blessings in such an excellent mother, and so many good neighbours and friends, and a home that wanted for nothing. The simplicity and cheerfulness of her nature, her contented and grateful spirit, were a recommendation to everybody, and a mine of felicity to herself. She was a great talker upon little matters, which exactly suited Mr. Woodhouse, full of trivial communications and harmless gossip.

Mrs. Goddard was the mistress of a school—not of a seminary, or an establishment, or anything which professed, in long sentences of refined nonsense, to combine liberal acquirements with elegant morality, upon new principles and new systems—and where young ladies for enormous pay might be screwed out of health and into vanity—but a real, honest, old-fashioned boarding-school, where a reasonable quantity of accomplishments were sold at a reasonable price, and where girls might be sent to be out of the way, and scramble themselves into a little education, without any danger of coming back prodigies. Mrs. Goddard's school was in high repute, and very deservedly; for Highbury was reckoned a particularly healthy spot: she had an ample house and garden, gave the children plenty of wholesome food, let them run about a great deal in the summer, and in winter dressed their chilblains with her own hands. It was no wonder that a train of twenty young couples now walked after her to church. She was a plain, motherly kind of woman, who had worked hard in her youth, and now thought herself entitled to the occasional holiday of a tea-visit; and having formerly

owed much to Mr. Woodhouse's kindness felt his particular claim on
her to leave her neat parlour, hung round with fancy work whenever
she could, and win or lose a few sixpences by his fireside.

These were the ladies who Emma found herself very frequently able
to collect; and happy was she, for her father's sake, in the power;
though, as far as she was herself concerned, it was no remedy for the
absence of Mrs. Weston. She was delighted to see her father look comfortable, and very much pleased with herself for contriving things so
well; but the quiet prosings of three such women made her feel that
every evening so spent was indeed one of the evenings she had fearfully
anticipated.

As she sat one morning, looking forward to exactly such a close of the
present day, a note was brought from Mrs. Goddard requesting, in most
respectful terms, to be allowed to bring Miss Smith with her; a most
welcome request; for Miss Smith was a girl of seventeen, whom Emma
knew very well by sight, and had long felt an interest in, on account of
her beauty. A very gracious invitation was returned, and the evening no
longer dreaded by the fair mistress of the mansion.

Harriet Smith was the natural daughter of somebody. Somebody had
placed her, several years back, at Mrs. Goddard's school, and somebody
had lately raised her from the condition of scholar to that of parlour
boarder. This was all that was generally known of her history. She had
no visible friends, but what had been acquired at Highbury, and was
now just returned from a long visit in the country to some young ladies
who had been at school there with her.

She was a very pretty girl, and her beauty happened to be of a sort
which Emma particularly admired. She was short, plump, and fair, with
a fine bloom, blue eyes, light hair, regular features, and a look of great
sweetness; and, before the end of the evening, Emma was as much pleased
with her manners as her person, and quite determined to continue the
acquaintance.

She was not struck by anything remarkably clever in Miss Smith's
conversation, but she found her altogether very engaging—not incon-
veniently shy, nor unwilling to talk—and yet so far from pushing, showing
so proper and becoming a deference, seeming so pleasantly grateful for
being admitted to Hartfield, and so artlessly impressed by the appearance
of everything in so superior a style to what she had been used to, that she
must have good sense, and deserve encouragement. Encouragement should
be given. Those soft blue eyes, and all those natural graces, should
not be wasted on the inferior society of Highbury and its connections. The
acquaintances she had already formed were unworthy of her. The friends
from whom she had just parted, though very good sort of people, must be
doing her harm. They were a family of the name of Martin, whom Emma
well knew by character, as renting a large farm of Mr. Knightley, and
residing in the parish of Donwell—very creditably, she believed; she knew
Mr. Knightley thought highly of them; but they must be coarse and

unpolished, and very unfit to be the intimates of a girl who wanted only
a little more knowledge and elegance to be quite perfect. *She* would notice
her; she would improve her; she would detach her from her bad acquaintances, and introduce her into good society; she would form her opinions
and her manners. It would be an interesting, and certainly a very kind
undertaking; highly becoming her own situation in life, her leisure, and
powers.

She was so busy in admiring those soft blue eyes, in talking and listening
and forming all these schemes in the inbetweens that the evening flew
away at a very unusual rate; and the supper-table, which always closed
such parties, and for which she had been used to sit and watch the due
time, was all set out and ready, and moved forwards to the fire, before she
was aware. With an alacrity beyond the common impulse of a spirit
which yet was never indifferent to the credit of doing everything well and
attentively, with the real good-will of a mind delighted with its own ideas,
did she then do all the honours of the meal, and help and recommend the
minced chicken and scalloped oysters, with an urgency which she knew
would be acceptable to the early hours and civil scruples of their guests.

Upon such occasions poor Mr. Woodhouse's feelings were in sad warfare. He loved to have the cloth laid, because it had been the fashion of his
youth, but his conviction of suppers being very unwholesome made him
rather sorry to see anything put on it; and while his hospitality would have
welcomed his visitors to everything, his care for their health made him
grieve that they would eat.

Such another small basin of thin gruel as his own was all that he could
with thorough self-approbation, recommend; though he might constraiı.
himself, while the ladies were comfortably clearing the nicer things, to
say—

"Mrs. Bates, let me propose your venturing on one of these eggs. Aɴ
egg boiled very soft is not unwholesome. Serle understands boiling an egg
better than anybody. I would not recommend an egg boiled by anybody
else—but you need not be afraid, they are very small, you see—one of our
small eggs will not hurt you. Miss Bates, let Emma help you to a *little* bit
of tart—a *very* little bit. Ours are all apple-tarts. You need not be afraid of
unwholesome preserves here. I do not advise the custard. Mrs. Goddard,
what say you to *half* a glass of wine? A *small* half-glass, put into a tumbler
of water? I do not think it could disagree with you."

Emma allowed her father to talk—but supplied her visitors in a much
more satisfactory style; and on the present evening had particular
pleasure in sending them away happy. The happiness of Miss Smith was
quite equal to her intentions. Miss Woodhouse was so great a personage
in Highbury, that the prospect of the introduction had given as much
panic as pleasure; but the humble, grateful little girl went off with highly
gratified feelings, delighted with the affability with which Miss Woodhouse had treated her all the evening, and actually shaken hands with
her at last!

Chapter 4

HARRIET SMITH's intimacy at Hartfield was soon a settled thing. Quick and decided in her ways, Emma lost no time in inviting, encouraging, and telling her to come very often; and as their acquaintance increased, so did their satisfaction in each other. As a walking companion, Emma had very early foreseen how useful she might find her. In that respect Mrs. Weston's loss had been important. Her father never went beyond the shrubbery, where two divisions of the ground sufficed him for his long walk, or his short, as the year varied; and since Mrs. Weston's marriage her exercise had been too much confined. She had ventured once alone to Randalls, but it was not pleasant; and a Harriet Smith, therefore, one whom she could summon at any time to a walk, would be a valuable addition to her privileges. But in every respect, as she saw more of her, she approved her, and was confirmed in all her kind designs.

Harriet certainly was not clever, but she had a sweet, docile, grateful disposition, was totally free from conceit, and only desiring to be guided by any one she looked up to. Her early attachment to herself was very amiable; and her inclination for good company, and power of appreciating what was elegant and clever, showed that there was no want of taste, though strength of understanding must not be expected. Altogether she was quite convinced of Harriet Smith's being exactly the young friend she wanted—exactly the something which her home required. Such a friend as Mrs. Weston was out of the question. Two such could never be granted. Two such she did not want. It was quite a different sort of thing, a sentiment distinct and independent. Mrs. Weston was the object of a regard which had its basis in gratitude and esteem. Harriet would be loved as one to whom she could be useful. For Mrs. Weston there was nothing to be done; for Harriet everything.

Her first attempts at usefulness were in an endeavour to find out who were the parents; but Harriet could not tell. She was ready to tell every thing in her power, but on this subject questions were vain. Emma was obliged to fancy what she liked; but she could never believe that in the same situation *she* should not have discovered the truth. Harriet had no penetration. She had been satisfied to hear and believe just what Mrs. Goddard chose to tell her; and looked no further.

Mrs. Goddard and the teachers, and the girls, and the affairs of the school in general, formed naturally a great part of the conversation—and but for her acquaintance with the Martins of Abbey-Mill Farm, it must have been the whole. But the Martins occupied her thoughts a good deal; she had spent two very happy months with them, and now loved to talk of the pleasures of her visit, and describe the many comforts and wonders of the place. Emma encouraged her talkativeness, amused by such a picture of another set of beings, and enjoying the youthful simplicity which could speak with so much exultation of Mrs. Martin's having *"two* parlours, two very good parlours, indeed; one of them quite as large as Mrs. Goddard's drawing-room; and of her having an upper maid who had lived five-and-twenty years with her; and of their having eight cows, two of them Alderneys, and one a little Welch cow, a very pretty little Welch cow, indeed; and of Mrs. Martin's saying, as she was so fond of it, it should be called *her* cow; and of their having a very handsome summer-house in their garden, where some day next year they were all to drink tea; a very handsome summer-house, large enough to hold a dozen people."

For some time she was amused, without thinking beyond the immediate cause; but as she came to understand the family better, other feelings arose. She had taken up a wrong idea, fancying it was a mother and daughter, a son and son's wife, who all lived together; but when it appeared that the Mr. Martin, who bore a part in the narrative, and was always mentioned with approbation for his great good-nature in doing something or other, was a single man—that there was no young Mrs. Martin, no wife in the case—she did suspect danger to her poor little friend from all this hospitality and kindness, and that, if she were not taken care of, she might be required to sink herself for ever.

With this inspiring notion, her questions increased in number and meaning; and she particularly led Harriet to talk more of Mr. Martin, and there was evidently no dislike to it. Harriet was very ready to speak of the share he had had in their moonlight walks and merry evening games; and dwelt a good deal upon his being so very good-humoured and obliging. "He had gone three miles round one day in order to bring her some walnuts, because she had said how fond she was of them, and in everything else he was so very obliging. He had his shepherd's son into the parlour one night on purpose to sing to her. She was very fond of singing. He could sing a little himself. She believed he was very clever, and understood everything. He had a very fine flock, and, while she was with them, he had been bid more for his wool than anybody in the country. She believed everybody spoke well of him. His mother and sisters were very fond of him. Mrs. Martin had told her one day (and there was a blush as she said it) that it was impossible for anybody to be a better son, and therefore she was sure, whenever he married, he would make a good husband. Not that she *wanted* him to marry. She was in no hurry at all."

"Well done, Mrs. Martin!" thought Emma. "You know what you are about."

"And when she had come away, Mrs. Martin was so very kind as to send Mrs. Goddard a beautiful goose—the finest goose Mrs. Goddard had ever seen. Mrs. Goddard had dressed it on a Sunday, and asked all the three teachers, Miss Nash, and Miss Prince, and Miss Richardson, to sup with her."

"Mr. Martin, I suppose, is not a man of information beyond the line of his own business? He does not read?"

"Oh, yes! that is, no—I do not know—but I believe he has read a good deal—but not what you would think anything of. He reads the Agricultural Reports, and some other books that lay in one of the window seats—but he reads all *them* to himself. But sometimes of an evening, before we went to cards, he would read something aloud out of the 'Elegant Extracts,' very entertaining. And I know he has read the 'Vicar of Wakefield.' He never read the 'Romance of the Forest,' nor the 'Children of the Abbey.' He had never heard of such books before I mentioned them, but he is determined to get them now as soon as ever he can."

The next question was—

"What sort of looking man is Mr. Martin?"

"Oh! not handsome—not at all handsome. I thought him very plain at first, but I do not think him so plain now. One does not, you know, after a time. But did you never see him? He is in Highbury every now and then, and he is sure to ride through every week on his way to Kingston. He has passed you very often."

"That may be, and I may have seen him fifty times, but without having any idea of his name. A young farmer, whether on horseback or on foot, is the very last sort of person to raise my curiosity. The yeomanry are precisely the order of people with whom I feel I can have nothing to do. A degree or two lower, and a creditable appearance might interest me; I might hope to be useful to their families in some way or other. But a farmer can need none of my help, and is, therefore, in one sense, as much above my notice, as in every other he is below it."

"To be sure. Oh, yes! it is not likely you should ever have observed him; but he knows you very well, indeed—I mean by sight."

"I have no doubt of his being a very respectable young man. I know, indeed, that he is so, and, as such, wish him well. What do you imagine his age to be?"

"He was four-and-twenty the 8th of last June, and my birthday is the 23rd—just a fortnight and a day's difference—which is very odd."

"Only four-and-twenty. That is too young to settle. His mother is perfectly right not to be in a hurry. They seem very comfortable as they are, and if she were to take any pains to marry him, she would probably repent it. Six years hence, if he could meet with a good sort of young woman in the same rank as his own, with a little money, it might be very desirable."

"Six years hence! dear Miss Woodhouse, he would be thirty years old!"

"Well, and that is as early as most men can afford to marry, who are not born to an independence. Mr. Martin, I imagine, has his fortune entirely to make—cannot be at all beforehand with the world. Whatever money he might come into when his father died, whatever his share of the family property, it is, I dare say, all afloat, all employed in his stock, and so forth; and though, with diligence and good luck, he may be rich in time it is next to impossible that he should have realised anything yet."

"To be sure, so it is. But they live very comfortably. They have no in-doors man, else they do not want for anything; and Mrs. Martin talks of taking a boy another year."

"I wish you may not get into a scrape, Harriet, whenever he-does marry —I mean, as to being acquainted with his wife; for though his sisters, from a superior education, are not to be altogether objected to, it does not follow that he might marry anybody at all fit for you to notice. The misfortune of your birth ought to make you particularly careful as to your associates. There can be no doubt of your being a gentleman's daughter, and you must support your claim to that station by everything within your own power, or there will be plenty of people who would take pleasure in degrading you."

"Yes, to be sure, I suppose there are. But while I visit at Hartfield, and you are so kind to me, Miss Woodhouse, I am not afraid of what anybody can do."

"You understand the force of influence pretty well, Harriet; but I would have you so firmly established in good society, as to be independent even of Hartfield and Miss Woodhouse. I want to see you permanently well connected, and to that end it will be advisable to have as few odd acquaintances as may be; and, therefore, I say, that if you should still be in this country when Mr. Martin marries, I wish you may not be drawn in by your intimacy with the sisters, to be acquainted with the wife, who will probably be some mere farmer's daughter, without education."

"To be sure. Yes. Not that I think Mr. Martin would ever marry any-body but what had had some education, and been very well brought up. However, I do not mean to set up my opinion against yours—and I am sure I shall not wish for the acquaintance of his wife. I shall always have a great regard for the Miss Martins, especially Elizabeth, and should be very sorry to give them up, for they are quite as well educated as me. But if he marries a very ignorant vulgar woman, certainly I had better not visit her, if I can help it."

Emma watched her through the fluctuations of this speech, and saw no alarming symptoms of love. The young man had been the first admirer, but she trusted there was no other hold, and that there would be no serious difficulty, on Harriet's side, to oppose any friendly arrangement of her own.

They met Mr. Martin the very next day, as they were walking on the Donwell road. He was on foot, and after looking very respectfully at her, looked with most unfeigned satisfaction at her companion. Emma was not sorry to have such an opportunity of survey; and walking a few yards forward, while they talked together, soon made her quick eye sufficiently acquainted with Mr. Robert Martin. His appearance was very neat and he looked like a sensible young man, but his person had no other advantage: and when he came to be contrasted with gentlemen, she thought he must lose all the ground he had gained in Harriet's inclination. Harriet was not insensible of manner; she had voluntarily noticed her father's gentleness with admiration as well as wonder. Mr. Martin looked as if he did not know what manner was.

They remained but a few minutes together, as Miss Woodhouse must not be kept waiting; and Harriet then came running to her with a smiling face, and in a flutter of spirits, which Miss Woodhouse hoped very soon to compose.

"Only think of our happening to meet him! How very odd. It was quite a chance, he said, that he had not gone round by Randalls. He did not think we ever walked this road. He thought we walked towards Randalls most days. He has not been able to get the 'Romance of the Forest' yet. He was so busy the last time he was at Kingston that he quite forgot it, but he goes again to-morrow. So very odd we should happen to meet! Well, Miss Woodhouse, is he like what you expected? What do you think of him? Do you think him so very plain?"

"He is very plain, undoubtedly; remarkably plain; but that is nothing compared with his entire want of gentility. I had no right to expect much, and I did not expect much; but I had no idea that he could be so very clownish, so totally without air. I had imagined him, I confess, a degree or two nearer gentility."

"To be sure," said Harriet, in a mortified voice, "he is not so genteel as real gentlemen."

"I think, Harriet, since your acquaintance with us, you have been repeatedly in the company of some such very real gentlemen, that you must yourself be struck with the difference in Mr. Martin. At Hartfield, you have had very good specimens of well-educated, well-bred men. I should be surprised if, after seeing them, you could be in company with Mr. Martin again without perceiving him to be a very inferior creature —and rather wondering at yourself for having ever thought him at all agreeable before. Do not you begin to feel that now? Were not you struck? I am sure you must have been struck by his awkward look and abrupt manner and the uncouthness of a voice which I heard to be wholly un-modulated as I stood here."

"Certainly, he is not like Mr. Knightley. He has not such a fine air and way of walking as Mr. Knightley. I see the difference plain enough. But Mr. Knightley is so very fine a man!"

"Mr. Knightley's air is so remarkably good that it is not fair to compare Mr. Martin with *him*. You might not see one in a hundred with *gentleman* so plainly written as in Mr. Knightley. But he is not the only gentleman you have been lately used to. What say you to Mr. Weston and Mr. Elton? Compare Mr. Martin with either of *them*. Compare their manner of carry-ing themselves, of walking, of speaking, of being silent. You must see the difference."

"Oh, yes, there is a great difference. But Mr. Weston is almost an old man. Mr. Weston must be between forty and fifty."

"Which makes his good manners the more valuable. The older a person grows, Harriet, the more important it is that their manners should not be bad; the more glaring and disgusting any loudness, or coarseness, or awk-wardness becomes. What is passable in youth is detestable in later age.

Mr. Martin is now awkward and abrupt; what will he be at Mr. Weston's time of life?"

"There is no saying, indeed," replied Harriet, rather solemnly.

"But there may be pretty good guessing. He will be a completely gross, vulgar farmer, totally inattentive to appearances, and thinking of nothing but profit and loss."

"Will he, indeed? that will be very bad."

"How much his business engrosses him already, is very plain from the circumstance of his forgetting to inquire for the book you recommended. He was a great deal too full of the market to think of anything else—which is just as it should be, for a thriving man. What has he to do with books? And I have no doubt that he *will* thrive, and be a very rich man in time; and his being illiterate and coarse need not disturb *us*."

"I wonder he did not remember the book," was all Harriet's answer, and spoken with a degree of grave displeasure which Emma thought might be safely left to itself. She, therefore, said no more for some time. Her next beginning was—

"In one respect, perhaps, Mr. Elton's manners are superior to Mr. Knightley's or Mr. Weston's. They have more gentleness. They might be more safely held up as a pattern. There is an openness, a quickness, almost a bluntness in Mr. Weston, which everybody likes in *him,* because there is so much good humour with it—but that would not do to be copied. Neither would Mr. Knightley's downright, decided, commanding sort of manner, though it suits *him* very well: his figure, and look, and situation in life seem to allow it; but if any young man were to set about copying him, he would not be sufferable. On the contrary, I think a young man might be very safely recommended to take Mr. Elton as a model. Mr. Elton is good-humoured, cheerful, obliging, and gentle. He seems to me to be grown particularly gentle of late. I do not know whether he has any design of ingratiating himself with either of us, Harriet, by additional softness, but it strikes me that his manners are softer than they used to be. If he means anything, it must be to please you. Did not I tell you what he said of you the other day?"

She then repeated some warm personal praise which she had drawn from Mr. Elton, and now did full justice to; and Harriet blushed and smiled, and said she had always thought Mr. Elton very agreeable.

Mr. Elton was the very person fixed on by Emma for driving the young farmer out of Harriet's head. She thought it would be an excellent match; and only too palpably desirable, natural, and probable, for her to have much merit in planning it. She feared it was what everybody else must think of and predict. It was not likely, however, that anybody should have equalled her in the date of the plan as it had entered her brain during the very first evening of Harriet's coming to Hartfield. The longer she considered it, the greater was her sense of its expediency. Mr. Elton's situation was most suitable, quite the gentleman himself, and without low connections; at the same time, not of any family that could fairly object to the doubtful birth of Harriet. He had a comfortable home for her, and Emma imagined a very sufficient income; for though the vicarage of Highbury was not large, he was known to have some independent property; and she thought very highly of him as a good-humoured, well-meaning, respectable young man, without any deficiency of useful understanding or knowledge of the world.

She had already satisfied herself that he thought Harriet a beautiful girl, which she trusted, with such frequent meetings at Hartfield, was foundation enough on his side; and on Harriet's there could be little doubt that the idea of being preferred by him would have all the usual weight and efficacy. And he was really a very pleasing young man, a young man whom any woman not fastidious might like. He was reckoned very handsome; his person much admired in general, though not by her, there being a want of elegance of feature which she could not dispense with: but the girl who could be gratified by a Robert Martin's riding about the country to get walnuts for her might very well be conquered by Mr. Elton's admiration.

Chapter 5

"I do not know what your opinion may be, Mrs. Weston," said Mr. Knightley, "of this great intimacy between Emma and Harriet Smith but I think it a bad thing."

"A bad thing! Do you really think it a bad thing? why so?"

"I think they will neither of them do the other any good."

"You surprise me! Emma must do Harriet good; and by supplying her with a new object of interest, Harriet may be said to do Emma good. I have been seeing their intimacy with the greatest pleasure. How very differently we feel! Not think they will do each other any good! This will certainly be the beginning of one of our quarrels about Emma, Mr. Knightley."

"Perhaps you think I am come on purpose to quarrel with you, knowing Weston to be out, and that you must still fight your own battle."

"Mr. Weston would undoubtedly support me, if he were here, for he thinks exactly as I do on the subject. We were speaking of it only yesterday, and agreeing how fortunate it was for Emma that there should be such a girl in Highbury for her to associate with. Mr. Knightley, I shall not allow you to be a fair judge in this case. You are so much used to live alone, that you do not know the value of a companion; and, perhaps, no man can be a good judge of the comfort a woman feels in the society of one of her own sex, after being used to it all her life. I can imagine your objection to Harriet Smith. She is not the superior young woman which Emma's friend ought to be. But, on the other hand, as Emma wants to see her better informed, it will be an inducement to her to read more herself. They will read together. She means it, I know."

"Emma has been meaning to read more ever since she was twelve years old. I have seen a great many lists of the drawing-up, at various times, of books that she meant to read regularly through—and very good lists they were, very well chosen, and very neatly arranged—sometimes alphabetically, and sometimes by some other rule. The list she drew up when only fourteen—I remember thinking it did her judgment so much credit, that I preserved it some time, and I dare say she may have made out a very good list now. But I have done with expecting any course of steady reading from Emma. She will never submit to anything requiring industry and patience, and a subjection of the fancy to the understanding. Where Miss Taylor failed to stimulate, I may safely affirm that Harriet Smith will do nothing. You never could persuade her to read half so much as you wished. You know you could not."

"I dare say," replied Mrs. Weston, smiling, "that I thought so *then;* but since we have parted, I can never remember Emma's omitting to do anything I wished."

"There is hardly any desiring to refresh such a memory as *that,*" said Mr. Knightley, feelingly; and for a moment or two he had done. "But I," he soon added, "who have had no such charm thrown over my senses, must still see, hear, and remember. Emma is spoiled by being the cleverest of her family. At ten years old she had the misfortune of being able to answer questions which puzzled her sister at seventeen. She was always quick and assured; Isabella slow and diffident. And ever since she was twelve, Emma has been mistress of the house and of you all. In her mother she lost the only person able to cope with her. She inherits her mother's talents, and must have been under subjection to her."

"I should have been sorry, Mr. Knightley, to be dependent on *your* recommendation, had I quitted Mr. Woodhouse's family and wanted another situation; I do not think you have spoken a good word for me to anybody. I am sure you always thought me unfit for the office I held."

"Yes," said he, smiling. "You are better placed *here*—very fit for a wife, but not at all for a governess. But you were preparing yourself to be an excellent wife all the time you were at Hartfield. You might not give Emma such a complete education as your powers would seem to promise; but you were receiving a very good education from *her,* on the very material matrimonial point of submitting your own will, and doing as you were bid; and if Weston had asked me to recommend him a wife, I should certainly have named Miss Taylor."

"Thank you. There will be very little merit in making a good wife to such a man as Mr. Weston."

"Why, to own the truth, I am afraid you are rather thrown away, and that with every disposition to bear, there will be nothing to be borne. We will not despair, however. Weston may grow cross from the wantonness of comfort, or his son may plague him."

"I hope not *that*. It is not likely. No, Mr. Knightley, do not foretell vexation from that quarter."

"Not I, indeed. I only name possibilities. I do not pretend to Emma's genius for foretelling and guessing. I hope, with all my heart, the young man may be a Weston in merit, and a Churchill in fortune. But Harriet Smith, I have not half done about Harriet Smith. I think her the very worst sort of companion that Emma could possibly have. She knows nothing herself, and looks upon Emma as knowing everything. She is a flatterer in all her ways; and so much the worse, because undesigned. Her ignorance is hourly flattery. How can Emma imagine she has anything to learn herself, while Harriet is presenting such a delightful inferiority? And as for Harriet, I will venture to say that *she* cannot gain by the acquaintance. Hartfield will only put her out of conceit with all the other places she belongs to. She will grow just refined enough to be uncomfortable with those among whom birth and circumstances have placed her home. I am much mistaken if Emma's doctrines give any strength of mind, or tend at all to make a girl adapt herself rationally to the varieties of her situation in life. They only give a little polish."

"I either depend more upon Emma's good sense than you do, or am more anxious for her present comfort; for I cannot lament the acquaintance. How well she looked last night!"

"Oh, you would rather talk of her person than her mind, would you? Very well; I shall not attempt to deny Emma's being pretty."

"Pretty! say beautiful rather. Can you imagine anything nearer perfect beauty than Emma altogether—face and figure?"

"I do not know what I could imagine, but I confess that I have seldom seen a face or figure more pleasing to me than hers. But I am a partial old friend."

"Such an eye!—the true hazel eye—and so brilliant! regular features, open countenance, with a complexion—oh, what a bloom of full health, and such a pretty height and size! such a firm and upright figure! There is health not merely in her bloom, but in her air, her head, her glance. One hears sometimes of a child being 'the picture of health'; now, Emma always gives me the idea of being the complete picture of grown-up health. She is loveliness itself. Mr. Knightley, is not she?"

"I have not a fault to find with her person," he replied. "I think her all you describe. I love to look at her; and I will add this praise, that I do not think her personally vain. Considering how very handsome she is, she appears to be little occupied with it; her vanity lies another way. Mrs. Weston, I am not to be talked out of my dislike of her intimacy with Harriet Smith, or my dread of its doing them both harm."

"And I, Mr. Knightley, am equally stout in my confidence of its not doing them any harm. With all dear Emma's little faults, she is an excellent creature. Where shall we see a better daughter, or a kinder sister, or a truer friend? No, no; she has qualities which may be trusted; she will never lead any one really wrong; she will make no lasting blunder; where Emma errs once, she is in the right a hundred times."

"Very well; I will not plague you any more. Emma shall be an angel, and I will keep my spleen to myself till Christmas brings John and Isa-

EMMA 785

bella. John loves Emma with a reasonable, and therefore not a blind affection, and Isabella always thinks as he does, except when he is not quite frightened enough about the children. I am sure of having their opinions with me."

"I know that you all love her really too well to be unjust or unkind; but excuse me, Mr. Knightley, if I take the liberty—(I consider myself, you know, as having somewhat of the privilege of speech that Emma's mother might have had)—the liberty of hinting that I do not think any possible good can arise from Harriet Smith's intimacy being made a matter of much discussion among you. Pray excuse me; but supposing any little inconvenience may be apprehended from the intimacy, it cannot be expected that Emma, accountable to nobody but her father, who perfectly approves the acquaintance, should put an end to it, so long as it is a source of pleasure to herself. It has been so many years my province to give advice, that you cannot be surprised, Mr. Knightley, at this little remains of office."

"Not at all," cried he; "I am much obliged to you for it. It is very good advice, and it shall have a better fate than your advice has often found; for it shall be attend to."

"Mrs. John Knightley is easily alarmed, and might be made unhappy about her sister."

"Be satisfied," said he, "I will not raise any outcry. I will keep my ill-humour to myself. I have a very sincere interest in Emma. Isabella does not seem more my sister; has never excited a greater interest; perhaps hardly so great. There is an anxiety, a curiosity in what one feels for Emma. I wonder what will become of her."

"So do I," said Mrs. Weston, gently, "very much."

"She always declares she will never marry, which, of course, means just nothing at all. But I have no idea that she has yet ever seen a man she cared for. It would not be a bad thing for her to be very much in love with a proper object. I should like to see Emma in love, and in some doubt of a return; it would do her good. But there is nobody hereabouts to attach her; and she goes so seldom from home."

"There does, indeed, seem as little to tempt her to break her resolution at present," said Mrs. Weston, "as can well be; and while she is so happy at Hartfield, I cannot wish her to be forming any attachment which would be creating such difficulties on poor Mr. Woodhouse's account. I do not recommend matrimony at present to Emma, though I mean no slight to the state, I assure you."

Part of her meaning was to conceal some favourite thoughts of her own and Mr. Weston's on the subject as much as possible. There were wishes at Randalls respecting Emma's destiny, but it was not desirable to have them suspected; and the quiet transition which Mr. Knightley soon afterwards made to "What does Weston think of the weather?—shall we have rain?"—convinced her that he had nothing more to say or surmise about Hartfield.

Chapter 6

EMMA could not feel a doubt of having given Harriet's fancy a proper direction, and raised the gratitude of her young vanity to a very good purpose; for she found her decidedly more sensible than before of Mr. Elton's being a remarkably handsome man, with most agreeable manners; and as she had no hesitation in following up the assurance of his admiration by agreeable hints, she was soon pretty confident of creating as much liking on Harriet's side as there could be any occasion for. She was quite convinced of Mr. Elton's being in the fairest way of falling in love, if not in love already. She had no scruple with regard to him. He talked of Harriet; and praised her so warmly that she could not suppose anything wanting which a little time would not add. His perception of the striking improvement of Harriet's manner, since her introduction at Hartfield, was not one of the least agreeable proofs of his growing attachment.

"You have given Miss Smith all that she required," said he; "you have made her graceful and easy. She was a beautiful creature when she came to you; but, in my opinion, the attractions you have added are infinitely superior to what she received from nature."

"I am glad you think I have been useful to her; but Harriet only wanted drawing out, and receiving a few, very few hints. She had all the natural grace of sweetness of temper and artlessness in herself. I have done very little."

"If it were admissible to contradict a lady——" said the gallant Mr. Elton.

"I have, perhaps, given her a little more decision of character—have taught her to think on points which had not fallen in her way before."

"Exactly so; that is what principally strikes me. So much superadded decision of character! Skilful has been the hand!"

"Great has been the pleasure, I am sure. I never met with a disposition more truly amiable."

"I have no doubt of it." And it was spoken with a sort of sighing animation which had a vast deal of the lover. She was not less pleased, another day, with the manner in which he seconded a sudden wish of hers—to have Harriet's picture.

"Did you ever have your likeness taken, Harriet?" said she; "did you ever sit for your picture?"

Harriet was on the point of leaving the room, and only stopped to say, with a very interesting naïveté—

"Oh dear, no—never."

No sooner was she out of sight than Emma exclaimed—

"What an exquisite possession a good picture of her would be! I would give any money for it. I almost long to attempt her likeness myself. You do not know it, I dare say, but two or three years ago I had a great passion for taking likenesses, and attempted several of my friends, and was thought to have a tolerable eye in general; but, from one cause or another, I gave it up in disgust. But, really, I could almost venture if Harriet would sit to me. It would be such a delight to have her picture!"

"Let me entreat you," cried Mr. Elton; "it would indeed be a delight; let me entreat you, Miss Woodhouse, to exercise so charming a talent in favour of your friend. I know what your drawings are. How could you suppose me ignorant? Is not this room rich in specimens of your land-scapes and flowers! and has not Mrs. Weston some inimitable figure pieces in her drawing-room at Randalls?"

Yes, good man! thought Emma, but what has all that to do with taking likenesses? You know nothing of drawing. Don't pretend to be in raptures about mine. Keep your raptures for Harriet's face. "Well, if you give me such kind encouragement, Mr. Elton, I believe I shall try what I can do. Harriet's features are very delicate, which makes a likeness difficult; and yet, there is a peculiarity in the shape of the eye, and the lines about the mouth, which one ought to catch."

"Exactly so, the shape of the eye and the lines about the mouth, I have not a doubt of your success. Pray, pray attempt it. As you will do it, it will indeed, to use your own words, be an exquisite possession."

"But I am afraid, Mr. Elton, Harriet will not like to sit, she thinks so little of her own beauty. Did not you observe her manner of answering me? How completely it meant 'Why should my picture be drawn?' "

"Oh, yes, I observed it, I assure you. It was not lost on me. But still I cannot imagine she would not be persuaded."

Harriet was soon back again, and the proposal almost immediately made; and she had no scruples which could stand many minutes against the earnest pressing of both the others. Emma wished to go to work directly, and therefore produced the portfolio containing her various attempts at portraits, for not one of them had ever been finished, that they might decide together on the best size for Harriet. Her many begin-nings were displayed. Miniatures, half-lengths, whole-lengths, pencil, crayon, and water-colours had been all tried in turn. She had always wanted to do everything, and had made more progress, both in drawing and music, than many might have done with so little labour as she would ever submit to. She played and sang, and drew in almost every style; but steadiness had always been wanting; and in nothing had she approached the degree of excellence which she would have been glad to command, and ought not to have failed of. She was not much deceived as to her own skill, either as an artist or a musician; but she was not unwilling to have others deceived, or sorry to know her reputation for accomplishment often higher than it deserved.

There was merit in every drawing, in the least finished, perhaps the most. Her style was spirited; but had there been much less, or had there been ten times more, the delight and admiration of her two companions would have been the same. They were both in ecstasies. A likeness pleases everybody; and Miss Woodhouse's performances must be capital.

"No great variety of faces for you," said Emma. "I had only my own family to study from. There is my father—another of my father—but the idea of sitting for his picture made him so nervous, that I could only take him by stealth, neither of them alike, therefore. Mrs. Weston again, and again, and again, you see. Dear Mrs. Weston—always my kindest friend on every occasion. She would sit whenever I asked her. There is my sister; and really quite her own little elegant figure—and the face not unlike. I should have made a good likeness of her, if she would have sat longer; but she was in such a hurry to have me draw her four children that she would not be quiet. Then, here come all my attempts at three of those four children—there they are, Henry, and John, and Bella, from one end of the sheet to the other, and any one of them might do for any one of the rest. She was so eager to have them drawn that I could not refuse; but there is no making children of three or four years old stand still, you know; nor can it be very easy to take any likeness of them, beyond the air and complexion, unless they are coarser featured than any mamma's children ever were. Here is my sketch of the fourth, who was a baby. I took him as he was sleeping on the sofa, and it is as strong a likeness of his cockade as you would wish to see. He had nestled down his head most conveniently: that's very like. I am rather proud of little George. The corner of the sofa is very good. Then here is my last," unclosing a pretty sketch of a gentleman in small size, whole-length—"my last and my best—my brother, Mr. John Knightley. This did not want much of being finished, when I put it away in a pet, and vowed I would never take another likeness. I could not help being provoked; for, after all my pains, and when I had really made a very good likeness of it—(Mrs. Weston and I were quite agreed in thinking it *very* like)—only too handsome—too flattering—but that was a fault on the right side—after all this, came poor dear Isabella's cold approbation of—'Yes, it was a little like; but, to be sure, it did not do him justice.' We had had a great deal of trouble in persuading him to sit at all. It was made a great favour of; and altogether it was more than I could bear; and so I never would finish it, to have it apologised over, as an unfavourable likeness, to every morning visitor in Brunswick Square; and, as I said, I did then forswear ever drawing anybody again. But, for Harriet's sake, or rather for my own, and as there are no husbands and wives in the case at present, I will break my resolution now."

Mr. Elton seemed very properly struck and delighted by the idea, and was repeating, "No husbands and wives in the case *at present* indeed, as you observe. Exactly so. No husbands and wives," with so interesting a consciousness that Emma began to consider whether she had not better leave them together at once. But as she wanted to be drawing, the declaration must wait a little longer.

She had soon fixed on the size and sort of portrait. It was to be a whole-length in water-colours, like Mr. John Knightley's, and was destined, if she could please herself, to hold a very honourable station over the mantelpiece.

The sitting began; and Harriet smiling and blushing, and afraid of not keeping her attitude and countenance, presented a very sweet mixture of youthful expression to the steady eye of the artist. But there was no doing anything, with Mr. Elton fidgeting behind her, and watching every touch. She gave him credit for stationing himself where he might gaze and gaze again without offence; but was really obliged to put an end to it, and request him to place himself elsewhere. It then occurred to her to employ him in reading.

"If he would be so good as to read to them, it would be a kindness indeed! It would amuse away the difficulties of her part, and lessen the irksomeness of Miss Smith's."

Mr. Elton was only too happy. Harriet listened, and Emma drew in peace. She must allow him to be still frequently coming to look; anything less would certainly have been too little in a lover; and he was ready at the smallest intermission of the pencil to jump up and see the progress, and be charmed. There was no being displeased with such an encourager, for his admiration made him discern a likeness almost before it was possible. She could not respect his eye, but his love and his complaisance were unexceptionable.

The sitting was altogether very satisfactory: she was quite enough pleased with the first day's sketch to wish to go on. There was no want of likeness; she had been fortunate in the attitude; and as she meant to throw in a little improvement to the figure, to give a little more height and considerably more elegance, she had great confidence of its being in every way a pretty drawing at last, and of its filling its destined place with credit to them both, a standing memorial of the beauty of the one, the skill of the other, and the friendship of both; with as many other agreeable associations as Mr. Elton's very promising attachment was likely to add.

Harriet was to sit again the next day; and Mr. Elton, just as he ought, entreated for the permission of attending and reading to them again.

"By all means. We shall be most happy to consider you as one of the party."

The same civilities and courtesies, the same success and satisfaction, took place on the morrow, and accompanied the whole progress of the picture, which was rapid and happy. Everybody who saw it was pleased, but Mr. Elton was in continual raptures, and defended it through every criticism.

"Miss Woodhouse has given her friend the only beauty she wanted," observed Mrs. Weston to him, not in the least suspecting that she was addressing a lover. "The expression of the eye is most correct, but Miss Smith has not those eyebrows and eyelashes. It is the fault of her face that she has them not."

"Do you think so?" replied he. "I cannot agree with you. It appears to me a most perfect resemblance in every feature. I never saw such a likeness in my life. We must allow for the effect of shade, you know."

"You have made her too tall, Emma," said Mr. Knightley.

Emma knew that she had, but would not own it; and Mr. Elton warmly added:

"Oh, no—certainly not too tall—not in the least too tall. Consider, she is sitting down, which naturally presents a different—which in short gives exactly the idea—and the proportions must be preserved, you know. Proportions, fore-shortening—oh, no! It gives one exactly the idea of such a height as Miss Smith's—exactly so, indeed."

"It is very pretty," said Mr. Woodhouse. "So prettily done! Just as your drawings always are, my dear. I do not know anybody who draws so well as you do. The only thing I do not thoroughly like is, that she seems to be sitting out of doors, with only a little shawl over her shoulders; and it makes one think she must catch cold."

"But, my dear papa, it is supposed to be summer; a warm day in summer. Look at the tree."

"But it is never safe to sit out of doors, my dear."

"You, sir, may say anything," cried Mr. Elton, "but I must confess that I regard it as a most happy thought, the placing of Miss Smith out of doors; and the tree is touched with such inimitable spirit! Any other situation would have been much less in character. The naïveté of Miss Smith's manners—and altogether—oh, it is most admirable! I cannot keep my eyes from it. I never saw such a likeness."

The next thing wanted was to get the picture framed; and here were a few difficulties. It must be done directly; it must be done in London; the order must go through the hands of some intelligent person whose taste could be depended on; and Isabella, the usual doer of all commissions, must not be applied to, because it was December, and Mr. Woodhouse could not bear the idea of her stirring out of her house in the fogs of December. But no sooner was the distress known to Mr. Elton than it was removed. His gallantry was always on the alert. "Might he be trusted with the commission, what infinite pleasure should he have in executing it! He could ride to London at any time. It was impossible to say how much he should be gratified by being employed on such an errand."

"He was too good! She could not endure the thought! She would not give him such a troublesome office for the world"—brought on the desired repetition of entreaties and assurances—and a very few minutes settled the business.

Mr. Elton was to take the drawing to London, choose the frame, and give the directions; and Emma thought she could so pack it as to ensure its safety without much incommoding him, while he seemed mostly fearful of not being incommoded enough.

"What a precious deposit!" said he, with a tender sigh, as he received it.

"This man is almost too gallant to be in love," thought Emma. "I should say so, but that I suppose there may be a hundred different ways of being in love. He is an excellent young man, and will suit Harriet exactly; it will be an 'exactly so,' as he says himself; but he does sigh and languish, and study for compliments rather more than I could endure as a principal. I come in for a pretty good share as a second. But it is his gratitude on Harriet's account."

Chapter 7

THE very day of Mr. Elton's going to London produced a fresh occasion for Emma's services towards her friend. Harriet had been at Hartfield, as usual, soon after breakfast; and, after a time, had gone home to return again to dinner; she returned, and sooner than had been talked of, and with an agitated, hurried look, announcing something extraordinary to have happened which she was longing to tell. Half a minute brought it all out. She had heard, as soon as she got back to Mrs. Goddard's, that Mr. Martin had been there an hour before, and finding she was not at home, nor particularly expected, had left a little parcel for her from one of his sisters, and gone away; and, on opening this parcel, she had actually found, besides the two songs which she had lent Elizabeth to copy, a letter to herself; and this letter was from him—from Mr. Martin—and contained a direct proposal of marriage. "Who could have thought it? She was so surprised she did not know what to do. Yes, quite a proposal of marriage; and a very good letter, at least she thought so. And he wrote as if he really loved her very much—but she did not know—and so, she was come as fast as she could to ask Miss Woodhouse what she should do." Emma was half ashamed of her friend for seeming so pleased and so doubtful.

"Upon my word," she cried, "the young man is determined not to lose anything for want of asking. He will connect himself well if he can."

"Will you read the letter?" cried Harriet. "Pray do, I'd rather you would."

Emma was not sorry to be pressed. She read, and was surprised. The style of the letter was much above her expectation. There were not merely no grammatical errors, but as a composition it would not have disgraced a gentleman; the language, though plain, was strong and unaffected, and the sentiments it conveyed very much to the credit of the writer. It was short, but expressed good sense, warm attachment, liberality, propriety, even delicacy of feeling. She paused over it while Harriet stood anxiously watching for her opinion, with a "Well, well," and was at last forced to add, "Is it a good letter, or is it too short?"

"Yes, indeed, a very good letter," replied Emma, rather slowly; "so good a letter, Harriet, that, everything considered, I think one of his sisters must have helped him. I can hardly imagine the young man whom I saw talking with you the other day could express himself so well, if left quite to his own powers, and yet it is not the style of a woman; no, certainly, it is too strong and concise; but diffuse enough for a woman. No doubt he is a sensible man, and I suppose may have a natural talent for—

thinks strongly and clearly—and when he takes a pen in hand, his thoughts naturally find proper words. It is so with some men. Yes, I understand the sort of mind. Vigorous, decided, with sentiments to a certain point not coarse. A better written letter, Harriet (returning it), than I had expected."

"Well," said the still waiting Harriet; "well—and—and what shall I do?"

"What shall you do—in what respect? Do you mean with regard to this letter?"

"Yes."

"But what are you in doubt of? You must answer it, of course, and speedily."

"Yes. But what shall I say? Dear Miss Woodhouse, do advise me."

"Oh, no, no; the letter had much better be all your own. You will express yourself very properly, I am sure. There is no danger of your not being intelligible, which is the first thing. Your meaning must be unequivocal; no doubts or demurs; and such expressions of gratitude and concern for the pain you are inflicting as propriety requires, will present themselves unbidden to *your* mind, I am persuaded. *You* need not be prompted to write with the appearance of sorrow for his disappointment."

"You think I ought to refuse him, then?" said Harriet, looking down.

"Ought to refuse him! My dear Harriet, what do you mean? Are you in any doubt as to that? I thought—but I beg your pardon, perhaps I have been under a mistake. I certainly have been misunderstanding you, if you feel in doubt as to the *purport* of your answer. I had imagined you were consulting me only as to the wording of it."

Harriet was silent. With a little reserve of manner, Emma continued:

"You mean to return a favourable answer, I collect?"

"No; I do not, that is, I do not mean—what shall I do? What would you advise me to do? Pray, dear Miss Woodhouse, tell me what I ought to do."

"I shall not give you any advice, Harriet. I will have nothing to do with it. This is a point which you must settle with your own feelings."

"I had no notion that he liked me so very much," said Harriet, contemplating the letter. For a little while Emma persevered in her silence; but, beginning to apprehend the bewitching flattery of that letter might be too powerful, she thought it best to say:

"I lay it down as a general rule, Harriet, that if a woman *doubts* as to whether she should accept a man or not, she certainly ought to refuse him. If she can hesitate as to 'Yes,' she ought to say 'No,' directly. It is not a state to be safely entered into with doubtful feelings, with half a heart. I thought it my duty as a friend, and older than yourself, to say this much to you. But do not imagine that I want to influence you."

"Oh, no, I am sure you are a great deal too kind to—but if you would just advise me what I had best do—no, no, I do not mean that—as you say, one's mind ought to be quite made up—one should not be hesitating

—it is a very serious thing. It will be safer to say 'No,' perhaps. Do you think I had better say 'No'?"

"Not for the world," said Emma, smiling graciously, "would I advise you either way. You must be the best judge of your own happiness. If you prefer Mr. Martin to every other person, if you think him the most agreeable man you have ever been in company with, why should you hesitate? You blush, Harriet. Does anybody else occur to you at this moment under such a definition? Harriet, Harriet, do not deceive yourself; do not be run away with by gratitude and compassion. At this moment whom are you thinking of?"

The symptoms were favourable. Instead of answering, Harriet turned away confused, and stood thoughtfully by the fire; and though the letter was still in her hand, it was now mechanically twisted about without regard. Emma waited the result with impatience, but not without strong hopes. At last, with some hesitation, Harriet said:

"Miss Woodhouse, as you will not give me your opinion, I must do as well as I can by myself; and I have now quite determined, and really almost made up my mind, to refuse Mr. Martin. Do you think I am right?"

"Perfectly, perfectly right, my dearest Harriet; you are doing just what you ought. While you were at all in suspense, I kept my feelings to myself, but now that you are so completely decided, I have no hesitation in approving. Dear Harriet, I give myself joy of this. It would have grieved me to lose your acquaintance, which must have been the consequence of your marrying Mr. Martin. While you were in the smallest degree wavering, I said nothing about it, because I would not influence; but it would have been the loss of a friend to me. I could not have visited Mrs. Robert Martin, of Abbey-Mill Farm. Now I am secure of you for ever."

Harriet had not surmised her own danger, but the idea of it struck her forcibly.

"You could not have visited me!" she cried, looking aghast. "No, to be sure you could not; but I never thought of that before. That would have been too dreadful! What an escape! Dear Miss Woodhouse, I would not give up the pleasure and honour of being intimate with you for anything in the world."

"Indeed, Harriet, it would have been a severe pang to lose you; but it must have been. You would have thrown yourself out of all good society. I must have given you up."

"Dear me! How should I ever have borne it? It would have killed me never to come to Hartfield any more."

"Dear, affectionate creature! *You* banished to Abbey-Mill Farm! *You* confined to the society of the illiterate and vulgar all your life! I wonder how the young man could have the assurance to ask it. He must have a pretty good opinion of himself."

"I do not think he is conceited either, in general," said Harriet, her conscience opposing such censure; "at least, he is very good-natured, and

I shall always feel much obliged to him, and have a great regard for—
but that is quite a different thing from—and you know, though he may
like me, it does not follow that I should—and, certainly, I must confess
that since my visiting here I have seen people—and if one comes to compare them, person and manners, there is no comparison at all, *one* is so
very handsome and agreeable. However, I do really think Mr. Martin a
very amiable young man, and have a great opinion of him; and his being
so much attached to me—and his writing such a letter—but as to leaving
you, it is what I would not do upon any consideration."

"Thank you, thank you, my own sweet little friend. We will not be
parted. A woman is not to marry a man merely because she is asked, or
because he is attached to her, and can write a tolerable letter."

"Oh no; and it is but a short letter, too."

Emma felt the bad taste of her friend, but let it pass with a "Very true:
and it would be a small consolation to her, for the clownish manner which
might be offending her every hour of the day, to know that her husband
could write a good letter."

"Oh yes, very. Nobody cares for a letter: the thing is, to be always
happy with pleasant companions. I am quite determined to refuse him.
But how shall I do? What shall I say?"

Emma assured her there would be no difficulty in the answer, and
advised its being written directly, which was agreed to, in the hope of her
assistance; and though Emma continued to protest against any assistance
being wanted, it was, in fact, given in the formation of every sentence.
The looking over his letter again, in replying to it, had such a softening
tendency, that it was particularly necessary to brace her up with a few
decisive expressions; and she was so very much concerned at the idea of
making him unhappy, and thought so much of what his mother and sisters
would think and say, and was so anxious that they should not fancy her
ungrateful, that Emma believed, if the young man had come in her way
at that moment, he would have been accepted after all.

This letter, however, was written, and sealed, and sent. The business
was finished, and Harriet safe. She was rather low all the evening; but
Emma could allow for her amiable regrets, and sometimes relieved them
by speaking of her own affection, sometimes by bringing forward the idea
of Mr. Elton.

"I shall never be invited to Abbey-Mill again," was said in rather a
sorrowful tone.

"Nor, if you were, could I ever bear to part with you, my Harriet. You
are a great deal too necessary at Hartfield to be spared to Abbey-Mill."

"And I am sure I should never want to go there; for I am never happy
but at Hartfield."

Some time afterwards it was, "I think Mrs. Goddard would be very
much surprised if she knew what had happened. I am sure Miss Nash
would; for Miss Nash thinks her own sister very well married, and it is
only a linen-draper."

"One should be sorry to see greater pride or refinement in the teacher of a school, Harriet. I dare say Miss Nash would envy you such an opportunity as this of being married. Even this conquest would appear valuable in her eyes. As to anything superior for you, I suppose she is quite in the dark. The attentions of a certain person can hardly be among the tittle-tattle of Highbury yet. Hitherto, I fancy you and I are the only people to whom his looks and manners have explained themselves."

Harriet blushed and smiled, and said something about wondering that people should like her so much. The idea of Mr. Elton was certainly cheering; but still, after a time, she was tender-hearted again towards the rejected Mr. Martin.

"Now he has got my letter," said she, softly. "I wonder what they are all doing—whether his sisters know—if he is unhappy, they will be unhappy too. I hope he will not mind it so very much."

"Let us think of those among our absent friends who are more cheerfully employed," cried Emma. "At this moment, perhaps, Mr. Elton is showing your picture to his mother and sisters, telling how much more beautiful is the original, and after being asked for it five or six times, allowing them to hear your name—your own dear name."

"My picture! But he has left my picture in Bond Street."

"Has he so! Then I know nothing of Mr. Elton. No, my dear little modest Harriet, depend upon it, the picture will not be in Bond Street till just before he mounts his horse to-morrow. It is his companion all this evening, his solace, his delight. It opens his designs to his family, it introduces you among them, it diffuses through the party those pleasantest feelings of our nature—eager curiosity and warm prepossession. How cheerful, how animated, how suspicious, how busy their imaginations all are!"

Harriet smiled again, and her smiles grew stronger.

Chapter 8

HARRIET slept at Hartfield that night. For some weeks past she had been spending more than half her time there, and gradually getting to have a bedroom appropriated to herself; and Emma judged it best in every respect, safest and kindest, to keep her with them as much as possible just at present. She was obliged to go the next morning for an hour or two to Mrs. Goddard's, but it was then to be settled that she should return to Hartfield, to make a regular visit of some days.

While she was gone, Mr. Knightley called, and sat some time with Mr. Woodhouse and Emma, till Mr. Woodhouse, who had previously made up his mind to walk out, was persuaded by his daughter not to defer it, and was induced by the entreaties of both, though against the scruples of his own civility, to leave Mr. Knightley for that purpose. Mr. Knightley, who had nothing of ceremony about him, was offering, by his short, decided answers, an amusing contrast to the protracted apologies and civil hesitations of the other.

"Well, I believe, if you will excuse me, Mr. Knightley, if you will not consider me as doing a very rude thing, I shall take Emma's advice and go out for a quarter of an hour. As the sun is out, I believe I had better take my three turns while I can. I treat you without ceremony, Mr. Knightley. We invalids think we are privileged people."

"My dear sir, do not make a stranger of me."

"I leave an excellent substitute in my daughter. Emma will be happy to entertain you. And therefore I think I will beg your excuse, and take my three turns—my winter walk."

"You cannot do better, sir."

"I would ask for the pleasure of your company, Mr. Knightley, but I am a very slow walker, and my pace would be tedious to you; and, besides, you have another long walk before you, to Donwell Abbey."

"Thank you, sir, thank you; I am going this moment myself; and I think the sooner *you* go the better. I will fetch your greatcoat and open the garden-door for you."

Mr. Woodhouse at last was off; but Mr. Knightley, instead of being immediately off likewise, sat down again, seemingly inclined for more chat. He began speaking of Harriet, and speaking of her with more voluntary praise than Emma had ever heard before.

"I cannot rate her beauty as you do," said he; "but she is a pretty little creature, and I am inclined to think very well of her disposition. Her character depends upon those she is with; but in good hands she will turn out a valuable woman."

"I am glad you think so; and the good hands, I hope, may not be wanting."

"Come," said he, "you are anxious for a compliment, so I will tell you that you have improved her. You have cured her of her schoolgirl's giggle; she really does you credit."

"Thank you. I should be mortified, indeed, if I did not believe I had been of some use; but it is not everybody who will bestow praise where they may. *You* do not often overpower me with it."

"You are expecting her again, you say, this morning?"

"Almost every moment. She has been gone longer already than she intended."

"Something has happened to delay her; some visitors, perhaps."

"Highbury gossips! Tiresome wretches!"

"Harriet may not consider everybody tiresome that you would."

Emma knew this was too true for contradiction, and, therefore, said nothing. He presently added, with a smile:

"I do not pretend to fix on times or places, but I must tell you that I have good reason to believe your little friend will soon hear of something to her advantage."

"Indeed! How so? Of what sort?"

"A very serious sort, I assure you," still smiling.

"Very serious! I can think of but one thing—who is in love with her? Who makes you their confidant?"

Emma was more than half in hopes of Mr. Elton's having dropped a hint. Mr. Knightley was a sort of general friend and adviser, and she knew Mr. Elton looked up to him.

"I have reason to think," he replied, "that Harriet Smith will soon have an offer of marriage, and from a most unexceptionable quarter—Robert Martin is the man. Her visit to Abbey-Mill, this summer, seems to have done his business. He is desperately in love, and means to marry her."

"He is very obliging," said Emma; "but is he sure that Harriet means to marry him?"

"Well, well, means to make her an offer, then. Will that do? He came to the Abbey two evenings ago, on purpose to consult me about it. He knows I have a thorough regard for him and all his family, and, I believe, considers me as one of his best friends. He came to ask me whether I thought it would be imprudent in him to settle so early; whether I thought her too young—in short, whether I approved his choice altogether; having some apprehension, perhaps, of her being considered (especially since *your* making so much of her) as in a line of society above him. I was very much pleased with all that he said. I never hear better sense from anyone than Robert Martin. He always speaks to the purpose; open, straightforward, and very well judging. He told me everything; his circumstances and plans, and what they all proposed doing in the event of his marriage. He is an excellent young man, both as son and brother. I had no hesitation in advising him to marry. He proved to me that he could afford it; and that being the case, I was convinced he could not do better. I praised the fair lady too, and altogether sent him away very happy. If he had never esteemed my opinion before, he would have thought highly of me then; and, I dare say, left the house thinking me the best friend and counsellor man ever had. This happened the night before last. Now, as we may fairly suppose, he would not allow much time to pass before he spoke to the lady, and as he does not appear to have spoken yesterday, it is not unlikely that he should be at Mrs. Goddard's to-day; and she may be detained by a visitor, without thinking him at all a tiresome wretch."

"Pray, Mr. Knightley," said Emma, who had been smiling to herself through a great part of this speech, "how do you know that Mr. Martin did not speak yesterday?"

"Certainly," replied he, surprised, "I do not absolutely know it, but it may be inferred. Was not she the whole day with you?"

"Come," said she, "I will tell you something in return for what you have told me. He did speak yesterday—that is, he wrote, and was refused."

This was obliged to be repeated before it could be believed; and Mr.

Knightley actually looked red with surprise and displeasure, as he stood up, in tall indignation, and said:

"Then she is a greater simpleton than I ever believed her. What is the foolish girl about?"

"Oh, to be sure," cried Emma, "it is always incomprehensible to a man, that a woman should ever refuse an offer of marriage. A man always imagines a woman to be ready for anybody who asks her."

"Nonsense! A man does not imagine any such thing. But what is the meaning of this? Harriet Smith refuse Robert Martin! Madness, if it is so; but I hope you are mistaken."

"I saw her answer! Nothing could be clearer."

"You saw her answer! You wrote her answer too. Emma, this is your doing. You persuaded her to refuse him."

"And if I did (which, however, I am far from allowing), I should not feel that I had done wrong. Mr. Martin is a very respectable young man, but I cannot admit him to be Harriet's equal; and am rather surprised, indeed, that he should have ventured to address her. By your account he does seem to have had some scruples. It is a pity that they were ever got over."

"Not Harriet's equal!" exclaimed Mr. Knightley, loudly and warmly; and with calmer asperity added, a few moments afterwards, "No, he is not her equal, indeed, for he is as much her superior in sense as in situation. Emma, your infatuation about that girl blinds you. What are Harriet Smith's claims, either of birth, nature, or education, to any connection higher than Robert Martin? She is the natural daughter of nobody knows whom, with probably no settled provision at all, and certainly no respectable relations. She is known only as parlour boarder at a common school. She is not a sensible girl, nor a girl of any information. She has been taught nothing useful, and is too young and too simple to have acquired anything herself. At her age she can have no experience; and, with her little wit, is not very likely ever to have any that can avail her. She is pretty, and she is good-tempered, and that is all. My only scruple in advising the match was on his account, as being beneath his deserts, and a bad connection for him. I felt that, as to fortune, in all probability he might do much better, and that, as to a rational companion or useful helpmate, he could not do worse. But I could not reason so to a man in love, and was willing to trust to there being no harm in her; to her having that sort of disposition which, in good hands like his, might be easily led aright, and turn out very well. The advantage of the match I felt to be all on her side; and had not the smallest doubt (nor have I now) that there would be a general cry out upon her extreme good luck. Even *your* satisfaction I made sure of. It crossed my mind immediately that you would not regret your friend's leaving Highbury, for the sake of her being settled so well. I remember saying to myself, 'Even Emma, with all her partiality for Harriet, will think this a good match.'"

"I cannot help wondering at your knowing so little of Emma as to say any such thing. What! Think a farmer (and with all his sense and all his merit Mr. Martin is nothing more) a good match for my intimate friend! Not regret her leaving Highbury, for the sake of marrying a man whom I could never admit as an acquaintance of my own! I wonder you should think it possible for me to have such feelings. I assure you mine are very different. I must think your statement by no means fair. You are not just to Harriet's claims. They would be estimated very differently by others as well as myself; Mr. Martin may be the richest of the two, but he is undoubtedly her inferior as to rank in society. The sphere in which she moves is much above his. It would be a degradation."

"A degradation to illegitimacy and ignorance to be married to a respectable, intelligent, gentleman-farmer!"

"As to the circumstances of her birth, though in a legal sense she may be called Nobody, it will not hold in common sense. She is not to pay for the offence of others, by being held below the level of those with whom she is brought up. There can scarcely be a doubt that her father is a gentleman—and a gentleman of fortune. Her allowance is very liberal; nothing has ever been grudged for her improvement or comfort. That she is a gentleman's daughter is indubitable to me; that she associates with gentlemen's daughters, no one, I apprehend, will deny. She is superior to Mr. Robert Martin."

"Whoever might be her parents," said Mr. Knightley, "whoever may have had the charge of her, it does not appear to have been any part of their plan to introduce her into what you would call good society. After receiving a very indifferent education, she is left in Mrs. Goddard's hands to shift as she can—to move, in short, in Mrs. Goddard's line, to have Mrs. Goddard's acquaintance. Her friends evidently thought this good enough for her; and it *was* good enough. She desired nothing better herself. Till you chose to turn her into a friend, her mind had no distaste for her own set, nor any ambition beyond it. She was as happy as possible with the Martins in the summer. She had no sense of superiority then. If she has it now, you have given it. You have been no friend to Harriet Smith, Emma. Robert Martin would never have proceeded so far, if he had not felt persuaded of her not being disinclined to him. I know him well. He has too much real feeling to address any woman on the haphazard of selfish passion. And as to conceit, he is the farthest from it of any man I know. Depend upon it, he had encouragement."

It was most convenient to Emma not to make a direct reply to this assertion; she chose rather to take up her own line of the subject again.

"You are a very warm friend of Mr. Martin; but, as I said before, are unjust to Harriet. Harriet's claims to marry well are not so contemptible as you represent them. She is not a clever girl, but she has better sense than you are aware of, and does not deserve to have her understanding spoken of so slightingly. Waiving that point, however, and supposing her to be, as you describe her, only pretty and good-natured, let me tell you, that in the degree she possesses them, they are not trivial recommenda-

tions to the world in general, for she is, in fact, a beautiful girl, and must
be thought so by ninety-nine people out of a hundred; and till it appears
that men are much more philosophic on the subject of beauty than they
are generally supposed, till they do fall in love with well-informed minds
instead of handsome faces, a girl, with such loveliness as Harriet, has a
certainty of being admired and sought after, of having the power of choosing from among many, consequently a claim to be nice. Her good nature,
too, is not so very slight a claim, comprehending, as it does, real, thorough
sweetness of temper and manner, a very humble opinion of herself, and
a great readiness to be pleased with other people. I am very much mistaken if your sex in general would not think such beauty, and such temper,
the highest claims a woman could possess."

"Upon my word, Emma, to hear you abusing the reason you have, is
almost enough to make me think so too. Better be without sense than
misapply it as you do."

"To be sure," cried she, playfully. "I know *that* is the feeling of you all.
I know that such a girl as Harriet is exactly what every man delights in—
what at once bewitches his senses and satisfies his judgment. Oh, Harriet
may pick and choose. Were you, yourself, ever to marry, she is the very
woman for you. And is she, at seventeen, just entering into life, just
beginning to be known, to be wondered at because she does not accept the
first offer she receives? No—pray let her have time to look about her."

"I have always thought it a very foolish intimacy," said Mr. Knightley
presently, "though I have kept my thoughts to myself; but I now perceive
that it will be a very unfortunate one for Harriet. You will puff her up
with such ideas of her own beauty, and of what she has a claim to, that,
in a little while, nobody within her reach will be good enough for her.
Vanity working on a weak head produces every sort of mischief. Nothing
so easy as for a young lady to raise her expectations too high. Miss Harriet Smith may not find offers of marriage flow in so fast, though she is a
very pretty girl. Men of sense, whatever you may choose to say, do not
want silly wives. Men of family would not be very fond of connecting
themselves with a girl of such obscurity—and most prudent men would
be afraid of the inconvenience and disgrace they might be involved in,
when the mystery of her parentage came to be revealed. Let her marry
Robert Martin, and she is safe, respectable, and happy for ever; but if
you encourage her to expect to marry greatly, and teach her to be satisfied
with nothing less than a man of consequence and large fortune, she may
be a parlour-boarder at Mrs. Goddard's all the rest of her life—or, at
least (for Harriet Smith is a girl who will marry somebody or other), till
she grow desperate, and is glad to catch at the old writing-master's son."

"We think so very differently on this point, Mr. Knightley, that there
can be no use in canvassing it. We shall only be making each other more
angry. But as to my *letting* her marry Robert Martin, it is impossible;
she has refused him, and so decidedly, I think, as must prevent any second
application. She must abide by the evil of having refused him, whatever

it may be; and as to the refusal itself, I will not pretend to say that I might not influence her a little; but I assure you there was very little for me or for anybody to do. His appearance is so much against him, and his manner so bad, that if she ever were disposed to favour him, she is not now. I can imagine, that, before she had seen anybody superior, she might tolerate him. He was the brother of her friends, and he took pains to please her; and altogether, having seen nobody better (that must have been his great assistant), she might not, while she was at Abbey-Mill, find him disagreeable. But the case is altered now. She knows now what gentlemen are; and nothing but a gentleman in education and manner has any chance with Harriet."

"Nonsense, arrant nonsense, as ever was talked!" cried Mr. Knightley. "Robert Martin's manners have sense, sincerity, and good humour to recommend them; and his mind more true gentility than Harriet Smith could understand."

Emma made no answer, and tried to look cheerfully unconcerned, but was really feeling uncomfortable, and wanting him very much to be gone. She did not repent what she had done; she still thought herself a better judge of such a point of female right and refinement than he could be; but yet she had a sort of habitual respect for his judgment in general, which made her dislike having it so loudly against her; and to have him sitting just opposite to her in angry state was very disagreeable. Some minutes passed in this unpleasant silence, with only one attempt on Emma's side to talk of the weather, but he made no answer. He was thinking. The result of his thoughts appeared at last in these words:

"Robert Martin has no great loss—if he can but think so; and I hope it will not be long before he does. Your views for Harriet are best known to yourself; but as you make no secret of your love of match-making, it is fair to suppose that views, and plans, and projects you have; and as a friend I shall just hint to you, that if Elton is the man, I think it will be all labour in vain."

Emma laughed and disclaimed. He continued:

"Depend upon it, Elton will not do. Elton is a very good sort of man, and a very respectable vicar of Highbury, but not at all likely to make an imprudent match. He knows the value of a good income as well as any-body. Elton may talk sentimentally, but he will act rationally. He is as well acquainted with his own claims as you can be with Harriet's. He knows that he is a very handsome young man, and a great favourite wherever he goes; and from his general way of talking in unreserved moments, when there are only men present, I am convinced that he does not mean to throw himself away. I have heard him speak with great ani-mation of a large family of young ladies that his sisters are intimate with, who have all twenty thousand pounds apiece."

"I am very much obliged to you," said Emma, laughing again. "If I had set my heart on Mr. Elton's marrying Harriet, it would have been very kind to open my eyes; but at present I only want to keep Harriet to

myself. I have done with matchmaking, indeed. I could never hope to
equal my own doings at Randalls. I shall leave off while I am well."

"Good morning to you," said he, rising and walking off abruptly. He
was very much vexed. He felt the disappointment of the young man, and
was mortified to have been the means of promoting it by the sanction he
had given; and the part which, he was persuaded, Emma had taken in the
affair was provoking him exceedingly.

Emma remained in a state of vexation too; but there was more indistinctness in the causes of hers than in his. She did not always feel so absolutely satisfied with herself, so entirely convinced that her opinions were
right and her adversary's wrong, as Mr. Knightley. He walked off in more
complete self-approbation than he left for her. She was not so materially
cast down, however, but that a little time and the return of Harriet were
very adequate restoratives. Harriet's staying away so long was beginning
to make her uneasy. The possibility of the young man's coming to Mrs.
Goddard's that morning, and meeting with Harriet, and pleading his own
cause, gave alarming ideas. The dread of such a failure, after all, became
the prominent uneasiness; and when Harriet appeared, and in very good
spirits, and without having any such reason to give for her long absence,
she felt a satisfaction which settled her with her own mind, and convinced
her that, let Mr. Knightley think or say what he would, she had done
nothing which woman's friendship and woman's feelings would not justify.

He had frightened her a little about Mr. Elton; but when she considered
that Mr. Knightley could not have observed him as she had done, neither
with the interest nor (she must be allowed to tell herself, in spite of Mr.
Knightley's pretensions) with the skill of such an observer on such a
question as herself, that he had spoken it hastily and in anger, she was
able to believe, that he had rather said what he wished resentfully to be
true, than what he knew anything about. He certainly might have heard
Mr. Elton speak with more unreserve than she had ever done, and Mr.
Elton might not be of an imprudent, inconsiderate disposition, as to
money matters: he might naturally be rather attentive than otherwise to
them; but then, Mr. Knightley did not make due allowance for the influence of a strong passion, at war with all interested motives. Mr. Knightley
saw no such passion, and of course thought nothing of its effects; but she
saw too much of it to feel a doubt of its overcoming any hesitations that a
reasonable prudence might originally suggest; and more than a reasonable, becoming degree of prudence, she was very sure did not belong to
Mr. Elton.

Harriet's cheerful look and manner established hers: she came back,
not to think of Mr. Martin, but to talk of Mr. Elton. Miss Nash had been
telling her something, which she repeated immediately with great delight.
Mr. Perry had been to Mrs. Goddard's to attend a sick child, and Miss
Nash had seen him; and he had told Miss Nash that as he was coming
back yesterday from Clayton Park he had met Mr. Elton, and found, to
his great surprise. that Mr. Elton was actually on his road to London, and

not meaning to return till the morrow, though it was the whist club night, which he had been never known to miss before; and Mr. Perry had remonstrated with him about it, and told him how shabby it was in him, their best player, to absent himself, and tried very much to persuade him to put off his journey only one day; but it would not do; Mr. Elton had been determined to go on, and had said, in a *very particular* way indeed, that he was going on business which he would not put off for any inducement in the world; and something about a very enviable commission, and being the bearer of something exceedingly precious. Mr. Perry could not quite understand him, but he was very sure there must be a *lady* in the case, and he told him so; and Mr. Elton only looked very conscious and smiling, and rode off in great spirits. Miss Nash had told her all this, and had talked a great deal more about Mr. Elton; and said, looking so very significantly at her, "that she did not pretend to understand what his business might be, but she only knew that any woman whom Mr. Elton could prefer, she should think the luckiest woman in the world; for, beyond a doubt, Mr. Elton had not his equal for beauty or agreeableness."

Chapter 9

MR. KNIGHTLEY might quarrel with her, but Emma could not quarrel with herself. He was so much displeased, that it was longer than usual before he came to Hartfield again; and when they did meet, his grave looks showed that she was not forgiven. She was sorry, but could not repent. On the contrary, her plans and proceedings were more and more justified, and endeared to her by the general appearances of the next few days.

The picture, elegantly framed, came safely to hand soon after Mr. Elton's return, and being hung over the mantelpiece of the common sitting-room, he got up to look at it, and sighed out his half sentences of admiration just as he ought; and as for Harriet's feelings, they were visibly forming themselves into as strong and steady an attachment as her youth and sort of mind admitted. Emma was soon perfectly satisfied of Mr. Martin's being no otherwise remembered, than as he furnished a contrast with Mr. Elton, of the utmost advantage to the latter.

Her views of improving her little friend's mind, by a great deal of useful reading and conversation, had never yet led to more than a few first chapters, and the intention of going on to-morrow. It was much easier to chat than to study; much pleasanter to let her imagination range and work at Harriet's fortune, than to be labouring to enlarge her comprehension, or exercise it on sober facts; and the only literary pursuit which engaged Harriet at present, the only mental provision she was making for the evening of life, was the collecting and transcribing all the riddles of every sort that she could meet with, into a thin quarto of hot-pressed paper, made up by her friend, and ornamented with cyphers and trophies.

In this age of literature, such collections on a very grand scale are not uncommon. Miss Nash, head teacher at Mrs. Goddard's, had written out at least three hundred; and Harriet, who had taken the first hint of it from her, hoped, with Miss Woodhouse's help, to get a great many more. Emma assisted with her invention, memory, and taste; and as Harriet wrote a very pretty hand, it was likely to be an arrangement of the first order, in form as well as quantity.

Mr. Woodhouse was almost as much interested in the business as the girls, and tried very often to recollect something worth their putting in. "So many clever riddles as there used to be when he was young—he wondered he could not remember them; but he hoped he should in time." And it always ended in "Kitty, a fair but frozen maid."

His good friend Perry, too, whom he had spoken to on the subject, did not at present recollect anything of the riddle kind; but he had desired Perry to be upon the watch, and as he went about so much, something, he thought, might come from that quarter.

It was by no means his daughter's wish that the intellects of Highbury in general should be put under requisition. Mr. Elton was the only one whose assistance she asked. He was invited to contribute any really good enigmas, charades or conundrums, that he might recollect; and she had the pleasure of seeing him most intently at work with his recollections; and at the same time, as she could perceive, most earnestly careful that nothing ungallant, nothing that did not breathe a compliment to the sex, should pass his lips. They owed to him their two or three politest puzzles; and the joy and exultation with which at last he recalled, and rather sentimentally recited, that well-known charade:

> My first doth affliction denote,
>   Which my second is destin'd to feel,
> And my whole is the best antidote
>   That affliction to soften and heal

made her quite sorry to acknowledge that they had transcribed it some pages ago already.

"Why will not you write one yourself for us, Mr. Elton?" said she; "that is the only security for its freshness; and nothing could be easier to you."

"Oh no; he had never written, hardly ever, anything of the kind in his life. The stupidest fellow! He was afraid not even Miss Woodhouse"—he stopped a moment—"or Miss Smith could inspire him."

The very next day, however, produced some proof of inspiration. He called for a few moments, just to leave a piece of paper on the table containing, as he said, a charade which a friend of his had addressed to a young lady, the object of his admiration; but which, from his manner, Emma was immediately convinced must be his own.

"I do not offer it for Miss Smith's collection," said he. "Being my friend's, I have no right to expose it in any degree to the public eye, but perhaps you may not dislike looking at it."

The speech was more to Emma than to Harriet, which Emma could understand. There was deep consciousness about him, and he found it easier to meet her eye than her friend's. He was gone the next moment. After another moment's pause:

"Take it," said Emma, smiling, and pushing the paper towards Harriet, "it is for you. Take your own."

But Harriet was in a tremor, and could not touch it; and Emma, never loth to be first, was obliged to examine it herself.

To Miss ———

CHARADE

My first displays the wealth and pomp of kings,
    Lords of the earth! their luxury and ease.
Another view of man my second brings,
    Behold him there, the monarch of the seas!

But ah! united, what reverse we have!
    Man's boasted power and freedom, all are flown:
Lord of the earth and sea, he bends a slave,
    And woman, lovely woman, reigns alone.

    Thy ready wit the word will soon supply,
    May its approval beam in that soft eye!

She cast her eye over it, pondered, caught the meaning, read it through again to be quite certain, and quite mistress of the lines, and then passing it to Harriet, sat happily smiling, and saying to herself, while Harriet was puzzling over the paper in all the confusion of hope and dullness, "Very well, Mr. Elton, very well, indeed. I have read worse charades. *Courtship* —a very good hint. I give you credit for it. This is feeling your way. This is saying very plainly, 'Pray, Miss Smith, give me leave to pay my addresses to you. Approve my charade and my intentions in the same glance.'

    May its approval beam in that soft eye!

Harriet exactly. Soft is the very word for her eye—of all epithets, the justest that could be given.

    Thy ready wit the word will soon supply.

Humph—Harriet's ready wit! All the better. A man must be very much in love, indeed, to describe her so. Ah! Mr. Knightley, I wish you had the benefit of this; I think this would convince you. For once in your life you would be obliged to own yourself mistaken. An excellent charade, indeed, and very much to the purpose. Things must come to a crisis soon now."

She was obliged to break off from these very pleasant observations, which were otherwise of a sort to run into great length, by the eagerness of Harriet's wondering questions.

"What can it be, Miss Woodhouse? What can it be? I have not an idea —I cannot guess it in the least. What can it possibly be? Do try to find it out, Miss Woodhouse. Do help me. I never saw anything so hard. Is it kingdom? I wonder who the friend was—and who could be the young lady. Do you think it is a good one? Can it be woman?

> And woman, lovely woman, reigns alone.

Can it be Neptune?

> Behold him there, the monarch of the seas!

Or a trident? Or a mermaid? Or a shark? Oh, no; shark is only one syllable. It must be very clever, or he would not have brought it. Oh, Miss Woodhouse, do you think we shall ever find it out?"

"Mermaids and sharks! Nonsense! My dear Harriet, what are you thinking of? Where would be the use of his bringing us a charade made by a friend upon a mermaid or a shark? Give me the paper and listen.

> "For Miss———, read Miss Smith.

> My first displays the wealth and pomp of kings,
>   Lords of the earth! their luxury and ease.

That is *court*.

> Another view of man, my second brings;
>   Behold him there, the monarch of the seas!

That is *ship*—plain as it can be. Now for the cream.

> But ah! united (*courtship*, you know), what reverse we have!
>   Man's boasted power and freedom, all are flown:
> Lord of the earth and sea, he bends a slave,
>   And woman, lovely woman, reigns alone.

A very proper compliment! and then follows the application which I think, my dear Harriet, you cannot find much difficulty in comprehending. Read it in comfort to yourself. There can be no doubt of its being written for you and to you."

Harriet could not long resist so delightful a persuasion. She read the concluding lines, and was all flutter and happiness. She could not speak. But she was not wanted to speak. It was enough for her to feel. Emma spoke for her.

"There is so pointed and so particular a meaning in this compliment," said she, "that I cannot have a doubt as to Mr. Elton's intentions. You are his object—and you will soon receive the completest proof of it. I thought it must be so. I thought I could not be so deceived; but now it is clear: the state of his mind is as clear and decided as my wishes on the subject have been ever since I knew you. Yes, Harriet, just so long have I been wanting the very circumstance to happen which has happened. I could never tell whether an attachment between you and Mr. Elton were most desirable or most natural. Its probability and its eligibility have really so equalled each other! I am very happy. I congratulate you, my dear Harriet, with all my heart. This is an attachment which a woman may well feel pride in creating. This is a connection which offers nothing but good. It will give you everything that you want—consideration, independence, a proper home—it will fix you in the centre of all your real friends, close to Hartfield and to me, and confirm our intimacy for ever. This, Harriet, is an alliance which can never raise a blush in either of us."

"Dear Miss Woodhouse!" and "Dear Miss Woodhouse!" was all that Harriet, with many tender embraces could articulate at first; but when they did arrive at something more like conversation, it was sufficiently clear to her friend that she saw, felt, anticipated, and remembered just as she ought. Mr. Elton's superiority had very ample acknowledgment.

"Whatever you say is always right," cried Harriet, "and therefore I suppose, and believe, and hope it must be so; but otherwise I could not have imagined it. It is so much beyond anything I deserve. Mr. Elton, who might marry anybody! There cannot be two opinions about *him*. He is so very superior. Only think of those sweet verses—'To Miss ——.' Dear me, how clever! Could it really be meant for me?"

"I cannot make a question, or listen to a question about that. It is a certainty. Receive it on my judgment. It is a sort of prologue to the play, a motto to the chapter; and will be soon followed by matter-of-fact prose."

"It is a sort of thing which nobody could have expected. I am sure, a month ago, I had no more idea myself! The strangest things do take place!"

"When Miss Smiths and Mr. Eltons get acquainted they do indeed— and really it is strange; it is out of the common course that what is so evidently, so palpably desirable—what courts the prearrangement of other people—should so immediately shape itself into the proper form. You and Mr. Elton are by situation called together; you belong to one another by every circumstance of your respective homes. Your marrying will be equal to the match at Randalls. There does seem to be a something in the air of Hartfield which gives love exactly the right direction, and sends it into the very channel where it ought to flow.

The course of true love never did run smooth—

A Hartfield edition of Shakespeare would have a long note on that passage."

"That Mr. Elton should really be in love with me—me, of all people, who did not know him, to speak to him, at Michaelmas. And he, the very handsomest man that ever was, and a man that everybody looks up to, quite like Mr. Knightley. His company so sought after, that everybody says he need not eat a single meal by himself if he does not choose it; that he has more invitations than there are days in the week. And so excellent in the Church! Miss Nash has put down all the texts he has ever preached from since he came to Highbury. Dear me! When I look back to the first time I saw him! How little did I think! The two Abbots and I ran into the front room, and peeped through the blind when we heard he was going by, and Miss Nash came and scolded us away, and stayed to look through herself; however, she called me back presently, and let me look too, which was very good-natured. And how beautiful we thought he looked! He was arm-in-arm with Mr. Cole."

"This is an alliance which, whoever—whatever your friends may be, must be agreeable to them, provided, at least, they have common sense; and we are not to be addressing our conduct to fools. If they are anxious to see you *happily* married, here is a man whose amiable character gives every assurance of it: if they wish to have you settled in the same country and circle which they have chosen to place you in, here it will be accomplished; and if their only object is that you should, in the common phrase, be *well* married, here is the comfortable fortune, the respectable establishment, the rise in the world which must satisfy them."

"Yes, very true. How nicely you talk! I love to hear you. You understand everything. You and Mr. Elton are one as clever as the other. This charade! If I had studied a twelvemonth I could never have made anything like it."

"I thought he meant to try his skill, by his manner of declining it yesterday."

"I do think it is, without exception, the best charade I ever read."

"I never read one more to the purpose, certainly."

"It is as long again as almost all we have had before."

"I do not consider its length as particularly in its favour. Such things in general cannot be too short."

Harriet was too intent on the lines to hear. The most satisfactory comparisons were rising in her mind.

"It is one thing," said she, presently, her cheeks in a glow, "to have very good sense in a common way, like everybody else, and if there is anything to say, to sit down and write a letter, and say just what you must, in a short way; and another, to write verses and charades like this."

Emma could not have desired a more spirited rejection of Mr. Martin's prose.

"Such sweet lines!" continued Harriet, "these two last! But how shall I ever be able to return the paper, to say I have found it out? Oh, Miss Woodhouse, what can we do about that?"

"Leave it to me. You do nothing. He will be here this evening, I dare

say, and then I will give it him back, and some nonsense or other will pass
between us, and you shall not be committed. Your soft eyes shall choose
their own time for beaming. Trust to me."

"Oh, Miss Woodhouse, what a pity that I must not write this beautiful
charade into my book; I am sure I have not got one half so good."

"Leave out the two last lines, and there is no reason why you should not
write it into your book."

"Oh, but those two lines are——"

"The best of all. Granted—for private enjoyment; and for private enjoyment keep them. They are not at all the less written, you know,
because you divide them. The couplet does not cease to be, nor does its
meaning change. But take it away, and all *appropriation* ceases, and a
very pretty gallant charade remains, fit for any collection. Depend upon
it, he would not like to have his charade slighted much better than his
passion. A poet in love must be encouraged in both capacities, or neither.
Give me the book. I will write it down, and then there can be no possible
reflection on you."

Harriet submitted, though her mind could hardly separate the parts, so
as to feel quite sure that her friend were not writing down a declaration of
love. It seemed too precious an offering for any degree of publicity.

"I shall never let that book go out of my own hands," said she.

"Very well," replied Emma, "a most natural feeling, and the longer it
lasts, the better I shall be pleased. But here is my father coming; you will
not object to my reading the charade to him. It will be giving him so much
pleasure. He loves anything of the sort, and especially anything that pays
woman a compliment. He has the tenderest spirit of gallantry towards us
all. You must let me read it to him."

Harriet looked grave.

"My dear Harriet, you must not refine too much upon this charade. You
will betray your feelings improperly, if you are too conscious and too
quick, and appear to affix more meaning, or even quite all the meaning
which may be affixed to it. Do not be overpowered by such a little tribute
of admiration. If he had been anxious for secrecy, he would not have left
the paper while I was by, but he rather pushed it towards me than towards
you. Do not let us be too solemn on the business. He has encouragement
enough to proceed, without our sighing out our souls over this charade."

"Oh no: I hope I shall not be ridiculous about it. Do as you please."

Mr. Woodhouse came in, and very soon led to the subject again, by the
recurrence of his very frequent inquiry of "Well, my dears, how does your
book go on? Have you got anything fresh?"

"Yes, papa; we have something to read you, something quite fresh. A
piece of paper was found on the table this morning (dropped, we suppose,
by a fairy), containing a very pretty charade, and we have just copied it
in."

She read it to him, just as he liked to have anything read, slowly and
distinctly, and two or three times over, with explanations of every part.

as she proceeded; and he was very much pleased, and, as she had foreseen, especially struck with the complimentary conclusion.

"Aye, that's very just, indeed; that's very properly said. Very true. 'Woman, lovely woman.' It is such a pretty charade, my dear, that I can easily guess what fairy brought it. Nobody could have written so prettily but you, Emma."

Emma only nodded and smiled. After a little thinking, and a very tender sigh, he added:

"Ah, it is no difficulty to see who you take after. Your dear mother was so clever at all those things. If I had but her memory. But I can remember nothing; not even that particular riddle which you have heard me mention; I can only recollect the first stanza; and there are several:

> Kitty, a fair but frozen maid,
>   Kindled a flame I yet deplore;
> The hoodwink'd boy I called to aid,
> Though of his near approach afraid,
>   So fatal to my suit before.

And that is all that I can recollect of it; but it is very clever all the way through. But I think, my dear, you said you had got it."

"Yes, papa, it is written out in our second page. We copied it from the 'Elegant Extracts.' It was Garrick's, you know."

"Aye, very true—I wish I could recollect more of it:

> Kitty, a fair but frozen maid—

The names make me think of poor Isabella; for she was very near being christened Catherine, after her grandmamma. I hope we shall have her here next week. Have you thought, my dear, where you shall put her, and what room there will be for the children?"

"Oh yes—she will have her own room, of course, the room she always has; and there is the nursery for the children—just as usual, you know. Why should there be any change?"

"I do not know, my dear—but it is so long since she was here—not since last Easter, and then only for a few days. Mr. John Knightley's being a lawyer is very inconvenient. Poor Isabella! she is sadly taken away from us all; and how sorry she will be, when she comes, not to see Miss Taylor here."

"She will not be surprised, papa, at least."

"I do not know, my dear. I am sure I was very much surprised when I first heard she was going to be married."

"We must ask Mr. and Mrs. Weston to dine with us, while Isabella is here."

"Yes, my dear, if there is time. But" (in a very depressed tone) "she is coming for only one week. There will not be time for anything."

"It is unfortunate that they cannot stay longer, but it seems a case of necessity. Mr. John Knightley must be in town again on the 28th; and we ought to be thankful, papa, that we are to have the whole of the time they can give to the country, that two or three days are not to be taken out for the Abbey. Mr. Knightley promises to give up his claim this Christmas, though you know it is longer since they were with him than with us."

"It would be very hard, indeed, my dear, if poor Isabella were to be anywhere but at Hartfield."

Mr. Woodhouse could never allow for Mr. Knightley's claims on his brother, or anybody's claims on Isabella, except his own. He sat musing a little while, and then said:

"But I do not see why poor Isabella should be obliged to go back so soon, though he does. I think, Emma, I shall try and persuade her to stay longer with us. She and the children might stay very well."

"Ah, papa, that is what you never have been able to accomplish, and I do not think you ever will. Isabella cannot bear to stay behind her husband."

This was too true for contradiction. Unwelcome as it was, Mr. Woodhouse could only give a submissive sigh; and as Emma saw his spirits affected by the idea of his daughter's attachment to her husband, she immediately led to such a branch of the subject as must raise them.

"Harriet must give us as much of her company as she can while my brother and sister are here. I am sure she will be pleased with the children. We are very proud of the children, are not we, papa? I wonder which she will think the handsomest, Henry or John?"

"Aye, I wonder which she will. Poor little dears, how glad they will be to come. They are very fond of being at Hartfield, Harriet."

"I dare say they are, sir. I am sure I do not know who is not."

"Henry is a fine boy, but John is very like his mamma. Henry is the eldest; he was named after me, not after his father. John, the second, is named after his father. Some people are surprised, I believe, that the eldest was not, but Isabella would have him called Henry, which I thought very pretty of her. And he is a very clever boy, indeed. They are all remarkably clever; and they have so many pretty ways. They will come and stand by my chair and say, 'Grandpapa, can you give me a bit of string?' and once Henry asked me for a knife, but I told him knives were only made for grandpapas. I think their father is too rough with them very often."

"He appears rough to you," said Emma, "because you are so very gentle yourself; but if you could compare him with other papas, you would not think him rough. He wishes his boys to be active and hardy; and if they misbehave, can give them a sharp word now and then; but he is an affectionate father—certainly Mr. John Knightley is an affectionate father. The children are all fond of him."

"And then their uncle comes in, and tosses them up to the ceiling in a very frightful way."

"But they like it, papa; there is nothing they like so much. It is such enjoyment to them, that if their uncle did not lay down the rule of their taking turns, whichever began would never give way to the other."

"Well, I cannot understand it."

"That is the case with us all, papa. One half of the world cannot understand the pleasures of the other."

Late in the morning, and just as the girls were going to separate, in preparation for the regular four o'clock dinner, the hero of this inimitable charade walked in again. Harriet turned away; but Emma could receive him with the usual smile, and her quick eye soon discerned in his the consciousness of having made a push—of having thrown a die; and she imagined he was come to see how it might turn up. His ostensible reason, however, was to ask whether Mr. Woodhouse's party could be made up in the evening without him, or whether he should be in the smallest degree necessary at Hartfield. If he were, everything else must give way; but otherwise his friend Cole had been saying so much about his dining with him—had made such a point of it—that he had promised him conditionally to come.

Emma thanked him, but could not allow of his disappointing his friend on their account; her father was sure of his rubber. He re-urged—she re-declined; and he seemed then about to make his bow, when, taking the paper from the table, she returned it.

"Oh, here is the charade you were so obliging as to leave with us; thank you for the sight of it. We admired it so much that I have ventured to write it into Miss Smith's collection. Your friend will not take it amiss, I hope. Of course, I have not transcribed beyond the first eight lines."

Mr. Elton certainly did not very well know what to say. He looked rather doubtingly—rather confused; said something about "honour," glanced at Emma and at Harriet, and then seeing the book open on the table, took it up, and examined it very attentively. With the view of passing off an awkward moment, Emma smilingly said:

"You must make my apologies to your friend; but so good a charade must not be confined to one or two. He may be sure of every woman's approbation while he writes with such gallantry."

"I have no hesitation in saying," replied Mr. Elton, though hesitating a good deal while he spoke—"I have no hesitation in saying—at least if my friend feels at all as *I* do—I have not the smallest doubt that, could he see his little effusion honoured as *I* see it (looking at the book again, and replacing it on the table), he would consider it as the proudest moment of his life."

After this speech he was gone as soon as possible. Emma could not think it too soon; for with all his good and agreeable qualities there was a sort of parade in his speeches which was very apt to incline her to laugh. She ran away to indulge the inclination, leaving the tender and the sublime of pleasure to Harriet's share.

Chapter 10

THOUGH now the middle of December, there had yet been no weather
to prevent the young ladies from tolerably regular exercise; and on the
morrow, Emma had a charitable visit to pay to a poor sick family who
lived a little way out of Highbury.

Their road to this detached cottage was down Vicarage Lane, a lane
leading at right-angles from the broad, though irregular, main street of
the place; and, as may be inferred, containing the blessed abode of Mr.
Elton. A few inferior dwellings were first to be passed, and then, about a
quarter of a mile down the line, rose the vicarage, an old and not very
good house, almost as close to the road as is could be. It had no advantage
of situation; but had been very much smartened up by the present proprietor; and, such as it was, there could be no possibility of the two
friends passing it without a slackened pace and observing eyes. Emma's
remark was:

"There it is. There go you and your riddle-book one of these days."
Harriet's was:

"Oh, what a sweet house! How very beautiful! There are the yellow
curtains that Miss Nash admires so much."

"I do not often walk this way *now*," said Emma, as they proceeded,
"but *then* there will be an inducement, and I shall gradually get intimately acquainted with all the hedges, gates, pools, and pollards, of this
part of Highbury."

Harriet, she found had never in her life been within side the vicarage;
and her curiosity to see it was so extreme, that, considering exteriors and
probabilities, Emma could only class it as a proof of love, with Mr. Elton's
seeing ready wit in her.

"I wish we could contrive it," said she; "but I cannot think of any
tolerable pretence for going in; no servant that I want to inquire about of
his housekeeper—no message from my father."

She pondered, but could think of nothing. After a mutual silence of
some minutes, Harriet thus began again:

"I do so wonder, Miss Woodhouse, that you should not be married, or
going to be married—so charming as you are."

Emma laughed, and replied,

"My being charming, Harriet, is not quite enough to induce me to
marry; I must find other people charming—one other person at least.
And I am not only not going to be married at present, but have very little
intention of ever marrying at all."

"Ah, so you say; but I cannot believe it."

"I must see somebody very superior to any one I have seen yet, to be
tempted: Mr. Elton, you know" (recollecting herself), "is out of the
question: and I do *not* wish to see any such person. I would rather not be

tempted. I cannot really change for the better. If I were to marry, I must expect to repent it."

"Dear me! it is so odd to hear a woman talk so!"

"I have none of the usual inducements of women to marry. Were I to fall in love, indeed, it would be a different thing; but I never have been in love; it is not my way, or my nature; and I do not think I ever shall. And, without love, I am sure I should be a fool to change such a situation as mine. Fortune I do not want; employment I do not want; consequence I do not want; I believe few married women are half as much mistress of their husband's house as I am of Hartfield; and never, never could I expect to be so truly beloved and important; so always first and always right in any man's eyes as I am in my father's."

"But then, to be an old maid at last, like Miss Bates!"

"That is as formidable an image as you could present, Harriet; and if I thought I should ever be like Miss Bates—so silly, so satisfied, so smiling, so prosing, so undistinguishing and unfastidious, and so apt to tell everything relative to everybody about me, I would marry to-morrow. But between *us*, I am convinced there never can be any likeness, except in being unmarried."

"But still, you will be an old maid—and that's so dreadful!"

"Never mind, Harriet, I shall not be a poor old maid; and it is poverty only which makes celibacy contemptible to a generous public! A single woman with a very narrow income must be a ridiculous, disagreeable old maid! the proper sport of boys and girls; but a single woman of good fortune is always respectable, and may be as sensible and pleasant as anybody else! And the distinction is not quite so much against the candour and common-sense of the world as appears at first; for a very narrow income has a tendency to contract the mind, and sour the temper. Those who can barely live, and who live perforce in a very small, and generally very inferior society, may well be illiberal and cross. This does not apply, however, to Miss Bates: she is only too good-natured and too silly to suit me; but, in general, she is very much to the taste of everybody, though single and though poor. Poverty certainly has not contracted her mind: I really believe, if she had only a shilling in the world, she would be very likely to give away sixpence of it; and nobody is afraid of her—that is a great charm."

"Dear me! but what shall you do? How shall you employ yourself when you grow old?"

"If I know myself, Harriet, mine is an active, busy mind, with a great many independent resources; and I do not perceive why I should be more in want of employment at forty or fifty than one-and-twenty. Woman's usual occupations of eye, and hand, and mind, will be as open to me then as they are now, or with no important variation. If I draw less, I shall read more; if I give up music, I shall take to carpet-work. And as for objects of interest, objects for the affections, which is, in truth, the great point of inferiority, the want of which is really the great evil to be avoided in *not* marrying, I shall be very well off, with all the children of a sister I love so much to care about. There will be enough of them, in all probability, to supply every sort of sensation that declining life can need. There will be enough for every hope and every fear; and though my attachment to none can equal that of a parent, it suits my ideas of comfort better than what is warmer and blinder. My nephews and nieces: I shall often have a niece with me."

"Do you know Miss Bates's niece? That is, I know you must have seen her a hundred times—but are you acquainted?"

"Oh, yes; we are always forced to be acquainted whenever she comes to Highbury. By-the-bye, *that* is almost enough to put one out of conceit with a niece. Heaven forbid, at least, that I should ever bore people half so much about all the Knightleys together as she does about Jane Fairfax. One is sick of the very name of Jane Fairfax. Every letter from her is read forty times over; her compliments to all friends go round and round again; and if she does but send her aunt the pattern of a stomacher, or knit a pair of garters for her grandmother, one hears of nothing else for a month. I wish Jane Fairfax very well, but she tires me to death."

They were now approaching the cottage, and all idle topics were superseded. Emma was very compassionate; and the distress of the poor were as sure of relief from her personal attention and kindness, her counsel and her patience, as from her purse. She understood their ways, could allow for their ignorance and their temptations, had no romantic expectations of extraordinary virtue from those for whom education had done so little, entered into their troubles with ready sympathy, and always gave her assistance with as much intelligence as good-will. In the present instance, it was sickness and poverty together which she came to visit; and after remaining there as long as she could give comfort or advice, she quitted the cottage with such an impression of the scene as made her say to Harriet, as they walked away:

"These are the sights, Harriet, to do one good. How trifling they make everything else appear! I feel now as if I could think of nothing but these poor creatures all the rest of the day; and yet who can say how soon it may all vanish from my mind?"

"Very true," said Harriet. "Poor creatures! one can think of nothing else."

"And really, I do not think the impression will soon be over," said Emma, as she crossed the low hedge, and tottering footstep which ended the narrow, slippery path through the cottage garden, and brought them into the lane again. "I do not think it will," stopping to look once more at all the outward wretchedness of the place, and recall the still greater within.

"Oh dear no," said her companion.

They walked on. The lane made a slight bend; and when that bend was passed, Mr. Elton was immediately in sight and so near as to give Emma time only to say further,

"Ah, Harriet, here comes a very sudden trial of our stability in good thoughts. Well" (smiling), "I hope it may be allowed that if compassion has produced exertion and relief to the sufferers, it has done all that is truly important. If we feel for the wretched enough to do all we can for them, the rest is empty sympathy, only distressing to ourselves."

Harriet could just answer, "Oh dear, yes," before the gentleman joined them. The wants and sufferings of the poor family, however, were the first subject on meeting. He had been going to call on them. His visit he would now defer; but they had a very interesting parley about what could be done and should be done. Mr. Elton then turned back to accompany them.

"To fall in with each other on such an errand as this," thought Emma; "to meet in a charitable scheme; this will bring a great increase of love on each side. I should not wonder if it were to bring on the declaration. It must, if I were not here. I wish I were anywhere else."

Anxious to separate herself from them as far as she could, she soon afterwards took possesion of a narrow footpath, a little raised on one side of the lane, leaving them together in the main road. But she had not been there two minutes when she found that Harriet's habits of dependence and imitation were bringing her up too, and that, in short, they would both be soon after her. This would not do; she immediately stopped, under pretence of having some alteration to make in the lacing of her half-boot, and stooping down in complete occupation of the footpath, begged them to have the goodness to walk on, and she would follow in half a minute. They did as they were desired; and by the time she judged it reasonable to have done with her boot, she had the comfort of further delay in her power, being overtaken by a child from the cottage, setting out, according to orders, with her pitcher, to fetch broth from Hartfield. To walk by the side of this child, and talk to and question her, was the most natural thing in the world, or would have been the most natural, had she been acting just then without design; and by this means the others were still able to keep ahead, without any obligation of waiting for her. She gained on them, however, involuntarily; the child's pace was quick, and theirs rather slow; and she was the more concerned at it, from their being evidently in a conversation which interested them. Mr. Elton was speaking with animation, Harriet listening with a very pleased attention; and Emma having sent the child on, was beginning to think how she might draw back a little more, when they both looked round, and she was obliged to join them.

Mr. Elton was still talking, still engaged in some interesting detail; and Emma experienced some disappointment when she found that he was only giving his fair companion an account of the yesterday's party at his friend Cole's, and that she was come in herself for the Stilton cheese, the North Wiltshire, the butter, the celery, the beetroot, and all the dessert.

"This would soon have led to something better, of course," was her consoling reflection; "anything interests between those who love; and anything will serve as introduction to what is near the heart. If I could but have kept longer away."

They now walked on together quietly till within view of the vicarage pales, when a sudden resolution of at least getting Harriet into the house, made her again find something very much amiss about her boot, and fall behind to arrange it once more. She then broke the lace off short, and dexterously throwing it into a ditch, was presently obliged to entreat them to stop and acknowledged her inability to put herself to rights so as to be able to walk home in tolerable comfort.

"Part of my lace is gone," said she, "and I do not know how I am to contrive. I really am a most troublesome companion to you both, but I hope I am not often so ill-equipped. Mr. Elton, I must beg leave to stop at your house, and ask your housekeeper for a bit of ribbon or string, or anything just to keep my boot on."

Mr. Elton looked all happiness at this proposition; and nothing could exceed his alertness and attention in conducting them into his house, and endeavouring to make everything appear to advantage. The room they were taken into was the one he chiefly occupied, and looking forwards; behind it was another with which it immediately communicated; the door between them was open, and Emma passed into it with the housekeeper, to receive her assistance in the most comfortable manner. She was obliged to leave the door ajar as she found it; but she fully intended that Mr. Elton should close it. It was not closed, however, it still remained ajar; but by engaging the housekeeper in incessant conversation, she hoped to make it practicable for him to choose his own subject in the adjoining room. For ten minutes she could hear nothing but herself. It could be protracted no longer. She was then obliged to be finished, and make her appearance.

The lovers were standing together at one of the windows. It had a most favourable aspect; and, for half a minute, Emma felt the glory of having schemed successfully. But it would not do; he had not come to the point. He had been most agreeable, most delightful; he had told Harriet that he had seen them go by, and had purposely followed them; other little gallantries and allusions had been dropped, but nothing serious.

"Cautious, very cautious," thought Emma; "he advances inch by inch, and will hazard nothing till he believes himself secure."

Still, however, though everything had not been accomplished by her ingenious device, she could not but flatter herself that it had been the occasion of much present enjoyment to both, and must be leading them forward to the great event.

Chapter 11

Mr. Elton must now be left to himself. It was no longer in Emma's power to superintend his happiness, or quicken his measures. The coming of her sister's family was so very near at hand, that first in anticipation, and then in reality, it became henceforth her prime object of interest; and during the ten days of their stay at Hartfield it was not to be expected—she did not herself expect—that anything beyond occasional, fortuitous assistance could be afforded by her to the lovers. They might advance rapidly if they would, however; they must advance somehow or other, whether they would or no. She hardly wished to have more leisure for them. There are people, who the more you do for them, the less they will do for themselves.

Mr. and Mrs. John Knightley, from having been longer than usual absent from Surrey, were exciting, of course, rather more than the usual interest. Till this year, every long vacation since their marriage had been divided between Hartfield and Donwell Abbey; but all the holidays of this autumn had been given to sea-bathing for the children; and it was therefore many months since they had been seen in a regular way by their Surrey connections, or seen at all by Mr. Woodhouse, who could not be induced to get so far as London, even for poor Isabella's sake; and who, consequently, was now most nervously and apprehensively happy in forestalling this too short visit.

He thought much of the evils of the journey for her, and not a little of the fatigues of his own horses and coachman, who were to bring some of the party the last half of the way; but his alarms were needless: the sixteen miles being happily accomplished, and Mr. and Mrs. John Knightley, their five children, and a competent number of nursery-maids, all reaching Hartfield in safety. The bustle and joy of such an arrival, the many to be talked to, welcomed, encouraged, and variously dispersed and disposed of, produced a noise and confusion which his nerves could not have borne under any other cause; nor have endured much longer even for this; but the ways of Hartfield and the feelings of her father were so respected by Mrs. John Knightley, that in spite of maternal solicitude for the immediate enjoyment of her little ones, and for their having instantly all the liberty and attendance, all the eating and drinking, and sleeping and playing, which they could possibly wish for, without the smallest delay, the children were never allowed to be long a disturbance to him, either in themselves or in any restless attendance on them.

Mrs. John Knightley was a pretty, elegant little woman, of gentle, quiet manners, and a disposition remarkably amiable and affectionate, wrapped up in her family, a devoted wife, a doting mother, and so tenderly attached to her father and sister that, but for these higher ties, a warmer love might have seemed impossible. She could never see a fault in any of them. She was not a woman of strong understanding or any quickness; and with this resemblance of her father, she inherited also much of his constitution; was delicate in her own health, over-careful of that of her children, had many fears and many nerves, and was as fond of her own Mr. Wingfield in town as her father could be of Mr. Perry. They were alike, too, in a general benevolence of temper, and a strong habit of regard for every old acquaintance.

Mr. John Knightley was a tall, gentleman-like, and very clever man, rising in his profession; domestic, and respectable in his private char-acter: but with reserved manners which prevented his being generally pleasing; and capable of being sometimes out of humour. He was not an ill-tempered man, not so often unreasonably cross as to deserve such a reproach: but his temper was not his great perfection; and, indeed, with such a worshipping wife, it was hardly possible that any natural defects in it should not be increased. The extreme sweetness of her temper must hurt his. He had all the clearness and quickness of mind which she wanted; and he could sometimes act an ungracious, or say a severe thing. He was not a great favourite with his fair sister-in-law. Nothing wrong in him escaped her. She was quick in feeling the little injuries to Isabella, which Isabella never felt herself. Perhaps she might have passed over more had his manners been flattering to Isabella's sister, but they were only those of a calmly kind brother and friend, without praise and with-out blindness; but hardly any degree of personal compliment could have made her regardless of that greatest fault of all in her eyes which he sometimes fell into, the want of respectful forbearance towards her father. There he had not always the patience that could have been wished. Mr. Woodhouse's peculiarities and fidgetiness were sometimes provoking him to a rational remonstrance or sharp retort equally ill bestowed. It did not often happen; for Mr. John Knightley had really a great regard for his father-in-law, and generally a strong sense of what was due to him: but it was too often for Emma's charity, especially as there was all the pain of apprehension frequently to be endured, though the offence came not. The beginning, however, of every visit displayed none but the properest feelings, and this being of necessity so short might be hoped to pass away in unsullied cordiality. They had not been long seated and composed when Mr. Woodhouse, with a melancholy shake of the head and a sigh, called his daughter's attention to the sad change at Hartfield since she had been there last.

"Ah, my dear," said he, "poor Miss Taylor! It is a grievous business."

"Oh yes, sir," cried she, with ready sympathy, "how you must miss her! And dear Emma too. What a dreadful loss to you both! I have been so grieved for you. I could not imagine how you could possibly do without her. It is a sad change, indeed; but I hope she is pretty well, sir."

"Pretty well, my dear—I hope—pretty well. I do not know but that the place agrees with her tolerably."

Mr. John Knightley here asked Emma, quietly, whether there were any doubts of the air of Randalls.

"Oh no: none in the least. I never saw Mrs. Weston better in my life—never looking so well. Papa is only speaking his own regret."

"Very much to the honour of both," was the handsome reply.

"And do you see her, sir, tolerably often?" asked Isabella, in the plaintive tone which just suited her father.

Mr. Woodhouse hesitated. "Not near so often, my dear, as I could wish."

"Oh, papa, we have missed seeing them but one entire day since they married. Either in the morning or evening of every day, excepting one, have we seen either Mr. Weston or Mrs. Weston, and generally both, either at Randalls or here; and as you may suppose, Isabella, most frequently here. They are very, very kind in their visits. Mr. Weston is really as kind as herself. Papa, if you speak in that melancholy way, you will be giving Isabella a false idea of us all. Everybody must be aware that Miss Taylor must be missed; but everybody ought also to be assured that Mr. and Mrs. Weston do really prevent our missing her by any means to the extent we ourselves anticipated—which is the exact truth."

"Just as it should be," said Mr. John Knightley, "and just at I hoped it was from your letters. Her wish of showing you attention could not be doubted, and his being a disengaged and social man makes it all easy. I have been always telling you, my love, that I had no idea of the change being so very material to Hartfield as you apprehended; and now you have Emma's account, I hope you will be satisfied."

"Why, to be sure," said Mr. Woodhouse—"yes, certainly. I cannot deny that Mrs. Weston—poor Mrs. Weston—does come and see us pretty often; but then, she is always obliged to go away again."

"It would be very hard upon Mr. Weston if she did not, papa. You quite forget poor Mr. Weston."

"I think, indeed," said John Knightley, pleasantly, "that Mr. Weston has some little claim. You and I, Emma, will venture to take the part of the poor husband. I being a husband, and you not being a wife, the claims of the man may very likely strike us with equal force. As for Isabella, she has been married long enough to see the convenience of putting all the Mr. Westons aside as much as she can."

"Me, my love?" cried his wife, hearing and understanding only in part. "Are you talking about me? I am sure nobody ought to be, or can be, a greater advocate for matrimony than I am; and if it had not been for the misery of her leaving Hartfield, I should never have thought of Miss Taylor but as the most fortunate woman in the world; and as to slighting Mr. Weston—that excellent Mr. Weston—I think there is nothing he does not deserve. I believe he is one of the very best-tempered men that ever existed. Excepting yourself and your brother, I do not know his equal for temper. I shall never forget his flying Henry's kite for him that very windy day last Easter; and ever since his particular kindness last September twelvemonth in writing that note, at twelve o'clock at night, on purpose to assure me that there was no scarlet fever at Cobham, I have been convinced there could not be a more feeling heart nor a better man in existence. If anybody can deserve him, it must be Miss Taylor."

"Where is the young man?" said John Knightley. "Has he been here on this occasion, or has he not?"

"He has not been here yet," replied Emma. "There was a strong expectation of his coming soon after the marriage, but it ended in nothing; and I have not heard him mentioned lately."

"But you should tell them of the letter, my dear," said her father. "He wrote a letter to poor Mrs. Weston, to congratulate her, and a very proper, handsome letter it was. She showed it to me. I thought it very well done of him, indeed. Whether it was his own idea, you know, one cannot tell. He is but young, and his uncle perhaps——"

"My dear papa, he is three-and-twenty. You forget how time passes."

"Three-and-twenty! is he, indeed? Well, I could not have thought it; and he was but two years old when he lost his poor mother. Well, time does fly, indeed! and my memory is very bad. However, it was an exceeding good, pretty letter, and gave Mr. and Mrs. Weston a great deal of pleasure. I remember it was written from Weymouth, and dated September 28th, and began, 'My dear Madam,' but I forget how it went on; and it was signed 'F. C. Weston Churchill.' I remember that perfectly."

"How very pleasing and proper of him!" cried the good-hearted Mrs. John Knightley. "I have no doubt of his being a most amiable young man. But how sad it is that he should not live at home with his father! There is something so shocking in a child's being taken away from his parents and natural home! I never could comprehend how Mr. Weston could part with him. To give up one's child! I really never could think well of anybody who proposed such a thing to anybody else."

"Nobody ever did think well of the Churchills, I fancy," observed Mr. John Knightley, coolly. "But you need not imagine Mr. Weston to have felt what you would feel in giving up Henry or John. Mr. Weston is rather an easy, cheerful-tempered man, than a man of strong feelings: he takes things as he finds them, and makes enjoyment of them somehow or other, depending, I suspect, much more upon what is called *society* for his comforts, that is, upon the power of eating and drinking, and playing whist with his neighbours five times a week, than upon family affection, or anything that home affords."

Emma could not like what bordered on a reflection on Mr. Weston, and had half a mind to take it up; but she struggled, and let it pass. She would keep the peace if possible; and there was something honourable and valuable in the strong domestic habits, the all-sufficiency of home to himself, whence resulted her brother's disposition to look down on the common rate of social intercourse, and those to whom it was important. It had a high claim to forbearance.

Chapter 12

Mr. Knightley was to dine with them, rather against the inclination of Mr. Woodhouse, who did not like that any one should share with him in Isabella's first day. Emma's sense of right, however, had decided it; and, besides the consideration of what was due to each brother, she had particular pleasure, from the circumstance of the late disagreement between Mr. Knightley and herself, in procuring him the proper invitation.

She hoped they might now become friends again. She thought it was time to make up. Making-up, indeed, would not do. *She* certainly had not been in the wrong, and *he* would never own that he had. Concession must be out of the question; but it was time to appear to forget that they had ever quarrelled; and she hoped it might rather assist the restoration of friendship, that when he came into the room she had one of the children with her—the youngest, a nice little girl about eight months old, who was now making her first visit to Hartfield, and very happy to be danced about in her aunt's arms. It did assist; for, though he began with grave looks and short questions, he was soon led on to talk of them all in the usual way, and to take the child out of her arms with all the unceremoniousness of perfect amity. Emma felt they were friends again; and the conviction giving her at first great satisfaction, and then a little sauciness, she could not help saying, as he was admiring the baby:

"What a comfort it is that we think alike about our nephews and nieces! As to men and women, our opinions are sometimes very different; but with regard to these children, I observe we never disagree."

"If you were as much guided by nature in your estimate of men and women, and as little under the power of fancy and whim in your dealings with them, as you are where these children are concerned, we might always think alike."

"To be sure—our discordancies must always arise from my being in the wrong."

"Yes," said he, smiling, "and reason good. I was sixteen years old when you were born."

"A material difference, then," she replied; "and no doubt you were much my superior in judgment at that period of our lives; but does not the lapse of one-and-twenty years bring our understandings a good deal nearer?"

"Yes, a good deal *nearer*."

"But still, not near enough to give me a chance of being right, if we think differently."

"I have still the advantage of you by sixteen years' experience, and by not being a pretty young woman and a spoiled child. Come, my dear Emma, let us be friends, and say no more about it. Tell your aunt, little Emma, that she ought to set you a better example than to be renewing old grievances, and that if she were not wrong before, she is now."

"That's true," she cried, "very true. Little Emma, grow up a better woman than your aunt. Be infinitely cleverer, and not half so conceited. Now, Mr. Knightley, a word or two more, and I have done. As far as good intentions went, we were *both* right, and I must say that no effects on my

side of the argument have yet proved wrong. I only want to know that
Mr. Martin is not very, very bitterly disappointed."

"A man cannot be more so," was his short, full answer.

"Ah! Indeed I am very sorry. Come, shake hands with me."

This had just taken place, and with great cordiality, when John
Knightley made his appearance; and "How d'ye do, George?" and "John,
how are you?" succeeded in the true English style, burying under a calmness that seemed all but indifference the real attachment which would
have led either of them, if requisite, to do everything for the good of the
other.

The evening was quiet and conversible, as Mr. Woodhouse declined
cards entirely, for the sake of comfortable talk with his dear Isabella,
and the little party made two natural divisions: on one side he and his
daughter; on the other the two Mr. Knightleys; their subjects totally
distinct, or very rarely mixing, and Emma only occasionally joining in
one or the other.

The brothers talked of their own concerns and pursuits, but principally
of those of the elder, whose temper was by much the most communicative, and who was always the greater talker. As a magistrate, he had
generally some point of law to consult John about, or, at least, some
curious anecdote to give; and as a farmer, as keeping in hand the home-
farm at Donwell, he had to tell what every field was to bear next year,
and to give all such local information as could not fail of being interesting
to a brother whose home it had equally been the longest part of his life,
and whose attachments were strong. The plan of a drain, the change of
a fence, the felling of a tree, and the destination of every acre for wheat,
turnips, or spring corn, was entered into with as much equality of interest
by John as his cooler manners rendered possible; and if his willing brother
ever left him anything to inquire about, his inquiries even approached a
tone of eagerness.

While they were thus comfortably occupied, Mr. Woodhouse was enjoying a full flow of happy regrets and fearful affection with his daughter.

"My poor dear Isabella," said he, fondly taking her hand, and interrupting, for a few moments, her busy labours for some one of her five
children, "how long it is, how terribly long since you were here! And how
tired you must be after your journey! You must go to bed early, my
dear—and I recommend a little gruel to you before you go. You and I
will have a nice basin of gruel together. My dear Emma, suppose we all
have a little gruel."

Emma could not suppose any such thing, knowing, as she did, that both
the Mr. Knightleys were as unpersuadable on that article as herself, and
two basins only were ordered. After a little more discourse in praise of
gruel, with some wondering at its not being taken every evening by
everybody, he proceeded to say, with an air of grave reflection:

"It was an awkward business, my dear, your spending the autumn at

Southend instead of coming here. I never had much opinion of the sea air."

"Mr. Wingfield most strenuously recommended it, sir, or we should not have gone. He recommended it for all the children, but particularly for the weakness in little Bella's throat—both sea air and bathing."

"Ah, my dear, but Perry had many doubts about the sea doing her any good; and as to myself, I have been long perfectly convinced, though perhaps I never told you so before, that the sea is very rarely of use to anybody. I am sure it almost killed me once."

"Come, come," cried Emma, feeling this to be an unsafe subject, "I must beg you not to talk of the sea. It makes me envious and miserable; I who have never seen it! Southend is prohibited, if you please. My dear Isabella, I have not heard you make one inquiry about Mr. Perry yet; and he never forgets you."

"Oh, good Mr. Perry, how is he, sir?"

"Why, pretty well; but not quite well. Poor Perry is bilious, and he has not time to take care of himself; he tells me he has not time to take care of himself—which is very sad—but he is always wanted all around the country. I suppose there is not a man in such practice anywhere. But then there is not so clever a man anywhere."

"And Mrs. Perry and the children, how are they? Do the children grow? I have a great regard for Mr. Perry. I hope he will be calling soon. He will be so pleased to see my little ones."

"I hope he will be here to-morrow, for I have a question or two to ask him about myself of some consequence. And, my dear, whenever he comes, you had better let him look at little Bella's throat."

"Oh, my dear sir, her throat is so much better that I have hardly any uneasiness about it. Either bathing has been of the greatest service to her, or else it is to be attributed to an excellent embrocation of Mr. Wingfield's, which we have been applying at times ever since August."

"It is not very likely, my dear, that bathing should have been of use to her; and if I had known you were wanting an embrocation, I would have spoken to——"

"You seem to me to have forgotten Mrs. and Miss Bates," said Emma; "I have not heard one inquiry after them."

"Oh! the good Bateses. I am quite ashamed of myself, but you mention them in most of your letters. I hope they are quite well. Good old Mrs. Bates! I will call upon her to-morrow, and take my children. They are always so pleased to see my children. And that excellent Miss Bates! such thorough worthy people! how are they, sir?"

"Why, pretty well, my dear, upon the whole. But poor Mrs. Bates had a bad cold about a month ago."

"How sorry I am! but colds were never so prevalent as they have been this autumn. Mr. Wingfield told me that he has never known them more general or heavy, except when it has been quite an influenza."

"That has been a good deal the case, my dear, but not to the degree you mention. Perry says that colds have been very general, but not so heavy as he has very often known them in November. Perry does not call it altogether a sickly season."

"No, I do not know that Mr. Wingfield considers it *very* sickly, ex-cept——"

"Ah, my poor dear child, the truth is, that in London it is always a sickly season. Nobody is healthy in London—nobody can be. It is a dreadful thing to have you forced to live there; so far off! and the air so bad!"

"No, indeed, *we* are not at all in a bad air. Our part of London is very superior to most others. You must not confound us with London in gen-eral, my dear sir. The neighbourhood of Brunswick Square is very different from almost all the rest. We are so very airy! I should be un-willing, I own, to live in any other part of the town; there is hardly any other that I could be satisfied to have my children in: but *we* are so remarkably airy! Mr. Wingfield thinks the vicinity of Brunswick Square decidedly the most favourable as to air."

"Ah, my dear, it is not like Hartfield. You make the best of it—but after you have been a week at Hartfield, you are all of you different creatures; you do not look like the same. Now I cannot say that I think you are any of you looking well at present."

"I am sorry to hear you say so, sir; but I assure you, excepting those little nervous headaches and palpitations which I am never entirely free from anywhere, I am quite well myself; and if the children were rather pale before they went to bed, it was only because they were a little more tired than usual, from their journey and the happiness of coming. I hope you will think better of their looks to-morrow; for I assure you Mr. Wing-field told me, that he did not believe he had ever sent us off altogether in such good case. I trust, at least, that you do not think Mr. Knightley looking ill," turning her eyes with affectionate anxiety towards her hus-band.

"Middling, my dear; I cannot compliment you. I think Mr. John Knightley very far from looking well."

"What is the matter, sir? Did you speak to me?" cried Mr. John Knightley, hearing his own name.

"I am sorry to find, my love, that my father does not think you looking well; but I hope it is only from being a little fatigued. I could have wished, however, as you know, that you had seen Mr. Wingfield before you left home."

"My dear Isabella," exclaimed he, hastily, "pray do not concern your-self about my looks. Be satisfied with doctoring and coddling yourself and the children, and let me look as I choose."

"I did not thoroughly understand what you were telling your brother," cried Emma, "about your friend Mr. Graham's intending to have a bailiff from Scotland, to look after his new estate. But will it answer? Will not the old prejudice be too strong?"

And she talked in this way so long and successfully that, when forced to give her attention again to her father and sister, she had nothing worse to hear than Isabella's kind inquiry after Jane Fairfax; and Jane Fairfax, though no great favourite with her in general, she was, at that moment, very happy to assist in praising.

"That sweet, amiable Jane Fairfax!" said Mrs. John Knightley. "It is so long since I have seen her, except now and then for a moment accidentally in town. What happiness it must be to her good old grandmother and excellent aunt, when she comes to visit them! I always regret excessively, on dear Emma's account, that she cannot be more at Highbury; but now their daughter is married, I suppose Colonel and Mrs. Campbell will not be able to part with her at all. She would be such a delightful companion for Emma."

Mr. Woodhouse agreed to it all, but added:

"Our little friend, Harriet Smith, however, is just such another pretty kind of young person. You will like Harriet. Emma could not have a better companion than Harriet."

"I am most happy to hear it; but only Jane Fairfax one knows to be so very accomplished and superior, and exactly Emma's age."

This topic was discussed very happily, and others succeeded of similar moment, and passed away with similar harmony; but the evening did not close without a little return of agitation. The gruel came, and supplied a great deal to be said—much praise and many comments—undoubting decision of its wholesomeness for every constitution, and pretty severe philippics upon the many houses where it was never met with tolerable; but, unfortunately, among the failures which the daughter had to instance, the most recent, and therefore most prominent, was in her own cook at Southend, a young woman hired for the time, who never had been able to understand what she meant by a basin of nice smooth gruel, thin, but not too thin. Often as she had wished for and ordered it, she had never been able to get anything tolerable. Here was a dangerous opening.

"Ah," said Mr. Woodhouse, shaking his head, and fixing his eyes on her with tender concern. The ejaculation in Emma's ear expressed, "Ah, there is no end of the sad consequences of your going to Southend. It does not bear talking of." And for a little while she hoped he would not talk of it, and that a silent rumination might suffice to restore him to the relish of his own smooth gruel. After an interval of some minutes, however, he began with:

"I shall always be very sorry that you went to the sea this autumn, instead of coming here."

"But why should you be sorry, sir? I assure you, it did the children a great deal of good."

"And, moreover, if you must go to the sea, it had better not have been to Southend. Southend is an unhealthy place. Perry was surprised to hear you had fixed upon Southend."

"I know there is such an idea with many people, but indeed it is quite a mistake, sir. We all had our health perfectly well there, never found the least inconvenience from the mud, and Mr. Wingfield says it is entirely a mistake to suppose the place unhealthy; and I am sure he may be depended on, for he thoroughly understands the nature of the air and his own brother and family have been there repeatedly."

"You should have gone to Cromer, my dear, if you went anywhere. Perry was a week at Cromer once, and he holds it to be the best of all the sea-bathing places. A fine open sea, he says, and very pure air. And, by what I understand, you might have had lodgings there quite away from the sea—a quarter of a mile off—very comfortable. You should have consulted Perry."

"But, my dear sir, the difference of the journey; only consider how great it would have been. A hundred miles, perhaps, instead of forty."

"Ah, my dear, as Perry says, where health is at stake nothing else should be considered: and if one is to travel, there is not much to choose between forty miles and a hundred. Better not move at all, better stay in London altogether, than travel forty miles to get into a worse air. This is just what Perry said. It seemed to him a very ill-judged measure."

Emma's attempts to stop her father had been vain; and when he had reached such a point as this, she could not wonder at her brother-in-law's breaking out.

"Mr. Perry," said he, in a voice of very strong displeasure, "would do as well to keep his opinion till it is asked for. Why does he make it any business of his to wonder at what I do? at my taking my family to one part of the coast or another? I may be allowed, I hope, the use of my judgment as well as Mr. Perry. I want his directions no more than his drugs." He paused, and growing cooler in a moment, added, with only sarcastic dryness, "If Mr. Perry can tell me how to convey a wife and five children a distance of a hundred and thirty miles with no greater expense or inconvenience than a distance of forty, I should be as willing to prefer Cromer to Southend as he could himself."

"True, true," cried Mr. Knightley, with most ready interposition—"very true. That's a consideration, indeed. But, John, as to what I was telling you of my idea of moving the path to Langham, of turning it more to the right that it may not cut through the home meadows, I cannot conceive any difficulty. I should not attempt it, if it were to be the means of inconvenience to the Highbury people, but if you call to mind exactly the present line of the path—the only way of proving it, however, will be to turn to our maps. I shall see you at the Abbey to-morrow morning, I hope, and then we will look them over, and you shall give me your opinion."

Mr. Woodhouse was rather agitated by such harsh reflections on his friend Perry, to whom he had in fact, though unconsciously, been attributing many of his own feelings and expressions; but the soothing attentions of his daughters gradually removed the present evil, and the immediate alertness of one brother, and better recollections of the other, prevented any renewal of it.

Chapter 13

THERE could hardly be a happier creature in the world than Mrs. John Knightley, in this short visit to Hartfield, going about every morning among her old acquaintances with her five children, and talking over what she had done every evening with her father and sister. She had nothing to wish otherwise, but that the days did not pass so swiftly. It was a delightful visit—perfect, in being much too short.

In general their evenings were less engaged with friends than their mornings: but one complete dinner engagement, and out of the house too, there was no avoiding, though at Christmas. Mr. Weston would take no denial: they must all dine at Randalls one day; even Mr. Woodhouse was persuaded to think it a possible thing in preference to a division of the party.

How they were all to be conveyed, he would have made a difficulty if he could, but as his son and daughter's carriage and horses were actually at Hartfield, he was not able to make more than a simple question on that head; it hardly amounted to a doubt; nor did it occupy Emma long to convince him that they might in one of the carriages find room for Harriet also.

Harriet, Mr. Elton, and Mr. Knightley, their own especial set, were the only persons invited to meet them—the hours were to be early as well as the numbers few; Mr. Woodhouse's habits and inclination being consulted in everything.

The evening before this great event (for it was a very great event that Mr. Woodhouse should dine out on the 24th of December) had been spent by Harriet at Hartfield, and she had gone home so much indisposed with a cold, that, but for her own earnest wish of being nursed by Mrs. Goddard Emma could not have allowed her to leave the house. Emma called on her the next day, and found her doom already signed with regard to Randalls. She was very feverish and had a bad sore throat: Mrs. Goddard was full of care and affection, Mr. Perry was talked of, and Harriet herself was too ill and low to resist the authority which excluded her from this delightful engagement, though she could not speak of her loss without many tears.

Emma sat with her as long as she could, to attend her in Mrs. Goddard's unavoidable absences, and raise her spirits by representing how much Mr. Elton's would be depressed when he knew her state; and left her at last tolerably comfortable, in the sweet dependence of his having a most comfortless visit, and of their all missing her very much. She had not advanced many yards from Mrs. Goddard's door, when she was met by Mr. Elton himself, evidently coming towards it, and as they walked on slowly together in conversation about the invalid—of whom he, on the rumour

of considerable illness, had been going to inquire, that he might carry
some report of her to Hartfield—they were overtaken by Mr. John
Knightley, returning from the daily visit to Donwell, with his two eldest
boys, whose healthy, glowing faces showed all the benefit of a country
run, and seem to ensure a quick despatch of the roast mutton and rice
pudding they were hastening home for. They joined company and proceeded together. Emma was just describing the nature of her friend's
complaint—"a throat very much inflamed, with a great deal of heat
about her, a quick low pulse, etc., and she was sorry to find from Mrs.
Goddard that Harriet was liable to very bad sore throats, and had often
alarmed her with them." Mr. Elton looked all alarm on the occasion, as
he exclaimed—

"A sore throat! I hope not infectious. I hope not of a putrid infectious
sort. Has Perry seen her? Indeed you should take care of yourself as well
as of your friend. Let me entreat you to run no risks. Why does not Perry
see her?"

Emma, who was not really at all frightened herself, tranquillised this
excess of apprehension by assurances of Mrs. Goddard's experience and
care; but as there must still remain a degree of uneasiness which she
could not wish to reason away, which she would rather feed and assist
than not, she added soon afterwards—as if quite another subject—

"It is so cold, so very cold, and looks and feels so very much like snow,
that if it were to any other place or with any other party, I should really
try not to go out to-day, and dissuade my father from venturing; but as
he has made up his mind, and does not seem to feel the cold himself, I do
not like to interfere, as I know it would be so great a disappointment to
Mr. and Mrs. Weston. But upon my word, Mr. Elton, in your case, I
should certainly excuse myself. You appear to me a little hoarse already;
and when you consider what demand of voice and what fatigues to-morrow
will bring, I think it would be no more than common prudence to stay at
home and take care of yourself to-night."

Mr. Elton looked as if he did not very well know what answer to make,
which was exactly the case; for though very much gratified by the kind
care of such a fair lady, and not liking to resist any advice of hers, he had
not really the least inclination to give up the visit; but Emma, too eager
and busy in her own previous conceptions and views to hear him impartially, or see him with clear vision, was very well satisfied with his muttering acknowledgment of its being "very cold, certainly very cold," and
walked on, rejoicing in having extricated him from Randalls, and secured
him the power of sending to inquire after Harriet every hour of the evening.

"You do quite right," said she; "we will make your apologies to Mr.
and Mrs. Weston."

But hardly had she so spoken, when she found her brother was civilly
offering a seat in his carriage, if the weather were Mr. Elton's only objection, and Mr. Elton actually accepting the offer with much prompt satis-

faction. It was a done thing; Mr. Elton was to go, and never had his broad handsome face expressed more pleasure than at this moment; never had his smile been stronger, nor his eyes more exulting than when he next looked at her.

"Well," she said to herself, "this is most strange! After I had got him off so well, to choose to go into company, and leave Harriet ill behind! Most strange indeed! But there is, I believe, in many men, especially single men, such an inclination—such a passion for dining out; a dinner engagement is so high in the class of their pleasures, their employments, their dignities, almost their duties, that everything gives way to it, and this must be the case with Mr. Elton—a most valuable, amiable, pleasing young man undoubtedly, and very much in love with Harriet; but still he cannot refuse an invitation, he must dine out wherever he is asked. What a strange thing love is! he can see ready wit in Harriet, but will not dine alone for her."

Soon afterwards, Mr. Elton quitted them, and she could not but do him the justice of feeling that there was a great deal of sentiment in his manner of naming Harriet at parting; in the tone of his voice, while assuring her that he should call at Mrs. Goddard's for news of her fair friend, the last thing before he prepared for the happiness of meeting her again, when he hoped to be able to give a better report; and he sighed and smiled himself off in a way that left the balance of approbation much in his favour.

After a few minutes of entire silence between them, John Knightley began with—

"I never in my life saw a man more intent on being agreeable than Mr. Elton. It is downright labour to him where ladies are concerned. With men he can be rational and unaffected, but when he has ladies to please, every feature works."

"Mr. Elton's manners are not perfect," replied Emma; "but where there is a wish to please, one ought to overlook, and one does overlook a great deal. Where a man does his best with only moderate powers, he will have the advantage over negligent superiority. There is such perfect good temper and good-will in Mr. Elton, as one cannot but value."

"Yes," said Mr. John Knightley presently, with some slyness, "he seems to have a great deal of good-will towards *you*."

"Me!" she replied with a smile of astonishment; "are you imagining me to be Mr. Elton's object?"

"Such an imagination has crossed me, I own, Emma; and if it never occurred to you before, you may as well take it into consideration now."

"Mr. Elton in love with me! What an idea!"

"I do not say it is so; but you will do well to consider whether it is so or not, and to regulate your behaviour accordingly. I think your manners to him encouraging. I speak as a friend, Emma. You had better look about you, and ascertain what you do, and what you mean to do."

"I thank you; but I assure you, you are quite mistaken. Mr. Elton and I are very good friends, and nothing more;" and she walked on, amusing herself in the consideration of the blunders which often arise from a partial knowledge of circumstances, of the mistakes which people of high pretensions to judgment are for ever falling into; and not very well pleased with her brother for imagining her blind and ignorant, and in want of counsel. He said no more.

Mr. Woodhouse had so completely made up his mind to the visit, that in spite of the increasing coldness, he seemed to have no idea of shrinking from it, and set forward at last most punctually with his eldest daughter in his own carriage, with less apparent consciousness of the weather than either of the others; too full of the wonder of his own going, and the pleasure it was to afford at Randalls, to see that it was cold, and too well wrapped up to feel it. The cold, however, was severe; and by the time the second carriage was in motion, a few flakes of snow were finding their way down, and the sky had the appearance of being so overcharged as to want only a milder air to produce a very white world in a very short time.

Emma soon saw that her companion was not in the happiest humour. The preparing and the going abroad in such weather, with the sacrifice of his children after dinner, were evils, were disagreeables at least, which Mr. John Knightley did not by any means like; he anticipated nothing in the visit that could be at all worth the purchase; and the whole of their drive to the vicarage was spent by him in expressing his discontent.

"A man," said he, "must have a very good opinion of himself when he asks people to leave their own fireside, and encounter such a day as this, for the sake of coming to see him. He must think himself a most agreeable fellow; I could not do such a thing. It is the greatest absurdity—actually snowing at this moment! The folly of not allowing people to be comfortable at home, and the folly of people's not staying comfortably at home when they can! If we were obliged to go out such an evening as this by any call of duty or business, what a hardship we should deem it; and here are we, probably with rather thinner clothing than usual, setting forward voluntarily, without excuse, in defiance of the voice of nature, which tells man, in everything given to his view or his feelings, to stay at home himself, and keep all under shelter that he can; here are we setting forward to spend five dull hours in another man's house, with nothing to say or to hear that was not said and heard yesterday, and may not be said and heard again to-morrow. Going in dismal weather, to return probably in worse; four horses and four servants taken out for nothing but to convey five idle, shivering creatures into colder rooms and worse company than they might have had at home."

Emma did not find herself equal to give the pleased assent, which no doubt he was in the habit of receiving, to emulate the "Very true, my love," which must have been usually administered by his travelling companion; but she had resolution enough to refrain from making any answer at all. She could not be complying; she dreaded being quarrelsome; her heroism reached only to silence. She allowed him to talk, and arranged the glasses, and wrapped herself up, without opening her lips.

They arrived, the carriage turned, the step was let down, and Mr. Elton, spruce, black, and smiling, was with them instantly. Emma thought with pleasure of some change of subject. Mr. Elton was all obligation and cheerfulness; he was so very cheerful in his civilities indeed, that she began to think he must have received a different account of Harriet from what had reached her. She had sent while dressing, and the answer had been, "Much the same—not better."

"*My* report from Mrs. Goddard's," said she, presently, "was not so pleasant as I had hoped: 'not better,' was *my* answer."

His face lengthened immediately, and his voice was the voice of sentiment as he answered:

"Oh no—I am grieved to find—I was on the point of telling you, that when I called at Mrs. Goddard's door, which I did the very last thing before I returned to dress, I was told that Miss Smith was not better, by no means better, rather worse. Very much grieved and concerned—I had flattered myself that she must be better after such a cordial as I knew had been given her in the morning."

Emma smiled, and answered: "My visit was of use to the nervous part of her complaint, I hope; but not even I can charm away sore throat; it is a most severe cold, indeed. Mr. Perry has been with her, as you probably heard."

"Yes—I imagined—that is—I did not——"

"He has been used to her in these complaints, and I hope to-morrow morning will bring us both a more comfortable report. But it is impossible not to feel uneasiness. Such a sad loss to our party to-day!"

"Dreadful! Exactly so, indeed. She will be missed every moment."

This was very proper; the sigh which accompanied it was really estimable; but it should have lasted longer. Emma was rather in dismay when only half a minute afterwards he began to speak of other things, and in a voice of the greatest alacrity and enjoyment.

"What an excellent device," said he, "the use of a sheep-skin for carriages. How very comfortable they make it; impossible to feel cold with such precautions. The contrivances of modern days, indeed, have rendered a gentleman's carriage perfectly complete. One is so fenced and guarded from the weather, that not a breath of air can find its way unpermitted. Weather becomes absolutely of no consequence. It is a very cold afternoon—but in this carriage we know nothing of the matter. Ha! Snows a little, I see."

"Yes," said John Knightley, "and I think we shall have a good deal of it."

"Christmas weather," observed Mr. Elton. "Quite seasonable; and extremely fortunate we may think ourselves that it did not begin yesterday, and prevent this day's party, which it might very possibly have done, for Mr. Woodhouse would hardly have ventured had there been much snow on the ground; but now it is of no consequence. This is quite the season, indeed, for friendly meetings. At Christmas everybody invites their friends about them, and people think little of even the worst weather. I was snowed up at a friend's house once for a week. Nothing could be pleasanter. I went for only one night, and could not get away till that very day sennight."

Mr. John Knightley looked as if he did not comprehend the pleasure, but said only, coolly:

"I cannot wish to be snowed up a week at Randalls."

At another time Emma might have been amused, but she was too much astonished now at Mr. Elton's spirit for other feelings. Harriet seemed quite forgotten in the expectation of a pleasant party.

"We are sure of excellent fires," continued he, "and everything in the greatest comfort. Charming people, Mr. and Mrs. Weston; Mrs. Weston indeed is much beyond praise, and he is exactly what one values, so hospitable, and so fond of society; it will be a small party, but where small parties are select, they are, perhaps, the most agreeable of any. Mr. Weston's dining-room does not accommodate more than ten comfortably; and for my part, I would rather, under such circumstances, fall short by two than exceed by two. I think you will agree with me (turning with a soft air to Emma), I think I shall certainly have your approbation, though Mr. Knightley, perhaps, from being used to the large parties of London, may not quite enter into our feelings."

"I know nothing of the large parties of London, sir—I never dine with anybody."

"Indeed!" (in a tone of wonder and pity). "I had no idea that the law had been so great a slavery. Well, sir, the time must come when you will be paid for all this, when you will have little labour and great enjoyment."

"My first enjoyment," replied John Knightley, as they passed through the sweep-gate, "will be to find myself safe at Hartfield again."

Chapter 14

SOME change of countenance was necessary for each gentleman as they walked into Mrs. Weston's drawing-room; Mr. Elton must compose his joyous looks, and Mr. John Knightley disperse his ill-humour. Mr. Elton must smile less, and Mr. John Knightley more, to fit them for the place. Emma only might be as nature prompted, and show herself just as happy as she was. To her, it was real enjoyment to be with the Westons. Mr. Weston was a great favourite, and there was not a creature in the world to whom she spoke with such unreserve as to his wife; not anyone, to whom she related with such conviction of being listened to and under-stood, of being always interesting and always intelligible, the little affairs, arrangements, perplexities, and pleasures of her father and herself. She could tell nothing of Hartfield, in which Mrs. Weston had not a lively concern: and half an hour's uninterrupted communication of all those little matters on which the daily happiness of private life depends, was one of the first gratifications of each.

This was a pleasure which perhaps the whole day's visit might not afford, which certainly did not belong to the present half-hour; but the very sight of Mrs. Weston, her smile, her touch, her voice, was grateful to Emma, and she determined to think as little as possible of Mr. Elton's oddities, or of anything else unpleasant, and enjoy all that was enjoyable to the utmost.

The misfortune of Harriet's cold had been pretty well gone through before her arrival. Mr. Woodhouse had been safely seated long enough to give the history of it, besides all the history of his own and Isabella's coming, and of Emma's being to follow; and had, indeed, just got to the end of his satisfaction that James should come and see his daughter, when the others appeared, and Mrs. Weston, who had been almost wholly engrossed by her attentions to him, was able to turn away and welcome her dear Emma.

Emma's project of forgetting Mr. Elton for a while made her rather sorry to find, when they had all taken their places, that he was close to her. The difficulty was great of driving this strange insensibility towards Harriet from her mind, while he not only sat at her elbow, but was continually obtruding his happy countenance on her notice, and solicitously addressing her upon every occasion. Instead of forgetting him, his behaviour was such that she could not avoid the internal suggestion of "Can it really be as my brother imagined? Can it be possible for this man to be beginning to transfer his affections from Harriet to me? Absurd and insufferable!" Yet he would be so anxious for her being perfectly warm, would be so interested about her father, and so delighted with Mrs. Weston; and, at last, would begin admiring her drawings with so much zeal and so little knowledge, as seemed terribly like a would-be lover, and made it some effort with her to preserve her good manners. For her own sake she could not be rude; and for Harriet's in the hope that all would yet turn out right, she was even positively civil; but it was an effort, especially as something was going on amongst the others, in the most overpowering period of Mr. Elton's nonsense, which she particularly wished to listen to. She heard enough to know that Mr. Weston was giving some information about his son: she heard the words "my son," and "Frank," and "my son," repeated several times over; and, from a few other half syllables, very much suspected that he was announcing an early visit from his son; but before she could quiet Mr. Elton, the subject was so completely past, that any reviving question from her would have been awkward.

Now it so happened, that, in spite of Emma's resolution of never marrying, there was something in the name, in the idea, of Mr. Frank Churchill, which always interested her. She had frequently thought— especially since his father's marriage with Miss Taylor—that if she *were* to marry, he was the very person to suit her in age, character, and condition. He seemed, by this connection between the families, quite to belong to her. She could not but suppose it to be a match that everybody who knew them must think of. That Mr. and Mrs. Weston did think of it, she was very strongly persuaded; and though not meaning to be induced by him, or by anybody else, to give up a situation which she believed more replete with good than any she could change it for, she had a great curiosity to see him, a decided intention of finding him pleasant, of being liked by him to a certain degree, and a sort of pleasure in the idea of their being coupled in their friends' imaginations.

With such sensations, Mr. Elton's civilities were dreadfully ill-timed; but she had the comfort of appearing very polite, while feeling very cross; and of thinking that the rest of the visit could not possibly pass without bringing forward the same information again, or the substance of it, from the open-hearted Mr. Weston. So it proved; for, when happily released from Mr. Elton, and seated by Mr. Weston at dinner, he made use of the very first interval in the cares of hospitality, the very first leisure from the saddle of mutton, to say to her:

"We want only two more to be just the right number. I should like to see two more here—your pretty little friend, Miss Smith, and my son—and then I should say we were quite complete. I believe you did not hear me telling the others in the drawing-room that we are expecting Frank. I had a letter from him this morning, and he will be with us within a fortnight."

Emma spoke with a very proper degree of pleasure, and fully assented to his proposition, of Mr. Frank Churchill and Miss Smith making their party quite complete.

"He has been wanting to come to us," continued Mr. Weston, "ever since September: every letter has been full of it; but he cannot command his own time. He has those to please who must be pleased, and who (between ourselves) are sometimes to be pleased only by a good many sacrifices. But now I have no doubt of seeing him here about the second week in January."

"What a very great pleasure it will be to you! And Mrs. Weston is so anxious to be acquainted with him, that she must be almost as happy as yourself."

"Yes, she would be, but that she thinks there will be another put-off. She does not depend upon his coming so much as I do; but she does not know the parties so well as I do. The case, you see, is—(but this is quite between ourselves; I did not mention a syllable of it in the other room. There are secrets in all families, you know)—the case is, that a party of friends are invited to pay a visit at Enscombe in January, and that Frank's coming depends upon their being put off. If they are not put off, he cannot stir. But I know they will, because it is a family that a certain lady, of some consequence at Enscombe, has a particular dislike to; and though it is thought necessary to invite them once in two or three years, they always are put off when it comes to the point. I have not the smallest doubt of the issue. I am as confident of seeing Frank here before the middle of January, as I am of being here myself; but your good friend there (nodding towards the upper end of the table) has so few vagaries herself, and has been so little used to them at Hartfield, that she cannot calculate on their effects, as I have been long in the practice of doing."

"I am sorry there should be anything like doubt in the case," replied Emma; " but am disposed to side with you, Mr. Weston. If you think he will come, I shall think so too; for you know Enscombe."

"Yes—I have some right to that knowledge; though I have never been at the place in my life. She is an odd woman! But I never allow myself to speak ill of her, on Frank's account; for I do believe her to be very fond of him. I used to think she was not capable of being fond of anybody except herself; but she has always been kind to him (in her way—allowing for little whims and caprices, and expecting everything to be as she likes). And it is no small credit, in my opinion, to him, that he should excite such an affection; for, though I would not say it to anybody else, she has no more heart than a stone to people in general, and the devil of a temper."

Emma liked the subject so well, that she began upon it to Mrs. Weston, very soon after their moving into the drawing-room, wishing her joy— yet observing that she knew the first meeting must be rather alarming. Mrs. Weston agreed to it; but added, that she should be very glad to be secure of undergoing the anxiety of a first meeting at the time talked of; "for I cannot depend upon his coming. I cannot be so sanguine as Mr. Weston. I am very much afraid that it will all end in nothing. Mr. Weston, I dare say, has been telling you exactly how the matter stands?"

"Yes—it seems to depend upon nothing but the ill-humour of Mrs. Churchill, which I imagine to be the most certain thing in the world."

"My, Emma!" replied Mrs. Weston, smiling. "what is the certainty of caprice?" Then turning to Isabella, who had not been attending before: "You must know, my dear Mrs. Knightley, that we are by no means so sure of seeing Mr. Frank Churchill, in my opinion, as his father thinks. It depends entirely upon his aunt's spirits and pleasure; in short, upon her temper. To you—to my two daughters—I may venture on the truth. Mrs. Churchill rules at Enscombe, and is a very odd-tempered woman; and his coming now depends upon her being willing to spare him."

"Oh, Mrs. Churchill! everybody knows Mrs. Churchill," replied Isabella, "and I am sure I never think of that poor young man without the greatest compassion. To be constantly living with an ill-tempered person must be dreadful. It is what we happily have never known anything of; but it must be a life of misery. What a blessing that she never had any children! Poor little creatures, how unhappy she would have made them!"

Emma wished she had been alone with Mrs. Weston. She should then have heard more. Mrs. Weston would speak to her with a degree of un- reserve which she would not hazard with Isabella; and, she really be- lieved, would scarcely try to conceal anything relative to the Churchills from her, excepting those views on the young man, of which her own imagination had already given her such instinctive knowledge. But at present there was nothing more to be said. Mr. Woodhouse very soon followed them into the drawing-room. To be sitting long after dinner was a confinement that he could not endure. Neither wine nor conversation was anything to him; and gladly did he move to those with whom he was always comfortable.

While he talked to Isabella, however, Emma found an opportunity of saying:

"And so you do not consider this visit from your son as by any means certain. I am sorry for it. The introduction must be unpleasant, whenever it takes place; and the sooner it could be over the better."

"Yes; and every delay makes one more apprehensive of other delays. Even if this family, the Braithwaites, are put off, I am still afraid that some excuse may be found for disappointing us. I cannot bear to imagine any reluctance on his side; but I am sure there is a great wish on the Churchills to keep him to themselves. There is jealousy. They are jealous even of his regard for his father. In short, I can feel no dependence on his coming, and I wish Mr. Weston were less sanguine."

"He ought to come," said Emma. "If he could stay only a couple of days, he ought to come; and one can hardly conceive a young man's not having it in his power to do as much as that. A young *woman*, if she fall into bad hands, may be teased, and kept at a distance from those she wants to be with; but one cannot comprehend a young *man's* being under such restraint, as not to be able to spend a week with his father, if he likes it."

"One ought to be at Enscombe, and know the ways of the family, before one decides upon what he can do," replied Mrs. Weston. "One ought to use the same caution, perhaps, in judging of the conduct of any one individual of any one family; but Enscombe, I believe, certainly must not be judged by general rules; *she* is so very unreasonable; and everything gives way to her."

"But she is so fond of the nephew; he is so very great a favourite. Now, according to my idea of Mrs. Churchill, it would be most natural, that while she makes no sacrifice for the comfort of the husband, to whom she owes everything, while she exercises incessant caprice towards *him*, she should frequently be governed by the nephew, to whom she owes nothing at all."

"My dearest Emma, do not pretend, with your sweet temper, to understand a bad one, or to lay down rules for it: you must let it go its own way. I have no doubt of his having, at times, considerable influence; but it may be perfectly impossible for him to know beforehand *when* it will be."

Emma listened, and then coolly said: "I shall not be satisfied unless he comes."

"He may have a great deal of influence on some points," continued

Mrs. Weston, "and on others, very little; and among those, on which she is beyond his reach, it is but too likely may be this very circumstance of his coming away from them to visit us."

Chapter 15

Mr. Woodhouse was soon ready for his tea; and when he had drank his tea he was quite ready to go home; and it was as much as his three companions could do, to entertain away his notice of the lateness of the hour before the other gentlemen appeared. Mr. Weston was chatty and convivial, and no friend to early separations of any sort; but at last the drawing-room party did receive an augmentation. Mr. Elton, in very good spirits, was one of the first to walk in. Mrs. Weston and Emma were sitting together on a sofa. He joined them immediately, and with scarcely an invitation, seated himself between them.

Emma, in good spirits too, from the amusement afforded her mind by the expectation of Mr. Frank Churchill, was willing to forget his late improprieties, and be as well satisfied with him as before, and on his making Harriet his very first subject, was ready to listen with most friendly smiles.

He professed himself extremely anxious about her fair friend—her fair, lovely, amiable friend. "Did she know? Had she heard anything about her, since their being at Randalls? He felt much anxiety—he must confess that the nature of her complaint alarmed him considerably." And in this style he talked on for some time very properly, not much attending to any answer, but altogether sufficiently awake to the terror of a bad sore throat; and Emma was quite in charity with him.

But at last there seemed a perverse turn; it seemed all at once as if he were more afraid of its being a bad sore throat on her account than on Harriet's—more anxious that she should escape the infection, than that there should be no infection in the complaint. He began with great earnestness to entreat her to refrain from visiting the sick chamber again, for the present, to entreat her to *promise him* not to venture into such hazard till he had seen Mr. Perry and learnt his opinion; and though she tried to laugh it off and bring the subject back into its proper course, there was no putting an end to his extreme solicitude about her. She was vexed. It did appear—there was no concealing it—exactly like the pretence of being in love with her instead of Harriet; an inconstancy, if real, the most contemptible and abominable! And she had difficulty in behaving with temper. He turned to Mrs. Weston to implore her assistance: "Would not she give him her support? Would not she add her persuasions to his, to induce Miss Woodhouse not to go to Mrs. Goddard's, till it were certain that Miss Smith's disorder had no infection? He could not be satisfied without a promise—would not she give him her influence in procuring it?"

"So scrupulous for others," he continued, "and yet so careless for herself! She wanted me to nurse my cold by staying at home to-day, and yet will not promise to avoid the danger of catching an ulcerated sore throat herself. Is this fair, Mrs. Weston? Judge between us. Have not I some right to complain? I am sure of your kind support and aid."

Emma saw Mrs. Weston's surprise, and felt that it must be great, at an address which, in words and manner, was assuming to himself the right of first interest in her; and as for herself, she was too much provoked and offended to have the power of directly saying anything to the purpose. She could only give him a look; but it was such a look as she thought must restore him to his senses, and then left the sofa, removing to a seat by her sister, and giving her all her attention.

She had not time to know how Mr. Elton took the reproof, so rapidly did another subject succeed; for Mr. John Knightley now came into the room from examining the weather, and opened on them all with the information of the ground being covered with snow, and of its still snowing fast, with a strong, drifting wind; concluding with these words to Mr. Woodhouse:

"This will prove a spirited beginning of your winter engagements, sir. Something new for your coachman and horses to be making their way through a storm of snow."

Poor Mr. Woodhouse was silent from consternation; but everybody else had something to say; everybody was either surprised, or not surprised, and had some question to ask, or some comfort to offer. Mrs. Weston and Emma tried earnestly to cheer him and turn his attention from his son-in-law, who was pursuing his triumph rather unfeelingly:

"I admired your resolution very much, sir," said he, "in venturing out in such weather, for of course you saw there would be snow very soon. Everybody must have seen the snow coming on. I admired your spirit; and I dare say we shall get home very well. Another hour or two's snow can hardly make the road impassable; and we are two carriages; if *one* is blown over in the bleak part of the common field there will be the other at hand. I dare say we shall be all safe at Hartfield before midnight."

Mr. Weston, with triumph of a different sort, was confessing that he had known it to be snowing some time, but had not said a word, lest it should make Mr. Woodhouse uncomfortable, and be an excuse for his hurrying away. As to there being any quantity of snow fallen or likely to fall to impede their return, that was a mere joke; he was afraid they would find no difficulty. He wished the road might be impassable, that he might be able to keep them all at Randalls; and with the utmost goodwill was sure that accommodation might be found for everybody, calling on his wife to agree with him, that, with a little contrivance, everybody might be lodged, which she hardly knew how to do, from the consciousness of there being but two spare rooms in the house.

"What is to be done, my dear Emma? What is to be done?" was Mr. Woodhouse's first exclamation, and all that he could say for some time. To her he looked for comfort: and her assurances of safety, her representation of the excellence of the horses, and of James, and of their having so many friends about them, revived him a little.

His eldest daughter's alarm was equal to his own. The horror of being blocked up at Randalls, while her children were at Hartfield, was full in her imagination; and fancying the road to be now just passable for adventurous people, but in a state that admitted no delay, she was eager to have it settled, that her father and Emma should remain at Randalls, while she and her husband set forward instantly, through all the possible accumulations of drifted snow that might impede them.

"You had better order the carriage directly, my love," said she; "I dare say we shall be able to get along, if we set off directly; and if we do come to anything very bad, I can get out and walk. I am not at all afraid. I should not mind walking half the way. I could change my shoes, you know, the moment I got home; and it is not the sort of thing that gives me cold."

"Indeed!" replied he. "Then, my dear Isabella, it is the most extraordinary sort of thing in the world, for in general everything does give you cold. Walk home! You are prettily shod for walking home, I dare say. It will be bad enough for the horses."

Isabella turned to Mrs. Weston for her approbation of the plan. Mrs. Weston could only approve. Isabella then went to Emma; but Emma could not so entirely give up the hope of their being all able to get away; and they were still discussing the point, when Mr. Knightley, who had left the room immediately after his brother's first report of the snow, came back again, and told them that he had been out of doors to examine, and could answer for there not being the smallest difficulty in their getting home, whenever they liked it, either now or an hour hence. He had gone beyond the sweep—some way along the Highbury road—the snow was nowhere above half an inch deep—in many places hardly enough to whiten the ground; a very few flakes were falling at present, but the clouds were parting, and there was every appearance of its being soon over. He had seen the coachmen, and they both agreed with him in there being nothing to apprehend.

To Isabella the relief of such tidings was very great, and they were scarcely less acceptable to Emma on her father's account, who was immediately set as much at ease on the subject as his nervous constitution allowed; but the alarm that had been raised could not be appeased, so as to admit of any comfort for him while he continued at Randalls. He was satisfied of their being no present danger in returning home, but no assurances could convince him that it was safe to stay; and while the others were variously urging and recommending, Mr. Knightley and Emma settled it in a few brief sentences—thus:

"Your father will not be easy; why do not you go?"

"I am ready, if the others are."

"Shall I ring the bell?"

"Yes, do."

And the bell was rung, and the carriages spoken for. A few minutes
more, and Emma hoped to see one troublesome companion deposited in
his own house, to get sober and cool, and the other recover his temper
and happiness when this visit of hardship were over.

The carriage came; and Mr. Woodhouse, always the first object on
such occasions, was carefully attended to his own by Mr. Knightley and
Mr. Weston; but not all that either could say could prevent some renewal
of alarm at the sight of the snow which had actually fallen, and the discovery of a much darker night than he had been prepared for. "He was
afraid they should have a very bad drive. He was afraid poor Isabella
would not like it. And there would be poor Emma in the carriage behind
He did not know what they had best do. They must keep as much together
as they could"; and James was talked to, and given a charge to go very
slow, and wait for the other carriage.

Isabella stepped in after her father; John Knightley, forgetting that he
did not belong to their party, stepped in after his wife very naturally; so
that Emma found, on being escorted and followed into the second carriage
by Mr. Elton, that the door was to be lawfully shut on them, and that they
were to have a *tête-à-tête* drive. It would not have been the awkwardness
of a moment, it would have been rather a pleasure, previous to the suspicions of this very day; she could have talked to him of Harriet, and the
three-quarters of a mile would have seemed but one. But now, she would
rather it had not happened. She believed he had been drinking too much
of Mr. Weston's good wine, and felt sure that he would want to be talking
nonsense.

To restrain him as much as might be, by her own manners, she was
immediately preparing to speak, with exquisite calmness and gravity, of
the weather and the night; but scarcely had she begun, scarcely had they
passed the sweep-gate and joined the other carriage, than she found her
subject cut up—her hand seized—her attention demanded, and Mr. Elton
actually making violent love to her: availing himself of the precious opportunity, declaring sentiments which must be already well known, hoping—fearing—adoring—ready to die if she refused him; but flattering
himself that his ardent attachment and unequalled love and unexampled
passion could not fail of having some effect, and, in short, very much resolved on being seriously accepted as soon as possible. It really was so.
Without scruple—without apology—without much apparent diffidence,
Mr. Elton, the lover of Harriet, was professing himself *her* lover. She tried
to stop him; but vainly; he would go on, and say it all. Angry as she was,
the thought of the moment made her resolve to restrain herself when she
did speak. She felt that half this folly must be drunkenness, and therefore
could hope that it might belong only to the passing hour. Accordingly,
with a mixture of the serious and the playful, which she hoped would best
suit his half-and-half state, she replied:

"I am much astonished, Mr. Elton. This to *me!* You forget yourself; you take me for my friend; any message to Miss Smith I shall be happy to deliver; but no more of this to *me*, if you please."

"Miss Smith!—message to Miss Smith! What could she possibly mean?" And he repeated her words with such assurance of accent, such boastful pretence of amazement, that she could not help replying with quickness:

"Mr. Elton, this is the most extraordinary conduct! And I can account for it only in one way: you are not yourself, or you could not speak either to me or of Harriet in such a manner. Command yourself enough to say no more, and I will endeavour to forget it."

But Mr. Elton had only drunk wine enough to elevate his spirits, not at all to confuse his intellects. He perfectly knew his own meaning; and having warmly protested against her suspicion as most injurious, and slightly touched upon his respect for Miss Smith as her friend, but acknowledging his wonder that Miss Smith should be mentioned at all, he resumed the subject of his own passion, and was very urgent for a favourable answer.

As she thought less of his inebriety, she thought more of his inconstancy and presumption, and with fewer struggles for politeness, replied:

"It is impossible for me to doubt any longer. You have made yourself too clear. Mr. Elton, my astonishment is much beyond anything I can express. After such behaviour as I have witnessed during the last month, to Miss Smith—such attentions as I have been in the daily habit of observing—to be addressing me in this manner: this is an unsteadiness of character, indeed, which I had not supposed possible. Believe me, sir, I am far, very far, from gratified in being the object of such professions."

"Good heaven!" cried Mr. Elton, "what can be the meaning of this? Miss Smith! I never thought of Miss Smith in the whole course of my existence; never paid her any attentions, but as your friend; never cared whether she were dead or alive, but as your friend. If she has fancied otherwise, her own wishes have misled her, and I am very sorry, extremely sorry. But, Miss Smith, indeed! Oh, Miss Woodhouse, who can think of Miss Smith when Miss Woodhouse is near? No, upon my honour, there is no unsteadiness of character. I have thought only of you. I protest against having paid the smallest attention to any one else. Everything that I have said or done, for many weeks past, has been with the sole view of marking my adoration of yourself. You cannot really seriously doubt it. No" (in an accent meant to be insinuating), "I am sure you have seen and understood me."

It would be impossible to say what Emma felt on hearing this; which of all her unpleasant sensations was uppermost. She was too completely overpowered to be immediately able to reply; and two moments of silence being ample encouragement, for Mr. Elton's sanguine state of mind, he tried to take her hand again, as he joyously exclaimed:

"Charming Miss Woodhouse! Allow me to interpret this interesting silence. It confesses that you have long understood me."

"No, sir," cried Emma, "it confesses no such thing. So far from having long understood you, I have been in a most complete error with respect to your views, till this moment. As to myself, I am very sorry that you should have been giving way to any feelings. Nothing could be further from my wishes—your attachment to my friend Harriet—your pursuit of her (pursuit it appeared) gave me great pleasure, and I have been very earnestly wishing you success; but had I supposed that she were not your attraction to Hartfield, I should certainly have thought you judged ill in making your visits so frequent. Am I to believe that you have never sought to recommend yourself particularly to Miss Smith—that you have never thought seriously of her?"

"Never, madam," cried he, affronted in his turn; "never, I assure you. *I* think seriously of Miss Smith! Miss Smith is a very good sort of girl; and I should be happy to see her respectably settled. I wish her extremely well; and, no doubt, there are men who might not object to—— Everybody has their level; but as for myself, I am not, I think, quite so much at a loss. I need not so totally despair of an equal alliance as to be addressing myself to Miss Smith! No, madam, my visits to Hartfield have been for yourself only; and the encouragement I received——"

"Encouragement! I give you encouragement! Sir, you have been entirely mistaken in supposing it. I have seen you only as the admirer of my friend. In no other light could you have been more to me than a common acquaintance. I am exceedingly sorry; but it is well that the mistake ends where it does. Had the same behaviour continued, Miss Smith might have been led into a misconception of your views; not being aware, probably, any more than myself, of the very great inequality which you are so sensible of. But, as it is, the disappointment is single, and, I trust, will not be lasting. I have no thoughts of matrimony at present."

He was too angry to say another word, her manner too decided to invite supplication; and in this state of swelling resentment, and mutually deep mortification, they had to continue together a few minutes longer, for the fears of Mr. Woodhouse had confined them to a foot-pace. If there had not been so much anger, there would have been desperate awkwardness; but their straightforward emotions left no room for the little zig-zags of embarrassment. Without knowing when the carriage turned into Vicarage Lane, or when it stopped, they found themselves, all at once, at the door of his house; and he was out before another syllable passed. Emma then felt it indispensable to wish him a good-night. The compliment was just returned, coldly and proudly; and, under indescribable irritation of spirits, she was then conveyed to Hartfield.

There she was welcomed, with the utmost delight, by her father, who had been trembling for the dangers of a solitary drive from Vicarage Lane —turning a corner which he could never bear to think of—and in strange hands—a mere common coachman—no James; and there it seemed as if her return only were wanted to make everything go well: for Mr. John Knightley, ashamed of his ill-humour, was now all kindness and attention:

and so particularly solicitous for the comfort of her father, as to seem—
if not quite ready to join him in a basin of gruel—perfectly sensible of its
being exceedingly wholesome; and the day was concluding in peace and
comfort to all their little party, except herself. But her mind had never
been in such perturbation; and it needed a very strong effort to appear
attentive and cheerful till the usual hour of separating allowed her the
relief of quiet reflection.

Chapter 16

THE hair was curled, and the maid sent away, and Emma sat down to
think and be miserable. It was a wretched business indeed. Such an overthrow of everything she had been wishing for. Such a development of
everything most unwelcome! Such a blow for Harriet!—that was the
worst of all. Every part of it brought pain and humiliation of some sort or
other; but, compared with the evil to Harriet, all was light; and she would
gladly have submitted to feel yet more mistaken—more in error—more
disgraced by misjudgment than she actually was, could the effects of her
blunders have been confined to herself.

"If I had not persuaded Harriet into liking the man, I could have borne
anything. He might have doubled his presumption to me—but poor
Harriet!"

How she could have been so deceived! He protested that he had never
thought seriously of Harriet—never! She looked back as well as she could;
but it was all confusion. She had taken up the idea, she supposed, and
made everything bend to it. His manners, however, must have been unmarked, wavering, dubious, or she could not have been so misled.

The picture! How eager he had been about the picture! And the charade! And a hundred other circumstances; how clearly they had seemed
to point at Harriet! To be sure, the charade, with its "ready wit"—but
then, the "soft eyes"—in fact it suited neither; it was a jumble without
taste or truth. Who could have seen through such thick-headed nonsense?

Certainly she had often, especially of late, thought his manners to herself unnecessarily gallant; but it had passed as his way, as a mere error of
judgment, of knowledge, of taste, as one proof, among others, that he had
not always lived in the best society; that, with all the gentleness of his
address, true elegance was sometimes wanting; but, till this very day, she
had never for an instant suspected it to mean anything but grateful respect to her as Harriet's friend.

To Mr. John Knightley was she indebted for her first idea on the subject, for the first start of its possibility. There was no denying that those
brothers had penetration. She remembered what Mr. Knightley had once
said to her about Mr. Elton, the caution he had given, the conviction he
had professed that Mr. Elton would never marry indiscreetly; and blushed
to think how much truer a knowledge of his character had been there

shown than any she had reached herself. It was dreadfully mortifying; but Mr. Elton was proving himself, in many respects, the very reverse of what she had meant and believed him—proud, assuming, conceited; very full of his own claims, and little concerned about the feelings of others.

Contrary to the usual course of things, Mr. Elton's wanting to pay his addresses to her had sunk him in her opinion. His professions and his proposals did him no service. She thought nothing of his attachment, and was insulted by his hopes. He wanted to marry well, and having the arrogance to raise his eyes to her, pretended to be in love; but she was perfectly easy as to his not suffering any disappointment that need be cared for. There had been no real affection either in his language or manners. Sighs and fine words had been given in abundance; but she could hardly devise any set of expressions, or fancy any tone of voice, less allied with real love. She need not trouble herself to pity him. He only wanted to aggrandise and enrich himself; and if Miss Woodhouse of Hartfield, the heiress of thirty thousand pounds, were not quite so easily obtained as he had fancied, he would soon try for Miss Somebody-else with twenty, or with ten.

But, that he should talk of encouragement, should consider her as aware of his views, accepting his attentions, meaning, in short, to marry him!—should suppose himself her equal in connection or mind!—look down upon her friend, so well understanding the gradations of rank below him, and be so blind to what rose above, as to fancy himself showing no presumption in addressing her!—it was most provoking.

Perhaps it was not fair to expect him to feel how very much he was her inferior in talent, and all the elegancies of mind. The very want of such equality might prevent his perception of it; but he must know that in fortune and consequence she was greatly his superior. He must know that the Woodhouses had been settled for several generations at Hartfield, the younger branch of a very ancient family, and that the Eltons were nobody. The landed property of Hartfield certainly was inconsiderable, being but a sort of notch in the Donwell Abbey estate, to which all the rest of Highbury belonged; but their fortune, from other sources, was such as to make them scarcely secondary to Donwell Abbey itself, in every other kind of consequence; and the Woodhouses had long held a high place in the consideration of the neighbourhood which Mr. Elton had first entered not two years ago, to make his way as he could, without any alliances but in trade, or anything to recommend him to notice but his situation and his civility. But he had fancied her in love with him; that evidently must have been his dependence; and after raving a little about the seeming incongruity of gentle manners and a conceited head, Emma was obliged in common honesty, to stop and admit that her own behaviour to him had been so complaisant and obliging, so full of courtesy and attention, as (supposing her real motive unperceived) might warrant a man of ordinary observation and delicacy, like Mr. Elton, in fancying himself a very decided favourite. If *she* had so misinterpreted his feelings, she had littl⟨

right to wonder that *he*, with self-interest to blind him, should have mistaken hers.

The first error, and the worst, lay at her door. It was foolish, it was wrong, to take so active a part in bringing any two people together. It was adventuring too far, assuming too much, making light of what ought to be serious—a trick of what ought to be simple. She was quite concerned and ashamed, and resolved to do such things no more.

"Here have I," said she, "actually talked poor Harriet into being very much attached to this man. She might never have thought of him but for me; and certainly never would have thought of him with hope, if I had not assured her of his attachment, for she is as modest and humble as I used to think him. Oh, that I had been satisfied with persuading her not to accept young Martin. There I was quite right: that was well done of me; but there I should have stopped, and left the rest to time and chance. I was introducing her into good company, and giving her the opportunity of pleasing someone worth having; I ought not to have attempted more. But now, poor girl! her peace is cut up for some time. I have been but half a friend to her! and if she were *not* to feel this disappointment so very much, I am sure I have not an idea of anybody else who would be at all desirable for her. William Coxe—oh, no, I could not endure William Coxe —a pert young lawyer."

She stopped to blush and laugh at her own relapse, and then resumed a more serious, more dispiriting cogitation upon what had been, and might be, and must be. The distressing explanation she had to make to Harriet, and all that poor Harriet would be suffering, with the awkwardness of future meetings, the difficulties of continuing or discontinuing the acquaintance, of subduing feelings, concealing resentment, and avoiding éclat, were enough to occupy her in most unmirthful reflections some time longer, and she went to bed at last with nothing settled but the conviction of her having blundered most dreadfully.

To youth and natural cheerfulness like Emma's, though under temporary gloom at night, the return of day will hardly fail to bring return of spirits. The youth and cheerfulness of morning are in happy analogy, and of powerful operation; and if the distress be not poignant enough to keep the eyes unclosed, they will be sure to open to sensations of softened pain and brighter hope.

Emma got up on the morrow more disposed for comfort than she had gone to bed; more ready to see alleviations of the evil before her, and to depend on getting tolerably out of it.

It was a great consolation that Mr. Elton should not be really in love with her, or so particularly amiable as to make it shocking to disappoint him; that Harriet's nature should not be of that superior sort in which the feelings are most acute and retentive; and that there could be no necessity for anybody's knowing what had passed except the three principals, and especially for her father's being given a moment's uneasiness about it.

These were very cheering thoughts; and the sight of a great deal of snow on the ground did her further service, for anything was welcome that might justify their all three being quite asunder at present.

The weather was most favourable for her; though Christmas Day, she could not go to church. Mr. Woodhouse would have been miserable had his daughter attempted it, and she was therefore safe from either exciting or receiving unpleasant and most unsuitable ideas. The ground covered with snow, and the atmosphere in that unsettled state between frost and thaw which is, of all others, the most unfriendly for exercise, every morning beginning in rain or snow, and every evening setting in to freeze, she was for many days a most honourable prisoner. No intercourse with Harriet possible but by note; no church for her on Sunday any more than on Christmas Day; and no need to find excuses for Mr. Elton's absenting himself.

It was weather which might fairly confine everybody at home; and though she hoped and believed him to be really taking comfort in some society or other, it was very pleasant to have her father so well satisfied with his being all alone in his own house, too wise to stir out; and to hear him say to Mr. Knightley, whom no weather could keep entirely from them:

"Ah, Mr. Knightley, why do not you stay at home like poor Mr. Elton?"

These days of confinement would have been, but for her private perplexities, remarkably comfortable, as such seclusion exactly suited her brother, whose feelings must always be of great importance to his companions; and he had, besides, so thoroughly cleared off his ill-humour at Randalls, that his amiableness never failed him during the rest of his stay at Hartfield. He was always agreeable and obliging, and speaking pleasantly of everybody. But with all the hopes of cheerfulness, and all the present comfort of delay, there was still such an evil hanging over her in the hour of explanation with Harriet, as made it impossible for Emma to be ever perfectly at ease.

Chapter 17

Mr. and Mrs. John Knightley were not detained long at Hartfield. The weather soon improved enough for those to move who must move; and Mr. Woodhouse having, as usual, tried to persuade his daughter to stay behind with all her children, was obliged to see the whole party set off, and return to his lamentations over the destiny of poor Isabella— which poor Isabella, passing her life with those she doted on, full of their merits, blind to their faults, and always innocently busy, might have been a model of right feminine happiness.

The evening of the very day on which they went brought a note from Mr. Elton to Mr. Woodhouse, a long, civil, ceremonious note, to say, with Mr. Elton's best compliments, "that he was proposing to leave Highbury

the following morning in his way to Bath; where, in compliance with the
pressing entreaties of some friends, he had engaged to spend a few weeks;
and very much regretted the impossibility he was under, from various
circumstances of weather and business, of taking a personal leave of Mr.
Woodhouse, of whose friendly civilities he should ever retain a grateful
sense; and had Mr. Woodhouse any commands, should be happy to attend
to them."

Emma was most agreeably surprised. Mr. Elton's absence just at this
time was the very thing to be desired. She admired him for contriving it,
though not able to give him much credit for the manner in which it was
announced. Resentment could not have been more plainly spoken than
in a civility to her father, from which she was so pointedly excluded. She
had not even a share in his opening compliments. Her name was not mentioned; and there was so striking a change in all this, and such an ill-
judged solemnity of leavetaking in his graceful acknowledgments, as she
thought, at first, could not escape her father's suspicion.

It did, however. Her father was quite taken up with the surprise of so
sudden a journey, and his fears that Mr. Elton might never get safely to
the end of it, and saw nothing extraordinary in his language. It was a very
useful note, for it supplied them with fresh matter for thought and conversation during the rest of their lonely evening. Mr. Woodhouse talked
over his alarms, and Emma was in spirits to persuade them away with all
her usual promptitude.

She now resolved to keep Harriet no longer in the dark. She had reason
to believe her nearly recovered from her cold, and it was desirable that
she should have as much time as possible for getting the better of her
other complaint before the gentleman's return. She went to Mrs. Goddard's, accordingly, the very next day, to undergo the necessary penance of
communication; and a severe one it was. She had to destroy all the hopes
which she had been so industriously feeding, to appear in the ungracious
character of the one preferred, and acknowledge herself grossly mistaken
and misjudging in all her ideas on one subject, all her observations, all her
convictions, all her prophecies for the last six weeks.

The confession completely renewed her first shame, and the sight of
Harriet's tears made her think that she should never be in charity with
herself again.

Harriet bore the intelligence very well, blaming nobody, and in everything testifying such an ingenuousness of disposition and lowly opinion
of herself as must appear with particular advantage at that moment to
her friend.

Emma was in the humour to value simplicity and modesty to the utmost; and all that was amiable, all that ought to be attaching, seemed on
Harriet's side, not her own. Harriet did not consider herself as having
anything to complain of. The affection of such a man as Mr. Elton would
have been too great a distinction. She never could have deserved him; and

nobody but so partial and kind a friend as Miss Woodhouse would have thought it possible.

Her tears fell abundantly; but her grief was so truly artless, that no dignity could have made it more respectable in Emma's eyes; and she listened to her, and tried to console her with all her heart and understanding—really for the time convinced that Harriet was the superior creature of the two, and that to resemble her would be more for her own welfare and happiness than all that genius or intelligence could do.

It was rather too late in the day to set about being simpleminded and ignorant; but she left her with every previous resolution confirmed of being humble and discreet, and repressing imagination all the rest of her life. Her second duty now, inferior only to her father's claims, was to promote Harriet's comfort, and endeavour to prove her own affection in some better method than by match-making. She got her to Hartfield, and showed her the most unvarying kindness, striving to occupy and amuse her, and by books and conversation to drive Mr. Elton from her thoughts.

Time, she knew, must be allowed for this being thoroughly done; and she could suppose herself but an indifferent judge of such matters in general, and very inadequate to sympathise in an attachment to Mr. Elton in particular; but it seemed to her reasonable that at Harriet's age, and with the entire extinction of all hope, such a progress might be made towards a state of composure by the time of Mr. Elton's return, as to allow them all to meet again in the common routine of acquaintance, without any danger of betraying sentiments or increasing them.

Harriet did think him all perfection, and maintain the non-existence of anybody equal to him in person or goodness, and did, in truth, prove herself more resolutely in love than Emma had foreseen; but yet it appeared to her so natural, so inevitable to strive against an inclination of that sort *unrequited,* that she could not comprehend its continuing very long in equal force.

If Mr. Elton, on his return, made his own indifference as evident and indubitable as she could not doubt he would anxiously do, she could not imagine Harriet's persisting to place her happiness in the sight or the recollection of him.

Their being fixed, so absolutely fixed, in the same place, was bad for each, for all three. Not one of them had the power of removal, or of effecting any material change of society. They must encounter each other, and make the best of it.

Harriet was further unfortunate in the tone of her companions at Mrs. Goddard's, Mr. Elton being the adoration of all the teachers and great girls in the school; and it must be at Hartfield only that she could have any chance of hearing him spoken of with cooling moderation or repellent truth. Where the wound had been given, there must the cure be found, if anywhere; and Emma felt that till she saw her in the way of cure, there could be no true peace for herself.

Chapter 18

MR. FRANK CHURCHILL did not come. When the time proposed drew near, Mrs. Weston's fears were justified in the arrival of a letter of excuse. For the present, he could not be spared, to his "very great mortification and regret; but still he looked forward with the hope of coming to Randalls at no distant period."

Mrs. Weston was exceedingly disappointed—much more disappointed, in fact, than her husband, though her dependence on seeing the young man had been so much more sober; but a sanguine temper, though for ever expecting more good than occurs, does not always pay for its hopes by any proportionate depression. It soon flies over the present failure, and begins to hope again. For half an hour Mr. Weston was surprised and sorry; but then he began to perceive that Frank's coming two or three months later would be a much better plan, better time of year, better weather; and that he would be able, without any doubt, to stay considerably longer with them than if he had come sooner.

These feelings rapidly restored his comfort, while Mrs. Weston, of a more apprehensive disposition, foresaw nothing but a repetition of excuses and delays; and after all her concern for what her husband was to suffer, suffered a great deal more herself.

Emma was not, at this time, in a state of spirits to care really about Mr. Frank Churchill's not coming, except as a disappointment at Randalls. The acquaintance, at present, had no charm for her. She wanted rather to be quiet and out of temptation; but still, as it was desirable that she should appear, in general, like her usual self, she took care to express as much interest in the circumstance, and enter as warmly into Mr. and Mrs. Weston's disappointment as might naturally belong to their friendship.

She was the first to announce it to Mr. Knightley; and exclaimed quite as much as was necessary (or, being acting a part, perhaps rather more), at the conduct of the Churchills in keeping him away. She then proceeded to say a good deal more than she felt of the advantage of such an addition to their confined society in Surrey; the pleasure of looking at somebody new; the gala-day to Highbury entire, which the sight of him would have made; and ending with reflections on the Churchills again, found herself directly involved in a disagreement with Mr. Knightley; and, to her great amusement, perceived that she was taking the other side of the question from her real opinion, and making use of Mrs. Weston's arguments against herself.

"The Churchills are very likely in fault," said Mr. Knightley coolly; "but I dare say he might come if he would."

"I do not know why you should say so. He wishes exceedingly to come; but his uncle and aunt will not spare him."

"I cannot believe that he has not the power of coming, if he made a point of it. It is too unlikely for me to believe it without proof."

"How odd you are! What has Mr. Frank Churchill done, to make you suppose him such an unnatural creature?"

"I am not supposing him at all an unnatural creature in suspecting that he may have learnt to be above his connections, and to care very little for anything but his own pleasure, from living with those who have always set him the example of it. It is a great deal more natural than one could wish, that a young man, brought up by those who are proud, luxurious, and selfish, should be proud, luxurious, and selfish too. If Frank Churchill had wanted to see his father, he would have contrived it between September and January. A man at his age—what is he? three or four-and-twenty—cannot be without the means of doing as much as that. It is impossible."

"That's easily said, and easily felt by you, who have always been your own master. You are the worst judge in the world, Mr. Knightley, of the difficulties of dependence. You do not know what it is to have tempers to manage."

"It is not to be conceived that a man of three or four-and-twenty should not have liberty of mind or limb to that amount. He cannot want money, he cannot want leisure. We know, on the contrary, that he has so much of both, that he is glad to get rid of them at the idlest haunts in the kingdom. We hear of him for ever at some watering-place or other; a little while ago he was at Weymouth. This proves that he can leave the Churchills."

"Yes, sometimes, he can."

"And those times are, whenever he thinks it worth his while; whenever there is any temptation of pleasure."

"It is very unfair to judge of anybody's conduct without an intimate knowledge of their situation. Nobody, who has not been in the interior of a family, can say what the difficulties of any individual of that family may be. We ought to be acquainted with Enscombe, and with Mrs. Churchill's temper before we pretend to decide upon what her nephew can do. He may, at times, be able to do a great deal more than he can at others."

"There is one thing, Emma, which a man can always do, if he chooses, and that is, his duty; not by manœuvring and finessing, but by vigour and resolution. It is Frank Churchill's duty to pay this attention to his father. He knows it to be so, by his promises and messages; but if he wished to do it, it might be done. A man who felt rightly would say at once, simply and resolutely, to Mrs. Churchill, 'Every sacrifice of mere pleasure you will always find me ready to make to your convenience; but I must go and see my father immediately. I know he would be hurt by my failing in such a mark of respect to him on the present occasion. I shall, therefore, set off to-morrow.' If he would say so to her at once in the tone of decision becoming a man, there would be no opposition made to his going."

"No," said Emma, laughing, "but perhaps there might be some made to his coming back again. Such language for a young man entirely dependent to use! Nobody but you, Mr. Knightley, would imagine it possible; but you have not an idea of what is requisite in situations directly opposite to your own. Mr. Frank Churchill to be making such a speech as that to the uncle and aunt who have brought him up, and are to provide for him! standing up in the middle of the room, I suppose, and speaking as loud as he could! How can you imagine such conduct practicable?"

"Depend upon it, Emma, a sensible man would find no difficulty in it. He would feel himself in the right; and the declaration, made, of course, as a man of sense would make it, in a proper manner, would do him more good, raise him higher, fix his interest stronger with the people he depended on, than all that a line of shifts and expedients can ever do. Respect would be added to affection. They would feel that they could trust him; that the nephew who had done rightly by his father would do rightly by them; for they know as well as he does, as well as all the world must know, that he ought to pay this visit to his father; and while meanly exerting their power to delay it are in their hearts not thinking the better of him for submitting to their whims. Respect for right conduct is felt by everybody: if he would act in this sort of manner on principle, consistently, regularly, their little minds would bend to his."

"I rather doubt that. You are very fond of bending little minds; but where little minds belong to rich people in authority, I think they have a knack of swelling out till they are quite as unmanageable as great ones. I can imagine that if you, as you are, Mr. Knightley, were to be transported and placed all at once in Mr. Frank Churchill's situation, you would be able to say and do just what you have been recommending for him; and it might have a very good effect. The Churchills might not have a word to say in return; but then you would have no habits of early obedience and long observance to break through. To him who has, it might not be so easy to burst forth at once into perfect independence, and set all their claims on his gratitude and regard at nought. He may have as strong a sense of what would be right as you can have, without being so equal, under particular circumstances, to act up to it."

"Then it would not be so strong a sense. If it failed to produce equal exertion, it could not be an equal conviction."

"Oh the difference of situation and habit! I wish you would try to understand what an amiable young man may be likely to feel in directly opposing those whom, as child and boy, he has been looking up to all his life."

"Your amiable young man is a very weak young man, if this be the first occasion of his carrying through a resolution to do right against the will of others. It ought to have been a habit with him, by this time, of following his duty, instead of consulting expediency. I can allow for the fears of the child, but not of the man. As he became rational, he ought to have roused himself, and shaken off all that was unworthy in their authority. He ought to have opposed the first attempt on their side to make him slight his father. Had he begun as he ought, there would have been no difficulty now."

"We shall never agree about him," cried Emma; "but that is nothing extraordinary. I have not the least idea of his being a weak young man; I feel sure that he is not. Mr. Weston would not be blind to folly, though in his own son; but he is very likely to have a more yielding, complying, mild disposition than would suit your notions of man's perfection. I dare say he has; and though it may cut him off from some advantages, it will secure him many others."

"Yes; all the advantages of sitting still when he ought to move, and of leading a life of mere idle pleasure, and fancying himself extremely expert in finding excuses for it. He can sit down and write a fine flourishing letter, full of professions and falsehoods, and persuade himself that he has hit upon the very best method in the world of preserving peace at home, and preventing his father's having any right to complain. His letters disgust me."

"Your feelings are singular. They seem to satisfy everybody else."

"I suspect they do not satisfy Mrs. Weston. They hardly can satisfy a woman of her good sense and quick feelings: standing in a mother's place, but without a mother's affection to blind her. It is on her account that attention to Randalls is doubly due, and she must doubly feel the omission. Had she been a person of consequence herself he would have come, I dare say! and it would not have signified whether he did or no. Can you think your friend behind-hand in these sort of considerations? Do you suppose she does not often say all this to herself? No, Emma; your amiable young man can be amiable only in French, not in English. He may be very 'amiable,' have very good manners, and be very agreeable; but he can have no English delicacy towards the feelings of other people—nothing really amiable about him."

"You seem determined to think ill of him."

"Me! not at all," replied Mr. Knightley, rather displeased; "I do not want to think ill of him. I should be as ready to acknowledge his merits as any other man; but I hear of none, except what are merely personal—that he is well-grown and good-looking, with smooth, plausible manners."

"Well, if he have nothing else to recommend him, he will be a treasure at Highbury. We do not often look upon fine young men, well-bred and agreeable. We must not be nice, and ask for all the virtues into the bargain. Cannot you imagine, Mr. Knightley, what a *sensation* his coming will produce? There will be but one subject throughout the parishes of Donwell and Highbury; but one interest—one object of curiosity; it will be all Mr. Frank Churchill; we shall think and speak of nobody else."

"You will excuse my being so much overpowered. If I find him conversable, I shall be glad of his acquaintance; but if he is only a chattering coxcomb, he will not occupy much of my time or thoughts."

"My idea of him is, that he can adapt his conversation to the taste of everybody, and has the power as well as the wish of being universally agreeable. To you, he will talk of farming; to me, of drawing or music; and so on to everybody, having that general information on all subjects which will enable him to follow the lead, or take the lead, just as propriety may require, and to speak extremely well on each; that is my idea of him."

"And mine," said Mr. Knightley warmly, "is, that if he turn out anything like it, he will be the most insufferable fellow breathing! What! at three-and-twenty to be the king of his company—the great man—the practised politician, who is to read everybody's character, and make everybody's talents conduce to the display of his own superiority; to be dispensing his flatteries around, that he may make all appear like fools compared with himself! My dear Emma, your own good sense could not endure such a puppy when it came to the point."

"I will say no more about him," cried Emma—"you turn everything to evil. We are both prejudiced! you against, I for him; and we have no chance of agreeing till he is really here."

"Prejudiced! I am not prejudiced."

"But I am very much, and without being at all ashamed of it. My love for Mr. and Mrs. Weston gives me a decided prejudice in his favour."

"He is a person I never think of from one month's end to another," said Mr. Knightley, with a degree of vexation, which made Emma immediately talk of something else, though she could not comprehend why he should be angry.

To take a dislike to a young man, only because he appeared to be of a different disposition from himself, was unworthy the real liberality of mind which she was always used to acknowledge in him; for, with all the high opinion of himself which she had often laid to his charge she had never before for a moment supposed it could make him unjust to the merit of another.

Chapter 19

EMMA and Harriet had been walking together one morning, and, in Emma's opinion, had been talking enough of Mr. Elton for that day. She could not think that Harriet's solace or her own sins required more; and she was therefore industriously getting rid of the subject as they returned, but it burst out again when she thought she had succeeded, and after speaking some time of what the poor must suffer in winter, and receiving no other answer than a very plaintive—"Mr. Elton is so good to the poor!" she found something else must be done.

EMMA

They were just approaching the house where lived Mrs. and Miss Bates. She determined to call upon them, and seek safety in numbers. There was always sufficient reason for such an attention; Mrs. and Miss Bates loved to be called on; and she knew she was considered by the very few who presumed ever to see imperfection in her, as rather negligent in that respect, and as not contributing what she ought to the stock of their scanty comforts.

She had had many a hint from Mr. Knightley, and some from her own heart, as to her deficiency, but none were equal to counteract the persuasion of its being very disagreeable—a waste of time—tiresome women —and all the horror of being in danger of falling in with the second rate and third rate of Highbury, who were calling on them for ever, and therefore she seldom went near them. But now she made the sudden resolution of not passing their door without going in; observing, as she proposed it to Harriet, that, as well as she could calculate, they were just now quite safe from any letter from Jane Fairfax.

The house belonged to people in business. Mrs. and Miss Bates occupied the drawing-room floor; and there, in the very moderate-sized apartment, which was everything to them, the visitors were most cordially and even gratefully welcomed; the quiet, neat old lady, who with her knitting was seated in the warmest corner, wanting even to give up her place to Miss Woodhouse, and her more active, talking daughter almost ready to overpower them with care and kindness, thanks for their visit, solicitude for their shoes, anxious inquiries after Mr. Woodhouse's health; cheerful communications about her mother's, and sweetcake from the buffet:—"Mrs. Cole had just been there, just called in for ten minutes, and had been so good as to sit an hour with them, and *she* had taken a piece of cake, and been so kind as to say she liked it very much; and, therefore, she hoped Miss Woodhouse and Miss Smith would do them the favour to eat a piece too."

The mention of the Coles was sure to be followed by that of Mr. Elton. There was intimacy between them, and Mr. Cole had heard from Mr. Elton since his going away. Emma knew what was coming: they must have the letter over again, and settle how long he had been gone, and how much he was engaged in company, and what a favourite he was wherever he went, and how full the Master of the Ceremonies' ball had been; and she went through it very well, with all the interest and all the commendation that could be requisite, and always putting forward to prevent Harriet's being obliged to say a word.

This she had been prepared for when she entered the house; but meant, having once talked him handsomely over, to be no further incommoded by any troublesome topic, and to wander at large amongst all the Mistresses and Misses of Highbury, and their card-parties. She had not been prepared to have Jane Fairfax succeed Mr. Elton; but he was actually hurried off by Miss Bates; she jumped away from him at last abruptly to the Coles, to usher in a letter from her niece.

"Oh yes—Mr. Elton, I understand—certainly as to dancing—Mrs. Cole was telling me that dancing at the rooms at Bath was—Mrs. Cole was so kind as to sit some time with us, talking of Jane; for as soon as she came in she began inquiring after her, Jane is so very great a favourite there. Whenever she is with us, Mrs. Cole does not know how to show her kindness enough; and I must say that Jane deserves it as much as anybody can. And so she began inquiring after her directly, saying, 'I know you cannot have heard from Jane lately, because it is not her time for writing;' and when I immediately said, 'But indeed we have, we had a letter this very morning,' I do not know that I ever saw anybody more surprised. 'Have you, upon your honour?' she said; 'well, that is quite unexpected. Do let me hear what she says.'"

Emma's politeness was at hand directly, to say, with smiling interest:

"Have you heard from Miss Fairfax so lately? I am extremely happy. I hope she is well?"

"Thank you. You are so kind!" replied the happily deceived aunt, while eagerly hunting for the letter. "Oh, here it is. I was sure it could not be far off; but I had put my housewife upon it, you see, without being aware, and so it was quite hid; but I had it in my hand so very lately that I was almost sure it must be on the table. I was reading it to Mrs. Cole, and, since she went away, I was reading it again to my mother, for it is such a pleasure to her—a letter from Jane—that she can never hear it often enough; so I knew it could not be far off, and here it is, only just under my housewife—and since you are so kind as to wish to hear what she says—but, first of all, I really must, in justice to Jane, apologise for her writing so short a letter—only two pages, you see hardly two, and in general she fills the whole paper and crosses half. My mother often wonders that I can make it out so well. She often says, when the letter is first opened, 'Well, Hetty, now I think you will be put to it to make out all that checker-work'—don't you, ma'am? And then I tell her, I am sure she would contrive to make it out herself, if she had nobody to do it for her, every word of it—I am sure she would pore over it till she had made out every word. And, indeed, though my mother's eyes are not so good as they were, she can see amazingly well still, thank God! with the help of spectacles. It is such a blessing! My mother's are really very good indeed. Jane often says, when she is here, 'I am sure, grandmamma, you must have had very strong eyes to see as you do, and so much fine work as you have done too! I only wish my eyes may last me as well.'"

All this, spoken extremely fast, obliged Miss Bates to stop for breath; and Emma said something very civil about the excellence of Miss Fairfax's handwriting.

"You are extremely kind," replied Miss Bates, highly gratified; "you, who are such a judge, and write so beautifully yourself. I am sure there is nobody's praise that could give us so much pleasure as Miss Woodhouse's. My mother does not hear; she is a little deaf, you know. Ma'am," addressing her, "do you hear what Miss Woodhouse is so obliging to say about Jane's handwriting?"

And Emma had the advantage of hearing her own silly compliment repeated twice over before the good old lady could comprehend it. She was pondering, in the meanwhile, upon the possibility, without seeming very rude, of making her escape from Jane Fairfax's letter, and had almost resolved on hurrying away directly, under some slight excuse when Miss Bates turned to her again and seized her attention.

"My mother's deafness is very trifling, you see, just nothing at all. By only raising my voice, and saying anything two or three times over, she is sure to hear; but then she is used to my voice. But it is very remarkable that she should always hear Jane better than she does me. Jane speaks so distinct! However, she will not find her grandmamma at all deafer than she was two years ago; which is saying a great deal at my mother's time of life; and it really is full two years, you know, since she was here. We never were so long without seeing her before; and, as I was telling Mrs. Cole, we shall hardly know how to make enough of her now."

"Are you expecting Miss Fairfax here soon?"

"Oh, yes; next week."

"Indeed! that must be a very great pleasure."

"Thank you. You are very kind. Yes, next week. Everybody is so surprised; and everybody says the same obliging things. I am sure she will be as happy to see her friends at Highbury as they can be to see her. Yes, Friday or Saturday; she cannot say which, because Colonel Campbell will be wanting the carriage himself one of those days. So very good of them to send her the whole way! But they always do, you know. Oh, yes, Friday or Saturday next. That is what she writes about. That is the reason of her writing out of rule, as we call it; for, in the common course, we should not have heard from her before next Tuesday or Wednesday."

"Yes, so I imagined. I was afraid there could be little chance of my hearing anything of Miss Fairfax to-day."

"So obliging of you! No, we should not have heard, if it had not been for this particular circumstance, of her being to come here so soon. My mother is so delighted! for she is to be three months with us at least. Three months, she says so, positively, as I am going to have the pleasure of reading to you. The case is, you see, that the Campbells are going to Ireland. Mrs. Dixon has persuaded her father and mother to come over and see her directly. They had not intended to go over till the summer, but she is so impatient to see them again; for till she married, last October, she was never away from them so much as a week, which must make it very strange to be in different kingdoms, I was going to say, but, however, different countries, and so she wrote a very urgent letter to her mother, or her father. I declare I do not know which it was, but we shall see presently in Jane's letter—wrote in Mr. Dixon's name as well as her own, to press their coming over directly; and they would give them the meeting in Dublin, and take them back to their country-seat, Baly-craig—a beautiful place, I fancy. Jane has heard a great deal of its beauty—from Mr. Dixon, I mean—I do not know that she ever heard about it from anybody else—but it was very natural, you know, that he should like to speak of his own place while he was paying his addresses—and as Jane used to be very often walking out with them—for Colonel and Mrs. Campbell were very particular about their daughter's not walking out often with only Mr. Dixon, for which I do not at all blame them; of course she heard everything he might be telling Miss Campbell about his own home in Ireland; and I think she wrote us word that he had shown them some drawing of the place, views that he had taken himself. He is a most amiable, charming young man, I believe. Jane was quite longing to go to Ireland, from his account of things."

At this moment, an ingenious and animating suspicion entering Emma's brain with regard to Jane Fairfax, this charming Mr. Dixon, and the not going to Ireland, she said, with the insidious design of further discovery:

"You must feel it very fortunate that Miss Fairfax should be allowed to come to you at such a time. Considering the very particular friendship between her and Mrs. Dixon you could hardly have expected her to be excused from accompanying Colonel and Mrs. Campbell."

"Very true, very true, indeed. The very thing that we have always been rather afraid of; for we should not have liked to have her at such a distance from us, for months together, not able to come if anything was to happen; but you see everything turns out for the best. They want her (Mr. and Mrs. Dixon) excessively to come over with Colonel and Mrs. Campbell; quite depend upon it; nothing can be more kind or pressing than their *joint* invitation Jane says, as you will hear presently. Mr. Dixon does not seem in the least backward in any attention. He is a most charming young man. Ever since the service he rendered Jane at Weymouth, when they were out in that party on the water, and she, by the sudden whirling round of something or other among the sails, would have been dashed into the sea at once, and actually was all but gone, if he had not with the greatest presence of mind, caught hold of her habit, I can never think of it without trembling! but ever since we had the history of that day, I have been so fond of Mr. Dixon!"

"But in spite of all her friends' urgency, and her own wish of seeing Ireland, Miss Fairfax prefers devoting the time to you and Mrs. Bates?"

"Yes—entirely her own doing, entirely her own choice; and Colonel and Mrs. Campbell think she does quite right, just what they should recommend; and indeed they particularly *wish* her to try her native air, as she has not been quite so well as usual lately."

"I am concerned to hear it. I think they judge wisely; but Mrs. Dixon must be very much disappointed. Mrs. Dixon, I understand, has no remarkable degree of personal beauty—is not, by any means, to be compared with Miss Fairfax?"

"Oh, no. You are very obliging to say such things, but certainly not;

there is no comparison between them. Miss Campbell always was ab-solutely plain, but extremely elegant and amiable."

"Yes, that of course."

"Jane caught a bad cold, poor thing! so long ago as the 7th of November (as I am going to read to you), and has never been well since. A long time, is it not, for a cold to hang upon her? She never mentioned it before, because she would not alarm us. Just like her! so considerate! But, how-ever, she is so far from well, that her kind friends the Campbells think she had better come home, and try an air that always agrees with her: and they have no doubt that three or four months at Highbury will entirely cure her; and it is certainly a great deal better that she should come here than go to Ireland, if she is unwell. Nobody could nurse her as we should do."

"It appears to me the most desirable arrangement in the world."

"And so she is to come to us next Friday or Saturday, and the Camp-bells leave town in their way to Holyhead the Monday following, as you will find from Jane's letter. So sudden! You may guess, dear Miss Wood-house, what a flurry it has thrown me in. If it was not for the drawback of her illness—but I am afraid we must expect to see her grown thin, and looking very poorly. I must tell you what an unlucky thing happened to me as to that. I always make a point of reading Jane's letters through to myself first, before I read them aloud to my mother, you know, for fear of there being anything in them to distress her. Jane desired me to do it, so I always do! and so I began to-day with my usual caution: but no sooner did I come to the mention of her being unwell, than I burst out, quite frightened, with 'Bless me! poor Jane is ill!' which my mother, being on the watch, heard distinctly, and was sadly alarmed at. How-ever, when I read on, I found it was not near so bad as I had fancied at first; and I make so light of it now to her that she does not think much about it: but I cannot imagine how I could be so off my guard. If Jane does not get well soon, we will call in Mr. Perry. The expense shall not be thought of; and though he is so liberal and so fond of Jane, that I dare say he would not mean to charge anything for attendance, we could not suffer it to be so, you know. He has a wife and family to maintain, and is not to be giving away his time. Well, now I have just given you a hint of what Jane writes about, we will turn to her letter, and I am sure she tells her own story a great deal better than I can tell it for her."

"I am afraid we must be running away," said Emma, glancing at Harriet, and beginning to rise, "my father will be expecting us. I had no intention, I thought I had no power, of staying more than five minutes when I first entered the house. I merely called because I would not pass the door without inquiring after Mrs. Bates; but I have been so pleasantly detained. Now, however, we must wish you and Mrs. Bates good morning."

And not all that could be urged to detain her succeeded. She regained the street, happy in this, that though much had been forced on her against her will; though she had, in fact, heard the whole substance of Jane Fairfax's letter, she had been able to escape the letter itself.

Chapter 20

JANE FAIRFAX was an orphan, the only child of Mrs. Bates's youngest daughter.

The marriage of Lieut. Fairfax, of the —— regiment of infantry, and Miss Jane Bates, had had its day of fame and pleasure, hope and interest; but nothing now remained of it save the melancholy remembrance of him dying in action abroad, of his widow sinking under consumption and grief soon afterwards, and this girl.

By birth she belonged to Highbury; and when, at three years old, on losing her mother she became the property, the charge, the consolation, the fondling of her grandmother and aunt, there had seemed every probability of her being permanently fixed there; of her being taught only what very limited means could command, and growing up with no advantages of connection or improvement, to be engrafted on what nature had given her in a pleasing person, good understanding, and warm-hearted, well-meaning relations.

But the compassionate feelings of a friend of her father gave a change to her destiny. This was Colonel Campbell, who had very highly regarded Fairfax, as an excellent officer and most deserving young man; and further had been indebted to him for such attentions, during a severe camp-fever, as he believed had saved his life. These were claims which he did not learn to overlook, though some years passed away from the death of poor Fairfax before his own return to England put anything in his power. When he did return, he sought out the child and took notice of her. He was a married man, with only one living child, a girl, about Jane's age; and Jane became their guest, paying them long visits and growing a favourite with all, and before she was nine years old, his daughter's great fondness for her, and his own wish of being a real friend, united to produce an offer from Colonel Campbell of undertaking the whole charge of her education. It was accepted; and from that period Jane had belonged to Colonel Campbell's family, and had lived with them entirely, only visiting her grandmother from time to time.

The plan was that she should be brought up for educating others; the very few hundred pounds which she inherited from her father making independence impossible. To provide for her otherwise was out of Colonel Campbell's power; for though his income, by pay and appointments, was handsome, his fortune was moderate, and must be all his daughter's; but, by giving her an education, he hoped to be supplying the means of respectable subsistence hereafter.

Such was Jane Fairfax's history. She had fallen into good hands, known nothing but kindness from the Campbells, and been given an excellent education. Living constantly with right-minded and well-informed people, her heart and understanding had received every advantage of discipline and culture; and Colonel Campbell's residence being in London, every lighter talent had been done full justice to, by the attendance of first-rate masters. Her disposition and abilities were equally worthy of all that friendship could do; and at eighteen or nineteen she was, as far as such an early age can be qualified for the care of children, fully competent to the office of instruction herself; but she was too much beloved to be parted with. Neither father nor mother could promote, and the daughter could not endure it. The evil day was put off. It was easy to decide that she was still too young; and Jane remained with them, sharing as another daughter, in all the rational pleasures of an elegant society, and a judicious mixture of home and amusement, with only the drawback of the future—the sobering suggestions of her own good understanding—to remind her that all this might soon be over.

The affection of the whole family, the warm attachment of Miss Campbell in particular, was the more honourable to each party from the circumstance of Jane's decided superiority, both in beauty and acquirements. That nature had given it in feature could not be unseen by the young woman, nor could her higher powers of mind be unfelt by the parents. They continued together with unabated regard, however, till the marriage of Miss Campbell, who, by that chance, that luck which so often defies anticipation in matrimonial affairs, giving attraction to what is moderate rather than to what is superior, engaged the affections of Mr. Dixon, a young man, rich and agreeable, almost as soon as they were acquainted; and was eligibly and happily settled, while Jane Fairfax had yet her bread to earn.

This event had very lately taken place; too lately for anything to be yet attempted by her less fortunate friend towards entering on her path of duty, though she had now reached the age which her own judgment had fixed on for beginning. She had long resolved that one-and-twenty should be the period. With the fortitude of a devoted novitiate, she had resolved at one-and-twenty to complete the sacrifice, and retire from all the pleasures of life, of rational intercourse, equal society, peace and hope, to penance and mortification for ever.

The good sense of Colonel and Mrs. Campbell could not oppose such a resolution, though their feelings did. As long as they lived, no exertions would be necessary, their home might be hers for ever; and for their own comfort they would have retained her wholly; but this would be selfishness: what must be at last had better be soon. Perhaps they began to feel it might have been kinder and wiser to have resisted the temptation of any delay, and spared her from a taste of such enjoyments of ease and leisure as must now be relinquished. Still, however, affection was glad to catch at any reasonable excuse for not hurrying on the wretched moment. She had never been quite well since the time of their daughter's marriage; and till she should have completely recovered her usual strength, they must forbid

her engaging in duties, which, so far from being compatible with a weakened frame and varying spirits, seemed, under the most favourable circumstances, to require something more than human perfection of body
and mind to be discharged with tolerable comfort.

With regard to her not accompanying them to Ireland her account to
her aunt contained nothing but truth, though there might be some truths
not told. It was her own choice to give the time of their absence to
Highbury; to spend, perhaps, her last months of perfect liberty with those
kind relations to whom she was so very dear; and the Campbells, whatever might be their motive or motives, whether single, or double, or
treble, gave the arrangement their ready sanction, and said that they
depended more on a few months spent in her native air, for the recovery
of her health, than on anything else. Certain it was that she was to come,
and that Highbury, instead of welcoming that perfect novelty which had
been so long promised it—Mr. Frank Churchill—must put up for the
present with Jane Fairfax, who could bring only the freshness of a two
years' absence.

Emma was sorry to have to pay civilities to a person she did not like
through three long months! to be always doing more than she wished,
and less than she ought! Why she did not like Jane Fairfax might be a
difficult question to answer; Mr. Knightley had once told her it was
because she saw in her the really accomplished young woman which she
wanted to be thought herself; and though the accusation had been eagerly
refuted at the time, there were moments of self-examination in which
her conscience could not quite acquit her. But "she could never get
acquainted with her; she did not know how it was, but there was such
coldness and reserve; such apparent indifference whether she pleased or
not; and then, her aunt was such an eternal talker!—and she was made
such a fuss with by everybody!—and it had been always imagined that
they were to be so intimate; because their ages were the same, everybody
had supposed they must be so fond of each other." These were her
reasons; she had no better.

It was a dislike so little just—every imputed fault was so magnified by
fancy— that she never saw Jane Fairfax, the first time after any considerable absence, without feeling that she had injured her; and now, when the
due visit was paid on her arrival, after a two years' interval, she was
particularly struck with the very appearance and manners which for
those two whole years she had been depreciating. Jane Fairfax was very
elegant, remarkably elegant, and she had herself the highest value for
elegance. Her height was pretty, just such as almost everybody would
think tall, and nobody could think very tall; her figure particularly
graceful; her size a most becoming medium, between fat and thin, though
a slight appearance of ill-health seemed to point out the likeliest evil of
the two. Emma could not but feel all this; and then, her face—her features—there was more beauty in them all together than she had remembered; it was not regular, but it was very pleasing beauty. Her eyes, a

deep grey, with dark eyelashes and eyebrows, had never been denied their praise; but the skin, which she had been used to cavil at, as wanting colour, had a clearness and delicacy which really needed no fuller bloom. It was a style of beauty of which elegance was the reigning character, and as such, she must, in honour, by all her principles, admire it; elegance which, whether of person or of mind, she saw so little in Highbury. There, not to be vulgar, was distinction and merit.

In short, she sat, during the first visit, looking at Jane Fairfax with twofold complacency—the sense of pleasure and the sense of rendering justice, and was determining that she would dislike her no longer. When she took in her history, indeed, her situation, as well as her beauty; when she considered what all this elegance was destined to, what she was going to sink from, how she was going to live, it seemed impossible to feel anything but compassion and respect; especially, if to every well-known particular, entitling her to interest, were added the highly probable circumstance of an attachment to Mr. Dixon, which she had so naturally started to herself. In that case, nothing could be more pitiable or more honourable than the sacrifices she had resolved on. Emma was very willing now to acquit her of having seduced Mr. Dixon's affections from his wife, or of anything mischievous which her imagination had suggested at first. If it were love, it might be simple, single, unsuccessful love on her side. She alone might have been unconsciously sucking in the sad poison, while a sharer of his conversation with her friend; and from the best, the purest of motives, might now be denying herself this visit to Ireland, and resolving to divide herself effectually from him and his connections by soon beginning her career of laborious duty.

Upon the whole, Emma left her with such softened, charitable feelings, as made her look around in walking home, and lament that Highbury afforded no young man worthy of giving her independence—nobody that she could wish to scheme about for her.

These were charming feelings, but not lasting. Before she had committed herself by any public profession of eternal friendship for Jane Fairfax, or done more towards a recantation of past prejudices and errors, than saying to Mr. Knightley, "She certainly is handsome: she is better than handsome!" Jane had spent an evening at Hartfield with her grandmother and aunt, and everything was relapsing much into its usual state. Former provocations reappeared. The aunt was as tiresome as ever; more tiresome, because anxiety for her health was now added to admiration of her powers; and they had to listen to the description of exactly how little bread and butter she ate for breakfast, and how small a slice of mutton for dinner, as well as to see exhibitions of new caps and new work-bags for her mother and herself; and Jane's offences rose again. They had music: Emma was obliged to play; and the thanks and praise which necessarily followed appeared to her an affectation of candour, an air of greatness, meaning only to show off in higher style her own very superior performance. She was, besides, which was the worst of all, so cold, so cautious! There was no getting at her real opinion. Wrapped up in a cloak of politeness, she seemed determined to hazard nothing. She was disgustingly, was suspiciously reserved.

If anything could be more, where all was most, she was more reserved on the subject of Weymouth and the Dixons than anything. She seemed bent on giving no real insight into Mr. Dixon's character, or her own value for his company, or opinion of the suitableness of the match. It was all general approbation and smoothness; nothing delineated or distinguished. It did her no service, however. Her caution was thrown away. Emma saw its artifice, and returned to her first surmises. There probably *was* something more to conceal than her own preference; Mr. Dixon, perhaps, had been very near changing one friend for the other, or been fixed only to Miss Campbell, for the sake of the future twelve thousand pounds.

The like reserve prevailed on other topics. She and Mr. Frank Churchill had been at Weymouth at the same time. It was known that they were a little acquainted, but not a syllable of real information could Emma procure as to what he truly was. "Was he handsome?" "She believed he was reckoned a very fine young man." "Was he agreeable?" "He was generally thought so." "Did he appear a sensible young man; a young man of information?" "At a watering-place, or in a common London acquaintance, it was difficult to decide on such points. Manners were all that could be safely judged of, under a much longer knowledge than they had yet had of Mr. Churchill. She believed everybody found his manners pleasing." Emma could not forgive her.

Chapter 21

EMMA could not forgive her; but as neither provocation nor resentment were discerned by Mr. Knightley, who had been of the party, and had seen only proper attention and pleasing behaviour on each side, he was expressing the next morning, being at Hartfield again on business with Mr. Woodhouse, his approbation of the whole, not so openly as he might have done had her father been out of the room, but speaking plain enough to be very intelligible to Emma. He had been used to think her unjust to Jane, and had now great pleasure in marking an improvement.

"A very pleasant evening," he began, as soon as Mr. Woodhouse had been talked into what was necessary, told that he understood, and the papers swept away—"particularly pleasant. You and Miss Fairfax gave us some very good music. I do not know a more luxurious state, sir, than sitting at one's ease to be entertained a whole evening by two such young women; sometimes with music and sometimes with conversation. I am sure Miss Fairfax must have found the evening pleasant, Emma. You left nothing undone. I was glad you made her play so much, for having no instrument at her grandmother's, it must have been a real indulgence."

"I am happy you approved," said Emma, smiling; "but I hope I am not often deficient in what is due to guests at Hartfield."

"No, my dear," said her father, instantly; "*that* I am sure you are not. There is nobody half so attentive and civil as you are. If anything you are too attentive. The muffin last night—if it had been handed round once, I think it would have been enough."

"No," said Mr. Knightley, nearly at the same time; "you are not often deficient; not often deficient, either in manner or comprehension. I think you understand me, therefore."

An arch look expressed—"I understand you well enough;" but she said only, "Miss Fairfax is reserved."

"I always told you she was—a little; but you will soon overcome all that part of her reserve which ought to be overcome, all that has its foundation in diffidence. What arises from discretion must be honoured."

"You think her diffident. I do not see it."

"My dear Emma," said he, moving from his chair into one close by her, "you are not going to tell me, I hope, that you had not a pleasant evening?"

"Oh no; I was pleased with my own perseverance in asking questions; and amused to think how little information I obtained."

"I am disappointed," was his only answer.

"I hope everybody had a pleasant evening," said Mr. Woodhouse, in his quiet way. "I had. Once, I felt the fire rather too much; but then I moved back my chair a little, a very little, and it did not disturb me. Miss Bates was very chatty and good-humoured, as she always is, though she speaks rather too quick. However, she is very agreeable, and Mrs. Bates, too, in a different way. I like old friends; and Miss Jane Fairfax is a very pretty sort of young lady; a very pretty and a very well-behaved young lady indeed. She must have found the evening agreeable, Mr. Knightley, because she had Emma."

"True, sir; and Emma, because she had Miss Fairfax."

Emma saw his anxiety, and wishing to appease it, at least for the present, said, and with a sincerity which no one could question—

"She is a sort of elegant creature that one cannot keep one's eyes from. I am always watching her to admire; and I do pity her from my heart."

Mr. Knightley looked as if he were more gratified than he cared to express; and before he could make any reply Mr. Woodhouse, whose thoughts were on the Bateses, said—

"It is a great pity that their circumstances should be so confined! a great pity indeed! and I have often wished—but it is so little one can venture to do—small, trifling presents, of anything uncommon. Now, we have killed a porker, and Emma thinks of sending them a loin or a leg; it is very small and delicate—Hartfield pork is not like any other pork—but still it is pork—and, my dear Emma, unless one could be sure of their making it into steaks, nicely fried, as ours are fried, without the smallest grease, and not roast it, for no stomach can bear roast pork—I think we had better send the leg—do not you think so, my dear?"

"My dear papa, I sent the whole hind-quarter. I knew you would wish it. There will be the leg to be salted, you know, which is so very nice, and the loin to be dressed directly, in any manner they like."

"That's right, my dear—very right. I had not thought of it before, but that is the best way. They must not oversalt the leg; and then, if it is not over-salted, and if it is very thoroughly boiled, just as Serle boils ours, and eaten very moderately of, with a boiled turnip, and a little carrot or parsnip, I do not consider it unwholesome."

"Emma," said Mr. Knightley, presently, "I have a piece of news for you. You like news—and I heard an article in my way hither that I think will interest you."

"News! Oh yes, I always like news. What is it? why do you smile so? where did you hear it? at Randalls?"

He had time only to say—

"No, not at Randalls; I have not been near Randalls," when the door was thrown open, and Miss Bates and Miss Fairfax walked into the room. Full of thanks, and full of news, Miss Bates knew not which to give quickest. Mr. Knightley soon saw that he had lost his moment, and that not another syllable of communication could rest with him.

"Oh, my dear sir, how are you this morning? My dear Miss Woodhouse—I come quite overpowered. Such a beautiful hind-quarter of pork! You are too bountiful! Have you heard the news? Mr. Elton is going to be married."

Emma had not had time even to think of Mr. Elton, and she was so completely surprised, that she could not avoid a little start, and a little blush, at the sound.

"There is my news—I thought it would interest you," said Mr. Knightley, with a smile, which implied a conviction of some part of what had passed between them.

"But where could *you* hear it?" cried Miss Bates. "Where could you possibly hear it, Mr. Knightley? For it is not five minutes since I received Mrs. Cole's note—no, it cannot be more than five—or at least ten—for I had got my bonnet and spencer on, just ready to come out—I was only gone down to speak to Patty again about the pork—Jane was standing in the passage—were not you, Jane?—for my mother was so afraid that we had not any saltingpan large enough. So I said, I would go down and see, and Jane said, 'Shall I go down instead? for I think you have a little cold, and Patty has been washing the kitchen.' 'Oh, my dear,' said I—well, and just then came the note. A Miss Hawkins—that's all I know. A Miss Hawkins of Bath. But, Mr. Knightley, how could you possibly have heard it, for the very moment Mr. Cole told Mrs. Cole of it, she sat down and wrote to me. A Miss Hawkins—"

"I was with Mr. Cole on business an hour and a half ago. He had just read Elton's letter as I was shown in, and handed it to me directly."

"Well! that is quite—I suppose there never was a piece of news more generally interesting. My dear sir, you really are too bountiful. My mother desires her very best compliments and regards, and a thousand thanks, and says you really oppress quite her."

"We consider our Hartfield pork," replied Mr. Woodhouse—"indeed it certainly is, so very superior to all other pork, that Emma and I cannot have a greater pleasure than—"

"Oh, my dear sir, as my mother says, our friends are only too good to us. If ever there were people who, without having great wealth themselves, had everything they could wish for, I am sure it is us. We may well say, that 'our lot is cast in a goodly heritage.' Well, Mr. Knightley, and so you actually saw the letter—well—"

"It was short—merely to announce—but cheerful, exulting, of course." Here was a sly glance at Emma. "He had been so fortunate as to—I forget the precise words—one has no business to remember them. The information was, as you state, that he was going to be married to a Miss Hawkins. By his style I should imagine it just settled."

"Mr. Elton going to be married!" said Emma, as soon as she could speak. "He will have everybody's wishes for his happiness."

"He is very young to settle," was Mr. Woodhouse's observation. "He had better not be in a hurry. He seemed to me very well off as he was. We were always glad to see him at Hartfield."

"A new neighbour for us all, Miss Woodhouse!" said Miss Bates joyfully; "my mother is so pleased! she says she cannot bear to have the poor old vicarage without a mistress. This is great news, indeed. Jane, you have never seen Mr. Elton; no wonder that you have such a curiosity to see him."

Jane's curiosity did not appear of that absorbing nature as wholly to occupy her.

"No, I have never seen Mr. Elton," she replied, starting on this appeal: "is he—is he a tall man?"

"Who shall answer that question?" cried Emma. "My father would say, 'Yes'; Mr. Knightley, 'No'; and Miss Bates and I, that he is just the happy medium. When you have been here a little longer, Miss Fairfax, you will understand that Mr. Elton is the standard of perfection in Highbury, both in person and mind."

"Very true, Miss Woodhouse, so she will. He is the very best young man; but, my dear Jane, if you remember, I told you yesterday he was precisely the height of Mr. Perry. Miss Hawkins!—I dare say, an excellent young woman. His extreme attention to my mother—wanting her to sit in the vicarage-pew, that she might hear the better, for my mother is a little deaf, you know—it is not much, but she does not hear quite quick. Jane says that Colonel Campbell is a little deaf. He fancied bathing might be good for it—the warm bath—but she says it did him no lasting benefit. Colonel Campbell, you know, is quite our angel. And Mr. Dixon seems a very charming young man, quite worthy of him. It is such a happiness when good people get together—and they always do. Now, here will be Mr. Elton and Miss Hawkins; and there are the Coles, such very good people; and the Perrys—I suppose there never was a happier or a better couple than Mr. and Mrs. Perry. I say, sir," turning to Mr. Woodhouse, "I think there are few places with such society as Highbury. I always say, we are quite blessed in our neighbours. My dear sir, if there is one thing my mother loves better than another, it is pork—a roast loint of pork——"

"As to who, or what, Miss Hawkins is, or how long he has been acquainted with her," said Emma, "nothing, I suppose, can be known. One feels that it cannot be a very long acquaintance. He has been gone only four weeks."

Nobody had any information to give; and, after a few more wonderings, Emma said—

"You are silent, Miss Fairfax—but I hope you mean to take an interest in this news. You, who have been hearing and seeing so much of late on these subjects, who must have been so deep in the business on Miss Campbell's account—we shall not excuse your being indifferent about Mr. Elton and Miss Hawkins."

"When I have seen Mr. Elton," replied Jane, "I dare say I shall be interested—but I believe it requires *that* with me. And as it is some months since Miss Campbell married, the impression may be a little worn off."

"Yes, he has been gone just four weeks, as you observe, Miss Woodhouse," said Miss Bates, "four weeks yesterday. A Miss Hawkins! Well, I had always rather fancied it would be some young lady hereabouts; not that I ever—Mrs. Cole once whispered to me—but I immediately said, 'No, Mr. Elton is a most worthy young man—but——' In short, I do not think I am particularly quick at those sort of discoveries. I do not pretend to it. What is before me, I see. At the same time, nobody could wonder if Mr. Elton should have aspired—Miss Woodhouse lets me chatter on, so good-humouredly. She knows I would not offend for the world. How does Miss Smith do? She seems quite recovered now. Have you heard from Mrs. John Knightley lately? Oh, those dear little children. Jane, do you know I always fancy Mr. Dixon like Mr. John Knightley. I mean in person—tall, and with that sort of look—and not very talkative."

"Quite wrong, my dear aunt; there is no likeness at all."

"Very odd! but one never does form a just idea of anybody beforehand. One takes up a notion and runs away with it. Mr. Dixon, you say, is not, strictly speaking, handsome?"

"Handsome! Oh no—far from it—certainly plain. I told you he was plain."

"My dear, you said that Miss Campbell would not allow him to be plain, and that you yourself——"

"Oh, as for me, my judgment is worth nothing. Where I have regard, I always think a person well-looking. But I gave what I believed the general opinion, when I called him plain."

"Well, my dear Jane. I believe we must be running away. The weather does not look well, and grandmamma will be uneasy. You are too obliging, my dear Miss Woodhouse; but we really must take leave. This has been a most agreeable piece of news indeed. I shall just go round by Mrs. Cole's; but I shall not stop three minutes; and, Jane, you had better go home directly—I would not have you out in a shower. We think she is the better for Highbury already. Thank you—we do indeed. I shall not attempt calling on Mrs. Goddard, for I really do not think she cares for anything but *boiled* pork; when we dress the leg it will be another thing. Good morning to you, my dear sir. Oh, Mr. Knightley is coming too. Well, that is so very—! I am sure if Jane is tired, you will be so kind as to give her your arm. Mr. Elton and Miss Hawkins! Good morning to you."

Emma, alone with her father, had half her attention wanted by him, while he lamented that young people would be in such a hurry to marry —and to marry strangers too—and the other half she could give to her own view of the subject. It was to herself an amusing and a very welcome piece of news, as proving that Mr. Elton could not have suffered long; but she was sorry for Harriet—Harriet must feel it—and all that she could hope was, by giving the first information herself, to save her from hearing it abruptly from others. It was now about the time that she was likely to call. If she were to meet Miss Bates in her way!—and upon its beginning to rain, Emma was obliged to expect that the weather would be detaining her at Mrs. Goddard's, and that the intelligence would undoubtedly rush upon her without preparation.

The shower was heavy, but short; and it had not been over five minutes, when in came Harriet, with just the heated, agitated look which hurrying thither with a full heart was likely to give; and the "Oh, Miss Woodhouse, what do you think has happened?" which instantly burst forth, had all the evidence of corresponding perturbation. As the blow was given, Emma felt that she could not now show greater kindness than in listening; and Harriet, unchecked, ran eagerly through what she had to tell. "She had set out from Mrs. Goddard's half an hour ago —she had been afraid it would rain—she had been afraid it would pour down every moment—but she thought she might get to Hartfield first —she had hurried on as fast as possible; but then, as she was passing by the house where a young woman was making up a gown for her, she thought she would just step in and see how it went on; and though she did not seem to stay half a moment there, soon after she came out it began to rain, and she did not know what to do; so she ran on directly, as fast as she could, and took shelter at Ford's." Ford's was the principal woollendraper, linendraper, and haberdasher's shop united —the shop first in size and fashion in the place. "And so there she had sat, without an idea of anything in the world, full ten minutes perhaps— when, all of a sudden, who should come in—to be sure it was so very odd! but they always dealt at Ford's—who should come in, but Elizabeth Martin and her brother! Dear Miss Woodhouse! only think. I thought I should have fainted. I did not know what to do. I was sitting near the door—Elizabeth saw me directly; but he did not; he was busy with the umbrella. I am sure she saw me, but she looked away directly, and took no notice; and they both went to quite the farther end of the shop; and I kept sitting near the door. Oh dear, I was so miserable! I am sure I must have been as white as my gown. I could not go away, you know, because of the rain; but I did so wish myself anywhere in the world but there. Oh dear, Miss Woodhouse! well at last, I fancy, he looked round and saw me; for instead of going on with her buyings, they began whispering to one another. I am sure they were talking of me; and I could not help thinking that he was persuading her to speak to me— (do you think he was, Miss Woodhouse?)—for presently she came forward—came quite up to me, and asked me how I did, and seemed ready to shake hands, if I would. She did not do any of it in the same way that she used: I could see she was altered; but, however, she seemed to *try* to be very friendly, and we shook hands, and stood talking some time; but I know no more what I said—I was in such a tremble! I remember she said she was sorry we never met now, which I thought almost too kind! Dear Miss Woodhouse, I was absolutely miserable! By that time, it was beginning to hold up, and I was determined that nothing should stop me from getting away—and then—only think! I found he was coming up towards me too—slowly, you know, and as if he did not quite know what to do; and so he came and spoke, and I answered— and I stood for a minute, feeling dreadfully, you know, one can't tell how; and then I took courage, and said it did not rain, and I must go; and so off I set; and I had not got three yards from the door, when he came after me, only to say, if I was going to Hartfield, he thought I had much better go round by Mr. Cole's stables, for I should find the near way quite floated by this rain. Oh dear, I thought it would have been the death of me! So I said I was very much obliged to him; you know I could not do less; and then he went back to Elizabeth, and I came round by the stables—I believe I did—but I hardly knew where I was, or anything about it. Oh, Miss Woodhouse, I would rather done anything than have had it happen; and yet, you know, there was a sort of satisfaction in seeing him behave so pleasantly and so kindly. And Elizabeth, too. Oh, Miss Woodhouse, do talk to me, and make me comfortable again."

Very sincerely did Emma wish to do so; but it was not immediately in her power. She was obliged to stop and think. She was not thoroughly comfortable herself. The young man's conduct, and his sister's, seemed the result of real feeling, and she could not but pity them. As Harriet described it, there had been an interesting mixture of wounded affection and genuine delicacy in their behaviour; but she had believed them to be well-meaning, worthy people before; and what difference did this make in the evils of the connection? It was folly to be disturbed by it.

Of course, he must be sorry to lose her—they must be all sorry—ambition, as well as love, had probably been mortified. They might all have hoped to rise by Harriet's acquaintance; and besides, what was the value of Harriet's description? So easily pleased—so little discerning—what signified her praise?

She exerted herself, and did try to make her comfortable, by considering all that had passed as a mere trifle, and quite unworthy of being dwelt on.

"It might be distressing for the moment," said she, "but you seem to have behaved extremely well; and it is over, and may never—can never, as a first meeting—occur again, and therefore you need not think about it."

Harriet said, "Very true," and she "would not think about it;" but still she talked of it—still she could talk of nothing else; and Emma, at last, in order to put the Martins out of her head, was obliged to hurry on the news, which she had meant to give with so much tender caution, hardly knowing herself whether to rejoice or be angry, ashamed, or only amused, at such a state of mind in poor Harriet—such a conclusion of Mr. Elton's importance with her!

Mr. Elton's rights, however, gradually revived. Though she did not feel the first intelligence as she might have done the day before, or an hour before, its interest soon increased; and before their first conversation was over, she had talked herself into all the sensations of curiosity, wonder and regret, pain and pleasure, as to this fortunate Miss Hawkins, which could conduce to place the Martins under proper subordination in her fancy.

Emma learned to be rather glad that there had been such a meeting It had been serviceable in deadening the first shock, without retaining any influence to alarm. As Harriet now lived, the Martins could not get at her, without seeking her where hitherto they had wanted either the courage or the condescension to seek her; for since her refusal of the brother, the sisters never had been at Mrs. Goddard's; and a twelvemonth might pass without their being thrown together again, with any necessity, or even any power of speech.

Chapter 22

HUMAN nature is so well disposed towards those who are in interesting situations, that a young person, who either marries or dies, is sure of being kindly spoken of.

A week had not passed since Miss Hawkins's name was first mentioned in Highbury, before she was, by some means or other, discovered to have every recommendation of person and mind—to be handsome, elegant, highly accomplished, and perfectly amiable; and when Mr. Elton himself arrived to triumph in his happy prospects, and circulate the fame of her merits, there was very little more for him to do than to tell her Christian name, and say whose music she principally played.

Mr. Elton returned, a very happy man. He had gone away rejected and mortified, disappointed in a very sanguine hope, after a series of what appeared to him strong encouragements; and not only losing the right lady, but finding himself debased to the level of a very wrong one. He had gone away deeply offended, he came back engaged to another; and to another as superior, of course, to the first, as under such circumstances what is gained always is to what is lost. He came back gay and self-satisfied, eager and busy, caring nothing for Miss Woodhouse, and defying Miss Smith.

The charming Augusta Hawkins, in addition to all the usual advantages of perfect beauty and merit, was in possession of an independent fortune, of so many thousands as would always be called ten—a point of some dignity, as well as some convenience. The story told well: he had not thrown himself away—he had gained a woman of ten thousand pounds, or thereabouts, and he had gained her with such delightful rapidity; the first hour of introduction had been so very soon followed by distinguishing notice; the history which he had to give Mrs. Cole of the rise and progress of the affair was so glorious; the steps so quick, from the accidental rencontre, to the dinner at Mr. Green's, and the party at Mrs. Brown's—smiles and blushes rising in importance—with consciousness and agitation richly scattered; the lady had been so easily impressed—so sweetly disposed; had, in short, to use a most intelligent phrase, been so very ready to have him, that vanity and prudence were equally contented.

He had caught both substance and shadow, both fortune and affection, and was just the happy man he ought to be; talking only of himself and his own concerns—expecting to be congratulated—ready to be laughed at—and, with cordial, fearless smiles, now addressing all the young ladies of the place, to whom, a few weeks ago, he would have been more cautiously gallant.

The wedding was no distant event, as the parties had only themselves to please, and nothing but the necessary preparations to wait for; and when he set out for Bath again, there was a general expectation, which a certain glance of Mrs. Cole's did not seem to contradict, that when he next entered Highbury he would bring his bride.

During his present short stay, Emma had barely seen him; but just enough to feel that the first meeting was over, and to give her the impression of his not being improved by the mixture of pique and pretension now spread over his air. She was, in fact, beginning very much to wonder that she had ever thought him pleasing at all; and his right was so inseparably connected with some very disagreeable feelings, that, except in a moral light, as a penance, a lesson, a source of profitable humiliation to her own mind, she would have been thankful to be assured of never seeing him again. She wished him very well; but he gave her pain; and his welfare twenty miles off would administer most satisfaction.

The pain of his continued residence in Highbury, however, must certainly be lessened by his marriage. Many vain solicitudes would be prevented—many awkwardnesses smoothed by it. A *Mrs. Elton* would be an excuse for any change of intercourse; former intimacy might sink without remark. It would be almost beginning their life of civility again.

Of the lady individually, Emma thought very little. She was good enough for Mr. Elton, no doubt; accomplished enough for Highbury—handsome enough—to look plain, probably, by Harriet's side. As to connection, there Emma was perfectly easy; persuaded that, after all his own vaunted claims and disdain of Harriet, he had done nothing. On that article, truth seemed attainable. *What* she was, must be uncertain; but *who* she was, might be found out; and setting aside the £10,000 it did not appear that she was at all Harriet's superior. She brought no name, no blood, no alliance. Miss Hawkins was the youngest of the two daughters of a Bristol—merchant, of course, he must be called; but, as the whole of the profits of his mercantile life appeared so very moderate, it was not unfair to guess the dignity of his line of trade had been very moderate also. Part of every winter she had been used to spend in Bath; but Bristol was her home, the very heart of Bristol; for though the father and mother had died some years ago, an uncle remained—in the law line: nothing more distinctly honourable was hazarded of him, than that he was in the law line; and with him the daughter had lived. Emma guessed him to be the drudge of some attorney, and too stupid to rise. And all the grandeur of the connection seemed dependent on the elder sister, who was *very well married,* to a gentleman in a *great way,* near Bristol, who kept two carriages! That was the wind-up of the history; that was the glory of Miss Hawkins.

Could she but have given Harriet her feelings about it all! She had talked her into love; but, alas! she was not so easily to be talked out of it. The charm of an object to occupy the many vacancies of Harriet's mind was not to be talked away. He might be superseded by another; he certainly would, indeed! nothing could be clearer; even a Robert Martin would have been sufficient; but nothing else, she feared, would cure her. Harriet was one of those, who, having once begun, would be always in love. And now, poor girl, she was considerably worse from this reappearance of Mr. Elton—she was always having a glimpse of him somewhere or other. Emma saw him only once; but two or three times every day Harriet was sure *just* to meet with him, or *just* to miss him, *just* to hear his voice, or see his shoulder, *just* to have something occur to preserve him in her fancy, in all the favouring warmth of surprise and conjecture. She was, moreover, perpetually hearing about him; for, excepting when at Hartfield, she was always among those who saw no fault in Mr. Elton, and found nothing so interesting as the discussion of his concerns; and every report, therefore, every guess—all that had already occurred, all that might occur in the arrangement of his affairs, comprehending income, servants, and furniture—was continually in agitation around her. Her regard was receiving strength by invariable praise of him, and her regrets kept alive, and feelings irritated by ceaseless repetitions of Miss Hawkins's happiness, and continual observation of how much he seemed attached! his air as he walked by the house, the very sitting of his hat, being all in proof of how much he was in love!

Had it been allowable entertainment, had there been no pain to her friend, or reproach to herself, in the waverings of Harriet's mind, Emma would have been amused by its variations. Sometimes Mr. Elton predominated, sometimes the Martins; and each was occasionally useful as a check to the other. Mr. Elton's engagement had been the cure of the agitation of meeting Mr. Martin. The unhappiness produced by the knowledge of that engagement had been a little put aside by Elizabeth Martin's calling at Mrs. Goddard's a few days afterwards. Harriet had not been at home; but a note had been prepared and left for her, written in the very style to touch—a small mixture of reproach with a great deal of kindness; and till Mr. Elton himself appeared, she had been much occupied by it, continually pondering over what could be done in return, and wishing to do more than she dared to confess. But Mr. Elton, in person, had driven away all such cares. While he stayed, the Martins were forgotten; and on the very morning of his setting off for Bath again, Emma, to dissipate some of the distress it occasioned, judged it best for her to return Elizabeth Martin's visit.

How that visit was to be acknowledged, what would be necessary, and what might be safest, had been a point of some doubtful considertation. Absolute neglect of the mother and sisters, when invited to come, would be ingratitude. It must not be; and yet the danger of a renewal of the acquaintance!

After much thinking, she could determine on nothing better than Harriet's returning the visit; but in a way that, if they had understanding, should convince them that it was to be only a formal acquaintance. She meant to take her in the carriage, leave her at the Abbey-Mill, while she drove a little further, and call for her again so soon as to allow no time for insidious applications or dangerous recurrences to the past, and give the most decided proof of what degree of intimacy was chosen for the future.

She could think of nothing better; and though there was something in it which her own heart could not approve—something of ingratitude, merely glossed over—it must be done, or what would become of Harriet?

Chapter 23

SMALL heart had Harriet for visiting. Only half an hour before her friend called for her at Mrs. Goddard's, her evil stars had led her to the very spot, where, at that moment, a trunk, directed to *The Rev. Philip Elton, White Hart, Bath,* was to be seen under the operation of being lifted into the butcher's cart, which was to convey it to where the coaches passed; and everything in this world, except that trunk and the direction, was consequently a blank.

She went, however; and when they reached the farm, and she was to be put down, at the end of the broad, neat gravel walk, which led between espalier apple-trees to the front door, the sight of everything which had given her so much pleasure the autumn before was beginning to revive a little local agitation; and when they parted, Emma observed her to be looking around with a sort of fearful curiosity, which determined her not to allow the visit to exceed the proposed quarter of an hour. She went on herself, to give that portion of time to an old servant who was married, and settled in Donwell.

The quarter of an hour brought her punctually to the white gate again; and Miss Smith receiving her summons, was with her without delay, and unattended by any alarming young man. She came solitarily down the gravel walk—a Miss Martin just appearing at the door, and parting with her seemingly with ceremonious civility.

Harriet could not very soon give an intelligible account. She was feeling too much; but at last Emma collected from her enough to understand the sort of meeting, and the sort of pain it was creating. She had seen only Mrs. Martin and the two girls. They had received her doubtingly, if not coolly; and nothing beyond the merest commonplace had been talked almost all the time—till just at last, when Mrs. Martin's saying all of a sudden, that she thought Miss Smith was grown, had brought on a more interesting subject, and a warmer manner. In that very room she had been measured last September with her two friends. There were the pencilled marks and memorandums on the wainscot by the window. *He* had done it. They all seemed to remember the day, the hour, the party, the occasion—to feel the same consciousness, the same regrets—to be ready to return to the same good understanding; and they were just growing again like themselves (Harriet, as Emma must suspect, as ready as the best of them to be cordial and happy) when the carriage reappeared, and all was over. The style of the visit, and the shortness of it, were then felt to be decisive. Fourteen minutes to be given to those with whom she had thankfully passed six weeks not six months ago! Emma could not but picture it all, and feel how justly they might resent, how naturally Harriet must differ. It was a bad business. She would have given a great deal, or endured a great deal, to have had the Martins in a higher rank of life. They were so deserving, that a *little* higher should have been enough; but as it was, how could she have done otherwise? Impossible! She could not repent. They must be separated; but there was a great deal of pain in the process—so much to herself at this time, that she soon felt the necessity of a little consolation, and resolved on going home by way of Randalls to procure it. Her mind was quite sick of Mr. Elton and the Martins. The refreshment of Randalls was absolutely necessary.

It was a good scheme; but on driving to the door they heard that neither "master nor mistress was at home;" they had both been out some time; the man believed they were gone to Hartfield.

"This is too bad," cried Emma, as they turned away. "And now we shall just miss them; too provoking. I do not know when I have been so disappointed." And she leaned back in the corner, to indulge her murmurs, or to reason them away; probably a little of both—such being the commonest process of a not ill-disposed mind. Presently the carriage stopped: she looked up; it was stopped by Mr. and Mrs. Weston, who were standing to speak to her. There was instant pleasure in the sight of them, and still greater pleasure was conveyed in sound; for Mr. Weston immediately accosted her with:

"How d'ye do? How d'ye do? We have been sitting with your father—glad to see him so well. Frank comes to-morrow—I had a letter this morning—we see him to-morrow by dinner-time to a certainty—he is at Oxford to-day, and he comes for a whole fortnight—I knew it would be so. If he had come at Christmas he could not have stayed three days. I was always glad he did not come at Christmas; now we are going to have just the right weather for him—fine, dry, settled weather. We shall enjoy him completely; everything has turned out exactly as we could wish."

There was no resisting such news, no possibility of avoiding the influence of such a happy face as Mr. Weston's, confirmed as it all was by the words and the countenance of his wife, fewer and quieter, but not less to the purpose. To know that *she* thought his coming certain was enough to make Emma consider it so, and sincerely did she rejoice in their joy. It was a most delightful reanimation of exhausted spirits. The worn-out past was sunk in the freshness of what was coming; and in the rapidity of half a moment's thought, she hoped Mr. Elton would now be talked of no more.

Mr. Weston gave her the history of the engagements at Enscombe, which allowed his son to answer for having an entire fortnight at his command, as well as the route and the method of his journey; and she listened, and smiled, and congratulated.

"I shall soon bring him over to Hartfield," said he, at the conclusion.

Emma could imagine she saw a touch of the arm at this speech, from his wife.

"We had better move on, Mr. Weston," said she; "we are detaining the girls."

"Well, well, I am ready;" and turning again to Emma—"but you must not be expecting such a *very* fine young man; you have only had *my* account, you know; I dare say he is really nothing extraordinary," though his own sparkling eyes at the moment were speaking a very different conviction.

Emma could look perfectly unconscious and innocent, and answer in a manner that appropriated nothing.

"Think of me to-morrow, my dear Emma, about four o'clock," was Mrs. Weston's parting injunction, spoken with some anxiety, and meant only for her.

"Four o'clock!—Depend upon it he will be here by three," was Mr. Weston's quick amendment; and so ended a most satisfactory meeting. Emma's spirits were mounted quite up to happiness. Everything wore a different air. James and his horses seemed not half so sluggish as before. When she looked at the hedges, she thought the elder, at least, must soon be coming out; and when she turned round to Harriet she saw something like a look of spring, a tender smile even there.

"Will Mr. Frank Churchill pass through Bath as well as Oxford?" was a question, however, which did not augur much.

But neither geography nor tranquillity could come all at once; and Emma was now in a humour to resolve that they should both come in time.

The morning of the interesting day arrived, and Mrs. Weston's faithful pupil did not forget either at ten, or eleven, or twelve o'clock, that she was to think of her at four.

"My dear, dear anxious friend," said she, in mental soliloquy, while walking downstairs from her own room, "always over-careful for everybody's comfort but your own; I see you now in all your little fidgets, going again and again into his room, to be sure that all is right." The clock struck twelve as she passed through the hall. " 'Tis twelve; I shall not forget to think of you four hours hence; and by this time to-morrow, perhaps, or a little later, I may be thinking of the possibility of their all calling here. I am sure they will bring him soon."

She opened the parlour door, and saw two gentlemen sitting with her father—Mr. Weston and his son. They had been arrived only a few minutes; and Mr. Weston had scarcely finished his explanation of Frank's being a day before his time, and her father was yet in the midst of his very civil welcome and congratulations, when she appeared, to have her share of surprise, introduction and pleasure.

The Frank Churchill so long talked of, so high in interest, was actually before her. He was presented to her, and she did not think too much had been said in his praise. He was a *very* good-looking young man—height, air, address, all were unexceptionable, and his countenance had a great deal of the spirit and liveliness of his father's—he looked quick and sensible. She felt immediately that she should like him; and there was a well-bred ease of manner, and a readiness to talk, which convinced her that he came intending to be acquainted with her, and that acquainted they soon must be.

He had reached Randalls the evening before. She was pleased with the eagerness to arrive which had made him alter his plan, and travel earlier, later and quicker, that he might gain half a day.

"I told you yesterday," cried Mr. Weston, with exultation, "I told you all that he would be here before the time named. I remembered what I used to do myself. One cannot creep upon a journey; one cannot help getting on faster than one has planned: and the pleasure of coming in upon one's friends before the look-out begins is worth a great deal more than any little exertion it needs."

"It is a great pleasure where one can indulge in it," said the young man, "though there are not many houses that I should presume on so far; but in coming *home* I felt I might do anything."

The word *home* made his father look on him with fresh complacency. Emma was directly sure that he knew how to make himself agreeable; the conviction was strengthened by what followed. He was very much pleased with Randalls, thought it a most admirably arranged house, would hardly allow it even to be very small, admired the situation, the walk to Highbury, Highbury itself, Hartfield still more, and professed himself to have always felt the sort of interest in the country, which none but one's *own* country gives, and the greatest curiosity to visit it. That he should never have been able to indulge so amiable a feeling before passed suspiciously through Emma's brain; but still if it were a falsehood, it was a pleasant one, and pleasantly handled. His manner had no air of study or exaggeration. He did really look and speak as if in a state of no common enjoyment.

Their subjects, in general, were such as belong to an opening acquaintance. On his side were the inquiries: "Was she a horsewoman? Pleasant rides? Pleasant walks? Had they a large neighbourhood? Highbury, perhaps, afforded society enough? There were several very pretty houses in and about it. Balls—had they balls? Was it a musical society?"

But when satisfied on all these points, and their acquaintance proportionately advanced, he contrived to find an opportunity, while their two fathers were engaged with each other, of introducing his mother-in-law, and speaking of her with so much handsome praise, so much warm admiration, so much gratitude for the happiness she secured to his father, and her very kind reception of himself, as was an additional proof of his knowing how to please—and of his certainly thinking it worth while to try to please her. He did not advance a word of praise beyond what she knew to be thoroughly deserved by Mrs. Weston; but, undoubtedly, he could know very little of the matter. He understood what would be welcome; he could be sure of little else. "His father's marriage," he said, "had been the wisest measure: every friend must rejoice in it; and the family from whom he had received such a blessing must be ever considered as having conferred the highest obligation on him."

He got as near as he could to thanking her for Miss Taylor's merits, without seeming quite to forget that, in the common course of things, it was to be rather supposed that Miss Taylor had formed Miss Woodhouse's character, than Miss Woodhouse Miss Taylor's. And at last, as if resolved to qualify his opinion completely for travelling around to its object, he wound it all up with astonishment at the youth and beauty of her person.

"Elegant, agreeable manners, I was prepared for," said he; "but I confess that, considering everything, I had not expected more than a very tolerably well-looking woman of a certain age; I did not know that I was to find a pretty young woman in Mrs. Weston."

"You cannot see too much perfection in Mrs. Weston, for my feelings," said Emma; "were you to guess her to be *eighteen*, I should listen with pleasure; but *she* would be ready to quarrel with you for using such words. Don't let her imagine that you have spoken of her as a pretty young woman."

"I hope I should know better," he replied; "no, depend upon it" (with a gallant bow), "that in addressing Mrs. Weston, I should understand whom I might praise without any danger of being thought extravagant in my terms."

Emma wondered whether the same suspicion of what might be expected from their knowing each other, which had taken strong possession of her mind, had ever crossed his; and whether his compliments were to be considered as marks of acquiescence or proofs of defiance. She must see more of him to understand his ways; at present she only felt they were agreeable.

She had no doubt of what Mr. Weston was often thinking about. His quick eye she detected again and again glancing towards them with a happy expression; and even when he might have determined not to look she was confident that he was often listening.

Her own father's perfect exemption from any thought of the kind, the entire deficiency in him of all such sort of penetration or suspicion, was a most comfortable circumstance. Happily he was not further from approving matrimony than from foreseeing it. Though always objecting to every marriage that was arranged, he never suffered beforehand from the apprehension of any; it seemed as if he could not think so ill of any two persons' understanding as to suppose they meant to marry till it were proved against them. She blessed the favouring blindness. He could now, without the drawback of a single unpleasant surmise, without a glance forward at any possible treachery in his guest, give way to all his natural kind-hearted civility, in solicitous inquiries after Mr. Frank Churchill's accommodation on his journey, through the sad evils of sleeping two nights on the road, and express very genuine unmixed anxiety to know that he had certainly escaped catching cold—which, however, he could not allow him to feel quite assured of himself, till after another night.

A reasonable visit paid, Mr. Weston began to move. "He must be going. He had business at the Crown about his hay, and a great many errands for Mrs. Weston at Ford's; but he need not hurry anybody else." His son, too well bred to hear the hint, rose immediately also, saying:

"As you are going further on business, sir, I will take the opportunity of paying a visit, which must be paid some day or other, and therefore may as well be paid now. I have the honour of being acquainted with a neighbour of yours" (turning to Emma), "a lady residing in or near Highbury; a family of the name of Fairfax. I shall have no difficulty, I suppose, in finding the house; though Fairfax, I believe, is not the proper name—I should rather say Barnes or Bates. Do you know any family of that name?"

"To be sure we do," cried his father; "Mrs. Bates—we passed her house—I saw Miss Bates at the window. True, true, you are acquainted with Miss Fairfax; I remember you knew her at Weymouth, and a fine girl she is. Call upon her, by all means."

"There is no necessity for my calling this morning," said the young man; "another day would do as well; but there was that degree of acquaintance at Weymouth, which——"

"Oh, go to-day, go to-day. Do not defer it. What is right to be done cannot be done too soon. And besides, I must give you a hint, Frank—any want of attention to her *here* should be carefully avoided. You saw her with the Campbells, when she was the equal of everybody she mixed with, but here she is with a poor old grandmother, who has barely enough to live on. If you do not call early it will be a slight."

The son looked convinced.

"I have heard her speak of the acquaintance," said Emma; "she is a very elegant young woman."

He agreed to it, but with so quiet a "Yes," as inclined her almost to doubt his real concurrence; and yet there must be a very distinct sort of elegance for the fashionable world if Jane Fairfax could be thought only ordinarily gifted with it.

"If you were never particularly struck by her manners before," said she, "I think you will to-day. You will see her to advantage; see her and hear her—no, I am afraid you will not hear her at all, for she has an aunt who never holds her tongue."

"You are acquainted with Jane Fairfax, sir, are you?" said Mr. Woodhouse, always the last to make his way in conversation; "then give me leave to assure you that you will find her a very agreeable young lady. She is staying here on a visit to her grandmamma and aunt, very worthy people; I have known them all my life. They will be extremely glad to see you, I am sure; and one of my servants shall go with you to show you the way."

"My dear sir, upon no account in the world; my father can direct me."

"But your father is not going so far; he is only going to the Crown, quite on the other side of the street, and there are a great many houses; you might be very much at a loss. and it is a very dirty walk, unless you keep on the footpath; but my coachman can tell you where you had best cross the street."

Mr. Frank Churchill still declined it, looking as serious as he could; and his father gave his hearty support, by calling out: "My good friend, this is quite unnecessary; Frank knows a puddle of water when he sees it, and as to Mrs. Bates's, he may get there from the Crown in a hop, step and jump."

They were permitted to go alone; and with a cordial nod from one, and a graceful bow from the other, the two gentlemen took leave. Emma remained very well pleased with this beginning of the acquaintance, and could now engage to think of them all at Randalls any hour of the day, with full confidence in their comfort.

Chapter 24

THE next morning brought Mr. Frank Churchill again. He came with Mrs. Weston, to whom and to Highbury he seemed to take very cordially. He had been sitting with her, it appeared, most companionably at home till her usual hour of exercise: and on being desired to choose their walk, immediately fixed on Highbury. "He did not doubt there being very pleasant walks in every direction, but if left to him, he should always choose the same. Highbury, that airy, cheerful, happy-looking Highbury, would be his constant attraction." Highbury, with Mrs. Weston, stood for Hartfield; and she trusted to its bearing the same construction with him. They walked thither directly.

Emma had hardly expected them: for Mr. Weston, who had called in for half a minute, in order to hear that his son was very handsome, knew nothing of their plans; and it was an agreeable surprise to her, therefore, to perceive them walking up to the house together, arm in arm. She was wanting to see him again; and especially to see him in company with Mrs. Weston, upon his behaviour to whom her opinion of him was to depend. If he were deficient there, nothing should make amends for it. But on seeing them together she became perfectly satisfied. It was not merely in fine words or hyperbolical compliment that he paid his duty; nothing could be more proper or pleasing than his whole manner to her—nothing could more agreeably denote his wish of considering her as a friend, and securing her affection. And there was time enough for Emma to form a reasonable judgment, as their visit included all the rest of the morning. They were all three walking about together for an hour or two—first round the shrubberies of Hartfield, and afterwards in Highbury. He was delighted with everything; admired Hartfield sufficiently for Mr. Woodhouse's ear; and when their going further was resolved on, confessed his wish to be made acquainted with the whole village, and found matter of commendation and interest much oftener than Emma could have supposed.

Some of the objects of his curiosity spoke very amiable feelings. He begged to be shown the house which his father had lived in so long, and which had been the home of his father's father, and on recollecting that an old woman who had nursed him was still living, walked in quest of her cottage, from one end of the street to the other; and though in some points of pursuit or observation there was no positive merit, they showed altogether a goodwill towards Highbury in general which must be very like a merit to those he was with.

Emma watched, and decided that with such feelings as were now shown it could not be fairly supposed that he had been ever voluntarily absenting himself; that he had not been acting a part, or making a parade of insincere professions; and that Mr. Knightley certainly had not done him justice.

Their first pause was at the Crown Inn, an inconsiderable house, though the principal one of the sort, where a couple of pair of post-horses were kept, more for the convenience of the neighbourhood than from any run on the road; and his companions had not expected to be detained by any interest excited there; but in passing it they gave the history of the large room visibly added. It had been built many years ago for a ballroom, and while the neighbourhood had been in a particularly populous, dancing state, had been occasionally used as such; but such brilliant days had long passed away; and now the highest purpose for which it was ever wanted was to accommodate a whist-club, established among the gentlemen and half-gentlemen of the place. He was immediately interested. Its character as a ballroom caught him; and instead of passing on, he stopped for several minutes at the two superior sashed windows which were open, to look in and contemplate its capabilities, and lament that its original purpose should have ceased. He saw no fault in the room; he would acknowledge none which they suggested. No; it was long enough, broad enough, handsome enough. It would hold the very number for comfort. They ought to have balls there at least every fortnight through the winter. Why had not Miss Woodhouse revived the former good old days of the room! She who could do anything in Highbury! The want of proper families in the place, and the conviction that none beyond the place and its immediate environs could be tempted to attend, were mentioned; but he was not satisfied. He could not be persuaded that so many good-looking houses as he saw around him could not furnish numbers enough for such a meeting; and even when particulars were given and families described, he was still unwilling to admit that the inconvenience of such a mixture would be anything, or that there would be the smallest difficulty in everybody's returning into their proper place the next morning. He argued like a young man very much bent on dancing; and Emma was rather surprised to see the constitution of the Weston prevail so decidedly against the habits of the Churchills. He seemed to have all the life and spirit, cheerful feelings, and social inclinations of his father, and nothing of the pride or reserve of Enscombe. Of pride, indeed, there was, perhaps, scarcely enough; his indifference to a confusion of rank bordered too much on inelegance of mind. He could be no judge, however, of the evil he was holding cheap. It was but an effusion of lively spirits.

At last he was persuaded to move on from the front of the Crown; and being now almost facing the house where the Bateses lived, Emma recollected his intended visit the day before, and asked him if he had paid it.

"Yes, oh yes!" he replied. "I was just going to mention it. A very successful visit. I saw all the three ladies; and felt very much obliged to you for your preparatory hint. If the talking aunt had taken me quite by surprise it must have been the death of me. As it was, I was only betrayed into paying a most unreasonable visit. Ten minutes would have been all that was necessary, perhaps all that was proper; and I had told my father I should certainly be at home before him, but there was no getting away, no pause; and, to my utter astonishment, I found, when he (finding me nowhere else) joined me there at last, that I had been actually sitting with them very nearly three-quarters of an hour. The good lady had not given me the possibility of escape before."

"And how did you think Miss Fairfax looking?"

"Ill, very ill—that is, if a young lady can ever be allowed to look ill; but the expression is hardly admissible, Mrs. Weston, is it? Ladies can never look ill; and seriously, Miss Fairfax is naturally so pale as almost always to give the appearance of ill-health—a most deplorable want of complexion.'

Emma would not agree to this, and began a warm defence of Miss Fairfax's complexion. "It was certainly never brilliant, but she would not allow it to have a sickly hue in general; and there was a softness and delicacy in her skin which gave peculiar elegance to the character of her face." He listened with all due deference; acknowledged that he had heard many people say the same; but yet he must confess that to him nothing could make amends for the want of the fine glow of health. Where features were indifferent, a fine complexion gave beauty to them all; and where they were good, the effect was—fortunately he need not attempt to describe what the effect was.

"Well," said Emma, "there is no disputing about taste. At least you admire her, except her complexion."

He shook his head and laughed. "I cannot separate Miss Fairfax and her complexion."

"Did you see her often at Weymouth? Were you often in the same society?"

At this moment they were approaching Ford's, and he hastily exclaimed, "Ha! this must be the very shop that everybody attends every day of their lives, as my father informs me. He comes to Highbury himself, he says, six days out of the seven, and has always business at Ford's. If it be not inconvenient to you, pray let us go in, that I may prove myself to belong to the place—to be a true citizen of Highbury. I must buy something at Ford's. It will be taking out my freedom. I dare say they sell gloves."

"Oh, yes, gloves and everything. I do admire your patriotism. You will be adored in Highbury. You were very popular before you came, because you were Mr. Weston's son; but lay out half a guinea at Ford's, and your popularity will stand upon your own virtues."

They went in; and while the sleek, well-tied parcels of "Men's Beavers" and "York Tan" were bringing down and displaying on the counter, he said: "But I beg your pardon, Miss Woodhouse; you were speaking to me, you were saying something at the very moment of this burst of my *amor patriæ*. Do not let me lose it; I assure you the utmost stretch of public fame would not make me amends for the loss of any happiness in private life."

"I merely asked, whether you had known much of Miss Fairfax and her party at Weymouth."

"And now that I understand your question I must pronounce it to be a very unfair one. It is always the lady's right to decide on the degree of acquaintance. Miss Fairfax must already have given her account. I shall not commit myself by claiming more than she may choose to allow."

"Upon my word, you answer as discreetly as she could do herself. But her account of everything leaves so much to be guessed; she is so very reserved, so very unwilling to give the least information about anybody, that I really think you may say what you like of your acquaintance with her."

"May I, indeed? Then I will speak the truth, and nothing suits me so well. I met her frequently at Weymouth. I had known the Campbells a little in town; and at Weymouth we were very much in the same set. Colonel Campbell is a very agreeable man, and Mrs. Campbell a friendly warm-hearted woman. I like them all."

"You know Miss Fairfax's situation in life, I conclude? What she is destined to be?"

"Yes"—(rather hesitatingly)—"I believe I do."

"You get upon delicate subjects, Emma," said Mrs. Weston, smiling; "remember that I am here. Mr. Frank Churchill hardly knows what to say when you speak of Miss Fairfax's situation in life. I will move a little further off."

"I certainly do forget to think of *her*," said Emma, "as having ever been anything but my friend and my dearest friend."

He looked as if he fully understood and honoured such a sentiment.

When the gloves were bought, and they had quitted the shop again: "Did you ever hear the young lady we were speaking of play?" said Frank Churchill.

"Ever hear her?" repeated Emma. "You forget how much she belongs to Highbury. I have heard her every year of our lives since we both began. She plays charmingly."

"You think so, do you? I wanted the opinion of some one who could really judge. She appeared to me to play well, that is, with considerable taste, but I know nothing of the matter myself. I am excessively fond of music, but without the smallest skill or right of judging of anybody's performance. I have been used to hear hers admired; and I remember one proof of her being thought to play well: a man, a very musical man, and in love with another woman—engaged to her—on the point of marriage—would yet never ask that other woman to sit down to the instrument, if the lady in question could sit down instead—never seemed to like to hear one if he could hear the other. That I thought, in a man of known musical talent, was some proof."

"Proof, indeed!" said Emma, highly amused. "Mr. Dixon is very musical, is he? We shall know more about them all, in half an hour, from you, than Miss Fairfax would have vouchsafed in half a year."

"Yes, Mr. Dixon and Miss Campbell were the persons; and I thought it a very strong proof."

"Certainly, very strong it was; to own the truth, a great deal stronger than, if *I* had been Miss Campbell, would have been at all agreeable to me. I could not excuse a man's having more music than love—more ear than eye—a more acute sensibility to fine sounds than to my feelings. How did Miss Campbell appear to like it?"

"It was her very particular friend, you know."

"Poor comfort!" said Emma, laughing. "One would rather have a stranger preferred than one's very particular friend; with a stranger it might not recur again, but the misery of having a very particular friend always at hand, to do everything better than one does one's self. Poor Mrs. Dixon! Well, I am glad she is gone to settle in Ireland."

"You are right. It was not very flattering to Miss Campbell; but she really did not seem to feel it."

"So much the better, or so much the worse; I do not know which. But be it sweetness, or be it stupidity in her—quickness of friendship, or dullness of feeling—there was one person, I think, who must have felt it—Miss Fairfax herself. *She* must have felt the improper and dangerous distinction."

"As to that—I do not——"

"Oh, do not imagine that I expect an account of Miss Fairfax's sensations from you, or from anybody else. They are known to no human being, I guess, but herself; but if she continued to play whenever she was asked by Mr. Dixon, one may guess what one chooses."

"There appeared such a perfectly good understanding among them all——" he began rather quickly, but checking himself, added: "However, it is impossible for me to say on what terms they really were—how it might all be behind the scenes. I can only say that there was smoothness outwardly. But you, who have known Miss Fairfax from a child, must be a better judge of her character, and of how she is likely to conduct herself in critical situations, than I can be."

"I have known her from a child, undoubtedly; we have been children and women together; and it is natural to suppose that we should be intimate—that we should have taken to each other whenever she visited her friends. But we never did. I hardly know how it has happened; a little, perhaps, from that wickedness on my side which was prone to take disgust towards a girl so idolised and so cried up as she always was, by her aunt and grandmother, and all their set. And then, her reserve! I never could attach myself to anyone so completely reserved."

"It is a most repulsive quality, indeed," said he. "Oftentimes very convenient, no doubt, but never pleasing. There is safety in reserve, but no attraction. One cannot love a reserved person."

"Not till the reserve ceases towards one's self; and then the attraction may be the greater. But I must be more in want of a friend, or an agreeable companion, than I have yet been, to take the trouble of conquering anybody's reserve to procure one. Intimacy between Miss Fairfax and me is quite out of the question. I have no reason to think ill of her—not the least—except that such extreme and perpetual cautiousness of word and manner, such a dread of giving a distinct idea about anybody, is apt to suggest suspicions of there being something to conceal."

He perfectly agreed with her; and after walking together so long, and thinking so much alike, Emma felt herself so well acquainted with him that she could hardly believe it to be only their second meeting. He was not exactly what she had expected; less of a man of the world in some of his notions, less of the spoiled child of fortune, therefore better than she had expected. His ideas seemed more moderate—his feelings warmer. She was particularly struck by his manner of considering Mr. Elton's house, which, as well as the church, he would go and look at, and would not join them in finding much fault with. No, he could not believe it a bad house; not such a house as a man was to be pitied for having. If it were to be shared with the woman he loved, he could not think any man to be pitied for having that house. There must be ample room in it for every real comfort. The man must be a blockhead who wanted more.

Mrs. Weston laughed, and said he did not know what he was talking about. Used only to a large house himself, and without ever thinking how many advantages and accommodations were attached to its size, he could be no judge of the privations inevitably belonging to a small one. But Emma, in her own mind, determined that he *did* know what he was talking about, and that he showed a very amiable inclination to settle early in life, and to marry from worthy motives. He might not be aware of the inroads on domestic peace to be occasioned by no housekeeper's room, or a bad butler's pantry; but no doubt he did perfectly feel that Enscombe could not make him happy, and that whenever he were attached he would willingly give up much of wealth to be allowed an early establishment.

Chapter 25

EMMA's very good opinion of Frank Churchill was a little shaken the following day by hearing that he was gone off to London, merely to have his hair cut. A sudden freak seemed to have seized him at breakfast, and he had sent for a chaise and set off, intending to return to dinner, but with no more important view that appeared than having his hair cut. There was certainly no harm in his travelling sixteen miles twice over on such an errand; but there was an air of foppery and nonsense in it which she could not approve. It did not accord with the rationality of plan, the moderation in expense, or even the unselfish warmth of heart, which she had believed herself to discern in him yesterday. Vanity, extravagance, love of change, restlessness of temper, which must be doing something, good or bad; heedlessness as to the pleasure of his father and Mrs. Weston, indifferent as to how his conduct might appear in general—he became liable to all these charges. His father only called him a coxcomb, and thought it a very good story; but that Mrs. Weston did not like it was clear enough by her passing it over as quickly as possible, and making no other comment than that "all young people would have their little whims."

With the exception of this little blot, Emma found that his visit hitherto had given her friend only good ideas of him. Mrs. Weston was very ready to say how attentive and pleasant a companion he made himself—how much she saw to like in his disposition altogether. He appeared to have a very open temper—certainly a very cheerful and lively one; she could observe nothing wrong in his notions—a great deal decidedly right; he spoke of his uncle with warm regard—was fond of talking of him; said he would be the best man in the world if he were left to himself; and though there was no being attached to the aunt, he acknowledged her kindness with gratitude, and seemed to mean always to speak of her with respect. This was all very promising; and but for such an unfortunate fancy for having his hair cut, there was nothing to denote him unworthy of the distinguished honour which her imagination had given him; the honour, if not of being really in love with her, of being at least very near it, and saved only by her own indifference—(for still her resolution held of never marrying)—the honour, in short, of being marked out for her by all their joint acquaintances.

Mr. Weston, on his side, added a virtue to the account which must have some weight. He gave her to understand that Frank admired her extremely —thought her very beautiful and very charming; and with so much to be said for him altogether, she found she must not judge him harshly: as Mrs. Weston observed, "all young people would have their little whims."

There was one person among his new acquaintances in Surrey not so leniently disposed. In general, he was judged, throughout the parishes of Donwell and Highbury with great candour; liberal allowances were made for the little excesses of such a handsome young man—one who smiled so often and bowed so well; but there was one spirit among them not to be softened, from its power of censure, by bows or smiles—Mr. Knightley. The circumstance was told him at Hartfield; for the moment he was silent; but Emma heard him almost immediately afterwards say to him-self, over a newspaper he held in his hand, "Hum! just the trifling, silly fellow I took him for." She had half a mind to resent; but an instant's observation convinced her that it was really said only to relieve his own feelings, and not meant to provoke; and therefore she let it pass.

Although in one instance the bearers of not good tidings, Mr. and Mrs. Weston's visit this morning was in another respect particularly opportune. Something occurred while they were at Hartfield to make Emma want their advice; and, which was still more lucky, she wanted exactly the advice they gave.

This was the occurrence: The Coles had been settled some years in Highbury, and were very good sort of people, friendly, liberal and unpretending; but, on the other hand, they were of low origin, in trade, and only moderately genteel. On their first coming into the country they had lived in proportion to their income, quietly, keeping little company, and that little unexpensively; but the last year or two had brought them a considerable increase of means—the house in town had yielded greater profits, and fortune in general had smiled on them. With their wealth their views increased; their want of a larger house, their inclination for more company. They added to their house, to their number of servants, to their expenses of every sort; and by this time were, in fortune and style of living, second only to the family at Hartfield. Their love of society, and their new dining-room, prepared everybody for their keeping dinner-company; and a few parties, chiefly among the single men, had already taken place. The regular and best families Emma could hardly suppose they would presume to invite—neither Donwell, nor Hartfield, nor Randalls. Nothing should tempt *her* to go, if they did; and she regretted that her father's known habits would be giving her refusal less meaning than she could wish. The Coles were very respectable in their way, but they ought to be taught that it was not for them to arrange the terms on which the superior families would visit them. This lesson, she very much feared, they would receive only from herself; she had little hope of Mr. Knightley, none of Mr. Weston.

But she had made up her mind how to meet this presumption so many weeks before it appeared, that when the insult came at last it found her very differently affected. Donwell and Randalls had received their invitation, and none had come for her father and herself; and Mrs. Weston's accounting for it with, "I suppose they will not take the liberty with you; they know you do not dine out," was not quite sufficient. She felt that she should like to have had the power of refusal; and afterwards, as the idea of the party to be assembled there, consisting precisely of those whose society was dearest to her, occurred again and again, she did not know that she might not have been tempted to accept. Harriet was to be there in the evening, and the Bateses. They had been speaking of it as they walked about Highbury the day before, and Frank Churchill had most earnestly lamented her absence. Might not the evening end in a dance? had been a question of his. The bare possibility of it acted as a further irritation on her spirits; and her being left in solitary grandeur, even supposing the omission to be intended as a compliment, was but poor comfort.

It was the arrival of this very invitation, while the Westons were at Hartfield, which made their presence so acceptable; for though her first remark on reading it was, that, "of course it must be declined," she so very soon proceeded to ask them what they advised her to do, that their advice for her going was most prompt and successful.

She owned that, considering everything, she was not absolutely without inclination for the party. The Coles expressed themselves so properly—there was so much real attention in the manner of it—so much consideration for her father. "They would have solicited the honour earlier, but had been waiting the arrival of a folding-screen from London, which they hoped might keep Mr. Woodhouse from any draught of air, and, therefore, induce him the more readily to give them the honour of his company." Upon the whole, she was very persuadable; and it being briefly settled among themselves how it might be done without neglecting his comfort—how certainly Mrs. Goddard, if not Mrs. Bates, might be depended on for bearing him company—Mr. Woodhouse was to be talked into an acquiescence of his daughter's going out to dinner on a day now near at hand, and spending the whole evening away from him. As for *his* going, Emma did not wish him to think it possible; the hours would be too late, and the party too numerous. He was soon pretty well resigned.

"I am not fond of dinner-visiting," said he; "I never was. No more is Emma. Late hours do not agree with us. I am sorry Mr. and Mrs. Cole should have done it. I think it would be much better if they would come in one afternoon next summer and take their tea with us; take us in their afternoon walk, which they might do, as our hours are so reasonable, and yet get home without being out in the damp of the evening. The dews of a summer evening are what I would not expose anybody to. However, as they are so very desirous to have dear Emma dine with them, and as you will both be there, and Mr. Knightley too, to take care of her, I cannot wish to prevent it, provided the weather be what it ought, neither damp, nor cold, nor windy." Then turning to Mrs. Weston, with a look of gentle reproach: "Ah, Miss Taylor, if you had not married, you would have stayed at home with me."

"Well, sir," cried Mr. Weston, "as I took Miss Taylor away, it is incumbent on me to supply her place, if I can; and I will step to Mrs. Goddard in a moment, if you wish it."

But the idea of anything to be done in a *moment* was increasing, not lessening Mr. Woodhouse's agitation. The ladies knew better how to allay it. Mr. Weston must be quiet, and everything deliberately arranged.

With this treatment Mr. Woodhouse was soon composed enough for talking as usual. "He should be happy to see Mrs. Goddard. He had a great regard for Mrs. Goddard; and Emma should write a line and invite her. James could take the note. But first of all there must be an answer written to Mrs. Cole.

"You will make my excuses, my dear, as civilly as possible. You will say that I am quite an invalid, and go nowhere. and therefore must decline their obliging invitation; beginning with my *compliments,* of course. But you will do everything right. I need not tell you what is to be done. We must remember to let James know that the carriage will be wanted on Tuesday. I shall have no fears for you with him. We have never been there above once since the new approach was made; but still I have no doubt that James will take you very safely; and when you get there you must tell him at which time you would have him come for you again; and you had better name an early hour. You will not like staying late. You will get very tired when tea is over."

"But you would not wish me to come away before I am tired, papa?"

"Oh no, my love; but you will soon be tired. There will be a great many people talking at once. You will not like the noise."

"But, my dear sir," cried Mr. Weston, "if Emma comes away early it will be breaking up the party."

"And no great harm if it does," said Mr. Woodhouse. "The sooner every party breaks up the better."

"But you do not consider how it may appear to the Coles. Emma's going away directly after tea might be giving offence. They are good-natured people, and think little of their own claims; but still they must feel that anybody's hurrying away is no great compliment; and Miss Woodhouse's doing it would be more thought of than any other person's in the room. You would not wish to disappoint and mortify the Coles, I am sure, sir; friendly, good sort of people as ever lived, and who have been your neighbours for *ten* years."

"No, upon no account in the world, Mr. Weston, I am much obliged to you for reminding me. I should be extremely sorry to be giving them any pain. I know what worthy people they are. Perry tells me that Mr. Cole never touches malt liquor. You would not think it to look at him, but he is bilious—Mr. Cole is very bilious. No, I would not be the means of giving them any pain. My dear Emma, we must consider this. I am sure rather than run the risk of hurting Mr. and Mrs. Cole you would stay a little longer than you might wish. You will not regard being tired. You will be perfectly safe, you know, among your friends."

"Oh yes, papa. I have no fears at all for myself; and I should have no scruples of staying as late as Mrs. Weston, but on your account. I am only afraid of your sitting up for me. I am not afraid of your not being exceedingly comfortable with Mrs. Goddard. She loves piquet, you know; but when she is gone home I am afraid you will be sitting up by yourself, instead of going to bed at your usual time; and the idea of that would entirely destroy my comfort. You must promise me not to sit up."

He did on the condition of some promises on her side; such as that, if she came home cold, she would be sure to warm herself thoroughly; if hungry that she would take something to eat; that her own maid should sit up for her; and that Serle and the butler should see that everything were safe in the house as usual.

Chapter 26

FRANK CHURCHILL came back again; and if he kept his father's dinner waiting it was not known at Hartfield; for Mrs. Weston was too anxious for his being a favourite with Mr. Woodhouse, to betray any imperfection which could be concealed.

He came back, had had his hair cut, and laughed at himself with a very good grace, but without seeming really at all ashamed of what he had done. He had no reason to wish his hair longer to conceal any confusion of face; no reason to wish the money unspent to improve his spirits. He was quite as undaunted and as lively as ever; and, after seeing him, Emma thus moralised to herself:

"I do not know whether it ought to be so, but certainly silly things do cease to be silly if they are done by sensible people in an impudent way. Wickedness is always wickedness, but folly is not always folly. It depends upon the character of those who handle it. Mr. Knightley, he is not a trifling, silly young man. If he were, he would have done this differently. He would either have gloried in the achievement, or been ashamed of it. There would have been either the ostentation of a coxcomb, or the evasions of a mind too weak to defend its own vanities. No, I am perfectly sure that he is not trifling or silly."

With Tuesday came the agreeable prospect of seeing him again, and for a longer time than hitherto; of judging of his general manners, and, by inference, of the meaning of his manners towards herself; of guessing how soon it might be necessary for her to throw coldness into her air; and of fancying what the observations of all those might be, who were now seeing them together for the first time.

She meant to be very happy, in spite of the scene being laid at Mr. Cole's; and without being able to forget that among the failings of Mr. Elton, even in the days of his favour, none had disturbed her more than his propensity to dine with Mr. Cole.

Her father's comfort was amply secured, Mrs. Bates as well as Mrs. Goddard being able to come; and her last pleasing duty, before she left the house, was to pay her respects to them as they sat together after dinner; and while her father was fondly noticing the beauty of her dress, to make the two ladies all the amends in her power, by helping them to large slices of cake and full glasses of wine, for whatever unwilling self-denial his care of their constitutions might have obliged them to practise during the meal. She had provided a plentiful dinner for them; she wished she could know that they had been allowed to eat it.

She followed another carriage to Mr. Cole's door; and was pleased to see that it was Mr. Knightley's; for Mr. Knightley, keeping no horses, having little spare money and a great deal of health, activity, and independence, was too apt, in Emma's opinion, to get about as he could, and not use his carriage so often as became the owner of Donwell Abbey.

She had an opportunity now of speaking her approbation while warm from her heart, for he stopped to hand her out.

"This is coming as you should do," said she; "like a gentleman. I am quite glad to see you."

He thanked her, observing, "How lucky that we should arrive at the same moment; for, if we had met first in the drawing-room, I doubt whether you would have discerned me to be more of a gentleman than usual. You might not have distinguished how I came by my look or manner."

"Yes, I should; I am sure I should. There is always a look of consciousness or bustle when people come in a way which they know to be beneath them. You think you carry it off very well, I dare say; but with you it is a sort of bravado, an air of affected unconcern; I always observe it whenever I meet you under those circumstances. *Now* you have nothing to try for. You are not afraid of being supposed ashamed. You are not striving to look taller than anybody else. *Now* I shall really be very happy to walk into the same room with you."

"Nonsensical girl!" was his reply, but not at all in anger.

Emma had as much reason to be satisfied with the rest of the party as with Mr. Knightley. She was received with a cordial respect which could not but please, and given all the consequence she could wish for. When the Westons arrived, the kindest looks of love, the strongest of admiration, were for her, from both husband and wife; the son approached her with a cheerful eagerness, which marked her as his peculiar object, and at dinner she found him seated by her; and, as she firmly believed, not without some dexterity on his side.

The party was rather large, as it included one other family—a proper unobjectionable country family, whom the Coles had the advantage of naming among their acquaintances—and the male part of Mr. Cox's family, the lawyer of Highbury. The less worthy females were to come in the evening, with Miss Bates, Miss Fairfax, and Miss Smith; but already, at dinner, they were too numerous for any subject of conversation to be general; and, while politics and Mr. Elton were talked over, Emma could fairly surrender all her attention to the pleasantness of her neighbour. The first remote sound to which she felt herself obliged to attend was the name of Jane Fairfax. Mrs. Cole seemed to be relating something of her that was expected to be very interesting. She listened, and found it well worth listening to. That very dear part of Emma, her fancy, received an amusing supply. Mrs. Cole was telling that she had been calling on Miss Bates; and as soon as she entered the room, had been struck by the sight of a pianoforte, a very elegant looking instrument; not a grand, but a large-sized square pianoforte; and the substance of the story, the end of all the dialogue which ensued of surprise, and inquiry, and congratulations on her side, and explanations on Miss Bates's, was, that this pianoforte had arrived from Broadwood's the day before, to the great astonishment of both aunt and niece, entirely unexpected; that, at first, by Miss Bates's

account, Jane herself was quite at a loss, quite bewildered to think who
could possibly have ordered it; but now they were both perfectly satisfied
that it could be from only one quarter—of course it must be from Colonel
Campbell.

"One can suppose nothing else," added Mrs. Cole; "and I was only
surprised that there could ever have been a doubt. But Jane, it seems, had
a letter from them very lately, and not a word was said about it. She
knows their ways best; but I should not consider their silence as any
reason for their not meaning to make the present. They might choose to
surprise her."

Mrs. Cole had many to agree with her; everybody who spoke on the
subject was equally convinced that it must come from Colonel Campbell,
and equally rejoiced that such a present had been made; and there were
enough ready to speak to allow Emma to think her own way, and still
listen to Mrs. Cole.

"I declare, I do not know when I have heard anything that has given
me more satisfaction. It always has quite hurt me that Jane Fairfax, who
plays so delightfully, should not have an instrument. It seemed quite a
shame, especially considering how many houses there are where fine
instruments are absolutely thrown away. This is like giving ourselves a
slap, to be sure; and it was but yesterday I was telling Mr. Cole I really
was ashamed to look at our new grand pianoforte in the drawing-room,
while I do not know one note from another, and our little girls, who are but
just beginning, perhaps may never make anything of it; and there is poor
Jane Fairfax, who is mistress of music, has not anything of the nature of an
instrument, not even the pitifullest old spinet in the world, to amuse
herself with. I was saying this to Mr. Cole but yesterday, and he quite
agreed with me; only he is so particularly fond of music that he could not
help indulging himself in the purchase, hoping that some of our good
neighbours might be so obliging occasionally to put it to a better use than
we can; and that really is the reason why the instrument was bought—or
else I am sure we ought to be ashamed of it. We are in great hopes that
Miss Woodhouse may be prevailed with to try it this evening."

Miss Woodhouse made the proper acquiescence, and finding that
nothing more was to be entrapped from any communication of Mrs. Cole's,
turned to Frank Churchill.

"Why do you smile?" said she.

"Nay, why do you?"

"Me! I suppose I smile for pleasure at Colonel Campbell's being so
rich and so liberal. It is a handsome present."

"Very."

"I rather wonder that it was never made before."

"Perhaps Miss Fairfax has never been staying here so long before."

"Or that he did not give her the use of their own instrument, which
must now be shut up in London, untouched by anybody."

"That is a grand pianoforte, and he might think it too large for Mrs. Bates's house."

"You may *say* what you choose, but your countenance testifies that your *thoughts* on this subject are very much like mine."

"I do not know. I rather believe you are giving me more credit for acuteness than I deserve. I smile because you smile, and shall probably suspect whatever I find you suspect; but at present I do not see what there is to question. If Colonel Campbell is not the person, who can be?"

"What do you say to Mrs. Dixon?"

"Mrs. Dixon! very true, indeed. I had not thought of Mrs. Dixon. She must know, as well as her father, how acceptable an instrument would be; and perhaps the mode of it, the mystery, the surprise, is more like a young woman's scheme than an elderly man's. It is Mrs. Dixon, I dare say. I told you that your suspicions would guide mine."

"If so, you must extend your suspicions, and comprehend *Mr.* Dixon in them."

"Mr. Dixon! very well. Yes. I immediately perceive that it must be the joint present of Mr. and Mrs. Dixon. We were speaking the other day, you know, of his being so warm an admirer of her performance."

"Yes, and what you told me on that head confirmed an idea which I had entertained before. I do not mean to reflect upon the good intentions of either Mr. Dixon or Miss Fairfax; but I cannot help suspecting either that, after making his proposals to her friend, he had the misfortune to fall in love with *her,* or that he became conscious of a little attachment on her side. One might guess twenty things without guessing exactly the right; but I am sure there must be a particular cause for her choosing to come to Highbury, instead of going with the Campbells to Ireland. Here, she must be leading a life of privation and penance; there it would have been all enjoyment. As to the pretence of trying her native air, I look upon that as a mere excuse. In the summer it might have passed; but what can anybody's native air do for them in the months of January, February, and March? Good fires and carriages would be much more to the purpose in most cases of delicate health, and I dare say in hers. I do not require you to adopt all my suspicions, though you make so noble a profession of doing it, but I honestly tell you what they are."

"And upon my word, they have an air of great probability. Mr. Dixon's preference of her music to her friend's I can answer for being very decided."

"And then, he saved her life. Did you ever hear of that? A water party; and by some accident she was falling overboard. He caught her."

"He did. I was there—one of the party."

"Were you really? Well! But you observed nothing, of course, for it seems to be a new idea to you. If I had been there, I think I should have made some discoveries."

"I dare say you would; but I, simple I, saw nothing but the fact, that Miss Fairfax was nearly dashed from the vessel, and that Mr. Dixon caught her—it was the work of a moment. And though the consequent shock and alarm was very great, and much more durable—indeed I believe it was half an hour before any of us were comfortable again—yet that was too general a sensation for anything of peculiar anxiety to be observable. I do not mean to say, however, that you might not have made discoveries."

The conversation was here interrupted. They were called on to share in the awkwardness of a rather long interval between the courses, and obliged to be as formal and as orderly as the others; but when the table was again safely covered, when every corner dish was placed exactly right, and occupation and ease were generally restored, Emma said:

"The arrival of this pianoforte is decisive with me. I wanted to know a little more, and this tells me quite enough. Depend upon it, we shall soon hear that it is a present from Mr. and Mrs. Dixon."

"And if the Dixons should absolutely deny all knowledge of it we must conclude it to come from the Campbells."

"No, I am sure it is not from the Campbells. Miss Fairfax knows it is not from the Campbells, or they would have been guessed at first. She would not have been puzzled had she dared fix on them. I may not have convinced you, perhaps, but I am perfectly convinced myself that Mr. Dixon is a principal in the business."

"Indeed you injure me if you suppose me unconvinced. Your reasonings carry my judgment along with them entirely. At first, while I supposed you satisfied that Colonel Campbell was the giver I saw it only as paternal kindness, and thought it the most natural thing in the world. But when you mentioned Mrs. Dixon, I felt how much more probable that it should be the tribute of warm female friendship. And now I can see it in no other light than as an offering of love."

There was no occasion to press the matter further. The conviction seemed real; he looked as if he felt it. She said no more—other subjects took their turn, and the rest of the dinner passed away; the dessert succeeded, the children came in, and were talked to and admired amid the usual rate of conversation; a few clever things said, a few downright silly, but by much the larger proportion neither the one nor the other—nothing worse than everyday remarks, dull repetitions, old news, and heavy jokes. The ladies had not been long in the drawing-room before the other ladies, in their different divisions, arrived. Emma watched the entrée of her own particular little friend; and if she could not exult in her dignity and grace she could not only love the blooming sweetness and the artless manner, but could most heartily rejoice in that light, cheerful, unsentimental disposition which allowed her so many alleviations of pleasure in the midst of the pangs of disappointed affection. There she sat—and who would have guessed how many tears she had been lately shedding? To be in company, nicely dressed herself, and seeing others nicely dressed, to sit and smile and look pretty and say nothing, was enough for the happiness of the present hour. Jane Fairfax did look and move superior; but Emma suspected she might have been glad to change feelings with Harriet—very glad to have purchased the mortification of having loved—yes, of having loved even Mr. Elton in vain by the surrender of all the dangerous pleasure of knowing herself beloved by the husband of her friend.

In so large a party it was not necessary that Emma should approach her. She did not wish to speak of the pianoforte, she felt too much in the secret herself to think the appearance of curiosity or interest fair, and therefore purposely kept at a distance; but by the others the subject was almost immediately introduced, and she saw the blush of consciousness with which congratulations were received, the blush of guilt which accompanied the name of "my excellent friend, Colonel Campbell."

Mrs. Weston, kind-hearted and musical, was particularly interested by the circumstance, and Emma could not help being amused at her perseverance in dwelling on the subject; and having so much to ask and to say as to tone, touch, and pedal, totally unsuspicious of that wish of saying as little about it as possible, which she plainly read in the fair heroine's countenance.

They were soon joined by some of the gentlemen; and the very first of the early was Frank Churchill. In he walked, the first and handsomest; and after paying his compliments, *en passant* to Miss Bates and her niece, made his way directly to the opposite side of the circle, where sat Miss Woodhouse; and till he could find a seat by her would not sit at all. Emma divined what everybody present must be thinking. She was his object, and everybody must perceive it. She introduced him to her friend Miss Smith, and, at convenient moments afterwards, heard what each thought of the other. "He had never seen so lovely a face, and was delighted with her naïveté." And she—"only to be sure it was paying him too great a compliment, but she did think there were some looks a little like Mr. Elton." Emma restrained her indignation, and only turned from her in silence.

Smiles of intelligence passed between her and the gentleman on first glancing towards Miss Fairfax; but it was most prudent to avoid speech. He told her that he had been impatient to leave the dining-room—hated sitting long—was always the first to move when he could—that his father, Mr. Knightley, Mr. Cox, and Mr. Cole, were left very busy over parish business—that as long as he had stayed, however, it had been pleasant enough, as he had found them in general a set of gentlemenlike, sensible men; and spoke so handsomely of Highbury altogether—thought it so abundant in agreeable families—that Emma began to feel she had been used to despise the place rather too much. She questioned him as to the society in Yorkshire, the extent of the neighbourhood about Enscombe, and the sort; and could make out from his answers that, as far as Enscombe was concerned, there was very little going on, that their visitings were among a range of great families, none very near; and that even when days were fixed, and invitations accepted, there was an even chance that Mrs. Churchill were not in health and spirits for going; that they made a point of visiting no fresh person; and that, though he had his separate engagements, it was not without difficulty, without considerable address, *at times*, that he could get away, or introduce an acquaintance for a night.

She saw that Enscombe could not satisfy, and that Highbury, taken at its best, might reasonably please a young man who had more retirement at home than he liked. His importance at Enscombe was very evident. He did not boast, but it naturally betrayed itself, that he had persuaded his aunt where his uncle could do nothing, and on her laughing and noticing it, he owned that he believed (excepting one or two points) he could *with time* persuade her to anything. One of those points on which his influence failed he then mentioned. He had wanted very much to go abroad—had been very eager indeed to be allowed to travel—but she would not hear of it. This had happened the year before. *Now,* he said, he was beginning to have no longer the same wish.

The unpersuadable point, which he did not mention, Emma guessed to be good behaviour to his father.

"I have made a most wretched discovery," said he, after a short pause. "I have been here a week to-morrow—half my time. I never knew days fly so fast. A week to-morrow! and I have hardly begun to enjoy myself. But just got acquainted with Mrs. Weston, and others. I hate the recollection."

"Perhaps you may now begin to regret that you spent one whole day, out of so few, in having your hair cut."

"No," said he smiling, "that is no subject of regret at all. I have no pleasure in seeing my friends, unless I can believe myself fit to be seen."

The rest of the gentlemen being now in the room, Emma found herself obliged to turn from him for a few minutes, and listen to Mr. Cole. When Mr. Cole had moved away, and her attention could be restored as before, she saw Frank Churchill looking intently across the room at Miss Fairfax, who was sitting exactly opposite.

"What is the matter?" said she.

He started. "Thank you for rousing me," he replied. "I believe I have been very rude; but really Miss Fairfax has done her hair in so odd a way —so very odd a way—that I cannot keep my eyes from her. I never saw anything so *outré!* Those curls! This must be a fancy of her own. I see nobody else looking like her. I must go and ask her whether it is an Irish fashion. Shall I? Yes, I will—I declare I will; and you shall see how she takes it—whether she colours."

He was gone immediately; and Emma soon saw him standing before Miss Fairfax, and talking to her; but as to its effect on the young lady, as he had improvidently placed himself exactly between them, exactly in front of Miss Fairfax, she could absolutely distinguish nothing.

Before he could return to his chair it was taken by Mrs. Weston.

"This is the luxury of a large party," said she; "one can get near everybody, and say everything. My dear Emma, I am longing to talk to you. I have been making discoveries and forming plans, just like yourself, and I must tell them while the idea is fresh. Do you know how Miss Bates and her niece came here?"

"How! They were invited, were not they?"

"Oh yes—but how they were conveyed hither? the manner of their coming?"

"They walked, I conclude. How else could they come?"

"Very true. Well, a little while ago it occurred to me how very sad it would be to have Jane Fairfax walking home again, late at night, and cold as the nights are now. And as I looked at her, though I never saw her appear to more advantage, it struck me that she was heated, and would therefore be particularly liable to take cold. Poor girl! I could not bear the idea of it; so, as soon as Mr. Weston came into the room, and I could get at him, I spoke to him about the carriage. You may guess how readily he came into my wishes; and having his approbation, I made my way directly to Miss Bates, to assure her that the carriage would be at her service before it took us home; for I thought it would be making her comfortable at once. Good soul! she was as grateful as possible, you may be sure. 'Nobody was ever so fortunate as herself!'—but with many, many thanks —'there was no occasion to trouble us, for Mr. Knightley's carriage had brought, and was to take them home again.' I was quite surprised; very glad, I am sure; but really quite surprised. Such a very kind attention— and so thoughtful an attention!—the sort of thing that so few men would think of. And, in short, from knowing his usual ways, I am very much inclined to think that it was for their accommodation the carriage was used at all. I do suspect he would not have had a pair of horses for himself, and that it was only as an excuse for assisting them."

"Very likely," said Emma, "nothing more likely. I know no man more likely than Mr. Knightley to do the sort of thing—to do anything really good-natured, useful, considerate, or benevolent. He is not a gallant man, but he is a very humane one; and this, considering Jane Fairfax's ill-health, would appear a case of humanity to him; and for an act of un-ostentatious kindness there is nobody whom I would fix on more than on Mr. Knightley. I know he had horses to-day, for we arrived together; and I laughed at him about it, but he said not a word that could betray."

"Well," said Mrs. Weston, smiling, "you give him credit for more simple, disinterested benevolence in this instance than I do; for while Miss Bates was speaking, a suspicion darted into my head, and I have never been able to get it out again. The more I think of it, the more prob-able it appears. In short, I have made a match between Mr. Knightley and Jane Fairfax. See the consequence of keeping you company! What do you say to it?"

"Mr. Knightley and Jane Fairfax!" exclaimed Emma. "Dear Mrs. Weston, how could you think of such a thing? Mr. Knightley! Mr. Knightley must not marry! You would not have little Henry cut out from Donwell? Oh no, no; Henry must have Donwell. I cannot at all consent to Mr. Knightley's marrying; and I am sure it is not at all likely. I am amazed that you should think of such a thing."

"My dear Emma, I have told you what led me to think of it. I do not want the match—I do not want to injure dear little Henry—but the idea has been given me by circumstances; and if Mr. Knightley really wished to marry, you would not have him refrain on Henry's account, a boy of six years old, who knows nothing of the matter?"

"Yes, I would. I could not bear to have Henry supplanted. Mr. Knightley marry! No, I have never had such an idea, and I cannot adopt it now. And Jane Fairfax, too, of all women!"

"Nay, she has always been a first favourite with him, as you very well know."

"But the imprudence of such a match!"

"I am not speaking of its prudence—merely its probability."

"I see no probability in it, unless you have any better foundation than what you mention. His good-nature, his humanity, as I tell you, would be quite enough to account for the horses. He has a great regard for the Bateses, you know, independent of Jane Fairfax—and is always glad to show them attention. My dear Mrs. Weston, do not take to match-making. You do it very ill. Jane Fairfax mistress of the Abbey? Oh no, no—every feeling revolts. For his own sake, I would not have had him do so mad a thing."

"Imprudent, if you please—but not mad. Excepting inequality of fortune, and perhaps a little disparity of age, I can see nothing unsuitable."

"But Mr. Knightley does not want to marry. I am sure he has not the least idea of it. Do not put it into his head. Why should he marry? He is as happy as possible by himself; with his farm, and his sheep, and his library, and all the parish to manage; and he is extremely fond of his brother's children. He has no occasion to marry, either to fill up his time or his heart."

"My dear Emma, as long as he thinks so, it is so; but if he really loves Jane Fairfax——"

"Nonsense! He does not care about Jane Fairfax. In the way of love, I am sure he does not. He would do any good to her, or her family; but——"

"Well," said Mrs. Weston, laughing, "perhaps the greatest good he could do them would be to give Jane such a respectable home."

"If it would be good to her I am sure it would be evil to himself—a very shameful and degrading connection. How would he bear to have Miss Bates belonging to him? To have her haunting the Abbey, and thanking him all day long for his great kindness in marrying Jane? 'So very kind and obliging! But he always had been such a very kind neighbour.' And then fly off, through half a sentence, to her mother's old petticoat. 'Not that it was such a very old petticoat either—for still it would last a great while—and, indeed, she must thankfully say that their petticoats were all very strong.' "

"For shame, Emma! Do not mimic her. You divert me against my conscience. And, upon my word, I do not think Mr. Knightley would be much disturbed by Miss Bates. Little things do not irritate him. She might talk on; and if he wanted to say anything himself, he would only talk louder, and drown her voice. But the question is not, whether it would be a bad connection for him, but whether he wishes it; and I think he does. I have heard him speak, and so must you, so very highly of Jane Fairfax! The interest he takes in her—his anxiety about her health—his concern that she should have no happier prospect! I have heard him express himself so warmly on those points. Such an admirer of her performance on the pianoforte, and of her voice. I have heard him say that he could listen to her for ever. Oh! and I had almost forgotten one idea that occurred to me—this pianoforte that has been sent here by somebody—though we have all been so well satisfied to consider it a present from the Campbells, may it not be from Mr. Knightley? I cannot help suspecting him. I think he is just the person to do it, even without being in love."

"Then it can be no argument to prove that he is in love. But I do not think it is at all a likely thing for him to do. Mr. Knightley does nothing mysteriously."

"I have heard him lamenting her having no instrument repeatedly; oftener than I should suppose such a circumstance would in the common course of things occur to him."

"Very well; and if he had intended to give her one, he would have told her so."

"There might be scruples of delicacy, my dear Emma. I have a very strong notion that it comes from him. I am sure he was particularly silent when Mrs. Cole told us of it at dinner."

"You take up an idea, Mrs. Weston, and run away with it, as you have many a time reproached me with doing. I see no sign of attachment. I believe nothing of the pianoforte, and proof only shall convince me that Mr. Knightley has any thought of marrying Jane Fairfax."

They combated the point some time longer in the same way, Emma rather gaining ground over the mind of her friend; for Mrs. Weston was the most used of the two to yield; till a little bustle in the room showed them that tea was over, and the instrument in preparation; and at the same moment, Mr. Cole approaching to entreat Miss Woodhouse would do them the honour of trying it. Frank Churchill, of whom, in the eagerness of her conversation with Mrs. Weston, she had been seeing nothing except that he had found a seat by Miss Fairfax, followed Mr. Cole, to add his very pressing entreaties; and as, in every respect, it suited Emma best to lead, she gave a very proper compliance.

She knew the limitations of her own powers too well to attempt more than she could perform with credit; she wanted neither taste nor spirit in the little things which are generally acceptable, and could accompany her own voice well. One accompaniment to her song took her agreeably by surprise; a second, slightly, but correctly taken by Frank Churchill. Her pardon was duly begged at the close of the song, and everything usual followed. He was accused of having a delightful voice, and a perfect knowledge of music, which was properly denied; and that he knew nothing of the matter, and had no voice at all, roundly asserted. They sang together once more, and Emma would then resign her place to Miss Fairfax, whose performance, both vocal and instrumental, she never could attempt to conceal from herself, was infinitely superior to her own.

With mixed feelings she seated herself at a little distance from the numbers round the instrument, to listen. Frank Churchill sang again. They had sung together once or twice, it appeared, at Weymouth. But the sight of Mr. Knightley among the most attentive soon drew away half Emma's mind; and she fell into a train of thinking on the subject of Mrs. Weston's suspicions, to which the sweet sounds of the united voices gave only momentary interruptions. Her objections to Mr. Knightley's marrying did not in the least subside. She could see nothing but evil in it. It would be a great disappointment to Mr. John Knightley, consequently to Isabella. A real injury to the children—a most mortifying change and material loss to them all—a very great deduction from her father's daily comfort—and, as to herself, she could not at all endure the idea of Jane Fairfax at Donwell Abbey. A Mrs. Knightley for them all to give way to! No—Mr. Knightley must never marry. Little Henry must remain the heir of Donwell.

Presently Mr. Knightley looked back, and came and sat down by her. They talked at first only of the performance. His admiration was certainly very warm; yet she thought, but for Mrs. Weston, it would not have struck her. As a sort of touchstone, however, she began to speak of his kindness in conveying the aunt and niece; and though his answer was in the spirit of cutting the matter short, she believed it to indicate only his disinclination to dwell on any kindness of his own.

"I often feel concern," said she, "that I dare not make *our* carriage more useful on such occasions. It is not that I am without the wish; but you know how impossible my father would deem it that James should put to for such a purpose."

"Quite out of the question, quite out of the question," he replied; "but you must often wish it, I am sure." And he smiled with such seeming pleasure at the conviction, that she must proceed another step.

"This present from the Campbells," said she—"this pianoforte is very kindly given."

"Yes," he replied, and without the smallest apparent embarrassment. "But they would have done better had they given her notice of it. Surprises are foolish things. The pleasure is not enhanced, and the inconvenience is often considerable. I should have expected better judgment in Colonel Campbell."

From that moment Emma could have taken her oath that Mr. Knightley had had no concern in giving the instrument. But whether he were entirely free from peculiar attachment—whether there were no actual preference—remained a little longer doubtful. Toward the end of Jane's second song her voice grew thick.

"That will do," said he, when it was finished, thinking aloud; "you have sung quite enough for one evening; now be quiet."

Another song, however, was soon begged for. "One more; they would not fatigue Miss Fairfax on any account, and would only ask for one more." And Frank Churchill was heard to say, "I think you could manage this without effort; the first part is so very trifling. The strength of the song falls on the second."

Mr. Knightley grew angry.

"That fellow," said he, indignantly, "thinks of nothing but showing off his own voice. This must not be." And touching Miss Bates, who at that moment passed near, "Miss Bates, are you mad, to let your niece sing herself hoarse in this manner? Go, and interfere. They have no mercy on her."

Miss Bates, in her real anxiety for Jane, could hardly stay even to be grateful, before she stepped forward and put an end to all further singing. Here ceased the concert part of the evening, for Miss Woodhouse and Miss Fairfax were the only young lady performers; but soon (within five minutes) the proposal of dancing—originating nobody exactly knew where—was so effectually promoted by Mr. and Mrs. Cole that everything was rapidly cleared away, to give proper space. Mrs. Weston, capital in her country-dances, was seated, and beginning an irresistible waltz; and Frank Churchill, coming up with most becoming gallantry to Emma, had secured her hand, and led her up to the top.

While waiting till the other young people could pair themselves off, Emma found time, in spite of the compliments she was receiving on her voice and her taste, to look about, and see what became of Mr. Knightley. This would be a trial. He was no dancer in general. If he were to be very alert in engaging Jane Fairfax now it might augur something. There was no immediate appearance. No; he was talking to Mrs. Cole—he was looking on unconcerned; Jane was asked by somebody else, and he was still talking to Mrs. Cole.

Emma had no longer an alarm for Henry; his interest was yet safe; and she led off the dance with genuine spirit and enjoyment. Not more than five couples could be mustered; but the rarity and the suddenness of it made it very delightful, and she found herself well matched in a partner. They were a couple worth looking at.

Two dances, unfortunately, were all that could be allowed. It was growing late, and Miss Bates became anxious to get home, on her mother's account. After some attempts, therefore, to be permitted to begin again, they were obliged to thank Mrs. Weston, look sorrowful, and have done.

"Perhaps it is as well," said Frank Churchill, as he attended Emma to her carriage. "I must have asked Miss Fairfax, and her languid dancing would not have agreed with me after yours."

Chapter 27

EMMA did not repent her condescension in going to the Coles. The visit afforded her many pleasant recollections the next day, and all that she might be supposed to have lost on the side of dignified seclusion must be amply repaid in the splendour of popularity. She must have delighted the Coles—worthy people; who deserve to be made happy! and left a name behind her that would not soon die away.

Perfect happiness, even in memory, is not common; and there were two points on which she was not quite easy. She doubted whether she had not transgressed the duty of woman by woman, in betraying her suspicions of Jane Fairfax's feelings to Frank Churchill. It was hardly right; but it had been so strong an idea that it would escape her, and his submission to all that she told was a compliment to her penetration, which made it difficult for her to be quite certain that she ought to have held her tongue.

The other circumstances of regret related also to Jane Fairfax, and there she had no doubt. She did unfeignedly and unequivocally regret the inferiority of her own playing and singing. She did most heartily grieve over the idleness of her childhood; and sat down and practised vigorously an hour and a half.

She was then interrupted by Harriet's coming in; and if Harriet's praise could have satisfied her, she might soon have been comforted.

"Oh, if I could but play as well as you and Miss Fairfax!"

"Don't class us together, Harriet. My playing is no more like hers than a lamp is like sunshine."

"Oh dear, I think you play the best of the two. I think you play quite as well as she does. I am sure I had much rather hear you. Everybody last night said how well you played."

"Those who knew anything about it must have felt the difference. The truth is, Harriet, that my playing is just good enough to be praised, but Jane Fairfax's is much beyond it."

"Well, I always shall think that you play quite as well as she does, or that if there is any difference nobody would ever find it out. Mr. Cole said how much taste you had! and Mr. Frank Churchill talked a great deal about your taste, and that he valued taste much more than execution."

"Ah, but Jane Fairfax has them both, Harriet."

"Are you sure? I saw she had execution, but I did not know she had any taste. Nobody talked about it; and I hate Italian singing; there is no understanding a word of it. Besides, if she does play so very well, you know, it is no more than she is obliged to do, because she will have to teach. The Coxes were wondering last night whether she would get into any great family. How did you think the Coxes looked?"

"Just as they always do—very vulgar."

"They told me something," said Harriet, rather hesitatingly, "but it is nothing of any consequence."

Emma was obliged to ask what they had told her, though fearful of its producing Mr. Elton.

"They told me that Mr. Martin dined with them last Saturday."

"Oh!"

"He came to their father upon some business, and he asked him to stay to dinner."

"Oh!"

"They talked a great deal about him, especially Anne Cox. I do not know what she meant, but she asked me if I thought I should go and stay there again next summer."

"She meant to be impertinently curious, just as such as Anne Cox should be."

"She said he was very agreeable the day he dined there. He sat by her at dinner. Miss Nash thinks either of the Coxes would be very glad to marry him."

"Very likely: I think they are, without exception, the most vulgar girls in Highbury."

Harriet had business at Ford's. Emma thought it most prudent to go with her. Another accidental meeting with the Martins was possible, and in her present state, would be dangerous.

Harriet, tempted by everything, and swayed by half a word, was always very long at a purchase; and while she was still hanging over muslins and changing her mind Emma went to the door for amusement. Much could not be hoped from the traffic of even the busiest part of Highbury:—Mr. Perry walking hastily by; Mr. William Cox letting himself in at the office-door; Mr. Cole's carriage horses returning from exercise; or a stray letter-boy on an obstinate mule, were the liveliest objects she could presume to expect; and when her eyes fell only on the butcher with his tray, a tidy old woman travelling homewards from shop with her full basket, two curs quarrelling over a dirty bone, and a string of dawdling children round the baker's little bow-window eyeing the ginger bread, she knew she had no reason to complain, and was amused enough; quite enough still to stand at the door. A mind lively and at ease can do with seeing nothing, and can see nothing that does not answer.

She looked down the Randalls road. The scene enlarged:—two persons appeared: Mrs. Weston and her son-in-law. They were walking into Highbury; to Hartfield of course; they were stopping, however, in the first place at Mrs. Bates's, whose house was a little nearer Randalls than Ford's, and had all but knocked when Emma caught their eye. Immediately they crossed the road and came forward to her; and the agreeableness of yesterday's engagement seemed to give fresh pleasure to the present meeting. Mrs. Weston informed her that she was going to call on the Bateses, in order to hear the new instrument.

"For my companion tells me," said she, "that I absolutely promised Miss Bates last night that I would come this morning. I was not aware of it myself. I did not know that I had fixed a day; but as he says I did I am going now."

"And while Mrs. Weston pays her visit, I may be allowed, I hope," said Frank Churchill, "to join your party and wait for her at Hartfield, if you are going home."

Mrs. Weston was disappointed.

"I thought you meant to go with me. They would be very much pleased."

"Me! I should be quite in the way. But, perhaps, I may be equally in the way here. Miss Woodhouse looks as if she did not want me. My aunt always sends me off when she is shopping. She says I fidget her to death; and Miss Woodhouse looks as if she could almost say the same. What am I to do?"

"I am here on no business of my own," said Emma, "I am only waiting for my friend. She will probably have soon done, and then we shall go home. But you had better go with Mrs. Weston and hear the instrument."

"Well, if you advise it. But" (with a smile) "if Colonel Campbell should have employed a careless friend, and if it should prove to have an indifferent tone, what shall I say? I shall be no support to Mrs. Weston. She might do very well by herself. A disagreeable truth would be palatable through her lips, but I am the wretchedest being in the world at a civil falsehood."

"I do not believe any such thing," replied Emma; "I am persuaded that you can be as insincere as your neighbours, when it is necessary; but there is no reason to suppose the instrument is indifferent. Quite otherwise, indeed, if I understood Miss Fairfax's opinion last night."

"Do come with me," said Mrs. Weston, "if it be not very disagreeable to you. It need not detain us long. We will go to Hartfield afterwards. We will follow them to Hartfield. I really wish you to call with me; it will be felt so great an attention—and I always thought you meant it."

He could say no more; and, with the hope of Hartfield to reward him, returned with Mrs. Weston to Mrs. Bates's door. Emma watched them in, and then joined Harriet at the interesting counter, trying with all the force of her own mind, to convince her that if she wanted plain muslin, it was of no use to look at figured: and that a blue ribbon, be it ever so beautiful, would still never match her yellow pattern. At last it was all settled, even to the destination of the parcel.

"Should I send it to Mrs. Goddard's, ma'am?" asked Mrs. Ford. "Yes—no—yes, to Mrs. Goddard's. Only my pattern gown is at Hartfield. No, you shall send it to Hartfield, if you please. But then Mrs. Goddard will want to see it. And I could take the pattern gown home any day. But I shall want the ribbon directly; so it had better go to Hartfield—at least the ribbon. You could make it into two parcels, Mrs. Ford, could not you?"

"It is not worth while, Harriet, to give Mrs. Ford the trouble of two parcels."

"No more it is."

"No trouble in the world, ma'am," said the obliging Mrs. Ford.

"Oh, but indeed I would much rather have it only in one. Then, if you please, you shall send it all to Mrs. Goddard's—I do not know—no, I think, Miss Woodhouse, I may just as well have it sent to Hartfield, and take it home with me at night. What do you advise?"

"That you do not give another half-second to the subject. To Hartfield, if you please, Mrs. Ford."

"Aye, that will be much best," said Harriet, quite satisfied; "I should not at all like to have it sent to Mrs. Goddard's."

Voices approached the shop, or rather, one voice and two ladies; Mrs. Weston and Miss Bates met them at the door.

"My dear Miss Woodhouse," said the latter, "I am just run across to entreat the favour of you to come and sit down with us a little while, and give us your opinion of our new instrument—you and Miss Smith. How do you do, Miss Smith? Very well, I thank you. And I begged Mrs. Weston to come with me, that I might be sure of succeeding."

"I hope Mrs. Bates and Miss Fairfax are——"

"Very well, I am much obliged to you. My mother is delightfully well; and Jane caught no cold last night. How is Mr. Woodhouse? I am so glad to hear such a good account. Mrs. Weston told me you were here. 'Oh, then,' said I, 'I must run across; I am sure Miss Woodhouse will allow me just to run across and entreat her to come in: my mother will be so very happy to see her; and now we are such a nice party, she cannot refuse.' 'Aye, pray do,' said Mr. Frank Churchill, 'Miss Woodhouse's opinion of the instrument will be worth having.' 'But,' said I, 'I shall be more sure of succeeding if one of you will go with me.' 'Oh,' said he, 'wait half a minute, till I have finished my job;' for, would you believe it, Miss Woodhouse, there he is, in the most obliging manner in the world, fastening in the rivet of my mother's spectacles. The rivet came out, you know, this morning; so very obliging! For my mother had no use of her spectables—could not put them on. And, by-the-bye, everybody ought to have two pair of spectacles: they should indeed. Jane said so. I meant to take them over to John Saunders the first thing I did, but something or other hindered me all the morning; first one thing, then another, there is no saying what: you know. At one time Patty came to say she thought the kitchen chimney wanted sweeping. 'Oh,' said I, 'Patty, do not come with your bad news to me. Here is the rivet of your mistress's spectacles out.' Then the baked apples came home; Mrs. Wallis sent them by her boy; they are extremely civil and obliging to us, the Wallises, always. I have heard some people say that Mrs. Wallis can be uncivil and give a very rude answer; but we have never known anything but the greatest attention from them. And it cannot be for the value of our custom now, for what is our consumption of bread, you know? only three of us. Besides, dear Jane at present—and she really eats nothing—makes such a shocking breakfast, you would be quite frightened if you saw it. I dare not let my mother know how little she eats; so I say one thing, and then I say another, and it passes off. But about the middle of the day she gets hungry, and there is nothing she likes so well as these baked apples, and they are extremely wholesome; for I took the opportunity the other day of asking Mr. Perry; I happened to meet him in the street. Not that I had any doubt before. I have so often heard Mr. Woodhouse recommend a baked apple. I believe it is the only way that Mr. Woodhouse thinks the fruit thoroughly wholesome. We have apple dumplings, however, very often. Patty makes an excellent apple dumpling. Well, Mrs. Weston, you have prevailed, I hope, and these ladies will oblige us."

Emma would be "very happy to wait on Mrs. Bates," etc., and they did at last move out of the shop, with no further delay from Miss Bates than:

"How do you do, Mrs. Ford? I beg your pardon; I did not see you before. I hear you have a charming collection of new ribbons from town. Jane came back delighted yesterday. Thank ye, the gloves do very well-- only a little too large about the wrist; but Jane is taking them in."

"What was I talking of?" said she, beginning again when they were all in the street.

Emma wondered on what, of all the medley, she would fix.

"I declare I cannot recollect what I was talking of. Oh, my mother's spectacles! So very obliging of Mr. Frank Churchill! 'Oh!' said he, 'I do think I can fasten the rivet; I like a job of this kind excessively.' Which, you know, showed him to be so very—Indeed I must say that, much as I had heard of him before, and much as I had expected, he very far exceeds anything—I do congratulate you, Mrs. Weston, most warmly. He seems everything the fondest parent could—'Oh!' said he, 'I can fasten the rivet. I like a job of that sort excessively.' I never shall forget his manner. And when I brought out the baked apples from the closet, and hoped our friends would be so very obliging as to take some, 'Oh!' said he, directly, 'there is nothing in the way of fruit half so good, and these are the finest-looking home-baked apples I ever saw in my life.' That, you know, was so very—And I am sure, by his manner, it was no compliment. Indeed they are very delightful apples, and Mrs. Wallis does them full justice, only we do not have them baked more than twice, and Mr. Woodhouse made us promise to have them done three times; but Miss Woodhouse will be so good as not to mention it. The apples themselves are the very finest sort for baking, beyond a doubt; all from Donwell—some of Mr. Knightley's most liberal supply. He sends us a sack every year; and certainly there never was such a keeping apple anywhere as one of his trees—I believe there is two of them. My mother says the orchard was always famous in her younger days. But I was really quite shocked the other day; for Mr. Knightley called one morning, and Jane was eating these apples, and we talked about them, and said how much she enjoyed them, and he asked whether we were not got to the end of our stock. 'I am sure you must be,' said he, 'and I will send you another supply; for I have a great many more than I can ever use. William Larkins let me keep a larger quantity than usual this year. I will send you some more, before they get good for nothing.' So I begged he would not—for really as to ours being gone, I

could not absolutely say that we had a great many left—it was but half a
dozen indeed; but they should be all kept for Jane; and I could not at all
bear that he should be sending us more, so liberal as he had been already;
and Jane said the same. And when he was gone she almost quarrelled with
me—no, I should not say quarrelled, for we never had a quarrel in our
lives—but she was quite distressed that I owned the apples were so nearly
gone; she wished I had made him believe we had a great many left. 'Oh,'
said I, 'my dear, I did say as much as I could.' However, the very same
evening William Larkins came over with a large basket of apples, the same
sort of apples, a bushel at least, and I was very much obliged, and went
down and spoke to William Larkins, and said everything, as you may
suppose. William Larkins is such an old acquaintance! I am always glad
to see him. But, however, I found afterwards from Patty that William said
it was all the apples of *that* sort his master had; he had brought them all—
and now his master had not one left to bake or boil. William did not seem
to mind it himself, he was so pleased to think his master had sold so many;
for William, you know, thinks more of his master's profit than anything;
but Mrs. Hodges, he said, was quite displeased at their being all sent away.
She could not bear that her master should not be able to have another
apple-tart this spring. He told Patty this, but bid her not mind it, and be
sure not to say anything to us about it, for Mrs. Hodges *would* be cross
sometimes and as long as so many sacks were sold it did not signify who
ate the remainder. And so Patty told me, and I was excessively shocked
indeed! I would not have Mr. Knightley know anything about it for the
world. He would be so very—I wanted to keep it from Jane's knowledge;
but, unluckily, I had mentioned it before I was aware."

Miss Bates had just done as Patty opened the door; and her visitors
walked upstairs, without having any regular narration to attend to, pursued only by the sounds of her desultory good-will.

"Pray, take care, Mrs. Weston, there is a step at the turning. Pray, take
care, Miss Woodhouse, ours is rather a dark staircase—rather darker and
narrower than one could wish. Miss Smith, pray take care. Miss Woodhouse, I am quite concerned, I am sure you hit your foot. Miss Smith, the
step at the turning."

Chapter 28

THE appearance of the little sitting-room as they entered was tranquillity itself; Mrs. Bates, deprived of her usual employment, slumber-
ing on one side of the fire, Frank Churchill, at a table, near her, most
deedily occupied about her spectacles, and Jane Fairfax, standing with
her back to them, intent on her pianoforte.

Busy as he was, however, the young man was yet able to show a most
happy countenance on seeing Emma again.

"This is a pleasure," said he, in rather a low voice, "coming at least ten minutes earlier than I had calculated. You find me trying to be useful; tell me if you think I shall succeed."

"What!" said Mrs. Weston, "have not you finished it yet? you would not earn a very good livelihood as a working silversmith at this rate."

"I have not been working uninterruptedly," he replied, "I have been assisting Miss Fairfax in trying to make her instrument stand steadily; it was not quite firm; an unevenness in the floor, I believe. You see we have been wedging one leg with paper. This was very kind of you to be persuaded to come. I was almost afraid you would be hurrying home."

He contrived that she should be seated by him; and was sufficiently employed in looking out the best baked apple for her, and trying to make her help or advise him in his work, till Jane Fairfax was quite ready to sit down to the pianoforte again. That she was not immediately ready Emma did suspect to arise from the state of her nerves; she had not yet possessed the instrument long enough to touch it without emotion; she must reason herself into the power of performance; and Emma could not but pity such feelings, whatever their origin, and could not but resolve never to expose them to her neighbour again.

At last Jane began, and though the first bars were feebly given, the powers of the instrument were gradually done full justice to. Mrs. Weston had been delighted before, and was delighted again; Emma joined her in all her praise; and the pianoforte, with every proper discrimination, was pronounced to be altogether of the highest promise.

"Whoever Colonel Campbell might employ," said Frank Churchill, with a smile at Emma, "the person has not chosen ill. I heard a good deal of Colonel Campbell's taste at Weymouth; and the softness of the upper notes I am sure is exactly what he and *all that party* would particularly prize. I dare say, Miss Fairfax, that he either gave his friend very minute directions, or wrote to Broadwood himself. Do not you think so?"

Jane did not look round. She was not obliged to hear. Mrs. Weston had been speaking to her at the same moment.

"It is not fair," said Emma, in a whisper; "mine was a random guess. Do not distress her."

He shook his head with a smile, and looked as if he had very little doubt and very little mercy. Soon afterwards he began again:

"How much your friends in Ireland must be enjoying your pleasure on this occasion, Miss Fairfax. I dare say they often think of you, and wonder which will be the day, the precise day, of the instrument's coming to hand. Do you imagine Colonel Campbell knows the business to be going forward just at this time? Do you imagine it to be the consequence of an immediate commission from him, or that he may have sent only a general direction, an order indefinite as to time, to depend upon contingencies and conveniences?"

He paused. She could not but hear; she could not avoid answering:

"Till I have a letter from Colonel Campbell," said she, in a voice of forced calmness, "I can imagine nothing with any confidence. It must be all conjecture."

"Conjecture! aye, sometimes one conjectures right, and sometimes one conjectures wrong. I wish I could conjecture how soon I shall make this rivet quite firm. What nonsense one talks, Miss Woodhouse, when hard at work, if one talks at all; your real workmen, I suppose, hold their tongues; but we, gentlemen labourers, if we get hold of a word—Miss Fairfax said something about conjecturing. There, it is done. I have the pleasure, madam" (to Mrs. Bates), "of restoring your spectacles, healed for the present."

He was very warmly thanked both by mother and daughter; to escape a little from the latter he went to the pianoforte, and begged Miss Fairfax, who was still sitting at it, to play something more.

"If you are very kind," said he, "it will be one of the waltzes we danced last night; let me live them over again. You did not enjoy them as I did: you appeared tired the whole time. I believe you were glad we danced no longer; but I would have given worlds—all the worlds one ever has to give —for another half-hour."

She played.

"What felicity it is to hear a tune again which *has* made one happy! If I mistake not, that was danced at Weymouth."

She looked up at him for a moment, coloured deeply, and played something else. He took some music from a chair near the pianoforte, and turning to Emma, said:

"Here is something quite new to me. Do you know it? Cramer. And here are a new set of Irish melodies. That, from such a quarter, one might expect. This was all sent with the instrument. Very thoughtful of Colonel Campbell, was not it? He knew Miss Fairfax could have no music here. I honour that part of the attention particularly; it shows it to have been so thoroughly from the heart. Nothing hastily done, nothing incomplete. True affection only could have prompted it."

Emma wished he would be less pointed, yet could not help being amused; and when, on glancing her eye towards Jane Fairfax, she caught the remains of a smile, when she saw that with all the deep blush of consciousness there had been a smile of secret delight, she had less scruple in the amusement, and much less compunction with respect to her. This amiable, upright, perfect Jane Fairfax was apparently cherishing very reprehensible feelings.

He brought all the music to her, and they looked it over together. Emma took the oportunity of whispering:

"You speak too plain. She must understand you."

"I hope she does. I would have her understand me. I am not in the least ashamed of my meaning."

"But really, I am half ashamed, and wish I had never taken up the idea."

"I am very glad you did, and that you communicated it to me. I have now a key to all her odd looks and ways. Leave shame to her. If she does wrong, she ought to feel it."

"She is not entirely without it, I think."

"I do not see much sign of it. She is playing 'Robin Adair' at this moment—*his* favourite."

Shortly afterwards Miss Bates, passing near the window, descried Mr. Knightley on horseback not far off.

"Mr. Knightley, I declare! I must speak to him, if possible, just to thank him. I will not open the window here; it would give you all cold; but I can go into my mother's room, you know. I dare say he will come in when he knows who is here. Quite delightful to have you all meet so! Our little room so honoured!"

She was in the adjoining chamber while she still spoke, and, opening the casement there, immediately called Mr. Knightley's attention, and every syllable of their conversation was as distinctly heard by the others as if it had passed within the same apartment.

"How d'ye do? How d'ye do? Very well, I thank you. So obliged to you for the carriage last night. We were just in time; my mother just ready for us. Pray come in; do come in. You will find some friends here."

So began Miss Bates; and Mr. Knightley seemed determined to be heard in his turn, for most resolutely and commandingly did he say—

"How is your niece, Miss Bates? I want to inquire after you all, but particularly your niece. How is Miss Fairfax? I hope she caught no cold last night? How is she to-day? Tell me how Miss Fairfax is."

And Miss Bates was obliged to give a direct answer before he would hear her in anything else. The listeners were amused; and Mrs. Weston gave Emma a look of particular meaning. But Emma still shook her head in steady scepticism.

"So obliged to you! so very much obliged to you for the carriage," resumed Miss Bates.

He cut her short with—

"I am going to Kingston. Can I do anything for you?"

"Oh, dear! Kingston—are you? Mrs. Cole was saying the other day she wanted something from Kingston."

"Mrs. Cole has servants to send; can I do anything for *you?*"

"No, I thank you. But do come in. Who do you think is here? Miss Woodhouse and Miss Smith; so kind as to call to hear the new pianoforte. Do put up your horse at the Crown, and come in."

"Well," said he, in a deliberating manner, "for five minutes, perhaps."

"And here is Mrs. Weston and Mr. Frank Churchill too! Quite delightful! so many friends!"

"No, not now, I thank you. I could not stay two minutes. I must get on to Kingston as fast as I can."

"Oh, do come in! They will be so very happy to see you."

"No, no; your room is full enough. I will call another day and hear the pianoforte."

"Well, I am so sorry! Oh, Mr. Knightley, what a delightful party last night! how extremely pleasant! Did you ever see such dancing? Was not it delightful? Miss Woodhouse and Mr. Frank Churchill; I never saw anything equal to it."

"Oh, very delightful, indeed! I can say nothing less, for I suppose Miss Woodhouse and Mr. Frank Churchill are hearing everything that passes. And" (raising his voice still more) "I do not see why Miss Fairfax should not be mentioned too. I think Miss Fairfax dances very well; and Mrs. Weston is the very best country-dance player, without exception, in England. Now, if your friends have any gratitude, they will say something pretty loud about you and me in return; but I cannot stay to hear it."

"Oh, Mr. Knightley, one moment more; something of consequence—so shocked! Jane and I are both so shocked about the apples!"

"What is the matter now?"

"To think of your sending us all your store of apples! You said you had a great many, and now you have not one left. We really are so shocked! Mrs. Hodges may well be angry. William Larkins mentioned it here. You should not have done it, indeed you should not. Ah, he is off! He never can bear to be thanked. But I thought he would have stayed now, and it would have been a pity not to have mentioned—well" (returning to the room), "I have not been able to succeed. Mr. Knightley cannot stop. He is going to Kingston. He asked me if he could do anything——"

"Yes." said Jane, "we heard his kind offers; we heard everything."

"Oh, yes, my dear, I dare say you might; because, you know, the door was open, and the window was open, and Mr. Knightley spoke loud. You must have heard everything, to be sure. 'Can I do anything for you at Kingston?' said he; so I just mentioned—Oh, Miss Woodhouse, must you be going? You seem but just come; so very obliging of you."

Emma found it really time to be at home; the visit had already lasted long; and, on examining watches, so much of the morning was perceived to be gone, that Mrs. Weston and her companion, taking leave also, could allow themselves only to walk with the two young ladies to Hartfield gates before they set off for Randalls.

Chapter 29

IT may be possible to do without dancing entirely. Instances have been known of young people passing many, many months successively without being at any ball of any description, and no material injury accrue either to body or mind; but when a beginning is made—when the felicities of rapid motion have once been, though slightly, felt—it must be a very heavy set that does not ask for more.

Frank Churchill had danced once at Highbury, and longed to dance again; and the last half-hour of an evening which Mr. Woodhouse was persuaded to spend with his daughter at Randalls was passed by the two young people in schemes on the subject. Frank's was the first idea, and his the greatest zeal in pursuing it; for the lady was the best judge of the difficulties, and the most solicitous for accommodation and appearance. But still she had inclination enough for showing people again how delightfully Mr. Frank Churchill and Miss Woodhouse danced—for doing that in which she need not blush to compare herself with Jane Fairfax—and even for simple dancing itself, without any of the wicked aids of vanity—to assist him first in pacing out the room they were in to see what it could be made to hold—and then in taking the dimensions of the other parlour, in the hope of discovering, in spite of all that Mr. Weston could say of their exactly equal size, that it was a little the largest.

His first proposition and request, that the dance begun at Mr. Cole's should be finished there—that the same party should be collected, and the same musician engaged—met with the readiest acquiescence. Mr. Weston entered into the idea with thorough enjoyment, and Mrs. Weston most willingly undertook to play as long as they could wish to dance; and the interesting employment had followed, of reckoning up exactly who there would be, and portioning out the indispensable division of space to every couple.

"You and Miss Smith and Miss Fairfax will be three, and the two Miss Coxes five," had been repeated many times over. "And there will be the two Gilberts, young Cox, my father, and myself, besides Mr. Knightley. Yes, that will be quite enough for pleasure. You and Miss Smith and Miss Fairfax will be three, and the two Miss Coxes five, and for five couple there will be plenty of room."

But soon it came to be on one side—

"But will there be good room for five couple? I really do not think there will."

On another—

"And, after all, five couple are not enough to make it worth while to stand up. Five couple are nothing when one thinks seriously about it. It will not do to *invite* five couple. It can be allowable only as the thought of the moment."

Somebody said that *Miss* Gilbert was expected at her brother's, and must be invited with the rest. Somebody else believed *Mrs.* Gilbert would have danced the other evening if she had been asked. A word was put in for a second young Cox! and at last, Mr. Weston naming one family of cousins who must be included, and another of very old acquaintance who could not be left out, it became a certainty that the five couple would be at least ten, and a very interesting speculation in what possible manner they could be disposed of.

The doors of the two rooms were just opposite each other. "Might not they use both rooms, and dance across the passage?" It seemed the best scheme; and yet it was not so good but that many of them wanted a better. Emma said it would be awkward; Mrs. Weston was in distress about the supper; and Mr. Woodhouse opposed it earnestly on the score of health.

It made him so very unhappy, indeed, that it could not be persevered in.

"Oh, no," said he, "it would be the extreme of imprudence. I could not bear it for Emma! Emma is not strong. She would catch a dreadful cold. So would poor little Harriet. So you would all. Mrs. Weston, you would be quite laid up; do not let them talk of such a wild thing; pray do not let them talk of it. That young man" (speaking lower) "is very thoughtless. Do not tell his father, but that young man is not quite the thing. He has been opening the doors very often this evening, and keeping them open very inconsiderately. He does not think of the draught. I do not mean to set you against him, but indeed he is not quite the thing."

Mrs. Weston was sorry for such a charge. She knew the importance of it, and said everything in her power to do it away. Every door was now closed, the passage plan given up, and the first scheme, of dancing only in the room they were in, resorted to again; and with such goodwill on Frank Churchill's part, that the space which a quarter of an hour before had been deemed barely sufficient for five couple was now endeavoured to be made out quite enough for ten.

"We were too magnificent," said he. "We allowed unnecessary room. Ten couple may stand here very well."

Emma demurred. "It would be a crowd—a sad crowd; and what could be worse than dancing without space to turn in?"

"Very true," he gravely replied; "it was very bad." But still he went on measuring, and still he ended with:

"I think there will be very tolerable room for ten couple."

"No, no," said she, "you are quite unreasonable. It would be dreadful to be standing so close. Nothing can be further from pleasure than to be dancing in a crowd—and a crowd in a little room."

"There is no denying it," he replied. "I agree with you exactly. A crowd in a little room—Miss Woodhouse, you have the art of giving pictures in a few words. Exquisite, quite exquisite! Still, however, having proceeded so far, one is unwilling to give the matter up. It would be a disappointment to my father—and altogether—I do not know that—I am rather of opinion that ten couple might stand here very well."

Emma perceived that the nature of his gallantry was a little self-willed, and that he would rather oppose than lose the pleasure of dancing with her; but she took the compliment, and forgave the rest. Had she intended ever to *marry* him, it might have been worth while to pause and consider and try to understand the value of his preference, and the character of his temper; but for all the purposes of their acquaintance he was quite amiable enough.

Before the middle of the next day he was at Hartfield; and he entered the room with such an agreeable smile as certified the continuance of the scheme. It soon appeared that he came to announce an improvement.

"Well, Miss Woodhouse," he almost immediately began, "your inclination for dancing has not been quite frightened away, I hope, by the terrors of my father's little rooms. I bring a new proposal on the subject: a thought of my father's, which waits only your approbation to be acted upon. May I hope for the honour of your hand for the two first dances of this little projected ball, to be given, not at Randalls, but at the Crown Inn?"

"The Crown!"

"Yes; if you and Mr. Woodhouse see no objection, and I trust you cannot, my father hopes his friends will be so kind as to visit him there. Better accommodations he can promise them, and not a less grateful welcome than at Randalls. It is his own idea. Mrs. Weston sees no objection to it, provided you are satisfied. This is what we all feel. Oh, you were perfectly right! Ten couple, in either of the Randalls rooms, would have been insufferable—dreadful! I felt how right you were the whole time, but was too anxious for securing *anything* to like to yield. Is not it a good exchange? You consent—I hope you consent?"

"It appears to me a plan that nobody can object to, if Mr. and Mrs. Weston do not. I think it admirable; and, as far as I can answer for myself, shall be most happy—it seems the only improvement that could be. Papa, do you not think it an excellent improvement?"

She was obliged to repeat and explain it before it was fully comprehended; and then, being quite new, further representations were necessary to make it acceptable.

"No; he thought it very far from an improvement—a very bad plan—much worse than the other. A room at an inn was always damp and dangerous, never properly aired, or fit to be inhabited. If they must dance, they had better dance at Randalls. He had never been in the room at the Crown in his life—did not know the people who kept it by sight. Oh no—a very bad plan. They would catch worse colds at the Crown than anywhere."

"I was going to observe, sir," said Frank Churchill, "that one of the great recommendations of this change would be the very little danger of anybody's catching cold—so much less danger at the Crown than at Randalls! Mr. Perry might have reason to regret the alteration, but nobody else could."

"Sir," said Mr. Woodhouse, rather warmly, "you are very much mistaken if you suppose Mr. Perry to be that sort of character. Mr. Perry is extremely concerned when any of us are ill. But I do not understand how the room at the Crown can be safer for you than your father's house."

"From the very circumstance of its being larger, sir. We shall have no occasion to open the windows at all—not once the whole evening; and it is that dreadful habit of opening the windows, letting in cold air upon heated bodies, which (as you well know, sir) does the mischief."

"Open the windows! But surely, Mr. Churchill, nobody would think of opening the windows at Randalls. Nobody could be so imprudent! I never heard of such a thing. Dancing with open windows! I am sure neither your father nor Mrs. Weston (poor Miss Taylor that was) would suffer it."

"Ah! sir—but a thoughtless young person will sometimes step behind a window-curtain, and throw up a sash, without its being suspected. I have often known it done myself."

"Have you, indeed, sir! Bless me! I never could have supposed it. But I live out of the world, and am often astonished at what I hear. However, this does make a difference; and perhaps, when we come to talk it over—but these sort of things require a good deal of consideration. One cannot resolve upon them in a hurry. If Mr. and Mrs. Weston will be so obliging as to call here one morning we may talk it over, and see what can be done."

"But, unfortunately, sir, my time is so limited——"

"Oh," interrupted Emma, "there will be plenty of time for talking everything over. There is no hurry at all. If it can be contrived to be at the Crown, papa, it will be very convenient for the horses. They will be so near their own stable."

"So they will, my dear. That is a great thing. Not that James ever complains; but it is right to spare our horses when we can. If I could be sure of the rooms being thoroughly aired—but is Mrs. Stokes to be trusted? I doubt it. I do not know her, even by sight."

"I can answer for everything of that nature, sir, because it will be under Mrs. Weston's care. Mrs. Weston undertakes to direct the whole."

"There, papa! Now you must be satisfied—our own dear Mrs. Weston, who is carefulness itself. Do not you remember what Mr. Perry said, so many years ago, when I had the measles? 'If *Miss Taylor* undertakes to wrap Miss Emma up, you need not have any fears, sir.' How often have I heard you speak of it as such a compliment to her!"

"Aye, very true, Mr. Perry did say so. I shall never forget it. Poor little Emma! You were very bad with the measles; that is, you would have been very bad, but for Perry's great attention. He came four times a day for a week. He said, from the first, it was a very good sort—which was our great comfort; but the measles are a dreadful complaint. I hope whenever poor Isabella's little ones have the measles she will send for Perry."

"My father and Mrs. Weston are at the Crown at this moment," said Frank Churchill, "examining the capabilities of the house. I left them there and came on to Hartfield, impatient for your opinion, and hoping you might be persuaded to join them and give your advice on the spot. I was desired to say so from both. It would be the greatest pleasure to them if you could allow me to attend you there. They can do nothing satisfactorily without you."

Emma was most happy to be called to such a council: and, her father engaging to think it all over while she was gone, the two young people set off together without delay for the Crown. There were Mr. and Mrs. Weston; delighted to see her and receive her approbation, very busy and very happy in their different way: she, in some little distress; and he, finding everything perfect.

"Emma," said she, "this paper is worse than I expected. Look! in places you see it is dreadfully dirty; and the wainscot is more yellow and forlorn than anything I could have imagined."

"My dear, you are too particular," said her husband. "What does all that signify? You will see nothing of it by candle-light. It will be as clean as Randalls by candle-light. We never see anything of it on our club-nights."

The ladies here probably exchanged looks which meant, "Men never know when things are dirty or not"; and the gentlemen perhaps thought each to himself, "Women will have their little nonsenses and needless cares."

One perplexity, however, arose, which the gentlemen did not disdain: it regarded a supper-room. At the time of the ball-room's being built suppers had not been in question; and a small card-room adjoining was the only addition. What was to be done? This card-room would be wanted as a card-room now; or, if cards were conveniently voted unnecessary by their four selves, still was it not too small for any comfortable supper? Another room of much better size might be secured for the purpose; but it was at the other end of the house, and a long awkward passage must be gone through to get at it. This made a difficulty. Mrs. Weston was afraid of draughts for the young people in that passage; and neither Emma nor the gentlemen could tolerate the prospect of being miserably crowded at supper.

Mrs. Weston proposed having no regular supper; merely sandwiches etc., set out in the little room; but that was scouted as a wretched suggestion. A private dance without sitting down to supper, was pronounced an infamous fraud upon the rights of men and women; and Mrs. Weston must not speak of it again. She then took another line of expediency, and looking into the doubtful room, observed:

"I do not think it *is* so very small. We shall not be many, you know."

And Mr. Weston at the same time, walking briskly with long steps through the passage, was calling out:

"You talk a great deal of the length of this passage, my dear. It is a mere nothing after all; and not the least draught from the stairs."

"I wish," said Mrs. Weston, "one could know which arrangement our guests in general would like best. To do what would be most generally pleasing must be our object—if one could but tell what that would be."

"Yes, very true," cried Frank, "very true. You want your neighbours' opinions. I do not wonder at you. If one could ascertain what the chief of them—the Coles, for instance, they are not far off. Shall I call upon them? Or Miss Bates? She is still nearer. And I do not know whether Miss Bates is not as likely to understand the inclinations of the rest of the people as anybody. I think we do want a larger council. Suppose I go and invite Miss Bates to join us?"

"Well—if you please," said Mrs. Weston, rather hesitating. "If you think she will be of any use."

"You will get nothing to the purpose from Miss Bates," said Emma;

"she will be all delight and gratitude, but she will tell you nothing. She will not even listen to your questions. I see no advantage in consulting Miss Bates."

"But she is so amusing, so extremely amusing! I am very fond of hearing Miss Bates talk. And I need not bring the whole family, you know."

Here Mr. Weston joined them, and on hearing what was proposed gave it his decided approbation.

"Aye, do, Frank; go and fetch Miss Bates, and let us end the matter at once. She will enjoy the scheme, I am sure; and I do not know a more proper person for showing us how to do away difficulties. Fetch Miss Bates. We are growing a little too nice. She is a standing lesson of how to be happy. But fetch them both. Invite them both."

"Both, sir? Can the old lady——?"

"The old lady! No, the young lady, to be sure! I shall think you a great blockhead, Frank, if you bring the aunt without the niece."

"Oh! I beg your pardon, sir. I did not immediately recollect. Undoubtedly, if you wish it, I will endeavour to persuade them both." And away he ran.

Long before he reappeared, attending the short, neat, brisk-moving aunt, and her elegant niece—Mrs. Weston, like a sweet-tempered woman and a good wife, had examined the passage again, and found the evils of it much less than she had supposed before—indeed, very trifling; and here ended the difficulties of decision. All the rest, in speculation at least, was perfectly smooth. All the minor arrangements of table and chair, lights and music, tea and supper, made themselves; or were left as mere trifles, to be settled at any time between Mrs. Weston and Mrs. Stokes. Everybody invited was certain to come; Frank had already written to Enscombe to propose staying a few days beyond his fortnight, which could not possibly be refused. And a delightful dance it was to be.

Most cordially, when Miss Bates arrived, did she agree that it must. As a counsellor she was not wanted; but as an approver (a much safer character) she was truly welcome. Her approbation, at once general and minute, warm and incessant, could not but please; and for another half-hour they were all walking to and fro between the different rooms, some suggesting, some attending, and all in happy enjoyment of the future. The party did not break up without Emma's being positively secured for the two first dances by the hero of the evening, nor without her overhearing Mr. Weston whisper to his wife, "He has asked her, my dear. That's right. I knew he would!"

Chapter 30

ONE thing only was wanting to make the prospect of the ball completely satisfactory to Emma—its being fixed for a day within the granted term of Frank Churchill's stay in Surrey; for, in spite of Mr. Weston's confidence, she could not think it so very impossible that the Churchills might not allow their nephew to remain a day beyond his fortnight. But this was not judged feasible. The preparations must take their time, nothing could be properly ready till the third week were entered on, and for a few days they must be planning, proceeding, and hoping in uncertainty, at the risk—in her opinion, the great risk—of its being all in vain.

Enscombe, however, was gracious—gracious in fact, if not in word. His wish of staying longer evidently did not please; but it was not opposed. All was safe and prosperous; and as the removal of one solicitude generally makes way for another, Emma being now certain of her ball, began to adopt as the next vexation Mr. Knightley's provoking indifference about it. Either because he did not dance himself, or because the plan had been formed without his being consulted, he seemed resolved that it should not interest him, determined against its exciting any present curiosity, or affording him any future amusement. To her voluntary communications Emma could get no more approving reply than:

"Very well. If the Westons think it worth while to be at all this trouble for a few hours of noisy entertainment I have nothing to say against it, but that they shall not choose pleasures for me. Oh, yes! I must be there; I could not refuse; and I will keep as much awake as I can; but I would rather be at home, looking over William Larkins's week's account; much rather, I confess. Pleasure in seeing dancing! Not I, indeed—I never look at it—I do not know who does. Fine dancing, I believe, like virtue, must be its own reward. Those who are standing by are usually thinking of something very different."

This Emma felt was aimed at her; and it made her quite angry. It was not in compliment to Jane Fairfax, however, that he was so indifferent, or so indignant; he was not guided by *her* feelings in reprobating the ball, for *she* enjoyed the thought of it to an extraordinary degree. It made her animated—open-hearted; she voluntarily said:

"Oh! Miss Woodhouse, I hope nothing may happen to prevent the ball! What a disappointment it would be! I do look forward to it, I own, with *very* great pleasure."

It was not to oblige Jane Fairfax, therefore, that he would have preferred the society of William Larkins. No!—she was more and more convinced that Mrs. Weston was quite mistaken in that surmise. There was a great deal of friendly and of compassionate attachment on his side—but no love.

Alas! there was soon no leisure for quarrelling with Mr. Knightley. Two days of joyful security were immediately followed by the overthrow of everything. A letter arrived from Mr. Churchill to urge his nephew's instant return. Mrs. Churchill was unwell—far too unwell to do without him; she had been in a very suffering state (so said her husband) when writing to her nephew two days before, though from her usual unwillingness to give pain, and constant habit of never thinking of herself, she had not mentioned it; but now she was too ill to trifle, and must entreat him to set off for Enscombe without delay.

The substance of this letter was forwarded to Emma, in a note from Mrs. Weston, instantly. As to his going, it was inevitable. He must be gone within a few hours, though without feeling any real alarm for his aunt, to lessen his repugnance. He knew her illnesses; they never occurred but for her own convenience.

Mrs. Weston added, "that he could only allow himself time to hurry to Highbury, after breakfast, and take leave of the few friends there whom he could suppose to feel any interest in him; and that he might be expected at Hartfield very soon."

This wretched note was the finale of Emma's breakfast. When once it had been read there was no doing anything but lament and exclaim. The loss of the ball—the loss of the young man—and all that the young man might be feeling! It was too wretched! Such a delightful evening as it would have been! Everybody so happy! And she and her partner the happiest! "I said it would be so," was the only consolation.

Her father's feelings were quite distinct. He thought principally of Mrs. Churchill's illness, and wanted to know how she was treated; and as for the ball, it was shocking to have dear Emma disappointed; but they would all be safer at home.

Emma was ready for her visitor some time before he appeared; but if this reflected at all upon his impatience, his sorrowful look and total want of spirits when he did come might redeem him. He felt the going away almost too much to speak of it. His dejection was most evident. He sat really lost in thought for the first few minutes; and when rousing himself it was only to say:

"Of all horrid things leave-taking is the worst."

"But you will come again," said Emma. "This will not be your only visit to Randalls."

"Ah!"—(shaking his head)—"the uncertainty of when I may be able to return! I shall try for it with a zeal! It will be the object of all my thoughts and cares! And if my uncle and aunt go to town this spring—but I am afraid—they did not stir last spring—I am afraid it is a custom gone for ever."

"Our poor ball must be quite given up."

"Ah! that ball! Why did we wait for anything? Why not seize the pleasure at once? How often is happiness destroyed by preparation, foolish preparation? You told us it would be so. Oh! Miss Woodhouse, why are you always so right?"

"Indeed, I am very sorry to be right in this instance. I would much rather have been merry than wise."

"If I can come again, we are still to have our ball. My father depends on it. Do not forget your engagement."

Emma looked graciously.

"Such a fortnight as it has been!" he continued; "every day more precious and more delightful than the day before! Every day making me less fit to bear any other place. Happy those who can remain at Highbury!"

"As you do us such ample justice now," said Emma, laughing, "I will venture to ask whether you did not come a little doubtfully at first? Do not we rather surpass your expectations? I am sure we do. I am sure you did not much expect to like us. You would not have been so long in coming if you had had a pleasant idea of Highbury."

He laughed rather consciously; and though denying the sentiment, Emma was convinced that it had been so.

"And you must be off this very morning?"

"Yes; my father is to join me here: we shall walk back together, and I must be off immediately. I am almost afraid that every moment will bring him."

"Not five minutes to spare even for your friends Miss Fairfax and Miss Bates? How unlucky! Miss Bates's powerful, argumentative mind might have strengthened yours."

"Yes—I *have* called there; passing the door, I thought it better. It was a right thing to do. I went in for three minutes, and was detained by Miss Bates's being absent. She was out; and I felt it impossible not to wait till she came in. She is a woman that one may, that one *must* laugh at; but that one would not wish to slight. It was better to pay my visit, then——"

He hesitated, got up, walked to a window.

"In short," said he, "perhaps, Miss Woodhouse—I think you can hardly be quite without suspicion——"

He looked at her, as if wanting to read her thoughts. She hardly knew what to say. It seemed like the forerunner of something absolutely serious, which she did not wish. Forcing herself to speak, therefore, in the hope of putting it by, she calmly said:

"You are quite in the right; it was most natural to pay your visit, then——"

He was silent. She believed he was looking at her; probably reflecting on what she had said, and trying to understand the manner. She heard him sigh. It was natural for him to feel that he had *cause* to sigh. He could not believe her to be encouraging him. A few awkward moments passed and he sat down again; and in a more determined manner said:

"It was something to feel that all the rest of my time might be given to Hartfield. My regard for Hartfield is most warm——"

He stopped again, rose again, and seemed quite embarrassed. He was more in love with her than Emma had supposed; and who can say how it might have ended, if his father had not made his appearance? Mr. Woodhouse soon followed; and the necessity of exertion made him composed.

A very few minutes more, however, completed the present trial. Mr.

Weston, always alert when business was to be done, and as incapable of procrastinating any evil that was inevitable as of foreseeing any that was doubtful, said, "It was time to go"; and the young man, though he might and did sigh, could not but agree, and rise to take leave.

"I shall hear about you all," said he; "that is my chief consolation. I shall hear of everything that is going on among you. I have engaged Mrs. Weston to correspond with me. She has been so kind as to promise it. Oh! the blessing of a female correspondent, when one is really interested in the absent! She will tell me everything. In her letters I shall be at dear Highbury again."

A very friendly shake of the hand, a very earnest "Good-bye," closed the speech, and the door had soon shut out Frank Churchill. Short had been the notice—short their meeting; he was gone; and Emma felt so sorry to part, and foresaw so great a loss to their little society from his absence as to begin to be afraid of being too sorry, and feeling it too much.

It was a sad change. They had been meeting almost every day since his arrival. Certainly his being at Randalls had given great spirit to the last two weeks—indescribable spirit; the idea, the expectation of seeing him which every morning had brought, the assurance of his attentions, his liveliness, his manners! It had been a very happy fortnight, and forlorn must be the sinking from it into the common course of Hartfield days. To complete every other recommendation, he had *almost* told her that he loved her. What strength or what constancy of affection he might be subject to was another point; but at present she could not doubt his having a decidedly warm admiration, a conscious preference of herself; and this persuasion, joined to all the rest, made her think that she *must* be a little in love with him, in spite of every previous determination against it.

"I certainly must," said she. "This sensation of listlessness, weariness, stupidity, this disinclination to sit down and employ myself, this feeling of everything's being dull and insipid about the house! I must be in love; I should be the oddest creature in the world if I were not—for a few weeks at least. Well, evil to some is always good to others. I shall have many fellow-mourners for the ball, if not for Frank Churchill; but Mr. Knightley will be happy. He may spend the evening with his dear William Larkins now if he likes."

Mr. Knightley, however, showed no triumphant happiness. He could not say that he was sorry on his own account; his very cheerful look would have contradicted him if he had; but he said, and very steadily, that he was sorry for the disappointment of the others, and with considerable kindness added:

"You, Emma, who have so few opportunities of dancing, you are really out of luck; you are very much out of luck!"

It was some days before she saw Jane Fairfax, to judge of her honest regret in this woeful change; but when they did meet her composure was odious. She had been particularly unwell, however, suffering from head-ache to a degree which made her aunt declare that, had the ball taken place, she did not think Jane could have attended it; and it was charity to impute some of her unbecoming indifference to the languor of ill-health.

Chapter 31

EMMA continued to entertain no doubt of her being in love. Her ideas only varied as to the how much. At first she thought it was a good deal; and afterwards but little. She had great pleasure in hearing Frank Churchill talked of; and, for his sake, greater pleasure than ever in seeing Mr. and Mrs. Weston; she was very often thinking of him, and quite impatient for a letter, that she might know how he was, how were his spirits, how was his aunt, and what was the chance of his coming to Randalls again this spring. But, on the other hand, she could not admit herself to be unhappy, nor, after the first morning, to be less disposed for employ-ment than usual; she was still busy and cheerful; and, pleasing as he was, she could yet imagine him to have faults; and further, though thinking of him so much, and, as she sat drawing or working, forming a thousand amusing schemes for the progress and close of their attachment, fancying interesting dialogues, and inventing elegant letters; the conclusion of every imaginary declaration on his side was that she *refused him*. Their affection was always to subside into friendship. Everything tender and charming was to mark their parting; but still they were to part. When she became sensible of this, it struck her that she could not be very much in love; for, in spite of her previous and fixed determination never to quit her father, never to marry, a strong attachment certainly must produce more of a struggle than she could foresee in her own feelings.

"I do not find myself making any use of the word *sacrifice*," said she. "In not one of all my clever replies, my delicate negatives, is there any allusion to making a sacrifice. I do suspect that he is not really necessary to my happiness. So much the better. I certainly will not persuade myself to feel more than I do. I am quite enough in love. I should be sorry to be more."

Upon the whole, she was equally contented with her view of his feelings.

"*He* is undoubtedly very much in love—everything denotes it—very much in love indeed!—and when he comes again, if his affection continue, I must be on my guard not to encourage it. It would be most inexcusable to do otherwise, as my own mind is quite made up. Not that I imagine he can think I have been encouraging him hitherto. No; if he had believed me at all to share his feelings he would not have been so wretched. Could he have thought himself encouraged, his looks and language at parting would have been different. Still, however, I must be on my guard. This is in the supposition of his attachment continuing what it now is; but I do not know that I expect it will; I do not look upon him to be quite the sort of man—I do not altogether build upon his steadiness or constancy. His feelings are warm, but I can imagine them rather changeable. Every consideration of the subject, in short, makes me thankful that my happiness is not more deeply involved. I shall do very well again after a little while—and then, it will be a good thing over; for they say everybody is in love once in their lives, and I shall have been let off easily."

When his letter to Mrs. Weston arrived Emma had the perusal of it; and she read it with a degree of pleasure and admiration which made her at first shake her head over her own sensations, and think she had under-valued their strength. It was a long, well-written letter, giving the particulars of his journey and of his feelings, expressing all the affection, gratitude and respect which was natural and honourable, and describing everything exterior and local that could be supposed attractive, with spirit and precision. No suspicious flourishes now of apology or concern; it was the language of real feeling towards Mrs. Weston; and the transition from Highbury to Enscombe, the contrast between the places in some of the first blessings of social life, was just enough touched on to show how keenly it was felt, and how much more might have been said but for the restraints of propriety. The charm of her own name was not wanting. *Miss Woodhouse* appeared more than once, and never without a something of pleasing connection, either a compliment to her taste, or a remembrance of what she had said; and in the very last time of its meeting her eye, unadorned as it was by any such broad wreath of gallantry, she yet could discern the effect of her influence, and acknowledge the greatest compliment perhaps of all conveyed. Compressed into the very lowest vacant corner were these words: "I had not a spare moment on Tuesday, as you know, for Miss Woodhouse's beautiful little friend. Pray make my excuses and adieux to her." This, Emma could not doubt, was all for herself. Harriet was remembered only from being *her* friend. His information and prospects, as to Enscombe, were neither worse nor better than had been anticipated; Mrs. Churchill was recovering, and he dared not yet, even in his own imagination, fix a time for coming to Randalls again.

Gratifying, however, and stimulative as was the letter in the material part, its sentiments, she yet found, when it was folded up and returned to Mrs. Weston, that it had not added any lasting warmth—that she could still do without the writer, and that he must learn to do without her. Her intentions were unchanged. Her resolution of refusal only grew more interesting by the addition of a scheme for his subsequent consolation and happiness. His recollection of Harriet, and the words which clothed it—the "beautiful little friend"—suggested to her the idea of Harriet's succeeding her in his affections. Was it impossible? No. Harriet undoubtedly was greatly his inferior in understanding; but he had been very much struck with the loveliness of her face and the warm simplicity of her manner; and all the probabilities of circumstance and connection were in her favour. For Harriet it would be advantageous and delightful indeed.

"I must not dwell upon it," said she; "I must not think of it. I know the danger of indulging such speculations. But stranger things have happened; and when we cease to care for each other as we do now, it will be the means of confirming us in that sort of true disinterested friendship which I can already look forward to with pleasure."

It was well to have a comfort in store on Harriet's behalf, though it might be wise to let the fancy touch it seldom; for evil in that quarter was at hand. As Frank Churchill's arrival had succeeded Mr. Elton's engagement in the conversation of Highbury, as the latest interest had entirely borne down the first, so now, upon Frank Churchill's disappearance, Mr. Elton's concerns were assuming the most irresistible form. His wedding-day was named. He would soon be among them again—Mr. Elton and his bride. There was hardly time to talk over the first letter from Enscombe before "Mr. Elton and his bride" was in everybody's mouth, and Frank Churchill was forgotten. Emma grew sick at the sound. She had had three weeks of happy exemption from Mr. Elton; and Harriet's mind, she had been willing to hope, had been lately gaining strength. With Mr. Weston's ball in view, at least, there had been a great deal of insensibility to other things; but it was now too evident that she had not attained such a state of composure as could stand against the actual approach—new carriage, bell-ringing, and all.

Poor Harriet was in a flutter of spirits which required all the reasonings, and soothings, and attentions of every kind that Emma could give. Emma felt that she could not do too much for her, that Harriet had a right to all her ingenuity and all her patience; but it was heavy work to be for ever convincing without producing any effect; for ever agreed to, without being able to make their opinions the same. Harriet listened submissively, and said, "It was very true; it was just as Miss Woodhouse described—it was not worth while to think about them—and she would not think about them any longer." But no change of subject could avail, and the next half-hour saw her as anxious and restless about the Eltons as before. At last Emma attacked her on another ground.

"Your allowing yourself to be so occupied and so unhappy about Mr. Elton's marrying, Harriet, is the strongest reproach you can make *me*. You could not give me a greater reproof for the mistake I fell into. It was all my doing, I know. I have not forgotten it, I assure you. Deceived myself, I did very miserably deceive you; and it will be a painful reflection to me for ever. Do not imagine me in danger of forgetting it."

Harriet felt this too much to utter more than a few words of eager exclamation. Emma continued:

"I have not said, exert yourself, Harriet, for my sake; think less, talk less of Mr. Elton for my sake; because, for your own sake rather, I would wish it to be done, for the sake of what is more important than my comfort—a habit of self-command in you, a consideration of what is your duty, an attention to propriety, an endeavour to avoid the suspicions of others, to save your health and credit and restore your tranquillity. These are the motives which I have been pressing on you. They are very important, and sorry I am that you cannot feel them sufficiently to act upon them. My being saved from pain is a very secondary consideration. I want you to save yourself from greater pain. Perhaps I may sometimes have felt that Harriet would not forget what was due—or rather, what would be kind by me."

This appeal to her affections did more than all the rest. The idea of wanting gratitude and consideration for Miss Woodhouse, whom she really loved extremely, made her wretched for a while; and when the violence of grief was comforted away, still remained powerful enough to prompt what was right, and support her in it very tolerably.

"You, who have been the best friend I ever had in my life! Want gratitude to you! Nobody is equal to you! I care for nobody as I do for you! Oh, Miss Woodhouse, how ungrateful I have been!"

Such expressions, assisted as they were by everything that look and manner could do, made Emma feel that she had never loved Harriet so well, nor valued her affection so highly before.

"There is no charm equal to tenderness of heart," said she afterwards to herself. "There is nothing to be compared to it. Warmth and tenderness of heart, with an affectionate, open manner, will beat all the clearness of head in the world, for attraction: I am sure it will. It is tenderness of heart which makes my dear father so generally beloved—which gives Isabella all her popularity. I have it not; but I know how to prize and respect it. Harriet is my superior in all the charm and all the felicity it gives. Dear Harriet! I would not change you for the clearest-headed, longest-sighted, best-judging female breathing. Oh, the coldness of a Jane Fairfax! Harriet is worth a hundred such: and for a wife—a sensible man's wife—it is invaluable. I mention no names; but happy the man who changes Emma for Harriet!"

Chapter 32

Mrs. Elton was first seen at church: but though devotion might be interrupted, curiosity could not be satisfied by a bride in a pew, and it must be left for the visits in form which were then to be paid, to settle whether she were very pretty indeed, or only rather pretty, or not pretty at all.

Emma had feelings, less of curiosity than of pride or propriety, to make her resolve on not being the last to pay her respects: and she made a point of Harriet's going with her, that the worst of the business might be gone through as soon as possible.

She could not enter the house again, could not be in the same room to which she had with such vain artifice retreated three months ago, to lace up her boot, without *recollecting*. A thousand vexatious thoughts would recur. Compliments, charades, and horrible blunders; and it was not to be supposed that poor Harriet should not be recollecting too; but she be-haved very well, and was only rather pale and silent. The visit was of course short! And there was so much embarrassment and occupation of mind to shorten it that Emma would not allow herself entirely to form an opinion of the lady, and on no account to give one, beyond the nothing-meaning terms of being "elegantly dressed, and very pleasing."

She did not really like her. She would not be in a hurry to find fault, but she suspected that there was no elegance; ease, but not elegance. She was almost sure that for a young woman, a stranger, a bride, there was too much ease. Her person was rather good; her face not unpretty; but neither feature nor air, nor voice, nor manner were elegant. Emma thought, at least, it would turn out so.

As for Mr. Elton, his manners did not appear—but no, she would not permit a hasty or a witty word from herself about his manners. It was an awkward ceremony at any time to be receiving wedding visits; and a man had need be all grace to acquit himself well through it. The woman was better off; she might have the assistance of fine clothes, and the privilege of bashfulness; but the man had only his own good sense to depend on; and when she considered how peculiarly unlucky poor Mr. Elton was in being in the same room at once with the woman he had just married, the woman he had wanted to marry, and the woman whom he had been expected to marry, she must allow him to have the right to look as little wise, and to be as much affectedly, and as little really, easy as could be.

"Well, Miss Woodhouse," said Harriet, when they had quitted the house and after waiting in vain for her friend to begin; "well, Miss Wood-house" (with a gentle sigh), "what do you think of her? Is not she very charming?"

There was a little hesitation in Emma's answer.

"Oh! yes—very—a very pleasing young woman."

"I think her beautiful, quite beautiful."

"Very nicely dressed, indeed; a remarkably elegant gown."

"I am not at all surprised that he should have fallen in love."

"Oh! no; there is nothing to surprise one at all; a pretty fortune, and she came in his way."

"I dare say," returned Harriet, sighing again, "I dare say she was very much attached to him."

"Perhaps she might; but it is not every man's fate to marry the woman who loves him best. Miss Hawkins, perhaps, wanted a home, and thought this the best offer she was likely to have."

"Yes," said Harriet, earnestly, "and well she might; nobody could ever have a better. Well, I wish them happy with all my heart. And now, Miss Woodhouse, I do not think I shall mind seeing them again. He is just as superior as ever; but being married, you know, it is quite a different thing. No, indeed, Miss Woodhouse, you need not be afraid; I can sit and admire him now without any great misery. To know that he has not thrown himself away is such a comfort! She does seem a charming young woman, just what he deserves. Happy creature! He called her 'Augusta.' How delightful!"

When the visit was returned Emma made up her mind. She could then see more and judge better. From Harriet's happening not to be at Hartfield, and her father's being present to engage Mr. Elton, she had a quarter of an hour of the lady's conversation to herself, and could composedly attend to her; and the quarter of an hour quite convinced her that Mrs. Elton was a vain woman, extremely well satisfied with herself, and thinking much of her own importance; that she meant to shine and be very superior; but with manners which had been formed in a bad school; pert and familiar; that all her notions were drawn from one set of people, and one style of living; that, if not foolish, she was ignorant, and that her society would certainly do Mr. Elton no good.

Harriet would have been a better match. If not wise or refined herself, she would have connected him with those who were; but Miss Hawkins, it might be fairly supposed, from her easy conceit, had been the best of her own set. The rich brother-in-law, near Bristol, was the pride of the alliance, and his place and his carriages were the pride of him.

The very first subject, after being seated, was Maple Grove, "My brother, Mr. Suckling's seat"; a comparison of Hartfield to Maple Grove. The grounds of Hartfield were small, but neat and pretty; and the house was modern and well built. Mrs. Elton seemed most favourably impressed by the size of the room, the entrance, and all that she could see or imagine. "Very like Maple Grove indeed! She was quite struck by the likeness! That room was the very shape and size of the morning-room at Maple Grove; her sister's favourite room." Mr. Elton was appealed to. "Was not it astonishingly like? She could really almost fancy herself at Maple Grove.

"And the staircase. You know, as I came in, I observed how very like the staircase was; placed exactly in the same part of the house. I really could not help exclaiming! I assure you, Miss Woodhouse, it is very delightful to me to be reminded of a place I am so extremely partial to as Maple Grove. I have spent so many happy months there!" (with a little sigh of sentiment). "A charming place, undoubtedly. Everybody who sees it is struck by its beauty; but to me it has been quite a home. Whenever you are transplanted, like me, Miss Woodhouse, you will understand how very delightful it is to meet with anything at all like what one has left behind. I always say this is quite one of the evils of matrimony."

Emma made as slight a reply as she could; but it was fully sufficient for Mrs. Elton, who only wanted to be talking herself.

"So extremely like Maple Grove! And it is not merely the house; the grounds, I assure you, as far as I could observe, are strikingly like. The laurels at Maple Grove are in the same profusion as here, and stand very much in the same way—just across the lawn; and I had a glimpse of a fine large tree, with a bench round it, which put me so exactly in mind! My brother and sister will be enchanted with this place. People who have extensive grounds themselves are always pleased with anything in the same style."

Emma doubted the truth of this sentiment. She had a great idea that people who had extensive grounds themselves cared very little for the extensive grounds of anybody else; but it was not worth while to attack an error so double-dyed, and therefore only said in reply:

"When you have seen more of this country I am afraid you will think you have overrated Hartfield. Surrey is full of beauties."

"Oh! yes, I am quite aware of that. It is the garden of England, you know. Surrey is the garden of England."

"Yes; but we must not rest our claims on that distinction. Many counties, I believe, are called the garden of England, as well as Surrey."

"No, I fancy not," replied Mrs. Elton, with a most satisfied smile. "I never heard any county but Surrey called so."

Emma was silenced.

"My brother and sister have promised us a visit in the spring, or summer at farthest," continued Mrs. Elton; "and that will be our time for exploring. While they are with us we shall explore a great deal, I dare say. They will have their barouche-landau, of course, which holds four perfectly; and therefore, without saying anything of *our* carriage, we should be able to explore the different beauties extremely well. They would hardly come in their chaise, I think, at that season of the year. Indeed, when the time draws on, I shall decidedly recommend their bringing the barouche-landau; it will be so very much preferable. When people come into a beautiful country of this sort, you know, Miss Woodhouse, one naturally wishes them to see as much as possible; and Mr. Suckling is extremely fond of exploring. We explored to King's-Weston twice last summer, in that way, most delightfully, just after their first having the barouche-landau. You have many parties of that kind here, I suppose, Miss Woodhouse, every summer?"

"No; not immediately here. We are rather out of distance of the very striking beauties which attract the sort of parties you speak of; and we are a very quiet set of people, I believe; more disposed to stay at home than engage in schemes of pleasure."

"Ah! there is nothing like staying at home for real comfort. Nobody can be more devoted to home than I am. I was quite a proverb for it at Maple Grove. Many a time has Selina said, when she has been going to Bristol, 'I really cannot get this girl to move from the house. I absolutely must go in by myself, though I hate being stuck up in the barouche-landau without a companion: but Augusta, I believe, with her own good-will, would never stir beyond the park paling.' Many a time has she said so; and yet I am no advocate for entire seclusion. I think, on the contrary, when people shut themselves up entirely from society, it is a very bad thing; and that it is much more advisable to mix in the world in a proper degree, without living in it either too much or too little. I perfectly understand your situation, however, Miss Woodhouse" (looking towards Mr. Woodhouse), "your father's state of health must be a great drawback. Why does not he try Bath? Indeed he should. Let me recommend Bath to you. I assure you I have no doubt of its doing Mr. Woodhouse good."

"My father tried it more than once, formerly, but without receiving any benefit, and Mr. Perry, whose name, I dare say, is not unknown to you, does not conceive it would be at all more likely to be useful now."

"Ah! that's a great pity; for I assure you, Miss Woodhouse, where the waters do agree, it is quite wonderful the relief they give. In my Bath life I have seen such instances of it! And it is so cheerful a place that it could not fail of being of use to Mr. Woodhouse's spirits, which, I understand, are sometimes much depressed. And as to its recommendations to *you*, I fancy I need not take much pains to dwell on them. The advantages of Bath to the young are pretty generally understood. It would be a charming introduction for you, who have lived so secluded a life; and I could immediately secure you some of the best society in the place. A line from me would bring you a little host of acquaintances; and my particular friend Mrs. Partridge, the lady I have always resided with when in Bath, would be most happy to show you any attentions, and would be the very person for you to go into public with."

It was as much as Emma could bear, without being impolite! The idea of her being indebted to Mrs. Elton for what was called an *introduction*— of her going into public under the auspices of a friend of Mrs. Elton's— probably some vulgar dashing widow—who, with the help of a boarder just made a shift to live! The dignity of Miss Woodhouse, of Hartfield, was sunk indeed!

She restrained herself, however, from any of the reproofs she could have given and only thanked Mrs. Elton coolly; "but their going to Bath was quite out of the question; and she was not perfectly convinced that the place might suit her better than her father." And then, to prevent further outrage and indignation, changed the subject directly.

"I do not ask whether you are musical, Mrs. Elton. Upon these occasions a lady's character generally precedes her; and Highbury has long known that you are a superior performer."

"Oh! no, indeed; I must protest against any such idea. A superior performer! Very far from it, I assure you: consider from how partial a quarter your information came. I am dotingly fond of music—passionately fond; and my friends say I am not entirely devoid of taste; but as to anything else, upon my honour my performance is *mediocre* to the last degree. You, Miss Woodhouse, I well know, play delightfully. I assure you it has been the greatest satisfaction, comfort, and delight to me to hear what a musical society I am got into. I absolutely cannot do without music; it is a necessary of life to me; and having always been used to a very musical society, both at Maple Grove and in Bath, it would have been a most serious sacrifice. I honestly said as much to Mr. E. when he was speaking of my future home, and expressing his fears lest the retirement of it should be disagreeable; and the inferiority of the house too—knowing what I had been accustomed to—of course he was not wholly without apprehension. When he was speaking of it in that way, I honestly said that *the world* I

could give up—parties, balls, plays—for I had no fear of retirement.
Blessed with so many resources within myself, the world was not necessary
to *me*. I could do very well without it. To those who had no resources it
was a different thing; but my resources made me quite independent. And
as to smaller-sized rooms than I had been used to, I really could not give
it a thought. I hoped I was perfectly equal to any sacrifice of that description. Certainly, I had been accustomed to every luxury at Maple Grove;
but I did assure him that two carriages were not necessary to my happiness, nor were spacious apartments. 'But,' said I, 'to be quite honest, I
do not think I can live without something of a musical society. I condition for nothing else; but, without music, life would be a blank to me.' "

"We cannot suppose," said Emma, smiling, "that Mr. Elton would
hesitate to assure you of there being a *very* musical society in Highbury;
and I hope you will not find he has outstepped the truth more than may be
pardoned, in consideration of the motive."

"No, indeed, I have no doubts at all on that head. I am delighted to find
myself in such a circle; I hope we shall have many sweet little concerts
together. I think, Miss Woodhouse, you and I must establish a musical
club, and have regular weekly meetings at your house, or ours. Will not it
be a good plan? If *we* exert ourselves, I think we shall not be long in want
of allies. Something of that nature would be particularly desirable for *me*,
as an inducement to keep me in practice; for married women, you know—
there is a sad story against them, in general. They are but too apt to give
up music."

"But you, who are so extremely fond of it—there can be no danger,
surely?"

"I should hope not; but really when I look around among my acquaintances, I tremble. Selina has entirely given up music; never touches the
instrument, though she played sweetly. And the same may be said of Mrs.
Jeffereys—Clara Partridge that was—and of the two Milmans, now Mrs.
Bird and Mrs. James Cooper; and of more than I can enumerate. Upon my
word, it is enough to put one in a fright. I used to be quite angry with
Selina; but, really, I begin now to comprehend that a married woman has
many things to call her attention. I believe I was half an hour this morning
shut up with my housekeeper."

"But everything of that kind," said Emma, "will soon be in so regular
a train——"

"Well," said Mrs. Elton, laughing, "we shall see."

Emma, finding her so determined upon neglecting her music, had
nothing more to say; and, after a moment's pause, Mrs. Elton chose
another subject.

"We have been calling at Randalls," said she, "and found them both
at home; and very pleasant people they seem to be. I like them extremely.
Mr. Weston seems an excellent creature—quite a first-rate favourite with
me already, I assure you. And *she* appears so truly good—there is some-

thing so motherly and kindhearted about her, that it wins upon one directly. She was your governess, I think?"

Emma was almost too much astonished to answer; but Mrs. Elton hardly waited for the affirmative before she went on.

"Having understood as much, I was rather astonished to find her so very ladylike. But she is really quite the gentlewoman."

"Mrs. Weston's manners," said Emma, "were always particularly good. Their propriety, simplicity, and elegance would make them the safest model for any young woman."

"And who do you think came in while we were there?"

Emma was quite at a loss. The tone implied some old acquaintance, and how could she possibly guess?

"Knightley!" continued Mrs. Elton; "Knightley himself! Was not it lucky? For, not being within when he called the other day, I had never seen him before; and of course, as so particular a friend of Mr. E.'s, I had a great curiosity. 'My friend Knightley' had been so often mentioned, that I was really impatient to see him; and I must do my *caro sposo* the justice to say that he need not be ashamed of his friend. Knightley is quite the gentleman; I like him very much. Decidedly, I think, a very gentlemanlike man."

Happily, it was now time to be gone. They were off, and Emma could breathe.

"Insufferable woman!" was her immediate exclamation. "Worse than I had supposed. Absolutely insufferable! Knightley! I could not have believed it. Knightley! never seen him in her life before and call him Knightley! and discover that he is a gentleman. A little upstart, vulgar being, with her Mr. E. and her *caro sposo*, and her resources, and all her air of pert pretension and underbred finery. Actually to discover that Mr. Knightley is a gentleman! I doubt whether he will return the compliment, and discover her to be a lady. I could not have believed it! And to propose that she and I should unite to form a musical club! One would fancy we were bosom friends! And Mrs. Weston! Astonished that the person who had brought me up should be a gentlewoman! Worse and worse! I never met with her equal. Much beyond my hopes! Harriet is disgraced by any comparison. Oh! what would Frank Churchill say to her if he were here? How angry and how diverted he would be! Ah! there I am thinking of him directly. Always the first person to be thought of! How I catch myself out! Frank Churchill comes as regularly into my mind——!"

All this ran so glibly through her thoughts, that by the time her father had arranged himself, after the bustle of the Eltons' departure, and was ready to speak, she was very tolerably capable of attending.

"Well, my dear," he deliberately began, "considering we never saw her before, she seems a very pretty sort of young lady; and I dare say she was very much pleased with you. She speaks a little too quick. A little quickness of voice there is which rather hurts the ear. But I believe I am nice; I do not like strange voices; and nobody speaks like you and poor Miss

Taylor. However, she seems a very obliging pretty-behaved young lady, and no doubt will make him a very good wife. Though I think he had better not have married. I made the best excuses I could for not having been able to wait on him and Mrs. Elton on this happy occasion: I said that I hoped I *should* in the course of the summer. But I ought to have gone before. Not to wait upon a bride is very remiss. Ah! it shows what a sad invalid I am! But I do not like the corner into Vicarage Lane."

"I dare say your apologies were accepted, sir. Mr. Elton knows you."

"Yes; but a young lady—a bride—I ought to have paid my respects to her if possible. It was being very deficient."

"But, my dear papa, you are no friend to matrimony; and therefore why should you be so anxious to pay your respects to a *bride?* It ought to be no recommendation to *you.* It is encouraging people to marry if you make so much of them."

"No, my dear, I never encouraged anybody to marry, but I would always wish to pay every proper attention to a lady—and a bride especially is never to be neglected. More is avowedly due to *her.* A bride, you know, my dear, is always the first in company, let the others be who they may."

"Well, papa, if this is not encouragement to marry I do not know what is. And I should never have expected you to be lending your sanction to such vanity-baits for poor young ladies."

"My dear, you do not understand me. This is a matter of mere common politeness and good-breeding, and has nothing to do with any encouragement to people to marry."

Emma had done. Her father was growing nervous, and could not understand *her.* Her mind returned to Mrs. Elton's offences and long, very long, did they occupy her.

Chapter 33

EMMA was not required, by any subsequent discovery, to retract her ill opinion of Mrs. Elton. Her observation had been pretty correct. Such as Mrs. Elton appeared to her on this second interview, such she appeared whenever they met again: self-important, presuming, familiar, ignorant, and ill-bred. She had a little beauty and a little accomplishment, but so little judgment that she thought herself coming with superior knowledge of the world, to enliven and improve a country neighbourhood; and conceived Miss Hawkins to have held such a place in society as Mrs. Elton's consequence only could surpass.

There was no reason to suppose Mr. Elton thought at all differently from his wife. He seemed not merely happy with her, but proud. He had the air of congratulating himself on having brought such a woman to Highbury as not even Miss Woodhouse could equal; and the greater part of her new acquaintance, disposed to commend, or not in the habit of judging, following the lead of Miss Bates's good-will, or taking it for granted that the bride must be as clever and as agreeable as she professed herself, were very well satisfied; so that Mrs. Elton's praise passed from one mouth to another as it ought to do, unimpeded by Miss Woodhouse, who readily continued her first contribution, and talked with a good grace of her being "very pleasant, and very elegantly dressed."

In one respect Mrs. Elton grew even worse than she had appeared at first. Her feelings altered towards Emma. Offended, probably, by the little encouragement which her proposals of intimacy met with, she drew back, in her turn, and gradually became much more cold and distant; and though the effect was agreeable, the ill-will which produced it was necessarily increasing Emma's dislike. Her manners, too—and Mr. Elton's—were unpleasant towards Harriet. They were sneering and negligent. Emma hoped it must rapidly work Harriet's cure; but the sensations which could prompt such behaviour sunk them both very much. It was not to be doubted that poor Harriet's attachment had been an offering to conjugal unreserve, and her own share in the story, under a colouring the least favourable to her, and the most soothing to him, had in all likelihood been given also. She was, of course, the object of their joint dislike. When they had nothing else to say, it must be always easy to begin abusing Miss Woodhouse; and the enmity which they dared not show in open disrespect to her found a broader vent in contemptuous treatment of Harriet.

Mrs. Elton took a great fancy to Jane Fairfax; and from the first. Not merely when a state of warfare with one young lady might be supposed to recommend the other, but from the very first; and she was not satisfied with expressing a natural and reasonable admiration, but without solicitation, or plea, or privilege, she must be wanting to assist and befriend her. Before Emma had forfeited her confidence, and about the third time of their meeting, she heard all Mrs. Elton's knight-errantry on the subject.

"Jane Fairfax is absolutely charming, Miss Woodhouse. I quite rave about Jane Fairfax. A sweet interesting creature. So mild and ladylike—and with such talents! I assure you I think she has very extraordinary talents. I do not scruple to say that she plays extremely well. I know enough of music to speak decidedly on that point. Oh! she is absolutely charming! You will laugh at my warmth, but, upon my word, I talk of nothing but Jane Fairfax—and her situation is so calculated to affect one! Miss Woodhouse, we must exert ourselves and endeavour to do something for her. We must bring her forward. Such talent as hers must not be suffered to remain unknown. I dare say you have heard those charming lines of the poet—

'Full many a flower is born to blush unseen
And waste its fragrance on the desert air.'

We must not allow them to be verified in sweet Jane Fairfax."

"I cannot think there is any danger of it," was Emma's calm answer "and when you are better acquainted with Miss Fairfax's situation, and understand what her home has been, with Colonel and Mrs. Campbell, I have no idea that you will suppose her talents can be unknown."

"Oh! but, dear Miss Woodhouse, she is now in such retirement, such obscurity, so thrown away. Whatever advantages she may have enjoyed with the Campbells are so palpably at an end! And I think she feels it. I am sure she does. She is very timid and silent. One can see that she feels the want of encouragement. I like her the better for it. I must confess it is a recommendation to me. I am a great advocate for timidity—and I am sure one does not often meet with it. But in those who are at all inferior it is extremely prepossessing. Oh! I assure you, Jane Fairfax is a very delightful character, and interests me more than I can express."

"You appear to feel a great deal; but I am not aware how you or any of Miss Fairfax's acquaintance here, any of those who have known her longer than yourself, can show her any other attention than——"

"My dear Miss Woodhouse, a vast deal may be done by those who dare to act. You and I need not be afraid. If *we* set the example, many will follow it as far as they can; though all have not our situations. *We* have carriages to fetch and convey her home; and *we* live in a style which could not make the addition of Jane Fairfax at any time the least inconvenient. I should be extremely displeased if Wright were to send us up such a dinner as could make me regret having asked *more* than Jane Fairfax to partake of it. I have no idea of that sort of thing. It is not likely that I *should,* considering what I have been used to. My greatest danger, perhaps, in housekeeping, may be quite the other way, in doing too much, and being too careless of expense. Maple Grove will probably be my model more than it ought to be—for we do not at all affect to equal my brother, Mr. Suckling, in income. However, my resolution is taken as to noticing Jane Fairfax. I shall certainly have her very often at my house, shall introduce her wherever I can, shall have musical parties to draw out her talents, and shall be constantly on the watch for an eligible situation. My acquaintance is so very extensive, that I have little doubt of hearing of something to suit her shortly. I shall introduce her, of course, very particularly to my brother and sister when they come to us. I am sure they will like her extremely; and when she gets a little acquainted with them, her fears will completely wear off, for there really is nothing in the manners of either but what is highly conciliating. I shall have her very often, indeed, while they are with me; and I dare say we shall sometimes find a seat for her in the barouche-landau in some of our exploring parties."

"Poor Jane Fairfax!" thought Emma, "you have not deserved this. You may have done wrong with regard to Mr. Dixon; but this is a punishment beyond what you can have merited. The kindness and protection of Mrs. Elton! 'Jane Fairfax and Jane Fairfax!' Heavens! let me suppose that she dares go about Emma Woodhouse-ing me! But, upon my honour, there seems no limits to the licentiousness of that woman's tongue!"

Emma had not to listen to such paradings again—to any so exclusively addressed to herself—so disgustingly decorated with a "dear Miss Wood-house." The change on Mrs. Elton's side soon afterwards appeared, and she was left in peace—neither forced to be the very particular friend of Mrs. Elton nor, under Mrs. Elton's guidance, the very active patroness of Jane Fairfax, and only sharing with others in a general way, in knowing what was felt, what was meditated, what was done.

She looked on with some amusement. Miss Bates's gratitude for Mrs. Elton's attentions to Jane was in the first style of guileless simplicity and warmth. She was quite one of her worthies—the most amiable, affable, delightful woman—just as accomplished and condescending as Mrs. Elton meant to be considered. Emma's only surprise was that Jane Fairfax should accept those attentions, and tolerate Mrs. Elton as she seemed to do. She heard of her walking with the Eltons, sitting with the Eltons, spending a day with the Eltons! This was astonishing! She could not have believed it possible that the taste or the pride of Miss Fairfax could endure such society and friendship as the Vicarage had to offer.

"She is a riddle, quite a riddle," said she. "To choose to remain here month after month, under privations of every sort. And now to choose the mortification of Mrs. Elton's notice, and the penury of her conversation, rather than return to the superior companions who have always loved her with such real, generous affection."

Jane had come to Highbury professedly for three months; the Camp-bells were gone to Ireland for three months; but now the Campbells had promised their daughter to stay at least till Midsummer, and fresh invitations had arrived for her to join them there. According to Miss Bates—it all came from her—Mrs. Dixon had written most pressingly. Would Jane but go, means were to be found, servants sent, friends contrived—no travelling difficulty allowed to exist; but still she had declined it.

"She must have some motive, more powerful than appears, for refusing this invitation," was Emma's conclusion. "She must be under some sort of penance, inflicted either by the Campbells or herself. There is great fear, great caution, great resolution somewhere. She is *not* to be with the *Dixons*. The decree is issued by somebody. But why must she consent to be with the Eltons? Here is quite a separate puzzle."

Upon her speaking her wonder aloud on that part of the subject, before the few who knew her opinion of Mrs. Elton, Mrs. Weston ventured this apology for Jane.

"We cannot suppose that she has any great enjoyment at the vicarage, my dear Emma—but it is better than being always at home. Her aunt is a good creature; but, as a constant companion, must be very tiresome. We must consider what Miss Fairfax quits, before we condemn her taste for what she goes to."

"You are right, Mrs. Weston," said Mr. Knightley warmly; "Miss Fairfax is as capable as any of us of forming a just opinion of Mrs. Elton. Could she have chosen with whom to associate, she would not have chosen her. But" (with a reproachful smile at Emma) "she receives attentions from Mrs. Elton, which nobody else pays her."

Emma felt that Mrs. Weston was giving her a momentary glance, and she was herself struck by his warmth. With a faint blush, she presently replied:

"Such attentions as Mrs. Elton's, I should have imagined, would rather disgust than gratify Miss Fairfax. Mrs. Elton's invitations I should have imagined anything but inviting."

"I should not wonder," said Mrs. Weston, "if Miss Fairfax were to have been drawn on beyond her own inclination, by her aunt's eagerness in accepting Mrs. Elton's civilities for her. Poor Miss Bates may very likely have committed her niece, and hurried her into a greater appearance of intimacy than her own good sense would have dictated, in spite of the very natural wish of a little change."

Both felt rather anxious to hear him speak again; and, after a few minutes' silence, he said:

"Another thing must be taken into consideration too—Mrs. Elton does not talk *to* Miss Fairfax as she speaks *of* her. We all know the difference between the pronouns he or she and thou, the plainest spoken amongst us; we all feel the influence of a something beyond common civility in our personal intercourse with each other—a something more early implanted. We cannot give anybody the disagreeable hints that we may have been very full of the hour before. We feel things differently. And besides the operation of this, as a general principle, you may be sure that Miss Fairfax awes Mrs. Elton by her superiority both of mind and manner; and that, face to face, Mrs. Elton treats her with all the respect which she has a claim to. Such a woman as Jane Fairfax probably never fell in Mrs. Elton's way before—and no degree of vanity can prevent her acknowledging her own comparative littleness in action, if not in consciousness."

"I know how highly you think of Jane Fairfax," said Emma. Little Henry was in her thoughts, and a mixture of alarm and delicacy made her irresolute what else to say.

"Yes," he replied, "anybody may know how highly I think of her."

"And yet," said Emma, beginning hastily, and with an arch look, but soon stopping—it was better, however, to know the worst at once—she hurried on, "and yet, perhaps, you may hardly be aware yourself how highly it is. The extent of your admiration may take you by surprise some day or other."

Mr. Knightley was hard at work upon the lower buttons of his thick leather gaiters, and either the exertion of getting them together, or some other cause, brought the colour into his face, as he answered:

"Oh! are you there? But you are miserably behindhand. Mr. Cole gave me a hint of it six weeks ago."

He stopped. Emma felt her foot pressed by Mrs. Weston, and did not herself know what to think. In a moment he went on:

"That will never be, however, I can assure you. Miss Fairfax, I dare say wouid not have me if I were to ask her; and I am very sure I shall never ask her."

Emma returned her friend's pressure with interest; and was pleased enough to exclaim:

"You are not vain, Mr. Knightley. I will say that for you."

He seemed hardly to hear her; he was thoughtful, and, in a manner which showed him not pleased, soon afterwards said:

"So you have been settling that I should marry Jane Fairfax?"

"No, indeed, I have not. You have scolded me too much for match-making for me to presume to take such a liberty with you. What I said just now meant nothing. One says those sort of things, of course, without any idea of a serious meaning. Oh! no; upon my word I have not the smallest wish for your marrying Jane Fairfax, or Jane anybody. You would not come in and sit with us in this comfortable way if you were married."

Mr. Knightley was thoughtful again. The result of his reverie was— "No, Emma, I do not think the extent of my admiration for her will ever take me by surprise. I never had a thought of her in that way, I assure you."

And soon afterwards, "Jane Fairfax is a very charming young woman— but not even Jane Fairfax is perfect. She has a fault. She has not the open temper which a man would wish for in a wife."

Emma could not but rejoice to hear that she had a fault.

"Well," said she, "and you soon silenced Mr. Cole, I suppose?"

"Yes, very soon. He gave me a quiet hint; I told him he was mistaken; he asked my pardon, and said no more. Cole does not want to be wiser or wittier than his neighbours."

"In that respect how unlike dear Mrs. Elton, who wants to be wiser and wittier than all the world! I wonder how she speaks of the Coles— what she calls them. How can she find any appellation for them, deep enough in familiar vulgarity? She calls you Knightley; what can she do for Mr. Cole? And so I am not to be surprised that Jane Fairfax accepts her civilities, and consents to be with her. Mrs. Weston, your argument weighs most with me. I can much more readily enter into the temptation of getting away from Miss Bates, than I can believe in the triumph of Miss Fairfax's mind over Mrs. Elton. I have no faith in Mrs. Elton's acknowledging herself the inferior in thought, word, or deed; or in her being under any restraint beyond her own scanty rule of good breeding. I cannot imagine that she will not be continually insulting her visitor with praise, encouragement, and offers of service; that she will not be continually detailing her magnificent intentions from the procuring her a permanent situation to the including her in those delightful exploring parties which are to take place in the barouche-landau."

"Jane Fairfax has feeling," said Mr. Knightley; "I do not accuse her of want of feeling. Her sensibilities, I suspect, are strong, and her temper excellent in its power of forbearance, patience, self-control; but it wants openness. She is reserved; more reserved, I think, than she used to be; and I love an open temper. No; till Cole alluded to my supposed attachment, it had never entered my head. I saw Jane Fairfax, and conversed with her, with admiration and pleasure always; but with no thought beyond."

"Well, Mrs. Weston," said Emma, triumphantly, when he left them, "what do you say now to Mr. Knightley's marrying Jane Fairfax?"

"Why, really, dear Emma, I say that he is so very much occupied by the idea of *not* being in love with her, that I should not wonder if it were to end in his being so at last. Do not beat me."

Chapter 34

EVERYBODY in and about Highbury, who had ever visited Mr. Elton, was disposed to pay him attention on his marriage. Dinner parties and evening parties were made for him and his lady; and invitations flowed in so fast that she had soon the pleasure of apprehending they were never to have a disengaged day.

"I see how it is," said she; "I see what a life I am to lead among you. Upon my word, we shall be absolutely dissipated. We really seem quite the fashion. If this is living in the country, it is nothing very formidable. From Monday next to Saturday I assure you we have not a disengaged day! A woman with fewer resources than I have need not have been at a loss."

No invitation came amiss to her. Her Bath habits made evening parties perfectly natural to her, and Maple Grove had given her a taste for dinners. She was a little shocked at the want of two drawing-rooms, at the poor attempt at rout-cakes, and there being no ice in the Highbury card-parties. Mrs. Bates, Mrs. Perry, Mrs. Goddard, and others, were a good deal behindhand in knowledge of the world, but *she* would soon show them how everything ought to be arranged. In the course of the spring she must return their civilities by one very superior party; in which her card-tables should be set out with their separate candles and unbroken packs in the true style, and more waiters engaged for the evening than their own establishment could furnish, to carry round the refreshments at exactly the proper hour, and in the proper order.

Emma, in the meanwhile, could not be satisfied without a dinner at Hartfield for the Eltons. They must not do less than others, or she should be exposed to odious suspicions, and imagined capable of pitiful resentment. A dinner there must be. After Emma had talked about it for ten minutes, Mr. Woodhouse felt no unwillingness, and only made the usual stipulation of not sitting at the bottom of the table himself, with the usual regular difficulty of deciding who should do it for him.

The persons to be invited required little thought. Besides the Eltons, it must be the Westons and Mr. Knightley; so far it was all of course: and it was hardly less inevitable that poor little Harriet must be asked to make the eighth; but this invitation was not given with equal satisfaction, and, on many accounts, Emma was particularly pleased by Harriet's begging to be allowed to decline it. "She would rather not be in *his* company more than she could help. She was not yet quite able to see him and his charming happy wife together, without feeling uncomfortable. If Miss Woodhouse would not be displeased, she would rather stay at home." It was precisely what Emma would have wished, had she deemed it possible enough for wishing. She was delighted with the fortitude of her little friend—for fortitude she knew it was in her to give up being in company, and stay at home; and she could now invite the very person whom she really wanted to make the eighth, Jane Fairfax. Since her last conversation with Mrs. Weston and Mr. Knightley, she was more conscience-stricken about Jane Fairfax than she had often been. Mr. Knightley's words dwelt with her. He had said that Jane Fairfax received attentions from Mrs. Elton which nobody else paid her.

"This is very true," said she, "at least as far as relates to me, which was all that was meant, and it is very shameful. Of the same age, and always knowing her, I ought to have been more her friend. She will never like me now. I have neglected her too long. But I will show her greater attention than I have done."

Every invitation was successful. They were all disengaged and all happy. The preparatory interest of this dinner, however, was not yet over. A circumstance rather unlucky occurred. The two eldest little Knightleys were engaged to pay their grandpapa and aunt a visit of some weeks in the spring and their papa now proposed bringing them, and staying one whole day at Hartfield—which one day would be the very day of the party. His professional engagements did not allow of his being put off, but both father and daughter were disturbed by its happening so. Mr. Woodhouse considered eight persons at dinner together as the utmost that his nerves could bear—and here would be a ninth—and Emma apprehended that it would be a ninth very much out of humour, at not being able to come even to Hartfield for forty-eight hours, without falling in with a dinner party.

She comforted her father better than she could comfort herself, by representing that though he certainly would make them nine, yet he always said so little, that the increase of noise would be very immaterial. She thought it in reality a sad exchange for herself, to have him, with his grave looks and reluctant conversation, opposed to her instead of his brother.

The event was more favourable to Mr. Woodhouse than to Emma. John Knightley came; but Mr. Weston was unexpectedly summoned to town, and must be absent on the very day. He might be able to join them in the evening, but certainly not to dinner. Mr. Woodhouse was quite at ease; and the seeing him so, with the arrival of the little boys, and the philosophic composure of her brother on hearing his fate, removed the chief of even Emma's vexation.

The day came, the party were punctually assembled and Mr. John Knightley seemed early to devote himself to the business of being agreeable. Instead of drawing his brother off to a window while they waited for dinner he was talking to Miss Fairfax. Mrs. Elton, as elegant as lace and pearls could make her, he looked at in silence—wanting only to observe enough for Isabella's information—but Miss Fairfax was an old acquaintance and a quiet girl, and he could talk to her. He had met her before breakfast as he was returning from a walk with his little boys, when it had been just beginning to rain. It was natural to have some civil hopes on the subject, and he said:

"I hope you did not venture far, Miss Fairfax, this morning, or I am sure you must have been wet. *We* scarcely got home in time. I hope you turned directly."

"I went only to the post-office," said she, "and reached home before the rain was much. It is my daily errand. I always fetch the letters when I am here. It saves trouble, and is a something to get me out. A walk before breakfast does me good."

"Not a walk in the rain, I should imagine."

"No; but it did not absolutely rain when I set out."

Mr. John Knightley smiled, and replied:

"That is to say, you chose to have your walk, for you were not six yards from your own door when I had the pleasure of meeting you; and Henry and John had seen more drops than they could count long before. The post-office had a great charm at one period of our lives. When you have lived to my age, you will begin to think letters are never worth going through the rain for."

There was a little blush, and then this answer—

"I must not hope to be ever situated as you are, in the midst of every dearest connection, and therefore I cannot expect that simply growing older should make me indifferent about letters."

"Indifferent! Oh no—I never conceived you could become indifferent. Letters are no matters of indifference; they are generally a very positive curse."

"You are speaking of letters of business; mine are letters of friendship."

"I have often thought them the worst of the two," replied he, coolly. "Business you know, may bring money, but friendship hardly ever does."

"Ah! you are not serious now. I know Mr. John Knightley too well—I am very sure he understands the value of friendship as well as anybody. I can easily believe that letters are very little to you, much less than to me; but it is not your being ten years older than myself which makes the difference; it is not age, but situation. You have everybody dearest to you always at hand, I, probably, never shall again; and therefore, till I have outlived all my affections, a post-office, I think, must always have power to draw me out, in worse weather than to-day."

"When I talked of your being altered by time, by the progress of years," said John Knightley, "I meant to imply the change of situation which time usually brings. I consider one as including the other. Time will generally lessen the interest of every attachment not within the daily circle—but that is not the change I had in view for you. As an old friend, you will allow me to hope, Miss Fairfax, that ten years hence you may have as many concentrated objects as I have."

It was kindly said, and very far from giving offence. A pleasant "thank you" seemed meant to laugh it off; but a blush, a quivering lip, a tear in the eye, showed that it was felt beyond a laugh. Her attention was now claimed by Mr. Woodhouse, who being, according to his custom on such occasions, making the circle of his guests, and paying his particular compliments to the ladies, was ending with her—and with all his mildest urbanity said:

"I am very sorry to hear, Miss Fairfax, of your being out this morning in the rain. Young ladies should take care of themselves. Young ladies are delicate plants. They should take care of their health and their complexion. My dear, did you change your stockings?"

"Yes, sir, I did indeed; and I am very much obliged by your kind solicitude about me."

"My dear Miss Fairfax, young ladies are very sure to be cared for. I hope your good grandmamma and aunt are well. They are some of my very old friends. I wish my health allowed me to be a better neighbour. You do us a great deal of honour to-day, I am sure. My daughter and I are both highly sensible of your goodness, and have the greatest satisfaction in seeing you at Hartfield."

The kind-hearted, polite old man might then sit down and feel that he had done his duty, and made every fair lady welcome and easy.

By this time the walk in the rain had reached Mrs. Elton, and her remonstrances now opened upon Jane.

"My dear Jane, what is this I hear? Going to the post-office in the rain! This must not be, I assure you. You sad girl, how could you do such a thing? It is a sign I was not there to take care of you."

Jane very patiently assured her that she had not caught any cold.

"Oh! do not tell *me*. You really are a very sad girl, and do not know how to take care of yourself. To the post-office indeed! Mrs. Weston, did you ever hear the like? You and I must positively exert our authority."

"My advice," said Mrs. Weston, kindly and persuasively, "I certainly do feel tempted to give. Miss Fairfax, you must not run such risks. Liable as you have been to severe colds, indeed you ought to be particularly careful, especially at this time of year. The spring I always think requires more than common care. Better wait an hour or two, or even half a day for your letters, than run the risk of bringing on your cough again. Now do not you feel that you had? Yes, I am sure you are much too reasonable. You look as if you would not do such a thing again."

"Oh, she *shall not* do such a thing again," eagerly rejoined Mrs. Elton. "We will not allow her to do such a thing again":—and nodding significantly—"there must be some arrangement made, there must indeed. I

shall speak to Mr. E. The man who fetches our letters every morning (one
of our men, I forget his name) shall inquire for yours too and bring them
to you. That will obviate all difficulties, you know; and from *us* I really
think, my dear Jane, you can have no scruple to accept such an accommodation."

"You are extremely kind," said Jane; "but I cannot give up my early
walk. I am advised to be out of doors as much as I can; I must walk
somewhere, and the post-office is an object; and, upon my word, I have
scarcely ever had a bad morning before."

"My dear Jane, say no more about it. The thing is determined, that is"
(laughing affectedly) "as far as I can presume to determine anything
without the concurrence of my lord and master. You know, Mrs. Weston,
you and I must be cautious how we express ourselves. But I do flatter
myself, my dear Jane, that my influence is not entirely worn out. If I meet
with no insuperable difficulties, therefore, consider that point as settled."

"Excuse me," said Jane earnestly, "I cannot by any means consent to
such an arrangement, so needlessly troublesome to your servant. If the
errand were not a pleasure to me, it could be done, as it always is when I
am not here, but my grandmamma's——"

"Oh! my dear; but so much as Patty has to do! And it is a kindness to
employ our men."

Jane looked as if she did not mean to be conquered; but, instead of
answering, she began speaking again to Mr. John Knightley.

"The post-office is a wonderful establishment!" said she. "The regularity and dispatch of it! If one thinks of all that it has to do, and all that
it does so well, it is really astonishing!"

"It is certainly very well regulated."

"So seldom that any negligence or blunder appears! So seldom that a
letter, among the thousands that are constantly passing about the kingdom, is even carried wrong—and not one in a million, I suppose, actually
lost! And when one considers the variety of hands, and of bad hands too,
that are to be deciphered, it increases the wonder."

"The clerks grow expert from habit. They must begin with some
quickness of sight and hand, and exercise improves them. If you want
any further explanation," continued he, smiling, "they are paid for it.
That is the key to a great deal of capacity. The public pays and must
be served well."

The varieties of handwriting were farther talked of, and the usual
observations made.

"I have heard it asserted," said John Knightley, "that the same sort
of handwriting often prevails in a family; and where the same master
teaches, it is natural enough. But for that reason, I should imagine the
likeness must be chiefly confined to the females, for boys have very
little teaching after an early age, and scramble into any hand they can
get. Isabella and Emma, I think, do write very much alike. I have not
always known their writing apart."

"Yes," said his brother, hesitatingly; "there is a likeness. I know what you mean—but Emma's hand is the strongest."

"Isabella and Emma both write beautifully," said Mr. Woodhouse; "and always did. And so does poor Mrs. Weston"—with half a sigh and half a smile at her.

"I never saw any gentleman's handwriting"—Emma began, looking also at Mrs. Weston; but stopped, on perceiving that Mrs. Weston was attending to someone else—and the pause gave her time to reflect. "Now, how am I going to introduce him?—Am I unequal to speaking his name at once before all these people? Is it necessary for me to use any round-about phrase? Your Yorkshire friend—your correspondent in Yorkshire; that would be the way, I suppose, if I were very bad. No, I can pronounce his name without the smallest distress. I certainly get better and better. Now for it."

Mrs. Weston was disengaged, and Emma began again—"Mr. Frank Churchill writes one of the best gentleman's hands I ever saw."

"I do not admire it," said Mr. Knightley. "It is too small—wants strength. It is like a woman's writing."

This was not submitted to by either lady. They vindicated him against the base aspersion. "No, it by no means wanted strength—it was not a large hand, but very clear, and certainly strong. Had not Mrs. Weston any letter about her to produce?" No, she had heard from him very lately, but having answered the letter, had put it away.

"If we were in the other room," said Emma—"if I had my writing-desk I am sure I could produce a specimen. I have a note of his. Do not you remember, Mrs. Weston, employing him to write for you one day?"

"He chose to say he was employed."

"Well, well, I have that note; and can show it after dinner to convince Mr. Knightley."

"Oh! when a gallant young man, like Mr. Frank Churchill," said Mr. Knightley drily, "writes to a fair lady like Miss Woodhouse, he will, of course, put forth his best."

Dinner was on table. Mrs. Elton, before she could be spoken to, was ready; and before Mr. Woodhouse had reached her, with his request to be allowed to hand her into the dining-parlour, was saying:

"Must I go first? I really am ashamed of always leading the way."

Jane's solicitude about fetching her own letters had not escaped Emma. She had heard and seen it all; and felt some curiosity to know whether the wet walk of this morning had produced any. She suspected that it *had;* that it would not have been so resolutely encountered but in full expectation of hearing from someone very dear, and that it had not been in vain. She thought there was an air of greater happiness than usual—a glow both of complexion and spirits.

She could have made an inquiry or two, as to the expedition and the expense of the Irish mails; it was at her tongue's end—but she abstained. She was quite determined not to utter a word that should hurt Jane

Fairfax's feelings: and they followed the other ladies out of the room, arm-in-arm, with an appearance of good-will highly becoming to the beauty and grace of each.

Chapter 35

WHEN the ladies returned to the drawing-room after dinner, Emma found it hardly possible to prevent their making two distinct parties, with so much perseverance in judging and behaving ill did Mrs. Elton engross Jane Fairfax and slight herself. She and Mrs. Weston were obliged to be almost always either talking together or silent together. Mrs. Elton left them no choice. If Jane repressed her for a little time she soon began again; and though much that passed between them was in a half-whisper, especially on Mrs. Elton's side, there was no avoiding a knowledge of their principal subjects:—the post-office—catching cold —fetching letters—and friendship, were long under discussion; and to them succeeded one which must be at least equally unpleasant to Jane—inquiries whether she had yet heard of any situation likely to suit her, and professions of Mrs. Elton's meditated activity.

"Here is April come," said she; "I get quite anxious about you. June will soon be here."

"But I have never fixed on June or any other month—merely looked forward to the summer in general."

"But have you really heard of nothing?"

"I have not even made any inquiry; I do not wish to make any yet."

"Oh! my dear, we cannot begin too early; you are not aware of the difficulty of procuring exactly the desirable thing."

"I not aware!" said Jane, shaking her head; "dear Mrs. Elton, who can have thought of it as I have done?"

"But you have not seen so much of the world as I have. You do not know how many candidates there always are for the *first* situations. I saw a vast deal of that in the neighbourhood round Maple Grove. A cousin of Mr. Suckling, Mrs. Bragge, had such an infinity of applications; everybody was anxious to be in her family, for she moves in the first circle. Wax-candles in the school-room! You may imagine how desirable! Of all houses in the kingdom, Mrs. Bragge's is the one I would most wish to see you in."

"Colonel and Mrs. Campbell are to be in town again by Midsummer," said Jane, "I must spend some time with them; I am sure they will want it; afterwards I may probably be glad to dispose of myself. But I would not wish you to take the trouble of making any inquiries at present."

"Trouble! aye, I know your scruples. You are afraid of giving me trouble; but I assure you, my dear Jane, the Campbells can hardly be more interested about you than I am. I shall write to Mrs. Partridge in a day or two, and shall give her a strict charge to be on the look-out for anything eligible."

"Thank you, but I would rather you did not mention the subject to her; till the time draws nearer, I do not wish to be giving anybody trouble."

"But, my dear child, the time *is* drawing near; here is April, and June, or say even July, is very near, with such business to accomplish before us. Your inexperience really amuses me! A situation such as you deserve, and your friends would require for you, is no everyday occurrence, is not obtained at a moment's notice; indeed, indeed, we must begin inquiring directly."

"Excuse me, ma'am, but this is by no means my intention; I make no inquiry myself, and should be sorry to have any made by my friends. When I am quite determined as to the time, I am not at all afraid of being long unemployed. There are places in town, offices, where inquiry would soon produce something—offices for the sale, not quite of human flesh, but of human intellect."

"Oh! my dear, human flesh! You quite shock me; if you mean a fling at the slave trade, I assure you Mr. Suckling was always rather a friend to the abolition."

"I did not mean—I was not thinking of the slave-trade," replied Jane; "governess-trade, I assure you, was all that I had in view; widely different, certainly, as to the guilt of those who carry it on; but as to the greater misery of the victims, I do not know where it lies. But I only mean to say that there are advertising offices, and that by applying to them I should have no doubt of very soon meeting with something that would do."

"Something that would do!" repeated Mrs. Elton. "Aye, *that* may suit your humble ideas of yourself; I know what a modest creature you are; but it will not satisfy your friends to have you taking up with anything that may offer, any inferior commonplace situation, in a family not moving in a certain circle, or able to command the elegancies of life."

"You are very obliging; but as to all that I am very indifferent; it would be no object to me to be with the rich; my mortifications, I think, would only be the greater; I should suffer more from comparison. A gentleman's family is all that I should condition for."

"I know you, I know you; you would take up with anything; but I shall be a little more nice, and I am sure the good Campbells will be quite on my side; with your superior talents, you have a right to move in the first circle. Your musical knowledge alone would entitle you to name your own terms, have as many rooms as you like, and mix in the family as much as you choose; that is—I do not know—if you knew the harp, you might do all that, I am very sure; but you sing as well as play; yes, I really believe you might; even without the harp, stipulate for what you choose; and you must and shall be delightfully, honourably, and comfortably settled before the Campbells or I have any rest."

"You may well class the delight, the honour, and the comfort of such a situation together," said Jane, "they are pretty sure to be equal; however, I am very serious in not wishing anything to be attempted at present for me. I am exceedingly obliged to you, Mrs. Elton; I am obliged to anybody who feels for me, but I am quite serious in wishing nothing to be done till the summer. For two or three months longer I shall remain where I am, and as I am."

"And I am quite serious too, I assure you," replied Mrs. Elton gaily, "in resolving to be always on the watch, and employing friends to watch also, that nothing really unexceptionable may pass us."

In this style she ran on; never thoroughly stopped by anything till Mr. Woodhouse came into the room; her vanity had then a change of object, and Emma heard her saying in the same half-whisper to Jane:

"Here comes this dear old beau of mine, I protest! Only think of his gallantry in coming away before the other men! what a dear creature he is! I assure you I like him excessively. I admire all that quaint, old-fashioned politeness; it is much more to my taste than modern ease; modern ease often disgusts me. But this good old Mr. Woodhouse, I wish you had heard his gallant speeches to me at dinner. Oh! I assure you I began to think my *caro sposo* would be absolutely jealous. I fancy I am rather a favourite; he took notice of my gown. How do you like it? Selina's choice—handsome, I think, but I do not know whether it is not over-trimmed; I have the greatest dislike to the idea of being overtrimmed; quite a horror of finery. I must put on a few ornaments *now*, because it is expected of me. A bride, you know, must appear like a bride, but my natural taste is all for simplicity; a simple style of dress is so infinitely preferable to finery. But I am quite in the minority, I believe; few people seem to value simplicity of dress—show and finery are everything. I have some notion of putting such a trimming as this to my white and silver poplin. Do you think it will look well?"

The whole party were but just reassembled in the drawing-room, when Mr. Weston made his appearance among them. He had returned to a late dinner, and walked to Hartfield as soon as it was over. He had been too much expected by the best judges, for surprise—but there was great joy. Mr. Woodhouse was almost as glad to see him now, as he would have been sorry to see him before. John Knightley only was in mute astonishment. That a man who might have spent his evening quietly at home after a day of business in London should set off again, and walk half a mile to another man's house for the sake of being in mixed company till bed-time, of finishing his day in the efforts of civility and the noise of numbers, was a circumstance to strike him deeply. A man who had been in motion since eight o'clock in the morning, and might now have been still—who had been long talking, and might have been silent—who had been in more than one crowd, and might have been alone! Such a man to quit the tranquillity and independence of his own fireside, and on the evening of a cold sleety April day rush out again into the world! Could he, by a touch of his finger, have instantly taken back his wife, there would have been a motive; but his coming would probably prolong rather than break up the party. John Knightley looked at him with amazement, then shrugged his shoulders, and said, "I could not have believed it even of *him*."

Mr. Weston, meanwhile, perfectly unsuspicious of the indignation he was exciting, happy and cheerful as usual, and with all the right of being principal talker, which a day spent anywhere from home confers, was making himself agreeable among the rest; and having satisfied the inquiries of his wife as to his dinner, convincing her that none of all her careful directions to the servants had been forgotten, and spread abroad what public news he had heard, was proceeding to a family communication which, though principally addressed to Mrs. Weston, he had not the smallest doubt of being highly interesting to everybody in the room. He gave her a letter—it was from Frank, and to herself; he had met with it in his way, and had taken the liberty of opening it.

"Read it, read it," said he—"it will give you pleasure; only a few lines—will not take you long; read it to Emma."

The two ladies looked over it together; and he sat smiling and talking to them the whole time, in a voice a little subdued, but very audible to everybody.

"Well, he is coming, you see; good news, I think. Well, what do you say to it? I always told you he would be here again soon, did not I? Anne, my dear, did not I always tell you so, and you would not believe me? In town next week, you see—at the latest, I dare say; for *she* is as impatient as the black gentleman when anything is to be done; most likely they will be there to-morrow or Saturday. As to her illness, all nothing, of course. But it is an excellent thing to have Frank among us again, so near as town. They will stay a good while when they do come, and he will be half his time with us. This is precisely what I wanted. Well, pretty good news, is not it? Have you finished it? Has Emma read it all? Put it up, put it up; we will have a good talk about it some other time, but it will not do now. I shall only just mention the circumstance to the others in a common way."

Mrs. Weston was most comfortably pleased on the occasion. Her looks and words had nothing to restrain them. She was happy, she knew she was happy, and knew she ought to be happy. Her congratulations were warm and open; but Emma could not speak so fluently. *She* was a little occupied in weighing her own feelings, and trying to understand the degree of her agitation, which she rather thought was considerable.

Mr. Weston, however, too eager to be very observant, too communicative to want others to talk, was very well satisfied with what she did say, and soon moved away to make the rest of his friends happy, by a partial communication of what the whole room must have overheard already.

It was well that he took everybody's joy for granted, or he might not have thought either Mr. Woodhouse or Mr. Knightley particularly delighted. They were the first entitled, after Mrs. Weston and Emma, to be made happy. From them he would have proceeded to Miss Fairfax; but she was so deep in conversation with John Knightley, that it would have been too positive an interruption; and, finding himself close to Mrs. Elton, and her attention disengaged, he necessarily began on the subject with her.

Chapter 36

"I hope I shall soon have the pleasure of introducing my son to you," said Mr. Weston.

Mrs. Elton, very willing to suppose a particular compliment intended her by such a hope, smiled most graciously.

"You have heard of a certain Frank Churchill, I presume," he continued, "and know him to be my son, though he does not bear my name."

"Oh, yes, and I shall be very happy in his acquaintance. I am sure Mr. Elton will lose no time in calling on him; and we shall both have great pleasure in seeing him at the vicarage."

"You are very obliging. Frank will be extremely happy, I am sure. He is to be in town next week, if not sooner. We have notice of it in a letter to-day. I met the letters in my way this morning, and seeing my son's hand, presumed to open it, though it was not directed to me—it was to Mrs. Weston. She is his principal correspondent, I assure you. I hardly ever get a letter."

"And so you absolutely opened what was directed to her! Oh, Mr. Weston" (laughing affectedly), "I must protest against that. A most dangerous precedent indeed! I beg you will not let your neighbours follow your example. Upon my word, if this is what I am to expect, we married women must begin to exert ourselves. Oh, Mr. Weston, I could not have believed it of you!"

"Aye, we men are sad fellows. You must take care of yourself, Mrs. Elton. This letter tells us—it is a short letter, written in a hurry, merely to give us notice—it tells us that they are all coming up to town directly, on Mrs. Churchill's account! she has not been well the whole winter, and thinks Enscombe too cold for her; so they are all to move southward without loss of time."

"Indeed! from Yorkshire, I think. Enscombe is in Yorkshire?"

"Yes, they are about one hundred and ninety miles from London: a considerable journey."

"Yes, upon my word, very considerable. Sixty-five miles farther than from Maple Grove to London. But what is distance, Mr. Weston, to people of large fortune? You would be amazed to hear how my brother, Mr. Suckling, sometimes flies about. You will hardly believe me, but twice in one week he and Mr. Bragge went to London and back again with four horses."

"The evil of the distance from Enscombe," said Mr. Weston, "is, that Mrs. Churchill, *as we understood,* has not been able to leave the sofa for a week together. In Frank's last letter she complained, he said, of being too weak to get into her conservatory without having both his arm and his uncle's. This, you know, speaks a great degree of weakness; but now she is so impatient to be in town, that she means to sleep only two nights on the road—so Frank writes word. Certainly, delicate ladies have very extraordinary constitutions, Mrs. Elton; you must grant me that."

"No, indeed, I shall grant you nothing. I always take the part of my own sex; I do, indeed. I give you notice, you will find me a formidable antagonist on that point. I always stand up for women; and I assure you, if you knew how Selina feels with respect to sleeping at an inn, you would not wonder at Mrs. Churchill's making incredible exertions to avoid it. Selina says it is quite horror to her; and I believe I have caught a little of her nicety. She always travels with her own sheets; an excellent precaution. Does Mrs. Churchill do the same?"

"Depend upon it, Mrs. Churchill does everything that any other fine lady ever did. Mrs. Churchill will not be second to any lady in the land for——"

Mrs. Elton eagerly interposed with—

"Oh, Mr. Weston, do not mistake me. Selina is no fine lady, I assure you. Do not run away with such an idea."

"Is not she? Then she is no rule for Mrs. Churchill, who is as thorough a fine lady as anybody ever beheld."

Mrs. Elton began to think she had been wrong in disclaiming so warmly. It was by no means her object to have it believed that her sister was *not* a fine lady; perhaps there was want of spirit in the pretence of it; and she was considering in what way she had best retract, when Mr. Weston went on:

"Mrs. Churchill is not much in my good graces, as you may suspect; but this is quite between ourselves. She is very fond of Frank, and therefore I would not speak ill of her. Besides, she is out of health now; but *that* indeed, by her own account, she had always been. I would not say so to everybody, Mrs. Elton; but I have not much faith in Mrs. Churchill's illness."

"If she is really ill, why not go to Bath, Mr. Weston? To Bath, or to Clifton?"

"She has taken it into her head that Enscombe is too cold for her. The fact is, I suppose, that she is tired of Enscombe. She has now been a longer time stationary there than she ever was before, and she begins to want change. It is a retired place. A fine place, but very retired."

"Aye, like Maple Grove, I dare say. Nothing can stand more retired from the road than Maple Grove. Such an immense plantation all round it! You seem shut out from everything—in the most complete retirement. And Mrs. Churchill probably has not health or spirits like Selina to enjoy that sort of seclusion. Or, perhaps, she may not have resources enough in herself to be qualified for a country life. I always say a woman cannot have too many resources—and I feel very thankful that I have so many myself as to be quite independent of society."

"Frank was here in February for a fortnight."

"So I remember to have heard. He will find an *addition* to the society of Highbury when he comes again; that is, if I may presume to call myself an addition. But perhaps he may never have heard of there being such a creature in the world."

This was too loud a call for a compliment to be passed by, and Mr. Weston, with a very good grace, immediately exclaimed:

"My dear madam! Nobody but yourself could imagine such a thing possible. Not heard of you! I believe Mrs. Weston's letters lately have been full of very little else than Mrs. Elton."

He had done his duty, and could return to his son.

"When Frank left us," continued he, "it was quite uncertain when we might see him again, which makes this day's news doubly welcome. It has been completely unexpected. That is, *I* always had a strong persuasion he would be here again soon; I was sure something favourable would turn up —but nobody believed me. He and Mrs. Weston were both dreadfully desponding. 'How could he contrive to come? And how could it be supposed that his uncle and aunt would spare him again?' and so forth. I always felt that something would happen in our favour, and so it has, you see. I have observed, Mrs. Elton, in the course of my life, that if things are going untowardly one month, they are sure to mend the next."

"Very true, Mr. Weston, perfectly true. It is just what I used to say to a certain gentleman in company in the days of courtship, when, because things did not go quite right—did not proceed with all the rapidity which suited his feelings—he was apt to be in despair, and exclaim that he was sure at this rate it would be *May* before Hymen's saffron robe would be put on for us! Oh! the pains I have been at to dispel those gloomy ideas, and give him cheerfuller views! The carriage—we had disappointments about the carriage—one morning, I remember, he came to me quite in despair."

She was stopped by a slight fit of coughing, and Mr. Weston instantly seized the opportunity of going on.

"You were mentioning May. May is the very month which Mrs. Churchill is ordered, or has ordered herself, to spend in some warmer place than Enscombe—in short, to spend in London; so that we have the agreeable prospect of frequent visits from Frank, the whole spring—precisely the season of the year which one should have chosen for it: days almost at the longest: weather genial and pleasant, always inviting one out, and never too hot for exercise. When he was here before, we made the best of it; but there was a good deal of wet, damp, cheerless weather; there always is in February, you know; and we could not do half that we intended. Now will be the time. This will be complete enjoyment; and I do not know, Mrs. Elton, whether the uncertainty of our meetings, the sort of constant expectation there will be of his coming in to-day or to-morrow, and at any hour, may not be more friendly to happiness than having him actually in the house. I think it is so. I think it is the state of mind which gives most spirit and delight. I hope you will be pleased with my son; but you must not expect a prodigy. He is generally thought a fine young man, but do not expect a prodigy. Mrs. Weston's partiality for him is very great, and, as you may suppose, most gratifying to me. She thinks nobody equal to him."

"And I assure you, Mr. Weston, I have very little doubt that my opinion will be decidedly in his favour. I have heard so much in praise of Mr. Frank Churchill. At the same time, it is fair to observe, that I am one of those who always judge for themselves, and are by no means implicitly guided by others. I give you notice, that as I find your son, so I shall judge of him. I am no flatterer."

Mr. Weston was musing.

"I hope," said he, presently, "I have not been severe upon poor Mrs. Churchill. If she is ill, I should be sorry to do her injustice; but there are some traits in her character which make it difficult for me to speak of her with the forbearance I could wish. You cannot be ignorant, Mrs. Elton, of my connection with the family, nor of the treatment I have met with; and, between ourselves, the whole blame of it is to be laid to her. She was the instigator. Frank's mother would never have been slighted as she was but for her. Mr. Churchill has pride; but his pride is nothing to his wife's; his is a quiet, indolent, gentlemanlike sort of pride, that would harm nobody, and only make himself a little helpless and tiresome; but her pride is arrogance and insolence. And what inclines one less to bear, she has no fair pretence of family or blood. She was nobody when he married her, barely the daughter of a gentleman; but ever since her being turned into a Churchill, she has out-Churchill'd them all in high and mighty claims; but in herself, I assure you, she is an upstart."

"Only think! well, that must be infinitely provoking! I have quite a horror of upstarts. Maple Grove has given me a thorough disgust to people of that sort; for there is a family in that neighbourhood who are such an annoyance to my brother and sister from the airs they give themselves! Your description of Mrs. Churchill made me think of them directly. People of the name of Tupman, very lately settled there, and encumbered with many low connections, but giving themselves immense airs, and expecting to be on a footing with the old established families. A year and a half is the very utmost that they can have lived at West Hall; and how they got their fortune nobody knows. They came from Birmingham, which is not a place to promise much, you know, Mr. Weston. One has not great hopes from Birmingham. I always say there is something direful in the sound; but nothing more is positively known of the Tupmans, though a good many things, I assure you, are suspected; and yet by their manners they evidently think themselves equal even to my brother, Mr. Suckling, who happens to be one of their nearest neighbours. It is infinitely too bad. Mr.

Suckling, who has been eleven years a resident at Maple Grove, and whose father had it before him—I believe, at least—I am almost sure that old Mr. Suckling had completed the purchase before his death."

They were interrupted. Tea was carrying round, and Mr. Weston, having said all that he wanted, soon took the opportunity of walking away.

After tea, Mr. and Mrs. Weston, and Mr. Elton, sat down with Mr. Woodhouse to cards. The remaining five were left to their own powers, and Emma doubted their getting on very well; for Mr. Knightley seemed little disposed for conversation; Mrs. Elton was wanting notice, which nobody had inclination to pay, and she was herself in a worry of spirits which would have made her prefer being silent.

Mr. John Knightley proved more talkative than his brother. He was to leave them early the next day; and he soon began with——

"Well, Emma, I do not believe I have anything more to say about the boys; but you have your sister's letter, and everything is down at full length there, we may be sure. My charge would be much more concise than hers, and probably not much in the same spirit; all that I have to recommend being comprised in—Do not spoil them, and do not physic them."

"I rather hope to satisfy you both," said Emma; "for I shall do all in my power to make them happy, which will be enough for Isabella; and happiness must preclude false indulgence and physic."

"And if you find them troublesome, you must send them home again.'

"That is very likely. You think so, do not you?"

"I hope I am aware that they may be too noisy for your father; or even may be some incumbrance to you, if your visiting engagements continue to increase as much as they have done lately."

"Increase!"

"Certainly; you must be sensible that the last half-year has made a great difference in your way of life."

"Difference! No, indeed, I am not."

"There can be no doubt of your being much more engaged with company than you used to be. Witness this very time. Here am I come down for only one day, and you are engaged with a dinner-party! When did it happen before, or anything like it? Your neighbourhood is increasing, and you mix more with it. A little while ago, every letter to Isabella brought an account of fresh gaieties, dinners at Mr. Cole's, or balls at the Crown. The difference which Randalls, Randalls alone, makes in your goings on is very great."

"Yes," said his brother, quickly, "it is Randalls that does it all."

"Very well; and as Randalls, I suppose, is not likely to have less influence than heretofore it strikes me as a possible thing, Emma, that Henry and John may be sometimes in the way. And if they are, I only beg you to send them home."

"No," cried Mr. Knightley; "that need not be the consequence. Let them be sent to Donwell. I shall certainly be at leisure."

"Upon my word," exclaimed Emma, "you amuse me! I should like to know how many of all my numerous engagements take place without your being of the party; and why I am to be supposed in danger of wanting leisure to attend to the little boys. These amazing engagements of mine—what have they been? Dining once with the Coles, and having a ball talked of, which never took place. I can understand you"—(nodding at Mr. John Knightley)—"your good fortune in meeting with so many of your friends at once here delights you too much to pass unnoticed. But you" (turning to Mr. Knightley), "who know how very, very seldom I am ever two hours from Hartfield—why you should foresee such a series of dissipation for me, I cannot imagine. And as to my dear little boys, I must say, that if Aunt Emma has not time for them, I do not think they would fare much better with Uncle Knightley, who is absent from home about five hours where she is absent one; and who, when he is at home, is either reading to himself or settling his accounts."

Mr. Knightley seemed to be trying not to smile; and succeeded without difficulty, upon Mrs. Elton's beginning to talk to him.

Chapter 37

A VERY little quiet reflection was enough to satisfy Emma as to the nature of her agitation on hearing this news of Frank Churchill. She was soon convinced that it was not for herself she was feeling at all apprehensive or embarrassed—it was for him. Her own attachment had really subsided into a mere nothing—it was not worth thinking of; but if he, who had undoubtedly been always so much the most in love of the two, were to be returning with the same warmth of sentiment which he had taken away, it would be very distressing. If a separation of two months should not have cooled him, there were dangers and evils before her: caution for him and for herself would be necessary. She did not mean to have her own affections entangled again, and it would be incumbent on her to avoid any encouragement of his.

She wished she might be able to keep him from an absolute declaration. That would be so very painful a conclusion of their present acquaintance; and yet she could not help rather anticipating something decisive. She felt as if the spring would not pass without bringing a crisis, an event, a something to alter her present composed and tranquil state.

It was not very long, though rather longer than Mr. Weston had foreseen, before she had the power of forming some opinion of Frank Churchill's feelings. The Enscombe family were not in town quite so soon as had been imagined, but he was at Highbury very soon afterwards. He rode down for a couple of hours; he could not yet do more; but as he came from Randalls immediately to Hartfield, she could then exercise all her quick observation, and speedily determine how he was influenced, and how she must act. They met with the utmost friendliness. There could be no doubt of his great pleasure in seeing her. But she had an almost instant doubt of his caring for her as he had done, of his feeling the same tenderness in the same degree. She watched him well. It was a clear thing he was less in love than he had been. Absence, with the conviction probably of her indifference, had produced this very natural and very desirable effect.

He was in high spirits; as ready to talk and laugh as ever; and seemed delighted to speak of his former visit, and recur to old stories; and he was not without agitation. It was not in his calmness that she read his comparative difference. He was not calm; his spirits were evidently fluttered; there was restlessness about him. Lively as he was, it seemed a liveliness that did not satisfy himself; but what decided her belief on the subject, was his staying only a quarter of an hour, and hurrying away to make other calls in Highbury. "He had seen a group of old acquaintance in the street as he passed—he had not stopped, he would not stop for more than a word—but he had the vanity to think they would be disappointed if he did not call; and, much as he wished to stay longer at Hartfield, he must hurry off."

She had no doubt as to his being less in love, but neither his agitated spirits nor his hurrying away seemed like a perfect cure; and she was rather inclined to think it implied a dread of her returning power, and a discreet resolution of not trusting himself with her long.

This was the only visit from Frank Churchill in the course of ten days. He was often hoping, intending to come; but was always prevented. His aunt could not bear to have him leave her. Such was his own account at Randalls. If he were quite sincere, if he really tried to come, it was to be inferred that Mrs. Churchill's removal to London had been of no service to the wilful or nervous part of her disorder. That she was really ill was very certain; he had declared himself convinced of it, at Randalls. Though much might be fancy, he could not doubt, when he looked back, that she was in a weaker state of health than she had been half a year ago. He did not believe it to proceed from anything that care and medicine might not remove, or at least that she might not have many years of existence before her; but he could not be prevailed on, by all his father's doubts, to say that her complaints were merely imaginary, or that she was as strong as ever.

It soon appeared that London was not the place for her. She could not endure its noise. Her nerves were under continual irritation and suffering; and by the ten days' end, her nephew's letter to Randalls communicated a change of plan. They were going to remove immediately to Richmond. Mrs. Churchill had been recommended to the medical skill of an eminent person there, and had otherwise a fancy for the place. A ready-furnished house in a favourite spot was engaged, and much benefit expected from the change.

Emma heard that Frank wrote in the highest spirits of this arrangement, and seemed most fully to appreciate the blessing of having two months before him of such near neighbourhood to many dear friends; for the house was taken for May and June. She was told that now he wrote with the greatest confidence of being often with them, almost as often as he could even wish.

Emma saw how Mr. Weston understood these joyous prospects. He was considering her as the source of all the happiness they offered. She hoped it was not so. Two months must bring it to the proof.

Mr. Weston's own happiness was indisputable. He was quite delighted. It was the very circumstance he could have wished for. Now, it would be really having Frank in their neighbourhood. What were nine miles to a young man? An hour's ride. He would be always coming over. The difference in that respect of Richmond and London was enough to make the whole difference of seeing him always and seeing him never. Sixteen miles—nay, eighteen—it must be full eighteen to Manchester Street—was a serious obstacle. Were he ever able to get away, the day would be spent in coming and returning. There was no comfort in having him in London; he might as well be at Enscombe; but Richmond was the very distance for easy intercourse. Better than nearer!

One good thing was immediately brought to a certainty by this removal —the ball at the Crown. It had not been forgotten before; but it had been soon acknowledged vain to attempt to fix a day. Now, however, it was absolutely to be; every preparation was resumed; and very soon after the Churchills had removed to Richmond, a few lines from Frank, to say that his aunt felt already much better for the change, and that he had no doubt of being able to join them for twenty-four hours at any given time, induced them to name as early a day as possible.

Mr. Weston's ball was to be a real thing. A very few to-morrows stood between the young people of Highbury and happiness.

Mr. Woodhouse was resigned. The time of year lightened the evil to him. May was better for everything than February. Mrs. Bates was engaged to spend the evening at Hartfield; James had due notice, and he sanguinely hoped that neither dear little Henry nor dear little John would have anything the matter with them while dear Emma were gone.

Chapter 38

No misfortune occurred again to prevent the ball. The day approached, the day arrived; and, after a morning of some anxious watching, Frank Churchill, in all the certainty of his own self, reached Randalls before dinner; and everything was safe.

No second meeting had there yet been between him and Emma. The room at the Crown was to witness it; but it would be better than a common meeting in a crowd. Mr. Weston had been so very earnest in his entreaties for her early attendance, for her arriving there as soon as possible after themselves, for the purpose of taking her opinion as to the propriety and comfort of the rooms before any other persons came, that she could not refuse him, and therefore must spend some quiet interval in the young man's company. She was to convey Harriet, and they drove to the Crown in good time, the Randalls party just sufficiently before them.

Frank Churchill seemed to have been on the watch; and though he did not say much, his eyes declared that he meant to have a delightful evening. They all walked about together, to see that everything was as it should be; and within a few minutes were joined by the contents of another carriage which Emma could not hear the sound of at first without great surprise. "So unreasonably early!" she was going to exclaim; but she presently found that it was a family of old friends, who were coming, like herself, by particular desire, to help Mr. Weston's judgment; and they were so very closely followed by another carriage of cousins, who had been entreated to come early with the same distinguishing earnestness, on the same errand that it seemed as if half the company might soon be collected together for the purpose of preparatory inspection.

Emma perceived that her taste was not the only taste on which Mr. Weston depended, and felt that to be the favourite and intimate of a man who had so many intimates and confidantes, was not the very first distinction in the scale of vanity. She liked his open manners, but a little less of open-heartedness would have made him a higher character. General benevolence, but not general friendship, made a man what he ought to be. She could fancy such a man.

The whole party walked about, and looked, and praised again; and then, having nothing else to do, formed a sort of half-circle round the fire, to observe in their various modes, till other subjects were started, that, though *May*, a fire in the evening was still very pleasant.

Emma found that it was not Mr. Weston's fault that the number of privy counsellors was not yet larger. They had stopped at Mrs. Bates's door to offer the use of their carriage, but the aunt and niece were to be brought by the Eltons.

Frank was standing by her, but not steadily; there was a restlessness, which showed a mind not at ease. He was looking about, he was going to the door, he was watching for the sound of other carriages—impatient to begin, or afraid of being always near her.

Mrs. Elton was spoken of. "I think she must be here soon," said he. "I have a great curiosity to see Mrs. Elton, I have heard so much of her. It cannot be long, I think, before she comes."

A carriage was heard. He was on the move immediately; but coming back, said:

"I am forgetting that I am not acquainted with her. I have never seen either Mr. or Mrs. Elton. I have no business to put myself forward."

Mr. and Mrs. Elton appeared; and all the smiles and the proprieties passed.

"But Miss Bates and Miss Fairfax!" said Mr. Weston, looking about. "We thought you were to bring them."

The mistake had been slight. The carriage was sent for them now. Emma longed to know what Frank's first opinion of Mrs. Elton might be; how he was affected by the studied elegance of her dress, and her smiles of graciousness. He was immediately qualifying himself to form an opinion, by giving her very proper attention, after the introduction had passed.

In a few minutes the carriage returned. Somebody talked of rain. "I will see that there are umbrellas, sir," said Frank to his father: "Miss Bates must not be forgotten;" and away he went. Mr. Weston was following: but Mrs. Elton detained him, to gratify him by her opinion of his son; and so briskly did she begin, that the young man himself, though by no means moving slowly, could hardly be out of hearing.

"A very fine young man, indeed, Mr. Weston. You know I candidly told you I should form my own opinion; and I am happy to say that I am extremely pleased with him. You may believe me. I never compliment. I think him a very handsome young man, and his manners are precisely what I like and approve, so truly the gentleman, without the least conceit or puppyism. You must know I have a vast dislike to puppies—quite a horror of them. They were never tolerated at Maple Grove. Neither Mr. Suckling nor me had ever any patience with them; and we used sometimes to say very cutting things. Selina, who is mild almost to a fault, bore with them much better."

While she talked of his son, Mr. Weston's attention was chained; but when she got to Maple Grove, he could recollect that there were ladies just arriving to be attended to, and with happy smiles must hurry away.

Mrs. Elton turned to Mrs. Weston. "I have no doubt of its being our carriage with Miss Bates and Jane. Our coachman and horses are so extremely expeditious! I believe we drive faster than anybody. What a pleasure it is to send one's carriage for a friend! I understand you were so kind as to offer, but another time it will be quite unnecessary. You may be very sure I shall always take care of *them*."

Miss Bates and Miss Fairfax, escorted by the two gentlemen, walked into the room; and Mrs. Elton seemed to think it as much her duty as Mrs. Weston's to receive them. Her gestures and movements might be understood by anyone who looked on like Emma; but her words, everybody's words, were soon lost under the incessant flow of Miss Bates, who came in talking, and had not finished her speech under many minutes after her being admitted into the circle at the fire. As the door opened she was heard—

"So very obliging of you! No rain at all. Nothing to signify. I do not care for myself. Quite thick shoes. And Jane declares—Well!" (as soon as she was within the door), "well! This is brilliant indeed! This is admirable! Excellently contrived, upon my word. Nothing wanting. Could not have imagined it. So well lighted up! Jane, Jane, look! did you ever see anything—? Oh! Mr. Weston, you must really have had Aladdin's lamp. Good Mrs. Stokes would not know her own room again. I saw her as I came in; she was standing in the entrance. 'Oh! Mrs. Stokes,' said I—but I had not time for more." She was now met by Mrs. Weston. "Very well, I thank you, ma'am. I hope you are quite well. Very happy to hear it. So afraid you might have a headache! seeing you pass by so often, and knowing how much trouble you must have. Delighted to hear it indeed! Ah! dear Mrs. Elton, so obliged to you for the carriage; excellent time; Jane and I quite ready. Did not keep the horses a moment. Most comfortable carriage. Oh! and I am sure our thanks are due to you, Mrs. Weston, on that score. Mrs. Elton had most kindly sent Jane a note, or we should have been. But two such offers in one day! Never were such neighbours. I said to my mother, 'Upon my word, ma'am—' Thank you, my mother is remarkably well. Gone to Mr. Woodhouse's. I made her take her shawl—for the evenings are not warm—her large new shawl, Mrs. Dixon's wedding present. So kind of her to think of my mother! Bought at Weymouth, you know; Mr. Dixon's choice. There were three others, Jane says, which they hesitated about some time. Colonel Campbell rather preferred an olive. My dear Jane, are you sure you did not wet your feet? It was but a drop or two, but I am so afraid; but Mr. Frank Churchill was so extremely—and there was a mat to step upon. I shall never forget his extreme politeness. Oh! Mr. Frank Churchill, I must tell you my mother's spectacles have never been in fault since; the rivet never came out again. My mother often talks of your good-nature; does not she, Jane? Do not we often talk of Mr. Frank Churchill? Ah, here's Miss Woodhouse. Dear Miss Woodhouse, how do you do? Very well, I thank you, quite well. This is meeting quite in fairy land. Such a transformation! Must not compliment, I know" (eyeing Emma most complacently)— "that would be rude; but upon my word, Miss Woodhouse, you do look— how do you like Jane's hair? You are a judge. She did it all herself. Quite wonderful how she does her hair! No hairdresser from London, I think, could—Ah! Dr. Hughes, I declare—and Mrs. Hughes. Must go and speak to Dr. and Mrs. Hughes for a moment. How do you do? How do you do? Very well, I thank you. This is delightful, is not it? Where's dear Mr. Richard? Oh! there he is. Don't disturb him. Much better employed talking to the young ladies. How do you do, Mr. Richard? I saw you the other day as you rode through the town. Mrs. Otway, I protest, and good Mr. Otway, and Miss Otway, and Miss Caroline. Such a host of friends! and Mr. George and Mr. Arthur! How do you do? How do you all do? Quite well, I am much obliged to you. Never better. Don't I hear another carriage? Who can this be? very likely the worthy Coles. Upon my word, this is charming, to be standing about among such friends! and such a noble fire! I am quite roasted. No coffee, I thank you, for me; never take coffee. A little tea, if you please, sir, by and by; no hurry. Oh! here it comes. Everything is so good!"

Frank Churchill returned to his station by Emma; and as soon as Miss Bates was quiet, she found herself necessarily overhearing the discourse of

Mrs. Elton and Miss Fairfax, who were standing a little way behind her. He was thoughtful. Whether he were overhearing too she could not determine. After a good many compliments to Jane on her dress and look —compliments very quietly and properly taken—Mrs. Elton was evidently wanting to be complimented herself—and it was, "How do you like my gown? How do you like my trimming! How has Wright done my hair?" with many other relative questions, all answered with patient politeness. Mrs. Elton then said:

"Nobody can think less of dress in general than I do: but upon such an occasion as this, when everybody's eyes are so much upon me, and in compliment to the Westons, who I have no doubt are giving this ball chiefly to do me honour—I would not wish to be inferior to others; and I see very few pearls in the room except mine. So Frank Churchill is a capital dancer, I understand. We shall see if our styles suit. A fine young man certainly is Frank Churchill. I like him very well."

At this moment Frank began talking so vigorously, that Emma could not but imagine he had overheard his own praises, and did not want to hear more; and the voices of the ladies were drowned for a while, till another suspension brought Mrs. Elton's tones again distinctly forward. Mr. Elton had just joined him, and his wife was exclaiming:

"Oh! you have found us out at last, have you, in our seclusion? I was this moment telling Jane, I thought you would begin to be impatient for tidings of us."

"Jane!" repeated Frank Churchill, with a look of surprise and displeasure. "That is easy; but Miss Fairfax does not disapprove it, I suppose."

"How do you like Mrs. Elton?" said Emma, in a whisper.

"Not at all."

"You are ungrateful."

"Ungrateful! What do you mean?" Then changing from a frown to a smile, "No, do not tell me, I do not want to know what you mean. Where is my father? When are we to begin dancing?"

Emma could hardly understand him; he seemed in an odd humour. He walked off to find his father, but was quickly back again with both Mr. and Mrs. Weston. He had met with them in a little perplexity, which must be laid before Emma. It had just occurred to Mrs. Weston that Mrs. Elton must be asked to begin the ball; that she would expect it; which interfered with all their wishes of giving Emma that distinction. Emma heard the sad truth with fortitude.

"And what are we to do for a proper partner for her?" said Mr. Weston. "She will think Frank ought to ask her."

Frank turned instantly to Emma, to claim her former promise; and boasted himself an engaged man, which his father looked his most perfect approbation of—and it then appeared that Mrs. Weston was wanting *him* to dance with Mrs. Elton himself, and that their business was to help to persuade him into it, which was done pretty soon. Mr. Weston and Mrs.

Elton led the way; Mr. Frank Churchill and Miss Woodhouse followed. Emma must submit to stand second to Mrs. Elton though she had always considered the ball as peculiarly for her. It was almost enough to make her think of marrying.

Mrs. Elton had undoubtedly the advantage, at this time, in vanity completely gratified; for though she had intended to begin with Frank Churchill, she could not lose by the change. Mr. Weston might be his son's superior. In spite of this little rub, however, Emma was smiling with enjoyment, delighted to see the respectable length of the set as it was forming, and to feel that she had so many hours of unusual festivity before her. She was more disturbed by Mr. Knightley's not dancing than by anything else. There he was, among the standers-by, where he ought not to be; he ought to be dancing, not classing himself with the husbands, and fathers, and whist-players, who were pretending to feel an interest in the dance till their rubbers were made up, so young as he looked! He could not have appeared to greater advantage perhaps anywhere, than where he had placed himself. His tall, firm, upright figure, among the bulky forms and stooping shoulders of the elderly men, was such as Emma felt must draw everybody's eyes; and, excepting her own partner, there was not one among the whole row of young men who could be compared with him. He moved a few steps nearer, and those few steps were enough to prove in how gentlemanlike a manner, with what natural grace, he must have danced, would he but take the trouble. Whenever she caught his eye, she forced him to smile; but in general he was looking grave. She wished he could love a ball-room better, and could like Frank Churchill better. He seemed often observing her. She must not flatter herself that he thought of her dancing; but if he were criticising her behaviour, she did not feel afraid. There was nothing like flirtation between her and her partner. They seemed more like cheerful, easy friends than lovers. That Frank Churchill thought less of her than he had done was indubitable.

The ball proceeded pleasantly. The anxious cares, the incessant attentions of Mrs. Weston were not thrown away. Everybody seemed happy; and the praise of being a delightful ball, which is seldom bestowed till after a ball has ceased to be, was repeatedly given in the very beginning of the existence of this. Of very important, very recordable events, it was not more productive than such meetings usually are. There was one, however, which Emma thought something of. The two last dances before supper were begun, and Harriet had no partner; the only young lady sitting down; and so equal had been hitherto the number of dancers, that how there could be any one disengaged was the wonder. But Emma's wonder lessened soon afterwards, on seeing Mr. Elton sauntering about. He would not ask Harriet to dance, if it were possible to be avoided; she was sure he would not—and she was expecting him every moment to escape into the card-room.

Escape, however, was not his plan. He came to the part of the room where the sitters-by were collected, spoke to some, and walked about in front of them, as if to show his liberty, and his resolution of maintaining it. He did not omit being sometimes directly before Miss Smith, or speaking to those who were close to her. Emma saw it. She was not yet dancing; she was working her way up from the bottom, and had therefore leisure to look around, and by only turning her head a little she saw it all. When she was half-way up the set, the whole group were exactly behind her, and she would no longer allow her eyes to watch; but Mr. Elton was so near, that she heard every syllable of a dialogue which just then took place between him and Mrs. Weston; and she perceived that his wife, who was standing immediately above her, was not only listening also, but even encouraging him by significant glances. The kind-hearted, gentle Mrs. Weston had left her seat to join him and say, "Do not you dance, Mr. Elton?" to which his prompt reply was, "Most readily, Mrs. Weston, if you will dance with me."

"Me! oh! no—I would get you a better partner than myself. I am no dancer."

"If Mrs. Gilbert wishes to dance," said he, "I shall have great pleasure I am sure; for, though beginning to feel myself rather an old married man, and that my dancing days are over, it would give me very great pleasure at any time to stand up with an old friend like Mrs. Gilbert."

"Mrs. Gilbert does not mean to dance, but there is a young lady disengaged whom I should be very glad to see dancing—Miss Smith."

"Miss Smith— Oh! I had not observed. You are extremely obliging— and if I were not an old married—but my dancing days are over, Mrs. Weston. You will excuse me. Anything else I should be most happy to do, at your command—but my dancing days are over."

Mrs. Weston said no more; and Emma could imagine with what surprise and mortification she must be returning to her seat. This was Mr. Elton! the amiable, obliging, gentle Mr. Elton. She looked round for a moment; he had joined Mr. Knightley at a little distance, and was arranging himself for settled conversation, while smiles of high glee passed between him and his wife. She would not look again. Her heart was in a glow, and she feared her face might be as hot.

In another moment a happier sight caught her—Mr. Knightley leading Harriet to the set! Never had she been more surprised, seldom more delighted, than at that instant. She was all pleasure and gratitude, both for Harriet and herself, and longed to be thanking him; and though too distant for speech, her countenance said much, as soon as she could catch his eye again.

His dancing proved to be just what she had believed it, extremely good; and Harriet would have seemed almost too lucky, if it had not been for the cruel state of things before, and for the very complete enjoyment and very high sense of the distinction which her happy features announced. It was not thrown away on her; she bounded higher than ever, flew farther down the middle, and was in a continual course of smiles.

Mr. Elton had retreated into the card-room, looking (Emma trusted) very foolish. She did not think he was quite so hardened as his wife, though growing very like her; *she* spoke some of her feelings, by observing audibly to her partner:

"Knightley has taken pity on poor little Miss Smith! Very good-natured, I declare."

Supper was announced. The move began; and Miss Bates might be heard from that moment without interruption, till her being seated at table and taking up her spoon.

"Jane, Jane, my dear Jane, where are you? Here is your tippet. Mrs. Weston begs you to put on your tippet. She says she is afraid there will be draughts in the passage, though everything has been done—one door nailed up—quantities of matting—my dear Jane, indeed you must. Mr. Churchill, oh! you are too obliging. How well you put it on—so gratified! Excellent dancing indeed. Yes, my dear, I ran home, as I said I should, to help grandmamma to bed, and got back again, and nobody missed me. I set off without saying a word, just as I told you. Grandmamma was quite well, had a charming evening with Mr. Woodhouse, a vast deal of chat, and backgammon. Tea was made downstairs, biscuits and baked apples, and wine before she came away: amazing luck in some of her throws: and she inquired a great deal about you, how you were amused, and who were your partners. 'Oh!' said I, 'I shall not forestall Jane; I left her dancing with Mr. George Otway; she will love to tell you all about it herself to-morrow: her first partner was Mr. Elton; I do not know who will ask her next, perhaps Mr. William Cox.' My dear sir, you are too obliging. Is there nobody you would not rather? I am not helpless. Sir, you are most kind. Upon my word, Jane on one arm, and me on the other. Stop, stop, let us stand a little back, Mrs. Elton is going; dear Mrs. Elton, how elegant she looks—beautiful lace. Now we all follow in her train. Quite the queen of the evening! Well, here we are at the passage. Two steps, Jane, take care of the two steps. Oh, no, there is but one. Well, I was persuaded there were two. How very odd! I was convinced there were two, and there is but one. I never saw anything equal to the comfort and style—candles everywhere. I was telling you of your grandmamma, Jane—there was a little disappointment. The baked apples and biscuits, excellent in their way, you know; but there was a delicate fricassee of sweetbread and some asparagus brought in at first, and good Mr. Woodhouse, not thinking the asparagus quite boiled enough, sent it all out again. Now there is nothing grandmamma loves better than sweetbread and asparagus—so she was rather disappointed; but we agreed we would not speak of it to anybody, for fear of its getting round to dear Miss Woodhouse, who would be so very much concerned. Well, this is brilliant! I am all amazement! could not have supposed anything—such elegance and profusion! I have seen nothing like it since—Well, where shall we sit? Where shall we sit? Anywhere, so that Jane is not in a draught. Where *I* sit is of no consequence. Oh! do you recommend this side? Well, I am sure, Mr. Churchill—only it seems too good—but just as you please. What you direct in this house cannot be wrong. Dear Jane, how shall we ever recollect half the dishes for grandmamma? Soup too! Bless me! I should not be helped so soon, but it smells most excellent, and I cannot help beginning."

Emma had no opportunity of speaking to Mr. Knightley till after supper; but, when they were all in the ball-room again, her eyes invited him irresistibly to come to her and be thanked. He was warm in his reprobation of Mr. Elton's conduct; it had been unpardonable rudeness; and Mrs. Elton's looks also received the due share of censure.

"They aimed at wounding more than Harriet," said he. "Emma, why is it that they are your enemies?"

He looked with smiling penetration; and, on receiving no answer, added, "*She* ought not to be angry with you, I suspect, whatever he may be. To that surmise, you say nothing, of course: but confess, Emma, that you did want him to marry Harriet."

"I did," replied Emma, "and they cannot forgive me."

He shook his head; but there was a smile of indulgence with it, and he only said:

"I shall not scold you. I leave you to your own reflections."

"Can you trust me with such flatterers? Does my vain spirit ever tell me I am wrong?"

"Not your vain spirit, but your serious spirit. If one leads you wrong, I am sure the other tells you of it."

"I do own myself to have been completely mistaken in Mr. Elton. There is a littleness about him which you discovered, which I did not: and I was fully convinced of his being in love with Harriet. It was through a series of strange blunders!"

"And, in return for your acknowledging so much, I will do you the justice to say, that you would have chosen for him better than he has chosen for himself. Harriet Smith has some first-rate qualities, which Mrs. Elton is totally without. An unpretending, single-minded, artless girl— infinitely to be preferred by any man of sense and taste to such a woman as Mrs. Elton. I found Harriet more conversable than I expected."

Emma was extremely gratified. They were interrupted by the bustle of Mr. Weston calling on everybody to begin dancing again.

"Come, Miss Woodhouse, Miss Otway, Miss Fairfax, what are you all doing? Come, Emma, set your companions the example. Everybody is lazy! Everybody is asleep!"

"I am ready," said Emma, "whenever I am wanted."

"Whom are you going to dance with?" asked Mr. Knightley.

She hesitated a moment, and then replied, "With you if you will ask me."

"Will you?" said he, offering his hand.

"Indeed I will. You have shown that you can dance, and you know we are not really so much brother and sister as to make it at all improper."

"Brother and sister! no, indeed."

Chapter 39

THIS little explanation with Mr. Knightley gave Emma considerable pleasure. It was one of the agreeable recollections of the ball, which she walked about the lawn the next morning to enjoy. She was extremely glad that they had come to so good an understanding respecting the Eltons, and that their opinions of both husband and wife were so much alike; and his praise of Harriet, his concession in her favour, was peculiarly gratifying. The impertinence of the Eltons, which for a few moments had threatened to ruin the rest of her evening, had been the occasion of some of its highest satisfactions; and she looked forward to another happy result— the cure of Harriet's infatuation. From Harriet's manner of speaking of the circumstance before they quitted the ball-room she had strong hopes. It seemed as if her eyes were suddenly opened, and she were enabled to see that Mr. Elton was not the superior creature she had believed him. The fever was over, and Emma could harbour little fear of the pulse being quickened again by injurious courtesy. She depended on the evil feelings of the Eltons for supplying all the discipline of pointed neglect that could be further requisite. Harriet rational, Frank Churchill not too much in love, and Mr. Knightley not wanting to quarrel with her, how very happy a summer must be before her.

She was not to see Frank Churchill this morning. He had told her that he could not allow himself the pleasure of stopping at Hartfield, as he was to be home by the middle of the day. She did not regret it.

Having arranged all these matters, looked them through, and put them all to rights, she was just turning to the house, with spirits freshened up for the demands of the two little boys, as well as of their grandpapa, when the great iron sweep-gate opened, and two persons entered whom she had never less expected to see together—Frank Churchill, with Harriet leaning on his arm—actually Harriet! A moment sufficed to convince her that something extraordinary had happened. Harriet looked white and frightened, and he was trying to cheer her. The iron gates and the front-door were not twenty yards asunder—they were all three soon in the hall; and Harriet, immediately sinking into a chair, fainted away.

A young lady who faints must be recovered; questions must be answered, and surprises be explained. Such events are very interesting; but the suspense of them cannot last long. A few minutes made Emma acquainted with the whole.

Miss Smith, and Miss Bickerton, another parlour boarder at Mrs. Goddard's, who had been also at the ball, had walked out together, and taken a road—the Richmond road, which, though apparently public enough for safety, had led them into alarm. About half a mile beyond Highbury, making a sudden turn, and deeply shaded by elms on each side, it became for a considerable stretch very retired; and when the young ladies had advanced some way into it, they had suddenly perceived, at a small distance before them, on a broader patch of greensward by the side, a party of gipsies. A child on the watch came towards them to beg; and Miss Bickerton, excessively frightened, gave a great scream, and calling on Harriet to follow her, ran up a steep bank, cleared a slight hedge at the top, and made the best of her way by a short cut back to Highbury. But poor Harriet could not follow. She had suffered very much from cramp after dancing, and her first attempt to mount the bank brought on such a return of it as made her absolutely powerless; and in this state, and exceedingly terrified, she had been obliged to remain.

How the trampers might have behaved, had the young ladies been more courageous, must be doubtful; but such an invitation for attack could not be resisted; and Harriet was soon assailed by half a dozen children, headed by a stout woman, and a great boy, all clamorous, and impertinent in look, though not absolutely in word. More and more frightened, she immediately promised them money, and taking out her purse, gave them a shilling, and begged them not to want more, or to use her ill. She was then able to walk, though but slowly, and was moving away—but her terror and her purse were too tempting; and she was followed, or rather surrounded, by the whole gang, demanding more.

In this state Frank Churchill had found her, she trembling and conditioning, they loud and insolent. By a most fortunate chance, his leaving Highbury had been delayed so as to bring him to her assistance at this critical moment. The pleasantness of the morning had induced him to walk forward, and leave his horses to meet him by another road, a mile or two beyond Highbury; and happening to have borrowed a pair of scissors the night before of Miss Bates, and to have forgotten to restore them, he had been obliged to stop at her door, and go in for a few minutes; he was therefore later than he had intended; and being on foot, was unseen by the whole party till almost close to them. The terror which the woman and boy had been creating in Harriet was then their own portion. He had left them completely frightened; and Harriet eagerly clinging to him, and hardly able to speak, had just strength enough to reach Hartfield, before her spirits were quite overcome. It was his idea to bring her to Hartfield; he had thought of no other place.

This was the amount of the whole story—of his communication and of Harriet's, as soon as she had recovered her senses and speech. He dared not stay longer than to see her well; these several delays left him not another minute to lose; and Emma engaging to give assurance of her safety to Mrs. Goddard, and notice of there being such a set of people in the neighbourhood to Mr. Knightley, he set off, with all the grateful blessings that she could utter for her friend and herself.

Such an adventure as this, a fine young man and a lovely young woman thrown together in such a way, could hardly fail of suggesting certain ideas to the coldest heart and the steadiest brain. So Emma thought, at least. Could a linguist, could a grammarian, could even a mathematician have seen what she did, have witnessed their appearance together, and heard their history of it, without feeling that circumstances had been at work to make them peculiarly interesting to each other? How much more must an imaginist, like herself, be on fire with speculation and foresight? especially with such a groundwork of anticipation as her mind had already made.

It was a very extraordinary thing! Nothing of the sort had ever occurred before to any young ladies in the place, within her memory; no rencontre, no alarm of the kind; and now it had happened to the very person, and at the very hour, when the other very person was chancing to pass by to rescue her! It certainly was very extraordinary! And knowing, as she did, the favourable state of mind of each at this period, it struck her the more. He was wishing to get the better of his attachment to herself, she just recovering from her mania for Mr. Elton. It seemed as if everything united to promise the most interesting consequences. It was not possible that the occurrence should not be strongly recommending each to the other.

In the few minutes' conversation which she had yet had with him, while Harriet had been partially insensible, he had spoken of her terror, her naïveté, her fervour as she seized and clung to his arm, with a sensibility amused and delighted; and just at last, after Harriet's own account had been given, he had expressed his indignation at the abominable folly of Miss Bickerton in the warmest terms. Everything was to take its natural course, however, neither impelled nor assisted. She would not stir a step nor drop a hint. No, she had had enough of interference. There could be no harm in a scheme, a mere passive scheme. It was no more than a wish. Beyond it she would on no account proceed.

Emma's first resolution was to keep her father from the knowledge of what had passed, aware of the anxiety and alarm it would occasion; but she soon felt that concealment must be impossible. Within half an hour it was known all over Highbury. It was the very event to engage those who talk most—the young and the low; and all the youth and servants in the place were soon in the happiness of frightful news. The last night's ball seemed lost in the gipsies. Poor Mr. Woodhouse trembled as he sat, and, as Emma had foreseen, would scarcely be satisfied without their promising never to go beyond the shrubbery again. It was some comfort to him that many inquiries after himself and Miss Woodhouse (for his neighbours knew that he loved to be inquired after), as well as Miss Smith, were coming in during the rest of the day; and he had the pleasure of returning for answer, that they were all very indifferent; which, though not exactly true, for she was perfectly well, and Harriet not much otherwise, Emma would not interfere with. She had an unhappy state of health in general for the child of such a man, for she hardly knew what indisposition was; and if he did not invent illnesses for her, she could make no figure in a message.

The gipsies did not wait for the operations of justice; they took themselves off in a hurry. The young ladies of Highbury might have walked again in safety before their panic began. and the whole history dwindled soon into a matter of little importance but to Emma and her nephews: in her imagination it maintained its ground; and Henry and John were still asking every day for the story of Harriet and the gipsies, and still tenaciously setting her right if she varied in the slightest particular from the original recital.

Chapter 40

A VERY few days had passed after this adventure, when Harriet came one morning to Emma with a small parcel in her hand, and after sitting down and hesitating, thus began:

"Miss Woodhouse—if you are at leisure, I have something that I should like to tell you: a sort of confession to make—and then, you know, it will be over."

Emma was a good deal surprised; but begged her to speak. There was a seriousness in Harriet's manner which prepared her, quite as much as her words, for something more than ordinary.

"It is my duty, and I am sure it is my wish," she continued, "to have no reserves with you on this subject. As I am, happily, quite an altered creature, in *one respect*, it is very fit that you should have the satisfaction of knowing it. I do not want to say more than is necessary; I am too much ashamed of having given way as I have done, and I dare say you understand me."

"Yes," said Emma, "I hope I do."

"How I could so long a time be fancying myself—" cried Harriet warmly. "It seems like madness! I can see nothing at all extraordinary in him now. I do not care whether I meet him or not, except that, of the two, I had rather not see him; and, indeed, I would go any distance round to avoid him; but I do not envy her, as I have done. She is very charming, I dare say, and all that; but I think her very ill-tempered and disagreeable: I shall never forget her look the other night. However, I assure you, Miss Woodhouse, I wish her no evil. No; let them be ever so happy together, it will not give me another moment's pang; and, to convince you that I have been speaking truth, I am now going to destroy—what I ought to have destroyed long ago—what I ought never to have kept: I know that very well" (blushing as she spoke). "However, now I will destroy it all; and it is my particular wish to do it in your presence, that you may see how rational I am grown. Cannot you guess what this parcel holds?" said she, with a conscious look.

"Not the least in the world. Did he ever give you anything?"

"No—I cannot call them gifts; but they are things that I have valued very much."

She held the parcel towards her, and Emma read the words *Most precious treasures* on the top. Her curiosity was greatly excited. Harriet unfolded the parcel, and she looked on with impatience. Within abundance of silver paper was a pretty little Tunbridge-ware box, which Harriet opened: it was well lined with the softest cotton; but, excepting the cotton, Emma saw only a small piece of court-plaster.

"Now," said Harriet, "you *must* recollect."

"No, indeed, I do not."

"Dear me! I should not have thought it possible you could forget what passed in this very room about court-plaster, one of the very last times we ever met in it. It was but a very few days before I had my sore throat— just before Mr. and Mrs. John Knightley came; I think the very evening. Do not you remember his cutting his finger with your new penknife, and your recommending court-plaster? But, as you had none about you, and knew I had, you desired me to supply him; and so I took mine out and cut him a piece: but it was a great deal too large, and he cut it smaller, and kept playing some time with what was left, before he gave it back to me. And so then, in my nonsense, I could not help making a treasure of it; so I put it by, never to be used, and looked at it now and then as a great treat."

"My dearest Harriet!" cried Emma, putting her hand before her face, and jumping up, "you make me more ashamed of myself than I can bear. Remember it? Aye, I remember it all now; all, except your saving this relic: I knew nothing of that till this moment, but the cutting the finger, and my recommending court-plaster, and saying I had none about me. Oh! my sins! my sins! And I had plenty all the while in my pocket! One of my senseless tricks. I deserve to be under a continual blush all the rest of my life. Well" (sitting down again), "go on: what else?"

"And had you really some at hand yourself? I am sure I never suspected it, you did it so naturally."

"And so you actually put this piece of court-plaster by for his sake!" said Emma, recovering from her state of shame, and feeling divided between wonder and amusement; and secretly she added to herself, "Lord bless me! when should I ever have thought of putting by in cotton a piece of court-plaster that Frank Churchill had been pulling about! I never was equal to this."

"Here," resumed Harriet, turning to her box again, "here is something still more valuable, I mean that *has been* more valuable, because this is what did really once belong to him, which the court-plaster never did."

Emma was quite eager to see this superior treasure. It was the end of an old pencil, the part without any lead.

"This was really his," said Harriet. "Do not you remember one morning? no, I dare say you do not. But one morning—I forget exactly the day —but perhaps it was the Tuesday or Wednesday before *that evening*, he wanted to make a memorandum in his pocket-book; it was about spruce-beer. Mr. Knightley had been telling him something about brewing spruce-beer, and he wanted to put it down; but when he took out his pencil, there was so little lead that he soon cut it all away, and it would not do, so you lent him another, and this was left upon the table as good for nothing. But I kept my eye on it; and, as soon as I dared, caught it up, and never parted with it again from that moment."

"I do remember it," cried Emma; "I perfectly remember it. Talking about spruce-beer. Oh! yes. Mr. Knightley and I both saying we liked it, and Mr. Elton's seeming resolved to learn to like it too. I perfectly remember it. Stop—Mr. Knightley was standing just here, was not he? I have an idea he was standing just here."

"Ah! I do not know. I cannot recollect. It is very odd, but I cannot recollect. Mr. Elton was sitting here, I remember, much about where I am now."

"Well, go on."

"Oh! that's all. I have nothing more to show you, or to say, except that I am now going to throw them both behind the fire, and I wish you to see me do it."

"My poor dear Harriet! and have you actually found happiness in treasuring up these things?"

"Yes, simpleton as I was! but I am quite ashamed of it now, and wish I could forget as easily as I can burn them. It was very wrong of me, you know, to keep any remembrances after he was married. I knew it was— but had not resolution enough to part with them."

"But, Harriet, is it necessary to burn the court-plaster? I have not a word to say for the bit of old pencil, but the court-plaster might be useful."

"I shall be happier to burn it," replied Harriet. "It has a disagreeable look to me. I must get rid of everything. There it goes, and there is an end, thank Heaven! of Mr. Elton."

"And when," thought Emma, "will there be a beginning of Mr. Churchill?"

She had soon afterwards reason to believe that the beginning was already made, and could not but hope that the gipsy, though she had *told* no fortune, might be proved to have made Harriet's. About a fortnight after the alarm they came to a sufficient explanation, and quite undesignedly Emma was not thinking of it at the moment, which made the information she received more valuable. She merely said in the course of some trivial chat, "Well, Harriet, whenever you marry, I would advise you to do so and so"—and thought no more of it, till, after a minute's silence she heard Harriet say, in a very serious tone, "I shall never marry." Emma then looked up, and immediately saw how it was; and after a moment's debate, as to whether it should pass unnoticed or not, replied:

"Never marry! This is a new resolution."

"It is one that I shall never change, however."

After another short hesitation, "I hope it does not proceed from—I hope it is not in compliment to Mr. Elton?"

"Mr. Elton, indeed!" cried Harriet, indignantly. "Oh! no"—and Emma could just catch the words, "so superior to Mr. Elton!"

She then took a longer time for consideration. Should she proceed no further? should she let it pass, and seem to suspect nothing? Perhaps

Harriet might think her cold or angry if she did; or perhaps, if she were totally silent, it might only drive Harriet into asking her to hear too much; and against anything like such an unreserve as had been, such an open and frequent discussion of hopes and chances, she was perfectly resolved. She believed it would be wiser for her to say and know at once all that she meant to say and know. Plain dealing was always best. She had previously determined how far she would proceed, on any application of the sort; and it would be safer for both to have the judicious law of her own brain laid down with speed. She was decided, and thus spoke:

"Harriet, I will not affect to be in doubt of your meaning. Your resolution, or rather your expectation of never marrying, results from an idea that the person whom you might prefer would be too greatly your superior in situation to think of you. Is not it so?"

"Oh, Miss Woodhouse, believe me, I have not the presumption to suppose—indeed I am not so mad. But it is a pleasure to me to admire him at a distance, and to think of his infinite superiority to all the rest of the world, with the gratitude, wonder, and veneration which are so proper, in me especially."

"I am not at all surprised at you, Harriet. The service he rendered you was enough to warm your heart."

"Service! oh, it was such an inexpressible obligation! The very recol lection of it, and all that I felt at the time, when I saw him coming—his noble look, and my wretchedness before. Such a change! In one moment such a change! From perfect misery to perfect happiness!"

"It is very natural. It is natural, and it is honourable. Yes, honourable, I think, to choose so well and so gratefully. But that it will be a fortunate preference is more than I can promise. I do not advise you to give way to it, Harriet. I do not by any means engage for its being returned. Consider what you are about. Perhaps it will be wisest in you to check your feelings while you can: at any rate do not let them carry you far, unless you are persuaded of his liking you. Be observant of him. Let his behaviour be the guide of your sensations. I give you this caution now, because I shall never speak to you again on the subject. I am determined against all interference. Henceforward, I know nothing of the matter. Let no name ever pass our lips. We were very wrong before; we will be cautious now. He is your superior, no doubt, and there do seem objections and obstacles of a very serious nature; but yet, Harriet, more wonderful things have taken place: there have been matches of greater disparity. But take care of yourself; I would not have you too sanguine; though, however it may end, be assured that your raising your thoughts to *him* is a mark of good taste which I shall always know how to value."

Harriet kissed her hand in silent and submissive gratitude. Emma was very decided in thinking such an attachment no bad thing for her friend. Its tendency would be to raise and refine her mind—and it must be saving her from the danger of degradation.

Chapter 41

In this state of schemes, and hopes, and connivance, June opened upon Hartfield. To Highbury, in general, it brought no material change. The Eltons were still talking of a visit from the Sucklings, and of the use to be made of their barouche-landau, and Jane Fairfax was still at her grandmother's; and as the return of the Campbells from Ireland was again delayed, and August, instead of Midsummer, fixed for it, she was likely to remain there full two months longer, provided at least she were able to defeat Mrs. Elton's activity in her service, and save herself from being hurried into a delightful situation against her will.

Mr. Knightley, who, for some reason best known to himself, had certainly taken an early dislike to Frank Churchill, was only growing to dislike him more. He began to suspect him of some double dealing in his pursuit of Emma. That Emma was his object appeared indisputable. Everything declared it; his own attentions, his father's hints, his stepmother's guarded silence; it was all in unison; words, conduct, discretion and indiscretion, told the same story. But while so many were devoting him to Emma, and Emma herself making him over to Harriet, Mr. Knightley began to suspect him of some inclination to trifle with Jane Fairfax. He could not understand it; but there were symptoms of intelligence between them—he thought so at least—symptoms of admiration on his side, which, having once observed, he could not persuade himself to think entirely void of meaning, however he might wish to escape any of Emma's errors of imagination. *She* was not present when the suspicion first arose. He was dining with the Randalls family and Jane at the Eltons'; and he had seen a look, more than a single look, at Miss Fairfax, which, from the admirer of Miss Woodhouse, seemed somewhat out of place. When he was again in their company, he could not help remembering what he had seen; nor could he avoid observations which, unless it were like Cowper and his fire at twilight,

"Myself creating what I saw,"

brought him yet stronger suspicion of there being a something of private liking, of private understanding even, between Frank Churchill and Jane.

He had walked up one day after dinner, as he very often did, to spend his evening at Hartfield. Emma and Harriet were going to walk; he joined them; and, on returning, they fell in with a larger party, who, like themselves, judged it wisest to take their exercise early as the weather threatened rain; Mr. and Mrs. Weston and their son, Miss Bates and her niece, who had accidentally met. They all united; and, on reaching Hartfield gates, Emma, who knew it was exactly the sort of visiting that would be welcome to her father, pressed them all to go in and drink tea with him. The Randalls party agreed to it immediately; and after a pretty long speech from Miss Bates, which few persons listened to, she also found it possible to accept dear Miss Woodhouse's most obliging invitation.

As they were turning into the grounds, Mr. Perry passed by on horseback. The gentlemen spoke of his horse.

"By the bye," said Frank Churchill to Mrs. Weston presently, "what became of Mr. Perry's plan of setting up his carriage?"

Mrs. Weston looked surprised, and said, "I did not know that he ever had any such plan."

"Nay, I had it from you. You wrote me word of it three months ago."

"Me! impossible!"

"Indeed you did. I remember it perfectly. You mentioned it as what was certainly to be very soon. Mrs. Perry had told somebody and was extremely happy about it. It was owing to *her* persuasion, as she thought his being out in bad weather did him a great deal of harm. You must remember it now?"

"Upon my word, I never heard of it till this moment."

"Never really never! Bless me! how could it be? Then I must have dreamt it—but I was completely persuaded—Miss Smith, you walk as if you were tired. You will not be sorry to find yourself at home."

"What is this? What is this?" cried Mr. Weston, "about Perry and a carriage? Is Perry going to set up his carriage, Frank? I am glad he can afford it. You had it from himself, had you?"

"No, sir," replied his son, laughing. "I seem to have had it from nobody. Very odd! I really was persuaded of Mrs. Weston's having mentioned it in one of her letters to Enscombe, many weeks ago, with all these particulars; but as she declares she never heard a syllable of it before, of course it must have been a dream. I am a great dreamer. I dream of everybody at Highbury, when I am away; and when I have gone through my particular friends, then I begin dreaming of Mr. and Mrs. Perry."

"It is odd, though," observed his father, "that you should have had such a regular connected dream about people whom it was not very likely you should be thinking of at Enscombe. Perry's setting up his carriage! and his wife's persuading him to it, out of care for his health—just what will happen, I have no doubt, some time or other; only a little premature. What an air of probability sometimes runs through a dream! And at others, what a heap of absurdities it is! Well, Frank, your dream certainly shows that Highbury is in your thoughts when you are absent. Emma, you are a great dreamer, I think?"

Emma was out of hearing. She had hurried on before her guests to prepare her father for their appearance, and was beyond the reach of Mr. Weston's hint.

"Why, to own the truth," cried Miss Bates, who had been trying in vain to be heard the last two minutes, "if I must speak on this subject, there is no denying that Mr. Frank Churchill might have—I do not mean to say that he did not dream it—I am sure I have sometimes the oddest dreams in the world—but if I am questioned about it, I must acknowledge that there was such an idea last spring; for Mrs. Perry herself mentioned it to my mother, and the Coles knew of it as well as ourselves—but it was quite a secret, known to nobody else, and only thought of about three days. Mrs. Perry was very anxious that he should have a carriage, and came to my mother in great spirits one morning because she thought she had prevailed. Jane, don't you remember grandmamma's telling us of it when we got home? I forget where we had been walking to—very likely to Randalls; yes, I think it was to Randalls. Mrs. Perry was always particularly fond of my mother—indeed I do not know who is not—and she had mentioned it to her in confidence; she had no objection to her telling us, of course, but it was not to go beyond; and from that day to this I never mentioned it to a soul that I know of. At the same time, I will not positively answer for my having never dropped a hint, because I know I do sometimes pop out a thing before I am aware. I am a talker, you know; I am rather a talker; and now and then I have let a thing escape me which I should not. I am not like Jane; I wish I were. I will answer for it *she* never betrayed the least thing in the world. Where is she? Oh! just behind. Perfectly remember Mrs. Perry's coming. Extraordinary dream, indeed!"

They were entering the hall. Mr. Knightley's eyes had preceded Miss Bates's in a glance at Jane. From Frank Churchill's face, where he thought he saw confusion suppressed or laughed away, he had involuntarily turned to hers; but she was indeed behind, and too busy with her shawl. Mr. Weston had walked in. The two other gentlemen waited at the door to let her pass. Mr. Knightley suspected in Frank Churchill the determination of catching her eye—he seemed watching her intently—in vain, however, if it were so. Jane passed between them into the hall, and looked at neither.

There was no time for further remark or explanation. The dream must be borne with, and Mr. Knightley must take his seat with the rest round the large modern circular table which Emma had introduced at Hartfield, and which none but Emma could have had power to place there and persuade her father to use, instead of the small-sized Pembroke, on which two of his daily meals had for forty years been crowded. Tea passed pleasantly, and nobody seemed in a hurry to move.

"Miss Woodhouse," said Frank Churchill, after examining a table behind him, which he could reach as he sat, "have your nephews taken away their alphabets—their box of letters? It used to stand here. Where is it? This is a sort of dull-looking evening, that ought to be treated rather as winter than summer. We had great amusement with those letters one morning. I want to puzzle you again."

Emma was pleased with the thought; and producing the box, the table was quickly scattered over with alphabets, which no one seemed so much disposed to employ as their two selves. They were rapidly forming words for each other, or for anybody else who would be puzzled. The quietness of the game made it particularly eligible for Mr. Woodhouse, who had often been distressed by the more animated sort, which Mr. Weston had occasionally introduced, and who now sat happily occupied in lamenting, with tender melancholy, over the departure of the "poor little boys," or in fondly pointing out, as he took up any stray letter near him, how beautifully Emma had written it.

Frank Churchill placed a word before Miss Fairfax. She gave a slight glance round the table, and applied herself to it. Frank was next to Emma, Jane opposite to them; and Mr. Knightley so placed as to see them all; and it was his object to see as much as he could, with as little apparent observation. The word was discovered, and with a faint smile pushed away. If meant to be immediately mixed with the others, and buried from sight, she should have looked on the table instead of looking just across, for it was not mixed; and Harriet, eager after every fresh word, and finding out none, directly took it up, and fell to work. She was sitting by Mr. Knightley, and turned to him for help. The word was *blunder;* and as Harriet exultingly proclaimed it, there was a blush on Jane's cheek which gave it a meaning not otherwise ostensible. Mr. Knightley connected it with the dream; but how it could all be, was beyond his comprehension. How the delicacy, the discretion of his favourite could have been so lain asleep! He feared there must be some decided involvement. Disingenuousness and double dealing seemed to meet him at every turn. These letters were but the vehicle for gallantry and trick. It was a child's play, chosen to conceal a deeper game on Frank Churchill's part.

With great indignation did he continue to observe him; with great alarm and distrust, to observe also his two blinded companions. He saw a short word prepared for Emma, and given to her with a look sly and demure. He saw that Emma had soon made it out, and found it highly entertaining, though it was something which she judged it proper to appear to censure; for she said, "Nonsense! for shame!" He heard Frank Churchill next say, with a glance towards Jane, "I will give it to her— shall I?" and as clearly heard Emma opposing it with eager laughing warmth, "No, no, you must not, you shall not, indeed."

It was done, however. This gallant young man, who seemed to love without feeling, and to recommend himself without complaisance, directly handed over the word to Miss Fairfax, and with a particular degree of sedate civility entreated her to study it. Mr. Knightley's excessive curiosity to know what this word might be, made him seize every possible moment for darting his eye towards it, and it was not long before he saw it to be *Dixon*. Jane Fairfax's perception seemed to accompany his; her comprehension was certainly more equal to the covert meaning, the superior intelligence, of those five letters so arranged. She was evidently displeased; looked up, and seeing herself watched, blushed more deeply than he had ever perceived her, and saying only, "I did not know that proper names were allowed," pushed away the letters with even an angry spirit, and looked resolved to be engaged by no other word that could be offered. Her face was averted from those who had made the attack, and turned towards her aunt.

"Aye very true, my dear," cried the latter, though Jane had not spoken a word: "I was just going to say the same thing. It is time for us to be going, indeed. The evening is closing in, and grandmamma will be looking for us. My dear sir, you are too obliging. We really must wish you good-night."

Jane's alertness in moving proved her as ready as her aunt had pre-conceived. She was immediately up, and wanting to quit the table; but so many were also moving, that she could not get away; and Mr. Knightley thought he saw another collection of letters, anxiously pushed towards her, and resolutely swept away by her unexamined. She was afterwards looking for her shawl—Frank Churchill was looking also: it was growing dusk, and the room was in confusion; and how they parted Mr. Knightley could not tell.

He remained at Hartfield after all the rest, his thoughts full of what he had seen; so full, that when the candles came to assist his observations, he must—yes, he certainly must, as a friend—an anxious friend—give Emma some hint, ask her some question. He could not see her in a situation of such danger without trying to preserve her. It was his duty.

"Pray, Emma," said he, "may I ask in what lay the great amusement, the poignant sting of the last word given to you and Miss Fairfax? I saw the word, and am curious to know how it could be so very entertaining to the one, and so very distressing to the other."

Emma was extremely confused. She could not endure to give him the true explanation; for though her suspicions were by no means removed, she was really ashamed of having ever imparted them.

"Oh!" she cried in evident embarrassment, "it all meant nothing, a mere joke among ourselves."

"The joke," he replied gravely, "seemed confined to you and Mr. Churchill."

He had hoped she would speak again, but she did not. She would rather busy herself about anything than speak. He sat a little while in doubt. A variety of evils crossed his mind. Interference—fruitless interference. Emma's confusion, and the acknowledged intimacy, seemed to declare her affection engaged. Yet he would speak. He owed it to her to risk anything that might be involved in an unwelcome interference, rather than her welfare; to encounter anything, rather than the remembrance of neglect in such a cause.

"My dear Emma," said he at last, with earnest kindness, "do you think you perfectly understand the degree of acquaintance between the gentle-man and lady we have been speaking of?"

"Between Mr. Frank Churchill and Miss Fairfax? Oh! yes, perfectly. Why do you make a doubt of it?"

"Have you never at any time had reason to think that he admired her, or that she admired him?"

"Never, never!" she cried with a most open eagerness. "Never, for the twentieth part of a moment, did such an idea occur to me. And how could it possibly come into your head?"

"I have lately imagined that I saw symptoms of attachment between them; certain expressive looks, which I did not believe meant to be public."

"Oh! you amuse me excessively. I am delighted to find that you can vouchsafe to let your imagination wander; but it will not do—very sorry to check you in your first essay, but indeed it will not do. There is no admiration between them, I do assure you; and the appearances which have caught you, have arisen from some peculiar circumstances; feelings rather of a totally different nature; it is impossible exactly to explain—there is a good deal of nonsense in it—but the part which is capable of being communicated, which is sense, is, that they are as far from any attachment or admiration for one another as any two beings in the world can be. That is, I *presume* it to be so on her side, and I can *answer* for its being so on his. I will answer for the gentleman's indifference."

She spoke with a confidence which staggered, with a satisfaction which silenced Mr. Knightley. She was in gay spirits, and would have prolonged the conversation, wanting to hear the particulars of his suspicions, every look described, and all the wheres and hows of a circumstance which highly entertained her; but his gaiety did not meet hers. He found he could not be useful, and his feelings were too much irritated for talking. That he might not be irritated into an absolute fever by the fire which Mr. Woodhouse's tender habits required almost every evening throughout the year, he soon afterwards took a hasty leave, and walked home to the coolness and solitude of Donwell Abbey.

Chapter 42

AFTER being long fed with hopes of a speedy visit from Mr. and Mrs. Suckling, the Highbury world were obliged to endure the mortification of hearing that they could not possibly come till the autumn. No such importation of novelties could enrich their intellectual stores at present. In the daily interchange of news, they must be again restricted to the other topics, with which for a while the Sucklings' coming had been united, such as the last accounts of Mrs. Churchill, whose health seemed every day to supply a different report, and the situation of Mrs. Weston, whose happiness, it was to be hoped, might eventually be as much increased by the arrival of a child, as that of all her neighbours was by the approach of it.

Mrs. Elton was very much disappointed. It was the delay of a great deal of pleasure and parade. Her introductions and recommendations must all wait, and every projected party be still only talked of. So she thought at first; but a little consideration convinced her that everything need not be put off. Why should not they explore to Box Hill though the Sucklings did not come? They could go there again with them in the autumn. It was settled that they should go to Box Hill. That there was to be such a party had been long generally known; it had even given the idea of another. Emma had never been to Box Hill; she wished to see what everybody found so well worth seeing, and she and Mr. Weston had agreed to choose some fine morning and drive thither. Two or three more of the chosen only were to be admitted to join them, and it was to be done in a quiet, unpretending, elegant way, infinitely superior to the bustle and preparation, the regular eating and drinking and picnic parade of the Eltons and the Sucklings.

This was so very well understood between them that Emma could not but feel some surprise, and a little displeasure, on hearing from Mr. Weston that he had been proposing to Mrs. Elton, as her brother and sister had failed her, that the two parties should unite, and go together; and that as Mrs. Elton had very readily acceded to it, so it was to be, if she had no objection. Now, as her objection was nothing but her very great dislike of Mrs. Elton, of which Mr. Weston must already be perfectly aware, it was not worth bringing forward again: it could not be done without a reproof to him, which would be giving pain to his wife; and she found herself, therefore, obliged to consent to an arrangement which she would have done a great deal to avoid; an arrangement which would, probably, expose her even to the degradation of being said to be of Mr. Elton's party! Every feeling was offended; and the forbearance of her outward submission left a heavy arrear due of secret severity in her reflections, on the unmanageable goodwill of Mr. Weston's temper.

"I am glad you approve of what I have done," said he, very comfortably. "But I thought you would. Such schemes as these are nothing without numbers. One cannot have too large a party. A large party secures its own amusement. And she is a good-natured woman after all. One could not leave her out."

Emma denied none of it aloud, and agreed to none of it in private.

It was now the middle of June and the weather fine; and Mrs. Elton was growing impatient to name the day, and settle with Mr. Weston as to pigeon-pies and cold lamb, when a lame carriage-horse threw everything into sad uncertainty. It might be weeks, it might be only a few days, before the horse were usable; but no preparations could be ventured on, and it was all melancholy stagnation. Mrs. Elton's resources were inadequate to such an attack.

"Is not this most vexatious, Knightley?" she cried; "and such weather for exploring! These delays and disappointments are quite odious. What are we to do? The year will wear away at this rate, and nothing done. Before this time last year, I assure you, we had a delightful exploring party from Maple Grove to King's Weston."

"You had better explore to Donwell," replied Mr. Knightley. "That may be done without horses. Come and eat my strawberries; they are ripening fast."

If Mr. Knightley did not begin seriously, he was obliged to proceed so; for his proposal was caught at with delight; and the "Oh! I should like it

of all things," was not plainer in words than manner. Donwell was famous
for its strawberry-beds, which seemed a plea for the invitation; but no
plea was necessary; cabbage-beds would have been enough to tempt the
lady, who only wanted to be going somewhere. She promised him again
and again to come—much oftener than he doubted—and was extremely
gratified by such a proof of intimacy, such a distinguishing compliment as
she chose to consider it.

"You may depend upon me," said she; "I certainly will come. Name
your day, and I will come. You will allow me to bring Jane Fairfax?"

"I cannot name a day," said he, "till I have spoken to some others,
whom I would wish to meet you."

"Oh, leave all that to me; only give me a *carte blanche*. I am Lady
Patroness, you know. It is my party. I will bring friends with me."

"I hope you will bring Elton," said he; "but I will not trouble you to
give any other invitations."

"Oh, now you are looking very sly; but consider—you need not be
afraid of delegating power to *me*. I am no young lady on her preferment.
Married women, you know, may be safely authorised. It is my party.
Leave it all to me. I will invite your guests."

"No," he calmly replied, "there is but one married woman in the world
whom I can ever allow to invite what guests she pleases to Donwell, and
that one is——"

"Mrs. Weston, I suppose," interrupted Mrs. Elton, rather mortified

"No—Mrs. Knightley; and till she is in being, I will manage such matters myself."

"Ah, you are an odd creature!" she cried, satisfied to have no one preferred to herself. "You are a humorist, and may say what you like. Quite
a humorist. Well, I shall bring Jane with me—Jane and her aunt. The
rest I leave to you. I have no objections at all to meeting the Hartfield
family. Don't scruple, I know you are attached to them."

"You certainly will meet them, if I can prevail; and I shall call on Miss
Bates in my way home."

"That's quite unnecessary; I see Jane every day; but as you like. It
is to be a morning scheme, you know, Knightley; quite a simple thing.
I shall wear a large bonnet, and bring one of my little baskets hanging on
my arm. Here—probably this basket with pink ribbon. Nothing can be
more simple, you see. And Jane will have such another. There is to be no
form or parade—a sort of gipsy party. We are to walk about your gardens,
and gather the strawberries ourselves, and sit under trees; and whatever
else you may like to provide, it is to be all out of doors; a table spread in
the shade, you know. Everything as natural and simple as possible. Is not
that your idea?"

"Not quite. My idea of the simple and the natural will be to have the
table spread in the dining-room. The nature and the simplicity of gentlemen and ladies, with their servants and furniture, I think is best observed

by meals within doors. When you are tired of eating strawberries in the garden, there shall be cold meat in the house."

"Well, as you please; only don't have a great set-out. And, by the bye, can I or my housekeeper be of any use to you with our opinion? Pray be sincere, Knightley. If you wish me to talk to Mrs. Hodges, or to inspect anything——"

"I have not the least wish for it, I thank you."

"Well—but if any difficulties should arise, my housekeeper is extremely clever."

"I will answer for it that mine thinks herself full as clever, and would spurn anybody's assistance."

"I wish we had a donkey. The thing would be for us all to come on donkeys, Jane, Miss Bates, and me, and my *caro sposo* walking by. I really must talk to him about purchasing a donkey. In a country life I conceive it to be a sort of necessary; for, let a woman have ever so many resources, it is not possible for her to be always shut up at home; and very long walks, you know—in summer there is dust, and in winter there is dirt."

"You will not find either between Donwell and Highbury. Donwell Lane is never dusty, and now it is perfectly dry. Come on a donkey, however, if you prefer it. You can borrow Mrs. Cole's. I would wish everything to be as much to your taste as possible."

"That I am sure you would. Indeed I do you justice, my good friend. Under that peculiar sort of dry, blunt manner, I know you have the warmest heart. As I tell Mr. E., you are a thorough humorist. Yes, believe me, Knightley, I am fully sensible of your attention to me in the whole of this scheme. You have hit upon the very thing to please me."

Mr. Knightley had another reason for avoiding a table in the shade. He wished to persuade Mr. Woodhouse, as well as Emma, to join the party; and he knew that to have any of them sitting down out of doors to eat would inevitably make him ill. Mr. Woodhouse must not, under the specious pretence of a morning drive, and an hour or two spent at Donwell, be tempted away to his misery.

He was invited on good faith. No lurking horrors were to upbraid him for his easy credulity. He did consent. He had not been at Donwell for two years. "Some very fine morning, he, and Emma, and Harriet could go very well; and he could sit still with Mrs. Weston while the dear girls walked about the garden. He did not suppose they could be damp now, in the middle of the day. He should like to see the old house again exceedingly, and should be very happy to meet Mr. and Mrs. Elton, and any other of his neighbours. He could not see any objection at all to his, and Emma's, and Harriet's going there some very fine morning. He thought it very well done of Mr. Knightley to invite them; very kind and sensible; much cleverer than dining out. He was not fond of dining out."

Mr. Knightley was fortunate in everybody's most ready concurrence. The invitation was everywhere so well received, that it seemed as if, like Mrs. Elton, they were all taking the scheme as a particular compliment to themselves. Emma and Harriet professed very high expectations of pleasure from it; and Mr. Weston, unasked, promised to get Frank over to join them, if possible; a proof of approbation and gratitude which could have been dispensed with. Mr. Knightley was then obliged to say that he should be glad to see him; and Mr. Weston engaged to lose no time in writing, and spare no arguments to induce him to come.

In the meanwhile the lame horse recovered so fast that the party to Box Hill was again under happy consideration; and at last Donwell was settled for one day; and Box Hill for the next, the weather appearing exactly right.

Under a bright midday sun, at almost Midsummer, Mr. Woodhouse was safely conveyed in his carriage, with one window down, to partake of this *alfresco* party; and in one of the most comfortable rooms in the Abbey, especially prepared for him by a fire all the morning, he was happily placed, quite at his ease, ready to talk with pleasure of what had been achieved, and advise everybody to come and sit down, and not to heat themselves. Mrs. Weston, who seemed to have walked there on purpose to be tired, and sit all the time with him, remained, when all the others were invited or persuaded out, his patient listener and sympathiser.

It was so long since Emma had been at the Abbey, that as soon as she was satisfied of her father's comfort, she was glad to leave him and look around her; eager to refresh and correct her memory with more particular observation, more exact understanding of a house and grounds which must ever be so interesting to her and all her family.

She felt all the honest pride and complacency which her alliance with the present and future proprietor could fairly warrant, as she viewed the respectable size and style of the building, its suitable, becoming, characteristic situation, low and sheltered; its ample gardens stretching down to meadows washed by a stream, of which the Abbey, with all the old neglect of prospect, had scarcely a sight—and its abundance of timber in rows and avenues, which neither fashion nor extravagance had rooted up. The house was larger than Hartfield, and totally unlike it, covering a good deal of ground, rambling and irregular, with many comfortable, and one or two handsome rooms. It was just what it ought to be, and it looked what it was; and Emma felt an increasing respect for it, as the residence of a family of such true gentility, untainted in blood and understanding. Some faults of temper John Knightley had; but Isabella had connected herself unexceptionally. She had given them neither men, nor names, nor places, that could raise a blush. These were pleasant feelings, and she walked about and indulged them till it was necessary to do as the others did, and collect round the strawberry-beds. The whole party were assembled, excepting Frank Churchill, who was expected every moment from Richmond; and Mrs. Elton, in all her apparatus of happiness, her large bonnet and her basket, was very ready to lead the way in gathering, accepting, or talking. Strawberries, and only strawberries, could now be thought or spoken of. "The best fruit in England—everybody's favourite—always wholesome. These the finest beds and finest sorts. Delightful to gather for one's self—the only way of really enjoying them. Morning decidedly the best time—never tired—every sort good—hautboy infinitely superior— no comparison—the others hardly eatable—hautboys very scarce—Chili preferred—white wood finest flavour of all—price of strawberries in Lon- don—abundance about Bristol—Maple Grove—cultivations—beds when to be renewed—gardeners thinking exactly different—no general rule— gardeners never to be put out of their way—delicious fruit—only too rich to be eaten much of—inferior to cherries—currants more refreshing— only objections to gathering strawberries the stooping—glaring sun—tired to death—could bear it no longer—must go and sit in the shade."

Such, for half an hour, was the conversation; interrupted only once by Mrs. Weston, who came out, in her solicitude after her son-in-law, to in- quire if he were come; and she was a little uneasy. She had some fears of his horse.

Seats tolerably in the shade were found; and now Emma was obliged to overhear what Mrs. Elton and Jane Fairfax were talking of. A situation, a most desirable situation, was in question. Mrs. Elton had received notice of it that morning, and was in raptures. It was not with Mrs. Suckling, it was not with Mrs. Bragge, but in felicity and splendour it fell short only of them: it was with a cousin of Mrs. Bragge, an acquaintance of Mrs. Suckling, a lady known at Maple Grove. Delightful, charming, superior, first circles, spheres, lines, ranks, everything; and Mrs. Elton was wild to have the offer closed with immediately. On her side, all was warmth, energy, and triumph; and she positively refused to take her friend's negative, though Miss Fairfax continued to assure her that she would not at present engage in anything—repeating the same motives which she had been heard to urge before. Still Mrs. Elton insisted on being authorised to write an acquiescence by the morrow's post. How Jane could bear it at all, was astonishing to Emma. She did look vexed, she did speak pointedly —and at last, with a decision of action unusual to her, proposed a removal. "Should not they walk? Would not Mr. Knightley show them the gardens —all the gardens? She wished to see the whole extent." The pertinacity of her friend seemed more than she could bear.

It was hot; and after walking some time over the gardens in a scattered, dispersed way, scarcely any three together, they insensibly followed one another to the delicious shade of a broad short avenue of limes, which, stretching beyond the garden at an equal distance from the river, seemed the finish of the pleasure ground. It led to nothing; nothing but a view at the end over a low stone wall with high pillars, which seemed intended, in their erection, to give the appearance of an approach to the house, which never had been there. Disputable, however, as might be the taste of such a termination, it was in itself a charming walk, and the view which closed it extremely pretty. The considerable slope, at nearly the foot of which the Abbey stood, gradually acquired a steeper form beyond its grounds; and at half a mile distant was a bank of considerable abruptness and

grandeur, well clothed with wood; and at the bottom of this bank, favourably placed and sheltered, rose the Abbey-Mill Farm, with meadows in
front, and the river making a close and handsome curve around it.

It was a sweet view—sweet to the eye and the mind. English verdure,
English culture, English comfort, seen under a bright sun, without being
oppressive.

In this walk Emma and Mr. Weston found all the others assembled;
and towards this view she immediately perceived Mr. Knightley and
Harriet distinct from the rest, quietly leading the way. Mr. Knightley and
Harriet! It was an odd *tête-à-tête;* but she was glad to see it. There had
been a time when he would have scorned her as a companion, and turned
from her with little ceremony. Now they seemed in pleasant conversation.
There had been a time also when Emma would have been sorry to see
Harriet in a spot so favourable for the Abbey-Mill Farm; but now she
feared it not. It might be safely viewed, with all its appendages of prosperity and beauty, its rich pastures, spreading flocks, orchard in blossom,
and light column of smoke ascending. She joined them at the wall, and
found them more engaged in talking than in looking around. He was giving Harriet information as to modes of agriculture, etc.; and Emma received a smile which seemed to say, "These are my own concerns. I have
a right to talk on such subjects, without being suspected of introducing
Robert Martin." She did not suspect him. It was too old a story. Robert
Martin had probably ceased to think of Harriet. They took a few turns
together along the walk. The shade was most refreshing, and Emma found
it the pleasantest part of the day.

The next remove was to the house; they must all go in and eat; and they
were all seated and busy, and still Frank Churchill did not come. Mrs.
Weston looked, and looked in vain. His father would not own himself
uneasy, and laughed at her fears; but she could not be cured of wishing
that he would part with his black mare. He had expressed himself as to
coming with more than common certainty. "His aunt was so much better,
that he had not a doubt of getting over to them." Mrs. Churchill's state,
however, as many were ready to remind her, was liable to such sudden
variation as might disappoint her nephew in the most reasonable dependence; and Mrs. Weston was at last persuaded to believe, or to say, that it
must be by some attack of Mrs. Churchill that he was prevented coming.
Emma looked at Harriet while the point was under consideration; she
behaved very well, and betrayed no emotion.

The cold repast was over, and the party were to go out once more to see
what had not yet been seen, the old Abbey fish-ponds; perhaps get as far
as the clover, which was to be begun cutting on the morrow, or, at any
rate, have the pleasure of being hot, and growing cool again. Mr. Woodhouse, who had already taken his little round in the highest part of the
gardens, where no damps from the river were imagined even by him,
stirred no more; and his daughter resolved to remain with him, that Mrs.

Weston might be persuaded away by her husband to the exercise and variety which her spirits seemed to need.

Mr. Knightley had done all in his power for Mr. Woodhouse's entertainment. Books of engravings, drawers of medals, cameos, corals, shells, and every other family collection within his cabinets, had been prepared for his old friend, to while away the morning; and the kindness had perfectly answered. Mr. Woodhouse had been exceedingly well amused. Mrs. Weston had been showing them all to him, and now he would show them all to Emma; fortunate in having no other resemblance to a child, than in a total want of taste for what he saw, for he was slow, constant, and methodical. Before this second looking over was begun, however, Emma walked into the hall for the sake of a few moments' free observation of the entrance and ground-plot of the house, and was hardly there when Jane Fairfax appeared, coming quickly in from the garden, and with a look of escape. Little expecting to meet Miss Woodhouse so soon, there was a start at first; but Miss Woodhouse was the very person she was in quest of.

"Will you be so kind," said she, "when I am missed, as to say that I am gone home! I am going this moment. My aunt is not aware how late it is, nor how long we have been absent; but I am sure we shall be wanted, and I am determined to go directly. I have said nothing about it to anybody. It would only be giving trouble and distress. Some are gone to the ponds, and some to the lime-walk. Till they all come in I shall not be missed; and when they do, will you have the goodness to say that I am gone?"

"Certainly, if you wish it; but you are not going to walk to Highbury alone?"

"Yes; what should hurt me? I walk fast. I shall be at home in twenty minutes."

"But it is too far, indeed it is, to be walking quite alone. Let my father's servant go with you. Let me order the carriage. It can be round in five minutes."

"Thank you, thank you—but on no account—I would rather walk. And for *me* to be afraid of walking alone!—I, who may so soon have to guard others!"

She spoke with great agitation; and Emma very feelingly replied: "That can be no reason for your being exposed to danger now. I must order the carriage. The heat even would be danger. You are fatigued already."

"I am," she answered, "I am fatigued; but it is not the sort of fatigue— quick walking will refresh me. Miss Woodhouse, we all know at times what it is to be wearied in spirits. Mine, I confess, are exhausted. The greatest kindness you can show me will be to let me have my own way, and only say that I am gone when it is necessary."

Emma had not another word to oppose. She saw it all; and entering into her feelings, promoted her quitting the house immediately, and watched her safely off with the zeal of a friend. Her parting look was grateful; and her parting words, "Oh! Miss Woodhouse, the comfort of being some-

EMMA

times alone!" seemed to burst from an overcharged heart, and to describe somewhat of the continual endurance to be practised by her, even towards some of those who loved her best.

"Such a home, indeed! Such an aunt!" said Emma, as she turned back into the hall again. "I do pity you. And the more sensibility you betray of their just horrors, the more I shall like you."

Jane had not been gone a quarter of an hour, and they had only accomplished some views of St. Mark's Place, Venice, when Frank Churchill entered the room. Emma had not been thinking of him; she had forgotten to think of him, but she was very glad to see him. Mrs. Weston would be at ease. The black mare was blameless; *they* were right who had named Mrs. Churchill as the cause. He had been detained by a temporary increase of illness in her—a nervous seizure which had lasted some hours; and he had quite given up every thought of coming till very late; and had he known how hot a ride he should have, and how late, with all his hurry, he must be, he believed he should not have come at all. The heat was excessive; he had never suffered anything like it—almost wished he had stayed at home—nothing killed him like heat—he could bear any degree of cold, etc., but heat was intolerable; and he sat down, at the greatest possible distance from the slight remains of Mr. Woodhouse's fire, looking very deplorable.

"You will soon be cooler, if you sit still," said Emma.

"As soon as I am cooler I shall go back again. I could very ill be spared; but such a point had been made of my coming! You will all be going soon, I suppose; the whole party breaking up. I met *one* as I came. Madness in such weather—absolute madness!"

Emma listened, and looked, and soon perceived that Frank Churchill's state might be best defined by the expressive phrase of being out of humour. Some people were always cross when they were hot. Such might be his constitution; and as she knew that eating and drinking were often the cure of such incidental complaints, she recommended his taking some refreshment; he would find abundance of everything in the dining-room; and she humanely pointed out the door.

"No; he should not eat. He was not hungry; it would only make him hotter." In two minutes, however, he relented in his own favour; and muttering something about spruce-beer, walked off. Emma returned all her attention to her father, saying in secret:

"I am glad I have done being in love with him. I should not like a man who is so soon discomposed by a hot morning. Harriet's sweet easy temper will not mind it."

He was gone long enough to have had a very comfortable meal, and came back all the better—grown quite cool, and with good manners, like himself, able to draw a chair close to them, take an interest in their employment, and regret, in a reasonable way, that he should be so late. He was not in his best spirits, but seemed trying to improve them; and, at last, made himself talk nonsense very agreeably. They were looking over views in Switzerland.

"As soon as my aunt gets well I shall go abroad," said he. "I shall never be easy till I have seen some of these places. You will have my sketches, some time or other, to look at—or my tour to read—or my poem. I shall do something to expose myself."

"That may be—but not by sketches in Switzerland. You will never go to Switzerland. Your uncle and aunt will never allow you to leave England."

"They may be induced to go too. A warm climate may be prescribed for her. I have more than half an expectation of our all going abroad. I assure you, I have. I feel a strong persuasion, this morning, that I shall soon be abroad. I ought to travel. I am tired of doing nothing. I want a change. I am serious, Miss Woodhouse, whatever your penetrating eyes may fancy—I am sick of England, and would leave it to-morrow if I could."

"You are sick of prosperity and indulgence! Cannot you invent a few hardships for yourself, and be contented to stay?"

"*I* sick of prosperity and indulgence! You are quite mistaken. I do not look upon myself as either prosperous or indulged. I am thwarted in everything material. I do not consider myself at all a fortunate person."

"You are not quite so miserable, though, as when you first came. Go and eat and drink a little more, and you will do very well. Another slice of cold meat, another draught of Madeira and water, will make you nearly on a par with the rest of us."

"No—I shall not stir. I shall sit by you. You are my best cure."

"We are going to Box Hill to-morrow; you will join us. It is not Switzerland, but it will be something for a young man so much in want of a change. You will stay and go with us?"

"No; certainly not. I shall go home in the cool of the evening."

"But you may come again in the cool of to-morrow morning."

"No—it will not be worth while. If I come, I shall be cross."

"Then pray stay at Richmond."

"But if I do, I shall be crosser still. I can never bear to think of you all there without me."

"These are difficulties which you must settle for yourself. Choose your own degree of crossness. I shall press you no more."

The rest of the party were now returning, and all were soon collected. With some there was great joy at the sight of Frank Churchill; others took it very composedly; but there was a very general distress and disturbance on Miss Fairfax's disappearance being explained. That it was time for everybody to go concluded the subject; and with a short final arrangement for the next day's scheme, they parted. Frank Churchill's little inclination to exclude himself increased so much, that his last words to Emma were:

"Well; if *you* wish me to stay and join the party, I will."

She smiled her acceptance; and nothing less than a summons from Richmond was to take him back before the following evening.

Chapter 43

THEY had a very fine day for Box Hill; and all the other outward circumstances of arrangement, accommodation, and punctuality, were in
favour of a pleasant party. Mr. Weston directed the whole, officiating
safely between Hartfield and the vicarage, and everybody was in good
time. Emma and Harriet went together; Miss Bates and her niece with
the Eltons; the gentlemen on horseback. Mrs. Weston remained with Mr.
Woodhouse. Nothing was wanting but to be happy when they got there.
Seven miles were travelled in expectation of enjoyment, and everybody
had a burst of admiration on first arriving; but in the general amount of
the day there was deficiency. There was a languor, a want of spirits, a
want of union, which could not be got over. They separated too much into
parties. The Eltons walked together; Mr. Knightley took charge of Miss
Bates and Jane; and Emma and Harriet belonged to Frank Churchill. And
Mr. Weston tried, in vain, to make them harmonise better. It seemed at
first an accidental division, but it never materially varied. Mr. and Mrs.
Elton, indeed, showed no unwillingness to mix, and be as agreeable as they
could; but during the two whole hours that were spent on the Hill, there
seemed a principle of separation between the other parties, too strong for
any fine prospects, or any cold collation, or any cheerful Mr. Weston, to
remove.

At first it was downright dullness to Emma. She had never seen Frank
Churchill so silent and stupid. He said nothing worth hearing—looked
without seeing—admired without intelligence—listened without knowing
what she said. While he was so dull, it was no wonder that Harriet should
be dull likewise; and they were both insufferable.

When they all sat down it was better—to her taste a great deal better—
for Frank Churchill grew talkative and gay, making her his first object
Every distinguishing attention that could be paid, was paid to her. To
amuse her, and be agreeable in her eyes, seemed all that he cared for—and
Emma, glad to be enlivened, not sorry to be flattered, was gay and easy
too, and gave him all the friendly encouragement, the admission to be
gallant, which she had ever given in the first and most animating period
of their acquaintance; but which now, in her own estimation, meant nothing, though in the judgment of most people looking on, it must have had
such an appearance as no English word but flirtation could very well
describe. "Mr. Frank Churchill and Miss Woodhouse flirted together excessively." They were laying themselves open to that very phrase—and
to having it sent off in a letter to Maple Grove by one lady, to Ireland by
another. Not that Emma was gay and thoughtless from any real felicity;
it was rather because she felt less happy than she had expected. She
laughed because she was disappointed; and though she liked him for his
attentions, and thought them all, whether in friendship, admiration, or

playfulness, extremely judicious, they were not winning back her heart. She still intended him for her friend.

"How much I am obliged to you," said he, "for telling me to come to-day! If it had not been for you, I should certainly have lost all the happiness of this party. I had quite determined to go away again."

"Yes, you were very cross; and I do not know what about, except that you were too late for the best strawberries. I was a kinder friend than you deserved. But you were humble. You begged hard to be commanded to come."

"Don't say I was cross. I was fatigued. The heat overcame me."

"It is hotter to-day."

"Not to my feelings. I am perfectly comfortable to-day."

"You are comfortable because you are under command."

"Your command? Yes."

"Perhaps I intended you to say so, but I meant self-command. You had, somehow or other, broken bounds yesterday, and run away from your own management; but to-day you are got back again—and as I cannot be always with you, it is best to believe your temper under your own command rather than mine."

"It comes to the same thing. I can have no self-command without a motive. You order me, whether you speak or not. And you can be always with me. You are always with me."

"Dating from three o'clock yesterday. My perpetual influence could not begin earlier, or you would not have been so much out of humour before."

"Three o'clock yesterday! That is your date. I thought I had seen you first in February."

"Your gallantry is really unanswerable. But" (lowering her voice), "nobody speaks except ourselves, and it is rather too much to be talking nonsense for the entertainment of seven silent people."

"I say nothing of which I am ashamed," replied he, with lively impudence. "I saw you first in February. Let everybody on the Hill hear me if they can. Let my accent swell to Mickleham on one side, and Dorking on the other. I saw you first in February." And then whispering: "Our companions are excessively stupid. What shall we do to rouse them? Any nonsense will serve. They *shall* talk. Ladies and gentlemen, I am ordered by Miss Woodhouse (who, wherever she is, presides) to say, that she desires to know what you are all thinking of."

Some laughed, and anwered good-humouredly. Miss Bates said a great deal; Mrs. Elton swelled at the idea of Miss Woodhouse's presiding; Mr. Knightley's answer was the most distinct.

"Is Miss Woodhouse sure that she would like to hear what we are all thinking of?"

"Oh, no, no!" cried Emma, laughing as carelessly as she could; "upon no account in the world. It is the very last thing I would stand the brunt of just now. Let me hear anything rather than what you are all thinking of. I will not say quite all. There are one or two perhaps" (glancing at Mr.

Weston and Harriet), "whose thoughts I might not be afraid of knowing."

"It is a sort of thing," cried Mrs. Elton emphatically, "which *I* should not have thought myself privileged to inquire into. Though, perhaps, as the *chaperone* of the party—*I* never was in any circle—exploring parties—young ladies—married women——"

Her mutterings were chiefly to her husband; and he murmured, in reply:

"Very true, my love, very true. Exactly so, indeed—quite unheard of—but some ladies say anything. Better pass it off as a joke. Everybody knows what is due to *you*."

"It will not do," whispered Frank to Emma, "they are most of them affronted. I will attack them with more address. Ladies and gentlemen, I am ordered by Miss Woodhouse to say, that she waives her right of knowing exactly what you may all be thinking of, and only requires something very entertaining from each of you, in a general way. Here are seven of you, besides myself (who, she is pleased to say, am very entertaining already), and she only demands from each of you, either one thing very clever, be it prose or verse, original or repeated; or two things moderately clever; or three things very dull indeed; and she engages to laugh heartily at them all."

"Oh! very well," exclaimed Miss Bates; "then I need not be uneasy. 'Three things very dull indeed.' That will just do for me, you know. I shall be sure to say three dull things as soon as ever I open my mouth, shan't I?" (looking round with the most good-humoured dependence on everybody's assent). "Do not you all think I shall?"

Emma could not resist.

"Ah! ma'am, but there may be a difficulty. Pardon me, but you will be limited as to number—only three at once."

Miss Bates, deceived by the mock ceremony of her manner, did not immediately catch her meaning; but, when it burst on her, it could not anger, though a slight blush showed that it could pain her.

"Ah! well—to be sure. Yes, I see what she means" (turning to Mr. Knightley), "and I will try to hold my tongue. I must make myself very disagreeable, or she would not have said such a thing to an old friend."

"I like your plan," cried Mr. Weston. "Agreed, agreed. I will do my best. I am making a conundrum. How will a conundrum reckon?"

"Low, I am afraid, sir, very low," answered his son; "but we shall be indulgent, especially to anyone who leads the way."

"No, no," said Emma, "it will not reckon low. A conundrum of Mr. Weston's shall clear him and his next neighbour. Come, sir, pray let me hear it."

"I doubt its being very clever myself," said Mr. Weston. "It is too much a matter of fact; but here it is: What two letters of the alphabet are there that express perfection?"

"What two letters—express perfection? I am sure I do not know."

"Ah! you will never guess. You" (to Emma), "I am certain, will never guess. I will tell you. M. and A. Emma. Do you understand?"

Understanding and gratification came together. It might be a very indifferent piece of wit, but Emma found a great deal to laugh at and enjoy in it: and so did Frank and Harriet. It did not seem to touch the rest of the party equally; some looked very stupid about it, and Mr. Knightley gravely said:

"This explains the sort of clever thing that is wanted, and Mr. Weston has done very well for himself; but he must have knocked up everybody else. *Perfection* should not have come quite so soon."

"Oh! for myself, I protest I must be excused," said Mrs. Elton. "*I* really cannot attempt—I am not at all fond of the sort of thing. I had an acrostic once sent to me upon my own name which I was not at all pleased with. I knew who it came from. An abominable puppy! You know who I mean" (nodding to her husband). "These kind of things are very well at Christmas, when one is sitting round the fire; but quite out of place, in my opinion, when one is exploring about the country in summer. Miss Woodhouse must excuse me. I am not one of those who have witty things at everybody's service. I do not pretend to be a wit. I have a great deal of vivacity in my own way, but I really must be allowed to judge when to speak, and when to hold my tongue. Pass us, if you please, Mr. Churchill. Pass Mr. E., Knightley, Jane, and myself. We have nothing clever to say —not one of us."

"Yes, yes, pray pass *me*," added her husband, with a sort of sneering consciousness; "*I* have nothing to say that can entertain Miss Woodhouse, or any other young lady. An old married man—quite good for nothing. Shall we walk, Augusta?"

"With all my heart. I am really tired of exploring so long on one spot. Come, Jane, take my other arm."

Jane declined it, however, and the husband and wife walked off. "Happy couple!" said Frank Churchill, as soon as they were out of hearing; "how well they suit one another! Very lucky—marrying as they did, upon an acquaintance formed only in a public place! They only knew each other, I think, a few weeks in Bath! Peculiarly lucky! For as to any real knowledge of a person's disposition that Bath, or any public place, can give—it is all nothing; there can be no knowledge. It is only by seeing women in their own homes, among their own set, just as they always are, that you can form any just judgment. Short of that, it is all guess and luck—and will generally be ill-luck. How many a man has committed himself on a short acquaintance, and rued it all the rest of his life!"

Miss Fairfax, who had seldom spoken before, except among her own confederates, spoke now.

"Such things do occur, undoubtedly." She was stopped by a cough. Frank Churchill turned towards her to listen.

"You were speaking," said he gravely. She recovered her voice.

"I was only going to observe, that though such unfortunate circumstances do sometimes occur both to men and women, I cannot imagine them to be very frequent. A hasty and imprudent attachment may arise—but there is generally time to recover from it afterwards. I would be understood to mean, that it can be only weak, irresolute characters (whose happiness must be always at the mercy of chance), who will suffer an unfortunate acquaintance to be an inconvenience, an oppression for ever."

He made no answer; merely looked, and bowed in submission; and soon afterwards said, in a lively tone:

"Well, I have so little confidence in my own judgment, that whenever I marry, I hope somebody will choose my wife for me? Will you?" (turning to Emma). "Will you choose a wife for me? I am sure I should like anybody fixed on by you. You provide for the family, you know" (with a smile at his father). "Find somebody for me. I am in no hurry. Adopt her; educate her."

"And make her like myself."

"By all means, if you can."

"Very well. I undertake the commission. You shall have a charming wife."

"She must be very lively and have hazel eyes. I care for nothing else. I shall go abroad for a couple of years—and when I return, I shall come to you for my wife. Remember."

Emma was in no danger of forgetting. It was a commission to touch every favourite feeling. Would not Harriet be the very creature described? Hazel eyes excepted, two years more might make her all that he wished. He might even have Harriet in his thoughts at the moment; who could say? Referring the education to her seemed to imply it.

"Now, ma'am," said Jane to her aunt, "shall we join Mrs. Elton?"

"If you please, my dear. With all my heart. *I* am quite ready. I was ready to have gone with her, but this will do just as well. We shall soon overtake her. There she is—no, that's somebody else. That's one of the ladies in the Irish car party, not at all like her. Well, I declare——"

They walked off, followed in half a minute by Mr. Knightley. Mr. Weston, his son, Emma, and Harriet only remained; and the young man's spirits now rose to a pitch almost unpleasant. Even Emma grew tired at last of flattery and merriment, and wished herself rather walking quietly about with any of the others, or sitting almost alone, and quite unattended to, in tranquil observation of the beautiful views beneath her. The appearance of the servants looking out for them to give notice of the carriages was a joyful sight; and even the bustle of collecting and preparing to depart, and the solicitude of Mrs. Elton to have *her* carriage first, were gladly endured, in the prospect of the quiet drive home which was to close the very questionable enjoyments of this day of pleasure. Such another scheme, composed of so many ill-assorted people, she hoped never to be betrayed into again.

While waiting for the carriage, she found Mr. Knightley by her side. He looked around, as if to see that no one were near, and then said:

"Emma, I must once more speak to you as I have been used to do; a privilege rather endured than allowed, perhaps, but I must still use it. I cannot see you acting wrong, without a remonstrance. How could you be so unfeeling to Miss Bates? How could you be so insolent in your wit to a woman of her character, age, and situation? Emma, I had not thought it possible."

Emma recollected, blushed, was sorry, but tried to laugh it off.

"Nay, how could I help saying what I did? Nobody could have helped it. It was not so very bad. I dare say she did not understand me."

"I assure you she did. She felt your full meaning. She has talked of it since. I wish you could have heard how she talked of it—with what candour and generosity. I wish you could have heard her honouring your forbearance, in being able to pay her such attentions, as she was for ever receiving from yourself and your father, when her society must be so irksome."

"Oh!" cried Emma, "I know there is not a better creature in the world; but you must allow, that what is good and what is ridiculous are most unfortunately blended in her."

"They are blended," said he, "I acknowledge; and, were she prosperous, I could allow much for the occasional prevalence of the ridiculous over the good. Were she a woman of fortune, I would leave every harmless absurdity to take its chance; I would not quarrel with you for any liberties of manner. Were she your equal in situation—but, Emma, consider how far this is from being the case. She is poor; she has sunk from the comforts she was born to; and if she live to old age must probably sink more. Her situation should secure your compassion. It was badly done, indeed! You, whom she had known from an infant, whom she had seen grow up from a period when her notice was an honour—to have you now, in thoughtless spirits, and the pride of the moment, laugh at her, humble her—and before her niece, too—and before others, many of whom (certainly *some*) would be entirely guided by *your* treatment of her. This is not pleasant to you, Emma—and it is very far from pleasant to me; but I must, I will—I will tell you truths while I can; satisfied with proving myself your friend by very faithful counsel and trusting that you will some time or other do me greater justice than you can do now."

While they talked they were advancing towards the carriage; it was ready; and, before she could speak again, he had handed her in. He had misinterpreted the feelings which had kept her face averted, and her tongue motionless. They were combined only of anger against herself, mortification, and deep concern. She had not been able to speak; and, on entering the carriage, sunk back for a moment overcome; then reproaching herself for having taken no leave, making no acknowledgment, parting in apparent sullenness, she looked out with voice and hand eager to show a difference; but it was just too late. He had turned away, and the horses were in motion. She continued to look back, but in vain; and soon, with what appeared unusual speed, they were half-way down the hill, and everything left far behind. She was vexed beyond what could have been expressed—almost beyond what she could conceal. Never had she felt so agitated, mortified, grieved, at any circumstance in her life. She was most forcibly struck. The truth of his representation there was no denying. She felt it at her heart. How could she have been so brutal, so cruel to Miss Bates! How could she have exposed herself to such ill opinion in any one she valued! And how suffer him to leave her without saying one word of gratitude, of concurrence, of common kindness!

Time did not compose her. As she reflected more, she seemed but to feel it more. She never had been so depressed. Happily it was not necessary to speak. There was only Harriet, who seemed not in spirits herself, fagged, and very willing to be silent; and Emma felt the tears running down her cheeks almost all the way home, without being at any trouble to check them, extraordinary as they were.

Chapter 44

THE wretchedness of a scheme to Box Hill was in Emma's thoughts all the evening. How it might be considered by the rest of the party she could not tell. They, in their different homes, and in their different ways, might be looking back on it with pleasure; but in her view it was a morning more completely misspent, more totally bare of rational satisfaction at the time, and more to be abhorred in recollection, than any she had ever passed. A whole evening of backgammon with her father was felicity to it. *There*, indeed, lay real pleasure, for there she was giving up the sweetest hours of the twenty-four to his comfort; and feeling that, unmerited as might be the degree of his fond affection and confiding esteem, she could not, in her general conduct, be open to any severe reproach. As a daughter, she hoped she was not without a heart. She hoped no one could have said to her, "How could you be so unfeeling to your father? I must, I will tell you truths while I can." Miss Bates should never again—no never! If attention in future could do away the past she might hope to be forgiven. She had been often remiss, her conscience told her so; remiss, perhaps, more in thought than fact; scornful, ungracious. But it should be so no more. In the warmth of true contrition she would call upon her the very next morning, and it should be the beginning, on her side, of a regular, equal, kindly intercourse.

She was just as determined when the morrow came and went early, that nothing might prevent her. It was not unlikely, she thought, that she might see Mr. Knightley in her way; or perhaps he might come in while she were paying her visit. She had no objection. She would not be ashamed of the appearance of the penitence, so justly and truly hers. Her eyes were towards Donwell as she walked, but she saw him not.

"The ladies were all at home." She had never rejoiced at the sound before, nor ever before entered the passage, nor walked up the stairs, with any wish of giving pleasure, but in conferring obligation, or of deriving it, except in subsequent ridicule.

There was a bustle on her approach; a good deal of moving and talking. She heard Miss Bates's voice; something was to be done in a hurry; the maid looked frightened and awkward; hoped she would be pleased to wait a moment, and then ushered her in too soon. The aunt and niece seemed both escaping into the adjoining room. Jane she had a distinct glimpse of, looking extremely ill; and, before the door had shut them out, she heard Miss Bates saying, "Well, my dear, I shall *say* you are laid down upon the bed, and I am sure you are ill enough."

Poor old Mrs. Bates, civil and humble as usual, looked as if she did not quite understand what was going on.

"I am afraid Jane is not very well," said she, "but *I* do not know; they *tell* me she is well. I dare say my daughter will be here presently, Miss Woodhouse. I hope you find a chair. I wish Hetty had not gone. I am very little able—have you a chair, ma'am? Do you sit where you like? I am sure she will be here presently."

Emma seriously hoped she would. She had a moment's fear of Miss Bates keeping away from her. But Miss Bates soon came—"Very happy and obliged"—but Emma's conscience told her that there was not the same cheerful volubility as before—less ease of look and manner. A very friendly inquiry after Miss Fairfax, she hoped, might lead the way to a return of old feelings. The touch seemed immediate.

"Ah, Miss Woodhouse, how kind you are! I suppose you have heard—and are come to give us joy. This does not seem much like joy, indeed, in me" (twinkling away a tear or two); "but it will be very trying for us to part with her, after having had her so long; and she has a dreadful headache just now, writing all the morning; such long letters, you know, to be written to Colonel Campbell and Mrs. Dixon. 'My dear,' said I, 'you will blind yourself,' for tears were in her eyes perpetually. One cannot wonder, one cannot wonder. It is a great change; and though she is amazingly fortunate—such a situation, I suppose, as no young woman before ever met with on first going out; do not think us ungrateful, Miss Woodhouse, for such surprising good fortune" (again dispersing her tears), "but, poor dear soul! If you were to see what a headache she has. When one is in great pain, you know one cannot feel any blessing quite as it may deserve. She is as low as possible. To look at her nobody would think how delighted and happy she is to have secured such a situation. You will excuse her not coming to you; she is not able, she is gone into her own room. I want her to lie down upon the bed. 'My dear,' said I, 'I shall say you are laid down upon the bed;' but, however, she is not; she is walking about the room. But, now that she has written her letters, she says she shall soon be well. She will be extremely sorry to miss seeing you, Miss Woodhouse, but your kindness will excuse her. You were kept waiting at the door: I was quite ashamed; but somehow there was a little bustle; for it so happened that we had not heard the knock; and, till you were on the stairs, we did not know

anybody was coming. 'It is only Mrs. Cole,' said I, 'depend upon it;
nobody else would come so early.' 'Well,' said she, 'it must be borne some
time or other, and it may as well be now.' But then Patty came in, and
said it was you. 'Oh!' said I, 'it is Miss Woodhouse, I am sure you will like
to see her.' 'I can see nobody,' said she, and up she got, and would go away;
and that was what made us keep you waiting; and extremely sorry and
ashamed we were. 'If you must go, my dear,' said I, 'you must, and I will
say you are laid down upon the bed.' "

Emma was most sincerely interested. Her heart had been long growing
kinder towards Jane; and this picture of her present sufferings acted as a
cure of every former ungenerous suspicion, and left her nothing but pity;
and the remembrance of the less just and less gentle sensations of the past
obliged her to admit that Jane might very naturally resolve on seeing Mrs.
Cole, or any other steady friend, when she might not bear to see herself.
She spoke as she felt, with earnest regret and solicitude—sincerely wishing
that the circumstances which she collected from Miss Bates to be now
actually determined on, might be as much for Miss Fairfax's advantage
and comfort as possible.

"It must be a severe trial to them all. She had understood it was to be
delayed till Colonel Campbell's return."

"So very kind!" replied Miss Bates; "but you are always kind."

There was no bearing such an "always"; and to break through her
dreadful gratitude Emma made the direct inquiry of·

"Where, may I ask, is Miss Fairfax going?"

"To a Mrs. Smallridge—charming woman—most superior—to have the
charge of her three little girls—delightful children! Impossible that any
situation could be more replete with comfort: if we except, perhaps, Mrs.
Suckling's own family, and Mrs. Bragge's, but Mrs. Smallridge is intimate
with both, and in the very same neighbourhood: lives only four miles from
Maple Grove. Jane will be only four miles from Maple Grove."

"Mrs. Elton, I suppose, has been the person to whom Miss Fairfax
owes——"

"Yes, our good Mrs. Elton. The most indefatigable, true friend. She
would not take a denial. She would not let Jane say 'No;' for when Jane
first heard of it (it was the day before yesterday, the very morning we were
at Donwell), when Jane first heard of it, she was quite decided against
accepting the offer, and for the reasons you mention; exactly as you say,
she had made up her mind to close with nothing till Colonel Campbell's
return, and nothing should induce her to enter into any engagement at
present—and so she told Mrs. Elton over and over again—and I am sure
I had no more idea that she would change her mind! But that good Mrs.
Elton, whose judgment never fails her, saw further than I did. It is not
everybody that would have stood out in such a kind way as she did, and
refuse to take Jane's answer; but she positively declared she would *not*
write any such denial yesterday, as Jane wished her; she would wait—
and, sure enough, yesterday evening it was all settled that Jane should go.

Quite a surprise to me! I had not the least idea! Jane took Mrs. Elton aside, and told her at once, that, upon thinking over the advantages of Mrs. Smallridge's situation, she had come to the resolution of accepting it. I did not know a word of it till it was all settled."

"You spent the evening with Mrs. Elton?"

"Yes, all of us; Mrs. Elton would have us come. It was settled so, upon the Hill, while we were walking about with Mr. Knightley. 'You *must all* spend your evening with us,' said she. 'I positively must have you all come.'"

"Mr. Knightley was there, too, was he?"

"No, not Mr. Knightley; he declined it from the first; and though I thought he would come, because Mrs. Elton declared she would not let him off, he did not; but my mother, and Jane, and I, were all there, and a very agreeable evening we had. Such kind friends, you know, Miss Woodhouse, one must always find agreeable, though everybody seemed rather fagged after the morning's party. Even pleasure, you know, is fatiguing—and I cannot say that any of them seemed very much to have enjoyed it. However, *I* shall always think it a very pleasant party, and feel extremely obliged to the kind friends who included me in it."

"Miss Fairfax, I suppose, though you were not aware of it, had been making up her mind the whole day?"

"I dare say she had."

"Whenever the time may come it must be unwelcome to her and all her friends—but I hope her engagement will have every alleviation that is possible—I mean, as to the character and manners of the family."

"Thank you, dear Miss Woodhouse. Yes, indeed, there is everything in the world that can make her happy in it. Except the Sucklings and Bragges, there is not such another nursery establishment, so liberal and elegant, in all Mrs. Elton's acquaintance. Mrs. Smallridge, a most delightful woman! A style of living almost equal to Maple Grove—and as to the children, except the little Sucklings and little Bragges, there are not such elegant sweet children anywhere. Jane will be treated with such regard and kindness! It will be nothing but pleasure—a life of pleasure. And her salary—I really cannot venture to name her salary to you, Miss Woodhouse. Even you, used as you are to great sums, would hardly believe that so much could be given to a young person like Jane."

"Ah, madam," cried Emma, "if other children are at all like what I remember to have been myself, I should think five times the amount of what I have ever yet heard named as a salary on such occasions dearly earned."

"You are so noble in your ideas!"

"And when is Miss Fairfax to leave you?"

"Very soon, very soon, indeed; that's the worst of it. Within a fortnight. Mrs. Smallridge is in a great hurry. My poor mother does not know how to bear it. So, then, I try to put it out of her thoughts, and say, 'Come, ma'am, do not let us think about it any more.'"

"Her friends must all be sorry to lose her; and will not Colonel and Mrs. Campbell be sorry to find that she has engaged herself before their return?"

"Yes; Jane says she is sure they will; but yet this is such a situation as she cannot feel herself justified in declining. I was so astonished when she first told me what she had been saying to Mrs. Elton, and when Mrs. Elton at the same moment came congratulating me upon it! It was before tea—stay—no, it could not be before tea, because we were just going to cards—and yet it was before tea, because I remember thinking—Oh, no, now I recollect, now I have it: something happened before tea, but not that. Mr. Elton was called out of the room before tea, old John Abdy's son wanted to speak with him. Poor old John—I have a great regard for him; he was clerk to my poor father twenty-seven years; and now, poor old man, he is bedridden, and very poorly with the rheumatic gout in his joints—I must go and see him to-day; and so will Jane, I am sure, if she gets out at all. And Poor John's son came to talk to Mr. Elton about relief from the parish: he is very well-to-do himself, you know, being head man at the Crown—ostler, and everything of that sort—but still he cannot keep his father without some help; and so, when Mr. Elton came back, he told us what John ostler had been telling him, and then it came out about the chaise having been sent to Randalls to take Mr. Frank Churchill to Richmond. That was what happened before tea. It was after tea that Jane spoke to Mrs. Elton."

Miss Bates would hardly give Emma time to say how perfectly new this circumstance was to her; but as, without supposing it possible that she could be ignorant of any of the particulars of Mr. Frank Churchill's going, she proceeded to give them all, it was of no consequence.

What Mr. Elton had learned from the ostler on the subject, being the accumulation of the ostler's own knowledge, and the knowledge of the servants at Randalls, was, that a messenger had come over from Richmond soon after the return of the party from Box Hill—which messenger, however, had been no more than was expected; and that Mr. Churchill had sent his nephew a few lines containing, upon the whole, a tolerable account of Mrs. Churchill, and only wishing him not to delay coming back beyond the next morning early; but that Mr. Frank Churchill having resolved to go home directly, without waiting at all, and his horse seeming to have got a cold, Tom had been sent off immediately for the Crown chaise, and the ostler had stood out and seen it pass by, the boy going a good pace, and driving very steady.

There was nothing in all this either to astonish or interest, and it caught Emma's attention only as it united with the subject which already engage l her mind. The contrast between Mrs. Churchill's importance in the world and Jane Fairfax's struck her; one was everything, the other nothing— and she sat musing on the difference of woman's destiny, and quite unconscious on what her eyes were fixed, till roused by Miss Bates saying:

"Aye, I see what you are thinking of. the pianoforte. What is to become of that? Very true. Poor dear Jane was talking of it just now. 'You must go,' said she. 'You and I must part. You will have no business here. Let it stay, however,' said she; 'give it house-room till Colonel Campbell comes back. I shall talk about it to him; he will settle for me; he will help me out of all my difficulties.' And to this day, I do believe, she knows not whether it was his present or his daughter's."

Now Emma was obliged to think of the pianoforte; and the remembrance of all her former fanciful and unfair conjectures was so little pleasing that she soon allowed herself to believe her visit had been long enough; and, with a repetition of everything that she could venture to say of the good wishes which she really felt, took leave.

Chapter 45

EMMA'S pensive meditations, as she walked home, were not interrupted; but on entering the parlour, she found those who must rouse her. Mr. Knightley and Harriet had arrived during her absence, and were sitting with her father. Mr. Knightley immediately got up, and, in a manner decidedly graver than usual, said:

"I would not go away without seeing you, but I have no time to spare, and therefore must now be gone directly. I am going to London, to spend a few days with John and Isabella. Have you anything to send or say, besides the 'love,' which nobody carries?"

"Nothing at all. But is not this a sudden scheme?"

"Yes—rather—I have been thinking of it some little time."

Emma was sure he had not forgiven her; he looked unlike himself. Time, however, she thought, would tell him that they ought to be friends again. While he stood, as if meaning to go, but not going—her father began his inquiries.

"Well, my dear, and did you get there safely? And how did you find my worthy old friend and her daughter? I dare say they must have been very much obliged to you for coming. Dear Emma has been to call on Mrs. and Miss Bates, Mr. Knightley, as I told you before. She is always so attentive to them."

Emma's colour was heightened by this unjust praise; and with a smile and shake of the head, which spoke much, she looked at Mr. Knightley. It seemed as if there were an instantaneous impression in her favour, as if his eyes received the truth from hers, and all that had passed of good in her feelings were at once caught and honoured. He looked at her with a glow of regard. She was warmly gratified—and in another moment still more so, by a little movement of more than common friendliness on his part. He took her hand; whether she had not herself made the first motion, she could not say—she might, perhaps, have rather offered it—but he took her hand, pressed it, and certainly was on the point of carrying it to his lips—when, from some fancy or other, he suddenly let it go. Why he should feel such a scruple, why he should change his mind when it was all but done, she could not perceive. He would have judged better, she thought, if he had not stopped. The intention, however, was indubitable; and whether it was that his manners had in general so little gallantry, or however else it happened, but she thought nothing became him more. It was with him of so simple, yet so dignified a nature. She could not but recall the attempt with great satisfaction. It spoke such perfect amity. He left them immediately afterwards—gone in a moment. He always moved with the alertness of a mind which could neither be undecided nor dilatory, but now he seemed more sudden than usual in his disappearance.

Emma could not regret her having gone to Miss Bates, but she wished she had left her ten minutes earlier; it would have been a great pleasure to talk over Jane Fairfax's situation with Mr. Knightley. Neither would she regret that he should be going to Brunswick Square, for she knew how much his visit would be enjoyed—but it might have happened at a better time—and to have had longer notice of it would have been pleasanter. They parted thorough friends, however; she could not be deceived as to the meaning of his countenance, and his unfinished gallantry; it was all done to assure her that she had fully recovered his good opinion. He had been sitting with them half an hour, she found. It was a pity that she had not come back earlier.

In the hope of diverting her father's thoughts from the disagreeableness of Mr. Knightley's going to London, and going so suddenly, and going on horseback, which she knew would be all very bad, Emma communicated her news of Jane Fairfax, and her dependence on the effect was justified; it supplied a very useful check—interested, without disturbing him. He had long made up his mind to Jane Fairfax's going out as governess, and could talk of it cheerfully, but Mr. Knightley's going to London had been an unexpected blow.

"I am very glad, indeed, my dear, to hear she is to be so comfortably settled. Mrs. Elton is very good-natured and agreeable, and I dare say her acquaintances are just what they ought to be. I hope it is a dry situation, and that her health will be taken good care of. It ought to be a first object, as I am sure poor Miss Taylor's always was with me. You know, my dear, she is going to be to this new lady what Miss Taylor was to us. And I hope she will be better off in one respect, and not be induced to go away after it has been her home so long."

The following day brought news from Richmond to throw everything else into the background. An express arrived at Randalls to announce the death of Mrs. Churchill. Though her nephew had had no particular reason to hasten back on her account, she had not lived above six-and-thirty hours after his return. A sudden seizure, of a different nature from anything foreboded by her general state, had carried her off after a short struggle. The great Mrs. Churchill was no more

It was felt as such things must be felt. Everybody had a degree of gravity and sorrow; tenderness towards the departed, solicitude for the surviving friends; and, in a reasonable time, curiosity to know where she would be buried. Goldsmith tells us, that when lovely woman stoops to folly, she has nothing to do but to die; and when she stoops to be disagreeable, it is equally to be recommended as a clearer of ill-fame. Mrs. Churchill, after being disliked at least twenty-five years, was now spoken of with compassionate allowances. In one point she was fully justified. She had never been admitted before to be seriously ill. The event acquitted her of all the fancifulness, and all the selfishness of imaginary complaints.

"Poor Mrs. Churchill! no doubt she had been suffering a great deal: more than anybody had ever supposed—and continual pain would try the temper. It was a sad event—a great shock—with all her faults, what would Mr. Churchill do without her? Mr. Churchill's loss would be dreadful, indeed, Mr. Churchill would never get over it." Even Mr. Weston shook his head, and looked solemn, and said, "Ah, poor woman, who would have thought it!" and resolved that his mourning should be as handsome as possible; and his wife sat sighing and moralizing over her broad hems with a commiseration and good sense true and steady. How it would affect Frank, was among the earliest thoughts of both. It was also a very early speculation with Emma. The character of Mrs. Churchill, the grief of her husband—her mind glanced over them both with awe and compassion—and then rested with lightened feelings on how Frank might be affected by the event, how benefited, how freed. She saw in a moment all the possible good. Now an attachment to Harriet Smith would have nothing to encounter. Mr. Churchill, independent of his wife, was feared by nobody; an easy, guidable man, to be persuaded into anything by his nephew. All that remained to be wished was that the nephew should form the attachment, as, with all her good-will in the cause, Emma could feel no certainty of its being already formed.

Harriet behaved extremely well on the occasion—with great self-command. Whatever she might feel of brighter hope she betrayed nothing. Emma was gratified to observe such a proof in her of strengthened character, and refrained from any allusion that might endanger its maintenance. They spoke, therefore, of Mrs. Churchill's death with mutual forbearance.

Short letters from Frank were received at Randalls, communicating all that was immediately important of their state and plans. Mr. Churchill was better than could be expected; and their first removal, on the departure of the funeral for Yorkshire, was to be to the house of a very old friend in Windsor, to whom Mr. Churchill had been promising a visit the last ten years. At present, there was nothing to be done for Harriet; good wishes for the future were all that could yet be possible on Emma's side.

It was a more pressing concern to show attention to Jane Fairfax, whose prospects were closing while Harriet's opened, and whose engagements now allowed of no delay in any one at Highbury who wished to show her kindness—and with Emma it was grown into a first wish. She had scarcely a stronger regret than for her past coldness; and the person, whom she had been so many months neglecting, was now the very one on whom she would have lavished every distinction of regard or sympathy. She wanted to be of use to her; wanted to show a value for her society, and testify respect and consideration. She resolved to prevail on her to spend a day at Hartfield. A note was written to urge it. The invitation was refused, and by a verbal message. "Miss Fairfax was not well enough to write;" and when Mr. Perry called at Hartfield, the same morning, it appeared that she was so much indisposed as to have been visited, though against her own consent, by himself, and that she was suffering under severe headaches, and a nervous fever to a degree which made him doubt the possibility of her going to Mrs. Smallridge's at the time proposed. Her health seemed for the moment completely deranged—appetite quite gone; and though there were no absolutely alarming symptoms, nothing touching the pulmonary complaint which was the standing apprehension of the family, Mr. Perry was uneasy about her. He thought she had undertaken more than she was equal to, and that she felt it so herself, though she would not own it. Her spirits seemed overcome. Her present home, he could not but observe, was unfavourable to a nervous disorder; confined always to one room; he could have wished it otherwise; and her good aunt, though his very old friend, he must acknowledge to be not the best companion for an invalid of that description. Her care and attention could not be questioned; they were, in fact, only too great. He very much feared that Miss Fairfax derived more evil than good from them. Emma listened with the warmest concern; grieved for her more and more, and looked around eager to discover some way of being useful. To take her—be it only an hour or two—from her aunt, to give her change of air and scene, and quiet, rational conversation, even for an hour or two, might do her good; and the following morning she wrote again to say, in the most feeling language she could command, that she would call for her in the carriage at any hour that Jane would name—mentioning that she had Mr. Perry's decided opinion in favour of such exercise for his patient. The answer was only in this short note:—

"Miss Fairfax's compliments and thanks, but is quite unequal to any exercise."

Emma felt that her own note had deserved something better; but it was impossible to quarrel with words, whose tremulous inequality showed indisposition so plainly, and she thought only of how she might best counteract this unwillingness to be seen or assisted. In spite of the answer, therefore, she ordered the carriage, and drove to Mrs. Bates's, in the hope that Jane would be induced to join her—but it would not do; Miss Bates came to the carriage door, all gratitude, and agreeing with her most earnestly in thinking an airing might be of the greatest service—and everything that message could do was tried—but all in vain. Miss Bates was obliged to return without success; Janes was quite unpersuadable; the mere proposal of going out seemed to make her worse. Emma wished she could have seen her, and tried her own powers; but, almost before she could hint the wish, Miss Bates made it appear that she had promised her niece on no acount to let Miss Woodhouse in. "Indeed, the truth was, that poor dear Jane could not bear to see anybody—anybody at all—Mrs. Elton, indeed, could not be denied—and Mrs. Cole had made such a point —and Mrs. Perry had said so much—but, except them, Jane would really see nobody."

Emma did not want to be classed with the Mrs. Eltons, the Mrs. Perrys, and the Mrs. Coles, who would force themselves anywhere; neither could she feel any right of preference herself—she submitted, therefore, and only questioned Miss Bates further as to her niece's appetite and diet, which she longed to be able to assist. On that subject poor Miss Bates was very unhappy, and very communicative; Jane would hardly eat anything. Mr. Perry recommended nourishing food; but everything they could command (and never had anybody such good neighbours) was distasteful.

Emma, on reaching home, called the housekeeper directly to an examination of her stores; and some arrowroot of very superior quality was speedily despatched to Miss Bates with a most friendly note. In half an hour the arrowroot was returned, with a thousand thanks from Miss Bates, but "dear Jane would not be satisfied without its being sent back; it was a thing she could not take—and, moreover, she insisted on her saying that she was not at all in want of anything."

When Emma afterwards heard that Jane Fairfax had been seen wandering about the meadows, at some distance from Highbury, on the afternoon of the very day on which she had, under the plea of being unequal to any exercise, so peremptorily refused to go out with her in the carriage, she could have no doubt—putting everything together—that Jane was resolved to receive no kindness from *her*. She was sorry, very sorry. Her heart was grieved for a state which seemed but the more pitiable from this sort of irritation of spirits, inconsistency of action, and inequality of powers: and it mortified her that she was given so little credit for proper feeling, or esteemed so little worthy as a friend: but she had the consolation of knowing that her intentions were good, and of being able to say to herself, that could Mr. Knightley have been privy to all her attempts of assisting Jane Fairfax, could he even have seen into her heart, he would not, on this occasion, have found anything to reprove.

Chapter 46

ONE morning, about ten days after Mrs. Churchill's decease, Emma was called downstairs to Mr. Weston, who "could not stay five minutes, and wanted particularly to speak with her." He met her at the parlour-door, and hardly asking her how she did, in the natural key of his voice, sunk it immediately, to say, unheard by her father:

"Can you come to Randalls at any time this morning? Do, if it be possible. Mrs. Weston wants to see you. She must see you."

"Is she unwell?"

"No, no; not at all; only a little agitated. She would have ordered the carriage and come to you, but she must see you *alone,* and that you know" (nodding towards her father)—"Humph! can you come?"

"Certainly. This moment, if you please. It is impossible to refuse what you ask in such a way, but what can be the matter? is she really not ill?"

"Depend upon me; but ask no more questions. You will know it all in time. The most unaccountable business! But hush, hush!"

To guess what all this meant was impossible even for Emma. Some-thing really important seemed announced by his looks; but, as her friend was well, she endeavoured not to be uneasy, and settling it with her father, that she would take her walk now, she and Mr. Weston were soon out of the house together, and on their way at a quick pace for Randalls.

"Now," said Emma, when they were fairly beyond the sweep-gates—"now, Mr. Weston, do let me know what has happened."

"No, no," he gravely replied. "Don't ask me. I promised my wife to leave it all to her. She will break it to you better than I can. Do not be impatient, Emma; it will all come out too soon."

"Break it to me!" cried Emma, standing still with terror. "Good God! Mr. Weston, tell me at once. Something has happened in Brunswick Square. I know it has. Tell me, I charge you, tell me this moment what it is."

"No, indeed, you are mistaken."

"Mr. Weston, do not trifle with me. Consider how many of my dearest friends are now in Brunswick Square. Which of them is it? I charge you by all that is sacred not to attempt concealment."

"Upon my word, Emma——"

"Your word! why not your honour! why not say upon your honour, that it has nothing to do with any of them? Good heavens! What can be to be *broke* to me, that does not relate to one of that family?"

"Upon my honour," said he very seriously, "it does not. It is not in the smallest degree connected with any human being of the name of Knightley."

Emma's courage returned, and she walked on.

"I was wrong," he continued, "in talking of its being *broke* to you. I should not have used the expression. In fact, it does not concern you, it concerns only myself;—that is, we hope. Humph!—In short, my dear Emma, there is no occasion to be so uneasy about it. I don't say that it is not a disagreeable business, but things might be much worse. If we walk fast, we shall soon be at Randalls." Emma found that she must wait; and now it required little effort. She asked no more questions therefore, merely employed her own fancy, and that soon pointed out to her the probability of its being some money concern—something just come to light, of a disagreeable nature, in the circumstances of the family; something which the late event at Richmond had brought forward. Her fancy was very active. Half a dozen natural children, perhaps, and poor Frank cut off! This, though very undesirable, would be no matter of agony to her. It inspired more than an animating curiosity.

"Who is that gentleman on horseback?" said she, as they proceeded; speaking more to assist Mr. Weston in keeping his secret than with any other view.

"I do not know. One of the Otways. Not Frank: it is not Frank, I assure you. You will not see him. He is half-way to Windsor by this time."

"Has your son been with you, then?"

"Oh! yes, did not you know? Well, well, never mind." For a moment he was silent; and then added, in a tone much more guarded and demure:

"Yes, Frank came over this morning just to ask us how we did."

They hurried on, and were speedily at Randalls. "Well, my dear," said he, as they entered the room, "I have brought her, and now I hope you will soon be better. I shall leave you together. There is no use in delay. I shall not be far off, if you want me." And Emma distinctly heard him add, in a lower tone, before he quitted the room—"I have been as good as my word. She has not the least idea."

Mrs. Weston was looking so ill, and had an air of so much perturbation, that Emma's uneasiness increased: and the moment they were alone, she eagerly said:

"What is it, my dear friend? Something of a very unpleasant nature, I find, has occurred; do let me know directly what it is. I have been walking all this way in complete suspense. We both abhor suspense. Do not let mine continue longer. It will do you good to speak of your distress, whatever it may be."

"Have you, indeed, no idea?" said Mrs. Weston in a trembling voice. "Cannot you, my dear Emma—cannot you form a guess as to what you are to hear?"

"So far as that it relates to Mr. Frank Churchill, I do guess."

"You are right. It does relate to him, and I will tell you directly" (resuming her work, and seeming resolved against looking up). "He has been here, this very morning, on a most extraordinary errand. It is impossible to express our surprise. He came to speak to his father on a subject—to announce an attachment——"

She stopped to breathe. Emma thought first of herself, and then of Harriet.

"More than an attachment, indeed," resumed Mrs. Weston: "an engagement—a positive engagement. What will you say, Emma—what will anybody say—when it is known that Frank Churchill and Miss Fairfax are engaged—nay, that they have been long engaged?"

Emma even jumped with surprise; and, horror-struck, exclaimed:

"Jane Fairfax! Good God! You are not serious? You do not mean it?"

"You may well be amazed," returned Mrs. Weston, still averting her eyes, and talking on with eagerness, that Emma might have time to recover—"you may well be amazed. But it is even so. There has been a solemn engagement between them ever since October—formed at Weymouth, and kept a secret from everybody. Not a creature knowing it but themselves—neither the Campbells, nor her family, nor his. It is so wonderful, that though perfectly convinced of the fact, it is yet almost incredible to myself. I can hardly believe it. I thought I knew him."

Emma scarcely heard what was said. Her mind was divided between two ideas; her own former conversations with him about Miss Fairfax and poor Harriet; and for some time she could only exclaim, and require confirmation, repeated confirmation.

"Well!" said she at last, trying to recover herself, "this is a circumstance which I must think of at least half a day before I can at all comprehend it. What! engaged to her all the winter—before either of them came to Highbury?"

"Engaged since October—secretly engaged. It has hurt me, Emma, very much. It has hurt his father equally. *Some part* of his conduct we cannot excuse."

Emma pondered a moment, and then replied: "I will not pretend *not* to understand you; and to give you all the relief in my power, be assured that no such effect has followed his attentions to me as you are apprehensive of."

Mrs. Weston looked up, afraid to believe; but Emma's countenance was as steady as her words.

"That you may have less difficulty in believing this boast of my present perfect indifference," she continued, "I will further tell you, that there was a period in the early part of our acquaintance when I did like him—when I was very much disposed to be attached to him; nay, was attached—and how it came to cease is perhaps the wonder. Fortunately, however, it did cease. I have really for some time past—for at least three months—cared nothing about him. You may believe me, Mrs. Weston. This is the simple truth."

Mrs. Weston kissed her with tears of joy; and when she could find utterance, assured her that this protestation had done her more good than anything else in the world could do.

"Mr. Weston will be almost as much relieved as myself," said she. "On this point we have been wretched. It was our darling wish that you might be attached to each other, and we were persuaded that it was so. Imagine what we have been feeling on your account."

"I have escaped; and that I should escape may be a matter of grateful wonder to you and myself. But this does not acquit *him*, Mrs. Weston; and I must say that I think him greatly to blame. What right had he to come among us with affection and faith engaged, and with manners so *very* disengaged? What right had he to endeavour to please, as he certainly did—to distinguish any one young woman with persevering attention, as he certainly did, while he really belonged to another? How could he tell what mischief he might be doing? How could he tell that he might not be making me in love with him? Very wrong, very wrong, indeed."

"From something that he said, my dear Emma, I rather imagine——"

"And how could *she* bear such behaviour? Composure with a witness! to look on, while repeated attentions were offering to another woman before her face, and not resent it. That is a degree of placidity which I can neither comprehend nor respect."

"There were misunderstandings between them, Emma; he said so expressly. He had no time to enter into much explanation. He was here only a quarter of an hour, and in a state of agitation which did not allow the full use even of the time he could stay—but that there had been misunderstandings, he decidedly said. The present crisis, indeed, seemed to be brought on by them; and those misunderstandings might very possibly arise from the impropriety of his conduct."

"Impropriety! Oh! Mrs. Weston, it is too calm a censure. Much, much beyond impropriety! It has sunk him—I cannot say how it has sunk him in my opinion. So unlike what a man should be! None of that upright integrity, that strict adherence to truth and principle, that disdain of trick and littleness, which a man should display in every transaction of his life."

"Nay, dear Emma, now I must take his part; for though he has been wrong in this instance, I have known him long enough to answer for his having many, very many good qualities; and——"

"Good God!" cried Emma, not attending to her, "Mrs. Smallridge too! Jane actually on the point of going as governess! What could he mean by such horrible indelicacy? To suffer her to engage herself—to suffer her even to think of such a measure!"

"He knew nothing about it, Emma. On this article I can fully acquit him. It was a private resolution of hers, not communicated to him, or at least not communicated in a way to carry conviction. Till yesterday, I know, he said he was in the dark as to her plans. They burst on him, I do not know how, but by some letter or message—and it was the discovery of what she was doing, of this very project of hers, which determined him to come forward at once, own it all to his uncle, throw himself on his kindness, and, in short, put an end to the miserable state of concealment that had been carrying on so long."

Emma began to listen better.

"I am to hear from him soon," continued Mrs. Weston. "He told me at parting that he should soon write; and he spoke in a manner which seemed to promise me many particulars that could not be given now. Let us wait, therefore, for this letter. It may bring many extenuations. It may make many things intelligible and excusable which now are not to be understood. Don't let us be severe; don't let us be in a hurry to condemn him. Let us have patience. I must love him; and now that I am satisfied on one point, the one material point, I am sincerely anxious for its all turning out well, and ready to hope that it may. They must both have suffered a great deal under such a system of secrecy and concealment."

"*His* sufferings," replied Emma drily, "do not appear to have done him much harm. Well, and how did Mr. Churchill take it?"

"Most favourably for his nephew—gave his consent with scarcely a difficulty. Conceive what the events of a week have done in that family! While poor Mrs. Churchill lived, I suppose there could not have been a hope, a chance, a possibility; but scarcely are her remains at rest in the family vault than her husband is persuaded to act exactly opposite to what she would have required. What a blessing it is, when undue influence does not survive the grave! He gave his consent with very little persuasion."

"Ah!" thought Emma, "he would have done as much for Harriet."

"This was settled last night, and Frank was off with the light this morning. He stopped at Highbury, at the Bates's, I fancy, some time, and then came on hither; but was in such a hurry to get back to his uncle, to whom he is just now more necessary than ever, that, as I tell you, he could stay with us but a quarter of an hour. He was very much agitated—very much indeed—to a degree that made him appear quite a different creature from anything I had ever seen him before. In addition to all the rest there had been the shock of finding her so very unwell, which he had had no previous suspicion of, and there was every appearance of his having been feeling a great deal."

"And do you really believe the affair to have been carrying on with such perfect secrecy? The Campbells, the Dixons—did none of them know of the engagement?"

Emma could not speak the name of Dixon without a little blush.

"None; not one. He positively said that it had been known to no being in the world but their two selves."

"Well," said Emma, "I suppose we shall gradually grow reconciled to the idea, and I wish them very happy. But I shall always think it a very abominable sort of proceeding. What has it been but a system of hypoc⋅ risy and deceit, espionage and treachery? To come among us with pro⋅ fessions of openness and simplicity; and such a league in secret to judge us all! Here have we been the whole winter and spring, completely duped, fancying ourselves all on an equal footing of truth and honour, with two people in the midst of us who may have been carrying round, comparing and sitting in judgment on sentiments and words that were never meant for both to hear. They must take the consequence, if they have heard each other spoken of in a way not perfectly agreeable."

"I am quite easy on that head," replied Mrs. Weston. "I am very sure that I never said anything of either to the other which both might not have heard."

"You are in luck. Your only blunder was confined to my ear, when you imagined a certain friend of ours in love with the lady."

"True. But as I have always had a thoroughly good opinion of Miss Fairfax, I never could, under any blunder, have spoken ill of her; and as to speaking ill of him, there I must have been safe."

At this moment Mr. Weston appeared at a little distance from the window, evidently on the watch. His wife gave him a look which invited him in; and, while he was coming round, added:

"Now, dearest Emma, let me entreat you to say and look everything that may set his heart at ease, and incline him to be satisfied with the match. Let us make the best of it—and, indeed, almost everything may be fairly said in her favour. It is not a connection to gratify; but if Mr. Churchill does not feel that, why should we? and it may be a very fortunate circumstance for him—for Frank, I mean—that he should have attached himself to a girl of such steadiness of character and good judgment as I have always given her credit for, and still am disposed to give her credit for, in spite of this one great deviation from the strict rule of right. And how much may be said, in her situation, for even that error!"

"Much, indeed!" cried Emma feelingly. "If a woman can ever be excused for thinking only of herself, it is in a situation like Jane Fairfax's. Of such, one may almost say, that 'the world is not theirs, nor the world's law.' "

She met Mr. Weston on his entrance with a smiling countenance, exclaiming:

"A very pretty trick you have been playing me, upon my word! This was a device, I suppose, to sport with my curiosity, and exercise my talent of guessing. But you really frightened me. I thought you had lost half your property, at least. And here, instead of its being a matter of condolence, it turns out to be one of congratulation. I congratulate you, Mr. Weston, with all my heart, on the prospect of having one of the most lovely and accomplished young women in England for your daughter."

A glance or two between him and his wife convinced him that all was as right as this speech proclaimed; and its happy effect on his spirits was immediate. His air and voice recovered their usual briskness; he shook her heartily and gratefully by the hand, and entered on the subject in a manner to prove that he now only wanted time and persuasion to think the engagement no very bad thing. His companions suggested only what could palliate imprudence or smooth objections; and by the time they had talked it all over together, and he had talked it all over again with Emma, in their walk back to Hartfield, he was become perfectly reconciled, and not far from thinking it the very best thing Frank could possibly have done.

Chapter 47

"HARRIET, poor Harriet!" Those were the words; in them lay the tormenting ideas which Emma could not get rid of, and which constituted the real misery of the business to her. Frank Churchill had behaved very ill by herself—very ill in many ways—but it was not so much *his* behaviour as her own which made her so angry with him. It was the scrape which he had drawn her into on Harriet's account, that gave the deepest hue to his offence. Poor Harriet! to be a second time the dupe of her misconceptions and flattery. Mr. Knightley had spoken prophetically when he once said, "Emma, you have been no friend to Harriet Smith." She was afraid she had done her nothing but disservice. It was true that she had not to charge herself in this instance, as in the former, with being the sole and original author of the mischief: with having suggested such feelings as might otherwise never have entered Harriet's imagination; for Harriet had acknowledged her admiration and preference of Frank Churchill before she had ever given her a hint on the subject; but she felt completely guilty of having encouraged what she might have repressed. She might have prevented the indulgence and increase of such sentiments. Her influence would have been enough. And now she was very conscious that she ought to have prevented them. She felt that she had been risking her friend's happiness on most insufficient grounds. Common sense would have directed her to tell Harriet that she must not allow herself to think of him, and that there were five hundred chances to one against his ever caring for her. "But with common sense," she added, "I am afraid I have had little to do."

She was extremely angry with herself. If she could not have been angry with Frank Churchill too, it would have been dreadful. As for Jane Fairfax, she might at least relieve her feelings from any present solicitude on her account. Harriet would be anxiety enough; she need no longer be unhappy about Jane, whose troubles and whose ill-health having, of course, the same origin, must be equally under cure. Her days of insignificance and evil were over. She would soon be well, and happy and prosperous. Emma could not imagine why her own attentions had been slighted. This discovery laid many smaller matters open. No doubt it had been from jealousy. In Jane's eyes she had been a rival; and well might anything she could offer of assistance or regard be repulsed. An airing in the Hartfield carriage would have been the rack, and arrowroot from the Hartfield store-room must have been poison. She understood it all; and as far as her mind could disengage itself from the injustice and selfishness of angry feelings, she acknowledged that Jane Fairfax would have neither elevation nor happiness beyond her desert. But poor Harriet was such an engrossing charge! There was little sympathy to be spared for anybody else. Emma was sadly fearful that this second disappointment would be more severe than the first. Considering the very superior claims of the object, it ought; and judging by its apparently stronger effect on Harriet's mind, producing reserve and self-command, it would. She must communicate the painful truth, however, and as soon as possible. An injunction of secrecy had been among Mr. Weston's parting words. "For the present the whole affair was to be completely a secret. Mr. Churchill had made a point of it, as a token of respect to the wife he had so very recently lost; and everybody admitted it to be no more than due decorum." Emma had promised; but still Harriet must be excepted. It was her superior duty.

In spite of her vexation, she could not help feeling it almost ridiculous, that she should have the very same distressing and delicate office to perform by Harriet which Mrs. Weston had just gone through by herself. The intelligence, which had been so anxiously announced to her, she was now to be anxiously announcing to another. Her heart beat quick on hearing Harriet's footstep and voice; so, she supposed, had poor Mrs Weston felt when *she* was approaching Randalls. Could the event of the disclosure bear an equal resemblance! But of that, unfortunately, there could be no chance.

"Well, Miss Woodhouse," cried Harriet, coming eagerly into the room, "is not this the oddest news that ever was?"

"What news do you mean?" replied Emma, unable to guess, by look or voice, whether Harriet could indeed have received any hint.

"About Jane Fairfax. Did you ever hear anything so strange? Oh! you need not be afraid of owning it to me, for Mr. Weston has told me himself. I met him just now. He told me it was to be a great secret; and, therefore, I should not think of mentioning it to anybody but you, but he said you knew it."

"What did Mr. Weston tell you?" said Emma, still perplexed.

"Oh! he told me all about it; that Jane Fairfax and Mr. Frank Churchill are to be married, and that they have been privately engaged to one another this long while. How very odd!"

It was, indeed, so odd, Harriet's behaviour was so extremely odd, that Emma did not know how to understand it. Her character appeared absolutely changed. She seemed to propose showing no agitation, or disappointment, or peculiar concern in the discovery. Emma looked at her, quite unable to speak.

"Had you any idea," cried Harriet, "of his being in love with her? You, perhaps, might. You" (blushing as she spoke), "who can see into everybody's heart; but nobody else——"

"Upon my word," said Emma, "I begin to doubt my having any such talent. Can you seriously ask me, Harriet, whether I imagined him attached to another woman at the very time that I was—tacitly if not openly—encouraging you to give way to your own feelings? I never had the slightest suspicion, till within the last hour, of Mr. Frank Churchill's having the least regard for Jane Fairfax. You may be very sure that, if I had, I should have cautioned you accordingly."

"Me!" cried Harriet, colouring, and astonished. "Why should you caution me? You do not think I care about Mr. Frank Churchill?"

"I am delighted to hear you speak so stoutly on the subject," replied Emma, smiling, "but you do not mean to deny that there was a time—and not very distant either—when you gave me reason to understand that you did care about him?"

"Him! never, never. Dear Miss Woodhouse, how could you so mistake me?" (turning away distressed).

"Harriet," cried Emma, after a moment's pause, "what do you mean? Good Heaven! what do you mean? Mistake you! Am I to suppose then—?"

She could not speak another word. Her voice was lost; and she sat down, waiting in great terror till Harriet should answer.

Harriet, who was standing at some distance and with face turned from her, did not immediately say anything; and when she did speak, it was in a voice nearly as agitated as Emma's.

"I should not have thought it possible," she began, "that you could have misunderstood me! I know we agreed never to name him—but considering how infinitely superior he is to everybody else, I should not have thought it possible that I could be supposed to mean any other person. Mr. Frank Churchill, indeed! I do not know who would ever look at him in the company of the other. I hope I have a better taste than to think of Mr. Frank Churchill, who is like nobody by his side. And that you should have been so mistaken, is amazing! I am sure, but for believing that you entirely approved and meant to encourage me in my attachment, I should have considered it at first too great a presumption almost to dare to think of him. At first, if you had not told me that more wonderful things had happened; that there had been matches of greater disparity (those were your very words)—I should not have dared to give way to—I should not have thought it possible; but if *you*, who had been always acquainted with him——"

"Harriet," cried Emma, collecting herself resolutely, "let us understand each other now, without the possibility of further mistake. Are you speaking of—Mr. Knightley?"

"To be sure I am. I never could have an idea of anybody else—and so I thought you knew. When we talked about him, it was as clear as possible."

"Not quite," returned Emma, with forced calmness; "for all that you then said appeared to me to relate to a different person. I could almost assert that you had *named* Mr. Frank Churchill. I am sure the service Mr. Frank Churchill had rendered you, in protecting you from the gipsies, was spoken of."

"Oh, Miss Woodhouse, how you do forget!"

"My dear Harriet, I perfectly remember the substance of what I said on the occasion. I told you that I did not wonder at your attachment; that, considering the service he had rendered you, it was extremely natu-

ral; and you agreed to it, expressing yourself very warmly as to your
sense of that service, and mentioning even what your sensations had
been in seeing him come forward to your rescue. The impression of it
is strong on my memory."

"Oh, dear," cried Harriet, "now I recollect what you mean; but I was
thinking of something very different at the time. It was not the gipsies—
it was not Mr. Frank Churchill that I meant. No!" (with some elevation) "I was thinking of a much more precious circumstance—of Mr.
Knightley's coming and asking me to dance, when Mr. Elton would
not stand up with me, and when there was no other partner in the room.
That was the kind action; that was the noble benevolence and generosity; that was the service which made me begin to feel how superior
he was to every other being upon earth."

"Good God!" cried Emma, "this has been a most unfortunate—most
deplorable mistake! What is to be done?"

"You would not have encouraged me, then, if you had understood
me? At least, however, I cannot be worse off than I should have been,
if the other had been the person; and now—it *is* possible——"

She paused a few moments. Emma could not speak.

"I do not wonder, Miss Woodhouse," she resumed, "that you should
feel a great difference between the two, as to me or as to anybody. You
must think one five hundred million times more above me than the
other. But I hope, Miss Woodhouse, that supposing—that if—strange
as it may appear— But you know they were your own words, that *more*
wonderful things had happened; matches of *greater* disparity had taken
place than between Mr. Frank Churchill and me; and, therefore, it
seems as if such a thing even as this may have occurred before—and
if I should be so fortunate, beyond expression, as to—if Mr. Knightley
should really—if *he* does not mind the disparity, I hope, dear Miss
Woodhouse, you will not set yourself against it and try to put difficulties in the way. But you are too good for that, I am sure."

Harriet was standing at one of the windows. Emma turned round to
look at her in consternation, and hastily said:

"Have you any idea of Mr. Knightley's returning your affection?"

"Yes," replied Harriet, modestly, but not fearfully; "I must say
that I have."

Emma's eyes were instantly withdrawn; and she sat silently meditating, in a fixed attitude, for a few minutes. A few minutes were sufficient
for making her acquainted with her own heart. A mind like hers, once
opening to suspicion, made rapid progress; she touched, she admitted,
she acknowledged the whole truth. Why was it so much worse that
Harriet should be in love with Mr. Knightley than with Frank Churchill? Why was the evil so dreadfully increased by Harriet's having some
hope of a return? It darted through her with the speed of an arrow
that Mr. Knightley must marry no one but herself!

Her own conduct, as well as her own heart, was before her in the same

few minutes. She saw it all with a clearness which had never blessed her
before. How improperly had she been acting by Harriet! How inconsiderate, how indelicate, how irrational, how unfeeling, had been her conduct!
What blindness, what madness had led her on! It struck her with dreadful
force, and she was ready to give it every bad name in the world. Some
portion of respect for herself, however, in spite of all these demerits, some
concern for her own appearance, and a strong sense of justice by Harriet
(there would be no need of *compassion* to the girl who believed herself
loved by Mr. Knightley—but justice required that she should not be made
unhappy by any coldness now), gave Emma the resolution to sit and
endure further with calmness, with even apparent kindness. For her own
advantage, indeed, it was fit that the utmost extent of Harriet's hopes
should be inquired into; and Harriet had done nothing to forfeit the regard
and interest which had been so voluntarily formed and maintained, or to
deserve to be slighted by the person whose counsels had never led her
right. Rousing from reflection, therefore, and subduing her emotion, she
turned to Harriet again, and in a more inviting accent renewed the conversation; for as to the subject which had first introduced it, the wonderful
story of Jane Fairfax, that was quite sunk and lost. Neither of them
thought but of Mr. Knightley and themselves.

Harriet, who had been standing in no unhappy reverie, was yet very
glad to be called from it by the now encouraging manner of such a judge,
and such a friend, as Miss Woodhouse; and only wanted invitation to give
the history of her hopes with great though trembling delight. Emma's
tremblings, as she asked, and as she listened, were better concealed than
Harriet's, but they were not less. Her voice was not unsteady; but her
mind was in all the perturbation that such a development of self, such a
burst of threatening evil, such a confusion of sudden and perplexing emotions, must create. She listened with much inward suffering, but with great
outward patience, to Harriet's detail. Methodical, or well arranged, or
very well delivered, it could not be expected to be; but it contained, when
separated from all the feebleness and tautology of the narration, a substance to sink her spirit; especially with the corroborating circumstances
which her own memory brought in favour of Mr. Knightley's most improved opinion of Harriet.

Harriet had been conscious of a difference in his behaviour ever since
those two decisive dances. Emma knew that he had, on that occasion,
found her much superior to his expectation. From that evening, or at least
from the time of Miss Woodhouse's encouraging her to think of him,
Harriet had begun to be sensible of his talking to her much more than he
had been used to do, and of his having, indeed, quite a different manner
towards her; a manner of kindness and sweetness. Latterly, she had been
more and more aware of it. When they had been all walking together, he
had so often come and walked by her, and talked so very delightfully! He
seemed to want to be acquainted with her. Emma knew it to have been
very much the case: she had often observed the change, to almost the

same extent. Harriet repeated expressions of approbation and praise from him—and Emma felt them to be in the closest agreement with what she had known of his opinion of Harriet. He praised her for being without art or affectation; for having simple, honest, generous feelings. She knew that he saw such recommendations in Harriet; he had dwelt on them to her more than once. Much that lived in Harriet's memory, many little particulars of the notice she had received from him, a look, a speech, a removal from one chair to another, a compliment implied, a preference inferred, had been unnoticed, because unsuspected, by Emma. Circumstances that might swell to half an hour's relation, and contained multiplied proofs to her who had seen them, had passed undiscerned by her who now heard them; but the two latest occurrences to be mentioned—the two of strongest promise to Harriet—were not without some degree of witness from Emma herself. The first was his walking with her apart from the others in the limewalk at Donwell, where they had been walking some time before Emma came, and he had taken pains (as she was convinced) to draw her from the rest to himself; and at first he had talked to her in a more particular way than he had ever done before—in a very particular way indeed! (Harriet could not recall it without a blush.) He seemed to be almost asking her whether her affections were engaged. But as soon as she (Miss Woodhouse) appeared likely to join them, he changed the subject, and began talking about farming. The second was his having sat talking with her nearly half an hour before Emma came back from her visit, the very last morning of his being at Hartfield—though, when he first came in, he had said that he could not stay five minutes—and his having told her, during their conversation, that though he must go to London, it was very much against his inclination that he left home at all, which was much more (as Emma felt) than he had acknowledged to *her*. The superior degree of confidence towards Harriet which this one article marked gave her severe pain.

On the subject of the first of the two circumstances, she did, after a little reflection, venture the following question: "Might he not? Is not it possible, that, when inquiring, as you thought, into the state of your affections, he might be alluding to Mr. Martin—he might have Mr. Martin's interest in view?" But Harriet rejected the suspicion with spirit.

"Mr. Martin! No, indeed! There was not a hint of Mr. Martin. I hope I know better now than to care for Mr. Martin, or to be suspected of it."

When Harriet had closed her evidence, she appealed to her dear Miss Woodhouse to say whether she had not good ground for hope.

"I never should have presumed to think of it at first," said she, "but for you. You told me to observe him carefully, and let his behaviour be the rule of mine—and so I have. But now I seem to feel that I may deserve him; and that if he does choose me, it will not be anything so very wonderful."

The bitter feelings occasioned by this speech, the many bitter feelings, made the utmost exertion necessary on Emma's side to enable her to say in reply:

"Harriet, I will only venture to declare, that Mr. Knightley is the last man in the world who would intentionally give any woman the idea of his feeling for her more than he really does."

Harriet seemed ready to worship her friend for a sentence so satisfactory; and Emma was only saved from raptures and fondness, which at that moment would have been dreadful penance, by the sound of her father's footsteps. He was coming through the hall. Harriet was too much agitated to encounter him. "She could not compose herself—Mr. Woodhouse would be alarmed—she had better go;" with most ready encouragement from her friend, therefore, she passed off through another door—and the moment she was gone, this was the spontaneous burst of Emma's feelings:—"O God! that I had never seen her!"

The rest of the day, the following night, were hardly enough for her thoughts. She was bewildered amidst the confusion of all that had rushed on her within the last few hours. Every moment had brought a fresh surprise; and every surprise must be matter of humiliation to her. How to understand it all! How to understand the deceptions she had been thus practising on herself, and living under! The blunders, the blindness of her own head and heart! She sat still, she walked about, she tried her own room, she tried the shrubbery—in every place, every posture, she perceived that she had acted most weakly; that she had been imposed on by others in a most mortifying degree; that she had been imposing on herself in a degree yet more mortifying; that she was wretched, and should probably find this day but the beginning of wretchedness.

To understand, thoroughly understand her own heart, was the first endeavour. To that point went every leisure moment which her father's claims on her allowed, and every moment of involuntary absence of mind.

How long had Mr. Knightley been so dear to her, as every feeling declared him now to be? When had his influence, such influence begun? When had he succeeded to that place in her affection which Frank Churchill had once, for a short period, occupied? She looked back; she compared the two—compared them, as they had always stood in her estimation, from the time of the latter's becoming known to her—and as they must at any time have been compared by her, had it—oh! had it, by any blessed felicity, occurred to her to institute the comparison. She saw that there never had been a time when she did not consider Mr. Knightley as infinitely the superior, or when his regard for her had not been infinitely the most dear. She saw, that in persuading herself, in fancying, in acting to the contrary, she had been entirely under a delusion, totally ignorant of her own heart—and, in short, that she had never really cared for Frank Churchill at all!

This was the conclusion of the first series of reflections. This was the knowledge of herself, on the first question of inquiry, which she reached; and without being long in reaching it. She was most sorrowfully indignant;

ashamed of every sensation but the one revealed to her—her affection for Mr. Knightley. Every other part of her mind was disgusting.

With insufferable vanity had she believed herself in the secret of everybody's feelings; with unpardonable arrogance proposed to arrange everybody's destiny. She was proved to have been universally mistaken; and she had not quite done nothing—for she had done mischief. She had brought evil on Harriet, on herself, and, she too much feared, on Mr. Knightley. Were this most unequal of all connections to take place, on her must rest all the reproach of having given it a beginning; for this attachment she must believe to be produced only by a consciousness of Harriet's; and even were this not the case, he would never have known Harriet at all but for her folly.

Mr. Knightley and Harriet Smith! It was a union to distance every wonder of the kind. The attachment of Frank Churchill and Jane Fairfax became commonplace, threadbare, stale in the comparison, exciting no surprise, presenting no disparity, affording nothing to be said or thought. Mr. Knightley and Harriet Smith! Such an elevation on her side! Such a debasement on his! It was horrible to Emma to think how it must sink him in the general opinion, to foresee the smiles, the sneers, the merriment it would prompt at his expense; the mortification and disdain of his brother, the thousand inconveniences to himself. Could it be? No; it was impossible. And yet it was far, very far, from impossible. Was it a new circumstance for a man of first-rate abilities to be captivated by very inferior powers? was it new for one, perhaps too busy to seek, to be the prize of a girl who would seek him? Was it new for anything in this world to be unequal, inconsistent, incongruous—or for chance and circumstance (as second causes) to direct the human fate?

Oh! had she never brought Harriet forward! Had she left her where she ought, and where he had told her she ought! Had she not, with a folly which no tongue could express, prevented her marrying the unexceptionable young man who would have made her happy and respectable in the line of life to which she ought to belong, all would have been safe; none of this dreadful sequel would have been.

How Harriet could ever have had the presumption to raise her thoughts to Mr. Knightley! How she could dare to fancy herself the chosen of such a man till actually assured of it! But Harriet was less humble, had fewer scruples than formerly. Her inferiority, whether of mind or situation, seemed little felt. She had seemed more sensible of Mr. Elton's being to stoop in marrying her, than she now seemed of Mr. Knightley's. Alas! was not that her own doing too? Who had been at pains to give Harriet notions of self-consequence but herself? Who but herself had taught her, that she was to elevate herself if possible, and that her claims were great to a high worldly establishment? If Harriet, from being humble, were grown vain, it was her doing too.

Chapter 48

TILL now that she was threatened with its loss, Emma had never
known how much of her happiness depended on being *first* with Mr.
Knightley, first in interest and affection. Satisfied that it was so, and
feeling it her due, she had enjoyed it without reflection; and only in the
dread of being supplanted, found how inexpressibly important it had
been. Long, very long, she felt she had been first; for, having no female
connections of his own, there had been only Isabella whose claims could be
compared with hers, and she had always known exactly how far he loved
and esteemed Isabella. She had herself been first with him for many
years past. She had not deserved it; she had often been negligent or
perverse, slighting his advice, or even wilfully opposing him, insensible of
half his merits, and quarrelling with him because he would not acknowledge her false and insolent estimate of her own—but still, from family
attachment and habit, and thorough excellence of mind, he had loved her,
and watched over her from a girl, with an endeavour to improve her, and
an anxiety for her doing right, which no other creature had at all shared.
In spite of all her faults, she knew she was dear to him; might she not say,
very dear? When the suggestions of hope, however, which must follow
here, presented themselves, she could not presume to indulge them.
Harriet Smith might think herself not unworthy of being peculiarly,
exclusively, passionately loved by Mr. Knightley. *She* could not. She could
not flatter herself with any idea of blindness in his attachment to *her*. She
had received a very recent proof of its impartiality. How shocked had he
been by her behaviour to Miss Bates! How directly, how strongly had he
expressed himself to her on the subject! Not too strongly for the offence—
but far, far too strongly to issue from any feeling softer than upright
justice and clear-sighted good-will. She had no hope, nothing to deserve
the name of hope, that he could have that sort of affection for herself
which was now in question; but there was a hope (at times a slight one, at
times much stronger) that Harriet might have deceived herself, and be
overrating his regard for *her*. Wish it she must, for his sake—be the
consequence nothing to herself, but his remaining single all his life. Could
she be secure of that, indeed, of his never marrying at all, she believed she
should be perfectly satisfied. Let him but continue the same Mr. Knightley
to her, and her father, the same Mr. Knightley to all the world; let
Donwell and Hartfield lose none of their precious intercourse of friendship
and confidence, and her peace would be fully secured. Marriage, in fact,
would not do for her. It would be incompatible with what she owed to her
father, and with what she felt for him. Nothing should separate her from
her father. She would not marry, even if she were asked by Mr. Knightley.

It must be her ardent wish that Harriet might be disappointed; and she
hoped, that when able to see them together again, she might at least be
able to ascertain what the chances for it were. She should see them

henceforward with the closest observance; and wretchedly as she had hitherto misunderstood even those she was watching, she did not know how to admit that she could be blinded here. He was expected back every day. The power of observation would be soon given—frightfully soon it appeared when her thoughts were in one course. In the meanwhile, she resolved against seeing Harriet. It would do neither of them good, it would do the subject no good, to be talking of it further. She was resolved not to be convinced, as long as she could doubt, and yet had no authority for opposing Harriet's confidence. To talk would be only to irritate. She wrote to her, therefore, kindly, but decisively, to beg that she would not, at present, come to Hartfield; acknowledging it to be her conviction that all further confidential discussion of *one* topic had better be avoided; and hoping, that if a few days were allowed to pass before they met again, except in the company of others—she objected only to a *tête-à-tête*—they might be able to act as if they had forgotten the conversation of yesterday. Harriet submitted, and approved, and was grateful.

This point was just arranged when a visitor arrived to tear Emma's thoughts a little from the one subject which had engrossed them, sleeping or waking, the last twenty-four hours—Mrs. Weston, who had been calling on her daughter-in-law elect, and took Hartfield in her way home, almost as much in duty to Emma as in pleasure to herself, to relate all the particulars of so interesting an interview.

Mr. Weston had accompanied her to Mrs. Bates's, and gone through his share of this essential attention most handsomely; but she having then induced Miss Fairfax to join her in an airing, was now returned with much more to say, and much more to say with satisfaction, than a quarter of an hour spent in Mrs. Bates's parlour, with all the incumbrance of awkward feelings, could have afforded.

A little curiosity Emma had, and she made the most of it while her friend related. Mrs. Weston had set off to pay the visit in a good deal of agitation herself; and in the first place had wished not to go at all at present; to be allowed merely to write to Miss Fairfax instead, and to defer this ceremonious call till a little time had passed, and Mr. Churchill could be reconciled to the engagement's becoming known; as, considering everything, she thought such a visit could not be paid without leading to reports; but Mr. Weston had thought differently; he was extremely anxious to show his approbation to Miss Fairfax and her family, and did not conceive that any suspicion could be excited by it; or if it were, that it would be of any consequence; for "such things," he observed, "always got about." Emma smiled, and felt that Mr. Weston had very good reason for saying so. They had gone, in short; and very great had been the evident distress and confusion of *the* lady. She had hardly been able to speak a word, and every look and action had shown how deeply she was suffering from consciousness. The quiet, heart-felt satisfaction of the old lady, and the rapturous delight of her daughter, who proved even too joyous to talk as usual, had been a gratifying, yet almost an affecting scene. They were both so truly respectable in their happiness, so disinterested in every sensation; thought so much of Jane, so much of everybody, and so little of themselves that every kindly feeling was at work for them. Miss Fairfax's recent illness had offered a fair plea for Mrs. Weston to invite her to an airing; she had drawn back and declined at first, but, on being pressed, had yielded; and, in the course of their drive, Mrs. Weston had, by gentle encouragement, overcome so much of her embarrassment, as to bring her to converse on the important subject. Apologies for her seemingly ungracious silence in their first reception, and the warmest expressions of the gratitude she was always feeling towards herself and Mr. Weston, must necessarily open the cause; but when these effusions were put by, they had talked a good deal of the present and of the future state of the engagement. Mrs. Weston was convinced that such conversation must be the greatest relief to her companion, pent up within her own mind as everything had so long been, and was very much pleased with all that she had said on the subject.

"On the misery of what she had suffered, during the concealment of so many months," continued Mrs. Weston, "she was energetic. This was one of her expressions: 'I will not say that since I entered into the engagement I have not had some happy moments; but I can say, that I have never known the blessing of one tranquil hour:' and the quivering lip, Emma, which uttered it was an attestation that I felt at my heart."

"Poor girl!" said Emma. "She thinks herself wrong, then, for having consented to a private engagement?"

"Wrong! No one, I believe, can blame her more than she is disposed to blame herself. 'The consequence,' said she, 'has been a state of perpetual suffering to me; and so it ought. But after all the punishment that misconduct can bring, it is still not less misconduct. Pain is no expiation. I never can be blameless. I have been acting contrary to all my sense of right; and the fortunate turn that everything has taken, and the kindness I am now receiving, is what my conscience tells me ought not to be. Do not imagine, madam,' she continued, 'that I was taught wrong. Do not let any reflection fall on the principles or the care of the friends who brought me up. The error has been all my own and I do assure you that, with all the excuse that the present circumstances may appear to give, I shall yet dread making the story known to Colonel Campbell.' "

"Poor girl!" said Emma, again. "She loves him, then, excessively, I suppose. It must have been from attachment only that she could be led to form the engagement. Her affection must have overpowered her judgment."

"Yes, I have no doubt of her being extremely attached to him."

"I am afraid," returned Emma, sighing, "that I must often have contributed to make her unhappy."

"On your side, my love, it was very innocently done. But she probably had something of that in her thoughts, when alluding to the misunderstandings which he had given us hints of before. One natural consequence of the evil she had involved herself in, she said, was that of making her *unreasonable*. The consciousness of having done amiss had exposed her to a thousand inquietudes, and made her captious and irritable to a degree that must have been—that had been—hard for him to bear. 'I did not make the allowances,' said she, 'which I ought to have done, for his temper and spirits—his delightful spirits, and that gaiety, that playfulness of disposition, which, under any other circumstances, would, I am sure, have been as constantly bewitching to me as they were at first.' She then began to speak of you, and of the great kindness you had shown her during her illness; and, with a blush which showed me how it was all connected, desired me, whenever I had an opportunity, to thank you—I could not thank you too much—for every wish and every endeavour to do her good. She was sensible that you had never received any proper acknowledgment from herself."

"If I did not know her to be happy now," said Emma, seriously, "which, in spite of every little drawback from her scrupulous conscience, she must be, I could not bear these thanks; for, oh! Mrs. Weston, if there were an account drawn up of the evil and the good I have done Miss Fairfax—— Well" (checking herself and trying to be more lively), "this is all to be forgotten. You are very kind to bring me these interesting particulars; they show her to the greatest advantage. I am sure she is very good; I hope she will be very happy. It is fit that the fortune should be on his side, for I think the merit will be all on hers."

Such a conclusion could not pass unanswered by Mrs. Weston. She thought well of Frank in almost every respect; and, what was more, she loved him very much, and her defence was, therefore, earnest. She talked with a great deal of reason, and at least equal affection; but she had too much to urge for Emma's attention; it was soon gone to Brunswick Square or to Donwell; she forgot to attempt to listen; and when Mrs. Weston ended with, "We have not yet had the letter we are so anxious for, you know, but I hope it will soon come," she was obliged to pause before she answered, and at last obliged to answer at random, before she could at all recollect what letter it was which they were so anxious for.

"Are you well, my Emma?" was Mrs. Weston's parting question.

"Oh, perfectly. I am always well, you know. Be sure to give me intelligence of the letter as soon as possible."

Mrs. Weston's communications furnished Emma with more food for unpleasant reflection, by increasing her esteem and compassion, and her sense of past injustice towards Miss Fairfax. She bitterly regretted not having sought a closer acquaintance with her, and blushed for the envious feelings which had certainly been, in some measure, the cause. Had she followed Mr. Knightley's known wishes, in paying that attention to Miss Fairfax which was every way her due; had she tried to know her better; had she done her part towards intimacy; had she endeavoured to find a friend there instead of in Harriet Smith, she must, in all probability, have been spared from every pain which pressed on her now. Birth, abilities, and education had been equally marking one as an associate for her, to be received with gratitude; and the other—what was she? Supposing even that they had never become intimate friends; that she had never been admitted into Miss Fairfax's confidence on this important matter—which was most probable—still, in knowing her as she ought, and as she might, she must have been preserved from the abominable suspicions of an improper attachment to Mr. Dixon, which she had not only so foolishly fashioned and harboured herself, but had so unpardonably imparted; an idea which she greatly feared had been made a subject of material distress to the delicacy of Jane's feelings, by the levity or carelessness of Frank Churchill's. Of all the sources of evil surrounding the former, since her coming to Highbury, she was persuaded that she must herself have been the worst. She must have been a perpetual enemy. They never could have been all three together, without her having stabbed Jane Fairfax's peace in a thousand instances; and on Box Hill, perhaps, it had been the agony of a mind that would bear no more.

The evening of this day was very long and melancholy at Hartfield. The weather added what it could of gloom. A cold stormy rain set in, and nothing of July appeared but in the trees and shrubs, which the wind was despoiling, and the length of the day, which only made such cruel sights the longer visible.

The weather affected Mr. Woodhouse; and he could only be kept tolerably comfortable by almost ceaseless attention on his daughter's side, and by exertions which had never cost her half so much before. It reminded her of their first forlorn *tête-à-tête*, on the evening of Mrs. Weston's wedding-day; but Mr. Knightley had walked in then, soon after tea, and dissipated every melancholy fancy. Alas! such delightful proofs of Hartfield's attraction, as those sort of visits conveyed, might shortly be over. The picture which she had then drawn of the privations of the approaching winter had proved erroneous; no friends had deserted them, no pleasures had been lost. But her present forebodings she feared would experience no similar contradiction. The prospect before her now was threatening to a degree that could not be entirely dispelled—that might not be even partially brightened. If all took place that might take place among the circle of her friends, Hartfield must be comparatively deserted; and she left to cheer her father with the spirits only of ruined happiness.

The child to be born at Randalls must be a tie there even dearer than herself; and Mrs. Weston's heart and time would be occupied by it. They should lose her; and probably, in great measure, her husband also. Frank Churchill would return among them no more; and Miss Fairfax, it was reasonable to suppose, would soon cease to belong to Highbury. They would be married, and settled either at or near Enscombe. All that were good would be withdrawn; and if to these losses the loss of Donwell were to be added, what would remain of cheerful or of rational society within their reach? Mr. Knightley to be no longer coming there for his evening comfort! No longer walking in at all hours, as if ever willing to change his

own home for theirs! How was it to be endured? And if he were to be lost
to them for Harriet's sake; if he were to be thought of hereafter, as finding
in Harriet's society all that he wanted! if Harriet were to be the chosen,
the first, the dearest, the friend, the wife to whom he looked for all the best
blessings of existence; what could be increasing Emma's wretchedness but
the reflection, never far distant from her mind, that it had been all her
own work?

When it came to such a pitch as this, she was not able to refrain from a
start, or a heavy sigh, or even from walking about the room for a few
seconds; and the only source whence anything like consolation or composure could be drawn, was in the resolution of her own better conduct,
and the hope that, however inferior in spirit and gaiety might be the
following and every future winter of her life to the past, it would yet find
her more rational, more acquainted with herself, and leave her less to
regret when it were gone.

Chapter 49

THE weather continued much the same all the following morning; and
the same loneliness, and the same melancholy, seemed to reign at Hartfield; but in the afternoon it cleared; the wind changed into a softer
quarter; the clouds were carried off: the sun appeared; it was summer
again. With all the eagerness which such a transition gives Emma resolved to be out of doors as soon as possible. Never had the exquisite sight,
smell, sensation of nature, tranquil, warm, and brilliant after a storm,
been more attractive to her. She longed for the serenity they might gradually introduce; and on Mr. Perry's coming in soon after dinner, with a
disengaged hour to give her father, she lost no time in hurrying into the
shrubbery. There, with spirits freshened, and thoughts a little relieved,
she had taken a few turns, when she saw Mr. Knightley passing through
the garden door, and coming towards her. It was the first intimation of his
being returned from London. She had been thinking of him the moment
before, as unquestionably sixteen miles distant. There was time only for
the quickest arrangement of mind. She must be collected and calm. In
half a minute they were together. The "How-d'ye-do's" were quiet and
constrained on each side. She asked after their mutual friends; they were
all well. When had he left them? Only that morning. He must have had a
wet ride. Yes! He meant to walk with her, she found. "He had just looked
into the dining-room, and as he was not wanted there, preferred being out
of doors." She thought he neither looked nor spoke cheerfully; and the
first possible cause for it, suggested by her fears, was, that he had perhaps
been communicating his plans to his brother, and was pained by the
manner in which they had been received.

They walked together. He was silent. She thought he was often looking
at her, and trying for a fuller view of her face than it suited her to give.
And this belief produced another dread. Perhaps he wanted to speak to

ner of his attachment to Harriet, he might be watching for encouragement
to begin. She did not, could not, feel equal to lead the way to any such subject. He must do it all himself. Yet she could not bear this silence. With
him it was most unnatural. She considered, resolved, and, trying to smile,
began:

"You have some news to hear, now you are come back, that will rather
surprise you."

"Have I?" said he quietly, and looking at her; "of what nature?"

"Oh, the best nature in the world—a wedding."

After waiting a moment, as if to be sure she intended to say no more,
he replied:

"If you mean Miss Fairfax and Frank Churchill, I have heard that
already."

"How is it possible?" cried Emma, turning her glowing cheeks towards
him; for, while she spoke, it occurred to her that he might have called at
Mrs. Gooddard's in his way.

"I had a few lines on parish business from Mr. Weston this morning,
and at the end of them he gave me a brief account of what had happened."

Emma was quite relieved, and could presently say, with a little more
composure:

"*You* probably have been less surprised than any of us, for you have
had your suspicions. I have not forgotten that you once tried to give me a
caution. I wish I had attended to it—but" (with a sinking voice and a
heavy sigh) "I seem to have been doomed to blindness."

For a moment or two nothing was said, and she was unsuspicious of
having excited any particular interest till she found her arm drawn within
his, and pressed against his heart, and heard him thus saying, in a tone of
great sensibility, speaking low:

"Time, my dearest Emma, time will heal the wound. Your own excellent sense; your exertions for your father's sake: I know you will not
allow yourself——" Her arm was pressed again, as he added, in a more
broken and subdued accent, "The feelings of the warmest friendship—
indignation—abominable scoundrel!" And in a louder, steadier tone, he
concluded with, "He will soon be gone. They will soon be in Yorkshire. I
am sorry for *her*. She deserves a better fate."

Emma understood him; and as soon as she could recover from the
flutter of pleasure, excited by such tender consideration, replied:

"You are very kind, but you are mistaken, and I must set you right.
I am not in want of that sort of compassion. My blindness to what was
going on led me to act by them in a way that I must always be ashamed
of, and I was very foolishly tempted to say and do many things which
may well lay me open to unpleasant conjectures, but I have no other
reason to regret that I was not in the secret earlier."

"Emma," cried he, looking eagerly at her, "are you indeed?" but
checking himself—"No, no, I understand you—forgive me—I am pleased
that you can say even so much. He is no object of regret, indeed! and it

will not be very long, I hope, before that becomes the acknowledgment of more than your reason. Fortunate that your affections were not further entangled! I could never, I confess, from your manners, assure myself as to the degree of what you felt—I could only be certain that there was a preference—and a preference which I never believed him to deserve. He is a disgrace to the name of man. And is he to be rewarded with that sweet young woman? Jane! Jane! you will be a miserable creature."

"Mr. Knightley," said Emma, trying to be lively, but really confused—"I am in a very extraordinary situation. I cannot let you continue in your error; and yet, perhaps, since my manners gave such an impression, I have as much reason to be ashamed of confessing that I never have been at all attached to the person we are speaking of, as it might be natural for a woman to feel in confessing exactly the reverse. But I never have."

He listened in perfect silence. She wished him to speak, but he would not. She supposed she must say more before she were entitled to his clemency; but it was a hard case to be obliged still to lower herself in his opinion. She went on, however:

"I have very little to say for my own conduct. I was tempted by his attentions, and allowed myself to appear pleased. An old story, probably—a common case—and no more than has happened to hundreds of my sex before; and yet it may not be the more excusable in one who sets up as I do for Understanding. Many circumstances assisted the temptation. He was the son of Mr. Weston—he was continually here—I always found him very pleasant—and, in short, for" (with a sigh) "let me swell out the causes ever so ingeniously, they all centre in this at last—my vanity was flattered, and I allowed his attentions. Latterly, however—for some time, indeed—I have had no idea of their meaning anything. I thought them a habit, a trick, nothing that called for seriousness on my side. He has imposed on me, but he has not injured me. I have never been attached to him. And now I can tolerably comprehend his behaviour. He never wished to attach me. It was merely a blind to conceal his real situation with another. It was his object to blind all about him; and no one, I am sure, could be more effectually blinded than myself—except that I was *not* blinded—that it was my good fortune—that, in short, I was somehow or other safe from him."

She had hoped for an answer here—for a few words to say that her conduct was at least intelligible; but he was silent; and, as far as she could judge, deep in thought. At last, and tolerably in his usual tone, he said:

"I have never had a high opinion of Frank Churchill. I can suppose, however, that I may have underrated him. My acquaintance with him has been but trifling. And even if I have not underrated him hitherto, he may yet turn out well. With such a woman he has a chance. I have no motive for wishing him ill—and for her sake, whose happiness will be involved in his good character and conduct, I shall certainly wish him well."

"I have no doubt of their being happy together," said Emma; "I believe them to be very mutually and very sincerely attached."

"He is a most fortunate man," returned Mr. Knightley, with energy. "So early in life—at three-and-twenty—a period when, if a man chooses a wife, he generally chooses ill. At three-and-twenty to have drawn such a prize! What years of felicity that man, in all human calculation, has before him! Assured of the love of such a woman—the disinterested love—for Jane Fairfax's character vouches for her disinterestedness; everything in his favour—equality of situation—I mean, as far as regards society, and all the habits and manners that are important; equality in every point but one—and that one, since the purity of her heart is not to be doubted, such as must increase his felicity, for it will be his to bestow the only advantages she wants. A man would always wish to give a woman a better home than the one he takes her from; and he who can do it, where there is no doubt of *her* regard, must, I think, be the happiest of mortals. Frank Churchill is, indeed, the favourite of fortune. Everything turns out for his good. He meets with a young woman at a watering-place, gains her affection, cannot even weary her by negligent treatment—and had he and all his family sought round the world for a perfect wife for him, they could not have found her superior. His aunt is in the way. His aunt dies. He has only to speak. His friends are eager to promote his happiness. He has used everybody ill—and they are all delighted to forgive him. He is a fortunate man, indeed!"

"You speak as if you envied him."

"And I do envy him, Emma. In one respect he is the object of my envy."

Emma could say no more. They seemed to be within half a sentence of Harriet, and her immediate feeling was to avert the subject, if possible. She made her plan; she would speak of something totally different—the children in Brunswick Square; and she only waited for breath to begin, when Mr. Knightley startled her by saying:

"You will not ask me what is the point of envy. You are determined, I see, to have no curiosity. You are wise—but *I* cannot be wise. Emma, I must tell what you will not ask, though I may wish it unsaid the next moment."

"Oh, then, don't speak it, don't speak it," she eagerly cried. "Take a little time, consider, do not commit yourself."

"Thank you," said he, in an accent of deep mortification, and not another syllable followed.

Emma could not bear to give him pain. He was wishing to confide in her—perhaps to consult her; cost her what it would, she would listen. She might assist his resolution, or reconcile him to it; she might give just praise to Harriet, or, by representing to him his own independence, relieve him from that state of indecision which must be more intolerable than any alternative to such a mind as his. They had reached the house.

"You are going in, I suppose?" said he.

"No," replied Emma, quite confirmed by the depressed manner in which he still spoke, "I should like to take another turn. Mr. Perry is not gone." And, after proceeding a few steps, she added: "I stopped you ungraciously just now, Mr. Knightley, and, I am afraid, gave you pain. But if you have any wish to speak openly to me as a friend, or to ask my opinion of anything that you may have in contemplation—as a friend, indeed, you may command me. I will hear whatever you like. I will tell you exactly what I think."

"As a friend!" repeated Mr. Knightley. "Emma, that, I fear, is a word—no, I have no wish. Stay, yes, why should I hesitate? I have gone too far already for concealment. Emma, I accept your offer, extraordinary as it may seem, I accept it, and refer myself to you as a friend. Tell me, then, have I no chance of ever succeeding?"

He stopped in his earnestness to look the question, and the expression of his eyes overpowered her.

"My dearest Emma," said he, "for dearest you will always be, whatever the event of this hour's conversation, my dearest, most beloved Emma—tell me at once. Say 'No,' if it is to be said." She could really say nothing. "You are silent," he cried, with great animation; "absolutely silent! At present I ask no more."

Emma was almost ready to sink under the agitation of this moment. The dread of being awakened from the happiest dream was perhaps the most prominent feeling.

"I cannot make speeches, Emma," he soon resumed, and in a tone of such sincere, decided, intelligible tenderness as was tolerably convincing. "If I loved you less, I might be able to talk about it more. But you know what I am. You hear nothing but truth from me. I have blamed you, and lectured you, and you have borne it as no other woman in England would have borne it. Bear with the truths I would tell you now, dearest Emma, as well as you have borne with them. The manner, perhaps, may have as little to recommend them. God knows, I have been a very indifferent lover. But you understand me. Yes, you see, you understand my feelings—and will return them if you can. At present, I ask only to hear—once to hear your voice."

While he spoke, Emma's mind was most busy, and, with all the wonderful velocity of thought, had been able—and yet without losing a word—to catch and comprehend the exact truth of the whole; to see that Harriet's hopes had been entirely groundless, a mistake, a delusion, as complete a delusion as any of her own—that Harriet was nothing; that she was everything herself; that what she had been saying relative to Harriet had been all taken as the language of her own feelings; and that her agitation, her doubts, her reluctance, her discouragement, had been all received as discouragement from herself. And not only was there time for these convictions, with all their glow of attendant happiness, there was time also to rejoice that Harriet's secret had not escaped her, and to resolve that it need not, and should not. It was all the service she could now render her

poor friend; for as to any of that heroism of sentiment which might have
prompted her to entreat him to transfer his affection from herself to
Harriet, as infinitely the most worthy of the two—or even the more simple
sublimity of resolving to refuse him at once and for ever, without vouch-
safing any motive because he could not marry them both, Emma had it
not. She felt for Harriet, with pain and with contrition; but no flight of
generosity run mad, opposing all that could be probable or reasonable,
entered her brain. She had led her friend astray, and it would be a reproach
to her for ever; but her judgment was as strong as her feelings, and as
strong as it had ever been before, in reprobating any such alliance for him,
as most unequal and degrading. Her way was clear, though not quite
smooth. She spoke then, on being so entreated. What did she say? Just
what she ought, of course. A lady always does. She said enough to show
there need not be despair—and to invite him to say more himself. He *had*
despaired at one period; he had received such an injunction to caution and
silence, as for the time crushed every hope—she had begun by refusing to
hear him. The change had perhaps been somewhat sudden—her proposal
of taking another turn, her renewing the conversation which she had just
put an end to, might be a little extraordinary. She felt its inconsistency;
but Mr. Knightley was so obliging as to put up with it, and seek no
further explanation.

Seldom, very seldom does complete truth belong to any human disclosure; seldom can it happen that something is not a little disguised, or
a little mistaken; but where, as in this case, though the conduct is mistaken, the feelings are not, it may not be very material. Mr. Knightley
could not impute to Emma a more relenting heart than she possessed,
or a heart more disposed to accept of his.

He had, in fact, been wholly unsuspicious of his own influence. He had
followed her into the shrubbery with no idea of trying it. He had come,
in his anxiety to see how she bore Frank Churchill's engagement, with no
selfish view, no view at all, but of endeavouring, if she allowed him an
opening, to soothe or to counsel her. The rest had been the work of the
moment, the immediate effect of what he heard, on his feelings. The delightful assurance of her total indifference towards Frank Churchill, of her
having a heart completely disengaged from him, had given birth to the
hope that, in time, he might gain her affection himself; but it had been no
present hope—he had only, in the momentary conquest of eagerness over
judgment, aspired to be told that she did not forbid his attempt to attach
her. The superior hopes which gradually opened were so much the more
enchanting. The affection which he had been asking to be allowed to
create, if he could, was already his. Within half an hour he had passed from
a thoroughly distressed state of mind, to something so like perfect happiness, that it could bear no other name.

Her change was equal. This one half-hour had given to each the same
precious certainty of being beloved, had cleared from each the same degree
of ignorance, jealousy, or distrust. On his side, there had been a long-

standing jealousy, old as the arrival, or even the expectation, of Frank Churchill. He had been in love with Emma, and jealous of Frank Churchill, from about the same period, one sentiment having probably enlightened him as to the other. It was his jealousy of Frank Churchill that had taken him from the country. The Box Hill party had decided him on going away. He would save himself from witnessing again such permitted, encouraged attentions. He had gone to learn to be indifferent. But he had gone to a wrong place. There was too much domestic happiness in his brother's house; women wore too amiable a form in it; Isabella was too much like Emma—differing only in those striking inferiorities which always brought the other in brilliancy before him, for much to have been done even had his time been longer. He had stayed on, however, vigorously, day after day—till this very morning's post had conveyed the history of Jane Fairfax. Then, with the gladness which must be felt, nay, which he did not scruple to feel, having never believed Frank Churchill to be at all deserving of Emma, was there so much fond solicitude, so much keen anxiety for her, that he could stay no longer. He had ridden home through the rain; and had walked up directly after dinner, to see how this sweetest and best of all creatures, faultless in spite of all her faults, bore the discovery.

He had found her agitated and low. Frank Churchill was a villain. He heard her declare that she had never loved him. Frank Churchill's character was not desperate. She was his own Emma, by hand and word, when they returned into the house; and if he could have thought of Frank Churchill then, he might have deemed him a very good sort of fellow.

Chapter 50

WHAT totally different feelings did Emma take back into the house from what she had brought out! She had then been only daring to hope for a little respite of suffering; she was now in an exquisite flutter of happiness—and such happiness, moreover, as she believed must still be greater when the flutter should have passed away.

They sat down to tea—the same party round the same table—how often it had been collected!—and how often had her eyes fallen on the same shrubs in the lawn, and observed the same beautiful effect of the western sun! But never in such a state of spirits, never in anything like it; and it was with difficulty that she could summon enough of her usual self to be the attentive lady of the house, or even the attentive daughter.

Poor Mr. Woodhouse little suspected what was plotting against him in the breast of that man whom he was so cordially welcoming, and so anxiously hoping might not have taken cold from his ride. Could he have seen the heart, he would have cared very little for the lungs; but without the most distant imagination of the impending evil, without the slightest perception of anything extraordinary, in the looks or ways of either, he repeated to them very comfortably all the articles of news he had received from Mr. Perry, and talked on with much self-contentment, totally unsuspicious of what they could have told him in return.

As long as Mr. Knightley remained with them, Emma's fever continued; but when he was gone she began to be a little tranquillised and subdued, and in the course of the sleepless night, which was the tax for such an evening, she found one or two such very serious points to consider, as made her feel that even her happiness must have some alloy. Her father—and Harriet. She could not be alone without feeling the full weight of their separate claims; and how to guard the comfort of both to the utmost was the question. With respect to her father, it was a question soon answered. She hardly knew yet what Mr. Knightley would ask; but a very short parley with her own heart produced the most solemn resolution of never quitting her father. She even wept over the idea of it, as a sin of thought. While he lived, it must be only an engagement; but she flattered herself that if divested of the danger of drawing her away, it might become an increase of comfort to him. How to do her best by Harriet was of more difficult decision; how to spare her from any unnecessary pain; how to make her any possible atonement; how to appear least her enemy? On these subjects her perplexity and distress were very great. —and her mind had to pass again and again through every bitter reproach and sorrowful regret that had ever surrounded it. She could only resolve at last that she would still avoid a meeting with her, and communicate all that need be told by letter; that it would be inexpressibly desirable to have her removed just now for a time from Highbury, and—indulging in one scheme more—nearly resolve that it might be practicable to get an invitation for her to Brunswick Square. Isabella had been pleased with Harriet; and a few weeks spent in London must give her some amusement. She did not think it in Harriet's nature to escape being benefited by novelty and variety, by the streets, the shops, and the children. At any rate, it would be a proof of attention and kindness in herself, from whom everything was due; a separation for the present; an averting of the evil day, when they must all be together again.

She rose early, and wrote her letter to Harriet; an employment which left her so very serious, so nearly sad, that Mr. Knightley, in walking up to Hartfield to breakfast, did not arrive at all too soon; and half an hour stolen afterwards to go over the same ground again with him, literally and figuratively, was quite necessary to reinstate her in a proper share of the happiness of the evening before.

He had not left her long—by no means long enough for her to have the slightest inclination for thinking of anybody else—when a letter was brought her from Randalls, a very thick letter; she guessed what it must contain, and deprecated the necessity of reading it. She was now in perfect charity with Frank Churchill: she wanted no explanations, she wanted only to have her thoughts to herself—and as for understanding anything he wrote, she was sure she was incapable of it. It must be waded through, however. She opened the packet; it was too surely so; a note from Mrs. Weston to herself, ushered in the letter from Frank to Mrs. Weston:

"I have the greatest pleasure, my dear Emma, in forwarding to you the enclosed. I know what thorough justice you will do it, and have scarcely a doubt of its happy effect. I think we shall never materially disagree about the writer again; but I will not delay you by a long preface. We are quite well. This letter has been the cure of all the little nervousness I have been feeling lately. I did not quite like your looks on Tuesday, but it was an ungenial morning; and though you will never own being affected by weather, I think everybody feels a north-east wind. I felt for your dear father very much in the storm of Tuesday afternoon and yesterday morning, but had the comfort of hearing last night, by Mr. Perry, that it had not made him ill.—Yours ever,

"A. W."

[*To Mrs. Weston.*]

"Windsor.—*July.*

"My Dear Madam,—If I made myself intelligible yesterday, this letter will be expected; but expected or not, I know it will be read with candour and indulgence. You are all goodness, and I believe there will be need of even all your goodness to allow for some parts of my past conduct. But I have been forgiven by one who had still more to resent. My courage rises while I write. It is very difficult for the prosperous to be humble. I have already met with such success in two applications for pardon, that I may be in danger of thinking myself too sure of yours, and of those among your friends who have had any ground of offence. You must all endeavour to comprehend the exact nature of my situation when I first arrived at Randalls; you must consider me as having a secret which was to be kept at all hazards. This was the fact. My right to place myself in a situation requiring such concealment is another question. I shall not discuss it here. For my temptation to *think* it a right, I refer every caviller to a brick house, sashed windows below, and casements above, in Highbury. I dared not address her openly; my difficulties in the then state of Enscombe must be too well known to require definition; and I was fortunate enough to prevail, before we parted at Weymouth, and to induce the most upright female mind in the creation to stoop in charity to a secret engagement. Had she refused, I should have gone mad. But you will be ready to say, What was your hope in doing this? What did you look forward to? To anything, everything—to time, chance, circumstance, slow effects, sudden bursts, perseverance, and weariness, health and sickness. Every possibility of good was before me, and the first of blessings secured, in obtaining her promises of faith and correspondence. If you need further explanation, I have the honour, my dear madam, of being your husband's son, and the advantage of inheriting a disposition to hope for good, which no inheritance of houses or lands can ever equal the value of. See me, then, under these circumstances, arriving on my first visit to Randalls; and here I am conscious of wrong, for that visit might have been sooner paid. You will look back, and see that I did not come till Miss Fairfax was in Highbury; and as *you* were the person slighted, you will forgive me instantly; but I must work on my father's compassion, by reminding him, that so long as I absented myself from his house, so long I lost the blessing of knowing you. My behaviour, during the very happy fortnight which I spent with you, did not, I hope, lay me open to reprehension, excepting on one point. And now I come to the principal, the only important part of my conduct, while belonging to you, which excites my own anxiety, or requires very solicitous explanation. With the greatest respect, and the warmest friendship, do I mention Miss Woodhouse; my father, perhaps, will think I ought to add, with the deepest humiliation. A few words which dropped from him yesterday spoke his opinion, and some censure I acknowledge myself liable to. My behaviour to Miss Woodhouse indicated, I believe, more than it ought. In order to assist a concealment so essential to me, I was led on to make more than an allowable use of the sort of intimacy into which we were immediately thrown. I cannot deny that Miss Woodhouse was my ostensible object; but I am sure you will believe the declaration, that had I not been convinced of her indifference, I would not have been induced by any selfish views to go on. Amiable and delightful as Miss Woodhouse is, she never gave me the idea of a young woman likely to be attached; and that she was perfectly free from any tendency to being attached to me, was as much my conviction as my wish. She received my attentions with an easy, friendly, good-humoured playfulness which exactly suited me. We seemed to understand each other. From our relative situation, those attentions were her due, and were felt to be so. Whether Miss Woodhouse began really to understand me before the expiration of that fortnight I cannot say; when I called to take leave of her, I remember that I was within a moment of confessing the truth, and I then fancied she was not without suspicion; but I have no doubt of her having since detected me—at least in some degree. She may not have surmised the whole, but her quickness must have penetrated a part. I cannot doubt it. You will find, whenever the subject becomes freed from its present restraints, that it did not take her wholly by surprise. She frequently gave me hints of it. I remember her telling me at the ball that I owed Mrs. Elton gratitude for her attentions to Miss Fairfax. I hope this history of my conduct towards her will be admitted by you and my father as great extenuation of what you saw amiss. While you considered me as having sinned against Emma Woodhouse, I could deserve nothing from either. Acquit me here, and procure for me, when it is allowable, the acquittal and good wishes of that said Emma Woodhouse, whom I regard with so much brotherly affection as to long to have her as deeply and as happily in love as myself. Whatever strange things I said or did during that fortnight you have now a key to. My heart was in Highbury, and my business was to get my body thither as often as might be, and with the least suspicion. If you remember any queernesses set them all to the right account. Of the pianoforte so much talked of, I feel it only necessary to say, that its being ordered was absolutely unknown to Miss Fairfax, who would never have allowed me to send it had any choice been given her. The delicacy of her mind throughout the whole engagement, my dear madam, is much beyond my power of doing justice to. You will soon, I earnestly hope, know her thoroughly yourself. No description can describe her. She must tell you herself what she is; yet not by word, for never was there a human creature who would so designedly suppress her own merit. Since I began this letter, which will be longer than I foresaw, I have heard from her. She gives a good account of her own health; but as she never complains, I dare not depend. I want to have your opinion of her looks. I know you will soon call on her; she is living in dread of the visit. Perhaps it is paid already. Let me hear from you without delay, I am impatient for a thousand particulars. Remember how few minutes I was at Randalls, and in how bewildered, how mad a state; and I am not much better yet; still insane either from happiness or misery. When I think of the kindness and favour I have met with, of her excellence and patience, and my uncle's generosity, I am mad with joy; but when I recollect all the uneasiness I occasioned her, and how little I deserve to be forgiven, I am mad with anger. If I could but see her again! But I must not propose it yet; my uncle has been too good for me to encroach. I must still add to this long letter. You have not heard all that you ought to hear. I could not give any connected detail yesterday; but the suddenness and, in one light, the unseasonableness with which the affair burst out, needs explanation; for, though the event of the 26th ult., as you will conclude, immediately opened to me the happiest prospects, I should not have presumed on such early measures, but from the very particular circumstances which left me not an hour to lose. I should myself have shrunk from anything so hasty, and she would have felt every scruple of mine with multiplied strength and refinement; but I had no choice. The hasty engagement she had entered into with that woman—here, my dear madam, I was obliged to leave off abruptly, to recollect and compose myself. I have been walking over the country, and am now, I hope, rational enough to make the rest of my letter what it ought to be. It is, in fact, a most mortifying retrospect for me. I behaved shamefully. And here I can admit that my manners to Miss W., in being unpleasant to Miss F., were highly blameable. *She* disapproved them, which ought to have been enough. My plea of concealing the truth she did not think sufficient. She was displeased: I thought unreasonably so; I thought her, on a thousand occasions, unnecessarily scrupulous and cautious; I thought her even cold. But she was always right. If I had followed her judgment, and subdued my spirits to the level of what she deemed proper, I should have escaped the greatest unhappiness I have ever known. We quarrelled. Do you remember the morning spent at Donwell? *There* every little dissatisfaction that had occurred before came to a crisis. I was late: I met her walking home by herself, and wanted to walk with her, but she would not suffer it. She absolutely refused to allow me, which I then thought most unreasonable. Now, however, I see nothing in it but a very natural and consistent degree of discretion. While I, to blind the world to our engagement, was behaving one hour with objectionable particularly to another woman, was she to be consenting the next to a proposal which might have made every previous caution useless? Had we been met walking together between Donwell and Highbury, the truth must have been suspected. I was mad enough, however, to resent. I doubted her affection. I doubted it more the next day on Box Hill; when, provoked by such conduct on my side, such shameful, insolent neglect of her, and such apparent devotion to Miss W., as it would have been impossible for any woman of sense to endure, she spoke her resentment in a form of words perfectly intelligible to me. In short, my dear madam, it was a quarrel blameless on her side, abominable on mine; and I returned the same evening to Richmond, though I might have stayed with you till the next morning, merely because I would be as angry with her as possible. Even then, I was not such a fool as not to mean to be reconciled in time; but I was the injured person—injured by her coldness—and I went away determined that she should make the first advances. I shall always congratulate myself that you were not of the Box Hill party. Had you witnessed my behaviour there, I can hardly suppose you would ever have thought well of me again. Its effect upon her appears in the immediate resolution it produced. As soon as she found I was really gone from Randalls, she closed with the offer of that officious Mrs. Elton; the whole system of whose treatment of her, by the bye, has ever filled me with indignation and hatred. I must not quarrel with a spirit of forbearance which has been so richly extended towards myself; but, otherwise, I should loudly protest against the share of it which that woman has known. 'Jane,' indeed! You will observe that I have not yet indulged myself in calling her by that name, even to you. Think, then, what I must have endured in hearing it bandied between the Eltons, with all the vulgarity of needless repetition, and all the insolence of imaginary superiority. Have patience with me, I shall soon have done. She closed with this offer, resolving to break with me entirely, and wrote the next day to tell me that we never were to meet again. *She felt the engagement to be a source of repentance and misery to each: she dissolved it.* This letter reached me on the very morning of my poor aunt's death. I answered it within an hour; but from the confusion of my mind, and the multiplicity of business falling on me at once, my answer, instead of being sent with all the many other letters of that day, was locked up in my writing-desk, and I, trusting that I had written enough, though but a few lines, to satisfy her, remained without any uneasiness. I was rather disappointed that I did not hear from her again speedily; but I made excuses for her, and was too busy, and—may I add?—too cheerful in my views to be captious. We removed to Windsor; and two days afterwards I received a parcel from her—my own letters all returned—and a few lines at the same time by the post, stating her extreme surprise at not having had the smallest reply to her last; and adding that as silence on such a point could not be misconstrued, and as it must be equally desirable to both to have every subordinate arrangement concluded as soon as possible, she now sent me, by a safe conveyance, all my letters, and requested, that if I could not directly command hers, so as to send them to Highbury within a week, I would forward them after that period to her at ———: in short, the full direction to Mr. Smallridge's, near Bristol, stared me in the face. I knew the name, the place, I knew all about it, and instantly saw what she had been doing. It was perfectly accordant with that resolution of character which I knew her to possess; and the secrecy she had maintained as to any such design in her former letter, was equally descriptive of its anxious delicacy. For the world would not she have seemed to threaten me. Imagine the shock; imagine how, till I had actually detected my own blunder, I raved at the blunders of the post. What was to be done? One thing only. I must speak to my uncle. Without his sanction I could not hope to be listened to again. I spoke; circumstances were in my favour; the late event had softened away his pride, and he was, earlier than I could have anticipated, wholly reconciled and complying; and could say at last, poor man! with a deep sigh, that he wished I might find as much happiness in the marriage state as he had done. I felt that it would be of a different sort. Are you disposed to pity me for what I must have suffered in opening the cause to him, for my suspense while all was at stake? No; do not pity me till I reached Highbury, and saw how ill I had made her. Do not pity me till I saw her wan, sick looks. I reached Highbury at the time of day when, from my knowledge of their late breakfast-hour, I was certain of a good chance of finding her alone. I was not disappointed; and at last I was not disappointed either in the object of my journey. A great deal of very reasonable, very just displeasure I had to persuade away. But it is done; we are reconciled, dearer, much dearer, than ever, and no moment's uneasiness can ever occur between us again. Now, my dear madam, I will release you; but I could not conclude before. A thousand and a thousand thanks for all the kindness you have ever shown me, and ten thousand for the attentions your heart will dictate towards her. If you think me in a way to be happier than I deserve, I am quite of your opinion. Miss W. calls me the child of good fortune. I hope she is right. In one respect my good fortune is undoubted, that of being able to subscribe myself, your obliged and affectionate Son,

"F. C. WESTON CHURCHILL."

Chapter 51

His letter must make its way to Emma's feelings. She was obliged, in spite of her previous determination to the contrary, to do it all the justice that Mrs. Weston foretold. As soon as she came to her own name, it was irresistible; every line relating to herself was interesting, and almost every line agreeable; and when this charm ceased, the subject could still maintain itself by the natural return of her former regard for the writer, and the very strong attraction which any picture of love must have for her at that moment. She never stopped till she had gone through the whole: and though it was impossible not to feel that he had been wrong, yet he had been less wrong than she had supposed; and he had suffered and was very sorry; and he was so grateful to Mrs. Weston, and so much in love with Miss Fairfax, and she was so happy herself, that there was no being severe; and could he have entered the room, she must have shaken hands with him as heartily as ever.

She thought so well of the letter, that when Mr. Knightley came again she desired him to read it. She was sure of Mrs. Weston's wishing it to be communicated; especially to one who, like Mr. Knightley, had seen so much to blame in his conduct.

"I shall be very glad to look it over," said he; "but it seems long. I will take it home with me at night."

But that would not do. Mr. Weston was to call in the evening, and she must return it by him.

"I would rather be talking to you," he replied; "but as it seems a matter of justice, it shall be done."

He began—stopping, however, almost directly to say, "Had I been offered the sight of one of this gentleman's letters to his mother-in-law a few months ago, Emma, it would not have been taken with such indifference."

He proceeded a little further, reading to himself; and then, with a smile, observed: "Humph! a fine complimentary opening: but it is his way. One man's style must not be the rule of another's. We will not be severe."

"It will be natural for me," he added shortly afterwards, "to speak my opinion aloud as I read. By doing it, I shall feel that I am near you. It will not be so great a loss of time; but if you dislike it——"

"Not at all. I should wish it."

Mr. Knightley returned to his reading with greater alacrity.

"He trifles here," said he, "as to the temptation. He knows he is wrong, and has nothing rational to urge. Bad. He ought not to have formed the engagement. 'His father's disposition'—he is unjust, however, to his father. Mr. Weston's sanguine temper was a blessing on all his upright and honourable exertions; but Mr. Weston earned every present comfort before he endeavoured to gain it. Very true; he did not come till Miss Fairfax was here."

"And I have not forgotten," said Emma, "how sure you were that he might have come sooner if he would. You pass it over very handsomely: but you were perfectly right."

"I was not quite impartial in my judgment, Emma; but yet, I think, had *you* not been in the case, I should still have mistrusted him."

When he came to Miss Woodhouse, he was obliged to read the whole
of it aloud—all that related to her—with a smile, a look, a shake of the
head, a word or two of assent, or disapprobation, or merely of love, as the
subject required; concluding, however, seriously, and, after steady reflection, thus:

"Very bad—though it might have been worse. Playing a most dangerous
game. Too much indebted to the event for his acquittal. No judge of his
own manners by you. Always deceived, in fact, by his own wishes, and regardless of little besides his own convenience. Fancying you to have fath-
omed his secret! Natural enough! His own mind full of intrigue, that he
should suspect it in others. Mystery—finesse—how they pervert the understanding! My Emma, does not everything serve to prove more and
more the beauty of truth and sincerity in all our dealings with each other?"

Emma agreed to it, and with a blush of sensibility on Harriet's account,
which she could not give any sincere explanation of.

"You had better go on," said she.

He did so, but very soon stopped again to say, "The pianoforte! Ah!
That was the act of a very, very young man, one too young to consider
whether the inconvenience of it might not very much exceed the pleasure.
A boyish scheme, indeed! I cannot comprehend a man's wishing to give a
woman any proof of affection which he knows she would rather dispense
with: and he did know that she would have prevented the instrument's
coming if she could."

After this, he made some progress without any pause. Frank Churchill's
confession of having behaved shamefully was the first thing to call for
more than a word in passing.

"I perfectly agree with you, sir," was then this remark. "You did behave
very shamefully. You never wrote a truer line." And having gone through
what immediately followed of the basis of their disagreement, and his
persisting to act in direct opposition to Jane Fairfax's sense of right, he
made a fuller pause to say, "This is very bad. He had induced her to place
herself, for his sake, in a situation of extreme difficulty and uneasiness, and
it should have been his first object to prevent her from suffering unnecessarily. She must have had much more to contend with in carrying on the
correspondence than he could. He should have respected even unreasonable scruples, had there been such; but hers were all reasonable. We must
look to her one fault, and remember that she had done a wrong thing in
consenting to the engagement; to bear that she should have been in such
a state of punishment."

Emma knew that he was now getting to the Box Hill party, and grew
uncomfortable. Her own behaviour had been so very improper! She was
deeply ashamed, and a little afraid of his next look. It was all read, however, steadily, attentively, and without the smallest remark; and, excepting one momentary glance at her, instantly withdrawn, in the fear of
giving pain, no remembrance of Box Hill seemed to exist.

"There is no saying much for the delicacy of our good friends, the

Eltons," was his next observation. "His feelings are natural. What? Actually resolve to break with him entirely! She felt the engagement to be a source of repentance and misery to each: she dissolved it. What a view this gives of her sense of his behaviour! Well, he must be a most extraordinary——"

"Nay, nay, read on. You will find how very much he suffers."

"I hope he does," replied Mr. Knightley coolly, and resuming the letter. " 'Smallridge!' What does this mean? What is all this?"

"She had engaged to go as governess to Mrs. Smallridge's children—a dear friend of Mrs. Elton's—a neighbour of Maple Grove; and, by the bye, I wonder how Mrs. Elton bears the disappointment?"

"Say nothing, my dear Emma, while you oblige me to read—not even of Mrs. Elton. Only one page more. I shall soon have done. What a letter the man writes!"

"I wish you would read it with a kinder spirit towards him."

"Well, there *is* feeling here. He does seem to have suffered in finding her ill. Certainly, I can have no doubt of his being fond of her. 'Dearer, much dearer, than ever.' I hope he may long continue to feel all the value of such a reconciliation. He is a very liberal thanker, with his thousands and tens of thousands. 'Happier than I deserve.' Come, he knows himself there. 'Miss Woodhouse calls me the child of good fortune.' Those were Miss Woodhouse's words, were they? And a fine ending—and there is the letter. 'The child of good fortune!' That was your name for him, was it?"

"You do not appear so well satisfied with his letter as I am; but still you must, at least I hope you must, think the better of him for it. I hope it does him some service with you."

"Yes, certainly it does. He has had great faults—faults of inconsideration and thoughtlessness; and I am very much of his opinion in thinking him likely to be happier than he deserves; but still as he is, beyond a doubt, really attached to Miss Fairfax, and will soon, it may be hoped, have the advantage of being constantly with her, I am very ready to believe his character will improve, and acquire from hers the steadiness and delicacy of principle that it wants. And now, let me talk to you of something else. I have another person's interest at present so much at heart, that I cannot think any longer about Frank Churchill. Ever since I left you this morning, Emma, my mind has been hard at work on one subject."

The subject followed; it was in plain, unaffected, gentlemanlike English, such as Mr. Knightley used even to the woman he was in love with, how to be able to ask her to marry him without attacking the happiness of her father. Emma's answer was ready at the first word. "While her dear father lived, any change of condition must be impossible for her. She could never quit him." Part only of this answer, however, was admitted. The impossibility of her quitting her father Mr. Knightley felt as strongly as herself; but the inadmissibility of any other change he could not agree to. He had been thinking it over most deeply, most intently; he had at first hoped to induce Mr. Woodhouse to remove with her to Donwell; he had wanted to believe it feasible, but his knowledge of Mr. Woodhouse would not suffer him to deceive himself long; and now he confessed his persuasion that such a transplantation would be a risk of her father's comfort, perhaps even of his life, which must not be hazarded. Mr. Woodhouse taken from Hartfield! No, he felt that it ought not to be attempted. But the plan which had arisen on the sacrifice of this, he trusted his dearest Emma would not find in any respect objectionable; it was, that he should be received at Hartfield! That so long as her father's happiness—in other words his life—required Hartfield to continue her home, it should be his likewise.

Of their all removing to Donwell, Emma had already had her own passing thoughts. Like him, she had tried the scheme and rejected it; but such an alternative as this had not occurred to her. She was sensible of all the affection it evinced. She felt that, in quitting Donwell, he must be sacrificing a great deal of independence of hours and habits; that in living constantly with her father, and in no house of his own, there would be much, very much, to be borne with. She promised to think of it, and advised him to think of it more; but he was fully convinced that no reflection could alter his wishes or his opinion on the subject. He had given it, he could assure her, very long and calm consideration; he had been walking away from William Larkins the whole morning to have his thoughts to himself.

"Ah! there is one difficulty unprovided for," cried Emma. "I am sure William Larkins will not like it. You must get his consent before you ask mine."

She promised, however, to think of it; and pretty nearly promised moreover, to think of it with the intention of finding it a very good scheme.

It is remarkable that Emma, in the many, very many, points of view in which she was now beginning to consider Donwell Abbey, was never struck with any sense of injury to her nephew Henry, whose rights as heir expectant had formerly been so tenaciously regarded. Think she must of the possible difference to the poor little boy; and yet she only gave herself a saucy conscious smile about it, and found amusement in detecting the real cause of that violent dislike of Mr. Knightley's marrying Jane Fairfax, or anybody else, which at the time she had wholly imputed to the amiable solicitude of the sister and the aunt.

This proposal of his, this plan of marrying and continuing at Hartfield—the more she contemplated it the more pleasing it became. His evils seemed to lessen, her own advantages to increase, their mutual good to outweigh every drawback. Such a companion for herself in the periods of anxiety and cheerlessness before her! Such a partner in all those duties and cares to which time must be giving increase of melancholy!

She would have been too happy but for poor Harriet; but every blessing of her own seemed to involve and advance the sufferings of her friend, who must now be even excluded from Hartfield. The delightful family party which Emma was securing for herself, poor Harriet must, in mere charitable caution, be kept at a distance from. She would be a loser in every way. Emma could not deplore her future absence as any deduction from her own enjoyment. In such a party, Harriet would be rather a dead weight than otherwise; but for the poor girl herself, it seemed a peculiarly cruel necessity that was to be placing her in such a state of unmerited punish‧ment.

In time, of course, Mr. Knightley would be forgotten, that is, sup‧planted; but this could not be expected to happen very early. Mr. Knight‧ley himself would be doing nothing to assist the cure; not like Mr. Elton. Mr. Knightley, always so kind, so feeling, so truly considerate for everybody, would never deserve to be less worshipped than now; and it really was too much to hope even of Harriet, that she could be in love with more than *three* men in one year.

Chapter 52

IT was a very great relief to Emma to find Harriet as desirous as herself to avoid a meeting. Their intercourse was painful enough by letter. How much worse had they been obliged to meet!

Harriet expressed herself very much, as might be supposed, without reproaches, or apparent sense of ill-usage; and yet Emma fancied there was a something of resentment, a something bordering on it in her style, which increased the desirableness of their being separate. It might be only her own consciousness; but it seemed as if only an angel could have been quite without resentment under such a stroke.

She had no difficulty in procuring Isabella's invitation; and she was fortunate in having a sufficient reason for asking it, without resorting to invention. There was a tooth amiss. Harriet really wished, and had wished some time, to consult a dentist. Mrs. John Knightley was delighted to be of use; anything of ill-health was a recommendation to her; and though not so fond of a dentist as of a Mr. Wingfield, she was quite eager to have Harriet under her care. When it was thus settled on her sister's side, Emma proposed it to her friend, and found her very persuadable. Harriet was to go; she was invited for at least a fortnight. She was to be conveyed in Mr. Woodhouse's carriage. It was all arranged, it was all completed, and Har‧riet was safe in Brunswick Square.

Now Emma could, indeed, enjoy Mr. Knightley's visits; now she could talk, and he could listen with true happiness, unchecked by that sense of injustice, of guilt, of something most painful, which had haunted her when remembering how disappointed a heart was near her, how much might at that moment, and at a little distance, be enduring by the feelings which she had led astray herself.

The difference of Harriet at Mrs. Goddard's, or in London made, per‧haps, an unreasonable difference in Emma's sensations; but she could not think of her in London without objects of curiosity and employment, which must be averting the past, and carrying her out of herself.

She would not allow any other anxiety to succeed directly to the place in her mind which Harriet had occupied. There was a communication before her, one which *she* only could be competent to make—the confession of her engagement to her father; but she would have nothing to do with it at present. She had resolved to defer the disclosure till Mrs. Weston were safe and well. No additional agitation should be thrown at this period among those she loved—and the evil should not act on herself by anticipation before the appointed time. A fortnight, at least, of leisure and peace of mind, to crown every warmer, but more agitating, delight, should be hers.

She soon resolved, equally as a duty and a pleasure, to employ half an hour of this holiday of spirits in calling on Miss Fairfax. She ought to go—and she was longing to see her; the resemblance of their present situations increasing every other motive of good-will. It would be a *secret* satisfaction; but the consciousness of a similarity of prospect would certainly add to the interest with which she should attend to anything Jane might communicate.

She went—she had driven once unsuccessfully to the door, but had not been into the house since the morning after Box Hill, when poor Jane had been in such distress as had filled her with compassion, though all the worst of her sufferings had been unsuspected. The fear of being still unwelcome determined her, though assured of their being at home, to wait in the passage, and send up her name. She heard Patty announcing it; but no such bustle succeeded as poor Miss Bates had before made so happily intelligible. No; she heard nothing but the instant reply of "Beg her to walk up"; and a moment afterwards she was met on the stairs by Jane herself coming eagerly forward, as if no other reception of her were felt sufficient. Emma had never seen her look so well, so lovely, so engaging. There was consciousness, animation, and warmth; there was everything which her countenance or manner could ever have wanted. She came forward with an offered hand; and said, in a low, but very feeling tone:

"This is most kind indeed! Miss Woodhouse, it is impossible for me to express—I hope you will believe— Excuse me for being so entirely without words."

Emma was gratified, and would soon have shown no want of words, if the sound of Mrs. Elton's voice from the sitting-room had not checked her, and made it expedient to compress all her friendly and all her congratulatory sensations into a very, very earnest shake of the hand.

Mrs. Bates and Mrs. Elton were together. Miss Bates was out, which accounted for the previous tranquillity. Emma could have wished Mrs. Elton elsewhere; but she was in a humour to have patience with everybody; and as Mrs. Elton met her with unusual graciousness, she hoped the rencontre would do them no harm.

She soon believed herself to penetrate Mrs. Elton's thoughts, and understand why she was, like herself, in happy spirits; it was being in Miss Fairfax's confidence, and fancying herself acquainted with what was still

a secret to other people. Emma saw symptoms of it immediately in the
expression of her face; and while paying her own compliments to Mrs.
Bates, and appearing to attend to the good old lady's replies, she saw her
with a sort of anxious parade of mystery fold up a letter which she had
apparently been reading aloud to Miss Fairfax, and return it into the
purple and gold reticule by her side, saying, with significant nods:

"We can finish this some other time, you know. You and I shall not
want opportunities; and, in fact, you have heard all the essential already.
I only wanted to prove to you that Mrs. S. admits our apology, and is not
offended. You see how delightfully she writes. Oh, she is a sweet creature!
You would have doted on her, had you gone. But not a word more. Let
us be discreet—quite on our good behaviour. Hush! You remember those
lines—I forget the poem at this moment:—

> 'For when a lady's in the case,
>   You know, all other things give place.'

Now I say, my dear, in *our* case, for *lady,* read—mum! a word to the wise.
I am in a fine flow of spirits, an't I? But I want to set your heart at ease as
to Mrs. S. *My* representation, you see, has quite appeased her."

And again, on Emma's merely turning her head to look at Mrs. Bates's
knitting, she added, in a half whisper:

"I mentioned no *names,* you will observe. Oh no! cautious as a minister
of state. I managed it extremely well."

Emma could not doubt. It was a palpable display, repeated on every
possible occasion. When they had all talked a little while in harmony of
the weather and Mrs. Weston, she found herself abruptly addressed with:

"Do not you think, Miss Woodhouse, our saucy little friend here is
charmingly recovered? Do not you think her cure does Perry the highest
credit?" (here was a side glance of great meaning at Jane). "Upon my
word, Perry has resorted her in a wonderful short time! Oh, if you had
seen her, as I did, when she was at the worst!" And when Mrs. Bates was
saying something to Emma, whispered further, "We do not say a word of
any *assistance* that Perry might have; not a word of a certain young
physician from Windsor. Oh! no, Perry shall have all the credit."

"I have scarce had the pleasure of seeing you, Miss Woodhouse," she
shortly afterwards began, "since the party to Box Hill. Very pleasant
party. But yet I think there was something wanting. Things did not seem
—that is, there seemed a little cloud upon the spirits of some. So it appeared to me, at least, but I might be mistaken. However, I think it answered so far as to tempt one to go again. What say you both to our
collecting the same party, and exploring to Box Hill again, while the fine
weather lasts? It must be the same party, you know—quite the same
party, not *one* exception."

Soon after this Miss Bates came in and Emma could not help being
diverted by the perplexity of her first answer to herself, resulting, she sup-

posed, from doubt of what might be said, and impatience to say everything.

"Thank you, dear Miss Woodhouse, you are all kindness. It is impossible to say— Yes, indeed, I quite understand—dearest Jane's prospects—
that is, I do not mean. But she is charmingly recovered. How is Mr. Woodhouse? I am so glad. Quite out of my power—such a happy little circle
as you find us here. Yes, indeed. Charming young man! that is—so very
friendly; I mean good Mr. Perry! such attention to Jane!" And from her
great, her more than commonly thankful delight towards Mrs. Elton for
being there, Emma guessed that there had been a little show of resentment towards Jane, from the vicarage quarter, which was now graciously
overcome. After a few whispers, indeed, which placed it beyond a guess,
Mrs. Elton, speaking louder, said:

"Yes, here I am, my good friend; and here I have been so long, that
anywhere else I should think it necessary to apologise; but the truth is,
that I am waiting for my lord and master. He promised to join me here,
and pay his respects to you."

"What! are we to have the pleasure of a call from Mr. Elton? That will
be a favour indeed; for I know gentlemen do not like morning visits, and
Mr. Elton's time is so engaged."

"Upon my word it is, Miss Bates. He really is engaged from morning to
night. There is no end of people's coming to him, on some pretence or
other. The magistrates, and overseers, and churchwardens, are always
wanting his opinion. They seem not able to do anything without him.
'Upon my word, Mr. E.,' I often say, 'rather you than I. I do not know
what would become of my crayons and my instrument if I had half so
many applicants.' Bad enough as it is, for I absolutely neglect them both
to an unpardonable degree. I believe I have not played a bar this fortnight.
However, he is coming, I assure you: yes, indeed, on purpose to wait on
you all." And putting up her head to screen her words from Emma—"A
congratulatory visit, you know. Oh! yes, quite indispensable."

Miss Bates looked about her, so happily.

"He promised to come to me as soon as he could disengage himself from
Knightley; but he and Knightley are shut up together in deep consultation. Mr. E. is Knightley's right hand."

Emma would not have smiled for the world, and only said, "Is Mr.
Elton gone on foot to Donwell? He will have a hot walk."

"Oh no, it is a meeting at the Crown—a regular meeting. Weston and
Cole will be there too; but one is apt to speak only of those who lead. I
fancy Mr. E. and Knightley have everything their own way."

"Have not you mistaken the day?" said Emma. "I am almost certain
that the meeting at the Crown is not till to-morrow. Mr. Knightley was at
Hartfield yesterday, and spoke of it as for Saturday."

"Oh no, the meeting is certainly to-day," was the abrupt answer, which
denoted the impossibility of any blunder on Mrs. Elton's side. "I do be-

lieve," she continued, "this is the most troublesome parish that ever was.
We never heard of such things at Maple Grove."

"Your parish there was small," said Jane.

"Upon my word, my dear, I do not know, for I never heard the subject
talked of."

"But it is proved by the smallness of the school, which I have heard you
speak of, as under the patronage of your sister and Mrs. Bragge; the only
school, and not more than five-and-twenty children."

"Ah! you clever creature, that's very true. What a thinking brain you
have! I say, Jane, what a perfect character you and I should make, if we
could be shaken together. My liveliness and your solidity would produce
perfection. Not that I presume to insinuate, however, that *some* people
may not think *you* perfection already. But hush! not a word, if you
please."

It seemed an unnecessary caution; Jane was wanting to give her words,
not to Mrs. Elton, but to Miss Woodhouse, as the latter plainly saw. The
wish of distinguishing her, as far as civility permitted, was very evident,
though it could not often proceed beyond a look.

Mr. Elton made his appearance. His lady greeted him with some of her
sparkling vivacity.

"Very pretty, sir, upon my word; to send me on here, to be an encumbrance to my friends, so long before you vouchsafe to come. But you knew
what a dutiful creature you had to deal with. You knew I should not stir
till my lord and master appeared. Here have I been sitting this hour, giving these young ladies a sample of true conjugal obedience; for who can
say, you know, how soon it may be wanted?"

Mr. Elton was so hot and tired, that all this wit seemed thrown away.
His civilities to the other ladies must be paid; but his subsequent object
was to lament over himself, for the heat he was suffering, and the walk he
had had for nothing.

"When I got to Donwell," said he, "Knightley could not be found. Very
odd! very unaccountable! after the note I sent him this morning, and the
message he returned, that he should certainly be at home till one."

"Donwell!" cried his wife. "My dear Mr. E., you have not been to
Donwell! you mean the Crown; you come from the meeting at the Crown."

"No, no, that's to-morrow; and I particularly wanted to see Knightley
to-day on that very account. Such a dreadful broiling morning! I went
over the fields too" (speaking in a tone of great ill-usage), "which made it
so much the worse. And then not to find him at home! I assure you I am
not at all pleased. And no apology left, no message for me. The housekeeper declared she knew nothing of my being expected. Very extraordinary! And nobody knew at all which way he was gone. Perhaps to
Hartfield, perhaps to the Abbey-Mill, perhaps into his woods. Miss Woodhouse, this is not like our friend Knightley! Can you explain it?"

Emma amused herself by protesting that it was very extraordinary
indeed, and that she had not a syllable to say for him.

"I cannot imagine," said Mrs. Elton (feeling the indignity as a wife ought to do), "I cannot imagine how he could do such a thing by you, of all people in the world! The very last person whom one should expect to be forgotten! My dear Mr. E., he must have left a message for you, I am sure he must. Not even Knightley could be so very eccentric; and his servants forgot it. Depend upon it that was the case; and very likely to happen with the Donwell servants, who are all, I have often observed, extremely awkward and remiss. I am sure I would not have such a creature as his Harry stand at our sideboard for any consideration. And as for Mrs. Hodges, Wright holds her very cheap indeed. She promised Wright a receipt, and never sent it."

"I met William Larkins," continued Mr. Elton, "as I got near the house, and he told me I should not find his master at home, but I did not believe him. William seemed rather out of humour. He did not know what was come to his master lately, he said, but he could hardly ever get the speech of him. I have nothing to do with William's wants, but it really is of very great importance that I should see Knightley to-day; and it becomes a matter, therefore, of very serious inconvenience that I should have had this hot walk to no purpose."

Emma felt that she could not do better than go home directly. In all probability she was at this very time waited for there; and Mr. Knightley might be preserved from sinking deeper in aggression towards Mr. Elton, if not towards William Larkins.

She was pleased, on taking leave, to find Miss Fairfax determined to attend her out of the room, to go with her even downstairs; it gave her an opportunity, which she immediately made use of, to say:

"It is as well, perhaps, that I have not had the possibility. Had you not been surrounded by other friends, I might have been tempted to introduce a subject, to ask questions, to speak more openly than might have been strictly correct. I feel that I should certainly have been impertinent."

"Oh!" cried Jane, with a blush and an hesitation which Emma thought infinitely more becoming to her than all the elegance of all her usual composure—"there would have been no danger. The danger would have been of my wearying you. You could not have gratified me more than by expressing an interest—— Indeed, Miss Woodhouse" (speaking more collectedly), "with the consciousness which I have of misconduct—very great misconduct—it is particularly consoling to me to know that those of my friends whose good opinion is most worth preserving, are not disgusted to such a degree as to—I have not time for half that I could wish to say. I long to make apologies, excuses, to urge something for myself. I feel it so very due. But, unfortunately—in short, if your compassion does not stand my friend——"

"Oh! you are too scrupulous, indeed you are," cried Emma warmly, and taking her hand. "You owe me no apologies; and everybody to whom you might be supposed to owe them is so perfectly satisfied, so delighted even——"

"You are very kind, but I know what my manners were to you So cold and artificial! I had always a part to act. It was a life of deceit! I know that I must have disgusted you."

"Pray say no more. I feel that all the apologies should be on my side. Let us forgive each other at once. We must do whatever is to be done quickest, and I think our feelings will lose no time there. I hope you have pleasant accounts from Windsor?"

"Very."

"And the next news, I suppose, will be, that we are to lose you—just as I begin to know you."

"Oh! as to all that, of course nothing can be thought of yet. I am here till claimed by Colonel and Mrs. Campbell."

"Nothing can be actually settled yet, perhaps," replied Emma, smiling —"but, excuse me, it must be thought of."

The smile was returned as Jane answered:

"You are very right; it has been thought of. And I will own to you (I am sure it will be safe), that so far as our living with Mr. Churchill at Enscombe, it is settled. There must be three months, at least, of deep mourning; but when they are over, I imagine there will be nothing more to wait for."

"Thank you, thank you. This is just what I wanted to be assured of. Oh! if you knew how much I love everything that is decided and open! Good-bye, good-bye."

Chapter 53

MRS. WESTON'S friends were all made happy by her safety; and if the satisfaction of her well-doing could be increased to Emma, it was by knowing her to be the mother of a little girl. She had been decided in wishing for a Miss Weston. She would not acknowledge that it was with any view of making a match for her, hereafter, with either of Isabella's sons; but she was convinced that a daughter would suit both father and mother best. It would be a great comfort to Mr. Weston, as he grew older—and even Mr. Weston might be growing older ten years hence—to have his fireside enlivened by the sports and the nonsense, the freaks and the fancies of a child never banished from home; and Mrs. Weston—no one could doubt that a daughter would be most to her; and it would be quite a pity that anyone who so well knew how to teach, should not have their powers in exercise again.

"She has had the advantage, you know, of practising on me," she continued—"like La Baronne d'Almane on La Comtesse d'Ostalis, in Madame de Genlis' 'Adelaide and Theodore,' and we shall now see her own little Adelaide educated on a more perfect plan."

"That is," replied Mr. Knightley, "she will indulge her even more than she did you, and believe that she does not indulge her at all. It will be the only difference."

"Poor child!" cried Emma; "at that rate what will become of her?"

"Nothing very bad. The fate of thousands. She will be disagreeable in infancy, and correct herself as she grows older. I am losing all my bitterness against spoilt children, my dearest Emma. I, who am owing all my happiness to *you*, would not it be horrible ingratitude in me to be severe on them?"

Emma laughed, and replied: "But I had the assistance of all your endeavours to counteract the indulgence of other people. I doubt whether my own sense would have corrected me without it."

"Do you? I have no doubt. Nature gave you understanding: Miss Taylor gave you principles. You must have done well. My interference was quite as likely to do harm as good. It was very natural for you to say 'What right has he to lecture me?' and I am afraid very natural for you to feel that it was done in a disagreeable manner. I do not believe I did you any good. The good was all to myself, by making you an object of the tenderest affection to me. I could not think about you so much without doting on you, faults and all; and by dint of fancying so many errors, have been in love with you ever since you were thirteen at least."

"I am sure you were of use to me," cried Emma. "I was very often influenced rightly by you—oftener than I would own at the time. I am very sure you did me good. And if poor little Anna Weston is to be spoiled, it will be the greatest humanity in you to do as much for her as you have done for me, except falling in love with her when she is thirteen."

"How often, when you were a girl, have you said to me, with one of your saucy looks—'Mr. Knightley, I am going to do so-and-so; papa says I may,' or 'I have Miss Taylor's leave'—something which, you knew, I did not approve. In such cases my interference was giving you two bad feelings instead of one."

"What an amiable creature I was! No wonder you should hold my speeches in such affectionate remembrance."

" 'Mr. Knightley,' you always called me. 'Mr. Knightley'; and, from habit, it has not so very formal a sound. And yet it is formal. I want you to call me something else, but I do not know what."

"I remember once calling you 'George,' in one of my amiable fits, about ten years ago. I did it because I thought it would offend you; but, as you made no objection, I never did it again."

"And cannot you call me 'George' now?"

"Impossible! I never can call you anything but 'Mr. Knightley.' I will not promise even to equal the elegant terseness of Mrs. Elton, by calling you Mr. K. But I will promise," she added presently, laughing and blushing, "I will promise to call you once by your Christian name. I do not say when, but perhaps you may guess where—in the building in which N. takes M. for better, for worse."

Emma grieved that she could not be more openly just to one important service which his better sense would have rendered her, to the advice which would have saved her from the worst of all her womanly follies--

her wilful intimacy with Harriet Smith; but it was too tender a subject. She could not enter on it. Harriet was very seldom mentioned between them.

This, on his side, might merely proceed from her not being thought of; but Emma was rather inclined to attribute it to delicacy, and a suspicion, from some appearances, that their friendship were declining. She was aware herself, that parting under any other circumstances, they certainly should have corresponded more, and that her intelligence would not have rested, as it now almost wholly did, on Isabella's letters. He might observe that it was so. The pain of being obliged to practise concealment towards him was very little inferior to the pain of having made Harriet unhappy.

Isabella sent quite as good an account of her visitor as could be expected; on her first arrival she had thought her out of spirits, which appeared perfectly natural, as there was a dentist to be consulted; but since that business had been over, she did not appear to find Harriet different from what she had known her before. Isabella, to be sure, was no very quick observer; yet if Harriet had not been equal to playing with the children, it would not have escaped her. Emma's comforts and hopes were most agreeably carried on, by Harriet's being to stay longer; her fortnight was likely to be a month at least. Mr. and Mrs. John Knightley were to come down in August, and she was invited to remain till they could bring her back.

"John does not even mention your friend," said Mr. Knightley. "Here is his answer, if you like to see it." It was the answer to the communication of his intended marriage. Emma accepted it with a very eager hand, with an impatience all alive to know what he would say about it, and not at all checked by hearing that her friend was unmentioned.

"John enters like a brother into my happiness," continued Mr. Knightley, "but he is no complimenter; and though I well know him to have, likewise, a most brotherly affection for you, he is so far from making flourishes, that any other young woman might think him rather cool in her praise. But I am not afraid of your seeing what he writes."

"He writes like a sensible man," replied Emma, when she had read the letter. "I honour his sincerity. It is very plain that he considers the good fortune of the engagement as all on my side, but that he is not without hope of my growing, in time, as worthy of your affection as you think me already. Had he said anything to bear a different construction, I should not have believed him."

"My Emma, he means no such thing. He only means——"

"He and I should differ very little in our estimation of the two," interrupted she, with a sort of serious smile—"much less, perhaps, than he is aware of it, if we could enter without ceremony or reserve on the subject."

"Emma, my dear Emma——"

"Oh!" she cried with more thorough gaiety, "if you fancy your brother does not do me justice, only wait till my dear father is in the secret, and hear his opinion. Depend upon it, he will be much further from doing *you* justice. He will think all the happiness, all the advantage on your side of the question; all the merit on mine. I wish I may not sink into 'poor Emma' with him at once. His tender compassion towards oppressed worth can go no further."

"Ah!" he cried, "I wish your father might be half as easily convinced as John will be, of our having every right that equal worth can give, to be happy together. I am amused by one part of John's letter—did you notice it? where he says that my information did not take him wholly by surprise, that he was rather in expectation of hearing something of the kind."

"If I understand your brother, he only means so far as your having some thoughts of marrying. He had no idea of me. He seems perfectly unprepared for that."

"Yes, yes—but I am amused that he should have seen so far into my feelings. What has he been judging by? I am not conscious of any difference in my spirits or conversation that could prepare him at this time for my marrying any more than at another. But it was so, I suppose. I dare say there was a difference when I was staying with them the other day. I believe I did not play with the children quite so much as usual. I remember one evening the poor boys saying, 'Uncle seems always tired now.' "

The time was coming when the news must spread further, and other persons' reception of it tried. As soon as Mrs. Weston was sufficiently recovered to admit Mr. Woodhouse's visits, Emma having it in view that her gentle reasonings should be employed in the cause, resolved first to announce it at home, and then at Randalls. But how to break it to her father at last! She had bound herself to do it, in such an hour of Mr. Knightley's absence, or when it came to the point her heart would have failed her, and she must have put it off; but Mr. Knightley was to come at such a time, and follow up the beginning she was to make. She was forced to speak, and to speak cheerfully too. She must not make it a more decided subject of misery to him, by a melancholy tone herself. She must not appear to think it a misfortune. With all the spirits she could command she prepared him first for something strange, and then, in a few words, said, that if his consent and approbation could be obtained—which, she trusted, would be attended with no difficulty, since it was a plan to promote the happiness of all—she and Mr. Knightley meant to marry; by which means Hartfield would receive the constant addition of that person's company, whom she knew he loved, next to his daughters and Mrs. Weston, best in the world.

Poor man! it was at first a considerable shock to him, and he tried earnestly to dissuade her from it. She was reminded, more than once, of having always said she would never marry, and assured that it would be a great deal better for her to remain single; and told of poor Isabella, and poor Miss Taylor. But it would not do. Emma hung about him affectionately, and smiled, and said it must be so; and that he must not class her with Isabella and Mrs. Weston, whose marriages taking them from Hartfield had, indeed, made a melancholy change: but she was not going from

Hartfield; she should be always there; she was introducing no change in their numbers or their comforts but for the better; and she was very sure that he would be a great deal the happier for having Mr. Knightley always at hand, when he were once got used to the idea. Did he not love Mr. Knightley very much? He would not deny that he did, she was sure. Whom did he ever want to consult on business but Mr. Knightley? Who was so useful to him, who so ready to write his letters, who so glad to assist him? Who so cheerful, so attentive, so attached to him? Would not he like to have him always on the spot? Yes. That was all very true. Mr. Knightley could not be there too often; he should be glad to see him every day; but they did see him every day as it was. Why could not they go on as they had done?

Mr. Woodhouse could not be soon reconciled; but the worst was overcome, the idea was given; time and continual repetition must do the rest. To Emma's entreaties and assurances succeeded Mr. Knightley's, whose fond praise of her gave the subject even a kind of welcome; and he was soon used to be talked to by each on every fair occasion. They had all the assistance which Isabella could give, by letters of the strongest approbation; and Mrs. Weston was ready, on the first meeting, to consider the subject in the most serviceable light; first as a settled, and secondly as a good one—well aware of the nearly equal importance of the two recommendations to Mr. Woodhouse's mind. It was agreed upon, as what was to be; and everybody by whom he was used to be guided assuring him that it would be for his happiness, and having some feelings himself which almost admitted it, he began to think that some time or other, in another year or two perhaps, it might not be so very bad if the marriage did take place.

Mrs. Weston was acting no part, feigning no feelings in all that she said to him in favour of the event. She had been extremely surprised, never more so, than when Emma first opened the affair to her; but she saw in it only increase of happiness to all, and had no scruple in urging him to the utmost. She had such a regard for Mr. Knightley, as to think he deserved even her dearest Emma; and it was in every respect so proper, suitable, and unexceptionable a connection, and in one respect, one point of the highest importance, so peculiarly eligible, so singularly fortunate, that now it seemed as if Emma could not safely have attached herself to any other creature, and that she had herself been the stupidest of beings in not having thought of it, and wished it long ago. How very few of those men in a rank of life to address Emma would have renounced their own home for Hartfield! And who but Mr. Knightley could know and bear with Mr. Woodhouse, as so to make such an arrangement desirable! The difficulty of disposing of poor Mr. Woodhouse had been always felt in her husband's plans and her own, for a marriage between Frank and Emma. How to settle the claims of Enscombe and Hartfield had been a continual impediment—less acknowledged by Mr. Weston than by herself—but even he had never been able to finish the subject better than by saying—"Those matters will take care of themselves; the young people will find a way." But here there was nothing to be shifted off in a wild speculation on the future. It was all right, all open, all equal. No sacrifice on any side worth the name. It was a union of the highest promise of felicity in itself, and without one real, rational difficulty to oppose or delay it.

Mrs. Weston, with her baby on her knee, indulging in such reflections as these, was one of the happiest women in the world. If anything could increase her delight, it was perceiving that the baby would soon have outgrown its first set of caps.

The news was universally a surprise wherever it spread; and Mr. Weston had his five minutes' share of it; but five minutes were enough to familiarize the idea to his quickness of mind. He saw the advantages of the match, and rejoiced in them with all the constancy of his wife; but the wonder of it was very soon nothing; and by the end of an hour he was not far from believing that he had always foreseen it.

"It is to be a secret, I conclude," said he. "These matters are always a secret, till it is found out that everybody knows them. Only let me be told when I may speak out. I wonder whether Jane has any suspicion?"

He went to Highbury the next morning, and satisfied himself on that point. He told her the news. Was not she like a daughter, his eldest daughter? he must tell her; and Miss Bates being present, it passed, of course, to Mrs. Cole, Mrs. Perry, and Mrs. Elton, immediately afterwards. It was no more than the principals were prepared for; they had calculated from the time of its being known at Randalls how soon it would be over Highbury; and were thinking of themselves, as the evening wonder in many a family circle, with great sagacity.

In general, it was a very well approved match. Some might think him, and others might think her, the most in luck. One set might recommend their all removing to Donwell, and leaving Hartfield for the John Knightleys; and another might predict disagreements among their servants; but yet, upon the whole, there was no serious objection raised, except in one habitation—the Vicarage. There, the surprise was not softened by any satisfaction. Mr. Elton cared little about it, compared with his wife; he only hoped "the young lady's pride would now be contented"; and supposed "she had always meant to catch Knightley if she could"; and, on the point of living at Hartfield, could daringly exclaim, "Rather he than I!" But Mrs. Elton was very much discomposed indeed. "Poor Knightley! poor fellow! sad business for him. She was extremely concerned; for though very eccentric, he had a thousand good qualities. How could he be so taken in? Did not think him at all in love—not in the least. Poor Knightley! There would be an end of all pleasant intercourse with him. How happy he had been to come and dine with them whenever they asked him! But that would be all over now. Poor fellow! No more exploring parties to Donwell made for *her*. Oh no; there would be a Mrs. Knightley to throw cold water on everything. Extremely disagreeable;

but she was not at all sorry that she had abused the housekeeper the other day. Shocking plan, living together. It would never do. She knew a family near Maple Grove who had tried it, and been obliged to separate before the end of the first quarter."

Chapter 54

TIME passed on. A few more to-morrows, and the party from London would be arriving. It was an alarming change; and Emma was thinking of it one morning, as what must bring a great deal to agitate and grieve her, when Mr. Knightley came in, and distressing thoughts were put by. After the first chat of pleasure, he was silent; and then, in a graver tone, began with:

"I have something to tell you, Emma; some news."

"Good or bad?" said she, quickly, looking up in his face.

"I do not know which it ought to be called."

"Oh, good I am sure. I see it in your countenance. You are trying not to smile."

"I am afraid," said he, composing his features, "I am very much afraid, my dear Emma, that you will not smile when you hear it."

"Indeed! but why so? I can hardly imagine that anything which pleases or amuses you should not please and amuse me too."

"There is one subject," he replied, "I hope but one, on which we do not think alike." He paused a moment, again smiling, with his eyes fixed on her face. "Does nothing occur to you? Do not you recollect? Harriet Smith."

Her cheeks flushed at the name, and she felt afraid of something, though she knew not what.

"Have you heard from her yourself this morning?" cried he. "You have, I believe, and know the whole."

"No, I have not; I know nothing; pray tell me."

"You are prepared for the worst, I see; and very bad it is. Harriet Smith marries Robert Martin."

Emma gave a start, which did not seem like being prepared; and her eyes, in eager gaze, said, "No, this is impossible!" but her lips were closed.

"It is so, indeed!" continued Mr. Knightley; "I have it from Robert Martin himself. He left me not half an hour ago."

She was still looking at him with the most speaking amazement.

"You like it, my Emma, as little as I feared—I wish our opinions were the same. But in time they will be. Time, you may be sure, will make one or the other of us think differently; and in the meanwhile, we need not talk much on the subject."

"You mistake me, you quite mistake me," she replied, exerting herself. "It is not that such a circumstance would now make me unhappy, but I cannot believe it. It seems an impossibility! You cannot mean to say that Harriet Smith has accepted Robert Martin! You cannot mean that he has even proposed to her again—yet! You only mean that he intends it."

"I mean that he has done it," answered Mr. Knightley with smiling but determined decision, "and been accepted."

"Good God!" she cried. "Well!" Then, having recourse to her work-basket in excuse for leaning down her face, and concealing all the exquisite feelings of delight and entertainment which she knew she must be expressing, she added, "Well, now, tell me everything; make this intelligible to me. How, where, when? Let me know it all. I never was more surprised—but it does not make me unhappy, I assure you. How —how has it been possible?"

"It is a very simple story. He went to town on business three days ago, and I got him to take charge of some papers which I was wanting to send to John. He delivered these papers to John, at his chambers, and was asked by him to join their party the same evening to Astley's. They were going to take the two eldest boys to Astley's. The party was to be our brother and sister, Henry, John—and Miss Smith. My friend Robert could not resist. They called for him in their way; were all extremely amused: and my brother asked him to dine with them the next day, which he did, and in the course of that visit (as I understand) he found an opportunity of speaking to Harriet; and certainly did not speak in vain. She made him, by her acceptance, as happy even as he is deserving. He came down by yesterday's coach, and was with me this morning, immediately after breakfast, to report his proceedings, first on my affairs, and then on his own. This is all that I can relate of the how, where, and when. Your friend Harriet will make a much longer history when you see her. She will give you all the minute particulars, which only woman's language can make interesting. In our communications we deal only in the great. However, I must say, that Robert Martin's heart seemed for *him*, and to *me*, very overflowing; and that he did mention, without its being much to the purpose, that on quitting their box at Astley's, my brother took charge of Mrs. John Knightley and little John, and he followed, with Miss Smith and Henry; and that at one time they were in such a crowd as to make Miss Smith rather uneasy."

He stopped. Emma dared not attempt any immediate reply. To speak, she was sure, would be to betray a most unreasonable degree of happiness. She must wait a moment, or he would think her mad. Her silence disturbed him; and after observing her a little while, he added:

"Emma, my love, you said that this circumstance would not now make you unhappy; but I am afraid it gives you more pain than you expected. His situation is an evil; but you must consider it as what satisfies your friend; and I will answer for your thinking better and better of him as you know him more; his good sense and good principles would delight you. As far as the man is concerned, you could not wish your friend in better hands. His rank in society I would alter if I could, which is saying a great deal, I assure you, Emma. You laugh at me about William Larkins; but I could quite as ill spare Robert Martin."

He wanted her to look up and smile; and having now brought herself not to smile too broadly, she did, cheerfully answering:

"You need not be at any pains to reconcile me to the match. I think Harriet is doing extremely well. *Her* connections may be worse than *his:* in respectability of character, there can be no doubt that they are. I have been silent from surprise, merely—excessive surprise. You cannot imagine how suddenly it has come on me: how peculiarly unprepared I was! for I had reason to believe her very lately more determined against him, much more than she was before."

"You ought to know your friend best," replied Mr. Knightley; "but I should say she was a good-tempered, soft-hearted girl, not likely to be very, very determined against any young man who told her he loved her."

Emma could not help laughing as she answered, "Upon my word, I believe you know her quite as well as I do. But, Mr. Knightley, are you perfectly sure that she has absolutely and downright *accepted* him? I could suppose she might in time, but can she already? Did not you misunderstand him? You were both talking of other things; of business, shows of cattle, or new drills; and might not you, in the confusion of so many subjects, mistake him? It was not Harriet's hand that he was certain of—it was the dimensions of some famous ox."

The contrast between the countenance and air of Mr. Knightley and Robert Martin was, at this moment, so strong to Emma's feelings, and so strong was the recollection of all that had so recently passed on Harriet's side, so fresh the sound of those words spoken with such emphasis, "No, I hope I know better than to think of Robert Martin," that she was really expecting the intelligence to prove, in some measure, premature. It could not be otherwise.

"Do you dare say this?" cried Mr. Knightley. "Do you dare to suppose me so great a blockhead as not to know what a man is talking of? What do you deserve?"

"Oh! I always deserve the best treatment, because I never put up with any other; and, therefore, you must give me a plain, direct answer. Are you quite sure that you understand the terms on which Mr. Martin and Harriet now are?"

"I am quite sure," he replied, speaking very distinctly, "that he told me she had accepted him; and that there was no obscurity, nothing doubtful, in the words he used; and I think I can give you a proof that it must be so. He asked my opinion as to what he was now to do. He knew of no one but Mrs. Goddard to whom he could apply for information of her relations or friends. Could I mention anything more fit to be done than to go to Mrs. Goddard? I assured him that I could not. Then, he said, he would endeavour to see her in the course of this day."

"I am perfectly satisfied," replied Emma, with the brightest smiles, "and most sincerely wish them happy."

"You are materially changed since we talked on this subject before."

"I hope so—for at that time I was a fool."

"And I am changed also; for I am now very willing to grant you all Harriet's good qualities. I have taken some pains for your sake, and for Robert Martin's sake (whom I have always had reason to believe as much in love with her as ever), to get acquainted with her. I have often talked to her a good deal. You must have seen that I did. Sometimes, indeed, I have thought you were half suspecting me of pleading poor Martin's cause, which was never the case; but, from all my observations, I am convinced of her being an artless, amiable girl, with very good notions, very seriously good principles, and placing her happiness in the affections and utility of domestic life. Much of this, I have no doubt, she may thank you for."

"Me!" cried Emma, shaking her head. "Ah, poor Harriet!"

She checked herself, however, and submitted quietly to a little more praise than she deserved.

Their conversation was soon afterwards closed by the entrance of her father. She was not sorry. She wanted to be alone. Her mind was in a state of flutter and wonder, which made it impossible for her to be collected. She was in dancing, singing, exclaiming spirits; and till she had moved about, and talked to herself, and laughed and reflected, she could be fit for nothing rational.

Her father's business was to announce James' being gone out to put the horses to, preparatory to their now daily drive to Randalls; and she had, therefore, an immediate excuse for disappearing.

The joy, the gratitude, the exquisite delight of her sensations may be imagined. The sole grievance and alloy thus removed in the prospect of Harriet's welfare, she was really in danger of becoming too happy for security. What had she to wish for? Nothing, but to grow more worthy of him, whose intentions and judgment had been ever so superior to her own. Nothing but that the lessons of her past folly might teach her humility and circumspection in future.

Serious she was, very serious, in her thankfulness and in her resolutions; and yet there was no preventing a laugh, sometimes in the very midst of them. She must laugh at such a close—such an end of the doleful disappointment of five weeks back—such a heart—such a Harriet!

Now there would be pleasure in her returning; everything would be a pleasure; it would be a great pleasure to know Robert Martin.

High in the rank of her most serious and heartfelt felicities was the reflection that all necessity of concealment from Mr. Knightley would soon be over. The disguise, equivocation, mystery, so hateful to her to practise, might soon be over. She could now look forward to giving him that full and perfect confidence which her disposition was most ready to welcome as a duty.

In the gayest and happiest spirits, she set forward with her father, not always listening, but always agreeing to what he said; and, whether in speech or silence, conniving at the comfortable persuasion of his being obliged to go to Randalls every day, or poor Mrs. Weston would be disappointed.

They arrived. Mr. Weston was alone in the drawing-room. But hardly had they been told of the baby, and Mr. Woodhouse received the thanks for coming, which he asked for, when a glimpse was caught through the blind of two figures passing near the window.

"It is Frank and Miss Fairfax," said Mrs. Weston. "I was just going to tell you of our agreeable surprise in seeing him arrive this morning. He stays till to-morrow, and Miss Fairfax has been persuaded to spend the day with us. They are coming in, I hope."

In half a minute they were in the room. Emma was extremely glad to see him; but there was a degree of confusion, a number of embarrassing recollections, on each side. They met readily and smiling, but with a consciousness which at first allowed little to be said; and having all sat down again, there was for some time such a blank in the circle that Emma began to doubt whether the wish now indulged, which she had long felt, of seeing Frank Churchill once more, and of seeing him with Jane, would yield its proportion of pleasure. When Mr. Weston joined the party, however, and when the baby was fetched, there was no longer a want of subject or animation, or of courage and opportunity for Frank Churchill to draw near her and say:

"I have to thank you, Miss Woodhouse, for a very kind, forgiving message in one of Mrs. Weston's letters. I hope time has not made you less willing to pardon; I hope you do not retract what you then said."

"No, indeed," cried Emma, most happy to begin; "not in the least. I am particularly glad to see and shake hands with you, and to give you joy in person."

He thanked her with all his heart, and continued some time to speak with serious feeling of his gratitude and happiness.

"Is not she looking well?" said he, turning his eyes towards Jane—"better than she ever used to do? You see how my father and Mrs. Weston dote upon her."

But his spirits were soon rising again; and, with laughing eyes, after mentioning the expected return of the Campbells, he named the name of Dixon. Emma blushed, and forbade its being pronounced in her hearing.

"I can never think of it," she cried, "without extreme shame."

"The shame," he answered, "is all mine, or ought to be. But is it possible that you had no suspicion? I mean of late: early, I know, you had none."

"I never had the smallest, I assure you."

"That appears quite wonderful. I was once very near—and I wish I had; it would have been better. But though I was always doing wrong things, they were very *bad* wrong things, and such as did me no service.

It would have been a much better transgression had I broken the bond of secrecy and told you everything."

"It is not now worth a regret," said Emma.

"I have some hope," resumed he, "of my uncle's being persuaded to pay a visit at Randalls; he wants to be introduced to her. When the Campbells are returned, we shall meet them in London, and continue there, I trust, till we may carry her northward; but now, I am at such a distance from her—is not it hard, Miss Woodhouse? Till this morning, we have not once met since the day of reconciliation. Do not you pity me?"

Emma spoke her pity so very kindly, that with a sudden accession of gay thought, he cried:

"Ah! by the bye," then sinking his voice, and looking demure for the moment, "I hope Mr. Knightley is well?" He paused. She coloured and laughed. "I know you saw my letter, and think you may remember my wish in your favour. Let me return your congratulations. I assure you that I have heard the news with the warmest interest and satisfaction. He is a man whom I cannot presume to praise."

Emma was delighted, and only wanted him to go on in the same style; but his mind was the next moment in his own concerns and with his own Jane, and his next words were:

"Did you ever see such a skin? such smoothness! such delicacy! and yet without being actually fair. One cannot call her fair. It is a most uncommon complexion, with her dark eyelashes and hair—a most distinguishing complexion! So peculiarly the lady in it. Just colour enough for beauty."

"I have always admired her complexion," replied Emma, archly; "but do not I remember the time when you found fault with her for being so pale? When we first began to talk of her. Have you quite forgotten?"

"Oh, no! what an impudent dog I was! how could I dare——"

But he laughed so heartily at the recollection that Emma could not help saying:

"I do suspect that in the midst of your perplexities at that time, you had very great amusement in tricking us all. I am sure you had. I am sure it was a consolation to you."

"Oh, no, no, no! how can you suspect me of such a thing? I was the most miserable wretch."

"Not quite so miserable as to be insensible to mirth. I am sure it was a source of high entertainment to you, to feel that you were taking us all in. Perhaps I am the readier to suspect, because, to tell you the truth, I think it might have been some amusement to myself in the same situation. I think there is a little likeness between us."

He bowed.

"If not in our dispositions," she presently added, with a look of true sensibility, "there is a likeness in our destiny; the destiny which bids fair to connect us with two characters so much superior to our own."

"True, true," he answered warmly. "No, not true on your side. You can have no superior, but most true on mine. She is a complete angel. Look at her. Is not she an angel in every gesture? Observe the turn of her throat. Observe her eyes, as she is looking up at my father. You will be glad to hear" (inclining his head, and whispering seriously) "that my uncle means to give her all my aunt's jewels. They are to be new set. I am resolved to have some in an ornament for the head. Will not it be beautiful in her dark hair?"

"Very beautiful, indeed," replied Emma; and she spoke so kindly that he gratefully burst out:

"How delighted I am to see you again! and to see you in such excellent looks! I would not have missed this meeting for the world. I should certainly have called at Hartfield had you failed to come."

The others had been talking of the child, Mrs. Weston giving an account of a little alarm she had been under the evening before, from the infant's appearing not quite well. She believed she had been foolish, but it had alarmed her, and she had been within half a minute of sending for Mr. Perry. Perhaps she ought to be ashamed but Mr. Weston had been almost as uneasy as herself. In ten minutes, however, the child had been perfectly well again. This was her history; and particularly interesting it was to Mr. Woodhouse, who commended her very much for thinking of sending for Perry, and only regretted that she had not done it. "She should always send for Perry, if the child appeared in the slightest degree disordered, were it only for a moment. She could not be too soon alarmed, nor send for Perry too often. It was a pity, perhaps, that he had not come last night; for, though the child seemed well now—very well considering—it would probably have been better if Perry had seen it."

Frank Churchill caught the name.

"Perry!" said he to Emma, and trying, as he spoke, to catch Miss Fairfax's eye. "My friend Mr. Perry! What are they saying about Mr. Perry? Has he been here this morning? And how does he travel now? Has he set up his carriage?"

Emma soon recollected, and understood him; and while she joined in the laugh, it was evident from Jane's countenance, that she too was really hearing him, though trying to seem deaf.

"Such an extraordinary dream of mine!" he cried. "I can never think of it without laughing. She hears us, she hears us, Miss Woodhouse. I see it in her cheek, her smile, her vain attempt to frown. Look at her. Do not you see that, at this instant, the very passage of her own letter, which sent me the report, is passing under her eye; that the whole blunder is spread before her; that she can attend to nothing else, though pretending to listen to the others?"

Jane was forced to smile completely for a moment; and the smile partly remained as she turned towards him, and said, in a conscious, low, yet steady voice:

"How you can bear such recollections is astonishing to me. They *will* sometimes obtrude; but how you can *court* them!"

He had a great deal to say in return, and very entertainingly; but Emma's feelings were chiefly with Jane in the argument; and on leaving Randalls, and falling naturally into a comparison of the two men, she felt, that pleased as she had been to see Frank Churchill, and really regarding him as she did with friendship, she had never been more sensible of Mr. Knightley's high superiority of character. The happiness of this most happy day received its completion in the animated contemplation of his worth which this comparison produced.

Chapter 55

IF Emma had still, at intervals, an anxious feeling for Harriet, a momentary doubt of its being possible for her to be really cured of her attachment to Mr. Knightley, and really able to accept another man from unbiassed inclination, it was not long that she had to suffer from the recurrence of any such uncertainty. A very few days brought the party from London; and she had no sooner an opportunity of being one hour alone with Harriet, than she became perfectly satisfied, unaccountable as it was, that Robert Martin had thoroughly supplanted Mr. Knightley; and was now forming all her views of happiness.

Harriet was a little distressed—did look a little foolish at first: but having once owned that she had been presumptuous and silly, and self-deceived before, her pain and confusion seemed to die away with the words, and leave her without a care for the past, and with the fullest exultation in the present and future: for as to her friend's approbation, Emma had instantly removed every fear of that nature, by meeting her with the most unqualified congratulations. Harriet was most happy to give every particular of the evening at Astley's, and the dinner the next day: she could dwell on it all with the utmost delight. But what did such particulars explain? The fact was, as Emma could now acknowledge, that Harriet had always liked Robert Martin; and that his continuing to love her had been irresistible. Beyond this, it must ever be unintelligible to Emma.

The event, however, was most joyful; and every day was giving her fresh reason for thinking so. Harriet's parentage became known. She proved to be the daughter of a tradesman, rich enough to afford her the comfortable maintenance which had ever been hers, and decent enough to have always wished for concealment. Such was the blood of gentility which Emma had formerly been so ready to vouch for! It was likely to be as untainted, perhaps, as the blood of many a gentleman: but what a connection had she been preparing for Mr. Knightley, or for the Churchills, or even for Mr. Elton! The stain of illegitimacy, unbleached by nobility or wealth, would have been a stain indeed.

No objection was raised on the father's side; the young man was treated liberally; it was all as it should be: and as Emma became acquainted with Robert Martin, who was now introduced at Hartfield, she fully acknowledged in him all the appearance of sense and worth which could bid fairest for her little friend. She had no doubt of Harriet's happiness with any good-tempered man; but with him, and in the home he offered, there would be the hope of more, of security, stability, and improvement. She would be placed in the midst of those who loved her, and who had better sense than herself; retired enough for safety, and occupied enough for cheerfulness. She would be never led into temptation, nor left for it to find her out. She would be respectable and happy; and Emma admitted her to be the luckiest creature in the world, to have created so steady and persevering an affection in such a man; or, if not the luckiest, to yield only to herself.

Harriet, necessarily drawn away by her engagements with the Martins, was less and less at Hartfield, which was not to be regretted. The intimacy between her and Emma must sink; their friendship must change into a calmer sort of good-will; and, fortunately, what ought to be, and must be, seemed already beginning, and in the most gradual, natural manner.

Before the end of September, Emma attended Harriet to church, and saw her hand bestowed on Robert Martin with so complete a satisfaction, as no remembrances even connected with Mr. Elton, as he stood before them, could impair. Perhaps indeed, at that time, she scarcely saw Mr. Elton, but as the clergyman whose blessing at the altar might next fall on herself. Robert Martin and Harriet Smith, the latest couple engaged of the three, were the first to be married.

Jane Fairfax had already quitted Highbury, and was restored to the comforts of her beloved home with the Campbells. The Mr. Churchills were also in town; and they were only waiting for November.

The intermediate month was the one fixed on, as far as they dared, by Emma and Mr. Knightley. They had determined that their marriage ought to be concluded, while John and Isabella were still at Hartfield, to allow them the fortnight's absence in a tour to the seaside, which was the plan. John and Isabella, and every other friend, were agreed in approving it. But Mr. Woodhouse—how was Mr. Woodhouse to be induced to consent? he, who had never yet alluded to their marriage but as a distant event.

When first sounded on the subject, he was so miserable that they were almost hopeless. A second allusion, indeed, gave less pain. He began to think it was to be, and that he could not prevent it—a very promising step of the mind on its way to resignation. Still, however, he was not happy. Nay, he appeared so much otherwise that his daughter's courage failed. She could not bear to see him suffering; to know him fancying himself neglected; and though her understanding almost acquiesced in the assurance of both the Mr. Knightleys, that when once the event was over his distress would be soon over too, she hesitated—she could not proceed.

In this state of suspense, they were befriended, not by any sudden illumination of Mr. Woodhouse's mind, or any wonderful change of his nervous system, but by the operation of the same system in another way. Mrs. Weston's poultry-house was robbed one night of all her turkeys—evidently by the ingenuity of man. Other poultry-yards in the neighbourhood also suffered. Pilfering was *house-breaking* to Mr. Woodhouse's fears. He was very uneasy; and but for the sense of his son-in-law's protection, would have been under wretched alarm every night of his life. The strength, resolution, and presence of mind of the Mr. Knightleys commanded his fullest dependence. While either of them protected him and his, Hartfield was safe. But Mr. John Knightley must be in London again by the end of the first week in November.

The result of this distress, was, that, with a much more voluntary, cheerful consent than his daughter had ever presumed to hope for at the moment, she was able to fix her wedding-day; and Mr. Elton was called on, within a month from the marriage of Mr. and Mrs. Robert Martin, to join the hands of Mr. Knightley and Miss Woodhouse.

The wedding was very much like other weddings, where the parties have no taste for finery or parade; and Mrs. Elton, from the particulars detailed by her husband, thought it all extremely shabby, and very inferior to her own. "Very little white satin, very few lace veils; a most pitiful business! Selina would stare when she heard of it." But, in spite of these deficiencies, the wishes, the hopes, the confidence, the predictions of the small band of true friends who witnessed the ceremony, were fully answered in the perfect happiness of the union.

FINIS

NORTHANGER ABBEY

(First Published 1818*)*

NORTHANGER ABBEY

Chapter 1

No one who had ever seen Catherine Morland in her infancy would have supposed her born to be an heroine. Her situation in life, the character of her father and mother, her own person and disposition, were all equally against her. Her father was a clergyman, without being neglected or poor, and a very respectable man, though his name was Richard, and he had never been handsome. He had a considerable independence, besides two good livings, and he was not in the last addicted to locking up his daughters. Her mother was a woman of useful plain sense, with a good temper, and, what is more remarkable, with a good constitution. She had three sons before Catherine was born; and, instead of dying in bringing the latter into the world, as anybody might expect, she still lived on—lived to have six children more—to see them growing up around her, and to enjoy excellent health herself. A family of ten children will be always called a fine family, where there are heads, and arms, and legs enough for the number; but the Morlands had little other right to the word, for they were in general very plain, and Catherine, for many years of her life, as plain as any. She had a thin awkward figure, a sallow skin without colour, dark lank hair, and strong features; so much for her person, and not less un propitious for heroism seemed her mind. She was fond of all boys' play and greatly preferred cricket, not merely to dolls, but to the more heroic enjoyments of infancy, nursing a dormouse, feeding a canary-bird, or watering a rose-bush. Indeed she had no taste for a garden, and if she gathered flowers at all, it was chiefly for the pleasure of mischief, at least so it was conjectured from her always preferring those which she was forbidden to take. Such were her propensities; her abilities were quite as extraordinary. She never could learn or understand anything before she was taught, and sometimes not even then, for she was often inattentive, and occasionally stupid. Her mother was three months in teaching her only to repeat the "Beggar's Petition," and, after all, her next sister Sally could say it better than she did. Not that Catherine was always stupid; by no means; she learnt the fable of "The Hare and many Friends," as quickly as any girl in England. Her mother wished her to learn music; and Catherine was sure she should like it, for she was very fond of tinkling the keys of the old forlorn spinnet, so at eight years old she began. She learnt a year and could not bear it; and Mrs. Morland, who did not insist on her daughters being accomplished in spite of incapacity or distaste, allowed her to leave off. The day which dismissed the music-master was one of the happiest of Catherine's life. Her taste for drawing was not superior; though whenever she could obtain the outside of a letter from her mother, or seize upon any other odd piece of paper, she did what she could in that way by drawing houses and trees, hens and chickens, all very much like one another. Writing and accounts she was taught by her father; French by her mother. Her proficiency in either was not remarkable, and she shirked her lessons in both whenever she could. What a strange unaccountable character! for with all these symptoms of profligacy at ten years old, she had neither a bad heart nor a bad temper, was seldom stubborn, scarcely ever quarrelsome, and very kind to the little ones, with few interruptions of tyranny. She was, moreover, noisy and wild, hated confinement and cleanliness, and loved nothing so well in the world as rolling down the green slope at the back of the house.

Such was Catherine Morland at ten. At fifteen appearances were mending; she began to curl her hair and long for balls, her complexion improved, her features were softened by plumpness and colour, her eyes gained more animation, and her figure more consequence. Her love of dirt gave way to an inclination for finery, and she grew clean as she grew smart; she had now the pleasure of sometimes hearing her father and mother remark on her personal improvement. "Catherine grows quite a good-looking girl; she is almost pretty to-day," were words which caught her ears now and then; and how welcome were the sounds! To look *almost* pretty is an acquisition of higher delight to a girl who has been looking plain the first fifteen years of her life than a beauty from her cradle can ever receive.

Mrs. Morland was a very good woman, and wished to see her children everything they ought to be: but her time was so much occupied in lying-in and teaching the little ones, that her elder daughters were inevitably left to shift for themselves; and it was not very wonderful that Catherine, who had by nature nothing heroic about her, should prefer cricket, baseball, riding on horseback, and running about the country, at the age of fourteen, to books, or at least books of information, for, provided that nothing like useful knowledge could be gained from them, provided they were all story and no reflection, she had never any objection to books at all. But from fifteen to seventeen she was in training for a heroine; she read all such works as heroines must read to supply their memories with those quotations which are so serviceable and so soothing in the vicissitudes of their eventful lives.

From Pope, she learnt to censure those who

> "bear about the mockery of woe."

From Gray, that

> "Many a flower is born to blush unseen.
> And waste its sweetness on the desert air."

From Thomson, that it is a

> "Delightful task . . .
> To teach the young idea how to shoot."

And from Shakespeare she gained a great store of information: amongst the rest, that

> "trifles light as air,
> Are, to the jealous, confirmations strong
> As proofs of Holy Writ."

That

> "The poor beetle, that we tread upon,
> In corporal sufferance finds a pang as great
> As when a giant dies."

And that a young woman in love always looks

> "like Patience on a monument
> Smiling at Grief."

So far her improvement was sufficient, and in many other points she came on exceedingly well; for though she could not write sonnets, she brought herself to read them; and though there seemed no chance of her throwing a whole party into raptures by a prelude on the pianoforte of her own composition, she could listen to other people's performance with very little fatigue. Her greatest deficiency was in the pencil—she had no notion of drawing—not enough even to attempt a sketch of her lover's profile, that she might be detected in the design. There she fell miserably short of the true heroic height. At present she did not know her own poverty, for she had no lover to portray. She had reached the age of seventeen without having seen one amiable youth who could call forth her sensibility: without having inspired one real passion, and without having excited even any admiration but what was very moderate and very transient. This was strange indeed! But strange things may be generally accounted for if their cause be fairly searched out. There was not one lord in the neighbour-hood; no, not even a baronet. There was not one family among their ac-quaintances who had reared and supported a boy accidentally found at their door; not one young man whose origin was unknown. Her father had no ward, and the squire of the parish no children.

But when a young lady is to be a heroine, the perverseness of forty surrounding families cannot prevent her. Something must and will happen to throw a hero in her way.

Mr. Allen, who owened the chief of the property about Fullerton, the village in Wiltshire where the Morlands lived, was ordered to Bath for the benefit of a gouty constitution; and his lady, a good-humoured woman, fond of Miss Morland, and probably aware that, if adventures will not befall a young lady in her own village, she must seek them abroad, invited her to go with them. Mr. and Mrs. Morland were all compliance, and Catherine all happiness.

Chapter 2

In addition to what has been already said of Catherine Morland's personal and mental endowments, when about to be launched into all the difficulties and dangers of a six weeks' residence in Bath, it may be stated, for the reader's more certain information, lest the following pages should otherwise fail of giving any idea of what her character is meant to be, that her heart was affectionate, her disposition cheerful and open, without conceit or affectation of any kind; her manners just removed from the awkwardness and shyness of a girl; her person pleasing, and, when in good looks, pretty; and her mind about as ignorant and uninformed as the female mind at seventeen usually is.

When the hour of departure drew near, the maternal anxiety of Mrs. Morland will be naturally supposed to be most severe. A thousand alarming presentiments of evil to her beloved Catherine from this terrific separation must oppress her heart with sadness, and drown her in tears for the last day or two of their being together; and advice of the most important and applicable nature must of course flow from her wise lips in their parting conference in her closet. Cautions against the violence of such noblemen and baronets as delight in forcing young ladies away to some remote farmhouse, must, at such a moment, relieve the fullness of her heart. Who would not think so? But Mrs. Morland knew so little of lords and baronets, that she entertained no notion of their general mischievousness, and was wholly unsuspicious of danger to her daughter from their machinations. Her cautions were confined to the following points: "I beg, Catherine, you will always wrap yourself up very warm about the throat when you come from the Rooms at night; and I wish you would try to keep some account of the money you spend; I will give you this little book on purpose."

Sally, or rather Sarah (for what young lady of common gentility will reach the age of sixteen without altering her name as far as she can?), must from situation be at this time the intimate friend and confidante of her sister. It is remarkable, however, that she neither insisted on Catherine's writing by every post, nor exacted her promise of transmitting the character of every new acquaintance, nor a detail of every interesting conversation that Bath might produce. Everything, indeed, relative to this important journey was done on the part of the Morlands with a degree of moderation and composure, which seemed rather consistent with the common feelings of common life, than with the refined susceptibilities —the tender emotions which the first separation of a heroine from her

family ought always to excite. Her father, instead of giving her an unlimited order on his banker, or even putting a hundred pounds' bank-
bill into her hands, gave her only ten guineas, and promised her more
when she wanted it.

Under these unpromising auspices, the parting took place and the
journey began. It was performed with suitable quietness and uneventful
safety. Neither robbers nor tempests befriended them, nor one lucky
overturn to introduce them to the hero. Nothing more alarming occurred
than a fear, on Mrs. Allen's side, of having once left her clogs behind
her at an inn, and that fortunately proved to be groundless.

They arrived at Bath. Catherine was all eager delight; her eyes were
here, there, everywhere, as they approached its fine and striking environs,
and afterwards drove through those streets which conducted them to the
hotel. She was come to be happy, and she felt happy already.

They were soon settled in comfortable lodgings in Pulteney Street.

It is now expedient to give some description of Mrs. Allen that the
reader may be able to judge in what manner her actions will hereafter
tend to promote the general distress of the work, and how she will probably contribute to reduce poor Catherine to all the desperate wretchedness
of which a last volume is capable—whether by her imprudence, vulgarity,
or jealousy—whether by intercepting her letters, ruining her character,
or turning her out of doors.

Mrs. Allen was one of that numerous class of females, whose society
can raise no other emotion than surprise at there being any men in the
world who could like them well enough to marry them. She had neither
beauty, genius, accomplishment, nor manner. The air of a gentlewoman,
a great deal of quiet, inactive good temper, and a trifling turn of mind,
were all that could account for her being the choice of a sensible, intelligent man, like Mr. Allen. In one respect she was admirably fitted to
introduce a young lady into public, being as fond of going everywhere
and seeing everything herself, as any young lady could be. Dress was
her passion. She had a most harmless delight in being fine; and our
heroine's entrée into life could not take place till after three or four
days had been spent in learning what was mostly worn, and her chaperon
was provided with a dress of the newest fashion. Catherine, too, made
some purchases herself, and when all these matters were arranged, the
important evening came which was to usher her into the Upper Rooms.
Her hair was cut and dressed by the best hand, her clothes put on with
care, and both Mrs. Allen and her maid declared she looked quite as
she should do. With such encouragement, Catherine hoped at least to
pass uncensured through the crowd; as for admiration, it was always
very welcome when it came, but she did not depend on it.

Mrs. Allen was so long in dressing that they did not enter the ballroom
till late. The season was full, the room crowded, and the two ladies
squeezed in as well as they could. As for Mr. Allen, he repaired directly
to the card-room, and left them to enjoy a mob by themselves. With

more care for the safety of her new gown than for the comfort of her protégée, Mrs. Allen made her way through the throng of men by the door, as swiftly as the necessary caution would allow; Catherine, however, kept close at her side, and linked her arm too firmly within her friend's to be torn asunder by any common effort of a struggling assembly. But, to her utter amazement, she found that to proceed along the room was by no means the way to disengage themselves from the crowd; it seemed rather to increase as they went on; whereas she had imagined that, when once fairly within the door, they should easily find seats, and be able to watch the dances with perfect convenience. But this was far from being the case; and though by unwearied diligence they gained even the top of the room, their situation was just the same; they saw nothing of the dancers but the high feathers of some of the ladies. Still they moved on: something better was yet in view; and by a continued exertion of strength and ingenuity, they found themselves at last in the passage behind the highest bench. Here there was something less of a crowd than below; and hence Miss Morland had a comprehensive view of all the company beneath her, and of all the dangers of her late passage through them. It was a splendid sight; and she began, for the first time that evening, to feel herself at a ball: she longed to dance, but she had not an acquaintance in the room. Mrs. Allen did all that she could do in such a case, by saying very placidly, every now and then, "I wish you could dance, my dear; I wish you could get a partner." For some time her young friend felt obliged to her for these wishes, but they were repeated so often, and proved so totally ineffectual, that Catherine grew tired at last, and would thank her no more.

They were not long able, however, to enjoy the repose of the eminence they had so laboriously gained. Everybody was shortly in motion for tea, and they must squeeze out like the rest. Catherine began to feel something of disappointment: she was tired of being continually pressed against by people, the generality of whose faces possessed nothing to interest, and with all of whom she was so wholly unacquainted that she could not relieve the irksomeness of imprisonment by the exchange of a syllable with any of her fellow-captives; and when at last arrived in the Tea Room, she felt yet more the awkwardness of having no party to join, no acquaintance to claim, no gentlemen to assist them. They saw nothing of Mr. Allen; and after looking about them in vain for a more eligible situation, were obliged to sit down at the end of a table, at which a large party were already placed, without having anything to do there, or anybody to speak to, except each other.

Mrs. Allen congratulated herself, as soon as they were seated, on having preserved her gown from injury. "It would have been very shocking to have it torn," said she, "would not it? It is such a delicate muslin. For my part, I have not seen anything I like so well in the whole room, I assure you."

"How uncomfortable it is," whispered Catherine, "not to have a single acquaintance here!"

"Yes, my dear," replied Mrs. Allen, with perfect serenity, "it is very uncomfortable, indeed."

"What shall we do? The gentlemen and ladies at this table look as if they wondered why we came here; we seem forcing ourselves into their party."

"Aye, so we do. That is very disagreeable. I wish we had a large acquaintance here."

"I wish we had *any;* it would be somebody to go to."

"Very true, my dear; and if we knew anybody, we would join them directly. The Skinners were here last year; I wish they were here now."

"Had not we better go away as it is? Here are no tea-things for us, you see."

"No more there are, indeed. How very provoking! But I think we had better sit still, for one gets so tumbled in such a crowd. How is my head, my dear? Somebody gave me a push that has hurt it, I am afraid."

"No, indeed, it looks very nice. But, dear Mrs. Allen, are you sure there is nobody you know in all this multitude of people? I think you *must* know somebody."

"I don't, upon my word; I wish I did. I wish I had a large acquaintance here with all my heart, and then I should get you a partner. I should be so glad to have you dance. There goes a strange-looking woman! What an odd gown she has got on! How old-fashioned it is! Look at the back."

After some time they received an offer of tea from one of their neighbours; it was thankfully accepted, and this introduced a light conversation with the gentleman who offered it, which was the only time that anybody spoke to them during the evening, till they were discovered and joined by Mr. Allen when the dance was over.

"Well, Miss Morland," said he, directly, "I hope you have had an agreeable ball."

"Very agreeable, indeed," she replied, vainly endeavouring to hide a great yawn.

"I wish she had been able to dance," said his wife; "I wish we could have got a partner for her. I have been saying how glad I should be if the Skinners were here this winter instead of last; or, if the Parrys had come, as they talked of once, she might have danced with George Parry. I am so sorry she has not had a partner."

"We shall do better another evening, I hope," was Mr. Allen's consolation.

The company began to disperse when the dancing was over: enough to leave space for the remainder to walk about in some comfort; and now was the time for a heroine, who had not yet played a very distinguished part in the events of the evening, to be noticed and admired. Every five minutes, by removing some of the crowd, gave greater openings for her charms. She was now seen by many young men who had not been **near** her before. Not one, however, started with rapturous wonder on beholding her, no whisper of eager inquiry ran round the room, nor was she once called a divinity by anybody. Yet Catherine was in very good looks, and had the company only seen her three years before, they would *now* have thought her exceedingly handsome.

She *was* looked at, however, and with some admiration; for, in her own hearing two gentlemen pronounced her to be a pretty girl. Such words had their due effect: she immediately thought the evening more pleasant than she had found it before, her humble vanity was contented; she felt more obliged to the two young men for this simple praise, than a true quality heroine would have been for fifteen sonnets in celebration of her charms, and went to her chair in good humour with everybody, and perfectly satisfied with her share of public attention.

Chapter 3

EVERY morning now brought its regular duties; shops were to be visited, some new part of the town to be looked at, and the Pump Room to be attended, where they paraded up and down for an hour, looking at every body and speaking to no one. The wish of a numerous acquaintance in Bath was still uppermost with Mrs. Allen, and she repeated it after every fresh proof, which every morning brought, of her knowing nobody at all.

They made their appearance in the Lower Rooms; and here fortune was more favourable to our heroine. The master of the ceremonies introduced to her a very gentleman-like young man as a partner; his name was Tilney. He seemed to be about four or five-and-twenty, was rather tall, had a pleasing countenance, a very intelligent and lively eye, and, if not quite handsome, was very near it. His address was good and Catherine felt herself in high luck. There was little leisure for speaking while they danced; but when they were seated at tea she found him as agreeable as she had already given him credit for being. He talked with fluency and spirit, and there was an archness and pleasantry in his manner which interested, though it was hardly understood by her. After chatting some time on such matters as naturally arose from the objects around them, he suddenly addressed her with: "I have hitherto been very remiss, madam, in the proper attentions of a partner here; I have not yet asked you how long you have been in Bath, whether you were ever here before, whether you have been at the Upper Rooms, the theatre, and the concert, and how you like the place altogether. I have been very negligent; but are you now at leisure to satisfy me in these particulars? If you are, I will begin directly."

"You need not give yourself that trouble, sir."

"No trouble, I assure you, madam." Then forming his features into a set smile, and affectedly softening his voice, he added, with a simpering air, "Have you been long in Bath, madam?"

"About a week, sir," replied Catherine, trying not to laugh.

"Really!" with affected astonishment.

"Why should you be surprised, sir?"

"Why indeed?" said he, in his natural tone; "but some emotion must appear to be raised by your reply, and surprise is more easily assumed, and not less reasonable, than any other. Now let us go on. Were you never here before, madam?"

"Never, sir."

"Indeed! Have you yet honoured the Upper Rooms?"

"Yes, sir; I was there last Monday."

"Have you been to the theatre?"

"Yes, sir; I was at the play on Tuesday."

"To the concert?"

"Yes, sir; on Wednesday."

"And are you altogether pleased with Bath?"

"Yes; I like it very well."

"Now I must give one smirk, and then we may be rational again."

Catherine turned away her head, not knowing whether she might venture to laugh.

"I see what you think of me," said he gravely; "I shall make but a poor figure in your journal to-morrow."

"My journal!"

"Yes; I know exactly what you will say: 'Friday, went to the Lower Rooms; wore my sprigged muslin robe with blue trimmings, plain black shoes; appeared to much advantage, but was strangely harassed by a queer half-witted man, who would make me dance with him, and distressed me by his nonsense.'"

"Indeed I shall say no such thing."

"Shall I tell you what you ought to say?"

"If you please."

"I danced with a very agreeable young man, introduced by Mr. King; had a great deal of conversation with him; seems a most extraordinary genius; hope I may know more of him. *That*, madam, is what I *wish* you to say."

"But perhaps I keep no journal."

"Perhaps you are not sitting in this room, and I am not sitting by you. These are points in which a doubt is equally possible. Not keep a journal! How are your absent cousins to understand the tenor of your life in Bath without one? How are the civilities and compliments of every day to be related as they ought to be unless noted down every evening in a journal? How are your various dresses to be remembered, and the particular state of your complexion, and curl of your hair to be described in all their diversities, without having constant recourse to a journal? My dear madam, I am not so ignorant of young ladies' ways as you wish to believe me. It is this delightful habit of journalising which largely contributes to form the easy style of writing for which ladies are so generally celebrated.

Everybody allows that the talent of writing agreeable letters is peculiarly female. Nature may have done something, but I am sure it must be essentially assisted by the practice of keeping a journal."

"I have sometimes thought," said Catherine, doubtingly, "whether ladies *do* write so much better letters than gentlemen. That is, I should not think the superiority was always on our side."

"As far as I have had opportunity of judging it appears to me that the usual style of letter-writing among women is faultless, except in three particulars."

"And what are they?"

"A general deficiency of subject, a total inattention to stops, and a very frequent ignorance of grammar."

"Upon my word, I need not have been afraid of disclaiming the compliment! You do not think too highly of us in that way."

"I should no more lay it down as a general rule that women write better letters than men, than that they sing better duets, or draw better landscapes. In every power of which taste is the foundation, excellence is pretty fairly divided between the sexes."

They were interrupted by Mrs. Allen. "My dear Catherine," said she, "do take this pin out of my sleeve. I am afraid it has torn a hole already. I shall be quite sorry if it has, for this is a favourite gown, though it cost but nine shillings a yard."

"That is exactly what I should have guessed it, madam," said Mr. Tinley, looking at the muslin.

"Do you understand muslins, sir?"

"Particularly well; I always buy my own cravats, and am allowed to be an excellent judge; and my sister has often trusted me in the choice of a gown. I bought one for her the other day, and it was pronounced to be a prodigious bargain by every lady who saw it. I gave but five shillings a yard for it, and a true Indian muslin."

Mrs. Allen was quite struck by his genius. "Men commonly take so little notice of those things," said she. "I can never get Mr. Allen to know one of my gowns from another. You must be a great comfort to your sister, sir."

"I hope I am, madam."

"And pray, sir, what do you think of Miss Morland's gown?"

"It is very pretty, madam," said he, gravely examining it; "but I do not think it will wash well. I am afraid it will fray."

"How can you," said Catherine, laughing, "be so——?" she had almost said "strange."

"I am quite of your opinion, sir," replied Mrs. Allen; "and so I told Miss Morland when she bought it."

"But then you know, madam, muslin always turns to some account or other; Miss Morland will get enough out of it for a handkerchief or a cap, or a cloak. Muslin can never be said to be wasted. I have heard my sister say so forty times, when she has been extravagant in buying more than she wanted, or careless in cutting it to pieces."

"Bath is a charming place, sir; there are so many good shops here. We are sadly off in the country; not but what we have very good shops in Salisbury, but it is so far to go; eight miles is a long way. Mr. Allen says it is nine, measured nine; but I am sure it cannot be more than eight; and it is such a fag; I come back tired to death. Now, here one can step out of doors, and get a thing in five minutes."

Mr. Tilney was polite enough to seem interested in what she said; and she kept him on the subject of muslin till the dancing recommenced. Catherine feared as she listened to their discourse, that he indulged himself a little too much with the foibles of others. "What are you thinking of so earnestly?" said he, as they walked back to the ball-room; "not of your partner, I hope, for by that shake of the head, your meditations are not satisfactory."

Catherine coloured, and said, "I was not thinking of anything."

"That is artful and deep, to be sure; but I had rather be told at once that you will not tell me."

"Well, then, I will not."

"Thank you; for now we shall soon be acquainted, as I am authorised to tease you on this subject whenever we meet, and nothing in the world advances intimacy so much."

They danced again; and when the assembly closed, parted on the lady's side at least with a strong inclination for continuing the acquaintance. Whether she thought of him so much, while she drank her warm wine and water, and prepared herself for bed, as to dream of him when there, cannot be ascertained, but I hope it was no more than in a slight slumber, or a morning doze at most; for if it be true, as a celebrated writer has maintained, that no young lady can be justified in falling in love before the gentleman's love is declared,* it must be very improper that a young lady should dream of a gentleman before the gentleman is first known to have dreamt of her. How proper Mr. Tilney might be as a dreamer or a lover, had not yet, perhaps, entered Mr. Allen's head, but that he was not objectionable as a common acquaintance for his young charge, he was on inquiry satisfied; for he had early in the evening taken pains to know who her partner was, and had been assured of Mr. Tilney's being a clergyman, and of a very respectable family in Gloucestershire.

Chapter 4

With more than usual eagerness did Catherine hasten to the Pump Room the next day, secure within herself of seeing Mr. Tilney there before the morning was over, and ready to meet him with a smile: but no smile

* *Vide* a letter from Mr. Richardson, No. 97, vol. ii, "Rambler."

was demanded—Mr. Tilney did not appear. Every creature in Bath, except himself, was to be seen in the Room at different periods of the fashionable hours; crowds of people were every moment passing in and out, up the steps and down; people whom nobody cared about, and nobody wanted to see; and he only was absent. "What a delightful place Bath is," said Mrs. Allen, as they sat down near the great clock, after parading the Room till they were tired; "and how pleasant it would be if we had any acquaintances here."

This sentiment had been uttered so often in vain, that Mrs. Allen had no particular reason to hope it would be followed with more advantage now; but we are told to "Despair of nothing we would attain," as "Unwearied diligence our point would gain," and the unwearied diligence with which she had every day wished for the same thing was at length to have its just reward; for hardly had she been seated ten minutes, before a lady of about her own age, who was sitting by her, and had been looking at her attentively for several minutes, addressed her with great complaisance in these words: "I think, madam, I cannot be mistaken; it is a long time since I had the pleasure of seeing you, but is not your name Allen?" This question answered, as it readily was, the stranger pronounced hers to be Thorpe; and Mrs. Allen immediately recognised the features of a former schoolfellow and intimate, whom she had seen only once since their respective marriages, and that many years ago. Their joy on this meeting was very great, as well as it might be, since they had been contented to know nothing of each other for the last fifteen years. Compliments on good looks now passed; and, after observing how time had slipped away since they were last together, how little they had thought of meeting in Bath, and what a pleasure it was to see an old friend, they proceeded to make inquiries and give intelligence as to their families, sisters and cousins, talking both together, far more ready to give than to receive information, and each hearing very little what the other said. Mrs. Thorpe, however, had one great advantage as a talker, over Mrs. Allen, in a family of children; and when she expatiated on the talents of her sons, and the beauty of her daughters, when she related their different situations and views, that John was at Oxford, Edward at Merchant Taylors', and William at sea, and all of them more beloved and respected in their different stations than any other three beings ever were, Mrs. Allen had no similar information to give, no similar triumphs to press on the unwilling and unbelieving ear of her friend; and was forced to sit and appear to listen to all these maternal effusions, consoling herself, however, with the discovery, which her keen eyes soon made, that the lace on Mrs. Thorpe's pelisse was not half so handsome as that on her own.

"Here come my dear girls," cried Mrs. Thorpe, pointing at three smart-looking females, who, arm-in-arm, were then moving towards her. "My dear Mrs. Allen, I long to introduce them; they will be so delighted to see you; the tallest is Isabella, my eldest; is not she a fine young woman? The others are very much admired too, but I believe Isabella is the hand-somest."

The Miss Thorpes were introduced, and Miss Morland, who had been for a short time forgotten, was introduced likewise. The name seemed to strike them all; and, after speaking to her with great civility, the eldest young lady observed aloud to the rest, "How excessively like her brother Miss Morland is!"

"The very picture of him, indeed!" cried the mother; and "I should have known her anywhere for his sister!" was repeated by them all, two or three times over. For a moment Catherine was surprised; but Mrs. Thorpe and her daughters had scarcely begun the history of their acquaintance with Mr. James Morland, before she remembered that her eldest brother had lately formed an intimacy with a young man of his own college, of the name of Thorpe, and that he had spent the last week of the Christmas vacation with his family near London.

The whole being explained, many obliging things were said by the Miss Thorpes of their wish of being better acquainted with her; of being considered as already friends, through the friendship of their brothers, etc., which Catherine heard with pleasure, and answered with all the pretty expressions she could command; and, as the first proof of amity, she was soon invited to accept an arm of the eldest Miss Thorpe, and take a turn with her about the Room. Catherine was delighted with this extension of her Bath acquaintance, and almost forgot Mr. Tilney while she talked to Miss Thorpe. Friendship is certainly the finest balm for the pangs of disappointed love.

Their conversation turned upon those subjects of which the free discussion had generally much to do in perfecting a sudden intimacy between two young ladies; such as dress, balls, flirtations and quizzes. Miss Thorpe, however, being four years older than Miss Morland, and at least four years better informed, had a very decided advantage in discussing such points. She could compare the balls of Bath with those of Tunbridge; its fashions with the fashions of London; could rectify the opinions of her new friend in many articles of tasteful attire; could discover a flirtation between any gentleman and lady who only smiled on each other; and point out a quiz through the thickness of a crowd. These powers received due admiration from Catherine, to whom they were entirely new; and the respect which they naturally inspired might have been too great for familiarity, had not the easy gaiety of Miss Thorpe's manners, and her frequent expressions of delight on this acquaintance with her, softened down every feeling of awe, and left nothing but tender affection. Their increasing attachment was not to be satisfied with half a dozen turns in the Pump Room, but required, when they all quitted it together, that Miss Thorpe should accompany Miss Morland to the very door of Mr. Allen's house; and that they should there part with a most affectionate and lengthened shake of hands, after learning, to their mutual relief, that they should see each other across the theatre at night, and say their prayers in the same chapel the next morning. Catherine then ran directly upstairs, and watched Miss Thorpe's progress down the street from the drawing-room window; admired the graceful spirit of her walk, the fashionable air of her figure and dress, and felt grateful, as well she might, for the chance which had procured her such a friend.

Mrs. Thorpe was a widow, and not a very rich one; she was a good-humoured, well-meaning woman, and a very indulgent mother. Her eldest daughter had great personal beauty, and the younger ones, by pretending to be as handsome as their sister, imitating her air, and dressing in the same style, did very well.

This brief account of the family is intended to supersede the necessity of a long and minute detail from Mrs. Thorpe herself, of her past adventures and sufferings, which might otherwise be expected to occupy the three or four following chapters, in which the worthlessness of lords and attornies might be set forth; and conversations which had passed twenty years before be minutely repeated.

Chapter 5

CATHERINE was not so much engaged at the theatre, that evening, in returning the nods and smiles of Miss Thorpe, though they certainly claimed much of her leisure, as to forget to look with an inquiring eye for Mr. Tilney in every box which her eye could reach; but she looked in vain. Mr. Tilney was no fonder of the play than the Pump Room. She hoped to be more fortunate the next day; and when her wishes for fine weather were answered by seeing a beautiful morning, she hardly felt a doubt of it; for a fine Sunday in Bath empties every house of its inhabitants, and all the world appears on such an occasion, to walk about, and tell their acquaintances what a charming day it is.

As soon as divine service was over, the Thorpes and Allens eagerly joined each other; and, after staying long enough in the Pump Room to discover that the crowd was unsupportable, and that there was not a genteel face to be seen, which everybody discovers every Sunday throughout the season, they hastened away to the Crescent, to breathe the fresh air of better company. Here Catherine and Isabella, arm-in-arm, again tasted the sweets of friendship in an unreserved conversation. They talked much, and with much enjoyment; but again was Catherine disappointed in her hope of re-seeing her partner. He was nowhere to be met with; every search for him was equally unsuccessful, in morning lounges or evening assemblies, neither at the Upper nor Lower rooms, at dressed or undressed balls was he perceivable; nor among the walkers, the horsemen, or the curricle-drivers of the morning. His name was not in the Pump Room book, and curiosity could do no more. He must be gone from Bath; yet he had not mentioned that his stay would be so short. This sort of mysteriousness, which is always so becoming in a hero, threw a fresh grace, in Catherine's imagination, around his person and manners, and increased her anxiety to know more of him. From the Thorpes she could learn nothing, for they had been only two days in Bath before they met with Mrs. Allen. It was a subject, however, in which she often indulged with her fair friend, from whom she received every possible encouragement to continue to think of him; and his impression on her fancy was not suffered therefore to weaken. Isabella was very sure that he must be a charming young man; and was equally sure that he must have been delighted with her dear Catherine, and would therefore shortly return. She liked him the better for being a clergyman, "for she must confess herself very partial to the profession"; and something like a sigh escaped her as she said it. Perhaps Catherine was wrong in not demanding the cause of that gentle emotion, but she was not experienced enough in the finesse of love, or the duties of friendship, to know when delicate raillery was properly called for, or when a confidence should be forced.

Mrs. Allen was now quite happy, quite satisfied with Bath. She had found some acquaintance; had been so lucky, too, as to find in them the family of a most worthy old friend; and, as the completion of good fortune, had found these friends by no means so expensively dressed as herself. Her daily expressions were no longer, "I wish we had some acquaintances in Bath." They were changed into, "How glad I am we have met with Mrs. Thorpe!" and she was as eager in promoting the intercourse of the two families as her young charge and Isabella themselves could be; never satisfied with the day unless she spent the chief of it by the side of Mrs. Thorpe, in what they called conversation; but in which there was scarcely ever any exchange of opinion, and not often any resemblance of sub-ject, for Mrs. Thorpe talked chiefly of her children, and Mrs. Allen of her gowns.

The progress of the friendship between Catherine and Isabella was quick as its beginning had been warm; and they passed so rapidly through every gradation of increasing tenderness, that there was shortly no fresh proof of it to be given to their friends or themselves. They called each other by their Christian name, were always arm-in-arm when they walked, pinned up each other's train for the dance, and were not to be divided in the set; and, if a rainy morning deprived them of other enjoyments, they were still resolute in meeting in defiance of wet and dirt, and shut themselves up to read novels together. Yes, novels; for I will not adopt that un-generous and impolitic custom, so common with novel writers, of de-grading, by their contemptuous censure, the very performances to the number of which they are themselves adding: joining with their greatest enemies in bestowing the harshest epithets on such works, and scarcely ever permitting them to be read by their own heroine, who, if she acci-dentally take up a novel, is sure to turn over its insipid pages with disgust Alas! If the heroine of one novel be not patronised by the heroine of another, from whom can she expect protection and regard? I cannot approve of it. Let us leave it to the Reviewers to abuse such effusions of fancy at their leisure, and over every new novel to talk in threadbare strains of the trash with which the press now groans. Let us not desert one another; we are an injured body. Although our productions have afforded more extensive and unaffected pleasure than those of any other literary corporation in the world, no species of composition has been so much decried. From pride, ignorance, or fashion, our foes are almost as many as our readers; and while the abilities of the nine-hundredth abridger of the History of England, or of the man who collects and publishes in a volume some dozen lines of Milton, Pope, and Prior, with a paper from the *Spectator*, and a chapter from Sterne, are eulogised by a thousand pens, there seems almost a general wish of decrying the capacity and undervaluing the labour of the novelist, and of slighting the performances which have only genius, wit and taste to recommend them. "I am no novel reader; I seldom look into novels; do not imagine that *I* often read novels; it is really very well for a novel." Such is the common cant. "And what are you reading, Miss ——?" "Oh! it is only a novel!" replies the young lady; while she lays down her book with affected indifference, or momentary shame. "It is only *Cecilia*, or *Camilla*, or *Belinda*"; or, in short, only some work in which the greatest powers of the mind are displayed, in which the most thorough knowledge of human nature, the happiest delineation of its varieties, the liveliest effusions of wit and humour, are conveyed to the world in the best chosen language. Now, had the same young lady been engaged with a volume of the *Spectator*, instead of such a work, how proudly would she have produced the book, and told its name! though the chances must be against her being occupied by any part of that voluminous publication, of which either the matter or manner would not disgust a young person of taste; the substance of its papers so often consisting in the statement of improbable circumstances, unnatural characters, and topics of conversation, which no longer concern any one living; and their language, too, frequently so coarse as to give no very favourable idea of the age that could endure it.

Chapter 6

THE following conversation, which took place between the two friends in the Pump Room one morning, after an acquaintance of eight or nine days, is given as a specimen of their very warm attachment, and of the delicacy, discretion, originality of thought, and literary taste which marked the reasonableness of that attachment.

They met by appointment; and as Isabella had arrived nearly five minutes before her friend, her first address naturally was: "My dearest creature, what can have made you so late? I have been waiting for you at least this age!"

"Have you, indeed? I am very sorry for it, but really I thought I was in very good time. It is but just one. I hope you have not been here long?"

"Oh! these ten ages at least. I am sure I have been here this half-hour. But now, let us go and sit down at the other end of the Room and enjoy ourselves. I have an hundred things to say to you. In the first place, I was so afraid it would rain this morning just as I wanted to set off; it looked very showery, and that would have thrown me into agonies! Do you know I saw the prettiest hat you can imagine in a shop window in Milsom Street just now; very like yours, only with coquelicot ribands instead of green; I quite longed for it. But, my dearest Catherine, what have you been doing with yourself all this morning? Have you gone on with *Udolpho?*"

"Yes, I have been reading it ever since I woke; and I am got to the black veil."

"Are you, indeed? How delightful! Oh! I would not tell you what is behind the black veil for the world! Are not you wild to know?"

"Oh! yes, quite; what can it be? But do not tell me: I would not be told upon any account. I know it must be a skeleton; I am sure it is Laurentina's skeleton. Oh! I am delighted with the book! I should like to spend my whole life in reading it, I assure you; if it had not been to meet you, I would not have come away from it for all the world."

"Dear creature, how much I am obliged to you; and when you have finished *Udolpho*, we will read the Italian together; and I have made out a list of ten or twelve more of the same kind for you."

"Have you, indeed? How glad I am! What are they all?"

"I will read you their names directly; here they are in my pocket-book. *Castle of Wolfenbach, Clermont, Mysterious Warnings, Necromancer of the Black Forest, Midnight Bell, Orphan of the Rhine,* and *Horrid Mysteries.* Those will last us some time."

"Yes; pretty well; but are they all horrid? Are you sure they are all horrid?"

"Yes, quite sure; for a particular friend of mine, a Miss Andrews, a sweet girl, one of the sweetest creatures in the world, has read every one of them. I wish you knew Miss Andrews, you would be delighted with her. She is netting herself the sweetest cloak you can conceive. I think her as beautiful as an angel, and I am so vexed with the men for not admiring her! I scold them all amazingly about it."

"Scold them! Do you scold them for not admiring her?"

"Yes, that I do. There is nothing I would not do for those who are really my friends. I have no notion of loving people by halves; it is not my nature. My attachments are always excessively strong. I told Captain Hunt, at one of our assemblies this winter, that if he was to tease me all night, I would not dance with him, unless he would allow Miss Andrews to be as beautiful as an angel. The men think us incapable of real friend-ship, you know, and i am determined to show them the difference. Now, if I were to hear anybody speak slightingly of you, I should fire up in a moment; but that is not at all likely, for *you* are just the kind of girl to be a great favourite with the men."

"Oh, dear!" cried Catherine, colouring, "how can you say so?"

"I know you very well; you have so much animation, which is exactly what Miss Andrews wants; for I must confess there is something amazingly insipid about her. Oh! I must tell you, that, just after we parted yesterday, I saw a young man looking at you so earnestly; I am sure he is in love with you." Catherine coloured, and disclaimed again. Isabella laughed. "It is very true, upon my honour; but I see how it is: you are indifferent to everybody's admiration, except that of one gentleman, who shall be nameless. Nay, I cannot blame you" (speaking more seriously)— "your feelings are easily understood. Where the heart is really attached, I know very well how little one can be pleased with the attention of anybody else. Everything is so insipid, so uninteresting, that does not relate to the beloved object! I can perfectly comprehend your feelings."

"But you should not persuade me that I think so very much about Mr. Tilney, for perhaps I may never see him again."

"Not see him again! My dearest creature, do not talk of it. I am sure you would be miserable if you thought so."

"No, indeed; I should not. I do not pretend to say that I was not very much pleased with him; but while I have *Udolpho* to read, I feel as if nobody could make me miserable. Oh! the dreadful black veil! My dear Isabella, I am sure there must be Laurentina's skeleton behind it."

"It is so odd to me, that you should never have read *Udolpho* before; but I suppose Mrs. Morland objects to novels."

"No, she does not. She very often reads *Sir Charles Grandison* herself; but new books do not fall in our way."

"*Sir Charles Grandison!* That is an amazingly horrid book, is it not? I remember Miss Andrews could not get through the first volume."

"It is not like *Udolpho* at all; but yet I think it is very entertaining."

"Do you indeed? You surprise me; I thought it had not been readable. But, my dearest Catherine, have you settled what to wear on your head to-night? I am determined, at all events, to be dressed exactly like you. The men take notice of *that* sometimes, you know."

"But it does not signify, if they do," said Catherine, very innocently.

"Signify! Oh heavens! I make it a rule never to mind what they say. They are very often amazingly impertinent, if you do not treat them with spirit, and make them keep their distance."

"Are they? Well, I never observed *that*. They always behave very well to me."

"Oh! They give themselves such airs. They are the most conceited creatures in the world, and think themselves of so much importance! By the bye, though I have thought of it an hundred times, I have always forgot to ask you what is your favourite complexion in a man. Do you like them best dark or fair?"

"I hardly know. I never much thought about it. Something between both, I think; brown: not fair, and not very dark."

"Very well, Catherine. That is exactly he. I have not forgot your description of Mr. Tilney: 'a brown skin, with dark eyes, and rather dark hair.' Well, my taste is different. I prefer light eyes; and as to complexion, do you know, I like a sallow better than any other. You must not betray me, if you should ever meet with one of your acquaintances answering that description."

"Betray you! What do you mean?"

"Nay, do not distress me. I believe I have said too much. Let us drop the subject."

Catherine, in some amazement, complied; and, after remaining a few moments silent, was on the point of reverting to what interested her at that time rather more than anything else in the world, Laurentina's skeleton, when her friend prevented her, by saying: "For Heaven's sake! let us move away from this end of the room. Do you know, there are two odious young men who have been staring at me this half-hour. They really put me quite out of countenance. Let us go and look at the arrivals. They will hardly follow us there."

Away they walked to the book; and while Isabella examined the names, it was Catherine's employment to watch the proceedings of these alarming young men.

"They are not coming this way, are they? I hope they are not so impertinent as to follow us. Pray let me know if they are coming. I am determined I will not look up."

In a few moments Catherine, with unaffected pleasure, assured her that she need not be long uneasy, as the gentlemen had just left the Pump Room.

"And which way are they gone?" said Isabella, turning hastily round. "One was a very good-looking young man."

"They went towards the churchyard."

"Well, I am amazingly glad I have got rid of them. And now, what say you to going to Edgar's Buildings with me, and looking at my new hat? You said you would like to see it."

Catherine readily agreed. "Only," she added, "perhaps we may overtake the two young men."

"Oh! never mind that. If we make haste, we shall pass by them presently, and I am dying to show you my hat."

"But if we only wait a few minutes, there will no danger of our seeing them at all."

"I shall not pay them any such compliment, I assure you. I have no notion of treating men with such respect. *That* is the way to spoil them."

Catherine had nothing to oppose against such reasoning; and therefore, to show the independence of Miss Thorpe, and her resolution of humbling the sex, they set off immediately, as fast as they could walk, in pursuit of the two young men.

Chapter 7

HALF a minute conducted them through the Pump-yard to the arch-way, opposite Union Passage; but here they were stopped. Everybody acquainted with Bath may remember the difficulties of crossing Cheap Street at this point; it is indeed a street of so impertinent a nature, so unfortunately connected with the great London and Oxford roads, and the principal inn of the city, that a day never passes in which parties of ladies, however important their business, whether in quest of pastry, millinery, or even (as in the present case) of young men, are not detained on one side or the other by carriages, horsemen, or carts. This evil had been felt and lamented, at least three times a day, by Isabella since her residence in Bath; and she was now fated to feel and lament it once more; for at the very moment of coming opposite to Union Passage, and within view of the two gentlemen who were proceeding through the crowds, and threading the gutters of that interesting alley, they were prevented cross-ing by the approach of a gig, driven along on bad pavement by a most knowing-looking coachman, with all the vehemence that could most fitly endanger the lives of himself, his companions, and his horse.

"Oh! these odious gigs!" said Isabella, looking up, "how I detest them!" But this detestation, though so just, was of short duration, for she looked again, and exclaimed, "Delightful! Mr. Morland and my brother!"

"Good heaven! 'tis James!" was uttered at the same moment by Catherine; and, on catching the young men's eyes, the horse was imme-diately checked with a violence which almost threw him on his haunches, and the servant having now scampered up, the gentlemen jumped out, and the equippage was delivered to his care.

Catherine by whom this meeting was wholly unexpected, received her brother with the liveliest pleasure; and he, being of a very amiable dis-position, and sincerely attached to her, gave every proof on his side of equal satisfaction, which he could have leisure to do, while the bright eyes of Miss Thorpe were incessantly challenging his notice; and to her his devoirs were speedily paid, with a mixture of joy and embarrassment which might have informed Catherine, had she been more expert in the development of other people's feelings, and less simply engrossed by her own, that her brother thought her friend quite as pretty as she could do herself.

John Thorpe, who, in the meantime, had been giving orders about the horses, soon joined them, and from him she directly received the amends which were her due; for while he slightly and carelessly touched the hand of Isabella, on her he bestowed a whole scrape and half a short bow. He was a stout young man, of middling height, who with a plain face and ungraceful form, seemed fearful of being too handsome, unless he wore the dress of a groom, and too much like a gentleman unless he were easy where he ought to be civil, and impudent where he might be allowed to be easy. He took out his watch: "How long do you think we have been running it from Tetbury, Miss Morland?"

"I do not know the distance." Her brother told her that it was twenty-three miles.

"*Three* and twenty!" cried Thorpe; "five and twenty if it is an inch." Morland remonstrated, pleaded the authority of road-books, innkeepers, and milestones; but his friend disregarded them all; he had a surer test of distance. "I know it must be five and twenty," said he, "by the time we have been doing it. It is now half after one; we drove out of the inn-yard at Tetbury as the town-clock struck eleven; and I defy any man in England to make my horse go less than ten miles in harness; that makes it exactly twenty-five."

"You have lost an hour," said Morland; "it was only ten o'clock when we came from Tetbury."

"Ten o'clock! It was eleven, upon my soul! I counted every stroke. This brother of yours would persuade me out of my senses, Miss Morland; do but look at my horse; did you ever see an animal so made for speed in your life?" (The servant had just mounted the carriage and was driving off.) "Such true blood! Three hours and a half indeed, coming only three and twenty miles! Look at that creature, and suppose it possible if you can."

"He *does* look very hot, to be sure!"

"Hot! He had not turned a hair till we came to Walcot church; but look at his forehead; look at his loins; only see how he moves; that horse *cannot* go less than ten miles an hour; tie his legs, and he will get on. What do you think of my gig, Miss Morland? A neat one, is it not? Well hung; town built. I have not had it a month. It was built for a Christ Church man, a friend of mine, a very good sort of fellow; he ran it a few weeks, till, I believe, it was convenient to have done with it. I happened just then to be looking out for some light thing of the kind, though I had pretty well determined on a curricle too; but I chanced to meet him on Magdalen Bridge, as he was driving into Oxford last term. 'Ah! Thorpe,' said he, 'do you happen to want such a little thing as this? It is a capital one of the kind, but I am cursed tired of it.' 'Oh! d——,' said I, 'I am your man; what do you ask?' And how much do you think he did, Miss Morland?"

"I am sure I cannot guess at all."

"Curricle-hung, you see; seat, trunk, sword-case, splashing-board, lamps, silver moulding, all, you see, complete; the ironwork as good as new, or better. He asked fifty guineas: I closed with him directly, threw down the money, and the carriage was mine."

"And I am sure," said Catherine, "I know so little of such things, that I cannot judge whether it was cheap or dear."

"Neither one nor t'other; I might have got it for less, I dare say; but I hate haggling, and poor Freeman wanted cash."

"That was very good-natured of you," said Catherine, quite pleased.

"Oh! d—— it, when one has the means of doing a kind thing by a friend, I hate to be pitiful."

An inquiry now took place into the intended movements of the young ladies; and, on finding whither they were going, it was decided that the gentlemen should accompany them to Edgar's Buildings, and pay their respects to Mrs. Thorpe. James and Isabella led the way; and so well satisfied was the latter with her lot, so contentedly was she endeavouring to ensure a pleasant walk to him who brought the double recommendation of being her brother's friend and her friend's brother, so pure and un-coquettish were her feelings, that, though they overtook and passed the two offending young men in Milsom Street, she was so far from seeking to attract their notice, that she looked back at them only three times.

John Thorpe kept of course with Catherine, and, after a few minutes' silence, renewed the conversation about his gig: "You will find, however, Miss Morland, it would be reckoned a cheap thing by some people, for I might have sold it for ten guineas more the next day; Jackson, of Oriel, bid me sixty at once; Morland was with me at the time."

"Yes," said Morland, who overheard this; "but you forget that your horse was included."

"My horse! Oh, d—— it! I would not sell my horse for a hundred. Are you fond of an open carriage, Miss Morland?"

"Yes, very; I have hardly ever an opportunity of being in one; but I am particularly fond of it."

"I am glad of it; I will drive you out in mine every day."

"Thank you," said Catherine, in some distress, from a doubt of the propriety of accepting such an offer.

"I will drive you up Lansdown Hill to-morrow."

"Thank you; but will not your horse want rest?"

"Rest! He has only come three and twenty miles to-day; all nonsense; nothing ruins horses so much as rest; nothing knocks them up so soon. No, no; I shall exercise mine at the average of four hours every day while I am here."

"Shall you, indeed?" said Catherine, very seriously, "that will be forty miles a day."

"Forty! aye, fifty for what I care. Well, I will drive you up Lansdown to-morrow; mind, I am engaged."

"How delightful that will be!" cried Isabella, turning round; "my dearest Catherine, I quite envy you; but I am afraid, brother, you will not have room for a third."

"A third, indeed! No, no; I did not come to Bath to drive my sisters about; that would be a good joke, faith! Morland must take care of you."

This brought on a dialogue of civilities between the other two; but Catherine heard neither the particulars nor the result. Her companion's discourse now sunk from its hitherto animated pitch, to nothing more than a short, decisive sentence of praise or condemnation on the face of every woman they met; and Catherine, after listening and agreeing as long as she could, with all the civility and deference of the youthful female mind, fearful of hazarding an opinion of its own in opposition to that of a self-assured man, especially where the beauty of her own sex is concerned, ventured at length to vary the subject by a question which had been long uppermost in her thoughts: it was, "Have you ever read *Udolpho*, Mr. Thorpe?"

"*Udolpho!* Oh, Lord! not I; I never read novels. I have something else to do."

Catherine, humbled and ashamed, was going to apologise for her question; but he prevented her by saying, "Novels are all so full of nonsense and stuff! There has not been a tolerably decent one come out since *Tom Jones*, except *The Monk*; I read that t'other day; but as for all the others, they are the stupidest things in creation."

"I think you must like *Udolpho*, if you were to read it. It is so very interesting."

"Not I, faith! No, if I read any, it shall be Mrs. Radcliffe's. Her novels are amusing enough; they are worth reading; some fun and nature in *them*."

"*Udolpho* was written by Mrs. Radcliffe," said Catherine, with some hesitation from the fear of mortifying him.

"No, sure; was it? Aye, I remember, so it was; I was thinking of that other stupid book, written by that woman they make such a fuss about; she who married the French emigrant."

"I suppose you mean *Camilla!*"

"Yes, that's the book; such unnatural stuff! An old man playing at see-saw. I took up the first volume once, and looked it over, but I soon found it would not do; indeed, I guessed what sort of stuff it must be before I saw it; as soon as I heard she had married an emigrant, I was sure I should never be able to get through it."

"I have never read it."

"You had no loss, I assure you; it is the horridest nonsense you can imagine; there is nothing in the world in it but an old man's playing at see-saw and learning Latin; upon my soul, there is not."

This critique, the justness of which was unfortunately lost on poor Catherine, brought them to the door of Mrs. Thorpe's lodgings, and the feelings of the discerning and unprejudiced reader of *Camilla* gave way to the feelings of the dutiful and affectionate son, as they met Mrs. Thorpe, who had descried them from above, in the passage. "Ah, Mother, how do you do?" said he, giving her a hearty shake of the hand. "Where did you get that quiz of a hat, it makes you look like an old witch? Here is Morland and I come to stay a few days with you; so you must look out for a couple of good beds somewhere near." And this address seemed to satisfy all the fondest wishes of the mother's heart, for she received him with the most delighted and exulting affection. On his two younger sisters he then bestowed an equal portion of his fraternal tenderness, for he asked each of them how they did, and observed that they both looked very ugly.

These manners did not please Catherine; but he was James's friend and Isabella's brother; and her judgment was further bought off by Isabella's assuring her, when they withdrew to see the new hat, that John thought her the most charming girl in the world, and by John's engaging her before they parted to dance with him that evening. Had she been older or vainer, such attacks might have done little; but where youth and diffidence are united, it requires uncommon steadiness of reason to resist the attraction of being called the most charming girl in the world, and being so very early engaged as a partner; and the consequence was, that when the two Morlands, after sitting an hour with the Thorpes, set off to walk together to Mr. Allen's, and James, as the door was closed on them, said, "Well, Catherine, how do you like my friend Thorpe?" instead of answering, as she probably would have done, had there been no friendship, and no flattery in the case, "I do not like him at all;" she directly replied, "I like him very much; he seems very agreeable."

"He is as good-natured a fellow as ever lived; a little of a rattle; but that will recommend him to your sex, I believe; and how do you like the rest of the family?"

"Very, very much indeed; Isabella particularly."

"I am very glad to hear you say so; she is just the kind of young woman I could wish to see you attached to; she has so much good sense, and is so thoroughly unaffected and amiable. I always wanted you to know her; and she seems very fond of you. She said the highest things in your praise that could possibly be; and the praise of such a girl as Miss Thorpe, even you, Catherine," taking her hand with affection, "may be proud of."

"Indeed I am," she replied; "I love her exceedingly, and am delighted to find that you like her too. You hardly mentioned anything of her when you wrote to me after your visit there."

"Because I thought I should soon see you myself. I hope you will be a great deal together while you are in Bath. She is a most amiable girl; such a superior understanding! How fond all the family are of her; she is evidently the general favourite; and how much she must be admired in such a place as this. Is not she?"

"Yes, very much, indeed, I fancy; Mr. Allen thinks her the prettiest girl in Bath."

"I dare say he does; and I do not know any man who is a better judge of beauty than Mr. Allen. I need not ask you whether you are happy here, my dear Catherine; with such a companion and friend as Isabella Thorpe, it would be impossible for you to be otherwise; and the Allens, I am sure, are very kind to you."

"Yes, very kind; I never was so happy before; and now you are come it will be more delightful than ever. How good it is of you to come so far on purpose to see *me*."

James accepted this tribute of gratitude, and qualified his conscience for accepting it too, by saying with perfect sincerity, "Indeed, Catherine, I love you dearly."

Inquiries and communications concerning brothers and sisters, the situation of some, the growth of the rest, and other family matters, now passed between them, and continued, with ony one small digression on James's part, in praise of Miss Thorpe, till they reached Pulteney Street, where he was welcomed with great kindness by Mr. and Mrs. Allen, invited by the former to dine with them, and summoned by the latter to guess the price and weigh the merits of a new muff and tippet. A pre-engagement in Edgar's Buildings prevented his accepting the invitation of one friend, and obliged him to hurry away as soon as he had satisfied the demands of the other. The time of the two parties' uniting in the Octagon Room being correctly adjusted, Catherine was then left to the luxury of a raised, restless, and frightened imagination over the pages of *Udolpho,* lost from all worldly concerns of dressing and dinner, incapable of soothing Mrs. Allen's fears on the delay of an expected dressmaker, and having only one minute in sixty to bestow even on the reflection of her own felicity, in being already engaged for the evening.

Chapter 8

In spite of *Udolpho* and the dressmaker, however, the party from Pulteney Street reached the Upper Rooms in very good time. The Thorpes and James Morland were there only two minutes before them; and Isabella having gone through the usual ceremonial of meeting her friend with the most smiling and affectionate haste, of admiring the set of her gown, and envying the curl of her hair, they followed their chaperons, arm-in-arm, into the ball-room, whispering to each other whenever a thought occurred, and supplying the place of many ideas by a squeeze of the hand or a smile of affection.

The dancing began within a few minutes after they were seated; and James, who had been engaged quite as long as his sister, was very importunate with Isabella to stand up; but John was gone into the cardroom to speak to a friend, and nothing, she declared, should induce her to join the set before her dear Catherine could join it too. "I assure you," said she, "I would not stand up without your dear sister for all the world; for if I did, we should certainly be separated the whole evening." Catherine accepted this kindness with gratitude and they continued as they were for three minutes longer, when Isabella, who had been talking to James on the other side of her, turned again to his sister and whispered, "My dear creature, I am afraid I must leave you, your brother is so amazingly impatient to begin; I know you will not mind my going away, and I dare say John will be back in a moment, and then you may easily find me out." Catherine, though a little disappointed, had too much good-nature to make any opposition, and the others rising up,

Isabella had only time to press her friend's hand and say, "Good-bye, my dear love," before they hurried off. The younger Miss Thorpes being also dancing, Catherine was left to the mercy of Mrs. Thorpe and Mrs. Allen, between whom she now remained. She could not help being vexed at the non-appearance of Mr. Thorpe: for she not only longed to be dancing, but was likewise aware that, as the real dignity of her situation could not be known, she was sharing with the scores of other young ladies still sitting down all the discredit of wanting a partner. To be disgraced in the eye of the world, to wear the appearance of infamy while her heart is all purity, her actions all innocence, and the misconduct of another the true source of her debasement, is one of those circumstances which peculiarly belong to the heroine's life, and her fortitude under it what particularly dignifies her character. Catherine had fortitude too; she suffered, but no murmur passed her lips.

From this state of humiliation she was roused at the end of ten minutes, to a pleasanter feeling, by seeing, not Mr. Thorpe, but Mr. Tilney, within three yards of the place where they sat; he seemed to be moving that way, but he did not see her, and, therefore, the smile and the blush, which his sudden reappearance raised in Catherine, passed away without sullying her heroic importance. He looked as handsome and as lively as ever, and was talking with interest to a fashionable and pleasing-looking young woman who leant on his arm, and whom Catherine immediately guessed to be his sister; thus unthinkingly throwing away a fair opportunity of considering him lost to her for ever, by being married already. But, guided only by what was simple and probable, it had never entered her head that Mr. Tilney could be married; he had not behaved, he had not talked, like the married men to whom she had been used; he had never mentioned a wife, and he had acknowledged a sister. From these circumstances sprang the instant conclusion of his sister's now being by his side; and, therefore, instead of turning of a deathlike paleness, and falling in a fit on Mrs. Allen's bosom, Catherine sat erect, in the perfect use of her senses, and with cheeks only a little redder than usual.

Mr. Tilney and his companion, who, continued, though slowly, to approach, were immediately preceded by a lady, an acquaintance of Mrs. Thorpe; and this lady stopping to speak to her, they, as belonging to her, stopped likewise, and Catherine, catching Mr. Tilney's eye, instantly received from him the smiling tribute of recognition. She returned it with pleasure, and then advancing still nearer, he spoke both to her and Mrs. Allen, by whom he was civilly acknowledged. "I am very happy to see you again, sir, indeed; I was afraid you had left Bath." He thanked her for her fears, and said that he had quitted it for a week on the very morning after his having had the pleasure of seeing her.

"Well, sir, and I dare say you are not sorry to be back again, for it is just the place for young people; and, indeed, for everybody else too. I tell Mr. Allen, when he talks of being sick of it, that I am sure he should not complain, for it is so very agreeable a place, that it is much better to be here than at home at this dull time of year. I tell him he is quite in luck to be sent here for his health."

"And I hope, madam, that Mr. Allen will be obliged to like the place from finding it of service to him."

"Thank you, sir. I have no doubt that he will. A neighbour of ours, Dr. Skinner, was here for his health last winter, and came away quite stout."

"This circumstance must give great encouragement."

"Yes, sir; and Dr. Skinner and his family were here three months; so I tell Mr. Allen he must not be in a hurry to get away."

Here they were interrupted by a request from Mrs. Thorpe to Mrs. Allen, that she would move a little to accommodate Mrs. Hughes and Miss Tilney with seats, as they had agreed to join their party. This was accordingly done, Mr. Tilney still continuing standing before them; and, after a few minutes' consideration, he asked Catherine to dance with him. This compliment, delightful as it was, produced severe mortification to the lady; and, in giving her denial, she expressed her sorrow on the occasion so very much as if she really felt it, that had Thorpe, who joined her just afterwards, been half a minute earlier, he might have thought her sufferings rather too acute. The very easy manner in which he then told her that he had kept her waiting, did not, by any means reconcile her more to her lot; nor did the particulars which he entered into while they were standing up, of the horses and dogs of the friend whom he had just left, and of a proposed exchange of terriers between them, interest her so much as to prevent her looking very often towards that part of the room where she had left Mr. Tilney. Of her dear Isabella, to whom she particularly longed to point out that gentleman, she could see nothing. They were in different sets. She was separated from all her party, and away from all her acquaintances; one mortification succeeded another, and from the whole she deduced their useful lesson, that to go previously engaged to a ball does not necessarily increase either the dignity or enjoyment of a young lady. From such a moralizing strain as this she was suddenly roused by a touch on the shoulder; and, turning round, perceived Mrs. Hughes directly behind her, attended by Miss Tilney and a gentleman. "I beg your pardon, Miss Morland," said she, "for this liberty, but I cannot anyhow get to Miss Thorpe; and Mrs. Thorpe said she was sure you would not have the least objection to letting in this young lady by you." Mrs. Hughes could not have applied to any creature in the room more happy to oblige her than Catherine. The young ladies were introduced to each other, Miss Tilney expressing a proper sense of such goodness; Miss Morland, with the real delicacy of a generous mind, making light of the obligation; and Mrs. Hughes, satisfied with having so respectably settled her young charge, returned to her party.

Miss Tilney had a good figure, a pretty face, and a very agreeable countenance; and her air, though it had not all the decided pretension, the resolute stylishness, of Miss Thorpe's, had more real elegance. Her manners showed good sense and good breeding; they were neither shy, nor affectedly open; and she seemed capable of being young, attractive, and at a ball, without wanting to fix the attention of every man near her, and without exaggerated feelings of ecstatic delight or inconceivable vexation on every little trifling occurrence. Catherine, interested at once by her appearance and her relationship to Mr. Tilney, was desirous of being acquainted with her, and readily talked, therefore, whenever she could think of anything to say, and had courage and leisure for saying it. But the hindrance thrown in the way of a very speedy intimacy by the frequent want of one or more of these requisites, prevented their doing more than going through the first rudiments of an acquaintance, by informing themselves how well the other liked Bath, how much she admired its buildings and surrounding country; whether she drew, or played, or sang, and whether she was fond of riding on horseback.

The two dances were scarcely concluded, before Catherine found her arm gently seized by her faithful Isabella, who in great spirits exclaimed, "At last I have got you. My dearest creature, I have been looking for you this hour. What could induce you to come into this set, when you knew I was in the other? I have been quite wretched without you."

"My dear Isabella, how was it possible for me to get at you? I could not even see where you were."

"So I told your brother all the time, but he would not believe me. Do go and seek for her, Mr. Morland, said I; but all in vain, he would not stir an inch. Was not it so, Mr. Morland? But you men are all so immoderately lazy! I have been scolding him to such a degree, my dear Catherine, you would be quite amazed. You know I never stand upon ceremony with such people."

"Look at that young lady with the white beads round her head," whispered Catherine, detaching her friend from James: "it is Mr. Tilney's sister."

"Oh heavens! you don't say so! Let me look at her this moment. What a delightful girl! I never saw anything half so beautiful! But where is her all-conquering brother? Is he in the room? Point him out to me this instant, if he is; I die to see him. Mr. Morland, you are not to listen; we are not talking about you."

"But what is all this whispering about? What is going on?"

"There now, I knew how it would be! You men have such restless curiosity! Talk of the curiosity of women, indeed! 'tis nothing. But be satisfied; for you are not to know anything at all of the matter."

"And is that likely to satisfy me, do you think?"

"Well, I declare, I never knew anything like you. What can it signify to you what we are talking of? Perhaps we are talking about you;

therefore I would advise you not to listen, or you may happen to hear something not very agreeable."

In this common-place chatter, which lasted some time, the original subject seemed entirely forgotten; and though Catherine was very well pleased to have it dropped for a while, she could not avoid a little suspicion at the total suspension of all Isabella's impatient desire to see Mr. Tilney. When the orchestra struck up a fresh dance, James would have led his fair partner away, but she resisted. "I tell you, Mr. Morland," she cried, "I would not do such a thing for all the world. How can you be so teasing! Only conceive, my dear Catherine, what your brother wants me to do? He wants me to dance with him again, though I tell him that it is a most improper thing, and entirely against the rules. It would make us the talk of the place, if we were not to change partners."

"Upon my honour," said James, "in these public assemblies it is as often done as not."

"Nonsense, how can you say so? But when you men have a point to carry, you never stick at anything. My sweet Catherine, do support me; persuade your brother how impossible it is. Tell him that it would quite shock you to see me do such a thing; now would not it?"

"No, not at all; but if you think it wrong, you had much better change."

"There," cried Isabella, "you hear what your sister says, and yet you will not mind her. Well, remember that it is not my fault, if we set all the old ladies in Bath in a bustle. Come along, my dearest Catherine, for heaven's sake, and stand by me." And off they went to regain their former place. John Thorpe, in the meanwhile, had walked away; and Catherine, ever willing to give Mr. Tilney an opportunity of repeating the agreeable request which had already flattered her once, made her way to Mrs. Allen and Mrs. Thorpe as fast as she could, in the hope of finding him still with them, a hope which, when it proved to be fruitless, she felt to have been highly unreasonable. "Well, my dear," said Mrs. Thorpe, impatient for praise of her son, "I hope you have had an agreeable partner."

"Very agreeable, madam."

"I am glad of it. John has charming spirits, has not he?"

"Did you meet Mr. Tilney, my dear?" said Mrs. Allen.

"No; where is he?"

"He was with us just now, and said he was so tired of lounging about, that he was resolved to go and dance; so I thought perhaps he would ask you, if he met with you."

"Where can he be?" said Catherine, looking round; but she had not looked around long, before she saw him leading a young lady to the dance.

"Ah! he has got a partner; I wish he had asked *you*," said Mrs. Allen; and after a short silence, she added, "he is a very agreeable young man."

"Indeed he is, Mrs. Allen," said Mrs. Thorpe, smiling complacently:

"I must say it, though I *am* his mother, that there is not a more agreeable young man in the world."

This inapplicable answer might have been too much for the comprehension of many; but it did not puzzle Mrs. Allen; for, after only a moment's consideration, she said, in a whisper, to Catherine, "I dare say she thought I was speaking of her son."

Catherine was disappointed and vexed. She seemed to have missed, by so little, the very object she had had in view; and this persuasion did not incline her to a very gracious reply, when John Thorpe came up to her soon afterwards, and said, "Well, Miss Morland, I suppose you and I are to stand up and jig it together again?"

"Oh, no! I am much obliged to you, our two dances are over; and besides, I am tired, and do not mean to dance any more."

"Do not you? then let us walk about and quiz people. Come along with me, and I will show you the four greatest quizzers in the room; my two younger sisters and their partners. I have been laughing at them this half-hour."

Again Catherine excused herself; and at last he walked off to quiz his sisters by himself. The rest of the evening she found very dull; Mr. Tilney was drawn away from their party at tea to attend that of his partner; Miss Tilney, though belonging to it, did not sit near her; and James and Isabella were so much engaged in conversing together that the latter had no leisure to bestow more on her friend than one smile, one squeeze, and one "dearest Catherine."

Chapter 9

THE progress of Catherine's unhappiness from the events of the evening was as follows. It appeared first in a general dissatisfaction with everybody about her, while she remained in the Rooms, which speedily brought on considerable weariness and a violent desire to go home. This, on arriving in Pulteney Street, took the direction of extraordinary hunger, and when that was appeased, changed into an earnest longing to be in bed. Such was the extreme point of her distress; for when there she immediately fell into sound sleep, which lasted nine hours, and from which she awoke perfectly revived, in excellent spirits, with fresh hopes and fresh schemes. The first wish of her heart was to improve her acquaintance with Miss Tilney, and almost her first resolution to seek her for that purpose in the Pump Room at noon. In the Pump Room one so newly arrived in Bath must be met with; and that building she had already found so favourable for the discovery of female excellence, and the completion of female intimacy, so admirably adapted for secret discourses and unlimited confidence, that she was most reasonably encouraged to expect another friend from within its walls. Her plan for the morning thus settled, she sat quietly down to her book after breakfast, resolving to remain in the same place and the same employment till the clock struck one; and from habitude very little incommoded by the remarks and ejaculations of Mrs. Allen, whose vacancy of mind, and incapacity for thinking, were such, that, as she never talked a great deal, so she could never be entirely silent; and, therefore, while she sat at her work, if she lost her needle, or broke her thread, if she heard a carriage in the street, or saw a speck upon her gown, she must observe it aloud, whether there were any one at leisure to answer her or not. About half-past twelve a remarkably loud rap drew her in haste to the window, and scarcely had she time to inform Catherine of their being two open carriages at the door, in the first only a servant, her brother driving Miss Thorpe in the second, before John Thorpe came running upstairs, calling out, "Well, Miss Morland, here I am. Have you been waiting long? We could not come before, the old devil of a coachmaker was such an eternity finding out a thing fit to be got into, and now it is ten thousand to one but they break down before we are out of the street. How do you do, Mrs. Allen? A famous ball last night, was not it? Come, Miss Morland, be quick, for the others are in a confounded hurry to be off. They want to get their tumble over."

"What do you mean?" said Catherine; "where are you all going to?"

"Going to! Why, you have not forgotten our engagement? Did not we agree together to take a drive this morning? What a head you have? We are going up Claverton Down."

"Something was said about it, I remember," said Catherine, looking at Mrs. Allen for her opinion; "but really I did not expect you."

"Not expect me! That's a good one! And what a dust you would have made if I had not come!"

Catherine's silent appeal to her friend, meanwhile, was entirely thrown away; for Mrs. Allen, not being at all in the habit of conveying any expression herself by a look, was not aware of its being ever intended by anybody else; and Catherine, whose desire of seeing Miss Tilney again, could at that moment bear a short delay in favour of a drive, and who thought there could be no impropriety in her going with Mr. Thorpe as Isabella was going at the same time with James, was therefore obliged to speak plainer. "Well, ma'am, what do you say to it? Can you spare me for an hour or two? Shall I go?"

"Do just as you please, my dear," replied Mrs. Allen, with the most placid indifference. Catherine took the advice, and ran off to get ready. In a very few minutes she reappeared, having scarcely allowed the two others time enough to get through a few short sentences in her praise, after Thorpe had procured Mrs. Allen's admiration of his gig, and then, receiving her friend's parting good wishes, they both hurried downstairs. "My dearest creature," cried Isabella, to whom the duty of friendship immediately called her before she could get into the carriage, "you have been at least three hours getting ready: I was afraid you were ill. What a delightful ball we had last night! I have a thousand things to say to you; but make haste and get in, for I long to be off."

Catherine followed her orders and turned away, but not too soon to hear her friend exclaim aloud to James, "What a sweet girl she is! I quite dote on her."

"You will not be frightened, Miss Morland," said Thorpe, as he handed her in, "if my horse should dance about a little at first setting off. He will most likely give a plunge or two, and perhaps take the rest for a minute; but he will soon know his master. He is full of spirits, playful as can be, but there is no vice in him."

Catherine did not think the portrait a very inviting one, but it was too late to retreat, and she was too young to own herself frightened; so, resigning herself to her fate, and trusting to the animal's boasted knowledge of its owner, she sat peaceably down, and saw Thorpe sit down by her. Everything being then arranged, the servant who stood at the horse's head was bid in an important voice "to let him go," and off they went in the quietest manner imaginable, without a plunge or caper, or anything like one. Catherine, delighted at so happy an escape, spoke her pleasure aloud with grateful surprise; and her companion immediately made the matter perfectly simple by assuring her that it was entirely owing to the peculiarly judicious manner in which he had then held the reins, and the singular discernment and dexterity with which he had directed his whip. Catherine, though she could not help wondering that, with such perfect command of his horse, he should think it necessary to alarm her with a relation of its tricks, congratulated herself sincerely on being under the care of so excellent a coachman; and perceiving that the animal continued to go on in the same quiet manner, without showing the smallest propensity towards any unpleasant vivacity, and (considering its inevitable pace was ten miles an hour) by no means alarmingly fast, gave herself up to all the enjoyment of air and exercise of the most invigorating kind in a fine mild day of February, with the consciousness of safety. A silence of several minutes succeeded their first short dialogue. It was broken by Thorpe's saying very abruptly, "Old Allen is as rich as a Jew, is not he?" Catherine did not understand him, and he repeated his question, adding in explanation, "Old Allen, the man you are with."

"Oh! Mr. Allen you mean. Yes, I believe he is very rich."

"And no children at all?"

"No, not any."

"A famous thing for his next heirs. He is *your* godfather, is not he?"

"My godfather! No."

"But you are always very much with them?"

"Yes, very much."

"Aye, that is what I meant. He seems a good kind of old fellow enough, and has lived very well in his time, I dare say; he is not gouty for nothing. Does he drink his bottle a day now?"

"His bottle a day! No. Why should you think of such a thing? He is a very temperate man, and you could not fancy him in liquor last night?"

"Lord help me! You women are always thinking of men's being in liquor. Why, you do not suppose a man is overset by a bottle? I am sure of *this*, that if everybody was to drink their bottle a day, there would not be half the disorders in the world there are now. It would be a famous good thing for us all."

"I cannot believe it."

"Oh! lord, it would be the saving of thousands. There is not the hundredth part of the wine consumed in this kingdom that there ought to be. Our foggy climate wants help."

"And yet I have heard that there is a great deal of wine drank in Oxford."

"Oxford! There is no drinking at Oxford now, I assure you. Nobody drinks there. You would hardly meet with a man who goes beyond his four pints at the utmost. Now, for instance, it was reckoned a remarkable thing at the last party in my rooms, that upon an average we cleared about five pints a head. It was looked upon as something out of the common way. *Mine* is famous good stuff, to be sure. You would not often meet with anything like it in Oxford, and that may account for it. But this will just give you a notion of the general rate of drinking there."

"Yes, it does give a notion," said Catherine, warmly, "and that is, that you all drink a great deal more wine than I thought you did. However, I am sure James does not drink so much."

This declaration brought on a loud and overpowering reply, of which no part was very distinct, except the frequent exclamations, amounting almost to oaths, which adorned it, and Catherine was left, when it ended, with rather a strengthened belief of there being a great deal of wine drank in Oxford, and the same happy conviction of her brother's comparative sobriety.

Thorpe's ideas then all reverted to the merits of his own equipage, and she was called on to admire the spirit and freedom with which his horse moved along, and the ease which his paces, as well as the excellence of the springs, gave the motion of the carriage. She followed him in all his admiration as well as she could. To go before, or beyond him, was impossible. His knowledge and her ignorance of the subject, his rapidity of expression and her diffidence of herself, put that out of her power; she could strike out nothing new in commendation but she readily echoed whatever he chose to assert, and it was finally settled between them, without any difficulty, that this equipage was altogether the most complete of its kind in England, his carriage the neatest, his horse the best goer, and himself the best coachman. "You do not really think, Mr. Thorpe," said Catherine, venturing after some time to consider the matter as entirely decided, and to offer some little variation on the subject, "that James's gig will break down?"

"Break down! Oh, lord! Did you ever see such a little tittuppy thing in your life? There is not a sound piece of iron about it. The wheels have been fairly worn out these ten years at least; and as for the body, upon my soul, you might shake it to pieces yourself with a touch. It is the most devilish little rickety business I ever beheld! Thank God! we have got a better. I would not be bound to go two miles in it for fifty thousand pounds."

"Good heavens!" cried Catherine, quite frightened, "then pray let us turn back; they will certainly meet with an accident if we go on. Do let us turn back, Mr. Thorpe; stop and speak to my brother, and tell him how very unsafe it is."

"Unsafe! Oh, lord! what is there in that? They will only get a roll if it does break down; and there is plenty of dirt, it will be excellent falling. Oh, curse it! the carriage is safe enough if a man knows how to drive it; a thing of that sort in good hands will last above twenty years after it is fairly worn out. Lord bless you! I would undertake for five pounds to drive it to York and back again without losing a nail."

Catherine listened with astonishment. She knew not how to reconcile two such very different accounts of the same thing; for she had not been brought up to understand the propensities of a rattle, nor to know to how many idle assertions and impudent falsehoods the excess of vanity will lead. Her own family were plain matter-of-fact people, who seldom aimed at wit of any kind; her father at the utmost being contented with a pun, and her mother with a proverb; they were not in the habit, therefore, of telling lies to increase their importance, or of asserting at one moment what they would contradict the next. She reflected on the affair for some time in much perplexity, and was more than once on the point of requesting from Mr. Thorpe a clearer insight into his real opinion on the subject; but she checked herself, because it appeared to her that he did not excel in giving those clearer insights, in making those things plain which he had before made ambiguous, and, joining to this the consideration that he would not really suffer his sister and his friend to be exposed to a danger from which he might easily preserve them, she concluded at last that he must know the carriage to be in fact perfectly safe, and therefore would alarm herself no longer. By him the whole matter seemed entirely forgotten; and all the rest of his conversation, or rather talk, began and ended with himself and his own concerns. He told her of horses which he had bought for a trifle and sold for incredible sums; of racing matches, in which his judgment had infallibly foretold the winner; of shooting parties, in which he had killed more birds (though without having one good shot) than all his companions together; and described to her some famous days' sport with the foxhounds, in which his foresight and skill in directing the dogs had repaired the mistakes of the most experienced huntsman, and in which the boldness of his riding, though it had never endangered his own life for a moment, had been constantly leading others into difficulties, which, he calmly concluded, had broken the necks of many.

Little as Catherine was in the habit of judging for herself, and unfixed as were her general notions of what men ought to be, she could not entirely repress a doubt, while she bore with the effusions of his endless conceit, of his being altogether completely agreeable. It was a bold surmise, for he was Isabella's brother, and she had been assured by James that his manners would recommend him to all her sex; but in spite of this, the extreme weariness of his company which crept over her before they had been out an hour, and which continued unceasingly to increase till they stopped in Pulteney Street again, induced her in some small degree to resist such high authority, and to distrust his powers of giving universal pleasure.

When they arrived at Mrs. Allen's door, the astonishment of Isabella was hardly to be expressed on finding that it was too late in the day for them to attend her friend into the house:—"Past three o'clock!" it was inconceivable, incredible, impossible, and she would neither believe her own watch, nor her brother's, nor the servant's, she would believe no assurance of it founded on reason or reality, till Morland produced his watch and ascertained the fact: to have doubted a moment longer *then*, would have been equally inconceivable, incredible, and impossible, and she could only protest over and over again, that no two hours and a half had ever gone off so swiftly before, as Catherine was called on to confirm; Catherine could not tell a falsehood even to please Isabella; but the latter was spared the misery of her friend's dissenting voice by not waiting for her answer. Her own feelings entirely engrossed her; her wretchedness was most acute on finding herself obliged to go directly home. It was ages since she had had a moment's conversation with her dearest Catherine, and though she had such thousands of things to say to her, it appeared as if they were never to be together again; so with smiles of most exquisite misery, and the laughing eye of utter despondency, she bade her friend adieu and went on.

Catherine found Mrs. Allen just returned from all the busy idleness of the morning, and was immediately greeted with, "Well, my dear, here you are!" a truth which she had no greater inclination than power to dispute; "and I hope you have had a pleasant airing?"

"Yes, ma'am, I thank you; we could not have had a nicer day."

"So Mrs. Thorpe said. She was vastly pleased at your all going."

"You have seen Mrs. Thorpe, then?"

"Yes; I went to the Pump Room as soon as you were gone, and there I met her, and we had a great deal of talk together. She says there was hardly any veal to be got at market this morning, it is so uncommonly scarce."

"Did you see anybody else of our acquaintance?"

"Yes, we agreed to take a turn in the Crescent, and there we met Mrs. Hughes, and Mr. and Miss Tilney walking with her."

"Did you, indeed? and did they speak to you?"

"Yes; we walked along the Crescent together for half an hour. They seem very agreeable people. Miss Tilney was in a very pretty spotted muslin, and I fancy, by what I can learn, that she always dresses very handsomely. Mrs. Hughes talked to me a great deal about the family."

"And what did she tell you of them?"

"Oh! a vast deal, indeed; she hardly talked of anything else."

"Did she tell you what part of Gloucestershire they come from?"

"Yes, she did, but I cannot recollect now. But they are very good kind of people, and very rich. Mrs. Tilney was a Miss Drummond, and she and Mrs. Hughes were school-fellows; and Miss Drummond had a very large fortune, and, when she married, her father gave her twenty thousand pounds, and five hundred to buy wedding clothes. Mrs. Hughes saw all the clothes after they came from the warehouse."

"And are Mr. and Mrs. Tilney in Bath?"

"Yes, I fancy they are, but I am not quite certain. Upon recollection, however, I have a notion they are both dead; at least the mother is; yes, I am sure Mrs. Tilney is dead, because Mrs. Hughes told me there was a very beautiful set of pearls that Mr. Drummond gave his daughter on her wedding-day, and that Miss Tilney has got now, for they were put by for her when her mother died."

"And is Mr. Tilney, my partner, the only son?"

"I cannot be quite positive about that, my dear; I have some idea he is; but, however, he is a very fine young man, Mrs. Hughes says, and likely to do very well."

Catherine inquired no further; she had heard enough to feel that Mrs. Allen had no real intelligence to give, and that she was most particularly unfortunate herself in having missed such a meeting with both brother and sister. Could she have foreseen such a circumstance, nothing should have persuaded her to go out with the others; and, as it was, she could only lament her ill-luck, and think over what she had lost, till it was clear to her that the drive had by no means been very pleasant, and that John Thorpe himself was quite disagreeable.

Chapter 10

THE Allens, Thorpes, and Morlands all met in the evening at the theatre; and, as Catherine and Isabella sat together, there was then an opportunity for the latter to utter some few of the many thousand things which had been collecting within her for communication in the immeasurable length of time which had divided them. "Oh, heavens! my beloved Catherine, have I got you at last?" was her address on Catherine's entering the box and sitting by her. "Now, Mr. Morland," for he was close to her on the other side, "I shall not speak another word to you all the rest of the evening; so I charge you not to expect it. My sweetest Catherine, how have you been this long age? but I need not ask you, for you look delightfully. You really have done your hair in a more heavenly style than ever; you mischievous creature, do you want to attract everybody? I assure you, my brother is quite in love with you already; and as for Mr. Tilney—but *that* is a settled thing—even *your* modesty cannot doubt his attachment now; his coming back to Bath makes it too plain. Oh! what would not I give to see him! I really am quite wild with impatience. My mother says he is the most delightful young man in the world; she saw him this morning, you know. You must introduce him to me. Is he in the house now? Look about, for heaven's sake! I assure you I can hardly exist till I see him."

"No," said Catherine, "he is not here. I cannot see him anywhere."

"Oh, horrid! am I never to be acquainted with him? How do you like my gown? I think it does not look amiss; the sleeves were entirely my own thought. Do you know, I get so immoderately sick of Bath! Your brother and I were agreeing this morning, that, though it is vastly well to be here for a few weeks, we would not live here for millions. We soon found out that our tastes were exactly alike in preferring the country to every other place; really our opinions were so exactly the same, it was quite ridiculous\ There was not a single point in which we differed. I would not have had you by for the world; you are such a sly thing, I am sure you would have made some droll remark or other about it."

"No, indeed, I should not."

"Oh, yes! you would, indeed. I know you better than you know yourself. You would have told us that we seemed born for each other, or some nonsense of that kind which would have distressed me beyond conception; my cheeks would have been as red as your roses; I would not have had you by for the world."

"Indeed, you do me injustice; I would not have made so improper a remark upon any account; and besides, I am sure it would never have entered my head."

Isabella smiled incredulously, and talked the rest of the evening to James.

Catherine's resolution of endeavouring to meet Miss Tilney again continued in full force the next morning; and till the usual moment of going to the Pump Room, she felt some alarm from the dread of a second prevention. But nothing of that kind occurred, no visitors appeared to delay them, and they all three set off in good time for the Pump Room, where the ordinary course of events and conversation took place. Mr. Allen, after drinking his glass of water, joined some gentlemen to talk over the politics of the day, and compare the accounts of their newspapers; and the ladies walked about together, noticing every new face, and almost every new bonnet in the room. The female part of the Thorpe family, attended by James Morland, appeared among the crowd in less than a quarter of an hour, and Catherine immediately took her usual place by the side of her friend. James, who was now in constant attendance, maintained a similar position, and separating themselves from the rest of their party, they walked in that manner for some time, till Catherine began to doubt the happiness of a situation which, confining her entirely to her friend and brother, gave her very little share in the notice of either. They were always engaged in some sentimental discussion or lively dispute, but their sentiment was conveyed in such whispering voices, and their vivacity attended with so much laughter, that though Catherine's supporting opinion was not unfrequently called for by one or the other, she was never able to give any, from not having heard a word of the subject. At length, however, she was empowered to disengage herself from her friend, by the avowed necessity of speaking to Miss Tilney, whom she most joyfully saw just entering the room with Mrs. Hughes, and whom she instantly joined, with a firmer determination to be acquainted, than she might have had courage to command, had she not been urged by the disappointment of the day before. Miss Tilney met her with great civility, returned her advances with equal good-will, and they continued talking together as long as both parties remained in the Room; and though in all probability not an observation was made, not an expression used by either which had not been made and used some thousands of time before, under that roof, in every Bath season, yet the merit of their being spoken with simplicity and truth, and without personal conceit, might be something uncommon.

"How well your brother dances!" was an artless exclamation of Catherine's towards the close of their conversation, which at once surprised and amused her companion.

"Henry!" she replied with a smile. "Yes, he does dance very well."

"He must have thought it very odd to hear me say I was engaged the other evening, when he saw me sitting down. But I really had been engaged the whole day to Mr. Thorpe." Miss Tilney could only bow. "You cannot think," added Catherine, after a moment's silence, "how surprised I was to see him again. I felt so sure of his being quite gone away."

"When Henry had the pleasure of seeing you before, he was in Bath but for a couple of days. He came only to engage lodgings for us."

"That never occurred to me; and of course, not seeing him anywhere, I thought he must be gone. Was not the young lady he danced with on Monday a Miss Smith?"

"Yes; an acquaintance of Mrs. Hughes."

"I dare say she was very glad to dance. Do you think her pretty?"

"Not very."

"He never comes to the Pump Room, I suppose?"

"Yes; sometimes; but he has rid out this morning with my father."

Mrs. Hughes now joined them, and asked Miss Tilney if she was ready to go. "I hope I shall have the pleasure of seeing you again soon," said Catherine. "Shall you be at the cotillion ball to-morrow?"

"Perhaps we—yes, I think we certainly shall."

"I am glad of it, for we shall all be there." This civility was duly returned and they parted: on Miss Tilney's side with some knowledge of her
new acquaintance's feelings, and on Catherine's without the smallest
consciousness of having explained them.

She went home very happy. The morning had answered all her hopes,
and the evening of the following day was now the object of expectation—
the future good. What gown and what head-dress she should wear on the
occasion became her chief concern. She cannot be justified in it. Dress is at
all times a frivolous distinction, and excessive solicitude about it often
destroys its own aim. Catherine knew all this very well; her great-aunt
had read her a lecture on the subject only the Christmas before; and yet
she lay awake ten minutes on Wednesday night debating between her
spotted and her tamboured muslin; and nothing but the shortness of the
time prevented her buying a new one for the evening. This would have
been an error in judgment, great though not uncommon, from which one
of the other sex rather than her own, a brother rather than a great-aunt,
might have warned her; for man only can be aware of the insensibility of
man towards a new gown. It would be mortifying to the feelings of many
ladies could they be made to understand how little the heart of man is
affected by what is costly or new in their attire; how little it is biased by
the texture of their muslin, and how unsusceptible of peculiar tenderness
towards the spotted, the sprigged, the mull, or the jackonet. Woman is
fine for her own satisfaction alone. No man will admire her the more, no
woman will like her the better for it. Neatness and fashion are enough for
the former, and a something of shabbiness or impropriety will be most
endearing to the latter. But not one of these grave reflections troubled
the tranquillity of Catherine.

She entered the Rooms on Thursday evening with feelings very different from what had attended her thither the Monday before. She had then
been exulting in her engagement to Thorpe, and was now chiefly anxious
to avoid his sight, lest he should engage her again; for though she could
not, dared not expect that Mr. Tilney should ask her a third time to
dance, her wishes, hopes, and plans, all centred on nothing less. Every
young lady may feel for my heroine in this critical moment, for every
young lady has at some time or other known the same agitation. All have
been, or at least all have believed themselves to be, in danger from the
pursuit of someone whom they wish to avoid; and all have been anxious
for the attentions of someone whom they wished to please. As soon as
they were joined by the Thorpes, Catherine's agony began; she fidgeted
about if John Thorpe came towards her, hid herself as much as possible
from his view, and when he spoke to her pretended not to hear him. The
cotillions were over, the country-dancing beginning, and she saw nothing
of the Tilneys. "Do not be frightened, my dear Catherine," whispered
Isabella, "but I am really going to dance with your brother again. I
declare positively it is quite shocking. I tell him he ought to be ashamed
of himself, but you and John must keep us in countenance. Make haste

my dear creature, and come to us. John is just walked off, but he will be back in a moment."

Catherine had neither time nor inclination to answer. The others walked away. John Thorpe was still in view, and she gave herself up for lost. That she might not appear, however, to observe or expect him, she kept her eyes intently fixed on her fan; and a self-condemnation for her folly, in supposing that among such a crowd they should even meet with the Tilneys in any reasonable time, had just passed through her mind, when she suddenly found herself addressed and again solicited to dance, by Mr. Tilney himself. With what sparkling eyes and ready motion she granted his request, and with how pleasing a flutter of heart she went with him to the set may be easily imagined! To escape, and as she believed, so narrowly escape John Thorpe, and to be asked, so immediately on his joining her, asked by Mr. Tilney, as if he had sought her on purpose! it did not appear to her that life could supply any greater felicity.

Scarcely had they worked themselves into the quiet possession of a place, however, when her attention was claimed by John Thorpe, who stood behind her. "Heyday, Miss Morland!" said he, "what is the meaning of this? I thought you and I were to dance together."

"I wonder you should think so, for you never asked me."

"That is a good one, by jove! I asked you as soon as I came into the room, and I was just going to ask you again, but when I turned round, you were gone! This is a cursed shabby trick! I only came for the sake of dancing with *you*, and I firmly believe you were engaged to me ever since Monday. Yes; I remember, I asked you while you were waiting in the lobby for your cloak; and here have I been telling all my acquaintances that I was going to dance with the prettiest girl in the room; and when they see you standing up with somebody else; they will quiz me famously."

"Oh! no; they will never think of *me*, after such a description as that."

"By heavens! if they do not, I will kick them out of the room for blockheads. What chap have you there?" Catherine satisfied his curiosity. "Tilney," he repeated; "hum; I do not know him. A good figure of a man; well put together. Does he want a horse? Here is a friend of mine, Sam Fletcher, has got one to sell that would suit anybody. A famous clever animal for the road; only forty guineas. I had fifty minds to buy it myself, for it is one of my maxims always to buy a good horse when I meet with one; but it would not answer my purpose, it would not do for the field. I would give any money for a real good hunter. I have three now, the best that ever were backed. I would not take eight hundred guineas for them. Fletcher and I mean to get a house in Leicestershire against the next season. It is so d—— uncomfortable living at an inn."

This was the last sentence by which he could weary Catherine's attention, for he was just then borne off by the resistless pressure of a long string of passing ladies. Her partner now drew near, and said, "That gentleman would have put me out of patience, had he stayed with you

half a minute longer. He has no business to withdraw the attention of my
partner from me. We have entered into a contract of mutual agreeableness for the space of an evening, and all our agreeableness belongs solely
to each other for that time. Nobody can fasten themselves on the notice
of one, without injuring the rights of the other. I consider a country-
dance as an emblem of marriage. Fidelity and complaisance are the principal duties of both; and those men who do not choose to dance or marry
themselves, have no business with the partners or wives of their neighbours."

"But they are such very different things!"

"That you think they cannot be compared together?"

"To be sure not. People that marry can never part, but must go and
keep house together. People that dance, only stand opposite to each other
in a long room for half an hour."

"And such is your definition of matrimony and dancing. Taken in that
light certainly, their resemblance is not striking; but I think I could place
them in such a view. You will allow that in both man has the advantage of
choice, woman only the power of refusal; that in both it is an engagement
between man and woman, formed for the advantage of each; and that
when once entered into, they belong exclusively to each other till the
moment of its dissolution; that it is their duty each to endeavour to give
no cause for wishing that he or she had bestowed themselves elsewhere,
and their best interest to keep their own imaginations from wandering
towards the perfections of their neighbours, or fancying that they should
have been better off with anyone else. You will allow all this?"

"Yes, to be sure, as you state it, all this sounds very well; but still they
are so very different. I cannot look upon them at all in the same light, nor
think the same duties belong to them."

"In one respect, there certainly is a difference. In marriage, the man
is supposed to provide for the support of the woman; the woman to make
the home agreeable to the man; he is to purvey, and she is to smile. But
in dancing, their duties are exactly changed; the agreeableness, the compliance are expected from him, while she furnishes the fan and the
lavender water. *That,* I suppose, was the difference of duties which
struck you, as rendering the conditions incapable of comparison."

"No, indeed, I never thought of that."

"Then I am quite at a loss. One thing, however, I must observe. This
disposition on your side is rather alarming. You totally disallow any
similarity in the obligations; and may I not thence infer, that your notions of the duties of the dancing state are not so strict as your partner
might wish? Have I not reason to fear, that if the gentleman who spoke
to you just now were to return, or if any gentleman were to address
you, there would be nothing to restrain you from conversing with him
as long as you choose?"

"Mr. Thorpe is such a very particular friend of my brother's, that if
he talks to me, I must talk to him again; but there are hardly three

young men in the room besides him that I have any acquaintance with."

"And is that to be my only security? alas! alas!"

"Nay, I am sure that you cannot have a better; for if I do not know anybody, it is impossible for me to talk to them; and, besides, I do not *want* to talk to anybody."

"Now you have given me a security worth having; and I shall proceed with courage. Do you find Bath as agreeable as when I had the honour of making the inquiry before?"

"Yes, quite; more so, indeed."

"More so! Take care, or you will forget to be tired of it at the proper time. You ought to be tired at the end of six weeks."

"I do not think I should be tired, if I were to stay here six months."

"Bath, compared with London, has little variety, and so everybody finds out every year. 'For six weeks, I allow, Bath is pleasant enough; but beyond *that*, it is the most tiresome place in the world.' You would be told so by people of all descriptions, who come regularly every winter, lengthen their six weeks into ten or twelve, and go away at last because they can afford to stay no longer."

"Well, other people must judge for themselves, and those who go to London may think nothing of Bath. But I, who live in a small retired village in the country, can never find greater sameness in such a place as this than in my own home; for here are a variety of amusements, a variety of things to be seen and done all day long, which I can know nothing of there."

"You are not fond of the country."

"Yes, I am. I have always lived there, and always been very happy. But certainly there is much more sameness in a country life than in a Bath life. One day in the country is exactly like another."

"But then you spend your time so much more rationally in the country."

"Do I?"

"Do you not?"

"I do not believe there is much difference."

"Here you are in pursuit only of amusement all day long."

"And so I am at home: only I do not find so much of it. I walk about here, and so I do there; but here I see a variety of people in every street, and there I can only go and call on Mrs. Allen."

Mr. Tilney was very much amused. 'Only go and call on Mrs. Allen!" he repeated. "What a picture of intellectual poverty! However, when you sink into this abyss again, you will have more to say. You will be able to talk of Bath, and of all that you did here."

"Oh, yes; I shall never be in want of something to talk of again to Mrs. Allen, or anybody else. I really believe I shall always be talking of Bath, when I am at home again; I *do* like it so very much. If I could have but papa and mamma, and the rest of them here, I suppose I should be too happy! James's coming (my eldest brother) is quite delightful; and espe-

cially as it turns out that the very family we are just got so intimate with
are his intimate friends already. Oh! who can ever be tired of Bath?"

"Not those who bring such fresh feelings of every sort to it as you do.
But papas and mammas, and brothers and intimate friends, are a good
deal gone by, to most of the frequenters of Bath; and the honest relish of
balls and plays, and every-day sights, is past with them."

Here their conversation closed; the demands of the dance becoming
now too importunate for a divided attention.

Soon after their reaching the bottom of the set, Catherine perceived
herself to be earnestly regarded by a gentleman who stood among the
lookers-on, immediately behind her partner. He was a very handsome
man, of a commanding aspect, past the bloom, but not past the vigour of
life; and with his eye still directed towards her, she saw him presently
address Mr. Tilney in a familiar whisper. Confused by his notice, and
blushing from the fear of its being excited by something wrong in her
appearance, she turned away her head. But while she did so, the gentleman
retreated, and her partner coming nearer, said, "I see that you guess what
I have just been asked. That gentleman knows your name, and you have a
right to know his. It is General Tilney, my father."

Catherine's answer was only "Oh!" but it was an "Oh!" expressing
everything needful: attention to his words, and perfect reliance on their
truth. With real interest and strong admiration did her eye now follow the
General, as he moved through the crowd, and "How handsome a family
they are!" was her secret remark.

In chatting with Miss Tilney before the evening concluded, a new
source of felicity arose to her. She had never taken a country walk since
her arrival in Bath. Miss Tilney, to whom all the commonly frequented
environs were familiar, spoke of them in terms which made her all eagerness to know them too; and on her openly fearing that she might find
nobody to go with her, it was proposed by the brother and sister that they
should join in a walk, some morning or other. "I shall like it," she cried,
"beyond anything in the world; and do not let us put it off; let us go
to-morrow." This was readily agreed to, with only a proviso of Miss
Tilney's, that it did not rain, which Catherine was sure it would not. At
twelve o'clock, they were to call for her in Pulteney Street, and "remember
twelve o'clock," was her parting speech to her new friend. Of her other,
her older, her more established friend, Isabella, of whose fidelity and
worth she had enjoyed a fortnight's experience, she scarcely saw anything
during the evening. Yet, though longing to make her acquainted with her
happiness, she cheerfully submitted to the wish of Mr. Allen, which took
them rather early away, and her spirits danced within her, as she danced in
her chair all the way home.

Chapter 11

THE morrow brought a very sober-looking morning, the sun making only a few efforts to appear; and Catherine augured from it everything most favourable to her wishes. A bright morning so early in the year, she allowed, would generally turn to rain; but a cloudy one foretold improvement as the day advanced. She applied to Mr. Allen for confirmation of her hopes, but Mr. Allen not having his own skies and barometer about him, declined giving any absolute promise of sunshine. She applied to Mrs. Allen, and Mrs. Allen's opinion was more positive. "She had no doubt in the world of its being a very fine day, if the clouds would go off, and the sun keep out."

At about eleven o'clock, however, a few specks of small rain upon the windows caught Catherine's watchful eye, and "Oh dear! I do believe it will be wet," broke from her in a most desponding tone.

"I thought how it would be," said Mrs. Allen.

"No walk for me to-day," sighed Catherine; "but perhaps it may come to nothing, or it may hold up before twelve."

"Perhaps it may; but then, my dear, it will be so dirty."

"Oh! that will not signify; I never mind dirt."

"No," replied her friend very placidly, "I know you never mind dirt."

After a short pause, "It comes on faster and faster!" said Catherine, as she stood watching at a window.

"So it does, indeed. If it keeps raining, the streets will be very wet."

"There are four umbrellas up already. How I hate the sight of an umbrella!"

"They are disagreeable things to carry. I would much rather take a chair at any time."

"It was such a nice looking morning! I felt so convinced it would be dry!"

"Anybody would have thought so, indeed. There will be very few people in the Pump Room, if it rains all morning. I hope Mr. Allen will put on his great-coat when he goes, but I dare say he will not, for he had rather do anything in the world than walk out in a great-coat; I wonder he should dislike it, it must be so comfortable."

The rain continued, fast though not heavy. Catherine went every five minutes to the clock, threatening, on each return, that, if it still kept on raining another five minutes, she would give up the matter as hopeless. The clock struck twelve, and it still rained. "You will not be able to go, my dear."

"I do not quite despair yet. I shall not give it up till a quarter after twelve. This is just the time of day for it to clear up, and I do think it looks a little lighter. There, it is twenty minutes after twelve, and now I *shall* give it up entirely. Oh! that we had such weather here as they had at

Udoipho, or at least in Tuscany and the south of France! the night that poor St. Aubin died! such beautiful weather!"

At half past twelve, when Catherine's anxious attention to the weather was over, and she could no longer claim any merit from its amendment, the sky began voluntarily to clear. A gleam of sunshine took her quite by surprise; she looked round, the clouds were parting, and she instantly returned to the window to watch over and encourage the happy appearance. Ten minutes more made it certain that a bright afternoon would succeed, and justified the opinion of Mrs. Allen, who had "always thought it would clear up." But whether Catherine might still expect her friends, whether there had not been too much rain for Miss Tilney to venture, must yet be a question.

It was too dirty for Mrs. Allen to accompany her husband to the Pump Room; he accordingly set off by himself, and Catherine had barely watched him down the street, when her notice was claimed by the approach of the same two open carriages, containing the same three people that had surprised her so much a few mornings back.

"Isabella, my brother, and, Mr. Thorpe, I declare! They are coming for me, perhaps; but I shall not go; I cannot go, indeed; for, you know, Miss Tilney may still call." Mrs. Allen agreed to it. John Thorpe was soon with them, and his voice was with them yet sooner, for on the stairs he was calling to Miss Morland to be quick. "Make haste! make haste!" as he threw open the door, "put on your hat this moment; there is no time to be lost; we are going to Bristol. How d'ye do, Mrs. Allen?"

"To Bristol! Is not that a great way off? But, however, I cannot go with you to-day, because I am engaged; I expect some friends every moment." This was of course vehemently talked down as no reason at all. Mrs. Allen was called on to second him, and the two others walked in, to give their assistance. "My sweetest Catherine, is not this delightful? We shall have a most heavenly drive. You are to thank your brother and me for the scheme: it darted into our heads at breakfast time, I verily believe at the same instant; and we should have been off two hours ago, if it had not been for this detestable rain. But it does not signify, the nights are moonlight, and we shall do delightfully. Oh! I am in such ecstasies at the thoughts of a little country air and quiet! so much better than going to the Lower Rooms. We shall drive directly to Clifton and dine there; and as soon as dinner is over, if there is time for it, go on to Kingsweston."

"I doubt our being able to do so much," said Morland.

"You croaking fellow!" cried Thorpe, "we shall be able to do ten times more. Kingsweston! aye, and Blaize Castle too, and anything else we can hear of; but here is your sister says she will not go."

"Blaize Castle!" cried Catherine; "what is that?"

"The finest place in England; worth going fifty miles at any time to see."

"What, is it really a castle, an old castle?"

"The oldest in the kingdom."

"But is it like what one reads of?"

"Exactly: the very same."

"But now, really, are there towers and long galleries?"

"By dozens."

"Then I should like to see it; but I cannot, I cannot go."

"Not go! my beloved creature, what do you mean?"

"I cannot go, because" (looking down as she spoke, fearful of Isabella's smile) "I expect Miss Tilney and her brother to call on me to take a country walk. They promised to come at twelve, only it rained; but now, as it is so fine, I dare say they will be here soon."

"Not they, indeed," cried Thorpe; "for as we turned into Broad Street, I saw them. Does he not drive a phaeton with bright chestnuts?"

"I do not know, indeed."

"Yes, I know he does; I saw him. You are talking of the man you danced with last night, are not you?"

"Yes."

"Well, I saw him at that moment turn up Lansdown Road, driving a smart-looking girl."

"Did you, indeed?"

"Did, upon my soul; knew him again directly; and he seemed to have got some very pretty cattle too."

"It is very odd! But I suppose they thought it would be too dirty for a walk."

"And well they might, for I never saw so much dirt in my life. Walk! you could no more walk than you could fly! It has not been so dirty the whole winter; it is ankle deep everywhere."

Isabella corroborated it:—"My dearest Catherine, you cannot form an idea of the dirt; come, you must go; you cannot refuse going now."

"I should like to see the castle; but may we go all over it? May we go up every staircase, and into every suite of rooms?"

"Yes, yes; every hole and corner."

"But then, if they should only be gone out for an hour till it is drier, and call by and by?"

"Make yourself easy, there is no danger of that; for I heard Tilney hallooing to a man who was just passing by on horseback, that they were going as far as Wick Rocks."

"Then I will. Shall I go, Mrs. Allen?"

"Just as you please, my dear."

"Mrs. Allen, you must persuade her to go," was the general cry. Mrs. Allen was not inattentive to it. "Well, my dear," said she, "suppose you go." And in two minutes they were off.

Catherine's feelings, as she got into the carriage, were in a very unsettled state; divided between regret for the loss of one great pleasure, and the hope of soon enjoying another, almost its equal in degree, however unlike in kind. She could not think the Tilneys had acted quite well by her, in so readily giving up their engagement, without sending her any message of excuse. It was now but an hour later than the time fixed on for the beginning of their walk; and, in spite of what she had heard of the prodigious accumulation of dirt in the course of that hour, she could not from her own observation help thinking that they might have gone with very little inconvenience. To feel herself slighted by them was very painful. On the other hand, the delight of exploring an edifice like Udolpho, as her fancy represented Blaize Castle to be, was such a counterpoise of good, as might console her for almost anything.

They passed briskly down Pulteney Street, and through Laura Place, without the exchange of many words. Thorpe talked to his horse, and she meditated by turns on broken promises and broken arches, phaetons and false hangings, Tilneys and trap-doors. As they entered Argyle Buildings, however, she was roused by this address from her companion, "Who is that girl who looked at you so hard as she went by?"

"Who? where?"

"On the right-hand pavement: she must be almost out of sight now." Catherine looked round, and saw Miss Tilney leaning on her brother's arm, walking slowly down the street. She saw them both looking back at her. "Stop, stop, Mr. Thorpe," she impatiently cried, "it is Miss Tilney; it is indeed. How could you tell me they were gone? Stop, stop, I will get out this moment and go to them." But to what purpose did she speak? Thorpe only lashed his horse into a brisker trot; the Tilneys, who had soon ceased to look after her, were in a moment out of sight round the corner of Laura Place, and in another moment, she was herself whisked into the Market Place. Still, however, and during the length of another street, she entreated him to stop. "Pray, pray stop, Mr. Thorpe. I cannot go on, I will not go on; I must go back to Miss Tilney." But Mr. Thorpe only laughed, smacked his whip, encouraged his horse, made odd noises, and drove on; and Catherine, angry and vexed as she was, having no power of getting away, was obliged to give up the point and submit. Her reproaches, how-ever, were not spared. "How could you deceive me so, Mr. Thorpe? How could you say that you saw them driving up the Lansdown Road? I would not have had it happen so for the world. They must think it so strange, so rude of me, to go by them, too, without saying a word! You do not know how vexed I am. I shall have no pleasure at Clifton, nor in anything else. I had rather, ten thousand times rather, get out now, and walk back to them. How could you say, you saw them driving out in a phaeton?" Thorpe defended himself very stoutly, declared he had never seen two men so much alike in his life, and would hardly give up the point of its having been Tilney himself.

Their drive, even when this subject was over, was not likely to be very agreeable. Catherine's complaisance was no longer what it had been in their former airing. She listened reluctantly, and her replies were short. Blaize Castle remained her only comfort; towards *that*, she still looked at intervals with pleasure; though rather than be disappointed of the prom-ised walk, and especially rather than be thought ill of by the Tilneys, she would willingly have given up all the happiness which its walls could supply: the happiness of a progress through a long suite of lofty rooms, exhibiting the remains of magnificent furniture, though now for many years deserted: the happiness of being stopped in their way along narrow, winding vaults, by a low, grated door; or even of having their lamp, their only lamp, extinguished by a sudden gust of wind, and of being left in total darkness. In the meanwhile, they proceeded on their journey without any mischance: and were within view of the town of Keynsham, when a halloo from Morland, who was behind them, made his friend pull up, to know what was the matter. The others then came close enough for conversation; and Morland said, "We had better go back, Thorpe; it is too late to go on to-day; your sister thinks so as well as I. We have been exactly an hour coming from Pulteney Street, very little more than seven miles; and, I suppose, we have at least eight more to go. It will never do. We set out a great deal too late. We had much better put it off till another day, and turn round."

"It is all one to me," replied Thorpe, rather angrily; and instantly turning his horse, they were on their way back to Bath.

"If your brother had not got such a d—— beast to drive," said he soon afterwards, "we might have done it very well. My horse would have trotted to Clifton within the hour, if left to himself, and I have almost broke my arm pulling him in to the cursed broken-winded jade's pace. Morland is a fool for not keeping a horse and gig of his own."

"No, he is not," said Catherine warmly; "for I am sure he could not afford it."

"And why cannot he afford it?"

"Because he has not money enough."

"And whose fault is that?"

"Nobody's that I know of." Thorpe then said something in the loud, incoherent way to which he had often recourse, about its being a d—— thing to be miserly; and that if people who rolled in money could not afford things, he did not know who could, which Catherine did not even endeavour to understand. Disappointed of what was to have been the consolation of her first disappointment, she was less and less disposed either to be agreeable herself, or to find her companion so; and they returned to Pulteney Street without her speaking twenty words.

As she entered the house, the footman told her, that a gentleman and lady had called and inquired for her a few minutes after setting off; that, when he told them she was gone out with Mr. Thorpe, the lady had asked whether any message had been left for her, and on saying no, had felt for a card, but said she had none about her, and went away. Pondering over these heart-rending tidings, Catherine walked slowly upstairs. At the head of them she was met by Mr. Allen, who, on hearing the reason of their speedy return, said, "I am glad your brother had so much sense; I am glad you are come back. It was a strange wild scheme."

They all spent the evening together at Thorpe's. Catherine was disturbed and out of spirits; but Isabella seemed to find a pool of commerce in the fate of which she shared, by private partnership, with Morland, a very good equivalent for the quiet and country air of an inn at Clifton. Her satisfaction, too, in not being at the Lower Rooms, was spoken more than once. "How I pity the poor creatures that are going there! How glad I am that I am not amongst them! I wonder whether it will be a full ball or not! They have not begun dancing yet. I would not be there for all the world. It is so delightful to have an evening now and then to one's self. I dare say it will not be a very good ball. I know the Mitchells will not be there. I am sure I pity everybody that is. But I dare say, Mr. Morland, you long to be at it, do not you? I am sure you do. Well, pray do not let anybody here be a restraint on you. I dare say we could do very well without you, but you men think yourselves of such consequence."

Catherine could almost have accused Isabella of being wanting in tenderness towards herself and her sorrows, so very little did they appear to dwell on her mind, and so very inadequate was the comfort she offered. "Do not be so dull, my dearest creature," she whispered. "You will quite break my heart. It was amazingly shocking, to be sure, but the Tilneys were entirely to blame. Why were they not more punctual? It was dirty, indeed, but what did that signify? I am sure John and I should have not minded it. I never mind going through anything where a friend is concerned; that is my disposition, and John is just the same; he has amazing strong feelings. Good heavens! what a delightful hand you have got! Kings, I vow! I never was so happy in my life! I would fifty times rather you should have them than myself."

And now I may dismiss my heroine to the sleepless couch which is the true heroine's portion; to a pillow strewed with thorns and wet with tears. And lucky may she think herself, if she get another good night's rest in the course of the next three months.

Chapter 12

"Mrs. Allen," said Catherine, the next morning, "will there be any harm in my calling on Miss Tilney to-day? I snall not be easy till I have explained everything."

"Go, by all means, my dear; only put on a white gown. Miss Tilney always wears white."

Catherine cheerfully complied; and, being properly equipped, was more impatient than ever to be at the Pump Room, that she might inform herself of General Tilney's lodgings; for though she believed they were in Milsom Street, she was not certain of the house, and Mrs. Allen's wavering convictions only made it more doubtful. To Milsom Street she was directed; and having made herself perfect in the number, hastened away with eager steps and a beating heart to pay her visit, explain her conduct, and be forgiven: tripping lightly through the churchyard, and resolutely turning away her eyes, that she might not be obliged to see her beloved Isabella, and her dear family, who, she had reason to believe, were in a shop hard by. She reached the house without any impediment, looked at the number, knocked at the door, and inquired for Miss Tilney. The man believed Miss Tilney to be at home, but was not quite certain. Would she be pleased to send up her name? She gave her card. In a few minutes the servant returned, and with a look which did not quite confirm his words, said he had been mistaken, for that Miss Tilney had walked out. Catherine, with a blush of mortification, left the house. She left almost persuaded that Miss Tilney *was* at home, and too much offended to admit her; and as she retired down the street, could not withhold one glance at the drawing-room windows, in expectation of seeing her there; but no one appeared at them. At the bottom of the street, however, she looked back again, and then, not at a window, but issuing from the door, she saw Miss Tilney herself. She was followed by a gentleman whom Catherine believed to be her father, and they turned up towards Edgar's Buildings. Catherine, in deep mortification, proceeded on her way. She could almost be angry herself at such angry incivility; but she checked the resentful sensation, she remembered her own ignorance. She knew not how such an offence as hers might be classed by the laws of worldly politeness, to what a degree of unforgiveness it might with propriety lead, nor to what rigours of rudeness in return it might justly make her amenable. Dejected and humbled, she had even some thoughts of not going with the others to the theatre that night; but, it must be confessed that they were not of long continuance; for she soon recollected, in the first place, that she was without any excuse for staying at home; and, in the second, that it was a play she wanted very much to see. To the theatre accordingly they all went; no Tilneys appeared to plague or please her; she feared that amongst the many perfections of the family a fondness for plays was not to be ranked, but perhaps it was because they were habituated to the finer performances of the London stage, which she knew, on Isabella's authority, rendered everything else of the kind "quite horrid." She was not deceived in her own expectation of pleasure: the comedy so well suspended her care, that no one observing her during the first four acts would have supposed she had any wretchedness about her. On the beginning of the fifth, however, the sudden view of Mr. Henry Tilney and his father joining a party in the opposite box recalled her to anxiety and distress. The stage could no longer excite genuine merriment, no longer keep her whole attention. Every other look upon an average was directed towards the opposite box; and for the space of two entire scenes did she thus watch Henry Tilney, without being once able to catch his eye. No longer could he be suspected of indifference for a play; his notice was never withdrawn from the stage during two whole scenes. At length, however, he did look towards her, and he bowed, but such a bow! No smile, no continued observance attended it: his eyes were immediately returned to their former direction. Catherine was restlessly miserable; she could almost have run round to the box in which he sat, and forced him to hear her explanation. Feelings rather natural than heroic possessed her. Instead of considering her own dignity injured by this ready condemnation; instead of proudly resolving in conscious innocence, to show her resentment towards him who could harbour a doubt of it, to leave to him all the trouble of seeking an explanation, and to enlighten him on the past only by avoiding his sight, or flirting with somebody else, she took to herself all the shame of misconduct, or, at least, of its appearance, and was only eager for an opportunity of explaining its cause.

The play concluded, the curtain fell; Henry Tilney was no longer to be seen where he had hitherto sat, but his father remained, and perhaps he might be now coming round to their box. She was right: in a few minutes he appeared, and making his way through the then thinning rows, spoke with like calm politeness to Mrs. Allen and her friend. Not with such calmness was he answered by the latter. "Oh, Mr. Tilney, I have been quite wild to speak to you, and make my apologies. You must have thought me so rude; but indeed it was not my own fault. Was it, Mrs. Allen? Did not they tell me that Mr. Tilney and his sister were gone out in a phaeton together? And then what could I do? But I had ten thousand times rather have been with you. Now, had not I, Mrs. Allen?"

"My dear, you tumble my gown," was Mrs. Allen's reply.

Her assurance, however, standing sole as it did, was not thrown away; it brought a more cordial, more natural smile into his countenance, and he replied in a tone which retained only a little affected reserve. "We were much obliged to you, at any rate, for wishing us a pleasant walk after our passing you in Argyle Street. You were so kind as to look back on purpose."

"But indeed, I did not wish you a pleasant walk, I never thought of such a thing; but I begged Mr. Thorpe so earnestly to stop; I called out to him as soon as ever I saw you. Now, Mrs. Allen, did not—— Oh! you were not there. But, indeed, I did; and, if Mr. Thorpe would only have stopped, I would have jumped out and run after you."

Is there a Henry in the world who could be insensible to such a declaration? Henry Tilney, at least, was not. With a yet sweeter smile, he said everything that need be said of his sister's concern, regret, and dependence on Catherine's honour. "Oh, do not say Miss Tilney was not angry," cried Catherine, "because I know she was; for she would not see me this morning when I called. I saw her walk out of the house the next minute after my leaving it. I was hurt, but I was not affronted. Perhaps you did not know I had been there."

"I was not within at the time; but I heard of it from Eleanor, and she has been wishing ever since to see you, to explain the reason of such incivility; but perhaps, I can do it as well. It was nothing more than that my father——. They were just preparing to walk out, and he being hurried for time, and not caring to have it put off, made a point of her being

denied. That was all, I do assure you. She was very much vexed, and
meant to make her apology as soon as possible."

Catherine's mind was greatly eased by this information, yet a something
of solicitude remained, from which sprang the following question, thoroughly artless in itself, though rather distressing to the gentleman: "But,
Mr. Tilney, why were *you* less generous than your sister? If she felt such
confidence in my good intentions, and could suppose it to be only a mistake, why should *you* be so ready to take offence?"

"Me! I take offence!"

"Nay, I am sure by your look, when you came into the box, you were
angry."

"I angry! I could have no right!"

"Well, nobody would have thought you had no right who saw your
face."

He replied by asking her to make room for him and talking of the play.
He remained with them some time, and was only too agreeable for Catherine to be contented when he went away. Before they parted, however,
it was agreed that the projected walk should be taken as soon as possible;
and, setting aside the misery of his quitting their box, she was, upon the
whole, left one of the happiest creatures in the world.

While talking to each other, she had observed with some surprise that
John Thorpe, who was never in the same part of the house for ten minutes
together, was engaged in conversation with General Tilney; and she felt
something more than surprise, when she thought she could perceive herself
the object of their attention and discourse. What could they have to say
of her? She feared General Tilney did not like her appearance. She found
it was implied in his preventing her admittance to his daughter, rather
than postpone his own walk a few minutes. "How came Mr. Thorpe to
know your father?" was her anxious inquiry, as she pointed them out to
her companion. He knew nothing about it: but his father, like every military man, had a very large acquaintance.

When the entertainment was over, Thorpe came to assist them in getting out. Catherine was the immediate object of his gallantry; and, while
they waited in the lobby for a chair, he prevented the inquiry which had
travelled from her heart almost to the tip of her tongue, by asking in a
consequential manner, whether she had seen him talking with General
Tilney. "He is a fine old fellow, upon my soul! Stout, active; looks as
young as his son. I have a great regard for him, I assure you. A gentlemanlike, good sort of fellow as ever lived."

"But how came you to know him?"

"Know him! There are few people much about town that I do not know.
I have met him for ever at the Bedford; and I knew his face again to-day
the moment he came into the billiard-room. One of the best players we
have, by the bye; and we had a little touch together, though I was almost
afraid of him at first. The odds were five to four against me; and, if I had
not made one of the cleanest strokes that perhaps ever was made in this

world—I took his ball exactly—but I could not make you understand it without a table: however, I *did* beat him. A very fine fellow; as rich as a Jew. I should like to dine with him. I dare say he gives famous dinners. But what do you think we have been talking of? You. Yes, by heavens, and the General thinks you the finest girl in Bath."

"Oh, nonsense! How can you say so?"

"And what do you think I said?" (lowering his voice). " 'Well done, General,' said I, 'I am quite of your mind.' "

Here Catherine, who was much less gratified by his admiration than by General Tilney's, was not sorry to be called away by Mr. Allen. Thorpe, however, would see her to her chair, and, till she entered it, continued the same kind of delicate flattery, in spite of her entreating him to have done.

That General Tilney, instead of disliking, should admire her, was very delightful; and she joyfully thought that there was not one of the family whom she need now fear to meet. The evening had done more, much more, for her than could have been expected.

Chapter 13

MONDAY, Tuesday, Wednesday, Thursday, Friday and Saturday have now passed in review before the reader; the events of each day, its hopes and fears, mortifications and pleasures, have been separately stated, and the pangs of Sunday only now remain to be described, and close the week. The Clifton scheme had been deferred, not relinquished; and on the afternoon's Crescent of this day it was brought forward again. In a private consultation between Isabella and James, the former of whom had particularly set her heart upon going, and the latter no less anxiously placed his upon pleasing her, it was agreed that, provided the weather was fair, the party should take place on the following morning; and they were to set off very early, in order to be at home in good time. The affair thus determined, and Thorpe's approbation secured, Catherine only remained to be apprised of it. She had left them for a few minutes to speak to Miss Tilney. In that interval the plan was completed, and as soon as she came again, her agreement was demanded; but instead of the gay acquiescence expected by Isabella, Catherine looked grave, was very sorry, but could not go. The engagement which ought to have kept her from joining in the former attempt would make it impossible for her to accompany them now. She had that moment settled with Miss Tilney to take their promised walk to-morrow; it was quite determined, and she would not, upon any account, retract. But that she *must* and *should* retract was instantly the eager cry of both the Thorpes; they must go to Clifton to-morrow, they would not go without her, it would be nothing to put off a mere walk for one day longer, and they would not hear of a refusal. Catherine was distressed, but not subdued. "Do not urge me, Isabella. I am engaged to Miss Tilney. I cannot go." This availed nothing. Th-

same arguments assailed her again; she must go, she should go, and they would not hear of a refusal. "It would be so easy to tell Miss Tilney that you had just been reminded of a prior engagement, and must only beg to put off the walk till Tuesday."

"No, it would not be easy. I could not do it. There has been no prior engagement." But Isabella became only more and more urgent; calling on her in the most affectionate manner; addressing her by the most endearing names. She was sure her dearest, sweetest Catherine would not seriously refuse such a trifling request to a friend who loved her so dearly. She knew her beloved Catherine to have so feeling a heart, so sweet a temper, to be easily persuaded by those she loved. But all in vain; Catherine felt herself to be in the right, and though pained by such tender, such flattering supplication, could not allow it to influence her. Isabella then tried another method. She reproached her with having more affection for Miss Tilney, though she had known her so little a while, than for her best and oldest friends; with being grown cold and indifferent, in short, towards herself. "I cannot help being jealous, Catherine, when I see myself slighted for strangers; I, who love you so excessively! When once my affections are placed, it is not in the power of anything to change them. But I believe my feelings are stronger than anybody's; I am sure they are too strong for my own peace; and to see myself supplanted in your friendship by strangers does cut me to the quick, I own. These Tilneys seem to swallow up everything else."

Catherine thought this reproach equally strange and unkind. Was it the part of a friend thus to expose her feelings to the notice of others? Isabella appeared to her ungenerous and selfish, regardless of everything but her own gratification. These painful ideas crossed her mind, though she said nothing. Isabella, in the meanwhile, had applied her handkerchief to her eyes; and Morland, miserable at such a sight, could not help saying, "Nay, Catherine, I think you cannot stand out any longer now. The sacrifice is not much; and to oblige such a friend, I shall think you quite unkind, if you still refuse."

This was the first time of her brother's openly siding against her; and anxious to avoid his displeasure, she proposed a compromise. If they would only put off their scheme till Tuesday, which they might easily do, as it depended only on themselves, she could go with them, and everybody might then be satisfied. But "No, no, no!" was the immediate answer; "that could not be, for Thorpe did not know that he might not go to town on Tuesday." Catherine was sorry, but could do no more; and a short silence ensued, which was broken by Isabella, who, in a voice of cold resentment, said, "Very well, then there is an end of the party. If Catherine does not go, I cannot. I cannot be the only woman. I would not upon any account in the world do so improper a thing."

"Catherine, you must go," said James.

"But why cannot Mr. Thorpe drive one of his other sisters? I dare say either of them would like to go."

"Thank ye," cried Thorpe; "but I did not come to Bath to drive my sisters about and look like a fool. No, if you do not go, d—— me if I do. I only go for the sake of driving you."

"That is a compliment which gives me no pleasure." But her words were lost on Thorpe, who had turned abruptly away.

The three others still continued together, talking in a most uncomfortable manner to poor Catherine; sometimes not a word was said, sometimes she was again attacked with supplications or reproaches, and her arm was still linked within Isabella's, though their hearts were at war. At one moment she was softened, at another irritated; always distressed, but always steady.

"I did not think you had been so obstinate, Catherine," said James; "you were not used to be so hard to persuade; you once were the kindest, best-tempered of my sisters."

"I hope I am not less so now," she replied, very feelingly; "but indeed I cannot go. If I am wrong, I am doing what I believe to be right."

"I suspect," said Isabella, in a low voice, "there is no great struggle."

Catherine's heart swelled; she drew away her arm, and Isabella made no opposition. Thus passed a long ten minutes, till they were again joined by Thorpe, who, coming to them with a gayer look, said, "Well, I have settled the matter, and now we may all go to-morrow with a safe conscience. I have been to Miss Tilney, and made your excuses."

"You have not!" cried Catherine.

"I have upon my soul. Left her this moment. Told her you had sent me to say, that having just recollected a prior engagement of going to Clifton with us to-morrow you could not have the pleasure of walking with her till Tuesday. She said very well, Tuesday was just as convenient to her; so there is an end of all our difficulties. A pretty good thought of mine, eh?"

Isabella's countenance was once more all smiles and good humour, and James, too, looked happy again.

"A most heavenly thought, indeed! Now, my sweet Catherine, all our distresses are over, you are honourably acquitted, and we shall have a most delightful party."

"This will not do," said Catherine; "I cannot submit to this. I must run after Miss Tilney directly and set her right."

Isabella, however, caught hold of one hand, Thorpe of the other; and remonstrances poured in from all three. Even James was quite angry. When everything was settled, when Miss Tilney herself said that Tuesday would suit her as well, it was quite ridiculous, quite absurd, to make any further objection.

"I do not care. Mr. Thorpe had no business to invent any such message. If I had thought it right to put it off, I could have spoken to Miss Tilney myself. This is only doing it in a ruder way; and how do I know that Mr. Thorpe has——; he may be mistaken again, perhaps. He led me into one act of rudeness by his mistake on Friday. Let me go, Mr. Thorpe; Isabella, do not hold me."

Thorpe told her it would be in vain to go after the Tilneys; they were turning the corner into Brook Street when he had overtaken them, and were at home by this time.

"Then I will go after them," said Catherine; "wherever they are, I will go after them. It does not signify talking. If I could not be persuaded into doing what I thought wrong, I never will be tricked into it." And with these words she broke away and hurried off. Thorpe would have darted after her, but Morland withheld him. "Let her go, let her go, if she will go. She is as obstinate as——"

Morland never finished the simile, for it could hardly have been a proper one.

Away walked Catherine in great agitation, as fast as the crowd would permit her, fearful of being pursued, yet determined to persevere. As she walked, she reflected on what had passed. It was painful to her to disappoint and displease them, particularly to displease her brother; but she could not repent her resistance. Setting her own inclination apart, to have failed a second time in her engagement to Miss Tilney, to have retracted a promise voluntarily made only five minutes before, and on a false pretence too, must have been wrong. She had not been withstanding them on selfish principles alone, she had not consulted merely her own gratification; *that* might have been ensured in some degree by the excursion itself, by seeing Blaize Castle; no, she had attended to what was due to others, and to her own character in their opinion. Her conviction of being right, however, was not enough to restore her composure; till she had spoken to Miss Tilney, she could not be at ease; and quickening her pace when she got clear of the Crescent, she almost ran over the remaining ground till she gained the top of Milsom Street. So rapid had been her movements, that in spite of the Tilneys' advantage in the outset, they were but just turning into their lodgings as she came within view of them; and the servant still remaining at the open door, she used only the ceremony of saying that she must speak with Miss Tilney that moment, and hurrying by him proceeded upstairs. Then, opening the first door before her, which happened to be the right, she immediately found herself in the drawing-room with General Tilney, his son and daughter. Her explanation, defective only in being—from her irritation of nerves, and shortness of breath—no explanation at all, was instantly given. "I am come in a great hurry—it was all a mistake; I never promised to go; I told them from the first I could not go; I ran away in a great hurry to explain it; I did not care what you thought of me; I would not stay for the servant."

The business, however, though not perfectly elucidated by this speech, soon ceased to be a puzzle. Catherine found that John Thorpe *had* given the message; and Miss Tilney had no scruples in owning herself greatly surprised by it. But whether her brother had still exceeded her in resentment, Catherine, though she instinctively addressed herself as much to one as to the other in her vindication, had no means of knowing. Whatever might have been felt before her arrival, her eager declarations immediately made every look and sentence as friendly as she could desire.

The affair thus happily settled, she was introduced by Miss Tilney to her father, and received by him with such ready, such solicitous polite-ness, as recalled Thorpe's information to her mind, and made her think with pleasure that he might be sometimes depended on. To such anxious attention was the General's civility carried, that, not aware of her extraordinary swiftness in entering the house, he was quite angry with the servant whose neglect had reduced her to open the door of the apart-ment herself. "What did William mean by it? He should make a point of inquiring into the matter." And if Catherine had not most warmly asserted his innocence, it seemed likely that William would lose the favour of his master for ever, if not his place, by her rapidity.

After sitting with them a quarter of an hour, she rose to take leave, and was then most agreeably surprised by General Tilney's asking her if if she would do his daughter the honour of dining and spending the rest of the day with her. Miss Tilney added her own wishes. Catherine was greatly obliged; but it was quite out of her power, Mr. and Mrs. Allen would expect her back every moment. The General declared he could say no more; the claims of Mr. and Mrs. Allen were not to be superseded; but on some other day, he trusted, when longer notice could be given, they would not refuse to spare her to her friend. "Oh, no; Catherine was sure they would not have the least objection and she should have great pleasure in coming." The General attended her himself to the street door, saying everything gallant as they went downstairs, admiring the elasticity of her walk, which corresponded exactly with the spirit of her dancing, and making her one of the most graceful bows she had ever be-held when they parted.

Catherine, delighted by all that had passed, proceeded gaily to Pulteney Street, walking, as she concluded, with great elasticity, though she had never thought of it before. She reached home without seeing anything more of the offended party; and now that she had been triumphant throughout, had carried her point, and was secure of her walk, she began (as the flutter of her spirits subsided) to doubt whether she had been perfectly right. A sacrifice was always noble; and if she had given way to their entreaties, she should have been spared the distressing idea of a friend displeased, a brother angry, and a scheme of great happiness to both destroyed, perhaps through her means. To ease her mind, and ascer-tain by the opinion of an unprejudiced person what her own conduct had really been, she took occasion to mention before Mr. Allen the half-settled scheme of her brother and the Thorpes for the following day. Mr. Allen caught at it directly. "Well," said he, "and do you think of going too?"

"No; I had just engaged myself to walk with Miss Tilney before they told me of it; and therefore, you know, I could not go with them, could I?"

"No, certainly not; and I am glad you do not think of it. These schemes are not at all the thing. Young men and women driving about the country in open carriages! Now and then it is very well; but going to inns and public places together! It is not right; and I wonder Mrs. Thorpe should allow it. I am glad you do not think of going; I am sure Mrs. Morland would not be pleased. Mrs. Allen, are not you of my way of thinking? Do not you think these kind of projects objectionable?"

"Yes, very much so, indeed. Open carriages are nasty things. A clean gown is not five minutes' wear in them. You are splashed getting in and getting out; and the wind takes your hair and your bonnet in every direction. I hate an open carriage myself."

"I know you do; but that is not the question. Do not you think it has an odd appearance, if young ladies are frequently driven about in them by young men, to whom they are not even related?"

"Yes, my dear, a very odd appearance indeed. I cannot bear to see it."

"Dear madam," cried Catherine, "then why did not you tell me so before? I am sure if I had known it to be improper I would not have gone with Mr. Thorpe at all; but I always hoped you would tell me, if you thought I was doing wrong."

"And so I should, my dear, you may depend on it; for, as I told Mrs. Morland at parting, I would always do the best for you in my power. But one must not be over particular. Young people *will* be young people, as your good mother says herself. You know I wanted you, when we first came, not to buy that sprigged muslin, but you would. Young people do not like to be always thwarted."

"But this was something of real consequence; and I do not think you would have found me hard to persuade."

"As far as it has gone hitherto, there is no harm done," said Mr. Allen: "and I would only advise you, my dear, not to go out with Mr. Thorpe any more."

"That is just what I was going to say," added his wife.

Catherine, relieved for herself, felt uneasy for Isabella; and after a moment's thought, asked Mr. Allen whether it would not be both proper and kind in her to write to Miss Thorpe, and explain the indecorum of which she must be as insensible as herself; for she considered that Isabella might otherwise perhaps be going to Clifton the next day, in spite of what had passed. Mr. Allen, however, discouraged her from doing any such thing. "You had better leave her alone, my dear, she is old enough to know what she is about: and if not, has a mother to advise her. Mrs. Thorpe is too indulgent beyond a doubt: but, however, you had better not interfere. She and your brother choose to go, and you will be only getting ill-will."

Catherine submitted; and though sorry to think that Isabella should be doing wrong, felt greatly relieved by Mr. Allen's approbation of her own conduct, and truly rejoiced to be preserved by his advice from the danger of falling into such an error herself. Her escape from being one or the party to Clifton was now an escape indeed; for what would the Tilneys have thought of her, if she had broken her promise to them in order to do what was wrong in itself—if she had been guilty of one breach of propriety only to enable her to be guilty of another?

Chapter 14

THE next morning was fair, and Catherine almost expected another attack from the assembled party. With Mr. Allen to support her, she felt no dread of the event; but she would gladly be spared a contest where victory itself was painful, and was heartily rejoiced, therefore, at neither seeing nor hearing anything of them. The Tilneys called for her at the appointed time, and no new difficulty arising, no sudden recollection, no unexpected summons, no impertinent intrusion to disconcert their measures, my heroine was most unnaturally able to fulfil her engagement, though it was made with the hero himself. They determined on walking round Beechen Cliff, that noble hill, whose beautiful verdure and hanging coppice render it so striking an object from almost every opening in Bath.

"I never look at it," said Catherine, as they walked along the side of the river, "without thinking of the south of France."

"You have been abroad, then?" said Henry, a little surprised.

"Oh! no, I only mean what I have read about. It always puts me in mind of the country that Emily and her father travelled through in *The Mysteries of Udolpho*. But you never read novels, I dare say?"

"Why not?"

"Because they are not clever enough for you; gentlemen read better books."

"The person, be it gentleman or lady, who has not pleasure in a good novel, must be intolerably stupid. I have read all Mrs. Radcliffe's works, and most of them with great pleasure. *The Mysteries of Udolpho*, when I had once begun it, I could not lay down again; I remember finishing it in two days, my hair standing on end the whole time."

"Yes," added Miss Tilney; "and I remember that you undertook to read it aloud to me; and that when I was called away for only five minutes to answer a note, instead of waiting for me, you took the volume into the Hermitage Walk, and I was obliged to stay till you had finished it."

"Thank you, Eleanor; a most honourable testimony. You see, Miss Morland, the injustice of your suspicions. Here was I, in my eagerness to get on, refusing to wait only five minutes for my sister; breaking the promise I had made of reading it aloud, and keeping her in suspense at a most interesting part, by running away with the volume, which, you are to observe, was her own, particularly her own. I am proud when I reflect on it, and I think it must establish me in your good opinion."

"I am very glad to hear it, indeed; and now I shall never be ashamed of liking *Udolpho* myself. But I really thought before, young men despised novels amazingly."

"It is *amazingly;* it may well suggest *amazement* if they do, for they read nearly as many as women. I, myself, have read hundreds and hundreds. Do not imagine that you can cope with me in a knowledge of Julias and Louisas. If we proceed to particulars, and engage in the never-ceasing inquiry of 'Have you read this?' and 'Have you read that?' I shall soon leave you as far behind me as—what shall I say? I want an appropriate simile; as far as your friend Emily herself left poor Valancourt when she went with her aunt into Italy. Consider how many years I have had the start of you. I had entered on my studies at Oxford, while you were a good little girl working your sampler at home!"

"Not very good, I am afraid. But now, really, do not you think *Udolpho* the nicest book in the world?"

"The nicest; by which I suppose you mean the neatest. That must depend upon the binding."

"Henry," said Miss Tilney, "you are very impertinent. Miss Morland, he is treating you exactly as he does his sister. He is for ever finding fault with me for some incorrectness of language, and now he is taking the same liberty with you. The word 'nicest,' as you used it, did not suit him; and you had better change it as soon as you can, or we shall be over-powered with Johnson and Blair all the rest of the way."

"I am sure," cried Catherine, "I did not mean to say anything wrong; but it *is* a nice book, and why should not I call it so?"

"Very true," said Henry, "and this is a very nice day; and we are taking a very nice walk; and you are two very nice young ladies. Oh! it is a very nice word, indeed! It does for everything. Originally, perhaps, it was applied only to express neatness, propriety, delicacy, or refinement; people were nice in their dress, in their sentiments, or their choice. But now every commendation on every subject is comprised in that one word."

"While, in fact," cried his sister, "it ought only to be applied to you, without any commendation at all. You are more nice than wise. Come, Miss Morland, let us leave him to meditate over our faults in the utmost propriety of diction, while we praise *Udolpho* in whatever terms we like best. It is a most interesting work. You are fond of that kind of reading?"

"To say the truth, I do not much like any other."

"Indeed!"

"That is, I can read poetry and plays, and things of that sort, and do not dsilike travels. But history, real solemn history, I cannot be interested in. Can you?"

"Yes, I am fond of history."

"I wish I were too. I read it a little as a duty; but it tells me nothing that does not either vex or weary me. The quarrels of popes and kings, with wars and pestilences in every page; the men all so good for nothing, and hardly any women at all, it is very tiresome; and yet I often think it odd that it should be so dull, for a great deal of it must be invention. The speeches that are put into the heroes' mouths, their thoughts and designs; the chief of all this must be invention, and invention is what delights me in other books."

"Historians you think," said Miss Tilney, "are not happy in their flights of fancy. They display imagination without raising interest. I am fond of history. and am very well contented to take the false with the true. In the principal facts they have sources of intelligence in former histories and records, which may be as much depended on, I conclude, as anything that does not actually pass under one's own observation; and as for the little embellishments you speak of, they are embellishments, and I like them as such. If a speech be well drawn up, I read it with pleasure, by whomsoever it may be made; and probably with much greater, if the production of Mr. Hume or Mr. Robertson, than if the genuine words of Caractacus, Agricola, or Alfred the Great."

"You are fond of history! And so are Mr. Allen and my father; and I have two brothers who do not dislike it. So many instances within my small circle of friends is remarkable! At this rate, I shall not pity the writers of history any longer. If people like to read their books, it is all very well; but to be at so much trouble in filling great volumes, which, as I used to think, nobody would willingly ever look into, to be labouring only for the torment of little boys and girls, always struck me as a hard fate; and though I know it is all very right and necessary, I have often wondered at the person's courage that could sit down on purpose to do it."

"That little boys and girls should be tormented," said Henry, "is what no one at all acquainted with human nature in a civilised state can deny; but in behalf of our most distinguished historians, I must observe, that they might well be offended at being supposed to have no higher aim; and that by their method and style they are perfectly well qualified to torment readers of the most advanced reason and mature time of life. I use the verb 'to torment,' as I observed to be your own method, instead of 'to instruct,' supposing them to be now admitted as synonymous."

"You think me foolish to call instruction a torment; but if you had been as much used as myself to hear poor little children first learning their letters, and then learning to spell, if you had ever seen how stupid they can be for a whole morning together, and how tired my poor mother is at the end of it, as I am in the habit of seeing almost every day of my life at home, you would allow, that to *torment* and to *instruct* might sometimes be used as synonymous words."

"Very probably. But historians are not accountable for the difficulty of learning to read; and even you yourself, who do not altogether seem particularly friendly to very severe, very intense application, may perhaps be brought to acknowledge that it is very well worth while to be tormented for two or three years of one's life, for the sake of being able to read all the rest of it. Consider, if reading had not been taught, Mrs. Radcliffe would have written in vain, or, perhaps, might not have written at all."

Catherine assented; and a very warm panegyric from her on that lady's merits closed the subject. The Tilneys were soon engaged in another, on which she had nothing to say. They were viewing the country with the eyes of persons accustomed to drawing, and decided on its capability of being formed into pictures, with all the eagerness of real taste. Here Catherine was quite lost. She knew nothing of drawing—nothing of taste; and she listened to them with an attention which brought her little profit, for they talked in phrases which conveyed scarcely any idea to her. The little which she could understand, however, appeared to contradict the very few notions she had entertained on the matter before. It seemed as if a good view were no longer to be taken from the top of a high hill, and that a clear blue sky was no longer a proof of a fine day. She was heartily ashamed of her ignorance—a misplaced shame. Where poeple wish to attach, they should always be ignorant. To come with a well-informed mind, is to come with an inability of administering to the vanity of others, which a sensible person would always wish to avoid. A woman, especially, if she have the misfortune of knowing anything, should conceal it as well as she can.

The advantages of natural folly in a beautiful girl have been already set forth by the capital pen of a sister author; and to her treatment of the subject I will only add, in justice to men, that though, to the larger and more trifling part of the sex, imbecility in females is a great enchancement of their personal charms, there is a portion of them too reasonable, and too well informed themselves, to desire anything more in woman than ignorance. But Catherine did not know her own advantages; did not know that a good-looking girl with an affectionate heart, and a very ignorant mind, cannot fail of attracting a clever young man, unless circumstances are particularly untoward. In the present instance, she confessed and lamented her want of knowledge; declared that she would give anything in the world to be able to draw; and a lecture on the picturesque immediately followed, in which his instructions were so clear that she soon began to see beauty in everything admired by him; and her attention was so earnest, that he became perfectly satisfied of her having a great deal of natural taste. He talked of foregrounds, distances, and second distances; side-screens and perspectives; lights and shades; and Catherine was so hopeful a scholar, that when they gained the top of Beechen Cliff, she voluntarily rejected the whole city of Bath, as unworthy to make part of a landscape. Delighted with her progress, and fearful of wearying her with too much wisdom at once, Henry suffered the subject to decline, and, by an easy transition from a piece of rocky fragment, and the withered oak which he had placed near its summit, to oaks in general—to forests, the enclosure of them, waste lands, crown lands and government—he shortly found himself arrived at politics; and from politics it was an easy step to silence. The general pause which succeeded his short disquisition on the state of the nation was put an end to by Catherine, who, in rather a solemn tone of voice, uttered these words, "I have heard that something very shocking indeed will soon come out in London."

Miss Tilney, to whom this was chiefly addressed, was startled, and hastily replied, "Indeed! And of what nature?"

"That I do not know, nor who is the author. I have only heard that it is to be more horrible than anything we have met with yet."

"Good heaven! Where could you hear of such a thing?"

"A particular friend of mine had an account of it in a letter from London yesterday. It is to be uncommonly dreadful. I shall expect murder and everything of the kind."

"You speak with astonishing composure. But I hope your friend's accounts have been exaggerated; and if such a design is known beforehand, proper measures will undoubtedly be taken by government to prevent its coming to effect."

"Government," said Henry, endeavouring not to smile, "neither desires nor dares to interfere in such matters. There must be murder, and government cares not how much."

The ladies stared. He laughed, and added, "Come, shall I make you understand each other, or leave you to puzzle out an explanation as you can? No, I will be noble. I will prove myself a man no less by the generosity of my soul, than the clearness of my head. I have no patience with such of my sex as disdain to let themselves sometimes down to the comprehension of yours. Perhaps the abilities of women are neither sound nor acute, neither vigorous nor keen. Perhaps they may want observation, discernment, judgment, fire, genius and wit."

"Miss Morland, do not mind what he says; but have the goodness to satisfy me as to this dreadful riot."

"Riot! What riot?"

"My dear Eleanor, the riot is only in your own brain. The confusion there is scandalous. Miss Morland has been talking of nothing more dreadful than a new publication which is shortly to come out, in three duodecimo volumes, two hundred and seventy-six pages in each, with a frontispiece to the first, of two tombstones and a lantern—do you understand? And you, Miss Morland—my stupid sister has mistaken all your clearest expressions. You talked of expected horrors in London; and instead of instantly conceiving, as any rational creature would have done, that such words could relate only to a circulating library, she immediately pictured to herself a mob of three thousand men assembling in St. George's Fields; the Bank attacked, the Tower threatened, the streets of London flowing with blood, a detachment of the 12th Light Dragoons (the hopes of the nation) called up from Northampton to quell the insurgents, and the gallant Captain Frederick Tilney, in the moment of charging at the head of his troop, knocked off his horse by a brick-bat from an upper window. Forgive her stupidity. The fears of the sister have added to the weakness of the woman, but she is by no means a simpleton in general."

Catherine looked grave. "And now, Henry," said Miss Tilney, "that you have made us understand each other, you may as well make Miss Morland understand yourself, unless you mean to have her think you intolerably rude to your sister, and a great brute in your opinion of women in general. Miss Morland is not used to your odd ways."

"I shall be most happy to make her better acquainted with them."

'No doubt; but that is no explanation of the present."

"What am I to do?"

"You know what you ought to do. Clear your character handsomely before her. Tell her that you think very highly of the understanding of women."

"Miss Morland, I think very highly of the understanding of all the women in the world, especially of those, whoever they may be, with whom I happen to be in company."

"That is not enough. Be more serious."

"Miss Morland, no one can think more highly of the understanding of women than I do. In my opinion, nature has given them so much that they never find it necessary to use more than half."

"We shall get nothing more serious from him now, Miss Morland. He is not in a sober mood. But I assure you that he must be entirely misunderstood if he can ever appear to say an unjust thing of any woman at all, or an unkind one of me."

It was no effort to Catherine to believe that Henry Tilney could never be wrong. His manner might sometimes surprise, but his meaning must always be just; and what she did not understand, she was almost as ready to admire, as what she did. The whole walk was delightful, and though it ended too soon, its conclusion was delightful too. Her friends attended her into the house, and Miss Tilney, before they parted, addressing herself with respectful form, as much to Mrs. Allen as to Catherine, petitioned for the pleasure of her company to dinner on the day after the next. No difficulty was made on Mrs. Allen's side, and the only difficulty on Catherine's was in concealing the excess of her pleasure.

The morning had passed away so charmingly as to banish all her friendship and natural affection; for no thought of Isabella or James crossed her mind during their walk. When the Tilneys were gone, she became amiable again, but she was amiable for some time to little effect; Mrs. Allen had no intelligence to give that could relieve her anxiety; she had heard nothing of any of them. Towards the end of the morning, however, Catherine having occasion for some indispensable yard of riband, which must be bought without a moment's delay, walked out into the town, and in Bond Street overtook the second Miss Thorpe, as she was loitering towards Edgar's Buildings between two of the sweetest girls in the world, who had been her dear friends all the morning. From her, she soon learned that the party to Clifton had taken place. "They set off at eight this morning," said Miss Anne, "and I am sure I do not envy them their drive. I think you and I are very well off to be out of the scrape. It must be the dullest thing in the world, for there is not a soul at Clifton at this time of the year. Belle went with your brother, and John drove Maria."

Catherine spoke the pleasure she really felt on hearing this part of the arrangement.

"Oh! yes," rejoined the other, "Maria is gone. She was quite wild to go. She thought it would be something very fine. I cannot say I admire her taste; and, for my part, I was determined from the first not to go, if they pressed me ever so much."

Catherine, a little doubtful of this, could not help answering, "I wish you could have gone too. It is a pity you could not all go."

"Thank you: but it is quite a matter of indifference to me. Indeed, I would not have gone on any account. I was saying so to Emily and Sophia when you overtook us."

Catherine was still unconvinced; but glad that Anne should have the friendship of an Emily and a Sophia to console her, she bade her adieu without much uneasiness, and returned home, pleased that the party had not been prevented by her refusing to join it, and very heartily wishing that it might be too pleasant to allow either James or Isabella to resent her resistance any longer.

Chapter 15

EARLY the next day, a note from Isabella, speaking peace and tenderness in every line, and entreating the immediate presence of her friend on a matter of the utmost importance, hastened Catherine, in the happiest state of confidence and curiosity, to Edgar's Buildings. The two youngest Miss Thorpes were by themselves in the parlour, and on Anne's quitting it to call her sister, Catherine took the opportunity of asking the other for some particulars of their yesterday's party.

Maria desired no greater pleasure than to speak of it; and Catherine immediately learned that it had been altogether the most delightful scheme in the world, that nobody could imagine how charming it had been, and that it had been more delightful than anybody could conceive. Such was the information of the first five minutes; the second unfolded thus much in detail, that they had driven directly to the York Hotel, ate some soup, and bespoke an early dinner, walked down to the Pump Room, tasted the water, and laid out some shillings in purses and spars; thence adjourned to eat ice at a pastrycook's, and hurrying back to the hotel, swallowed their dinner in haste, to prevent being in the dark, and then had a delightful drive back, only the moon was not up, and it rained a little, and Mr. Morland's horse was so tired he could hardly get it along.

Catherine listened with heartfelt satisfaction. It appeared that Blaize Castle had never been thought of, and as for all the rest, there was nothing to regret for half an instant. Maria's intelligence concluded with a tender effusion of pity for her sister Anne, whom she represented as insupportably cross from being excluded the party.

"She will never forgive me, I am sure; but, you know, how could I help it? John would have me go, for he vowed he would not drive her because she had such thick ankles. I dare say she will not be in good humour again this month; but I am determined I will not be cross; it is not a little matter that puts me out of temper."

Isabella now entered the room with so eager a step, and a look of such happy importance, as engaged all her friend's notice. Maria was without ceremony sent away, and Isabella, embracing Catherine, thus began: "Yes, my dear Catherine, it is so, indeed; your penetration has not deceived you. Oh, that arch eye of yours! It sees through everything."

Catherine replied only by a look of wondering ignorance.

"Nay, my beloved, sweetest friend," continued the other, "compose yourself. I am amazingly agitated, as you perceive. Let us sit down and talk in comfort. Well, and so you guessed it the moment you had my note? Sly creature! Oh! my dear Catherine, you alone who know my heart can judge of my present happiness. Your brother is the most charming of men. I only wish I were more worthy of him. But what will your excellent father and mother say? Oh, heavens! When I think of them, I am so agitated!"

Catherine's understanding began to awake; an idea of the truth suddenly darted into her mind; and, with the natural blush of so new an emotion, she cried out, "Good heaven! my dear Isabella, what do you mean? Can you—can you really be in love with James?"

This bold surmise, however, she soon learnt comprehended but half the fact. The anxious affection which she was accused of having continually watched in Isabella's every look and action, had, in the course of their yesterday's party, received the delightful confession of an equal love. Her heart and faith were alike engaged to James. Never had Catherine listened to anything so full of interest, wonder, and joy. Her brother and her friend engaged! New to such circumstances, the importance of it appeared unspeakably great, and she contemplated it as one of those grand events of which the ordinary course of life can hardly afford a return. The strength of her feelings she could not express; the nature of them, however, contented her friend. The happiness of having such a sister was their first effusion, and the fair ladies mingled in embraces and tears of joy.

Delighting, however, as Catherine sincerely did, in the prospect of the connection, it must be acknowledged that Isabella far surpassed her in tender anticipations. "You will be so infinitely dearer to me, my Catherine, than either Anne or Maria. I feel that I shall be so much more attached to my dear Morland's family than to my own."

This was a pitch of friendship beyond Catherine.

"You are so like your dear brother," continued Isabella, "that I quite doted on you the first moment I saw you. But so it always is with me: the first moment settles everything. The very first day that Morland came to us last Christmas, the very first moment I beheld him, my heart was irrevocably gone. I remember I wore my yellow gown, with my hair done up in braids; and when I came into the drawing-room, and John introduced him, I thought I never saw anybody so handsome before."

Here Catherine secretly acknowledged the power of love; for though exceedingly fond of her brother, and partial to all his endowments, she had never in her life thought him handsome.

"I remember, too, Miss Andrews drank tea with us that evening, and wore her puce-coloured sarsenet; and she looked so heavenly that I thought your brother must certainly fall in love with her; I could not sleep a wink all night for thinking of it. Oh! Catherine, the many sleepless nights I have had on your brother's account! I would not have you suffer half what I have done! I am grown wretchedly thin, I know; but I will not pain you by describing my anxiety; you have seen enough of it. I feel that I have betrayed myself perpetually; so unguarded in speaking of my partiality for the church! But my secret I was always sure would be safe with *you*."

Catherine felt that nothing could have been safer; but ashamed of an ignorance little expected, she dared no longer contest the point, nor refuse to have been as full of arch penetration and affectionate sympathy as Isabella chose to consider her. Her brother, she found, was preparing to set off with all speed to Fullerton, to make known his situation and ask consent; and here was a source of some real agitation to the mind of Isabella. Catherine endeavoured to persuade her, as she was herself persuaded, that her father and mother would never oppose their son's wishes. "It is impossible," said she, "for parents to be more kind, or more desirous of their children's happiness; I have no doubt of their consenting immediately."

"Morland says exactly the same," replied Isabella; "and yet I dare not expect it; my fortune will be so small; they never can consent to it. Your brother, who might marry anybody!"

Here Catherine again discerned the force of love.

"Indeed, Isabella, you are too humble. The difference of fortune can be nothing to signify."

"Oh! my sweet Catherine, in *your* generous heart I know it would signify nothing, but we must not expect such disinterestedness in many. As for myself, I am sure I only wish our situations were reversed. Had I the command of millions, were I mistress of the whole world, your brother would be my only choice."

This charming sentiment, recommended as much by sense as novelty, gave Catherine a most pleasing remembrance of all the heroines of her acquaintance; and she thought her friend never looked more lovely than in uttering the grand idea. "I am sure they will consent," was her frequent declaration; "I am sure they will be delighted with you."

"For my own part," said Isabella, "my wishes are so moderate, that the smallest income in nature would be enough for me. Where people are really attached, poverty itself is wealth: grandeur I detest: I would not settle in London for the universe. A cottage in some retired village would be ecstasy. There are some charming little villas about Richmond."

"Richmond!" cried Catherine. "You must settle near Fullerton. You must be near us."

"I am sure I shall be miserable if we do not. If I can but be near *you*, I shall be satisfied. But this is idle talking! I will not allow myself to think of such things till we have your father's answer. Morland says that by sending it to-night to Salisbury, we may have it to-morrow. To-morrow! I know I shall never have courage to open the letter. I know it will be the death of me."

A reverie succeeded this conviction, and when Isabella spoke again, it was to resolve on the quality of her wedding-gown.

Their conference was put an end to by the anxious young lover him-self, who came to breathe his parting sigh before he set off for Wiltshire. Catherine wished to congratulate him, but knew not what to say, and her eloquence was only in her eyes. From them, however, the eight parts of speech shone out most expressively, and James could combine them with ease. Impatient for the realisation of all that he hoped at home, his adieux were not long, and they would have been yet shorter had he not been frequently detained by the urgent entreaties of his fair one that he would go. Twice was he called almost from the door by her eagerness to have him gone. "Indeed, Morland, I must drive you away. Consider how far you have to ride. I cannot bear to see you linger so. For heaven's sake, waste no more time. There, go, go—I insist on it."

The two friends, with hearts now more united than ever, were in-separable for the day; and in schemes of sisterly happiness the hours flew along. Mrs. Thorpe and her son, who were acquainted with every-thing, and who seemed only to want Mr. Morland's consent to consider Isabella's engagement as the most fortunate circumstance imaginable for their family, were allowed to join their counsels, and add their quota of significant looks and mysterious expressions, to fill up the measure of curiosity to be raised in the unprivileged younger sisters. To Catherine's simple feelings, this odd sort of reserve seemed neither kindly meant, nor consistently supported; and its unkindness she would hardly have for-borne pointing out, had its inconsistency been less their friend; but Anne and Maria soon set her heart at ease by the sagacity of their "I know what"; and the evening was spent in a sort of war of wit, a display of family ingenuity; on one side in the mystery of an affected secret, on the other of undefined discovery, all equally acute.

Catherine was with her friend again the next day, endeavouring to support her spirits, and while away the many tedious hours before the delivery of the letters: a needful exertion; for as the time of reasonable expectation drew near, Isabella became more and more desponding, and before the letter arrived, had worked herself into a state of real distress. But when it did come, where could distress be found? "I have had no difficulty in gaining the consent of my kind parents, and am promised that everything in their power shall be done to forward my happiness," were the first three lines, and in one moment all was joyful security. The brightest glow was instantly spread over Isabella's features—all care and anxiety seemed removed, her spirits became almost too high for control, and she called herself without scruple the happiest of mortals.

Mrs. Thorpe, with tears of joy, embraced her daughter, her son, her visitor, and could have embraced half the inhabitants of Bath with satisfaction. Her heart was overflowing with tenderness It was "dear John," and "dear Catherine," at every word; "dear Anne and dear Maria," must immediately be made sharers in their felicity; and two "dears" at once before the name of Isabella were not more than that beloved child had now well earned. John himself was no skulker in joy. He not only bestowed on Mr. Morland the high commendation of being one of the finest fellows in the world, but swore off many sentences in his praise.

The letter whence sprang all this felicity was short, containing little more than this assurance of success; and every particular was deferred till James could write again. But for particulars Isabella could well afford to wait. The needful was comprised in Mr. Morland's promise: his honour was pledged to make everything easy; and by what means their income was to be formed, whether landed property were to be resigned, or funded money made over, was a matter in which her disinterested spirit took no concern. She knew enough to feel secure of an honourable and speedy establishment, and her imagination took a rapid flight over its intended felicities. She saw herself, at the end of a few weeks, the gaze and admiration of every new acquaintance at Fullerton, the envy of every valued old friend in Putney, with a carriage at her command, a new name on her tickets, and a brilliant exhibition of hoop-rings on her finger.

When the contents of the letter were ascertained, John Thorpe, who had only waited its arrival to begin his journey to London, prepared to set off. "Well, Miss Morland," said he, on finding her alone in the parlour, "I am come to bid you good-bye." Catherine wished him a good journey. Without appearing to hear her, he walked to the window, fidgeted about, hummed a tune, and seemed wholly self-occupied.

"Shall not you be late at Devizes?" said Catherine. He made no answer; but after a minute's silence burst out with, "A famous good thing this marrying scheme, upon my soul! A clever fancy of Morland's and Belle's. What do you think of it, Miss Morland? *I* say it is no bad notion."

"I am sure I think it a very good one."

"Do you? That's honest, by heavens! I am glad you are no enemy to matrimony, however. Did you ever hear the old song, 'Going to one wedding brings on another'? I say, you will come to Belle's wedding, I hope."

"Yes; I have promised your sister to be with her, if possible."

"And then you know"—twisting himself about, and forcing a foolish laugh—"I say, then you know, we may try the truth of this same old song."

"May we? But I never sing. Well, I wish you a good journey. I dine with Miss Tilney to-day, and must now be going home."

"Nay, but there is no such confounded hurry. Who knows when we may be together again! Not but that I shall be down again by the end of a fortnight, and a devilish long fortnight it will appear to me."

"Then why do you stay away so long?" replied Catherine, finding that he waited for an answer.

"That is kind of you, however; kind and good-natured. I shall not forget it in a hurry. But you have more good-nature, and all that, than anybody living, I believe. A monstrous deal of good-nature, and it is not only good-nature, but you have so much—so much of everything; and then you have such—upon my soul, I do not know anybody like you."

"Oh, dear! There are a great many people like me, I dare say, only a great deal better. Good morning to you."

"But I say, Miss Morland, I shall come and pay my respects at Fullerton before it is long, if not disagreeable."

"Pray do; my father and mother will be very glad to see you."

"And I hope—I hope, Miss Morland, *you* will not be sorry to see me."

"Oh dear, not at all! There are very few people I am sorry to see. Company is always cheerful."

"That is just my way of thinking. Give me but a little cheerful company, let me only have the company of the people I love, let me only be where I like and with whom I like, and the devil take the rest, say I; and I am heartily glad to hear you say the same. But I have a notion, Miss Morland, you and I think pretty much alike upon most matters."

"Perhaps we may; but it is more than I ever thought of. And as to *most matters*, to say the truth, there are not many that I know my own mind about."

"By Jove, no more do I! It is not my way to bother my brains with what does not concern me. My notion of things is simple enough. Let me only have the girl I like, say I, with a comfortable house over my head, and what care I for all the rest? Fortune is nothing. I am sure of a good income of my own; and if she had not a penny, why so much the better."

"Very true. I think like you there. If there is a good fortune on one side, there can be no occasion for any on the other. No matter which has it, so that there is enough. I hate the idea of one great fortune looking out for another; and to marry for money I think the wickedest thing in existence. Good day. We shall be very glad to see you at Fullerton, whenever it is convenient." And away she went. It was not in the power of all his gallantry to detain her longer. With such news to communicate, and such a visit to prepare for, her departure was not to be delayed by anything in his nature to urge; and she hurried away, leaving him to the

undivided consciousness of his own happy address and her explicit encouragement.

The agitation which she had herself experienced on first learning her
brother's engagement made her expect to raise no inconsiderable emotion
in Mr. and Mrs. Allen, by the communication of the wonderful event.
How great was her disappointment! The important affair, which many
words of preparation ushered in, had been foreseen by them both ever
since her brother's arrival; and all that they felt on the occasion was
comprehended in a wish for the young people's happiness, with a remark,
on the gentleman's side, in favour of Isabella's beauty, and on the lady's
of her great good luck. It was to Catherine the most surprising insensibility. The disclosure, however, of the great secret of James's going to
Fullerton the day before did raise some emotion in Mrs. Allen. She could
not listen to that with perfect calmness, but repeatedly regretted the
necessity of its concealment, wished she could have known his intention,
wished she could have seen him before he went, as she should certainly
have troubled him with her best regards to his father and mother, and
her kind compliments to all the Skinners.

Chapter 16

CATHERINE's expectations of pleasure from her visit in Milsom Street
were so very high, that disappointment was inevitable; and, accordingly,
though she was most politely received by General Tilney, and kindly
welcomed by his daughter; though Henry was at home, and no one else
of the party, she found on her return, without spending many hours in
the examination of her feelings, that she had gone to her appointment
preparing for happiness which it had not afforded. Instead of finding
herself improved in acquaintance with Miss Tilney, from the intercourse
of the day, she seemed hardly so intimate with her as before. Instead of
seeing Henry Tilney to greater advantage than ever, in the ease of a
family party, he had never said so little nor been so little agreeable; and,
in spite of their father's great civilities to her, in spite of his thanks, invitations and compliments, it had been a release to get away from him. It
puzzled her to account for all this. It could not be General Tilney's fault.
That he was perfectly agreeable and good-natured, and altogether a
very charming man, did not admit of a doubt, for he was tall and handsome, and Henry's father. *He* could not be accountable for his children's
want of spirits, or for her want of enjoyment in his company. The former
she hoped at last might have been accidental, and the latter she could
only attribute to her own stupidity. Isabella, on hearing the particulars
of the visit, gave a different explanation. "It was all pride, pride; insufferable haughtiness and pride. She had long suspected the family to
be very high, and this made it certain. Such insolence of behaviour as
Miss Tilney's she had never heard in her life! Not to do the honours of

her house with common good breeding! To behave to her guest with such superciliousness! Hardly even to speak to her!"

"But it was not so bad as that, Isabella; there was no superciliousness; she was very civil."

"Oh, don't defend her! And then the brother, he who had appeared so attached to you! Good heavens! Well, some people's feelings are incomprehensible. And so he hardly looked once at you the whole day?"

"I do not say so; but he did not seem in good spirits."

"How contemptible! Of all things in the world inconstancy is my aversion. Let me entreat you never to think of him again, my dear Catherine; indeed, he is unworthy of you."

"Unworthy! I do not suppose he ever thinks of me."

"That is exactly what I say; he never thinks of you. Such fickleness! Oh, how different to your brother and to mine! I really believe John has the most constant heart."

"But as for General Tilney, I assure you it would be impossible for anybody to behave to me with greater civility and attention; it seemed to be his only care to entertain and make me happy."

"Oh! I know no harm of him; I do not suspect him of pride. I believe he is a very gentlemanlike man. John thinks very well of him, and John's judgment——"

"Well, I shall see how they behave to me this evening; we shall meet them at the Rooms."

"And must I go?"

"Do not you intend it? I thought it was all settled."

"Nay, since you make such a point of it, I can refuse you nothing. But do not insist upon my being very agreeable, for my heart, you know, will be some forty miles off; and as for dancing, do not mention it, I beg; *that* is quite out of the question. Charles Hodges will plague me to death, I daresay; but I shall cut him very short. Ten to one but he guesses the reason, and that is exactly what I want to avoid; so I shall insist on his keeping his conjecture to himself."

Isabella's opinion of the Tilneys did not influence her friend; she was sure there had been no insolence in the manners either of brother or sister; and she did not credit there being any pride in their hearts. The evening rewarded her confidence; she was met by one with the same kindness, and by the other with the same attention as heretofore. Miss Tilney took pains to be near her, and Henry asked her to dance.

Having heard the day before in Milsom Street that their elder brother, Captain Tilney, was expected almost every hour, she was at no loss for the name of a very fashionable-looking, handsome young man, whom she had never seen before, and who now evidently belonged to their party. She looked at him with great admiration; and even supposed it possible, that some people might think him handsomer than his brother, though, in her eyes, his air was more assuming, and his countenance less prepossessing. His taste and manners were, beyond a doubt, decidedly inferior; for, within her hearing, he not only protested against every thought of dancing himself, but even laughed openly at Henry for finding it possible. From the latter circumstance it may be presumed that, what-ever might be our heroine's opinion of him, his admiration of her was not of a very dangerous kind; not likely to produce animosities between the brothers, nor persecutions to the lady. *He* cannot be the instigator of the three villains in horsemen's great-coats, by whom she will hereafter be forced into a travelling chaise and four, which will drive off with incredible speed. Catherine, meanwhile, undisturbed by presentiments of such an evil, or of any evil at all, except that of having but a short set to dance down, enjoyed her usual happiness with Henry Tilney, listening with sparkling eyes to everything he said; and, in finding him irresistible, becoming so herself.

At the end of the first dance, Captain Tilney came towards them again, and, much to Catherine's dissatisfaction, pulled his brother away. They retired whispering together; and, though her delicate sensibility did not take immediate alarm, and lay it down as fact, that Captain Tilney must have heard some malevolent misrepresentation of her, which he now hastened to communicate to his brother, in the hope of separating them for ever, she could not have her partner conveyed from her sight without very uneasy sensations. Her suspense was of full five minutes' duration; and she was beginning to think it a very long quarter of an hour, when they both returned; and an explanation was given by Henry's requesting to know if she thought her friend Miss Thorpe would have any objection to dancing, as his brother would be most happy to be introduced to her. Catherine, without hesitation, replied that she was very sure Miss Thorpe did not mean to dance at all. The cruel reply was passed on to the other, and he immediately walked away.

"Your brother will not mind it, I know," said she, "because I heard him say before that he hated dancing; but it was very good-natured in him to think of it. I suppose he saw Isabella sitting down, and fancied she might wish for a partner; but he is quite mistaken, for she would not dance upon any account in the world."

Henry smiled, and said, "How very little trouble it can give you to understand the motive of other people's actions."

"Why? What do you mean?"

"With you it is not, How is such a one likely to be influenced? What is the inducement most likely to act upon such a person's feelings, age, situation, and probable habits of life considered? But, How should *I* be influenced; and what would be *my* inducement in acting so and so?"

"I do not understand you."

"Then we are on very unequal terms, for I understand you perfectly well."

"Me? Yes; I cannot speak well enough to be unintelligible."

"Bravo! An excellent satire on modern language."

"But pray tell me what you mean."

"Shall I, indeed? Do you really desire it? But you are not aware or the consequences; it will involve you in a very cruel embarrassment, and certainly bring on a disagreement between us."

"No, no; it shall not do either; I am not afraid."

"Well, then, I only meant that your attributing my brother's wish of dancing with Miss Thorpe to good nature alone, convinced me of you being superior in good nature yourself to all the rest of the world."

Catherine blushed and disclaimed, and the gentleman's predictions were verified. There was a something, however, in his words which repaid her for the pain of confusion; and that something occupied her mind so much, that she drew back for some time, forgetting to speak or to listen, and almost forgetting where she was; till, roused by the voice of Isabella, she looked up and saw her with Captain Tilney preparing to give them hands across.

Isabella shrugged her shoulders and smiled, the only explanation of this extraordinary change which could at that time be given; but as it was not quite enough for Catherine's comprehension, she spoke her astonishment in very plain terms to her partner.

"I cannot think how it could happen! Isabella was so determined not to dance."

"And did Isabella never change her mind before?"

"Oh! but, because—— And your brother! After what you told him from me, how could he think of going to ask her?"

"I cannot take surprise to myself on that head. You bid me be surprised on your friend's account, and therefore I am; but as for my brother, his conduct in the business, I must own, has been no more than I believed him perfectly equal to. The fairness of your friend was an open attraction; her firmness, you know, could only be understood by yourself."

"You are laughing; but, I assure you, Isabella is very firm in general."

"It is as much as should be said of anyone. To be always firm must be to be often obstinate. When properly to relax is the trial of judgment; and, without reference to my brother, I really think Miss Thorpe has by no means chosen ill in fixing on the present hour."

The friends were not able to get together for any confidential discourse till all the dancing was over; but then, as they walked about the room arm-in-arm, Isabella thus explained herself: "I do not wonder at your surprise; and I am really fatigued to death. He is such a rattle! Amusing enough, if my mind had been disengaged; but I would have given the world to sit still."

"Then why did not you?"

"Oh! my dear, it would have looked so particular; and you know how I abhor doing that. I refused him as long as I possibly could, but he would take no denial. You have no idea how he pressed me. I begged him to excuse me, and get some other partner; but no, not he; after aspiring to my hand, there was nobody else in the room he could bear to think of; and it was not that he wanted merely to dance, he wanted to be with *me*.

Oh, such nonsense! I told him he had taken a very unlikely way to prevail upon me; for, of all things in the world, I hated fine speeches and compliments; and so—and so then I found there would be no peace if I did not stand up. Besides, I thought Mrs. Hughes, who introduced him, might take it ill if I did not; and your dear brother, I am sure he would have been miserable if I had sat down the whole evening. I am so glad it is over! My spirits are quite jaded with listening to his nonsense; and then, being such a smart young fellow, I saw every eye was upon us."

"He is very handsome, indeed."

"Handsome! Yes, I suppose he may. I dare say people would admire him in general; but he is not at all in my style of beauty. I hate a florid complexion and dark eyes in a man. However, he is very well. Amazingly conceited, I am sure. I took him down several times, you know, in my way."

When the young ladies next met, they had a far more interesting subject to discuss. James Morland's second letter was then received, and the kind intentions of his father fully explained. A living, of which Mr. Morland was himself patron and incumbent, of about four hundred pounds' yearly value, was to be resigned to his son as soon as he should be old enough to take it; no trifling deduction from the family income, no niggardly assignment to one of ten children. An estate of at least equal value, moreover, was assured as his future inheritance.

James expressed himself on the occasion with becoming gratitude; and the necessity of waiting between two and three years before they could marry being, however unwelcome, no more than he had expected, was borne by him without discontent. Catherine, whose expectations had been as unfixed as her ideas of her father's income, and whose judgment was now entirely led by her brother, felt equally well satisfied, and heartily congratulated Isabella on having everything so pleasantly settled.

"It is very charming, indeed," said Isabella, with a grave face.

"Mr. Morland has behaved vastly handsome, indeed," said the gentle Mrs. Thorpe, looking anxiously at her daughter. "I only wish I could do as much. One could not expect more from him, you know. If he finds he *can* do more, by the bye, I dare say he will; for I am sure he must be an excellent, good-hearted man. Four hundred is but a small income to begin on, indeed; but your wishes, my dear Isabella, are so moderate, you do not consider how little you ever want, my dear."

"It is not on my account I wish for more; but I cannot bear to be the means of injuring my dear Morland, making him sit down upon an income hardly enough to find one in the common necessaries of life. For myself, it is nothing; I never think of myself."

"I know you never do, my dear; and you will always find your reward in the affection it makes everybody feel for you. There never was a young woman so beloved as you are by everybody that knows you; and I dare say when Mr. Morland sees you, my dear child—but do not let us distress our dear Catherine by talking of such things. Mr. Morland has behaved so very handsome, you know. I always heard he was a most excellent man; and you know, my dear, we are not to suppose but what, if you had had a suitable fortune, he would have come down with something more; for I am sure he must be a most liberal-minded man."

"Nobody can think better of Mr. Morland than I do, I am sure. But everybody has their failing, you know; and everybody has a right to do what they like with their own money."

Catherine was hurt by these insinuations. "I am very sure," said she, "that my father has promised to do as much as he can afford."

Isabella recollected herself. "As to that, my sweet Catherine, there cannot be a doubt, and you know me well enough to be sure that a much smaller income would satisfy me. It is not the want of more money that makes me just at present a little out of spirits. I hate money; and if our union could take place now upon only fifty pounds a year, I should not have a wish unsatisfied. Ah! my Catherine, you have found me out. There's the sting. The long, long, endless two years and a half that are to pass before your brother can hold the living."

"Yes, yes, my darling Isabella," said Mrs. Thorpe, "we perfectly see into your heart. You have no disguise. We perfectly understood the present vexation; and everybody must love you the better for such a noble, honest affection."

Catherine's uncomfortable feelings began to lessen. She endeavoured to believe that the delay of the marriage was the only source of Isabella's regret; and when she saw her at their next interview as cheerful and amiable as ever, endeavoured to forget that she had for a minute thought otherwise. James soon followed his letter, and was received with the most gratifying kindness.

Chapter 17

THE Allens had now entered on the sixth week of their stay in Bath; and whether it should be the last, was for some time a question, to which Catherine listened with a beating heart. To have her acquaintance with the Tilneys end so soon, was an evil which nothing could counterbalance. Her whole happiness seemed at stake, while the affair was in suspense, and everything secured when it was determined that the lodgings should be taken for another fortnight. What this additional fortnight was to produce to her beyond the pleasure of sometimes seeing Henry Tilney, made but a small part of Catherine's speculation. Once or twice, indeed, since James's engagement had taught her what *could* be done, she had got so far as to indulge in a secret "perhaps," but in general the felicity of being with him for the present bounded her views: the present was now comprised in another three weeks, and her happiness being certain for that period, the rest of her life was at such a distance as to excite but little interest. In the course of the morning which saw this business arranged, she visited Miss Tilney, and poured forth her joyful feelings. It was doomed to be a day of trial. No sooner had she expressed her delight in Mr. Allen's lengthened stay, than Miss Tilney told her of her father's having just determined upon quitting Bath by the end of another week. Here was a blow! The past suspense of the morning had been ease and quiet to the present disappointment. Catherine's countenance fell; and in a voice of most sincere concern she echoed Miss Tilney's concluding words, "By the end of another week!"

"Yes; my father can seldom be prevailed on to give the waters what I think a fair trial. He has been disappointed of some friends' arrival whom he expected to meet here, and as he is now pretty well, is in a hurry to get home."

"I am very sorry for it," said Catherine dejectedly; "if I had known this before——"

"Perhaps," said Miss Tilney in an embarrassed manner, "you would be so good—it would make me very happy if——"

The entrance of her father put a stop to the civility which Catherine was beginning to hope might introduce a desire of their corresponding. After addressing her with his usual politeness, he turned to his daughter, and said, "Well, Eleanor, may I congratulate you on being successful in your application to your fair friend?"

"I was just beginning to make the request, sir, as you came in."

"Well, proceed by all means. I know how much your heart is in it. My daughter, Miss Morland," he continued, without leaving his daughter time to speak, "has been forming a very bold wish. We leave Bath, as she has perhaps told you, on Saturday se'nnight. A letter from my steward tells me that my presence is wanted at home; and being disappointed in my hope of seeing the Marquis of Longtown and General Courtenay here, some of my very old friends, there is nothing to detain me longer in Bath. And could we carry our selfish point with you, we should leave it without a single regret. Can you, in short, be prevailed on to quit this scene of public triumph, and oblige your friend Eleanor with your company in Gloucestershire? I am almost ashamed to make the request, though its presumption would certainly appear greater to every creature in Bath than yourself. Modesty such as yours—but not for the world would I pain it by open praise. If you can be induced to honour us with a visit, you will make us happy beyond expression. 'Tis true we can offer you nothing like the gaieties of this lively place; we can tempt you neither by amusement nor splendour, for our mode of living, as you see, is plain and unpretending, yet no endeavours shall be wanting on our side to make Northanger Abbey not wholly disagreeable."

Northanger Abbey! These were thrilling words, and wound up Catherine's feelings to the highest points of ecstasy. Her grateful and gratified heart could hardly restrain its expressions within the language of tolerable calmness. To receive so flattering an invitation! To have her company so warmly solicited! Everything honourable and soothing, every present enjoyment and every future hope was contained in it, and her acceptance, with only the saving clause of papa and mamma's approbation, was eagerly given. "I will write home directly," said she, "and if they do not object, as I dare say they will not——"

General Tilney was not less sanguine, having already waited on her excellent friends in Pulteney Street, and obtained their sanction of his wishes. "Since they can consent to part with you," said he, "we may expect philosophy from all the world."

Miss Tilney was earnest, though gentle, in her secondary civilities, and the affair became in a few minutes as nearly settled as this necessary reference to Fullerton would allow.

The circumstances of the morning had led Catherine's feelings through the varieties of suspense, security, and disappointment: but they were now safely lodged in perfect bliss; and with spirits elated to rapture, with Henry at her heart, and Northanger Abbey on her lips, she hurried home to write her letter. Mr. and Mrs. Morland, relying on the discretion of the friends to whom they had already entrusted their daughter, felt no doubt of the propriety of an acquaintance which had been formed under their eye, and sent, therefore, by return of post, their ready consent to her visit in Gloucestershire. This indulgence, though not more than Catherine had hoped for, completed her conviction of being favoured beyond every other human creature, in friends and fortune, circumstances and chance. Everything seemed to co-operate for her advantage. By the kindness of her first friends, the Allens, she had been introduced into scenes where pleasures of every kind had met her. Her feelings, her preferences had each known the happiness of a return. Wherever she felt attachment, she had been able to create it. The affection of Isabella was to be secured to her in a sister. The Tilneys, they by whom above all she desired to be favourably thought of, outstripped even her wishes in the flattering measures by which their intimacy was to be continued. She was to be their chosen visitor, she was to be for weeks under the same roof with the person whose society she mostly prized; and, in addition to all the rest, this roof was to be the roof of an abbey! Her passion for ancient edifices was next in degree to her passion for Henry Tilney, and castles and abbeys made usually the charm of those reveries which his image did not fill. To see and explore either the ramparts and keep of the one, or the cloisters of the other, had been for many weeks a darling wish, though to be more than the visitor of an hour had seemed too nearly impossible for desire; and yet this was to happen. With all the chances against her of house, hall, place, park, court and cottage, Northanger turned up an abbey, and she was to be its inhabitant. Its long, damp passages, its narrow cells and ruined chapel, were to be within her daily reach, and she could not entirely subdue the hope of some traditional legends, some awful memorials of an injured and ill-fated nun.

It was wonderful that her friends should seem so little elated by the possession of such a home; that the consciousness of it should be so meekly borne. The power of early habit only could account for it. A distinction to which they had been born gave no pride. Their superiority of abode was no more to them than their superiority of person.

Many were the inquiries she was eager to make of Miss Tilney; but so active were her thoughts, that when these inquiries were answered, she was hardly more assured than before of Northanger Abbey having been a richly endowed convent at the time of the Reformation, of its having fallen into the hands of an ancestor of the Tilneys on its dissolution, of a large portion of the ancient building still making a part of the present dwelling although the rest was decayed, or of its standing low in a valley, sheltered from the north and east by rising woods of oak.

Chapter 18

WITH a mind thus full of happiness, Catherine was hardly aware that two or three days had passed away without her seeing Isabella for more than a few minutes together. She began first to be sensible of this, and to sigh for her conversation, as she walked along the Pump Room one morning, by Mrs. Allen's side, without anything to say or to hear; and scarcely had she felt a five minutes' longing of friendship, before the object of it appeared, and inviting her to a secret conference, led the way to a seat. "This is my favourite place," said she, as they sat down on a bench between the doors, which commanded a tolerable view of everybody entering at either, "it is so out of the way."

Catherine, observing that Isabella's eyes were continually bent towards one door or the other, as in eager expectation, and remembering how often she had been falsely accused of being arch, thought the present a fine opportunity for being really so, and therefore gaily said, "Do not be uneasy, Isabella. James will soon be here."

"Psha! my dear creature," she replied, "do not think me such a simpleton as to be always wanting to confine him to my elbow. It would be hideous to be always together; we should be the jest of the place. And so you are going to Northanger! I am amazingly glad of it. It is one of the finest old places in England, I understand. I shall depend upon a most particular description of it."

"You shall certainly have the best in my power to give. But who are you looking for? Are your sisters coming?"

"I am not looking for anybody. One's eyes must be somewhere, and you know what a foolish trick I have of fixing mine, when my thoughts are a hundred miles off. I am amazingly absent; I believe I am the most absent creature in the world. Tilney says it is always the case with minds of a certain stamp."

"But I thought, Isabella, you had something in particular to tell me?"

"Oh, yes! and so I have. But here is a proof of what I was saying. My poor head! I had quite forgot it. Well, the thing is this: I have just had a letter from John. You can guess the contents."

"No, indeed, I cannot."

"My sweet love, do not be so abominably affected. What can he write about but yourself? You know he is over head and ears in love with you."

"With me, dear Isabella?"

"Nay, my sweetest Catherine, this is being quite absurd. Modesty, and all that, is very well in its way, but really a little common honesty is sometimes quite as becoming. I have no idea of being so overstrained. It is fishing for compliments. His attentions were such that a child must have noticed, and it was but half an hour before he left Bath that you gave him the most positive encouragement. He says so in this letter; says that he as good as made you an offer, and that you received his advances in the kindest way, and now he wants me to urge his suit, and say all manner of pretty things to you. So it is in vain to affect ignorance."

Catherine, with all the earnestness of truth, expressed her astonishment at such a charge, protesting her innocence of every thought of Mr. Thorpe's being in love with her, and the consequent impossibility of her having ever intended to encourage him. "As to any attentions on his side, I do declare, upon my honour, I never was sensible of them for a moment, except just his asking me to dance the first day of his coming; and as to making me an offer, or anything like it, there must be some unaccountable mistake. I could not have misunderstood a thing of that kind, you know; and, as I ever wish to be believed, I solemnly protest that no syllable of such a nature ever passed between us. The last half-hour before he went away! It must be all and completely a mistake, for I did not see him once that whole morning."

"But *that* you certainly did, for you spent the whole morning in Edgar's Buildings. It was the day your father's consent came, and I am pretty sure that you and John were alone in the parlour some time before you left the house."

"Are you? Well, if you say it, it was so, I dare say; but for the life of me I cannot recollect it. I *do* remember now being with you, and seeing him as well as the rest; but that we were alone for five minutes—— However, it is not worth arguing about, for whatever might pass on his side, you must be convinced, by my having no recollection of it, that I never thought, nor expected, nor wished for anything of the kind from him. I am excessively concerned that he should have any regard for me, but indeed it has been quite unintentional on my side; I never had the smallest idea of it. Pray undeceive him as soon as you can, and tell him I beg his pardon; that is——I do not know what I ought to say——but make him understand what I mean in the properest way. I would not speak disrespectfully of a brother of yours, Isabella, I am sure, but you know very well that if I could think of one man more than another, *he* is not the person." Isabella was silent. "My dear friend, you must not be angry with me. I cannot suppose your brother cares so very much about me; and, you know, we shall still be sisters."

"Yes, yes" (with a blush), "there are more way than one of our being sisters. But where am I wandering to? Well, my dear Catherine, the case seems to be, that you are determined against poor John, is not it so?"

"I certainly cannot return his affection, and as certainly never meant to encourage it."

"Since that is the case, I am sure I shall not tease you any further. John desired me to speak to you on the subject, and therefore I have. But I confess, as soon as I read his letter, I thought it a very foolish, imprudent business, and not likely to promote the good of either; for what were you to live upon, supposing you came together? You have both of you something, to be sure, but it is not a trifle that will support a family nowadays; and after all that romancers may say, there is no doing without money. I only wonder John could think of it; he could not have received my last."

"You *do* acquit me then of anything wrong? You are convinced that I never meant to deceive your brother, never suspected him of liking me till this moment?"

"Oh! as to that," answered Isabella, laughingly, "I do not pretend to determine what your thoughts and designs in time past may have been. All that is best known to yourself. A little harmless flirtation or so will occur, and one is often drawn on to give more encouragement than one wishes to stand by. But you may be assured that I am the last person in the world to judge you severely. All those things should be allowed for in youth and high spirits. What one means one day, you know, one may not mean the next. Circumstances change, opinions alter."

"But my opinion of your brother never did alter; it was always the same. You are describing what never happened."

"My dearest Catherine," continued the other without at all listening to her, "I would not for all the world be the means of hurrying you into an engagement before you knew what you were about. I do not think anything would justify me in wishing you to sacrifice all your happiness merely to oblige my brother, because he is my brother, and who perhaps, after all, you know, might be just as happy without you; for people seldom know what they would be at, young men especially, they are so amazingly changeable and inconstant. What I say is, why should a brother's happiness be dearer to me than a friend's? You know I carry my notions of friendship pretty high. But, above all things, my dear Catherine, do not be in a hurry. Take my word for it, that if you are in too great a hurry, you will certainly live to repent it. Tilney says, there is nothing people are so often deceived in as the state of their own affections; and I believe he is very right. Ah! here he comes; never mind, he will not see us, I am sure."

Catherine, looking up, perceived Captain Tilney; and Isabella, earnestly fixing her eye on him as she spoke, soon caught his notice. He ap-

proached immediately, and took the seat to which her movements invited
him. His first address made Catherine start. Though spoken low, she could
distinguish, "What! always to be watched, in person or by proxy!"

"Psha, nonsense!" was Isabella's answer, in the same half whisper.
"Why do you put such things into my head? If I could believe it!—my
spirit, you know, is pretty independent."

"I wish your heart was independent. That would be enough for me."

"My heart, indeed! What can you have to do with hearts? You men
have none of you any hearts."

"If we have not hearts, we have eyes; and they give us torment enough."

"Do they? I am sorry for it; I am sorry they find anything so disagreeable in me. I will look another way. I hope this pleases you" (turning her
back on him); "I hope your eyes are not tormented now."

"Never more so: for the edge of a blooming cheek is still in view—at
once too much and too little."

Catherine heard all this and, quite out of countenance, could listen no
longer. Amazed that Isabella could endure it, and jealous for her brother,
she rose up, and saying she should join Mrs. Allen, proposed their walking.
But for this Isabella showed no inclination. She was so amazingly tired,
and it was so tedious to parade about the Pump Room; and if she moved
from her seat, she should miss her sisters; she was expecting her sisters
every moment, so that her dearest Catherine must excuse her, and must
sit quietly down again. But Catherine could be stubborn too; and Mrs.
Allen just then coming up to propose their returning home, she joined her
and walked out of the Pump Room, leaving Isabella still sitting with
Captain Tilney. With much uneasiness did she thus leave them. It seemed
to her that Captain Tilney was falling in love with Isabella, and Isabella
unconsciously encouraging him; unconsciously it must be, for Isabella's
attachment to James was as certain and well acknowledged as her engagement. To doubt her truth or good intentions was impossible; and yet,
during the whole of their conversation, her manner had been odd. She
wished Isabella had talked more like her usual self, and not so much
about money; and had not looked so well pleased at the sight of Captain
Tilney. How strange that she should not perceive his admiration! Catherine longed to give her a hint of it, to put her on her guard, and prevent
all the pain which her too lively behaviour might otherwise create both for
him and her brother.

The compliment of John Thorpe's affection did not make amends for
this thoughtlessness in his sister. She was almost as far from believing as
from wishing it to be sincere; for she had not forgotten that he could
mistake; and his assertion of the offer, and of her encouragement, convinced her that his mistakes could sometimes be very egregious. In vanity,
therefore, she gained but little: her chief profit was in wonder. That he
should think it worth his while to fancy himself in love with her was a
matter of lively astonishment. Isabella talked of his attentions; *she* had
never been sensible of any; but Isabella had said many things which she

hoped had been spoken in haste, and would never be said again; and upon this she was glad to rest altogether for present ease and comfort.

Chapter 19

A FEW days passed away, and Catherine, though not allowing herself to suspect her friend, could not help watching her closely. The result of her observations was not agreeable. Isabella seemed an altered creature. When she saw her indeed surrounded only by their immediate friends in Edgar's Buildings or Pulteney Street, her change of manners was so trifling that, had it gone no further, it might have passed unnoticed. A something of languid indifference, or of that boasted absence of mind which Catherine had never heard of before, would occasionally come across her; but had nothing worse appeared, *that* might only have spread a new grace and inspired a warmer interest. But when Catherine saw her in public, admitting Captain Tilney's attentions as readily as they were offered, and allowing him almost an equal share with James in her notice and smiles, the alteration became too positive to be passed over. What could be meant by such unsteady conduct, what her friend could be at, was beyond her comprehension. Isabella could not be aware of the pain she was inflicting; but it was a degree of wilful thoughtlessness which Catherine could not but resent. James was the sufferer. She saw him grave and uneasy; and however careless of his present comfort the woman might be who had given him her heart, to *her* it was always an object. For poor Captain Tilney too she was greatly concerned. Though his looks did not please her, his name was a passport to her goodwill, and she thought with sincere compassion of his approaching disappointment; for, in spite of what she had believed herself to overhear in the Pump Room, his behaviour was so incompatible with a knowledge of Isabella's engagement, that she could not, upon reflection, imagine him aware of it. He might be jealous of her brother as a rival, but if more had seemed implied, the fault must have been in her misapprehension. She wished, by a gentle remonstrance, to remind Isabella of her situation, and make her aware of this double unkindness; but for remonstrance, either opportunity or comprehension was always against her. If able to suggest a hint, Isabella could never understand it. In this distress, the intended departure of the Tilney family became her chief consolation; their journey into Gloucestershire was to take place within a few days, and Captain Tilney's removal would at least restore peace to every heart but his own. But Captain Tilney had at present no intention of removing; he was not to be of the party to Northanger, he was to continue at Bath. When Catherine knew this, her resolution was directly made. She spoke to Henry Tilney on the subject, regretting his brother's evident partiality for Miss Thorpe, and entreating him to make known her prior engagement.

"My brother does know it," was Henry's answer.

"Does he; then why does he stay here?"

He made no reply, and was beginning to talk of something else; but she eagerly continued: "Why did not you persuade him to go away? The longer he stays, the worse it will be for him at last. Pray advise him for his own sake, and for everybody's sake, to leave Bath directly. Absence will in time make him comfortable again; but he can have no hope here, and it is only staying to be miserable."

Henry smiled, and said: "I am sure my brother would not wish to do that."

"Then you will persuade him to go away."

"Persuasion is not at command; but pardon me, if I cannot even endeavour to persuade him. I have myself told him that Miss Thorpe is engaged. He knows what he is about, and must be his own master."

"No, he does not know what he is about," cried Catherine; "he does not know the pain he is giving my brother. Not that James has ever told me so, but I am sure he is very uncomfortable."

"And are you sure it is my brother's doing?"

"Yes, very sure."

"Is it my brother's attentions to Miss Thorpe, or Miss Thorpe's admission of them, that gives the pain?"

"Is not it the same thing?"

"I think Mr. Morland would acknowledge a difference. No man is offended by another man's admiration of the woman he loves; it is the woman only who can make it a torment."

Catherine blushed for her friend, and said: "Isabella is wrong. But I am sure she cannot mean to torment, for she is very much attached to my brother. She has been in love with him ever since they first met, and while my father's consent was uncertain, she fretted herself almost into a fever. You know she must be attached to him."

"I understand: she is in love with James, and flirts with Frederick."

"Oh no, not flirts! A woman in love with one man cannot flirt with another."

"It is probable that she will neither love so well, nor flirt so well, as she might do either singly. The gentlemen must each give up a little."

After a short pause, Catherine resumed with: "Then you do not believe Isabella so very much attached to my brother?"

"I can have no opinion on that subject."

"But what can your brother mean? If he knows her engagement, what can he mean by his behaviour?"

"You are a very close questioner."

"Am I? I only ask what I want to be told."

"But do you only ask what I can be expected to tell?"

"Yes, I think so; for you must know your brother's heart."

"My brother's heart, as you term it, on the present occasion, I assure you I can only guess at."

"Well?"

"Well! Nay, if it is to be guess-work, let us all guess for ourselves. To be guided by secondhand conjecture is pitiful. The premises are before you. My brother is a lively, and perhaps sometimes a thoughtless, young man; he has had about a week's acquaintance with your friend, and he has known her engagement almost as long as he has known her."

"Well," said Catherine, after some moments' consideration, "*you* may be able to guess at your brother's intentions from all this; but I am sure I cannot. But is not your father uncomfortable about it? Does not he want Captain Tilney to go away? Sure, if your father were to speak to him he would go."

"My dear Miss Morland," said Henry, "in this amiable solicitude for your brother's comfort, may you not be a little mistaken? Are you not carried a little too far? Would he thank you, either on his own account or Miss Thorpe's, for supposing that her affection, or at least her good behaviour, is only to be secured by her seeing nothing of Captain Tilney? Is he safe only in solitude? Or is her heart constant to him only when unsolicited by anyone else? He cannot think this, and you may be sure that he would not have you think it. I will not say, 'Do not be uneasy,' because I know that you are so at this moment; but be as little uneasy as you can. You have no doubt of the mutual attachment of your brother and your friend; depend upon it, therefore, that real jealousy never can exist between them; depend upon it that no disagreement between them can be of any duration. Their hearts are open to each other, as neither heart can be to you; they know exactly what is required and what can be borne; and you may be certain, that one will never tease the other beyond what is known to be pleasant."

Perceiving her still to look doubtful and grave, he added: "Though Frederick does not leave Bath with us he will probably remain but a very short time, perhaps only a few days behind us. His leave of absence will soon expire, and he must return to his regiment. And what will then be their acquaintance? The mess-room will drink Isabella Thorpe for a fortnight, and she will laugh with your brother over poor Tilney's passion for a month."

Catherine would contend no longer against comfort. She had resisted its approaches during the whole length of a speech, but it now carried her captive. Henry Tilney must know best. She blamed herself for the extent of her fears, and resolved never to think so seriously on the subject again.

Her resolution was supported by Isabella's behaviour in their parting interview. The Thorpes spent the last evening of Catherine's stay in Pulteney Street, and nothing passed between the lovers to excite her uneasiness, or make her quit them in apprehension. James was in excellent spirits, and Isabella most engagingly placid. Her tenderness for her friend seemed rather the first feeling of her heart, but that at such a moment was allowable; and once she gave her lover a flat contradiction, and once she drew back her hand, but Catherine remembered Henry's instructions, and placed it all to judicious affection. The embraces, tears, and promises of the parting fair ones may be fancied.

Chapter 20

MR. AND MRS. ALLEN were sorry to lose their young friend, whose good humour and cheerfulness had made her a valuable companion, and in the promotion of whose enjoyment their own had been greatly increased. Her happiness in going with Miss Tilney, however, prevented their wishing it otherwise; and, as they were to remain only one more week in Bath themselves, her quitting them now would not long be felt. Mr. Allen attended her to Milsom Street, where she was to breakfast, and saw her seated with the kindest welcome among her new friends; but so great was her agitation in finding herself as one of the family, and so fearful was she of not doing exactly what was right, and of not being able to preserve their good opinion, that, in the embarrassment of the first five minutes, she could almost have wished to return with him to Pulteney Street.

Miss Tilney's manners, and Henry's smile, soon did away some of her unpleasant feelings: but still she was far from being at ease; nor could the incessant attentions of the General himself entirely reassure her. Nay, perverse as it seemed, she doubted whether she might not have felt less, had she been less attended to. His anxiety for her comfort, his continual solicitations that she would eat, and his often-expressed fears of her seeing nothing to her taste, though never in her life before had she beheld half such variety on a breakfast-table, made it impossible for her to forget for a moment that she was a visitor. She felt utterly unworthy of such respect, and knew not how to reply to it. Her tranquillity was not improved by the General's impatience for the appearance of his eldest son, nor by the displeasure he expressed at his laziness when Captain Tilney at last came down. She was quite pained by the severity of his father's reproof, which seemed disproportionate to the offence; and much was her concern increased, when she found herself the principal cause of the lecture; and that his tardiness was chiefly resented from being disrespectful to her. This was placing her in a very uncomfortable situation, and she felt great compassion for Captain Tilney, without being able to hope for his good will.

He listened to his father in silence, and attempted not any defence, which confirmed her in fearing that the inquietude of his mind, on Isabella's account, might, by keeping him long sleepless, have been the real cause of his rising late. It was the first time of her being decidedly in his company, and she had hoped to be now able to form her opinion of him; but she scarcely heard his voice while his father remained in the room; and even afterwards, so much were his spirits affected, she could distinguish nothing but these words, in a whisper to Eleanor, "How glad I shall be when you are all off!"

The bustle of going was not pleasant. The clock struck ten while the trunks were carrying down, and the General had fixed to be out of Milsom Street by that hour. His great-coat, instead of being brought for him to put on directly, was spread out in the curricle in which he was to accompany his son. The middle seat of the chaise was not drawn out, though there were three people to go in it, and his daughter's maid had so crowded it with parcels that Miss Morland would not have room to sit; and so much was he influenced by this apprehension when he handed her in, that she had some difficulty in saving her own new writing-desk from being thrown out into the street. At last, however, the door was closed upon the three females, and they set off at the sober pace in which the handsome, highly-fed four horses of a gentleman usually perform a journey of thirty miles: such was the distance of Northanger from Bath, to be now divided into two equal stages. Catherine's spirits revived as they drove from the door; for with Miss Tilney she felt no restraint; and with the interest of a road entirely new to her, of an abbey before, and a curricle behind, she caught the last view of Bath without any regret and met with every milestone before she expected it. The tediousness of a two hours' wait at Petty France, in which there was nothing to be done but to eat without being hungry, and loiter about without anything to see, next followed; and her admiration of the style in which they travelled, of the fashionable chaise and four, postillions handsomely liveried, rising so regularly in their stirrups, and numerous outriders, properly mounted, sunk a little under this consequent inconvenience. Had their party been perfectly agreeable, the delay would have been nothing; but General Tilney, though so charming a man, seemed always a check upon his children's spirits, and scarcely anything was said but by himself; the observation of which, with his discontent at whatever the inn afforded, and his angry impatience at the waiters, made Catherine grow every moment more in awe of him, and appeared to lengthen the two hours into four. At last, however, the order of release was given; and much was Catherine then surprised by the General's proposal of her taking his place in his son's curricle for the rest of the journey: "The day was fine, and he was anxious for her seeing as much of the country as possible."

The remembrance of Mr. Allen's opinion respecting young men's open carriages made her blush at the mention of such a plan, and her first thought was to decline it; but her second was of greater deference for General Tilney's judgment: he could not propose anything improper for her; and in the course of a few minutes she found herself with Henry in the curricle, as happy a being as ever existed. A very short trial convinced her that a curricle was the prettiest equipage in the world; the chaise and four wheeled off with some grandeur, to be sure, but it was a heavy and troublesome business, and she could not easily forget its having stopped two hours at Petty France. Half the time would have been enough for the curricle; and so nimbly were the light horses disposed to move, that, had not the General chosen to have his own carriage lead the way, they could have passed it with ease in half a minute. But the merit of the curricle did not all belong to the horses: Henry drove so well, so quietly, without making any disturbance, without parading to her, or swearing at them; so different from the only gentleman-coachman whom it was in her power to compare him with! And then his hat sat so well, and the innumerable capes of his great-coat looked so becomingly important! To be driven by him, next to being dancing with him, was certainly the greatest happiness in the world. In addition to every other delight, she had now that of listening to her own praise, of being thanked at least, on his sister's account, for her kindness in thus becoming her visitor; of hearing it ranked as real friendship, and described as creating real gratitude. His sister, he said, was uncomfortably circumstanced; she had no female companion, and in the frequent absence of her father, was sometimes without any companion at all.

"But how can that be?" said Catherine; "are not you with her?"

"Northanger is not more than half my home; I have an establishment at my own house in Woodston, which is nearly twenty miles from my father's, and some of my time is necessarily spent there."

"How sorry you must be for that!"

"I am always sorry to leave Eleanor."

"Yes; but besides your affection for her, you must be so fond of the Abbey! After being used to such a home as the Abbey, an ordinary parsonage house must be very disagreeable."

He smiled and said: "You have formed a very favourable idea of the Abbey."

"To be sure I have. Is not it a fine old place, just like what one reads about?"

"And are you prepared to encounter all the horrors that a building such as 'what one reads about' may produce? Have you a stout heart? Nerves fit for sliding panels and tapestry?"

"Oh! yes, I do not think I should be easily frightened, because there would be so many people in the house; and besides, it has never been uninhabited and left deserted for years, and then the family come back to it unawares without giving any notice, as generally happens."

"No, certainly. We shall not have to explore our way into a hall dimly lighted by the expiring embers of a wood fire, nor be obliged to spread our beds on the floor of a room without windows, doors or furniture. But you must be aware that when a young lady is (by whatever means) introduced into a dwelling of this kind, she is always lodged apart from the rest of the family. While they snugly repair to their own end of the house, she is formally conducted by Dorothy, the ancient housekeeper, up a different staircase, and along many gloomy passages, into an apartment never used since some cousin of kin died in it about twenty years before. Can you stand such a ceremony as this? Will not your mind misgive you, when you find yourself in this gloomy chamber, too lofty and extensive for you, with only the feeble rays of a single lamp to take in its size, its

walls hung with tapestry exhibiting figures as large as life, and the bed
of dark green stuff or purple velvet, presenting even a funereal appearance. Will not your heart sink within you?"

"Oh! but this will not happen to me, I am sure."

"How dreadfully will you examine the furniture of your apartment?
And what will you discern? Not tables, toilettes, wardrobes, or drawers,
but on one side perhaps the remains of a broken lute, on the other a
ponderous chest whrich no efforts can open, and over the fire-place the
portrait of some handsome warrior, whose features will so incompre-
hensibly strike you, that you will not be able to withdraw your eyes from
it. Dorothy, meanwhile, no less struck by your appearance, gazes on you
in great agitation, and drops a few unintelligible hints. To raise your
spirits, moreover, she gives you reason to suppose that the part of the
Abbey you inhabit is undoubtedly haunted, and informs you that you will
not have a single domestic within call. With this parting cordial, she
curtseys off: you listen to the sound of her receding footsteps as long as
the last echo can reach you; and when, with fainting spirits, you attempt
to fasten your door, you discover, with increased alarm, that it has no
lock."

"Oh! Mr. Tilney, how frightful! This is just like a book! But it cannot
really happen to me. I am sure your housekeeper is not really Dorothy.
Well, what then?"

"Nothing further to alarm, perhaps, may occur the first night. After
surmounting your *unconquerable* horror of the bed, you will retire to rest,
and get a few hours' unquiet slumber. But on the second, or at farthest
the *third* night after your arrival, you will probably have a violent storm.
Peals of thunder so loud as to seem to shake the edifice to its foundation
will roll round the neighbouring mountains; and during the frightful
gusts of wind which accompany it, you will probably think you discern
(for your lamp is not extinguished) one part of the hanging more violently
agitated than the rest. Unable of course to repress your curiosity in so
favourable a moment for indulging it, you will instantly arise, and throwing your dressing-gown around you, proceed to examine this mystery.
After a very short search you will discover a division in the tapestry so
artfully constructed as to defy the minutest inspection, and on opening
it a door will immediately appear, which door being only secured by
massy bars and a padlock, you will, after a few efforts, succeed in opening,
and with your lamp in your hand, will pass through it into a small vaulted
room."

"No, indeed; I should be too much frightened to do any such thing."

"What! not when Dorothy has given you to understand that there is a
secret subterraneous communication between your apartment and the
chapel of St. Anthony, scarcely two miles off? Could you shrink from so
simple an adventure? No, no; you will proceed into this small vaulted
room, and through this into several others, without perceiving anything
very remarkable in either. In one, perhaps, there may be a dagger, in

another, a few drops of blood, and in a third the remains of some instru‹ ment of torture; but there being nothing in all this out of the common way, and your lamp being nearly exhausted, you will return towards your own apartment. In repassing through the small vaulted room, however, your eyes will be attracted towards a large, old-fashioned cabinet of ebony and gold, which, though narrowly examining the furniture before, you had passed unnoticed. Impelled by an irresistible presentiment you will eagerly advance to it, unlock its folding doors, and search into every drawer; but for some time without discovering anything of importance; perhaps nothing but a considerable hoard of diamonds. At last, however, by touching a secret spring, an inner compartment will open, a roll of paper appears, you seize it—it contains many sheets of manuscript; you hasten with the precious treasure into your own chamber, but scarcely have you been able to decipher, 'Oh, thou, whomsoever thou mayst be, into whose hands these memoirs of the wretched Matilda may fall,' when your lamp suddenly expires in the socket, and leaves you in total darkness."

"Oh no, no! do not say so. Well, go on."

But Henry was too much amused by the interest he had raised to be able to carry it farther; he could no longer command solemnity either of subject or voice, and was obliged to entreat her to use her own fancy in the perusal of Matilda's woes. Catherine, recollecting herself, grew ashamed of her eagerness, and began earnestly to assure him that her attention had been fixed without the smallest apprehension of really meeting with what he related. Miss Tilney, she was sure, would never put her into such a chamber as he had described. She was not at all afraid.

As they drew near the end of their journey, her impatience for a sight of the Abbey, for some time suspended by his conversation on subjects very different, returned in full force, and every bend in the road was expected, with solemn awe, to afford a glimpse of its massy walls of grey stone, rising amidst a grove of ancient oaks, with the last beams of the sun playing in beautiful splendour on its high Gothic windows. But so low did the building stand, that she found herself passing through the great gates of the lodge, into the very grounds of Northanger, without having discerned even an antique chimney.

She knew not that she had any right to be surprised, but there was something in this mode of approach which she certainly had not expected. To pass between lodges of a modern appearance, to find herself with such ease in the very precincts of the Abbey, and driven so rapidly along a smooth, level road of fine gravel, without obstacle, alarm, or solemnity of any kind, struck her as odd and inconsistent. She was not long at leisure, however, for such considerations. A sudden scud of rain driving full in her face made it impossible for her to observe anything further, and fixed all her thoughts on the welfare of her new straw bonnet; and she was actually under the Abbey walls, was springing, with Henry's assistance, from the carriage, was beneath the shelter of the old porch, and had even passed on to the hall, where her friend and the General were waiting to welcome her, without feeling one awful foreboding of future misery to herself, or one moment's suspicion of any past scenes of horror being acted within the solemn edifice. The breeze had not seemed to waft the sighs of the murderer to her; it had wafted nothing worse than a thick mizzling rain, and having given a good shake to her habit, she was ready to be shown into the common drawing-room, and capable of considering where she was.

An Abbey! Yes, it was delightful to be really in an Abbey! But she doubted, as she looked round the room, whether anything within her observation would have given her the consciousness. The furniture was in all the profusion and elegance of modern taste. The fire-place where she had expected the ample and ponderous carving of former times, was contracted to a Rumford, with slabs of plain, though handsome, marble, and ornaments over it of the prettiest English china. The windows, to which she looked with peculiar dependence, from having heard the General talk of his preserving them in their Gothic form with reverential care, were yet less what her fancy had portrayed. To be sure the pointed arch was preserved, the form of them was Gothic, they might be even casements, but every pane was so large, so clear, so light! To an imagination which had hoped for the smallest divisions and the heaviest stone work, for painted glass, dirt, and cobwebs, the difference was very distressing.

The General, perceiving how her eye was employed, began to talk of the smallness of the room and simplicity of the furniture, where everything being for daily use, pretended only to comfort, &c., flattering himself, however, that there were some apartments in the Abbey not unworthy her notice, and was proceeding to mention the costly gilding of one in particular, when, taking out his watch, he stopped short, to pronounce it, with surprise, within twenty minutes of five! This seemed the word of separation and Catherine found herself hurried away by Miss Tilney, in such a manner as convinced her that the strictest punctuality to the family hours would be expected at Northanger.

Returning through the large and lofty hall, they ascended a broad staircase of shining oak, which, after many flights and many landing-places, brought them upon a long wide gallery. On one side it had a range of doors, and it was lighted on the other by windows, which Catherine had only time to discover looked into a quadrangle, before Miss Tilney led the way into a chamber, and, scarcely staying to hope she would find it comfortable, left her with an anxious entreaty that she would make as little alteration as possible in her dress.

Chapter 21

A MOMENT'S glance was enough to satisfy Catherine that her apartment was very unlike the one which Henry had endeavoured to alarm her by the description of. It was by no means unreasonably large, and

contained neither tapestry nor velvet. The walls were papered, the floor
was carpeted, the windows were neither less perfect nor more dim than
those of the drawing-room below; the furniture, though not of the latest
fashion, was handsome and comfortable, and the air of the room altogether far from uncheerful. Her heart instantaneously at ease on this
point, she resolved to lose no time in particular examination of anything,
as she greatly dreaded disobliging the General by any delay. Her habit
therefore was thrown off with all possible haste, and she was preparing to
unpin the linen package, which the chaise-seat had conveyed for her immediate accommodation, when her eye suddenly fell on a large high chest,
standing back in a deep recess on one side of the fire-place. The sight of
it made her start; and, forgetting everything else, she stood gazing on it
in motionless wonder, while these thoughts crossed her:—

"This is strange, indeed! I did not expect such a sight as this! An
immense heavy chest! what can it hold? Why should it be placed here?
Pushed back, too, as if meant to be out of sight! I will look into it; cost me
what it may, I will look into it, and directly too—by daylight. If I stay till
evening my candle may go out." She advanced and examined it closely; it
was cedar, curiously inlaid with some darker wood, and raised about a
foot from the ground on a carved stand of the same. The lock was silver,
though tarnished from age; at each end were the imperfect remains of
handles also of silver, broken perhaps prematurely by some strange violence; and on the centre of the lid was a mysterious cipher in the same
metal. Catherine bent over it intently, but without being able to distinguish anything with certainty. She could not, in whatever direction she
took it, believe the last letter to be a *T*; and yet that it should be anything
else in that house was a circumstance to raise no common degree of
astonishment. If not originally theirs, by what strange events could it
have fallen into the Tilney family?

Her fearful curiosity was every moment growing greater; and seizing,
with trembling hands, the clasp of the lock, she resolved, at all hazards, to
satisfy herself at least as to its contents. With difficulty, for something
seemed to resist her efforts, she raised the lid a few inches; but at that
moment a sudden knocking at the door of the room made her, starting,
quit her hold, and the lid closed with alarming violence. This ill-timed
intruder was Miss Tilney's maid, sent by her mistress to be of use to Miss
Morland; and though Catherine immediately dismissed her, it recalled her
to the sense of what she ought to be doing, and forced her, in spite of her
anxious desire to penetrate this mystery, to proceed in her dressing without further delay. Her progress was not quick, for her thoughts and
her eyes were still bent on the object so well calculated to interest and
alarm; and though she dared not waste a moment upon a second attempt,
she could not remain many paces from the chest. At length, however,
having slipped one arm into her gown, her toilet seemed so nearly finished,
that the impatience of her curiosity might safely be indulged. One moment
surely might be spared; and so desperate should be the exertion of her

strength that, unless secured by supernatural means, the lid in one moment should be thrown back. With this spirit she sprang forward, and her confidence did not deceive her. Her resolute effort threw back the lid, and gave to her astonished eyes the view of a white cotton counter-pane, properly folded, reposing at one end of the chest in undisputed possession!

She was gazing on it with the first blush of surprise, when Miss Tilney, anxious for her friend's being ready, entered the room, and to the rising shame of having harboured for some minutes an absurd expectation was then added the shame of being caught in so idle a search. "That is a curious old chest, is not it?" said Miss Tilney, as Catherine hastily closed it and turned away to the glass. "It is impossible to say how many generations it has been here. How it came to be first put in this room I know not, but I have not had it moved, because I thought it might sometimes be of use in holding hats and bonnets. The worst of it is, that its weight makes it difficult to open. In that corner, however, it is at least out of the way."

Catherine had no leisure for speech, being at once blushing, tying her gown, and forming wise resolutions with the most violent despatch. Miss Tilney gently hinted her fear of being late; and in half a minute they ran down stairs together, in an alarm not wholly unfounded, for General Tilney was pacing the drawing-room, his watch in his hand, and having, on the very instant of their entering, pulled the bell with violence, ordered, "Dinner to be on table *directly!*"

Catherine trembled at the emphasis with which he spoke, and sat pale and breathless, in a most humble mood, concerned for his children, and detesting old chests; and the General recovering his politeness as he looked at her, spent the rest of his time in scolding his daughter for so foolishly hurrying her fair friend, who was absolutely out of breath from haste, when there was not the least occasion for hurry in the world; but Catherine could not at all get over the double distress of having involved her friend in a lecture and been a great simpleton herself, till they were happily seated at the dinner-table, when the General's complacent smiles, and a good appetite of her own, restored her to peace. The dining-parlour was a noble room, suitable in its dimensions to a much larger drawing-room than the one in common use, and fitted up in a style of luxury and expense which was almost lost on the unpractised eye of Catherine, who saw little more than its spaciousness and the number of their attendants. Of the former, she spoke aloud her admiration; and the General, with a very gracious countenance, acknowledged that it was by no means an ill-sized room; and further confessed, that, though as careless on such subjects as most people, he did look upon a tolerably large eating-room as one of the necessaries of life; he supposed, however, "that she must have been used to much better sized apartments at Mr. Allen's?"

"No, indeed," was Catherine's honest assurance; "Mr. Allen's dining-parlour was not more than half as large;" and she had never seen so large a room as this in her life. The General's good-humour increased. Why, as he had such rooms, he thought it would be simple not to make use of them; but, upon his honour, he believed there might be more comfort in rooms of only half their size. Mr. Allen's house, he was sure, must be exactly of the true size for rational happiness.

The evening passed without any further disturbance, and, in the occasional absence of General Tilney, with much positive cheerfulness. It was only in his presence that Catherine felt the smallest fatigue from her journey; and even then, even in moments of languor, or restraint, a sense of general happiness preponderated, and she could think of her friends in Bath without one wish of being with them.

The night was stormy; the wind had been rising at intervals the whole afternoon; and by the time the party broke up, it blew and rained violently. Catherine, as she crossed the hall, listened to the tempest with sensations of awe; and when she heard it rage round a corner of the ancient building, and close with sudden fury a distant door, felt for the first time that she was really in an Abbey. Yes, these were characteristic sounds: they brought to her recollection a countless variety of dreadful situations and horrid scenes which such buildings had witnessed, and such storms ushered in; and most heartily did she rejoice in the happier circumstances attending her entrance within walls so solemn! *She* had nothing to dread from midnight assassins or drunken gallants. Henry had certainly been only in jest in what he had told her that morning. In a house so furnished, and so guarded, she could have nothing to explore or to suffer, and might go to her bedroom as securely as if it had been her own chamber at Fullerton. Thus wisely fortifying her mind, as she proceeded upstairs, she was enabled, especially on perceiving that Miss Tilney slept only two doors from her, to enter her room with a tolerably stout heart; and her spirits were immediately assisted by the cheerful blaze of a wood fire. "How much better is this," said she, as she walked to the fender; "how much better to find a fire ready lit, than to have to wait shivering in the cold, till all the family are in bed, as so many poor girls have been obliged to do, and then to have a faithful old servant frightening one by coming in with a faggot! How glad I am that Northanger is what it is! If it had been like some other places, I do not know that, in such a night as this, I could have answered for my courage; but now, to be sure, there is nothing to alarm one."

She looked round the room. The window curtains seemed in motion. It could be nothing but the violence of the wind penetrating through the divisions of the shutters; and she stepped boldly forward, carelessly humming a tune, to assure herself of its being so, peeped courageously behind each curtain, saw nothing on either low window-seat to scare her, and on placing a hand against the shutter, felt the strongest conviction of the wind's force. A glance at the old chest, as she turned away from this examination, was not without its use; she scorned the causeless fears of an idle fancy, and began with a most happy indifference to prepare herself for bed. "She should take her time; she should not hurry herself; she did not care if she were the last person up in the house. But she would not make up her fire: *that* would seem cowardly, as if she wished for the protection of light after she were in bed." The fire, therefore, died away; and Catherine, having spent the best part of an hour in her arrangements, was beginning to think of stepping into bed, when, on giving a parting glance round the room, she was struck by the appearance of a high, old-fashioned black cabinet, which though in a situation conspicuous enough, had never caught her notice before. Henry's words, the description of the ebony cabinet which was to escape her observation at first, immediately rushed across her; and though there could be nothing really in it, there was something whimsical, it was certainly a very remarkable coincidence! She took her candle and looked closely at the cabinet. It was not absolutely ebony and gold; but it was Japan, black and yellow Japan of the handsomest kind; and as she held her candle, the yellow had very much the effect of gold.

The key was in the door, and she had a strange fancy to look into it; not, however, with the smallest expectation of finding anything, but it was so very odd, after what Henry had said. In short, she could not sleep till she had examined it. So, placing the candle with great caution on a chair, she seized the key with a very tremulous hand, and tried to turn it, but it resisted her utmost strength. Alarmed but not discouraged, she tried it another way; a bolt flew, and she believed herself successful; but how strangely mysterious! the door was still immovable. She paused a moment in breathless wonder. The wind roared down the chimney, the rain beat in torrents against the windows, and everything seemed to speak the awfulness of her situation. To retire to bed, however, unsatisfied on such a point, would be in vain, since sleep must be impossible with the consciousness of a cabinet so mysteriously closed in her immediate vicinity. Again, therefore, she applied herself to the key, and after moving it in every possible way, for some instants, with the determined celerity of hope's last effort, the door suddenly yielded to her hand: her heart leaped with exultation at such a victory, and having thrown open each folding door, the second being secured only by bolts of less wonderful construction than the lock, though in that her eye could not discern anything unusual, a double range of small drawers appeared in view, with some larger drawers above and below them, and in the centre, a small door, closed also with lock and key, secured in all probability a cavity of importance.

Catherine's heart beat quick, but her courage did not fail her. With a cheek flushed by hope, and an eye straining with curiosity, her fingers grasped the handle of a drawer and drew it forth. It was entirely empty. With less alarm and greater eagerness she seized a second, a third, a fourth—each was equally empty. Not one was left unsearched, and in not one was anything found. Well read in the art of concealing a treasure, the possibility of false linings to the drawers did not escape her, and she felt round each with anxious acuteness in vain. The place in the middle alone remained now unexplored; and though she had "never from the first had

the smallest idea of finding anything in any part of the cabinet, and was
not in the least disappointed at her ill success thus far, it would be foolish
not to examine it thoroughly while she was about it." It was some time,
however, before she could unfasten the door, the same difficulty occurring
in the management of this inner lock as of the outer; but at length it did
open; and not vain, as hitherto, was her search; her quick eyes directly
fell on a roll of paper pushed back into the further part of the cavity,
apparently for concealment, and her feelings at that moment were indescribable. Her heart fluttered, her knees trembled, and her cheeks grew
pale. She seized, with an unsteady hand, the precious manuscript, for half
a glance sufficed to ascertain written characters; and while she acknowledged with awful sensations this striking exemplification of what Henry
had foretold, resolved instantly to peruse every line before she attempted
to rest.

The dimness of the light her candle emitted made her turn to it with
alarm; but there was no danger of its sudden extinction, it had yet some
hours to burn; and that she might not have any greater difficulty in
distinguishing the writing than what its ancient date might occasion, she
hastily snuffed it. Alas! it was snuffed and extinguished in one. A lamp
could not have expired with more awful effect. Catherine, for a few moments, was motionless with horror. It was done completely; not a remnant of light in the wick could give hope to the rekindling breath. Darkness
impenetrable and immovable filled the room. A violent gust of wind, rising
with sudden fury, added fresh horror to the moment. Catherine trembled
from head to foot. In the pause which succeeded, a sound like receding
footsteps and the closing of a distant door struck on her affrighted ear.
Human nature could support no more. A cold sweat stood on her forehead,
the manuscript fell from her hand, and groping her way to the bed, she
jumped hastily in, and sought some suspensions of agony by creeping
far underneath the clothes. To close her eyes in sleep that night she felt
must be entirely out of the question. With a curiosity so justly awakened,
and feelings in every way so agitated, repose must be absolutely impossible. The storm, too, abroad so dreadful! She had not been used to
feel alarm from wind, but now every blast seemed fraught with awful
intelligence. The manuscript so wonderfully found, so wonderfully ac-
complishing the morning's prediction, how was it to be accounted for?
What could it contain? to whom could it relate? by what means could
it have been so long concealed? and how singularly strange that it should
fall to her lot to discover it! Till she had made herself mistress of its
contents, however, she could have neither repose nor comfort; and with
the sun's first rays she was determined to peruse it. But many were the
tedious hours which must yet intervene. She shuddered, tossed about in
her bed, and envied every quiet sleeper. The storm still raged, and various
were the noises, more terrific even than the wind, which struck at intervals
on her startled ear. The very curtains of her bed seemed at one moment in
motion, and at another the lock of her door was agitated, as if by the

attempt of somebody to enter. Hollow murmurs seemed to creep along the gallery, and more than once her blood was chilled by the sound of distant moans. Hour after hour passed away, and the wearied Catherine had heard three proclaimed by all the clocks in the house, before the tempest subsided, or she unknowingly fell fast asleep.

Chapter 22

THE housemaid's folding back her window-shutters at eight o'clock the next day was the sound which first roused Catherine; and she opened her eyes, wondering that they could ever have been closed, on objects of cheerfulness; her fire was already burning, and a bright morning had succeeded the tempest of the night. Instantaneously with the consciousness of existence, returned her recollection of the manuscript; and springing from the bed in the very moment of the maid's going away, she eagerly collected every scattered sheet which had burst from the roll on its falling to the ground, and flew back to enjoy the luxury of their perusal on her pillow. She now plainly saw that she must not expect a manuscript of equal length with the generality of what she had shuddered over in books, for the roll, seeming to consist entirely of small disjointed sheets, was altogether but of trifling size, and much less than she had supposed it to be at first.

Her greedy eye glanced rapidly over a page. She started at its import. Could it be possible, or did not her senses play her false? An inventory of linen, in coarse and modern characters, seemed all that was before her! If the evidence of sight might be trusted, she held a washing-bill in her hand. She seized another sheet, and saw the same articles with little variation; a third, a fourth, and a fifth, presented nothing new. Shirts, stockings, cravats, and waistcoats, faced her in each. Two others, penned by the same hand, marked an expenditure scarcely more interesting, in letters, hair-powders, shoe-string, and breeches-ball; and the larger sheet, which had enclosed the rest, seemed by its first cramped line, "To poultice chestnut mare," a farrier's bill! Such was the collection of papers (left, perhaps, as she could then suppose, by the negligence of a servant, in the place whence she had taken them) which had filled her with expectation and alarm, and robbed her of half her night's rest! She felt humbled to the dust. Could not the adventure of the chest have taught her wisdom? A corner of it catching her eye as she lay, seemed to rise up in judgment against her. Nothing could now be clearer than the absurdity of her recent fancies. To suppose that a manuscript of many generations back could have remained undiscovered in a room such as that, so modern, so habitable! or that she could be the first to possess the skill of unlocking a cabinet, the key of which was open to all.

How could she have so imposed on herself? Heaven forbid that Henry Tilney should ever know her folly! And it was in great measure his own doing, for had not the cabinet appeared so exactly to agree with his description of her adventures, she should never have felt the smallest curiosity about it. This was the only comfort that occurred. Impatient to get rid of those hateful evidences of her folly, those detestable papers then scattered over the bed, she rose directly; and folding them up as nearly as possible in the same shape as before, returned them to the same spot within the cabinet, with a very hearty wish that no untoward accident might ever bring them forward again, to disgrace her even with herself.

Why the locks should have been so difficult to open, however, was still something remarkable, for she could now manage them with perfect ease. In this there was surely something mysterious, and she indulged in the flattering suggestion for half a minute, till the possibility of the door's having been at first unlocked, and of being herself its fastener, darted into her head and cost her another blush.

She got away as soon as she could from a room in which her conduct produced such unpleasant reflections, and found her way with all speed to the breakfast-parlour, as it had been pointed out to her by Miss Tilney the evening before. Henry was alone in it; and his immediate hope of her having been undisturbed by the tempest, with an arch reference to the character of the building they inhabited, was rather distressing. For the world would she not have her weakness suspected; and yet, unequal to an absolute falsehood, was constrained to acknowledge that the wind had kept her awake a little. "But we have a charming morning after it," she added, desiring to get rid of the subject; "and storms and sleeplessness are nothing when they are over. What beautiful hyacinths! I have just learnt to love a hyacinth."

"And how might you learn? By accident or argument?"

"Your sister taught me: I cannot tell how. Mrs. Allen used to take pains, year after year, to make me like them; but I never could, till I saw them the other day in Milsom Street; I am naturally indifferent about flowers."

"But now you love a hyacinth. So much the better. You have gained a new source of enjoyment, and it is well to have as many holds upon happiness as possible. Besides, a taste for flowers is always desirable in your sex, as a means of getting you out of doors, and tempting you to more frequent exercise than you would otherwise take: and though the love of a hyacinth may be rather domestic, who can tell, the sentiment once raised, but you may in time come to love a rose?"

"But I do not want any such pursuit to get me out of doors. The pleasure of walking and breathing fresh air is enough for me, and in fine weather I am out more than half my time. Mamma says I am never within."

"At any rate, however, I am pleased that you have learnt to love a hyacinth. The mere habit of learning to love is the thing; and a teachableness of disposition in a young lady is a great blessing. Has my sister a pleasant mode of instruction?"

Catherine was saved the embarrassment of attempting an answer by the entrance of the General, whose smiling compliments announced a happy state of mind, but whose gentle hint of sympathetic early rising did not advance her composure.

The elegance of the breakfast-set forced itself on Catherine's notice when they were seated at table; and, luckily, it had been the General's choice. "He was enchanted by her approbation of his taste, confessed it to be neat and simple, thought it right to encourage the manufacture of his country; and for his part, to his uncritical palate, the tea was as well flavoured from the clay of Staffordshire as from that of Dresden or Sevres. But this was quite an old set, purchased two years ago. The manufacture was much improved since that time: he had seen some beautiful specimens when last in town and, had he not been perfectly without vanity of that kind, might have been tempted to order a new set. He trusted, however, that an opportunity might ere long occur of selecting one, though not for himself." Catherine was probably the only one of the party who did not understand him.

Shortly after breakfast Henry left them for Woodston, where business required and would keep him two or three days. They all attended in the hall to see him mount his horse, and immediately on re-entering the breakfast-room, Catherine walked to a window in the hope of catching another glimpse of his figure. "This is a somewhat heavy call upon your brother's fortitude," observed the General to Eleanor. "Woodston will make but a sombre appearance to-day."

"Is it a pretty place?" asked Catherine.

"What say you, Eleanor? Speak your opinion; for ladies can best tell the taste of ladies in regard to places as well as men. I think it would be acknowledged by the most impartial eye to have many recommendations. The house stands among fine meadows facing the south-east, with an excellent kitchen-garden in the same aspect; the walls surrounding which I built and stocked myself about ten years ago, for the benefit of my son. It is a family living, Miss Morland; and, the property in the place being chiefly my own, you may believe I take care that it shall not be a bad one. Did Henry's income depend solely on this living, he would not be ill provided for. Perhaps it may seem odd, that with only two younger children, I should think any profession necessary for him; and certainly there are moments when we could all wish him disengaged from every tie of business. But though I may not exactly make converts of you young ladies, I am sure your father, Miss Morland, would agree with me in thinking it expedient to give every young man some employment. The money is nothing, it is not an object; but employment is the thing. Even Frederick, my eldest son, you see, who will perhaps inherit as considerable a landed property as any private man in the county, has his profession."

The imposing effect of this last argument was equal to his wishes. The silence of the lady proved it to be unanswerable.

Something had been said the evening before of her being shown over the house, and he now offered himself as her conductor; and though Catherine

had hoped to explore it accompanied only by his daughter, it was a proposal of too much happiness in itself, under any circumstances not to be
gladly accepted; for she had been already eighteen hours in the Abbey,
and had seen only a few of its rooms. The netting-box just leisurely drawn
forth was closed with joyful haste, and she was ready to attend him in a
moment. "And when they had gone over the house, he promised himself,
moreover, the pleasure of accompanying her into the shrubberies and
garden." She curtsied her acquiescence. "But perhaps it might be more
agreeable to her to make those her first object. The weather was at present
favourable, and at this time of year the uncertainty was very great of its
continuing so. Which would she prefer? He was equally at her service.
Which did his daughter think would most accord with her fair friend's
wishes? But he thought he could discern. Yes, he certainly read in Miss
Morland's eyes a judicious desire of making use of the present smiling
weather. But when did she judge amiss? The Abbey would be always safe
and dry. He yielded implicitly and would fetch his hat and attend them in
a moment." He left the room, and Catherine, with a disappointed anxious
face, began to speak of her unwillingness that he should be taking them
out of doors against his own inclination, under a mistaken idea of pleasing
her; but she was stopped by Miss Tilney's saying, with a little confusion,
"I believe it will be wisest to take the morning while it is so fine; and do
not be uneasy on my father's account: he always walks out at this time
of day."

Catherine did not exactly know how this was to be understood. Why was
Miss Tilney embarrassed? Could there be any unwillingness on the
General's side to show her over the Abbey? The proposal was his own.
And was it not odd that he should *always* take his walk so early? Neither
her father nor Mr. Allen did so. It was certainly very provoking. She was
all impatience to see the house, and had scarcely any curiosity about the
grounds. If Henry had been with them, indeed! but now she should not
know what was picturesque when she saw it. Such were her thoughts; but
she kept them to herself, and put on her bonnet in patient discontent.

She was struck, however, beyond her expectation, by the grandeur of the
Abbey as she saw it for the first time from the lawn. The whole building
enclosed a large court, and two sides of the quadrangle, rich in Gothic
ornaments, stood forward for admiration. The remainder was shut off by
knolls of old trees, or luxuriant plantations, and the steep woody hills
rising behind to give it shelter were beautiful even in the leafless month of
March. Catherine had seen nothing to compare with it; and her feelings
of delight were so strong, that without waiting for any better authority,
she boldly burst forth in wonder and praise. The General listened with
assenting gratitude, and it seemed as if his own estimation of Northanger
had awaited unfixed till that hour.

The kitchen-garden was to be next admired, and he led the way to it
across a small portion of the park.

The number of acres contained in this garden was such as Catherine could not listen to without dismay, being more than double the extent of all Mr. Allen's as well as her father's, including churchyard and orchard. The walls seemed countless in number, endless in length; a village of hot-houses seemed to arise among them, and a whole parish to be at work within the enclosure. The General was flattered by her looks of surprise, which told him almost as plainly, as he soon forced her to tell him in words, that she had never seen any gardens at all equal to them before; and he then modestly owned that, "without any ambition of that sort himself, without any solicitude about it, he did believe them to be un-rivalled in the kingdom. If he had a hobby-horse, it was *that*. He loved a garden. Though careless enough in most matters of eating, he loved good fruit; or if he did not, his friends and children did. There were great vexations, however, attending such a garden as his. The utmost care could not always secure the most valuable fruits. The pinery had yielded only one hundred in the last year. Mr. Allen, he supposed, must feel these inconveniences as well as himself."

"No, not at all. Mr. Allen did not care about the garden and never went into it."

With a triumphant smile of self-satisfaction, the General wished he could do the same, for he never entered his without being vexed in one way or other, by its falling short of his plan.

"How were Mr. Allen's succession-houses worked?" describing the nature of his own as they entered them.

"Mr. Allen had only one small hot-house, which Mrs. Allen had the use of for her plants in winter, and there was a fire in it now and then."

"He is a happy man!" said the General, with a look of very happy contempt.

Having taken her into every division, and led her under every wall, till she was heartily weary of seeing and wondering, he suffered the girls at last to seize the advantage of an outer door, and then expressing his wish to examine the effect of some recent alterations about the tea-house, pro-posed it as no unpleasant extension of their walk, if Miss Morland were not tired. "But where are you going, Eleanor? Why do you choose that cold, damp path to it? Miss Morland will get wet. Our best way is across the park."

"This is so favourite a walk of mine," said Miss Tilney, "that I always think it the best and nearest way. But perhaps it may be damp."

It was a narrow winding path through a thick grove of old Scotch firs; and Catherine, struck by its gloomy aspect, and eager to enter it, could not, even by the General's disapprobation, be kept from stepping forward. He perceived her inclination, and having again urged the plea of health in vain, was too polite to make further opposition. He excused himself, however, from attending them: The rays of the sun were not too cheerful for him, and he would meet them by another course. He turned away; and Catherine was shocked to find how much her spirits were relieved by the separation. The shock, however, being less real than the relief, offered it no injury; and she began to talk with easy gaiety of the delightful melancholy which such a grove inspired.

"I am particularly fond of this spot," said her companion, with a sigh. "It was my mother's favourite walk."

Catherine had never heard Mrs. Tilney mentioned in the family before; and the interest excited by this tender remembrance showed itself directly in her altered countenance, and in the attentive pause with which she waited for something more.

"I used to walk here so often with her," added Eleanor; "though I never loved it then as I have loved it since. At that time, indeed, I used to wonder at her choice. But her memory endears it now."

"And ought it not," reflected Catherine, "to endear it to her husband? Yet the General would not enter it." Miss Tilney continuing silent, she ventured to say, "Her death must have been a great affliction."

"A great and increasing one," replied the other, in a low voice. "I was only thirteen when it happened; and though I felt my loss perhaps as strongly as one so young could feel it, I did not, I could not then know what a loss it was." She stopped for a moment, and then added with great firmness: "I have no sister, you know; and though Henry—though my brothers are very affectionate, and Henry is a great deal here, which I am most thankful for, it is impossible for me not to be often solitary."

"To be sure, you must miss him very much."

"A mother would have been always present; a mother would have been a constant friend; her influence would have been beyond all other."

"Was she a very charming woman? Was she handsome? Was there any picture of her in the Abbey? And why had she been so partial to that grove? Was it from dejection of spirits?" were questions now eagerly poured forth. The first three received a ready affirmative, the two others were passed by; and Catherine's interest in the deceased Mrs. Tilney augmented with every question, whether answered or not. Of her unhappiness in marriage she felt persuaded. The General certainly had been an unkind husband. He did not love her walk; could he, therefore, have loved her? And besides, handsome as he was, there was a something in the turn of his features which spoke his not having behaved well to her.

"Her picture, I suppose," blushing at the consummate art of her own question, "hangs in your father's room?"

"No; it was intended for the drawing-room; but my father was dissatisfied with the painting, and for some time it had no place. Soon after her death I obtained it for my own, and hung it in my bedchamber, where I shall be happy to show it you: it is very like." Here was another proof. A portrait, very like, of a departed wife, not valued by her husband. He must have been dreadfully cruel to her.

Catherine attempted no longer to hide from herself the nature of the feelings which, in spite of all his attentions, he had previously excited; and what had been terror and dislike before, was now absolute aversion. Yes, aversion! His cruelty to such a charming woman made him odious to her.

She had often read of such characters; characters, which Mr. Allen had been used to call unnatural and overdrawn; but here was proof positive to the contrary.

She had just settled this point, when the end of the path brought them directly upon the General; and in spite of all her virtuous indignation, she found herself again obliged to walk with him, listen to him, and even to smile when he smiled. Being no longer able, however, to receive pleasure from the surrounding objects, she soon began to walk with lassitude; the General perceived it, and with a concern for her health, which seemed to reproach her for her opinion of him, was most urgent for returning with his daughter to the house. He would follow them in a quarter of an hour. Again they parted; but Eleanor was called back in half a minute to receive a strict charge against taking her friend round the Abbey till his return. This second instance of his anxiety to delay what she so much wished for struck Catherine as very remarkable.

Chapter 23

AN hour passed away before the General came in, spent, on the part of his young guest, in no very favourable consideration of his character. "This lengthened absence, these solitary rambles, did not speak a mind at ease, or a conscience void of reproach." At length he appeared; and whatever might have been the gloom of his meditations, he could still smile with *them*. Miss Tilney, understanding, in part, her friend's curiosity to see the house, soon revived the subject; and her father being, contrary to Catherine's expectations, unprovided with any pretence for further delay, beyond that of stopping five minutes to order refreshments to be in the room by their return, was at last ready to escort them.

They set forward; and, with a grandeur of air, a dignified step, which caught the eye, but could not shake the doubts of the well-read Catherine, he led the way across the hall through the common drawing-room and one useless ante-chamber, into a room magnificent both in size and furniture, the real drawing-room, used only with company of consequence. It was very noble, very grand, very charming, was all that Catherine had to say, for her indiscriminating eye scarcely discerned the colour of the satin; and all minuteness of praise, all praise that had such meaning, was supplied by the General: the costliness or elegance of any room's fitting up could be nothing to her; she cared for no furniture of a more modern date than the fifteenth century. When the General had satisfied his own curiosity, in a close examination of every well-known ornament, they proceeded to the library, an apartment, in its way, of equal magnificence, exhibiting a collection of books, on which an humble man might have looked with pride. Catherine heard, admired, and wondered with more genuine feeling than before, gathered all that she could from this storehouse of knowledge by running over the titles of half a shelf, and was ready to proceed. But suites of apartments did not spring up with her wishes. Large as was the building, she had already visited the greatest part; though, on being told that, with the addition of the kitchen, the six or seven rooms she had now seen surrounded three sides of the court, she could scarcely believe it, or overcome the suspicion of there being many chambers secreted. It was some relief, however, that they were to return to the rooms in common use by passing through a few of less importance, looking into the court, which with occasional passages, not wholly unintricate, connected the different sides; and she was further soothed in her progress by being told that she was treading what had once been a cloister, having traces of cells pointed out, and observing several doors that were neither opened nor explained to her; by finding herself successively in a billiard-room and in the General's private apartment, without comprehending their connection, or being able to turn aright when she left them; and lastly by passing through a dark little room, owning Henry's authority, and strewed with his litter of books, guns, and great-coats.

From the dining-room, of which, though already seen, and always to be seen at five o'clock, the General could not forego the pleasure of pacing out the length for the more certain information of Miss Morland, as to what she neither doubted nor cared for, they proceeded by quick communication to the kitchen—the ancient kitchen of the convent, rich in the massy walls and smoke of former days and in the stoves and hot closets of the present. The General's improving hand had not loitered here: every modern invention to facilitate the labour of the cooks had been adopted within this their spacious theatre; and, when the genius of others had failed, his own had often produced the perfection wanted. His endowments of this spot alone might at any time have placed him high among the benefactors of the convent.

With the walls of the kitchen ended all the antiquity of the Abbey; the fourth side of the quadrangle having, on account of its decaying state, been removed by the General's father and the present erected in its place. All that was venerable ceased here. The new building was not only new, but declared itself to be so; intended only for offices, and enclosed behind by stable-yards, no uniformity of architecture had been thought necessary. Catherine could have raved at the hand which had swept away what must have been beyond the value of all the rest, for the purpose of mere domestic economy; and would willingly have been spared the mortification of a walk through scenes so fallen, had the General allowed it: but if he had a vanity, it was in the arrangement of his offices; and as he was convinced that, to a mind like Miss Morland's, a view of the accommodations and comforts by which the labours of her inferiors were softened, must always be gratifying, he should make no apology for leading her on. They took a slight survey of all; and Catherine was impressed, beyond her expectation, by their multiplicity and their convenience. The purposes for which a few shapeless pantries and a comfortless scullery, were deemed sufficient at Fullerton, were here carried on in appropriate divisions, commodious and roomy. The number of servants continually appearing, did not strike her less than the number of their offices. Wherever they went, some pattened girl stopped to curtsey, or some footman in dishabille sneaked off. Yet this was an Abbey! How inexpressibly different in these domestic arrangements from such as she had read about: from abbeys and castles, in which, though certainly larger than Northanger, all the dirty work of the house was to be done by two pair of female hands at the utmost. How they could get through it all, had often amazed Mrs. Allen; and, when Catherine saw what was necessary here, she began to be amazed herself.

They returned to the hall, that the chief staircase might be ascended, and the beauty of its wood and ornaments of rich carving might be pointed out: having gained the top, they turned in an opposite direction from the gallery in which her room lay, and shortly entered one on the same plan, but superior in length and breadth. She was here shown successively into three large bed-chambers, with their dressing-rooms, most completely and handsomely fitted up: everything that money and taste could do, to give comfort and elegance to apartments, had been bestowed on these; and, being furnished within the last five years, they were perfect in all that would be generally pleasing, and wanting in all that could give pleasure to Catherine. As they were surveying the last, the General, after slightly naming a few of the distinguished characters by whom they had at times been honoured, turned with a smiling countenance to Catherine, and ventured to hope that henceforward some of the earliest tenants might be "our friends from Fullerton." She felt the unexpected compliment, and deeply regretted the impossibility of thinking well of a man so kindly disposed towards herself, and so full of civility to all her family.

The gallery was terminated by folding doors, which Miss Tilney, advancing, had thrown open, and passed through, and seemed on the point of doing the same by the first door to the left, in another long reach of gallery, when the General, coming forwards, called her hastily, and, as Catherine thought, rather angrily back, demanding whither she were going? And what was there more to be seen? Had not Miss Morland already seen all that could be worth her notice? And did she not suppose her friend might be glad of some refreshment after so much exercise? Miss Tilney drew back directly, and the heavy doors were closed upon the mortified Catherine, who, having seen, in a momentary glance beyond them, a narrower passage, more numerous openings, and symptoms of a winding staircase, believed herself at last within the reach of something worth her notice; and felt, as she unwillingly paced back the gallery, that she would rather be allowed to examine that end of the house than see all the finery of all the rest. The General's evident desire of preventing such an examination was an additional stimulant. Something was certainly to be concealed: her fancy, though it had trespassed lately once or twice, could not mislead her here; and what that something was, a short sentence of Miss Tilney's as they followed the General at some distance downstairs, seemed to point out:—"I was going to take you into what was my mother's room. the room in which she died——" were all her words; but few as they were, they conveyed pages of intelligence to Catherine. It was no wonder that the General should shrink from the sight of such objects as that room must contain—a room, in all probability, never entered by him since the dreadful scene had passed which released his suffering wife, and left him to the stings of conscience.

She ventured, when next alone with Eleanor, to express her wish of being permitted to see it, as well as all the rest of that side of the house; and Eleanor promised to attend her there, whenever they should have a convenient hour. Catherine understood her: the General must be watched from home, before that room could be entered. "It remains as it was, I suppose?" said she, in a tone of feeling.

"Yes, entirely."

"And how long ago may it be that your mother died?"

"She has been dead these nine years." And nine years, Catherine knew, was a trifle of time, compared with what generally elapsed after the death of an injured wife, before her room was put to rights.

"You were with her, I suppose, to the last?"

"No," said Miss Tilney, sighing: "I was unfortunately from home. Her illness was sudden and short; and before I arrived, it was all over."

Catherine's blood ran cold with the horrid suggestions which naturally sprang from these words. Could it be possible? Could Henry's father——? And yet how many were the examples to justify even the blackest suspicions! And when she saw him in the evening, while she worked with her friend, slowly pacing the drawing-room for an hour together in silent thoughtfulness, with downcast eyes and contracted brow, she felt secure from all possibility of wronging him. It was the air and attitude of a Montoni! What could more plainly speak the gloomy workings of a mind not wholly dead to every sense of humanity, in its fearful review of past scenes of guilt! Unhappy man! And the anxiousness of her spirits directed her eyes towards his figure so repeatedly, as to catch Miss Tilney's notice. "My father," she whispered, "often walks about the room in this way; it is nothing unusual."

"So much the worse!" thought Catherine: such ill-timed exercise was of a piece with the strange unseasonableness of his morning walks, and boded nothing good.

After an evening, the little variety and seeming length of which made her peculiarly sensible of Henry's importance among them, she was heartily glad to be dismissed; though it was a look from the General not designed for her observation which sent his daughter to the bell. When the butler would have lit his master's candle, however, he was forbidden. The latter was not going to retire. "I have many pamphlets to finish," said he to Catherine, "before I can close my eyes; and perhaps may be poring over the affairs of the nation for hours after you are asleep. Can either of us be more meetly employed? *My* eyes will be blinding for the good of others; and *yours* preparing by rest for future mischief."

But neither the business alleged, nor the magnificent compliment, could win Catherine from thinking that some very different object must occasion so serious a delay of proper repose. To be kept up for hours, after the family were in bed, by stupid pamphlets, was not very likely. There must be some deeper cause: something was to be done which could be done only when the household slept; and the probability that Mrs. Tilney yet lived, shut up for causes unknown, and receiving from the pitiless hands of her husband a nightly supply of coarse food, was the conclusion which necessarily followed. Shocking as was the idea, it was at least better than a death unfairly hastened, as in the natural course of things she must ere long be released. The suddenness of her reputed illness, the absence of her daughter, and probably of her other children, at the time, all favoured the supposition of her imprisonment. Its origin—jealousy, perhaps, or wanton cruelty—was yet to be unravelled.

In revolving these matters while she undressed, it suddenly struck her as not unlikely that she might that morning have passed near the very spot of this unfortunate woman's confinement; might have been within a few paces of the cell in which she languished out her days; for what part of the Abbey could be more fitted for the purpose than that which yet bore the traces of monastic division? In the high-arched passage, paved with stone, which already she had trodden with peculiar awe, she well remembered the doors of which the General had given no account. To what might not these doors lead? In support of the plausibility of this conjecture, it further occurred to her that the forbidden gallery in which lay the apartments of the unfortunate Mrs. Tilney, must be, as certainly as her memory could guide her, exactly over this suspected range of cells; and the staircase by the side of those apartments of which she had caught a transient glimpse, communicating by some secret means with those cells, might well have favoured the barbarous proceedings of her husband. Down that staircase she had perhaps been conveyed in a state of well-prepared insensibility.

Catherine sometimes started at the boldness of her own surmises, and sometimes hoped or feared that she had gone too far; but they were supported by such appearances as made their dismissal impossible.

The side of the quadrangle, in which she supposed the guilty scene to be acting, being, according to her belief, just opposite her own, it struck her that, if judiciously watched, some rays of light from the General's lamp might glimmer through the lower windows, as he passed to the prison of his wife; and, twice before she stepped into bed, she stole gently from her room, to the corresponding window in the gallery, to see if it appeared; but all abroad was dark, and it must yet be too early. The various ascending noises convinced her that the servants must still be up. Till midnight, she supposed it would be in vain to watch; but then, when the clock had struck twelve, and all was quiet, she would, if not appalled by darkness, steal out and look once more. The clock struck twelve, and Catherine had been half an hour asleep.

Chapter 24

THE next day afforded no opportunity for the proposed examination of the mysterious apartments. It was Sunday, and the whole time between morning and afternoon service was required by the General in exercise abroad or eating cold meat at home; and great as was Catherine's curiosity, her courage was not equal to a wish of exploring them after dinner, either by the fading light of the sky between six and seven o'clock, or by the yet more partial though stronger illumination of a treacherous lamp. The day was unmarked, therefore, by anything to interest her imagination beyond the sight of a very elegant monument to the memory of Mrs. Tilney, which immediately fronted the family pew. By that her eye was instantly caught and long retained; and the perusal of the highly strained epitaph, in which every virtue was ascribed to her by the inconsolable husband, who must have been in some way or other her destroyer, affected her even to tears.

That the General, having erected such a monument, should be able to face it, was not perhaps very strange, and yet that he could sit so boldly collected within its view, maintain so elevated an air, look so fearlessly around, nay, that he should even enter the church, seemed wonderful to Catherine. Not, however, that many instances of being equally hardened in guilt might not be produced. She could remember dozens who had persevered in every possible vice, going on from crime to crime, murdering whomsoever they chose, without any feeling of humanity or remorse, till a violent death or a religion retirement closed their black career. The erection of the monument itself could not in the smallest degree affect her doubts of Mrs. Tilney's actual decease. Were she even to descend into the family vault where her ashes were supposed to slumber, were she to behold the coffin in which they were said to be enclosed, what could it avail in such a case? Catherine had read too much not to be perfectly aware of the ease with which a waxen figure might be introduced, and a supposititious funeral carried on.

The succeeding morning promised something better. The General's early walk, ill-timed as it was in every other view, was favourable here; and when she knew him to be out of the house, she directly proposed to Miss Tilney the accomplishment of her promise. Eleanor was ready to oblige her; and Catherine reminding her as they went of another promise, their first visit in consequence was to the portrait in her bed-chamber. It represented a very lovely woman, with a mild and pensive countenance, justifying so far, the expectations of its new observer; but they were not in every respect answered, for Catherine had depended upon meeting with features, air, complexion, that should be the very counterpart, the very image, if not of Henry's, of Eleanor's; the only portraits of which she had been in the habit of thinking, bearing always an equal resemblance of mother and child. A face once taken was taken for generations. But here she was obliged to look, and consider, and study for a likeness. She contemplated it, however, in spite of this drawback, with much emotion; and, but for a yet stronger interest, would have left it unwillingly.

Her agitation, as they entered the great gallery, was too much for any endeavour at discourse; she could only look at her companion. Eleanor's countenance was dejected, yet sedate; and its composure spoke her enured to all the gloomy objects to which they were advancing. Again she passed through the folding-doors, again her hand was upon the important lock, and Catherine, hardly able to breathe, was turning to close the former with fearful caution, when the figure, the dreaded figure of the General himself at the further end of the gallery stood before her! The name of "Eleanor" at the same moment, in his loudest tone, resounded through the building, giving to his daughter the first intimation of his presence, and to Catherine terror upon terror. An attempt at concealment had been her first instinctive movement on perceiving him, yet she could scarcely hope to have escaped his eye; and when her friend, who with an apologizing look darted hastily by her, had joined and disappeared with him, she ran for safety to her own room, and, locking herself in, believed that she should never have courage to go down again. She remained there at least an hour, in the greatest agitation, deeply commiserating the state of her poor friend, and expecting a summons herself from the angry General, to attend him in his own apartment. No summons, however, arrived; and at last on seeing a carriage drive up to the Abbey, she was emboldened to descend and meet him under the protection of visitors. The breakfast-room was gay with company; and she was named to them by the General as the friend of his daughter, in a complimentary style, which so well concealed his resentful ire, as to make her feel secure at least of life for the present. And Eleanor, with a command of countenance which did honour to her concern for his character, taking an early occasion of saying to her, "My father only wanted me to answer a note," she began to hope that she had either been unseen by the General, or that from some consideration of policy she should be allowed to suppose herself so. Upon this trust she dared still to remain in his presence after the company left them, and nothing occurred to disturb it.

In the course of this morning's reflections, she came to a resolution of making her next attempt on the forbidden door alone. It would be much better in every respect that Eleanor should know nothing of the matter. To involve her in the danger of a second detection, to court her into an apartment which must wring her heart, could not be the office of a friend. The General's utmost anger could not be to herself what it might be to a daughter, and besides, she thought the examination itself would be more satisfactory if made without any companion. It would be impossible to explain to Eleanor the suspicions, from which the other had in all likelihood been hitherto happily exempt; nor could she therefore, in *her* presence, search for those proofs of the General's cruelty, which however they might yet have escaped discovery, she felt confident of somewhere drawing forth, in the shape of some fragmented journal, continued to the last gasp. Of the way to the apartment she was now perfectly mistress, and as she wished to get it over before Henry's return, who was expected on the morrow, there was no time to be lost. The day was bright, her courage high; at four o'clock the sun was now two hours above the horizon, and it would be only her retiring to dress half an hour earlier than usual.

It was done; and Catherine found herself alone in the gallery before the clocks had ceased to strike. It was no time for thought: she hurried on, slipped with the least possible noise through the folding doors, and without stopping to look or breathe, rushed forward to the one in question. The lock yielded to her hand, and luckily with no sullen sound that could alarm a human being. On tiptoe she entered: the room was before her: but it was some minutes before she could advance another step. She beheld what fixed her to the spot, and agitated every feature. She saw a large, well-proportioned apartment, a handsome dimity bed, arranged as unoccupied, with a housemaid's care, a bright Bath stove, mahogany wardrobes and neatly-painted chairs, on which the warm beams of a western sun gaily poured through two sash windows. Catherine had expected to have her feelings worked, and worked they were. Astonishment and doubt first seized them, and a shortly succeeding ray of common sense added some bitter emotions of shame. She could not be mistaken as to the room; but how grossly mistaken in everything else, in Miss Tilney's meaning, in her own calculation! This apartment, to which she had given a date so ancient, a position so awful, proved to be one end of what the General's father had built. There were two other doors in the chamber, leading probably into dressing-closets, but she had no inclination to open either. Would the veil in which Mrs. Tilney had last walked, or the volume in which she had last read, remain to tell what nothing else was allowed to whisper? No; whatever might have been the General's crimes, he had certainly too much wit to let them sue for detection. She was sick of exploring, and desired but to be safe in her own room, with her own heart only privy to its folly, and she was on the point of retreating as softly as she had entered, when the sound of footsteps, she could hardly tell where, made her pause and tremble. To be found there, even by a servant, would be unpleasant, but by the General (and he seemed always at hand when least wanted) much worse. She listened, the sound had ceased, and resolving not to lose a moment she passed through and closed the door. At that instant a door underneath was hastily opened, some one seemed with swift steps to ascend the stairs, by the head of which she had yet to pass before she could gain the gallery. She had no power to move. With a feeling of terror not very definable, she fixed her eyes on the staircase, and in a few moments it gave Henry to her view. "Mr. Tilney?" she exclaimed, in a voice of more than common astonishment. He looked astonished too. "Good God!" she continued, not attending to his address, "how came you here? How came you up that staircase?"

"How came I up that staircase?" he replied, greatly surprised. "Because it is my nearest way from the stable-yard to my own chamber; and why should I not come up it?"

Catherine recollected herself, blushed deeply, and could say no more. He seemed to be looking in her countenance for that explanation which her lips did not afford. She moved on towards the gallery. "And may I not, in my turn," said he, as he pushed back the folding doors, "ask how *you* came here? This passage is at least as extraordinary a road from the breakfast-parlour to your apartment, as that staircase can be from the stables to mine."

"I have been," said Catherine, looking down, "to see your mother's room."

"My mother's room! Is there anything extraordinary to be seen there?"

"No, nothing at all. I thought you did not mean to come back till to-morrow."

"I did not expect to be able to return sooner, when I went away; but three hours ago I had the pleasure of finding nothing to detain me. You look pale. I am afraid I alarmed you by running so fast up those stairs. Perhaps you did not know—you were not aware of their leading from the offices in common use?"

"No, I was not. You have had a very fine day for your ride?"

"Very; and does Eleanor leave you to find your way into all the rooms in the house by yourself?"

"Oh, no! she showed me over the greatest part on Saturday, and we were coming here to these rooms, but only" (dropping her voice), "your father was with us."

"And that prevented you," said Henry, earnestly regarding her. "Have you looked into all the rooms in that passage?"

"No; I only wanted to see—— Is not it very late? I must go and dress."

"It is only a quarter past four" (showing his watch); "and you are not now in Bath. No theatre, no Rooms to prepare for. Half an hour at Northanger must be enough."

She could not contradict it, and therefore suffered herself to be detained, though her dread of further questions made her, for the first time in their acquaintance, wish to leave him. They walked slowly up the gallery. "Have you had any letter from Bath since I saw you?"

"No, and I am very much surprised. Isabella promised so faithfully to write directly."

"Promised so faithfully! A faithful promise! That puzzles me. I have heard of a faithful performance; but a faithful promise—the fidelity of promising! It is a power little worth knowing, however, since it can deceive and pain you. My mother's room is very commodious, is it not? Large and cheerful looking, and the dressing-closets so well disposed. It always strikes me as the most comfortable apartment in the house; and I rather wonder that Eleanor should not take it for her own. She sent you to look at it, I suppose?"

"No."

"It has been your own doing entirely?" Catherine said nothing. After a short silence during which he had closely observed her, he added: "As there is nothing in the room in itself to raise curiosity, this must have proceeded from a sentiment of respect for my mother's character, as described by Eleanor, which does honour to her memory. The world, I believe, never saw a better woman. But it is not often that virtue can boast an interest such as this. The domestic, unpretending merits of a person never known, do not often create that kind of fervent, venerating tenderness which would prompt a visit like yours. Eleanor, I suppose, has talked of her a great deal?"

"Yes, a great deal. That is—no, not much, but what she did say, was very interesting. Her dying so suddenly" (slowly, and with hesitation it was spoken), "and you—none of you being at home; and your father, I thought, perhaps, had not been very fond of her."

"And from these circumstances," he replied (his quick eye fixed on hers), "you infer, perhaps, the probability of some negligence—some—" (involuntarily she shook her head), "or it may be, of something still less pardonable." She raised her eyes towards him more fully than she had ever done before. "My mother's illness," he continued, "the seizure which ended in her death, *was* sudden. The malady itself one from which she had often suffered: a bilious fever: its cause therefore constitutional. On the third day, in short, as soon as she could be prevailed on, a physician attended her; a very respectable man, and one in whom she had always placed great confidence. Upon his opinion of her danger, two others were called in the next day, and remained in almost constant attendance for four-and-twenty hours. On the fifth day she died. During the progress of her disorder, Frederick and I (*we* were both at home) saw her repeatedly; and from our own observation can bear witness to her having received every possible attention which could spring from the affection of those about her, or which her situation in life could command. Poor Eleanor *was* absent, and at such a distance as to return only to see her mother in her coffin."

"But your father," said Catherine, "was *he* afflicted?"

"For a time, greatly so. You have erred in supposing him not attached to her. He loved her, I am persuaded, as well as it was possible for him to—— We have not all, you know, the same tenderness of disposition; and I will not pretend to say that while she lived, she might not often have had much to bear; but though his temper injured her, his judgment never did. His value of her was sincere; and, if not permanently, he was truly afflicted by her death."

"I am very glad of it," said Catherine; "it would have been very shocking——"

"If I understand you rightly, you had formed a surmise of such horror as I have hardly words to—— Dear Miss Morland, consider the dreadful nature of the suspicions you have entertained. What have you been judging from? Remember the country and the age in which we live. Remember that we are English: that we are Christians. Consult your own understanding, your own sense of the probable, your own observation of what is passing around you. Does our education prepare us for such atrocities? Do our laws connive at them? Could they be perpetrated without being known in a country like this, where social and literary intercourse is on such a footing, where every man is surrounded by a neighbourhood of voluntary spies, and where roads and newspapers lay everything open? Dearest Miss Morland, what ideas have you been admitting?"

They had reached the end of the gallery; and with tears of shame she ran off to her own room.

Chapter 25

THE visions of romance were over. Catherine was completely awakened. Henry's address, short as it had been, had more thoroughly opened her eyes to the extravagance of her late fancies than all their several disappointments had done. Most grievously was she humbled. Most bitterly did she cry. It was not only with herself that she was sunk, but with Henry. Her folly, which now seemed even criminal, was all exposed to him, and he must despise her for ever. The liberty which her imagination had dared to take with the character of his father, could he ever forgive it? The absurdity of her curiosity and her fears, could they ever be forgotten? She hated herself more than she could express. He had, she thought he had, once or twice before this fatal morning, shown something like affection for her. But now—in short, she made herself as miserable as possible for about half an hour, went down, when the clock struck five, with a broken heart, and could scarcely give an intelligible answer to Eleanor's inquiry if she was well. The formidable Henry soon followed her into the room, and the only difference in his behaviour to her was, that he paid her rather more attention than usual. Catherine had never wanted comfort more, and he looked as if he was aware of it.

The evening wore away with no abatement of this soothing politeness; and her spirits were gradually raised to a modest tranquillity. She did not learn either to forget or defend the past; but she learned to hope that it would never transpire further, and that it might not cost her Henry's entire regard. Her thoughts being still chiefly fixed on what she had with such causeless terror felt and done, nothing could shortly be clearer, than that it had been all a voluntary, self-created delusion, each trifling circumstance receiving importance from an imagination resolved on alarm, and everything forced to bend to one purpose by a mind which, before she entered the Abbey, had been craving to be frightened. She remembered with what feelings she had prepared for a knowledge of Northanger. She saw that the infatuation had been created, the mischief settled, long before her quitting Bath, and it seemed as if the whole might be traced to the influence of that sort of reading which she had there indulged.

Charming as were all Mrs. Radcliffe's works, and charming even as were the works of all her imitators, it was not in them perhaps that human nature, at least in the midland counties of England was to be looked for. Of the Alps and Pyrenees, with their pine forests and their vices, they might give a faithful delineation; and Italy, Switzerland, and the South of France, might be as fruitful in horrors as they were there represented. Catherine dared not doubt beyond her own country, and even of that, if hard pressed, would have yielded the northern and western extremities. But in the central part of England there was surely some security for the existence even of a wife not beloved, in the laws of the land, and the manners of the age. Murder was not tolerated, servants were not slaves, and neither poison nor sleeping potions to be procured, like rhubarb, from every druggist. Among the Alps and Pyrenees, perhaps, there were no mixed characters. There, such as were not as spotless as an angel, might have the dispositions of a fiend. But in England it was not so; among the English, she believed, in their hearts and habits, there was a general though unequal mixture of good and bad. Upon this conviction, she would not be surprised if even in Henry and Eleanor Tilney some slight imperfection might hereafter appear; and upon this conviction she need not fear to acknowledge some actual specks in the character of their father, who, though cleared from the grossly injurious suspicions which she must ever blush to have entertained, she did believe, upon serious consideration, to be not perfectly amiable.

Her mind made up on these several points, and her resolution formed, of always judging and acting in future with the greatest good sense, she had nothing to do but to forgive herself and be happier than ever; and the lenient hand of time did much for her by insensible gradations in the course of another day. Henry's astonishing generosity and nobleness of conduct, in never alluding in the slightest way to what had passed, was of the greatest assistance to her; and sooner than she could have supposed it possible, in the beginning of her distress, her spirits became absolutely comfortable, and capable, as heretofore, of continual improvement by anything he said. There were still some subjects, indeed, under which she believed they must always tremble; the mention of a chest or a cabinet, for instance, and she did not love the sight of japan in any shape; but even *she* could allow that an occasional memento of past folly, however painful, might not be without use.

The anxieties of common life began soon to succeed to the alarms of romance. Her desire of hearing from Isabella grew every day greater. She was quite impatient to know how the Bath world went on, and how the Rooms were attended; and especially was she anxious to be assured of Isabella's having matched some fine netting cotton, on which she had left her intent; and of her continuing on the best terms with James. Her only dependence for information of any kind was on Isabella. James had protested against writing to her till his return to Oxford; and Mrs. Allen had given her no hopes of a letter till she had got back to Fullerton. But Isabella had promised and promised again; and when she promised a thing she was so scrupulous in performing it; this made it so particularly strange!

For nine successive mornings Catherine wondered over the repetition of a disappointment which each morning became more severe; but on the tenth, when she entered the breakfast-room, her first object was a letter, held out by Henry's willing hand. She thanked him as heartily as if he had written it himself. " 'Tis only from James, however," as she looked at the direction. She opened it: it was from Oxford, and to this purpose:

"DEAR CATHERINE,—Though, God knows, with little inclination for writing, I think it my duty to tell you, that everything is at an end between Miss Thorpe and me. I left her and Bath yesterday, never to see either again. I shall not enter into particulars, they would only pain you more. You will soon hear enough from another quarter to know where lies the blame; and I hope will acquit your brother of everything but the folly of too easily thinking his affection returned. Thank God! I am undeceived in time! But it is a heavy blow! After my father's consent had been so kindly given—but no more of this. She has made me miserable for ever! Let me soon hear from you, dear Catherine; you are my only friend; *your* love I do build upon. I wish your visit at Northanger may be over before Captain Tilney makes his engagement known, or you will be uncomfortably circumstanced. Poor Thorpe is in town: I dread the sight of him; his honest heart would feel so much. I have written to him and my father. Her duplicity hurts me more than all; till the very last, if I reasoned with her, she declared herself as much attached to me as ever, and laughed at my fears. I am ashamed to think how long I bore with it; but if ever man had reason to believe himself loved, I was that man. I cannot understand, even now, what she would be at, for there could be no need of my being played off to make her secure of Tilney. We parted at last by mutual consent. Happy for me had we never met! I can never expect to know such another woman! Dearest Catherine, beware how you give your heart.—Believe me, etc."

Catherine had not read three lines before her sudden change of countenance, and short exclamations of sorrowing wonder, declared her to be receiving unpleasant news; and Henry, earnestly watching her through the whole letter, saw plainly that it ended no better than it began. He was prevented, however, from even looking in surprise, by his father's entrance. They went to breakfast directly; but Catherine could hardly eat anything. Tears filled her eyes, and even ran down her cheeks as she sat. The letter was one moment in her hand, then in her lap, and then in her pocket; and she looked as if she knew not what she did. The General, between his cocoa and his newspaper, had luckily no leisure for noticing her; but to the other two her distress was equally visible. As soon as she dared leave the table, she hurried away to her own room; but the housemaids were busy in it, and she was obliged to come down again. She turned into the drawing-room for privacy, but Henry and Eleanor had likewise retreated thither, and were at that moment deep in consultation about her. She drew back, trying to beg their pardon, but was, with gentle violence, forced to return; and the others withdrew, after Eleanor had affectionately expressed a wish of being of use or comfort to her.

After half an hour's free indulgence of grief and reflection, Catherine felt equal to encountering her friends; but whether she should make her distress known to them was another consideration. Perhaps, if particularly questioned, she might just give an idea—just distantly hint at it—but not more. To expose a friend, such a friend as Isabella had been to her; and then their own brother so closely concerned in it! She believed she must waive the subject altogether. Henry and Eleanor were by themselves in the breakfast-room; and each, as she entered it, looked at her anxiously. Catherine took her place at the table, and after a short silence, Eleanor said: "No bad news from Fullerton, I hope? Mr. and Mrs. Morland, your brothers and sisters, I hope they are none of them ill?"

"No, I thank you" (sighing as she spoke); "they are all very well. My letter was from my brother at Oxford."

Nothing further was said for a few minutes; and then, speaking through her tears, she added: "I do not think I shall ever wish for a letter again!"

"I am sorry," said Henry, closing the book he had just opened; "if I had suspected the letter containing anything unwelcome, I should have given it with very different feelings."

"It contained something worse than anybody could suppose! Poor James is so unhappy! You will soon know why."

"To have so kind-hearted, so affectionate a sister," replied Henry, warmly, "must be a comfort to him under any distress."

"I have one favour to beg," said Catherine, shortly afterwards, in an agitated manner, "that, if your brother should be coming here, you will give me notice of it, that I may go away."

"Our brother! Frederick!"

"Yes; I am sure I should be very sorry to leave you so soon, but something has happened that would make it very dreadful for me to be in the same house with Captain Tilney."

Eleanor's work was suspended while she gazed with increasing astonishment; but Henry began to suspect the truth, and something in which Miss Thorpe's name was included, passed his lips.

"How quick you are!" cried Catherine; "you have guessed it, I declare! And yet, when we talked about it in Bath, you little thought of its ending so. Isabella—no wonder *now* I have not heard from her—Isabella has deserted my brother, and is to marry yours! Could you have believed there had been such inconstancy and fickleness, and everything that is bad in the world?"

"I hope, so far as concerns my brother, you are misinformed. I hope he has not had any material share in bringing on Mr. Morland's disappointment. His marrying Miss Thorpe is not probable. I think you must be deceived so far. I am very sorry for Mr. Morland; sorry that anyone you love should be unhappy; but my surprise would be greater at Frederick's marrying her, than at any other part of the story."

"It is very true, however; you shall read James's letter yourself. Stay, there is one part"—recollecting, with a blush, the last line.

"Will you take the trouble of reading to us the passages which concern my brother?"

"No, read it yourself," cried Catherine, whose second thoughts were clearer. "I do not know what I was thinking of" (blushing again that she had blushed before). "James only means to give me good advice."

He gladly received the letter; and, having read it through with close attention, returned it, saying, "Well, if it is to be so, I can only say that I am sorry for it. Frederick will not be the first man who has chosen a wife with less sense than his family expected. I do not envy his situation, either as a lover or a son."

Miss Tilney, at Catherine's invitation, now read the letter likewise; and, having expressed also her concern and surprise, began to inquire into Miss Thorpe's connections and fortune.

"Her mother is a very good sort of woman," was Catherine's answer.

"What was her father?"

"A lawyer, I believe. They live at Putney."

"Are they a wealthy family?"

"No, not very. I do not believe Isabella has any fortune at all; but that will not signify in your family. Your father is so very liberal! He told me the other day that he only valued money as it allowed him to promote the happiness of his children."

The brother and sister looked at each other. "But," said Eleanor, after a short pause, "would it be to promote his happiness to enable him to marry such a girl? She must be an unprincipled one, or she could not have used your brother so. And how strange an infatuation on Frederick's side! A girl who, before his eyes, is violating an engagement voluntarily entered into with another man! Is not it inconceivable, Henry? Frederick, too, who always wore his heart so proudly! Who found no woman good enough to be loved."

"That is the most unpromising circumstance, the strongest presumption against him. When I think of his past declarations, I give him up. Moreover, I have too good an opinion of Miss Thorpe's prudence, to suppose that she would part with one gentleman before the other was secured. It is all over with Frederick, indeed! He is a deceased man; defunct in understanding. Prepare for your sister-in-law, Eleanor; and such a sister-in-law as you must delight in. Open, candid, artless, guileless, with affections strong, but simple, forming no pretensions, and knowing no disguise."

"Such a sister-in-law, Henry, I should delight in," said Eleanor, with a smile.

"But, perhaps," observed Catherine, "though she has behaved so ill by our family, she may behave better by yours. Now she has really got the man she likes, she may be constant."

"Indeed, I am afraid she will," replied Henry; "I am afraid she will be very constant, unless a baronet should come in her way; that is Frederick's only chance. I will get the Bath paper, and look over the arrivals."

"You think it is all for ambition, then? And upon my word, there are some things that seem very like it. I cannot forget that, when she first knew what my father would do for them, she seemed quite disappointed that it was not more. I never was so deceived in anyone's character in my life before."

"Among all the great variety that you have known and studied."

"My own disappointment and loss in her is very great; but, as for poor James, I suppose he will hardly ever recover it."

"Your brother is certainly very much to be pitied at present; but we must not, in our concern for his sufferings, undervalue yours. You feel, I suppose, that in losing Isabella you lose half yourself; you feel a void in your heart which nothing else can occupy. Society is becoming irksome; and as for the amusements in which you were wont to share at Bath, the very idea of them without her is abhorrent. You would not, for instance, now go to a ball for the world. You feel that you have no longer any friend to whom you can speak with unreserve; on whose regard you can place dependence; or whose counsel, in any difficulty, you could rely on. You feel all this?"

"No," said Catherine, after a few moments' reflection, "I do not—ought I? To say the truth, though I am hurt and grieved that I cannot still love her, that I am never to hear from her, perhaps never to see her again, I do not feel so very much afflicted as one would have thought."

"You feel, as you always do, what is most to the credit of human nature. Such feelings ought to be investigated, that they may know themselves."

Catherine, by some chance or other, found her spirits so very much relieved by this conversation, that she could not regret her being led on, though so unaccountably, to mention the circumstance which had produced it.

Chapter 26

From this time the subject was frequently canvassed by the three young people; and Catherine found, with some surprise, that her two young friends were perfectly agreed in considering Isabella's want of consequence and fortune as likely to throw great difficulties in the way of her marrying their brother. Their persuasion that the General would, upon this ground alone, independent of the objection that might be raised against her character, oppose the connection, turned her feelings moreover with some alarm towards herself. She was as insignificant, and perhaps as portionless as Isabella; and if the heir of the Tilney property had not grandeur and wealth enough in himself, at what point of interest were the demands of his younger brother to rest! The very painful reflections to which this thought led could only be dispersed by a dependence on the effect of that particular partiality, which, as she was given to understand by his words as well as his actions, she had from the first been so fortunate as to excite in the General; and by a recollection of some most generous and disinterested sentiments on the subject of money, which she had more than once heard him utter, and which tempted her to think his disposition in such matters misunderstood by his children.

They were so fully convinced, however, that their brother would not have the courage to apply in person for his father's consent, and so repeatedly assured her that he had never in his life been less likely to come to Northanger than at the present time, that she suffered her mind to be at ease as to the necessity of any sudden removal of her own. But as it was not to be supposed that Captain Tilney, whenever he made his application, would give his father any just idea of Isabella's conduct, it occurred to her as highly expedient that Henry should lay the whole business before him as it really was, enabling the General by that means to form a cool and impartial opinion, and prepare his objections on a fairer ground than inequality of situations. She proposed it to him accordingly; but he did not catch at the measure so eagerly as she had expected. "No," said he; "my father's hands need not be strengthened, and Frederick's confession of folly need not be forestalled. He must tell his own story."

"But he will only tell half of it."

"A quarter would be enough."

A day of two passed away and brought no tidings of Captain Tilney. His brother and sister knew not what to think. Sometimes it appeared to them as if his silence would be the natural result of the suspected engagement, and at others that it was wholly incompatible with it. The General, meanwhile, though offended every morning by Frederick's remissness in writing, was free from any real anxiety about him; and had no more pressing solicitude than that of making Miss Morland's time at Northanger pass pleasantly. He often expressed his uneasiness on this head, "feared the sameness of every day's society and employment would disgust her with the place, wished the Lady Frasers had been in the country," talked every now and then of having a large party to dinner, and once or twice began even to calculate the number of young dancing people in the neighbourhood. "But then it was such a dead time of year, no wild-fowl, no game, and the Lady Frasers were not in the country." And it all ended, at last, in his telling Henry, one morning, that when he next went to Woodston, they would take him by surprise there some day or other, and eat their mutton with him. Henry was greatly honoured and very happy, and Catherine was quite delighted with the scheme. "And when do you think, sir, I may look forward to this pleasure? I must be at Woodston on Monday to attend the parish meeting, and shall probably be obliged to stay two or three days."

"Well, well, we will take our chance some one of those days. There is no need to fix. You are not to put yourself at all out of your way. Whatever you may happen to have in the house will be enough. I think I can answer for the young ladies making allowance for a bachelor's table. Let me see; Monday will be a busy day with you; we will not come on Monday; and Tuesday will be a busy one with me. I expect my surveyor from Brockham with his report in the morning; and afterwards I cannot, in decency, fail attending the club. I really could not face my acquaintance if I stayed away now; for, as I am known to be in the country, it would be taken exceedingly amiss; and it is a rule with me, Miss Mordand, never to give offence to any of my neighbours if a small sacrifice of time and attention can prevent it. They are a set of very worthy men. They have half a buck from Northanger twice a year; and I dine with them whenever I can. Tuesday, therefore, we may say, is out of the question But on Wednesday, I think, Henry, you may expect us; and we shall be with you early, that we may have time to look about us. Two hours and three-quarters will carry us to Woodston, I suppose; we shall be in the carriage by ten; so, about a quarter before one on Wednesday, you may look for us."

A ball itself could not have been more welcome to Catherine than this little excursion, so strong was her desire to be acquainted with Woodston; and her heart was still bounding with joy, when Henry, about an hour afterwards came booted and great-coated into the room where she and Eleanor were sitting, and said, "I am come, young ladies, in a very moralising strain, to observe that our pleasures in this world are always to be paid for, and that we often purchase them at a great disadvantage, giving ready-monied, actual happiness for a draft on the future that may not be honoured. Witness myself at this present hour. Because I am to hope for the satisfaction of seeing you at Woodston on Wednesray, which bad weather, or twenty other causes may prevent, I must go away directly, two days before I intended it."

"Go away," said Catherine, with a very long face, "and why?"

"Why! How can you ask the question? Because no time is to be lost in frightening my old housekeeper out of her wits; because I must go and prepare a dinner for you, to be sure."

"Oh! not seriously!"

"Aye, and sadly too; for I had much rather stay."

"But how can you think of such a thing after what the General said? When he so particularly desired you not to give yourself any trouble, because *anything* would do."

Henry only smiled. "I am sure it is quite unnecessary upon your sister's account, and mine. You must know it to be so; and the General made such a point of your providing nothing extraordinary; besides, if he had not said half so much as he did, he has always such an axcellent dinner at home, that sitting down to a middling one for one day could not signify."

"I wish I could reason like you, for his sake and my own Good-bye. As to-morrow is Sunday, Eleanor, I shall not return."

He went; and it being at any time a much simpler operation to Catherine to doubt her own judgment than Henry's, she was very soon obliged to give him credit for being right, however disagreeable to her his going, But the inexplicability of the General's conduct dwelt much on her thoughts. That he was very particular in his eating, she had, by her own unassisted observation, already discovered; but why he should say one thing so positively, and mean another all the while, was most unaccountable! How were people, at that rate, to be understood? Who but Henry could have been aware of what his father was at?

From Saturday to Wednesday, however, they were now to be without Henry. This was the sad finale of every reflection; and Captain Tilney's letter would certainly come in his absence, and Wednesday, she was very sure, would be wet. The past, present and future were all equally in gloom. Her brother so unhappy, and her loss in Isabella so great; and Eleanor's spirits always affected by Henry's absence! What was there to interest or amuse her? She was tired of the woods and the shrubberies, always so smooth and so dry; and the Abbey in itself was no more to her now than any other house. The painful remembrance of the folly it had helped to nourish and perfect was the only emotion which could spring from a consideration of the building. What a revolution in her ideas! She, who had so longed to be in an Abbey. Now, there was nothing so charming to her imagination as the unpretending comfort of a well-connected parsonage, something like Fullerton but better. Fullerton had its faults, but Woodston probably had none. If Wednesday should ever come!

It did come, and exactly when it might be reasonably looked for. It came; it was fine, and Catherine trod on air. By ten o'clock the chaise-and-four conveyed the two from the Abbey, and after an agreeable drive of almost twenty miles they entered Woodston, a large and populous village, in a situation not unpleasant. Catherine was ashamed to say how pretty she thought it, as the General seemed to think an apology necessary for the flatness of the country, and the size of the village; but in her heart she preferred it to any place she had ever been at, and looked with great admiration at every neat house above the rank of a cottage, and at all the little chandler's shops which they passed. At the further end of the village, and tolerably disengaged from the rest of it, stood the parsonage, a new-built substantial stone house, with its semi-circular sweep and green gates; and as they drove up to the door, Henry, with the friends of his solitude, a large Newfoundland puppy and two or three terriers, was ready to receive and make much of them.

Catherine's mind was too full, as she entered the house, for her either to observe or to say a great deal; and, till called on by the General for her opinion of it, she had very little idea of the room in which she was sitting. Upon looking round it then, she perceived in a moment that it

was the most comfortable room in the world; but she was too guarded to
say so, and the coldness of her praise disappointed him.

"We are not calling it a good house," said he. "We are not comparing
it with Fullerton and Northanger. We are considering it as a mere parsonage, small and confined we allow, but decent perhaps and habitable;
and altogether not inferior to the generality; or, in other words, I believe
there are few country parsonages in England half so good. It may admit
of improvement, however. Far be it from me to say otherwise; and anything in reason—a bow thrown out, perhaps; though, between ourselves,
if there is one thing more than another my aversion, it is a patched-on
bow."

Catherine did not hear enough of this speech to understand or be pained
by it; and other subjects being studiously brought forward and supported
by Henry, at the same time that a tray full of refreshments was introduced
by his servant, the General was shortly restored to his complacency, and
Catherine to all her usual ease of spirits.

The room in question was of a commodious, well-proportioned size,
and handsomely fitted up as a dining parlour; and on their quitting it to
walk round the grounds, she was shown, first into a smaller apartment
belonging peculiarly to the master of the house, and made unusually tidy
on the occasion; and afterwards into what was to be the drawing-room,
with the appearance of which, though unfurnished, Catherine was delighted enough even to satisfy the General. It was prettily-shaped room,
the windows reaching to the ground, and a view from them pleasant,
though over only green meadows; and she expressed her admiration at
the moment with all the honest simplicity with which she felt it. "Oh! why
do not you fit up this room, Mr. Tilney? What a pity not to have it fitted
up! It is the prettiest room I ever saw; it is the prettiest room in the
world!"

"I trust," said the General, with a most satisfied smile, "that it will
very speedily be furnished: it waits only for a lady's taste."

"Well, if it was my house, I should never sit anywhere else. Oh, what a
sweet little cottage there is among the trees; apple-trees too! It is the
prettiest cottage——"

"You like it: you approve it as an object; it is enough. Henry, remember that Robinson is spoken to about it. The cottage remains."

Such a compliment recalled all Catherine's consciousness, and silenced
her directly; and, though pointedly applied to by the General for her
choice of the prevailing colour of the paper and hangings, nothing like an
opinion on the subject could be drawn from her. The influence of fresh
objects and fresh air, however, was of great use in dissipating these embarrassing associations; and, having reached the ornamental part of the
premises, consisting of a walk round two sides of a meadow, on which
Henry's genius had begun to act about half a year ago, she was sufficiently
recovered to think it prettier than any pleasure-ground she had ever been

in before, though there was not a shrub in it higher than the green bench in the corner.

A saunter into other meadows, and through part of the village, with a visit to the stables to examine some improvements, and a charming game of play with a litter of puppies just able to roll about, brought them to four o'clock, when Catherine scarcely thought it could be three. At four they were to dine, and at six to set off on their return. Never had any day passed so quickly!

She could not but observe that the abundance of the dinner did not seem to create the smallest astonishment in the General, nay, that he was even looking at the side-table for cold meat which was not there. His son and daughter's observations were of a different kind. They had seldom seen him eat so heartily at any table but his own; and never before known him so little disconcerted by the melted butter's being oiled.

At six o'clock, the General having taken his coffee, the carriage again received them; and so gratifying had been the tenor of his conduct throughout the whole visit, so well assured was her mind on the subject of his expectations, that, could she have felt equally confident of the wishes of his son, Catherine would have quitted Woodston with little anxiety as to the How or the When she might return to it.

Chapter 27

THE NEXT morning brought the following very unexpected letter from Isabella:

"Bath, April——

"MY DEAREST CATHERINE—I received your two kind letters with the greatest delight, and have a thousand apologies to make for not answering them sooner. I really am quite ashamed of my idleness; but in this horrid place one can find time for nothing. I have had my pen in my hand to begin a letter to you almost every day since you left Bath, but have always been prevented by some silly trifle or other. Pray write to me soon, and direct to my own home. Thank God! we leave this vile place to-morrow. Since you went away I have had no pleasure in it; the dust is beyond anything; and everybody one cares for is gone. I believe if I could see you I should not mind the rest, for you are dearer to me than anybody can conceive. I am quite uneasy about your dear brother, not having heard from him since he went to Oxford; and am fearful of some mis-understanding. Your kind offices will set all right: he is the only man I ever did or could love, and I trust you will convince him of it. The spring fashions are partly down, and the hats the most frightful you can imagine. I hope you spend your time pleasantly, but am afraid you never think of me. I will not say all that I could of the family you are with, because I would not be ungenerous, or set you against those you esteem; but it is very difficult to know whom to trust, and young men never know their minds two days together. I rejoice to say that the young man whom, of all others, I particularly abhor, has left Bath. You will know, from this description, I must mean Captain Tilney, who, as you may remember, was amazingly disposed to follow and tease me, before you went away. Afterwards he got worse, and became quite my shadow. Many girls might have been taken in, for never were such attentions; but I knew the fickle sex too well. He went away to his regiment two days ago, and I trust I shall never be plagued with him again. He is the greatest coxcomb I ever saw, and amazingly disagreeable. The last two days he was always by the side of Charlotte Davis: I pitied his taste, but took no notice of him. The last time we met was in Bath Street, and I turned directly into a shop that he might not speak to me: I would not even look at him. He went into the Pump Room afterwards, but I would not have followed him for all the world. Such a contrast between him and your brother! Pray send me some news of the latter; I am quite unhappy about him, he seemed so uncomfortable when he went away, with a cold, or something that affected his spirits. I would write to him myself, but have mislaid his direction, and, as I hinted above, am afraid he took something in my conduct amiss. Pray explain everything to his satisfaction; or, if he still harbours any doubt, a line from himself to me, or a call at Putney when next in town, might set all to rights. I have not been to the Rooms this age, nor to the Play, except going in last night with the Hodges's, for a frolic, at half-price: they teased me into it; and I was determined they should not say I shut myself up because Tilney was gone. We happened to sit by the Mitchells, and they pretended to be quite surprised to see me out. I knew their spite: at one time they could not be civil to me, but now they are all friendship; but I am not such a fool as to be taken in by them. You know I have a pretty good spirit of my own. Anne Mitchell had tried to put on a turban like mine, as I wore it the week before at the Concert, but made wretched work of it. It happened to become my odd face, I believe, at least Tilney told me so at the time, and said every eye was upon me; but he is the last man whose word I would take. I wear nothing but purple now: I know I look hideous in it, but no matter; it is your dear brother's favourite colour. Lose no time, my dearest, sweetest Catherine, in writing to him and to me.—Who ever am, &c."

Such a strain of shallow artifice could not impose even upon Catherine. Its inconsistencies, contradictions, and falsehood, struck her from the very first. She was ashamed of Isabella, and ashamed of having ever loved her. Her professions of attachment were now as disgusting as her excuses were empty, and her demands impudent. "Write to James on her behalf! No! James should never hear Isabella's name mentioned by her again."

On Henry's arrival from Woodston she made known to him and Eleanor their brother's safety, congratulating them with sincerity on it, and reading aloud the most material passages of her letter with strong indignation. When she had finished it:—"So much for Isabella," she cried, "and for all our intimacy! She must think me an idiot, or she could not have written so; but perhaps this has served to make her character better known to me than mine is to her. I see what she has been about. She is a vain coquette, and her tricks have not answered. I do not believe she had ever any regard either for James or for me, and I wish I had never known her."

"It will soon be as if you never had," said Henry.

"There is but one thing that I cannot understand. I see that she has had designs on Captain Tilney which have not succeeded; but I do not understand what Captain Tilney has been about all this time. Why should he pay her such attentions as to make her quarrel with my brother, and then fly off himself?"

"I have very little to say for Frederick's motives, such as I believe them to have been. He has his vanities as well as Miss Thorpe, and the chief difference is, that having a stronger head they have not yet injured himself. If the *effect* of his behaviour does not justify him with you, we had better not seek after the cause."

"Then you do not suppose he ever really cared about her?"

"I am persuaded that he never did."

"And only made believe to do so for mischief's sake?"

Henry bowed his assent.

"Well then, I must say that I do not like him at all. Though it has turned out so well for us, I do not like him at all. As it happens, there is no great harm done, because I do not think Isabella has any heart to lose. But suppose he had made her very much in love with him?"

"But we must first suppose Isabella to have had a heart to lose, consequently to have been a very different creature; and, in that case, she would have met with very different treatment."

"It is very right that you should stand by your brother."

"And if you would stand by *yours*, you would not be much distressed by the disappointment of Miss Thorpe. But your mind is warped by an innate principle of general integrity, and, therefore, not accessible to the cool reasonings of family partiality, or a desire of revenge."

Catherine was complimented out of further bitterness. Frederick could not be unpardonably guilty while Henry made himself so agreeable. She resolved on not answering Isabella's letter, and tried to think no more of it.

Chapter 28

Soon after this, the General found himself obliged to go to London for a week; and he left Northanger, earnestly regretting that any necessity should rob him, even for an hour, of Miss Morland's company, and anxiously recommending the study of her comfort and amusement to his children, as their chief object in his absence. His departure gave Catherine the first experimental conviction that a loss may be sometimes a gain. The happiness with which their time now passed, every employment voluntary, every laugh indulged, every meal a scene of ease and good-humour, walking where they liked and when they liked, their hours, pleasures, and fatigues at their own command, made her thoroughly sensible of the restraint which the General's presence had imposed, and most thankfully feel their present release from it. Such ease and such delights made her love the place and the people more and more every day; and had it not been for a dread of its soon becoming expedient to leave the one, and an apprehension of not being equally beloved by the other, she would at each moment of each day have been perfectly happy; but she was now in the fourth week of her visit; before the General came home, the fourth week would be turned, and perhaps it might seem an intrusion if she stayed much longer. This was a painful consideration whenever it occurred; and eager to get rid of such a weight on her mind, she very soon resolved to speak to Eleanor about it at once, propose going away, and be guided in her conduct by the manner in which her proposal might be taken.

Aware that if she gave herself much time, she might feel it difficult to bring forward so unpleasant a subject, she took the first opportunity of being suddenly alone with Eleanor, and of Eleanor's being in the middle of a speech about something very different, to start forth her obligation of going away very soon. Eleanor looked and declared herself much concerned. She had "hoped for the pleasure of her company for a much longer time—had been misled (perhaps by her wishes) to suppose that a much longer visit had been promised, and could not but think that if Mr. and Mrs. Morland were aware of the pleasure it was to have her there, they would be too generous to hasten her return." Catherine explained. "Oh! as to *that*, papa and mamma were in no hurry at all. As long as she was happy, they would always be satisfied."

"Then why, might she ask, in such a hurry herself to leave them?"

"Oh! because she had been there so long."

"Nay, if you can use such a word, I can urge you no farther. If you think it long——"

"Oh no! I do not, indeed. For my own pleasure, I could stay with you as long again." And it was directly settled that, till she had, her leaving them was not even to be thought of. In having this cause of uneasiness so pleasantly removed, the force of the other was likewise weakened. The kindness, the earnestness of Eleanor's manner in pressing her to stay, and Henry's gratified look on being told that her stay was determined, were such sweet proofs of her importance with them, as left her only just so much solicitude as the human mind can never do comfortably without. She did, almost always, believe that Henry loved her, and quite always that his father and sister loved and even wished her to belong to them; and believing so far, her doubts and anxieties were merely sportive irritations.

Henry was not able to obey his father's injunction of remaining wholly at Northanger, in attendance on the ladies, during his absence in London;

the engagements of his curate at Woodston obliging him to leave them on Saturday for a couple of nights. His loss was not now what it had been while the General was at home; it lessened their gaiety, but did not ruin their comforts; and the two girls, agreeing in occupation, and improving in intimacy, found themselves so well-sufficient for the time to themselves, that it was eleven o'clock, rather a late hour at the Abbey, before they quitted the supper-room on the day of Henry's departure. They had just reached the head of the stairs, when it seemed, as far as the thickness of the walls would allow them to judge, that a carriage was driving up to the door, and the next moment confirmed the idea by the loud noise of the house-bell. After the first perturbation of surprise had passed away, in a "Good Heaven! what can be the matter?" it was quickly decided by Eleanor to be her eldest brother, whose arrival was often as sudden, if not quite so unseasonable, and accordingly she hurried down to welcome him.

Catherine walked on to her chamber, making up her mind, as well as she could, to a further acquaintance with Captain Tilney, and comforting herself under the unpleasant impression his conduct had given her, and the persuasion of his being by far too fine a gentleman to approve of her, that at least they should not meet under such circumstances as would make their meeting materially painful. She trusted he would never speak of Miss Thorpe, and, indeed, as he must by this time be ashamed of the part he had acted, there could be no danger of it; and as long as all mention of Bath scenes were avoided, she thought she could behave to him very civilly. In such considerations time passed away, and it was certainly in his favour that Eleanor should be so glad to see him, and have so much to say, for half an hour was almost gone since his arrival, and Eleanor did not come up.

At that moment Catherine thought she heard her step in the gallery, and listened for its continuance, but all was silent. Scarcely, however, had she convicted her fancy of error, when the noise of something moving close to her door made her start; it seemed as if someone was touching the very doorway, and in another moment a slight motion of the lock proved that some hand must be on it. She trembled a little at the idea of anyone's approaching so cautiously, but resolving not to be again overcome by trivial appearances of alarm, or misled by a raised imagination, she stepped quietly forward, and opened the door. Eleanor, and only Eleanor, stood there. Catherine's spirits, however, were tranquillised but for an instant, for Eleanor's cheeks were pale, and her manner greatly agitated. Though evidently intending to come in, it seemed an effort to enter the room, and a still greater to speak when there. Catherine, supposing some uneasiness on Captain Tilney's account, could only express her concern by silent attention, obliged her to be seated, rubbed her temples with lavender water, and hung over her with affectionate solicitude. "My dear Catherine, you must not, you must not, indeed——" were Eleanor's first connected words. "I am quite well. This kindness distracts me. I cannot bear it. I come to you on such an errand."

"Errand! to me!"

"How shall I tell you? Oh! how shall I tell you?"

A new idea now darted into Catherine's mind, and turning as pale as her friend, she exclaimed, " 'Tis a messenger from Woodston!"

"You are mistaken, indeed," returned Eleanor, looking at her most compassionately, "it is no one from Woodston. It is my father himself." Her voice faltered, and her eyes were turned to the ground as she mentioned his name. His unlooked-for return was enough in itself to make Catherine's heart sink, and for a few moments she hardly supposed there were anything worse to be told.

She said nothing; and Eleanor, endeavouring to collect herself and speak with firmness, but with eyes still cast down, soon went on. "You are too good, I am sure, to think the worse of me for the part I am obliged to perform. I am, indeed, a most unwilling messenger. After what has so lately passed, so lately been settled between us, how joyfully, how thankfully, on my side! as to your continuing here, as I hoped, for many weeks longer, how can I tell you that your kindness is not to be accepted, and that the happiness your company has hitherto given us is to be repaid by ——but I must not trust myself with words. My dear Catherine, we are to part. My father has recollected an engagement that takes our whole family away on Monday; we are going to Lord Longtown's, near Hereford, for a fortnight. Explanation and apology are equally impossible. I cannot attempt either."

"My dear Eleanor," cried Catherine, suppressing her feelings as well as she could, "do not be so distressed. A second engagement must give way to a first. I am very, very sorry we are to part so soon, and so suddenly too, but I am not offended, indeed I am not. I can finish my visit here, you know, at any time; or I hope you will come to me. Can you, when you return from this lord's, come to Fullerton?"

"It will not be in my power, Catherine."

"Come when you can, then."

Eleanor made no answer; and Catherine's thoughts recurring to something more directly interesting, she added, thinking aloud, "Monday; so soon as Monday; and you *all* go! Well, I am certain of—— I shall be able to take leave, however; I need not go till just before you do, you know. Do not be distressed, Eleanor; I can go on Monday very well. My father and mother's having no notice of it is of very little consequence. The General will send a servant with me, I dare say, half the way; and then I shall soon be at Salisbury, and then I am only nine miles from home."

"Ah, Catherine! were it settled so, it would be somewhat less intolerable; though in such common attentions, you would have received but half what you ought. But, how can I tell you? To-morrow morning is fixed for your leaving us, and not even the hour is left to your choice; the very carriage is ordered, and will be here at seven o'clock, and no servant will be offered you."

Catherine sat down breathless and speechless. "I could hardly believe my senses when I heard it; and no displeasure, no resentment that you can feel at this moment, however justly great, can be more than I myself ——but I must not talk of what I felt. Oh, that I could suggest anything in extenuation! Good God! what will your father and mother say? After courting you from the protection of real friends to this, almost double distance from your home, to have you driven out of the house, without the considerations even of decent civility! Dear, dear Catherine, in being the bearer of such a message, I seem guilty myself of all its insult; yet I trust you will acquit me, for you must have been long enough in this house to see that I am but a nominal mistress of it, that my real power is nothing."

"Have I offended the General?" said Catherine, in a faltering voice.

"Alas! for my feelings as a daughter, all that I know, all that I answer for is, that you can have given him no just cause of offence. He certainly is greatly, very greatly discomposed; I have seldom seen him more so. His temper is not happy, and something has now occurred to ruffle it in an uncommon degree; some disappointment, some vexation, which just at this moment seems important; but which I can hardly suppose you to have any concern in; for how is it possible?"

It was with pain that Catherine could speak at all; and it was only for Eleanor's sake that she attempted it. "I am sure," said she, "I am very sorry if I have offended him. It was the last thing I would willingly have done. But do not be unhappy, Eleanor. An engagement, you know, must be kept. I am only sorry it was not recollected sooner, that I might have written home. But it is of very little consequence."

"I hope, I earnestly hope that to your real safety it will be of none; but to everything else it is of the greatest consequence; to comfort, appearance, propriety, to your family, to the world. Were your friends, the Allens, still in Bath, you might go to them with comparative ease; a few hours would take you there; but a journey of seventy miles, to be taken post by you, at your age, alone, unattended!"

"Oh! the journey is nothing. Do not think about that. And if we are to part, a few hours sooner or later, you know, makes no difference. I can be ready by seven. Let me be called in time." Eleanor saw that she wished to be alone; and believing it better for each that they should avoid any further conversation, now left her with, "I shall see you in the morning."

Catherine's swelling heart needed relief. In Eleanor's presence friendship and pride had equally restrained her tears, but no sooner was she gone than they burst forth in torrents. Turned from the house, and in such a way! Without any reason that could justify, any apology that could atone for the abruptness, the rudeness, nay, the insolence of it. Henry at a distance; not able even to bid him farewell. Every hope, every expectation from him suspended, at least, and who could say how long? Who could say when they might meet again? And all this by such a man as General Tilney: so polite, so well-bred, and heretofore so particularly fond of her! It was as incomprehensible as it was mortifying and grievous. From what it could arise, and where it would end, were considerations of equal perplexity and alarm. The manner in which it was done so grossly uncivil: hurrying her away without any reference to her own convenience, or allowing her even the appearance of choice as to the time or mode of her travelling; of two days, the earliest fixed on, and of that almost the earliest hour, as if resolved to have her gone before he was stirring in the morning, that he might not be obliged even to see her. What could all this mean but an intentional affront? By some means or other she must have had the misfortune to offend him. Eleanor had wished to spare her from so painful a notion, but Catherine could not believe it possible that any injury or any misfortune could provoke such ill-will against a person not connected, or, at least, not supposed to be connected with it.

Heavily passed the night. Sleep, or repose that deserved the name of sleep, was out of the question. That room, in which her disturbed imagination had tormented her on her first arrival, was again the scene of agitated spirits and unquiet slumbers. Yet how different now the source of her inquietude from what it had been then; how mournfully superior in reality and substance! Her anxiety had foundation in fact, her fears in probability; and with a mind so occupied in the contemplation of actual and natural evil, the solitude of her situation, the darkness of her chamber, the antiquity of the building, were felt and considered without the smallest emotion; and though the wind was high, and often produced strange and sudden noises throughout the house, she heard it all as she lay awake, hour after hour, without curiosity or terror.

Soon after six Eleanor entered her room, eager to show attention, or give assistance where it was possible; but very little remained to be done. Catherine had not loitered; she was almost dressed, and her packing almost finished. The possibility of some conciliatory message from the General occurred to her as his daughter appeared. What so natural, as that anger should pass away and repentance succeed it? and she only wanted to know how far, after what had passed, an apology might properly be received by her. But the knowledge would have been useless here, it was not called for; neither clemency nor dignity was put to the trial; Eleanor brought no message. Very little passed between them on meeting: each found her greatest safety in silence; and few and trivial were the sentences exchanged while they remained upstairs; Catherine in busy agitation completing her dress, and Eleanor, with more good-will than experience, intent upon filling the trunk. When everything was done, they left the room, Catherine lingering only half a minute behind her friend to throw a parting glance on every well-known cherished object, and went down to the breakfast-parlour, where breakfast was prepared. She tried to eat, as well to save herself from the pain of being urged as to make her friend comfortable; but she had no appetite, and could not swallow many mouthfuls. The contrast between this and her last breakfast in that room gave her fresh misery, and strengthened her distaste for everything before her. It was not four-and-twenty hours ago since they had met there to the same repast, but in circumstances how different! With what cheerful ease,

what happy, though false security, had she then looked around her, enjoying everything present, and fearing little in future, beyond Henry's going
to Woodston for a day! Happy, happy breakfast! for Henry had been
there; Henry had sat by her and helped her. These reflections were long
indulged undisturbed by any address from her companion, who sat as
deep in thought as herself; and the appearance of the carriage was the
first thing to startle and recall them to the present moment. Catherine's
colour rose at the sight of it; and the indignity with which she was treated
striking, at that instant, on her mind with peculiar force, made her for a
short time sensible only of resentment. Eleanor seemed now impelled into
resolution and speech.

"You *must* write to me, Catherine," she cried; "you *must* let me hear
from you as soon as possible. Till I know you to be safe at home, I shall
not have an hour's comfort. For *one* letter, at all risks, all hazards, I must
entreat. Let me have the satisfaction of knowing that you are safe at
Fullerton, and have found your family well; and then, till I can ask for
your correspondence as I ought to do, I will not expect more. Direct to me
at Lord Longtown's, and, I must ask it, under cover to Alice."

"No, Eleanor, if you are not allowed to receive a letter from me, I am
sure I had better not write. There can be no doubt of my getting home
safe."

Eleanor only replied, "I cannot wonder at your feelings. I will not
importune you. I will trust to your own kindness of heart when I am at a
distance from you." But this, with the look of sorrow accompanying it,
was enough to melt Catherine's pride in a moment, and she instantly
said, "Oh! Eleanor, I *will* write to you, indeed!"

There was yet another point which Miss Tilney was anxious to settle,
though somewhat embarrassed in speaking of. It had occurred to her, that
after so long an absence from home, Catherine might not be provided with
money enough for the expenses of her journey, and, upon suggesting it to
her with most affectionate offers of accommodation, it proved to be exactly
the case. Catherine had never thought on the subject till that moment;
but, upon examining her purse, was convinced that but for this kindness
of her friend, she might have been turned from the house without even the
means of getting home; and the distress in which she must have been
thereby involved filling the minds of both, scarcely another word was said
by either during the time of their remaining together. Short, however, was
that time. The carriage was soon announced to be ready; and Catherine
instantly rising, a long and affectionate embrace supplied the place of
language in bidding each other adieu; and, as they entered the hall, unable
to leave the house without some mention of one whose name had not yet
been spoken by either, she paused a moment, and with quivering lips just
made it intelligible that she left "her kind remembrance for her absent
friend." But with this approach to his name ended all possibility of
restraining her feelings; and, hiding her face as well as she could with her

handkerchief, she darted across the hall, jumped into the chaise, and in a moment was driven from the door.

Chapter 29

CATHERINE was too wretched to be fearful. The journey in itself had no terrors for her; and she began it without either dreading its length or feeling its solitariness. Leaning back in one corner of the carriage, in a violent burst of tears, she was conveyed some miles beyond the walls of the Abbey before she raised her head; and the highest point of ground within the park was almost closed from her view before she was capable of turning her eyes towards it. Unfortunately, the road she now travelled was the same which only ten days ago she had so happily passed along in going to and from Woodston; and, for fourteen miles, every bitter feeling was rendered more severe by the review of objects on which she had first looked under impressions so different. Every mile, as it brought her nearer Woodston, added to her sufferings; and when within the distance of five she passed the turning which led to it, and thought of Henry, so near, yet so unconscious, her grief and agitation were excessive.

The day which she had spent at that place had been one of the happiest of her life. It was there, it was on that day that the General had made use of such expressions with regard to Henry and herself, had so spoken and so looked as to give her the most positive conviction of his actually wishing their marriage. Yes, only ten days ago had he elated her by his pointed regard—had he even confused her by his too significant reference! And now, what had she done, or what had she omitted to do, to merit such a change?

The only offence against him, of which she could accuse herself, had been such as was scarcely possible to reach his knowledge. Henry and her own heart only were privy to the shocking suspicions which she had so idly entertained; and equally safe did she believe her secret with each. Designedly, at least, Henry could not have betrayed her. If, indeed, by any strange mischance his father should have gained intelligence of what she had dared to think and look for, of her causeless fancies and injurious examinations, she could not wonder at any degree of his indignation. If aware of her having viewed him as a murderer, she could not wonder at his even turning her from his house. But a justification so full of torture to herself she trusted would not be in his power.

Anxious as were all her conjectures on this point, it was not, however, the one on which she dwelt most. There was a thought yet nearer; a more prevailing, more impetuous concern; how Henry would think, and feel, and look, when he returned on the morrow to Northanger, and heard of her being gone, was a question of force and interest to rise over every other, to be never-ceasing, alternately irritating and soothing: it sometimes suggested the dread of his calm acquiescence, and at others was answered by the sweetest confidence in his regret and resentment. To the General, of course, he would not dare to speak; but to Eleanor, what might he not say to Eleanor about her?

In this unceasing recurrence of doubts and inquiries, on any one article of which her mind was incapable of more than momentary repose, the hours passed away, and her journey advanced much faster than she looked for. The pressing anxieties of thought which prevented her from noticing anything before her, when once beyond the neighbourhood of Woodston, saved her at the same time from watching her progress; and though no object on the road could engage a moment's attention, she found no stage of it tedious. From this she was preserved, too, by another cause: by feeling no eagerness for her journey's conclusion; for to return in such a manner to Fullerton was almost to destroy the pleasure of a meeting with those she loved best, even after an absence such as hers: an eleven weeks' absence. What had she to say that would not humble herself and pain her family; that would not increase her own grief by the confession of it; extend a useless resentment, and perhaps involve the innocent with the guilty in undistinguishing ill-will? She could never do justice to Henry and Eleanor's merit: she felt it too strongly for expression, and should a dislike be taken against them, should they be thought of unfavourably on their father's account, it would cut her to the heart.

With these feelings, she rather dreaded than sought for the first view of that well-known spire which would announce her within twenty miles of home. Salisbury she had known to be her point on leaving Northanger, but after the first stage she had been indebted to the postmasters for the names of the places which were then to conduct her to it; so great had been her ignorance of her route. She met with nothing, however, to distress or frighten her. Her youth, civil manner, and liberal pay, procured her all the attention that a traveller like herself could require; and stopping only to change horses, she travelled on for about eleven hours without accident or alarm, and between six and seven o'clock in the evening found herself entering Fulleton.

A heroine returning at the close of her career, to her native village, in all the triumph of recovered reputation, and all the dignity of a countess, with a long train of noble relations in their several phaetons, and three waiting-maids in a travelling chaise-and-four behind her, is an event on which the pen of the contriver may well delight to dwell; it gives credit to every conclusion, and the author must share in the glory she so liberally bestows. But my affair is widely different; I bring back my heroine to her home in solitude and disgrace, and no sweet elation of spirits can lead me into minuteness. A heroine in a hack post-chaise is such a blow upon sentiment as no attempt at grandeur or pathos can withstand. Swiftly, therefore, shall her post-boy drive through the village, amid the gaze of Sunday groups, and speedy shall be her descent from it.

But whatever might be the distress of Catherine's mind as she thus advanced towards the parsonage, and whatever the humiliation of her biographer in relating it, she was preparing enjoyment of no every-day nature for those to whom she went; first, in the appearance of her carriage, and secondly, in herself. The chaise of a traveller being a rare sight in Fullerton, the whole family were immediately at the window; and to have it stop at the sweep-gate was a pleasure to brighten every eye, and occupy every fancy; a pleasure quite unlooked for by all but the two youngest children, a boy and girl of six and four years old, who expected a brother or sister in every carriage. Happy the glance that first distinguished Catherine! Happy the voice that proclaimed the discovery! but whether such happiness were the lawful property of George or Harriet, could never be exactly understood.

Her father, mother, Sarah, George, and Harriet, all assembled at the door, to welcome her with affectionate eagerness, was a sight to awaken the best feelings of Catherine's heart; and in the embrace of each, as she stepped from the carriage, she found herself soothed beyond anything she had believed possible. So surrounded, so caressed, she was even happy! In the joyfulness of family love, everything, for a short time, was subdued; and the pleasure of seeing her, leaving them at first little leisure for calm curiosity, they were all seated round the tea-table, which Mrs. Morland had hurried for the comfort of the poor traveller, whose pale and jaded looks soon caught her notice, before any inquiry so direct as to demand a positive answer was addressed to her.

Reluctantly, and with much hesitation, did she then begin what might, perhaps, at the end of half an hour, be termed by the courtesy of her hearers an explanation; but scarcely, within that time, could they at all discover the cause, or collect the particulars of her sudden return. They were far from being an irritable race; far from any quickness in catching, or bitterness in resenting affronts; but here, when the whole was unfolded, was an insult not to be overlooked, nor, for the first half-hour, to be easily pardoned. Without suffering any romantic alarm in the consideration of their daughter's long and lonely journey, Mr. and Mrs. Morland could not but feel that it might have been productive of much unpleasantness to her; that it was what they could never have voluntarily suffered; and that, in forcing her on such a measure, General Tilney had acted neither honourably nor feelingly, neither as a gentleman nor as a parent. Why he had done it, what could have provoked him to such a breach of hospitality, and so suddenly turned all his partial regard for their daughter into actual ill-will, was a matter which they were at least as far from divining as Catherine herself: but it did not oppress them by any means so long; and, after a due course of useless conjecture, that "it was a strange business, and that he must be a very strange man," grew enough for all their indignation and wonder; though Sarah, indeed, still indulged in the sweets of incomprehensibility, exclaiming and conjecturing with youthful ardour—— "My dear, you give yourself a great deal of needless trouble," said her mother at last; "depend upon it, it is something not at all worth understanding."

"I can allow for his wishing Catherine away when he recollected this engagement," said Sarah; "but why not do it civilly?"

"I am sorry for the young people," returned Mrs. Morland; "they must have a sad time of it; but as for anything else, it is no matter now: Catherine is safe at home, and our comfort does not depend upon General Tilney." Catherine sighed. "Well," continued her philosophic mother, "I am glad I did not know of your journey at the time; but now it is all over, perhaps there is no great harm done. It is always good for young people to be put upon exerting themselves; and you know, my dear Catherine, you always were a sad little shatter-brained creature: but now you must have been forced to have your wits about you, with so much changing of chaises and so forth; and I hope it will appear that you have not left anything behind you in any of the pockets."

Catherine hoped so too, and tried to feel an interest in her own amendment, but her spirits were quite worn down; and to be silent and alone becoming soon her only wish, she readily agreed to her mother's next counsel of going early to bed. Her parents seeing nothing in her ill-looks and agitation but the natural consequence of mortified feelings, and of the unusual exertion and fatigue of such a journey, parted from her without any doubt of their being soon slept away; and though when they all met the next morning, her recovery was not equal to their hopes, they were still perfectly unsuspicious of there being any deeper evil. They never once thought of her heart, which for the parents of a young lady of seventeen, just returned from her first excursion from home, was odd enough!

As soon as breakfast was over she sat down to fulfil her promise to Miss Tilney, whose trust in the effect of time and distance on her friend's disposition was already justified, for already did Catherine reproach herself with having parted from Eleanor coldly; with having never enough valued her merits or kindness; and never enough commiserated her for what she had been yesterday left to endure. The strength of these feelings, however, was far from assisting her pen; and never had it been harder for her to write than in addressing Eleanor Tilney. To compose a letter which might at once do justice to her sentiments and her situation, convey gratitude without servile regret, be guarded without coldness, and honest without resentment; a letter which Eleanor might not be pained by the perusal of; and, above all, which she might not blush herself, if Henry should chance to see, was an undertaking to frighten away all her powers of performance; and, after long thought and much perplexity, to be very brief was all that she could determine on with any confidence of safety. The money, therefore, which Eleanor had advanced was enclosed with little more than grateful thanks, and the thousand good wishes of a most affectionate heart.

"This has been a strange acquaintance," observed Mrs. Morland, as the letter was finished; "soon made and soon ended. I am sorry it happens so, for Mrs. Allen thought them very pretty kind of young people; and you were sadly out of luck, too, in your Isabella. Ah, poor James! Well, we must live and learn; and the next new friends you make I hope will be better worth keeping."

Catherine coloured as she warmly answered, "No friend can be better worth keeping than Eleanor."

"If so, my dear, I dare say you will meet again some time or other; do not be uneasy. It is ten to one but you are thrown together again in the course of a few years; and then, what a pleasure it will be!"

Mrs. Morland was not happy in her attempt at consolation. The hope of meeting again in the course of a few years could only put into Catherine's head what might happen within that time to make a meeting dreadful to her. She could never forget Henry Tilney, or think of him with less tenderness than she did at that moment, but he might forget her, and in that case to meet——! Her eyes filled with tears as she pictured her acquaintance so renewed; and her mother perceiving her comfortable suggestions to have had no good effect, proposed as another expedient for restoring her spirits, that they should call on Mrs. Allen.

The two houses were only a quarter of a mile apart; and, as they walked, Mrs. Morland quickly despatched all that she felt on the score of James's disappointment. "We are sorry for him," said she; "but otherwise there is no harm done in the match going off; for it could not be a desirable thing to have him engaged to a girl whom we had not the smallest acquaintance with, and who was so entirely without fortune; and now after such behaviour, we cannot think at all well of her. Just at present it comes hard to poor James, but that will not last for ever; and I dare say he will be a discreeter man all his life, for the foolishness of his first choice."

This was just such a summary view of the affair as Catherine could listen to: another sentence might have endangered her complaisance, and made her reply less rational; for soon were all her thinking powers swallowed up in the reflection of her own change of feelings and spirits since last she had trodden that well-known road. It was not three months ago since, wild with joyful expectations, she had there run backward and forwards some ten times a day, with a heart light, gay, and independent; looking forward to pleasures untasted and unalloyed, and free from the apprehension of evil as from the knowledge of it. Three months ago had seen her all this, and now, how altered a being did she return!

She was received by the Allens with all the kindness which her unlooked-for appearance, acting on a steady affection, would naturally call forth; and great was their surprise, and warm their displeasure, on hearing how she had been treated, though Mrs. Morland's account of it was no inflated representation, no studied appeal to their passions. "Catherine took us quite by surprise yesterday evening," said she. "She travelled all the way post by herself, and knew nothing of coming till Saturday night; for General Tilney, from some odd fancy or other, all of a sudden grew tired of having her there, and almost turned her out of the house. Very unfriendly, certainly; and he must be a very odd man; but we are so glad to have her amongst us again! And it is a great comfort to find that she is not a poor helpless creature but can shift very well for herself."

Mr. Allen expressed himself on the occasion with the reasonable resentment of a sensible friend; and Mrs. Allen thought his expression quite good enough to be immediately made use of again by herself. His wonder, his conjectures, and his explanations, became in succession hers, with the addition of this single remark: "I really have not patience with the General," to fill up every accidental pause; and "I really have not patience with the General," was uttered twice after Mr. Allen left the room, without any relaxation of anger, or any material digression of thought. A more considerable degree of wandering attended the third repetition; and, after completing the fourth, she immediately added, "Only think, my dear, of my having got that frightful great rent in my best Mechlin so charmingly mended, before I left Bath, that one can hardly see where it was. I must show it you some day or other. Bath is a nice place, Catherine, after all I assure you I did not above half like coming away. Mrs. Thorpe's being there was such a comfort to us, was not it? You know, you and I were quite forlorn at first."

"Yes, but *that* did not last long," said Catherine, her eyes brightening at the recollection of what had first given spirit to her existence.

"Very true: we soon met with Mrs. Thorpe, and then we wanted for nothing. My dear, do not you think these silk gloves wear very well? I put them on new the first time of our going to the Lower Rooms, you know, and I have worn them a great deal since. Do you remember that evening?"

"Do I! Oh, perfectly."

"It was very agreeable, was not it? Mr. Tilney drank tea with us, and I always thought him a great addition; he is so very agreeable. I have a notion you danced with him, but am not quite sure. I remember I had my favourite gown on."

Catherine could not answer; and, after a short trial of other subjects, Mrs. Allen again returned to—"I really have not patience with the General! Such an agreeable worthy man as he seemed to be! I do not suppose, Mrs. Morland, you ever saw a better-bred man in your life. His lodgings were taken the very day after he left them, Catherine. But no wonder; Milsom Street, you know."

As they walked home again, Mrs. Morland endeavoured to impress on her daughter's mind the happiness of having such steady well-wishers as Mr. and Mrs. Allen, and the very little consideration which the neglect or unkindness of slight acquaintance like the Tilneys ought to have with her, while she could preserve the good opinion and affection of her earliest friends. There was a great deal of good sense in all this; but there are some situations of the human mind in which good sense has very little power; and Catherine's feelings contradicted almost every position her mother advanced. It was upon the behaviour of these very slight acquaintance that all her present happiness depended; and while Mrs. Morland was successfully confirming her own opinions by the justness of her own representations, Catherine was silently reflecting that *now* Henry must have arrived at Northanger; *now* he must have heard of her departure; and *now*, perhaps, they were all setting off for Hereford.

Chapter 30

CATHERINE'S disposition was not naturally sedentary, nor had her habits been ever very industrious; but, whatever might hitherto have been her defects of that sort, her mother could not but perceive them now to be greatly increased. She could neither sit still nor employ herself for ten minutes together; walking round the garden and orchard again and again, as if nothing but motion was voluntary; and it seemed as if she could even walk about the house rather than remain fixed for any time in the parlour. Her loss of spirits was a yet greater alteration. In her rambling and her idleness, she might only be a caricature of herself; but in her silence and sadness, she was the very reverse of all that she had been before.

For two days Mrs. Morland allowed it to pass even without a hint; but when a third night's rest had neither restored her cheerfulness, improved her in useful activity, nor given her a greater inclination for needlework, she could no longer refrain from the gentle reproof of, "My dear Catherine, I am afraid you are growing quite a fine lady. I do not know when poor Richard's cravats would be done, if he had no friend but you. Your head runs too much upon Bath; but there is a time for everything—a time for balls and plays, and a time for work. You have had a long run of amusement, and now you must try to be useful."

Catherine took up her work directly, saying, in a dejected voice, that "her head did not run upon Bath—much."

"Then you are fretting about General Tilney, and that is very simple of you; for ten to one whether you ever see him again. You should never fret about trifles." After a short silence: "I hope, my Catherine, you are not getting out of humour with home, because it is not so grand as Northanger. That would be turning your visit into an evil, indeed. Wherever you are, you should always be contented, but especially at home, because there you must spend the most of your time. I did not quite like, at breakfast, to hear you talk so much about the French bread at Northanger."

"I am sure I do not care about the bread. It is all the same to me what I eat."

"There is a very clever essay in one of the books upstairs upon much such a subject, about young girls who have been spoilt for home by great acquaintance: *The Mirror*, I think. I will look it out for you some day or other, because I am sure it will do you good."

Catherine said no more; and, with an endeavour to do right, applied to her work; but, after a few minutes, sunk again, without knowing it herself, into languor and listlessness; moving herself in her chair, from the irritation of weariness, much oftener than she moved her needle. Mrs. Morland watched the progress of this relapse; and seeing, in her daughter's absent and dissatisfied look, the full proof of that repining spirit to which she had now begun to attribute her want of cheerfulness, hastily left the room to fetch the book in question, anxious to lose no time in attacking so dreadful a malady. It was some time before she could find what she looked for; and other family matters occurring to detain her, a quarter of an hour had elapsed ere she returned downstairs with the volume from which so much was hoped. Her avocations above having shut out all noise but what she created herself, she knew not that a visitor had arrived within the last few minutes, till, on entering the room, the first object she beheld was a young man whom she had never seen before. With a look of much respect, he immediately rose, and being introduced to her by her conscious daughter as "Mr. Henry Tilney," with the embarrassment of real sensibility began to apologise for his appearance there, acknowledging that after what had passed he had little right to expect a welcome at Fullerton, and stating his impatience to be assured of Miss Morland's having reached her home in safety, as the cause of his intrusion. He did not address himself to an uncandid judge or a resentful heart. Far from comprehending him or his sister in their father's misconduct, Mrs. Morland had been always kindly disposed towards each; and instantly, pleased by his appearance, received him with the simple professions of unaffected benevolence; thanking him for such an attention to her daughter; assuring him that the friends of her children were always welcome there, and intreated him to say not another word of the past.

He was not ill inclined to obey this request; for though his heart was greatly relieved by such unlooked-for mildness, it was not, just at that moment, in his power to say anything to the purpose. Returning in silence to his seat, therefore, he remained for some minutes most civilly answering all Mrs. Morland's common remarks about the weather and roads. Catherine, meanwhile, the anxious, agitated, happy, feverish Catherine, said not a word: but her glowing cheek and brightened eye made her mother trust that this good-natured visit would, at least, set her heart at ease for a time; and gladly, therefore, did she lay aside the first volume of *The Mirror* for a future hour.

Desirous of Mr. Morland's assistance, as well in giving encouragement as in finding conversation for her guest, whose embarrassment on his father's account she earnestly pitied, Mrs. Morland had very early despatched one of the children to summon him; but Mr. Morland was from home, and being thus without any support, at the end of a quarter of an hour she had nothing to say. After a couple of minutes' unbroken silence, Henry, turning to Catherine for the first time since her mother's entrance, asked her, with sudden alacrity, if Mr. and Mrs. Allen were now at Fullerton? and on developing, from amidst all her perplexity of words in reply, the meaning, which one short syllable would have given, immediately expressed his intention of paying his respects to them, and with a rising

colour, asked her if she would have the goodness to show him the way.
"You may see the house from this window, sir," was information, on
Sarah's side, which produced only a bow of acknowledgment from the
gentleman, and a silencing nod from her mother; for Mrs. Morland,
thinking it probable, as a secondary consideration in his wish of waiting
on their worthy neighbours, that he might have some explanation to give
of his father's behaviour, which it must be more pleasant for him to
communicate only to Catherine, would not, on any account, prevent her
accompanying him. They began their walk, and Mrs. Morland was not
entirely mistaken in his object in wishing it. Some explanation on his
father's account he had to give; but his first purpose was to explain himself; and before they reached Mr. Allen's grounds he had done it so well
that Catherine did not think it could ever be repeated too often. She was
assured of his affection; and that heart in return was solicited, which,
perhaps, they pretty equally knew was already entirely his own; for,
though Henry was now sincerely attached to her—though he felt and
delighted in all the excellencies of her character, and truly loved her
society—I must confess that his affection originated in nothing better
than gratitude; or, in other words, that a persuasion of her partiality for
him had been the only cause of giving her a serious thought. It is a new
circumstance in romance, I acknowledge, and dreadfully derogatory of an
heroine's dignity; but if it be as new in common life, the credit of a wild
imagination will at least be all my own.

A very short visit to Mrs. Allen, in which Henry talked at random,
without sense or connection, and Catherine, wrapt in the contemplation
of her own unutterable happiness, scarcely opened her lips, dismissed
them to the ecstasies of another tête-à-tête; and before it was suffered to
close, she was enabled to judge how far he was sanctioned by parental
authority in his present application. On his return from Woodston, two
days before, he had been met near the Abbey by his impatient father,
hastily informed in angry terms of Miss Morland's departure, and ordered
to think of her no more.

Such was the permission upon which he had now offered her his hand.
The affrighted Catherine, amidst all the terrors of expectation, as she
listened to this account, could not but rejoice in the kind caution with
which Henry had saved her from the necessity of a conscientious rejection,
by engaging her faith before he mentioned the subject; and as he proceeded to give the particulars, and explain the motives of his father's
conduct, her feelings soon hardened into even a triumphant delight. The
General had had nothing to accuse her of, nothing to lay to her charge,
but her being the involuntary, unconscious object of a deception which
his pride could not pardon, and which a better pride would have been
ashamed to own. She was guilty only of being less rich than he had supposed her to be. Under a mistaken persuasion of her possessions and claims
he had courted her acquaintance in Bath, solicited her company at Northanger, and designed her for his daughter-in-law. On discovering his error,

to turn her from the house seemed the best, though to his feelings, an inadequate proof, of his resentment towards herself, and his contempt of her family.

John Thorpe had first misled him. The General perceiving his son one night, at the theatre, to be paying considerable attention to Miss Morland, had accidentally inquired of Thorpe if he knew more of her than her name. Thorpe, most happy to be on speaking terms with a man of General Tilney's importance, had been joyfully and proudly communicative; and being at that time not only in daily expectation of Morland's engaging Isabella, but likewise pretty well resolved upon marrying Catherine himself, his vanity induced him to represent the family as yet more wealthy than his vanity and avarice had made him believe them. With whomsoever he was, or was likely to be connected, his own consequence always required that theirs should be great; and as his intimacy with any acquaintance grew, so regularly grew their fortune. The expectations of his friend Moland, therefore, from the first over-rated, had, ever since his introduction to Isabella, been gradually increasing; and by merely adding twice as much for the grandeur of the moment, by doubling what he chose to think the amount of Mr. Morland's preferment, trebling his private fortune, bestowing a rich aunt, and sinking half the children, he was able to represent the while family to the General in a most respectable light. For Catherine, however, the peculiar object of the General's curiosity and his own speculations, he had yet something more in reserve; and the ten or fifteen thousand pounds which her father could give her, would be a pretty addition to Mr. Allen's estate. Her intimacy there had made him seriously determined on her being handsomely legacied hereafter; and to speak of her, therefore, as the most acknowledged future heiress of Fullerton, naturally followed. Upon such intelligence the General had proceeded, for never had it occurred to him to doubt its authority. Thorpe's interest in the family, by his sister's approaching connection with one of its members, and his own views on another (circumstances of which he boasted with almost equal openness), seemed sufficient vouchers for his truth; and to these were added the absolute facts of the Allens being wealthy and childless, of Miss Morland's being under their care, and, as soon as his acquaintance allowed him to judge, of their treating her with parental kindness. His resolution was soon formed. Already had he discerned a liking towards Miss Morland in the countenance of his son; and thankful for Mr. Thorpe's communication, he almost instantly determined to spare no pains in weakening his boasted interest, and ruining his dearest hopes. Catherine herself could not be more ignorant at the time of all this than his own children. Henry and Eleanor, perceiving nothing in her situation likely to engage their father's particular respect, had seen with astonishment the suddenness, continuance, and extent of his attention; and though latterly, from some hints which had accompanied an almost positive command to his son of doing everything in his power to attach her, Henry was convinced of his father's believing it to be an advantageous connection, it was not till the late explanation at Northanger that they had the smallest idea of the false calculations which had hurried him on. That they were false, the General had learned from the very person who had suggested them, from Thorpe himself, whom he had chanced to meet again in town; and who, under the influence of exactly opposite feelings, irritated by Catherine's refusal, and yet more by the failure of a very recent endeavour to accomplish a reconciliation between Morland and Isabella, convinced that they were separated for ever, and spurning a friendship which could be no longer serviceable, hastened to contradict all that he had said before to the advantage of the Morlands: confessed himself to have been totally mistaken in his opinion of their circumstances and character, misled by the rodomontade of his friend to believe his father a man of substance and credit, whereas the transactions of the two or three last weeks proved him to be neither; for, after coming eagerly forward on the first overture of a marriage between the families, with the most liberal proposals, he had, on being brought to the point, by the shrewdness of the relator been constrained to acknowledge himself incapable of giving the young people even a decent support. They were, in fact, a necessitous family; numerous too, almost beyond example; by no means respected in their own neighbourhood, as he had lately had particulor opportunities of discovering; aiming at a style of life which their fortune could not warrant; seeking to better themselves by wealthy connections; a forward, bragging, scheming race.

The terrified General pronounced the name of Allen with an inquiring look, and here, too, Thorpe had learnt his error. The Allens, he believed, had lived near them too long, and he knew the young man on whom the Fullerton estate must devolve. The General needed no more. Enraged with almost everybody in the world but himself, he set out the day next for the Abbey, where his performances have been seen.

I leave it to my reader's sagacity to determine how much of all this it was possible for Henry to communicate at this time to Catherine; how much of it he could have learnt from his father, in what points his own conjectures might assist him, and what portion must yet remain to be told in a letter from James. I have united for their ease what they must divide for mine. Catherine, at any rate heard enough to feel, that, in suspecting General Tilney of either murdering or shutting up his wife, she had scarcely sinned against his character or magnified his cruelty.

Henry, in having such things to relate of his father, was almost as pitiable as in their first avowal to himself. He blushed for the narrow-minded counsel which he was obliged to expose. The conversation between them at Northanger had been of the most unfriendly kind. Henry's indignation on hearing how Catherine had been treated on comprehending his father's views, and being ordered to acquiesce in them, had been open and bold. The General, accustomed on every ordinary occasion to give the law in his family, prepared for no reluctance but of feeling, no opposing desire that should dare to clothe itself in words, could ill brook the opposition of his son, steady as the sanction of reason and the dictate of conscience could make it. But, in such a cause, his anger, though it must shock, could not intimidate Henry, who was sustained in his purpose by a conviction of its justice. He felt himself bound as much in honour as in affection to Miss Morland, and believing that heart to be his own which he had been directed to gain, no unworthy retraction of a tacit consent, no reversing decree of unjustifiable anger, could shake his fidelity, or influence the resolutions it prompted.

He steadily refused to accompany his father into Herefordshire, an engagement formed almost at the moment, to promote the dismissal of Catherine, and as steadily declared his intention of offering her his hand. The General was furious in his anger, and they parted in dreadful disagreement. Henry, in an agitation of mind which many solitary hours were required to compose, had returned almost instantly to Woodston; and on the afternoon of the following day had begun his journey to Fullerton.

Chapter 31

MR. AND MRS. MORLAND'S suprise on being applied to by Mr. Tilney for their consent to his marrying their daughter, was, for a few minutes, considerable; it having never entered their heads to suspect an attachment on either side; but as nothing, after all, could be more natural than Catherine's being beloved, they soon learnt to consider it with only the happy agitation of gratified pride; and, as far as they alone were concerned, had not a single objection to start. His pleasing manners and good sense were self-evident recommendations; and having never heard evil of him, it was not their way to suppose any evil could be told. Goodwill supplying the place of experience, his character needed no attestation. "Catherine would make a sad, heedless young housekeeper, to be sure," was her mother's foreboding remark; but quick was the consolation of there being nothing like practice.

There was but one obstacle, in short, to be mentioned; but till that one was removed it must be impossible for them to sanction the engagement. Their tempers were mild, but their principles were steady; and while his parent so expressly forbade the connection, they could not allow themselves to encourage it. That the General should come forward to solicit the alliance, or that he should even very heartily approve it, they were not refined enough to make any parading stipulation, but the decent appearance of consent must be yielded, and that once obtained, and their own hearts made them trust that it could not be very long denied, their willing approbation was instantly to follow. His *consent* was all that they wished for. They were no more inclined than entitled to demand his *money*. Of a very considerable fortune, his son was, by marriage settlements, eventually secure; his present income was an income of independence and comfort.

and under every pecuniary view it was a match beyond the claims of their daughter.

The young people could not be surprised at a decision like this. They felt and they deplored, but they could not resent it; and they parted, endeavouring to hope that such a change in the General, as each believed almost impossible, might speedily take place, to unite them again in the fullness of privileged affection. Henry returned to what was now his only home, to watch over his young plantations, and extend his improvements for her sake, to whose share in them he looked anxiously forward; and Catherine remained at Fullerton to cry. Whether the torments of absence were softened by a clandestine correspondence, let us not inquire. Mr. and Mrs. Morland never did; they had been too kind to exact any promise, and whenever Catherine received a letter, as at that time happened pretty often, they always looked another way.

The anxiety which in this state of their attachment must be the portion of Henry and Catherine, and of all who loved either, as to its final event, can hardly extend, I fear, to the bosom of my readers, who will see in the tell-tale compression of the pages before them, that we are all hastening together to perfect felicity. The means by which their early marriage was effected can be the only doubt: what probable circumstance could work upon a temper like the General's? The circumstance which chiefly availed was the marriage of his daughter with a man of fortune and consequence, which took place in the course of the summer: an accession of dignity that threw him into a fit of good humour, from which he did not recover till after Eleanor had obtained his forgiveness of Henry, and his permission for him "to be a fool if he liked it."

The marriage of Eleanor Tilney, her removal from all the evils of such a home as Northanger had been made by Henry's banishment, to the home of her choice and the man of her choice, is an event which I expect to give general satisfaction among all her acquaintance. My own joy on the occasion is very sincere. I know no one more entitled by unpretending merit, or better prepared by habitual suffering, to receive and enjoy felicity. Her partiality for this gentleman was not of recent origin, and he had been long withheld only by inferiority of situation from addressing her. His unexpected accession to title and fortune had removed all his difficulties; and never had the General loved his daughter so well in all her hours of companionship, utility, and patient endurance, as when he first hailed her, "Your Ladyship!" Her husband was really deserving of her, independent of his peerage, his wealth, and his attachment, being to a precision the most charming young man in the world. Any further definition of his merits must be unnecessary: the most charming young man in the world is instantly before the imagination of us all. Concerning the one in question, therefore, I have only to add (aware that the rules of composition forbid the introduction of a character not connected with my fable) that this was the very gentleman whose negligent servant left behind him that collection of washing-bills, resulting from a long visit at

Northanger, by which my heroine was involved in one of her most alarming adventures.

The influence of the Viscount and Viscountess in their brother's behalf
was assisted by that right understanding of Mr. Morland's circumstances,
which, as soon as the General would allow himself to be informed, they
were qualified to give. It taught him that he had been scarcely more
misled by Thorpe's first boast of the family wealth than by his subsequent
malicious overthrow of it; that in no sense of the word were they necessitous or poor, and that Catherine would have three thousand pounds
This was so material an amendment of his late expectations, that it greatly
contributed to smooth the descent of his pride; and by no means without
its effect was the private intelligence which he was at some pains to procure, that the Fullerton estate, being entirely at the disposal of its present
proprietor, was consequently open to every greedy speculation.

On the strength of this the General, soon after Eleanor's marriage,
permitted his son to return to Northanger, and thence made him the bearer
of his consent, very courteously worded in a page full of empty professions, to Mr. Morland. The event which it authorised soon followed:
Henry and Catherine were married, the bells rang and everybody smiled:
and, as this took place within a twelvemonth from the first day of their
meeting, it will not appear, after all the dreadful delays occasioned by the
General's cruelty, that they were essentially hurt by it. To begin perfect
happiness at the respective ages of twenty-six and eighteen is to do pretty
well; and professing myself, moreover, convinced that the General's
unjust interference, so far from being really injurious to their felicity, was
perhaps rather conducive to it, by improving their knowledge of each
other, and adding strength to their attachment, I leave it to be settled by
whomsoever it may concern, whether the tendency of this work be
altogether to recommend parental tyranny or reward filial disobedience.

THE END

PERSUASION

(First Published 1818)

PERSUASION

Chapter 1

SIR WALTER ELLIOT, of Kellynch Hall, in Somersetshire, was a man who, for his own amusement, never took up any book but the Baronetage; there he found occupation for an idle hour, and consolation in a distressed one; there his faculties were roused into admiration and respect by contemplating the limited remnant of the earliest patents; there any unwelcome sensations arising from domestic affairs changed naturally into pity and contempt as he turned over the almost endless creations of the last century; and there, if every other leaf were powerless, he could read his own history with an interest which never failed. This was the page at which the favourite volume always opened:—

"ELLIOT OF KELLYNCH HALL

"Walter Elliot, born March 1, 1760, married July 15, 1784, Elizabeth, daughter of James Stevenson, Esq., of South Park, in the county of Gloucester; by which lady (who died 1800) he has issue, Elizabeth, born June 1, 1785; Anne, born August 9, 1787; a still-born son, November 5, 1789; Mary, born November 20, 1791."

Precisely such had the paragraph originally stood from the printer's hands; but Sir Walter had improved it by adding, for the information of himself and his family, these words, after the date of Mary's birth:— "Married, December 16, 1810, Charles, son and heir of Charles Musgrove, Esq., of Uppercross, in the county of Somerset," and by inserting most accurately the day of the month on which he had lost his wife.

Then followed the history and rise of the ancient and respectable family in the usual terms; how it had been first settled in Cheshire, how mentioned in Dugdale, serving the office of high sheriff, representing a borough in three successive parliaments, exertions of loyalty, and dignity of baronet, in the first year of Charles II with all the Marys and Elizabeths they had married; forming altogether two handsome quarto pages, and concluding with the arms and motto:—"Principal seat, Kellynch Hall, in the county of Somerset," and Sir Walter's handwriting again in this finale:—

"Heir presumptive, William Walter Elliot, Esq., great-grandson of the second Sir Walter."

Vanity was the beginning and end of Sir Walter Elliot's character: vanity of person and of situation. He had been remarkably handsome in his youth, and at fifty-four was still a very fine man. Few women could think more of their personal appearance than he did, nor could the valet of any new-made lord be more delighted with the place he held in society. He considered the blessing of beauty as inferior only to the blessing of a baronetcy; and the Sir Walter Elliot, who united these gifts, was the constant object of his warmest respect and devotion.

His good looks and his rank had one fair claim on his attachment, since to them he must have owed a wife of very superior character to anything deserved by his own. Lady Elliot had been an excellent woman, sensible and amiable, whose judgment and conduct, if they might be pardoned the youthful infatuation which made her Lady Elliot, had never required indulgence afterwards. She had humoured, or softened, or concealed his failings, and promoted his real respectability for seventeen years; and though not the very happiest being in the world herself, had found enough in her duties, her friends, and her children, to attach her to life, and make it no matter of indifference to her when she was called on to quit them. Three girls, the two eldest sixteen and fourteen, was an awful legacy for a mother to bequeath, an awful charge rather, to confide to the authority and guidance of a conceited, silly father. She had, however, one very intimate friend, a sensible, deserving woman, who had been brought, by strong attachment to herself, to settle close by her, in the village of Kellynch; and on her kindness and advice Lady Elliot mainly relied for the best help and maintenance of the good principles and instruction which she had been anxiously giving her daughters.

This friend and Sir Walter did *not* marry, whatever might have been anticipated on that head by their acquaintance. Thirteen years had passed away since Lady Elliot's death, and they were still near neighbours and intimate friends, and one remained a widower, the other a widow.

That Lady Russell, of steady age and character, and extremely well provided for, should have no thought of a second marriage, needs no apology to the public, which is rather apt to be unreasonably discontented when a woman *does* marry again, than when she does *not*; but Sir Walter's continuing in singleness requires explanation. Be it known, then, that Sir Walter, like a good father (having met with one or two private disappointments in very unreasonable applications), prided himself on remaining single for his dear daughter's sake. For one daughter, his eldest, he would really have given up anything, which he had not been very much tempted to do. Elizabeth had succeeded at sixteen to all that was possible of her mother's rights and consequence; and being very handsome, and very like himself, her influence had always been great, and they had gone on together most happily. His two other children were of very inferior value. Mary had acquired a little artificial importance by becoming Mrs. Charles Musgrove; but Anne, with an elegance of mind and sweetness of character, which must have placed her high with any people of real understanding, was nobody with either father or sister; her word had no weight, her convenience was always to give way—she was only Anne.

To Lady Russell, indeed, she was a most dear and highly valued god-daughter, favourite, and friend. Lady Russell loved them all, but it was only in Anne that she could fancy the mother to revive again.

A few years before Anne Elliot had been a very pretty girl, but her bloom had vanished early; and as, even in its height, her father had found little to admire in her (so totally different were her delicate features and mild dark eyes from his own), there could be nothing in them, now that she was faded and thin, to excite his esteem. He had never indulged much hope, he had now none, of ever reading her name in any other page of his favourite work. All equality of alliance must rest with Elizabeth, for Mary had merely connected herself with an old country family of respectability and large fortune, and had, therefore, *given* all the honour and received none: Elizabeth would, one day or other, marry suitably.

It sometimes happens that a woman is handsomer at twenty-nine than she was ten years before; and, generally speaking. if there has been neither ill-health nor anxiety, it is a time of life at which scarcely any charm is lost. It was so with Elizabeth, still the same handsome Miss Elliot that she had begun to be thirteen years ago, and Sir Walter might be excused, therefore, in forgetting her age, or, at least, be deemed only half a fool, for thinking himself and Elizabeth as blooming as ever, amidst the wreck of the good looks of everybody else; for he could plainly see how old all the rest of his family and acquaintance were growing. Anne haggard, Mary coarse, every face in the neighbourhood worsting, and the rapid increase of the crow's foot about Lady Russell's temples had long been a distress to him.

Elizabeth did not quite equal her father in personal contentment. Thirteen years had seen her mistress of Kellynch Hall, presiding and directing with a self-possession and decision which could never have given the idea of her being younger than she was. For thirteen years had she been doing the honours, and laying down the domestic law at home, and leading the way to the chaise and four, and walking immediately after Lady Russell out of all the drawing-rooms and dining-rooms in the country. Thirteen winters' revolving frosts had seen her opening every ball of credit which a scanty neighbourhood afforded, and thirteen springs shown their blossoms, as she travelled up to London with her father, for a few weeks' annual enjoyment of the great world. She had the remem-brance of all this, she had the consciousness of being nine-and-twenty to give her some regrets and some apprehensions; she was fully satisfied of being still quite as handsome as ever, but she felt her approach to the years of danger, and would have rejoiced to be certain of being properly solicited by baronet-blood within the next twelvemonth or two. Then might she again take up the book of books with as much enjoyment as in her early youth, but now she liked it not. Always to be presented with the date of her own birth and see no marriage follow but that of a youngest sister, made the book an evil; and more than once, when her father had left it open on the table near her, had she closed it, with averted eyes, and pushed it away.

She had had a disappointment, moreover, which that book and especially the history of her own family, must ever present the remembrance of. The heir presumptive, the very William Walter Elliot, Esq., whose rights had been so generally supported by her father, had disappointed her.

She had, while a very young girl, as soon as she had known him to be, in the event of her having no brother, the future baronet, meant to marry him, and her father had always meant that she should. He had not been known to them as a boy; but soon after Lady Elliot's death, Sir Walter had sought the acquaintance, and though his overtures had not been met with any warmth, he had persevered in seeking it, making allowance for the modest drawing-back of youth; and, in one of their spring excursions to London, when Elizabeth was in her first bloom, Mr. Elliot had been forced into the introduction.

He was at that time a very young man, just engaged in the study of the law; and Elizabeth found him extremely agreeable, and every plan in his favour was confirmed. He was invited to Kellynch Hall; he was talked of and expected all the rest of the year; but he never came. The following spring he was seen again in town, found equally agreeable, again encouraged, invited, and expected, and again he did not come; and the next tidings were that he was married. Instead of pushing his fortune in the line marked out for the heir of the house of Elliot, he had purchased independence by uniting himself to a rich woman of inferior birth.

Sir Walter had resented it. As the head of the house, he felt that he ought to have been consulted, especially after taking the young man so publicly by the hand; "For they must have been seen together," he observed, "once at Tattersalls, and twice in the lobby of the House of Commons." His disapprobation was expressed, but apparently very little regard. Mr. Elliot had attempted no apology, and shown himself as unsolicitous of being longer noticed by the family, as Sir Walter considered him unworthy of it: all acquaintance between them had ceased.

This very awkward history of Mr. Elliot was still, after an interval of several years, felt with anger by Elizabeth, who had liked the man for himself, and still more for being her father's heir, and whose strong family pride could see only in *him* a proper match for Sir Walter Elliot's eldest daughter. There was not a baronet from A to Z whom her feelings could have so willingly acknowledged as an equal. Yet so miserably had he conducted himself, that though she was at this present time (the summer of 1814) wearing black ribbons for his wife, she could not admit him to be worth thinking of again. The disgrace of his first marriage might, perhaps, as there was no reason to suppose it perpetuated by offspring, have been got over, had he not done worse; but he had, as by the accustomary intervention of kind friends they had been informed, spoken most disrespectfully of them all, most slightingly and contemptuously of the very ɔlood he belonged to, and the honours which were hereafter to be his own. This could not be pardoned.

Such were Elizabeth Elliot's sentiments and sensations; such the cares to alloy, the agitations to vary, the sameness and the elegance, the prosperity and the nothingness of her scene of life; such the feelings to give interest to a long, uneventful residence in one country circle, to fill the vacancies which there were no habits of utility abroad, no talents or accomplishments for home, to occupy.

But now, another occupation and solicitude of mind was beginning to be added to these. Her father was growing distressed for money. She knew, that when he now took up the Baronetage, it was to drive the heavy bills of his tradespeople, and the unwelcome hints of Mr. Shepherd, his agent, from his thoughts. The Kellynch property was good, but not equal to Sir Walter's apprehension of the state required in its possessor. While Lady Elliot lived, there had been method, moderation, and economy, which had just kept him within his income; but with her had died all such right-mindedness, and from that period he had been constantly exceeding it. It had not been possible for him to spend less: he had done nothing but what Sir Walter Elliot was imperiously called on to do; but blameless as he was, he was not only growing dreadfully in debt, but was hearing of it so often, that it became vain to attempt concealing it longer, even partially, from his daughter. He had given her some hints of it the last spring in town; he had gone so far even as to say, "Can we retrench? Does it occur to you that there is any one article in which we can retrench?" and Elizabeth, to do her justice, had, in the first ardour of female alarm, set seriously to think what could be done, and had finally proposed these two branches of economy, to cut off some unnecessary charities, and to refrain from new furnishing the drawing-room; to which expedients she afterwards added the happy thought of their taking no present down to Anne, as had been the usual yearly custom. But these measures, however good in themselves, were insufficient for the real extent of the evil, the whole of which Sir Walter found himself obliged to confess to her soon afterwards. Elizabeth had nothing to propose of deeper efficacy. She felt herself ill-used and unfortunate, as did her father; and they were neither of them able to devise any means of lessening their expenses without compromising their dignity, or relinquishing their comforts in a way not to be borne.

There was only a small part of his estate that Sir Walter could dispose of, but had every acre been alienable, it would have made no difference. He had condescended to mortgage as far as he had the power, but he would never condescend to sell. No; he would never disgrace his name so far. The Kellynch estate should be transmitted whole and entire, as he had received it.

Their two confidential friends, Mr. Shepherd who lived in the neighbouring market town, and Lady Russell, were called on to advise them; and both father and daughter seemed to expect that something should be struck out by one or the other to remove their embarrassments and reduce their expenditure, without involving the loss of any indulgence of taste or pride.

Chapter 2

MR. SHEPHERD, a civil, cautious lawyer, who, whatever might be his hold or his views on Sir Walter, would rather have the *disagreeable* prompted by anybody else, excused himself from offering the slightest hint, and only begged leave to recommend an implicit reference to the excellent judgment of Lady Russell, from whose known good sense he fully expected to have just such resolute measures advised as he meant to see finally adopted.

Lady Russell was most anxiously zealous on the subject, and gave it much serious consideration. She was a woman rather of sound than of quick abilities, whose difficulties in coming to any decision in this instance were great, from the opposition of two leading principles. She was of strict integrity herself, with a delicate sense of honour; but she was as desirous of saving Sir Walter's feelings, as solicitous for the credit of the family, as aristocratic in her ideas of what was due to them, as anybody of sense and honesty could well be. She was a benevolent, charitable, good woman, and capable of strong attachments, most correct in her conduct, strict in her notions of decorum, and with manners that were held a standard of good-breeding. She had a cultivated mind, and was, generally speaking, rational and consistent; but she had prejudices on the side of ancestry; she had a value for rank and consequence, which blinded her a little to the faults of those who possessed them. Herself the widow of only a knight, she gave the dignity of a baronet all its due; and Sir Walter, independent of his claims as on old acquaintance, an attentive neighbour, an obliging land-lord, the husband of her very dear friend, the father of Anne and her sisters, was, as being Sir Walter in her apprehension, entitled to a great deal of compassion and consideration under his present difficulties.

They must retrench; that did not admit of a doubt. But she was very anxious to have it done with the least possible pain to him and Elizabeth. She drew up plans of economy, she made exact calculations, and she did what nobody else thought of doing: she consulted Anne, who never seemed considered by the others as having any interest in the question. She consulted, and in a degree was influenced by her in marking out the scheme of retrenchment which was at last submitted to Sir Walter. Every emendation of Anne's had been on the side of honesty against importance. She wanted more vigorous measures, a more complete reformation, a quicker release from debt, a much higher tone of indifference for every-thing but justice and equity.

"If we can persuade your father to all this," said Lady Russell, looking over her paper, "much may be done. If he will adopt these regulations, in seven years he will be clear; and I hope we may be able to convince him and Elizabeth that Kellynch Hall has a respectability in itself which cannot be affected by these reductions; and that the true dignity of Sir Walter Elliot will be very far from lessened in the eyes of sensible people, by his acting like a man of principle. What will he be doing, in fact, but what very many of our first families have done, or ought to do? There will be nothing singular in his case; and it is singularity which often makes the worst part of our suffering, as it always does of our conduct. I have great hope of our prevailing. We must be serious and decided; for after all, the person who has contracted debts must pay them; and though a great deal is due to the feelings of the gentleman, and the head of a house, like your father, there is still more due to the character of an honest man."

This was the principle on which Anne wanted her father to be proceed-ing, his friends to be urging him. She considered it as an act of indispens-able duty to clear away the claims of creditors with all the expedition which the most comprehensive retrenchments could secure, and saw no dignity in anything short of it. She wanted it to be prescribed and felt as a duty. She rated Lady Russell's influence highly; and as to the severe degree of self-denial which her own conscience prompted, she believed there might be little more difficulty in persuading them to a complete, than to half a reformation. Her knowledge of her father and Elizabeth inclined her to think that the sacrifice of one pair of horses would be hardly less painful than of both, and so on, through the whole list of Lady Russell's too gentle reductions.

How Anne's more rigid requisitions might have been taken is of little consequence. Lady Russell's had no success at all: could not be put up with, were not to be borne. "What! every comfort of life knocked off! Journeys, London, servants, horses, table—contractions and restrictions everywhere! To live no longer with the decencies even of a private gentle-man! No, he would sooner quit Kellynch Hall at once, than remain in it on such disgraceful terms."

"Quit Kellynch Hall!" The hint was immediately taken up by Mr. Shepherd, whose interest was involved in the reality of Sir Walter's retrenching, and who was perfectly persuaded that nothing would be done without a change of abode. "Since the idea had been started in the very quarter which ought to dictate, he had no scruple," he said, "in confessing his judgment to be entirely on that side. It did not appear to him that Sir Walter could materially alter his style of living in a house which had such a character of hospitality and ancient dignity to support. In any other place Sir Walter might judge for himself; and would be looked up to, as regulating the modes of life in whatever way he might choose to model his household."

Sir Walter would quit Kellynch Hall; and after a very few days more of doubt and indecision, the great question of whither he should go was settled, and the first outline of this important change made out.

There had been three alternatives, London, Bath, or another house in the country. All Anne's wishes had been for the latter. A small house in their own neighbourhood, where they might still have Lady Russell's society, still be near Mary, and still have the pleasure of sometimes seeing the lawns and groves of Kellynch, was the object of her ambition. But the usual fate of Anne attended her, in having something very opposite from her inclination fixed on. She disliked Bath, and did not think it agreed with her; and Bath was to be her home.

Sir Walter had at first thought more of London; but Mr. Shepherd felt that he could not be trusted in London, and had been skilful enough to dissuade him from it, and make Bath preferred. It was a much safer place for a gentleman in his predicament: he might there be important at comparatively little expense. Two material advantages of Bath over London had of course been given all their weight: its more convenient distance from Kellynch, only fifty miles, and Lady Russell's spending some part of every winter there; and to the very great satisfaction of Lady Russell, whose first views on the projected change had been for Bath, Sir Walter and Elizabeth were induced to believe that they should lose neither consequence nor enjoyment by settling there.

Lady Russell felt obliged to oppose her dear Anne's known wishes. It would be too much to expect Sir Walter to descend into a small house in his own neighbourhood. Anne herself would have found the mortifications of it more than she foresaw, and to Sir Walter's feelings they must have been dreadful. And with regard to Anne's dislike of Bath, she considered it as a prejudice and mistake arising, first from the circumstance of her having been three years at school there, after her mother's death; and secondly, from her happening to be not in perfectly good spirits the only winter which she had afterwards spent there with herself.

Lady Russell was fond of Bath, in short, and disposed to think it must suit them all; and as to her young friend's health, by passing all the warm months with her at Kellynch Lodge, every danger would be avoided; and it was, in fact, a change which must do both health and spirits good. Anne had been too little from home, too little seen. Her spirits were not high. A larger society would improve them. She wanted her to be more known.

The undesirableness of any other house in the same neighbourhood for Sir Walter was certainly much strengthened by one part, and a very material part of the scheme, which had been happily engrafted on the beginning. He was not only to quit his home, but to see it in the hands of others: a trial of fortitude which stronger heads than Sir Walter's have found too much. Kellynch Hall was to be let. This, however, was a profound secret, not to be breathed beyond their own circle.

Sir Walter could not have borne the degradation of being known to design letting his house. Mr. Shepherd had once mentioned the word "advertise," but never dared approach it again. Sir Walter spurned the idea of its being offered in any manner; forbade the slightest hint being dropped of his having such an intention; and it was only on the supposition of his being spontaneously solicited by some most unexceptionable applicant, on his own terms, and as a great favour, that he would let it at all.

How quick come the reasons for approving what we like! Lady Russell had another excellent one at hand, for being extremely glad that Sir Walter and his family were to remove from the country. Elizabeth had been lately forming an intimacy, which she wished to see interrupted. It was with a daughter of Mr. Shepherd, who had returned, after an unprosperous marriage, to her father's house, with the additional burden of two children. She was a clever young woman, who understood the art of pleasing—the art of pleasing, at least, at Kellynch Hall; who had made herself so acceptable to Miss Elliot, as to have been already staying there more than once, in spite of all that Lady Russell, who thought it a friendship quite out of place, could hint of caution and reserve.

Lady Russell, indeed, had scarcely any influence with Elizabeth, and seemed to love her, rather because she would love her, than because Elizabeth deserved it. She had never received from her more than outward attention, nothing beyond the observances of complaisance; had never succeeded in any point which she wanted to carry, against previous inclination. She had been repeatedly very earnest in trying to get Anne included in the visit to London, sensibly open to all the injustice and all the discredit of the selfish arrangements which shut her out, and on many lesser occasions had endeavoured to give Elizabeth the advantage of her own better judgment and experience; but always in vain: Elizabeth would go her own way; and never had she pursued it in more decided opposition to Lady Russell than in this selection of Mrs. Clay; turning from the society of so deserving a sister, to bestow her affection and confidence on one who ought to have been nothing to her but the object of distant civility.

From situation, Mrs. Clay was, in Lady Russell's estimate, a very unequal, and in her character, she believed, a very dangerous companion; and a removal that would leave Mrs. Clay behind, and bring a choice of more suitable intimates within Miss Elliot's reach, was therefore an object of first-rate importance.

Chapter 3

"I must take leave to observe, Sir Walter," said Mr. Shepherd one morning at Kellynch Hall, as he laid down the newspaper, "that the present juncture is much in our favour. This peace will be turning all our rich naval officers ashore. They will be all wanting a home. Could not be a better time, Sir Walter, for having a choice of tenants, very responsible tenants. Many a noble fortune has been made during the war. If a rich admiral were to come in our way, Sir Walter——"

"He would be a very lucky man, Shepherd," replied Sir Walter; "that's all I have to remark. A prize indeed, would Kellynch Hall be to him;

rather the greatest prize of all, let him have taken ever so many before; hey, Shepherd?"

Mr. Shepherd laughed, as he knew he must, at this wit, and then added:

"I presume to observe, Sir Walter, that, in the way of business, gentlemen of the navy are well to deal with. I have had a little knowledge of their methods of doing business; and I am free to confess that they have very liberal notions, and are as likely to make desirable tenants as any set of people one should meet with. Therefore, Sir Walter, what I would take leave to suggest is, that if in consequence of any rumours getting abroad of your intention; which must be contemplated as a possible thing, because we know how difficult it is to keep the actions and designs of one part of the world from the notice and curiosity of the other; consequence has its tax; I, John Shepherd, might conceal any family-matters that I chose, for nobody would think it worth their while to observe me; but Sir Walter Elliot has eyes upon him which it may be very difficult to elude; and, therefore, thus much I venture upon, that it will not greatly surprise me if, with all our caution, some rumour of the truth should get abroad; in the supposition of which, as I was going to observe, since applications will unquestionably follow, I should think any from our wealthy naval commanders particularly worth attending to; and beg leave to add, that two hours will bring me over at any time, to save you the trouble of replying."

Sir Walter only nodded. But soon afterwards, rising and pacing the room, he observed sarcastically:

"There are few among the gentlemen of the navy, I imagine, who would not be surprised to find themselves in a house of this description."

"They would look around them, no doubt, and bless their good fortune," said Mrs. Clay, for Mrs. Clay was present: her father had driven her over, nothing being of so much use to Mrs. Clay's health as a drive to Kellynch: "but I quite agree with my father in thinking a sailor might be a very desirable tenant. I have known a good deal of the profession; and besides their liberality, they are so neat and careful in all their ways! These valuable pictures of yours, Sir Walter, if you choose to leave them, would be perfectly safe. Everything in and about the house would be taken such excellent care of! The gardens and shrubberies would be kept in almost as high order as they are now. You need not be afraid, Miss Elliot, of your own sweet flower gardens being neglected."

"As to all that," rejoined Sir Walter coolly, "supposing I were induced to let my house, I have by no means made up my mind as to the privileges to be annexed to it. I am not particularly disposed to favour a tenant. The park would be open to him of course, and few navy officers, or men of any other description, can have had such a range; but what restrictions I might impose on the use of the pleasure-grounds is another thing. I am not fond of the idea of my shrubberies being always approachable; and I should recommend Miss Elliot to be on her guard with respect to her flower garden. I am very little disposed to grant a tenant of Kellynch Hall any extraordinary favour, I assure you, be he sailor or soldier."

After a short pause, Mr. Shepherd presumed to say:

"In all these cases there are established usages which make everything plain and easy between landlord and tenant. Your interest, Sir Walter, is in pretty safe hands. Depend upon me for taking care that no tenant has more than his just rights. I venture to hint, that Sir Walter Elliot cannot be half so jealous for his own, as John Shepherd will be for him."

Here Anne spoke:

"The navy, I think, who have done so much for us, have at least an equal claim with any other set of men, for all the comforts and all the privileges which any home can give. Sailors work hard enough for their comforts, we must all allow."

"Very true, very true. What Miss Anne says is very true," was Mr. Shepherd's rejoinder, and "Oh! certainly," was his daughter's; but Sir Walter's remark was, soon afterwards:

"The profession has its utility, but I should be sorry to see any friend of mine belonging to it."

"Indeed!" was the reply, and with a look of surprise.

"Yes; it is in two points offensive to me; I have two strong grounds of objection to it. First, as being the means of bringing persons of obscure birth into undue distinction, and raising men to honours which their fathers and grandfathers never dreamt of; and, secondly, as it cuts up a man's youth and vigour most horribly; a sailor grows old sooner than any other man. I have observed it all my life. A man is in greater danger in the navy of being insulted by the rise of one whose father his father might have disdained to speak to, and of becoming prematurely an object of disgust himself, than in any other line. One day last spring, in town, I was in company with two men, striking instances of what I am talking of: Lord St. Ives, whose father we all know to have been a country curate, without bread to eat: I was to give place to Lord St. Ives, and a certain Admiral Baldwin, the most deplorable-looking personage you can imagine; his face the colour of mahogany, rough and rugged to the last degree; all lines and wrinkles, nine grey hairs of a side, and nothing but a dab of powder at top. 'In the name of heaven, who is that old fellow?' said I to a friend of mine who was standing near (Sir Basil Morley). 'Old fellow!' cried Sir Basil, 'it is Admiral Baldwin. What do you take his age to be?' 'Sixty,' said I, 'or perhaps sixty-two.' 'Forty,' replied Sir Basil, 'forty, and no more.' Picture to yourselves my amazement: I shall not easily forget Admiral Baldwin. I never saw quite so wretched an example of what a sea-faring life can do; but to a degree. I know it is the same with them all: they are all knocked about, and exposed to every climate, and every weather, till they are not fit to be seen. It is a pity they are not knocked on the head at once, before they reach Admiral Baldwin's age."

"Nay, Sir Walter," cried Mrs. Clay, "this is being severe indeed. Have a little mercy on the poor men. We are not all born to be handsome. The sea is no beautifier, certainly; sailors do grow old betimes; I have often observed it: they soon lose the look of youth. But then, is not it the same with many other professions, perhaps most others? Soldiers, in active service, are not at all better off; and even in the quieter professions, there is a toil and a labour of the mind, if not of the body, which seldom leaves a man's looks to the natural effect of time. The lawyer plods, quite care-worn: the physician is up at all hours, and travelling in all weather; and even the clergyman—" she stopped a moment to consider what might do for the clergyman—"and even the clergyman, you know, is obliged to go into infected rooms, and expose his health and looks to all the injury of a poisonous atmosphere. In fact, as I have long been convinced, though every profession is necessary and honourable in its turn, it is only the lot of those who are not obliged to follow any, who can live in a regular way, in the country, choosing their own hours, following their own pursuits, and living on their own property, without the torment of trying for more; it is only *their* lot, I say, to hold the blessings of health and a good appearance to the utmost: I know no other set of men but what lose something of their personableness when they cease to be quite young."

It seemed as if Mr. Shepherd, in this anxiety to bespeak Sir Walter's good will towards a naval officer as tenant, had been gifted with foresight; for the very first application for the house was from an Admiral Croft, with whom he shortly afterwards fell into company in attending the quarter sessions at Taunton; and, indeed, he had received a hint of the Admiral from a London correspondent. By the report which he hastened over to Kellynch to make, Admiral Croft was a native of Somersetshire, who having acquired a very handsome fortune, was wishing to settle in his own country, and had come down to Taunton in order to look at some advertised places in that immediate neighbourhood, which, however, had not suited him; that accidentally hearing—(it was just as he had foretold, Mr. Shepherd observed, Sir Walter's concerns could not be kept a secret)— accidentally hearing of the possibility of Kellynch Hall being to let, and understanding his (Mr. Shepherd's) connection with the owner, he had introduced himself to him in order to make particular inquiries, and had, in the course of a pretty long conference, expressed as strong an inclination for the place as a man who knew it only by description could feel; and given Mr. Shepherd, in his explicit account of himself, every proof of his being a most responsible, eligible tenant.

"And who is Admiral Croft?" was Sir Walter's cold, suspicious inquiry.

Mr. Shepherd answered for his being of a gentleman's family, and mentioned a place; and Anne, after the little pause which followed, added:

"He is rear-admiral of the white. He was in the Trafalgar action, and has been in the East Indies since; he has been stationed there, I believe, several years."

"Then I take it for granted," observed Sir Walter, "that his face is about as orange as the cuffs and capes of my livery."

Mr. Shepherd hastened to assure him, that Admiral Croft was a very hale, hearty, well-looking man, a little weather-beaten, to be sure, but not much, and quite the gentleman in all his notions and behaviour; not likely to make the smallest difficulty about terms, only wanted a comfortable home, and to get into it as soon as possible; knew he must pay for his convenience; knew what rent a ready-furnished house of that consequence might fetch; should not have been surprised if Sir Walter had asked more; had inquired about the manor; would be glad of the deputation certainly, but made no great point of it; said he sometimes took out a gun but never killed; quite the gentleman.

Mr. Shepherd was eloquent on the subject, pointing out all the circumstances of the Admiral's family, which made him peculiarly desirable as a tenant. He was a married man, and without children; the very state to be wished for. A house was never taken good care of, Mr. Shepherd observed, without a lady: he did not know whether furniture might not be in danger of suffering as much where there was no lady, as where there were many children. A lady without a family was the very best preserver of furniture in the world. He had seen Mrs. Croft too; she was at Taunton with the Admiral, and had been present almost all the time they were talking the matter over.

"And a very well-spoken, genteel, shrewd lady, she seemed to be," continued he; "asked more questions about the house, and terms, and taxes, than the Admiral himself, and seemed more conversant with business; and moreover, Sir Walter, I found she was not quite unconnected in this country, any more than her husband; that is to say, she is sister to a gentleman who did live amongst us once; she told me so herself; sister to the gentleman who lived a few years back at Monkford. Bless me! what was his name? At this moment I cannot recollect his name, though I have heard it so lately. Penelope, my dear, can you help me to the name of the gentleman who lived at Monkford: Mrs. Croft's brother?"

But Mrs. Clay was talking so eagerly with Miss Elliot that she did not hear the appeal.

"I have no conception whom you can mean, Shepherd; I remember no gentleman resident at Monkford since the time of old Governor Trent."

"Bless me! how very odd! I shall forget my own name soon, I suppose. A name that I am so very well acquainted with; knew the gentleman so well by sight; seen him a hundred times; came to consult me once, I remember, about a trespass of one of his neighbours; farmer's man breaking into his orchard; wall torn down; apples stolen; caught in the fact; and afterwards, contrary to my judgment, submitted to an amicable compromise. Very odd, indeed!"

After waiting another moment:

"You mean Mr. Wentworth, I suppose?" said Anne.

Mr. Shepherd was all gratitude.

"Wentworth was the very name! Mr. Wentworth was the very man. He had the curacy of Monkford, you know, Sir Walter, some time back, for two or three years. Came there about the year —5, I take it. You remember him, I am sure."

"Wentworth? Oh ay! Mr. Wentworth, the curate of Monkford. You misled me by the term *gentleman*. I thought you were speaking of some man of property: Mr. Wentworth was nobody, I remember; quite unconnected; nothing to do with the Strafford family. One wonders how the names of many of our nobility become so common."

As Mr. Shepherd perceived that this connection of the Crofts did them no service with Sir Walter, he mentioned it no more; returning, with all his zeal, to dwell on the circumstances more indisputably in their favour; their age, and number, and fortune; the high idea they had formed of Kellynch Hall, and extreme solicitude for the advantage of renting it; making it appear as if they ranked nothing beyond the happiness of being the tenants of Sir Walter Elliot: an extraordinary taste, certainly, could they have been supposed in the secret of Sir Walter's estimate of the dues of a tenant.

It succeeded, however; and though Sir Walter must ever look with an evil eye on any one intending to inhabit that house, and think them infinitely too well off in being permitted to rent it on the highest terms, he was talked into allowing Mr. Shepherd to proceed in the treaty, and authorizing him to wait on Admiral Croft, who still remained at Taunton, and fix a day for the house being seen.

Sir Walter was not very wise; but still he had experience enough of the world to feel, that a more unobjectionable tenant, in all essentials, than Admiral Croft bid fair to be, could hardly offer. So far went his understanding; and his vanity supplied a little additional soothing, in the Admiral's situation in life, which was just high enough, and not too hgh. "I have let my house to Admiral Croft," would sound extremely well; very much better than to any mere *Mr.* ———; a *Mr.* (save, perhaps, some half dozen in the nation) always needs a note of explanation. An admiral speaks his own consequence, and, at the same time, can never make a baronet look small. In all their dealings and intercourse, Sir Walter Elliot must ever have the precedence.

Nothing could be done without a reference to Elizabeth: but her inclination was growing so strong for a removal, that she was happy to have it fixed and expedited by a tenant at hand; and not a word to suspend decision was uttered by her.

Mr. Shepherd was completely empowered to act; and no sooner had such an end been reached, than Anne, who had been a most attentive listener to the whole, left the room, to seek the comfort of cool air for her flushed cheeks; and as she walked along a favourite grove, said, with a gentle sigh, "A few months more, and *he*, perhaps, may be walking here."

Chapter 4

HE was not Mr. Wentworth, the former curate of Monkford, however suspicious appearances may be, but a Captain Frederick Wentworth, his brother, who being made commander in consequence of the action off

St. Domingo, and not immediately employed, had come into Somersetshire, in the summer of 1806; and having no parent living, found a home
for half a year at Monkford. He was, at that time, a remarkably fine
young man, with a great deal of intelligence, spirit, and brilliancy; and
Anne an extremely pretty girl, with gentleness, modesty, taste, and feeling.
Half the sum of attraction, on either side, might have been enough, for
he had nothing to do, and she had hardly anybody to love; but the encounter of such lavish recommendations could not fail. They were gradually acquainted, and when acquainted, rapidly and deeply in love. It
would be difficult to say which had seen highest perfection in the other, or
which had been the happiest: she, in receiving his declarations and proposals, or he in having them accepted.

A short period of exquisite felicity followed, and but a short one.
Troubles soon arose. Sir Walter, on being applied to, without actually
withholding his consent, or saying it should never be, gave it all the negative of great astonishment, great coldness, great silence, and a professed
resolution of doing nothing for his daughter. He thought it a very degrading alliance; and Lady Russell, though with more tempered and pardonable pride, received it as a most unfortunate one.

Anne Elliot, with all her claims of birth, beauty and mind, to throw
herself away at nineteen; involve herself, at nineteen, in an engagement
with a young man who had nothing but himself to recommend him, and no
hopes of attaining affluence, but in the chances of a most uncertain profession, and no connections to secure even his further rise in that profession, would be, indeed, a throwing away, which she grieved to think of!
Anne Elliot, so young; known to so few, to be snatched off by a stranger
without alliance or fortune; or rather sunk by him into a state of most
wearing, anxious, youth-killing dependence! It must not be, if by any fair
interference of friendship, any representations from one who had almost a
mother's love and mother's rights, it would be prevented.

Captain Wentworth had no fortune. He had been lucky in his profession; but spending freely what had come freely, had realised nothing. But
he was confident that he should soon be rich: full of life and ardour, he
knew that he should soon have a ship, and soon be on a station that would
lead to everything he wanted. He had always been lucky; he knew he
should be so still. Such confidence, powerful in its own warmth, and bewitching in the wit which often expressed it, must have been enough for
Anne; but Lady Russell saw it very differently. His sanguine temper, and
fearlessness of mind, operated very differently on her. She saw in it but
an aggravation of the evil. It only added a dangerous character to himself.
He was brilliant, he was headstrong. Lady Russell had little taste for wit,
and of anything approaching to imprudence a horror. She deprecated the
connection in every light.

Such opposition as these feelings produced was more than Anne could
combat. Young and gentle as she was, it might yet have been possible
withstand her father's ill-will, though unsoftened by one kind word

look on the part of her sister; but Lady Russell, whom she had always loved and relied on, could not, with such steadiness of opinion, and such tenderness of manner, be continually advising her in vain. She was persuaded to believe the engagement a wrong thing: indiscreet, improper, hardly capable of success, and not deserving it. But it was not a merely selfish caution under which she acted, in putting an end to it. Had she not imagined herself consulting his good, even more than her own, she could hardly have given him up. The belief of being prudent and self-denying, principally for *his* advantage, was her chief consolation under the misery of a parting, a final parting; and every consolation was required, for she had to encounter all the additional pain of opinions, on his side, totally unconvinced and unbending, and of his feeling himself ill-used by so forced a relinquishment. He had left the country in consequence.

A few months had seen the beginning and the end of their acquaintance; but not with a few months ended Anne's share of suffering from it. Her attachment and regrets had, for a long time, clouded every enjoyment of youth, and an early loss of bloom and spirits had been their lasting effect.

More than seven years were gone since this little history of sorrowful interest had reached its close; and time had softened down much, perhaps nearly all of peculiar attachment to him, but she had been too dependent on time alone; no aid had been given in change of place (except in one visit to Bath soon after the rupture), or in any novelty or enlargement of society. No one had ever come within the Kellynch circle, who could bear a comparison with Frederick Wentworth, as he stood in her memory. No second attachment, the only thoroughly natural, happy, and sufficient cure at her time of life, had been possible to the nice tone of her mind, the fastidiousness of her taste, in the small limits of the society around them. She had been solicited, when about two-and-twenty, to change her name by the young man who not long afterwards found a more willing mind in her younger sister: and Lady Russell had lamented her refusal: for Charles Musgrove was the eldest son of a man whose landed property and general importance were second in that country only to Sir Walter's, and of good character and appearance; and however Lady Russell might have asked yet for something more while Anne was nineteen, she would have rejoiced to see her at twenty-two so respectably removed from the partialities and injustice of her father's house, and settled so permanently near herself. But in this case Anne had left nothing for advice to do; and though Lady Russell, as satisfied as ever with her own discretion, never wished the past undone, she began now to have the anxiety which borders on hopelessness for Anne's being tempted, by some man of talents and independence, to enter a state for which she held her to be peculiarly fitted by her warm affections and domestic habits.

They knew not each other's opinion, either its constancy or its change, on the one leading point of Anne's conduct, for the subject was never alluded to; but Anne, at seven-and-twenty, thought very differently from what she had been made to think at nineteen. She did not blame Lady

Russell, she did not blame herself for having been guided by her; but she felt that were any young person in similar circumstances to apply to her for counsel, they would never receive any of such certain immediate wretchedness, such uncertain future good. She was persuaded that under every disadvantage of disapprobation at home, and every anxiety attending his profession, all their probable fears, delays, and disappointments, she should yet have been a happier woman in maintaining the engagement, than she had been in the sacrifice of it; and this, she fully believed had the usual share, had even more than a usual share of all such solicitudes and suspense been theirs, without reference to the actual results of their case, which, as it happened, would have bestowed earlier prosperity than could be reasonably calculated on. All his sanguine expectations, all his confidence, had been justified. His genius and ardour had seemed to foresee and to command his prosperous path. He had, very soon after their engagement ceased, got employ; and all that he had told her would follow had taken place. He had distinguished himself, and early gained the other step in rank, and must now, by successive captures, have made a handsome fortune. She had only navy lists and newspapers for her authority, but she could not doubt his being rich; and, in favour of his constancy, she had no reason to believe him married.

How eloquent could Anne Elliot have been! how eloquent, at least, were her wishes on the side of early warm attachment, and a cheerful confidence in futurity, against that over-anxious caution which seems to insult exertion and distrust Providence! She had been forced into prudence in her youth, she learned romance as she grew older: the natural sequel of an unnatural beginning.

With all these circumstances, recollections, and feelings, she could not hear that Captain Wentworth's sister was likely to live at Kellynch without a revival of former pain; and many a stroll, and many a sigh, were necessary to dispel the agitation of the idea. She often told herself it was folly, before she could harden her nerves sufficiently to feel the continual discussion of the Crofts and their business no evil. She was assisted, however, by that perfect indifference and apparent unconsciousness, among the only three of her own friends in the secret of the past, which seemed almost to deny any recollection of it. She could do justice to the superiority of Lady Russell's motives in this, over those of her father and Elizabeth; she could honour all the better feelings of her calmness; but the general air of oblivion among them was highly important from whatever it sprung; and in the event of Admiral Croft's really taking Kellynch Hall, she rejoiced anew over the conviction which had always been most grateful to her, of the past being known to those three only among her connections, by whom no syllable, she believed, would ever be whispered, and in the trust that among his, the brother only with whom he had been residing had received any information of their shortlived engagement. That brother had been long removed from the country, and being a sensible man, and.

moreover, a single man at the time, she had a fond dependence on no human creature's having heard of it from him.

The sister, Mrs. Croft, had then been out of England, accompanying her husband on a foreign station, and her own sister, Mary, had been at school while it all occurred; and never admitted by the pride of some, and the delicacy of others, to the smallest knowledge of it afterwards.

With these supports, she hoped that the acquaintance between herself and the Crofts, which, with Lady Russell still resident in Kellynch, and Mary fixed only three miles off, must be anticipated, need not involve any particular awkwardness.

Chapter 5

ON the morning appointed for Admiral and Mrs. Croft's seeing Kellynch Hall, Anne found it most natural to take her almost daily walk to Lady Russell's, and keep out of the way till all was over; when she found it most natural to be sorry that she had missed the opportunity of seeing them.

This meeting of the two parties proved highly satisfactory, and decided the whole business at once. Each lady was previously well disposed for an agreement, and saw nothing, therefore, but good manners in the other; and with regard to the gentlemen, there was such a hearty good humour, such an open, trusting liberality on the Admiral's side, as could not but influence Sir Walter, who had besides been flattered into his very best and most polished behaviour by Mr. Shepherd's assurances of his being known, by report, to the Admiral, as a model of good breeding.

The house, and grounds, and furniture, were approved, the Crofts were approved, terms, time, everything, and everybody, was right; and Mr. Shepherd's clerks were set to work, without there having been a single preliminary difference to modify of all that "This indenture showeth."

Sir Walter without hesitation, declared the Admiral to be the best-looking sailor he had ever met with, and went so far as to say, that if his own man might have had the arranging of his hair, he should not be ashamed of being seen with him anywhere; and the Admiral, with sympathetic cordiality, observed to his wife as they drove back through the park, "I thought we should soon come to a deal, my dear, in spite of what they told us at Taunton. The Baronet will never set the Thames on fire, but there seems no harm in him:" reciprocal compliments which would have been esteemed about equal.

The Crofts were to have possession at Michaelmas; and as Sir Walter proposed removing to Bath in the course of the preceding month, there was no time to be lost in making every dependent arrangement.

Lady Russell, convinced that Anne would not be allowed to be of any use, or any importance, in the choice of the house which they were going to secure, was very unwilling to have her hurried away so soon, and wanted to make it possible for her to stay behind till she might convey her to Bath herself after Christmas; but having engagements of her own which must take her from Kellynch for several weeks, she was unable to give the full invitation she wished, and Anne, though dreading the possible heats of September in all the white glare of Bath, and grieving to forego all the influence so sweet and so sad of the autumnal months in the country, did not think that, everything considered, she wished to remain. It would be most right, and most wise, and therefore must involve least suffering to go with the others.

Something occurred, however, to give her a different duty. Mary, often a little unwell, and always thinking a great deal of her own complaints, and always in the habit of claiming Anne when anything was the matter, was indisposed; and foreseeing that she should not have a day's health all the autumn, entreated, or rather required her, for it was hardly entreaty, to come to Uppercross Cottage, and bear her company as long as she could want her, instead of going to Bath.

"I cannot possibly do without Anne," was Mary's reasoning; and Elizabeth's reply was, "Then I am sure Anne had better stay, for nobody will want her in Bath."

To be claimed as a good, though in an improper style, is at least better than being rejected as no good at all; and Anne, glad to be thought of some use, glad to have anything marked out as a duty, and certainly not sorry to have the scene of it in the country, and her own dear country readily agreed to stay.

This invitation of Mary's removed all Lady Russell's difficulties, and it was consequently soon settled that Anne should not go to Bath till Lady Russell took her, and that all the intervening time should be divided between Uppercross Cottage and Kellynch Lodge.

So far all was perfectly right; but Lady Russell was almost startled by the wrong of one part of the Kellynch Hall plan, when it burst on her, which was, Mrs. Clay's being engaged to go to Bath with Sir Walter and Elizabeth, as a most important and valuable assistant to the latter in all the business before her. Lady Russell was extremely sorry that such a measure should have been resorted to at all, wondered, grieved, and feared; and the affront it contained to Anne, in Mrs. Clay's being of so much use, while Anne could be of none, was a very sore aggravation.

Anne herself was become hardened to such affronts, but she felt the imprudence of the arrangement quite as keenly as Lady Russell. With a great deal of quiet observation, and a knowledge, which she often wished less, of her father's character, she was sensible that results the most serious to his family from the intimacy were more than possible. She did not imagine that her father had at present an idea of the kind. Mrs. Clay had freckles, and a projecting tooth, and a clumsy wrist, which he was continually making severe remarks upon her in absence, but she was young, and certainly altogether well-looking, and possessed, in an acute mind and assiduous pleasing manners, infinitely more dangerous attractions than any merely personal might have been. Anne was so impressed by the degree of their danger, that she could not excuse herself from trying to make it perceptible to her sister. She had little hope of success, but Elizabeth, who in the event of such a reverse would be so much more to be pitied than herself, should never, she thought, have reason to reproach her for giving no warning.

She spoke, and seemed only to offend. Elizabeth could not conceive how such an absurd suspicion should occur to her, and indignantly answered for each party's perfection, knowing their situation.

"Mrs. Clay," said she, warmly, "never forgets who she is; and as I am rather better acquainted with her sentiments than you can be, I can assure you, that upon the subject of marriage they are particularly nice, and that she reprobates all inequality of condition and rank more strongly than most people. And as to my father, I really should not have thought that he who has kept himself single so long for our sakes need be suspected now. If Mrs. Clay were a very beautiful woman, I grant you it might be wrong to have her so much with me; not that anything in the world, I am sure, would induce my father to make a degrading match, but he might be rendered unhappy. But poor Mrs. Clay, who with all her merits, can never have been reckoned tolerably pretty, I really think poor Mrs. Clay may be staying here in perfect safety. One would imagine you had never heard my father speak of her personal misfortunes, though I know you must fifty times. That tooth of hers and those freckles. Freckles do not disgust me so very much as they do him. I have known a face not materially disfigured by a few, but he abominates them. You must have heard him notice Mrs. Clay's freckles."

"There is hardly any personal defect," replied Anne, "which an agreeable manner might not gradually reconcile one to."

"I think very differently," answered Elizabeth, shortly; "an agreeable manner may set off handsome features, but can never alter plain ones. However, at any rate, as I have a great deal more at stake on this point than anybody else can have, I think it rather unnecessary in you to be advising me."

Anne had done; glad that it was over, and not absolutely hopeless of doing good. Elizabeth, though resenting the suspicion, might yet be made observant by it.

The last office of the four carriage-horses was to draw Sir Walter, Miss Elliot, and Mrs. Clay to Bath. The party drove off in very good spirits; Sir Walter prepared with condescending bows for all the afflicted tenantry and cottagers who might have had a hint to show themselves, and Anne walked up at the same time in a sort of desolate tranquillity to the Lodge, where she was to spend the first week.

Her friend was not in better spirits than herself. Lady Russell felt this break-up of the family exceedingly. Their respectability was as dear to her as her own, and a daily intercourse had become precious by habit. It was painful to look upon their deserted grounds, and still worse to anticipate the new hands they were to fall into; and to escape the solitariness and the melancholy of so altered a village, and be out of the way when Admiral and Mrs. Croft first arrived, she had determined to make her own absence from home begin when she must give up Anne. Accordingly their removal was made together, and Anne was set down at Uppercross Cottage, in the first stage of Lady Russell's journey.

Uppercross was a moderate-sized village, which a few years back had been completely in the old English style, containing only two houses superior in appearance to those of the yeomen and labourers; the mansion of the squire, with its high walls, great gates, and old trees, substantial and unmodernized, and the compact, tight parsonage, enclosed in its own neat garden, with a vine and a pear-tree trained round its casements; but upon the marriage of the young squire, it had received the improvement of a farmhouse, elevated into a cottage, for his residence, and Uppercross Cottage, with its verandah, French windows, and other prettinesses, was quite as likely to catch the traveller's eye as the more consistent and considerable aspect and premises of the Great House, about a quarter of a mile further on.

Here Anne had often been staying. She knew the ways of Uppercross as well as those of Kellynch. The two families were so continually meeting, so much in the habit of running in and out of each other's house at all hours, that it was rather a surprise to her to find Mary alone; but being alone, her being unwell and out of spirits was almost a matter of course. Though better endowed than the elder sister, Mary had not Anne's understanding nor temper. While well, and happy, and properly attended to, she had great good humour and excellent spirits; but any indisposition sunk her completely. She had no resources for solitude; and, inheriting a considerable share of the Elliot self-importance, was very prone to add to every other distress that of fancying herself neglected and ill-used. In person, she was inferior to both sisters, and had, even in her bloom, only reached the dignity of being "a fine girl." She was now lying on the faded sofa of the pretty little drawing-room, the once elegant furniture of which had been gradually growing shabby under the influence of four summers and two children; and, on Anne's appearing, greeted her with:

"So you are come at last! I began to think I should never see you. I am so ill I can hardly speak. I have not seen a creature the whole morning!"

"I am sorry to find you unwell," replied Anne. "You sent me such a good account of yourself on Thursday."

"Yes, I made the best of it; I always do: but I was very far from well at the time; and I do not think I ever was so ill in my life as I have been all this morning: very unfit to be left alone, I am sure. Suppose I were to be seized of a sudden in some dreadful way, and not able to ring the bell! So Lady Russell would not get out. I do not think she has been in this house three times this summer."

Anna said what was proper, and enquired after her husband. "Oh!

Charles is out shooting. I have not seen him since seven o'clock. He would go, though I told him how ill I was. He said he should not stay out long; but he has never come back, and now it is almost one. I assure you I have not seen a soul this whole long morning."

"You have had your little boys with you?"

"Yes, as long as I could bear their noise; but they are so unmanageable that they do me more harm than good. Little Charles does not mind a word I say, and Walter is growing quite as bad."

"Well, you will soon be better now," replied Anne, cheerfully. "You know I always cure you when I come. How are your neighbours at the Great House?"

"I can give you no account of them. I have not seen one of them to-day, except Mr. Musgrove, who just stopped and spoke though the window, but without getting off his horse; and though I told him how ill I was, not one of them have been near me. It did not happen to suit the Miss Musgroves, I suppose, and they never put themselves out of their way."

"You will see them yet, perhaps, before the morning is gone. It is early."

"I never want them, I assure you. They talk and laugh a great deal too much for me. Oh! Anne, I am so very unwell! It was quite unkind of you not to come on Thursday."

"My dear Mary, recollect what a comfortable account you sent me of yourself ! You wrote in the cheerfullest manner, and said you were perfectly well, and in no hurry for me; and that being the case, you must be aware that my wish would be to remain with Lady Russell to the last: and besides what I felt on her account, I have really been so busy, have had so much to do, that I could not very conveniently have left Kellynch sooner."

"Dear me! what can *you* possibly have to do?"

"A great many things, I assure you. More than I can recollect in a moment; but I can tell you some. I have been making a duplicate of the catalogue of my father's books and pictures. I have been several times in the garden with Mackenzie, trying to understand, and make him understand, which of Elizabeth's plants are for Lady Russell. I have had all my own little concerns to arrange, books and music to divide, and all my trunks to repack, from not having understood in time what was intended as to the waggons: and one thing I have had to do, Mary, of a more trying nature: going to almost every house in the parish, as a sort of take-leave. I was told that they wished it; but all these things took up a great deal of time."

"Oh, well!" and after a moment's pause, "but you have never asked me one word about our dinner at the Pooles yesterday."

"Did you go, then? I have made no enquiries, because I concluded you must have been obliged to give up the party."

"Oh, yes! I went. I was very well yesterday; nothing at all the matter with me till this morning. It would have been strange if I had not gone."

"I am very glad you were well enough and I hope you had a pleasant party."

"Nothing remarkable. One always knows beforehand what the dinner will be, and who will be there; and it is so very uncomfortable not having a carriage of one's own. Mr. and Mrs. Musgrove took me, and we were so crowded! They are both so very large, and take up so much room; and Mr. Musgrove always sits forward. So there was I crowded into the back seat with Henrietta and Louisa; and I think it very likely that my illness to-day may be owing to it."

A little further perseverance in patience and forced cheerfulness on Anne's side produced nearly a cure on Mary's. She could soon sit upright on the sofa, and began to hope she might be able to leave it by dinner-time. Then, forgetting to think of it, she was at the other end of the room, beautifying a nosegay; then she ate her cold meat; and then she was well enough to propose a little walk.

"Where shall we go?" said she, when they were ready. "I suppose you will not like to call at the Great House before they have been to see you?"

"I have not the smallest objection on that account," replied Anne. "I should never think of standing on such ceremony with people I know so well as Mrs. and the Miss Musgroves "

"Oh! but they ought to call upon you as soon as possible. They ought to feel what is due to you as *my* sister. However, we may as well go and sit with them a little while, and when we have got that over, we can enjoy our walk."

Anne had always thought such a style of intercourse highly imprudent; but she had ceased to endeavour to check it, from believing that, though there were on each side continual subjects of offence, neither family could now do without it. To the Great House accordingly they went, to sit the full half hour in the old-fashioned square parlour, with a small carpet and shining floor, to which the present daughters of the house were gradually giving the proper air of confusion by a grand pianoforte and a harp, flowerstands, and little tables placed in every direction. Oh! could the originals of the portraits against the wainscot, could the gentlemen in brown velvet and the ladies in blue satin have seen what was going on, have been consicous of such an overthrow of all order and neatness! The portraits themselves seemed to be staring in astonishment.

The Musgroves, like their houses, were in a state of alteration, perhaps of improvement. The father and mother were in the old English style, and the young people in the new. Mr. and Mrs. Musgrove were a very good sort of people; friendly and hospitable, not much educated, and not at all elegant. Their children had more modern minds and manners. There was a numerous family; but the only two grown up, excepting Charles, were Henrietta and Louisa, young ladies of nineteen and twenty, who had brought from a school at Exeter all the usual stock of accomplishments, and were now, like thousands of other young ladies, living to be fashionable, happy, and merry. Their dress had every advantage, their faces were rather pretty, their spirits extremely good, their manners unembarrassed and pleasant; they were of consequence at home, and favourites abroad. Anne always contemplated them as some of the happiest creatures of her acquaintance: but still, saved as we all are, by some comfortable feeling of superiority from wishing for the possibility of exchange, she would not have given up her own more elegant and cultivated mind for all their enjoyments; and envied them nothing but that seemingly perfect good understanding and agreement together, that good-humoured mutual affection, of which she had known so little herself with either of her sisters.

They were received with great cordiality. Nothing seemed amiss on the side of the Great House family, which was generally, as Anne very well knew, the least to blame. The half hour was chatted away pleasantly enough; and she was not at all surprised, at the end of it, to have their walking party joined by both the Miss Musgroves, at Mary's particular invitation.

Chapter 6

ANNE had not wanted this visit to Uppercross to learn that a removal from one set of people to another, though at a distance of only three miles, will often include a total change of conversation, opinion, and idea. She had never been staying there before, without being struck by it, or without wishing that other Elliots could have her advantage in seeing how unknown, or unconsidered there, were the affairs which at Kellynch Hall were treated as of such general publicity and pervading interest; yet, with all this experience, she believed she must now submit to feel that another lesson, in the art of knowing our own nothingness beyond our own circle, was become necessary for her; for certainly, coming as she did, with a heart full of the subject which had been completely occupying both houses in Kellynch for many weeks, she had expected rather more curiosity and sympathy than she found in the separate, but very similar remark of Mr. and Mrs. Musgrove: "So, Miss Anne, Sir Walter and your sister are gone; and what part of Bath do you think they will settle in?" and this, without much waiting for an answer; or in the young ladies' addition of, "I hope *we* shall be in Bath in the winter; but remember, papa, if we do go, we must be in a good situation: none of your Queen Squares for us!" or in the anxious supplement from Mary, of—"Upon my word, I shall be pretty well off, when you are all gone away to be happy at Bath!"

She could only resolve to avoid such self-delusion in future, and think with heightened gratitude of the extraordinary blessing of having one such truly sympathising friend as Lady Russell.

The Mr. Musgroves had their own game to guard and to destroy, their own horses, dogs, and newspapers to engage them, and the females were fully occupied in all the other common subjects of housekeeping, neighbours, dress, dancing and music. She acknowledged it to be very fitting, that every little social commonwealth should dictate its own matters of discourse; and hoped, ere long, to become a not unworthy member of the one she was now transplanted into. With the prospect of spending at least two months at Uppercross, it was highly incumbent on her to clothe her imagination, her memory, and all her ideas in as much of Uppercross as possible.

She had no dread of these two months. Mary was not so repulsive and unsisterly as Elizabeth, nor so inaccessible to all influence of hers; neither was there anything among the other component parts of the Cottage inimical to comfort. She was always on friendly terms with her brother-in-law; and in the children, who loved her nearly as well, and respected her a great deal more than their mother, she had an object of interest, amusement, and wholesome exertion.

Charles Musgrove was civil and agreeable; in sense and temper he was undoubtedly superior to his wife, but not of powers, or conversation, or grace to make the past, as they were connected together, at all a dangerous contemplation; though, at the same time, Anne could believe, with Lady Russell, that a more equal match might have greatly improved him; and that a woman of real understanding might have given more consequence to his character, and more usefulness, rationality, and elegance to his habits and pursuits. As it was, he did nothing with much zeal, but sport; and his time was otherwise trifled away, without benefit from books or anything else. He had very good spirits, which never seemed much affected by his wife's occasional lowness, bore with her unreasonableness sometimes to Anne's admiration, and upon the whole, though there was very often a little disagreement (in which she had sometimes more share than she wished, being appealed to by both parties), they might pass for a happy couple. They were always perfectly agreed in the want of more money, and a strong inclination for a handsome present from his father; but here, as on most topics, he had the superiority, for while Mary thought it a great shame that such a present was not made, he always contended for his father's having many other uses for his money, and a right to spend it as he liked.

As to the management of their children, his theory was much better than his wife's, and his practice not so bad. "I could manage them very well, if it were not for Mary's interference," was what Anne often heard him say, and had a good deal of faith in; but when listening in turn to Mary's reproach of, "Charles spoils the children so that I cannot get them into any order," she never had the smallest temptation to say, "Very true."

One of the least agreeable circumstances of her residence there was her being treated with too much confidence by all parties, and being too much in the secret of the complaints of each house. Known to have some influence with her sister, she was continually requested, or at least receiving hints to exert it, beyond what was practicable. "I wish you could persuade Mary not to be always fancying herself ill," was Charles's language; and, in an unhappy mood, thus spoke Mary: "I do believe if Charles were to see me dying, he would not think there was anything the matter with me. I am sure, Anne, if you would, you might persuade him that I really am very ill—a great deal worse than I ever own."

Mary's declaration was, "I hate sending the children to the Great House, though their grandmamma is always wanting to see them, for she humours and indulges them to such a degree, and gives them so much trash and sweet things, that they are sure to come back sick and cross for the rest of the day." And Mrs. Musgrove took the first opportunity of being alone with Anne, to say, "Oh! Miss Anne, I cannot help wishing Mrs. Charles had a little of your method with those children. They are quite different creatures with you! But to be sure, in general, they are so spoilt! It is a pity you cannot put your sister in the way of managing them. They are as fine healthy children as ever were seen, poor little dears! without partiality; but Mrs. Charles knows no more how they should be treated——! Bless me! how troublesome they are sometimes. I assure you, Miss Anne, it prevents my wishing to see them at our house so often as I otherwise should. I believe Mrs. Charles is not quite pleased with my not inviting them oftener; but you know it is very bad to have children with one that one is obliged to be checking every moment; 'don't do this,' and 'don't do that'; or that one can only keep in tolerable order by more cake than is good for them."

She had this communication, moreover, from Mary: "Mrs. Musgrove thinks all her servants so steady, that it would be high treason to call it in question; but I am sure, without exaggeration, that her upper housemaid and laundrymaid, instead of being in their business, are gadding about the village all day long. I meet them wherever I go; and I declare I never go twice into my nursery without seeing something of them. If Jemima were not the trustiest, steadiest creature in the world, it would be enough to spoil her; for she tells me they are always tempting her to take a walk with them." And on Mrs. Musgrove's side it was, "I make a rule of never interfering in any of my daughter-in-law's concerns, for I know it would not do; but I shall tell *you*, Miss Anne, because you may be able to set things to rights, that I have no very good opinion of Mrs. Charles's nurserymaid: I hear strange stories of her; she is always upon the gad; and from my own knowledge, I can declare, she is such a fine-dressing lady, that she is enough to ruin any servants she comes near. Mrs. Charles quite swears by her, I know; but I just give you this hint, that you may be upon the watch; because, if you see anything amiss, you need not be afraid of mentioning it."

Again, it was Mary's complaint that Mrs. Musgrove was very apt not to give her the precedence that was her due, when they dined at the Great House with other families; and she did not see any reason why she was to be considered so much at home as to lose her place. And one day when Anne was walking with only the Miss Musgroves, one of them, after talking of rank, people of rank, and jealousy of rank, said, "I have no scruple of observing to *you*, how nonsensical some persons are about their

place, because all the world knows how easy and indifferent you are about
it; but I wish anybody would give Mary a hint that it would be a great
deal better if she were not so very tenacious, especially if she would not
be always putting herself forward to take place of mamma. Nobody
doubts her right to have precedence of mamma, but it would be more
becoming in her not to be always insisting on it. It is not that mamma
cares about it the least in the world, but I know it is taken notice of by
many persons."

How was Anne to set all these matters to rights? She could do little
more than listen patiently, soften every grievance, and excuse each to the
other; give them all hints of the forbearance necessary between such
near neighbours, and make those hints broadest which were meant for her
sister's benefit.

In all other respects, her visit began and proceeded very well. Her own
spirits improved by change of place and subject, by being removed three
miles from Kellynch; Mary's ailments lessened by having a constant companion, and their daily intercourse with the other family, since there was
neither superior affection, confidence nor employment in the Cottage to
be interrupted by it, was rather an advantage. It was certainly carried
nearly as far as possible, for they met every morning, and hardly ever
spent an evening asunder; but she believed they should not have done so
well without the sight of Mr. and Mrs. Musgrove's respectable forms in
the usual places, or without the talking, laughing, and singing of their
daughters.

She played a great deal better than either of the Miss Musgroves, but
having no voice, no knowledge of the harp, and no fond parents, to sit
by and fancy themselves delighted, her performance was little thought
of, only out of civility, or to refresh the others, as she was well aware.
She knew that when she played she was giving pleasure only to herself;
but this was no new sensation. Excepting one short period of her life,
she had never, since the age of fourteen, never since the loss of her dear
mother, known the happiness of being listened to, or encouraged by any
just appreciation or real taste. In music she had been always used to feel
alone in the world; and Mr. and Mrs. Musgrove's fond partiality for their
own daughters' performance, and total indifference to any other person's,
gave her much more pleasure for their sakes, than mortification for
her own.

The party at the Great House was sometimes increased by other company. The neighbourhood was not large, but the Musgroves were visited
by everybody, and had more dinner-parties, and more callers, more
visitors by invitation and by chance, than any other family. They were
more completely popular.

The girls were wild for dancing; and the evenings ended, occasionally,
in an unpremeditated little ball. There was a family of cousins within a
walk of Uppercross, in less affluent circumstances, who depended on the
Musgroves for all their pleasures; they would come at any time, or help

to play at anything, or dance anywhere; and Anne, very much preferring the office of musician to a more active post, played country dances to them by the hour together; a kindness which always recommended her musical powers to the notice of Mr. and Mrs. Musgrove more than anything else, and often drew this compliment—"Well done, Miss Anne! very well done, indeed! Lord bless me! how those little fingers of yours fly about!"

So passed the first three weeks, Michaelmas came; and now Anne's heart must be in Kellynch again. A beloved home made over to others; all the precious rooms and furniture, groves and prospects, beginning to own other eyes and other limbs! She could not think of much else on the 29th of September; and she had this sympathetic touch in the evening from Mary, who, on having occasion to note down the day of the month, exclaimed, "Dear me, is not this the day the Crofts were to come to Kellynch? I am glad I did not think of it before. How low it makes me!"

The Crofts took possession with true naval alertness, and were to be visited. Mary deplored the necessity for herself. "Nobody knew how much she should suffer. She should put it off as long as she could"; but was not easy till she had talked Charles into driving her over on an early day, and was in a very animated, comfortable state of imaginary agitation when she came back. Anne had very sincerely rejoiced in there being no means of her going. She wished, however, to see the Crofts, and was glad to be within when the visit was returned. They came: the master of the house was not at home, but the two sisters were together; and as it chanced that Mrs. Croft fell to the share of Anne, while the Admiral sat by Mary, and made himself very agreeable by his good-humoured notice of her little boys, she was well able to watch for a likeness, and if it failed her in the features, to catch it in the voice, or in the turn of sentiment and expression.

Mrs. Croft, though neither tall nor fat, had a squareness, uprightness, and vigour of form, which gave importance to her person. She had bright dark eyes, good teeth, and altogether an agreeable face; though her reddened and weather-beaten complexion, the consequence of her having been almost as much at sea as her husband, made her seem to have lived some years longer in the world than her real eight-and-thirty. Her manners were open, easy, and decided, like one who had no distrust of herself, and no doubts of what to do; without any approach to coarseness, however, or any want of good humour. Anne gave her credit, indeed, for feelings of great consideration towards herself, in all that related to Kellynch, and it pleased her: especially, as she had satisfied herself in the very first half minute, in the instant even of introduction, that there was not the smallest symptom of any knowledge or suspicion on Mrs. Croft's side to give a bias of any sort. She was quite easy on that head, and consequently full of strength and courage, till for a moment electrified by Mrs. Croft's suddenly saying:

"It was you, and not your sister, I find, that my brother had the pleasure of being acquainted with, when he was in this country."

Anne hoped she had outlived the age of blushing; but the age of emotion she certainly had not.

"Perhaps you may not have heard that he is married?" added Mrs. Croft.

She could now answer as she ought; and was happy to feel, when Mrs. Croft's next words explained it to be Mr. Wentworth of whom she spoke, that she had said nothing which might not do for either brother. She immediately felt how reasonable it was, that Mrs. Croft should be thinking and speaking of Edward, and not of Frederick; and with shame at her own forgetfulness, applied herself to the knowledge of their former neighbour's present state with proper interest.

The rest was all tranquillity; till, just as they were moving, she heard the Admiral say to Mary:

"We are expecting a brother of Mrs. Croft's here soon; I dare say you know him by name?"

He was cut short by the eager attacks of the little boys, clinging to him like an old friend, and declaring he should not go; and being too much engrossed by proposals of carrying them away in his coat pocket, etc., to have another moment for finishing or recollecting what he had begun, Anne was left to persuade herself, as well as she could, that the same brother must still be in question. She could not, however, reach such a degree of certainty as not to be anxious to hear whether anything had been said on the subject at the other house, where the Crofts had previously been calling.

The folks of Great House were to spend the evening of this day at the Cottage; and it being now too late in the year for such visits to be made on foot, the coach was beginning to be listened for, when the youngest Miss Musgrove walked in. That she was coming to apologise, and that they should have to spend the evening by themselves, was the first black idea; and Mary was quite ready to be affronted, when Louisa made all right by saying, that she only came on foot, to leave more room for the harp, which was bringing in the carriage.

"And I will tell you our reason," she added, "and all about it. I am come on to give you notice, that papa and mamma are out of spirits this evening, especially mamma; she is thinking so much of poor Richard! And we agreed it would be best to have the harp, for it seems to amuse her more than the pianoforte. I will tell you why she is out of spirits. When the Crofts called this morning (they called here afterwards, did not they?), they happened to say that her brother, Captain Wentworth, is just returned to England, or paid off, or something, and is coming to see them almost directly; and most unluckily it came into mamma's head, when they were gone, that Wentworth, or something very like it, was the name of poor Richard's captain, at one time; I do not know when or where, but a great while before he died, poor fellow! And upon looking over his letters and things, she found it was so, and is perfectly sure that this must be the very man, and her head is quite full of it, and of poor Richard! So we must all be as merry as we can, that she may not be dwelling upon such gloomy things."

The real circumstances of this pathetic piece of family history were, that the Musgroves had had the ill fortune of a very troublesome, hopeless son, and the good fortune to lose him before he reached his twentieth year; that he had been sent to sea because he was stupid and unmanageable on shore; that he had been very little cared for at any time by his family, though quite as much as he deserved; seldom heard of, and scarcely at all regretted, when the intelligence of his death abroad had worked its way to Uppercross, two years before.

He had, in fact, though his sisters were now doing all they could for him, by calling him "poor Richard," been nothing better than a thickheaded, unfeeling, unprofitable Dick Musgrove, who had never done anything to entitle himself to more than the abbreviation of his name, living or dead.

He had been several years at sea, and had, in the course of those removals to which all midshipmen are liable, and especially such midshipmen as every captain wishes to get rid of, been six months on board Captain Frederick Wentworth's frigate, the *Laconia;* and from the *Laconia* he had, under the influence of his captain, written the only two letters which his father and mother had ever received from him during the whole of his absence; that is to say, the only two disinterested letters: all the rest had been mere applications for money.

In each letter he had spoken well of his captain; but yet, so little were they in the habit of attending to such matters, so unobservant and incurious were they as to the names of men or ships, that it had made scarcely any impression at the time, and that Mrs. Musgrove should have been suddenly struck, this very day, with a recollection of the name of Wentworth, as connected with her son, seemed one of those extraordinary bursts of mind which do sometimes occur.

She had gone to her letters, and found it all as she supposed; and the re-perusal of these letters, after so long an interval, her poor son gone for ever, and all the strength of his faults forgotten, had affected her spirits exceedingly, and thrown her into greater grief for him than she had known on first hearing of his death. Mr. Musgrove was, in a lesser degree, affected likewise; and when they reached the Cottage, they were evidently in want, first, of being listened to anew on this subject, and afterwards, of all the relief which cheerful companions could give.

To hear them talking so much of Captain Wentworth, repeating his name so often, puzzling over past years, and at last ascertaining that it *might,* that it probably *would,* turn out to be the very same Captain Wentworth whom they recollected meeting, once or twice, after their coming back from Clifton—a very fine young man—but they could not say whether it was seven or eight years ago, was a new sort of trial to Anne's nerves. She found, however, that it was one to which she must inure herself. Since he actually was expected in the country, she must

teach herself to be insensible on such points. And not only did it appear
that he was expected, and speedily, but the Musgroves, in their warm
gratitude for the kindness he had shown poor Dick, and very high respect
for his character, stamped as it was by poor Dick's having been six
months under his care, and mentioning him in strong, though not perfectly well-spelt praise, as "a fine dashing fellow, only two perticular
about the schoolmaster," were bent on introducing themselves, and seeking his acquaintance as soon as they could hear of his arrival.

The resolution of doing so helped to form the comfort of their evening.

Chapter 7

A VERY few days more, and Captain Wentworth was known to be at
Kellynch, and Mr. Musgrove had called on him, and come back warm in
his praise, and he was engaged with the Crofts to dine at Uppercross by
the end of another week. It had been a great disappointment to Mr.
Musgrove to find that no earlier day could be fixed, so impatient was he to
show his gratitude, by seeing Captain Wentworth under his own roof, and
welcoming him to all that was strongest and best in his cellars. But a
week must pass; only a week, in Anne's reckoning, and then, she supposed,
they must meet; and soon she began to wish that she could feel secure
even for a week.

Captain Wentworth made a very early return to Mr. Musgrove's
civility and she was all but calling there in the same half hour. She and
Mary were actually setting forward for the Great House, where, as she
afterwards learnt, they must inevitably have found him, when they were
stopped by the eldest boy's being at that moment brought home in consequence of a bad fall. The child's situation put the visit entirely aside; but
she could not hear of her escape with indifference, even in the midst of
the serious anxiety which they afterwards felt on his account.

His collar-bone was found to be dislocated, and such injury received in
the back, as roused the most alarming ideas. It was an afternoon of distress, and Anne had everything to do at once; the apothecary to send for,
the father to have pursued and informed, the mother to support and keep
from hysterics, the servants to control, the youngest child to banish, and
the poor suffering one to attend and soothe; besides sending, as soon as
she recollected it, proper notice to the other house, which brought her an
accession rather of frightened inquiring companions, than of very useful assistants.

Her brother's return was the first comfort; he could take best care of
his wife: and the second blessing was the arrival of the apothecary. Till
he came and had examined the child, their apprehensions were the worse
for being vague; they suspected great injury, but knew not where; but
now the collar-bone was soon replaced, and though Mr. Robinson felt and
felt, and rubbed, and looked grave, and spoke low words both to the father

and the aunt, still they were all to hope the best, and to be able to part and eat their dinner in tolerable ease of mind; and then it was, just before they parted, that the two young aunts were able so far to digress from their nephew's state, as to give the information of Captain Wentworth's visit; staying five minutes behind their father and mother, to endeavour to express how perfectly delighted they were with him, how much handsomer, how infinitely more agreeable they thought him than any individual among their male acquaintance, who had been at all a favourite before. How glad they had been to hear papa invite him to stay to dinner, how sorry when he said it was quite out of his power, and how glad again when he had promised to reply to papa and mamma's further pressing invitations to come and dine with them on the morrow—actually on the morrow; and he had promised it in so pleasant a manner, as if he felt all the motive of their attention just as he ought. And in short, he had looked and said everything with such exquisite grace, that they could assure them all, their heads were both turned by him; and off they ran, quite as full of glee as of love, and apparently more full of Captain Wentworth than of little Charles.

The same story and the same raptures were repeated, when the two girls came with their father, through the gloom of the evening, to make enquiries; and Mr. Musgrove no longer under the first uneasiness about his heir, could add his confirmation and praise, and hope there would be now no occasion for putting Captain Wentworth off, and only be sorry to think that the Cottage party, probably, would not like to leave the little boy, to give him the meeting. "Oh! no; as to leaving the little boy," both father and mother were in much too strong and recent alarm to bear the thought; and Anne, in the joy of the escape, could not help adding her warm protestations to theirs.

Charles Musgrove, indeed, afterwards, showed more of inclination: "the child was going on so well, and he wished so much to be introduced to Captain Wentworth, that, perhaps, he might join them in the evening; he would not dine from home, but he might walk in for half an hour." But in this he was eagerly opposed by his wife, with "Oh! no, indeed, Charles, I cannot bear to have you go away. Only think, if anything should happen?"

The child had a good night, and was going on well the next day. It must be a work of time to ascertain that no injury had been done to the spine; but Mr. Robinson found nothing to increase alarm, and Charles Musgrove began, consequently, to feel no necessity for longer confinement. The child was to be kept in bed and amused as quietly as possible; but what was there for a father to do? This was quite a female case, and it would be highly absurd in him, who could be of no use at home, to shut himself up. His father very much wished him to meet Captain Wentworth, and there being no sufficient reason against it, he ought to go; and it ended in his making a bold, public declaration, when he came in from shooting, of his meaning to dress directly, and dine at the other house.

"Nothing can be going on better than the child," said he; "so I told my father, just now, that I would come, and he thought me quite right. Your sister being with you, my love, I have no scruple at all. You would not like to leave him yourself, but you see I can be of no use. Anne will send for me if anything is the matter."

Husbands and wives generally understand when opposition will be vain. Mary knew, from Charles's manner of speaking, that he was quite determined on going, and that it would be of no use to tease him. She said nothing, therefore, till he was out of the room; but as soon as there was only Anne to hear——

"So you and I are to be left to shift by ourselves, with this poor sick child; and not a creature coming near us all the evening! I knew how it would be. This is always my luck. If there is anything disagreeable going on men are always sure to get out of it, and Charles is as bad as any of them. Very unfeeling! I must say it is very unfeeling of him to be running away from his poor little boy. Talks of his being going on so well! How does he know that he is going on well, or that there may not be a sudden change half an hour hence? I did not think Charles would have been so unfeeling. So here he is to go away and enjoy himself, and because I am the poor mother, I am not to be allowed to stir; and yet, I am sure, I am more unfit than anybody else to be about the child. My being the mother is the very reason why my feelings should not be tried. I am not at all equal to it. You saw how hysterical I was yesterday."

"But that was only the effect of the suddenness of your alarm—of the shock. You will not be hysterical again. I dare say we shall have nothing to distress us. I perfectly understand Mr. Robinson's directions, and have no fears; and, indeed, Mary, I cannot wonder at your husband. Nursing does not belong to a man; it is not his province. A sick child is always the mother's property: her own feelings generally make it so."

"I hope I am as fond of my child as any mother, but I do not know that I am of any more use in the sick-room than Charles, for I cannot be always scolding and teasing a poor child when it is ill; and you saw, this morning, that if I told him to keep quiet, he was sure to begin kicking about. I have not nerves for the sort of thing."

"But could you be comfortable yourself, to be spending the whole evening away from the poor boy?"

"Yes; you see his papa can, and why should not I? Jemima is so careful; and she could send us word every hour how he was. I really think Charles might as well have told his father we would all come. I am not more alarmed about little Charles now than he is. I was dreadfully alarmed yesterday, but the case is very different to-day."

"Well, if you do not think it too late to give notice for yourself, suppose you were to go, as well as your husband. Leave little Charles to my care. Mr. and Mrs. Musgrove cannot think it wrong while I remain with him."

"Are you serious?" cried Mary, her eyes brightening. "Dear me! that's a very good thought, very good, indeed. To be sure, I may just as well go as not, for I am of no use at home—am I? and it only harasses me. You, who have not a mother's feelings, are a great deal the properest person. You can make little Charles do anything; he always minds you at a word. It will be a great deal better than leaving him with only Jemima. Oh! I will certainly go; I am sure I ought if I can, quite as much as Charles, for they want me excessively to be acquainted with Captain Wentworth, and I know you do not mind being left alone. An excellent thought of yours, indeed, Anne. I will go and tell Charles, and get ready directly. You can send for us, you know, at a moment's notice, if anything is the matter; but I dare say there will be nothing to alarm you. I should not g , you may be sure, if I did not feel quite at ease about my dear child."

The next moment she was tapping at her husband's dressing-room door, and as Anne followed her upstairs, she was in time for the whole conversation, which began with Mary's saying, in a tone of great exultation:

"I mean to go with you, Charles, for I am of no more use at home than you are. If I were to shut myself up for ever with the child, I should not be able to persuade him to do anything he did not like. Anne will stay; Anne undertakes to stay at home and take care of him. It is Anne's own proposal, and so I shall go with you, which will be a great deal better, for I have not dined at the other house since Tuesday."

"This is very kind of Anne," was her husband's answer, "and I should be very glad to have you go; but it seems rather hard that she should be left at home by herself, to nurse our sick child."

Anne was now at hand to take up her own cause, and the sincerity of her manner being soon sufficient to convince him, where conviction was at least very agreeable, he had no further scruples as to her being left to dine alone, though he still wanted her to join them in the evening, when the child might be at rest for the night, and kindly urged her to let him come and fetch her, but she was quite unpersuadable; and this being the case, she had ere long the pleasure of seeing them set off together in high spirits. They were gone, she hoped, to be happy, however oddly constructed such happiness might seem; as for herself, she was left with as many sensations of comfort, as were, perhaps, ever likely to be hers. She knew herself to be of the first utility to the child; and what was it to her if Frederick Wentworth were only half a mile distant, making himself agreeable to others?

She would have liked to know how he felt as to a meeting. Perhaps indifferent, if indifference could exist under such circumstances. He must be either indifferent or unwilling. Had he wished ever to see her again, he need not have waited till this time; he would have done what she could not but believe that in his place she should have done long ago, when events had been early giving him the independence which alone had been wanting.

Her brother and sister came back delighted with their new acquaintance, and their visit in general. There had been music, singing, talking, laughing, all that was most agreeable; charming manners in Captain

Wentworth, no shyness or reserve; they seemed all to know each other perfectly, and he was coming the very next morning to shoot with Charles. He was to come to breakfast, but not at the Cottage, though that had been proposed at first; but then he had been pressed to come to the Great House instead, and he seemed afraid of being in Mrs. Charles Musgrove's way, on account of the child, and therefore somehow, they hardly knew how, it ended in Charles's being to meet him to breakfast at his father's.

Anne understood it. He wished to avoid seeing her. He had inquired after her, she found, slightly, as might suit a former slight acquaintance, seeming to acknowledge such as she had acknowledged, actuated, perhaps, by the same view of escaping introduction when they were to meet.

The morning hours of the Cottage were always later than those of the other house, and on the morrow the difference was so great that Mary and Anne were not more than beginning breakfast when Charles came in to say that they were just setting off, that he was come for his dogs, that his sisters were following with Captain Wentworth; his sisters meaning to visit Mary and the child, and Captain Wentworth proposing also to wait on her for a few minutes if not inconvenient; and though Charles had answered for the child's being in no such state as could make it inconvenient, Captain Wentworth would not be satisfied without his running on to give notice.

Mary, very much gratified by this attention, was delighted to receive him, while a thousand feelings rushed on Anne, of which this was the most consoling, that it would soon be over. And it was soon over. In two minutes after Charles's preparation, the others appeared; they were in the drawing-room. Her eye half met Captain Wentworth's, a bow, a curtsey passed; she heard his voice; he talked to Mary, said all that was right, said something to the Miss Musgroves, enough to mark an easy footing; the room seemed full, full of persons and voices, but a few minutes ended it. Charles showed himself at the window, all was ready, their visitor had bowed and was gone, the Miss Musgroves were gone too, suddenly resolving to walk to the end of the village with the sportsmen; the room was cleared, and Anne might finish her breakfast as she could.

"It is over! It is over!" she repeated to herself again and again, in nervous gratitude. "The worst is over!"

Mary talked, but she could not attend. She had seen him. They had met. They had been once more in the same room.

Soon, however, she began to reason with herself, and try to be feeling less. Eight years, almost eight years had passed, since all had been given up. How absurd to be resuming the agitation which such an interval had banished into distance and indistinctness! What might not eight years do? Events of every description, changes, alienations, removals—all, all must be comprised in it, and oblivion of the past—how natural, how certain too! It included nearly a third part of her own life.

Alas! with all her reasonings she found that to retentive feelings eight years may be little more than nothing.

Now, how were his sentiments to be read? Was this like wishing to avoid her? And the next moment she was hating herself for the folly which asked the question.

On one other question, which perhaps her utmost wisdom might not have prevented, she was soon spared all suspense; for, after the Miss Musgroves had returned and finished their visit at the Cottage, she had this spontaneous information from Mary:

"Captain Wentworth is not very gallant by you, Anne, though he was so attentive to me. Henrietta asked him what he thought of you, when they went away, and he said: 'You were so altered he should not have known you again.'"

Mary had no feelings to make her respect her sister's in a common way, but she was perfectly unsuspicious of being inflicting any peculiar wound.

"Altered beyond his knowledge." Anne fully submitted, in silent, deep mortification. Doubtless it was so, and she could take no revenge, for he was not altered, or not for the worse. She had already acknowledged it to herself, and she could not think differently, let him think of her as he would. No: the years which had destroyed her youth and bloom had only given him a more glowing, manly, open look, in no respect lessening his personal advantages. She had seen the same Frederick Wentworth.

"So altered that he should not have known her again!" These were words which could not but dwell with her. Yet she soon began to rejoice that she had heard them. They were of sobering tendency; they allayed agitation; they composed, and consequently must make her happier.

Frederick Wentworth had used such words, or something like them, but without an idea that they would be carried round to her. He had thought her wretchedly altered, and in the first moment of appeal, had spoken as he felt. He had not forgiven Anne Elliot. She had used him ill, deserted and disappointed him; and worse, she had shown a feebleness of character in doing so, which his own decided, confident temper could not endure. She had given him up to oblige others. It had been the effect of over-persuasion. It had been weakness and timidity.

He had been most warmly attached to her, and had never seen a woman since whom he thought her equal; but, except from some natural sensation of curiosity, he had no desire of meeting her again. Her power with him was gone for ever.

It was now his object to marry. He was rich, and being turned on shore, fully intended to settle as soon as he could be properly tempted; actually looking round, ready to fall in love with all the speed which a clear head and quick taste could allow. He had a heart for either of the Miss Musgroves, if they could catch it; a heart, in short, for any pleasing young woman who came in his way, excepting Anne Elliot. This was his only secret exception, when he said to his sister, in answer to her suppositions:

"Yes, here I am, Sophia, quite ready to make a foolish match. Anybody between fifteen and thirty may have me for asking. A little beauty, and a few smiles, and a few compliments to the navy, and I am a lost man.

Should not this be enough for a sailor, who has had no society among women to make him nice?"

He said it, she knew, to be contradicted. His bright proud eye spoke the happy conviction that he was nice; and Anne Elliot was not out of his thoughts, when he more than seriously described the woman he should wish to meet with. "A strong mind, with sweetness of manner," made the first and the last of the description.

"That is the woman I want," said he. "Something a little inferior I shall of course put up with, but it must not be much. If I am a fool, I shall be a fool indeed, for I have thought on the subject more than m)st men."

Chapter 8

FROM this time Captain Wentworth and Anne Elliot were repeatedly in the same circle. They were soon dining in company together at Mr. Musgrove's, for the little boy's state could no longer supply his aunt with a pretence for absenting herself; and this was but the beginning of other dinings and other meetings.

Whether former feelings were to be renewed must be brought to the proof; former times must undoubtedly be brought to the recollection of each; *they* could not but be reverted to; the year of their engagement could not but be named by him, in the little narratives or descriptions which conversation called forth. His profession qualified him, his disposition led him to talk; and "*That* was in the year six"; "*That* happened before I went to sea, in the year six," occurred in the course of the first evening they spent together; and though his voice did not falter, and though she had no reason to suppose his eye wandering towards her while he spoke, Anne felt the utter impossibility, from her knowledge of his mind, that he could be unvisited by remembrance any more than herself. There must be the same immediate association of thought, though she was very far from conceiving it to be of equal pain.

They had no conversation together, no intercourse but what the commonest civility required. Once so much to each other! Now nothing! There *had* been a time, when of all the large party now filling the drawing-room at Uppercross, they would have found it most difficult to cease to speak to one another. With the exception, perhaps, of Admiral and Mrs. Croft, who seemed particularly attached and happy (Anne could allow no other exception, even among the married couples), there could have been no two hearts so open, no tastes so similar, no feelings so in unison, no countenances so beloved. Now they were as strangers; nay, worse than strangers, for they could never become acquainted. It was a perpetual estrangement.

When he talked, she heard the same voice, and discerned the same mind. There was a very general ignorance of all naval matters throughout the party: and he was very much questioned, and especially by the two

Miss Musgroves, who seemed hardly to have any eyes but for him, as to the manner of living on board, daily regulations, food, hours, etc.; and their surprise at his accounts, at learning the degree of accommodation and arrangement which was practicable, drew from him some pleasant ridicule, which reminded Anne of the early days when she too had been ignorant, and she too had been accused of supposing sailors to be living on board without anything to eat, or any cook to dress it if there were, or any servant to wait, or any knife and fork to use.

From thus listening and thinking, she was roused by a whisper of Mrs. Musgrove's, who, overcome by fond regrets, could not help saying:

"Ah! Miss Anne, if it had pleased Heaven to spare my poor son, I dare say he would have been just such another by this time."

Anne suppressed a smile, and listened kindly, while Mrs. Musgrove relieved her heart a little more; and for a few minutes, therefore, could not keep pace with the conversation of the others.

When she could let her attention take its natural course again, she found the Miss Musgroves just fetching the Navy List (their own Navy List, the first that had ever been at Uppercross), and sitting down together to pore over it, with the professed view of finding out the ships which Captain Wentworth had commanded.

"Your first was the *Asp*, I remember; we will look for the *Asp*."

"You will not find her there. Quite worn out and broken up. I was the last man who commanded her. Hardly fit for service then. Reported fit for home service for a year or two, and so I was sent off to the West Indies."

The girls looked all amazement.

"The Admiralty," he continued, "entertain themselves now and then, with sending a few hundred men to sea in a ship not fit to be employed. But they have a great many to provide for; and among the thousands that may just as well go to the bottom as not, it is impossible for them to distinguish the very set who may be least missed."

"Phoo! phoo!" cried the Admiral, "what stuff these young fellows talk! Never was there a better sloop than the *Asp* in her day. For an old built sloop, you would not see her equal. Lucky fellow to get her! He knows there must have been twenty better men than himslf applying for her at the same time. Lucky fellow to get anything so soon, with no more interest than his."

"I felt my luck, Admiral, I assure you," replied Captain Wentworth, seriously. "I was as well satisfied with my appointment as you can desire. It was a great object with me at that time to be at sea; a very great object, I wanted to be doing something."

"To be sure you did. What should a young fellow like you do ashore for half a year together? If a man has not a wife, he soon wants to be afloat again."

"But, Captain Wentworth," cried Louisa, "how vexed you must have been when you came to the *Asp,* to see what an old thing they had given you!"

"I knew pretty well what she was before that day," said he, smiling. "I had no more discoveries to make than you would have as to the fashion and strength of any old pelisse, which you had seen lent about among half your acquaintances ever since you could remember, and which at last, on some very wet day, is lent to yourself. Ah! she was a dear old *Asp* to me. She did all that I wanted. I knew she would. I knew that we should either go to the bottom together, or that she would be the making of me; and I never had two days of foul weather all the time I was at sea in her; and after taking privateers enough to be very entertaining, I had the good luck in my passage home, the next autumn to fall in with the very French frigate I wanted. I brought her into Plymouth; and here was another instance of luck. We had not been six hours in the Sound, when a gale came on, which lasted four days and nights, and which would have done for poor old *Asp* in half the time; our touch with the Great Nation not having much improved our condition. Four-and-twenty hours later, and I should only have been a gallant Captain Wentworth, in a small paragraph at one corner of the newspapers; and being lost in only a sloop, nobody would have thought about me."

Anne's shudderings were to herself alone; but the Miss Musgroves could be as open as they were sincere, in their exclamations of pity and horror.

"And so then, I suppose," said Mrs. Musgrove, in a low voice, as if thinking aloud, "so then he went away to the *Laconia,* and there he met with our poor boy. Charles, my dear" (beckoning him to her), "do ask Captain Wentworth where it was he first met with your poor brother. I always forget."

"It was at Gibraltar, mother, I know. Dick had been left ill at Gibraltar, with a recommendation from his former captain to Captain Wentworth."

"Oh! but Charles, tell Captain Wentworth, he need not be afraid of mentioning poor Dick before me, for it would be rather a pleasure to hear him talked of by such a good friend."

Charles being somewhat more mindful of the probabilities of the case, only nodded in reply, and walked away.

The girls were now hunting for the *Laconia;* and Captain Wentworth could not deny himself the pleasure of taking the precious volume into his own hands to save them the trouble, and once more read aloud the little statement of her name and rate, and present non-commissioned class, observing over it that she too had been one of the best friends man ever had.

"Ah, those were pleasant days when I had the *Laconia.* How fast I made money in her! A friend of mine and I had such a lovely cruise together off the Western Islands. Poor Harville, sister! You know how much he wanted money; worse than myself. He had a wife. Excellent fellow! I shall never forget his happiness. He felt it all, so much for her sake. I wished for him again the next summer, when I had still the same luck in the Mediterranean."

"And I am sure, sir," said Mrs. Musgrove, "it was a lucky day for *us,* when you were put captain into that ship. *We* shall never forget what you did."

Her feelings made her speak low; and Captain Wentworth, hearing only in part, and probably not having Dick Musgrove at all near his thoughts, looked rather in suspense, and as if waiting for more.

"My brother," whispered one of the girls; "mamma is thinking of poor Richard."

"Poor dear fellow!" continued Mrs. Musgrove; "he was grown so steady, and such an excellent correspondent, while he was under your care! Ah! it would have been a happy thing, if he had never left you. I assure you, Captain Wentworth, we are very sorry he ever left you."

There was a momentary expression in Captain Wentworth's face at this speech, a certain glance of his bright eye, and curl of his handsome mouth, which convinced Anne, that instead of sharing in Mrs. Musgrove's kind wishes, as to her son, he had probably been at some pains to get rid of him; but it was too transient an indulgence of self-amusement to be detected by any who understood him less than herself; in another moment he was perfectly collected and serious, and almost instantly afterwards coming up to the sofa, on which she and Mrs. Musgrove were sitting, took a place by the latter, and entered into conversation with her, in a low voice, about her son, doing it with so much sympathy and natural grace, as showed the kindest consideration for all that was real and unabsurd in the parent's feelings.

They were actually on the same sofa, for Mrs. Musgrove had most readily made room for him: they were divided only by Mrs. Musgrove. It was no insignificant barrier, indeed. Mrs. Musgrove was a comfortable substantial size, infinitely more fitted by nature to express good cheer and good humour than tenderness and sentiment; and while the agitations of Anne's slender form and pensive face may be considered as very completely screened, Captain Wentworth should be allowed some credit for the self-command with which he attended to her large fat sighings over the destiny of a son, whom alive nobody had cared for.

Personal size and mental sorrow have certainly no necessary proportions. A large bulky figure has as good a right to be in deep affliction as the most graceful set of limbs in the world. But, fair or not fair, there are unbecoming conjunctions, which reason will patronise in vain—which taste cannot tolerate—which ridicule will seize.

The Admiral, after taking two or three refreshing turns about the room with his hands behind him, being called to order by his wife, now came up to Captain Wentworth, and without any observation of what he might be interrupting, thinking only of his own thoughts, began with—

"If you had been a week later at Lisbon, last spring, Frederick, you would have been asked to give a passage to Lady Mary Grierson and her daughters."

"Should I? I am glad I was not a week later then!"

The Admiral abused him for his want of gallantry. He defended himself; though professing that he would never willingly admit any ladies on board a ship of his, excepting for a ball, or a visit, which a few hours might comprehend.

"But, if I know myself," said he, "this is from no want of gallantry towards them. It is rather from feeling how impossible it is, with all one's efforts, and all one's sacrifices, to make the accommodations on board such as women ought to have. There can be no want of gallantry, Admiral, in rating the claims of women to every personal comfort *high*, and this is what I do. I hate to hear of women on board; or to see them on board; and no ship under my command shall ever convey a family of ladies anywhere, if I can help it."

This brought his sister upon him.

"Oh! Frederick! But I cannot believe it of you. All idle refinement! Women may be as comfortable on board as in the best house in England. I believe I have lived as much on board as most women, and I know nothing superior to the accommodations of a man-of-war. I declare I have not a comfort or an indulgence about me, even at Kellynch Hall" (with a kind bow to Anne), "beyond what I always had in most of the ships I have lived in; and they have been five altogether."

"Nothing to the purpose," replied her brother. "You were living with your husband, and were the only woman on board."

"But you, yourself, brought Mrs. Harville, her sister, her cousin, and the three children, round from Portsmouth to Plymouth. Where was this superfine, extraordinary sort of gallantry of yours then?"

"All merged in my friendship, Sophia. I would assist any brother officer's wife that I could, and I would bring anything of Harville's from the world's end, if he wanted it. But do not imagine that I did not feel it an evil in itself."

"Depend upon it, they were all perfectly comfortable."

"I might not like them the better for that, perhaps. Such a number of women and children have no *right* to be comfortable on board."

"My dear Frederick, you are talking quite idly. Pray, what would become of us poor sailor's wives, who often want to be conveyed to one port or another, after our husbands, if everybody had your feelings?"

"My feelings, you see, did not prevent my taking Mrs. Harville and all her family to Plymouth."

"But I hate to hear you talking so like a fine gentleman, and as if women were all fine ladies, instead of rational creatures. We none of us expect to be in smooth water all our days."

"Ah! my dear," said the Admiral, "when he has got a wife, he will sing a different tune. When he is married, if we have the good luck to live to another war, we shall see him do as you and I, and a great many others, have done. We shall have him very thankful to anybody that will bring him his wife."

"Ay, that we shall."

"Now I have done," cried Captain Wentworth. "When once married people begin to attack me with—'Oh! you will think very differently when you are married,' I can only say, 'No, I shall not'; and then they say again, 'Yes, you will,' and there is an end of it."

He got up and moved away.

"What a great traveller you must have been, ma'am!" said Mrs. Musgrove to Mrs. Croft.

"Pretty well, ma'am, in the fifteen years of my marriage; though many women have done more. I have crossed the Atlantic four times, and have been once to the East Indies and back again, and only once; besides being in different places about home: Cork, and Lisbon, and Gibraltar. But I never went beyond the Streights, and never was in the West Indies. We do not call Bermuda or Bahama, you know, the West Indies."

Mrs. Musgrove had not a word to say in dissent; she could not accuse herself of having ever called them anything in the whole course of her life.

"And I do assure you, ma'am," pursued Mrs. Croft, "that nothing can exceed the accommodations of a man-of-war; I speak, you know, of the higher rates. When you come to a frigate, of course, you are more confined; though any reasonable woman may be perfectly happy in one of them; and I can safely say that the happiest part of my life has been spent on board a ship. While we were together, you know, there was nothing to be feared. Thank God! I have always been blessed with excellent health, and no climate disagrees with me. A little disordered always the first twenty-four hours of going to sea, but never knew what sickness was afterwards. The only time that I ever really suffered in body or mind, the only time that I ever fancied myself unwell, or had any ideas of danger— was the winter that I passed by myself at Deal, when the Admiral (*Captain* Croft then) was in the North Seas. I lived in perpetual fright at that time, and had all manner of imaginary complaints from not knowing what to do with myself, or when I should hear from him next; but as long as we could be together, nothing ever ailed me, and I never met with the smallest inconvenience."

"Ay, to be sure. Yes, indeed, oh yes! I am quite of your opinion, Mrs. Croft," was Mrs. Musgrove's hearty answer. "There is nothing so bad as a separation. I am quite of your opinion. *I* know what it is, for Mr. Musgrove always attends the assizes, and I am so glad when they are over, and he is safe back again."

The evening ended with dancing. On its being proposed, Anne offered her services, as usual; and though her eyes would sometimes fill with tears as she sat at the instrument, she was extremely glad to be employed, and desired nothing in return but to be unobserved.

It was a merry, joyous party, and no one seemed in higher spirits than

Captain Wentworth. She felt that he had everything to elevate him, which general attention and deference, and especially the attention of all the young women, could do. The Miss Hayters, the females of the family of cousins already mentioned were apparently admitted to the honour of being in love with him; and as for Henrietta and Louisa, they both seemed so entirely occupied by him, that nothing but the continued appearance of the most perfect good-will between themselves could have made it credible that they were not decided rivals. If he were a little spoilt by such universal, such eager admiration, who could wonder?

These were some of the thoughts which occupied Anne, while her fingers were mechanically at work, proceeding for half an hour together, equally without error, and without consciousness. *Once* she felt that he was looking at herself, observing her altered features, perhaps, trying to trace in them the ruins of the face which had once charmed him; and *once* she knew that he must have spoken of her; she was hardly aware of it till she heard the answer; but then she was sure of his having asked his partner whether Miss Elliot never danced? The answer was, "Oh, no! never; she has quite given up dancing. She had rather play. She is never tired of playing." Once, too, he spoke to her. She had left the instrument on the dancing being over, and he had sat down to try to make out an air which he wished to give the Miss Musgroves an idea of. Unintentionally she returned to that part of the room; he saw her, and instantly rising, said, with studied politeness:

"I beg your pardon, madam, this is your seat;" and though she immediately drew back with a decided negative, he was not to be induced to sit down again.

Anne did not wish for more of such looks and speeches. His cold politeness, his ceremonious grace, were worse than anything.

Chapter 9

CAPTAIN WENTWORTH was come to Kellynch as to a home, to stay as long as he liked, being as thoroughly the object of the Admiral's fraternal kindness as of his wife's. He had intended, on first arriving, to proceed very soon into Shropshire, and visit the brother settled in that country, but the attractions of Uppercross induced him to put this off. There was so much of friendliness, and of flattery, and of everything most bewitching in his reception there; the old were so hospitable, the young so agreeable, that he could not but resolve to remain where he was, and take all the charms and perfections of Edward's wife upon credit a little longer.

It was soon Uppercross with him almost every day. The Musgroves could hardly be more ready to invite than he to come, particularly in the morning, when he had no companion at home; for the Admiral and Mrs. Croft were generally out of doors together, interesting themselves in their new possessions, their grass, and their sheep, and dawdling about in a way not endurable to a third person, or driving out in a gig, lately added to their establishment.

Hitherto there had been but one opinion of Captain Wentworth among the Musgroves and their dependencies. It was unvarying, warm admiration everywhere; but this intimate footing was not more than established, when a certain Charles Hayter returned among them, to be a good deal disturbed by it, and to think Captain Wentworth very much in the way.

Charles Hayter was the eldest of all the cousins, and a very amiable, pleasing young man, between whom and Henrietta there had been a considerable appearance of attachment previous to Captain Wentworth's introduction. He was in orders; and having a curacy in the neighbourhood, where residence was not required, lived at his father's house, only two miles from Uppercross. A short absence from home had left his fair one unguarded by his attentions at this critical period, and when he came back he had the pain of finding very altered manners, and of seeing Captain Wentworth.

Mrs. Musgrove and Mrs. Hayter were sisters. They had each had money, but their marriages had made a material difference in their degree of consequence. Mr. Hayter had some property of his own, but it was insignificant compared with Mr. Musgrove's; and while the Musgroves were in the first class of society in the country, the young Hayters would, from their parents' inferior, retired, and unpolished way of living, and their own defective education, have been hardly in any class at all, but for their connection with Uppercross, this eldest son of course excepted, who had chosen to be a scholar and a gentleman, and who was very superior in cultivation and manners to all the rest.

The two families had always been on excellent terms, there being no pride on one side, and no envy on the other, and only such a consciousness of superiority in the Miss Musgroves, as made them pleased to improve their cousins. Charles's attentions to Henrietta had been observed by her father and mother without any disapprobation. "It would not be a great match for her; but if Henrietta liked him,"—and Henrietta *did* seem to like him.

Henrietta fully thought so herself, before Captain Wentworth came; but from that time Cousin Charles had been very much forgotten.

Which of the two sisters was preferred by Captain Wentworth was as yet quite doubtful, as far as Anne's observation reached. Henrietta was perhaps the prettiest, Louisa had the higher spirits; and she knew not *now*, whether the more gentle or the more lively character were most likely to attract him.

Mr. and Mrs. Musgrove, either from seeing little, or from an entire confidence in the discretion of both their daughters, and of all the young men who came near them, seemed to leave everything to take its chance. There was not the smallest appearance of solicitude or remark about them in the Mansion House; but it was different at the Cottage; the young couple there were more disposed to speculate and wonder; and Captain

Wentworth had not been above four or five times in the Miss Musgroves'
company, and Charles Hayter had but just reappeared, when Anne had to
listen to the opinions of her brother and sister, as to *which* was the one
liked best. Charles gave it for Louisa, Mary for Henrietta, but quite
agreeing that to have him marry either would be extremely delightful.

Charles "had never seen a pleasanter man in his life; and from what he
had once heard Captain Wentworth himself say, was very sure that he had
not made less than twenty thousand pounds by the war. Here was a fortune at once: besides which, there would be the chance of what might be
done in any future war; and he was sure Captain Wentworth was as likely
a man to distinguish himself as any officer in the navy. Oh! it would be a
capital match for either of his sisters."

"Upon my word it would," replied Mary. "Dear me! If he should rise to
any very great honours! If he should ever be made a baronet! 'Lady Wentworth' sounds very well. That would be a noble thing, indeed, for Henrietta! She would take place of me then, and Henrietta would not dislike
that. Sir Frederick and Lady Wentworth! It would be but a new creation,
however, and I never think much of your new creations."

It suited Mary best to think Henrietta the one preferred on the very
account of Charles Hayter, whose pretensions she wished to see put an end
to. She looked down very decidedly upon the Hayters, and thought it
would be quite a misfortune to have the existing connection between the
families renewed—very sad for herself and her children.

"You know," said she, "I cannot think him at all a fit match for Henrietta; and considering the alliances which the Musgroves have made, she
has no right to throw herself away. I do not think any young woman has a
right to make a choice that may be disagreeable and inconvenient to the
principal part of her family, and be giving bad connections to those who
have not been used to them. And, pray, who is Charles Hayter? Nothing
but a country curate. A most improper match for Miss Musgrove of
Uppercross."

Her husband, however, would not agree with her here; for besides having a regard for his cousin, Charles Hayter was an eldest son, and he saw
things as an eldest son himself.

"Now you are talking nonsense, Mary," was therefore his answer. "It
would not be a *great* match for Henrietta, but Charles has a very fair
chance, through the Spicers, of getting something from the Bishop in the
course of a year or two; and you will please to remember that he is the
eldest son; whenever my uncle dies, he steps into very pretty property.
The estate at Winthrop is not less than two hundred and fifty acres,
besides the farm near Taunton, which is some of the best land in the country. I grant you, that any of them but Charles would be a very shocking
match for Henrietta, and indeed it could not be; he is the only one that
could be possible; but he is a very good-natured, good sort of a fellow; and
whenever Winthrop comes into his hands, he will make a different sort of
place of it, and live in a very different sort of way; and with that property

he will never be a contemptible man—good freehold property. No, no; Henrietta might do worse than marry Charles Hayter; and if she has him and Louisa can get Captain Wentworth, I shall be very well satisfied."

"Charles may say what he pleases," cried Mary to Anne, as soon as he was out of the room, "but it would be shocking to have Henrietta marry Charles Hayter: a very bad thing for *her*, and still worse for *me;* and therefore it is very much to be wished that Captain Wentworth may soon put him quite out of her head, and I have very little doubt that he has. She took hardly any notice of Charles Hayter yesterday. I wish you had been there to see her behaviour. And as to Captain Wentworth's liking Louisa as well as Henrietta, it is nonsense to say so; for he certainly *does* like Henrietta a great deal the best. But Charles is so positive! I wish you had been with us yesterday, for then you might have decided between us; and I am sure you would have thought as I did, unless you had been determined to give it against me."

A dinner at Mr. Musgrove's had been the occasion when all these things should have been seen by Anne; but she had stayed at home, under the mixed plea of a headache of her own, and some return of indisposition in little Charles. She had thought only of avoiding Captain Wentworth; but an escape from being appealed to as umpire was now added to the advantages of a quiet evening.

As to Captain Wentworth's views, she deemed it of more consequence that he should know his own mind early enough not to be endangering the happiness of either sister, or impeaching his own honour, than that he should prefer Henrietta to Louisa, or Louisa to Henrietta. Either of them would, in all probability, make him an affectionate, good-humoured wife. With regard to Charles Hayter, she had delicacy which must be pained by any lightness of conduct in a well-meaning young woman, and a heart to sympathise in any of the sufferings it occasioned; but if Henrietta found herself mistaken in the nature of her feelings, the alteration could not be understood too soon.

Charles Hayter had met with much to disquiet and mortify him in his cousin's behaviour. She had too old a regard for him to be so wholly estranged as might in two meetings extinguish every past hope, and leave him nothing to do but to keep away from Uppercross: but there was such a change as became very alarming, when such a man as Captain Wentworth was to be regarded as the probable cause. He had been absent only two Sundays, and when they parted, had left her interested, even to the height of his wishes, in his prospect of soon quitting his present curacy, and obtaining that of Uppercross instead. It had then seemed the object nearest her heart, that Dr. Shirley, the rector, who for more than forty years had been zealously discharging all the duties of his office, but was now growing too infirm for many of them, should be quite fixed on engaging a curate; should make his curacy quite as good as he could afford, and should give Charles Hayter the promise of it. The advantage of his having to come only to Uppercross, instead of going six miles another way; of

his having, in every respect, a better curacy; of his belonging to their dear
Dr. Shirley; and of dear, good Dr. Shirley's being relieved from the duty
which he could no longer get through without most injurious fatigue, had
been a great deal, even to Louisa, but had been almost everything to
Henrietta. When he came back, alas! the zeal of the business was gone by.
Louisa could not listen at all to his account of a conversation which he had
just held with Dr. Shirley: she was at the window, looking out for Captain
Wentworth; and even Henrietta had at best only a divided attention to
give, and seemed to have forgotten all the former doubt and solicitude of
the negotiation.

"Well, I am very glad, indeed; but I always thought you would have it;
I always thought you sure. It did not appear to me that—in short, you
know, Dr. Shirley *must* have a curate, and you had secured his promise. Is
he coming, Louisa?"

One morning, very soon after the dinner at the Musgroves', at which
Anne had not been present, Captain Wentworth walked into the drawing-
room at the Cottage, where were only herself and the little invalid Charles,
who was lying on the sofa.

The surprise of finding himself almost alone with Anne Elliot deprived
his manners of their usual composure: he started, and could only say, "I
thought the Miss Musgroves had been here: Mrs. Musgrove told me I
should find them here," before he walked to the window to recollect himself, and feel how he ought to behave.

"There are upstairs with my sister: they will be down in a few moments,
I dare say," had been Anne's reply, in all the confusion that was natural;
and if the child had not called her to come and do something for him, she
would have been out of the room the next moment, and released Captain
Wentworth as well as herself.

He continued at the window; and after calmly and politely saying, "I
hope the little boy is better," was silent.

She was obliged to kneel down by the sofa, and remain there to satisfy
her patient; and thus they continued a few minutes, when, to her very
great satisfaction, she heard some other person crossing the little vestibule.
She hoped, on turning her head, to see the master of the house; but it
proved to be one much less calculated for making matters easy—Charles
Hayter, probably not at all better pleased by the sight of Captain Wentworth, than Captain Wentworth had been by the sight of Anne.

She only attempted to say, "How do you do? Will not you sit down?
The others will be here presently."

Captain Wentworth, however, came from his window, apparently not
ill-disposed for conversation; but Charles Hayter soon put an end to his
attempts, by seating himself near the table, and taking up the newspaper;
and Captain Wentworth returned to his window.

Another minute brought another addition. The younger boy, a remarkable stout, forward child, of two years old, having got the door opened for
him by some one without, made his determined appearance among them.

and went straight to the sofa to see what was going on, and put in his claim
to anything good that might be giving away.

There being nothing to be eat, he could only have some play; and as his
aunt would not let him tease his sick brother, he began to fasten himself
upon her, as she knelt, in such a way that, busy as she was about Charles,
she could not shake him off. She spoke to him, ordered, intreated, and
insisted in vain. Once did she contrive to push him away, but the boy had
the greater pleasure in getting upon her back again directly.

"Walter," said she, "get down this moment. You are extremely troublesome. I am very angry with you."

"Walter," cried Charles Hayter, "why do you not do as you are bid?
Do not you hear your aunt speak? Come to me, Walter; come to cousin
Charles."

But not a bit did Walter stir.

In another moment, however, she found herself in the state of being
released from him; some one was taking him from her, though he had bent
down her head so much, that his little sturdy hands were unfastened from
around her neck, and he was resolutely borne away, before she knew that
Captain Wentworth had done it.

Her sensations on the discovery made her perfectly speechless. She
could not even thank him. She could only hang over little Charles, with
most disordred feelings. His kindness in stepping forward to her relief,
the manner, the silence in which it had passed, the little particulars of the
circumstance, with the conviction soon forced on her by the noise he was
studiously making with the child, that he meant to avoid hearing her
thanks, and rather sought to testify that her conversation was the last of
his wants, produced such a confusion of varying, but very painful agitation as she could not recover from, till enabled, by the entrance of Mary
and the Miss Musgroves, to make over her little patient to their cares, and
leave the room. She could not stay. It might have been an opportunity
of watching the loves and jealousies of the four—they were now all together; but she could stay for none of it. It was evident that Charles
Hayter was not well inclined towards Captain Wentworth. She had a
strong impression of his having said, in a vexed tone of voice, after Captain Wentworth's interference, "You ought to have minded *me*, Walter; I
told you not to tease your aunt;" and could comprehend his regretting
that Captain Wentworth should do what he ought to have done himself.
But neither Charles Hayter's feelings, nor anybody's feelings, could interest her, till she had a little better arranged her own. She was ashamed
of herself, quite ashamed of being so nervous, so overcome by such a trifle;
but so it was, and it required a long application of solitude and reflection
to recover her.

Chapter 10

OTHER opportunities of making her observations could not fail to occur. Anne had soon been in company with all the four together often enough to have an opinion, though too wise to acknowledge as much at home, where she knew it would have satisfied neither husband nor wife; for while she considered Louisa to be rather the favourite, she could not but think, as far as she might dare to judge from memory and experience, that Captain Wentworth was not in love with either. They were more in love with him; yet there it was not love. It was a little fever of admiration; but it might, probably must, end in love with some. Charles Hayter seemed aware of being slighted, and yet Henrietta had sometimes the air of being divided between them. Anne longed for the power of representing to them all what they were about, and of pointing out some of the evils they were exposing themselves to. She did not attribute guile to any. It was the highest satisfaction to her to believe Captain Wentworth not in the least aware of the pain he was occasioning. There was no triumph, no pitiful triumph in his manner. He had, probably, never heard, and never thought of any claims of Charles Hayter. He was only wrong in accepting the attentions (for accepting must be the word) of two young women at once.

After a short struggle, however, Charles Hayter seemed to quit the field. Three days had passed without his coming once to Uppercross; a most decided change. He had even refused one regular invitation to dinner; and having been found on the occasion by Mr. Musgrove with some large books before him, Mr. and Mrs. Musgrove were sure all could not be right, and talked, with grave faces, of his studying himself to death. It was Mary's hope and belief that he had received a positive dismissal from Henrietta, and her husband lived under the constant dependence of seeing him to-morrow. Anne could only feel that Charles Hayter was wise.

One morning, about this time, Charles Musgrove and Captain Wentworth being gone a-shooting together, as the sisters in the Cottage were sitting quietly at work, they were visited at the window by the sisters from the Mansion House.

It was a very fine November day, and the Miss Musgroves came through the little grounds, and stopped for no other purpose than to say, that they were going to take a *long* walk, and therefore concluded Mary could not like to go with them; and when Mary immediately replied, with some jealousy at not being supposed a good walker, "Oh, yes! I should like to join you very much, I am very fond of a long walk," Anne felt persuaded, by the looks of the two girls, that it was precisely what they did not wish, and admired again the sort of necessity which the family habits seemed to produce, of everything being to be communicated, and everything being to be done together, however undesired and inconvenient. She tried to dissuade Mary from going, but in vain; and that being the case, thought it best to accept the Miss Musgroves' much more cordial invitation to herself to go likewise, as she might be useful in turning back with her sister, and lessening the interference in any plan of their own.

"I cannot imagine why they should suppose I should not like a long walk," said Mary, as she went upstairs. "Everybody is always supposing that I am not a good walker; and yet they would not have been pleased if we had refused to join them. When people come in this manner on purpose to ask us, how can one say no?"

Just as they were setting off, the gentlemen returned. They had taken out a young dog, which had spoilt their sport, and sent them back early. Their time, and strength, and spirits, were, therefore, exactly ready for this walk, and they entered into it with pleasure. Could Anne have foreseen such a junction, she would have stayed at home; but, from some feelings of interest and curiosity, she fancied now that it was too late to retract, and the whole six set forward together in the direction chosen by the Miss Musgroves, who evidently considered the walk as under their guidance.

Anne's object was, not to be in the way of anybody; and where the narrow paths across the fields made many separations necessary, to keep with her brother and sister. Her *pleasure* in the walk must arise from the exercise and the day, from the view of the last smiles of the year upon the tawny leaves and withered hedges, and from repeating to herself some few of the thousand poetical descriptions extant of autumn, that season of peculiar and inexhaustible influence on the mind of taste and tenderness, that season which has drawn from every poet, worthy of being read, some attempt at description, or some lines of feeling. She occupied her mind as much as possible in such like musings and quotations; but it was not possible, that when within reach of Captain Wentworth's conversation with either of the Miss Musgroves, she should not try to hear it; yet she caught little very remarkable. It was mere lively chat, such as any young persons, on an intimate footing, might fall into. He was more engaged with Louisa, than with Henrietta. Louisa certainly put more forward for his notice than her sister. This distinction appeared to increase, and there was one speech of Louisa's which struck her. After one of the many praises of the day, which were continually bursting forth, Captain Wentworth added:

"What glorious weather for the Admiral and my sister! They meant to take a long drive this morning; perhaps we may hail them from some of these hills. They talked of coming into this side of the country. I wonder whereabouts they will upset to-day. Oh! it does happen very often, I assure you; but my sister makes nothing of it; she would as lieve be tossed out as not."

"Ah! you make the most of it, I know," cried Louisa; "but if it were really so, I should do just the same in her place. If I loved a man as she loves the Admiral, I would always be with him, nothing should ever separate us, and I would rather be overturned by him, than driven safely by anybody else."

It was spoken with enthusiasm.

"Had you?" cried he, catching the same tone; "I honour you!" And there was silence between them for a little while.

Anne could not immediately fall into a quotation again. The sweet scenes of autumn were for a while put by, unless some tender sonnet, fraught with the apt analogy of the declining year with declining happiness, and the images of youth, and hope, and spring, all gone together, blessed her memory. She roused herself to say, as they struck by order into another path, "Is not this one of the ways to Winthrop?" But nobody heard, or, at least, nobody answered her.

Winthrop, however, or its environs—for young men are sometimes to be met with, strolling about near home—was their destination; and after another half mile of gradual ascent through large enclosures, where the ploughs at work, and the fresh made path spoke the farmer counteracting the sweets of poetical despondence, and meaning to have spring again, they gained the summit of the most considerable hill, which parted Uppercross and Winthrop, and soon commanded a full view of the latter, at the foot of the hill on the other side.

Winthrop, without beauty and without dignity, was stretched before them—an indifferent house, standing low, and hemmed in by the barns and buildings of a farmyard.

Mary exclaimed, "Bless me! here is Winthrop. I declare I had no idea! Well now, I think we had better turn back; I am excessively tired."

Henrietta, conscious and ashamed, and seeing no cousin Charles walking along any path, or leaning against any gate, was ready to do as Mary wished; but "No!" said Charles Musgrove, and "No, no!" cried Louisa, more eagerly, and taking her sister aside, seemed to be arguing the matter warmly.

Charles, in the meanwhile, was very decidedly declaring his resolution of calling on his aunt, now that he was so near; and very evidently, though more fearfully, trying to induce his wife to go too. But this was one of the points on which the lady showed her strength; and when he recommended the advantage of resting herself a quarter of an hour at Winthrop, as she felt so tired, she resolutely answered, "Oh, no, indeed! walking up that hill again would do her more harm than any sitting down could do her good;" and in short, her look and manner declared, that go she would not.

After a little succession of these sort of debates and consultations, it was settled between Charles and his two sisters, that he and Henrietta should just run down for a few minutes, to see their aunt and cousins, while the rest of the party waited for them at the top of the hill. Louisa seemed the principal arranger of the plan; and, as she went a little way with them down the hill, still talking to Henrietta, Mary took the opportunity of looking scornfully around her, and saying to Captain Wentworth:

"It is very unpleasant having such connections! But, I assure you, I have never been in the house above twice in my life."

She received no other answer than an artificial, assenting smile, followed by a contemptuous glance, as he turned away, which Anne perfectly knew the meaning of.

The brow of the hill, where they remained, was a cheerful spot; Louisa returned; and Mary, finding a comfortable seat for herself on the step of a stile, was very well satisfied so long as the others all stood about her; but when Louisa drew Captain Wentworth away, to try for a gleaning of nuts in an adjoining hedge-row, and they were gone by degrees quite out of sight and sound, Mary was happy no longer: she quarrelled with her own seat, was sure Louisa had got a much better somewhere, and nothing could prevent her from going to look for a better also. She turned through the same gate, but could not see them. Anne found a nice seat for her, on a dry sunny bank, under the hedge-row, in which she had no doubt of their still being, in some spot or other. Mary sat down for a moment, but it would not do; she was sure Louisa had found a better seat somewhere else, and she would go on till she overtook her.

Anne, really tired herself, was glad to sit down; and she very soon heard Captain Wentworth and Louisa in the hedge-row behind her, as if making their way back along the rough, wild sort of channel, down the centre. They were speaking as they drew near. Louisa's voice was the first distinguished. She seemed to be in the middle of some eager speech. What Anne first heard was:

"And so, I made her go. I could not bear that she should be frightened from the visit by such nonsense. What! would I be turned back from doing a thing that I had determined to do, and that I knew to be right, by the airs and interference of such a person, or of any persons, I may say? No, I have no idea of being so easily persuaded. When I have made up my mind, I have made it; and Henrietta seemed entirely to have made up hers to call at Winthrop to-day; and yet, she was as near giving it up out of nonsensical complaisance!"

"She would have turned back, then, but for you?"

"She would indeed. I am almost ashamed to say it."

"Happy for her, to have such a mind as yours at hand! After the hints you gave just now, which did but confirm my own observations, the last time I was in company with him, I need not affect to have no comprehension of what is going on. I see that more than a mere dutiful morning visit to your aunt was in question; and woe betide him, and her too, when it comes to things of consequence, when they are placed in circumstances requiring fortitude and strength of mind, if she have not resolution enough to resist idle interference in such a trifle as this. Your sister is an amiable creature; but *yours* is the character of decision and firmness, I see. If you value her conduct or happiness, infuse as much of your own spirit into her as you can. But this, no doubt, you have been always doing. It is the worst evil of too yielding and indecisive a character, that no influence over it can be depended on. You are never sure of a good impression being durable; everybody may sway it. Let those who would be happy be firm. Here is a nut," said he, catching one down from an upper bough, "to exemplify: a beautiful glossy nut, which, blessed with original strength, has outlived all the storms of autumn. Not a puncture, not a weak spot anywhere. This nut," he continued, with playful solemnity, "while so many of its brethren have fallen and been trodden under foot, is still in possession of all the happiness that a hazel nut can be supposed capable of." Then returning to his former earnest tone—"My first wish for all whom I am interested in, is that they should be firm. If Louisa Musgrove would be beautiful and happy in her November of life, she will cherish all her present powers of mind."

He had done, and was unanswered. It would have surprised Anne if Louisa could have readily answered such a speech: words of such interest, spoken with such serious warmth! She could imagine what Louisa was feeling. For herself, she feared to move, lest she should be seen. While she remained, a bush of low rambling holly protected her, and they were moving on. Before they were beyond her hearing, however, Louisa spoke again.

"Mary is good-natured enough in many respects," said she; "but she does sometimes provoke me excessively by her nonsense and pride—the Elliot pride. She has a great deal too much of the Elliot pride. We do so wish that Charles had married Anne instead. I suppose you know he wanted to marry Anne?"

After a moment's pause, Captain Wentworth said:

"Do you mean that she refused him?"

"Oh! yes; certainly."

"When did that happen?"

"I do not exactly know, for Henrietta and I were at school at the time; but I believe about a year before he married Mary. I wish she had accepted him. We should all have liked her a great deal better; and papa and mamma always think it was her great friend Lady Russell's doing that she did not. They think Charles might not be learned and bookish enough to please Lady Russell, and that, therefore, she persuaded Anne to refuse him."

The sounds were retreating, and Anne distinguished no more. Her own emotions still kept her fixed. She had much to recover from before she could move. The listener's proverbial fate was not absolutely hers: she had heard no evil of herself, but she had heard a great deal of very painful import. She saw how her own character was considered by Captain Wentworth, and there had been just that degree of feeling and curiosity about her in his manner which must give her extreme agitation.

As soon as she could, she went after Mary, and having found and walked back with her to their former station by the stile, felt some comfort in their whole party being immediately afterwards collected, and once more in motion together. Her spirits wanted the solitude and silence which only numbers could give.

Charles and Henrietta returned, bringing, as may be conjectured, Charles Hayter with them. The minutiæ of the business Anne could not attempt to understand; even Captain Wentworth did not seem admitted to perfect confidence here; but that there had been a withdrawing on the gentleman's side, and a relenting on the lady's, and that they were now very glad to be together again, did not admit a doubt. Henrietta looked a little ashamed, but very well pleased; Charles Hayter exceedingly happy: and they were devoted to each other almost from the first instant of their all setting forward for Uppercross.

Everything now marked out Louisa for Captain Wentworth: nothing could be plainer; and where many divisions were necessary, or even where they were not, they walked side by side nearly as much as the other two. In a long strip of meadow land, where there was ample space for all, they were thus divided, forming three distinct parties; and to that party of the three which boasted least animation, and least complaisance, Anne necessarily belonged. She joined Charles and Mary, and was tired enough to be very glad of Charles's other arm; but Charles, though in very good humour with her, was out of temper with his wife. Mary had shown herself disobliging to him, and was now to reap the consequence, which consequence was his dropping her arm almost every moment to cut off the heads of some nettles in the hedge with his switch; and when Mary began to complain of it, and lament her being ill-used, according to custom, it being on the hedge side, while Anne was never incommoded on the other, he dropped the arms of both, to hunt after a weasel, which he had a momentary glance of, and they could hardly get him along at all.

This long meadow bordered a lane which their footpath, at the end of it, was to cross, and when the party had all reached the gate of exit, the carriage advancing in the same direction, which had been some time heard, was just coming up, and proved to be Admiral Croft's gig. He and his wife had taken their intended drive, and were returning home. Upon hearing how long a walk the young people had engaged in, they kindly offered a seat to any lady who might be particularly tired; it would save her full a mile, and they were going through Uppercross. The invitation was general and generally declined. The Miss Musgroves were not at all tired, and Mary was either offended by not being asked before any of the others, or what Louisa called the Elliot pride could not endure to make a third in a one-horse chaise.

The walking party had crossed the lane, and were surmounting an opposite stile, and the Admiral was putting his horse into motion again, when Captain Wentworth cleared the hedge in a moment, to say something to his sister. The something might be guessed by its effects.

"Miss Elliot, I am sure *you* are tired," cried Mrs. Croft. "Do let us have the pleasure of taking you home. Here is excellent room for three, I assure you. If we were all like you, I believe we might sit four. You must, indeed, you must."

Anne was still in the lane, and though instinctively beginning to decline, she was not allowed to proceed. The Admiral's kind urgency came in support of his wife's: they would not be refused: they compressed themselves into the smallest possible space to leave her a corner, and Captain Wentworth, without saying a word, turned to her, and quietly obliged her to be assisted into the carriage.

Yes; he had done it. She was in the carriage, and felt that he had placed her there, that his will and his hands had done it, that she owed it to his perception of her fatigue, and his resolution to give her rest. She was very much affected by the view of his disposition towards her, which all these things made apparent. This little circumstance seemed the completion of all that had gone before. She understood him. He could not forgive her, but he could not be unfeeling. Though condemning her for the past, and considering it with high and unjust resentment, though perfectly careless of her, and though becoming attached to another, still he could not see her suffer without the desire of giving her relief. It was a remainder of former sentiment; it was an impulse of pure, though unacknowledged friendship; it was a proof of his own warm and amiable heart, which she could not contemplate without emotions so compounded of pleasure and pain, that she knew not which prevailed.

Her answers to the kindness and the remarks of her companions were at first unconsciously given. They had travelled half their way along the rough lane before she was quite awake to what they said. She then found them talking of "Frederick."

"He certainly means to have one or other of those two girls, Sophy," said the Admiral; "but there is no saying which. He has been running after them, too, long enough, one would think, to make up his mind. Ay, this comes of the peace. If it were war now, he would have settled it long ago. We sailors, Miss Elliot, cannot afford to make long courtships in time of war. How many days was it, my dear, between the first time of my seeing you and our sitting down together in our lodgings at North Yarmouth?"

"We had better not talk about it, my dear," replied Mrs. Croft, pleasantly; "for if Miss Elliot were to hear how soon we came to an understanding, she would never be persuaded that we could be happy together. I had known you by character, however, long before."

"Well, and I had heard of you as a very pretty girl, and what were we to wait for besides? I do not like having such things so long in hand. I wish Frederick would spread a little more canvas, and bring us home one of these young ladies to Kellynch. Then there would always be company for them. And very nice young ladies they both are; I hardly know one from the other."

"Very good humoured, unaffected girls, indeed," said Mrs. Croft, in a tone of calmer praise, such as made Anne suspect that her keener powers might not consider either of them as quite worthy of her brother; "and a very respectable family. One could not be connected with better people. My dear Admiral, that post; we shall certainly take that post."

But by coolly giving the reins a better direction herself they happily passed the danger; and by once afterwards judiciously putting out her hand they neither fell into a rut, nor ran foul of a dung-cart; and Anne, with some amusement at their style of driving, which she imagined no bad representation of the general guidance of their affairs, found herself safely deposited by them at the Cottage.

Chapter 11

THE time now approached for Lady Russell's return: the day was even fixed; and Anne, being engaged to join her as soon as she was resettled, was looking forward to an early removal to Kellynch, and beginning to think how her own comfort was likely to be affected by it.

It would place her in the same village with Captain Wentworth, within half a mile of him; they would have to frequent the same church, and there must be intercourse between the two families. This was against her; but on the other hand, he spent so much of his time at Uppercross that in removing thence she might be considered rather as leaving him behind, than as going towards him; and upon the whole, she believed she must, on this interesting question, be the gainer, almost as certainly as in her change of domestic society, in leaving poor Mary for Lady Russell.

She wished it might be possible for her to avoid ever seeing Captain Wentworth at the Hall: those rooms had witnessed former meetings which would be brought too painfully before her; but she was yet more anxious for the possibility of Lady Russell and Captain Wentworth never meeting anywhere. They did not like each other, and no renewal of acquaintance now could do any good; and were Lady Russell to see them together, she might think that he had too much self-possession, and she too little.

These points formed her chief solicitude in anticipating her removal from Uppercross, where she felt she had been stationed quite long enough. Her usefulness to little Charles would always give some sweetness to the memory of her two months' visit there, but he was gaining strength apace, and she had nothing else to stay for.

The conclusion of her visit, however, was diversified in a way which she had not at all imagined. Captain Wentworth, after being unseen and unheard of at Uppercross for two whole days, appeared again among them to justify himself by a relation of what had kept him away.

A letter from his friend, Captain Harville, having found him out at last, had brought intelligence of Captain Harville's being settled with his family at Lyme for the winter; of their being, therefore, quite unknowingly, within twenty miles of each other. Captain Harville had never been in good health since a severe wound which he received two years before, and Captain Wentworth's anxiety to see him had determined him to go immediately to Lyme. He had been there for four-and-twenty hours. His acquittal was complete, his friendship warmly honoured, a lively interest excited for his friend, and his description of the fine country about Lyme so feelingly attended to by the party, that an earnest desire to see Lyme themselves, and a project for going thither was the consequence.

The young people were all wild to see Lyme. Captain Wentworth talked of going there again himself, it was only seventeen miles from Uppercross; though November, the weather was by no means bad; and, in short, Louisa, who was the most eager of the eager, having formed the resolution to go, and besides the pleasure of doing as she liked, being now armed with the idea of merit in maintaining her own way, bore down all the wishes of her father and mother for putting it off till summer; and to Lyme they were to go—Charles, Mary, Anne, Henrietta, Louisa, and Captain Wentworth.

The first heedless scheme had been to go in the morning and return at night; but to this Mr. Musgrove, for the sake of his horses, would not consent; and when it came to be rationally considered, a day in the middle of November would not leave much time for seeing a new place, after deducting seven hours, as the nature of the country required, for going and returning. They were, consequently, to stay the night there, and not to be expected back till the next day's dinner. This was felt to be a considerable amendment; and though they all met at the Great House at rather an early breakfast hour, and set off very punctually, it was so much past noon before the two carriages, Mr. Musgrove's coach containing the four ladies, and Charles's curricle, in which he drove Captain Wentworth, were descending the long hill into Lyme, and entering upon the still steeper street of the town itself, that it was very evident they would not have more than time for looking about them, before the light and warmth of the day were gone.

After securing accommodations, and ordering a dinner at one of the inns, the next thing to be done was unquestionably to walk directly down to the sea. They were come too late in the year for any amusement or variety which Lyme, as a public place, might offer. The rooms were shut up, the lodgers almost all gone, scarcely any family but of the residents left; and, as there is nothing to admire in the buildings themselves, the remarkable situation of the town, the principal street almost hurrying into the water, the walk to the Cobb, skirting round the pleasant little bay, which, in the season, is animated with bathing machines and company; the Cobb itself, its old wonders and new improvements, with the very beautiful line of cliffs stretching out to the east of the town, are what the stranger's eye will seek; and a very strange stranger it must be, who does not see charms in the immediate environs of Lyme, to make him wish to know it better. The scenes in its neighbourhood, Charmouth, with its high grounds and extensive sweeps of country, and still more, its sweet, retired bay, backed by dark cliffs, where fragments of low rock among the sands make it the happiest spot for watching the flow of the tide, for sitting in unwearied contemplation; the wooded varieties of the cheerful village of Up Lyme; and, above all, Pinny, with its green chasms between romantic rocks, where the scattered forest trees and orchards of luxuriant growth declare that many a generation must have passed away since the first partial falling of the cliff prepared the ground for such a state, where a scene so wonderful and so lovely is exhibited as may more than equal any of the resembling scenes of the far-famed Isle of Wight: these places must be visited, and visited again to make the worth of Lyme understood.

The party from Uppercross passing down by the now deserted and melancholy looking rooms, and still descending, soon found themselves on the sea-shore; and lingering only, as all must linger and gaze on a first return to the sea, who ever deserve to look on it at all, proceeded towards the Cobb, equally their object in itself and on Captain Wentworth's account: for in a small house, near the foot of an old pier of unknown date, were the Harvilles settled. Captain Wentworth turned in to call on his friend: the others walked on, and he was to join them on the Cobb.

They were by no means tired of wondering and admiring; and not even Louisa seemed to feel that they had parted with Captain Wentworth long, when they saw him coming after them with three companions, all well known already, by description, to the Captain and Mrs. Harville, and a Captain Benwick, who was staying with them.

Captain Benwick had some time ago been first lieutenant of the *Laconia;* and the account which Captain Wentworth had given of him, on his return from Lyme before, his warm praise of him as an excellent young man and an officer whom he had always valued highly, which must have stamped him well in the esteem of every listener, had been followed by a little history of his private life, which rendered him perfectly interesting in the eyes of all the ladies. He had been engaged to Captain Harville's sister, and was now mourning her loss. They had been a year or two waiting for fortune and promotion. Fortune came, his prize-money as lieutenant being great; promotion, too, came at *last;* but Fanny Harville did not live to know it. She had died the preceding summer while he was at sea. Captain Wentworth believed it impossible for man to be more attached to woman than poor Benwick had been to Fanny Harville, or to be more deeply afflicted under the dreadful change. He considered his disposition as of the sort which must suffer heavily, uniting very strong feelings with quiet, serious, and retiring manners, and a decided taste for reading, and sedentary pursuits. To finish the interest of the story, the friendship between him and the Harvilles seemed, if possible, augmented by the event which closed all their views of alliance, and Captain Benwick was now living with them entirely. Captain Harville had taken his present house for half a year; his taste, and his health, and his fortune, all directing him to a residence unexpensive, and by the sea; and the grandeur of the country, and the retirement of Lyme in the winter, appeared exactly adapted to Captain Benwick's state of mind. The sympathy and good-will excited towards Captain Benwick was very great.

"And yet," said Anne to herself, as they now moved forward to meet the party, "he has not, perhaps, a more sorrowing heart than I have. I cannot believe his prospects so blighted for ever. He is younger than I am; younger in feeling, if not in fact; younger as a man. He will rally again, and be happy with another."

They all met, and were introduced. Captain Harville was a tall, dark man, with a sensible, benevolent countenance: a little lame; and from strong features and want of health, looking much older than Captain Wentworth. Captain Benwick looked, and was, the youngest of the three, and, compared with either of them, a little man. He had a pleasing face and a melancholy air, just as he ought to have, and drew back from conversation.

Captain Harville, though not equalling Captain Wentworth in manners, was a perfect gentleman, unaffected, warm, and obliging. Mrs. Harville, a degree less polished than her husband, seemed, however, to have the same good feelings; and nothing could be more pleasant than their desire of considering the whole party as friends of their own, because the friends of Captain Wentworth, or more kindly hospitable than their entreaties for their all promising to dine with them. The dinner, already ordered at the inn, was at last, though unwillingly, accepted as an excuse; but they seemed almost hurt that Captain Wentworth should have brought any such party to Lyme without considering it as a thing of course that they should dine with them.

There was so much attachment to Captain Wentworth in all this, and such a bewitching charm in a degree of hospitality so uncommon, so unlike the usual style of give-and-take invitations, and dinners of formality and display, that Anne felt her spirits not likely to be benefitted by an increasing acquaintance among his brother-officers. "These would have been all my friends," was her thought; and she had to struggle against a great tendency to lowness.

On quitting the Cobb, they all went indoors with their new friends, and found rooms so small as none but those who invite from the heart could think capable of accommodating so many. Anne had a moment's astonishment on the subject herself; but it was soon lost in the pleasanter feelings which sprang from the sight of all the ingenious contrivances and nice arrangements of Captain Harville, to turn the actual space to the best possible account, to supply the deficiencies of lodging-house furniture, and defend the windows and doors against the winter storms to be expected. The varieties in the fitting up of the rooms, where the common necessaries provided by the owner, in the common indifferent plight, were contrasted with some few articles of a rare species of wood, excellently worked up, and with something curious and valuable from all the distant countries Captain Harville had visited, were more than amusing to Anne: connected as it all was with his profession, the fruit of its labours, the effect of its influence on his habits, the picture of repose and domestic happiness it presented, made it to her a something more, or less, than gratification.

Captain Harville was no reader; but he had contrived excellent ac-

commodations, and fashioned very pretty shelves, for a tolerable collection of well-bound volumes, the property of Captain Benwick. His lame-
ness prevented him from taking much exercise; but a mind of usefulness
and ingenuity seemed to furnish him with constant employment within.
He drew, he varnished, he carpentered, he glued; he made toys for the
children; he fashioned new netting-needles and pins with improvements;
and if everything else was done, sat down to his large fishing-net at one
corner of the room.

Anne thought she left great happiness behind her when they quitted the
house; and Louisa, by whom she found herself walking, burst forth into
raptures of admiration and delight on the character of the navy; their
friendliness, their brotherliness, their openness, their uprightness; protesting that she was convinced of sailors having more worth and warmth
than any other set of men in England; that they only knew how to live,
and they only deserved to be respected and loved.

They went back to dress and dine; and so well had the scheme answered
already that nothing was found amiss; though its being "so entirely out
of the season," and the "no thoroughfare of Lyme," and the "no expectation of company," had brought many apologies from the heads of the inn.

Anne found herself by this time growing so much more hardened to
being in Captain Wentworth's company than she had at first imagined
could ever be, that the sitting down to the same table with him now, and
the interchange of the common civilities attending on it (they never got
beyond), was become a mere nothing.

The nights were too dark for the ladies to meet again till the morrow,
but Captain Harville had promised them a visit in the evening; and he
came, bringing his friend also, which was more than had been expected,
it having been agreed that Captain Benwick had all the appearance of
being oppressed by the presence of so many strangers. He ventured among
them again, however, though his spirits certainly did not seem fit for the
mirth of the party in general.

While Captains Wentworth and Harville led the talk on one side of the
room, and by recurring to former days, supplied anecdotes in abundance
to occupy and entertain the others, it fell to Anne's lot to be placed rather
apart with Captain Benwick; and a very good impulse of her nature
obliged her to begin an acquaintance with him. He was shy, and disposed
to abstraction; but the engaging mildness of her countenance, and gentleness of her manner, soon had their effect; and Anne was well repaid the
first trouble of exertion. He was evidently a young man of considerable
taste in reading, though principally in poetry; and besides the persuasion
of having given him at least an evening's indulgence in the discussion of
subjects, which his usual companions had probably no concern in, she had
the hope of being of real use to him in some suggestions as to the duty and
benefit of struggling against affliction, which had naturally grown out of
their conversation. For, though shy, he did not seem reserved: it had
rather the appearance of feelings glad to burst their usual restraints; and

having talked of poetry, the richness of the present age, and gone through a brief comparison of opinion as to the first-rate poets, trying to ascertain whether *Marmion* or *The Lady of the Lake* were to be preferred, and how ranked the *Giaour* and *The Bride of Abydos*, and moreover, how the *Giaour* was to be pronounced, he showed himself so intimately acquainted with all the tenderest songs of the one poet, and all the impassioned descriptions of hopeless agony of the other; he repeated, with such tremulous feeling, the various lines which imaged a broken heart, or a mind destroyed by wretchedness, and looked so entirely as if he meant to be understood, that she ventured to hope he did not always read only poetry, and to say that she thought it was the misfortune of poetry to be seldom safely enjoyed by those who enjoyed it completely; and that the strong feelings which alone could estimate it truly were the very feelings which ought to taste it but sparingly.

His looks showing him not pained, but pleased with this allusion to his situation, she was emboldened to go on; and feeling in herself the right of seniority of mind, she ventured to recommend a larger allowance of prose in his daily study; and on being requested to particularise, mentioned such works of our best moralists, such collections of the finest letters, such memoirs of characters of worth and suffering, as occurred to her at the moment as calculated to rouse and fortify the mind by the highest precepts and the strongest examples of moral and religious endurances.

Captain Benwick listened attentively, and seemed grateful for the interest implied; and though with a shake of the head, and sighs which declared his little faith in the efficacy of any books on grief like his, noted down the names of those she recommended, and promised to procure and read them.

When the evening was over, Anne could not but be amused at the idea of her coming to Lyme to preach patience and resignation to a young man whom she had never seen before; nor could she help fearing, on more serious reflection, that, like many other great moralists and preachers, she had been eloquent on a point in which her own conduct would ill bear examination.

Chapter 12

ANNE and Henrietta, finding themselves the earliest of the party the next morning, agreed to stroll down to the sea before breakfast. They went to the sands, to watch the flowing of the tide, which a fine southeasterly breeze was bringing in with all the grandeur which so flat a shore admitted. They praised the morning; gloried in the sea; sympathised in the delight of the fresh-feeling breeze—and were silent; till Henrietta suddenly began again, with:

"Oh, yes! I am quite convinced that, with very few exceptions, the sea-air always does good. There can be no doubt of its having been of the greatest service to Dr. Shirley, after his illness, last spring twelvemonth.

He declares himself, that coming to Lyme for a month did him more good than all the medicine he took; and that being by the sea always makes him feel young again. Now, I cannot help thinking it a pity that he does not live entirely by the sea. I do think he had better leave Uppercross entirely, and fix at Lyme. Do not you, Anne? Do not you agree with me, that it is the best thing he could do, both for himself and Mrs. Shirley? She has cousins here, you know, and many acquaintances, which would make it cheerful for her, and I am sure she would be glad to get a place where she could have medical attendance at hand, in case of his having another seizure. Indeed, I think it quite melancholy to have such excellent people as Dr. and Mrs. Shirley, who have been doing good all their lives, wearing out their last days in a place like Uppercross, where, excepting our family, they seem shut out from all the world. I wish his friends would propose it to him. I really think they ought. And, as to procuring a dispensation, there could be no difficulty at his time of life and with his character. My only doubt is, whether anything could persuade him to leave his parish. He is so very strict and scrupulous in his notions; over-scrupulous I must say. Do not you think, Anne, it is being over-scrupulous? Do not you think it is quite a mistaken point of conscience, when a clergyman sacrifices his health for the sake of duties which may be just as well performed by another person? And at Lyme, too, only seventeen miles off, he would be near enough to hear if people thought there was anything to complain of."

Anne smiled more than once to herself during this speech, and entered into the subject, as ready to do good by entering into the feelings of a young lady as of a young man, though here it was good of a lower standard, for what could be offered but general acquiescence? She said all that was reasonable and proper on the business; felt the claims of Dr. Shirley to repose as she ought; saw how very desirable it was that he should have some active, respectable young man as a resident curate, and was even courteous enough to hint at the advantage of such resident curate's being married.

"I wish," said Henrietta, very well pleased with her companion, "I wish Lady Russell lived at Uppercross, and were intimate with Dr. Shirley. I have always heard of Lady Russell as a woman of the greatest influence with everybody! I always look upon her as able to persuade a person to anything! I am afraid of her, as I told you before, quite afraid of her, because she is so very clever; but I respect her amazingly, and wish we had such a neighbour at Uppercross."

Anne was amused by Henrietta's manner of being grateful, and amused also that the course of events and the new interest of Henrietta's views should have placed her friend at all in favour with any of the Musgrove family; she had only time, however, for a general answer, and a wish that such another woman were at Uppercross, before all subjects suddenly ceased, on seeing Louisa and Captain Wentworth coming towards them. They came also for a stroll till breakfast was likely to be ready; but Louisa recollecting immediately afterwards that she had something to procure at a snop, invited them all to go back with her into the town. They were all at her disposal.

When they came to the steps, leading upwards from the beach, a gentleman, at the same moment preparing to come down, politely drew back, and stopped to give them way. They ascended and passed him; and as they passed, Anne's face caught his eye, and he looked at her with a degree of earnest admiration which she could not be insensible of. She was looking remarkably well; her very regular, very pretty features, having the bloom and freshness of youth restored by the fine wind which had been blowing on her complexion, and by the animation of eye which it had also produced. It was evident that the gentleman (completely a gentleman in manner) admired her exceedingly. Captain Wentworth looked round at her instantly in a way which showed his noticing of it. He gave her a momentary glance, a glance of brightness, which seemed to say, "That man is struck with you, and even I, at this moment, see something like Anne Elliot again."

After attending Louisa through her business, and loitering about a little longer, they returned to the inn; and Anne, in passing afterwards quickly from her own chamber to their dining-room, had nearly run against the very same gentleman, as he came out of an adjoining apartment. She had before conjectured him to be a stranger like themselves, and determined that a well-looking groom, who was strolling about near the two inns as they came back, should be his servant. Both master and man being in mourning assisted the idea. It was now proved that he belonged to the same inn as themselves; and this second meeting, short as it was, also proved again, by the gentleman's looks, that he thought hers very lovely, and by the readiness and propriety of his apologies, that he was a man of exceedingly good manners. He seemed about thirty, and though not handsome, had an agreeable person. Anne felt that she should like to know who he was.

They had nearly done breakfast, when the sound of a carriage (almost the first they had heard since entering Lyme), drew half the party to the window. It was a gentleman's carriage, a curricle, but only coming round from the stable-yard to the front door; somebody must be going away. It was driven by a servant in mourning.

The word curricle made Charles Musgrove jump up that he might compare it with his own; the servant in mourning roused Anne's curiosity, and the whole six were collected to look, by the time the owner of the curricle was to be seen issuing from the door, amidst the bows and civilities of the household, and taking his seat, to drive off.

"Ah!" cried Captain Wentworth, instantly, and with half a glance at Anne, "it is the very man we passed."

The Miss Musgroves agreed to it; and having all kindly watched him as far up the hill as they could, they returned to the breakfast table. The waiter came into the room soon afterwards.

"Pray," said Captain Wentworth, immediately, "can you tell us the name of the gentleman who is just gone away?"

"Yes, sir, a Mr. Elliot, a gentleman of large fortune, came in last night from Sidmouth. Dare say you heard the carriage, sir, while you were at dinner; and going on now for Crewkherne, on his way to Bath and London."

"Elliot!" Many had looked on each other, and many had repeated the name, before all this had been got through, even by the smart rapidity of a waiter.

"Bless me!" cried Mary, "it must be our cousin; it must be our Mr. Elliot, it must, indeed! Charles, Anne, must not it? In mourning, you see, just as our Mr. Elliot must be. How very extraordinary! In the very same inn with us! Anne, must not it be our Mr. Elliot? My father's next heir? Pray, sir," turning to the waiter, "did not you hear, did not his servant say whether he belonged to the Kellynch family?"

"No, ma'am, he did not mention no particular family; but he said his master was a very rich gentleman, and would be a baronet some day."

"There! you see!" cried Mary in an ecstasy; "just as I said! Heir to Sir Walter Elliot! I was sure that would come out, if it was so. Depend upon it, that is a circumstance which his servants take care to publish, wherever he goes. But, Anne, only conceive how extraordinary! I wish I had looked at him more. I wish we had been aware in time who it was, that he might have been introduced to us. What a pity that we should not have been introduced to each other! Do you think he had the Elliot countenance? I hardly looked at him, I was looking at the horses; but I think he had something of the Elliot countenance. I wonder the arms did not strike me! Oh! the great-coat was hanging over the panel, and hid the arms, so it did; otherwise, I am sure, I should have observed them, and the livery too; if the servant had not been in mourning, one should have known him by the livery."

"Putting all these very extraordinary circumstances together," said Captain Wentworth, "we must consider it to be the arrangement of Providence that you should not be introduced to your cousin."

When she could command Mary's attention, Anne quietly tried to convince her that their father and Mr. Elliot had not, for many years, been on such terms as to make the power of attempting an introduction at all desirable.

At the same time, however, it was a secret gratification to herself to have seen her cousin, and to know that the future owner of Kellynch was undoubtedly a gentleman, and had an air of good sense. She would not, upon any account, mention her having met with him the second time; luckily Mary did not much attend to their having passed close by him in their early walk, but she would have felt quite ill-used by Anne's having actually run against him in the passage, and received his very polite excuses, while she had never been near him at all; no, that cousinly little interview must remain a perfect secret.

"Of course," said Mary, "you will mention our seeing Mr. Elliot the next time you write to Bath. I think my father certainly ought to hear of it; do mention all about him."

Anne avoided a direct reply, but it was just the circumstance which she considered as not merely unnecessary to be communicated, but as what ought to be suppressed. The offence which had been given her father, many years back, she knew; Elizabeth's particular share in it she suspected; and that Mr. Elliot's idea always produced irritation in both was beyond a doubt. Mary never wrote to Bath herself; all the toil of keeping up a slow and unsatisfactory correspondence with Elizabeth fell on Anne.

Breakfast had not been long over when they were joined by Captain and Mrs. Harville and Captain Benwick; with whom they had appointed to take their last walk about Lyme. They ought to be setting off for Uppercross by one, and in the meanwhile were to be all together, and out of doors as long as they could.

Anne found Captain Benwick getting near her, as soon as they were all fairly in the street. Their conversation the preceding evening did not disincline him to seek her again; and they walked together some time, talking as before of Mr. Scott and Lord Byron, and still as unable as before, and as unable as any other two readers, to think exactly alike of the merits of either, till something occasioned an almost general change amongst their party, and instead of Captain Benwick, she had Captain Harville by her side.

"Miss Eliot," said he, speaking rather low, "you have done a good deed in making that poor fellow talk so much. I wish he could have such company oftener. It is bad for him, I know, to be shut up as he is; but what can we do? We cannot part."

"No," said Anne, "that I can easily believe to be impossible; but in time, perhaps—we know what time does in every case of affliction, and you must remember, Captain Harville, that your friend may yet be called a young mourner—only last summer, understand."

"Ay, true enough" (with a deep sigh), "only June."

"And not known to him, perhaps, so soon."

"Not till the first week in August, when he came home from the Cape, just made into the *Grappler*. I was at Plymouth dreading to hear of him; he sent in letters, but the *Grappler* was under orders for Portsmouth. There the news must follow him, but who was to tell it? Not I. I would as soon have been run up to the yard-arm. Nobody could do it, but that good fellow" (pointing to Captain Wentworth). "The *Laconia* had come into Plymouth the week before; no danger of her being sent to sea again. He stood his chance for the rest; wrote up for leave of absence, but without waiting the return, travelled night and day till he got to Portsmouth, rowed off to the *Grappler* that instant, and never left the poor fellow for a week. That's what he did, and nobody else could have saved poor James. You may think, Miss Elliot, whether he is dear to us!"

Anne did think on the question with perfect decision, and said as much in reply as her own feelings could accomplish, or as his seemed able to bear, for he was too much affected to renew the subject, and when he spoke again, it was of something totally different.

Mrs. Harville's giving it as her opinion that her husband would have quite walking enough by the time he reached home, determined the direction of all the party in what was to be their last walk; they would accompany them to their door, and then return and set off themselves. By all their calculations there was just time for this; but as they drew near the Cobb, there was such a general wish to walk along it once more, all were so inclined, and Louisa soon grew so determined, that the difference of a quarter of an hour, it was found, would be no difference at all; so with all the kind leave-taking, and all the kind interchange of invitations and promises which may be imagined, they parted from Captain and Mrs. Harville at their own door, and still accompained by Captain Benwick, who seemed to cling to them to the last, proceeded to make the proper adieux to the Cobb.

Anne found Captain Benwick again drawing near her. Lord Byron's "dark blue seas" could not fail of being brought forward by their present view, and she gladly gave him all her attention as long as attention was possible. It was soon drawn, perforce, another way.

There was too much wind to make the high part of the new Cobb pleasant for the ladies, and they agreed to get down the steps to the lower, and all were contented to pass quietly and carefully down the steep flight, excepting Louisa; she must be jumped down them by Captain Wentworth. In all their walks he had had to jump her from the stiles; the sensation was delightful to her. The hardness of the pavement for her feet made him less willing upon the present occasion; he did it, however. She was safely down, and instantly, to show her enjoyment, ran up the steps to be jumped down again. He advised her against it, thought the jar too great; but no, he reasoned and talked in vain, she smiled and said, "I am determined I will:" he put out his hands; she was too precipitate by half a second, she fell on the pavement on the Lower Cobb, and was taken up lifeless! There was no wound, no blood, no visible bruise; but her eyes were closed, she breathed not, her face was like death. The horror of that moment to all who stood around!

Captain Wentworth, who had caught her up, knelt with her in his arms, looking on her with a face as pallid as her own in an agony of silence. "She is dead! She is dead!" screamed Mary, catching hold of her husband, and contributing with his own horror to make him immovable; and in another moment, Henrietta, sinking under the conviction, lost her senses too, and would have fallen on the steps but for Captain Benwick and Anne, who caught and supported her between them.

"Is there no one to help me?" were the first words which burst from Captain Wentworth, in a tone of despair, and as if all his own strength were gone.

"Go to him, go to him," cried Anne, "for heaven's sake, go to him. I can support her myself. Leave me, and go to him. Rub her hands, rub her temples; here are salts: take them, take them."

Captain Benwick obeyed, and Charles at the same moment disengaging himself from his wife, they were both with him; and Louisa was raised up and supported more firmly between them, and everything was done that Anne had prompted, but in vain; while Captain Wentworth, staggering against the wall for his support, exclaimed in the bitterest agony:

"Oh God! her father and mother!"

"A surgeon!" said Anne.

He caught the word: it seemed to rouse him at once; and saying only: "True, true, a surgeon this instant," was darting away, when Anne eagerly suggested:

"Captain Benwick, would not it better for Captain Benwick? He knows where a surgeon is to be found."

Every one capable of thinking felt the advantage of the idea, and in a moment (it was all done in rapid moments) Captain Benwick had resigned the poor corpse-like figure entirely to the brother's care, and was off for the town with the utmost rapidity.

As to the wretched party left behind, it could scarcely be said which of the three, who were completely rational, was suffering most: Captain Wentworth, Anne, or Charles, who, really a very affectionate brother, hung over Louisa with sobs of grief, and could only turn his eyes from one sister to see the other in a state as insensible, or to witness the hysterical agitations of his wife, calling on him for help which he could not give.

Anne, attending with all the strength, and zeal, and thought, which instinct supplied, to Henrietta, still tried, at intervals, to suggest comfort to the others, tried to quiet Mary, to animate Charles, to assuage the feelings of Captain Wentworth. Both seemed to look to her for directions.

"Anne, Anne," cried Charles, "what is to be done next? What, in heaven's name, is to be done next?"

Captain Wentworth's eyes were also turned towards her.

"Had not she better be carried to the inn? Yes, I am sure: carry her gently to the inn."

"Yes, yes, to the inn," repeated Captain Wentworth, comparatively collected, and eager to be doing something. "I will carry her myself. Musgrove, take care of the others."

By this time the report of the accident had spread among the workmen and boatmen about the Cobb, and many were collected near them, to be useful if wanted; at any rate, to enjoy the sight of a dead young lady, nay, two dead young ladies, for it proved twice as fine as the first report. To some of the best-looking of these good people Henrietta was consigned, for, though partially revived, she was quite helpless; and in this manner, Anne walking by her side, and Charles attending to his wife, they set forward, treading back, with feelings unutterable, the ground which so lately, so very lately, and so light of heart, they had passed along.

They were not off the Cobb before the Harvilles met them. Captain

Benwick had been seen flying by their house, with a countenance which showed something to be wrong; and they had set off immediately, informed and directed as they passed, towards the spot. Shocked as Captain Harville was, he brought senses and nerves that could be instantly useful; and a look between him and his wife decided what was to be done. She must be taken to their house; all must go to their house; and wait the surgeon's arrival there. They would not listen to scruples: he was obeyed: they were all beneath his roof; and while Louisa, under Mrs. Harville's direction, was conveyed upstairs, and given possession of her own bed, assistance, cordials, restoratives were supplied by her husband to all who needed them.

Louisa had once opened her eyes, but soon closed them again, without apparent consciousness. This had been a proof of life, however, of service to her sister; and Henrietta, though perfectly incapable of being in the same room with Louisa, was kept, by the agitation of hope and fear, from a return of her own insensibility. Mary, too, was growing calmer.

The surgeon was with them almost before it had seemed possible. They were sick with horror, while he examined; but he was not hopeless. The head had received a severe contusion, but he had seen greater injuries recovered from; he was by no means hopeless; he spoke cheerfully.

That he did not regard it as a desperate case, that he did not say a few hours must end it, was at first felt beyond the hope of most; and the ecstasy of such a reprieve, the rejoicing, deep and silent, after a few fervent ejaculations of gratitude to Heaven had been offered, may be conceived.

The tone, the look, with which "Thank God!" was uttered by Captain Wentworth, Anne was sure could never be forgotten by her; nor the sight of him afterwards, as he sat near a table, leaning over it with folded arms, and face concealed, as if overpowered by the various feelings of his soul, and trying by prayer and reflection to calm them.

Louisa's limbs had escaped. There was no injury but to the head.

It now became necessary for the party to consider what was best to be done, as to their general situation. They were now able to speak to each other and consult. That Louisa must remain where she was, however distressing to her friends to be involving the Harvilles in such trouble, did not admit a doubt. Her removal was impossible. The Harvilles silenced all scruples, and, as much as they could, all gratitude. They had looked forward and arranged everything before the others began to reflect. Captain Benwick must give up his room to them and get a bed elsewhere; and the whole was settled. They were only concerned that the house could accommodate no more; and yet, perhaps, by "putting the children away in the maid's room, or swinging a cot somewhere," they could hardly bear to think of not finding room for two or three besides, supposing they might wish to stay; though, with regard to any attendance on Miss Musgrove, there need not be the least uneasiness in leaving her to Mrs. Harville's care entirely. Mrs. Harville was a very experienced nurse, and her nurserymaid, who had lived with her long, and gone about with her everywhere, was just such another. Between those two she could want no possible attendance by day or night. And all this was said with a truth and sincerity of feeling irresistible.

Charles, Henrietta, and Captain Wentworth were the three in consulta-- tion, and for a little while it was only an interchange of perplexity and terror. "Uppercross, the necessity of someone's going to Uppercross, the news to be conveyed; how it could be broken to Mr. and Mrs. Musgrove; the lateness of the morning; an hour already gone since they ought to have been off; the impossibility of being in tolerable time." At first they were capable of nothing more to the purpose than such exclamations; but after a while Captain Wentworth, exerting himself, said:

"We must be decided, and without the loss of another minute. Every minute is valuable. Someone must resolve on being off for Uppercross instantly. Musgrove, either you or I must go."

Charles agreed, but declared his resolution of not going away. He would be as little encumbrance as possible to Captain and Mrs. Harville; but as to leaving his sister in such a state, he neither ought nor would. So far it was decided; and Henrietta at first declared the same. She, however, was soon persuaded to think differently. The usefulness of her staying! She, who had not been able to remain in Louisa's room, or to look at her, without sufferings which made her worse than helpless! She was forced to acknowledge that she could do no good, yet was still unwilling to be away, till, touched by the thought of her father and mother, she gave it up; she consented, she was anxious to be at home.

The plan had reached this point, when Anne, coming quietly down from Louisa's room, could not but hear what followed, for the parlour door was open.

"Then it is settled, Musgrove," cried Captain Wentworth, "that you stay, and that I take care of your sister home. But as to the rest, as to the others, if one stays to assist Mrs. Harville, I think it need be only one. Mrs. Charles Musgrove will, of course, wish to get back to her children; but if Anne will stay, no one so proper, so capable as Anne."

She paused a moment to recover from the emotion of hearing herself so spoken of. The other two warmly agreed to what he said, and she then appeared.

"You will stay, I am sure; you will stay and nurse her," cried he, turn- ing to her and speaking with a glow, and yet a gentleness, which seemed almost restoring the past. She coloured deeply, and he recollected himself and moved away. She expressed herself most willing, ready, happy to re- main. "It was what she had been thinking of, and wishing to be allowed to do. A bed on the floor in Louisa's room would be sufficient for her, if Mrs. Harville would but think so."

One thing more, and all seemed arranged. Though it was rather de- sirable that Mr. and Mrs. Musgrove should be previously alarmed by some share of delay; yet the time required by the Uppercross horses to take them back, would be a dreadful extension of suspense; and Captain Wentworth proposed, and Charles Musgrove agreed, that it would be much better for him to take a chaise from the inn, and leave Mr. Musgrove's carriage and horses to be sent home the next morning early, when there could be the further advantage of sending an account of Louisa's night.

Captain Wentworth now hurried off to get everything ready on his part, and to be soon followed by the two ladies. When the plan was made known to Mary, however, there was an end of all peace in it. She was so wretched, and so vehement, complained so much of injustice in being expected to go away instead of Anne; Anne, who was nothing to Louisa, while she was her sister, and had the best right to stay in Henrietta's stead! Why was not she to be as useful as Anne? And to go home without Charles, too, without her husband! No, it was too unkind. And in short, she said more than her husband could long withstand, and as none of the others could oppose when he gave way, there was no help for it: the change of Mary for Anne was inevitable.

Anne had never submitted more reluctantly to the jealous and ill-judging claims of Mary; but so it must be, and they set off for the town, Charles taking care of his sister, and Captain Benwick attending to her. She gave a moment's recollection, as they hurried along, to the little circumstances which the same spots had witnessed earlier in the morning. There she had listened to Henrietta's schemes for Dr. Shirley's leaving Uppercross; farther on, she had first seen Mr. Elliot; a moment seemed all that could now be given to anyone but Louisa, or those who were wrapped up in her welfare.

Captain Benwick was most considerately attentive to her; and, united as they all seemed by the distress of the day, she felt an increasing degree of goodwill towards him, and a pleasure even in thinking that it might, perhaps, be the occasion of continuing their acquaintance.

Captain Wentworth was on the watch for them, and a chaise and four in waiting, stationed for their convenience in the lowest part of the street; but his evident surprise and vexation at the substitution of one sister for the other, the change of his countenance, the astonishment, the expressions begun and suppressed, with which Charles was listened to, made but a mortifying reception of Anne; or must at least convince her that she was valued only as she could be useful to Louisa.

She endeavoured to be composed, and to be just. Without emulating the feelings of an Emma towards her Henry, she would have attended on Louisa with a zeal above the common claims of regard, for his sake; and she hoped he would not long be so unjust as to suppose she would shrink unnecessarily from the office of a friend.

In the meanwhile she was in the carriage. He had handed them both in, and placed himself between them; and in this manner, under these circumstances, full of astonishment and emotion to Anne, she quitted Lyme. How the long stage would pass; how it was to affect their manners; what was to be their sort of intercourse, she could not foresee. It was all

quite natural, however. He was devoted to Henrietta; always turning
towards her; and when he spoke at all, always with the view of supporting
her hopes and raising her spirits. In general, his voice and manner were
studiously calm. To spare Henrietta from agitation seemed the governing
principle. Once only, when she had been grieving over the last ill-judged,
ill-fated walk to the Cobb, bitterly lamenting that it ever had been thought
of, he burst forth, as if wholly overcome:

"Don't talk of it, don't talk of it," he cried. "Oh, God! that I had not
given way to her at the fatal moment! Had I done as I ought! But so
eager and so resolute! Dear, sweet Louisa!"

Anne wondered whether it ever occurred to him now, to question the
justness of his own previous opinion as to the universal felicity and advantage of firmness of character; and whether it might not strike him that,
like all other qualities of the mind, it should have its proportions and
limits. She thought it could scarcely escape him to feel that a persuadable
temper might sometimes be as much in favour of happiness as a very
resolute character.

They got on fast. Anne was astonished to recognise the same hills and
the same objects so soon. Their actual speed, heightened by some dread
of the conclusion, made the road appear but half as long as on the day
before. It was growing quite dusk, however, before they were in the
neighbourhood of Uppercross, and there had been total silence among
them for some time, Henrietta leaning back in the corner, with a shawl
over her face, giving the hope of her having cried herself to sleep; when,
as they were going up their last hill, Anne found herself all at once addressed by Captain Wentworth. In a low cautious voice, he said:

"I have been considering what we had best do. She must not appear at
first. She could not stand it. I have been thinking whether you had not
better remain in the carriage with her, while I go in and break it to Mr.
and Mrs. Musgrove. Do you think this a good plan?"

She did: he was satisfied, and said no more. But the remembrance of
the appeal remained a pleasure to her, as a proof of friendship, and of
deference for her judgment, a great pleasure; and when it became a sort
of parting proof, its value did not lessen.

When the distressing communication at Uppercross was over, and he
had seen the father and mother quite as composed as could be hoped, and
the daughter all the better for being with them, he announced his intention
of returning in the same carriage to Lyme; and when the horses were
baited, he was off.

Chapter 13

THE remainder of Anne's time at Uppercross, comprehending only two
days, was spent entirely at the Mansion House; and she had the satisfaction of knowing herself extremely useful there, both as an immediate
companion, and as assisting in all those arrangements for the future,

which, in Mr. and Mrs. Musgrove's distressed state of spirits, would have
been difficulties.

They had an early account from Lyme the next morning. Louisa was
much the same. No symptoms worse than before had appeared. Charles
came a few hours afterwards to bring a later and more particular account.
He was tolerably cheerful. A speedy cure must not be hoped, but everything was going on as well as the nature of the case admitted. In speaking
of the Harvilles, he seemed unable to satisfy his own sense of their kindness, especially of Mrs. Harville's exertions as a nurse. "She really left
nothing for Mary to do. He and Mary had been persuaded to go early to
their inn last night. Mary had been hysterical again this morning. When
he came away, she was going to walk out with Captain Benwick, which
he hoped would do her good. He almost wished she had been prevailed on
to come home the day before; but the truth was, that Mrs. Harville left
nothing for anybody to do."

Charles was to return to Lyme the same afternoon, and his father had
at first half a mind to go with him, but the ladies could not consent. It
would be going only to multiply trouble to the others, and increase his
own distress; and a much better scheme followed, and was acted upon. A
chaise was sent for from Crewkherne, and Charles conveyed back a far
more useful person in the old nurserymaid of the family, one who, having
brought up all the children, and seen the very last, the lingering and long-
petted Master Harry, sent to school after his brothers, was now living in
her deserted nursery to mend stockings, and dress all the blains and bruises
she could get near her, and who, consequently, was only too happy in being
allowed to go and help nurse dear Miss Louisa. Vague wishes of getting
Sarah thither had occurred before to Mrs. Musgrove and Henrietta; but
without Anne, it would hardly have been resolved on, and found practicable so soon.

They were indebted, the next day, to Charles Hayter, for all the minute
knowledge of Louisa, which it was so essential to obtain every twenty-four
hours. He made it his business to go to Lyme, and his account was still
encouraging. The intervals of sense and consciousness were believed to be
stronger. Every report agreed in Captain Wentworth's appearing fixed in
Lyme.

Anne was to leave them on the morrow, an event which they all dreaded.
"What should they do without her? They were wretched comforters for
one another." And so much was said in this way, that Anne thought she
could not do better than impart among them the general inclination to
which she was privy, and persuade them all to go to Lyme at once. She
had little difficulty; it was soon determined that they would go: go to-
morrow, fix themselves at the inn, or get into lodgings, as it suited, and
there remain till dear Louisa could be moved. They must be taking off
some trouble from the good people she was with: they might at least
relieve Mrs. Harville from the care of her own children: and in short, they
were so happy in the decision, that Anne was delighted with what she had

done, and felt that she could not spend her last morning at Uppercross better than in assisting their preparations, and sending them off at an early hour, though her being left to the solitary range of the house was the consequence.

She was the last, excepting the little boys at the Cottage, she was the very last, the only remaining one of all that had filled and animated both houses, of all that had given Uppercross its cheerful character. A few days had made a change indeed!

If Louisa recovered, it would all be well again. More than former happiness would be restored. There could not be a doubt, to her mind there was none, of what would follow her recovery. A few months hence and the room now so deserted, occupied but by her silent, pensive self, might be filled again with all that was happy and gay, all that was glowing and bright in prosperous love, all that was most unlike Anne Elliot!

An hour's complete leisure for such reflections as these, on a dark November day, a small thick rain almost blotting out the very objects ever to be discerned from the windows, was enough to make the sound of Lady Russell's carriage exceedingly welcome; and yet, though desirous to be gone, she could not quit the Mansion House, or look an adieu to the Cottage, with its black, dripping and comfortless verandah, or even notice through the misty glasses the last humble tenements of the village, without a saddened heart. Scenes had passed in Uppercross which made it precious. It stood the record of many sensations of pain, once severe, but now softened; and of some instances of relenting feeling, some breathings of friendship and reconciliation, which could never be looked for again, and which could never cease to be dear. She left it all behind her, all but the recollection that such things had been.

Anne had never entered Kellynch since her quitting Lady Russell's house in September. It had not been necessary, and the few occasions of its being possible for her to go to the Hall she had contrived to evade and escape from. Her first return was to resume her place in the modern and elegant apartments of the Lodge, and to gladden the eyes of its mistress.

There was some anxiety mixed with Lady Russell's joy in meeting her. She knew who had been frequenting Uppercross. But happily, either Anne was improved in plumpness and looks, or Lady Russell fancied her so; and Anne, in receiving her compliments on the occasion, had the amusement of connecting them with the silent admiration of her cousin, and of hoping that she was to be blessed with a second spring of youth and beauty.

When they came to converse, she was soon sensible of some mental change. The subjects of which her heart had been full on leaving Kellynch, and which she had felt slighted, and been compelled to smother among the Musgroves, were now become but of secondary interest. She had lately lost sight even of her father, and sister, and Bath. Their concerns had been sunk under those of Uppercross; and when Lady Russell reverted to their former hopes and fears, and spoke her satisfaction in the house in Camden Place which had been taken, and her regret that Mrs. Clay should still be with them, Anne would have been ashamed to have it known how much more she was thinking of Lyme and Louisa Musgrove, and all her acquaintances there; how much more interesting to her was the home and the friendship of the Harvilles and Captain Benwick, than her own father's house in Camden Place, or her own sister's intimacy with Mrs. Clay. She was actually forced to exert herself to meet Lady Russell with anything like the appearance of equal solicitude, on topics which had by nature the first claim on her.

There was a little awkwardness at first in their discourse on another subject. They must speak of the accident at Lyme. Lady Russell had not been arrived five minutes the day before, when a full account of the whole had burst on her; but still it must be talked of, she must make enquiries, she must regret the imprudence, lament the result, and Captain Wentworth's name must be mentioned by both. Anne was conscious of not doing it so well as Lady Russell. She could not speak the name, and look straight forward to Lady Russell's eye, till she had adopted the expedient of telling her briefly what she thought of the attachment between him and Louisa. When this was told, his name distressed her no longer.

Lady Russell had only to listen composedly, and wish them happy, but internally her heart revelled in angry pleasure, in pleased contempt, that the man who at twenty-three had seemed to understand somewhat of the value of an Anne Elliot, should, eight years afterwards, be charmed by a Louisa Musgrove.

The first three or four days passed most quietly, with no circumstance to mark them excepting the receipt of a note or two from Lyme, which found their way to Anne, she could not tell how, and brought a rather improving account of Louisa. At the end of that period, Lady Russell's politeness could repose no longer, and the fainter self-threatenings of the past became in a decided tone, "I must call on Mrs. Croft; I really must call upon her soon. Anne, have you courage to go with me and pay a visit in that house? It will be some trial to us both."

Anne did not shrink from it: on the contrary, she truly felt as she said, in observing:

"I think you are very likely to suffer the most of the two; your feelings are less reconciled to the change than mine. By remaining in the neighbourhood, I am become enured to it."

She could have said more on the subject, for she had in fact so high an opinion of the Crofts, and considered her father so very fortunate in his tenants, felt the parish to be so sure of a good example, and the poor of the best attention and relief, that however sorry and ashamed for the necessity of the removal, she could not but in conscience feel that they were gone who deserved not to stay, and that Kellynch Hall had passed into better hands than its owners. These convictions must unquestionably have their own pain, and severe was its kind; but they precluded that pain which Lady Russell would suffer in entering the house again, and returning through the well-known apartments.

In such moments Anne had no power of saying to herself, "These rooms ought to belong only to us. Oh, how fallen in their destination! How unworthily occupied! An ancient family to be so driven away! Strangers filling their place!" No, except when she thought of her mother, and remembered where she had been used to sit and preside, she had no sigh of that description to heave.

Mrs. Croft always met her with a kindness which gave her the pleasure of fancying herself a favourite, and on the present occasion, receiving her in that house, there was particular attention.

The sad accident at Lyme was soon the prevailing topic, and on comparing their latest accounts of the invalid, it appeared that each lady dated her intelligence from the same hour of yestermorn; that Captain Wentworth had been in Kellynch yesterday (the first time since the accident), had brought Anne the last note, which she had not been able to trace the exact steps of; and stayed a few hours, and then returned again to Lyme, and without any present intention of quitting it any more. He had enquired after her, she found particularly; had expressed his hope of Miss Elliot's not being the worse for her exertions, and had spoken of those exertions as great. This was handsome, and gave her more pleasure than almost anything else could have done.

As to the sad catastrophe itself, it could be canvassed only in one style by a couple of steady, sensible women, whose judgments had to work on ascertained events; and it was perfectly decided that it had been the consequence of much thoughtlessness and much imprudence; that its effects were most alarming, and that it was frightful to think how long Miss Musgrove's recovery might yet be doubtful, and how liable she would still remain to suffer from the concussion hereafter! The Admiral wound it all up summarily by exclaiming:

"Ay, a very bad business, indeed. A new sort of way this, for a young fellow to be making love, by breaking his mistress's head, is not it, Miss Elliot? This is breaking a head and giving a plaster, truly!"

Admiral Croft's manners were not quite of the tone to suit Lady Russell, but they delighted Anne. His goodness of heart and simplicity of character were irresistible.

"Now, this must be very bad for you," said he, suddenly rousing from a little reverie, "to be coming and finding us here. I had not recollected it before, I declare, but it must be very bad. But now, do not stand upon ceremony. Get up and go over all the rooms in the house, if you like it."

"Another time, sir, I thank you; not now."

"Well, whenever it suits you. You can slip in from the shrubbery at any time; and there you will find we keep our umbrellas hanging up by that door. A good place, is not it? But" (checking himself), "you will not think it a good place, for yours were always kept in the butler's room. Ay, so it always is, I believe. One man's ways may be as good as another's, but we all like our own best; and so you must judge for yourself, whether it would be better for you to go about the house or not."

Anne, finding she might decline it, did so very gratefully.

"We have made very few changes either," continued the Admiral, after thinking a moment. "Very few. We told you about the laundry-door at Uppercross. That has been a very great improvement. The wonder was, how any family upon earth could bear with the inconvenience of its opening as it did so long! You will tell Sir Walter what we have done, and that Mr. Shepherd thinks it the greatest improvement the house ever had. Indeed, I must do ourselves the justice to say, that the few alterations we have made have been all very much for the better. My wife should have the credit of them, however. I have done very little besides sending away some of the large looking-glasses from my dressing-room, which was your father's. A very good man, and very much the gentleman, I am sure; but I should think, Miss Elliot" (looking with serious reflection), "I should think he must be rather a dressy man for his time of life. Such a number of looking-glasses! oh, Lord! there was no getting away from one's self. So I got Sophy to lend me a hand, and we soon shifted their quarters; and now I am quite snug, with my little shaving-glass in one corner, and another great thing that I never go near."

Anne, amused in spite of herself, was rather distressed for an answer; and the Admiral, fearing he might not have been civil enough, took up the subject again, to say:

"The next time you write to your good father, Miss Elliot, pray give my compliments and Mrs. Croft's, and say that we are settled here quite to our liking, and have no fault at all to find with the place. The breakfast-room chimney smokes a little, I grant you, but it is only when the wind is due north and blows hard, which may not happen three times a winter. And take it altogether, now that we have been into most of the houses hereabouts and can judge, there is not one that we like better than this. Pray say so, with my compliments. He will be glad to hear it."

Lady Russell and Mrs. Croft were very well pleased with each other: but the acquaintance which this visit began was fated not to proceed far at present; for when it was returned, the Crofts announced themselves to be going away for a few weeks, to visit their connections in the north of the county, and probably might not be at home again before Lady Russell would be removing to Bath.

So ended all danger to Anne of meeting Captain Wentworth at Kellynch Hall, or of seeing him in company with her friend. Everything was safe enough, and she smiled over the many anxious feelings she had wasted on the subject.

Chapter 14

THOUGH Charles and Mary had remained at Lyme much longer after Mr. and Mrs. Musgrove's going than Anne conceived they could have been at all wanted, they were yet the first of the family to be at home again; and as soon as possible after their return to Uppercross they drove over to the Lodge. They had left Louisa beginning to sit up; but her head, though clear, was exceedingly weak, and her nerves susceptible to the highest extreme of tenderness; and though she might be pronounced to be altogether doing very well, it was still impossible to say when she might be able to bear the removal home; and her father and mother, who must return in time to receive their younger children for the Christmas holidays, had hardly a hope of being allowed to bring her with them.

They had been all in lodgings together. Mrs. Musgrove had got Mrs. Harville's children away as much as she could, every possible supply from Uppercross had been furnished, to lighten the inconvenience to the Harvilles, while the Harvilles had been wanting them to come to dinner every day; and, in short, it seemed to have been only a struggle on each side, as to which should be most disinterested and hospitable.

Mary had had her evils; but upon the whole, as was evident by her staying so long, she had found more to enjoy than to suffer. Charles Hayter had been at Lyme oftener than suited her; and when they dined with the Harvilles there had been only a maid-servant to wait, and at first Mrs. Harville had always given Mrs. Musgrove precedence; but then she had received so very handsome an apology from her on finding out whose daughter she was, and there had been so much going on every day, there had been so many walks between their lodgings and the Harvilles, and she had got books from the library, and changed them so often, that the balance had certainly been much in favour of Lyme. She had been taken to Charmouth too, and she had bathed, and she had gone to church, and there were a great many more people to look at in the church at Lyme than at Uppercross; and all this, joined to the sense of being so very useful, had made really an agreeable fortnight.

Anne inquired after Captain Benwick. Mary's face was clouded directly. Charles laughed.

"Oh! Captain Benwick is very well, I believe, but he is a very odd young man. I do not know what he would be at. We asked him to come home with us for a day or two: Charles undertook to give him some shooting, and he seemed quite delighted, and, for my part, I thought it was all settled, when, behold! on Tuesday night, he made a very awkward sort of an excuse; 'he never shot,' and he had 'been quite misunderstood,' and he had promised this and he had promised that, and the end of it was, I found, that he did not mean to come. I suppose he was afraid of finding it dull; but upon my word I should have thought we were lively enough at the Cottage for such a heartbroken man as Captain Benwick."

Charles laughed again, and said, "Now, Mary, you know very well how it really was. It was all your doing" (turning to Anne). "He fancied that if he went with us he should find you close by: he fancied everybody to be living in Uppercross; and when he discovered that Lady Russell lived three miles off, his heart failed him, and he had not courage to come. That is the fact, upon my honour. Mary knows it is."

But Mary did not give into it very graciously. whether from not considering Captain Benwick entitled by birth and situation to be in love with an Elliot, or from not wanting to believe Anne a greater attraction to Uppercross than herself, must be left to be guessed. Anne's goodwill, however, was not to be lessened by what she heard. She boldly acknowledged herself flattered, and continued her enquiries.

"Oh! he talks of you," cried Charles, "in such terms——" Mary interrupted him. "I declare, Charles I never heard him mention Anne twice all the time I was there. I declare, Anne, he never talks of you at all."

"No," admitted Charles, "I do not know that he ever does, in a general way; but, however, it is a very clear thing that he admires you exceedingly. His head is full of some books that he is reading upon your recommendation, and he wants to talk to you about them; he has found out something or other in one of them which he thinks—oh! I cannot pretend to remember it, but it was something very fine—I overheard him telling Henrietta all about it; and then 'Miss Elliot' was spoken of in the highest terms! Now, Mary, I declare it was so, I heard it myself, and you were in the other room. 'Elegance, sweetness, beauty.' Oh! there was no end of Miss Elliot's charms."

"And I am sure," cried Mary, warmly, "it was very little to his credit if he did. Miss Harville only died last June. Such a heart is very little worth having, is it, Lady Russell? I am sure you will agree with me."

"I must see Captain Benwick before I decide," said Lady Russell, smiling.

"And that you are very likely to do very soon, I can tell you, ma'am," said Charles. "Though he had not nerves for coming away with us, and setting off again afterwards to pay a formal visit here, he will make his way over to Kellynch one day by himself, you may depend on it. I told him the distance and the road, and I told him of the church's being so very well worth seeing; for as he has a taste for those sort of things, I thought that would be a good excuse, and he listened with all his understanding and soul; and I am sure, from his manner, that you will have him calling here soon. So, I give you notice, Lady Russell."

"Any acquaintance of Anne's will be always welcome to me," was Lady Russell's kind answer.

"Oh! as to being Anne's acquaintance," said Mary, "I think he is rather my acquaintance, for I have been seeing him every day this last fortnight."

"Well, as your joint acquaintance, then, I shall be very happy to see Captain Benwick."

"You will not find anything very agreeable in him, I assure you, ma'am. He is one of the dullest young men that ever lived. He has walked with me, sometimes, from one end of the sands to the other, without saying a word. He is not at all a well-bred young man. I am sure you will not like him."

"There we differ, Mary," said Anne. "I think Lady Russell would like him. I think she would be so much pleased with his mind, that she would very soon see no deficiency in his manner."

"So do I, Anne," said Charles. "I am sure Lady Russell would like him. He is just Lady Russell's sort. Give him a book, and he will read all day long."

"Yes, that he will!" exclaimed Mary, tauntingly. "He will sit poring over his book, and not know when a person speaks to him, or when one drops one's scissors, or anything that happens. Do you think Lady Russell would like that?"

Lady Russell could not help laughing. "Upon my word," said she, "I should not have supposed that my opinion of any one could have admitted of such difference of conjecture, steady and matter of fact as I may call myself. I have really a curiosity to see the person who can give occasion to such directly opposite notions. I wish he may be induced to call here. And when he does, Mary, you may depend upon hearing my opinion; but I am determined not to judge him beforehand."

"You will not like him; I will answer for it."

Lady Russell began talking of something else. Mary spoke with animation of their meeting with, or rather missing Mr. Elliot so extraordinarily.

"He is a man," said Lady Russell, "whom I have no wish to see. His declining to be on cordial terms with the head of his family has left a very strong impression in his disfavour with me."

This decision checked Mary's eagerness, and stopped her short in the midst of the Elliot countenance.

With regard to Captain Wentworth, though Anne hazarded no enquiries, there was voluntary communication sufficient. His spirits had been greatly recovering lately, as might be expected. As Louisa improved, he had improved, and he was now quite a different creature from what he had been the first week. He had not seen Louisa; and was so extremely fearful of any ill consequence to her from an interview, that he did not press for it at all; and, on the contrary, seemed to have a plan of going away for a week or ten days, till her head was stronger. He had talked of going down to Plymouth for a week, and wanted to persuade Captain Benwick to go with him; but, as Charles maintained to the last, Captain Benwick seemed much more disposed to ride over to Kellynch.

There can be no doubt that Lady Russell and Anne were both occasionally thinking of Captain Benwick, from this time. Lady Russell could not hear the door-bell without feeling that it might be his herald; nor could Anne return from any stroll of solitary indulgence in her father's grounds, or any visit of charity in the village, without wondering whether she might see him or hear of him. Captain Benwick came not, however. He was either less disposed for it than Charles had imagined, or he was too shy; and after giving him a week's indulgence, Lady Russell determined him to be unworthy of the interest which he had been beginning to excite.

The Musgroves came back to receive their happy boys and girls from school, bringing with them Mrs. Harville's little children, to improve the noise of Uppercross, and lessen that of Lyme. Henrietta remained with Louisa, but all the rest of the family were again in their usual quarters.

Lady Russell and Anne paid their compliments to them once, when Anne could not but feel that Uppercross was already quite alive again. Though neither Henrietta, nor Louisa, nor Charles Hayter, nor Captain Wentworth were there, the room presented as strong a contrast as could be wished to the last state she had seen it in.

Immediately surrounding Mrs. Musgrove were the little Harvilles, whom she was sedulously guarding from the tyranny of the two children from the Cottage, expressly arrived to amuse them. On one side was a table occupied by some chattering girls, cutting up silk and gold paper; and on the other were tressels and trays, bending under the weight of brawn and cold pies, where riotous boys were holding high revel; the whole completed by a roaring Christmas fire, which seemed determined to be heard in spite of all the noise of the others. Charles and Mary also came in, of course, during their visit, and Mr. Musgrove made a point of paying his respects to Lady Russell, and sat down close to her for ten minutes, talking with a very raised voice, but, from the clamour of the children on his knees, generally in vain. It was a fine family-piece.

Anne, judging from her own temperament, would have deemed such a domestic hurricane a bad restorative of the nerves, which Louisa's illness must have so greatly shaken. But Mrs. Musgrove, who got Anne near her on purpose to thank her most cordially, again and again, for all her attentions to them, concluded a short recapitulation of what she had suffered herself by observing, with a happy glance round the room, that after all she had gone through, nothing was so likely to do her good as a little quiet cheerfulness at home.

Louisa was now recovering apace. Her mother could even think of her being able to join their party at home before her brothers and sisters went to school again. The Harvilles had promised to come with her and stay at Uppercross whenever she returned. Captain Wentworth was gone for the present, to see his brother in Shropshire.

"I hope I shall remember, in future," said Lady Russell, as soon as they were reseated in the carriage, "not to call at Uppercross in the Christmas holidays."

Everybody has their taste in noises as well as in other matters; and sounds are quite innoxious or most distressing, by their sort rather than their quantity. When Lady Russell, not long afterwards, was entering Bath on a wet afternoon, and driving through the long course of streets from the Old Bridge to Camden Place, midst the dash of other carriages, the heavy rumble of carts and drays, the bawling of newsmen, muffin-men, and milkmen, and the ceaseless clink of pattens, she made no complaint. No, these were noises which belonged to the winter pleasures; her spirits rose under their influence; and like Mrs. Musgrove, she was feeling, though not saying, that after being long in the country, nothing could be so good for her as a little quiet cheerfulness.

Anne did not share these feelings. She persisted in a very determined, though very silent disinclination for Bath; caught the first dim view of the extensive buildings, smoking in rain, without any wish of seeing them better; felt their progress through the streets to be, however disagreeable, yet too rapid; for who would be glad to see her when she arrived? And looked back with fond regret to the bustles of Uppercross and the seclusion of Kellynch.

Elizabeth's last letter had communicated a piece of news of some interest. Mr. Elliot was in Bath. He had called in Camden Place; had called a second time, a third; had been pointedly attentive. If Elizabeth and her father did not deceive themselves, had been taking as much pains to seek the acquaintance, and proclaim the value of the connection, as he had formerly taken pains to show neglect. This was very wonderful if it were true; and Lady Russell was in a state of very agreeable curiosity and perplexity about Mr. Elliot, already recanting the sentiment she had so lately expressed to Mary, of his being "a man whom she had no wish to see." She had a great wish to see him. If he really sought to reconcile himself like a dutiful branch, he must be forgiven for having dismembered himself from the paternal tree.

Anne was not animated to an equal pitch by the circumstance, but she felt that she would rather see Mr. Elliot again than not, which was more than she could say for many other persons in Bath.

She was put down in Camden Place, and Lady Russell then drove to her own lodgings in Rivers Street.

Chapter 15

Sir Walter had taken a very good house in Camden Place, a lofty, dignified situation, such as becomes a man of consequence; and both he and Elizabeth were settled there, much to their satisfaction.

Anne entered it with a sinking heart, anticipating an imprisonment of many months, and anxiously saying to herself, "Oh! when shall I leave you again?" A degree of unexpected cordiality, however, in the welcome she received, did her good. Her father and sister were glad to see her, for the sake of showing her the house and furniture, and met her with kindness. Her making a fourth, when they sat down to dinner, was noticed as an advantage.

Mrs. Clay was very pleasant and very smiling, but her courtesies and smiles were more a matter of course. Anne had always felt that she would pretend what was proper on her arrival, but the complaisance of the others was unlooked for. They were evidently in excellent spirits, and she was soon to listen to the causes. They had no inclination to listen to her. After laying out for some compliments of being deeply regretted in their old neighbourhood, which Anne could not pay, they had only a few faint enquiries to make, before the talk must be all their own. Uppercross excited no interest, Kellynch very little: it was all Bath.

They had the pleasure of assuring her that Bath more than answered their expectations in every respect. Their house was undoubtedly the best in Camden Place, their drawing-rooms had many decided advantages over all the others which they had either seen or heard of, and the superiority was not less in the style of the fitting-up or the taste of the furniture. Their acquaintance was exceedingly sought after. Everybody was wanting to visit them. They had drawn back from many introductions, and still were perpetually having cards left by people of whom they knew nothing.

Here were funds of enjoyment! Could Anne wonder that her father and sister were happy? She might not wonder, but she must sigh that her father should feel no degradation in his change, should see nothing to regret in the duties and dignity of the resident landholder, should find so much to be vain of in the littlenesses of a town; and she must sigh, and smile, and wonder too, as Elizabeth threw open the folding-doors, and walked with exultation from one drawing-room to the other, boasting of their space: at the possibility of that woman, who had been mistress of Kellynch Hall, finding extent to be proud of between two walls, perhaps thirty feet asunder.

But this was not all which they had to make them happy. They had Mr. Elliot too. Anne had a great deal to hear of Mr. Elliot. He was not only pardoned, they were delighted with him. He had been in Bath about a fortnight (he had passed through Bath in November, in his way to London, when the intelligence of Sir Walter's being settled there had of course reached him, though only twenty-four hours in the place, but he had not been able to avail himself of it) ; but he had now been a fortnight in Bath, and his first object on arriving had been to leave his card in Camden Place, following it up by such assiduous endeavours to meet, and when they did meet, by such great openness of conduct, such readiness to apologize for the past, such solicitude to be received as a relation again, that their former good understanding was completely re-established.

They had not a fault to find in him. He had explained away all the appearance of neglect on his own side. It had originated in misapprehension entirely. He had never had an idea of throwing himself off; he had feared that he was thrown off, but knew not why, and delicacy had kept him silent. Upon the hint of having spoken disrespectfully or carelessly of the family and the family honours, he was quite indignant. He, who had ever boasted of being an Elliot, and whose feelings, as to connection, were only too strict to suit the unfeudal tone of the present day. He was astonished, indeed, but his character and general conduct must refute it. He could refer Sir Walter to all who knew him; and certainly, the pains he had been taking on this, the first opportunity of reconciliation, to be restored to the footing of a relation and heir-presumptive, was a strong proof of his opinions on the subject.

The circumstances of his marriage, too, were found to admit of much extenuation. This was an article not to be entered on by himself; but a very intimate friend of his, a Colonel Wallis, a highly respectable man, perfectly the gentleman (and not an ill-looking man, Sir Walter added), who was living in very good style in Marlborough Buildings, and had, at his own particular request, been admitted to their acquaintance through Mr. Elliot, had mentioned one or two things relative to the marriage, which made a material difference in the discredit of it.

Colonel Wallis had known Mr. Elliot long, had been well acquainted also with his wife, had perfectly understood the whole story. She was certainly not a woman of family, but well educated, accomplished, rich, and excessively in love with his friend. There had been the charm. She had sought him. Without that attraction, not all her money would have tempted Elliot, and Sir Walter was, moreover, assured of her having been a very fine woman Here was a great deal to soften the business. A very fine woman with a large fortune, in love with him! Sir Walter seemed to admit it as complete apology; and though Elizabeth could not see the circumstance in quite so favourable a light, she allowed it to be a great extenuation.

Mr. Elliot had called repeatedly, had dined with them once, evidently delighted by the distinction of being asked for they gave no dinners in general; delighted, in short, by every proof of cousinly notice, and placing his whole happiness in being on intimate terms in Camden Place.

Anne listened, but without quite understanding it. Allowances, large allowances, she knew, must be made for the ideas of those who spoke. She heard it all under embellishment. All that sounded extravagant or irrational in the progress of the reconciliation might have no origin but in the language of the relators. Still, however, she had the sensation of there being something more than immediately appeared, in Mr. Elliot's wishing, after an interval of so many years. to be well received by them. In a worldly view, he had nothing to gain by being on terms with Sir Walter; nothing to risk by a state of variance. In all probability he was already the richer of the two, and the Kellynch estate would as surely be his hereafter as the title. A sensible man, and he had looked like a *very* sensible man, why should it be an object to him? She could only offer one solution: it was, perhaps, for Elizabeth's sake. There might really have been a liking formerly, though convenience and accident had drawn him a different way; and now that he could afford to please himself, he might mean to pay his addresses to her. Elizabeth was certainly very handsome, with well-bred, elegant manners, and her character might never have been penetrated by Mr. Elliot, knowing her but in public, and when very young himself. How her temper and understanding might bear the investigation of his present keener time of life was another concern and rather a fearful one. Most earnestly did she wish that he might not be too nice, or too observant if Elizabeth were his object; and that Elizabeth was disposed to believe herself so, and that her friend, Mrs. Clay, was encouraging

the idea, seemed apparent by a glance or two between them, while Mr.
Elliot's frequent visits were talked of.

Anne mentioned the glimpses she had had of him at Lyme, but without
being much attended to. "Oh! yes, perhaps, it had been Mr. Elliot. They
did not know. It might be him, perhaps." They could not listen to her
description of him. They were describing him themselves; Sir Walter
especially. He did justice to his very gentleman-like appearance, his air
of elegance and fashion, his good-shaped face, his sensible eye; but, at the
same time, "must lament his being very much under-hung, a defect which
time seemed to have increased; nor could he pretend to say that the years
had not altered almost every feature for the worse. Mr. Elliot appeared to
think that he (Sir Walter) was looking exactly as he had done when they
last parted;" but Sir Walter had "not been able to return the compliment
entirely, which had embarrassed him. He did not mean to complain, however. Mr. Elliot was better to look at than most men, and he had no
objection to being seen with him anywhere."

Mr. Elliot, and his friends in Marlborough Buildings, were talked of
the whole evening. "Colonel Wallis had been so impatient to be introduced to them! and Mr. Elliot so anxious that he should!" and there was
a Mrs. Wallis, at present known only to them by description, as she was in
daily expectation of her confinement; but Mr. Elliot spoke of her as "a
most charming woman, quite worthy of being known in Camden Place,"
and as soon as she recovered they were to be acquainted. Sir Walter
thought much of Mrs. Wallis; she was said to be an excessively pretty
woman, beautiful. "He longed to see her. He hoped she might make some
amends for the many very plain faces he was continually passing in the
streets. The worst of Bath was the number of its plain women. He did
not mean to say that there were no pretty women, but the number of the
plain was out of all proportion. He had frequently observed, as he walked,
that one handsome face would be followed by thirty, or five-and-thirty
frights; and once, as he had stood in a shop in Bond Street, he had counted
eighty-seven women go by, one after another, without there being a
tolerable face among them. It had been a frosty morning, to be sure, a
sharp frost, which hardly one woman in a thousand could stand the test
of. But still, there certainly were a dreadful multitude of ugly women in
Bath; and as for the men! they were infinitely worse. Such scarecrows
as the streets were full of! It was evident how little the women were
used to the sight of anything tolerable, by the effect which a man of
decent appearance produced. He had never walked anywhere arm-in-
arm with Colonel Wallis (who was a fine military figure, though sandy-
haired) without observing that every woman's eye was upon him; every
woman's eye was sure to be upon Colonel Wallis." Modest Sir Walter!
He was not allowed to escape, however. His daughter and Mrs. Clay
united in hinting that Colonel Wallis' companion might have as good
a figure as Colonel Wallis, and certainly was not sandy-haired.

"How is Mary looking?" said Sir Walter, in the height of his good humour. "The last time I saw her she had a red nose, but I hope that may not happen every day."

"Oh! no, that must have been quite accidental. In general she has been in very good health and very good looks since Michaelmas."

"If I thought it would not tempt her to go out in sharp winds, and grow coarse, I would send her a new hat and pelisse."

Anne was considering whether she should venture to suggest that a gown, or a cap, would not be liable to any such misuse, when a knock at the door suspended everything. "A knock at the door! and so late! It was ten o'clock. Could it be Mr. Elliot? They knew he was to dine in Lansdown Crescent. It was possible that he might stop in his way home to ask them how they did. They could think of no one else. Mrs. Clay decidedly thought it Mr. Elliot's knock." Mrs. Clay was right. With all the state which a butler and foot-boy could give, Mr. Elliot was ushered into the room.

It was the same, the very same man, with no difference but of dress. Anne drew a little back, while the others received his compliments, and her sister his apologies for calling at so unusual an hour, but "he could not be so near without wishing to know that neither she nor her friend had taken cold the day before," etc., etc.; which was all as politely done, and as politely taken, as possible, but her part must follow then. Sir Walter talked of his youngest daughter; "Mr. Elliot must give him leave to present him to his youngest daughter" (there was no occasion for remembering Mary); and Anne, smiling and blushing, very becomingly showed to Mr. Elliot the pretty features which he had by no means forgotten, and instantly saw, with amusement at his little start of surprise, that he had not been at all aware of who she was. He looked completely astonished, but not more astonished than pleased: his eyes brightened! and with the most perfect alacrity he welcomed the relationship, alluded to the past, and entreated to be received as an acquaintance already. He was quite as good-looking as he had appeared at Lyme, his countenance improved by speaking, and his manners were so exactly what they ought to be, so polished, so easy, so particularly agreeable, that she could compare them in excellence to only one person's manners. They were not the same, but they were, perhaps, equally good.

He sat down with them, and improved their conversation very much. There could be no doubt of his being a sensible man. Ten minutes were enough to certify that. His tone, his expressions, his choice of subject, his knowing where to stop: it was all the operation of a sensible, discerning mind. As soon as he could, he began to talk to her of Lyme, wanting to compare opinions respecting the place, but especially wanting to speak of the circumstance of their happening to be guests in the same inn at the same time; to give his own route, understand something of hers, and regret that he should have lost such an opportunity of paying his respects to her. She gave him a short account of her party and business at Lyme. His regret increased as he listened. He had spent his whole solitary evening in the room adjoining theirs; had heard voices, mirth continually; thought they must be a most delightful set of people, longed to be with them, but certainly without the smallest suspicion of his possessing the shadow of a right to introduce himself. If he had but asked who the party were! The name of Musgrove would have told him enough. "Well, it would serve to cure him of an absurd practice of never asking a question at an inn, which he had adopted, when quite a young man, on the principle of its being very ungenteel to be curious."

"The notions of a young man of one or two and twenty," said he, "as to what is necessary in manners to make him quite the thing, are more absurd, I believe, than those of any other set of beings in the world. The folly of the means they often employ is only to be equalled by the folly of what they have in view."

But he must not be addressing his reflections to Anne alone: he knew it; he was soon diffused again among the others, and it was only at intervals that he could return to Lyme.

His enquiries, however, produced at length an account of the scene she had been engaged in there, soon after his leaving the place. Having alluded to "an accident," he must hear the whole. When he questioned, Sir Walter and Elizabeth began to question also, but the difference in their manner of doing it could not be unfelt. She could only compare Mr. Elliot to Lady Russell, in the wish of really comprehending what had passed, and in the degree of concern for what she must have suffered in witnessing it.

He stayed an hour with them. The elegant little clock on the mantelpiece had struck "eleven with its silver sounds," and the watchman was beginning to be heard at a distance telling the same tale, before Mr. Elliot or any of them seemed to feel that he had been there long.

Anne could not have supposed it possible that her first evening in Camden Place could have passed so well.

Chapter 16

THERE was one point which Anne, on returning to her family, would have been more thankful to ascertain even than Mr. Elliot's being in love with Elizabeth, which was, her father's not being in love with Mrs. Clay; and she was very far from easy about it, when she had been at home a few hours. On going down to breakfast the next morning she found there had just been a decent pretence on the lady's side of meaning to leave them. She could imagine Mrs. Clay to have said, that "now Miss Anne was come, she could not suppose herself at all wanted;" for Elizabeth was replying in a sort of whisper, "That must not be any reason, indeed. I assure you I feel it none. She is nothing to me, compared with you;" and she was in full time to hear her father say, "My dear madam, this must not be. As yet, you have seen nothing of Bath. You have been here only to be useful. You must not run away from us now. You must stay to be acquainted with Mrs. Wallis, the beautiful Mrs. Wallis. To your fine mind, I well know the sight of beauty is a real gratification."

He spoke and looked so much in earnest, that Anne was not surprised to see Mrs. Clay stealing a glance at Elizabeth and herself. Her countenance, perhaps, might express some watchfulness; but the praise of the fine mind did not appear to excite a thought in her sister. The lady could not but yield to such joint entreaties, and promise to stay.

In the course of the same morning, Anne and her father chancing to be alone together, he began to compliment her on her improved looks; he thought her "less thin in her person, in her cheeks; her skin, her complexion greatly improved; clearer, fresher. Had she been using anything in particular?" "No, nothing." "Merely Gowland," he supposed. "No, nothing at all." "Ha! he was surprised at that;" and added, "certainly you cannot do better than continue as you are; you cannot be better than well; or I should recommend Gowland, the constant use of Gowland, during the spring months. Mrs. Clay has been using it at my recommendation, and you see what it has done for her. You see how it has carried away her freckles."

If Elizabeth could but have heard this! Such personal praise might have struck her, especially as it did not appear to Anne that the freckles were at all lessened. But everything must take its chance. The evil of the marriage would be much diminished, if Elizabeth were also to marry. As for herself, she might always command a home with Lady Russell.

Lady Russell's composed mind and polite manners were put to some trial on this point, in her intercourse in Camden Place. The sight of Mrs. Clay in such favour, and of Anne so overlooked, was a perpetual provocation to her there; and vexed her as much when she was away, as a person in Bath who drinks the water, gets all the new publications, and has a very large acquaintance, has time to be vexed.

As Mr. Elliot became known to her, she grew more charitable, or more indifferent, towards the others. His manners were an immediate recommendation; and on conversing with him she found the solid so fully supporting the superficial, that she was at first, as she told Anne, almost ready to exclaim: "Can this be Mr. Elliot?" and could not seriously picture to herself a more agreeable or estimable man. Everything united in him; good understanding, correct opinions, knowledge of the world, and a warm heart. He had strong feelings of family attachment and family honour, without pride or weakness; he lived with the liberality of a man of fortune, without display; he judged for himself in everything essential, without defying public opinion in any point of world decorum. He was steady, observant, moderate, candid; never run away with by spirits or by selfishness, which fancied itself strong feeling; and yet, with a sensibility to what was amiable and lovely, and a value for all the felicities of domestic life, which characters of fancied enthusiasm and violent agitation seldom really possess. She was sure that he had not been happy in marriage. Colonel Wallis said it, and Lady Russell saw it; but it had been no unhappiness to sour his mind, nor (she began pretty soon to suspect) to prevent his thinking of a second choice. Her satisfaction in Mr. Elliot outweighed all the plague of Mrs. Clay.

It was now some years since Anne had begun to learn that she and her excellent friend could sometimes think differently; and it did not surprise her, therefore, that Lady Russell should see nothing suspicious or inconsistent, nothing to require more motives than appeared in Mr. Elliot's great desire of a reconciliation. In Lady Russell's view, it was perfectly natural that Mr. Elliot, at a mature time of life, should feel it a most desirable object, and what would very generally recommend him among all sensible people, to be on good terms with the head of his family; the simplest process in the world of time upon a head naturally clear, and only erring in the heyday of youth. Anne presumed, however, still to smile about it, and at last to mention "Elizabeth." Lady Russell listened, and looked, and made only this cautious reply:—"Elizabeth! very well; time will explain."

It was a reference to the future, which Anne, after a little observation, felt she must submit to. She could determine nothing at present. In that house Elizabeth must be first; and she was in the habit of such general observance as "Miss Elliot," that any particularity of attention seemed almost impossible. Mr. Elliot, too, it must be remembered, had not been a widower seven months. A little delay on his side might be very excusable. In fact, Anne could never see the crape round his hat, without fearing that she was the inexcusable one, in attributing to him such imaginations; for though his marriage had not been very happy, still it had existed so many years that she could not comprehend a very rapid recovery from the awful impression of its being dissolved.

However it might end, he was without any question their pleasantest acquaintance in Bath: she saw nobody equal to him; and it was a great indulgence now and then to talk to him about Lyme, which he seemed to have as lively a wish to see again, and to see more of, as herself. They went through the particulars of their first meeting a great many times. He gave her to understand that he had looked at her with some earnestness. She knew it well; and she remembered another person's look also.

They did not always think alike. His value for rank and connection she perceived to be greater than hers. It was not merely complaisance, it must be a liking to the cause, which made him enter warmly into her father and sister's solicitudes on a subject which she thought unworthy to excite them. The Bath paper one morning announced the arrival of the Dowager Viscountess Dalrymple, and her daughter, the Honourable Miss Carteret; and all the comfort of No. —— Camden Place, was swept away for many days; for the Dalrymples (in Anne's opinion, most unfortunate) were cousins of the Elliots; and the agony was how to introduce themselves properly.

Anne had never seen her father and sister before in contact with nobility, and she must acknowledge herself disappointed. She had hoped better things from their high ideas of their own situation in life, and was reduced to form a wish which she had never foreseen; a wish that they had more pride; for "our cousins, Lady Dalrymple and Miss Carteret;" "our cousins the Dalrymples," sounded in her ears all day long.

Sir Walter had once been in company with the late viscount, but had never seen any of the rest of the family; and the difficulties of the case arose from there having been a suspension of all intercourse by letters of ceremony, ever since the death of that said late viscount, when, in consequence of a dangerous illness of Sir Walter's at the same time, there had been an unlucky omission at Kellynch. No letter of condolence had been sent to Ireland. The neglect had been visited on the head of the sinner; for when poor Lady Elliot died herself, no letter of condolence was received at Kellynch, and, consequently, there was but too much reason to apprehend that the Dalrymples considered the relationship as closed. How to have this anxious business set to rights, and be admitted as cousins again, was the question: and it was a question which, in a more rational manner, neither Lady Russell nor Mr. Elliot thought unimportant. "Family connections were always worth preserving, good company always worth seeking; Lady Dalrymple had taken a house, for three months, in Laura Place, and would be living in style. She had been at Bath the year before, and Lady Russell had heard her spoken of as a charming woman. It was very desirable that the connection should be renewed, if it could be done, without any compromise of propriety on the side of the Elliots."

Sir Walter, however, would choose his own means and at last wrote a very fine letter of ample explanation, regret, and entreaty, to his right honourable cousin. Neither Lady Russell nor Mr. Elliot could admire the letter; but it did all that was wanted, in bringing three lines of scrawl from the Dowager Viscountess. "She was very much honoured, and should be happy in their acquaintance." The toils of the business were over, the sweets began. They visited in Laura Place, they had the cards of Dowager Viscountess Dalrymple, and the Honourable Miss Carteret, to be arranged wherever they might be most visible: and "Our cousins in Laura Place,"—"Our cousins, Lady Dalrymple and Miss Carteret," were talked of to everybody.

Anne was ashamed. Had Lady Dalrymple and her daughter even been very agreeable, she would still have been ashamed of the agitation they created, but they were nothing. There was no superiority of manner, accomplishment, or understanding. Lady Dalrymple had acquired the name of "a charming woman," because she had a smile and a civil answer for everybody. Miss Carteret, with still less to say, was so plain and so awkward, that she would never have been tolerated in Camden Place but for her birth.

Lady Russell confessed that she had expected something better; but yet "it was an acquaintance worth having;" and when Anne ventured to speak her opinion of them to Mr. Elliot, he agreed to their being nothing in themselves, but still maintained that, as a family connection, as good company, as those who would collect good company around them, they had their value. Anne smiled and said:

"My idea of good company, Mr. Elliot, is the company of clever, well-informed people, who have a great deal of conversation; that is what I call good company."

"You are mistaken," said he, gently, "that is not good company; that is the best. Good company requires only birth, education, and manners, and with regard to education is not very nice. Birth and good manners are essential; but a little learning is by no means a dangerous thing in good company; on the contrary, it will do very well. My cousin Anne shakes her head. She is not satisfied. She is fastidious. My dear cousin" (sitting down by her), "you have a better right to be fastidious than almost any other woman I know; but will it answer? Will it make you happy? Will it not be wiser to accept the society of these good ladies in Laura Place, and enjoy all the advantages of the connection as far as possible? You may depend upon it, that they will move in the first set in Bath this winter, and as rank is rank, your being known to be related to them will have its use in fixing your family (our family let me say) in that degree of consideration which we must all wish for."

"Yes," sighed Anne, "we shall, indeed, be known to be related to them!" then recollecting herself, and not wishing to be answered she added, "I certainly do think there has been by far too much trouble taken to procure the acquaintance. I suppose" (smiling) "I have more pride than any of you; but I confess it does vex me, that we should be so solicitous to have the relationship acknowledged, which we may be very sure is a matter of perfect indifference to them."

"Pardon me, my dear cousin, you are unjust to your own claims. In London, perhaps, in your present quiet style of living, it might be as you say; but in Bath, Sir Walter Elliot and his family will always be worth knowing: always acceptable as acquaintance."

"Well," said Anne, "I certainly am proud, too proud to enjoy a welcome which depends so entirely upon place."

"I love your indignation," said he; "it is very natural. But here you are in Bath, and the object is to be established here with all the credit and dignity which ought to belong to Sir Walter Elliot. You talk of being proud; I am called proud, I know, and I shall not wish to believe myself otherwise; for our pride, if investigated, would have the same object, I have no doubt, though the kind may seem a little different. In one point I am sure, my dear cousin" (he continued, speaking lower, though there was no one else in the room), "in one point I am sure we must feel alike. We must feel that every addition to your father's society, among his equals or superiors, may be of use in diverting his thoughts from those who are beneath him."

He looked as he spoke, to the seat which Mrs. Clay had been lately occupying: a sufficient explanation of what he particularly meant; and

though Anne could not believe in their having the same sort of pride, she
was pleased with him for not liking Mrs. Clay; and her conscience admitted that his wishing to promote her father's getting great acquaintance
was more than excusable in the view of defeating her.

Chapter 17

WHILE Sir Walter and Elizabeth were assiduously pushing their good
fortune in Laura Place, Anne was renewing an acquaintance of a very
different description.

She had called on her former governess, and had heard from her of there
being an old schoolfellow in Bath, who had the two strong claims on her
attention of past kindness and present suffering. Miss Hamilton, now Mrs.
Smith, had shown her kindness in one of those periods of her life when it
had been most valuable. Anne had gone unhappy to school, grieving for
the loss of a mother whom she had dearly loved, feeling her separation
from home, and suffering as a girl of fourteen, of strong sensibility and not
high spirits, must suffer at such a time; and Miss Hamilton, three years
older than herself, but still from the want of near relations and a settled
home, remaining another year at school, had been useful and good to her
in a way which had considerably lessened her misery, and could never be
remembered with indifference.

Miss Hamilton had left school, had married not long afterwards, was
said to have married a man of fortune, and this was all that Anne had
known of her, till now that their governess's account brought her situation
forward in a more decided but very different form.

She was a widow and poor. Her husband had been extravagant; and at
his death, about two years before, had left his affairs dreadfully involved.
She had had difficulties of every sort to contend with, and in addition to
these distresses had been afflicted with a severe rheumatic fever, which,
finally settling in her legs, had made her for the present a cripple. She had
come to Bath on that account, and was now in lodgings near the hot baths,
living in a very humble way, unable even to afford herself the comfort of
a servant, and of course almost excluded from society.

Their mutual friend answered for the satisfaction which a visit from
Miss Elliot would give Mrs. Smith, and Anne therefore lost no time in
going. She mentioned nothing of what she had heard, or what she intended
at home. It would excite no proper interest there. She only consulted Lady
Russell, who entered thoroughly into her sentiments, and was most happy
to convey her as near to Mrs. Smith's lodgings, in Westgate Buildings, as
Anne chose to be taken.

The visit was paid, their acquaintance re-established, their interest in
each other more than rekindled. The first ten minutes had its awkwardness and its emotion. Twelve years were gone since they had parted, and
each presented a somewhat different person from what the other had

imagined. Twelve years had changed Anne from the blooming, silent unformed girl of fifteen, to the elegant little woman of seven-and-twenty, with every beauty excepting bloom, and with manners as consciously right as they were invariably gentle; and twelve years had transformed the fine-looking, well-grown Miss Hamilton, in all the glow of health and confidence of superiority, into a poor, infirm, helpless widow, receiving the visit of her former protégée as a favour; but all that was uncomfortable in the meeting had soon passed away, and left only the interesting charm of remembering former partialities and talking over old times.

Anne found in Mrs. Smith the good sense and agreeable manners which she had almost ventured to depend on, and a disposition to converse and be cheerful beyond her expectation. Neither the dissipations of the past—and she had lived very much in the world—nor the restrictions of the present, neither sickness nor sorrow seemed to have closed her heart or ruined her spirits.

In the course of a second visit she talked with great openness, and Anne's astonishment increased. She could scarcely imagine a more cheerless situation in itself than Mrs. Smith's. She had been very fond of her husband: she had buried him. She had been used to affluence: it was gone. She had no child to connect her with life and happiness again, no relations to assist in the arrangement of perplexed affairs, no health to make all the rest supportable. Her accommodations were limited to a noisy parlour, and a dark bedroom behind, with no possibility of moving from one to the other without assistance, which there was only one servant in the house to afford, and she never quitted the house but to be conveyed into the warm bath. Yet, in spite of all this, Anne had reason to believe that she had moments only of languor and depression to hours of occupation and enjoyment. How could it be? She watched, observed, reflected, and finally determined that this was not a case of fortitude or of resignation only. A submissive spirit might be patient, a strong understanding would supply resolution, but here was something more; here was that elasticity of mind, that disposition to be comforted, that power of turning readily from evil to good, and of finding employment which carried her out of herself, which was from nature alone. It was the choicest gift of Heaven; and Anne viewed her friend as one of those instances in which, by a merciful appointment, it seems designed to counterbalance almost every other want.

There had been a time, Mrs. Smith told her, when her spirits had nearly failed. She could not call herself an invalid now, compared with her state on first reaching Bath. Then she had, indeed, been a pitiable object; for she had caught cold on the journey, and had hardly taken possession of her lodgings before she was again confined to her bed, and suffering under severe and constant pain; and all this among strangers, with the absolute necessity of having a regular nurse, and finances at that moment particularly unfit to meet any extraordinary expense. She had weathered it, however, and could truly say that it had done her good. It had increased her comforts by making her feel herself to be in good hands. She had seen

too much of the world to expect sudden or disinterested attachment anywhere, but her illness had proved to her that her landlady had a character
to preserve, and would not use her ill; and she had been particularly
fortunate in her nurse, as a sister of her landlady, a nurse by profession,
and who had always a home in that house when unemployed, chanced to
be at liberty just in time to attend her. "And she," said Mrs. Smith,
"besides nursing me most admirably, has really proved an invaluable
acquaintance. As soon as I could use my hands she taught me to knit,
which has been a great amusement; and she put me in the way of making
these little thread-cases, pin-cushions, and card-racks, which you always
find me so busy about, and which supply me with the means of doing a
little good to one or two very poor families in this neighbourhood. She
has a large acquaintance, of course professionally, among those who can
afford to buy, and she disposes of my merchandise. She always takes the
right time for applying. Everybody's heart is open, you know, when they
have recently escaped from severe pain, or are recovering the blessing of
health, and Nurse Rooke thoroughly understands when to speak. She is a
shrewd, intelligent, sensible woman. Hers is a line for seeing human
nature; and she has a fund of good sense and observation, which, as a
companion, make her infinitely superior to thousands of those who, having
only received 'the best education in the world,' know nothing worth
attending to. Call it gossip, if you will, but when Nurse Rooke has half an
hour's leisure to bestow on me, she is sure to have something to relate that
is entertaining and profitable: something that makes one know one's
species better. One likes to hear what is going on, to be *au fait* as to the
newest modes of being trifling and silly. To me, who live so much alone,
her conversation, I assure you, is a treat."

Anne, far from wishing to cavil at the pleasure, replied, "I can easily
believe it. Women of that class have great opportunities, and if they are
intelligent may be well worth listening to. Such varieties of human nature
as they are in the habit of witnessing! And it is not merely in its follies
that they are well read; for they see it occasionally under every circumstance that can be most interesting or affecting. What instances must pass
before them of ardent, disinterested, self-denying attachment, of heroism,
fortitude, patience, resignation; of all the conflicts and all the sacrifices
that ennoble us most. A sick chamber may often furnish the worth of
volumes."

"Yes," said Mrs. Smith, more doubtingly, "sometimes it may, though I
fear its lessons are not often in the elevated style you describe. Here and
there, human nature may be great in times of trial; but generally speaking
it is its weakness and not its strength that appears in a sick chamber: it is
selfishness and impatience, rather than generosity and fortitude, that one
hears of. There is so little real friendship in the world! and unfortunately"
(speaking low and tremulously), "there are so many who forget to think
seriously till it is almost too late."

Anne saw the misery of such feelings. The husband had not been what he ought, and the wife had been led among that part of mankind which made her think worse of the world than she hoped it deserved. It was but a passing emotion, however, with Mrs. Smith; she shook it off, and soon added in a different tone:

"I do not suppose the situation my friend Mrs. Rooke is in at present will furnish much either to interest or edify me. She is only nursing Mrs. Wallis, of Marlborough Buildings; a mere pretty, silly, expensive, fashionable woman, I believe; and of course will have nothing to report but of lace and finery. I mean to make my profit of Mrs. Wallis, however. She has plenty of money, and I intend she shall buy all the high-priced things I have in hand now."

Anne had called several times on her friend, before the existence of such a person was known in Camden Place. At last, it became necessary to speak of her. Sir Walter, Elizabeth and Mrs. Clay, returned one morning from Laura Place, with a sudden invitation from Lady Dalrymple for the same evening, and Anne was already engaged to spend that evening in Westgate Buildings. She was not sorry for the excuse. They were only asked, she was sure, because Lady Dalrymple, being kept at home by a bad cold, was glad to make use of the relationship which had been so pressed on her; and she declined on her own account with great alacrity: "She was engaged to spend the evening with an old schoolfellow." They were not much interested in anything relative to Anne; but still there were questions enough asked to make it understood what this old schoolfellow was; and Elizabeth was disdainful! and Sir Walter severe.

"Westgate Buildings!" said he; "and who is Miss Anne Elliott to be visiting in Westgate Buildings? A Mrs. Smith. A widow Mrs. Smith; and who was her husband? One of the five thousand Mr. Smiths whose names are to be met with everywhere. And what is her attraction? That she is old and sickly. Upon my word, Miss Anne Elliot, you have the most extraordinary taste! Everything that revolts other people, low company, paltry rooms, foul air, disgusting associations, are inviting to you. But surely you may put off this old lady till to-morrow; she is not so near her end, I presume, but that she may hope to see another day. What is her age? Forty?"

"No, sir, she is not one-and-thirty; but I do not think I can put off my engagement, because it is the only evening for some time which will at once suit her and myself. She goes into the warm bath to-morrow; and for the rest of the week, you know, we are engaged."

"But what does Lady Russell think of this acquaintance?" asked Elizabeth.

"She sees nothing to blame in it," replied Anne; "on the contrary, she approves it, and has generally taken me when I have called on Mrs. Smith."

"Westgate Buildings must have been rather surprised by the appearance of a carriage drawn up near its pavement," observed Sir Walter. "Sir Henry Russell's widow, indeed, has no honours to distinguish her arms, but still it is a handsome equipage, and no doubt is well known to convey a Miss Elliot. A widow Mrs. Smith, lodging in Westgate Buildings! A poor widow, barely able to live, between thirty and forty; a mere Mrs. Smith, an every-day Mrs. Smith, of all people and all names in the world, to be the chosen friend of Miss Anne Elliot, and to be preferred by her to her own family connections among the nobility of England and Ireland! Mrs. Smith! Such a name!"

Mrs. Clay, who had been present while all this passed, now thought it advisable to leave the room, and Anne could have said much, and did long to say a little in defence of *her* friend's not very dissimilar claims to theirs, but her sense of personal respect to her father prevented her. She made no reply. She left it to himself to recollect, that Mrs. Smith was not the only widow in Bath between thirty and forty, with little to live on, and no surname of dignity.

Anne kept her appointment, the others kept theirs, and of course she heard the next morning that they had had a delightful evening. She had been the only one of the set absent, for Sir Walter and Elizabeth had not only been quite at her ladyship's service themselves, but had actually been happy to be employed by her in collecting others, and had been at the trouble of inviting both Lady Russell and Mr. Elliot; and Mr. Elliot had made a point of leaving Colonel Wallis early, and Lady Russell had fresh arranged all her evening engagements, in order to wait on her. Anne had the whole history of all that such an evening could supply from Lady Russell. To her, its greatest interest must be, in having been very much talked of between her friend and Mr. Elliot; in having been wished for, regretted, and at the same time honoured for staying away in such a cause. Her kind, compassionate visits to this old schoolfellow, sick and reduced, seemed to have quite delighted Mr. Elliot. He thought her a most extraordinary young woman: in her temper, manners, mind, a model of female excellence. He could meet even Lady Russell in a discussion of her merits; and Anne could not be given to understand so much by her friend, could not know herself to be so highly rated by a sensible man, without many of those agreeable sensations which her friend meant to create.

Lady Russell was now perfectly decided in her opinion of Mr. Elliot. She was as much convinced of his meaning to gain Anne in time as of his deserving her, and was beginning to calculate the number of weeks which would free him from all the remaining restraints of widowerhood, and leave him at liberty to exert his most open powers of pleasing. She would not speak to Anne with half the certainty she felt on the subject, she would venture on little more than hints of what might be hereafter, of a possible attachment on his side, of the desirableness of the alliance, supposing such an attachment to be real and returned. Anne heard her, and made no violent exclamations; she only smiled, blushed, and gently shook her head.

"I am no match-maker, as you well know," said Lady Russell, "being much too well aware of the uncertainty of all human events and calcu lations. I only mean that if Mr. Elliot should some time hence pay his addresses to you, and if you should be disposed to accept him, I think there would be every possibility of your being happy together. A most suitable connection everybody must consider it, but I think it might be a very happy one."

"Mr. Elliot is an exceedingly agreeable man, and in many respects I think highly of him," said Anne; "but we should not suit."

Lady Russell let this pass, and only said in rejoinder, "I own that to be able to regard you as the future mistress of Kellynch, the future Lady Elliot, to look forward and see you occupying your dear mother's place, succeeding to all her rights, and all her popularity, as well as to all her virtues, would be the highest possible gratification to me. You are your mother's self in countenance and disposition; and if I might be allowed to fancy you such as she was, in situation, and name, and home, presiding and blessing in the same spot, and only superior to her in being more highly valued, my dearest Anne, it would give me more delight than is often felt at my time of life."

Anne was obliged to turn away, to rise, to walk to a distant table, and, leaning there in pretended employment, try to subdue the feelings this picture excited. For a few moments her imagination and her heart were bewitched. The idea of becoming what her mother had been; of having the precious name of "Lady Elliot" first revived in herself; of being restored to Kellynch, calling it her home again, her home for ever, was a charm which she could not immediately resist. Lady Russell said not another word, willing to leave the matter to its own operation; and believing that, could Mr. Elliot at that moment with propriety have spoken for himself! —she believed, in short, what Anne did not believe. The same image of Mr. Elliot speaking for himself brought Anne to composure again. The charm of Kellynch and of "Lady Elliot" all faded away. She never could accept him. And it was not only that her feelings were still adverse to any man save one; her judgment, on a serious consideration of the possibilities of such a case, was against Mr. Elliot.

Though they had now been acquainted a month, she could not be satisfied that she really knew his character. That he was a sensible man, an agreeable man, that he talked well, professed good opinions, seemed to judge properly and as a man of principle, this was all clear enough. He certainly knew what was right, nor could she fix on any one article of moral duty evidently transgressed; but yet she would have been afraid to answer for his conduct. She distrusted the past, if not the present. The names which occasionally dropped of former associates, the allusions to former practices and pursuits, suggested suspicions not favourable of what he had been. She saw that there had been bad habits; that Sunday travelling had been a common thing; that there had been a period of his life (and probably not a short one) when he had been, at least, careless on all serious matters; and, though he might now think very differently, who could answer for the true sentiments of a clever, cautious man, grown old enough to appreciate a fair character? How could it ever be ascertained that his mind was truly cleansed?

Mr. Elliot was rational, discreet, polished, but he was not open. There was never any burst of feeling, any warmth of indignation or delight, at the evil or good of others. This, to Anne, was a decided imperfection. Her early impressions were incurable. She prized the frank, the open-hearted, the eager character beyond all others. Warmth and enthusiasm did captivate her still. She felt that she could so much more depend upon the sincerity of those who sometimes looked or said a careless or a hasty thing, than of those whose presence of mind never varied, whose tongue never slipped.

Mr. Elliot was too generally agreeable. Various as were the tempers in her father's house, he pleased them all. He endured too well, stood too well with everybody. He had spoken to her with some degree of openness of Mrs. Clay; had appeared completely to see what Mrs. Clay was about, and to hold her in contempt; and yet Mrs. Clay found him as agreeable as anybody.

Lady Russell saw either less or more than her young friend, for she saw nothing to excite distrust. She could not imagine a man more exactly what he ought to be than Mr. Elliot; nor did she ever enjoy a sweeter feeling than the hope of seeing him receive the hand of her beloved Anne in Kellynch church, in the course of the following autumn.

Chapter 18

It was the beginning of February; and Anne, having been a month in Bath, was growing very eager for news from Uppercross and Lyme. She wanted to hear much more than Mary communicated. It was three weeks since she had heard at all. She only knew that Henrietta was at home again; and that Louisa, though considered to be recovering fast, was still at Lyme; and she was thinking of them all very intently one evening, when a thicker letter than usual from Mary was delivered to her; and, to quicken the pleasure and surprise, with Admiral and Mrs. Croft's compliments.

The Crofts must be in Bath! A circumstance to interest her. They were people whom her heart turned to very naturally.

"What is this?" cried Sir Walter. "The Crofts arrived in Bath? The Crofts who rent Kellynch? What have they brought you?"

"A letter from Uppercross Cottage, sir."

"Oh! those letters are convenient passports. They secure an introduction. I should have visited Admiral Croft, however, at any rate. I know what is due to my tenant."

Anne could listen no longer; she could not even have told how the poor Admiral's complexion escaped; her letter engrossed her. It had been begun several days back.

February 1st——.

"MY DEAR ANNE,—I make no apology for my silence, because I know how little people think of letters in such a place as Bath. You must be a great deal too happy to care for Uppercross, which, as you well know, affords little to write about. We have had a very dull Christmas; Mr. and Mrs. Musgrove have not had one dinner-party all the holidays. I do not reckon the Hayters as anybody. The holidays, however, are over at last: I believe no children ever had such long ones. I am sure I had not. The house was cleared yesterday, except of the little Harvilles; but you will be surprised to hear that they have never gone home. Mrs. Harville must be an odd mother to part with them so long. I do not understand it. They are not at all nice children, in my opinion; but Mrs. Musgrove seems to like them quite as well, if not better, than her grandchildren. What dreadful weather we have had! It may not be felt in Bath, with your nice pavements; but in the country it is of some consequence. I have not had a creature call on me since the second week in January, except Charles Hayter, who has been calling much oftener than was welcome. Between ourselves, I think it a great pity Henrietta did not remain at Lyme as long as Lousia; it would have kept her a little out of his way. The carriage is gone to-day, to bring Lousia and the Harvilles to-morrow. We are not asked to dine with them, however, till the day after, Mrs. Musgrove is so afraid of her being fatigued by the journey, which is not very likely, considering the care that will be taken of her; and it would be much more convenient to me to dine there to-morrow. I am glad you find Mr. Elliot so agreeable, and wish I could be acquainted with him too; but I have my usual luck: I am always out of the way when anything desirable is going on; always the last of my family to be noticed. What an immense time Mrs. Clay has been staying with Elizabeth! Does she never mean to go away? But, perhaps, if she were to leave the room vacant, we might not be invited. Let me know what you think of this. I do not expect my children to be asked, you know. I can leave them at the Great House very well, for a month or six weeks. I have this moment heard that the Crofts are going to Bath almost immediately: they think the Admiral gouty. Charles heard it quite by chance: they have not had the civility to give me any notice, or offer to take anything. I do not think they improve at all as neighbours. We see nothing of them, and this is really an instance of gross inattention. Charles joins me in love, and everything proper. Yours affectionately,

"MARY M——.

"I am sorry to say that I am very far from well; and Jemima has just told me that the butcher says there is a bad sore-throat very much about. I dare say I shall catch it; and my sore-throats, you know, are always worse than anybody's."

So ended the first part, which had been afterwards put into an envelope, containing nearly as much more.

"I kept my letter open, that I might send you word how Lousia bore her journey, and now I am extremely glad I did, having a great deal to add. In the first place, I had a note from Mrs. Croft yesterday, offering to convey anything to you; a very kind, friendly note indeed, addressed to me, just as it ought; I shall therefore be able to make my letter as long as I like. The Admiral does not seem very ill, and I sincerely hope Bath will do him all the good he wants. I shall be truly glad to have them back again. Our neighbourhood cannot spare such a pleasant family. But now for Louisa. I have something to communicate that will astonish you not a little. She and the Harvilles came on Tuesday very safely, and in the evening we went to ask her how she did, when we were rather surprised not to find Captain Benwick of the party, for he had been invited as well as the Harvilles; and what do you think was the reason? Neither more nor less than his being in love with Louisa, and not choosing to venture to Uppercross till he had had an answer from Mr. Musgrove; for it was all settled between him and her before she came away, and he had written to her father by Captain Harville. True, upon my honour! Are not you astonished? I shall be surprised at least if you ever received a hint of it, for I never did. Mrs. Musgrove protests solemnly that she knew nothing of the matter. We are all very well pleased, however; for though it is not equal to her marrying Captain Wentworth, it is infinitely better than Charles Hayter; and Mr. Musgrove has written his consent, and Captain Benwick is expected to-day. Mrs. Harville says her husband feels a good deal on his poor sister's account; but, however, Louisa is a great favourite with both. Indeed, Mrs. Harville and I quite agree that we love her the better for having nursed her. Charles wonders what Captain Wentworth will say; but if you remember, I never thought him attached to Louisa; I never could see anything of it. And this is the end, you see, of Captain Benwick's being supposed to be an admirer of yours. How Charles could take such a thing into his head was always incomprehensible to me. I hope he will be more agreeable now. Certainly not a great match for Louisa Musgrove, but a million times better than marrying among the Hayters."

Mary need not have feared her sister's being in any degree prepared for the news. She had never in her life been more astonished. Captain Benwick and Louisa Musgrove! It was almost too wonderful for belief, and it was with the greatest effort that she could remain in the room, preserve an air of calmness, and answer the common questions of the moment. Happily for her, they were not many. Sir Walter wanted to know whether the Crofts travelled with four horses, and whether they were likely to be situated in such a part of Bath as it might suit Miss Elliot and himself to visit in; but had little curiosity beyond.

"How is Mary?" said Elizabeth; and without waiting for an answer, "And pray what brings the Crofts to Bath?"

"They come on the Admiral's account. He is thought to be gouty."

"Gout and decrepitude!" said Sir Walter. "Poor old gentleman!"

"Have they any acquaintances here?" asked Elizabeth.

"I do not know; but I can hardly suppose that, at Admiral Croft's time of life, and in his profession, he should not have many acquaintances in such a place as this."

"I suspect," said Sir Walter, coolly, "that Admiral Croft will be best known in Bath as the renter of Kellynch Hall. Elizabeth, may we venture to present him and his wife in Laura Place?"

"Oh no! I think not. Situated as we are with Lady Dalrymple, cousins, we ought to be very careful not to embarrass her with acquaintances she might not approve. If we were not related it would not signify; but as cousins, she would feel scrupulous as to any proposal of ours. We had better leave the Crofts to find their own level. There are several odd-looking men walking about here, who, I am told, are sailors. The Crofts will associate with them."

This was Sir Walter and Elizabeth's share of interest in the letter; when Mrs. Clay had paid her tribute of more decent attention, in an enquiry after Mrs. Charles Musgrove and her fine little boys, Anne was at liberty.

In her own room she tried to comprehend it. Well might Charles wonder how Captain Wentworth would feel! Perhaps he had quitted the field, had given Louisa up, had ceased to love, had found he did not love her. She could not endure the idea of treachery or levity, or anything akin to ill usage between him and his friend. She could not endure that such a friendship as theirs should be severed unfairly.

Captain Benwick and Louisa Musgrove! The high-spirited, joyous-talking Louisa Musgrove, and the dejected, thinking, feeling, reading Captain Benwick, seemed each of them everything that would not suit the other. Their minds most dissimilar! Where could have been the attraction? The answer soon presented itself. It had been in situation. They had been thrown together several weeks; they had been living in the same small family party: since Henrietta's coming away, they must have been depending almost entirely on each other, and Louisa, just recovering from illness, had been in an interesting state, and Captain Benwick was not inconsolable. That was a point which Anne had not been able to avoid suspecting before; and instead of drawing the same conclusion as Mary, from the present course of events, they served only to confirm the idea of his having felt some dawning of tenderness toward herself. She did not mean, however, to derive much more from it to gratify her vanity than Mary might have allowed. She was persuaded that any tolerably pleasing young woman who had listened and seemed to feel for him would have received the same compliment. He had an affectionate heart. He must love somebody.

She saw no reason against their being happy. Louisa had fine naval fervour to begin with, and they would soon grow more alike. He would gain cheerfulness, and she would learn to be an enthusiast for Scott and Lord Byron; nay, that was probably learnt already; of course they had fallen in love over poetry. The idea of Lo   Musgrove turned into a person of literary taste and sentimental reflection was amusing, but she had no doubt of its being so. The day at Lyme, the fall from the Cobb, might influence her health, her nerves, her courage, her character to the end of her life, as thoroughly as it appeared to have influenced her fate.

The conclusion of the whole was, that if the woman who had been sensible of Captain Wentworth's merits could be allowed to prefer another man, there was nothing in the engagement to excite lasting wonder; and if Captain Wentworth lost no friend by it, certainly nothing to be regretted. No, it was not regret which made Anne's heart beat in spite of herself, and brought the colour into her cheeks when she thought of Captain Wentworth unshackled and free. She had some feelings which she was ashamed to investigate. They were too much like joy, senseless joy!

She longed to see the Crofts; but when the meeting took place, it was evident that no rumour of the news had yet reached them. The visit of ceremony was paid and returned; and Louisa Musgrove was mentioned, and Captain Benwick, too, without even half a smile.

The Crofts had placed themselves in lodgings in Gay Street, perfectly to Sir Walter's satisfaction. He was not at all ashamed of the acquaintance, and did, in fact, think and talk a great deal more about the Admiral than the Admiral ever thought or talked about him.

The Crofts knew quite as many people in Bath as they wished for, and considered their intercourse with the Elliots as a mere matter of form, and not in the least likely to afford them any pleasure. They brought with them their country habit of being always together. He was ordered to walk to keep off the gout, and Mrs. Croft seemed to go shares with him in everything, and to walk for her life to do him good. Anne saw them wherever she went. Lady Russell took her out in her carriage almost every morning, and she never failed to think of them, and never failed to see them. Knowing their feelings as she did, it was a most attractive picture of happiness to her. She always watched them as long as she could, delighted to fancy she understood what they might be talking of, as they walked along in happy independence, or equally delighted to see the Admiral's hearty shake of the hand when he encountered an old friend, and observe their eagerness of conversation when occasionally forming into a little knot of the navy, Mrs. Croft looking as intelligent and keen as any of the officers around her.

Anne was too much engaged with Lady Russell to be often walking herself; but it so happened that one morning, about a week or ten days after the Crofts' arrival, it suited her best to leave her friend, or her friend's carriage, in the lower part of the town, and return alone to Camden Place, and in walking up Milsom Street she had the good fortune to meet with the Admiral. He was standing by himself, at a printshop window, with his hands behind him, in earnest contemplation of some print, and she not only might have passed him unseen, but was obliged to touch as well as address him before she could catch his notice. When he did perceive and acknowledge her, however, it was done with all his usual frankness and good-humour. "Ha! is it you? Thank you, thank you. This is treating me like a friend. Here I am, you see, staring at a picture. I can never get by this shop without stopping. But what a thing here is, by way of a boat! Do look at it. Did you ever see the like? What queer fellows your fine painters must be, to think that anybody would venture their lives in such a shapeless old cockle-shell as that? And yet here are two gentlemen stuck up in it mightily at their ease, and looking about them at the rocks and mountains, as if they were not to be upset the next moment, which they certainly must be. I wonder where that boat was built!" (laughing heartily); "I would not venture over a horsepond in it. Well" (turning away), "now, where are you bound? Can I go anywhere for you, or with you? Can I be of any use?"

"None, I thank you, unless you will give me the pleasure of your company the little way our road lies together. I am going home."

"That I will, with all my heart, and further too. Yes, yes, we will have a snug walk together, and I have something to tell you as we go along. There, take my arm; that's right; I do not feel comfortable if I have not a woman there. Lord! what a boat it is!" taking a last look at the picture, as they began to be in motion.

"Did you say that you had something to tell me, sir?"

"Yes, I have, presently. But here comes a friend, Captain Brigden; I shall only say, 'How d'ye do?' as we pass, however. I shall not stop. 'How d'ye do?' Brigden stares to see anybody with me but my wife. She, poor soul, is tied by the leg. She has a blister on one of her heels, as large as a three-shilling piece. If you look across the street, you will see Admiral Brand coming down and his brother. Shabby fellows, both of them! I am glad they are not on this side of the way. Sophy cannot bear them. They played me a pitiful trick once: got away some of my best men. I will tell you the whole story another time. There comes old Sir Archibald Drew and his grandson. Look, he sees us; he kisses his hand to you; he takes you for my wife. Ah! the peace has come too soon for that younker. Poor old Sir Archibald! How do you like Bath, Miss Elliot? It suits us very well. We are always meeting with some old friend or other; the streets full of them every morning; sure to have planty of chat; and then we get away from them all, and shut ourselves into our lodgings, and draw in our chairs, and are as snug as if we were at Kellynch, ay, or as we used to be even at North Yarmouth and Deal. We do not like our lodgings here the worse, I can tell you, for putting us in mind of those we first had at North Yarmouth. The wind blows through one of the cupboards just in the same way."

When they were got a little further, Anne ventured to press again for what he had to communicate. She had hoped when clear of Milsom Street to have her curiosity gratified; but she was still obliged to wait, for the Admiral had made up his mind not to begin till they had gained the greater space and quiet of Belmont; and as she was not really Mrs. Croft, she must let him have his own way. As soon as they were fairly ascending Belmont, he began:

"Well, now you shall hear something that will surprise you. But first of all, you must tell me the name of the young lady I am going to talk about. That young lady, you know, that we have all been so concerned for. The Miss Musgrove that all this has been happening to. Her Christian name: I always forget her Christian name."

Anne had been ashamed to appear to comprehend so soon as she really did; but now she could safely suggest the name of "Louisa."

"Ay, ay, Miss Louisa Musgrove, that is the name. I wish young ladies had not such a number of fine Christian names. I should never be out if they were all Sophys, or something of that sort. Well, this Miss Louisa, we all thought, you know, was to marry Frederick. He was courting her week after week. The only wonder was, what they could be waiting for, till the business at Lyme came; then, indeed, it was clear enough that they must wait till her brain was set to right. But even then there was something odd in their way of going on. Instead of staying at Lyme, he went off to Plymouth, and then he went off to see Edward. When we came back from Minehead he was gone down to Edward's, and there he has been ever since. We have seen nothing of him since November. Even Sophy could not understand it. But now, the matter has taken the strangest turn of all; for this young lady, this same Miss Musgrove, instead of being to marry Frederick, is to marry James Benwick. You know James Benwick?"

"A little. I am a little acquainted with Captain Benwick."

"Well, she is to marry him. Nay, most likely they are married already, for I do not know what they should wait for."

"I thought Captain Benwick a very pleasing young man," said Anne, "and I understand that he bears an excellent character."

"Oh! yes, yes, there is not a word to be said against James Benwick. He is only a commander, it is true, made last summer, and these are bad times for getting on, but he has not another fault that I know of. An excellent, good-hearted fellow, I assure you; a very active, zealous officer, too, which is more than you would think for, perhaps, for that soft sort of manner does not do him justice."

"Indeed, you are mistaken there, sir; I should never augur want of spirit from Captain Benwick's manners. I thought them particularly pleasing, and I will answer for it, they would generally please."

"Well, well, ladies are the best judges; but James Benwick is rather too piano for me; and though very likely it is all our partiality, Sophy and I cannot help thinking Frederick's manners better than his. There is something about Frederick more to our taste."

Anne was caught. She had only meant to oppose the too common idea of spirit and gentleness being incompatible with each other, not at all to represent Captain Benwick's manners as the very best that could possibly be; and, after a little hesitation, she was beginning to say, "I was not entering into any comparison of the two friends;" but the Admiral inter-rupted her with:

"And the thing is certainly true. It is not a mere bit of gossip. We have it from Frederick himself. His sister had a letter from him yesterday, in which he tells us of it, and he had just had it in a letter from Harville, written upon the spot, from Uppercross. I fancy they are all at Upper-cross."

This was an opportunity which Anne could not resist; she said, there-fore, "I hope, Admiral, I hope there is nothing in the style of Captain Wentworth's letter to make you and Mrs. Croft particularly uneasy. It did certainly seem, last autumn, as if there were an attachment between him and Louisa Musgrove; but I hope it may be understood to have worn out on each side equally, and without violence. I hope his letter does not breathe the spirit of an ill-used man."

"Not at all, not at all; there is not an oath or a murmur from beginning to end."

Anne looked down to hide her smile.

"No, no; Frederick is not a man to whine and complain; he has too much spirit for that. If the girl likes another man better, it is very fit she should have him."

"Certainly. But what I mean is, that I hope there is nothing in Captain Wentworth's manner of writing to make you suppose he thinks himself ill-used by his friend, which might appear, you know, without its being absolutely said. I should be very sorry that such a friendship as has sub-sisted between him and Captain Benwick should be destroyed, or even wounded by a circumstance of this sort."

"Yes, yes, I understand you. But there is nothing at all of that nature in the letter. He does not give the least fling at Benwick; does not so much as say, 'I wonder at it. I have a reason of my own for wondering at it.' No, you would not guess, from his way of writing, that he had ever thought of this Miss (what's her name?) for himself. He very handsomely hopes they will be happy together; and there is nothing very unforgiving in that, I think."

Anne did not receive the perfect conviction which the Admiral meant to convey, but it would have been useless to press the enquiry further. She therefore satisfied herself with commonplace remarks or quiet atten-tion, and the Admiral had it all his own way.

"Poor Frederick!" said he, at last. "Now he must begin all over again with somebody else. I think we must get him to Bath. Sophy must write, and beg him to come to Bath. Here are pretty girls enough, I am sure. It would be of no use to go to Uppercross again, for that other Miss Musgrove, I find, is bespoken by her cousin, the young parson. Do not you think, Miss Elliot, we had better try to get him to Bath?"

Chapter 19

WHILE Admiral Croft was taking this walk with Anne, and expressing his wish of getting Captain Wentworth to Bath, Captain Wentworth was already on his way thither. Before Mrs. Croft had written, he was arrived, and the very next time Anne walked out, she saw him.

Mr. Elliot was attending his two cousins and Mrs. Clay. They were in Milsom Street. It began to rain, not much, but enough to make shelter desirable for women, and quite enough to make it very desirable for Miss Elliot to have the advantage of being conveyed home in Lady Dalrymple's carriage, which was seen waiting at a little distance: she, Anne, and Mrs. Clay, therefore, turned into Molland's, while Mr. Elliot stepped to Lady Dalrymple, to request her assistance. He soon joined them again, success-ful, of course; Lady Dalrymple would be most happy to take them home, and would call for them in a few minutes.

Her ladyship's carriage was a barouche, and did not hold more than four with any comfort. Miss Carteret was with her mother; consequently it was not reasonable to expect accommodation for all the three Camden Place ladies. There could be no doubt as to Miss Elliot. Whoever suffered incon-venience, she must suffer none, but it occupied a little time to settle the point of civility between the other two. The rain was a mere trifle, and Anne was most sincere in preferring a walk with Mr. Elliot. But the rain was also a mere trifle to Mrs. Clay; she would hardly allow it even to drop at all, and her boots were so thick! much thicker than Miss Anne's; and, in short, her civility rendered her quite as anxious to be left to walk with Mr. Elliot as Anne could be, and it was discussed between them with a generosity so polite and so determined, that the others were obliged to settle it for them; Miss Elliot maintaining that Mrs. Clay had a little cold already, and Mr. Elliot, deciding, on appeal, that his cousin Anne's boots were rather the thickest.

It was fixed, accordingly, that Mrs. Clay should be of the party in the carriage; and they had just reached this point, when Anne, as she sat near the window, descried, most decidedly and distinctly, Captain Wentworth walking down the street.

Her start was perceptible only to herself; but she instantly felt that she was the greatest simpleton in the world, the most unaccountable and absurd! For a few minutes she saw nothing before her: it was all confusion. She was lost, and when she had scolded back her senses, she found the others still waiting for the carriage, and Mr. Elliot (always obliging) just setting off for Union Street on a commission of Mrs. Clay's.

She now felt a great inclination to go to the outer door; she wanted to see if it rained. Why was she to suspect herself of another motive? Captain Wentworth must be out of sight. She left her seat, she would go; one half of her should not be always so much wiser than the other half, or always suspecting the other of being worse than it was. She would see if it rained.

She was sent back, however, in a moment, by the entrance of Captain Wentworth himself, among a party of gentlemen and ladies, evidently his acquaintances, and whom he must have joined a little below Milsom Street. He was more obviously struck and confused by the sight of her than she had ever observed before; he looked quite red. For the first time since their renewed acquaintance, she felt that she was betraying the least sensibility of the two. She had the advantage of him in the preparation of the last few moments. All the overpowering, blinding, bewildering, first effects of strong surprise were over with her. Still, however, she had enough to feel! It was agitation, pain, pleasure; a something between delight and misery.

He spoke to her, and then turned away. The character of his manner was embarrassment. She could not have called it either cold or friendly, or anything so certainly as embarrassed.

After a short interval, however, he came towards her, and spoke again. Mutual enquiries on common subjects passed: neither of them, probably, much the wiser for what they heard, and Anne continuing fully sensible of his being less at ease than formerly. They had, by dint of being so very much together, got to speak to each other with a considerable portion of apparent indifference and calmness; but he could not do it now. Time had changed him, or Louisa had changed him. There was consciousness of some sort or other. He looked very well, not as if he had been suffering in health or spirits, and he talked of Uppercross, of the Musgroves, nay, even of Louisa, and had even a momentary look of his own arch significance as he named her; but yet it was Captain Wentworth not comfortable, not easy, not able to feign that he was.

It did not surprise, but it grieved Anne to observe that Elizabeth would not know him. She saw that he saw Elizabeth, that Elizabeth saw him, that there was complete internal recognition on each side; she was convinced that he was ready to be acknowledged as an acquaintance, expecting it, and she had the pain of seeing her sister turn away with unalterable coldness.

Lady Dalrymple's carriage, for which Miss Elliot was growing very impatient, now drew up; the servant came to announce it. It was beginning to rain again, and altogether there was a delay, and a bustle, and a talking, which must make all the little crowd in the shop understand that Lady Dalrymple was calling to convey Miss Elliot. At last Miss Elliot and her friend, unattended but by the servant (for there was no cousin returned), were walking off; and Captain Wentworth, watching them, turned again to Anne, and by manner, rather than words, was offering his services to her.

"I am much obliged to you," was her answer, "but I am not going with them. The carriage would not accommodate so many. I walk: I prefer walking."

"But it rains."

"Oh! very little. Nothing that I regard."

After a moment's pause, he said: "Though I came only yesterday, I have equipped myself properly for Bath already, you see" (pointing to a new umbrella); "I wish you would make us of it, if you are determined to walk; though I think it would be more prudent to let me get you a chair."

She was very much obliged to him, but declined it all, repeating her conviction that the rain would come to nothing at present, and adding, "I am only waiting for Mr. Elliot. He will be here in a moment, I am sure."

She had hardly spoken the words when Mr. Elliot walked in. Captain Wentworth recollected him perfectly. There was no difference between him and the man who had stood on the steps at Lyme, admiring Anne as she passed, except in the air and look, and manner of the privileged relation and friend. He came in with eagerness, appeared to see and think only of her, apologised for his stay, was grieved to have kept her waiting, and anxious to get her away without further loss of time, and before the rain increased; and in another moment they walked off together, her arm under his, a gentle and embarrassed glance, and a "Good morning to you!" being all that she had time for, as she passed away.

As soon as they were out of sight, the ladies of Captain Wentworth's party began talking of them.

"Mr. Elliot does not dislike his cousin, I fancy?"

"Oh! no, that is clear enough. One can guess what will happen there. He is always with them; half lives in the family, I believe. What a very good-looking man!"

"Yes, and Miss Atkinson, who dined with him once at the Wallises, says he is the most agreeable man she ever was in company with."

"She is pretty, I think, Anne Elliot; very pretty when one comes to look at her. It is not the fashion to say so, but I confess I admire her more than her sister."

"Oh! so do I."

"And so do I. No comparison. But the men are all wild after Miss Elliot. Anne is too delicate for them."

Anne would have been particularly obliged to her cousin if he would have walked by her side all the way to Camden Place without saying a word. She had never found it so difficult to listen to him, though nothing could exceed his solicitude and care, and though his subjects were principally such as were wont to be always interesting: praise, warm, just and discriminating, of Lady Russell, and insinuations highly rational against Mrs. Clay. But just now she could think only of Captain Wentworth. She could not understand his present feelings, whether he were really suffering much from disappointment or not; and till that point were settled, she could not be quite herself.

She hoped to be wise and reasonable in time; but alas! alas! she must confess to herself that she was not wise yet.

Another circumstance very essential for her to know was, how long he meant to be in Bath; he had not mentioned it, or she could not recollect it. He might be only passing through. But it was more probable that he should be come to stay. In that case, so liable as everybody was to meet everybody in Bath, Lady Russell would in all likelihood see him somewhere. Would she recollect him? How would it all be?

She had already been obliged to tell Lady Russell that Louisa Musgrove was to marry Captain Benwick. It had cost her something to encounter Lady Russell's surprise; and now, if she were by any chance to be thrown into company with Captain Wentworth, her imperfect knowledge of the matter might add another shade of prejudice against him.

The following morning Anne was out with her friend, and for the first hour, in an incessant and fearful sort of watch for him in vain; but at last, in returning down Pulteney Street, she distinguished him on the right hand pavement at such a distance as to have him in view the greater part of the street. There were many other men about him, many groups walking the same way, but there was no mistaking him. She looked instinctively at Lady Russell, but not from any mad idea of her recognising him so soon as she did herself. No, it was not to be supposed that Lady Russell would perceive him till they were nearly opposite. She looked at her, however, from time to time, anxiously; and when the moment approached which must point him out, though not daring to look again (for her own countenance she knew was unfit to be seen), she was yet perfectly conscious of Lady Russell's eyes being turned exactly in the direction for him—of her being, in short, intently observing him. She could thoroughly comprehend the sort of fascination he must possess over Lady Russell's mind, the difficulty it must be for her to withdraw her eyes, the astonishment she must be feeling that eight or nine years should have passed over him, and in foreign climes and in active service too, without robbing him of one personal grace!

At last, Lady Russell drew back her head. "Now, how would she speak of him?"

"You will wonder," said she, "what has been fixing my eye so long; but I was looking after some window-curtains, which Lady Alicia and Mrs. Frankland were telling me of last night. They described the drawing-room window-curtains of one of the houses on this side of the way, and this part of the street, as being the handsomest and best hung of any in Bath, but could not recollect the exact number, and I have been trying to find out which it could be; but I confess I can see no curtains hereabouts that answer their description."

Anne sighed, and blushed, and smiled, in pity and disdain, either at her friend or herself. The part which provoked her most, was that in all this waste of foresight and caution, she should have lost the right moment for seeing whether he saw them.

A day or two passed without producing anything. The theatre or the rooms, where he was most likely to be, were not fashionable enough for 'he Elliots, whose evening amusements were solely in the elegant stupidity of private parties, in which they were getting more and more engaged; and Anne, wearied of such a state of stagnation, sick of knowing nothing, and fancying herself stronger because her strength was not tried, was quite impatient for the concert evening. It was a concert for the benefit of a person patronised by Lady Dalrymple. Of course they must attend. It was really expected to be a good one, and Captain Wentworth was very fond of music. If she could only have a few minutes' conversation with him again, she fancied she should be satisfied; and as to the power of addressing him, she felt all over courage if the opportunity occurred. Elizabeth had turned from him, Lady Russell overlooked him; her nerves were strengthened by these circumstances; she felt that she owed him attention.

She had once partly promised Mrs. Smith to spend the evening with her; but in a short hurried call she excused herself and put it off, with the more decided promise of a longer visit on the morrow. Mrs. Smith gave a most good-humoured acquiescence.

"By all means," said she; "only tell me all about it, when you do come. Who is your party?"

Anne named them all. Mrs. Smith made no reply; but when she was leaving her said, and with an expression half serious, half arch, "Well, I heartily wish your concert may answer; and do not fail me to-morrow if you can come; for I begin to have a foreboding that I may not have many more visits from you."

Anne was startled and confused; but after standing in a moment's suspense, was obliged, and not sorry to be obliged, to hurry away.

Chapter 20

SIR WALTER, his two daughters, and Mrs. Clay, were the earliest of all their party at the rooms in the evening; and as Lady Dalrymple must be waited for, they took their station by one of the fires in the Octagon Room. But hardly were they so settled, when the door opened again, and Captain Wentworth walked in alone. Anne was the nearest to him, and making a little advance, she instantly spoke. He was preparing only to bow and pass on, but her gentle "How do you do?" brought him out of the straight line to stand near her, and make enquiries in return, in spite of the formidable father and sister in the background. Their being in the background was a support to Anne; she knew nothing of their looks, and felt equal to everything which she believed right to be done.

While they were speaking, a whispering between her father and Elizabeth caught her ear. She could not distinguish, but she must guess the subject; and on Captain Wentworth's making a distant bow, she comprehended that her father had judged so well as to give him that simple acknowledgment of acquaintance, and she was just in time by a side glance to see a slight curtsey from Elizabeth herself. This, though late, and reluctant, and ungracious, was yet better than nothing and her spirits improved.

After talking, however, of the weather, and Bath, and the concert, their conversation began to flag, and so little was said at last, that she was expecting him to go every moment, but he did not; he seemed in no hurry to leave her; and presently with renewed spirit, with a little smile, a little glow, he said:

"I have hardly seen you since our day at Lyme. I am afraid you must have suffered from the shock, and the more from its not overpowering you at the time."

She assured him that she had not.

"It was a frightful hour," said he, "a frightful day!" and he passed his hand across his eyes, as if the remembrance were still too painful, but in a moment, half smiling again, added, "The day has produced some effects, however; has had some consequences which must be considered as the very reverse of frightful. When you had the presence of mind to suggest that Benwick would be the properest person to fetch a surgeon, you could have little idea of his being eventually one of those most concerned in her recovery."

"Certainly I could have none. But it appears—I should hope it would be a very happy match. There are on both sides good principles and good temper."

"Yes," said he, looking not exactly forward; "but there, I think, ends the resemblance. With all my soul I wish them happy, and rejoice over every circumstance in favour of it. They have no difficulties to contend with at home, no opposition, no caprice, no delays. The Musgroves are behaving like themselves, most honourably and kindly, only anxious with true parental hearts to promote their daughter's comfort. All this is much, very much in favour of their happiness; more than perhaps——"

He stopped. A sudden recollection seemed to occur, and to give him some taste of that emotion which was reddening Anne's cheeks and fixing her eyes on the ground. After clearing his throat, however, he proceeded thus:

"I confess that I do think there is a disparity, too great a disparity, and in a point no less essential than mind. I regard Louisa Musgrove as a very amiable, sweet-tempered girl, and not deficient in understanding, but Benwick is something more. He is a clever man, a reading man; and I confess, that I do consider his attaching himself to her with some surprise. Had it been the effect of gratitude, had he learnt to love her, because he believed her to be preferring him, it would have been another thing. But I have no reason to suppose it so. It seems, on the contrary, to have been a perfectly spontaneous, untaught feeling on his side, and this surprises me. A man like him, in his situation! with a heart pierced, wounded, almost broken! Fanny Harville was a very superior creature, and his attachment to her was indeed attachment. A man does not recover from such a devotion of the heart to such a woman! He ought not; he does not."

Either from the consciousness, however, that his friend had recovered, or from some other consciousness, he went no further; and Anne who, in spite of the agitated voice in which the latter part had been uttered, and in spite of all the various noises of the room, the almost ceaseless slam of the door, and ceaseless buzz of persons walking through, had distinguished every word, was struck, gratified, confused, and beginning to breathe very quick, and feel a hundred things in a moment. It was impossible for her to enter on such a subject; and yet, after a pause, feeling the necessity of speaking, and having not the smallest wish for a total change, she only deviated so far as to say :

"You were a good while at Lyme, I think?"

"About a fortnight. I could not leave it till Louisa's doing well was quite ascertained. I had been too deeply concerned in the mischief to be soon at peace. It had been my doing, solely mine. She would not have been obstinate if I had not been weak. The country round Lyme is very fine. I walked and rode a great deal, and the more I saw, the more I found to admire."

"I should very much like to see Lyme again," said Anne.

"Indeed! I should not have supposed that you could have found any-thing in Lyme to inspire such a feeling. The horror and distress you were involved in, the stretch of mind, the wear of spirits! I should have thought your last impressions of Lyme must have been strong disgust."

"The last few hours were certainly very painful," replied Anne; "but when pain is over, the remembrance of it often becomes a pleasure. One does not love a place the less for having suffered in it, unless it has been all suffering, nothing but suffering, which was by no means the case at Lyme. We were only in anxiety and distress during the last two hours, and previously there had been a great deal of enjoyment. So much novelty and beauty! I have travelled so little, that every fresh place would be interesting to me; but there is real beauty at Lyme, and in short," with a faint blush at some recollections, "altogether my impressions of the place are very agreeable."

As she ceased, the entrance door opened again, and the very party appeared for whom they were waiting. "Lady Dalrymple, Lady Dal-rymple!" was the rejoicing sound; and with all the eagerness compatible with anxious elegance, Sir Walter and his two ladies stepped forward to meet her. Lady Dalrymple and Miss Carteret, escorted by Mr. Elliot and Colonel Wallis, who had happened to arrive nearly at the same instant, advanced into the room. The others joined them, and it was a group in which Anne found herself also necessarily included. She was divided from Captain Wentworth. Their interesting, almost too interesting conversa-tion, must be broken up for a time, but slight was the penance compared with the happiness which brought it on! She had learnt, in the last ten minutes, more of his feelings towards Louisa, more of all his feelings, than she dared to think of; and she gave herself up to the demands of the party, to the needful civilities of the moment, with exquisite, though agitated sensations. She was in good humour with all. She had received ideas which disposed her to be courteous and kind to all, and to pity every one, as being less happy than herself.

The delightful emotions were a little subdued, when on stepping back from the group, to be joined again by Captain Wentworth, she saw that he was gone. She was just in time to see him turn into the Concert Room. He was gone; he had disappeared, she felt a moment's regret. But "they should meet again. He would look for her, he would find her out long before the evening was over, and at present, perhaps, it was as well to be asunder. She was in need of a little interval for recollection."

Upon Lady Russell's appearance soon afterwards, the whole party was collected, and all that remained was to marshal themselves, and proceed into the Concert Room; and be of all the consequence in their power, draw as many eyes, excite as many whispers, and disturb as many people as they could.

Very, very happy were both Elizabeth and Anne Elliot as they walked in. Elizabeth arm-in-arm with Miss Carteret, and looking on the broad back of the dowager Viscountess Dalrymple before her, had nothing to wish for which did not seem within her reach; and Anne—but it would be an insult to the nature of Anne's felicity to draw any comparison between it and her sister's; the origin of one all selfish vanity, of the other all generous attachment.

Anne saw nothing, thought nothing of the brilliancy of the room. Her happiness was from within. Her eyes were bright, and her cheeks glowed; but she knew nothing about it. She was thinking only of the last half hour, and as they passed to their seats, her mind took a hasty range over it. His choice of subjects, his expressions, and still more his manner and look, had been such as she could see in only one light. His opinion of Louisa Musgrove's inferiority, an opinion which he had seemed solicitous to give, his wonder at Captain Benwick, his feelings as to a first, strong attachment; sentences begun which he could not finish, his half-averted eyes and more than half-expressive glance, all, all declared that he had a heart returning to her at least; that anger, resentment, avoidance, were no more; and that they were succeeded, not merely by friendship and regard, but by the tenderness of the past. Yes, some share of the tenderness of the past! She could not contemplate the change as implying less. He must love her.

These were thoughts, with their attendant visions, which occupied and flurried her too much to leave her any power of observation; and she passed along the room without having a glimpse of him, without even trying to discern him. When their places were determined on, and they were all properly arranged, she looked round to see if he should happen to be in the same part of the room, but he was not; her eye could not reach him; and the concert being just opening, she must consent for a time to be happy in a humbler way.

The party was divided and disposed of on two contiguous benches:

Anne was among those on the foremost, and Mr. Elliot had manœuvred
so well, with the assistance of his friend Colonel Wallis, as to have a seat
by her. Miss Elliot, surrounded by her cousins, and the principal object
of Colonel Wallis's gallantry, was quite contented.

Anne's mind was in a most favourable state for the entertainment of
the evening; it was just occupation enough: she had feelings for the tender,
spirits for the gay, attention for the scientific, and patience for the wearisome; and had never liked a concert better, at least during the first act.
Towards the close of it, in the interval succeeding an Italian song, she
explained the words of the song to Mr. Elliot. They had a concert bill
between them.

"This," said she, "is nearly the sense, or rather the meaning of the
words, for certainly the sense of an Italian love-song must not b talked
of, but it is as nearly the meaning as I can give; for I do not pretend to
understand the language. I am a very poor Italian scholar."

"Yes, yes, I see you are. I see you know nothing of the matter. You
have only knowledge enough of the language to translate at sight these
inverted, transposed, curtailed Italian lines, into clear, comprehensbile,
elegant English. You need not say anything more of your ignorance. Here
is complete proof."

"I will not oppose such kind politeness; but I should be sorry to be
examined by a real proficient."

"I have not had the pleasure of visiting in Camden Place so long,"
replied he, "without knowing something of Miss Anne Elliot; and I do
regard her as one who is too modest for the world in general to be aware
of half her accomplishments, and too highly accomplished for modesty
to be natural in any other woman."

"For shame! For shame! This is too much of flattery. I forget what we
are to have next," turning to the bill.

"Perhaps," said Mr. Elliot, speaking low, "I have had a longer acquaintance with your character than you are aware of."

"Indeed! How so? You can have been acquainted with it only since I
came to Bath, excepting as you might hear me previously spoken of in
my own family."

"I knew you by report long before you came to Bath. I had heard you
described by those who knew you intimately. I have been acquainted with
you by character many years. Your person, your disposition, accomplishments, manner; they were all described, they were all present to me."

Mr. Elliot was not disappointed in the interest he hoped to raise. No
one can withstand the charm of such a mystery. To have been described
long ago to a recent acquaintance, by nameless people, is irresistible; and
Anne was all curiosity. She wondered, and questioned him eagerly; but
in vain. He delighted in being asked, but he would not tell.

"No, no, some time or other, perhaps, but not now. He would mention
no names now; but such, he could assure her, had been the fact. He had
many years ago received such a description of Miss Anne Elliot as had

inspired him with the highest idea of her merit, and excited the warmest curiosity to know her."

Anne could think of no one so likely to have spoken with partiality of her many years ago as the Mr. Wentworth of Monkford, Captain Wentworth's brother. He might have been in Mr. Elliot's company, but she had not courage to ask the question.

"The name of Anne Elliot," said he, "has long had an interesting sound to me. Very long has it possessed a charm over my fancy; and, if I dared, I would breathe my wishes that the name might never change."

Such, she believed, were his words; but scarcely had she received their sound, than her attention was caught by other sounds immediately behind her, which rendered everything else trivial. Her father and Lady Dalrymple were speaking.

"A well-looking man," said Sir Walter, "a very well-looking man."

"A very fine young man, indeed!" said Lady Dalrymple. "More air than one often sees in Bath. Irish, I dare say?"

"No, I just know his name. A bowing acquaintance. Wentworth, Captain Wentworth of the navy. His sister married my tenant in Somersetshire, the Croft, who rents Kellynch."

Before Sir Walter had reached this point, Anne's eyes had caught the right direction, and distinguished Captain Wentworth, standing among a cluster of men at a little distance. As her eyes fell on him, his seemed to be withdrawn from her. It had that appearance. It seemed as if she had been one moment too late; and as long as she dared observe, he did not look again; but the performance was recommencing, and she was forced to seem to restore her attention to the orchestra, and look straight forward.

When she could give another glance, he had moved away. He could not have come nearer to her if he would; she was so surrounded and shut in: but she would rather have caught his eye.

Mr. Elliot's speech, too, distressed her. She had no longer any inclination to talk to him. She wished him not so near her.

The first act was over. Now she hoped for some beneficial change; and, after a period of nothing-saying amongst the party, some of them did decide on going in quest of tea. Anne was one of the few who did not choose to move. She remained in her seat, and so did Lady Russell; but she had the pleasure of getting rid of Mr. Elliot ; and she did not mean, whatever she might feel on Lady Russell's account, to shrink from conversation with Captain Wentworth, if he gave her the opportunity. She was persuaded by Lady Russell's countenance that she had seen him.

He did not come, however. Anne sometimes fancied she discerned him at a distance, but he never came. The anxious interval wore away unproductively. The others returned, the room filled again, benches were reclaimed and repossessed, and another hour of pleasure or of penance was to be sat out, another hour of music was to give delight or the gapes, as real or affected taste for it prevailed. To Anne it chiefly wore the prospect of an hour of agitation. She could not quit that room in peace without

seeing Captain Wentworth once more, without the interchange of one
friendly look.

In re-settling themselves there were now many changes, the result of
which was favourable for her. Colonel Wallis declined sitting down again,
and Mr. Elliot was invited by Elizabeth and Miss Carteret, in a manner
not to be refused, to sit between them; and by some other removals, and
a little scheming of her own, Anne was enabled to place herself much
nearer the end of the bench than she had been before, much more within
reach of a passer-by. She could not do so, without comparing herself with
Miss Larolles, the inimitable Miss Larolles; but still she did it, and not
with much happier effect; though by what seemed prosperity in the shape
of an early abdication in her next neighbours, she found herself at the
very end of the bench before the concert closed.

Such was her situation, with a vacant space at hand, when Captain
Wentworth was again in sight. She saw him not far off. He saw her too;
yet he looked grave, and seemed irresolute, and only by very slow degrees
came at last near enough to speak to her. She felt that something must be
the matter. The change was indubitable. The difference between his
present air and what it had been in the Octagon Room was strikingly
great. Why was it? She thought of her father, of Lady Russell. Could there
have been any unpleasant glances? He began by speaking of the concert
gravely, more like the Captain Wentworth of Uppercross; owned himself
disappointed, had expected better singing; and, in short, must confess that
he should not be sorry when it was over. Anne replied, and spoke in defence of the performance so well, and yet in allowance for his feelings so
pleasantly, that his countenance improved, and he replied again with
almost a smile. They talked for a few minutes more; the improvement
held; he even looked down towards the bench, as if he saw a place on it
well worth occupying; when at that moment a touch on her shoulder
obliged Anne to turn round. It came from Mr. Elliot. He begged her
pardon, but she must be applied to, to explain Italian again. Miss Carteret
was very anxious to have a general idea of what was next to be sung.
Anne could not refuse; but never had she sacrificed to politeness with a
more suffering spirit.

A few minutes, though as few as possible, were inevitably consumed;
and when her own mistress again, when able to turn and look as she had
done before, she found herself accosted by Captain Wentworth, in a
reserved yet hurried sort of farewell. "He must wish her good night; he
was going; he should get home as fast as he could."

"Is not this song worth staying for?" said Anne, suddenly struck by an
idea which made her yet more anxious to be encouraging.

"No!" he replied, impressively, "there is nothing worth my staying
for;" and he was gone directly.

Jealousy of Mr. Elliot! It was the only intelligible motive. Captain
Wentworth jealous of her affection! Could she have believed it a week
ago; three hours ago! For a moment the gratification was exquisite. But,

alas! there were very different thoughts to succeed. How was such jealousy to be quieted? How was the truth to reach him? How, in all the peculiar disadvantages of their respective situations, would he ever learn her real sentiments? It was misery to think of Mr. Elliot's attentions. Their evil was incalculable.

Chapter 21

ANNE recollected with pleasure the next morning her promise of going to Mrs. Smith, meaning that it should engage her from home at the time when Mr. Elliot would be most likely to call, for to avoid Mr. Elliot was almost a first object.

She felt a great deal of goodwill towards him. In spite of the mischief of his attentions, she owed him gratitude and regard, perhaps compassion. She could not help thinking much of the extraordinary circumstances attending their acquaintance, of the right which he seemed to have to interest her, by everything in situation, by his own sentiments, by his early prepossession. It was altogether very extraordinary; flattering, but painful. There was much to regret. How she might have felt had there been no Captain Wentworth in the case, was not worth enquiry; for there was a Captain Wentworth; and be the conclusion of the present suspense good or bad, her affection would be his for ever. Their union, she believed, could not divide her more from other men than their final separation.

Prettier musings of high-wrought love and eternal constancy could never have passed along the streets of Bath than Anne was sporting with from Camden Place to Westgate Buildings. It was almost enough to spread purification and perfume all the way.

She was sure of a pleasant reception; and her friend seemed this morning particularly obliged to her for coming, seemed hardly to have expected her, though it had been an appointment.

An account of the concert was immediately claimed; and Anne's recollections of the concert were quite happy enough to animate her features and make her rejoice to talk of it. All that she could tell she told most gladly, but the all was little for one who had been there, and unsatisfactory for such an enquirer as Mrs. Smith, who had already heard, through the short cut of a laundress and a waiter, rather more of the general success and produce of the evening than Anne could relate, and who now asked in vain for several particulars of the company. Everybody of any consequence or notoriety in Bath was well known by name to Mrs. Smith.

"The little Durands were there, I conclude," said she, "with their mouths open to catch the music, like unfledged sparrows ready to be fed. They never miss a concert."

"Yes; I did not see them myself, but I heard Mr. Elliot say they were in the room."

"The Ibbotsons, were they there? and the two new beauties, with the tall Irish officer, who is talked of for one of them?"

"I do not know. I do not think they were."

"Old Lady Mary MacLean? I need not ask after her. She never misses, I know; and you must have seen her. She must have been in your own circle; for as you went with Lady Dalrymple, you were in the seats of grandeur, round the orchestra, of course."

"No, that was what I dreaded. It would have been very unpleasant to me in every respect. But happily Lady Dalrymple always chooses to be farther off; and we were exceedingly well placed, that is, for hearing; I must not say for seeing, because I appear to have seen very little."

"Oh! you saw enough for your own amusement. I can understand. There is a sort of domestic enjoyment to be known even in a crowd, and this you had. You were a large party in yourselves, and you wanted nothing beyond."

"But I ought to have looked about me more," said Anne, conscious while she spoke that there had in fact been no want of looking about, that the object only had been deficient.

"No, no; you were better employed. You need not tell me that you had a pleasant evening. I see it in your eye. I perfectly see how the hours passed: that you had always something agreeable to listen to. In the intervals of the concert it was conversation."

Anne half smiled and said, "Do you see that in my eye?"

"Yes, I do. Your countenance perfectly informs me that you were in company last night with the person whom you think the most agreeable in the world, the person who interests you at this present time more than all the rest of the world put together."

A blush overspread Anne's cheeks. She could say nothing.

"And such being the case," continued Mrs. Smith, after a short pause, "I hope you believe that I do know how to value your kindness in coming to me this morning. It is really very good of you to come and sit with me, when you must have so many pleasanter demands upon your time."

Anne heard nothing of this. She was still in the astonishment and confusion excited by her friend's penetration, unable to imagine how any report of Captain Wentworth could have reached her. After another short silence:

"Pray," said Mrs. Smith, "is Mr. Elliot aware of your acquaintance with me? Does he know that I am in Bath?"

"Mr. Elliot!" repeated Anne, looking up surprised. A moment's reflection showed her the mistake she had been under. She caught it instantaneously; and recovering courage with the feeling of safety, soon added, more composediy, "Are you acquainted with Mr. Elliot?"

"I have been a good deal acquainted with him," replied Mrs. Smith, gravely, "but it seems worn out now. It is a great while since we met."

"I was not at all aware of this. You never mentioned it before. Had I known it, I would have had the pleasure of talking to him about you."

"To confess the truth," said Mrs. Smith, assuming her usual air of cheerfulness, "that is exactly the pleasure I want you to have. I want you to talk about me to Mr. Elliot. I want your interest with him. He can be of essential service to me; and if you would have the goodness, my dear Miss Elliot, to make it an object to yourself, of course it is done."

"I should be extremely happy; I hope you cannot doubt my willingness to be of even the slightest use to you," replied Anne; "but I suspect that you are considering me as having a higher claim on Mr. Elliot, a greater right to influence him, than is really the case. I am sure you have, somehow or other, imbibed such a notion. You must consider me only as Mr. Elliot's relation. If in that light there is anything which you suppose his cousin might fairly ask of him, I beg you would not hesitate to employ me."

Mrs. Smith gave her a penetrating glance, and then, smiling, said:

"I have been a little premature, I perceive; I beg your pardon. I ought to have waited for official information. But now, my dear Miss Elliot, as an old friend, do give me a hint as to when I may speak. Next week? To be sure by next week I may be allowed to think it all settled, and build my own selfish schemes on Mr. Elliot's good fortune."

"No," replied Anne, "nor next week, nor next, nor next. I assure you that nothing of the sort you are thinking of will be settled any week. I am not going to marry Mr. Elliot. I should like to know why you imagine I am?"

Mrs. Smith looked at her again, looked earnestly, smiled, shook her head, and exclaimed:

"Now, how I do wish I understood you! How I do wish I knew what you were at! I have a great idea that you do not design to be cruel, when the right moment comes. Till it does come, you know, we women never mean to have anybody. It is a thing of course among us, that every man is refused, till he offers. But why should you be cruel? Let me plead for my—present friend I cannot call him, but for my former friend. Where can you look for a more suitable match? Where could you expect a more gentlemanlike, agreeable man? Let me recommend Mr. Elliot. I am sure you hear nothing but good of him from Colonel Wallis; and who can know him better than Colonel Wallis?"

"My dear Mrs. Smith, Mr. Elliot's wife has not been dead much above half a year. He ought not to be supposed to be paying his addresses to anyone."

"Oh, if these are your only objections," cried Mrs. Smith, archly, "Mr. Elliot is safe, and I shall give myself no more trouble about him. Do not forget me when you are married, that's all. Let him know me to be a friend of yours, and then he will think little of the trouble required, which it is very natural for him now, with so many affairs and engagements of his own, to avoid and get rid of as he can; very natural, perhaps. Ninety-nine out of a hundred would do the same. Of course, he cannot be aware of the importance to me. Well, my dear Miss Elliot, I hope and trust you will be very happy. Mr. Elliot has sense to understand the value of such

a woman. Your peace will not be shipwrecked as mine has been. You are safe in all worldly matters, and safe in his character. He will not be led astray; he will not be misled by others to his ruin."

"No," said Anne, "I can readily believe all that of my cousin. He seems to have a calm decided temper, not at all open to dangerous impressions. I consider him with great respect. I have no reason, from anything that has fallen within my observation, to do otherwise. But I have not known him long; and he is not a man, I think, to be known intimately soon. Will not this manner of speaking of him, Mrs. Smith, convince you that he is nothing to me? Surely this must be calm enough. And, upon my word, he is nothing to me. Should he ever propose to me (which I have very little reason to imagine he has any thought of doing), I shall not accept him. I assure you I shall not. I assure you, Mr. Elliot had not the share, which you have been supposing, in whatever pleasure the concert of last night might afford: not Mr. Elliot; it is not Mr. Elliot that——"

She stopped, regretting, with a deep blush, that she had implied so much; but less would hardly have been sufficient. Mrs. Smith would hardly have believed so soon in Mr. Elliot's failure, but from the perception of there being a somebody else. As it was, she instantly submitted, and with all the semblance of seeing nothing beyond; and Anne, eager to escape further notice, was impatient to know why Mrs. Smith should have fancied she was to marry Mr. Elliot; where she could have received the idea, or from whom she could have heard it.

"Do tell me how it first came into your head?"

"It first came into my head," replied Mrs. Smith, "upon finding how much you were together, and feeling it to be the most profitable thing in the world to be wished for by everybody belonging to either of you; and you may depend upon it, that all your acquaintances have disposed of you in the same way. But I never heard it spoken of till two days ago."

"And has it, indeed, been spoken of?"

"Did you observe the woman who opened the door to you when you called yesterday?"

"No. Was not it Mrs. Speed, as usual, or the maid? I observed no one in particular."

"It was my friend Mrs. Rooke; Nurse Rooke; who, by-the-bye, had a great curiosity to see you, and was delighted to be in the way to let you in. She came away from Marlborough Buildings only on Sunday; and she it was who told me you were to marry Mr. Elliot. She had had it from Mrs. Wallis herself, which did not seem bad authority. She sat an hour with me on Monday evening, and gave me the whole history."

"The whole history!" repeated Anne, laughing. "She could not make a very long history, I think, of one such little article of unfounded news."

Mrs. Smith said nothing.

"But," continued Anne, presently, "though there is no truth in my having this claim on Mr. Elliot, I should be extremely happy to be of use to you, in any way that I could. Shall I mention to him your being in Bath? Shall I take any message?"

"No, I thank you; no, certainly not. In the warmth of the moment, and under a mistaken impression, I might, perhaps, have endeavoured to interest you in some circumstances; but not now. No, I thank you, I have nothing to trouble you with."

"I think you spoke of having known Mr. Elliot many years?"

"I did."

"Not before he married, I suppose?"

"Yes; he was not married when I knew him first."

"And—were you much acquainted?"

"Intimately."

"Indeed! Then do tell me what he was at that time of life. I have a great curiosity to know what Mr. Elliot was as a very young man. Was he at all such as he appears now?"

"I have not seen Mr. Elliot these three years," was Mrs. Smith's answer, given so gravely that it was impossible to pursue the subject further; and Anne felt that she had gained nothing but an increase of curiosity. They were both silent: Mrs. Smith very thoughtful. At last—

"I beg your pardon, my dear Miss Elliot," she cried in her natural tone of cordiality, "I beg your pardon for the short answers I have been giving you, but I have been uncertain what I ought to do. I have been doubting and considering as to what I ought to tell you. There were many things to be taken into the account. One hates to be officious, to be giving bad impressions, making mischief. Even the smooth surface of a family union seems worth preserving, though there may be nothing durable beneath. However, I have determined; I think I am right; I think you ought to be made acquainted with Mr. Elliot's real character. Though I fully believe that at present you have not the smallest intention of accepting him, there is no saying what may happen. You might, some time or other, be differently affected towards him. Hear the truth, therefore, now, while you are unprejudiced. Mr. Elliot is a man without heart or conscience; a designing, wary, cold-blooded being, who thinks only of himself; who, for his own interest or ease, would be guilty of any cruelty, or any treachery, that could be perpetrated without risk of his general character. He has no feeling for others. Those whom he has been the chief cause of leading into ruin, he can neglect and desert without the smallest compunction. He is totally beyond the reach of any sentiment of justice or compassion. Oh! he is black at heart; hollow and black!"

Anne's astonished air, and exclamation of wonder, made her pause, and in a calmer manner, she added:

"My expressions startle you. You must allow for an injured, angry woman. But I will try to command myself. I will not abuse him. I will only tell you what I have found him. Facts shall speak. He was the intimate friend of my dear husband, who trusted and loved him, and thought him as good as himself. The intimacy had been formed before our marriage. I found them most intimate friends; and I, too, became excessively pleased with Mr. Elliot, and entertained the highest opinion of him. At nineteen, you know, one does not think very seriously; but Mr. Elliot appeared to me quite as good as others, and much more agreeable than most others, and we were almost always together. We were principally in town, living in very good style. He was then the inferior in circumstances; he was then the poor one; he had chambers in the Temple, and it was as much as he could do to support the appearance of a gentleman. He had always a home with us whenever he chose it; he was always welcome; he was like a brother. My poor Charles, who had the finest, most generous spirit in the world, would have divided his last farthing with him; I know that his purse was open to him; I know that he often assisted him."

"This must have been about that very period of Mr. Elliot's life," said Anne, "which has always excited my particular curiosity. It must have been about the same time that he became known to my father and sister. I never knew him myself, I only heard of him; but there was a something in his conduct then, with regard to my father and sister, and afterwards in the circumstances of his marriage, which I never could quite reconcile with present times. It seemed to announce a different sort of man."

"I know it all, I know it all," cried Mrs. Smith. "He had been introduced to Sir Walter and your sister before I was acquainted with him, but I heard him speak of them for ever. I know he was invited and encouraged, and I know he did not choose to go. I can satisfy you, perhaps, on points which you would little expect; and as to his marriage, I knew all about it at the time. I was privy to all the fors and againsts; I was the friend to whom he confided his hopes and plans; and though I did not know his wife previously, her inferior situation in society, indeed, rendered that impossible, yet I knew her all her life afterwards, or at least till within the last two years of her life, and can answer any question you wish to put."

"Nay," said Anne, "I have no particular enquiry to make about her. I have always understood they were not a happy couple. But I should like to know why, at that time of his life, he should slight my father's acquaintance as he did. My father was certainly disposed to take very kind and proper notice of him. Why did Mr. Elliot draw back?"

"Mr. Elliot," replied Mrs. Smith, "at that period of his life had one object in view: to make his fortune, and by a rather quicker process than the law. He was determined to make it by marriage. He was determined, at least, not to mar it by an imprudent marriage; and I know it was his belief (whether justly or not, of course I cannot decide), that your father and sister, in their civilities and invitations, were designing a match between the heir and the young lady, and it was impossible that such a match should have answered his ideas of wealth and independence. That was his motive for drawing back, I can assure you. He told me the whole story. He had no concealments with me. It was curious, that having just left you behind me in Bath, my first and principal acquaintance on marrying should be your cousin: and that, through him, I should be continually hearing of your father and sister. He described one Miss Elliot, and I thought very affectionately of the other."

"Perhaps," cried Anne, struck by a sudden idea, "you sometimes spoke of me to Mr. Elliot?"

"To be sure I did; very often. I used to boast of my own Anne Elliot, and vouch for your being a very different creature from——"

She checked herself just in time.

"This accounts for something which Mr. Elliot said last night," cried Anne. "This explains it. I found he had been used to hear of me. I could not comprehend how. What wild imaginations one forms where dear self is concerned! How sure to be mistaken! But I beg your pardon; I have interrupted you. Mr. Elliot married then completely for money? The circumstance, probably, which first opened your eyes to his character?"

Mrs. Smith hesitated a little here. "Oh! those things are too common. When one lives in the world, a man or woman's marrying for money is too common to strike one as it ought. I was very young, and associated only with the young, and we were a thoughtless, gay set, without any strict rules of conduct. We lived for enjoyment. I think differently now; time and sickness and sorrow have given me other notions; but at that period, I must own I saw nothing reprehensible in what Mr. Elliot was doing. 'To do the best for himself' passed as a duty."

"But was not she a very low woman?"

"Yes; which I objected to, but he would not regard. Money, money, was all that he wanted. Her father was a grazier, her grandfather had been a butcher, but that was all nothing. She was a fine woman, had had a decent education, was brought forward by some cousins, thrown by chance into Mr. Elliot's company, and fell in love with him; and not a difficulty or a scruple was there on his side with respect to her birth. All his caution was spent in being secured of the real amount of her fortune, before he committed himself. Depend upon it, whatever esteem Mr. Elliot may have for his own situation in life now, as a young man he had not the smallest value for it. His chance of the Kellynch estate was something, but all the honour of the family he held as cheap as dirt. I have often heard him declare, that if baronetcies were saleable, anybody should have his for fifty pounds, arms and motto, name and livery included; but I will not pretend to repeat half that I used to hear him say on that subject. It would not be fair; and yet you ought to have proof, for what is all this but assertion, and you shall have proof."

"Indeed, my dear Mrs. Smith, I want none," cried Anne. "You have asserted nothing contradictory to what Mr. Elliot appeared to be some years ago. This is all in confirmation, rather, of what we used to hear and believe. I am more curious to know why he should be so different now."

"But for my satisfaction, if you will have the goodness to ring for Mary; stay: I am sure you will have the still greater goodness of going yourself into my bedroom, and bringing me the small inlaid box which you will find on the upper shelf of the closet."

Anne seeing her friend to be earnestly bent on it, did as she was desired.
The box was brought and placed before her, and Mrs. Smith, sighing over
it as she unlocked it, said:

"This is full of papers belonging to him, to my husband; a small portion
only of what I had to look over when I lost him. The letter I am looking
for was one written by Mr. Elliot to him before our marriage, and happened to be saved; why, one can hardly imagine. But he was careless and
unmethodical, like other men, about those things; and when I came to
examine his papers, I found it with others, still more trivial, from different
people scattered here and there, while many letters and memorandums
of real importance had been destroyed. Here it is; I would not burn it,
because being even then very little satisfied with Mr. Elliot, I was determined to preserve every document of former intimacy. I have now another
motive for being glad that I can produce it."

This was the letter, directed to "Charles Smith, Esq., Tunbridge Wells,"
and dated from London, as far back as July, 1803:—

"DEAR SMITH,—I have received yours. Your kindness almost overpowers me. I wish nature had made such hearts as yours more common,
but I have lived three-and-twenty years in the world, and have seen none
like it. At present, believe me, I have no need of your services, being in
cash again. Give me joy: I have got rid of Sir Walter and Miss. They are
gone back to Kellynch, and almost made me swear to visit them this
summer; but my first visit to Kellynch will be with a surveyor, to tell
me how to bring it with best advantage to the hammer. The baronet,
nevertheless, is not unlikely to marry again; he is quite fool enough. If he
does, however, they will leave me in peace, which may be a decent equivalent for the reversion. He is worse than last year.

"I wish I had any name but Elliot. I am sick of it. The name of Walter
I can drop, thank God! and I desire you will never insult me with my
second W. again, meaning, for the rest of my life, to be only yours truly,—
WM. ELLIOT."

Such a letter could not be read without putting Anne in a glow; and
Mrs. Smith, observing the high colour in her face, said:

"The language, I know, is highly disrespectful. Though I have forgot
the exact terms, I have a perfect impression of the general meaning. But it
shows you the man. Mark his professions to my poor husband. Can anything be stronger?"

Anne could not immediately get over the shock and mortification of
finding such words applied to her father. She was obliged to recollect that
her seeing the letter was a violation of the laws of honour, that no one
ought to be judged or to be known by such testimonies, that no private
correspondence could bear the eye of others, before she could recover
calmness enough to return the letter which she had been meditating over,
and say:

"Thank you. This is full proof undoubtedly: proof of everything you were saying. But why be acquainted with us now?"

"I can explain this too," cried Mrs. Smith, smiling.

"Can you really?"

"Yes. I have shown you Mr. Elliot as he was a dozen years ago, and I will show him as he is now. I cannot produce written proof again, but I can give as authentic oral testimony as you can desire, of what he is now wanting, and what he is now doing. He is no hypocrite now. He truly wants to marry you. His present attentions to your family are very sincere: quite from the heart. I will give you my authority: his friend Colonel Wallis."

"Colonel Wallis! are you acquainted with him?"

"No. It does not come to me in quite so direct a line as that; it takes a bend or two, but nothing of consequence. The stream is as good as at first; the little rubbish it collects in the turnings is easily moved away. Mr. Elliot talks unreservedly to Colonel Wallis of his views on you, which said Colonel Wallis, I imagine to be, in himself a sensible, careful, discerning sort of character; but Colonel Wallis has a very pretty silly wife, to whom he tells things which he had better not, and he repeats it all to her. She in the overflowing spirits of her recovery, repeats it all to her nurse; and the nurse knowing my acquaintance with you, very naturally brings it all to me. On Monday evening, my good friend Mrs. Rooke let me thus much into the secrets of Marlborough Buildings. When I talked of a whole history, therefore, you see I was not romancing so much as you supposed."

"My dear Mrs. Smith, your authority is deficient. This will not do. Mr. Elliot's having any views on me will not in the least account for the efforts he made towards a reconciliation with my father. That was all prior to my coming to Bath. I found them on the most friendly terms when I arrived."

"I know you did; I know it all perfectly, but——"

"Indeed, Mrs. Smith, we must not expect to get real information in such a line. Facts or opinions which are to pass through the hands of so many, to be misconceived by folly in one, and ignorance in another, can hardly have much truth left."

"Only give me a hearing. You will soon be able to judge of the general credit due, by listening to some particulars which you can yourself immediately contradict or confirm. Nobody supposes that you were his first inducement. He had seen you, indeed, before he came to Bath, and admired you, but without knowing it to be you. So says my historian, at least. Is this true? Did he see you last summer or autumn 'somewhere down in the west,' to use her own words, without knowing it to be you?"

"He certainly did. So far it is very true. At Lyme. I happened to be at Lyme."

"Well," continued Mrs. Smith, triumphantly, "grant my friend the credit due to the establishment of the first point asserted. He saw you then

at Lyme, and liked you so well as to be exceedingly pleased to meet with
you again in Camden Place, as Miss Anne Elliot, and from that moment,
I have no doubt, had a double motive in his visits there. But there was
another, and an earlier, which I will now explain. If there is anything in
my story which you know to be either false or improbable, stop me. My
account states, that your sister's friend, the lady now staying with you,
whom I have heard you mention, came to Bath with Miss Elliot and Sir
Walter as long ago as September (in short when they first came themselves), and has been staying there ever since; that she is a clever, insinuating, handsome woman, poor and plausible, and altogether such in
situation and manner, as to give a general idea, among Sir Walter's
acquaintances, of her meaning to be Lady Elliot, and as general a surprise
that Miss Elliot should be, apparently, blind to the danger."

Here Mrs. Smith paused a moment; but Anne had not a word to say,
and she continued:

"This was the light in which it appeared to those who knew the family,
long before you returned to it; and Colonel Wallis had his eye upon your
father enough to be sensible of it, though he did not then visit in Camden
Place; but his regard for Mr. Elliot gave him an interest in watching all
that was going on there, and when Mr. Elliot came to Bath for a day or
two, as he happened to do a little before Christmas, Colonel Wallis made
him acquainted with the appearance of things, and the reports beginning
to prevail. Now you are to understand, that time had worked a very
material change in Mr. Elliot's opinions as to the value of a baronetcy.
Upon all points of blood and connection he is a completely altered man.
Having long had as much money as he could spend, nothing to wish for
on the side of avarice or indulgence, he has been gradually learning to pin
his happiness upon the consequence he is heir to. I thought it coming on
before our acquaintance ceased, but it is now a confirmed feeling. He cannot bear the idea of not being Sir William. You may guess, therefore,
that the news he heard from his friend could not be very agreeable, and
you may guess what it produced; the resolution of coming back to Bath
as soon as possible, and of fixing himself there for a time, with the view
of renewing his former acquaintance, and recovering such a footing in the
family as might give him the means of ascertaining the degree of his danger, and of circumventing the lady if he found it material. This was
agreed upon between the two friends as the only thing to be done; and
Colonel Wallis was to assist in every way that he could. He was to be
introduced, and Mrs. Wallis was to be introduced, and everybody was to
be introduced. Mr. Elliot came back accordingly; and on application was
forgiven, as you know, and re-admitted into the family; and there it was
his constant object, and his only object (till your arrival added another
motive), to watch Sir Walter and Mrs. Clay. He omitted no opportunity
of being with them, threw himself in their way, called at all hours; but
I need not be particular on this subject. You can imagine what an artful

man would do; and with this guide, perhaps, may recollect what you have
seen him do."

"Yes," said Anne, "you tell me nothing which does not accord with
what I have known, or could imagine. There is always something offensive
in the details of cunning. The manœuvres of selfishness and duplicity must
ever be revolting, but I have heard nothing which really surprises me. I
know those who would be shocked by such a representation of Mr. Elliot,
who would have difficulty in believing it, but I have never been satisfied.
I have always wanted some other motive for his conduct than appeared.
I should like to know his present opinion, as to the probability of the event
he has been in dread of; whether he considers the danger to be lessening
or not."

"Lessening, I understand," replied Mrs. Smith. "He thinks Mrs. Clay
afraid of him, aware that he sees through her, and not daring to proceed
as she might do in his absence. But since he must be absent some time or
other, I do not perceive how he can ever be secure while she holds her
present influence. Mrs. Wallis has an amusing idea, as nurse tells me, that
it is to be put into the marriage articles when you and Mr. Elliot marry,
that your father is not to marry Mrs. Clay. A scheme worthy of Mrs.
Wallis's understanding, by all accounts; but my sensible Nurse Rooke sees
the absurdity of it. 'Why, to be sure, ma'am,' said she, 'it would not
prevent his marrying anybody else.' And, indeed, to own the truth, I do
not think nurse, in her heart, is a very strenuous opposer of Sir Walter's
making a second match. She must be allowed to be a favourer of matrimony you know; and (since self will intrude) who can say that she may
not have some flying visions of attending the next Lady Elliot. through
Mrs. Wallis's recommendation?"

"I am very glad to know all this," said Anne, after a little thoughtfulness. "It will be more painful to me in some respects to be in company
with him, but I shall know better what to do. My line of conduct will be
more direct. Mr. Elliot is evidently a disingenuous, artificial, worldly man.
who has had never any better principle to guide him than selfishness."

But Mr. Elliot was not yet done with. Mrs. Smith had been carried away
from her first direction, and Anne had forgotten, in the interest of her
own family concerns, how much had been originally implied against him;
but her attention was now called to the explanation of those first hints,
and she listened to a recital which, if it did not perfectly justify the unqualified bitterness of Mrs. Smith, proved him to have been very unfeeling
in his conduct towards her; very deficient both in justice and compassion.

She learned that (the intimacy between them continuing unimpaired by
Mr. Elliot's marriage) they had been as before always together, and Mr.
Elliot had led his friend into expenses much beyond his fortune. Mrs.
Smith did not want to take the blame to herself, and was most tender of
throwing any on her husband; but Anne could collect that their income
had never been equal to their style of living, and that from the first there
had been a great deal of general and joint extravagance. From his wife's

account of him she could discern Mr. Smith to have been a man of warm feelings, easy temper, careless habits, and not strong understanding; much more amiable than his friend, and very unlike him, led by him, and probably despised by him. Mr. Elliot, raised by his marriage to great affluence, and disposed to every gratification of pleasure and vanity which could be commanded without involving himself (for with all his self-indulgence he had become a prudent man), and beginning to be rich, just as his friend ought to have found himself to be poor, seemed to have had no concern at all for that friend's probable finances, but, on the contrary, had been prompting and encouraging expenses which could end only in ruin: and the Smiths accordingly had been ruined.

The husband had died just in time to be spared the full knowledge of it. They had previously known embarrassments enough to try the friendship of their friends, and to prove that Mr. Elliot's had better not be tried; but it was not till his death that the wretched state of his affairs was fully known. With a confidence in Mr. Elliot's regard, more creditable to his feelings than his judgment, Mr. Smith had appointed him the executor of his will; but Mr. Elliot would not act, and the difficulties and distresses which this refusal had heaped on her, in addition to the inevitable sufferings of her situation, had been such as could not be related without anguish of spirit, or listened to without corresponding indignation.

Anne was shown some letters of his on the occasion, answers to urgent applications from Mrs. Smith, which all breathed the same stern resolution of not engaging in a fruitless trouble, and, under a cold civility, the same hard-hearted indifference to any of the evils it might bring on her. It was a dreadful picture of ingratitude and inhumanity; and Anne felt, at some moments, that no flagrant open crime could have been worse. She had a great deal to listen to; all the particulars of past sad scenes, all the minutiæ of distress upon distress, which in former conversations had been merely hinted at, were dwelt on now with a natural indulgence. Anne could perfectly comprehend the exquisite relief, and was only the more inclined to wonder at the composure of her friend's usual state of mind.

There was one circumstance in the history of her grievances of particular irritation. She had good reason to believe that some property of her husband in the West Indies, which had been for many years under a sort of sequestration for the payment of its own incumbrances, might be recoverable by proper measures; and this property, though not large, would be enough to make her comparatively rich. But there was nobody to stir in it. Mr. Elliot would do nothing, and she could do nothing herself, equally disabled from personal exertion by her state of bodily weakness, and from employing others by her want of money. She had no natural connections to assist her even with their counsel, and she could not afford to purchase the assistance of the law. This was a cruel aggravation of actually straightened means. To feel that she ought to be in better circumstances, that a little trouble in the right place might do it, and to fear that delay might be even weakening her claims was hard to bear.

It was on this point that she had hoped to engage Anne's good offices with Mr. Elliot. She had previously, in the anticipation of their marriage, been very apprehensive of losing her friend by it; but on being assured that he could have made no attempt of that nature, since he did not even know her to be in Bath, it immediately occurred that something might be done in her favour by the influence of the woman he loved, and she had been hastily preparing to interest Anne's feelings as far as the observances due to Mr. Elliot's character would allow, when Anne's refutation of the supposed engagement changed the face of everything; and while it took from her the new-formed hope of succeeding in the object of her first anxiety, left her at least the comfort of telling the whole story her own way.

After listening to this full description of Mr. Elliot, Anne could not but express some surprise at Mrs. Smith's having spoken of him so favourably in the beginning of their conversation. "She had seemed to recommend and praise him!"

"My dear," was Mrs. Smith's reply, "there was nothing else to be done. I considered your marrying him as certain, though he might not yet have made the offer, and I could no more speak the truth of him, than if he had been your husband. My heart bled for you as I talked of happiness; and yet he is sensible, he is agreeable, and with such a woman as you, it was not absolutely hopeless. He was very unkind to his first wife. They were wretched together. But she was too ignorant and giddy for respect, and he had never loved her. I was willing to hope that you must fare better."

Anne could just acknowledge within herself such a possibility of having been induced to marry him, as made her shudder at the idea of the misery which must have followed. It was just possible that she might have been persuaded by Lady Russell! And under such a supposition, which would have been most miserable, when time had disclosed all, too late?

It was very desirable that Lady Russell should be no longer deceived; and one of the concluding arrangements of this important conference, which carried them through the greater part of the morning, was, that Anne had full liberty to communicate to her friend everything relative to Mrs. Smith, in which his conduct was involved.

Chapter 22

ANNE went home to think over all that she had heard. In one point, her feelings were relieved by this knowledge of Mr. Elliot. There was no longer anything of tenderness due to him. He stood as opposed to Captain Wentworth, in all his own unwelcome obtrusiveness; and the evil of his attentions last night, the irremediable mischief he might have done, was considered with sensations unqualified, unperplexed. Pity for him was all over. But this was the only point of relief. In every other respect, in looking around her, or penetrating forward, she saw more to distrust and to apprehend. She was concerned for the disappointment and pain Lady Russell would be feeling; for the mortifications which must be hanging over her father and sister, and had all the distress of foreseeing many evils without knowing how to avert any one of them. She was most thankful for her own knowledge of him. She had never considered herself as entitled to reward for not slighting an old friend like Mrs. Smith, but here was a reward, indeed, springing from it! Mrs. Smith had been able to tell her what no one else could have done. Could the knowledge have been extended through her family? But this was a vain idea. She must talk to Lady Russell, tell her, consult with her, and having done her best, wait the event with as much composure as possible; and after all, her greatest want of composure would be in that quarter of the mind which could not be opened to Lady Russell; in that flow of anxieties and fears which must be all to herself.

She found on reaching home, that she had, as she intended, escaped seeing Mr. Elliot; that he had called and paid them a long morning visit; but hardly had she congratulated herself, and felt safe, when she heard that he was coming again in the evening.

"I had not the smallest intention of asking him," said Elizabeth, with affected carelessness, "but he gave so many hints; so Mrs. Clay says, at least."

"Indeed, I do say it. I never saw anybody in my life spell harder for an invitation. Poor man! I was really in pain for him; for your hard-hearted sister, Miss Anne, seems bent on cruelty."

"Oh!" cried Elizabeth, "I have been rather too much used to the game to be soon overcome by a gentleman's hints. However, when I found how excessively he was regretting that he should miss my father this morning, I gave way immediately, for I would never really omit an opportunity of bringing him and Sir Walter together. They appear to so much advantage in company with each other. Each behaving so pleasantly. Mr. Elliot looking up with so much respect."

"Quite delightful!" cried Mrs. Clay, not daring, however, to turn her eyes towards Anne. "Exactly like father and son! Dear Miss Elliot, may I not say father and son?"

"Oh! I lay no embargo on anybody's words. If you will have such ideas! But, upon my word, I am scarcely sensible of his attentions being beyond those of other men."

"My dear Miss Elliot!" exclaimed Mrs. Clay, lifting up her hands and eyes, and sinking all the rest of her astonishment in a convenient silence.

"Well, my dear Penelope, you need not be so alarmed about him. I did invite him, you know. I sent him away with smiles. When I found he was really going to his friends at Thornberry Park for the whole day to-morrow, I had compassion on him."

Anne admired the good acting of the friend, in being able to show such pleasure, as she did, in the expectation and in the actual arrival of the very person whose presence must really be interfering with her prime object. It was impossible but that Mrs. Clay must hate the sight of Mr. Elliot; and yet she could assume a most obliging, placid look, and appear quite satisfied with the curtailed licence of devoting herself only half as much to Sir Walter as she would have done otherwise.

To Anne herself it was most distressing to see Mr. Elliot enter the room; and quite painful to have him approach and speak to her. She had been used before to feel that he could not be always quite sincere, but now she saw insincerity in everything. His attentive deference to her father, contrasted with his former language, was odious; and when she thought of his cruel conduct towards Mrs. Smith, she could hardly bear the sight of his present smiles and mildness, or the sound of his artificial good sentiments.

She meant to avoid any such alteration of manners as might provoke a remonstrance on his side. It was a great object with her to escape all enquiry or éclat; but it was her intention to be as decidedly cool to him as might be compatible with their relationship; and to retract, as quietly as she could, the few steps of unnecessary intimacy she had been gradually led along. She was accordingly more guarded, and more cool, than she had been the night before.

He wanted to animate her curiosity again as to how and where he could have heard her formerly praised; wanted very much to be gratified by more solicitation; but the charm was broken: he found that the heat and animation of a public room was necessary to kindle his modest cousin's vanity; he found, at least, that it was not to be done now, by any of those attempts which he could hazard among the too-commanding claims of the others. He little surmised that it was a subject acting now exactly against his interest, bringing immediately to her thoughts all those parts of his conduct which were least excusable.

She had some satisfaction in finding that he was really going out of Bath the next morning, going early, and that he would be gone the greater part of two days. He was invited again to Camden Place the very evening of his return; but from Thursday to Saturday evening his absence was certain. It was bad enough that a Mrs. Clay should be always before her; but that a deeper hypocrite should be added to their party, seemed the destruction of everything like peace and comfort. It was so humiliating to reflect on the constant deception practised on her father and Elizabeth; to consider the various sources of mortification preparing for them! Mrs. Clay's selfishness was not so complicate nor so revolting as his; and Anne would have compounded for the marriage at once, with all its evils, to be clear of Mr. Elliot's subtleties in endeavouring to prevent it.

On Friday morning she meant to go very early to Lady Russell, and accomplish the necessary communication; and she would have gone directly after breakfast, but that Mrs. Clay was also going out on some obliging purpose of saving her sister trouble, which determined her to wait till she might be safe from such a companion. She saw Mrs. Clay fairly off, therefore, before she began to talk of spending the morning in Rivers Street.

"Very well," said Elizabeth, "I have nothing to send but my love. Oh! you may as well take back that tiresome book she would lend me, and pretend I have read it through. I really cannot be plaguing myself for ever with all the new poems and states of the nation that come out. Lady Russell quite bores one with her new publications. You need not tell her so, but I thought her dress hideous the other night. I used to think she had some taste in dress, but I was ashamed of her at the concert. Something so formal and *arrangé* in her air! and she sits so upright! My best love, of course."

"And mine," added Sir Walter. "Kindest regards. And you may say, that I mean to call upon her soon. Make a civil message; but I shall only leave my card. Morning visits are never fair by women at her time of life, who make themselves up so little. If she would only wear rouge she would not be afraid of being seen; but last time I called, I observed the blinds were let down immediately."

While her father spoke, there was a knock at the door. Who could it be? Anne, remembering the preconcerted visits, at all hours, of Mr. Elliot, would have expected him, but for his known engagement seven miles off. After the usual period of suspense, the usual sounds of approach were heard, and "Mr. and Mrs. Charles Musgrove" were ushered into the room.

Surprise was the strongest emotion raised by their appearance; but Anne was really glad to see them; and the others were not so sorry but that they could put on a decent air of welcome; and as soon as it became clear that these, their nearest relations, were not arrived with any views of accommodation in that house, Sir Walter and Elizabeth were able to rise in cordiality, and do the honours of it very well. They were come to Bath for a few days with Mrs. Musgrove, and were at the White Hart. So much was pretty soon understood; but till Sir Walter and Elizabeth were walking Mary into the other drawing-room, and regaling themselves with her admiration, Anne could not draw upon Charles's brain for a regular history of their coming, or an explanation of some smiling hints of particular business, which had been ostentatiously dropped by Mary, as well as of some apparent confusion as to whom their party consisted of.

She then found that is consisted of Mrs. Musgrove, Henrietta, and Captain Harville, beside her two selves. He gave her a very plain, intelligible account of the whole; a narration in which she saw a great deal of most characteristic proceeding. The scheme had received its first impulse by Captain Harville's wanting to come to Bath on business. He had begun to talk of it a week ago; and by way of doing something, as shooting was over, Charles had proposed coming with him, and Mrs. Harville had seemed to like the idea of it very much, as an advantage to her husband; but Mary could not bear to be left, and had made herself so unhappy about it, that for a day or two everything seemed to be in suspense, or at an end. But then, it had been taken up by his father and mother. His mother had some old friends in Bath whom she wanted to see; it was thought a good opportunity for Henrietta to come and buy wedding-clothes for herself and her sister; and, in short, it ended in being his mother's party, that everything might be comfortable and easy to Captain Harville; and he and Mary were included in it by way of general convenience. They had arrived late the night before. Mrs. Harville, her children, and Captain Benwick, remained with Mr. Musgrove and Louisa at Uppercross.

Anne's only surprise was, that affairs should be in forwardness enough for Henrietta's wedding-clothes to be talked of. She had imagined such difficulties of fortune to exist there as must prevent the marriage from being near at hand; but she learned from Charles that, very recently (since Mary's last letter to herself), Charles Hayter had been applied to by a friend to hold a living for a youth who could not possibly claim it under many years; and that on the strength of this present income, with almost a certainty of something more permanent long before the term in question, the two families had consented to the young people's wishes, and that their marriage was likely to take place in a few months, quite as soon as Louisa's. "And a very good living it was," Charles added: "only five-and-twenty miles from Uppercross, and in a very fine country: fine part of Dorsetshire. In the centre of some of the best preserves in the kingdom, surrounded by three great proprietors, each more careful and jealous than the other; and to two of the three at least, Charles Hayter might get a special recommendation. Not that he will value is as he ought," he observed: "Charles is too cool about sporting. That's the worst of him."

"I am extremely glad, indeed," cried Anne; "particularly glad that this should happen; and that of two sisters who both deserve equally well, and who have always been such good friends, the pleasant prospects of one should not be dimming those of the other—that they should be so equal in their prosperity and comfort. I hope your father and mother are quite happy with regard to both."

"Oh yes! My father would be as well pleased if the gentlemen were richer, but he has no other fault to find. Money, you know, coming down with money—two daughters at once—it cannot be a very agreeable operation, and it streightens him as to many things. However, I do not mean to say they have not a right to it. It is very fit they should have daughters' shares; and I am sure he has always been a very kind, liberal father to me. Mary does not above half like Henrietta's match. She never did, you know. But she does not do him justice, nor think enough about Winthrop. I cannot make her attend to the value of the property. It is a very fair match as times go; and I have liked Charles Hayter all my life, and I shall not leave off now."

"Such excellent parents as Mr. and Mrs. Musgrove," exclaimed Anne, "should be happy in their children's marriages. They do everything to confer happiness, I am sure. What a blessing to young people to be in such hands! Your father and mother seem totally free from all those ambitious feelings which have led to so much misconduct and misery, both in young and old. I hope you think Louisa perfectly recovered now?"

He answered rather hesitatingly, "Yes, I believe I do; very much recovered; but she is altered; there is no running or jumping about, no laughing or dancing; it is quite different. If one happens only to shut the door a little hard, she starts and wriggles like a young dab-chick in the water; and Benwick sits at her elbow, reading verses, or whispering to her, all day long."

Anne could not help laughing. "That cannot be much to your taste, I know," said she; "but I do believe him to be an excellent young man."

"To be sure he is: nobody doubts it; and I hope you do not think I am so illiberal as to want every man to have the same objects and pleasures as myself. I have a great value for Benwick; and when one can but get him to talk, he has plenty to say. His reading has done him no harm, for he has fought as well as read. He is a brave fellow. I got more acquainted with him last Monday than ever I did before. We had a famous set-to at rat-hunting all the morning in my father's great barns; and he played his part so well that I have liked him the better ever since."

Here they were interrupted by the absolute necessity of Charles's following the others to admire mirrors and china: but Anne had heard enough to understand the present state of Uppercross, and rejoice in its happiness; and though she sighed as she rejoiced, her sigh had none of the ill-will of envy in it. She would certainly have risen to their blessings if she could, but she did not want to lessen theirs.

The visit passed off altogether in high good humour. Mary was in excellent spirits, enjoying the gaiety and the change, and so well satisfied with the journey in her mother-in-law's carriage with four horses, and with her own complete independence of Camden Place, that she was exactly in a temper to admire everything as she ought, and enter most readily into all the superiorities of the house, as they were detailed to her. She had no demands on her father or sister, and her consequence was just enough increased by their handsome drawing-rooms.

Elizabeth was, for a short time, suffering a good deal. She felt that Mrs. Musgrove and all her party ought to be asked to dine with them; but she could not bear to have the difference of style, the reduction of servants, which a dinner must betray, witnessed by those who had been always so inferior to the Elliots of Kellynch. It was a struggle between propriety and vanity; but vanity got the better, and then Elizabeth was happy again. These were her internal persuasions: "Old-fashioned notions; country hospitality; we do not profess to give dinners; few people in Bath do; Lady Alicia never does; did not even ask her own sister's family, though they were here a month; and I daresay it would be very inconvenient to Mrs. Musgrove; put her quite out of her way. I am sure she would rather not come; she cannot feel easy with us. I will ask them all for an evening; that will be much better; that will be a novelty and a treat. They have not seen two such drawing-rooms before. They will be delighted to come

to-morrow evening. It shall be a regular party, small, but most elegant."
And this satisfied Elizabeth; and when the invitation was given to the
two present, and promised for the absent, Mary was as completely satisfied. She was particularly asked to meet Mr. Elliot, and be introduced to
Lady Dalrymple and Miss Carteret, who were fortunately already engaged to come; and she could not have received a more gratifying attention. Miss Elliot was to have the honour of calling on Mrs. Musgrove in the
course of the morning; and Anne walked off with Charles and Mary, to go
and see her and Henrietta directly.

Her plan of sitting with Lady Russell must give way for the present.
They all three called in Rivers Street for a couple of minutes; but Anne
convinced herself that a day's delay of the intended communication could
be of no consequence, and hastened forward to the White Hart, to see
again the friends and companions of the last autumn, with an eagerness of
good-will which many associations contributed to form.

They found Mrs. Musgrove and her daughter within, and by themselves, and Anne had the kindest welcome from each. Henrietta was exactly
in that state of recently-improved views, of fresh-formed happiness,
which made her full of regard and interest for everybody she had ever
liked before at all; and Mrs. Musgrove's real affection had been won by
her usefulness when they were in distress. It was a heartiness, and a
warmth, and a sincerity which Anne delighted in the more, from the sad
want of such blessings at home. She was entreated to give them as much of
her time as possible, invited for every day and all day long, or rather
claimed as a part of the family; and, in return, she naturally fell into all
her wonted ways of attention and assistance, and on Charles's leaving
them together, was listening to Mrs. Musgrove's history of Louisa, and
to Henrietta's of herself, giving opinions on business, and recommendations to shops; with intervals of every help which Mary required, from
altering her ribbon to settling her accounts; from finding her keys, and
assorting her trinkets, to trying to convince her that she was not ill-used
by anybody; which Mary, well amused as she generally was, in her station
at a window overlooking the entrance to the Pump Room, could not but
have her moments of imagining.

A morning of thorough confusion was to be expected. A large party in
an hotel ensured a quick-changing, unsettled scene. One five minutes
brought a note, the next a parcel; and Anne had not been there half an
hour, when their dining-room, spacious as it was, seemed more than half
filled; a party of steady old friends were seated round Mrs. Musgrove,
and Charles came back with Captains Harville and Wentworth. The
appearance of the latter could not be more than the surprise of the moment.
It was impossible for her to have forgotten to feel that this arrival of their
common friends must be soon bringing them together again. Their last
meeting had been most important in opening his feelings: she had derived
from it a delightful conviction; but she feared from his looks, that the same
unfortunate persuasion, which had hastened him away from the concert

room, still governed. He did not seem to want to be near enough for conversation.

She tried to be calm, and leave things to take their course, and tried to dwell much on this argument of rational dependence:—"Surely, if there be constant attachment on each side, our hearts must understand each other ere long. We are not boy and girl, to be captiously irritable, misled by every moment's inadvertence, and wantonly playing with our own happiness." And yet, a few minutes afterwards, she felt as if their being in company with each other, under their present circumstances, could only be exposing them to inadvertencies and misconstructions of the most mischievous kind.

"Anne," cried Mary, still at her window, "there is Mrs. Clay, I am sure, standing under the colonnade, and a gentleman with her. I saw them turn the corner from Bath Street just now. They seem deep in talk. Who is it? Come, and tell me. Good heavens! I recollect. It is Mr. Elliot himself."

"No," cried Anne, quickly, "it cannot be Mr. Elliot, I assure you. He was to leave Bath at nine this morning, and does not come back till to-morrow."

As she spoke, she felt that Captain Wentworth was looking at her, the consciousness of which vexed and embarrassed her, and made her regret that she had said so much, simple as it was.

Mary, resenting that she should be supposed not to know her own cousin, began talking very warmly about the family features, and protesting still more positively that it was Mr. Elliot, calling again upon Anne to come and look herself, but Anne did not mean to stir, and tried to be cool and unconcerned. Her distress returned however, on perceiving smiles and intelligent glances pass between two or three of the lady visitors, as if they believed themselves quite in the secret. It was evident that the report concerning her had spread, and a short pause succeeded, which seemed to ensure that it would now spread further.

"Do come, Anne," cried Mary, "come and look yourself. You will be too late if you do not make haste. They are parting: they are shaking hands. He is turning away. Not know Mr. Elliot, indeed! You seem to have forgot all about Lyme."

To pacify Mary, and perhaps screen her own embarrassment, Anne did move quietly to the window. She was just in time to ascertain that it really was Mr. Elliot, which she had never believed, before he disappeared on one side, as Mrs. Clay walked quickly off on the other; and checking the surprise which she could not but feel at such an appearance of friendly conference between two persons of totally opposite interests, she calmly said, "Yes, it is Mr. Elliot, certainly. He has changed his hour of going, I suppose, that is all, or I may be mistaken, I might not attend;" and walked back to her chair, recomposed, and with the comfortable hope of having acquitted herself well.

The visitors took their leave; and Charles, having civilly seen them off, and then made a face at them, and abused them for coming, began with:

"Well, mother, I have done something for you that you will like. I have
been to the theatre, and secured a box for to-morrow night. A'n't I a good
boy? I know you love a play; and there is room for us all. It holds nine. I
have engaged Captain Wentworth. Anne will not be sorry to join us, I am
sure. We all like a play. Have not I done well, mother?"

Mrs. Musgrove was good humouredly beginning to express her perfect
readiness for the play, if Henrietta and all the others like it, when Mary
eagerly interrupted her by exclaiming:

"Good heavens! Charles, how can you think of such a thing? Take a
box for to-morrow night! Have you forgot that we are engaged to Camden
Place to-morrow night? and that we were most particularly asked to
meet Lady Dalrymple and her daughter, and Mr. Elliot, all the principal
family connections, on purpose to be introduced to them? How can you be
so forgetful?"

"Phoo! phoo!" replied Charles, "what's an evening party? Never worth
remembering. Your father might have asked us to dinner, I think, if he
had wanted to see us. You may do as you like, but I shall go to the play."

"Oh! Charles, I declare it will be too abominable if you do, when you
promised to go."

"No, I did not promise. I only smirked and bowed, and said the word
'happy.' There was no promise."

"But you must go, Charles. It would be unpardonable to fail. We were
asked on purpose to be introduced. There was always such a great connection between the Dalrymples and ourselves. Nothing ever happened
on either side that was not announced immediately. We are quite near
relations, you know; and Mr. Elliot too, whom you ought so particularly
to be acquainted with! Every attention is due to Mr. Elliot. Consider, my
father's heir: the future representative of the family."

"Don't talk to me about heirs and representatives," cried Charles. "I
am not one of those who neglect the reigning power to bow to the rising
sun. If I would not go for the sake of your father, I should think it scandalous to go for the sake of his heir. What is Mr. Elliot to me?" The careless
expression was life to Anne, who saw that Captain Wentworth was all
attention, looking and listening with his whole soul; and that the last
words brought his enquiring eyes from Charles to herself.

Charles and Mary still talked on in the same style; he, half serious and
half jesting, maintaining the scheme for the play, and she, invariably
serious, most warmly opposing it, and not omitting to make it known that,
however determined to go to Camden Place herself, she should not think
herself very well used, if they went to the play without her. Mrs. Musgrove
interposed.

"We had better put it off. Charles, you had much better go back and
change the box for Tuesday. It would be a pity to be divided, and we
should be losing Miss Anne too, if there is a party at her father's; and I am
sure neither Henrietta not I should care at all for the play if Miss Anne
could not be with us."

Anne felt truly obliged to her for such kindness; and quite as much s(
for the opportunity it gave her of decidedly saying:

"If it depended only on my inclination, ma'am, the party at hom(
(excepting on Mary's account) would not be the smallest impediment.
I have no pleasure in the sort of meeting, and should be too happy to
change it for a play, and with you. But it had better not be attempted,
perhaps." She had spoken it; but she trembled when it was done, conscious that her words were listened to, and daring not even to try to
observe their effect.

It was soon generally agreed that Tuesday should be the day; Charles
only reserving the advantage of still teasing his wife, by persisting that he
would go to the play to-morrow, if nobody else would.

Captain Wentworth left his seat, and walked to the fireplace; probably
for the sake of walking away from it soon afterwards, and taking a station,
with less barefaced design, by Anne.

"You have not been long enough in Bath," said he, "to enjoy the
evening parties of the place."

"Oh! no. The usual character of them has nothing for me. I am no
card-player."

"You were not formerly, I know. You did not use to like cards; but
time makes many changes."

"I am not yet so much changed," cried Anne, and stopped, fearing she
hardly knew what misconstruction. After waiting a few moments he said,
and as if it were the result of immediate feeling, "It is a period indeed!
Eight years and a half is a period!"

Whether he would have proceeded further was left to Anne's imagination to ponder over in a calmer hour; for while still hearing the sounds
he had uttered she was startled to other subjects by Henrietta, eager to
make use of the present leisure for getting out, and calling on her companions to lose no time, lest somebody else should come in.

They were obliged to move. Anne talked of being perfectly ready, and
tried to look it; but she felt that could Henrietta have known the regret
and reluctance of her heart in quitting that chair, in preparing to quit
the room, she would have found, in all her own sensations for her cousin,
in the very security of his affection, wherewith to pity her.

Their preparations, however, were stopped short. Alarming sounds
were heard; other visitors approached and the door was thrown open for
Sir Walter and Miss Elliot, whose entrance seemed to give a general chill.
Anne felt an instant oppression, and wherever she looked saw symptoms
of the same. The comfort, the freedom, the gaiety of the room was over,
hushed into cold composure, determined silence, or insipid talk, to meet
the heartless elegance of her father and sister. How mortifying to feel that
it was so!

Her jealous eye was satisfied in one particular. Captain Wentworth was
acknowledged again by each, by Elizabeth more graciously than before.
She even addressed him once, and looked at him more than once. Elizabeth

was, in fact, revolving a great measure. The sequel explained it. After the waste of a few minutes in saying the proper nothings, she began to give the invitation which was to comprise all the remaining dues of the Musgroves. "To-morrow evening, to meet a few friends: no formal party." It was all said very gracefully, and the cards with which she had provided herself, the "Miss Elliot at home," were laid on the table, with a courteous, comprehensive smile to all, and one smile and one card more decidedly for Captain Wentworth. The truth was, that Elizabeth had been long enough in Bath to understand the importance of a man of such an air and appearance as his. The past was nothing. The present was that Captain Wentworth would move about well in her drawing-room. The card was pointedly given, and Sir Walter and Elizabeth arose and disappeared.

The interruption had been short though severe, and ease and animation returned to most of those they left as the door shut them out, but not to Anne. She could think only of the invitation she had with such astonishment witnessed, and of the manner in which it had been received: a manner of doubtful meaning, of surprise rather than gratification, of polite acknowledgment rather than acceptance. She knew him: she saw disdain in his eyes, and could not venture to believe that he had determined to accept such an offering as an atonement for all the insolence of the past. Her spirits sank. He held the card in his hand after they were gone, as if deeply considering it.

"Only think of Elizabeth's including everybody!" whispered Mary, very audibly. "I do not wonder Captain Wentworth is delighted! You see he cannot put the card out of his hand."

Anne caught his eye, saw his cheeks glow, and his mouth form itself into a momentary expression of contempt, and turned away, that she might neither see nor hear more to vex her.

The party separated. The gentlemen had their own pursuits, the ladies proceeded on their own business, and they met no more while Anne belonged to them. She was earnestly begged to return and dine, and give them all the rest of the day, but her spirits had been so long exerted that at present she felt unequal to more, and fit only for home, where she might be sure of being as silent as she chose.

Promising to be with them the whole of the following morning, therefore, she closed the fatigues of the present by a toilsome walk to Camden Place, there to spend the evening chiefly in listening to the busy arrangements of Elizabeth and Mrs. Clay for the morrow's party, the frequent enumeration of the persons invited, and the continually improving detail of all the embellishments which were to make it the most completely elegant of its kind in Bath, while harassing herself in secret with the never-ending question of whether Captain Wentworth would come or not? They were reckoning him as certain, but with her it was a gnawing solicitude never appeased for five minutes together. She generally thought he would come, because she generally thought he ought; but it was a case which she could not so shape into any positive act of duty or discretion, as inevitably to defy the suggestions of very opposite feelings.

She only roused herself from the broodings of this restless agitation, to let Mrs. Clay know that she had been seen with Mr. Elliot three hours after his being supposed to be out of Bath, for, having watched in vain for some intimation of the interview from the lady herself, she determined to mention it, and it seemed to her that there was guilt in Mrs. Clay's face as she listened. It was transient: cleared away in an instant; but Anne could imagine she read there the consciousness of having, by some complication of mutual trick, or some overbearing authority of his, been obliged to attend (perhaps for half an hour) to his lectures and restrictions on her designs on Sir Walter. She exclaimed, however, with a very tolerable imitation of nature:

"Oh, dear! very true. Only think, Miss Elliot, to my great surprise I met with Mr. Elliot in Bath Street. I was never more astonished. He turned back and walked with me to the Pump Yard. He had been prevented setting off for Thornberry, but I really forget by what; for I was in a hurry, and could not much attend, and I can only answer for his being determined not to be delayed in his return. He wanted to know how early he might be admitted to-morrow. He was full of 'to-morrow,' and it is very evident that I have been full of it too, ever since I entered the house and learned the extension of your plan and all that had happened, or my seeing him could never have gone so entirely out of my head."

Chapter 23

ONE day only had passed since Anne's conversation with Mrs. Smith; but a keener interest had succeeded, and she was now so little touched by Mr. Elliot's conduct, except by its effects in one quarter, that it became a matter of course the next morning still to defer her explanatory visit in Rivers Street. She had promised to be with the Musgroves from breakfast to dinner. Her faith was plighted, and Mr. Elliot's character, like the Sultaness Scheherazade's head, must live another day.

She could not keep her appointment punctually, however; the weather was unfavourable, and she had grieved over the rain on her friend's account, and felt it very much on her own, before she was able to attempt the walk. When she reached the White Hart, and made her way to the proper apartment, she found herself neither arriving quite in time, nor the first to arrive. The party before her were, Mrs. Musgrove talking to Mrs. Croft, and Captain Harville to Captain Wentworth; and she immediately heard that Mary and Henrietta, too impatient to wait, had gone out the moment it had cleared, but would be back again soon, and that the strictest injunctions had been left with Mrs. Musgrove to keep her there till they returned. She had only to submit, sit down, be outwardly composed, and feel herself plunged at once in all the agitations which she had merely laid her account of tasting a little before the morning closed. There was no delay, no waste of time. She was deep in the happiness of such misery, or the misery of such happiness, instantly. Two minutes after her entering the room, Captain Wentworth said:

"We will write the letter we were talking of, Harville, now, if you will give me materials."

Materials were all at hand, on a separate table; he went to it, and nearly turning his back on them all, was engrossed by writing.

Mrs. Musgrove was giving Mrs. Croft the history of her eldest daughter's engagement, and just in that inconvenient tone of voice which was perfectly audible while it pretended to be a whisper. Anne felt that she did not belong to the conversation, and yet, as Captain Harville seemed thoughtful and not disposed to talk, she could not avoid hearing many undesirable particulars; such as, "how Mr. Musgrove and my brother Hayter had met again and again to talk it over; what my brother Hayter had said one day, and what Mr. Musgrove had proposed the next, and what had occurred to my sister Hayter, and what the young people had wished, and what I said at first I never could consent to, but was afterwards persuaded to think might do very well," and a great deal in the same style of open-hearted communication: minutiæ which, even with every advantage of taste and delicacy good Mrs. Musgrove could not give, could be properly interesting only to the principals. Mrs. Croft was attending with great good-humour, and whenever she spoke at all it was very sensibly. Anne hoped the gentlemen might each be too much self-occupied to hear.

"And so, ma'am, all these things considered," said Mrs. Musgrove, in her powerful whisper, "though we could have wished it different, yet, altogether, we did not think it fair to stand out any longer, for Charles Hayter was quite wild about it, and Henrietta was pretty near as bad; and so we thought they had better marry at once, and make the best of it, as many others have done before them. At any rate, said I, it will be better than a long engagement."

"That is precisely what I was going to observe," cried Mrs. Croft. "I would rather have young people settle on a small income at once, and have to struggle with a few difficulties together, than be involved in a long engagement. I always think that no mutual——"

"Oh! dear Mrs. Croft," cried Mrs. Musgrove, unable to let her finish her speech, "there is nothing I so abominate for young people as a long engagement. It is what I always protested against for my children. It is all very well, I used to say, for young people to be engaged, if there is a certainty of their being able to marry in six months, or even in twelve; but a long engagement——!"

"Yes, dear ma'am," said Mrs. Croft, "or an uncertain engagement, an engagement which may be long. To begin without knowing that at such a time there will be the means of marrying, I hold to be very unsafe and unwise, and what I think all parents should prevent as far as they can."

Anne found an unexpected interest here. She felt its application to herself, felt it in a nervous thrill all over her; and at the same moment that her eyes instinctively glanced towards the distant table, Captain Wentworth's pen ceased to move, his head was raised pausing, listening, and he turned round the next instant to give a look, one quick, conscious look at her.

The two ladies continued to talk, to re-urge the same admitted truths, and enforce them with such examples of the ill effect of a contrary practice as had fallen within their observation, but Anne heard nothing distinctly; it was only a buzz of words in her ear, her mind was in confusion.

Captain Harville, who had in truth been hearing none of it, now left his seat and moved to a window, and Anne seeming to watch him, though it was from thorough absence of mind, became gradually sensible that he was inviting her to join him where he stood. He looked at her with a smile, and a little motion of the head, which expressed, "Come to me, I have something to say;" and the unaffected, easy kindness of manner which denoted the feelings of an older_ acquaintance than he really was, strongly enforced the invitation. She roused herself and went to him. The window at which he stood was at the other end of the room from where the two ladies were sitting, and though nearer to Captain Wentworth's table, not very near. As she joined him, Captain Harville's countenance re-assumed the serious, thoughtful expression, which seemed its natural character.

"Look here," said he, unfolding a parcel in his hand, and displaying a small miniature painting; "do you know who that is?"

"Certainly; Captain Benwick."

"Yes, and you may guess who it is for. But" (in a deep tone), "it was not done for her. Miss Elliot, do you remember our walking together at Lyme, and grieving for him? I little thought then—but no matter. This was drawn at the Cape. He met with a clever young German artist at the Cape in compliance with a promise to my poor sister, sat to him, and was bringing it home for her; and I have now the charge of getting it properly set for another! It was a commission to me! But who else was there to employ? I hope I can allow for him. I am not sorry, indeed, to make it over to another. He undertakes it;" (looking towards Captain Wentworth) "he is writing about it now." And with a quivering lip he wound up the whole by adding, "Poor Fanny! she would not have forgotten him so soon."

"No," replied Anne, in a low feeling voice, "that I can easily believe."

"It was not in her nature. She doted on him."

"It would not be the nature of any woman who truly loved."

Captain Harville smiled, as much as to say, "Do you claim that for your sex?" and she answered the question, smiling also, "Yes. We cer tainly do not forget you so soon as you forget us. It is, perhaps, our fate rather than our merit. We cannot help ourselves. We live at home, quiet, confined, and our feelings prey upon us. You are forced on exertion. You have always a profession, pursuits, business of some sort or other, to take you back into the world immediately, and continual occupation and change soon weaken impressions."

"Granting your assertion that the world does all this so soon for men (which, however, I do not think I shall grant), it does not apply to Benwick. He has not been forced upon any exertion. The peace turned him on shore at the very moment, and he has been living with us, in our little family circle, ever since."

"True," said Anne, "very true; I did not recollect; but what shall we say now, Captain Harville? If the change be not from outward circumstances, it must be from within; it must be nature, man's nature, which has done the business for Captain Benwick."

"No, no, it is not man's nature. I will not allow it to be more man's nature than woman's to be inconstant and forget those they do love, or have loved. I believe the reverse. I believe in a true analogy between our bodily frames and our mental; and that as our bodies are the strongest, so are our feelings; capable of bearing most rough usage, and riding out the heaviest weather."

"Your feelings may be the strongest," replied Anne, "but the same spirit of analogy will authorise me to assert that ours are the most tender. Man is more robust than woman, but he is not longer lived; which exactly explains my view of the nature of their attachments. Nay, it would be too hard upon you, if it were otherwise. You have difficulties, and privations, and dangers enough to struggle with. You are always labouring and toiling, exposed to every risk and hardship. Your home, country, friends, all quitted. Neither time, nor health, nor life, to be called your own. It would be too hard, indeed" (with a faltering voice), "if woman's feelings were to be added to all this."

"We shall never agree upon this question," Captain Harville was beginning to say, when a slight noise called their attention to Captain Wentworth's hitherto perfectly quiet division of the room. It was nothing more than that his pen had fallen down; but Anne was startled at finding him nearer than she had supposed, and half inclined to suspect that the pen had only fallen because he had been occupied by them, striving to catch sounds, which yet she did not think he could have caught.

"Have you finished your letter?" said Captain Harville.

"Not quite, a few lines more. I shall have done in five minutes."

"There is no hurry on my side. I am only ready whenever you are. I am in very good anchorage here" (smiling at Anne), "well supplied, and want for nothing. No hurry for a signal at all. Well, Miss Elliot" (lowering his voice), "as I was saying, we shall never agree, I suppose,

upon this point. No man and woman would, probably. But let me
observe that all histories are against you—all stories, prose and verse.
If I had such a memory as Benwick, I could bring you fifty quotations
in a moment on my side the argument, and I do not think I ever opened
a book in my life which had not something to say upon woman's inconstancy. Songs and proverbs all talk of woman's fickleness. But, perhaps, you will say, these were all written by men."

"Perhaps I shall. Yes, yes, if you please, no reference to examples in
books. Men have had every advantage of us in telling their own story.
Education has been theirs in so much higher a degree; the pen has
been in their hands. I will not allow books to prove anything."

"But how shall we prove anything?"

"We never shall. We never can expect to prove anything upon such a
point. It is a difference of opinion which does not admit of proof. We
each begin, probably, with a little bias towards our own sex; and upon
that bias build every circumstance in favour of it which has occurred
within our own circle; many of which circumstances (perhaps those
very cases which strike us the most) may be precisely such as cannot
be brought forward without betraying a confidence, or in some respect,
saying what should not be said."

"Ah!" cried Captain Harville, in a tone of strong feeling, "if I could
but make you comprehend what a man suffers when he takes a last
look at his wife and children, and watches the boat that he has sent
them off in, as long as it is in sight, and then turns away and says,
'God knows whether we ever meet again!' And then, if I could convey
to you the glow of his soul when he does see them again; when, coming
back after a twelvemonth's absence, perhaps, and obliged to put into
another port, he calculates how soon it be possible to get them there,
pretending to deceive himself, and saying, 'They cannot be here till
such a day,' but all the while hoping for them twelve hours sooner,
and seeing them arrive at last, as if Heaven had given them wings, by
many hours sooner still! If I could explain to you all this, and all that
a man can bear and do, and glories to do, for the sake of these treasures
of his existence! I speak, you know, only of such men as have hearts!"
pressing his own with emotion.

"Oh!" cried Anne, eagerly, "I hope to do justice to all that is felt by
you, and by those who resemble you. God forbid that I should undervalue the warm and faithful feelings of any of my fellow creatures! I
should deserve utter contempt if I dared to suppose that true attachment
and constancy were known only by woman. No, I believe you capable
of everything great and good in your married lives. I believe you equal
to every important exertion, and to every domestic forbearance, so
long as—if I may be allowed the expression, so long as you have an
object. I mean while the woman you love lives, and lives for you. All
the privilege I claim for my own sex (it is not a very enviable one: you

need not covet it), is that of loving longest, when existence or when hope is gone!"

She could not immediately have uttered another sentence; her heart was too full, her breath too much oppressed.

"You are a good soul," cried Captain Harville, putting his hand on her arm, quite affectionately. "There is no quarrelling with you. And when I think of Benwick, my tongue is tied."

Their attention was called towards the others. Mrs. Croft was taking leave.

"Here, Frederick, you and I part company, I believe," said she. "I am going home, and you have an engagement with your friend. To-night we may have the pleasure of all meeting again at your party" (turning to Anne). "We had your sister's card yesterday, and I understood Frederick had a card too, though I did not see it; and you are disengaged, Frederick, are you not, as well as ourselves?"

Captain Wentworth was folding up a letter in great haste, and either could not or would not answer fully.

"Yes," said he, "very true; here we separate, but Harville and I shall soon be after you; that is, Harville, if you are ready, I am in half a minute. I know you will not be sorry to be off. I shall be at your service in half a minute."

Mrs. Croft left them, and Captain Wentworth, having sealed his letter with great rapidity, was indeed ready, and had even a hurried, agitated air, which showed impatience to be gone. Anne knew not how to understand it. She had the kindest "Good morning, God bless you!" from Captain Harville, but from him not a word, nor a look! He had passed out of the room without a look!

She had only time, however, to move closer to the table where he had been writing, when footsteps were heard returning; the door opened, it was himself. He begged their pardon, but he had forgotten his gloves, and instantly crossing the room to the writing table, and standing with his back towards Mrs. Musgrove, he drew out a letter from under the scattered paper, placed it before Anne with eyes of glowing entreaty fixed on her for a time, and hastily collecting his gloves, was again out of the room, almost before Mrs. Musgrove was aware of his being in it: the work of an instant!

The revolution which one instant had made in Anne was almost beyond expression. The letter, with a direction hardly legible, to "Miss A. E——," was evidently the one which he had been folding so hastily. While supposed to be writing only to Captain Benwick he had been also addressing her! On the contents of that letter depended all which this world could do for her. Anything was possible, anything might be defied rather than suspense. Mrs. Musgrove had little arrangements of her own at her own table; to their protection she must trust, and, sinking into the chair which he had occupied, succeeding to the very spot where he had leaned and written, her eyes devoured the following words:

"I can listen no longer in silence. I must speak to you by such means as are within my reach. You pierce my soul. I am half agony, half hope. Tell me not that I am too late, that such precious feelings are gone for ever. I offer myself to you again with a heart even more your own than when you almost broke it, eight years and a half ago. Dare not say that man forgets sooner than woman, that his love has an earlier death. I have loved none but you. Unjust I may have been, weak and resentful I have been, but never inconstant. You alone have brought me to Bath. For you alone, I think and plan. Have you not seen this? Can you fail to have understood my wishes? I had not waited even these ten days, could I have read your feelings, as I think you must have penetrated mine. I can hardly write. I am every instant hearing something which overpowers me. You sink your voice, but I can distinguish the tones of that voice when they would be lost on others. Too good, too excellent creature! You do us justice, indeed. You do believe that there is true attachment and constancy among men. Believe it to be most fervent, most undeviating, in

                                              "F. W.

"I must go, uncertain of my fate; but I shall return hither, or follow your party, as soon as possible. A word, a look, will be enough to decide whether I enter your father's house this evening or never."

Such a letter was not to be soon recovered from. Half an hour's solitude and reflection might have tranquillised her; but the ten minutes only which now passed before she was interrupted, with all the restraints of her situation, could do nothing towards tranquillity. Every moment rather brought fresh agitation. It was an overpowering happiness. And before she was beyond the first stage of full sensation, Charles, Mary, and Henrietta, all came in.

The absolute necessity of seeming like herself produced then an immediate struggle; but after a while she could do no more. She began not to understand a word they said, and was obliged to plead indisposition and excuse herself. They could then see that she looked very ill, were shocked and concerned, and would not stir without her for the world. This was dreadful. Would they only have gone away, and left her in the quiet possession of that room it would have been her cure; but to have them all standing or waiting around her was distracting, and in desperation, she said she would go home.

"By all means, my dear," cried Mrs. Musgrove, "go home directly, and take care of yourself, that you may be fit for the evening. I wish Sarah was here to doctor you, but I am no doctor myself. Charles, ring and order a chair. She must not walk."

But the chair would never do. Worse than all! To lose the possibility of speaking two words to Captain Wentworth in the course of her quiet, solitary progress up the town (and she felt almost certain of meeting him) could not be borne. The chair was earnestly protested against, and Mrs. Musgrove, who thought only of one sort of illness, having assured herself with some anxiety, that there had been no fall in the case; that Anne had not at any time lately slipped down, and got a blow on her head; that she was perfectly convinced of having had no fall; could part with her cheerfully, and depend on finding her better at night.

Anxious to omit no precaution, Anne struggled, and said:

"I am afraid, ma'am, that it is not perfectly understood. Pray be so good as to mention to the other gentlemen that we hope to see your whole party this evening. I am afraid there has been some mistake; and I wish you particularly to assure Captain Harville and Captain Wentworth, that we hope to see them both."

"Oh; my dear, it is quite understood, I give you my word. Captain Harville has no thought but of going."

"Do you think so? But I am afraid; and I should be so very sorry. Will you promise me to mention it when you see them again? You will see them both again this morning, I dare say. Do promise me."

"To be sure I will, if you wish it. Charles, if you see Captain Harville anywhere, remember to give Miss Anne's message. But, indeed, my dear, you need not be uneasy. Captain Harville holds himself quite engaged, I'll answer for it; and Captain Wentworth the same, I dare say."

Anne could do no more; but her heart prophesied some mischance to damp the perfection of her felicity. It could not be very lasting, however. Even if he did not come to Camden Place himself, it would be in her power to send an intelligible sentence by Captain Harville. Another momentary vexation occurred. Charles, in his real concern and good nature, would go home with her; there was no preventing him. This was almost cruel. But she could not be long ungrateful; he was sacrificing an engagement at a gunsmith's to be of use to her, and she set off with him, with no feeling but gratitude apparent.

They were in Union Street, when a quicker step behind, a something of familiar sound, gave her two moments' preparation for the sight of Captain Wentworth. He joined them; but, as if irresolute whether to join or to pass on, said nothing, only looked. Anne could command herself enough to receive that look, and not repulsively. The cheeks which had been pale now glowed, and the movements which had hesitated were decided. He walked by her side. Presently, struck by a sudden thought, Charles said:

"Captain Wentworth, which way are you going? Only to Gay Street, or farther up the town?"

"I hardly know," replied Captain Wentworth, surprised.

"Are you going as high as Belmont? Are you going near Camden Place? Because, if you are, I shall have no scruple in asking you to take my place, and give Anne your arm to her father's door. She is rather done for this morning, and must not go so far without help, and I ought to be at that fellow's in the Market Place. He promised me the sight of a capital gun he is just going to send off; said he would keep it unpacked to the last possible moment, that I might see it; and if I do not turn back now, I have no chance. By his description, a good deal like the second sized double-barrel of mine, which you shot with one day round Winthrop."

There could not be an objection. There could be only a most proper alacrity, a most obliging compliance for public view; and smiles reined in and spirits dancing in private rapture. In half a minute Charles was at the bottom of Union Street again, and the other two proceeding together: and soon words enough had passed between them to decide their direction towards the comparatively quiet and retired gravel walk, where the power of conversation would make the present hour a blessing indeed, and prepare it for all the immortality which the happiest recollections of their own future lives could bestow. There they exchanged again those feelings and those promises which had once before seemed to secure everything, but which had been followed by so many, many years of division and estrangement. There they returned again into the past, more exquisitely happy, perhaps, in their reunion, than when it had been first projected; more tender, more tried, more fixed in a knowledge of each other's character, truth, and attachment; more equal to act, more justified in acting. And there, as they slowly paced the gradual ascent, heedless of every group around them, seeing neither sauntering politicians, bustling housekeepers, flirting girls, nor nurserymaids and children, they could indulge in those retrospections and acknowledgments, and especially in those explanations of what had directly preceded the present moment, which were so poignant and so ceaseless in interest. All the little variations of the last week were gone through; and of yesterday and to-day there could scarcely be an end.

She had not mistaken him. Jealousy of Mr. Elliot had been the retarding weight, the doubt, the torment. That had begun to operate in the very hour of first meeting her in Bath; that had returned, after a short suspension, to ruin the concert; and that had influenced him in everything he had said and done, or omitted to say and do, in the last four-and-twenty hours. It had been gradually yielding to the better hopes which her looks, or words, or actions occasionally encouraged; it had been vanquished at last by those sentiments and those tones which had reached him while she talked with Captain Harville; and under the irresistible governance of which he had seized a sheet of paper, and poured out his feelings.

Of what he had then written nothing was to be retracted or qualified. He persisted in having loved none but her. She had never been supplanted. He never even believed himself to see her equal. Thus much, indeed, he was obliged to acknowledge: that he had been constant unconsciously, nay unintentionally; that he had meant to forget her, and believed it to be done. He had imagined himself indifferent, when he had only been angry; and he had been unjust to her merits, because he had been a sufferer from them. Her character was now fixed on his mind as perfection itself, maintaining the loveliest medium of fortitude and gentleness; but he was obliged to acknowledge that only at Uppercross had he learnt to do her justice, and only at Lyme had he begun to understand himself. At Lyme he had received lessons of more than one sort. The passing admiration of Mr. Elliot had at least roused him, and the scenes on the Cobb and at Captain Harville's had fixed her superiority.

In his preceding attempts to attach himself to Louisa Musgrove (the attempts of angry pride), he protested that he had for ever felt it to be impossible; that he had not cared, could not care, for Louisa; though till that day, till the leisure for reflection which followed it, he had not understood the perfect excellence of the mind with which Louisa's could so ill bear a comparison, or the perfect unrivalled hold it possessed over his own. There, he had learnt to distinguish between the steadiness of principle and the obstinacy of self-will, between the darings of heedlessness and the resolution of a collected mind. There he had seen everything to exalt in his estimation the woman he had lost; and there begun to deplore the pride, the folly, the madness of resentment, which had kept him from trying to regain her when thrown in his way.

From that period his penance had become severe. He had no sooner been free from the horror and remorse attending the first few days of Louisa's accident, no sooner begun to feel himself alive again, than he had begun to feel himself, though alive, not at liberty.

"I found," said he, "that I was considered by Harville an engaged man! That neither Harville nor his wife entertained a doubt of our mutual attachment. I was startled and shocked. To a degree, I could contradict this instantly; but, when I began to reflect that others might have felt the same—her own family, nay, perhaps herself—I was no longer at my own disposal. I was hers in honour if she wished it. I had been unguarded. I had not thought seriously on this subject before. I had not considered that my excessive intimacy must have its danger of ill consequence in many ways; and that I had no right to be trying whether I could attach myself to either of the girls, at the risk of raising even an unpleasant report, were there no other ill effects. I had been grossly wrong, and must abide the consequences."

He found too late, in short, that he had entangled himself; and that precisely as he became fully satisfied of his not caring for Louisa at all, he must regard himself as bound to her, if her sentiments for him were what the Harvilles supposed. It determined him to leave Lyme, and await her complete recovery elsewhere. He would gladly weaken, by any fair means, whatever feelings or speculations concerning him might exist; and he went, therefore, to his brother's, meaning after a while to return to Kellynch, and act as circumstances might require.

"I was six weeks with Edward," said he, "and saw him happy. I could have no other pleasure. I deserved none. He enquired after you very particularly; asked even if you were personally altered, little suspecting that to my eye you could never alter."

Anne smiled, and let it pass. It was too pleasing a blunder for a reproach. It is something for a woman to be assured, in her eight-and-twentieth year, that she has not lost one charm of earlier youth: but the value of such homage was inexpressibly increased to Anne, by comparing it with former words, and feeling it to be the result, not the cause, of a revival of his warm attachment.

He had remained in Shropshire, lamenting the blindness of his own pride, and the blunders of his own calculations, till at once released from Louisa by the astonishing and felicitous intelligence of her engagement with Benwick.

"Here," said he, "ended the worst of my state; for now I could at least put myself in the way of happiness; I could exert myself; I could do something. But to be waiting so long in inaction, and waiting only for evil, had been dreadful. Within the first five minutes I said, 'I will be at Bath on Wednesday,' and I was. Was it unpardonable to think it worth my while to come? and to arrive with some degree of hope? You were single. It was possible that you might retain the feelings of the past, as I did: and one encouragement happened to be mine. I could never doubt that you would be loved and sought by others, but I knew to a certainty that you had refused one man, at least, of better pretensions than myself; and I could not help often saying, 'Was this for me?' "

Their first meeting in Milsom Street afforded much to be said, but the concert still more. That evening seemed to be made up of exquisite moments. The moment of her stepping forward in the Octagon Room to speak to him: the moment of Mr. Elliot's appearing and tearing her away, and one or two subsequent moments, marked by returning hope or increasing despondency, were dwelt on with energy.

"To see you," cried he, "in the midst of those who could not be my well-wishers; to see your cousin close by you, conversing and smiling, and feel all the horrible eligibilities and proprieties of the match! To consider it as the certain wish of every being who could hope to influence you! Even if your own feelings were reluctant or indifferent, to consider what powerful supports would be his! Was it not enough to make the fool of me which I appeared? How could I look on without agony? Was not the very sight of the friend who sat behind you, was not the recollection of what had been, the knowledge of her influence, the indelible, immovable impression of what persuasion had once done—was it not all against me?"

"You should have distinguished," replied Anne. "You should not have suspected me now; the case so different, and my age so different. If I was wrong in yielding to persuasion once, remember that it was to persuasion exerted on the side of safety, not of risk. When I yielded, I thought it was to duty, but no duty could be called in aid here. In marrying a man indifferent to me, all risk would have been incurred, and all duty violated."

"Perhaps I ought to have reasoned thus," he replied, "but I could not. I could not derive benefit from the late knowledge I had acquired of your character. I could not bring it into play; it was overwhelmed, buried, lost in those earlier feelings which I had been smarting under year after year. I could think of you only as one who had yielded, who had given me up, who had been influenced by anyone rather than by me. I saw you with the very person who had guided you in that year of misery. I had no reason to believe her of less authority now. The force of habit was to be added."

"I should have thought," said Anne, "that my manner to yourself might have spared you much or all of this."

"No, no! Your manner might be only the ease which your engagement to another man would give. I left you in this belief; and yet, I was determined to see you again. My spirits rallied with the morning, and I felt that I had still a motive for remaining here."

At last Anne was at home again, and happier than any one in that house could have conceived. All the surprise and suspense, and every other painful part of the morning dissipated by this conversation, she re-entered the house so happy as to be obliged to find an alloy in some momentary apprehensions of its being impossible to last. An interval of meditation, serious and grateful, was the best corrective of everything dangerous in such high-wrought felicity; and she went to her room, and grew steadfast and fearless in the thankfulness of her enjoyment.

The evening come, the drawing-rooms were lighted up, the company assembled. It was but a card party, it was but a mixture of those who had never met before, and those who met too often: a commonplace business, too numerous for intimacy, too small for variety; but Anne had never found an evening shorter. Glowing and lovely in sensibility and happiness, and more generally admired than she thought about or cared for, she had cheerful or forbearing feelings for every creature around her. Mr. Elliot was there; she avoided, but she could pity him. The Wallises, she had amusement in understanding them. Lady Dalrymple and Miss Carteret—they would soon be innoxious cousins to her. She cared not for Mrs. Clay, and had nothing to blush for in the public manners of her father and sister. With the Musgroves there was the happy chat of perfect ease; with Captain Harville, the kind-hearted intercourse of brother and sister; with Lady Russell, attempts at conversation, which a delicious consciousness cut short; with Admiral and Mrs. Croft, everything of peculiar cordiality and fervent interest, which the same consciousness sought to conceal; and with Captain Wentworth, some moments of communication continually occurring, and always the hope of more, and always the knowledge of his being there.

It was in one of these short meetings, each apparently occupied in admiring a fine display of greenhouse plants, that she said:

"I have been thinking over the past, and trying impartially to judge of the right and wrong, I mean with regard to myself; and I must believe that I was right, much as I suffered from it, that I was perfectly right in being guided by the friend whom you will love better than you do now. To me, she was in the place of a parent. Do not mistake me, however. I am not saying that she did not err in her advice. It was, perhaps, one of those cases in which advice is good or bad only as the event decides; and for myself, I certainly never should, in any circumstance of tolerable similarity, give such advice. But I mean, that I was right in submitting to her, and that if I had done otherwise, I should have suffered more in continuing the engagement than I did even in giving it up, because I should have suffered in my conscience. I have now, as far as such a senti- ment is allowable in human nature, nothing to reproach myself with; and if I mistake not, a strong sense of duty is no bad part of a woman's portion."

He looked at her, looked at Lady Russell, and looking again at her, replied, as if in cool deliberation:

"Not yet, but there are hopes of her being forgiven in time. I trust to being in charity with her soon. But I too have been thinking over the past, and a question has suggested itself, whether there may not have been one person more my enemy even than that lady? My own self. Tell me if, when I returned to England, in the year eight, with a few thousand pounds, and was posted into the *Laconia,* if I had then written to you, would you have answered my letter? Would you, in short, have renewed the engagement then?"

"Would I?" was all her answer; but the accent was decisive enough.

"Good God!" he cried, "you would! It is not that I did not think of it, or desire it, as what could alone crown all my other success; but I was proud, too proud to ask again. I did not understand you. I shut my eyes, and would not understand you, or do you justice. This is a recollection which ought to make me forgive everyone sooner than myself. Six years of separation and suffering might have been spared. It is a sort of pain, too, which is new to me. I have been used to the gratification of believing myself to earn every blessing that I enjoyed. I have valued myself on honourable toils and just rewards. Like other great men under reverses," he added, with a smile, "I must endeavour to subdue my mind to my fortune. I must learn to brook being happier than I deserve."

Chapter 24

Who can be in doubt of what followed? When any two young people take it into their heads to marry, they are pretty sure by perseverance to carry their point, be they ever so poor, or ever so imprudent, or ever so little likely to be necessary to each other's ultimate comfort. This may be bad morality to conclude with, but I believe it to be truth, and if such parties succeed, how should a Captain Wentworth and an Anne Elliot, with the advantage of maturity of mind, consciousness of right, and one independent fortune between them, fail of bearing down every opposition? They might, in fact, have borne down a great deal more than they met with, for there was little to distress them beyond the want of graciousness and warmth. Sir Walter made no objection, and Elizabeth did nothing worse than look cold and unconcerned. Captain Wentworth, with five-and-twenty thousand pounds, and as high in his profession as merit and activity could place him, was no longer nobody. He was now esteemed quite worthy to address the daughter of a foolish, spendthrift baronet, who had not had principle or sense enough to maintain himself in the situation in which Providence had placed him, and who could give his daughter at present but a small part of the share of ten thousand pounds which must be hers hereafter.

Sir Walter, indeed, though he had no affection for Anne, had no vanity flattered, to make him really happy on the occasion, was very far from thinking it a bad match for her. On the contrary, when he saw more of Captain Wentworth, saw him repeatedly by daylight, and eyed him well, he was very much struck by his personal claims, and felt that his superiority of appearance might not be unfairly balanced against her superiority of rank; and all this, assisted by his well-sounding name, enabled Sir Walter, at last, to prepare his pen, with a very good grace, for the insertion of the marriage in the volume of honour.

The only one among them whose opposition of feeling could excite any serious anxiety was Lady Russell. Anne knew that Lady Russell must be suffering some pain in understanding and relinquishing Mr. Elliot, and by making some struggles to become truly acquainted with, and do justice to Captain Wentworth. This, however, was what Lady Russell had now to do. She must learn to feel that she had been mistaken with regard to both; that she had been unfairly influenced by appearances in each; that because Captain Wentworth's manners had not suited her own ideas she had been too quick in suspecting them to indicate a character of dangerous impetuosity; and that because Mr. Elliot's manners had precisely pleased her in their propriety and correctness, their general politeness and suavity, she had been too quick in receiving them as the certain result of the most correct opinions and well-regulated mind. There was nothing less for Lady Russell to do than to admit that she had been pretty completely wrong, and to take up a new set of opinions and of hopes.

There is a quickness of perception in some, a nicety in the discernment of character, a natural penetration, in short, which no experience in others can equal, and Lady Russell had been less gifted in this part of understanding than her young friend. But she was a very good woman, and if her second object was to be sensible and well-judging, her first was to see Anne happy. She loved Anne better than she loved her own abilities; and, when the awkwardness of the beginning was over, found little hardship in attaching herself as a mother to the man who was securing the happiness of her other child.

Of all the family, Mary was probably the one most immediately gratified by the circumstance. It was creditable to have a sister married, and she might flatter herself with having been greatly instrumental to the connection, by keeping Anne with her in the autumn; and as her own sister must be better than her husband's sisters, it was very agreeable that Captain Wentworth should be a richer man than either Captain Benwick or Charles Hayter. She had something to suffer, perhaps, when they came into contact again, in seeing Anne restored to the rights of seniority, and the mistress of a very pretty landaulette; but she had a future to look forward to of powerful consolation. Anne had no Uppercross Hall before her, no landed estate, no headship of a family; and if they could but keep Captain Wentworth from being made a baronet, she would not change situations with Anne.

It would be well for the eldest sister if she were equally satisfied with her situation, for a change is not very probable there. She had soon the mortification of seeing Mr. Elliot withdraw, and no one of proper condition has since presented himself to raise even the unfounded hopes which sunk with him.

The news of his cousin Anne's engagement burst on Mr. Elliot most unexpectedly. It deranged his best plan of domestic happiness, his best hope of keeping Sir Walter single by the watchfulness which a son-in-law's rights would have given. But, though discomfited and disappointed, he could still do something for his own interest and his own enjoyment. He soon quitted Bath; and on Mrs. Clay's quitting it soon afterwards, and being next heard of as established under his protection in London, it was evident how double a game he had been playing, and how determined he was to save himself from being cut out by one artful woman, at least.

Mrs. Clay's affections had overpowered her interest, and she had sacrificed, for the young man's sake, the possibility of scheming longer for Sir Walter. She has abilities, however, as well as affections; and it is now a doubtful point whether his cunning, or hers, may finally carry the day; whether, after preventing her from being the wife of Sir Walter, he may not be wheedled and caressed at last into making her the wife of Sir William.

It cannot be doubted that Sir Walter and Elizabeth were shocked and mortified by the loss of their companion, and the discovery of their deception in her. They had their great cousins, to be sure, to resort to for comfort; but they must long feel that to flatter and follow others, without being flattered and followed in turn, is but a state of half enjoyment.

Anne, satisfied at a very early period of Lady Russell's meaning to love Captain Wentworth as she ought, had no other alloy to the happiness of her prospects than what arose from the consciousness of having no relations to bestow on him which a man of sense could value. There she felt her own inferiority keenly. The disproportion in their fortune was nothing; it did not give her a moment's regret; but to have no family to receive and estimate him properly, nothing of respectability, of harmony, of goodwill, to offer in return for all the worth and all the prompt welcome which met her in his brothers and sisters, was a source of as lively pain as her mind could well be sensible of under circumstances of otherwise strong felicity. She had but two friends in the world to add to his list, Lady Russell and Mrs. Smith. To those, however, he was very well disposed to attach himself. Lady Russell, in spite of all her former transgressions, he could now value from his heart. While he was not obliged to say that he believed her to have been right in originally dividing them, he was ready to say almost everything else in her favour, and as for Mrs. Smith, she had claims of various kinds to recommend her quickly and permanently.

Her recent good offices by Anne had been enough in themselves, and their marriage, instead of depriving her of one friend, secured her two. She was their earliest visitor in their settled life, and Captain Wentworth, by putting her in the way of recovering her husband's property in the West Indies, by writing for her, acting for her, and seeing her through all the petty difficulties of the case with the activity and exertion of a fearless man and a determined friend, fully requited the services which she had rendered, or ever meant to render, to his wife.

Mrs. Smith's enjoyments were not spoiled by this improvement of income, with some improvement of health, and the acquisition of such friends to be often with, for her cheerfulness and mental alacrity did not fail her; and while these prime supplies of good remained, she might have bid defiance even to greater accessions of worldly prosperity. She might have been absolutely rich and perfectly healthy, and yet be happy. Her spring of felicity was in the glow of her spirits, as her friend Anne's was in the warmth of her heart. Anne was tenderness itself, and she had the full worth of it in Captain Wentworth's affection. His profession was all that could ever make her friends wish that tenderness less, the dread of a future war all that could dim her sunshine. She gloried in being a sailor's wife, but she must pay the tax of quick alarm for belonging to that profession which is, if possible, more distinguished in its domestic virtues than in its national importance.

THE END

MODERN LIBRARY GIANTS

A series of sturdily bound and handsomely printed, full-sized library editions of books formerly available only in expensive sets. These volumes contain from 600 to 1,400 pages each.

THE MODERN LIBRARY GIANTS REPRESENT A
SELECTION OF THE WORLD'S GREATEST BOOKS